CLARE

Clare Francis is the author of five internationally bestselling thrillers, *Night Sky*, *Red Crystal*, *Wolf Winter*, *Requiem* and *Deceit*. She has also written three non-fiction books, about her voyages across the oceans of the world.

CLARE FRANCIS

REQUIEM
WOLF WINTER

PAN BOOKS
in association with Heinemann

Requiem first published 1991 by William Heinemann Ltd
and first published by Pan Books 1992
in association with William Heinemann Ltd
Published in a revised edition 1994 by Pan Books
Wolf Winter first published 1987 by William Heinemann Ltd
and first published by Pan Books 1988
in association with William Heinemann Ltd

This combined edition published 1995 by Pan Books
an imprint of Macmillan General Books
25 Eccleston Place, London SW1W 9NF
in association with William Heinemann Ltd

Associated companies throughout the world

ISBN 0 330 34585 0

1 3 5 7 9 10 8 6 4 2

A CIP catalogue record for this book is available from
the British Library

Printed and bound in Great Britain

REQUIEM

For those patient and loving friends who have sustained me through the struggles of the last five years; and for all my fellow sufferers who are still fighting their way up the long path to recovery.

ONE

It was just after midnight when Nick slipped away from the house. The moon cast shards of pale light across the wide parkland and illuminated the beeches like giant white-sailed ships. The shadows were very deep, and he wondered if he would be able to find his way up through the glen. He'd never walked the glen in darkness before; usually he drove, and then in daylight with Alusha or Duncan, the estate manager, at his side. He could have done with Duncan's special knowledge to guide him now, but Duncan had been told nothing of this little expedition: he wouldn't approve.

From the post-and-wire fence marking the end of the park, rough pasture rose gently towards the dense woodland which covered the lower slopes of the hills. The direct route to the glen led diagonally across the pasture, but anxious to avoid the obvious paths, Nick struck off at a tangent, making for a dark mass of oak trees on the fringe of the woodland.

He paced himself for the long climb ahead. The shotgun in his hand felt awkward, absurd and rather obscene. He wasn't sure why he'd brought it. Maybe because here, in what was possibly the safest place in the world, he still felt unsafe. Time had done nothing to alleviate the unease; if anything, it had increased it, and he needed the reassurance of the weight in his hand, even if the idea of ever firing the thing frightened him to death. He had no skill with the weapon. Duncan had given him some rudimentary tuition on pointing it in the right direction and not accidentally shooting friends in the backside, but even Duncan, with his boundless optimism, had given up hope of making a good shot of him. Alusha hated him even

1

to pick up a gun. She would be far from happy if she knew he was carrying one now – and far from happy if she knew he was out here, playing cops and robbers in the middle of the night.

But he couldn't have stayed away, the chances were too good. For a week the weather had been foul even by West Highland standards, with blustery westerlies, lowering clouds and almost continuous rain. Then early that evening the sky had cleared, the wind had died, and a brittle blue-washed moon had risen over the hills of Cowal. It was then that Duncan's prediction had flashed into his mind, the prophecy that they would come after the rain, as soon as there was a touch of moon to light their way up the glen.

Almost as he thought it, the outline of the approaching woods became less distinct, blurring into the sky, and he saw that fingers of cloud were creeping across the moon from the west. Would the cloud be enough to put them off? The thought brought him a mixture of disappointment and relief. But it didn't make him turn back; it was too late for that now.

On reaching the woods, he had intended to follow a small footpath that wound between a succession of overgrown dells and hazel thickets, but the darkness was so great that he lost the path almost as soon as he found it and was forced back to the pasture, to skirt the edge of the wood.

At first he had been conscious of few sounds except his own breathing and the soft squelch of his feet on the sodden ground, but now, close under the trees, the night came alive with faint rustlings and scratchings and suggestions of movement. He felt an absurd pride, as if the untouched forest, complete with its small unseen residents, was his very own creation. And in a sense it was. Duncan was forbidden to touch this part of the estate, apart from cutting the worst of the bracken and erecting protective fences around rare plants. Fallen trees rotted where they lay, saplings were left to compete for light in tangled thickets. In the early days this non-interference policy had driven Duncan mad but, despite dark mutterings, he had never actually quit. Nick liked to think that, after eight years, Duncan was beginning to see the point of it all.

The clouds slid past the moon and the trees sprang into relief again. Coming to the corner of the pasture, he re-entered the woods, taking the path that would lead him west towards the deep cut of the glen. Now the forest was mainly oak and sycamore with the occasional Scots pine, the trees high and well-spaced, so that the moon filtered down onto the ground in delicate droppings of light.

As he hurried on, the distant whisper of the river grew steadily until the rush of fast-falling water drowned all but the most distinct sounds.

A pale ribbon appeared through the trees: the track that ran up the glen in a long lazy loop from the house. Stopping just short of it, he crouched in the shadows and, glancing up and down the empty road, strained to hear over the gush and rumble of the water. He became aware of how ludicrous he must look, hiding there like an overgrown boy scout, and, whether from nerves or amusement, he chuckled aloud. The chuckle died in his throat as the shadows at the bend in the track shifted and sent his heart thudding against his ribs. The shadows quickly settled into the benign shapes of trees and shrubs, but after that nothing seemed remotely funny.

Once his heart was back under some sort of control, he tried to plan his next move. How would the men come? By car? If so, there was only one way they could get onto the track without driving past the house itself – something even they, brass-nerved as they were, wouldn't dare. Some quarter of a mile down the glen a narrow overgrown track, hardly more than a wide path, ran off the main track towards the lochside road. Entry to this path was barred by a gate which Duncan had reinforced and locked with a massive padlock and chain. This hadn't stopped their visitors from entering in the past of course; they'd merely used larger bolt cutters. Nor had a three-night stakeout by Duncan and the local constabulary – all two of them. The enemy had merely bypassed the gate and trailed up the glen on foot.

So what would they do tonight? Would they break the padlock and drive up? Or come on foot?

Whichever way they chose, they were bound to use the track, which followed the glen and the racing river for miles, up through the forest to the high moorlands. It wouldn't be a good idea for him to be spotted dawdling along the middle of the road. On the other hand, he wasn't too sure he could manage the full commando approach, crawling through the undergrowth with a mud-daubed face.

Taking a final look both ways, he crossed the stony surface

3

of the track and entered the woods on the far side. Here the ground fell steeply away to the river. Clambering down through the undergrowth, he made for the narrow path that ran close beside the rushing water, and began to follow it up the glen. Now and again, when the moon slipped behind the clouds, he had to reach a hand out in front of him to feel his way forward. Once he stumbled, jarring his shoulder against a rock and the shotgun barrel struck the surface with a loud crack. The sound was quickly swallowed up by the thundering water, but he paused, sweating coldly, before pressing on. Finally Macinley's Rock came into view, a massive outcrop that obtruded into the river, deflecting the flow against the far bank and squeezing the water into a thundering cataract. Above the rock was the Great Pool. According to Duncan, this was where the vermin, as he called them, were to be found. Twice since April Duncan had found evidence of their visits in the form of trampled ground, cigarette butts and peg holes.

It took some time for Nick to find a suitable spot for his watch. Finally he picked a rocky ledge a few yards up the sloping bank, opposite the widest section of the pool. It was rather open, but if he'd gone higher the trees would have obscured his view of the approaches.

He lay on his stomach on the damp grassy earth, and peered over the edge. The Ashard was by no means a broad river – for much of its ten-mile length it was only a few yards wide – but after heavy rain the Great Pool flooded into a wide basin some fifteen yards across. After the commotion of the lower reaches, the pool was quiet, its surface satin-smooth in the moonlight, only the occasional ripple hinting at movement and eddies beneath.

A mournful bird-cry made him start slightly. It sounded again, a cross between a moan and a hoot. A tawny owl – well, an owl anyway. He wasn't quite up to positive identifications; *The Oxford Book of Birds* wasn't something one got to grips with overnight.

He rolled onto his side and felt something sharp dig into his hip: the shotgun cartridges in his jacket pocket. He pulled one out and fingered it. An unpleasant thought came to him. Might they be carrying a shotgun too? As he understood it, there was a sort of unwritten code in these parts, the sporting men's version of the Queensberry Rules, which said that gamekeepers waved shotguns and sometimes even fired them in anger, but that poachers remained unarmed and bolted when caught. He hoped the rules would be in full operation tonight.

If they weren't carrying anything, would they turn and fight? He nursed the idea with a mixture of fear and unexpected excitement. He'd been no hero in the early days. Once, years and years ago, after a gig in Sunderland, a group of the local lads had decided to exhibit their particular brand of machismo by lying in wait for him at the stage door and beating him up. He'd put up the best fight he could muster, which wasn't saying a great deal, but all that his meagre bravery had got him was a broken jaw and the lost earnings from five cancelled gigs. Not long after, he'd sworn a personal non-aggression pact with the world. It had lasted a long time – something like fifteen years – until six years ago and the incident in the Fifth Avenue apartment.

After that, all sorts of things had developed the power to make him angry. Most of all anybody or anything that threatened Alusha. Then, as a close second, anything that threatened this fabulous patch of earth that had somehow become his own. Yet it wasn't because Glen Ashard belonged to him that he was up here playing games in the middle of the night – though that would have been enough for most landowners hereabouts – it wasn't even the idea of all his and Duncan's painstaking work being ruined, it was the thought of having his space and peace invaded by money-grubbing oiks that he really couldn't stomach.

He never admitted as much of course; he talked about responsibility, a word he used to avoid like the plague but which he now said quite often, along with other words like obligation and conservation, which in these feudal parts were usually bandied about by tweedy aristos and retired army officers. According to Alusha, it was all to do with middle age. She said he was finally growing up.

He put the cartridges back in his pocket. There didn't seem much point in keeping them out, when he had no intention of loading them.

It was well after one when the moon dimmed for the last time, lost behind the rim of the hills. The darkness wouldn't last – the midsummer night up here was barely three hours long – but would they have the gall to come in the light? He resigned himself to the possibility that, if they were coming at all, they'd have shown by now. Yet he wouldn't leave, not while there was still the slightest chance. He rested his head on the crook of his arm, pulled his jacket higher round his neck and, ignoring the damp chill of the earth, tried to doze.

He woke after what seemed a very short time. Shifting his body a little, he tried to settle again but was seized by a tickle in the back of his nose. He drew breath, waiting for the itch to trigger the satisfaction of a good sneeze, and it was then that he heard it. A sharp sound. His mouth still poised for the sneeze, his lungs full, he jerked his head up. The sneeze hovered, refusing to die. He clamped his fingers over his nose and squeezed viciously until his eyes watered. Finally, reluctantly, the sneeze faded and died.

Another sound. A scrape, like metal against stone. Then the murmur of a human voice some way off. A second later, a second voice, much closer. Slowly Nick rolled onto his stomach and peered over the edge. At first he could see nothing. Then he spotted a movement – a black shadow against the gleaming surface – and heard the sloshing sound of someone wading into the water.

For a while he was frozen by indecision. He hadn't thought this bit through. Should he stand up and yell? Should he creep up on them and give them a fright? Though it was questionable as to who would be getting the bigger fright. He decided it was worth the risk of heart failure for the satisfaction of seeing them jump.

Taking the shotgun, he rose into a crouch and began to creep slowly down the bank, testing each footstep for loose ground, reaching a steadying hand out to the slope above him, all the time keeping his eye on the man in the water. It wasn't hard to follow him: he was splashing a good deal and leaving a long trail of ripples. There was one nasty moment when a voice called out, but it was only to say: 'Loose off.' A moment later a reply came floating on the air, but the words were muffled by the water.

A filigree of shimmering light rose above the pool as a thin line broke the surface: that would be the net. The excitement rose in Nick as he realised he was going to catch them right in the act.

They appeared to be dragging the deepest part of the pool

immediately behind Macinley's Rock. But where would they pull in the catch?

Nick decided on the likeliest spot and, keeping in a deep crouch, worked his way round to a point nearby and waited.

But they weren't bringing in the net, not yet. There was a tapping, like a mallet on wood, and he realised they were pegging the net to the ground, leaving the current to do some of their work for them. If he stayed where he was, it was likely to be a long wait.

He crept closer. He saw the shape of a man's head against the night sky. A moment later he heard a sloshing sound as a second man emerged from the water. Were there more than two? He couldn't be sure.

There was the flicker of a match and the glow of a cigarette, and the low murmur of voices.

It was now or never. Gripping the shotgun, aware of a quite ridiculous fear which had somehow turned to elation, with his heart exploding against his ribs, Nick stood upright and walked steadily towards them. He felt amazingly conspicuous: they must see him, must hear him at any moment, but by some miracle no shout came, no challenge; there was only the glowing cigarette end and the suggestion of two shadows in the darkness. With only a few steps left, he was overcome by a bizarre sense of unreality – was he really going through with this?

Suddenly they saw him. There was a sharp exclamation, a loud oath, and the two men jumped apart. One of them dropped into a crouch, as if to make a run for it.

'Stop or I shoot!' Nick heard his voice come out of the distance, as if it belonged to someone else. Had he really said that? It sounded like something out of a B-Western. They made no move. Then the one who'd been crouching straightened up slowly. There was a long electric pause. Nick tried to make out their faces, but it was too dark. What did one say next?

He began: 'What the hell do you think you're doing?'

One of them, the much taller of the two, relaxed his stance. There was something insolent in the gesture, as if he no longer considered himself at risk. That was it, of course: the fellow had realised that, far from facing the dreaded Duncan, who never had any compunction about peppering poachers' backsides with shot, he was dealing with an altogether softer opponent.

7

Nick held the gun higher to be sure the tall man could see it. 'Who are you?'

The man gave a grunt which was almost a laugh. 'I'd say that's for me to know an' you to find out.'

Nick's anger rose over him like a hot sea. 'I wouldn't take that attitude, if I were you.'

'No?' The man sounded unconvinced. 'What attitude should I take with a weapon pointin' at me? Intendin' murder, are you?'

'Why not – you're murdering the river!'

'I've never heard of a river bein' murdered. It doesna' look dead to me.' He was sounding very sure of himself now.

'But it soon bloody well will be. Then you'll have a chance to see what it looks like – when it's too bloody late!'

'Och well. Somethin' to see then.'

'You don't give a shit, do you?'

'I wouldna' say that,' came the cool reply. 'But then, why should I? An' then again, why should *you*? They say you're rich enough, eh?'

'What the hell's that got to do with it?' Nick's wrath wasn't helped by the realisation that the tall man knew exactly who he was.

The man pushed his head forward and spoke in fierce virtuous tones. 'You come in here, you buy up the place an' you think you own the entire country. You've no knowledge of our ways, no notion of our customs – '

'Your customs! You call years of wholesale poaching a custom! Christ – '

'No notion – '

'It's you who's got no notion, chum. The world won't put up with your sort any longer. Perhaps you haven't heard of conservation up here, but believe me the rest of the world has.' Nick waved the gun in a vaguely southerly direction.

'The rest of the world? Och, I beg your pardon.' The voice was heavy with sarcasm. 'It's in the name of conservation, is it, that your friends come up from London in their grand cars an' lord it over the place an' boast how they caught a salmon all by theirselves, eh? It's in the name of con-ser-vation' – he drew out the syllables scornfully – 'that we have to put up with your kind tellin' *us* what to do, is it?'

'There's been no fishing on this river for three years,' Nick cried in exasperation. 'And there'll be no fishing for years to

8

come either – not while you go on draining the bloody river dry.'

'No fishin', eh? Is that a fact?' The voice was both mocking and uncompromising. 'The folks round here will believe that when they see it. Let me tell you' – he raised a hand and Nick took a step backwards, momentarily misreading the gesture in the darkness – 'we've been comin' to this river for longer than any of us can remember. It's our right. We're not about to stop, not for the wild ideas of some loony pop star.'

Trembling with rage, Nick heard himself snap hotly: 'Song-writer.' No sooner said than regretted: what a time for accuracy.

A bow. 'Och, I beg your pardon.'

Nick flushed in the darkness, and let his anger carry him forward again. 'As for wild ideas, Christ, you can talk. You can't see any farther than the next easy buck. You don't give a damn about what happens to the river – '

'That we do!' the rough voice interjected, sounding injured. 'We want the fish back. It's not been good for us – '

'But they're not your fish!' Nick cried.

'An' what makes you think they're yours?'

'Damn it, they *are* mine!'

The other man didn't reply and Nick had the impression he was pulling a contemptuous face, even a laughing one.

Nick rushed on: 'Not good for you – God, you've a bloody nerve. If we're going to talk money, how much do you make a night, eh? Three hundred, five hundred? Who's the rich guy, then, eh?'

The comparison was a mistake, Nick knew it as soon as he said it. But the tall man wasn't about to bother with words, not when action would do, not when Nick had forgotten all about the gun and let the barrel drop. He came for the gun with a speed and confidence that caught Nick totally offguard. Grab-bing the barrel, he drove his body against Nick's and carried him backwards until Nick staggered, fighting for balance.

Finding his feet again, Nick held grimly on to the gun. But the tall man had the better grip and the better leverage, and as they grappled Nick could feel the weapon being slowly wrenched from his grasp. In his blind determination to hold on to the weapon, it was a moment before the vital realisation seeped dimly into his brain. The gun wasn't loaded, so why the hell was he battling for it? Even then it took a conscious

9

effort to overcome the instinctive urge to clutch on to it at all costs, and let go.

He was an instant too late. Just as he released his fingers, a powerful blow hit the back of his knees, knocking his legs from under him. He had the sensation of falling, then a jarring explosion came up and hit the side of his head and his brain was filled with flashes of brilliant light.

He had no sense of time when he woke. It took him a long while to remember where he was and why he was there. His head hurt with the sort of intense dagger-like pain that he remembered from spectacular bicycle crashes in his youth.

By screwing open one eye he registered the fact that the surface of the pool was reflecting the grey light of dawn. By swivelling the eye very carefully – he wasn't about to move his head, not yet anyway – he saw that the pool was deserted. The men had gone, and the net, and with them what would inevitably be a ruinous number of salmon.

His pride hurt almost as much as his skull. As a victim, he had been a gift. The tall man was probably laughing at this very moment.

The daggers began stabbing at his skull in earnest. He concentrated on feeling sorry for himself, an emotion he felt he richly deserved. He pulled his jacket closer round his neck and dimly registered the fact that something else had been placed over him, a coat of some sort. The coverings didn't prevent the cold from seeping up through the ground into his body, nor the sharp lump of rock from digging into the small of his back. But despite these aggravations, he no sooner closed his eyes than he fell into a heavy drug-like sleep.

Duggan was not at his best in the mornings, and certainly not when forced to get up at such an ungodly hour. It was four thirty when the alarm went off, and it was only the recollection of his precarious financial position that persuaded him to sit up and face the ugly little room with its single overhead light. He felt rotten. Having heard the favourable weather forecast the previous evening he'd been careful to keep off the booze – even in his most despondent moments, and there were all too many of those, he wasn't so stupid as to risk his licence – but he'd been hitting it hard earlier in the week, and for some obscure reason the hangover seemed to have caught up with him a few days late.

It took him ten minutes to dress, run an electric razor over his face and get downstairs. The landlady had said she would leave some food out for him and he peered expectantly into the darkened dining room, hoping for a pile of bacon sandwiches and a flask of coffee, but the shaft of light from the hall revealed a loaf of Mother's Pride, a pot of garish yellow margarine and a jar of runny marmalade. With weary resignation he slapped a sandwich together and went out to the car.

It was a ten-minute drive to the airfield. Automatically Duggan cast an eye at the dawn sky. No cloud, very little wind. He breathed a prayer of thanks. It was high time the weather went his way. He was paid piece rate – no flying, no money – although Acorn Flying Services Ltd did provide what was laughingly called a bad-weather retainer, a derisory sum that barely covered the cost of beer.

As he drove alongside the field he saw that the mechanic had got the generator and the two floodlights going, and was already poking around inside the Porter's engine. Outside the Portakabin which served as the local office of Acorn Flying Services (AFS) Ltd, Duggan was surprised to see a smart BMW, very shiny and very black. He could think of only one person who might have such a flash wagon, and when he had parked and stomped into the cabin his suspicions were confirmed.

Keen was at the table, poring over some papers. He was the executive director of AFS Ltd. According to the company's letterhead there were two other directors, who were so non-executive as to be invisible. At least Duggan had never met them, and he'd been here about three times as long as was good for him. But then Keen wasn't exactly a familiar face either; Duggan had seen him only once before when Keen had interviewed him at what was glowingly referred to as company head office – a couple of rooms in the converted stables of a country house north of Glasgow. During the interview Keen had spent all his time rattling orders down the phone to what appeared to be a host of operational offices at airfields all over Scotland. It was only later that Duggan had heard the rumours, which like all worrying gossip had proved to be absolutely true, that AFS was down to two aircraft, both of which were leased on short-term contracts, and, until the recent upsurge in business, had had severe financial

11

problems. The mention of financial difficulties had made Duggan nervous – he had quite enough of his own, thank you very much – but as long as the pay cheques kept coming through on time, then it was no concern of his.

Keen acknowledged him with a brusque nod and a frown at his gold Rolex. 'About time. Here – ' He tapped the chart spread out on the table. 'We've got a lot to cover today. Got to make up for all the bloody weather. Take off at six, preferably sooner. First job is the Drunour Estate. Three hundred acres of pine.' His finger stabbed a red-ringed area on the chart.

'What about the schedule? I thought – '

'No, Drunour first,' Keen interrupted testily and without explanation. 'Then we'll go back to the schedule.' He flicked through the typed sheets. 'Yes – job number 563 next. Then 568 if there's time.'

Duggan glanced over the job sheets and knew without making calculations that the three jobs would take him well over his official flying time, but made no comment. He needed the money too badly.

'No,' came Keen's voice. 'Forget that last one. We'll wind up with a little job by Loch Fyne.'

Duggan liked the way Keen talked about 'we', as if he himself was going to be up there all day, sweating it out in the poky cockpit of the Porter. Keen was red-pencilling a block of forest on the north side of Loch Fyne. Duggan cast an eye over it. A little job it was not. A hundred and fifty acres at least, and bloody hilly. Could be tricky. And tricky or not, he'd be lucky to get it finished that night. He glanced at the schedule: the job wasn't even typed up.

'It's not typed up,' he said.

'I'll write a job card now,' Keen said heavily.

'I won't have time to recce the site. And what about placing the Hi-Fix?' The electronic spray guidance system required two black box transmitters to be placed on high ground so as to give cross-bearings over the target area and thence, by means of a decoder in the cockpit, to guide the plane along corridors of precisely the right angle and width. Normally the black boxes were put in position by the second member of the ground crew, a singularly brainless oaf named Reggie.

Keen said with elaborate forbearance: 'You can do it on reciprocals, can't you?'

It wasn't worth arguing. Things had been hectic for weeks, ever since the panic about this new bug or moth or whatever it was that was gobbling up all the local forests. Duggan said: 'Allow me an extra fifteen minutes' flying time then.'

'Fifteen minutes?' Keen threw him a pitying glance. 'I thought you ex-fighter boys could do it backwards with your mind in neutral.' Duggan ignored this; he was used to facetious remarks from small-time flyers like Keen.

'What about the notifications?' he asked.

'I had assumed that Jeannie could just about manage that,' Keen said with heavy sarcasm.

Jeannie, who would drift in later, constituted the complete staff of the Portakabin office. Normally she sent the prior notifications to the local police, the local Health and Safety Executive and the properties adjacent to the spraying area by post a good couple of weeks before the expected spraying date, although in all the recent rush Duggan knew she had got behind. How she would cope with the need to leap into sudden and urgent action remained to be seen; even by local standards she wasn't exactly dynamite on the telephone.

Keen scribbled on the job card then, muttering something about going to see Davie the mechanic, hurried out of the Portakabin, leaving Duggan to ponder on the reason for his master's unexpected visit. Money troubles, probably: he had the look about him. Duggan should know; he saw a man with money troubles in the mirror every morning. He made a mental note to ask for his next week's money in cash.

Lighting another cigarette, Duggan settled down to look through the job descriptions and match them against the Ordnance Survey maps. The idea of double checking was to try to get the details right, details like spraying the correct forest, which was always a good start. Only a month before, he'd drenched a large corner of Forestry Commission land by mistake. Then, just last week, he'd showered a flock of sheep in a field that shouldn't have been there.

The sheep episode had refused to leave his mind, not because it was the first time such a thing had happened – it wasn't: cattle, sheep, horses, he'd given them all a dusting in his time – but because of the small dot of colour that had imprinted itself on the periphery of his memory – a dot glimpsed before it vanished under the wing, a dot that wasn't in the slightest sheep-like, a dot that should not under any reasonable circumstances have been there.

He got up to make a coffee and drank it with his fourth cigarette of the morning.

He reckoned up the flying time for the day. Even if he cut short his lunch break to the bare minimum, he'd be hard-pressed to finish all the jobs before nine that evening, uncomfortably close to twilight, and so far over his permitted flying time that it wasn't worth calculating.

As he glanced through the job card Keen had just scribbled, something caught his eye. It was the specification for the Loch Fyne job, a new chemical Keen had sent them out of the blue the week before, something which Jeannie had been writing up as ZXP, but which Duggan, congenitally allergic to technicalia, referred to as the new gunk. Duggan saw that Keen had used what must be the full name: Silveron ZXP.

The question was, would it be compatible with the old gunk they were using during the first half of the day? If not, they'd have to flush out the tanks, which would waste valuable time. He supposed he should ask Keen, since he seemed to be the only one who knew anything about the Loch Fyne job, but when Keen reappeared he was in a flap to get the show on the road and Duggan, not taking kindly to being goaded along, wasn't in the mood to ask.

In fact, what with having to fold an unusual number of charts and failing to find an aspirin for his growing headache and having to put up with Keen breathing down his neck and, most irritating of all, discovering that there was only one Mars Bar left in the box under Jeannie's desk, Duggan's temper was at rock bottom. And the day had only just begun.

At the edge of the forest Nick leaned against a tree and recovered his breath. Gingerly, he fingered the lump on his head and hoped it wasn't going to show. It would be better not to get embroiled in explanations. Alusha wouldn't understand. She'd give him that sideways look of hers, the one that asked him how he could have been such a fool, and he wouldn't be able to give her much of an answer.

It'd been hopelessly naive of him to think he could have a discussion, even an angry one, with a man in the act of breaking the law. And quoting conservation at him, that had been pie in the sky. The tall man was as likely to think green as to donate salmon to the poor and needy. As for the idea that everyone was going to stick to the quaint rules of conduct which required villains to turn and bolt – well, that cosy little myth looked pretty stupid now.

It wasn't the only myth looking shaky in the first light of day. He'd harboured this ridiculous idea that nothing unpleasant would ever happen at Ashard, that by settling his mind to it, by putting all his energies and emotions into the place, Ashard could become exactly what he wanted it to be – beautiful, flawless, safe. Now, with the night still fresh in his mind, nothing felt too safe any more, and some of the old bitterness and guilt come sourly into his mouth, and he remembered the suppressed rage that had haunted him when he and Alusha first left New York.

Yet, even as he looked out over the enormous panorama before him, he felt the place begin to work its old magic again. Light was expanding over the eastern hills in a brilliant show of gold and yellow that radiated into the tall blue dome of sky above the loch. The water itself was hidden under a thin grey mist, its surface dusted with gold as it caught the early light. There was a wonderful stillness to the air, broken only by birdsong and a sort of vibrant whisper, like the sound of the earth coming awake.

As the familiar delight began to creep through him, he folded the poacher's jacket into a cushion and settled down at the base of the tree. It was five thirty; until the rest of the world awoke this all belonged to him alone. Beneath him, the ground sloped gently away in a long sweep of rough pasture to the richer green of the wide park, with its tall beeches, oaks and cedars, standing like scattered sentries. Then, where the land flattened out slightly before continuing its onward fall to the loch, the house itself stood in its circle of gardens and lawns. There was a faint mist around the house, giving it an even more unreal and extravagant air than usual, like a castle created for a film set. A product of the nineteenth-century baronial building boom, Ashard came complete with mock keep, flagstaff and crenellations. It was not a beautiful house – the stonework was heavy, with reddish tone, the effect dark and sombre – but it had a solidity to it, a dependability that gave it the air of a large and ancient family pet. It was what Alusha called a house of character.

Despite encouragement from his friends, Nick had refrained

from flying anything from the flagstaff. A local heraldry expert had assured him that with a good Scots name like Mackenzie there'd be no trouble in finding a coat of arms, but having been born and raised in Chertsey, the depths of green-belt London suburbia, having come nowhere near Scotland for the first thirty-five years of his life, he felt that stuff like flags and coats of arms was not only inappropriate but ludicrously sentimental. Also, flags and pageantry might make Ashard look something of a joke, which it most certainly wasn't, a point on which he was particularly sensitive. Ashard was a working estate, the house his home, and he liked people to know it.

He'd never really wanted to live anywhere else, not since first seeing the place. Certainly not in the house in Provence that he'd owned briefly and visited three or four times, nor the place in the Bahamas he'd kept until last year and secretly hated, and certainly not the apartment in New York. Getting rid of them was the best thing he'd ever done. The only place he'd kept, apart from Ashard, was Caycoo, a small island in the Seychelles, where he and Alusha went every winter. Much as he loved Ashard, winter was not its best season.

He got up and stretched. He decided to walk the long way home, mainly to kill time. If he was going to pretend he'd gone for an early walk, he could hardly return yet.

He picked up the poacher's jacket and, taking the gun in his other hand, set off along the edge of the trees, heading east across the top of the pasture. His head ached at each step and he winced as his feet jarred over rough ground.

At the eastern corner of the pasture he came to the small dark round hill known as Meall Dhu – which meant, in the way of Gaelic names, dark round hill – and climbed it. It wasn't very high, but from its summit he could look out over the whole of this side of the estate and see high above him, rising over the tree line, the moorlands, daubed gold by the first splashes of sun; and beneath them, reaching as if to his feet, the wide band of mixed deciduous forest that was so much a feature of the Ashard Estate.

To the east the woodland curved round in a narrower band from one to three hundred yards wide, marking the estate boundary on that side. Beyond was the next-door Fincharn Estate. Owned by a London-based insurance company and

16

run solely for profit, it had been turned over to plantations of fast-growing Sitka spruce. Rising over a prominent hill, the dense regimented rows dominated and overshadowed the soft woodland and, to Nick's mind at least, spoilt the view.

He made his way slowly down the hill towards the railed paddock and Alusha's pony Rona. Rona, normally sedate and unexcitable, tossed her head at the sight of him. 'No treats,' he called out to her. 'Sorry.' Coming to the rail, she inspected his empty hands before turning her substantial buttocks on him and trotting off towards her stable.

He continued down, heading directly for the house. The mist was rising from the loch revealing waters the colour of gun-metal, very still and very dark. The loch was long, some forty miles from its head just beyond Inverary to the Firth of Clyde. Though Ashard was a long way from the open sea, he could often smell the salt in the air and sometimes, when up on the moors, he liked to imagine he could glimpse the open ocean beyond the distant Kintyre Peninsula, although he'd been told it was impossible.

He strolled down the steep slope that led from the paddock towards the walled garden, and stopped abruptly. A figure had appeared at the back of the house. It was Alusha, walking in that slow purposeful way of hers, her head high, her hair loose, a basket in one hand, like something out of a pre-Raphaelite painting.

Nick hesitated. He'd been intending to slip the shotgun unobtrusively into the house. Now, he realised, he'd have to think again.

Breaking the gun open, he hung it high over the branch of a rowan tree where it would be hidden behind a screen of foliage, then, after a moment's thought, hung the poacher's jacket alongside it.

Alusha had gone into the walled garden below him. He could see the top of her head as she bent to pick some vegetables. After a moment, she straightened up and stood very still, her face upturned. He knew exactly what she was doing: looking at the light spreading across the sky. The scene was so perfect, she looked so lovely, that his despondency lifted.

He touched the side of his head, checking the lump. It hadn't got any smaller. To cover it he agitated his hair into some sort of uniform confusion, then, brushing down his clothes, entered the walled garden by the nearest gate. Alusha was picking spinach.

'Well!' she exclaimed with a laugh. 'There you are! Where were you when I needed you?'

He gave her a brief kiss. 'Oh? What happened?'

She gave an expressive little shrug. 'Too late now.'

She had a way of being both suggestive and innocent all at the same time. A tantalising smile hovered on her mouth, and he kissed it again. What he really wanted to do was hug her very hard, not only because he loved her, and today more than ever, but because just looking at her was enough to make him feel the night had been nothing but a bad dream.

He settled on a small squeeze. Normally he wasn't at his most demonstrative before noon and anything more would have made her suspicious.

'What do you think our guests would like for breakfast?' she asked.

Nick had forgotten about them. 'Mel's never been a great one for breakfast,' he said. 'As for David – coffee I should think.'

'And you?' She looked up at him and her smile turned into a small frown. 'What have you been up to? Digging with the rabbits? You're covered in dirt.'

Nick ran a hand over his cheek. 'Don't laugh,' he said. 'I fell over.'

She laughed. 'What were you doing?'

'Tripped over a bramble,' he said, avoiding the question.

'Next you'll tell me you grazed your knee and need a sticky bandage.'

'A sticky plaster,' he automatically corrected her. It was a habit from the days when Alusha's English was fragmentary.

'Poor love,' she murmured with a soft laugh, and reached up as if to stroke his head.

He ducked quickly away. 'Must go and shower.' He blew her a kiss to stifle the faint surprise in her face. She watched him for a moment, narrowing her eyes in a sidelong glance that was both affectionate and suspicious at the same time, then gave a small wave, a slow fluttering of the fingers, before turning back to her vegetables.

It took him a while to find something for his headache. Pills

18

and potions, though not exactly banned at Ashard House, weren't encouraged either.

As Nick crossed the hall, the phone rang.

'Mr Mackenzie, if you please.' It was a male voice with a local accent.

'Yes.'

There was a pause. 'Is that you yourself, Mr Mackenzie?'

'It is.'

'You're back then,' the voice said.

Nick stiffened, then, as realisation came, he almost laughed with incredulity. 'You've got a bloody nerve!'

'An unfortunate mishap, Mr Mackenzie. Ma friend, he didna' mean for you to fall on the rock. He wasna' thinkin'.'

'Wasn't thinking! He almost killed me.'

'It was the gun,' the voice chided. 'If it hadna' been for the gun nothin' would have occurred, I think you'll agree.'

'Agree! My mistake was not using the bloody thing. Next time I won't make the same mistake.'

A short pause. 'In that case, Mr Mackenzie, it might be wise to try loadin' it.'

Nick gripped the side of the table. 'I'll remember that. Thank you for mentioning it.'

'Not at all. I trust your head mends good an' quick. An' if you'd leave ma coat by the back there, I'd be obliged. You've a wood store, have you not. If you would leave it there, just inside the door.' There was a soft click as he rang off.

Nick wrenched the receiver from his ear and, holding it inches from his face, stared at it, unable to speak.

Then he gave a short exasperated cry. He was still muttering when he stepped under the shower.

TWO

Saturday, Saturday. Daisy awoke feeling guilty, and it was a moment before she remembered that there was no need. She felt a wash of relief. No need to jump out of bed to push oranges through the expensive Californian juicer, which took hours to clean, no need to pound down the street to fetch newly baked croissants, nor feed freshly roasted coffee into the grinder whose screech carved right into her brain.

But then Richard would have put up with anything to get these things right. She knew the end had come when he decided it was time to get into heavy opera, and, not being one to do things by halves, had made her sit through over five hours of *Götterdämmerung*. She wouldn't have minded if opera had been a genuine passion, but like most things with Richard, it was a matter of social éclat. Something that had to be endured to get his lifestyle into shape.

At the opera, during one of the all-too-short intervals, Daisy had failed to live up to cultural expectations in front of Richard's friends by allowing her south London accent out of its cage – as often happened in times of exasperation or stress – and asking who this Wagner geezer thought he was anyway, rambling on for longer than *Ben Hur*, giving people stiff bums and tired brains?

She was so used to waking to the sound of Richard showering – a signal that the rush to create the perfect breakfast must begin – that it was a moment before she identified what had woken her. It was, she realised, the ring, click and buzz of the answering machine. A little early for a social call, which was the only sort she was interested in, but she got out of bed and checked the machine anyway.

'Daisy, something's come up – '

'Oh no, it hasn't,' she said switching the machine firmly off. She didn't need Alan's voice first thing on a Saturday morning, not when she'd heard it all week in the office. What she needed was some calls from her friends, an invitation to a party or two, and while she was waiting for that, a bit of self-indulgence. Now that it was no longer an offence to be a slob, she wanted to go the whole hog – milky Nescafé, the *Sun* and the blare of Capital Radio while reclining on her uncoordinated sheets. And for afters – yes, a bowl of Coco Pops with full-cream milk – none of your skimmed stuff – and a heavy lacing of white sugar, followed by toast made from steam-baked sliced muck from Gateways.

She pottered off to the rabbit-hutch of a kitchen and five minutes later was back in bed with a steaming mug of coffee which, coming straight from the jar, tasted like nectar. The newspapers, despite being yesterday's, weren't bad either, mainly because for the first time in months she passed straight over the *Guardian* and the *Independent* in favour of the tabloids and read all the silly bits.

Skimming through the papers was a regular item in her life, and when pushed she could get through all eight of the main rags in twenty minutes without missing anything very important. She took cuttings on most environmental articles, whether or not they related directly to Catch. Three years ago, when she'd started with Catch, she'd been lucky to find as many as three Green articles in a week of tabloid-reading. Now the office files fairly bulged with Green news, views and opinions.

Anything on chemicals or toxicity was of special interest, of course, but then she usually knew when something like that was coming up. The press, being short on time and information, and lazy to boot, often contacted her for their facts. After she'd done all their work for them she'd give them an earful on the government's environment policy – not a subject she ever felt reticent about – before spelling out Catch's name in full – the Campaign Against Toxic Chemicals – and telling them to put it in big letters near the top of the article, preferably with an appeal for funds. They never did, of course, but she lived in hope. If she hadn't been a dedicated career optimist she wouldn't have been in this job in the first place.

At eleven, when she'd exhausted the last gossip column, she finally got up and, pulling on some jeans and a sweater, went down the hill to Mr Patel's to fetch the Saturday papers.

She still wasn't quite sure why she'd chosen to live here on the borders of Tufnell Park and Upper Holloway. To the east was a ragbag of two-roomed flats and bedsits and crumbling terraces that housed every nationality, and a few more besides. To the west, ranks of grey-brick villas undulated over the switchback of hills that led up to Highgate. Inhabited by writers and academics, classless *Guardian*-readers and women who did pottery – professionally, mind you – and precocious chess-playing kids, it was another continent after the conspicuous consumption of SW3.

And Richard's consumption had been particularly conspicuous – designer haircuts, hand-made shirts, car phones, restaurants six nights a week – though, pig that she was, she'd miss the food all right – and a BMW convertible, for God's sake, which had taken a bit of explaining away at Catch, where the employees – a grand total of three including Daisy herself – were on wages that would have caused the tightest employer to blush.

Daisy hadn't always been poor. In fact until she gave up her job as a solicitor specialising in family law her salary, being firmly tied to the divorce rate, had been buoyant and rising fast. But three years ago, taken by the thought that there had to be more to life than the breakdown of the family unit she'd decided to go for broke, quite literally, by joining the anti-chemical group. She hadn't regretted it. Well, only when she was stupid enough to worry about money.

The newspapers didn't get any lighter, not even when Mr Patel handed them over with an apologetic smile. By the time she had bought Coco Pops, milk, jam, butter (a cholesterol no-no in SW3), a tin of mackerel, fruit, and a sticky cream cake (roughage-free), the walk back up the hill to number 50C Augustus Road became something of a trek.

Climbing, she planned her day. Coco Pops, papers, then work on the flat. The word flat was estate agent's hyperbole really: it was more of a one-roomed space with cubbyholes daringly described as bathroom and kitchen. The place was a new conversion of a Victorian house in a shabby terrace, and it was only after she'd moved in that she began to understand why the rent was affordable. The ceiling was so thin you could hear the two Greek waiters in the flat above arguing, which, being lovers, they did frequently; the fittings were so flimsy that the lever-type plastic door handles had assumed permanent downward curves, there was a chronic shortage of hanging space, and there wasn't a single door that wasn't slightly warped. That said, it was on the first floor with a large bay window which faced south, and the girl she shared it with, a social worker called Anthea, spent four days out of every seven at her boyfriend's.

She struggled in through the flat door just as the phone rang. A social call. One lived in hope anyway.

It was Alan again.

'Don't want to hear from you.'

'Didn't you get my message?' he asked. 'Listen – your Mrs Knowles. Something's come up.'

'Oh?'

'She's planning a one-woman demo at some agricultural show in Berkshire.'

Daisy groaned softly and said, more to herself than to Alan: 'What does she want to go and do that for?'

'Don't know, but it could spoil your coverage.'

Daisy didn't need reminding. She'd been working on the Knowles story for two months and now it was within a week of being ready to tout round the quality press as a subject for a serious investigative piece. The last thing it needed was Mrs Knowles making scenes at some agricultural show, and having the tabloids make her look like some kind of agitator.

'How did you hear?' she asked.

'Local pressman. Left a message on the office machine. Wanted some background. Apparently Mrs Knowles has talked to him and promised him the whole story. He says he's going to try to string it to a national.'

Daisy sat down heavily on the bed. 'Why, for God's sake?'

She could almost see Alan shrugging at the other end of the line. 'Finally got to her?' he suggested. 'Flipped her lid?'

'Don't even mention it.' But the thought had already occurred to her. Alice Knowles was under intolerable pressure; many lesser people would have cracked before now. 'When's this meant to be happening?' she asked.

'At three this afternoon.'

End of quiet Saturday.

Daisy tried calling Alice Knowles, but there was no reply. Already left for the show, perhaps. Or lying low, avoiding the phone.

There was nothing for it then, not if all the work wasn't going to go up the spout. Quite apart from anything else, she rather liked Mrs Knowles; it would be dreadful to see her disappointed, maybe even humiliated.

The case was typical of many that came Catch's way. The Knowleses were a farming family with seven hundred acres of good arable land not far from Newbury. Nice hard-working people, reasonably prosperous, distinctly law-abiding. Like most farmers, they worked with large quantities of chemicals. But unlike most other families they had been unlucky or not careful enough, or both, and now things had gone wrong.

But was a demonstration going to help? Daisy tried to imagine what sort of protest Alice Knowles might be planning. Handing out leaflets, setting up a stall? Not so bad. Banner waving, shouting, speech making? Not so good. In the minds of much of the press any sort of jumping up and down was still firmly associated with weirdos and political agitators, and while they might print a two-line protest story, they were unlikely to give the item the space it deserved. Alice would be written off as an isolated old woman with a grievance, and Daisy's chances of getting a serious investigative piece would be that much reduced.

But there might still be time to pre-empt things. Leafing through her address book, she found the number of Simon Calthrop, a *Sunday Times* journalist she'd just met. Simon was a committed environmental reporter, just as he'd been a committed consumer affairs correspondent two years before, and a dedicated investigative reporter the year before that.

He sounded grumpy when he answered the phone. 'Can't do anything this week,' he began unpromisingly.

'As a human interest story then,' Daisy suggested. 'You know, how ordinary people are driven to desperate acts. It could make a good photo feature.'

'Mmm.' He sounded unconvinced. 'So tell me about it.'

Daisy told him about the family and how the medical tests had shown them to have high levels of pesticide residues in their bodies – the residue of several pesticides unfortunately, and not just one or two, so that it was impossible to know

24

which particular chemical or cocktail of chemicals might have caused their troubles. But Daisy had her suspicions. For years the Knowleses had been using the pesticide Aldeb on their potato crop. She reminded Simon that Aldeb was under notice of withdrawal in the US because of fears that it was carcinogenic.

'And in Britain?' he asked.

'Here?' Daisy gave a derisive laugh. 'You know how it is – everything takes a little longer. The ministry did their usual trick and rejected the US research on the grounds that it was inconclusive. Aldeb's still heading the best-sellers' list.'

'Mmm.' He wasn't sounding enthralled by the story so far. 'Aldeb's who, remind me?'

'Morton-Kreiger. They've just announced their results. Worldwide profits of three hundred million, give or take the odd million. Pounds, that is.'

'And what's their response been? You've contacted them, presumably.'

Daisy was beginning to realise that, for all his erudite environmental articles, Simon still didn't know everything about the workings of agrochemical companies. 'What response?' she replied caustically. 'You must be joking. I'm always referred to their legal department.'

He took the point, though she could sense that he didn't appreciate it being made so forcefully. Tactlessness – and instant regret – were such a regular feature of her life that she automatically backtracked, adding quickly: 'What I mean is, they've been less helpful than they could have been.'

'Listen, this isn't exactly straightforward,' Simon said. 'If there's a story, it could take weeks to dig out. I really don't think there'd be much point in covering this woman and her demonstration this afternoon, not at this stage – '

'Maybe not, but let me come over with the file,' Daisy urged. 'It's impressive, I promise you. The story could be an important one. At least we think so. And if we're right, then a lot of farmers could be at risk.' He was silent, but Daisy could sense a flicker of interest. 'Needless to say,' she added, 'you'd have full access to all our material.'

Another pause. She'd almost got him.

'Where do you live?' she asked.

He lived in Islington. After a detour to the office at King's Cross to pick up the Knowles file and the draft press releases,

25

she made it in forty minutes. His flat was on the third floor of a tall house in a rubbish-strewn street off the Pentonville Road. The main room was basic but comfortable, with a couple of deep sofas, a Habitat dining-table and an expensive-looking Scandinavian hi-fi system. There were a few good etchings on the walls, a dying fig tree in the window and on the floor several piles of magazines and newspapers. A functional if untidy kitchen was visible through a half-open door.

A typical bachelor flat – or was it? She found herself casting around for signs of female occupation, and was surprised at herself. Was she making room for a new man in her life? More to the point, was she considering the rather dry, unemotional Simon?

He emerged from the kitchen with two mugs of coffee. He was wearing the rumpled but carefully assembled uniform of the north London intellectual: well-worn jeans, open-necked safari-style shirt which, if it had encountered an iron at all, had met it only briefly, and old tennis shoes. He had a pale face, glasses with minimal gold frames, dark eyebrows that feathered over the bridge of his nose and heavy black hair which kept falling over his eyes.

She took him through the file, item by item. Eventually he said wearily: 'It could make a small item, I suppose . . . Or a major investigative piece. But I can't see anything in between.'

'Okay then,' Daisy said immediately. 'Make it a major investigative piece.'

He gave a weighty sigh. 'I've got two big features on the go at the moment . . . I couldn't possibly start on anything yet. Not for some time, in fact.'

'But soonish?' She was pressing him, she knew it, but it was vital to screw some sort of commitment out of him, however tenuous. 'We could get more data, I'm sure of it,' she said more out of hope than certainty. 'Other victims and that sort of thing.'

'Oh? Where from?'

She had to think quickly. 'Umm, the unions. The NFU, the Transport and General Workers.' She had in fact already spent long hours with the health-and-safety officers of the two unions, combing their files. The National Farmers' Union had produced a number of cases which might be traceable to Aldeb, but the evidence had been sketchy even by Daisy's

26

undemanding standards. There were hundreds of cases out there, Daisy was sure of it; the victims just didn't know what had hit them.

'Okay.' Simon gave another, sharper sigh. 'Find what you can and when I've got the time I'll have a look at it.'

She had to settle for that. She took another coffee off him all the same, partly to satisfy her curiosity about him, partly to argue her case again should the chance arise, which it soon did. If she was being dogged, it was because in this line of work opportunites had to be grabbed as they arose and then shaken into life. It wasn't enough to have right on your side; that never got anyone anywhere.

'Of course it *has* been known for the Americans to get it wrong,' Simon said. 'They can over-react.'

'What, on Aldeb?' Daisy exclaimed. 'Have you seen the evidence?'

He shrugged, as if nobody of any sense could seriously believe that anything, even scientific evidence, could be taken at face value. 'To provide balance I'd have to interview Morton-Kreiger. Get their side of things.'

'I wish you luck,' she said drily. 'I'd be interested to know what they have to say.'

Simon, making an obvious effort to be sociable, asked about her background. She told him about being brought up in Catford, famous for the greyhound stadium, how her father had encouraged her to get some A-levels and try for a law scholarship to Birmingham, which she didn't get. Her parents had sent her all the same, though it was a strain financially. They thought education set you apart. It did, in Catford at least. None of my school friends ever spoke to me again. I had a best friend called Samantha who thought I'd got totally above myself. The last I heard, she was earning a thousand quid a week as a nude model. My only consolation is that my assets are likely to hold up longer than hers.'

Simon's forehead creased. 'Assets?'

Daisy studied him carefully but he wasn't having her on.

Comprehension finally slid over his face and his mouth cracked into a nominal grin. 'I'm a bit slow this morning. Late night,' he said with a hint of pride, and she wondered what – or who – had been keeping him up so late.

Letting it pass, she went on with the story, about her years at Birmingham and coming back to London and all the divorces she'd processed and how she'd despaired at married people's general desire to tear each other apart, and how she'd wanted to bash their heads together when they fought over the children. 'The only thing that kept me going was the light relief. After five years, what I didn't know about sexual proclivities wasn't worth stamping on a pinhead.'

Her life story had never been particularly exciting, even when she spiced it up a bit, but it was still disconcerting to find Simon staring past her towards the window, looking preoccupied. If there was potential in a relationship with Simon, then it was failing to reveal itself.

'Well,' she said, 'a pity to cut this short, but I must be going.'

He looked mildly sorry, which was a surprise. 'Ah.'

'I've got to go and see Alice Knowles.'

'I'll give you a ring next week then, shall I?' He shot her a quick glance. 'There's a good film on at the Screen.'

So it was to be social? Was he keen after all? If so, he'd done a brilliant job of concealing it. More to the point, how keen was she?

Perhaps he caught the doubt in her eyes, because he blinked at her through his spectacles and said: 'Sorry if I've been less than . . . er . . . *compos*, you know. But I was up till four. Working.'

'Till four? God, they push you hard.'

'No, no. I was working on . . . well, my novel.' He looked defensive, as if he'd just let her into a devastating secret and wasn't sure how she'd take it.

'Your novel?'

'Yes. Nights are the only chance I get.'

This explained the preoccupied look, and in her mind his image underwent an instantaneous metamorphosis from harassed journalist to tortured novelist. She agreed to go the cinema with him later in the week.

Daisy's W-registration Metro was perfectly adequate for London, but in recent months it had started to balk at motorways, and, reaching the M4, it began to grumble. A mechanic had told her the suspension was on its way out, a problem which hadn't sounded too serious in Chelsea, but which here on the open road was definitely ominous. She stuck to the slow lane, ambling along with the family traffic and swaying caravans, and hoped there wouldn't be too many jams getting into the show.

A few miles short of Newbury it began to rain, solid permeable stuff that seeped in through the bodywork, but it eased off a little as she took the slip-road and followed the signs towards the showground at Newbury racecourse. The traffic, though heavy, was still moving and she made it into the field-cum-car park by a few minutes before three. The rain, choosing its moment, fell heavily again. She did not have an umbrella. Getting out, her feet sank ominously into the sodden grass. She pulled her jacket over her head, mainly to protect the sheaf of press releases that she had under her arm.

Green wellies, dun-coloured waxed jackets, headscarves with chains and anchors; horsy women who talked in loud authoritative voices, farming types with jutting chins and grouchy expressions who looked as if they shot everything that moved, and probably did; also people, like Daisy, in unsuitable shoes, men in thin shirts and women in summer dresses sheltering from the rain. It was a big show and she had to ask the way to the agrochemical merchants' stand a couple of times before finally locating it half-way down an aisle of large marquees, lodged between a bank and a brewery.

Nothing. No Mrs Knowles chained to the railings. No Mrs Knowles brandishing a large placard. But there was a young man dripping quietly under the porch, sheltering a camera under his jacket, wearing the watchful lugubrious expression of a pro.

Daisy retreated to the bank next door and waited beneath their tented porch on a boardwalk. Three fifteen. Still no sign of Mrs Knowles. Then Daisy spotted the small purposeful figure in brogues and a long raincoat marching up the avenue of stands with a flat parcel under one arm. She was flanked by four men, and Daisy recognised the long waterproof jackets and energetic strides of provincial pressmen.

Alice was travelling fast. Daisy hurried to intercept her before she reached the agrochemical stand.

She didn't seem surprised at the sight of her. She even managed a faint smile. 'Oh, hullo, Daisy,' she said, stepping neatly past her and continuing her onward progress.

'Mrs Knowles – Alice – look, are you sure this is a good idea?' Daisy said, hurrying to keep up.

29

She didn't slow down. 'Well, something's got to be done, hasn't it?'

'Yes, but . . .' Eyeing the reporters, Daisy dropped her voice. 'What about our press release? What about the evidence and the meeting with the man from the ministry? I thought we were going to wait, like we agreed.'

Alice narrowed her lips and said firmly: 'Can't wait any longer.'

'But why now, Alice? Why so suddenly?'

She snorted and shook her head. 'Got a letter from the government safety people. Told me I was talking rubbish.'

'But, Alice – one letter.'

'Four years' hell and the blighters aren't even listening,' Alice retorted. 'Can't wait any longer.'

Daisy took her arm and whispered: 'I know how you feel, Alice, but listen – people aren't going to understand something like this . . . It might actually put them off, you know. They're going to think – well, that you're overdoing it a bit.'

'Oh?' Alice Knowles stuck her chin out. 'Well, we'll see, won't we?' Her hair, normally grey and bouncy, was plastered darkly over her forehead. Rivulets of water ran down her cheeks and hung from her nose in droplets. With her square face and jutting jaw, she looked like a bull terrier, small and very determined.

'Alice – I really don't think this is the best way.'

'If Jane Fonda can protest and get her picture in the paper, why can't I?'

Oh my Lord, Daisy thought, there's no answer to that. About the only thing Alice Knowles and Jane Fonda had in common was their age.

'Alice –'

But Alice wasn't listening any more. Having given her face an abrupt wipe on her sleeve, she was tackling the wrapping on her parcel, which looked uncomfortably like a placard.

'What's the story?' a reporter murmured in Daisy's ear.

Where did one start? Tragedy sounded trite when reduced to a few sentences. Instead, Daisy fumbled under her jacket and pulled out one of her press releases.

'Thanks.' The reporter skimmed through it. 'Can this be proved? I mean is it certain that this stuff killed her husband?'

'Depends what you mean by proof,' Daisy said. 'We've got

30

two doctors' opinions. Aldeb was found in his blood and body tissue – '

'But is that proof? You know . . .'

She knew all right. He meant, was it signed and sealed and agreed upon by the entire scientific community, the whole medical profession and all the various government departments. The answer was, of course, no. In fact: no, no and no. Not one body or group agreed on anything. Quite the opposite in fact: many so-called experts would rather die than admit to the possibility of agreeing with other experts in their own field.

'As much proof as one can ever get,' she said truthfully.

'Oh.' By the sound of his voice, he had lost interest and would probably have slipped away if the action, such as it was, hadn't been about to start.

The wrapping was off what was indeed a placard. Alice Knowles turned to face her audience, which consisted of the small knot of reporters and photographers, and a group of unsuspecting show-goers sheltering from the rain. She clasped the placard against her body, message inwards, so that no one could read it until she was ready.

She cleared her throat and began in a fierce emotional voice: 'I've come here today out of desperation. I've come to make myself heard because no one'll listen . . .' The show-goers began to shuffle imperceptibly backwards, as if this sudden burst of sincerity and passion might be dangerous. '. . . I couldn't let this thing go unchallenged any more. I have already lost my husband. Now I'm in danger of losing my son . . .' The crowd had stopped shuffling and was now rigid with amazement. '. . . They were both perfectly healthy men, nothing wrong with them, never been to a doctor in their lives. Not until they made the mistake of believing wholesale lies. Not until they made the mistake of believing the totally meaningless assurances they were given by the manufacturers of Aldeb and the Ministry of Agriculture . . .' The listeners weren't sure about that; nor, for that matter, was Daisy. *Too much, Alice; too strong, too moralistic.* The onlookers began to exchange glances and dive off into the rain in search of fresh shelter.

Sensing the crowd's restlessness, Alice faltered and seemed to lose her thread but then, fixing the reporters with her intense stare, she got a second wind and launched forth again. 'I want to prevent this happening to other families. I want to make sure no one has to suffer as we have suffered. I want these dangerous untested chemicals banned, and not just to protect people like us, farmers who have to work with these poisons, but to save every man, woman and child in this country. To save everyone who's eating and drinking these dreadful things and doesn't realise it.'

She went on for a bit, talking about the unrealised menace of pesticides, their role in disease – she quoted almost every incurable disease in the book, though where she'd got those ideas from, Daisy couldn't imagine – then, having repeated herself a few times, tailed off.

Daisy thought: Oh, *Alice*. It was a gallant little speech, bravely delivered but seriously misjudged. Daisy gave her a little cheer all the same. The pressmen looked less than bowled over.

Suddenly remembering the placard, Alice Knowles turned it round and held it up. It read: BAN DEADLY CHEMICALS – BAN ALDEB – BAN POISONS THAT KILL INNOCENT FARMERS.

A photographer dutifully took a picture or two. A local radio reporter advanced on Alice and pointed a microphone at her. Daisy handed out press releases. But it was no good, she knew it was no good. The popular press didn't like one-woman demos any more than they liked stories about obscure chemicals, shadowy unseen things neither they nor their readers knew or cared to know about, not when there were good old bogey men like nuclear power to pick on, not when they had tear-jerking pictures of children with leukaemia, not when they had villainous substances that were certified guaranteed all-bad, things like PCPs, CFCs and leaded petrol.

Poor Alice. Husband dead of cancer. Only son fighting the disease. She'd believed that her evidence, with the opinion of two doctors, would be enough to get her some sort of justice; she'd imagined that the world would listen. Well, she'd learnt differently, and now she was going to be disappointed all over again.

Not that the event was over. The agrochemical merchants had finally woken up to the fact that someone was saying nasty things about one of the products on their stand. A small bullish man had shoved his way through the onlookers and pushed his face close to Alice's. Daisy couldn't hear what was said, but Alice drew back, looking at once nervous and defiant, then, rallying, pulled herself up to her full height, which wasn't very much, and stood her ground.

Daisy stepped forward. 'Can I help?'

The bullish man spun round. 'She's got to go, or I'll have to call the police.'

Daisy was soothing. 'She's finished now, I think. Just making a point. Quite peaceably.'

But he wasn't having any of that. 'Off – *now*. This minute.'

'Well, of course, if that's – '

Alice cut in: 'I refuse to leave, I'm afraid.'

'Right,' said the bullish man, vibrating with sudden rage. 'If that's the way you want it, no problem. I'll get the police to remove you forcibly.' And elbowing his way past Daisy, he swept off into the rain.

Not surprisingly, the pressmen had changed their minds about going and were now waiting patiently for their police-remove-lady pictures. They weren't disappointed. It was an ugly little scene, and Daisy felt a lurch of humiliation for Alice Knowles. Once the two policemen had established that she wasn't going to go willingly, they took an elbow each and marched her towards the showground entrance. As Daisy set off after them, she looked back and saw the bullish man pick up the placard and break it across his knee.

It took quite a while to get Alice Knowles back into some sort of shape. Despite her brave front, she was badly shaken. She'd never experienced the police in anger before. Daisy drove her to a motorway café and fed her tea and biscuits for over an hour before deciding it was safe to take her back to the ground to collect her car.

They sat in the Metro for a while, watching the rain course down the windscreen.

Alice gave a deep sigh. 'I suppose I've been a bit of an ass,' she said.

'I wouldn't say that!' Daisy said quickly. 'A bit of an optimist maybe.'

'I had to do something.'

'I know.'

'What next then?'

'Well, I'll have another go at the live wires in the ministry,' said Daisy. 'Beat them over the head, you know. Interrupt their tea break, remind them we're not going to go away and give up.'

'Do you really think they'll listen?'

It was hard to explain to people like Alice just how obtuse and convoluted were the workings of the Ministry of Agriculture, Fisheries and Food. MAFF had until a few years ago worked entirely on the principle that pesticide manufacturers were all frightfully good honest chaps, and should be allowed to run their own chemical safety scheme on a voluntary basis, administered by the ministry's Advisory Committee on Pesticides. The safety scheme was now legally enforced, which was a step in the right direction, but that didn't prevent the activities of the ACP from being secretive, and their findings unchallengeable. Worse, there was no proper watchdog in the UK, nothing like the USA's Environmental Protection Agency, no one to re-examine the manufacturer's safety tests to make sure they had been sufficiently thorough, no one to challenge the widespread official view that chemicals were all right until they turned round and bit you. Ludicrously, the Ministry of Agriculture, Fisheries and Food was meant to represent not only the farmer and the agrochemical industry – groups whose interests were often diametrically opposed – but also the consumer. And though consumers might have a number of vague worries about the amount of chemicals in their food, it was the farming and agrochemical lobbies that had all the clout. Outsiders, people like the Knowleses, found it hard to understand just how low consumer interests came in the pecking order. Getting information out of the ACP or MAFF was like extracting a tasty bone from the teeth of a fierce dog: almost impossible without a large stick and a lot of muscle. Catch had neither.

'We'll get to them in the end,' Daisy said with a conviction she didn't entirely feel. 'There's our tame MP, Jimmy. He's had four shots at getting a question at prime minister's question time. Might be fifth time lucky.'

'But it's no good, is it? Any of it.'

Daisy laughed. 'Blimey, Alice, if I thought that, I might as well tie my ankles together and jump in the river. Honestly, I'd give up tomorrow if I thought I was getting nowhere. It's just *slow* that's all. Like swimming through wet concrete. But we'll get there in the end. I do believe that, Alice, I do, really, otherwise I wouldn't be bothering.'

Alice was slumped in the seat. Her hair had dried into a grey frizz. She looked exhausted. 'But they won't even speak to us, will they? Won't tell us anything. That's not going to change, is it?'

'Well – no, not for the moment,' Daisy admitted. Incredibly, information on certain types of pesticides came under the Official Secrets Act because the chemicals had been developed from nerve gases. No good pointing out that almost every belligerent country in the world – and there were enough of them, God only knew – was well aware of how to produce nerve gases. No good arguing that information on this type of pesticide was freely available in the US. The British loved secrets. Correction: the British *Establishment* loved secrets – a different thing. The information that wasn't protected by the Official Secrets Act was covered by that old stalwart of profit-making prevaricators – commercial confidentiality. MAFF and the pesticide manufacturers looked after each other very nicely, thank you. From the rosy picture the two of them painted, you'd never have thought there'd ever been a mishap, far less a disaster. No DDT, no 2,4,5-T, no dioxins. Very cosy, very frustrating, and very difficult to comprehend when all you wanted was the answer to a few simple questions like why and how, and can't this be prevented from happening again.

Alice blew into a handkerchief with a blast like a ship's siren, and shook her head. 'Just what will it take?'

Daisy knew the answer to that. Cast-iron scientific proof in triplicate. A silenced agrochemical lobby (that would be the day). Further disaster.

'They're banning it in the States,' Daisy reminded her. 'It'll get banned here in the end too.'

'But when?'

Daisy sighed. 'Good question.'

'What will it take?' Alice repeated, almost to herself.

'Money, I'm afraid, Alice. Pots of dough. On a scale I don't even dare think about.'

Alice nodded with weary resignation. She began to get out of the car. 'I'll send you a cheque when I can.'

Daisy's throat tightened. 'Oh, Alice, don't. Keep your money. You'll be needing it.'

Alice didn't reply but climbed out and slammed the door.

Daisy wound the window down and called after her: 'Sure you'll be all right?'

Alice gave a small wave and got into her car. Daisy watched

to make sure she got away all right, thinking that if only worthiness and dedication were enough, then the Alices of this world would keep Catch going for ever. But Catch ran on hard cash, and it took a shocking number of small cheques from the likes of Alice to keep it afloat. And that was without any wild notions about an independent research programme.

Put off by the rain, people were going home early and there were long queues of cars leaving the ground.

A research programme or two . . . And a proper press office, professional parliamentary lobbyists, a national membership organisation, a glossy newsletter . . . Well, the list was endless. All it needed was what Catch's accountant liked to call a healthy injection of cash. But then what campaigning organisation didn't need that? The few outfits that had managed to trap a tame environmentally minded millionaire kept good and quiet about it – and who could blame them – and those that hadn't, which was an awful lot, sat like alley cats, waiting to pounce on a passing moneypots, fully prepared to scratch each other's eyes out in the process. Green campaigning wasn't quite the benevolent business people imagined it to be.

Finally getting away from the showground, Daisy pointed the Metro in the direction of London, thinking about money, wondering what she could salvage from her press campaign on the Knowles story, and doing her best to ignore the grinding noises coming from the suspension.

THREE

David Weinberg awoke with a sense of alarm. It was a moment before he was able to identify the reason. It was the quiet; a pervasive and sinister sort of hush. For David, a Londoner born and bred, silence was unsettling: it was the world standing still, someone else getting a deal, and being dead and knowing all about it, all rolled into one.

The sound of a car in the drive reassured him sufficiently to get up. His instinct was to reach for the phone and start worrying his way through the day, but he remembered this was Saturday, he was in the middle of Scotland and this was supposed to be a break, something people like him were meant to need, though he could never understand why, since leisure had never done anything for him except upset his stomach.

Once dressed, he wandered downstairs in search of Nick. The house was quiet, the doors around the large flag-stoned hall open, no sounds issuing from the sunlit rooms. Only in the kitchen were there signs of life: coffee on a hot stand, croissants in a warming dish, butter and marmalade on the table. He helped himself to coffee, added forbidden sugar, and looked for the newspapers. Then he remembered: Nick had told him they didn't arrive before late morning.

Without the *Financial Times* the croissant tasted bland, the coffee flat. The kitchen was pleasant enough – Nick had always spent a lot of money on his homes – but if David couldn't look at the share index then he would like some company. Shoving the last of the croissant into his mouth, picking up his coffee cup, he went in search of the household.

37

The formal living room was, as expected, empty. The room was high and vaulted, with polished wood floors, Persian rugs, Victorian-style high-backed chairs, long damask-covered settees and a vast baronial fireplace crying out for stags' heads which, this being Nick's and Alusha's house, it would never get.

Nick called this the drawing room – a bit grand, David thought, even for such a grand room. There was something delightfully incongruous about Nick, whose family had never inhabited anything more impressive than a small lounge, talking about a drawing room as if he'd lived in one all his life. But then the Nick of Ashard House wasn't the same boy that David had first met in the poky Chertsey semi all those years ago – and that was just as it should be. Of all his people, David had been – perhaps still was – proudest of Nick. Nick had made the most of himself; Nick, as David's mother used to say, had made good. He'd never allowed himself to be taken in by the lunacy of fame and the endless flow of cash. Nick had gone his own way, in his own way.

Standing behind one of the long settees was a large drinks trolley, thickly forested with bottles. At one time Nick's way had included the drink, of course; but even then he had drunk with style, unobtrusively, almost secretively. Unlike Mel and Joe, there'd been no benders, no downhill races towards self-destruction, no stoking up on chemical cocktails. Not to say the drinking hadn't been a big problem: it had. Nick had drunk steadily and with singleminded concentration, as if mastering a new skill, and it was only after two unproductive years that he'd frightened himself into doing something about it. But once he'd made up his mind to stop, that was it. As David knew to his cost, Nick could be determined when he chose to be.

It was typical of Nick both to have such a lavishly stocked bar, and to have it in full view, where it would provide a constant reminder and maximum temptation.

On the other side of the hall was the library, now a television and video room, which looked altogether more lived in than the drawing room. This too was empty. Back in the hall, David paused to glance at the visitors' book, a thick leather-bound volume, already more than half full of signatures and comments from what seemed to be a fairly constant stream of guests. There were a few big names – actors, writers, new rich – but in the main it was Nick's carefully chosen inner circle, none of whom, as David well knew, came from the music world. The dining room he didn't bother to check, but went straight along the adjoining passage to the studio. The padded door was open, a sure sign that Nick was not at work, but David looked in all the same, just in case. He was curious to see if the setup had changed and, though he hardly admitted it even to himself, to see if there were signs of work in progress. In the twenty-eight years he'd handled Nick, David had never once asked when the next song was coming. He liked to think that that was one of the reasons he was still around.

The studio was a fairly recent addition to the house, built when Nick had decided to move in permanently six years before. Like everything else Nick had a hand in, it was beautifully designed, though, unusually for him, the room was untidy. In the old days Nick had always been neat to the point of obsession, especially when it came to his work places, yet there were books scattered over almost every working surface, even the piano and synthesiser.

David peered at the titles. There were books on organic farming, broadleaf forestry and environmental protection. Nick had been interested in things Green for a long time. As far back as the early seventies he'd marched in protest against whaling – or was it sealing?

On another surface were two large expensive-looking books on, of all things, birds. The books were lying open to show large colour illustrations of such feathered friends as – David had to peer at the unfamiliar names – kites, buzzards and ospreys. Beside them was a loose-leaf student's pad covered in Nick's spidery scrawl. David couldn't help glancing at it. Under the heading 'Habitat' were various notes on, as far as David could make out, the nesting habits of ospreys.

He scanned the rest of the room. There was no sign of anything like work, no scattering of sheet manuscript. Sipping the last of his coffee, he returned to the open pad and stared thoughtfully at the bird notes. When Nick had first thought of burying himself up here David had been as keen as anyone for him and Alusha to find a place where they could get over the unpleasantness of the New York incident, and had gone out on a limb to encourage him, something he would normally have avoided. It was one thing to be responsible for people's working lives – money and deals had neat conclusions – and quite another to interfere in their private affairs, which were always, but always, minefields of the most lethal kind. The mildest suggestion, the slightest offer of help, earned you nothing but resentment, hostility and a lifetime's blame.

Having broken his own rule and encouraged Nick, he had long since regretted it. He'd hoped this Scottish jaunt would mark the beginning of a new era of productivity, but far from stimulating Nick the place seemed gradually to have stultified him. The first three years had been all right – there'd been enough material for two albums – but more recently the flow had dropped to a trickle. Three songs in two years, not enough for an album, and worst of all, unrecorded because, try as David might, he couldn't get Nick near a recording studio.

Nick had hinted that he was working on some experimental material – there was a chilling rumour that it was a modern opera-type piece using a choir, or something else equally uncommercial. Whatever, it was a project rarely mentioned and never seen, and consequently written off by David. Yet Nick seemed perfectly happy. To David, this was totally mystifying. How could Nick be happy if he wasn't producing albums, wasn't using his gift? How could he live without work?

There was a sound from the passage, the door swung wide, and Nick strode in. He gave a start like a nervous animal, then a characteristically quiet smile spread across his face. 'David! Looking for the action, were you?' He gave a wry laugh. 'Well, you won't find it here, I'm afraid.' This admission didn't seem to upset him.

David gave a slow shrug. 'Just wondering where everyone was.'

'We were down in the new garden, looking at the roses.' Nick shot him an oblique glance. 'You found some breakfast all right?'

David raised his coffee cup in reply.

'Sleep well?'

David made a so-so gesture. 'I was a bit worried when I woke up. It was so quiet I thought I might have bought it in my sleep.'

Nick laughed at that. 'No chance. You'll die at ninety. Doing a deal with the undertaker.'

'Don't *you* find it quiet?'

Nick perched himself on the edge of a table. 'Too much to do. The estate, the gardens – you know. And people to stay. Alusha loves that. And so do I, of course,' he added quickly in case David should think otherwise.

Nick glanced towards the door and whispered in a theatrical voice: 'Got a smoke?'

'I gave up. Five years ago.'

'Of course. So you did. I gave up – when was it?'

'Four years ago. The year after me.'

Nick shook his head, surprised that David should remember such details of his life. 'I wouldn't mind a smoke now. I didn't sleep much last night.' He patted the side of his head and screwed up his face, as if in pain.

'That's not like you.'

'It's your visit, David, it makes me nervous.'

He didn't look in the slightest bit nervous. David made a mild gesture of astonishment. 'Me? Why?

'Because you never say anything.'

'What about, Nick?'

'You know. About the next album. You should be beating me over the head and giving me a hard time. And you don't. It makes me feel guilty as hell.'

David didn't take this accusation too seriously. 'Nick – when did I ever beat you over the head?'

'I've just been too busy, David. There's been all the forestry work. That took an age. Then there was the farm to get off the ground.'

'Nick, you don't have to apologise to me, you know.'

He conceded this with a small laugh. 'I know, but . . . I feel everyone's hovering quietly on the sidelines, waiting for me to produce the goods.'

'I don't think anyone's complaining.'

'Not complaining. But *expecting*, which is worse.' He paused apologetically. 'They might have a long wait, David. I'm not sure when there'll be another album. Or even *if* there'll be another album.'

'Well, if that's the way it is, then that's fine with me,' David lied, hiding a sudden swoop of disappointment. He could understand Nick's reluctance to get together with Amazon again – it was thirteen years since the band was at its peak and ten since it was more or less disbanded – but to give up

41

his solo career? After the last two albums had gone platinum? It tortured David even to think about it.

'But it's not so fine with Mel and Joe, I take it?' Nick asked, sounding beleaguered.

'Joe, he's got his Medea tour. I don't think he minds one way or the other. Mel, well . . .'

'What is it he wants? To get back together again?'

'I think so.'

This evasion earned David a mildly reproving look. 'The two of you coming up here. Looks like a deputation to me.'

'It was Mel's idea.'

Nick gave a slow nod as if he'd suspected this from the beginning. He went across to the window and stood staring out at the garden. 'I can't do the old stuff any more, David. I've moved on. I'm just not interested. I couldn't . . .' He lost momentum and trailed off. 'What does Mel want – an album?'

David moved across to a deep leather chair and sat down. 'I think so.'

'What – Amazon Ten Years On?'

'An album was one idea.'

Nick threw him a sharp glance. 'What was the other?'

David looked pained that he should even have to speak the word. 'A tour.'

'You're kidding? You are, aren't you?' Reading David's expression, he gasped: 'You're not. God. I never thought I'd hear that coming from Mel. Of all people.' He gave an incredulous laugh. 'I thought that was the one thing we were all agreed on. No more tours. What's made him change his mind, for heaven's sake?'

'I honestly don't know. You'll have to ask him yourself.'

Nick frowned for a moment then left the window and flopped into the chair opposite, stretching his long legs across the carpet.

'Kids don't want to see middle-aged trendies,' he argued. 'What's Mel – forty-eight? I'm almost forty-seven. That's as good as a hundred to them. They don't want to watch wrinkles and bulging tums and grey hairs peeking through gold medallions. Hell, they've got fathers of our age on their second coronary bypass.'

David knew the argument wasn't really about age or restarting Amazon or a shortage of the right material. It was all about touring being agony for Nick, who was too private a person to find the hysteria and clamour of the circuit anything but ridiculous.

'The Stones' US tour was a sell-out,' David ventured.

'They're different.'

'The Who, the –'

'Okay, okay. But turning back the clock? Trying to act twenty. Worse – trying to *look* it. They'd have a hell of a job tarting up my mug anyway.' Laughing, he rubbed a hand mercilessly over his face.

'You look fine,' David said, and meant it. Nick had never been good-looking – that accolade, such as it was, had always gone to Mel – but he was a striking man, with his broad strong features, sandy hair and pale eyes, made remarkable by having one of the most lived-in faces David had ever seen.

'It makes my blood run cold,' Nick added reflectively, 'to think of being sprayed into leather jeans and having my hair tangled each morning . . .'

David said: 'That's the biz though, isn't it?'

'I suppose so,' he agreed heavily.

'You'll have to talk to Mel.'

Nick gave a sigh of resignation or perhaps weariness. David didn't envy him the chat with Mel. Although Amazon had disbanded amicably, both Mel and Joe had regretted opting out. While Nick's solo career had rocketed, their attempts to go it alone had been less than successful. Which didn't come as any surprise to David, who'd never had any doubts as to who was the lynchpin of the group. Without Amazon, Mel and Joe were nothing, because they were nothing without Nick. Everyone knew it. 'It's not as if we needed the money,' Nick said almost to himself. He turned suddenly. 'We don't, do we?'

David shrugged. In his book one always needed more money because money was the only reliable measure of success. 'No one *needs* the bread,' he conceded. 'Except perhaps Joe, but then I warned him about getting married in California.'

'Is it the live gigs then? I mean, is that what Mel's hankering after?'

David was careful to make a non-committal face, but Nick wasn't fooled.

'You know, don't you?' he accused gently. Suspicion darted into his face. 'What is it – a woman?'

David went through a last gesture of reticence, then gave a slow nod. 'She's eighteen.'

Nick rolled his eyes. 'Dear Lord. What *is* he thinking of? No' – he held up a hand – 'don't answer that!' He pushed his head hard against the back of the chair, his eyes screwed up against some non-existent glare. 'It's no good.'

'But with new material, new ideas?'

'What new material? There is no new material. I've been writing solo stuff, David. Or stuff Mel or Joe wouldn't want to use.'

David was curious to know more about this experimental material and what made it so unperformable – was it lyrical, like most of Nick's solo material, or was the horrid rumour correct and it was opera stuff? And, just as relevant, did it exist on paper or was it still an unrealised idea in Nick's head?

Before he could think of a way of framing an appropriate question, Nick stood up abruptly and smiled his gentle sidelong smile. 'Come on, David, I'll show you round the estate.' He said it with such anticipation that David got to his feet and, looking suitably enthusiastic, asked him to lead on.

It was one by the time they had inspected the forest, the new broadleaf plantation and the farm which Nick had added to the estate three years before. As Nick liked to recount it, he'd had to buy the farm to obtain manure for the vegetable garden. Being a purist, only chemical-free manure would do, so the farm was slowly being turned into an all-organic showpiece.

It was costing, of course. Though the estate was a limited company which Nick ran more or less independently, David had a pretty good idea of what was being put into it in the way of hard cash. Nick didn't stint when it came to staff: there was a workforce of three on the farm; four estate workers including the manager; two gardeners, and a couple for the house. But then apart from Caycoo Nick had no other drain on his income. There was no reason why he shouldn't amuse himself in this or any other way he chose.

Hopefully the fascination with this place wouldn't last for ever. Nick might never return to touring – that would be too much to hope for – but the regular albums, recording studios, London, must lure him back eventually. Even as David tried to convince himself of this, he looked across at Nick in the driving seat, his face a picture of contentment, and wasn't so sure.

When they returned to the house, a large cold lunch had been laid out in the dining room. David had forgotten what a wonderful housekeeper Alusha was. The food was a mixture of Scottish feudal – cold wild salmon with mayonnaise, tender cold beef with horseradish sauce – and Seychellian exotica – spiced fish, devilled chicken with a variety of sweet spicy sauces. David's diet suffered another postponement.

After helping himself from the sideboard he made for the nearest place at the table but Alusha, sweeping up behind him, waved him to the far end, near the window. 'The sun, we must sit in the sun,' she exclaimed. 'It's too good to waste.' She sat next to him and, though the others had not yet appeared, urged him to start. As they ate, she chattered brightly, breathlessly, charmingly. She was one of those people who had the rare gift of intimacy, the ability to make you feel you were the most important friend in the world. David was flattered to remember that she bestowed this gift with considerable discretion.

Her looks, both exotic and unusual, had seemed entirely appropriate for Nick when he was at the height of his touring career but here, in the richly panelled dining room, amid the tartans, watercolours and heavy oak furniture, against the soft northern background of trees, mountains and water, she could not have looked more incongruous. David had never enquired about her parentage, but it was said her father was French, her mother Chinese or Indian or, much more likely, a mixture of both. The result was arresting rather than beautiful, but that, to David, was a recommendation rather than a fault.

'Can't you stay another day, David?' she asked, widening her eyes at him. 'It's Sunday tomorrow.'

'I've got a meeting.'

'And if you didn't have one, you would make one up.' The reprimand was delivered with such a beautiful smile that it was impossible to take offence.

'You know how it is.'

'Nick would have loved you to stay. So would I. Can't you really?' Alusha, for all her gentleness, had a streak of tenacity. But it was just this mixture of charm and quiet determination that seemed to make her relationship with Nick such a

45

success. Not many women would have made the move from New York to the back-of-beyond; fewer still would have stuck a life of organic farming and long country walks.

It was another ten minutes before Nick and Mel joined them. Mel looked stormy, Nick quietly pained: they had obviously had their discussion, complete with predictably unsatisfactory outcome.

Mel's mood didn't bother David; he'd been desensitised by eighteen years of Mel-instigated dramas. Alusha was not so hardhearted. She directed all her attention towards Mel, trying to soothe his ruffled feathers. Typically Mel was not to be placated so easily, and after a time even Alusha had to admit temporary defeat.

Nick, a peacemaker by nature, did his best to make conversation. Then, without warning, he said: 'What about that charity concert Amazon were offered some time ago, David? The one in aid of the rain forests. Are we still considering that?'

David could hardly believe his ears. The concert invitation had actually been for Nick, but that wasn't the point. Nick was talking about 'we', he was talking about Amazon. 'Well – no. You said . . . You . . . I turned it down. They've advertised it now.'

'Is there something else we could do? A one-off charity thing.' Nick shot a guileless look in Mel's direction. 'If it's all right with everyone else, of course. And if it could be fitted in on our way to Caycoo in the autumn.'

David recovered himself. 'It could be fixed, sure,' he said swiftly.

'Something worthwhile,' Nick continued. 'You know, something we all feel strongly about.' This wasn't just a small conciliatory gesture on Nick's part, it was a massive act of generosity, and David was relieved to see from Mel's expression that he had the grace to realise it.

'You name the charity, they've been asking for you,' David said. 'You only have to choose.' He immediately flicked his memory through the large quantity of requests that regularly flowed into the office and, inventing what he couldn't remember, listed a few ideas. The discussion roamed from whales to the ozone layer and back again, without decision.

'What about the clean water campaign?' Nick suggested. 'I don't imagine it gets much attention. Not glamorous enough.'

Mel dug himself out of his mood sufficiently to make a typically unhelpful comment. 'Clean water – isn't that the government's bag? I mean, where would our money be going?'

Not surprisingly, Nick knew something about the subject and patiently took Mel through it. Not for the first time David was struck by the contrast between the two: Nick, articulate, rational, restrained; Mel, thorny, mercurial, forever a victim of his own instincts and therefore life. Nick had had some education – grammar school and a year at Newcastle University – while Mel, like Joe, had left school at fifteen. But the contrast went far beyond that. Sometimes David wondered how Amazon had held together for as long as it did.

Mel announced himself unconvinced on the clean water campaign and, it seemed, on most other ideas as well. 'Everyone's on that bandwagon,' he kept saying. 'It'd look like we were desperate to cash in or something.'

There was an inconclusive pause. Determined not to let the idea wither, David dredged his memory further. 'There's always famine. That's got a good image. Even better, famine and children. The Save the Children Fund are having a famine-relief drive for the Sudan, I think it is. You can't go wrong with Save the Children. Worthy. Caring image. One of their fund raisers has been after you for months.' The fund raiser had actually been after Nick solo, but he didn't mention that.

No one expressed wild enthusiasm, but then no one looked unhappy about it either. In an effort to leave no stone unturned, David said to Nick: 'She says she's an old friend of yours. The fund-raising lady, that is. Wife of an MP. Driscoll, is it?'

Nick gave a shrug. 'Could be.' Like everyone in his position, he'd met thousnds of people for a few minutes each. It was impossible to remember them by name.

'Perhaps you *do* know her,' teased Alusha, narrowing her eyes. 'Perhaps she's an old flame.' She rolled her tongue round the idiom with obvious pleasure, as if she'd just learnt it.

Nick gave her a broad smile. 'Before you, my love, it's all a great big blank.'

Alusha laughed with great delight, as if hearing the remark for the first time, although to David's certain knowledge Nick

47

had used the same phrase several times before. Perhaps this was the secret of a happy marriage: repetition, ritual and feigned delight at each other's jokes. He wondered how they were getting on with their attempts to have babies. He would be careful not to ask. The last he'd heard Alusha was about to try yet another fertility treatment.

'Is it agreed then?' David pressed. 'Shall I pursue the Save-the-Children idea?'

Nick gave him an imperceptible wink of encouragement. Mel shrugged in what was not, apparently, disagreement. David breathed a sigh of pleasure and profound relief; against all expectations it seemed that Amazon was back on the road again. And from one charity concert, who knew what might grow?

Duggan felt the sweat dripping down the side of his face. His eyes flicked over the instrument panel: engine temperature normal, no malfunctions. Cockpit heating off; vents discharging cool air. What the hell, he was just hot. Hot and tired. The headache had settled into a sharp stabbing pain behind the eyes. He put the Porter into a steep turn and lined up for the next run. Only three more runs before the end of this job, thank the Lord, then back for a feet-up. He pulled the throttle back, dropping the machine quickly towards spraying height. This was a little game of his, to see how quickly and profi-ciently he could level out at the magic spraying height after a rapid drop. On a good day he could hit it in one, on a bad day – and there were plenty of those – he levelled out too high and had to ease her down. Now and again he gave himself a fright and dipped a bit too low. One way or the other, it relieved the boredom.

As usual, the job was forest. The terrain was almost flat and the trees of fairly uniform height, a doddle compared to ground crops, which were apt to be surrounded by tall trees, roads, telephone wires and houses with irate people.

He found his height at about fifteen feet over the treetops, throttled down to a steady ninety-five knots, located a visual marker at the far end of the run, and, fifty yards from the edge of the plantation, engaged the atomisers. He glanced briefly back through the scratched Perspex, saw the answering cloud of vapour, and looked ahead to the marker. The marker was less than adequate, but since dear gormless Reggie had somehow managed to cock up the placing of the black boxes and the Hi-Fix wasn't working, he had no choice but to rely on eyeball fixes, reciprocal bearings and old-fashioned seat-of-the-pants stuff. He had to estimate the spray widths, calculate what he'd already covered and find some landmark to keep him straight on the next run. Inevitably the spraying would overlap a bit. Just as inevitably there would be the occasional gaps. But he'd only get to hear about them when the angry proprietor complained about swathes of rampant bugs.

He completed the run, and the next. He noticed that the wind had got up. That was all he needed. Not only did it make flying more difficult but it caused excessive drift, blowing the spray off-target. His theoretical wind limit was eight knots. It might be close to that now, but since he had almost finished he wasn't going to let that get in his way. One more run, then it was back to the Portakabin for a couple of well-earned cigarettes, a large cup of coffee and one of Jeannie's lead-lined ham sandwiches.

He turned and came in for the last time. He switched on the atomisers, automatically glancing at the flow meter as he did so. He did a double-take. No spray. Red light. Cursing, he disengaged and re-engaged the atomisers several times. Still a red. He fiddled the control valve. Nothing. He spun it again, then punched at it viciously. Finally he was rewarded with a feeble green light and the sight of vapour when he glanced back. Too late for most of the run: the end of the plantation was approaching fast. The question now was, would the blasted spray turn off?

Only with great difficulty, he discovered. It took several flicks of the switch and a fast turn of the control valve before the spray trail finally thinned and vanished. Looking down, he saw he was overflying a clearing with a fleeing deer.

'Sorry about that, old girl.'

Gaining height, he turned sharply and headed back to the air strip. Hot and weary, he half hoped the mechanic would be unable to fix the trouble so that, though it would mean the loss of much-needed loot, he could take the rest of the day off.

FOUR

As soon as lunch was over, Nick slipped away and strode briskly up through the park to the rowan tree. Wrapping the shotgun in the poacher's jacket, he made his way back to the house, feeling conspicuous as he walked stiffly and unnaturally with the gun clamped firmly against his thigh. But there was no Alusha to see him this time, nor anyone else, and he managed to return the gun to the secure cupboard in the corner of the boot room unobserved.

As for the jacket, he couldn't make up his mind about that. To leave it in the wood store would be to suggest that last night was forgiven and forgotten, which it most certainly was not. To keep the damn thing would be equally unsatisfactory. Putting the decision off, he finally hung it on a peg behind the door.

On his way out he met Alusha in the hall and almost gave himself away with a guilty laugh. Duplicity had never been his strong point. But if Alusha noticed, she chose not to mention it. Instead she invited him to walk with her to the paddock while Mel was watching the American football on TV and David was, inevitably, phoning London.

They stepped into air that was unexpectedly fresh. He stood looking around him, as he always did when leaving the house. The sky was clear, the hills were bathed in a light which seemed to have burnt the high moors an unaccustomed shade of ochre. The trees sparkled and shimmered, their leaves tinkling and rustling in the breeze.

They walked past the walled garden, through the rhododendron grove and began the climb towards the paddock.

Nick looped his arm firmly in Alusha's. Already the events of the previous night seemed a long way off and, if he tried really hard, he could persuade himself that none of it had happened.

Clear of the gardens the breeze was stronger and cooler, and he realised that, unusually for the time of year, it was coming from the north, maybe even a little east of north.

From the house came the distant sound of a car crunching across the gravel and a moment later Nick glanced back to see the unmistakable figure of Duncan coming round the side of the house. Nick whistled to him and Duncan, waving a brief acknowledgement, started after them. Even at that distance Nick could see that Duncan was using his angry walk: stride rapid, head down, arms pumping. By the time he caught up with them at the paddock rail, his complexion was a deep and dangerous shade of red.

'They've been at it again!' Duncan panted through clenched teeth. 'They've been at it again!'

Nick caught Alusha stifling a slight smile and frowned at her. 'Who has?' he asked.

'Those damned poachers! Up at Macinley's Pool, curse their eyes! Just when I was away for the evening.' Duncan had been in the business of outmanoeuvring poachers for thirty years, but it never seemed to occur to him that the opposition's intelligence-gathering system might be better than his own.

'We'll get them next time,' Nick said soothingly.

'Of that you may be sure! If it's the very last thing I do. Oh yes!' Duncan was momentarily silenced by his own indignation.

Alusha had entered the paddock and was calling Rona, who was going through an elegant charade of evading capture. 'I could get some of those image-intensifying things,' Nick suggested. 'You know, sort of night binoculars. Would that help?' This offering was made to mollify Duncan, but also to assuage his own guilt at having cocked up a perfectly good opportunity for capture.

Duncan's eyes sparkled. 'Those things they use in the SAS?'

Nick hadn't thought of Duncan as a military enthusiast. He couldn't resist teasing him. 'I've only ever seen them in nature films,' he said innocently. 'But what do you think?'

Duncan chortled with unconcealed glee. 'Now that would

do the trick very nicely! Oh yes. I could set myself up on the hill-side, with a two-mile stretch of river in my sights. Oh yes!'

The pony, after a last coquettish dance, had allowed herself to be captured and was following Alusha meekly to the rail. Duncan, his optimism restored, said brightly: 'Not riding today, Mrs Mackenzie?'

Alusha stroked Rona's neck rhythmically. 'No, not today.' She looked away slyly, secretively. This small evasion was so uncharacteristic of her that Nick allowed himself to read an unmistakable message into her decision, and felt his stomach tighten.

Turning quickly to Duncan he said: 'Anyway, I thought you were taking the evening off. Going to Oban.'

Duncan admitted to the possibility with a dismissive grunt. 'But I'll be back later,' he said significantly. 'And every night, by God. Until the river falls.'

Nick heard this with some alarm. A stakeout wasn't likely to be too productive; the tall poacher, for all his artfulness, surely wouldn't come back so soon, not after a fracas like that. Hastily, he invented a job which would require Duncan to be in Oban early the next morning, so that it wouldn't be worth his while to come back from the evening with his sister. They argued gently for a while. Duncan vacillated, looked unhappy, but finally agreed.

'It's that Alistair Campbell from Inveraray, you know,' Duncan said over his shoulder as he started back down the hill.

'Who is?'

'The damned poacher.'

Alistair Campbell. Nick didn't know the name, but he turned it carefully over in his mind, fitting it to the voice and the dark faceless figure by the pool. 'You're sure?' he called after Duncan.

'Och, I'm sure,' Duncan said heavily, and, giving a rueful wave of farewell, plodded back towards the house.

Alusha said: 'The police, can't they arrest this Campbell?'

'They'd need proof.'

'What about the salmon? His house, it must be full of them.'

Nick regarded her fondly. 'Sold on by now.'

She gave him a narrow cat-like stare. 'And after you so nearly caught him.'

He was completely taken aback. 'I . . . caught him?'

Alusha unclipped Rona's halter and the pony shimmied away, picking up her feet and showing the whites of her eyes like some affronted spinster. Alusha ducked under the rail. 'You were out all night, weren't you? And there's that bump in your head.'

'On. *On* my head,' he corrected her. 'Does it show?' He put a hand to the lump.

'You've been touching it all day. And blood – I can see blood. Not much, but enough.' She gave him a triumphant grin. 'See? Easy.'

Alusha, as always, had an unfailing talent for rooting out the truth. Far from minding about this, Nick was rather proud of her for it.

Putting on a suitably sheepish expression, he said: 'It seemed a good idea at the time.'

'If you like to go falling over in the dark or whatever you did, well' – she gave a small shrug – 'what can I say? Playing cowboys and Indians. It's *almost* funny.' She raised her eyebrows to show how unfunny she thought it was.

A Wild West comparison wasn't the first Nick would have made, but considering the gun and the ridiculous tussle by the pool she wasn't so far wrong.

Alusha prodded his shoulder. 'So long as no one gets silly, Nick. As long as no one gets hurt. That's all I ask.'

He thought for an appalling moment that she knew about the gun. But reading her expression, he saw that there was nothing deeper in her remark and pulled her into his arms so that she wouldn't see the guilt and relief in his face.

Breathing the musky scent of her hair, feeling the familiar shape of her body against his, he wondered not for the first time how it was possible to foul up so much of one's life and still end up with the first prize.

Then her last words drifted back into his mind, and he complained mildly: 'But I *am* hurt.'

'No sympathy,' she said firmly, pulling away from him. 'Serves you right.' But she couldn't have been too cross with him because she put her hand into his as they walked down the hill.

Nearing the house, Nick could make out David's figure in the rose garden, wandering between the beds, examining the flowers, but stiffly as if he wasn't quite sure what to make of it all.

From long habit, Nick and Alusha made a detour through the walled kitchen garden. But unusually, they walked in silence as they made their inspection of the vegetables, the burgeoning raspberry canes and the vine in its long glasshouse.

Nick gathered his courage. This was the obvious moment to ask the question that had been hovering between them for days, since the time Alusha had stopped riding Rona.

He got to the point of opening his mouth then, hesitating disastrously, turned away to examine the grapes. His courage ebbed away. It was superstition, it was nameless fear, but he felt that asking the question would only invite disappointment, and he wasn't sure he was quite ready to face that yet. Postponement offered a sort of promise that seemed to go hand in hand with the perfection of the day. Anything, perhaps, was better than the blunt certainty of failure, although in some curious way the hope of children had been with them so long that it was almost enough in itself.

The sun was warmer here, the breeze soft, the day perfect. Later, when everyone had gone, the moment would come.

Squeezing her hand, he talked instead about the visit to Perthshire they were planning for the coming week.

David was first into the car, getting into the back with his briefcase at his side, doing his best to look sorry the visit was over.

Mel came next, sauntering jauntily out of the house, chattering with Alusha, kissing her warmly, as if the weekend had been an unqualified success. An afternoon in front of the television seemed to have restored his humour. As he climbed in, Nick started up the Mercedes. Alusha put her head to the open window. 'You'll come back soon, both of you – promise?'

She had pulled back her hair into a long plait and donned her workman's kit, a pair of baggy overalls. Nick tried to remember what she was planning to do for the remainder of the afternoon. Painting perhaps – she'd taken a watercolour course – or renovating an old lamp she'd bought in London.

As the car rattled over the cattle grid Nick glanced in the mirror and saw that Alusha was still there, waving slowly.

Something about the sight of her small figure standing in the wide expanse of the front sweep bothered him, but he couldn't pin it down. He slowed the car to give himself time to think, but Mel shot him a questioning glance and, remembering that they had a plane to catch, he pressed on.

'I can see the attraction of this place, you know,' Mel said as he surveyed the spectacular beauty of the loch. 'Unadulterated escapism.'

'Escapism? I wouldn't have called it that,' Nick replied amiably. Purposely choosing to misunderstand, he added: 'There's no need to escape from anything here.'

'No, I mean it's places like this you escape *to*,' Mel explained, impatiently. Then, catching Nick's expression, he closed his mouth abruptly before commenting: 'I wouldn't mind a place like this myself, mind. No aggravation. No pollution. No stress. And all that organic food – I tell you, you'll live for ever if you're not careful.'

Nick smiled. Sometimes, when he thought back to the early days, he could persuade himself that he missed the companionship, the running gags, the buzz one got after a good show. On the other hand, he only had to remember the horrors of the attendant nonsense, the tensions and disagreements and crises that used to spring up with unbelievable regularity to miss nothing at all. 'Is this for ever?' Mel asked suddenly.

'What?'

'This stopping the world and getting off.'

'I haven't got off. Not the world, not anything. You make me sound like a recluse or something.'

'I'm only asking if it's for ever.'

Nick was aware of David in the back making a poor job of pretending not to listen. 'I don't know, Mel,' he replied honestly. 'I really don't know.'

He knew what they were thinking. That the New York incident was years ago now, that he should have put that behind him, that he should be back where he belonged, producing an album a year and, while he was about it, throwing in a few gigs and an album or two to get Amazon off the ground again and put Mel and Joe back in the way of money and success.

One charity show wouldn't be enough to satisfy them. He

should have realised that. They didn't understand, either of them, that he was quite happy alone at Ashard with Alusha and his work.

They came into Inveraray, with its main street of neat white-painted shops and hotels. A string of tourists dawdled along, staring into windows packed with tartan dolls, plastic bag-pipes and miniature haggises.

A car drew out from in front of the Spa grocery shop on the other side of the street and came towards them. He recognised the car, and saw one of the occupants wave. It was his housekeeper, Mrs Alton, and her husband. He waved back. The vague concern about Alusha clarified. He realised that, with Mrs Alton here in town, all the staff were either off-duty or away. Even Duncan, who lived barely half a mile from the house, would be on his way to Oban by now. Alusha was on her own at Glen Ashard.

He calmed himself. He hadn't chosen a house in a remote corner of Scotland with automatic gates and high fences for nothing. Nevertheless, he felt guilt. Years ago, he'd made himself a promise never to leave her alone again. Now after all this time, he'd broken it and he couldn't for the life of him think why.

He pushed his foot down and the Mercedes leapt forward, accelerating out of Inveraray and along the winding lochside road. Another fifty minutes to the airport if he stepped on it and went in for some adventurous overtaking. He could be back at Glen Ashard by eight.

The afternoon sunlight was spreading a golden glow over the hills, like molten honey. Away to the right, above the ruffled waters of the loch, a small black dot appeared, moving smoothly across the absolute clarity of the sky. For a moment Nick thought that Helen in the estate office might have got it wrong and ordered a helicopter to take his visitors to the airport, but then he saw that it was not a helicopter but a light plane, and turned his attention back to the road.

The plane carried straight on, heading south-west, down the loch towards Glen Ashard.

Duggan wrestled with the Ordnance Survey map. The damned thing was not designed for small cockpits, nor for much else as far as he could tell. The multitudinous folds did not lend themselves to being pulled open and refolded. Though he'd prepared the blasted thing back in the Porta-kabin, he now needed to take a closer look at the terrain around the target area, specifically the area to the north-west, a patch he'd not planned on overflying, and would, under normal circumstances, have avoided.

But since his backup was as usual nil, and the weather information he'd been given by Jeannie as good as useless, he was having to think again. The north-westerly he'd been promised on take-off had developed a distinct north-easterly slant, and increased from a light wind to a firm breeze. The easterly twist might possibly result from the funnelling effect of the hills, but more likely the weather information was simply hours out of date. Whatever, he would have to look carefully at the approach angle. As far as he could estimate, the wind strength was ten knots or so. Well, maybe it was a touch more, but as long as he could fly crosswind on an east–west slant without hitting a hill on the way out, then it shouldn't be too much of a bother. Inveraray was down to starboard. The target area would be coming up shortly. With a last angry punch at an obdurate crease he finally got the map into some sort of order and started comparing the symbols with the landmarks below. The target area was immediately obvious, a large block of high-standing conifers, planted in serried ranks with occasional fire breaks.

The northern and eastern perimeters were clear-cut – the forest ended in rising moorland – but to the west and the south the conifers blended into broadleaf forest with no obvious boundary, excepting the contrast in colour. There was some broadleaf forest in the south-west corner too, but it soon gave way to pasture, paddocks and, beyond, a large castle-type house belonging to the neighbouring estate.

Duggan made a couple of passes over the timber, assessing the local wind conditions, gauging the lie of the land, checking for livestock. The obvious run was parallel to the high land, on a line south-west to north-east. The approach was long and reasonably level, and the exit even kinder, the land dropping gently away to the open pasture. Plenty of turning room. A doddle in a northwesterly.

The only problem was he didn't bloody well have a north-westerly. And, trying a dummy run, he soon discovered that the northeasterly that he did have was powering over a wide cleft in the hills in nasty gusts, causing the Porter to crab sideways.

He considered the possibility of flying on a south-to-north line. But while it might be easier to control the aircraft that way, it would also in all probability kill him. Quite apart from an approach over sharply rising ground, which was bound to be prone to down draughts, the way out was steep and craggy.

This was not the sort of job Duggan needed at the end of a long day. Not after an inadequate recce, not with the corking headache that refused to go away, not with the dodgy spray mechanism that might or might not have been fixed. Davie had sworn it would be okay, but then he would. Mechanics always said they'd fixed things even when they'd patched them up with sticky tape.

For the umpteenth time he cursed Keen who, after creating the maximum disruption and aggravation, had pissed off back to Glasgow in his vulgar little motor, throwing a last Hitlerite command over his shoulder to the effect that everyone had better pull harder or else they'd all be in trouble.

If anything, the wind seemed to be freshening. No point in hanging about then.

He took a swig of lemonade, pushed a toffee into his mouth and banked steeply to port to line up for a dummy run.

Rona snorted in sudden agitation. Alusha paused in her work to shush her. 'What's the matter with you? Go away.'

The mare stamped her feet, her shoes ringing on the hard standing in front of the stable.

'Away,' Alusha Mackenzie repeated. 'You're being a nuisance.' She waved her paintbrush at Rona and shooed her into the paddock. 'Off with you.'

The pony trotted off and stopped a short distance away, tossing her head. Turning back to the stable door, Alusha dipped her brush in the preservative and slapped some more onto the bare wooden door. The thin green mixture had an evil smell and instinctively she pulled back to avoid inhaling it.

Somewhere an engine buzzed lazily in the sky, like an insect in the sun. Rona snorted again.

Alusha laughed at her. 'What do you want this time, eh?' She finished the door and, fetching a large metal bucket, upended it and positioned it in the doorway. Balancing on it, she could just reach the lintel.

When it came to it, there was no decision really. It had to be the south-west–north-east line; Duggan wasn't about to kill himself to earn a mention in anyone's rule book. Besides, he should be able to adjust his course to allow for drift. It couldn't be that difficult.

He found his height, lined up on an imaginary line a width inside the southern perimeter of the plantation, and, holding a steady course, hovered his thumb over the spray switch.

The conifers sped towards and under him. He switched on. There was an answering billow of vapour from under the wings. That was something anyway; he supposed he should be grateful. Eyes front again, he was surprised to see broadleaf trees moving in under his port wing. The gust must be stronger than he'd thought. He compensated, touching the rudder once and again, only to find that either he'd overdone it or else the crosswind had dropped suddenly, because he was too far into the conifers now. Cursing, he eased the Porter back on line, only for the same thing to happen again. He was weaving about like a bloody amateur.

Not a moment too soon, the end of the plantation loomed up and vanished beneath. He switched off the spray and swivelled his head back.

No change: the spray continued to course lavishly from the atomisers. He felt a vicious choking anger. Swearing loud and long, he flicked the switch rapidly back and forth, kicking the heel of his hand against it, then leant down and rapidly rotated the control valve beside his feet until, quite suddenly, the indicator light went off and, an instant later, the trail of vapour finally thinned and died.

He looked up. *Christ!* He was almost over the parkland; the big house was not far ahead to port. Instinctively he took the Porter into a tight turn to starboard, rapidly gaining height to clear the rising ground beneath.

He twisted in his seat to press his face against the Perspex and look back towards the park. Nothing. Thank God. No sheep. No small figure, face upturned, like that child the other week.

59

The relief left him exhausted. He knew exactly what he was going to do now: give up and return to base. And he knew precisely what he was going to do once he got there: telephone Keen. Rehearsing the exact combination of expletives kept him occupied all the way home.

The buzzing hung languorously in the air, faded, then got louder again. Rona, unseen by her mistress, sidled silently back towards the stable and, blowing loudly in Alusha's ear, gave her a terrible fright.

'That's it!' Alusha exclaimed, stepping off the bucket. She made a grab for Rona's bridle, but the mare was too quick for her and danced away.

Alusha held out some sugar. 'Come on, you greedy pig.'

The pony, despite her uncharacteristic nervousness, couldn't resist the sugar and within a minute Alusha had caught her and hitched her to the ring on the stable wall. 'And here you stay until I've finished.'

The soft drone grew louder again. Alusha shaded her eyes and looked up but, seeing nothing, returned to her brush and her pot and dabbed some more green fluid on the door frame.

For some reason the smell of the stuff suddenly clutched at her throat. It was incredibly strong, like ammonia or worse. She clamped a hand over her mouth and nose and tried not to breathe, but the stuff seeped into her nose and throat. She staggered off the bucket and retreated onto the apron. She coughed, and the act of coughing made her pull a deep draught of air into her lungs. Air that wasn't air; air that was sharp and burning. Inexplicably, the fumes seemed to have followed her across the apron. By the time she had raised her collar over her mouth, it was too late. The acrid vapour was eating at her lungs, her eyes were streaming, her head was weaving violently.

She tried to find her way back to the stable. She was dimly aware of noise, of a clattering of hooves and sounds of alarm from Rona. But the collision, when it came, caught her by surprise. One moment she was groping her way back towards the stable, the next moment the bulk of Rona's hindquarters was barrelling into her, a solid weight that cannoned into her shoulder and toppled her over.

Her head didn't hit the concrete terribly hard – in fact, the impact was more like a hard knock than a solid thud – but it was enough to send her sliding into a grey land somewhere between panic and nightmare, a land in which her eyes saw nothing, in which every breath drew her deeper into some terrible darkness.

FIVE

Fifteen column-inches. Daisy pasted up the fourth and final cutting, already worn and ageing from the cutting agency's tardy service, and held the finished montage at arm's length. Not bad if one overlooked the origin of the stories – the *Newbury Chronicle*, the *Reading News* and such like – and imagined that the items had appeared in the national dailies. Alice Knowles' demonstration hadn't merited the attention of the nation, not in print, not on radio or TV. Nor had it, apparently, justified the undivided concentration of the journalists who'd covered it. One described Aldeb as a fumigant instead of a fungicide, while another talked vaguely about the dangers of processing potatoes as if the Knowleses ran a chip factory instead of a farm. All in all, the coverage was no better or worse than she'd expected.

The street door banged as someone arrived and Daisy heard the unmistakable sound of Alan clearing his throat, something he did so regularly first thing in the morning that she suspected him of being a secret smoker. Not that she dared say so; Alan wasn't too good with jokes.

She heard him enter the cubicle next door and shuffle around, the rubber soles of his shoes squelching softly on the lino-tiled floor. Catch didn't run to carpets or other such luxuries. Under normal circumstances it wouldn't have run to an office near King's Cross either, but the place had been let to them by a sympathetic developer at a peppercorn rent. Situated in the rambling basement of an Edwardian house due for demolition in a couple of years' time, with high barred windows and woefully little daylight, it was not the ideal workplace, and certainly not in winter when, for lack of central heating, they had to suffer the fumes of mobile gas heaters, an expedient which did little for their corporate image let alone their lungs.

Alan appeared round the door and, sorting through the mail, dropped a batch onto Daisy's desk. 'Can we have a talk some time?' he said.

'Now, if you like.'

He hesitated as if he'd rather have put the moment off, then sank into the chair beside her desk. Alan, dark and slightly built with the stoic tenacity of the seasoned campaigner, had come to Catch by way of Greenpeace, the anti-fur campaign Lynx and, for a brief time ten years before, his own environmentally friendly cleaning products company which had folded after six months, a victim of being ahead of its time.

Picking up a bulldog grip, he started operating the jaws. 'The Knowles case. What exactly *are* we recommending to the Committee?'

Daisy was on her guard. The two of them had discussed this only the previous afternoon. Alan was well aware of her views on the subject, so this could only be the opening gambit in an attempt to shift her.

'We're going to recommend full backing for the Knowleses, in their legal action and whatever else is needed,' she reminded him.

Alan closed the bulldog grip on his finger, screwed up his mouth in mild pain. Withdrawing the finger, he examined it carefully. 'I think it would be a mistake.'

'What – to help them?' Daisy tried to smooth any exasperation out of her voice. 'But why, for God's sake? We agreed – we should do everything we could – '

'Their case won't succeed.'

This needed to be taken gently, not an approach that came naturally to Daisy. 'How can you say it's doomed? We don't know till we try, do we?'

'A case like that – it'll take years and God only knows how many thousands of pounds.'

'I know, but we're not promising the family a lot of cash, are we? Just a token offering to get them going.'

'*And* back-up – data, information, research, liaison . . .'

'Well, of course . . .'

'Which means a helluva lot of time and money.' Alan

agitated the jaws of the grip so rapidly that they made a loud clacking noise, like the teeth of a mad animal. He looked up, wearing his most resolute expression. 'We decided right at the beginning, when Catch was first set up, that it would be absolutely futile to take on the agrochemical industry direct while we had such limited funds, that confrontation would be a sure way of defeating *ourselves*. Nothing's changed since then, Daisy. In fact, if anything there's even *more* reason to avoid getting bogged down in something like this. We're just as stretched as before, if not more so. Committed on too many fronts – the new newsletter, setting up all the regional groups . . . well – you *know* how it is. But a legal fight . . . it'd be a minefield, Daisy. We can't afford to go pioneering, not over totally untested ground. We just don't have the resources. The media – *that*'s our battlefield, *that*'s what we understand, it's the only place where we know how to win.'

Daisy let this flow over her; it was familiar, not to say well-trodden, ground. 'But it's not us who're taking on the case,' she pointed out. 'It's the Knowles family.'

'Quite.' He waved the bulldog grip in the air, as if he had just succeeded in explaining everything. 'The Knowleses should never have been encouraged to take legal action in the first place. The scientists are still totally divided, the evidence is too weak for any British court of law. You know that, I know that, but it seems the Knowleses of all people don't know it.'

'You're making it sound as if I pushed them into it,' she said defensively. 'You're making it sound as if I encouraged them. Which isn't true, and you know it.'

Alan shot her a stern look. 'Put it this way, perhaps you could have done a better job of discouraging them.'

'Thanks,' Daisy said sharply. 'And how exactly do you tell people that the law is a total waste of time? How do you tell them that their whole experience has been for nothing?'

'You tell them, that's what you do. You tell them because it's true.'

Daisy was losing ground but couldn't see how to fight her way out of it.

'Oh, the case'd get some publicity all right,' Alan went on remorselessly. 'On the last day of the case, that is. And maybe the first. But in the middle, all through the weeks and weeks of expert evidence and the months waiting for the second appeal, there'd be zilch. The only sure thing would be the catastophic expense and almost certain bankruptcy for the family.' He finished with a flourish: 'It seems rather a high price to pay for a little publicity.'

Daisy leant back in her chair and folded her arms tightly across her chest. 'So what on earth are we doing here then?' she said, unable to suppress the frustration in her voice. 'I mean, if we can't help people like the Knowleses?'

Alan stood up. 'You know the answer to that – to campaign. It's the only game we can play. More to the point, it's the only game we can – '

'Yes, yes,' she said wearily, 'I know, I *know* – it's the only game we can afford.'

A phone began to ring. Neither of them was in a hurry to answer it and it continued to sound eerily through the dingy rooms. Suddenly the street door banged and they heard the rapid tap of Jenny's metal-heeled boots as she ran into the general office to snatch up the phone.

In the silence, Daisy picked up her argument again. 'We should be doing both. Campaigning *and* offering support. Honestly, Alan, what's the point otherwise?'

He gave an exasperated laugh. 'But, Daisy . . . It's always a mistake to get too . . .' He hesitated. She had the feeling he had been about to say emotional, not a word she would have appreciated. Instead he murmured: '. . . *involved* in these things.'

Jenny's voice called from the outer office, summoning Alan to the phone. Before disappearing he gave a gesture of regret, an affirmation that, according to his reckoning, he had won his point.

Daisy stood up and took a couple of turns round the filing cabinets, trying to make sense of her anger. It wasn't just the lack of money, though that was a continual problem, it wasn't even Alan's habit of putting a dampener on her most precious ideas, though he did that often enough to make her suspect that he got a perverse satisfaction from it. No, the worst part was the knowledge that he had a point, that much as she longed to see a case brought against the agrochemical camp it would be wrong to let it go ahead at the Knowleses' expense. However determined Alice Knowles was, however keen her son to find a purpose in his illness, it was doubtful that a case fought with such meagre resources would be worth the emotional and financial strain. Reluctant though she was to admit it, Alan could have been right, and she should have done a better job of talking the Knowleses out of it.

Dropping dejectedly back into her chair, she leafed through her diary, looking for a date when she could go and see Alice again. The weekend, as usual, was the only time she had free.

She started on the mail, automatically flipping the discarded envelopes into the box earmarked for recycling. Magazines, journals, reports, scientific papers, members' letters, non-members' letters: too much of it, always too much of it.

Opening a large envelope, she pulled out three smaller ones, each addressed to a box number at *Farmers Weekly*. In a guilty reflex, Daisy glanced over her shoulder. This was a little idea she'd forgotten to mention to Alan, but now was not, she felt, the moment to come clean. The ad had been simple enough: ALDEB. *Anyone experiencing health problems from exposure to this fungicide, please write Box No. . . .* Normally Catch accumulated their case histories through people like the Farmers' Union Health Executive, through newspaper articles or contacts made on Catch's behalf by friendly toxicologists. To Daisy these haphazard methods had always seemed inadequate, and she'd long been haunted by the almost certain knowledge that there were dozens of other cases out there, just waiting to be uncovered.

The first letter was not promising. It was from a lady in Wiltshire who'd worked on a chicken farm and wanted to know if Aldeb was the medicine they were always feeding the chickens, because if so, she thought it was responsible for her 'hormones'. She'd been under the doctor for months, had had several operations, but was still suffering all her old troubles.

Daisy put the letter to one side. Investigating chickenfeed wasn't within Catch's present brief, though if anyone bothered to analyse a modern broiler hen's intestines, it probably would be.

The next letter was from a Lincolnshire farmer whose wife had developed cancer. Their main crop was potatoes and, until they'd been alerted to the dangers of Aldeb the previous year, they'd been using the chemical continuously. The wife had been in charge of warehousing and storage, which involved regular applications of fungicide in enclosed conditions. Daisy felt a small spark of optimism: this was more like it.

66

The third letter was from a man with a Hertfordshire address. Daisy wasn't quite sure what to make of it. He said he'd come across Aldeb and would like to tell her about it. He was in London for a few days, staying at a friend's in Battersea, and suggested they meet for tea. No details, no suggestion of how he'd come into contact with Aldeb; it was all rather vague and unsatisfactory.

She went back to the farmer's letter and read it again. Definitely worth following up. She started to dial the number then, remembering that farmers were rarely home at nine in the morning, called Simon instead. He was generally in the flat at this time of day, bashing out his articles before going in to the *Sunday Times* at about eleven to do his telephone research at the newspaper's expense. The later part of the day was for interviews and meetings, the evenings for the novel. Between all this came Daisy, at least she thought she fitted into the picture somewhere, though it was difficult to be sure.

'Is there any medical evidence of a link?' he asked as soon as Daisy told him about the letter. 'She might have got ill anyway.'

'Not yet,' Daisy conceded. 'But if we run some tests on her and the results tally with the Knowles family – well, we might have something.'

'Even then . . .'

'Well, what?'

'Not enough, is it?'

'It's a start.'

'You could do with some more cases.'

Daisy thought of the Hertfordshire man who wanted to meet her for tea. 'I'm working on it,' she said. She almost asked Simon if he was working on the story too, but she didn't like to press him, not when she'd given him a second hard sell only the previous week. She didn't want him to think she was obsessive, not when she'd hardly got into her stride.

'How about that Truffaut film?' she asked lightly, putting a low inviting note into her voice. But if there were ways to entice Simon into sudden acts of recklessness this, apparently, was not one of them.

'I'm working tonight and through the weekend,' he said. There was a pause. 'Umm – Tuesday?'

Tuesday was four days away. 'No chance of a quick meal in between? Like Monday?'

'Can't. I'm going to the Ritz.'

'The life you lead,' she said. 'What is it – a discussion on North Sea pollution washed down with a dozen oysters?'

'Not quite,' he said disapprovingly. 'Morton-Kreiger are unveiling some plans. For an environmentally friendly chemical plant, something like that.'

'Not so far wrong. Champagne and canapés in the lion's den.'

'Well, they're trying at least.'

'You could put it that way.'

'They try harder than most.'

'That's because they've got more to hide.'

Simon put on his authoritative voice, the one he used to counter emotional and ill-argued opinions. 'You can't look at everything in black and white, Daisy.'

'Maybe not, but even in colour Morton-Kreiger looks pretty murky.'

'I'll see you on Tuesday, Daisy.'

'Don't forget to ask them about Aldeb,' she called, but he'd already rung off. Unfinished conversations seemed to be a feature of whatever relationship she was establishing with Simon. She had the feeling that, when it came to discussions, she failed to come up to his rigorous intellectual standards of debate. Well, she'd never pretended to be Oxford Union material. Jenny poked her head through the door, a fax dangling from her fingers. Jenny was a punkette, complete with gold nose-ring, leather miniskirt, black tights and hair the colour of an iridescent tropical bird. She had a degree in sociology and laughed a lot, which was just as well considering her working conditions. 'It's your Washington friend Paul Erlinger,' she said.

'Why do you say *friend* like that?'

'I think he fancies you.'

'I've never met him.'

'Well, I wouldn't let a small thing like that get in the way,' Jenny said archly, closing the door.

The fax read: *Dear Daisy, The good news – the EPA won the Aldeb appeal. The bad news – by only two-one, and Morton-Kreiger International have been quick to file for a rehearing in the Federal Court of Appeal, and a stay of order. At the appeal hearing MKI pleaded bias in the testing procedures at the research company they used for the retesting demanded by the EPA. Rich, huh? The mind boggles at what comes next. More bad news – they've got a hold on the publication of the complete retest data, so I've nothing more to send you.* Daisy muttered to herself, a quiet heartfelt oath. She had been banking on that data. She had been hoping to be the first to send it to the Advisory Committee on Pesticides, prior to pressing for an urgent UK ban. *At this rate the whole thing will get to the Supreme Court some time next century. I dreamed about you the other night – crazy, huh? Something to do with having your picture (courtesy the Catch newsletter) pinned over my desk. Will you ever make it over this side? Love, Paul.*

Morton-Kreiger would fight the Aldeb ban to the bitter end – she wouldn't have expected them to do otherwise – but what surprised her was how successful their tactics were proving, and in the States of all places, where the balance was more heavily weighted in favour of consumer safety than anywhere else. Delays, appeals, hearings; Morton-Kreiger didn't seem to run short of ideas.

She swore again, though it was more of a sigh this time, and felt her disappointment drift into something approaching acceptance. She began to draft a reply to Paul Erlinger, asking when he guessed the data might finally be released, and if there might be a dirty-tricks story in there somewhere, a few unsavoury facts about Morton-Kreiger's tactics which might be suitable for leaking to the investigative press. She also asked for details of EarthForce's most recent case histories, in case there was an obvious overlap with the Knowles case. His reply would make for a lengthy fax, but EarthForce could afford it. Their supporters numbered a healthy two-point-five million, rising fast.

She read the last part of Paul's message again. It was hard to know how to respond. She'd seen a picture of Paul Erlinger in the EarthForce newsletter, and she didn't have it pinned over her desk.

After some thought, she scribbled: *I'll meet anyman anytime anywhere who gets me that Aldeb report.*

She took the letter out to Jenny for typing and faxing, and, after sifting the papers for cuttings, spent the next few hours working on a report on the aerial application of pesticides, breaking off only to take a couple of calls, and, at eleven, to phone the Hertfordshire man who'd sent the odd reply to her ad in the farming magazine. In his letter he said he was staying in Battersea for a few days, at a friend's flat, and he had given times when he could be contacted there. Eleven to eleven-thirty was the first slot.

It was answered immediately, almost as if he'd been waiting by the phone.

'Is this Colin Maynard?'

'It is.'

'About your letter. From the ad in *Farmers Weekly*.'

'Ah.' There was a pause and a rustling, and she imagined him sitting down and getting himself comfortable. 'Yes . . .' He sounded distant, as if he was holding the instrument away from his mouth. 'Your advertisement was most interesting.' The voice drew close again.

'You've had personal contact with Aldeb, have you?' asked Daisy.

'Forgive me,' he slid in, 'but before answering that question I hope you don't mind my asking who's asking.' He gave a nervous little chuckle like a bank clerk smoothing away any awkwardness.

'Of course not,' Daisy said hurriedly. 'My name is Daisy Field and – ' She wasn't sure why, but she was reluctant to mention Catch. 'I'm gathering information for a research project,' she said, which wasn't too far from the truth.

'Really? A research project? That sounds most interesting. May I ask, is this something you're doing as a – Oh, you know, what is it? – for one of those things, those – what *do* they call them?' The nervous little chuckle again, a click of the tongue. 'A thesis – that's it, a *thesis*.' He said the word with satisfaction as if he'd just answered a question on *Mastermind*.

'No, it's an independent project funded by a charitable trust.' This, too, had a grain of truth, since a large charitable trust had once funded one of Catch's few research projects.

'How interesting,' he repeated, his voice dipping obsequiously. 'I hope you don't mind my asking but it's as well to know who you're dealing with, don't you think?'

'Of course.' Daisy tried to guess what Colin Maynard might look like, how old he might be, but his voice gave nothing away. 'And what would the name of the trust be exactly?' he asked in a tone that was at once insistent and ingratiating.

Daisy hesitated. Even allowing for normal curiosity, the

conversation was disconcertingly one-sided. 'You suggested meeting for tea,' she said. 'How about this afternoon?'

'Oh.' A show of surprise, as if he hadn't expected to be so honoured. 'If you like. Why not. Yes – how about the Waldorf? I'm rather fond of the Waldorf. The foxtrot, all those *wonderful* Thirties tunes. Four o'clock all right for you? The Palm Court. I'll book. It's always best to book.'

Daisy rang off, wondering how a man so familiar with the Waldorf and things cosmopolitan matched up with Aldeb. He might not be anything to do with farming, of course; he might be on the marketing and distribution side of Aldeb, or even – the very thought – a renegade ministry man, complete with unpublished evidence of Aldeb's carcinogenic properties and cast-iron proof of the attendant cover-up. Well, one could always hope.

After lunch Jenny, who'd been out of the office on an errand for Alan, dropped in brandishing a magazine. 'Something for you,' she announced.

The magazine, a glossy gossip magazine with luscious 'pix' of stars reclining in their Hollywood homes, was not something Daisy normally got around to reading. Jenny had opened it at a page of news snippets and was pointing towards the lead story. It was about the singer-songwriter Nick Mackenzie and his wife Alusha. According to the report there'd been an accident on their Argyll estate. His wife – they referred to her as an exotic Seychellian – had been admitted to hospital after inhaling dangerous fumes.

Daisy murmured: 'Plenty of people inhale fumes.'

'But not many rock stars' wives,' declared Jenny.

'She's probably better by now.'

'They wouldn't have mentioned it if she was.'

Daisy was unconvinced. 'Most likely it was gas fumes or petrol or something like that.'

Jenny gave an expressive shrug. 'No harm in finding out though, is there?'

There would be no harm in finding out, but these things weren't that easy. By some peculiarity of human nature, people often preferred to remain in ignorance of the true nature of the risks they'd been exposed to, as if by ignoring them the dangers would in some magical way disappear.

It might be a waste of time, but she reached for the phone

anyway. She had quite a few Nick Mackenzie albums back in the flat. In fact she was rather a fan of his. There was something about his songs, an intriguing quality. Also, he wrote songs about the environment and, as far as she could remember, had done so for many years.

A contact on the staff of a rock magazine gave her the name of Nick Mackenzie's management company, which was listed at an address in Covent Garden. Getting this far had taken five minutes; the next part took a lot longer. David Weinberg Management was not the most friendly of organisations, nor the most forthcoming, and it took Daisy ten minutes to get through the first line of defence which came in the form of a girl with all the impenetrable indifference of a minor official unleashed on a position of unlimited power. But Daisy was used to wearing people down – it was part of her job: nonetheless it took a determined this-is-really-rather-important approach and a firm assurance that she wasn't trying to sell anything before she finally got through to the next bastion. This was some sort of personal assistant and, Daisy realised, as far as she was ever likely to get. Keeping the conversation short, Daisy introduced herself and asked what the chances might be of getting a letter through to Nick Mackenzie.

'We can't make any promises,' said the clipped female voice.

'If he doesn't read it himself, will he be told about it?'

'I really couldn't say.'

'Suppose I asked you to forward it to him wherever he was, would you? I wouldn't ask except it really is important and I've got to find someone I can trust to pass it on.' Daisy heard the sycophantic tone in her voice. 'I'll be sending information – nothing more – but it's information he might be very pleased to have.'

There was a pause. 'I'll do what I can,' the assistant finally conceded with great reluctance. Then, just in case Daisy should feel too confident, she added: 'Though I really can't promise.'

When Daisy came to write the letter there wasn't a great deal to say. She pointed out that Catch had access to most of the available information on common chemicals and their effects on health, and could, if necessary, recommend some good toxicologists. She also said she was sorry.

She sent two copies, one care of the assistant at David Weinberg Management and the second to Nick Mackenzie,

Argyll, Scotland. Correctly addressed mail was sometimes mislaid by the Post Office for no apparent reason at all but, incited by the flagrant challenge of a two-word address, the service could produce miracles.

Daisy wasn't sure what you wore to a tea dance at the Waldorf but she was fairly certain it wasn't tight jeans, patterned leather boots and a sweater of idiosyncratic design and clashing colours. Her jacket, short and soberly black, toned things down a bit, and she made a special attempt to brush her hair into some sort of order, not a simple matter when it was naturally curly and sprang out from her head.

The Waldorf was a massive grey elephant of a building, a Palladian–French-château hybrid in the Edwardian style. It seemed to sit on the curve of the Aldwych with reluctance, as if it had realised its mistake in being built bang on a noisy unattractive street.

A short flight of stairs with solid brass rails led to the foyer and the entrance to the Palm Court. A queue of people snaked out from the doorway, waiting to be seated. The tinny strains of 'There's A Small Hotel' floated out over their heads, and Daisy glimpsed a lone couple shuffling gently across a sunken dance floor.

As the queue inched forward she saw a room decorated in flat Wedgwood colours, dusty pinks and greyish greens, with marble floors and pilasters and a raised terrace around three sides of the room. There were a few palms all right, but they were small and emaciated.

The head waiter had been well primed: Maynard's name produced immediate recognition and a small bow. A young waiter led her round the terrace between tables of elderly ladies whispering across their teacups, giggly young people in Thirties-style hats, and terminally jetlagged tourists staring dully about them. Rounding a corner, the waiter stopped at a small table tucked in beside the balustrade and indicated a small grey-suited figure rising from the shadows of his chair.

He was young, in his twenties, and Daisy realised that she had pictured him as much older.

'What a pleasure.' He bowed obsequiously before straightening up to a height that was a good half inch shorter than Daisy's, and she wasn't that tall. She caught a strong whiff of the sort of heavy musk-like scent that Italians and Arabs splash on with impunity, but which Englishmen wear only at the risk of comments on their masculinity.

He hovered attentively while the waiter pushed in her chair. 'Now, first things first,' he began, settling back in his seat. 'The full tea or the not-so-full tea? I can't recommend the full tea highly enough. Sandwiches – very delicate, very dainty – scones, muffins. Nothing like it.' He gave a short laugh. 'A real touch of the good old days, I tell you. Then there are the teas to choose from – Earl Grey, Darjeeling, Lapsang Souchong.'

He couldn't have been more than twenty-eight or -nine, she decided, though he might have been even younger. He had a round fleshy face with a broad nose, pasty cheeks, a red full-lipped mouth and thick gingery hair that had been slicked back from his face with a lavish coating of wet-look gel. He was leaning forward in his seat, his pale indistinct eyes staring keenly across the table at her as if he were anxious not to miss her slightest movement or gesture.

Daisy chose the full tea although, at seventeen pounds, she rather hoped she wasn't going to be picking up the bill.

'I've been so looking forward to meeting you, Miss Field. I've never met a scientist before.' He spoke in the same mixture of servility and enquiry that had marked their telephone conversation.

'I'm not a scientist, I'm a researcher.'

He screwed his face up in an expression of apology. 'Oh, I do beg your pardon. Very remiss of me. One shouldn't make wild guesses, should one?'

'And you, Mr Maynard? What do you do?'

He blinked modestly, though it seemed to Daisy that he was overdoing it a bit. 'Ah. Now that's another story. Not a lot to tell, I'm afraid. How I wish there were. A modest accountant, that's all. With an insurance firm.'

Very Heep-like in his humility. Daisy tried to imagine Maynard bent over a ledger, working on columns of figures. The nondescript grey suit fitted the picture, as did the abject manner, but the plastering of hair gel and the heavy gold signet ring that adorned a thick finger appeared rather too flashy.

'And what's your interest exactly?' Daisy asked.

'Oh, I have many interests – golf, that sort of thing. Yes, golf mainly.'

'I meant in relation to Aldeb.'

He pressed a hand to his chest. 'Oh. *Oh*. Forgive me. How silly.' He screwed his face up and smiled at himself. 'Aldeb. Yes, of course, of course.' But he didn't answer her question. Instead he leant on the brass-capped balustrade and smiled indulgently towards the dance floor. 'Isn't this wonderful? All these old tunes.'

The band, who looked about the same vintage as the songs they were playing, had swung into a stately interpretation of 'The Blue Danube', a number whose higher notes were providing a considerable challenge to the trombone player.

The sandwiches and tea arrived. When she turned back it was to find Maynard staring at her. 'You were telling me about Aldeb,' she prompted.

'Of course. Well, it's like this, Miss Field. I've a sister, name of Jancis. Unusual name, isn't it? Most people call her Jan of course. Except me. I like to call her Jancis – such a pretty name, pity not to use it, don't you think?' He glanced at her constantly, watching her face, gauging her reaction. 'Quite a bit older than me,' he continued through the abject smile which seemed to be an almost permanent feature of his face. 'In fact, my half-sister, though you'd never know it. I mean, we're very close.' He creased up his ginger-lashed eyes to emphasise how close they were. 'She married a farmer, went to live in Northumberland. Then – oh, four years ago, she got sick. Her old man couldn't deal with it, couldn't cope at all. Went off with the neighbour's wife.'

He paused and, wrapping his lips delicately around a sandwich, chewed it rapidly.

'When you say sick, what exactly was the problem?'

He swallowed. His expression was unchanging, the eyes constantly searching her face, the smile expanding the corners of the heavy overblown mouth. For a moment Daisy thought he hadn't heard her question. 'They were never sure,' he said eventually. 'But she'd been working with Aldeb all right. Oh yes, she never had any doubt that it was Aldeb that had been the problem.'

Daisy caught the faintest hint of an accent. It wasn't one she knew, certainly nothing that came from anywhere near

South London. The only feature she could pin down was a guttural twang to his c's and k's. 'You say they weren't sure what was wrong,' she said, 'but she must have had some symptoms, surely?'

He started on a muffin, eating with the rapidity and determination of a compulsive eater. Below the fleshy cheeks, a heavy neck strained at its collar and the loose shirt could not hide the swell of a well-padded belly. 'Oh, plenty of symptoms. Aches, pains, that sort of thing. Bad aches and pains, mind. Very bad. Had to take pills and potions all the time. An absolute slave to them.'

'I see,' said Daisy, trying to sort her way through this morass of vague information. 'Would she be willing to come and see us, do you think? To undergo some tests? They're quite painless. Just blood, that sort of thing.'

'She would have, I'm sure. In fact she'd have been only too pleased. Sadly, though . . .' He paused, frowning deeply, and continued in an unsteady voice: '. . . it won't be possible.'

'Oh. Why not? Is she too ill?'

'Not exactly,' he said with evident difficulty. 'No, you see she died last year.'

It was Daisy's turn to stare. Until just a moment ago he had been using the present tense. 'How awful,' she murmured.

Momentarily overcome, Maynard looked down at his hands. The fingers were blunt, she noticed, and there were gingery hairs growing thickly along the backs.

Breaking free of his grief, he picked up the teapot. 'More tea, Miss Field?' he asked solicitously.

'It must have been awful, Mr Maynard. I'm so sorry.'

'Colin. Please call me Colin.' He did the trick with his eyes again, crinkling them at the edges to demonstrate his sincerity, before topping up her cup and offering her a muffin. 'Yes, it was sad, very sad indeed.'

'But surely the matter was investigated. Did they establish the cause of death?'

'Ah. There's no doubt about how she died, I'm afraid.' Adopting a reverential tone he confided: 'Her car went into a tree.'

Daisy took a moment to absorb this. 'I see.' She didn't like to ask if this mishap was likely to have been a complete accident or not. 'How awful,' she said. 'I'm sorry.'

He accepted her sympathy with a small bow of the head.

'One has to bear these things, doesn't one? One has to be brave. No choice really.' Almost immediately the ingratiating smile was back.

Daisy made an effort to like him and failed. His desire to please was so palpable, so overdone that her instinctive reaction was to pull up her drawbridge.

'Tell me,' she said, 'what exactly did you want from me, Mr Maynard?'

'From you?' He gave a humble little shrug. 'I thought maybe you could make something of what happened. You know, do something useful with the information. So her death won't have been in vain.'

The orchestra sprang into a noisy Charleston. Some of the younger dancers hurled themselves into a frenzy of leg kicking and arm waving. Every table in the room was taken, Daisy noticed, and people were being turned away at the door. Maynard had been lucky to get a booking.

Daisy raised her voice over the blare of the music. 'Quite honestly, I'm not sure we can do very much with what you've given me. There's so little to go on, you see.'

'Little to go on? Oh, I see. I hadn't realised.' He chewed thoughtfully on a pastry. 'But now you come to mention it, I suppose there isn't.' A regretful chuckle. 'Oh dear, oh dear. I'm disappointed of course. I mean, I had hoped . . . She was my sister, after all.' He popped the last of the pastry into his mouth. 'Well, well. There we are. There we are. One has to accept these things.' The smile slid back into place, and Daisy suppressed a sudden urge to wipe it off his face. 'So tell me, Miss Field, normally – when the person's available, so to speak – you can do these blood tests, can you? And what do they show exactly?'

'If we're lucky, if we catch the person soon enough, high levels of pesticide.'

'Just floating around in the blood, are they?'

'More or less.'

'And you've come across a lot of cases, have you?'

'Not as many as I'd like.' His accent: she had it at last. Unless she was mistaken it was South African or something very similar, an accent that time or determination had all but eradicated.

'Forgive me, but would that be tens of cases? Or hundreds?'

'We're not sure.' She explained how some people had been

77

exposed to several pesticides and it was hard to know which individual agent or combination of agents had caused their illness.

'But Aldeb's the number-one suspect, eh?' It seemed to Daisy that there was a hint of slyness in his eyes.

'Not necessarily.'

If he was disappointed in her answers he didn't show it. He offered her the last pastry. When she refused it he slid it onto his plate and raised his pale eyebrows in disapproval at his own self-indulgence. 'And the organisation you work for, Miss Field. I don't believe you mentioned it.'

'Didn't I?'

'You said you worked for a charitable organisation.'

'Yes, so I did.' She was tempted to skirt the truth again. There was something about Maynard that did not invite trust, and his questioning, for all its caution, had an edge of relentlessness to it. At the same time she had nothing to apologise for, and certainly nothing to hide.

'I work for Catch,' she told him. 'The Campaign Against Toxic Chemicals. We monitor all sorts of chemicals and their impact on health.'

A look of wonderment came over his face. 'Really?'

'Some of our work is funded by charitable trusts, as I told you, but mostly we rely on subscriptions.'

'You have a membership, do you?'

'Certainly. Would you like to join? It's twelve pounds fifty.'

He gave the briefest hesitation and, though it might have been Daisy's imagination, she thought she saw a flicker of calculation pass over his face. He beamed: 'Why, I'd be delighted.'

He insisted on paying in cash and drew fifteen pounds in notes from his wallet. She couldn't help noticing that the wallet was well stocked. He wouldn't accept any change. 'Let it be an extra little donation,' he said proudly. 'You will keep me in touch?'

She explained about the quarterly newsletters.

'And might I phone you just occasionally?' he asked. 'To see how things are going on the Aldeb front. If it wouldn't be too much trouble? It would mean so much.' He inclined his head timidly, though Daisy had got the feeling that timidity didn't come easily to Colin Maynard.

'There won't be much to report, not for some months anyway.'

He said hastily: 'In due course then. In due course.' He summoned the waiter and paid the thirty-five-pound bill without a murmur. Daisy couldn't help noticing that his lips moved as he calculated the tip.

SIX

Susan Driscoll waited for the driver to hurry round the
back of the car and open the door for her. She was perfectly
capable of opening it herself, of course, but such perks were
still novel enough to gratify and entertain her. Having stepped
out, she walked slowly into the house, leaving the driver to
unload the baggage and carry it into the hall after her.

Once inside, any fleeting illusion of high living came to an
abrupt end, and her mood darkened. She looked irritatedly
for something on which to focus her dissatisfaction, but the
hall and the drawing room, glimpsed through the open door
beyond, were just as she had left them, the scatter of cushions
unruffled, the carefully arranged bric-à-brac unmolested, the
picture frames straight. Even the dried flower-burst on the
Queen Anne occasional table by the door, which the cleaner
usually managed to displace, was for once undisturbed. The
place, her painstaking and loving creation of five years, was
perfect, and she felt an angry unreasoned resentment against
it. However much guests admired it – and they did, lavishly –
there was never any escaping the fact that she had exerted all
her creativity on a house that was small, hemmed in by
ugliness of immense proportion, and wildly inconvenient,
being deep in an area which, up-and-coming in the great
property boom of five years before, had failed to arrive. This
street and two of its neighbours formed an island of yuppifi-
cation in a sea of depressing council estates, run-down Victorian terraces and menacing inhabitants, most of whom were
coloured, a fact which Susan wasn't allowed to mention now
that Tony was a junior minister. Over the years guests had

become infrequent – it was easier and, though Tony wouldn't admit it, safer to meet them in town – and now the house seemed a laughable, lamentable waste of effort.

The driver asked if there was anything else she wanted, but she knew better than to take him up on the offer. A shopping trip to Knightsbridge would have been nice – her wardrobe had failed to stand up to the test of two days in Paris – but Tony would need to make cabinet rank before she could get away with anything as frivolous as that. As the other wives had allowed her to discover the hard way, the lines of privilege were not to be overstepped.

With the driver gone, she flicked through the bills and wandered into the kitchen. Even a cursory glance revealed the reason the dried flowers had been undisturbed: the cleaner, due yesterday morning, had failed to show up. Susan felt a deeper depression: it was really impossible to get things done around here.

A pan lay in the sink, clumps of congealed spaghetti floating in its oily waters. This meant that Camilla, her student daughter, must be in residence, an unexpected but largely pleasant surprise confirmed by the fact that the answering machine had been turned off and replaced by a stack of pencilled messages.

Susan brightened up a little and, going into the hall, called up the stairwell to the top floor. It was ten, still a little early for Camilla, and Susan was preparing to call again when her daughter's head suddenly appeared over the banister rail.

'Mummy! Who's a clever girl then?' Camilla shrieked.

'Oh? Am I? That makes a change.'

'And I thought you were kidding.'

'What are you talking about?' Susan said, slightly irritated.

'I'm talking about Nick Mackenzie!'

It took a moment for Susan to absorb the implications of this statement. Incredulous, she said: 'You mean – he's called?'

'His agent. Phoned yesterday.'

Susan hurried back to the kitchen and shuffled through the messages. There it was: David Weinberg Management had called. They wanted to discuss a date for a concert. Would she please call back.

She stared at the message, read it again, then sat down on the nearest stool.

Nick hadn't forgotten her then. He had realised that the unfamiliar-sounding Mrs Susan Driscoll was really her and had said yes; agreed to the impossible, to the one thing they'd said he'd never do.

The thought filled Susan with vivid exhilaration and a sort of bitter-sweet triumph. It had been a long time since she had seen Nick – incredibly, almost twenty years – but despite everything, despite the number of women who must have been through his life in all that time, despite his marriage to the woman with the strange name, he'd remembered.

And remembered her kindly, it seemed, despite – no, why did she say that? – *because* of what had happened so long ago. Yes, and why not? They had been very young. That said it all, really: very young, very selfish. Looking back now, he must feel guilty – *yes*, and rightly so. He had been awful, *awful* at the end. Yet she was happy to forgive and forget – it was such a long time ago, after all.

Even as she convinced herself of this she felt an echo of pain and anxiety, like an old wound. Would he really remember her kindly? Would he?

Camilla breezed in and enveloped her mother in an embrace that was mostly long hair and floppy T-shirt. Susan kissed her absentmindedly and disentangled herself.

Camilla gazed admiringly through oversize spectacles. 'Mummy, you *are* a dark horse. I'm afraid I didn't really believe you. I mean, it sounded so unlikely.'

Susan smoothed out the message and tucked it into her bag. 'What do you mean – unlikely?'

'Well, you knowing Nick Mackenzie.'

'But I told you. I knew him well.'

Camilla giggled delightedly. 'Mummy!'

Susan gave her a long cool look. 'We were very close for a time.'

The laughter fell away from Camilla's face. She looked respectful. 'Mummy, I had no idea.'

Susan gave a small secretive smile. 'Why should you?'

'Was it . . . Were you . . .?'

'We were lovers, if that's what you're getting at.' Susan looked away, out to the small enclosed patio with its scattering of geraniums. She noticed that the white walls, painted only a few months before, were already streaked with grime. 'We met at a party in Chelsea. It was one of those instant things, across a crowded room. The sort of thing you don't believe in until it happens to you. Within a week we were living together. It was – well, special. For both of us. We were very much in love.' She was aware of Camilla's incredulous stare. Children, selfish creatures that they were, always chose the images of their parents which suited them, and youth and desirability they found very uncomfortable indeed.

'What happened?' Camilla asked in a hushed voice.

Susan half turned so her face was in profile. 'I ended it. I didn't want that sort of life. It may sound glamorous, a non-stop succession of concerts and parties and travel but, believe me, it was soul-destroying. The band was always touring. The pace was mad, the pressure awful. No one could survive that. It started to destroy me and it certainly started to destroy Nick. He hit the drink, you know. I couldn't bear to watch it. I wanted it to end while we still had something going for us.'

'Mummy, I can't bear it. It's so sad.'

'Oh, not sad really.' Susan gave a brave little smile. 'These things happen all the time. Right person, wrong timing. And vice versa. It's the story of most people's lives.'

Camilla gave an agonised groan. 'But, Mummy, if he'd been anyone else, I mean if he'd been *ordinary*, would you – well, still be together?'

Only an eighteen-year-old could ask a question like that. 'Darling, who knows?' she answered enigmatically. 'One can never tell about these things.'

'Of course, I should be glad – that you married Daddy, I mean. Otherwise I wouldn't be here.'

Susan's mind was back on Nick Mackenzie. What memories came into his mind when he thought about her? Good ones hopefully. The others – well, they faded with time, didn't they? She gave a small shiver.

'Not that Daddy's ordinary, of course,' Camilla rattled on.

'No, darling,' Susan murmured vaguely. 'Of course not.'

'And he *is* a minister. Which isn't at all ordinary, is it?'

'A *government* minister, Camilla,' she said briskly. 'If you say minister people will think he's a parson.'

Camilla burst out laughing. 'Daddy a parson! What a thought!'

Susan didn't reply. She was thinking ahead to the night of the concert and the moment when she would face Nick again. She would dress very carefully. None of the staid government wife look, yet nothing too glitzy either. A designer dress, very simple, very dramatic. Very expensive. She would buy it first and argue with Tony later.

'Will you have lots of meetings beforehand?' Camilla asked. 'If so, can I be your assistant? Notebook in hand.'

Susan hadn't thought of meetings, but of course there would have to be several, maybe as many as three or four. Perhaps one with Nick himself. In which case she might well take Camilla along. But not the entire committee; they didn't deserve it. Though they were far, far too well bred to say so, they hadn't really believed she could pull this thing off. She would enjoy announcing her coup at the next meeting.

Pointing Camilla in the direction of the sink and the unwashed spaghetti pan, Susan hurried upstairs to unpack. Only a few hours before, everything about her clothes had disheartened her: frumpy, frowsy, second-rate. Now she sang as she hung them up. Pausing in front of a mirror, she cast a critical eye at her reflection, pushing her chin forward, turning to half profile to find her best angle. Not bad, really. She had good bones, and bones always stood the test of time. She didn't look forty-something, more like thirty-five. There were laugh-lines around her eyes, of course, and the eyelids were going a bit crêpy, but what could you expect. The hair needed attention though. The style, layered but long, like a shaggy lion, really didn't suit her. Too middle-class. Too middle-aged. She would go for something sleeker, simpler, more classical.

Normally she made it a rule never to unpack for Tony, just as she made it a rule never to wash and iron his shirts – laundries were the best people to field complaints about creases and late deliveries – but after this news she was feeling light-hearted and decidedly generous. Tony had to work hard in this new job of his; the three-day conference in Paris had been preceded by two days in Strasbourg and, before that, a hectic week in Parliament dispelling fears about contaminated water in Lancashire.

His case contained a pile of dirty shirts, socks and underclothes. There were an enormous number of them; he must have changed shirts at least twice a day. She bundled them into the laundry basket, hung his spare suit in the wardrobe and placed his unused clean shirts neatly on a shelf. In the bottom of the case were a few loose papers – brochures and circulars – and these she placed on his bedside table.

His sponge bag she put beside the basin in the bathroom, then, feeling really noble, opened it and hung out his flannel. She noticed his toothpaste was nearly finished and made a mental note to buy him some more.

She glanced at the brochure on top of the pile. A five-star converted château somewhere in France, complete with moat and drawbridge. Tony must have stayed there on his way from Strasbourg to Paris, before she flew out to join him. It looked gorgeous. How strange that he had said nothing about it. She opened the brochure out. Lying inside it was a slip, the sort they hand you with your key, confirming the room rate. At the top in French script was written: *Mme. Smith*, and a room number.

Susan sat down on the bed. It was several minutes before she moved. Then she got up and, going to the wardrobe, systematically went through the pockets of Tony's suits. Running quickly downstairs, she searched his overcoats hanging in the hall. Returning to the bedroom, she sat on the bed again for quite a time before going into the bathroom and staring at herself in the mirror.

This would take some thinking about.

As she turned to leave, something made her pause and look at the sponge bag again. At first she wasn't sure what it was that had caught her eye. Then she identified it. Just beyond the toothpaste, peeping out from a side pocket, was the corner of a small carton. Even as she stared at it, even as she reached to draw it slowly out, she knew exactly what it was, although that did nothing to prevent the rush of shock and anger.

The brand name was from the let's-make-condoms-jolly school. The packaging was bright and simple, as brash and innocent as a packet of sweets, designed to go with the bright young things' Porsches and post-modernist life-plans. Wishful thinking on Tony's part, perhaps. A middle-aged man's lustful little daydreams. Slowly she opened the packet. Her hand was shaking slightly. Out of a packet of three, there was only one left. No daydream, then. *Christ*.

Was she a bright young thing, this woman Tony was screwing? Had she been in Strasbourg with him as well as the château? Or even Paris? If Paris, she'd have had to be quick;

Tony had been there barely twenty-four hours before Susan herself arrived.

Was it a long-standing affair? Did they meet regularly? Was she young and pretty?

God – was it a friend of hers? Worst of all, was it someone Tony actually cared for?

Mrs Smith. She might have been more original. Such a shabby little name.

As far as Susan knew none of her female friends or acquaintances had been at either the Strasbourg or Paris conferences, nor had any of the female research assistants or secretaries from Tony's office. Unlikely, then, to be anyone she knew. In which case Tony couldn't possibly see the woman with any regularity. He was too busy, his movements too well accounted for.

But someone he cared about all the same? Surely not. There would have been signs: he would have been tense, or particularly attentive or unaccountably excited. She cast her mind back, but for as long as she could remember Tony had been nothing but his normal plodding reasonably affectionate self.

She relaxed a little. This couldn't be anything too serious. In which case, did she really need or even want to know more? She was surprised to find that, mixed with her shock and anger, was genuine amazement that bordered on admiration. The cunning devil. Who would have believed it? For years their love-life had been so-so, very so-so in fact. She had put this down to the channelling of Tony's energies into politics and his impossibly long working hours. But now she realised that she had been rather naive to think this state of affairs could continue unnoticed and unheeded, at least on his part. In the final analysis, no man could resist all the little extras that power brought with it. Weren't people always saying – and with monotonous regularity – that power was the greatest aphrodisiac of all?

She replaced the carton carefully in the side pocket, along with the damp flannel she had recently hung out, and carefully zipped the bag up again.

'Mummy, I quite forgot – '

Susan gave a great start and clamped a hand to her chest. Camilla was peering in from the bedroom. Susan shook with rage. 'Never do that again! Never!'

Camilla put on her sulkiest expression, the sort children

keep exclusively for their parents. 'Sorry. I only wanted to show you the paper. There's something about Daddy in it.' She gave a resentful shrug and tossed the newspaper onto the floor. 'Excuse me for trying to help,' she added with unnecessary sarcasm, and flounced out.

Angry with Camilla, angry with herself for having reacted so sharply, still catching her breath from the surprise, Susan reached for the paper. It was *The Times*. It took her a moment to find the item, tucked away in a political diary column.

> One dark horse is the fast-rising junior minister, Tony Driscoll. Dubbed grey and undistinguished in his first post in Transport, he quickly bloomed at the Environment office, and has been credited with singlehandedly getting the government out of the Lancashire water pollution fiasco almost unscathed. Until recently considered a rank outsider in the Cabinet stakes, Driscoll's unsuspected talent with the media, his readiness to take on thankless tasks, and his quick wit on the floor of the Commons have the pundits tipping him for a more senior post after the next election.

Were they serious? Quick wit. Talent with the media. Susan reread it with bemusement. It was hard to believe they were talking about Tony. His jokes were museum-pieces, his wit schoolboyish. As for the media, she had to brace herself to watch him on television. His desire to impress was so transparent, his concern so palpably laid on, that she felt sure everyone must see through him at any moment.

'Unbelievable,' she said aloud.

She was still murmuring her disbelief when she dressed for dinner that evening. She wore her favourite black suit with a tailored jacket and a skirt of decorous length that came to just above the knee: shorter skirts, though fashionable, had been forbidden. Tony said they looked tarty. He was a fine one to talk, Susan decided, when he had a tart of his own tucked away somewhere.

She'd a good mind to embarrass him in the restaurant, to drop a hint over the soup. That would serve him damn well right. At the same time, now that she had got over her shock and was feeling an almost perverse satisfaction in having caught the silly fool out, her more cautious instincts told her to do nothing of the sort. Like something let loose from its bottle, a revelation, once made, might expand and take on all sorts of ugly shapes. Besides, they were going to the Caprice, and she didn't want to spoil her meal.

The doorbell rang just before seven thirty. She opened the door to a uniformed chauffeur who tipped his hat to her. Behind him was a Rolls, the large-bodied type of thirty years ago that sat high above the road and was usually packed with Arabs on their way to Harrods. She sank into the dark recesses of the interior, feeling suitably indulged, and thought: Bully for Mr What's-his-name. Directed to the reading light by the chauffeur she checked her pocket diary for the name of their host for the evening. R.B. Schenker, chief executive, Morton-Kreiger International, Agrochemical Division. Morton-Kreiger was one of those vast corporations that made chemicals and pharmaceuticals, that she knew, but Mr Schenker she had never met, not so far as she could remember anyway.

Tony had told her the man's first name on the way back from Paris but she couldn't remember that either. R.B. – Robert? Richard? But certainly not Bob or Dick. These corporate men didn't like abbreviations: it invited people to take them less than seriously. Robert or Bob or whatever it was would be a bore, there was no getting away from that, and she would have to survive the evening as best she might.

His name, as it turned out, was Ronald. He was a slight man in his early forties, with dark hair which he brushed over to one side to cover his sharply receding hairline. He had a narrow high-boned face, a pointed chin and very white skin. His eyes, which were quick and dark, were set close together and stared at you with great intensity, as if he was watching for your every move. He was attentive and courteous, but without charm, as if he had taken a half-day course in etiquette and had forgotten the lesson about looking as though you were enjoying it. His manner first embarrassed then irritated Susan. Mr Schenker had obviously read in some how-to-succeed book that, on the path to influence, no stone was to be left unturned.

Most of the time Tony and he talked politics, or rather, Tony talked and Ronald Schenker listened. Mr Schenker, it appeared, was not married – at least he hadn't brought a wife with him – so that Susan often found herself left out of the conversation. She used the time to think about Nick Mackenzie and her husband, though not simultaneously. Her mind flittered schizophrenically between euphoria, biting uncertainties over the concert and wonder at the sight of her cheating husband, butter incapable of melting in any part of his anatomy.

As usual in company, Tony was animated, very – what was that awful word? – forceful. It was all laid on, of course, all part of his political persona. Away from the limelight he was quite a subdued person. At least, with her he was.

Susan had always regarded him as safe and sturdy, the sort of quietly successful, middle-of-the-road Englishman who never let you down – but didn't give you too many surprises either. The success of his political career had been a little unexpected, to put it mildly, but then the most unlikely people often make it in politics. She was constantly struck by the number of dull, narrow-minded bores she met in the Commons.

Until today she'd always believed that Tony's staunch Thatcherite qualities extended to their relationship. Never, during the nineteen years they had been together, had it ever occurred to her that Tony would rock the boat. Even after what she'd discovered today, she couldn't imagine that anything would ever seriously undermine their marriage.

But that, of course, was precisely what all unsuspecting wives thought, right until the moment their husbands walked out of the door. She would have to watch her step.

Tony caught her stare, and gave her a perfunctory grin. She tried to decide whether he could possibly appear good-looking to other women. He was very ordinary, so very ordinary that she sometimes wondered if he hadn't come out of a mould marked standard middle-aged mark-one Englishman. He had always had a tendency to put on weight, a battle that had ebbed and flowed through their marriage, but which, with the frequent lunches and dinners, was finally being lost. He had thinning hair of a nondescript colour, large rimless glasses, rather pudgy cheeks and a neck that was beginning to squeeze out over the edge of his collar.

Yet he must have something special, something that gave him the edge on the political platform and, so it would appear, with this woman in France.

Perhaps Susan was missing something, perhaps she had missed it right from the beginning. Perhaps Tony had charisma, that much overused word which always sounded to Susan like an unpleasant socially transmitted disease. But it was a hard idea to swallow. Charisma depended on sex appeal and Tony lacked the edge of danger that is the essential ingredient of sex appeal. Tony had always been unutterably safe.

She hadn't married him for sexual chemistry – she'd had quite enough of that and its attendant disasters in her early twenties – no, she'd married Tony for his dependability, his merchant banker's income, and because she was tired of having to look after herself. The merchant banker's income had disappeared soon after they married, when Tony had decided to earn his Brownie points by going to work for a big charity, but by then Camilla was on the way and she was rather taken by the idea of motherhood.

'Do you like opera, Mrs Driscoll?' Schenker asked with his rather stiff smile. 'We'd be delighted if you'd come to Glyndebourne with us next month.'

Susan glanced at Tony for affirmation and smiled graciously. 'That would be lovely,' she said. She didn't like opera, but she knew Tony would be keen to go, and everyone said the gardens were lovely.

'Good. I'll send you a programme then. There are four operas to choose from – Donizetti, Mozart, Tchaikovsky and Strauss.' There was a hint of hesitation and rehearsal in this speech, and Susan guessed Schenker had memorised the list especially for her benefit.

'We also take seats at Covent Garden. I don't know if you'd like that?' He watched her face carefully. 'Or the theatre?'

He spotted her flicker of interest and quietly seized on it. 'The theatre then? Just let me know what you'd like to see.' He waited, and Susan realised he was expecting her to name a play there and then. Mr Schenker was obviously someone who liked to nail things down.

'I'm not sure,' Susan replied. 'Any ideas, Tony?'

'Oh, you decide, my dear. You're more up to date with these things than I am. Besides, I always like the things that you like.' He raised his eyebrows at Schenker in a quick conspiratorial smile, as if they, as men, had conceived this ploy to keep the little woman happy.

Susan managed a thin smile, and named a popular musical you had to kill to get tickets for.

'Good. That'll be arranged then,' said Schenker, and Susan had no doubt that it would. 'The minister's kindly agreed to visit our new plant in Newcastle in September,' he continued, and for an instant Susan had to remind herself that this grand personage he was referring to was Tony. 'We would be delighted if you would come too. But of course, we'd quite understand if you'd prefer not to . . .' Schenker trailed off politely, awaiting his next cue.

Susan tried to think of something she'd hate more than a visit to a factory in Newcastle and failed. She put on an interested expression. 'A new plant?'

'Fertilisers. It's the largest and most modern fertiliser plant in Europe. We're very proud of it.'

'Really? How wonderful.' For a moment she was lost for anything else to say. 'But fertilisers aren't exactly environmentally friendly, are they?' She rolled her eyes in mock disapproval. 'I'm surprised at Tony having anything to do with it.'

It was not much of a joke, but she expected a favourable response. Tony did chuckle slightly, but Schenker was silent, the tight-lipped smile fastened to his face with difficulty, his small eyes unamused. Susan realised she had made the classic error of imagining that such a grey little man would have a sense of humour.

'Fertilisers have had a bad name in the past, of course,' Schenker said in a voice that was at once earnest and slightly reproachful. 'But as I'm sure you're aware, the agricultural industry in this country couldn't function without them. In fact food would cost four times as much, maybe more, if farmers were forced to do without them. But that isn't to say we don't take our environmental responsibilities very seriously. We do. Very seriously indeed.' The unblinking eyes stared into hers, as if he could convince her by willpower alone. 'In the last ten years Morton-Kreiger have spent millions and millions on developing fertilisers which are less likely to leach away through the soil and find their way into water sources – fertilisers which are kinder to the environment. Millions and millions. No one else has done as much as we have. No one.'

Susan said hastily: 'I'm sure that's true – '

'And it's the same story with pesticides. We lead the world in pesticide safety. Morton-Kreiger undertake more research than any other major company into producing safer products. Not only in terms of pounds and dollars, but in terms of the quality and thoroughness of the tests we run – '

This was getting tiresome. Susan said firmly: 'Mr Schenker, it was a joke. Really. Just a joke.'

The idea seemed to take him by surprise. He hesitated, absorbing the information, then nodded slowly. 'I see.'

'I think Susan was just echoing most people's misconceptions about my job,' Tony stepped in smoothly. 'They seem to think that an environment minister should go around banning everything in sight, rather than persuading manufacturers to adapt and modify existing products. If we banned everything the Greens wanted us to ban, then we'd be back in the Dark Ages, living in hovels and eating porridge three times a day.'

Schenker swivelled his eyes back to Susan.

'I'm not much of a one for porridge,' she said.

Schenker seemed to take her remark as a sign of approval, not only for what Tony had just said, but for himself and all his chemicals.

'Porridge.' He nodded and smiled, and Susan realised this was probably the closest he ever came to laughing. 'And what sort of cuisine do you like, Mrs Driscoll?'

Susan suspected she was meant to say: do call me Susan, but she resisted. 'Well, I'm not complaining at this,' she said, indicating the newly arrived dessert, an artistic array of sorbet, fruit, raspberry *coulis* and sugar wafers.

'I see,' said Mr Schenker, filing the information away. 'Then we'll come here again, shall we? After the theatre.'

Irritated at being parcelled up so tidily, Susan had the sudden urge to disturb Mr Schenker's meticulous little world. 'What about you?' she enquired politely. 'Do you like French food?'

'Yes, indeed.' Anticipating the drift her questions might take, he pulled back a little. 'But nothing too rich.'

'What sort of things exactly?'

His courteous expression slipped into something altogether more guarded, as if he was beginning to realise he was on thin ice. 'Oh . . . their soups.'

'Vichyssoise?'

He gave the faintest of nods, and looked away, trying to close the subject. It was just as she had suspected: he knew nothing about food.

'And what else?' Susan persisted.

He did not like being pressed, not when he was being

shown up. Moreover, he was beginning to suspect her motives. With good reason, of course. She was rather enjoying herself.

'The fish soups. They're very good too,' he said eventually. 'Bouillabaisse?'

This time he made no attempt to reply, but stared at her, the little eyes gleaming darkly. Mr Schenker did not enjoy being disconcerted.

'But you're not so good with the shellfish, eh?' Tony said. 'Made you sick as a dog, didn't they, Ronald?'

'Oh dear. What happened?' Susan asked pleasantly.

'Oysters,' Tony said. 'That's what happened. And it was me who persuaded him to try them. Not my finest recommendation. But you should have told me they were no good, Ronald. I would have called the hotel doctor. It could have been serious. Salmonella or something.'

'Where was this?' Susan asked.

There was a small pause. Susan looked up from her plate to see a shimmer of realisation slide over Tony's eyes, a flicker of caution as if he were thinking his way rapidly out of something. But the shift, which was so small that no one else would have noticed it, was gone as quickly as it had come and he said with his usual ease: 'At this hotel in France.'

For once Ronald Schenker was not staring at her, but examining his coffee cup.

So the two of them had been in France together, had they? Dining together, staying at the same hotel. Was it at the château, she wondered, or in Paris? One way or the other, they seemed to be spending a lot of time together. And when Tony was so busy; and when he had to be so careful to be impartial and objective and all the other things ministers were meant to be.

And where did the woman fit into all this? When, in the middle of all these cosy evenings with Schenker, would Tony have had time to see *her*?

She put down her spoon and abandoned the last of her dessert. One way and another, this day had really been too much.

'Everything all right?' Schenker asked solicitously.

Susan looked up and realised she had been frowning.

'Delicious,' she said. 'Absolutely delicious.'

*

93

'Have we sent the flowers to Mrs Driscoll?'

'Yes, Mr Schenker.'

'What did we send?'

'A mixed bouquet of seasonal flowers.'

Schenker looked up from his desk. 'A mixed bouquet. But what was in it?'

The secretary flipped through her notebook, and Schenker knew immediately that she was stalling. He said briskly: 'Find out, would you? And next time, make sure there are plenty of roses. I think Mrs Driscoll would like roses.'

When the secretary had gone Schenker buzzed the intercom and a moment later his personal assistant Peter Cramm entered. Schenker always felt invigorated when Cramm arrived. Cramm, tall, fit and well turned-out, was the only person whose energy matched his own, the only person with enough imagination to get things done unprompted.

'Find out what charity work Susan Driscoll does, will you?' Schenker said immediately. 'She must be on some committee or another. It might be a cause we could support.'

Cramm, sitting in his customary seat at one side of Schenker's modernistic desk, did not reply but made a brief note on his pocket jotter.

'Now – Aldeb,' said Schenker. 'What's the update?'

'Still stuck on Senator Brisco.'

'Do we really need him?'

'He's on the Senate Appropriations Committee.'

'I know, I know, but haven't we got anyone else?'

'Our people are working on it.'

Like all large conglomerates, Morton-Kreiger employed a considerable number of lobbyists to look after its interests in Washington and other major capitals. When things were quiet the Morton-Kreiger board questioned the necessity for spending hundreds of thousands in this way, but when things got rough, as they had been with Aldeb, the board were only too happy to have made the investment.

'It's the re-test data that's the problem with Brisco,' Cramm said. 'The environmentalists got hold of some of it, as you know, and they must have sent it to the senator, because he keeps quoting the figures at us. He sees himself as rather a science buff, I'm afraid. He's says even an idiot could see the data gaps and that he'd find it difficult to help until they can be explained.'

'What about the original tests? Hasn't he been shown a summary or something?'

'He says it's impossible to be sure they're unbiased.'

'Not unbiased?' Schenker echoed in an offended voice. 'What does he think he is, an expert? Does he have the slightest evidence for that sort of allegation?'

'He says TroChem is an industry-controlled laboratory and therefore incapable of delivering impartial data.'

'But everybody uses TroChem. Half the products on the US market have been tested at TroChem.' An exaggeration, of course – TroChem hadn't been going that long – but truthful enough for the purposes of the argument. Schenker tapped his fingers delicately on the desk. 'He must have been nobbled,' he declared. He didn't have to say who by.

The eco-mafia, as many people called them – and Schenker never discouraged the term – had loomed large in the lives of the agrochemical industry for some time. If the eco-mafia had their way, products would cost ten times as much and take ten times as long to bring to market, and this at a time when the number of new products getting through the system had already been squeezed to a trickle. These people also wanted to see products withdrawn on the most flimsy and far-fetched evidence, the sort of data that came from feeding rats virtually undiluted chemical for a month and getting a point-one per cent cancer rate.

'You know, I'd almost like the supply of products to dry up,' he remarked to Cramm, 'just to witness the anti-Green backlash.'

The anti-Green backlash was an old hope of Schenker's, one he had harboured ever since the Environmental Protection Agency had first moved to ban Aldeb in the US – since, as he liked to put it, environmental fever had taken over the Western world and bludgeoned the media into submission.

Swivelling his chair, Schenker pushed himself smoothly to his feet and walked over to the window to stretch his spine. His back always gave him trouble first thing in the morning, the left-over of a water-skiing injury sustained when staying with the chief executive of Morton-Kreiger Incorporated in the Bahamas. Water skiing, sports fishing, game shooting, snow skiing: Schenker had tried them all during his occasional and necessarily brief holidays. But the learning curves were too steep for his temperament and the available time.

Far below, the Thames flowed grey and sluggish. Even from this height he could see the whorls of polystyrene, plastic and aluminium cans swirling around the moored vessels. Soon the tide would turn and carry the debris back down-river in long ugly trails towards the East End, where doubtless it had originated. He bent over and touched his toes to ease the pressure on the lower vertebrae. 'That Senator Brisco should learn not to meddle,' he blew over his shoulder.

'Our people are working on one possibility that might swing him.'

'Yes?'

'It involves trading a few favours.'

That was always the way in American politics. 'And what are the chances?'

'Good, I'd say,' Cramm replied, and Schenker experienced the satisfaction he always felt when Cramm and the rest of the team had been beavering away behind the scenes. He didn't enquire further. It was quite enough to know that his people were working on it. The how and why did not concern him. Feeling brighter, he did some side bends, raising one arm in the air, putting the other hand on his hip and pushing over as far as he could go.

'A pity we never had conclusive data,' Schenker said more to himself than to Cramm, dredging up possibilities again. Although he, better than anyone, knew that Morton-Kreiger's scientific staff had been squeezed dry in the hunt for data favourable to Aldeb. 'Anyone else on that appropriations committee we should be attending to?' He breathed through a series of controlled pants.

Cramm shook his head. 'No one we haven't tried.'

'Keep at it,' Schenker said in the tone of a scoutmaster. 'This is still a number-one priority and I don't want anyone to forget it.'

Privately Schenker had already written Aldeb off in the US. That didn't mean that the battle wasn't to be fought to the bitter end, almost irrespective of cost. Not only was it a matter of principle to continue the fight, but it was essential to keep the environmentalists at bay and their resources stretched to the limit, if only to keep their attention from straying to other products.

Schenker had had plenty of time to get used to the idea of

losing Aldeb in the US. The filing of the original EPA case, the unsuccessful appeal and the move for a rehearing had taken four years. Time enough to make contingency plans, salvage whatever could be salvaged, and divert remaining stocks of Aldeb elsewhere. Very sensibly, the poorer countries weren't so hysterical about overinflated cancer risks. They only cared about feeding their people. Schenker often reminded himself about the enormous contribution that agrochemicals made to the developing world. It made him feel his job was worthwhile.

After a few more side bends, a couple of toe touches and a number of deep breaths, Schenker returned briskly to his desk. 'Globally, we're still okay, are we?'

Cramm nodded. 'No change.'

'No more nasty surprises then.'

'I don't think so. Though that campaigning group Catch are trying to dredge something up.'

'Something?' There was reproof in his tone; he disliked inexactitude.

'They're advertising in farming magazines for people who've supposedly been affected by Aldeb.'

'Can they do that?'

Cramm shrugged. 'Nothing to stop them.'

'I'm surprised it's allowed. And how are these people meant to know they've been harmed by Aldeb?'

'Presumably they'll be self-diagnosed.'

Schenker raised an eyebrow. 'Self-deluded.'

'One interesting thing though,' Cramm offered with the tiny degree of dramatic emphasis he sometimes allowed himself. 'Catch advertised anonymously.'

'And that's allowed, too, is it?'

'Apparently.'

Schenker sighed in wonder at the magnanimity of English law. 'This secrecy, they're frightened of attention or what?'

'I think they've finally realised that farmers aren't great fans of radical lefties, and won't have anything to do with them if they announce themselves.'

'So what sort of a response have they had?'

'We don't know that.'

'And do we know what they're planning to do with this information once – if – they get it?'

'More media stories, presumably. Like the one on the potato farmers in Berkshire – they've been trying to push that as an Aldeb-caused-cancer story to the nationals.'

'And how are they getting on?'

'Nothing's appeared yet. But we're keeping an eye on it.'

Schenker pondered for a moment. It was all very well keeping a watch on the activities of these people, but that didn't stop them scoring heavily and without warning, as he knew to his cost.

'Where does Catch's money come from?'

'Membership. Fifteen thousand, fairly static.'

Schenker turned his palms up and gestured amazement. 'In admin terms, that must cost them almost as much as it brings in. Sure there's nothing else?'

'Unlikely. It's a shoestring operation. Just data-gathering and media pressurisation. Nothing more ambitious.'

Schenker wasn't entirely convinced. 'Keep tabs on their financial situation, will you?' He pointed a long slow finger at Cramm, his favourite way of emphasising a point. 'Lack of cash – that's the key to that lot.'

He sat back in the soft leather of his chair. It was time to move on.

'Silveron okay?' he asked Cramm, adding with heavy irony: 'No problems with the EPA on that, I trust?'

Cramm gave his small tight laugh. 'No.'

'And we're ready to go?'

'We're ready to go,' Cramm echoed.

Silveron, a new broad-spectrum pesticide, promised to be very profitable. Which was just as well because it had taken six years and sixty million dollars to develop, cash the division needed to pull back in a hurry. Silveron was Schenker's baby. He'd been in at the start of its development, had rooted for it all the way along the line, had overseen its progress.

'Any more feedback on UK performance?' Silveron was already on the UK market under a restricted licence, which allowed limited use for a period of two years, prior to the grant of a full licence.

'Just the normal sort of thing.'

'What does that mean?' snapped Schenker. Statements needed quantifying, tying down, putting in context.

'There's been a small amount of negative feedback, but

according to Marketing it's nothing – statistically insignificant.'

'They're sure?'

'They're sure.'

'Anything else?' Schenker asked.

A slight pause, then: 'Miss Kershaw called.'

Schenker felt a touch of alarm. 'Here? For me?'

'Oh no.' Cramm gave an astonished smile. 'Gracious, no. My home. Last night.'

'What did she want?'

'It was just a friendly call, to keep in touch.'

Schenker's fears were far from allayed. 'She didn't want anything?'

'No, nothing.'

'She didn't mention Driscoll?'

'Oh no. She wouldn't do that.' Cramm sounded very sure. 'No, I only mention it because I thought we might like to ask her to the opening of the Newcastle plant.'

Schenker was very still. Had Cramm gone mad? 'I don't think that would be a good idea,' he said coldly.

The very thought of Miss Kershaw made him uneasy – but then he felt uneasy about women at the best of times. He had always found them difficult and disturbingly unpredictable, and his brief marriage and unpleasant divorce ten years before had done everything to confirm his opinion. When he was forced to deal with them now, it was cautiously.

Angela Kershaw was the most difficult kind of female, pretty and vivacious, a combination which, in his limited experience, was likely to make her doubly unpredictable.

She'd first turned up at a cocktail party during a clean water conference in Birmingham some weeks before, an event partly sponsored by Morton-Kreiger. He gathered from Cramm that she was employed on a stand there, one of the army of pretty girls who made the rounds of motor shows and exhibitions, demonstrating products and attracting business. No one seemed to know how she had come to be invited to Morton-Kreiger's party but, whoever brought her, it was Cramm who introduced her to Driscoll and asked her to join them for dinner. To Schenker, she seemed indistinguishable from dozens of other rather silly young women, with her identikit smile, bright makeup and inane conversation interspersed with gasps of girlish laughter, but to his amazement the evening was an enormous success. The minister had been transfixed by her, almost embarrassingly so.

Schenker had quickly forgotten about her until a month later, when Cramm mentioned that she would be in Paris during the European conference. Schenker's first reaction had been alarm.

'What? Who invited her?'

'She's working there,' Cramm had replied.

'I don't think we need concern ourselves with her.'

'But it would be a pity, wouldn't it, not to repeat the other evening? I mean, when she's going to be there anyway, in Paris, and the minister has a free evening. I know he'd enjoy seeing her again.'

There was something in the way Cramm said this that made Schenker pause. He was not always terribly perceptive about these things, but his imagination weaved inexorably towards an inescapable and disturbing conclusion.

'God – has she been seeing Driscoll?'

Cramm's impassive expression didn't falter. 'I really couldn't say.'

This, doubtless, was the truth, although it left too much unsaid. Schenker hesitated. He hated having to voice these things openly, but it was necessary to be clear. 'Has Driscoll said he'd like to see her?'

'Not in so many words, no, but . . .' His shrug was an answer in itself.

Schenker felt resentment, distaste and a sense of opportunity in about equal measures, but opportunity, based as it was on Driscoll's burgeoning political career, won the day.

In the event Cramm's arrangements for the evening were discreet, though there were few arrangements that could be discreet enough for Schenker. They had gone to a château on the Marne near Epernay. To make up a tidy foursome, a second girl was found to accompany Schenker. Everyone arrived separately, the Kershaw girl registered as Mrs Smith, the dinner was held in a private room, the party remained sober, nobody attracted attention, and when it came to leaving the next morning, the cars arrived on time. Driscoll seemed delighted. Schenker was not so easily satisfied – he took up a couple of minor administrative details with Cramm later – but all in all the project could be judged to have achieved its objectives.

But invite Angela Kershaw to Newcastle for an official event? With the local press all over the place? Cramm was losing his sense of proportion.

Schenker said: 'No, Peter. Not Newcastle.'

'Oh,' said Cramm, lifting his voice slightly in unspoken dissatisfaction. 'A private dinner, then?'

'If you like.'

'A celebration in London perhaps? Shall I arrange it?'

Schenker shuffled the papers on his desk, suddenly impatient to be rid of these disconcerting trivialities and get on with the real business of the day. 'Do as you think fit,' he said curtly, waving Cramm away. 'But don't bother me with the details.'

SEVEN

'Y ou should be pleased, Mr Mackenzie. It's good news.'
The doctor gave a professional smile, the sort designed to
inspire, reassure and subtly reassert authority all at the same
time.

Something dark and painful pulled at Nick's stomach, a
lurking unvoiced anger. He did his best to suppress it: after
all this man, a consultant physician named Plumb, meant well
– all of them meant well – yet their habit of reducing
everything to platitudes, of exuding this misplaced confidence, baffled and exasperated him.

'I wouldn't have called it good news,' Nick said evenly.

Plumb angled his head politely to one side.

'What you're saying is that you don't know what's wrong,'
Nick said.

There was a pause. The juddering roar of accelerating traffic
rose from the Marylebone Road below, reverberating through
the room. The toxicologist sitting on Plumb's right, imported
from a university especially for the meeting, studied his
hands.

'We're saying that we believe there's nothing physically
wrong with your wife,' Plumb explained gently.

'That you know of.'

'I'm sorry?'

Was it worth creating antagonism? Nick debated for a
moment, then repeated quietly: 'Nothing wrong with her that
you know of.'

'Mr Mackenzie' – Plumb gave a look of understanding and
compassion – 'we have very sophisticated tests nowadays.

Your wife's been through all we can think of – and a few more. If there'd been anything seriously wrong, we would have found it, believe me.'

'But chemicals don't always show up in tests, do they?' Nick said.

The toxicologist blinked into life. 'It depends on the type of chemical, the dosage and how soon after the event you can run a test. And of course it helps to know what you're looking for. Then you know which tests to run.'

'And we've run all the obvious tests,' Plumb said in his plodding delivery. 'Several times. But with no trace of chemicals or chemical damage.'

Arguing technical points with this man was like playing tennis without a racquet: it was difficult to return even the most basic shot. Like all specialists, he was paid to have an opinion, and he wasn't about to admit that there might be the occasional yawning chasm in his knowledge, that, just possibly, he might simply be wrong. Nick rubbed a hand over his eyes. He felt dreadfully tired.

Aware that he was repeating himself for perhaps the twentieth time, he said wearily: 'My wife was overcome by fumes. She inhaled a large quantity of dangerous chemicals. You can't possibly say they had no effect.'

Plumb put on a serious but kindly face. 'Mr Mackenzie, your worries are very understandable, but this particular chemical that your wife inhaled, the wood preservative . . .'

'Reldane.'

'. . . Yes – Reldane – has no known harmful effects. Isn't that so, Blair?'

The toxicologist tore his eyes away from his hands. 'As wood preservers go, it's pretty benign really.'

Nick tried to remember what the people from Catch had told him over the phone. 'But that's not absolutely certain, is it?' he said. 'I understand that the research is fairly thin.'

Plumb frowned at that. 'But Reldane's been passed for use by the safety people. It must have been. It wouldn't be allowed on the market otherwise, would it, Blair?' He flung a glance at the toxicologist.

'But I'm told that means very little,' Nick said before Blair had a chance to come in. 'The testing was done years ago. It could well be out of date.'

Plumb drew a deep breath. 'But there's no scientific basis

for saying it's dangerous. No hard evidence to suggest it has any long-term effects. Quite the contrary. Isn't that correct, Blair?'

Given his cue, the toxicologist spouted facts. 'When ingested by mouth in any significant quantity, more than a millilitre, Reldane can cause nausea and dizziness, but it has no other known toxic effects. It's not carcinogenic or tetrogenic. And it doesn't affect the nervous system, not like the cholinesterase inhibitors.'

'What're they when they're at home?' Nick asked, beginning to lose patience.

'Substances that cause damage to the nervous system by inhibiting nerve transmitters. You find them in powerful pesticides. But not Reldane.'

'But when it's breathed in? That must be damaging, surely?'

'The Reldane was definitely inhaled, was it?'

'Yes. It was spilt on the ground, next to my wife's head. She was breathing it all the time she lay unconscious.'

'In that case, I have to say that it's even more unlikely that Reldane was to blame. You see, the effects of inhalation are invariably *less* severe than those of direct ingestion.'

If it was a trap, it had been neatly laid. Nick heard his voice rise: 'So you're saying it's harmless?'

Blair looked to Plumb for help.

'Not harmless exactly,' Plumb said. 'But not harm*ful* either. One has to accept that if Reldane had had any serious long-term effects in the population they would have come to light by now.'

Something in Nick died a little every time he heard a statement like that. Every answer was so plausible, every explanation so utterly reasonable, that gradually but relentlessly they wore you down and swamped your own instincts. He was weary of text-book solutions and standard assurances, weary of beating his head against the wall of scientific fact.

Plumb added: 'And the amount your wife inhaled was really quite small. After all, she was discovered in a reasonably short time, wasn't she?'

Nick didn't reply.

'Don't misunderstand me,' Plumb said. 'The chemical incident – contamination, if you prefer – might well have contributed to the trauma and the miscarriage. I'm not discounting that possibility, far from it.'

Nick looked away to the window, reaching for his breath. Even now he couldn't hear mention of the lost pregnancy without experiencing a mixture of conflicting emotions, all strong, all painful. He dimly recognised that there was a large dose of guilt in there somewhere, guilt at not having been there to prevent the accident, guilt at not being able to share or alleviate Alusha's anguish, misery that was all the worse for her attempts to hide it.

He forced himself back to Plumb's words. 'So you're saying it was trauma?'

Plumb settled back in the chair, a gleam of relief in his eyes now that that he was on the safer ground of his own expertise. 'I do indeed. The bump on the head, the inhalation, the miscarriage – I don't think they can be separated. One alone probably wouldn't have caused too much bother, but all three together – well, they'd be sufficient to cause significant trauma. And trauma – shock – whatever you want to call it, has profound physical effects.'

He paused for a moment to ensure that he had been understood. Nick understood all right; he was saying there was nothing wrong with Alusha. Overcome by the now familiar sense of helplessness, he was silent, not trusting himself to speak.

'There's no doubt your wife has endured a very *testing* experience,' Plumb continued in a voice tinged with sympathy. 'But what has to be understood, Mr Mackenzie, is that all this was a long time ago. Three months ago, to be precise. After such a time there's absolutely no reason why your wife shouldn't have recovered. At least, be well on the way – '

'Then why in hell hasn't she recovered?' Nick said in sudden exasperation.

'Ah. Now, the best person to talk to you about that is my colleague, Dr Carter. He's *the* expert. He should be here any moment – '

'But I want *you* to explain.'

'I assure you – Carter's the best person.'

Something shifted in Nick, a final thread broke in the thin web of his control and his anger rose into his throat like sickness. 'No. *You.*' His voice wavered and he fought to control it. 'I want *you* to tell me.'

Plumb blinked at this unexpected show of emotion. Finally

he said awkwardly: 'Very well,' and, muttering thanks to Blair, waited for him to leave.

'Please understand,' Plumb said when they were alone, 'there's no suggestion that your wife doesn't have physical symptoms. Not for a moment. Her illness is very – real.'

'But you just said there was nothing wrong with her.'

'Well – ' Plumb glanced to the door as if for assistance but it remained stubbornly closed. Looking back, he began to feel his way slowly into his argument. 'Often, after some physical trauma or disease, the brain remembers the symptoms of the disease and keeps producing them in the body, even after the illness itself has gone. It's a well-known syndrome. Pain is a common manifestation. Pain from injury, pain from an accident. The brain gets so used to receiving pain signals that it continues to manufacture them long after the injury has healed.' He attempted a heartening smile which didn't quite come off. 'The good news is that this sort of syndrome usually responds well to treatment.'

Nick felt an icy calm, an absolute clarity. 'What you're saying is that it's all in her mind.'

Plumb gave a short bray of a laugh. 'Well – not in the way you mean, not in the sense that she's imagining it. Not at all, no, no. No, what happens is that the brain gets wrongly programmed and keeps sending out inappropriate signals – it's as simple as that.'

All Nick's instincts rebelled against this idea. This, surely, was nothing more than hot air wrapped up in elegant theory, intellectual verbiage invented to fill an inconvenient gap in the text books. But he resisted the impulse to say so. Instead, haunted by his responsibilities to Alusha and the need to consider every possibility, he tried to make sense of what Plumb was saying, to consider the idea rationally. Was it possible? Was there really no reason why Alusha shouldn't get well?

He thought back over the months, to the accident itself, to her fuddled brain, her streaming eyes and grey skin. There could be no doubting that. Nor the fact that her weight loss had started immediately, even before the miscarriage. All the other things – the sweating, the diarrhoea, the memory problems, the jumpiness – they too had started straight away. Since then little had changed. If anything she'd got worse.

How could such awful symptoms come out of nothing?

How could there be no real cause? These people kept forgetting one vital thing – that apart from the few days after the miscarriage Alusha had never given in to her illness, never stopped trying to get better, making the effort to walk even when she was exhausted which was nearly all the time, forcing herself to eat when it sickened her, putting on a bright smile when she must have longed to scream in despair.

No, he couldn't buy the idea that Alusha's brain was in some devious way blocking the way to a miraculous recovery. Quite apart from anything else, such a belief would be a betrayal.

Anyway, there was something about Plumb's little speech that made him wary; it had been too assertive, too facile, almost as if Plumb were convincing himself of his own argument.

And what was he really saying? What did the diagnosis actually boil down to?

Nick came full circle. 'So you *do* think it's in her mind.'

The other man's face reflected disappointment, but also lack of surprise. 'A lot of people have the same reaction,' he said. 'They think that any suggestion of, well, a *mental* component to a disease is some kind of a slur. But all illnesses have a mental component. Even a dose of flu. Really – all illness.'

If he hadn't been so close to despair, Nick would have laughed. He'd last had flu two years before, caught after crossing too many time zones. The only mental component he'd felt at the time was a desire to stop travelling in badly ventilated aircraft.

'Would you mind explaining that?' Nick asked with exaggerated courtesy. 'About the flu.'

'Well – people who have a positive attitude, their immune systems function better.'

'Ah, I get the idea. You mean people who are feeling good recover quicker?'

'Something like that.' Plumb nodded unsuspectingly.

'You mean people who are in good health, with no worries, no emotional problems and good strong bodies recover faster than other people?'

Seeing the way things were going, Plumb began to look cautious. He didn't reply.

'My wife was all those things, doctor. Strong in mind and body. So why isn't she better?'

107

Plumb drew a deep breath and began to wade through the morass of arguments again. Now, however, his tone was brisker, more uncompromising.

The sound of muffled female laughter floated in from the nursing station outside, then rose sharply as the door swung open and someone came in. Even before the new arrival had exchanged nods with Plumb, Nick knew this would be Carter. The man moved with the curious mixture of confidence and animal caution peculiar to specialists in private clinics, like a cat on a thick-pile carpet.

Nick shook the proffered hand but did not attempt to return the smile.

Plumb hurried into a rapid explanation of the conversation so far.

Seating himself elegantly in a chair, Carter nodded sagely, rubbing a finger across his upper lip in a practised gesture of concentration.

Carter turned to him. 'I'm sure we can help your wife, Mr Mackenzie.' His voice was beautifully modulated, like an actor's. For no apparent reason Nick took an instant dislike to him

'And what exactly is your angle, Dr Carter?'

'I'm a psychiatrist.' Carter watched for a reaction and, finding one, added smoothly: 'But from what you might call the new school. Not exclusively drug-based, you understand. We favour a multi-faceted approach. I deal with diseases with a mental component,' Carter continued. 'That is to say, *all* disease. Though sadly I don't have the opportunity to deal with half the cases I'd like to.' He gave a modest little shrug, as if he was in such demand that he had difficulty in allocating his time. 'Nowadays my sort of medicine gets called holistic. It approaches disease from the point of view of the whole person: mind, body and spirit. You really can't separate those three things, you see, though I have to admit modern medicine is slow to absorb the fact.'

'So what do you think caused my wife's illness?'

He went through the motions of considering the question. 'In a word – trauma.' The voice was low-pitched for reassurance. 'The fall, the knock on the head. The lost pregnancy. And I understand your wife suffered an assault some years ago. These events – all serious shocks – were bound to take

108

their toll. It's been established that these things can have long-term repercussions – '

Nick was so incredulous it took him a moment to interrupt. 'You're saying that something that happened six years ago could be making her ill now?'

'Not directly, not perhaps in the way you think. I'm suggesting a cumulative effect. It's been shown that shock can have profound physiological effects for many years after the event.'

Nick felt the beginnings of a quiet but total despair. 'So . . . how exactly would you treat my wife?'

It was a moment before Carter replied. 'Our main approach would be cognitive therapy,' he said.

'Which is?'

'Basically, we'd concentrate on getting your wife up and about again. We'd draw up a programme of measured exercise involving a variety of activities.'

'What sort of activities?'

'Oh – things she enjoys. You know. Swimming. Walking. Getting out and about.' He sounded like a seedy salesman pushing two weeks at a holiday camp. 'And some physio-therapy, of course. As I'm sure you're aware, there's a danger that too much inactivity can lead to muscle wastage and fatigue, and then the patient gets caught in a downward spiral which is twice as difficult to break out of.'

A picture of Alusha pushed to exhaustion on a relentless exercise machine came into Nick's mind. He murmured: 'She doesn't like swimming.'

'Really? We'd take her to a lovely warm pool. It's really very pleasant.'

Now Nick saw Alusha out of her depth, foundering. Shaking himself free, he asked, 'And drugs. Would you use drugs?'

'Some. But the minimum possible.'

'Which? What kind?'

'Well – antidepressants mainly.'

'But my wife's not depressed.'

'No, of course not,' he agreed hastily. 'It's an unfortunate name, a misleading name. You see, alleviating depression is only one function of this type of drug. They have many other uses. Sometimes the hormones and neurotransmitters in the brain get out of balance and block the pathways . . .'

109

He elaborated at some length. The scientific terms came in a steady flow, the words at once impressive and chilling. Nick made the effort to listen with great care so that he should miss no detail.

Eventually he cut Carter short by standing up. 'I think I've got the picture.'

Plumb, who'd been fidgeting with his hands for some time, got thankfully to his feet. Carter, too, stood up, and stretched out his hand. They both looked relieved because Nick had finally understood.

Nick stared down at Alusha. She was asleep, her breathing shallow, her face thin and pale. She lay with one arm over the covers, her fingers clutching the edge of the sheet, as if for support. Her hair, which had lost its distinctive shine, looked tangled and unwashed. The nurse must have overlooked it; he would mention it when he saw them.

He longed for her to wake up so they could talk. He wanted to know what she thought of Carter's ideas, though he was pretty sure what her reaction would be; she would give a small snort of disbelief, a derisive smile and say the madmen were loose again. She called most medics madmen, often to their faces. He knew what she would say, but he needed to be sure.

He stared down at her as if the very act of examining her face might make her wake up. Her skin, taut, translucent and devoid of lines, was like a mask; her features, smooth and expressionless, were curiously inanimate as if she had slipped away somewhere.

After a time the strangeness of the mask-like face began to frighten him, and he went across to the window and looked out. Even four storeys up he could smell the stench of the traffic fumes. He allowed himself a brief moment of longing for Ashard.

He waited another ten minutes in case Alusha should wake, then went in search of the staff. Leona, a plump Jamaican staff nurse, was behind the desk. Seeing him, she grinned and called a cheerful hullo. He told her about Alusha's hair.

'I know. And I'm sorry. It doesn't look very good, does it? But she didn't want bothering,' Leona explained.

'But she's usually awake by now.'

110

'She wanted to go back to sleep.' Leona tutted in friendly remonstration: 'We're not meant to let her, of course, but you know . . .'

Nick was instantly alert. 'Not meant to? What do you mean?'

'She needs to get up and about a bit. Sleeping's no good, is it? Not if you have too much of it.'

'You've been told she mustn't sleep?'

Leona's normally open expression clouded slightly. She said solemnly: 'She's meant to keep active, Mr Mackenzie. Get the circulation going and that sort of thing. All patients are, unless there are medical reasons against it.'

What had the staff been told? Nick wondered. Had the doctors already labelled Alusha a neurotic? Was Leona secretly planning to put Alusha on an exercise machine?

He pulled himself up short. He was getting paranoid. Leona was a perfectly nice straightforward girl who wouldn't force anyone to do anything. He managed a smile. 'Tell my wife I'll be in this afternoon, will you, Leona?'

He left by the stairs to avoid the public scrutiny of the lifts. As he approached the main lobby, he employed his usual technique for getting through busy places, putting his head down, keeping his eyes on the floor in front of him, and walking very fast. Half-way across the lobby, just as he was beginning to think he'd made it, a female voice called his name. Without breaking his stride he gave the briefest of glances over his shoulder to establish that he'd never seen her before in his life. Then, accelerating, he punched open the swing door and made it to the kerb in five seconds.

His car was nowhere in sight.

He heard panting at his elbow.

'I'm Daisy Field,' came the voice. 'We were going to meet.'

Nick stared obdurately ahead. There wasn't a single opening gambit in the entire world that he hadn't heard – it was astonishing what people would do to get his attention.

'Daisy Field, from Catch,' the girl persisted.

A memory stirred in his brain. Frowning, he looked down at her.

'The Campaign Against Toxic Chemicals,' she explained, reading the mystification in his face. 'We were due to meet at eleven, but they told me you were held up. Your manager suggested I come and wait here.'

Nick pressed his fingers against his forehead in a gesture of forgetfulness and apology. 'Sorry.'

'That's okay,' she said quickly. 'I mean really okay. You must be having an appalling time.'

Nick was silent. He had learned to cope with disbelief and puzzlement, but pity and understanding were altogether more difficult.

The car appeared at last, racing up to the kerb and swaying to a sudden halt. He was aware of wanting to be alone, yet not alone.

She must have sensed his uncertainty, because she offered: 'We could make it another time if that'd be easier.'

She was young, with an open face and a steady gaze. Making up his mind, he shook his head and gestured her into the car. She slid across the seat and settled in the far corner. As he climbed in after her he saw her inspect the car interior with open interest. 'How's it going with the doctors?' she asked. 'Are they saying there's nothing wrong?'

Nick hesitated, surprised that she should have guessed, but not sure that he was quite ready to discuss it. The car moved off; he looked ahead and gave a noncommittal shrug.

'It's their usual answer, I'm afraid,' she went on. 'Saying there's nothing wrong. That's what they told a forestry worker in Dumfries who'd inhaled 2,4,5-T. Not to mention a farmer's wife in Norfolk who miscarried after the next-door property had been sprayed with some cocktail or other – we never discovered what exactly.'

There was a pause; he was expected to respond. He shot her a quick glance, taking in those steady eyes, and an expression that was sympathetic but eager.

'Or are they saying it's all in her mind?' she asked in a sudden burst. 'That's another favourite, I'm afraid.'

She must have read the answer in his face, because she exclaimed: 'You mustn't believe it, you know. They only say that when they haven't a clue. And most of the time they haven't a clue, I'm afraid. That's what we're up against – a total failure to understand what chemicals can do to people.'

She was obviously very sincere and very idealistic. He dimly remembered feeling the same at that age, though his ire, directed as it was towards the Vietnam war and the arms race, appeared in retrospect altogether more aggressive and far less attractive. 'They're very . . . convincing,' he commented.

'Of course. That's their job, isn't it, to create confidence, to make you believe they have all the answers. It keeps the system going.'

He wondered how far to take this discussion. In his long experience of strangers it was best to be cautious until one was absolutely certain how far it was safe to go. It was amazing how little confidences got blown up into major items that ended up as so-called stories in the gutter press. On the other hand, this girl was a professional, she was offering help, and if he was going to take advantage of that he was going to have to trust her sooner or later.

He took another look at her. She was nice looking in a fresh unaffected sort of way. She was dressed carelessly, in a loose sweater and long flowing skirt with a diaphanous scarf of muted blues and purples tied round her shoulders. Her hair, which was copper-coloured and curly, almost bushy, was tied back to the nape of her neck with a loose bow, though several strands had escaped to form a soft frame for her face. Her skin was clear and slightly freckled, her eyes light-brown and very bright. She had a quick smile, a glowing energy and the sort of spontaneous sincerity that seems to leap out at you.

She was just the type to be an environmental campaigner, he decided: young – still in her twenties, he guessed – tenacious, unafraid and too sure by half.

'They say it's just trauma,' he said, and the admission was like a wrench. 'And when I try to argue they make me feel like I'm being difficult.'

'I can imagine,' she said, rolling her eyes expressively. 'Modern medicine's like an ancient religion. Full of mumbo-jumbo and powerful witchcraft, and anyone who dares to question it gets labelled a heretic.' She had a chirpy voice with a slight accent that he couldn't quite place – south or maybe east London.

'Talking to them, I feel like I'm back in school,' Nick said. 'They keep trying to explain the thing to me, first one way then the other, and when I refuse to accept it I know they're giving me another bad mark. One step nearer to being chucked out of class.'

The driver wove the car expertly through the traffic clogging Cavendish Square before grinding to a halt in the inevitable jam behind Oxford Circus.

'But there are other doctors in the world,' Daisy said.

113

'Are there?' Nick gave a short sharp laugh, which sounded caustic even to his own ears. He thought back over the long weeks of tests and opinions and referrals. 'We seem to have tried most of medical London,' he said. 'I've even spoken to people in the US. They form a fairly united front, believe me. None of them can say for sure what's wrong.'

'What about the alternative doctors?' Daisy argued. 'They've been into environmental illness for years.'

'Oh, I've talked to them all right,' he replied.

'And?'

'And they said, sure they could help. But when it came down to it, they couldn't offer much – vitamins, detoxification, herbs, that sort of thing.'

'But holistic medicine's all about being gentle with the body, letting it heal itself in its own time,' she said with a conviction that bordered on the evangelical. 'You take the load off the body and – '

'We've done all that,' Nick interrupted softly. 'Alusha's used alternative medicine for years. She went on a total health kick as soon as she could.'

'Oh.' Daisy withdrew, momentarily chastened before flinging him an uncertain smile. 'Well, there's still the scientific data. That might produce something.'

'On the phone you said the scientific evidence was thin, that it didn't mean much.'

'I meant the original toxicology data. That's bound to be suspect, simply because it was done so long ago. Chemicals like Reldane, stuff that's been around for years, it all got waved through on a nod and a wink. Trials that would be a joke today. You know, they'd feed the stuff to a couple of mice for a week and, eureka, when they didn't immediately keel over and die, it was given the green stamp and put straight on the market.'

'That bad?'

'Yep. Well – not far off anyway.'

Was this as much of an exaggeration as it sounded? he wondered. Was she just saying this to help win him over? And if so, what else was she prepared to say to persuade him to her point of view? It occurred to him, not for the first time, that she was latching on to him purely for his publicity value to her campaign, and his heart sank, as it always did when people wanted something out of him.

114

'But there might well be something tucked away in the literature somewhere,' Daisy remarked with blithe confidence, 'something that shows Reldane has damaging effects.'

'But if anything like that had been published, surely the doctors would know about it?'

She sucked in her breath. 'Oh dear,' she said gently. 'You do have a lot to learn.'

Nick looked stiffly ahead, feeling rebuked and suddenly and inappropriately close to anger.

Turning abruptly, as if she had just appreciated her gaffe, Daisy added hastily: 'We have contacts with all the experts. Really – I'm sure we can find someone who can understand your wife's illness. We'll follow it through, I assure you. We'll back you all the way, for as long as it takes.'

He thought: Or until my publicity value runs out. Her support was a little too unconditional, her outlook too optimistic to be entirely believable. Aloud, he murmured a cursory: 'Thanks.'

'I think the press coverage went well, don't you?' she said breathlessly, rushing the conversation forward. 'Have you seen the cuttings?'

The truth was, he hadn't dared look at a single newspaper since he'd agreed in what he now realised to be a rash and ill-judged moment to go public on what had happened. Despair, the ache for crude revenge, the terrible piercing fear that Alusha would never recover, had overridden his natural caution, and, as he was doubtless about to discover, he had probably paid the price.

Daisy Field pulled a collection of newspaper cuttings out of a voluminous bag. 'The *Star* ran something on Friday. Did you see it? A full-page feature. It means we've made a clean sweep of the tabloids – every single one.' Her voice shifted into a minor key. 'Though I have to admit, the qualities weren't quite so good. Nothing in the *Guardian* or *Independent*. But the *Sunday Times* ran a good piece – the environment correspondent's a friend of mine. I thought *The Times* would run something too – they seemed so sure – but their medical correspondent probably killed it off. He's one of the psychosomatic school. You know, life events and all that – thinks everything stems from getting a nasty fright in the woodshed as a child.'

Suddenly she laughed, an earthy chuckle that came from the back of her throat, and he turned in surprise.

115

She was already on to the next cutting. 'And here – a front page, no less.'

Nick glanced at it and shuddered. The headline ran: *Popstar Wife in Poison Horror*.

'God, I can do without this sort of stuff,' he said with feeling.

'Oh.' Her voice fell.

He was about to tell her exactly what was wrong with that sort of coverage, but stopped himself. It was he, after all, who, having given Catch permission to push the story, had failed to tell David or his own PR people about it, effectively ruining any chance of the story being handled properly.

Daisy was looking puzzled; she thought she'd done a good job.

He said: 'Not your fault. It's just – them.' He flicked a hand at the cuttings. 'If they didn't use photographs you'd have trouble recognising yourself.'

'But they've got most of the facts right.'

Bracing himself, Nick glanced at the first few lines.

Ex-Amazon megastar Nick Mackenzie announced today that his Bahamian model wife is gravely ill after a poisoning accident. Alusha, 35, was found unconscious in a pool of poisonous chemicals on their hideaway West Highland estate in June, and has been lying in a coma at a London clinic ever since.

Close to tears, Nick, 46, stated yesterday . . .

Nick flung the paper down. Close to tears – Christ. He was only close to tears when he realised he'd never be able to get hold of the reporter who'd written that garbage and squeeze him by the throat until he screamed for mercy. It was extraordinary how they always got your age right but precious little else. Alusha was not and never had been Bahamian, nor a model, nor was she in a coma. He'd never even spoken to the reporter, let alone cried.

Daisy picked up the paper, read it, and said in a quiet ironic voice: 'Well – they spelt your name right.'

He gave a rueful grunt. She had a point: it was absurd to worry about the press. They simply weren't worth it.

'We're going the wrong way,' Daisy announced suddenly.

They were crossing Oxford Street, heading south towards David Weinberg's office. 'Where should we be going then?' Nick asked.

'To Gower Street. To see Dr Peasedale.'

Nick wondered if he should know who Peasedale was. Grasping the problem, Daisy explained: 'He's our toxicologist at University College. The one I told you about on the phone. Our tame pesticide expert.'

'Ah,' Nick said, though he remembered nothing about it. Leaning forward, he redirected the driver. 'A toxicologist?' he murmured. 'I met one of those this morning.' He told her what had been said in the hot airless room high in the clinic.

'Ah, well, they only know what they're given the opportunity to know,' Daisy declared, moving into her polemic mode. 'And that's only what other people have told them, isn't it? They believe in research, but they forget that the only research that's being done is what the chemical companies and the governments *choose* to have done.'

So clear-cut again; so sure. 'There must be other research programmes,' he argued half-heartedly.

'But why should there be? Who's going to fund them? Groups like ours don't have the money, and the big charities only support the projects the doctors advise them to support. And the doctors aren't interested in the idea of wide-ranging non-specific chemical damage. It upsets their neat little theories of disease. They want tidy little boxes – viral disease, bacterial disease, neurological disease, *any* disease as long as it can be seen under a microscope – and when their box theories won't fit, they throw up their hands and say the problem doesn't exist. What's failing, of course, is Western medicine itself – stuck in tight compartments, totally reliant on drugs and drug companies, spineless, *visionless*.' In full flood, she had an extraordinary almost hypnotic fluency, so that her words flowed without break or hesitation. She gave an impression of both rehearsal and spontaneity, as well as vibrant indignation.

'And if things don't fit,' she went on, 'you throw them into a convenient catch-all, which in Western medicine is psychiatry, which has to have pulled off the greatest intellectual coup of the twentieth century, by passing itself off as scientifically based when in fact it's the only totally non-scientific speciality, based as it is on almost complete ignorance of the organ it's meant to know about.' She paused, as if to remind herself of what she had set out to say. 'No, they're simply not interested in difficult untreatable diseases. Untreatable

117

diseases make them feel powerless, and powerlessness makes them resentful and uncooperative. If they can't fire drugs at something, then they don't want to know about it. And I tell you' – she waved a finger, emphasising her point like a seasoned politician – 'they certainly don't want to know about anything that suggests we're on the brink of widespread trouble, not to mention environmental disaster.'

But one disaster was more than enough for Nick; he couldn't take on responsibility for the rest of humanity as well. He let Daisy talk on for a while until, realising she had lost her audience, she broke off quite amiably and lapsed into silence for the rest of the journey.

EIGHT

Peasedale, a young bird-like man with thinning hair and spectacles, was summing up. 'Not much to offer you, I'm afraid,' he said. 'Consumed in large quantities Reldane would, of course, poison anybody. But in a small dose – I can't find any evidence to suggest it could cause such catastrophic symptoms.'

Daisy glanced across to Nick Mackenzie by the window. He was sprawled gracefully in his chair, one elbow on the sill, gazing intently out at the blank walls of the building opposite. Daisy, who for once had been keeping commendably silent, now burst out: 'But what about inhalation? Surely if you breathe something for an *hour* . . .'

Peasedale shook his head apologetically. He was perched on a high stool, his long limbs entwined in its legs like a double-jointed insect. 'If you breathe enough of almost anything over a long period, then you'll get adverse effects. That's true of even the commonest fumes – petrol, glue, spirit-based substances. And of course cigarettes. But you wouldn't get such dire symptoms after just an hour, not when the substance is mixed with plenty of air, as it was in this case. The only circumstance I can think of that might change that would be previous exposure to a chemical or chemicals that create extreme sensitivity, then – well, I suppose even something as modest as Reldane could provoke a strong reaction.'

There was a silence as they waited for Nick to respond. But he seemed to be completely absorbed by the view from the window, and it was left to Peasedale to prompt him.

119

'Has your wife been exposed to any strong chemicals in the past, Mr Mackenzie?'

'What?' He seemed to wake up only with an effort. 'No. Nothing unusual. Just the usual hotchpotch.'

'You mean . . .?'

He half turned. 'Oh, antibiotics, that sort of thing. But not recently – she won't take anything like that now – when she was younger.'

That was it then. Mixed with Daisy's disappointment was a creeping sense of guilt. All that chatter, all that confidence – she regretted it, not only because it now looked totally misplaced, but because normally she would have known better than to raise false hopes. Something had gone wrong; she had misplayed the scene in the car. It was partly that old demon of hers, optimism; partly her uncharacteristic nervousness at meeting Nick Mackenzie. She'd banged on like an inane schoolgirl.

'Can't you run some tests?' she asked Peasedale.

'What sort of thing? If you mean standard toxicology tests, they were done on Reldane's active ingredient years ago. I looked it up. There was some evidence that, given in massive doses, the active ingredient might eventually cause cancer in a tiny proportion of rats.'

Nick's voice drifted in from the window. 'They test these things on animals?'

There was a short silence. 'Certainly,' Peasedale said.

'That can't be necessary, surely?'

'There's no other way, not if you're going to be absolutely certain.'

Nick gave a visible shudder and resumed his study of the scene outside the window.

'The original tests,' said Daisy, picking up the argument again. 'If they show cancer, surely that's significant.'

But Peasedale wasn't going to have words put into his mouth. 'Almost anything will cause cancer, given in sufficient quantity for a long enough period. But we're not talking cancer here, are we? We're talking about another sort of illness, a different set of symptoms. Now, if we were looking at something like 2,4,5-T, as found in Agent Orange, then we might have something. It causes all sorts of weird symptoms which don't show up in standard tests – immune dysfunction, enzyme and hormonal imbalance, that sort of thing.' He turned to Nick. 'You *are* sure it was Reldane and not something else?'

The sun had emerged from behind a cloud, driving golden shafts into the room and illuminating Nick Mackenzie's face in harsh brilliance.

Eventually he stirred. 'It was definitely Reldane,' he said in a soft voice.

'She's seen a toxicologist?'

A slight pause. 'A couple.'

'And the symptoms – these guys couldn't suggest anything?'

'Not really. They got excited about her memory loss, about mixing up her words – getting her sentences back to front, you know – and about her gut troubles. Then just as quickly they got unexcited again. Said they couldn't find anything.'

'Did they do a biopsy?'

'I'm not sure – '

'It involves taking a minute amount of tissue, usually with a needle.'

'Oh – that. Yes, they did it once – no, twice. I wouldn't let them do it again. Hurt her too much.'

'What about enzyme levels? Did they measure those?'

'I suppose so – yes. They said they'd looked at everything, anyway.'

Peasedale gave a wide shrug. 'In that case, I don't know what to suggest. And you say your wife hadn't been taking any prescription drugs recently?'

Nick shook his head. 'Neither of us ever took anything.' He added wryly: 'We went up to Scotland to escape all that, you see. Chemicals, pollution . . . Funny, when you think about it.'

No one smiled.

'What about water? Could she have drunk contaminated water?' Peasedale suggested.

Nick didn't reply, so Daisy answered for him. 'Mr Mackenzie had a sample sent down from the house supply. We had it tested. Nothing wrong with it.'

'Tell him the rest,' Nick said to Daisy, looking at her for the first time in a long while. 'Tell him what you told me on the phone.'

Daisy drew a breath. 'They said it was some of the best water they'd ever tested.'

'You see,' Nick said with gentle irony. 'Clean air. Clean water. Perfect.' With a last look at the sky, he stood up. 'Thank you, Dr Peasedale. You've been most helpful. Very informative.' There was no sarcasm in his tone, only resignation, and Daisy had the feeling that it was only by this rather forced show of manners that he was managing to keep himself together.

She followed him towards the lift. His expression didn't invite conversation. When they came out into the street he strode towards the waiting car in the same cannon-shot way that he had emerged from the clinic. When she caught up with him he was holding the car door open and waiting for her to get in.

She murmured: 'But my office – it's out of your way.'

'Your – ' He frowned suddenly. 'Oh? I thought – lunch? You haven't time?' He asked it tentatively, with an awkward sideways look, as if he wasn't at all sure of getting a positive response.

'Of course – yes. If you want to. Of course.'

He gave a sudden fleeting smile, a look that flickered up to her eyes and away again, and she realised that for all his apparent confidence and bodily grace he was essentially a reserved man. It was hard to reconcile this with the image of the seasoned stage performer who stood up in front of thousands of people, but as they set off, she realised her first instinct had been right. He hardly ever looked people in the eye for very long, not when he could possibly avoid it, and when he was forced to, he screwed up his eyes into a tight frown, as if this could offer him some degree of camouflage.

He said: 'I appreciate all you've done.'

Done? She caught the past tense with a twinge of alarm. 'I've done eff-all,' she said firmly. 'Yet.'

He was silent for a moment, then began haltingly: 'You know . . . in the old days – in the Sixties anyway – we all used to blame everything on the system. It was very . . . well, convenient, I suppose.' He shot her a quick glance. 'But you wouldn't remember that. You're only – what?'

'Thirty-two.'

He squinted at her. 'Oh? You look younger.' He said it as a statement of fact, not flattery.

He continued thoughtfully: 'Blaming the system used to be a great let-out. It covered everything – the government, the law, the welfare state – anything you liked. When Alusha became ill I was desperate to find an *it* or a *someone* to blame, just like in the old days. I longed to come face to come face with the person or *thing* that could let this happen. I wanted to – well, create stink, show them – I don't know. I just wanted *them* to suffer like Alusha was suffering.' He gave a gesture of resignation. His hands were long and slender. 'But really – what would be the use? Even if such a person existed, or an organisation or a *thing*, and even if they were exposed or whatever, it wouldn't change much, would it?'

'But it would!' she said emphatically, forgetting her intention to show restraint. 'It *could*. It might prevent this sort of thing happening again.'

His mouth turned down into a look that she was beginning to recognise, an expression that suggested she was being naive and idealistic.

'But it wouldn't get Alusha better, would it?' he pointed out, looking at her for the first time without frowning. She noticed the vivid blueness of his eyes, and how the skin at the edges was crinkled into islands of strong lines, as if under happier circumstances he smiled a lot.

'But it might,' she continued doggedly. 'Once they find out what happened – how this stuff actually caused the damage – then they might be able to find a treatment.'

'But they're never going to find out exactly how the stuff did what it did, are they?' he said patiently. 'Not if one's to believe Peasedale – which I do. So there's not much point in . . .' He paused, choosing his words. '. . . Well, going on with it. I'm sorry. I really feel my wife has to be my first priority. I have to concentrate on finding a doctor who can help her, a doctor who can find out what's wrong. I can't spend more time on this sort of thing.' He waved a hand apologetically. 'I don't mean your campaign's not *worthwhile* – far from it. It's just . . . I really can't get involved.'

'You mean – ?'

'Your campaign – I wouldn't be able to do it justice.'

He was giving up, she realised. He was telling her that, despite everything – his apparent interest in Catch, his agreement to publicise the case – he didn't want to be involved any more. In which case the campaign had, within the space of just two weeks, won and lost the most valuable asset it had ever possessed. The odd thing was she didn't blame him at all, although this didn't stop her from feeling an unaccountable sense of loss, as if something really important had been taken from her.

'I understand,' she said, managing a small smile.

'I'll be pleased to help when this is all over, when my wife's better. Tell me over lunch, what I might be able to do.'

'Of course.'

The car drew up outside a sparkling neo-classical building behind Covent Garden. Nick got out and, holding the door open for her, led the way inside at his customary pace. As they sped through the main lobby, heading for an open lift, Daisy saw a wall sign and realised they were making for the David Weinberg office.

'I'll be about ten minutes,' Nick explained as the lift started upwards. 'Just a few calls to make. You don't mind?'

'Not at all.'

The doors opened to reveal a stage-lit reception area, all chrome and muted greys and arrays of large glossy photographs and golden discs. The place was surprisingly crowded. Two delivery men in overalls stood by a trolley loaded with cartons, apparently waiting for orders, various people were sitting on low sofas along two sides of the room, looking as if they'd been there for some time, while a party of four smartly dressed women was grouped around the reception desk.

Even as Nick launched himself across the room towards a door on the far side, Daisy could see that he wasn't going to make it. One of the well-dressed women was nudging her neighbours and, as Nick advanced, the four turned to face him. One was a young girl of about twenty, the other three were quite a bit older.

Seeing Nick, the older women's faces lit up like awed teenagers. Their ludicrous smiles, their round-eyed stares were both fascinating and rather embarrassing.

One of the older women stepped forward to intercept Nick. She was smiling hard, too hard, although, if you took away the smile, she was good-looking in a slightly overstated way. Her makeup, though well applied, was a little on the heavy side, and her fair hair, which was longish and layered like feathers, had that solid impenetrable look that comes from long hours with a hairdresser and a tall can of hairspray.

'Nick,' she sang, standing in his path. 'Hullo! How *are* you?'

124

Nick jerked to a halt like a cornered animal. Finding no escape, he produced a polite though unconvincing smile.

'It's been such a long time, I can't believe it,' the woman persisted, subtly but firmly blocking his way. She gave a nervous laugh, aware of the audience behind her.

Nick was grappling with his memory, and it showed.

'Twenty years,' she hurried on, the first hint of panic in her voice. 'It seems unbelievable!'

Nick blinked rapidly. 'Yes, of course . . .'

But it was obvious that he hadn't placed her and there was an awkward pause, the sort that seems to stretch out for ever. The woman's smile faltered, then, attempting to carry the thing off, she made a joke of it. 'Good God, I didn't think I'd changed that much! At least, most people tell me I haven't changed at all.' If she was hoping for some sort of affirmation, she was quickly disappointed.

She laughed again, a sharp discordant sound, then, before the situation deteriorated any further, announced: 'It's Suki Armitage. Well, that's what you'd remember me as. I'm not that any more, of course. My name's Driscoll. And nowadays people seem to call me Susan. The Suki got lost somewhere along the line . . .' She went on for a bit, rather too fast, and after repeating herself a couple of times, trailed off.

A shot of recognition had flickered over Nick's face. 'Good Lord,' he murmured, and shifted his weight, on the point of flight again.

But Susan Driscoll wasn't about to give up. 'I was thinking about you only the other day,' she blundered on in her breathless Knightsbridge accent. 'I saw Annie and Roger Fenner. You remember them? And all those wonderful parties they used to give?'

The Fenners, as Daisy and everyone else in the world knew, were leading fashion designers. Susan Driscoll, it seemed, was rather practised at dropping names because she managed to squeeze in a few more as she rattled breathlessly through the brilliant people and parties of the good old days.

Daisy could tell that Nick had finally placed Susan Driscoll, though, from his expression, the realisation did not seem to have thrilled him nearly as much as Susan Driscoll had hoped it would.

The one-sided conversation lurched on. Susan Driscoll's voice became shrill at the edges, and Daisy had the feeling she was less than pleased at not having been instantly remembered. Nick was looking increasingly hunted, and Daisy was not surprised when he flicked a glance at her, signalling his intention to escape.

'Well, it's good to see you again,' he muttered to Susan Driscoll.

'I'm so sorry to hear about your wife,' she said to his retreating back. 'I do hope she'll recover soon.' Nick gave a brief backward glance of acknowledgement.

'And we're so thrilled about the concert. I can't tell you what it means.'

Nick paused in the doorway. 'Concert?' He looked back at her in mystification. 'Concert?'

A pause, little short of electric. 'For Save the Children,' Susan Driscoll said bravely. 'I'm organising it.'

He stared at her. 'What – ' He shook his head abruptly. 'There isn't going to be any concert.' For an instant he seemed to hover on the point of explanation then, thinking better of it, he turned and was gone.

There was a long moment while no one spoke and no one moved. Mrs Driscoll looked as if she'd got a very nasty taste in her mouth. Her lips were taut, her eyes narrow as a cat's. Humiliation then anger crossed over her face in quick succession, followed by something altogether more guarded.

Unobtrusively Daisy made for the door through which Nick had vanished. As she reached it, she heard a young voice saying: 'Oh, Mummy . . . Perhaps there's a mistake . . .'

Daisy looked back. Susan Driscoll was managing a brilliant recovery job. She was shrugging her daughter off, lifting her chin, putting on a smile. Only her eyes, in the instant before they swung round to face her friends, showed a last flash of bitter light.

Daisy escaped into a short corridor. There were several doors leading off it. The first stood open, revealing an empty office. The next was also open, and contained a young woman who seemed to know who Daisy was, and waved her to a seat.

After fifteen minutes Daisy's stomach started to rumble. After twenty she began to wonder if lunch might possibly have been forgotten.

She passed some of the time thinking about the rest of her week. She and Simon had been planning to go to a new film

126

that evening but he'd cancelled. It was the novel again. The novel had become a fixture, like the lover in a *ménage à trois*, mysterious, vaguely threatening, but best left alone. Looking at the relationship coolly – and it contained precious little heat even in its warmer moments – it had not developed a great deal. They liked the same things all right: they went to environmental awareness parties and political conferences, they saw art films and exhibitions, they ate in wine bars and went to parties in Islington. But when it came down to it, the only thing that had really changed was that she was now the one feeling beleaguered, while Simon was increasingly relaxed and carefree. Well, who wouldn't look happier when he had someone to collect his laundry, and cook and wash up twice a week?

Now there was an unworthy thought. She was forgetting how Simon had come and fixed her kitchen door and cooked Sunday lunch two weeks running. She was forgetting the conversations, the evenings out and the occasional smiles. Perhaps that was all you could ever ask or expect.

She thought of Nick Mackenzie and tried to imagine Simon in his place, fighting for her as she lay in some hospital bed, searching the world for some way to cure her, but the picture wouldn't come alive and she abandoned it.

The time crept on. The secretary unwrapped a sandwich. Daisy began to wonder if Nick Mackenzie wasn't quite as unspoilt as he seemed and didn't perhaps make a habit of keeping people waiting.

At last, after what must have been half an hour, there was a murmur of voices, the door opened and Nick Mackenzie finally appeared. Behind him was a dark plump balding man – presumably David Weinberg – who, spotting Daisy, peered at her briefly as if to confirm she was of no great importance, before saying a hasty goodbye to Nick and disappearing into the corridor.

Nick flopped down on the seat beside her.

'Sorry, but I had to sort out that schemozzle,' he said companionably. 'For some reason my manager had decided not to tell that lady that the concert had been cancelled. He seemed to think I would change my mind.'

'And did you?'

'No.'

'I don't think the lady was too pleased.'

'I think you're right.'

Daisy couldn't resist asking: 'Did you remember her?'

He shot her a grin which quite transformed his face. 'To be honest, no, not to begin with. She looked completely different. I mean, like someone *else*. Then . . . yes, I realised who she was.' He looked away and shook his head, as if some memory had just come back to him.

'Come on,' he said abruptly. 'Let's go and eat.'

They got as far as the end of the corridor – Daisy was just allowing herself a vision of a nice restaurant somewhere off the Covent Garden Piazza – when the secretary called Nick back to say his wife was on the phone. A look of surprise and pleasure leapt into his face as he turned to go. Calmly Daisy settled back against the wall and began a thorough inspection of the framed golden discs that decorated the corridor.

This time she didn't have to wait long; it was only a couple of minutes before he reappeared, emerging so quickly into the corridor that he was almost past her before she had realised.

Something had happened: his face was like thunder. She hesitated, uncertain whether to chase after him.

She caught up with him at the lift. As they both stepped inside, he flung her a fierce but impersonal look.

'Is there something the matter?' she asked. 'Can I do anything?'

He shook his head. 'No. No . . .' His voice was trembling with suppressed rage. 'No, no,' he repeated harshly. 'It's just that . . . I've got to go and move my wife.'

'Move her?'

'They made her swim. Made her swim when she hates it, absolutely hates it! And they've given her some drug, something that makes her feel terrible. They didn't even tell her what it was. Didn't even *tell* her! I can't believe it's possible. I can't – ' He broke off and screwed up his mouth, not trusting himself to say any more.

The lift was slowing down. Daisy tried to think of something useful to suggest. 'What about wheelchairs, ambulances and things? Can I – '

'No time for that. I'll carry her myself.' He said it as if it was the obvious thing to do, and Daisy thought: Lucky Alusha Mackenzie, having a husband like that.

The lift doors opened and he strode rapidly away, shoulders hunched, head down in that wary walk of his. As he stepped into the street, the sun caught him, illuminating his head with sudden light. It occurred to Daisy, not without an odd little pang, that she would probably never see him again.

After four visits to the Coach and Horses, Colin Hillyard had become quite a regular. It had got to the stage where the landlord, who went by the exotic name of Lionel Meredith-Peacock, greeted him warmly by name – Hillyard was using the name Meynell, a variation on Maynard, which was another favourite of his – and leant an elbow on the bar to exchange comments on the vagaries of the weather as if such things were quite unique to west Berkshire.

It was a Thursday. Hillyard made a point of arriving at more or less the same time every week and staying half an hour or so before leaving in a hurry, lending credence to the idea that he squeezed time out of his busy week to visit an ancient relative living nearby. He'd never elaborated on the elderly aunt or where she lived, nor had he said exactly what he did for a living; he spent too much time expressing quiet, almost languid interest in the local community and listening to the landlord's repertoire of well-worn anecdotes. Not that he ever pushed the local interest. Apart from establishing right at the outset that the Knowles family, who'd been featured in the local papers over an incident at the Berkshire Show, lived not far away and had been regular users of the pub, he hardly brought up a subject worth mentioning. In fact he'd once listened to the landlord holding forth on the merits of a cruise to Turkey over a package to the Canaries for all of twenty minutes before steering things gently back towards more parochial matters. He made such manoeuvres seem effortless, though he said so himself.

'People go for Turkey round here, do they?' he said to Meredith-Peacock, looking ready to be impressed. And then he'd got chapter and verse on the holidays the locals took, and the likely price of them, and how even when farming was meant to be in deep trouble some of them were still off to Kenya and the 'Sea-shells' islands, as Meredith-Peacock liked to pronounce them.

Once it came up, Hillyard had pursued the farmers-in-trouble avenue, of course; it was too good to miss. But he went ever so gently, expressing just the right blend of vague commiseration and glaring ignorance befitting a true town-dweller. But though the opening was leading him nicely up to the subject of the Knowles family, which was precisely where he wanted to be, the conversation had had to be aborted. The landlord had gone to serve another customer and when he ambled back along the bar his mind had diverted, by some mysterious progression, onto the subject of rheumatism.

Now it was Thursday again and he was back feeling rather pleased with life, though no thanks to the weather, which was blustery with racing clouds and a sudden sneaky chill which on leaving the car had flipped at the vents of the tweedy sports jacket he had bought specially for the job from a countryman's outfitters in Hungerford.

It was three and the pub was quiet. There was only one customer at the bar, a ruddy-faced man in heavy boots, work trousers and waxed jacket. Hillyard sat at the next stool, exchanged ritual head-shakes about the gale-force wind with the landlord and ordered a pint of best. The farmer-figure – the landlord called him Bill – waited impatiently to regain the landlord's attention and resume the conversation that Hillyard had interrupted. He was complaining to the landlord about the sale of some farm, though why it should displease him Hillyard couldn't make out, since he seemed neither to know nor care about the owners of the property who, it appeared, had been forced to sell at a bad price.

This time Hillyard plunged straight in. No pussy-footing, as Beryl often said, not once you've laid the groundwork; no skulking in the woodwork. He came straight out and asked if it was the Knowleses who were selling. The farmer nipped gently at the bait, took the taste of it, and let himself be led forward, jerking only once at the line when something alerted him to Hillyard's curiosity, and he demanded: 'What's it to you, anyway?'

'I read about them in the paper, didn't I, Lionel? Sad business. Sort of stuck in my mind.'

'Well, it's not them that's selling,' said the farmer. 'Not Mrs Knowles, oh no. She'll stick it out. Family been there too long. As long as anyone can remember. Though she won't get much out of the place, not this year, oh no,' he added to the landlord. 'Hiring all the help in. Not cheap.'

The landlord pulled the conversation towards cancer statistics then, providentially, a new customer diverted his attention and Hillyard was able to lead Farmer Bill onwards, through backwaters of maize and wheat and into the mainstream of the Knowleses' future.

'Going to sue, of course.'

'Sue?'

The beady eyes shot Hillyard a confiding glance. 'Going to sue the chemical makers. Been advised not to, they've all tried to put her off, the lawyers and everyone, but she won't have it. Off her head if you ask me. Ain't going to bring her husband back, is it? Not in a month of Sundays.'

'No.' Hillyard shook his head solemnly. 'And the law –' He sucked in his breath in a pitying hiss. 'Well, the only people who get rich are the lawyers, aren't they?'

'You're telling me,' gasped the farmer emphatically, and the idea triggered a blast of legal grievances that emerged blistering from the barrel of his memory. His protests finally spent, he murmured: 'That's what makes it crazy, see. She hasn't the money – well, not to spare. They'll bleed her dry.'

Hillyard made a commiserating face. 'No insurance money. Nothing like that?'

'Nope. Not that I've heard of, at any rate.'

And you would have heard, thought Hillyard. He said: 'You'd have thought she'd be able to get help. Some sort of legal aid.'

'Nothing handed out on a tray, is it? Not nowadays. Each man for himself.' He drained his beer and clunked the glass onto the bar with finality. He straightened up and patted his pockets. 'Right you are, Lionel,' he said, raising a farewell hand to the landlord.

He faced Hillyard for a moment. 'Not that people round here don't do what they can,' he said. 'The neighbours help out. They're in there right now.'

Hillyard maintained a look of polite interest. 'Right now?'

'Gone to the West Country for the week, Mrs Knowles and her son. First holiday in two years.'

Pure icing.

Hillyard almost danced his way to the car, checking his stride only with reluctance.

As he unlocked the car a silky-haired bundle pressed its nose to the glass and, as the door opened, hurled itself into his arms. 'Precious – were you waiting for your mum, were you? There, I wasn't so long, was I?'

The Pekinese snorted and snuffled and agitated its plume of tail like an uncontrolled metronome. Climbing in, Hillyard cradled it in his arms and sighed into its long coat: 'Did Beji miss me, did she? Of *course* she did, my little baby.' He gave the dog a rough squeeze and placed it on the sheepskin. 'Now be a good baby. Mummy's going to work.'

He didn't in fact get to work until eight that night. He parked in the spot he'd used before, by a gate on a quiet lane overlooking the Knowleses' farmhouse. It wasn't ideal – the house was too far away to see much with the naked eye and he had to clamp the binoculars to the window arch – but it gave as good a view as he was likely to get without camping under a soggy hedge, which really wasn't his style unless absolutely necessary. At six thirty a Land Rover drew up in the farm yard and a figure got out and went into one of the outbuildings, reappearing from time to time, fetching and carrying between barns and outbuildings.

At seven Hillyard changed into what Beryl called his Action Man kit – a dark track suit and trainers – and he and Beji had their respective suppers. Beji's, being the best marrow-bone chunks that money could buy, looked almost the more appetising. That wicked Beryl and her picnics; always forgetting the cling-film so that the bread got terminal dehydration, throwing in a couple of slabs of processed cheese, a dab of pickle and, no doubt, a splash of cigarette ash, and boasting she was doing him proud. He'd give her a piece of his mind when he got back. Much good it would do him.

At seven thirty he let Beji out to pee and almost missed the Land Rover leaving.

He gave it another half an hour to be on the safe side, and it was dark by the time he drove slowly along the rutted drive towards the farmhouse. Lights had been left shining on a couple of the outbuildings. One of the upstairs windows of the house was also lit, but he guessed this was merely a burglar deterrent.

He drew up just short of the house, turned the car round and killed the lights. Beji growled.

'Quiet, you little bitch.'

The growl grew into the beginnings of a yap. Hillyard clamped his hand over the back of the dog's neck and squeezed hard. The growl changed into a whimper. *'That'll teach you,'* he hissed.

Releasing his grip, he reached into the back for his bird-watching bag and hitched it diagonally over his head and shoulder. He opened the door and closed it almost noiselessly. With a bit of luck the farm dogs would be in a barn or locked in a back scullery. If they had the run of the house, things would be a bit more tricky. He could deal with one of the hounds, but not both, and he knew there were two, a collie and a Labrador-cross of some sort.

He approached the front door silently and listened for a few seconds before ringing the bell. An immediate frenetic barking came from the depths of the house. For a moment he thought he was in luck and the brutes were locked in a back room, but of course this was too much to hope for. The sound of wildly scrabbling claws on stone flags approached, and a dog threw its weight against the door with such force that it shook under his touch. Hillyard tutted and rolled his eyes in disgust. This door would have been easy – it had a single Yale lock – but on the principle that the dogs were unlikely to be permitted the run of the bedrooms, he would have to go to the infinitely greater trouble of an upstairs window instead.

Finding and extricating a ladder took twenty minutes. The only specimen he could locate was a long and ancient wooden relic with dubious treads. It was extremely heavy and it took all his strength to lift it against the side of the house without rasping the ends against the brickwork.

He rested for a while, listening hard, then climbed towards the window he'd selected, a wooden-framed casement job with what looked like a basic fastening.

Reaching the window, he flashed his torch through the glass and saw a bathroom with its door wide open. Well, he'd just have to risk that, because it was a dream of an entry: the catch was not fully engaged and, threading his bendy plastic through, he was able to slide it down without any trouble and pull the frame open noiselessly. There was all sorts of garbage on the sill – shampoos, toothpastes, old plastic mugs that would make one hell of a noise if they bounced around on the basin beneath. Painstakingly he moved them aside. In and over the basin. He took pride in the way he moved despite his build: smoothly, lightly, weight properly distributed, poised for sudden changes of plan. Beryl called him a bleedin' ballet dancer.

He had a good listen. His own panting was loud in his ears.

He might be a bleedin' ballet dancer, but he wasn't as fit as he should be, a result of Beryl's daily expeditions to the cake shop. He'd have to get back to some sparring and weights.

Everything back in its place: window down, tall mug to the right, shorter one to the left and the clutter reassembled in between. Creep, creep across the lino floor and another listen, short truncheon, military-police issue, ready at his belt, just in case. He could hear the dogs prowling restlessly below and waited until the clack of their claws faded and ceased.

All the bedroom doors were closed. Quick recce inside each. Ma Knowles' bedroom had the light burning. Her bedside table looked promising but yielded nothing. Have to be downstairs then. Enough to give a girl the vapours.

He left the door to Ma Knowles' bedroom open and tying a thin cord round the handle led it diagonally across the landing and in through the bathroom door. Then he whistled from the top of the stairs and retreated behind the almost closed bathroom door. The dogs barked and stampeded around downstairs before coming tentatively up. From their furtive behaviour it was obvious this was forbidden territory. The collie trotted into the mum's bedroom, but the Lab-cross paused outside the door, its nose to the air. It had smelled a rat – or rather it had smelled him, which boiled down to the same thing.

He yanked on the cord, closing the bedroom door and trapping the collie inside, then, while the Lab-cross barked in bemusement at the closed door, he stepped smartly out from behind the bathroom door and gave it a sharp tap on the head. The animal was stunned but conscious, which was just how he wanted it, and he was able to take it by the collar and cajole and drag it downstairs to a sort of scullery and close the door.

There was a large kitchen, a living room, a dining room, cold and musty from lack of use, and a study-cum-office, which was quite the most untidy room Hillyard had ever seen, and that was saying something.

The cascades of paper emanated from an old roll-top desk, its every orifice stuffed with rolls of documents, its open flap piled high with correspondence, much of it unopened.

He settled down for a long night. The curtains were too flimsy to risk the overhead light, so he took a small battery-operated book-light from his bird-watcher's bag and clipped it to the top of the desk.

The bank statements were jammed into two pigeonholes. Ma Knowles had two accounts, the farm another two, and all four were overdrawn. Letters from the bank manager, which had been relegated to the floor, followed an unyielding tone, kindly but firm. The overdrafts had exceeded agreed limits and could under no circumstances remain unsecured.

The correspondence with the lawyers lay in a thick folder on the top of the desk. It took Hillyard an hour to photograph everything. As always he took pains – each page lined up, the exposure carefully monitored, the light adjusted – but was well rewarded because he got the lot: the letters from the lawyers, the evidence from the experts, the opinions of doctors and scientists, complete with names, addresses and dates.

There was even a letter or two from Miss Field, she of the Waldorf tea dance. Advising Mrs Knowles to give up, then in the very next letter, saying that she understood her reasons for wanting to carry on and could rely totally on Catch's support.

He was so absorbed in his work that when he sat back at the end of the job he hardly noticed that a full gale had blown up and was buffeting at the window.

Releasing the dogs took some ingenuity. The Lab-cross had recovered sufficiently to howl as he approached the kitchen. He found a tin of dog food and emptied it into the bowl. He opened the door a crack and after a token growl the animal buried its head in the bowl and was still gobbling as he ran up the stairs. He pushed open the door of the main bedroom and stepped neatly out of view as the collie shook itself out of its sleep and loped out, ready if it had but known it for its ration of short truncheon. He must have hit it a bit harder than the Lab because it nosedived onto the floor, out cold. But he didn't have time to worry about that because the Lab had finished guzzling and was on its way up, growling hard.

Bedroom door closed again, as he had found it, skirt round the poleaxed collie and across the landing into the bathroom again. A moment for a breather then out over the sill again, toiletries rearranged for a second time, down into the yard, ladder back into the outhouse.

It was ten thirty. Two miles clear of the farm he treated himself to a swig of brandy and a cuddle with Beji. Then he stepped on it, in a hurry to get home and bask in the old trout's praise.

NINE

'Who is this person?' Schenker held up the newspaper cutting between two forefingers.

'He was a rock star back in the early Seventies,' Cramm said. 'With a group called Amazon. Then he went solo. Very successful. Writes good stuff.'

'Good stuff?' Schenker asked doubtfully, narrowing his mouth.

'Sort of lyrical, a bit sad. Though some are a bit happier, I suppose. But good anyway. Intelligent sort of words, memorable tunes. Often got a message to them – conservation, save the world, you know the sort of thing.'

Schenker didn't know the sort of thing, not at all. It sounded like pseudo-Green nonsense to him.

'Well, he should stick to writing songs and stop spreading hysterical stuff he knows nothing about,' Schenker said firmly, flicking through the sheaf of cuttings. 'This preservative, it's definitely not one of ours?'

'No – Reldane, apparently.'

'Well, it doesn't make much difference whose it is, does it? This sort of thing does none of us any good. What I want to know is why the hell the federation didn't get quoted? They must have been contacted, surely.' The UK Agrochemical Federation was the trade organisation of the pesticide manufacturers. One of its main functions was to counter the screechings of the Green lobby, though in Schenker's opinion it was largely ineffectual; it never moved without a committee decision and he, more than anyone, knew that committees nipped most effective action in the bud.

'They say they didn't have time to reply,' Cramm explained.

'How long do they need? A week? A year? Good God, this sort of thing can be answered in two minutes flat.' He shook his head irritably. 'Make sure the newspapers get a suitable complaint about unbalanced reporting. Make sure the federation gets *some* sort of statement in. We can't have this sort of thing splashed all over the papers and not put the record straight. Containment, Cramm. *Containment.*' He glanced anxiously at the time – he had to prepare for an important board meeting later in the morning – and reached across his desk for the next problem, which came in the form of a heavy document from the UK division. But Cramm hadn't quite finished.

'Catch was behind this,' he said, slipping the cuttings into a file.

'Mmm?' Schenker said vaguely, already absorbed by his reading. 'So?'

'They must have their claws into Nick Mackenzie. They'll try to milk him for funds.'

Tearing himself away, Schenker looked up. 'So?'

'This is a man with millions. He could – '

'Millions?' Schenker echoed with distaste. 'No wonder the country's in recession.' He waved a dismissive hand. He wasn't interested, not this morning, not when Research were manoeuvring for extra finance, which, if he wasn't very careful indeed, would be taken from his own marketing development budget. Research, under McNeill, had an independence from the executive which was intended to ensure that it retained a certain detachment and impartiality, but which only succeeded in splitting the power base and reducing effective decision making. McNeill was the thorn in Schenker's flesh, the one irritant that was impossible to shift.

'Deal with it,' he said vaguely.

Cramm seemed about to speak, but thought better of it.

Schenker returned to the notes which accompanied the fat document. The document, drawn up by Morton-Kreiger's UK Agrochemicals Division, dealt with the implications of a proposed new Food and Environment Protection Act. The changes brought by the last Act, in 1985, had been harsh but not, on the whole, unreasonable. But these new proposals went much further; in fact, they went so far as to be absurd. If enacted, it would become compulsory for certain foods to

138

carry what amounted to a health warning. The mind boggled: what were these warnings going to say? 'These potatoes have been sprayed with X, Y and Z'? They might as well say: 'These potatoes will endanger your health.' Or 'These potatoes contain dangerous chemicals.' Lunatic.

According to the Green lobby, this labelling was needed to discourage growing methods that resulted in the build-up of pesticide residues. But it was these very growing methods that had been encouraged by the Ministry of Agriculture for decades, and which were still practised by vast numbers of growers. Were they seriously going to put all those growers out of business? More to the point, where was the scientific proof to back the contention that pesticides were dangerous? There was absolutely no firm evidence that residues were in the slightest bit harmful.

As usual, it was alarmism based on the scantiest of research. A typical Green stratagem.

But if the idea for food labelling was a nuisance, the other legislative proposals were deeply worrying, for the simple reason they had a much better chance of getting through. The amount of food sampling was to be increased – that is, more products lifted off the supermarket shelves, tested for residues and the growers held responsible – and the maximum permissible levels of pesticide residues were to be put in line with those of other countries. This, Schenker feared, would put a real squeeze on the UK market. Until now, the UK market had been much freer of petty restrictions than other countries in the developed world. There were something like thirty-eight pesticides still in use in the UK which had been banned or restricted elsewhere, and that included 2,4,5-T of Agent Orange fame, aldrin, dieldrin and lindane.

Of course the British market was only a fifth the size of the US market, but that wasn't the point. One compromise, a single concession, and before you knew it, customers would be paying through the nose for rotting, unattractive produce.

'How are we getting on with this?' he asked Cramm. The question wasn't intended to elicit information about the glossy presentation document sent to the parliamentary committee by the Federation, nor the slim fact-file sent to every member of parliament, nor the seminar and lavish lunch already held for scientific journalists, nor the generous grants and personal softeners handed out to leading scientists: all this (initiated and overseen by Schenker) was just basic groundwork. What Schenker wanted to know was how they were getting on where it really mattered: with the government and, in particular, the Minister of Agriculture, Fisheries and Food, a tough-minded wet called Cranbourne.

'Can't get near Cranbourne,' Cramm said. 'Keep getting frozen off by his staff.'

'Why?' Schenker asked simply. '*Why?*'

Cramm shrugged. 'The official line is that they've got all the facts they need. But the problem is still Cranbourne himself. He seems determined to stick to his guns.'

'What's wrong with the man?' Schenker exclaimed. 'He seems to have got a serious blind spot. Why else would he shut us out? He's meant to be a senior minister, for God's sake. He's meant to have an open mind.' Schenker chewed his upper lip, a habit of which he was unaware, but which Cramm and the rest of his staff recognised as a sign of deep irritation.

Schenker's back was hurting. He got up from his chair and, stretching hard, went to the window. A thin drizzle was falling from a leaden sky, so that the grey of the river was indistinguishable from that of the sky. Schenker noticed the weather only in so far as it caused the traffic to clog up and slow his progress to meetings, or when, as now, it obscured his view of the City and the Stock Exchange, where even at this moment the market analysts would be reading indicators of Morton-Kreiger's soon-to-be-published half-year results.

'Still one of the PM's blue-eyed boys, Cranbourne, is he?' Schenker asked. 'Hasn't blotted his copy book?'

'No. Keeps his head down and his nose clean. Toes the line. Always has.'

'And no reshuffle before the next election?'

'Very unlikely. Though there are plenty of rumours of a snap election.'

'The spring. If they go early, they'll go in the spring. But assuming the worst scenario, Cranbourne could be sitting in that chair for another eighteen months. And he might just do it, you know. Push the Bill through.' Schenker turned to Cramm. 'No whispers about him? No rumblings of dissatisfaction?'

Cramm shook his head.

Schenker frowned. 'What – nothing?'

A look of understanding came over Cramm's quick face. 'I'll find out.'

Schenker sat down. 'You do just that. With a bit of luck, Driscoll will get Agriculture next time round and we'll be on to a better wicket. But in the meantime we've got to find a strategy for Cranbourne.'

'Containment,' offered Cramm, not without a faint smile.

The mention of Driscoll reminded Schenker of something. He buzzed his secretary. 'Contact Mrs Driscoll, would you, Elaine? See if she'd like a car on the morning of the opera. She might want to go to her hairdresser or something. And the flowers, Elaine, the ones for the next morning? Roses.'

He hadn't lost his certainty that Susan Driscoll would like roses. All real women liked roses. Real women dressed in feminine style, had tidy hair, pink lipstick and were a support to their husbands. Modern women, with their distorted values and almost masculine aggression, were unattractive, often alarmingly so. Fortunately career women were thin on the ground in the agrochemical industry.

Schenker surveyed his memo pad, and saw there was nothing more to discuss with Cramm. 'That's it then, is it?'

'Not quite.' Cramm rearranged the files on his lap. 'A small problem in Chicago. A report from one of our scientists.'

Schenker spread his fingers over the desk in two wide arcs. 'That's Research's problem, isn't it?' he said testily.

'Strictly speaking. But I thought you'd better see a copy of the report immediately, before it came to you through the normal channels. This scientist, Dublensky – if I've pronounced it right – he's gathered some data on the workers at the Aurora plant and – '

'Is that his job? To get data on the Aurora plant?' Schenker snapped.

'Well – no, I wouldn't have thought so.'

'What *is* his job then?'

'He's a toxicologist.'

'In charge of?'

'Er – ' Cramm glanced at some notes. 'Well, monitoring toxicology trials, I believe.'

'Then what the hell's he doing writing a report about the Aurora plant?' The Aurora Chemical Company of Aurora, Illinois, was a wholly-owned subsidiary of MKI – Morton-Kreiger International of Chicago. It manufactured three of the company's best-selling US products, but as far as day-to-day management went, it was a separate entity.

'Aurora's got a chief executive, hasn't it?' Schenker said crisply. 'And a chief chemist?'

'Yes. Why this Dublensky got involved, I don't know. But he seems to have got hold of this data – '

'What data?'

'Medical reports on some of the workers on the Silveron production line.'

'Production line? It's hardly *in* production.'

Cramm looked at his notes. 'Two lines, all export.'

'I know, I know.' He had meant, hardly in production compared to the way it would be in the future. He waved Cramm on.

'Well, apparently a few of these people have been experiencing medical problems which, according to this Dublensky, should be treated as a serious cause for concern.'

'What's his game, huh? I mean, he isn't medically qualified, is he?'

Cramm shrugged. 'I wouldn't have thought so. I'll find out . . .'

'Of course he's not medically qualified,' Schenker leapt in. 'He's a scientist, isn't he? Come on, Cramm – what's the Aurora management saying about this? Have we got a report?'

Cramm shook his head. 'Nothing. Apparently, the company medical advisors are saying that the workers' complaints – and there're just three people involved, I believe – are nothing to do with Silveron at all. Just normal illnesses.'

'So in effect there's no problem at all!'

'MKI don't think so, certainly. But I understand they're authorising a simple backup test on Silveron, just to be on the safe side. A repeat of one of the basic toxicology trials. The results should be through prior to launch. That should put paid to . . .' Cramm paused, choosing his words carefully. '. . . to any possible doubts.'

'So what the hell's this Dublensky moaning about, for God's sake?'

'He thinks the product launch should be delayed and a completely new set of trials undertaken.'

'Delayed!' Schenker protested. 'New trials! He must be joking. The trials would take years. The man's crazy. Listen – so long as MKI are happy, I don't want to hear another word about this.' He added reproachfully: 'Frankly I'm amazed it's got this far.'

Cramm gave it a moment, then said: 'I think it'd be wise to take a more cautious attitude.'

Sometimes Cramm spoke like that, quietly and insistently, and when he did so Schenker knew that he'd be foolish not to listen.

'Go on,' he said.

'The report came direct from this Dublensky. He bypassed the MKI management and somehow got it straight to us here in London. Not that he didn't try to get himself heard in Chicago. According to him he tried very hard. He says he sent a succession of memos and letters to the MKI board, but got palmed off, then threatened. He doesn't say how he was threatened. Dismissal perhaps.'

'So what's wrong with firing him?' Schenker asked. 'I would have thought it was an ideal solution for someone who's not prepared to follow proper procedures – for a scientist sounding off on matters that don't concern him.'

'My point is that this Dublensky must be a highly motivated man,' Cramm explained. 'He keeps at it when he's ignored. Then he jumps over his bosses' heads and risks his job. He might not appreciate being fired. He might run to the environmentalists.' Cramm added unnecessarily: 'Or the EPA.'

Schenker was silent for a moment. He needed to feel his way around this one. People like this Dublensky were almost beyond his understanding. What made a man turn on the company that provided his livelihood? What made him want to cause trouble for everyone? A grievance, lack of promotion? Leftist leanings? Or simply a perverse and mean-spirited nature hidden under that all-embracing guise, idealism? He had a strong urge to send these visionary types to live in a communist state for a while, so they'd catch a heavy and incurable dose of realism.

At the same time he needed no reminding of what would happen to Silveron's launch if the Environmental Protection Agency got wind of this and filed suit.

'So what do you think we should do with him?'

Cramm answered straight away, and Schenker realised he'd had it all worked out from the beginning. 'Perhaps we should think about congratulating him. Then promoting him.'

Schenker considered this for a moment. It went against the

grain to keep on a troublesome employee. At the same time Cramm's idea had certain advantages.

Yet the liturgy wasn't quite complete. Cramm should have said: congratulate him, promote him, then, most important of all, make him inactive. But then, being Cramm, this was undoubtedly what he had meant.

'Do it,' Schenker said and, seeing the time, hunched his shoulders over the desk and began reading to show that the session was over.

John Dublensky watched the first snowflakes of an unseasonally early winter swirl out of the darkness. A few stuck to the glass before melting into inconsequential droplets, defeated by the heating system of Morton-Kreiger International which was programmed to keep the staff in shirt sleeves right through till spring, when they were forced into sweaters by the air conditioning.

During Dublensky's college days at Columbia and his post-doc years at Syracuse, he'd looked forward to the snow; the eastern winters had a comforting enveloping quality that appealed to what he liked to think of as the mystical side of his nature, a side which Anne, his wife, constantly encouraged as an antidote to the absurdities of corporate life.

But the Chicago winters were different. Here the winds howled unchecked off the lake, the cold had a vicious edge, and the prairie landscape, open and urbanised, was bleak under its wrap of snow. He did not love the winters here. Come to that, he didn't much love Chicago, though he tried not to let that interfere with his enjoyment of life, which was considerable.

Shortly before five he began to tidy his desk. He did not usually leave on time, preferring to finish whatever he was doing at his own pace, but his son Tad's eighth birthday was coming up the next week and he wanted to get down to the sports store and look at a few things.

'What's this? Not staying late today?'

He recognised the strident voice of Don Reedy, his immediate superior.

Dublensky peered myopically at him. 'Hi.'

'Hi,' Reedy said, coming into the office. 'There must be a reason for this. Don't tell me – you're going on vacation!'

'That would be a little rash,' he smiled, searching his desk for his spare spectacles which he had seen only a moment ago. MKI operated a clean-desk policy, though no one would have believed it to look at Dublensky's desk.

'People have been known to benefit, you know. From vacations.'

Reedy perched on the edge of an adjacent desk watching Dublensky pack his briefcase. He was a large avuncular man, overweight by a good thirty pounds, with a benign smile which belied the very considerable committee skills that provided a welcome buffer between the senior management and the scientific staff. Reedy was tough but straight; Dublensky got on well with him.

Dublensky found his spectacles on the chair behind him. 'Well . . . I have to go now. Unless you . . .?'

His internal phone rang. In what was intended to be a practised move, Dublensky twisted the receiver up to his shoulder, but it slipped and he had to grab at it before it crashed to the desk. Anne, his wife, always said he was the clumsiest man she had ever met, a charge he gently refuted but which he had to admit had a grain of truth.

'Dublensky,' he said breathlessly.

'So glad to have caught you, Mr Dublensky,' the female voice said, and Dublensky felt a stab of surprise. Though he'd heard the clipped east-coast voice only a couple of times before, he recognised it immediately. It was Gertholm's secretary. Gertholm, president-in-chief of Morton-Kreiger International (US).

'Mr Gertholm was wondering if it would be convenient for you to see him in half an hour, at five thirty?'

It was convenient. It could hardly be otherwise. Ringing off, Dublensky sat slowly down at his desk, abandoning his briefcase to the floor. So. This was it. He shouldn't be surprised, of course. He'd stuck his neck out, and here was the guillotine, dropping fast. He supposed it was the report to London that had finally done it. The MKI management were not the kind of people to overlook a misdemeanour of that magnitude.

Well, there were worse things than being out of work, though the thought of Christmas without a pay cheque created an unpleasant sensation in the pit of his stomach.

'You okay?' Reedy asked.

'I've been summoned to Gertholm. It must be the axe. Has to be.'

'What? John, are you sure? No . . . *No!* You're mistaken. I would have known. Really. They would have told me.'

Dublensky wanted to believe him, but he wasn't sure what to believe just now. 'I don't think I quite share your optimism,' he said unhappily. 'Why else would Gertholm want to see me?'

'Listen, John . . . There could be other reasons, you know. Besides, why would he want to fire you?'

Dublensky looked at him in surprise. 'Hell, Don, we both know why. The Aurora business. Overstepping the mark. Exceeding my responsibilities.'

Reedy pulled up a chair and sat down. 'But that was a . . . well, a brave report, John. A fine thing. I always said so. It can't be held against you.'

'It can't? Remember the Greek messenger?'

'I'm sorry?'

'Killed for bringing the news.'

Reedy leaned forward and patted his arm awkwardly. 'Listen, you're wrong. I'm quite sure you're wrong. Wait and see.'

Dublensky shook his head. Reedy was just trying to soften the blow. 'I'd like to be alone, Don, if you don't mind.'

Reedy shook his head firmly. 'I'll stay. Otherwise you're going to talk yourself into believing your own worst fears.'

Dublensky didn't want to argue – in most respects he was a mild man – but on this occasion he was going to have to insist. Dublensky got up and stood by the open door. 'Thanks, Don, but really . . .'

Reedy gave a long slow shake of his head and said, with a half laugh of disbelief: 'If that's what you want . . .'

Dublensky closed the door behind Reedy and sat down again. His first instinct was to call Anne – he always discussed everything with her – but he realised that she'd be on her way from work to collect Tad. Lifting his spectacles, he rubbed a hand viciously over his eyes. He suddenly felt very alone. He tried to imagine himself in conversation with Anne, tried to hear her arguments. What would she recommend? They'd long since decided that it was essential for him to expose the facts about the Aurora workers. How could he have acted otherwise? The situation was impossible to ignore. One of the workers on the Silveron production line had been paid off, permanently sick, two more were on indefinite sick leave. There was the medical evidence of Burt, the local physician who had originally contacted Dublensky with his suspicions, evidence which, though clinical and in a sense circumstantial, was impressive. And then there were the testimonials of the victims themselves, which made the most alarming reading of all.

Anne always used to say he wasn't tough or worldly enough for corporate life, and in some senses that may have been true, but Dublensky hadn't been so naive as to think his initial report would be well received. No one wanted bad news, far less a successful company like MKI. Up till now Dublensky had thought himself prepared for the consequences of his actions. Yet he'd never quite believed it would come to this. However you looked at it, however limited corporate vision was inclined to be, something was seriously wrong when a guy got fired for doing what was right.

He had less than twenty minutes before starting for Gertholm's eyrie in the main tower. He realised this might be the last time he sat at his desk, the last time he handled the projects which had become so familiar to him. He opened his briefcase and removed the work he had been planning to take home for the evening. For a while he stared at the empty case, miserable with indecision. Then, quickly, before he changed his mind, he stood up and lifted a thick pile of papers off one of the shelves. Here was the file that he had built up on the Aurora affair: the testimonials, the physician's notes, Dublensky's original report and copies of his memos and letters to the MKI management.

He fingered the papers thoughtfully. He should make a copy – he must make a copy – but it would be crazy to do it here. Quite apart from the time factor, such a thing might well be noticed, particularly if he'd just been fired. No, far better to take the documents out of the building and copy them in a late-night office supply store.

Alert to the sounds from the corridor, his heart kicking against his ribs, he placed the dossier in his briefcase and closed it. Then he sat down again.

Yet the decision-making wasn't over. The health of Aurora workers wasn't the only disturbing thing he'd come across;

147

quite by chance he'd discovered another matter which also concerned Silveron. Until now he'd left this new difficulty on the back burner, progressing it slowly, almost reluctantly and, it had to be said, secretively. He had planned on doing a great deal more research on the matter, on assembling more facts, before putting his head on the block again; he was grimly aware that, if the state of the Aurora workers' health was unwelcome news for MKI, then this new information would be total anathema.

He opened a lower drawer and slid out a file. Though slimmer than the Aurora file, this bundle of papers weighed more heavily in his hands. For one thing the data was company property. Its removal from the MKI premises for the sort of purposes he had in mind would be a serious offence; the company could undoubtedly bring charges. And if he did manage to get the data out and copy it, what then? Hand it to the EPA? He tried to think through the consequences of such an action, but they were too enormous, too cataclysmic to settle easily in his mnd.

The immediate decision was both impossible and disturbing. He postponed it by gazing out of the window. The snow was thicker now, swirling past the glass in whorls and eddies, the flakes illuminated by the hundreds of brilliantly lit windows of the Morton-Kreiger building.

Five minutes to go. Impatient at his own indecision, Dublensky moved with sudden speed, opening the briefcase, placing the second file on top of the Aurora dossier and shutting the lid with a snap.

It was done. He was committed. Curiously, he didn't feel as terrified as he'd thought he would. If anything, his heart had lifted, buoyed by the certainty that he had done the right thing.

He stood the briefcase at the side of his desk, ready to retrieve immediately after the interview. Then, like the Greek messenger, he went to receive his punishment.

The interview was brief – a bare five minutes. It passed for Dublensky in a haze of astonishment. MKI in all its might, embodied by the thin expressionless face of Gertholm, was pleased with him. His initiative and persistence were commendable. He was to be promoted. Chief chemist at the Allentown Chemical Works in Virginia and a raise of fifteen thousand dollars a year. With immediate effect. Removal expenses, hotel bills, relocation payment.

He was so astounded that the interview was almost over before the still small voice of caution made itself heard. What would happen to the Aurora dossier, he asked. Would it be acted upon?

This question was met with immediate reassurances. Although it would be impossible to postpone the launch, the company was going to commission an independent rerun of one of the basic toxicology trials. It was also going to keep a close check on health and safety procedures at the Aurora plant.

Dublensky returned to the south tower in a state of exaltation and stupefaction. He entered his office to find that Reedy had returned and was sitting in his chair. On hearing the door, the senior chemist swung sharply round and got hastily to his feet.

It was a moment before Dublensky, numb with disbelief, was capable of communicating his news.

'I knew it,' Reedy said with a congratulatory smile. 'I knew they'd never let someone of your calibre go.'

After a while Dublensky, settling into a pleasant state of shock, allowed Reedy to help him on with his jacket and walk him down the corridor. He was hardly aware of setting off on the drive home to Evanston. The road conditions were treacherous, the visibility poor, but he registered little until he passed the sports store and remembered his son's birthday. He turned back and bought Tad a Prince tennis racquet. Then, because this was a day for celebration, he added a set of Adidas tennis shoes, socks, shorts and shirt.

He arrived home jubilant. His exhilaration lasted twenty minutes, the time it took to tell Anne and Tad the full story, and for Tad to ask questions about Allentown, Virginia.

'They're buying your silence,' Anne said quietly.

Dublensky, taking some wine from the ice box, pulled an aggrieved face. 'Why d'you say that? I told you – they've followed up my report.'

'That's what they're telling you. But how do you know they'll progress it? You won't be around to find out, will you? You'll be tucked away in Virginia.'

Dublensky felt a flutter of resentment at the swiftness with which she had managed to put a dampener on things. At the same time he had great respect for his wife's judgement. Slowly, almost reluctantly, he considered the possibility. 'You're saying that all this is just a way of getting me to keep my mouth shut? But there's no reason to say that. They haven't asked me to drop the Aurora report. They haven't suggested a deal. I mean . . . you'd have to have an abysmal opinion of people to believe something like that.'

'Not of people. Of large corporations dedicated to profit.'

It was typical of Anne to be categorical. In fact, if Dublensky didn't love and respect her so much, he'd say she had a tendency to oversimplify things. 'You're seeing villains round every corner, sweetheart. I mean, they wouldn't go to all this trouble in the hope of keeping me quiet.'

'Wouldn't they? I'd have thought it was exactly the kind of thing they would do.'

Dublensky pulled the cork on the wine and poured two glasses. Already the celebration had gone a little flat. Now that the seeds of uncertainty were sown, doubts were beginning to creep in on him, each one weightier than the last. 'But I'll soon hear if nothing gets done,' he said in an attempt to reassure himself as much as Anne. 'I'll keep in touch with the sick production workers, with some of the other Aurora people. *And* with that doctor, Burt . . . One way or another, I'll know what's going on.'

Anne took her glass but did not drink. 'Oh, I've no doubt they'll introduce some puny new safety measures at the Aurora plant and go ahead with trials of some description. But what does that prove? The trials will probably be meaningless.'

'Meaningless?' Now she had provoked him in so far as it was ever possible to provoke Dublensky. 'A trial is a trial. You can't alter results.'

Anne didn't reply but gave him a dry look. Dublensky was on the point of arguing until he remembered the slim file he'd put in his briefcase. The contents effectively challenged his own argument, and, throwing back a great gulp of wine, he sank despondently onto a kitchen chair.

Anne sat down next to him. 'How about keeping a copy of all the documentation?' she suggested earnestly. 'And using it if nothing gets done?'

'I was going to,' he admitted. 'I got the files ready – that was when I thought I was going to get fired.'

'Where are they? Have you got them with you?'

Dublensky had to think for a moment. In the confusion of leaving the office and Reedy's kindness in seeing him off, he realised what had happened. 'They're still at the office. In my briefcase.'

Anne sat back with a harsh sigh. 'Well, that's the last we'll see of them then.'

Dublensky shot her a horrified look, dismayed at the implication. 'This isn't the Mob, you know. This isn't some kind of Mafia that makes things disappear overnight. Those documents will be there in the morning. Believe me. I'll bet my last dollar on it. They'll be there.' Even as he said it, the doubts flourished. Was it possible? Would someone actually remove the documents? If so, who? MKI's security people? No, they wouldn't know what to look for. Reedy then? No. Tough he might be, but a collaborator in dark matters of chicanery he was not.

'Listen,' Dublensky added. 'If those documents aren't there in the morning I'll make one hell of a stink, believe me! One hell of a stink.' Dublensky had never made a real stink in his life – he preferred to raise awkward matters on paper – but on this issue he was pretty certain he could raise enough steam to propel himself into action.

Anne was silent; but then her silences were far worse than anything she might say because she reserved them for her moments of greatest displeasure.

Dublensky drained his glass and poured himself another. A moderate drinker, he had the sudden urge to throw prudence aside and take the consequences. 'Listen, let's just wait until tomorrow, shall we?' he said plaintively. 'Let's just wait and see.'

He woke early the next morning with an unfamiliar headache and a dry mouth, and hurried out of the house before seven. The ploughs were barely out, the dawn little more than a glimmer, but the snow had stopped and the sky was hard and clear. Apart from a section of uncleared drift on Lincoln Avenue, he had a smooth run across town to the familiar copper roofs of the MKI building.

The security man in the main lobby glanced up and gave

him a perfunctory nod. Dublensky felt a small burst of relief. In some of the wilder nightmares that had haunted him during the long night, the security men had refused him entry to the building. Now, amid the sounds of floor polishers and the chatter of the cleaners, his fears seemed absurd. They were promoting him, weren't they? They'd hardly give him the lock-out treatment reserved for abrupt departures.

Nevertheless his heart beat a little harder as he approached the security gate. He inserted his card. The green light flashed on, the gate opened, and he was through. When the elevator disgorged him at the sixth floor, his confidence had returned. Anne would be proved wrong; the documents would still be there.

The door of his office was open, an electrical cable snaking in from the passage. A cleaner was in the centre of the room, vacuuming in a desultory manner. Dublensky side-stepped the cleaning trolley and the cleaner and peered at the side of his desk. The briefcase stood there, just as he'd left it. He pulled it onto the desk and opened it. He allowed himself a small smile of relief and triumph.

Untouched.

He pulled the Aurora file to the top and opened it, just to be sure.

Complete. He'd known it. Anne had overreacted. There was nothing sinister going on at all. There never had been.

Nevertheless he would take the documents to the office supply store on his way home that evening, and get them copied, just in case.

After the uncertainties of the night, he felt a surge of euphoria which manifested itself in a spurt of manic energy, and he set about putting his papers into some sort of order, ready for the new incumbent, whoever that might be.

It wasn't long before he found out. Soon after eight thirty there was a knock and Don Reedy entered with a young woman.

'Well, how's our new man in Virginia?' Reedy said with forced joviality. Dublensky thought he looked strained. 'John – meet Mary Cummins,' said Reedy. 'She'll be taking over from you here.'

'Where have you come from, Mary?' Dublensky asked.

'Pharmaceuticals.'

'Been there long?'

'A couple of years.'

She seemed rather young for the job, though Dublensky was far too polite to say so. 'Welcome,' he said amiably. 'I wish I'd had longer to get things straight for you.' He glanced apologetically at the disorder of his desk. 'If you can give me a couple of hours . . .'

'Sure,' Reedy answered for her. 'In the meantime it would help Mary if she could get on with some reading.'

'Of course, of course,' Dublensky said, surveying his cluttered shelves. 'Where would you like to start?'

They picked their way through product performance reports, field reports and projects in hand – mainly toxicology trials on development products.

'That should keep you busy,' Dublensky smiled.

'It'll make a good start,' Mary Cummins said earnestly.

Reedy looked over the selection. 'Oh, and do you have the Aurora file, John? I need to have a look at it. Then I'll pass it on to Mary. Now we're doing this rerun.'

Dublensky's smile faltered. 'Sure.' His eyes were held by Reedy's, and for an instant he felt like a rabbit caught in the lights of a car. He forced himself to look away, only to find he was staring down at his open briefcase. The Aurora file, complete with inscribed title, gazed up at him.

Dublensky felt his heart banging against his chest just as it used to when, in his teens, he'd attempted to challenge his father's awesome authority. He felt the same sort of paralysis, too, a progressive deadening of the will that always seemed to overcome him in moments of stress.

'Er . . . give me a moment, would you?' With an enormous effort, he lifted his head and made a show of looking over the shelves. 'I'll have to think . . .'

No one spoke. The pause extended and intensified. Reedy stood back, waiting stoically; Dublensky could almost sense his determination. What was behind this doggedness? Was it just a matter of professional competence? Or was Reedy forcing the matter? In which case . . . Dublensky shied from some of the more uncomfortable conclusions.

Moving back along the shelf, Dublensky stole a glance at Reedy. He was beginning to look irritated, though this could well have been in response to Dublensky's embarrassing display of inefficiency.

The next moment Reedy gave an unexpected laugh and

153

said to Mary Cummins: 'I'm afraid John here is not the most organised of people.' Approaching, he clapped a friendly hand on Dublensky's shoulder and beamed at him. 'But he's done a fine job, and we shall miss him.'

Dublensky stared dumbly. Even before Reedy glanced down towards the desk, Dublensky knew what was going to happen, and his heart squeezed painfully.

'Here!' Reedy exclaimed. 'What's this?' He picked up the Aurora file. He gave a small indulgent shake of the head. 'Wasn't so far away after all.'

Dublensky could hardly breathe. Watching the file being removed was like seeing his own child kidnapped. The suddenness of it, the loss of all his painstaking work, overwhelmed him.

Yet – wasn't he overreacting? The file was coming to no harm, after all; it was just changing hands. But even as he tried to convince himself of this, he could hear Anne's weary sigh and harsh reproaches. She would say he'd been gullible and foolish. And he was depressingly aware that she might be right.

Reedy tucked the file under his arm and made for the door. Dublensky realised that, by some tacit arrangement, Mary was to remain in his office.

Reedy paused. 'Oh, and there are some documents which I can't seem to lay my hands on,' he said pleasantly. 'I thought you may have them, John. Perhaps you could look them out for me later this morning?'

He handed a sheet to Dublensky. On it was a list and there, among the ten or more items, were three documents belonging to the slim file still remaining in Dublensky's briefcase.

'Sure.' Dublensky tried to sound normal. 'Sure. By the end of the morning.'

It was two hours before Dublensky could persuade himself that it was safe to tuck the file in among some other documents and slip away. He remembered having seen a large automatic photocopier in the anonymous recesses of the west tower when he had visited the sales department some months before.

Perspiring, unable to prevent himself from glancing over his shoulder, he made his way across. Twice he had to ask for directions and then, having located the copier, he found himself explaining his visit to the clerk. A mumbled story about broken copiers and a meeting in the west tower seemed to suffice and, five minutes later, he had a duplicate in his hands.

Returning to his office, he waited until Mary Cummins went for a coffee then, rolling the duplicate into a scroll, slid it into the inner pocket of his overcoat.

Something, at least, had been salvaged. Anne couldn't accuse him of complete failure.

Now, only the doubts remained. Had Reedy been genuine? Had his request for the lost paperwork been the natural fruit of a tidy mind? Or had his apparent concern for Dublensky's welfare been fabricated from the outset?

Worse, had he been aware of what was in the briefcase? Had he been told to retrieve the missing documents?

It was possible. But if Dublensky accepted that, then the implications were almost too painful to think about.

TEN

Nick had forgotten how very long the nights were. He
woke early, before six, and lay staring out through the
uncurtained window, waiting for the dawn to light the giant
beeches in the park and reveal, far beyond, the faint line of
the hills of Cowal. But the darkness clung stubbornly to the
house, dense and unmoving. Even at seven when, careful not
to wake Alusha, he dressed noiselessly and slipped downstairs, no glimmering of light showed through the tall windows of the lower rooms.

Whenever he'd imagined Ashard in midwinter he'd pictured bare trees, grey landscape, snow, even a certain bleakness, but not darkness. In the old days he and Alusha had
always left Scotland by early October when the dawns were
still respectable early-morning occasions.

He gave up his plan for a pre-breakfast walk and wandered
slowly from room to room, turning on lights, pausing in
doorways. Everything was the same, yet disconcertingly
unfamiliar. Not a thing was out of place, every cushion had
been plumped, flowers had been placed on the tables, the
polished surfaces of the furniture gleamed immaculately; and
yet the effect was dark and cold and curiously lifeless.

Even his studio, which in his imagination was always as he
had left it – cluttered with his favourite books and gadgets –
was so tidy that it looked as if it had never seen a person, let
alone a note of music. The sight rather depressed him.

Some non-essential bags still stood in the hall, waiting to be
taken upstairs. Among them was a case belonging to the
nurse who'd accompanied them from Boston. He hoped she

wasn't planning on unpacking because she wouldn't be staying long. Nothing personal, but he never wanted to see another medical professional as long as he lived.

Sounds issued from the kitchen and he found Mrs Alton making coffee and laying out the breakfast things. She asked in a hushed reverential voice if Mrs Mackenzie would be wanting all her meals upstairs, and if so, would he be wanting to take them with her.

He got a fairly good picture of what Mrs Alton was thinking. Well, she'd have to think again.

'Of course not,' he said firmly. 'Only breakfast.'

'I see,' said Mrs Alton, nodding uncertainly. 'But if you'd like her to have something on a tray, in the library or wherever, you only have to say.'

'But she can tell you herself, Mrs Alton. Just like before.'

'Oh.' She blinked. 'Of course. It was just . . . I wanted to make everything as easy as possible . . .'

But he wasn't having any of this. 'Mrs Mackenzie's fine, Mrs Alton. Getting better all the time. And she's extremely happy to be back. So am I. We're really looking forward to Christmas.'

'Christmas,' she echoed, brightening a little. 'I've made the pudding. And a cake.'

'Good,' he said briskly. 'So – everything's fine then, isn't it, Mrs Alton?'

'Oh yes . . .' She was finally getting the idea. 'Yes, of course.'

Nick started to prepare Alusha's breakfast tray.

'Let me do that,' said Mrs Alton.

But he refused; he found an extraordinary satisfaction in choosing the food for Alusha, laying out the china, making the tray look attractive. He enjoyed the rhythm of the daily preparations and the challenge of finding new and exotic things to tempt Alusha's appetite. During the months in America it had made him feel useful.

He put out organic oranges ready for squeezing, some sesame thins, unhydrogenated vegetable margarine, organic marmalade and camomile tea, then added a slice of watermelon and half a papaya – also organic: everything was organic. He'd had it flown up specially from London.

When the food was set out, he opened the medicine box and started on the supplements, placing Alusha's morning dose of vitamins, minerals and amino acids in a small bowl on one side of the tray. Medicine box was actually a bit of a misnomer because it contained almost no medicines. Just before leaving Boston, he and Alusha had emptied every extraneous drug, antibiotic and allopathic medicine into the hotel waste bin. The cartons and bottles numbered an incredible fifty-eight, and that wasn't counting the stuff that'd been pumped into Alusha during her various spells in clinics and hospitals. Now, apart from vitamins and minerals, a few Chinese herbal medicines and some homeopathic drops, there were no drugs except for a few standard pain killers and sleeping tablets. And the morphine, of course. He kept that separately, with his own things. Originally the morphine had gone into the waste bin along with everything else, but a few hours later, when Alusha was asleep, he had retrieved it, despising himself for the deception, hating himself for admitting that there might be a need for it, yet doing it all the same. Doubter. Judas. Snake in the grass.

Dawn began to come at last, a grudging grey murk that seeped reluctantly through the kitchen windows. Chewing on some toast, he pulled on a jacket and, leaving Mrs Alton and the bright kitchen, escaped into the grounds.

The air tasted sweet and damp, heavy with the scent of decaying leaves fused with some indefinable tang – the peaty earth perhaps, or pine resin, or the faint salt breeze off the loch. Whatever, it was like nectar after the dry plasticky smell of aircraft and the stifling air of hermetically sealed service apartments.

Setting off at a cracking pace, he walked up through the park without pausing or looking back, delaying his first view of the landscape as a child postpones for a few agonising minutes the opening of a present, in anticipation of pleasure, but also half afraid of disappointment.

Clear of the trees, he stopped at last and turned and looked out over the loch. A vast bed of thin mist lay enclosed in the long dark scoop of the hills, obscuring water, trees, everything in a dank grey blur. The murk of the sky was balanced by the gloom of the mist, grey and dark and chill. The very air seemed to be dripping silently with something like foreboding.

Yet in spite of this a sense of homecoming began to creep up on him. There was a comforting familiarity in the reach of the pasture, the pattern of the trees in the park and the sight of the house itself, squatting in its nest of gardens, its lights glowing brightly.

He walked a long way, up through the western woods to the glen, following the cascading river as far as the high moorlands, and returning through the northern woods to emerge at Meall Dhu. The mist was dispersing, and plumes of vapour rose from the loch like steam. Beyond on the hills opposite, bands of snow made white slashes against the dull brown of the winter grasslands.

He picked up the path which led down to the upper paddock. The paddock was empty now; Rona had gone months ago, sold to people near Oban who, after a month, had been forced to put her down. She had pined for Alusha, so they said, had refused to eat. There had been nothing they could do. He had not told Alusha.

He steeled himself to look at the stable. It looked innocent, as if nothing terrible had ever happened there.

As he turned to continue down the hill he paused, his attention caught by a slight movement, a flicker at the periphery of his vision, somewhere across the paddock at the edge of the trees. He stared for a long time, trying to make out what it might have been, but there was nothing, just the dark forest, the phalanx of silent trees and the distant ticking of dripping leaves.

He was about to walk on when something made him look back – an irregularity in the pattern of the trees, a paler shape against the shadows – and then at last he saw it: a man. Wearing countryman's tweeds so that he almost blended into the background.

Was it Duncan? From this distance it was impossible to tell. One of the foresters perhaps?

The figure was standing perfectly still, yet Nick felt sure the man had seen him.

Maybe it was Duncan after all. Nick waved. For a long while the man did not move, and Nick began to wonder if the man hadn't seen him after all when, abruptly, the figure raised his arm and waved back, a brief hesitant gesture that was more like a salute. The next moment he turned into the forest and was swallowed up by the trees.

Not Duncan – who then? At the thought of intruders, all Nick's defensive reflexes returned with a vengeance, and he was tempted to start off across the paddock in hot pursuit. Almost immediately he thought better of it. This was Ashard, for heaven's sake. The man was probably a rambler who'd strayed off the path, or someone from the next-door estate.

Nevertheless, he set off down the hill in a sombre mood.

Emerging from the vegetable garden, he saw Duncan standing by the kitchen door. Beside him was Alusha. He was both surprised and pleased to see her up so early. It confirmed what he already knew: that coming home had been the best decision they'd made in the whole miserable time they'd been away.

Nick greeted Duncan then turned to Alusha.

'You're up early,' he said, kissing her lightly.

'I'm going for a walk!' she announced cheerfully. There was a hint of determination in her voice, like a child who won't be denied something she's set her heart on.

'What about breakfast?'

'I've had it. Thank you for making it for me.' Her eyes shone firmly, a smile danced resolutely on her lips. She looked transformed; Nick's heart twisted to see her so happy.

'Don't overdo it,' he said, thinking of the chill air.

At this public show of concern, she raised an eyebrow and ticked him off with her eyes. Then, with a small wave, she set off towards the rose garden. At first she walked briskly but soon the effort was too much for her, as Nick had known it would be, and she slowed to a gentler pace.

Duncan was watching her too, a deep frown on his face, and for a moment Nick saw Alusha as others must see her: far too thin, eyes unnaturally large, hair a shadow of its former glorious self. But then Duncan couldn't see what Nick saw, an Alusha vastly relieved at being home again.

The two men decided on a tour of the estate, and walked round the house towards the Range Rover.

'By the way, I saw someone up by Meall Dhu, lurking in the trees,' Nick remarked.

Duncan stopped in his tracks, looking mortified. 'A stranger?'

'I'm not sure.'

'Well, it couldn't be one of ours. Joe and Fergus are away by the loch, clearing brush. And the farmhands – well, they wouldn't be up in those parts.'

That's what Nick had thought. 'Oh well. Probably just a rambler.'

They climbed into the Range Rover. Nick added: 'Or a poacher.'

'But there's been no poaching!' Duncan exclaimed triumphantly. 'Not a dabble.'

'No?'

'Not since you left. Not a net, nor a peg, nor even a cigarette butt to be found. And not a fish disturbed, or I'm a Dutchman.'

'Well done.'

'Och, I'm not so certain it was my doing, to be perfectly honest. I rather think our friends decided to give up for some reason.'

Nick thought of the tall man and his partner by the pool. 'That was kind of them. They've reformed then, have they?'

'Not a bit of it!' Duncan shot him a guilty but not altogether serious glance. 'I rather think that those fancy managing agents next door are having their work cut out for them.' He gestured towards the Fincharn Estate.

'Oh dear,' Nick said straight-faced.

In mid afternoon, when Alusha was sleeping and the daylight was fading again, Nick ventured into the studio and tried to get the feel of the place again. He opened a few drawers, glanced at some abandoned songs and tapped out one of his old hits from years before. He remembered having thought it was rather good when he'd written it, but now it sounded flat and glib and rather pretentious.

His drawings looked all right though – the osprey series and some sketches he'd started making of the buzzards that inhabited the upper reaches of Ashard – and the sight of all his books cheered him further.

He wandered down the passage past the back stairs to the estate office, which had its main entrance off the courtyard to the east side of the house, a courtyard which housed Mr and Mrs Alton in a converted outhouse on the far side, and one of the forestry workers in a flat over the stables.

There was a pile of opened letters in the tray reserved for his mail. These would be letters that had come direct to Scotland and which Helen, who did the secretarial work in the estate office, thought he would like to see personally.

There was a letter from a writer friend who'd heard he and Alusha were coming back and wanted to know how they were. There was a note from an acquaintance in television asking about the possibility of making a TV programme about Nick's solo career. He apologised for not going through Nick's manager but, if Nick didn't mind him saying so, the man was totally impossible to deal with, since he never replied to letters or phone messages. Nick thought: That's David all right.

The next was a letter on Save the Children notepaper, written in a slanting female hand. He glanced at the signature. Susan Driscoll. Ever since his drinking years his memory for names and faces – sometimes even the words of his own songs – had been appalling. But he soon had it: it was Suki Armitage-that-was, organiser of charity concerts, and a touchy lady when she wasn't instantly remembered. She said she hadn't realised his wife was so ill. She was extremely sorry to hear about it, and of course quite understood why he couldn't do the concert. There was a PS. If at any time in the future things changed and he was ever interested in doing anything for her charity, she would of course be delighted to discuss it.

The next letter was also on headed notepaper. It was from the anti-chemical campaign, Catch. The signature was scrawled and it took him a moment to decipher it. Daisy, the eco-freak. He smiled, he wasn't sure why. He wondered if the realities of a heartless world had rubbed off on her yet.

The letter was short. She'd heard he might be returning. She hadn't stopped looking into Reldane, searching for evidence that it might have damaging effects, but she'd had no joy. However, she'd had some new thoughts. Could he send some more earth and water samples?

He put the letter on one side. She was a nice girl; he'd drop her a line. No, he'd call her. It would be easier to explain on the phone.

But something made him put it off; perhaps it was the thought of her persuasiveness and enthusiasm, which might prove altogether too powerful.

When after a week he still hadn't got round to calling, he finally scrawled her a note. *It's good of you to keep trying, but my wife and I really need to leave the past behind. That may seem selfish and irresponsible to you – and maybe it is – but it takes everything we have just to keep going. Hope you understand . . .*

He meant to finish there, but felt he owed her more of an

162

explanation. *We've been making the rounds of the doctors and clinics for months now. The medics tried everything they could think of, and I know we should be grateful for that, but nothing helped. In fact, I don't think any of them really had the faintest clue of how to treat my wife. All they did was pump her full of drugs, which seemed to have terrible side-effects and to make her worse.*

He thought: I'm sounding bitter. I really mustn't.

Though it's impossible to know how she would have been without the drugs, of course. The same, maybe even worse. Impossible to tell. Anyway, it doesn't seem to matter now, because –

But he couldn't go on. How could he put the rest down on paper, and to a virtual stranger, when he couldn't even voice it to Alusha?

He crossed out the unfinished sentence, scribbled some best wishes and put it out for posting.

Concern over the cause of Alusha's illness seemed to be surprisingly widespread because two days later Nick got another letter on the same subject. This time the signature, which was small and childish, read A. Campbell. The address was Inveraray. Nick didn't know any A. Campbell, either male or female, but whoever it was, he or she thought Nick would be interested to know that some other people in the Argyll area had been suffering a mysterious illness, just like Mrs Mackenzie's.

For a moment Nick considered the wild possibility that Alusha's illness might be contagious, but immediately dismissed it. If it had been catching, someone else would have got it by now.

He skimmed on through the letter. Mr or Mrs Campbell knew a young lad who'd been fit and well but was now unable to leave the house. The boy slept all day, couldn't eat, had lost weight, had an aversion to sunlight and suffered badly from 'weeping attacks'.

Nick began to lose interest. This wasn't the same illness at all. He felt a curious almost guilty relief; he was glad to be spared the complications of other people's problems.

The letter ended with the description of another case further down the loch at Lochgilphead. But again, the symptoms didn't tally. Along with a number of vague-sounding problems, this man apparently suffered vertigo, skin rashes and panic attacks.

Nick had the picture: here were the local nutters and

hypochondriacs and depressives coming out of the wood-work, trying to win respectability and attention for their illnesses, and finding a champion in the well-meaning but deluded A. Campbell.

He scribbled a pencilled message across the letter, asking Helen to thank A. Campbell for his interest, etc. Then, chucking the letter thankfully into the out-tray, he forgot about it.

The driving rain and gales came first, over Christmas and the New Year, then, almost as a welcome relief, the snow. Wet, slushy, damp stuff to begin with then, in late January, crisp dry snow that fell and fell, forming a thick blanket over the lower slopes of the hills and forests so that the trees groaned and creaked with the weight. After a few days a salty sou'westerly roared up the loch from the Gulf Stream waters and shook the trees free, blowing the snow into drifts and melting the surface into a heavy crust.

At Ashard House the days varied little. A few friends came to stay around Christmas, but after that, while no one was actually discouraged from coming, no one was openly invited either, and the trickle of company dried up. Nick was glad. Alusha wasn't up to it, and he wasn't sure he was either. People were very kind, but, being kind, they were also very wearing. Everyone was careful not to mention Alusha's appearance and to pretend she looked just fine, and questions about her health, if asked at all, were blatantly tactful. But they knew, and the worry and pity showed in their eyes, and it was like a ghastly game.

In the end it was easier to be alone, just him and Alusha, wrapped in the cocoon of the Glen Ashard winter. Being alone also gave Nick the opportunity to work again, or at least to attempt some sort of routine. Every morning at seven he crept out of bed and went down to the studio for a couple of hours' thought. In the old days thought itself, in enough quantity, had always resulted in a song or two but now, though he tinkered with a few ideas, nothing came. Even his great indulgence, the choral work that he'd been working on spasmodically for the past four years, didn't respond to this or any other approach. He gave it time – no point in forcing it – but even that didn't seem to do the trick. It was a situation he'd never encountered before and he began to feel a corrosive frustration. He was well aware that frustration itself could be highly counter-productive, and did his best to ignore it, but it ate slowly away at him, paralysing his will and deadening his mind.

He began to get headaches. His limbs began to ache, and he started to get irritable. He had no doubt it was psychosomatic. Too much stress – or how did the therapists put it? – the burden of suppressed emotion. Well, there was plenty of that. He lost some of his appetite, too, and his jeans started to get loose at the waist. He took to going to the studio late at night and, aided by forbidden cigarettes, tried working into the early hours, to see if that would hit the mental trigger. But though he went through the motions, tapping out one or two bars, he knew it was hopeless. After a few minutes, he'd start to read something light – the latest *Melody Maker*, or a Sunday colour magazine. Sometimes he'd try a sketch or, more usually, work on a detailed copy of an osprey illustration. Pencilling in the intricate featherwork of the wings was, he found, profoundly calming.

During these nights he also listened to the radio, to plays, discussion programmes, music – anything, in fact, to fill the long hours while Alusha slept. While she was awake, he could cope; there were the meals and the long ritualistic sessions in the kitchen with complex recipes and finicky ingredients, and the walks with Alusha – increasingly short – and in the evenings the videos and games of backgammon.

But in the night there was nothing, just the grinding truth, and his inability to deal with it. He came to the studio to escape. Escape? From Alusha? It was true. He knew it, yet couldn't bring himself to face it, just as he couldn't bring himself to face the reason. It had got to the point where he almost avoided touching her. In bed, when she curved her back into his stomach and drew his arm round her, he was filled with such misery that he could hardly speak, far less sleep. He waited in despair and self-hatred until she slept, so that he could ease away from her and escape the sharp points of bone where the soft roundness of her bottom had been, avoid the stick-like arms and the shrunken breasts where there had once been smooth firm flesh. In the day he could eliminate the picture of her wasting body from his mind and look her in the face and feel immense love and real bursting hope; he could, simply, believe. But the nights were impossible, because it was then that the evidence was at its most stark and inescapable.

In late February there was a change. She stopped sleeping at night. She began to mutter and turn, often for hours at a time. If he tried to touch her, she pushed him away and, still half-asleep, swore at him in French. At other times he woke and knew she was awake too. When he reached out to her he found her skin cold with sweat, her hands clenched. She'd murmur about dreams and feeling restless, but he knew it was the pain. She never mentioned it of course, but when she thought he was asleep, she'd flick on the light and wash down some pain killers.

He stopped his late night visits to the studio then, and a week or so later, his early morning ones as well. Curiously, he didn't mind; it was a relief to give up the farcical attempts to work. Now at least his course was clear, and his life revolved more than ever round Alusha's needs. When she woke in the night he'd ask if she wanted anything, and though she never did, she'd squeeze his hand and keep hold of it, and he liked to think he was helping to ease her pain.

To pass the long nights while he lay at her side he took to reading celebrity biographies, because they were straightforward and held his attention better than anything else. Often, though, he would just lie awake in the darkness, awed by Alusha's iron will and staggering perseverance. Where did this strength come from? How could she keep it up, day after day? How could she smile at him and chatter away and joke with him through the pain and sickness and despondency? Sometimes he caught her eyeing him thoughtfully, as if he were the one in need of inspection, and then the dogged uncompromising look disappeared from her eyes and was replaced by something altogether darker and angrier and softer.

She was amazing. He only wished he could be the same.

The thing came to him quite suddenly. It was on a day in early March or, more precisely, an early morning. He woke at five and there it was in his head: the choral work – theme, words, and orchestration, a whole bloody section, as if some ghostly superscribe had composed the entire thing, and, in case that wasn't enough for him, had obligingly written out the words and music in manuscript.

Checking that Alusha was asleep, he pulled on a robe and went straight down to the studio. He scribbled out some of the words, tried the melody on the piano, then the variation, and squirmed in anguish. Something was wrong; it didn't sound the same.

He tried again, but now something else wasn't right. The main theme had gone. Closing his eyes, maintaining his calm, he tried to recapture the sound that had been so vivid in his mind just ten minutes before. One phrase was crucial, he knew: a haunting minor cadence. If he could get that . . . He tried several ways, none of them right, and felt the mixture of elation and despair that always came at moments like this. Then, abruptly, the phrase came swooping back into his mind. At first it hovered there, amorphous and tantalisingly difficult to grasp, but slowly, patiently he began to pin it down until, quite suddenly, there it was: utterly complete, absolutely perfect. Well – as perfect as it was ever likely to be.

Once it was down on paper it began to look rather ordinary, and he could see plenty of imperfections – were the words a bit trite perhaps? Was the melody an unconscious rehash of an existing song?

Problems like these weren't new, of course. They came up all the time and, from long habit, he had learnt to ignore them, at least until the work was finished. The work . . . Having never written a choral work before, he wasn't too sure what to call it.

He scribbled down a few more words, fragments, phrases, then started to work on the baritone and bass harmonies for the main theme.

At seven the ideas ran out and he realised he'd have to come back to it later in the day.

As he eased his way gently back into bed he sensed the stiff watchfulness of Alusha's body beside him, and knew she was awake. As the silence stretched out, he felt all his old helplessness slip over him, familiar as an old coat, heavy as lead.

'All right?' he whispered finally in the direction of the back of her head. She had been particularly bad in the last few days, stiff with pain, and withdrawn and irritable.

'Yes.' Her voice was low and rough. 'Yes . . . And you? Were you writing? Did you have some ideas?'

'Mmm. Maybe.'

167

'I know that maybe of yours,' she said in her increasingly halting speech. 'Good. I'm happy. It's been too long.' She paused and he knew she was sorting out her next batch of thoughts and assembling her words in the right order, something that she no longer found easy. 'You should write another album,' she said eventually. 'It would be good for you.'

This was so unlike her that he raised his head to peer at her in the darkness. Normally, she never commented on the pace or, more recently, the total absence of his work.

'You're right,' he said. 'I should.'

'I worry about you.' Another pause. 'About what will happen to you.'

If her earlier remark had surprised him, this gave him a ripple of alarm. Ever since the accident any conversation that touched on defeat, on the idea of Alusha not getting well, was never to be mentioned.

'Plans,' she said. 'You need plans.'

'What plans?' he said lightly. 'Since when have we ever made plans?'

'Always,' she said crossly. 'Always. And we need some now. Listen – ' She paused, then gave a harsh little sigh of frustration because the words would not come out right. 'We've been doing things wrong, haven't we? Don't you think?'

He felt sick. 'What?' But he knew. He knew exactly what she meant.

'We never talk,' she said doggedly, 'about what will happen.'

He didn't reply. Although he'd thought about little else for the last few months, he couldn't begin to discuss it. He felt chilled, emotionally suspended.

The silence stretched out. Then she said: 'Thank you for the pain killer . . . for getting some more. It helps.' Her voice was low, laboured, and totally matter-of-fact.

'Does it?' This was the first time they had ever mentioned the fact that Alusha had found the morphine and was using it regularly.

'I tried without for a day or so . . . But no good. So I start again tonight. It makes me a little high, I think. And rather silly. Or more silly than usual.' She gave a snort of amusement that was almost a sigh. 'You'll just have to put up with that.'

168

Nick pulled her closer to him. 'I'll try.'

'You know . . .' She didn't finish.

After a minute, when she still hadn't replied, he prompted gently: 'Mmm?'

'You really must get on and finish that song or whatever it is,' she said.

He sensed that she'd been intending to say something quite different, but he didn't press her. 'I will,' he whispered. 'I promise.'

She pulled his arm further round her body, and tucked it under hers. Later she fell asleep again. Dressing quietly, he crept down to the studio to have another look at the song.

He played it several times but it didn't sound right. The magic, such as it was, had gone. The grand chords, the mystical quality he was so sure he'd captured had degenerated into something tawdry and uninspired.

The dawn when it finally appeared was grey, dark and cold. He leant his elbows on the desk, thrust his head into his hands and wept.

ELEVEN

A road to the edge of nowhere. Narrow and unmetalled, riddled with potholes, the track climbed tortuously through rough grassland and geometric blocks of forest towards empty hills. Then, just when Daisy felt certain nothing but wilderness could lie ahead, a patch of green appeared above, nestling in a crescent of forest, with a solitary dwelling at its edge.

The car bounced and weaved over the last few potholes, and Brayfield brought the car to a halt in front of a sagging picket fence. Daisy got out and, meeting the wind, pulled her jacket close around her. She wandered across the track and looked out over the broad landscape. The ground sloped gently away from her in a long sweep of newly planted forest and bracken towards a valley dotted with sheep and a meandering river marked by a snaking avenue of black trees.

She had never been anywhere like this before. She couldn't get over how quiet it was. No people, no noise. No real noise, that was. She didn't count the whistling of the wind, which sounded unreal, like the whooshing noises made by the special effects department in an old film. But beneath the wind, and almost as loud in its way, was a kind of mysterious silence, which was both weird and compelling.

After the sounds, the next thing she noticed was the space. Nothing but rolling hills, forest and water; miles and miles of emptiness. As she'd remarked to Brayfield on the drive up from Glasgow, it was hard to believe that this was the same country that contained London and Birmingham. It wasn't, Brayfield had reminded her sharply, not the same country at all. This was Scotland, quite a different country, and she'd best not forget it. Daisy had almost smiled until she saw he was deadly serious.

Presumably it was this very emptiness that brought the super-rich here. At five or six million for a nice little estate they probably thought the peace and quiet was cheap at the price. Nick Mackenzie's place was no more than fifteen miles from here; she knew – she'd looked it up on the map. She'd sent him a note to say she was coming and left a phone message with the David Weinberg office, but there had been no reply. Too concerned with his wife. Too reluctant to go over old ground. His original reply had, after all, been clear enough. But it would have been nice to have had a go at changing his mind.

She turned to find Brayfield waiting patiently by the gate. Brayfield, a heavy Highlander with a congenial manner and a terrifying smoker's cough, was her contact from the local branch of the Transport and General Workers' Union.

The house was small and single-storey, built of grey stone with small windows sheltering under deep eaves, a modern replica of a Highland croft. In the perverse way of small dwellings it had turned a blank side-wall to the view down the valley and chosen to face a stand of dense pines.

Brayfield led the way up a short path which ran through a patch of unkempt grass and dead plants. The curtains in the window to the left of the porch were drawn; as Daisy watched, one of them quivered and fell still. Brayfield knocked and the door swung open immediately. A stout grey-haired woman stood there, wearing a mauve sweater and grey tweed skirt with lace-up shoes. She had a square face with small eyes and a thin-pressed mouth. She looked about fifty but could have been less. Brayfield introduced her as Mrs Bell.

Mrs Bell gave Daisy's jeans, boots and bomber jacket a long dubious stare before standing back to let them in. The interior was dark and smelled of damp and fumes from some heating fuel. Mrs Bell led the way into a cluttered living room with a dralon three-piece suite adorned with sunflowers, a gold and orange rug over a threadbare brown carpet and fading pink rose-patterned wallpaper. In one corner was a television showing a football match with the sound turned down; in the other, a bed which was masked by the high back of the settee so that, from where they were standing, its occupant was almost hidden from view. Mrs Bell went up to the bed and bent over it, smoothing the bedcovers and talking in a low murmur. Finally she came back to them and said in a studiously low voice: 'Just five minutes now. He gets dreadful tired. And keep your voices down. He cannot manage with the noise.'

Daisy and Brayfield advanced. Brayfield had already told her a little about Mrs Bell's son, Adrian. His father, a forestry worker, had died suddenly eighteen months before, since when Adrian and his mother had been threatened with eviction. He had been ill for about nine months, and was now almost fourteen years old, though it would have been hard to judge his age from his looks. His face was narrow and angular, and the skin, which was stretched tightly across the bones, was extraordinarily white, with a scattering of livid pustular spots over the cheeks. His hands were long and thin and brittle-looking, and his frame, clothed in old-fashioned striped pyjamas, was sharp with bones.

He looked awful, and it suddenly occurred to Daisy that he might be dying. Yet his eyes were bright, and though he seemed to find the smallest movement a terrible effort, he managed a small wave.

Brayfield did most of the talking. 'Adrian was up in a field at the back here when it happened. This was in June last, wasn't it, Adrian? Up with the sheep, he was.'

Daisy asked softly: 'You were in charge of the sheep, were you, Adrian?'

Adrian hadn't heard. He was staring at Daisy with blank puzzlement, as if some exotic and unexpected creature had suddenly alighted by his bed. Becoming aware of their stares, he glanced away, looking embarrassed.

Brayfield took over again, calling over his shoulder: 'Just the three ewes, were there not, Mrs Bell?' A soft assent came from behind. 'Kept for their milk. Sent for cheese.' Looking back at Adrian, he continued: 'So there he was, young Adrian, up in back there, and he notices a strong smell drifting across the field. Coming from the forest. A plantation of young trees, were they not, Adrian? And then he sees the plane. A light plane. He remembers a red flash on the wing, going diagonal – a sort of stripe. Anyways, the plane passes right over. And after it comes the spray, and he's no hope of avoiding it. Very

172

strong, it was. Made the lad ill directly, did it not, Adrian? Coughing and feeling dizzy, were you not?'

Adrian gave a faint nod. Daisy encouraged him with a smile, but he refused to meet her gaze.

'Right-thinking chap that Adrian was,' Brayfield went on, 'as soon as he stopped coughing, he went directly to find the estate manager. The man admitted to the spraying on *that* occasion – but it was the last time he ever did. And what did he say, Adrian?'

A pause then the voice came, soft as a whisper. 'Told me I shouldna' have been there. Said . . . I should have kept clear. I . . .' He trailed off, as if he had lost the thread.

Brayfield nodded, urging him on. 'And then what happened?'

'I said about the sheep.'

'And he said to move them?'

Adrian blinked his agreement.

'What happened to the sheep?' Daisy asked.

'They took sick,' Brayfield said. 'Though it took some time. How long was it, Adrian, some months?'

Adrian took a breath that was almost a sigh. 'Aye. Two, three months.'

'They were taken for slaughter and examination.'

'And what did that show?' Daisy asked, trying to capture Adrian's attention.

Adrian stared fixedly at a point somewhere between the bedcovers and the window. He seemed to be shutting himself off from the conversation, as if the visit was already too much for him.

'There were no laboratories that could do the right tests,' Brayfield explained.

'Why not?'

'The veterinarians, they use the Ministry of Agriculture labs, but they're not equipped for pesticide tests.'

'Wouldn't you know it!' declared Daisy for Adrian's benefit. She caught him stealing a glance at her and, before he could look away, pulled a conspiratorial face at him. 'And what about you, Adrian? Did they do any tests on you?'

It was a moment before he responded, raising one of his thin fingers to point at his arm. 'Blood,' he whispered.

'And they tested it for pesticides?'

'We arranged it,' said Brayfield. 'In November.'

'And they found nothing?' Daisy guessed. 'Well, they wouldn't, I'm afraid, not so long after the event. You really have to be tested straight away. What about a tissue biopsy, Adrian, did they do that?' She explained: 'A bit of your arm. Or sometimes your bum, if you'll excuse the expression.'

A glimmer of a smile.

'Not even a sliver? Didn't sit you on a bacon slicer?'

He gave a small giggle and she risked reaching forward to touch his hand. He still wouldn't look at her, but he didn't pull away either.

'They did all the standard tests,' Brayfield said. 'Or so they informed Mrs Bell.' He spoke over his shoulder: 'Is that not right, Mrs Bell?'

'And?' Daisy asked.

Brayfield shook his head.

'So they found nothing?' she said to Adrian.

The smile had gone, he was looking blank again.

'So what have they decided is wrong with you?' Daisy had never believed in beating about the bush with sick people or children.

Coming up behind Daisy, Adrian's mother said firmly: 'They canna' be sure. But they do know he'll mend in time.' She spoke in the uplifting tone people use to convince themselves, as much as others, of something they desperately want to be true.

'And treatment? What have they given you?'

Adrian's eyes travelled towards a table at the head of the bed. Daisy had already spotted the rows of prescription drugs, and had only been waiting for an excuse to examine them. Anti-depressants. Tranquillisers. Antibiotics. Not what Pease-dale or any half-knowledgeable physician would have recommended, and that was putting it mildly. In fact they would have been horrified. But this wasn't the moment to say so.

Mrs Bell, looking defensive, her eyes on Daisy, had come to sit at the foot of the bed.

'And your symptoms, Adrian?' Daisy asked the boy. 'What did you notice first?'

He had to think about that. 'I felt just . . . terrible. Dreadful sick.' He frowned, and there was that puzzlement again, as if he were attempting to dredge a memory that refused to deliver.

174

'His memory hasna' recovered,' confirmed Mrs Bell. 'Half the time he has no knowledge of what month it is, let alone the day. He was never like that before, *never*.' Her voice quivered with anger or bitterness, or both. 'Then there was the sickness. He couldna' eat, not for weeks. Lost a terrible amount of weight. We've got some back on him since, but not enough as you'd notice. Some foods don't suit him any more. He canna' take the things he used to love.'

Brayfield prompted: 'And you say he was dizzy, Mrs Bell?'

'Aye. Terrible unsteady on his legs. Kept fallin' over. An' weak. Could barely lift his arms above his head. Feeble as a bairn. Terrible, terrible.'

Daisy jotted the details in her notebook.

'An' sleep,' Mrs Bell went on, 'he slept all the hours God sent and a few more. I could never wake him. Sleep in the morning, sleep in the afternoon, an' all the night too.'

'Anything else, Mrs Bell?'

'Eh . . .' She considered. 'His talkin'. Words – he couldna' say his words.'

'In what way exactly?'

'Back about face. He'd say white an' mean black. Or chair instead of table. Dinner instead of tea.'

A memory stirred in Daisy's brain, a connection to something in the past, though she couldn't quite pin it down.

Mrs Bell leaned towards Adrian and brushed her fingers lightly over his hair. She didn't have to tell them he'd had enough. He looked drained, his skin grey beneath the bloom of ghastly spots. His eyelids were drooping, his mouth slack.

In the hall Mrs Bell asked in her stolid way if they could continue their talk later, when she'd given Adrian his dinner. Daisy and Brayfield used the time to climb the hill and inspect the site of Adrian's accident.

Brayfield indicated the forest at the top of the field. 'That is the place,' he said, raising his voice above the wind. 'It's not Commission land, I need hardly say.'

'Why wouldn't it be?'

'If it was, there would not be any problem in knowing what happened. The Forestry Commission are not perfect, but they are a sight more safety conscious than the private landowners. The Commission is unionised, and there's not one of our members who is not aware of who comes first in the firing line with these chemicals.'

175

Daisy hobbled over the grass tussocks in her slippery-soled ankle-boots. She had imagined she'd dressed for the country, but had obviously been mistaken. 'Who does the forest belong to then?'

'An insurance outfit. The Salmon Group. One of those firms that invested in forestry a few years back when there were the tax incentives.'

'But surely,' Daisy panted, trying unsuccessfully to keep her hair from blowing into her eyes, 'they could tell us. I mean, they must know what spray they used.'

'Them? Och, no.'

'What – they're refusing?'

'Not refusing. They are "anxious to assist us in our enquiries" – that is the way they put it at any rate. Which means they refer us to their forestry managers.'

'Who are – ?'

'Willis Bain.' He spoke the name with contempt. 'And *they* say it was fenitrothion.'

'But you don't think so?'

'No.' It was a long hoot of disbelief. 'Fenitrothion has never done that sort of harm.'

'So you think they're lying?'

'I think they are not telling the whole story.'

They had reached the edge of the plantation of firs – or were they pines? Some thirty feet tall, they were planted in ranks so dense that their upper branches were interwoven like a thatch, and their lower branches were shrivelled and brown from the permanent darkness around their feet.

'Lodgepole pine,' Brayfield said. 'See the crowns there, and the way the new growth is eaten back? That's the pine beauty moth. The larvae, they eat the young needles.'

'The trees don't recover?'

'Oh, they recover, so they tell me, but it takes years, and that is all lost income to the owners.'

'But I thought spraying caused more problems than it solved. I thought you killed the natural predators and the bugs got resistant.'

Brayfield snorted, and Daisy sensed the working man's scorn for all theory, Green or otherwise. 'One of our foresters took a look here. He says whatever they used on these trees, it worked fine.'

176

Daisy swung her bag down from her shoulder, and pulled out her sampling kit. 'Well, let's see what we've got.'

She cut a three-inch square block of grass and topsoil, placed it in a container, sealed the lid, then, climbing into the plantation, repeated the operation, taking soil from under the branches of the trees.

They set off down the hill again. The wind was blowing straight into their faces. Daisy, stiff with cold, a Kleenex clamped to her dripping nose, had to strain to hear what Brayfield was saying.

'Willis Bain are denying the conversation with Adrian took place. They are saying they never sprayed this part of the forest at the time Adrian got his dose. They say they sprayed it back in May.' Brayfield gave an exclamation of disgust. 'When I pressed them again over what they had sprayed it with when they *did* spray it, they would not confirm the fenitrothion. Said it was not company policy to give that sort of information.'

'How can they justify that?' She had to raise her voice to be heard over the wind.

Brayfield shrugged. 'Who can say?'

Daisy blew her nose, which had gone dead at the end. 'Who would have done the spraying itself? Do Willis Bain have a plane?'

'No, no. The work would have been contracted out.'

'Another contractor?' Daisy retorted. 'Blimey, doesn't anybody do anything themselves around here?'

'Willis Bain would not say which company they used for the job. They said it was irrelevant.'

'So the owners don't know anything,' she shouted, 'and the managing agents say there was no spraying, no pilot, no plane and no damage to Adrian?'

'We tried the local authorities and the local Health and Safety Executive to find out if and when they received the obligatory spray notifications, and they said what Willis Bain said, that this estate was done in May. Though they did at least give us the name of the flying company. We found them easily enough. They seemed right enough. They confirmed the May date. They even showed me their records.'

'What was the chemical?'

'They said that was for Willis Bain to tell me. Although they

177

did go so far as to say the chemical was approved for aerial use.'

They paused by the fence at the side of the house. 'The only conclusion I can come to,' Brayfield said, 'is that the original spraying job did not cover this part of the forest, and that the moth suddenly spread and that someone panicked and called in another outfit in a hurry. Cowboys.'

Low clouds raced overhead, obscuring the hills, sending giant shadows chasing across the valley. Daisy's toes had lost all feeling, the cold seemed to have reached into her chest. 'Wouldn't there be some trace of them?' she managed through clenched teeth.

He shrugged. 'You would think so. We tried the local air traffic control people. Nothing. So long as agricultural pilots keep below the commercial air lanes, then they do not have to tell anyone except the military. And the military controllers, they have no record of a crop-spraying aircraft at the right time and place.'

They walked round to the gate. Brayfield held it open for her. 'A dead end, I fear.'

Well, that was nothing new, Daisy reflected. Investigations into chemical accidents were all about a succession of hurdles interspersed with dead ends.

As they entered the house Daisy noticed that another car had appeared in the lane, parked behind their own.

A man, presumably the car-owner, was sitting at the table in the kitchen. He was a big-boned fellow with a square face, a raw complexion and the broad bent nose and dog-eared features of a sporting man. His hair, which was an indistinct sandy-grey, was thin and clung to the mass of his considerable head. His eyes were small and quick-moving and creased up into a fierce expression, as if he regularly used it to frighten people.

He rose from his seat, an exercise that took his head within inches of the ceiling. He was both tall and broad, a giant of a man.

'My brother, Mr Campbell,' said Mrs Bell.

'Alistair Campbell,' the big man grunted. He didn't offer a hand, but dropped heavily back into his chair. 'So? What's to be done?' he demanded, elbows thrust onto the table. Before they had the chance to take off their coats or sit down he persisted: 'What are you proposin'?'

Daisy raised her eyebrows imperceptibly at Brayfield. She had met aggressive barn-storming types before.

As Daisy and Brayfield took chairs opposite each other on either side of Campbell, he threw yet more questions. Mrs Bell handed out cups of tea and retreated to the stove. Brayfield, who seemed unruffled by the verbal bludgeoning, calmly ran through a summary of the position, from the unhelpful response of the landowners to the evasiveness of Willis Bain.

Campbell swept all this aside with an impatient gesture. 'That's all very fine but where does it get the lad, eh? Where does it get him? Nowhere, that's where!' He spoke in a strong accent. 'He will be in need of care an' good food. That takes money.' He indicated his sister. 'Meg here canna' work, canna' leave him, so what's to be done, eh?'

Brayfield looked to Daisy for help.

'Well, there are two possible approaches, Mr Campbell,' Daisy said cautiously. 'First, we could use publicity, which is really all about shaming the opposition into coming to an arrangement –'

'But the money, what about the money?'

'I was just getting to that, Mr Campbell. The idea is that the opposition would eventually decide that some sort of ex-gratia payment is preferable to having their names spread all over the papers the whole time.'

Campbell swivelled on his chair and raised his shoulders at his sister. Neither of them seemed overly impressed by the idea.

Daisy pressed on. 'Another possibility is to go for a civil action in the courts, but I have to warn you that it could take years and an enormous amount of money, and even then – well, as things stand at present, it's simply Adrian's word against the managing agents'.'

Campbell gave her a truculent stare. 'So you're sayin' we should sit back and do nothin'!'

'I didn't quite say that,' Daisy explained patiently. 'What I'm saying is that the chances of getting full damages are not good. First, there's the problem of proving that the events happened as Adrian says they did, which means finding evidence that a chemical was sprayed on this particular section of forest on the day Adrian says the accident happened. Even if we managed to establish those events, in the absence of the aircraft operators and a precise identification of the chemical, we'd only have Willis Bain to go for, and the judge might decide that the company were only, say, fifty per cent liable, which means Adrian's award would get marked down by a half.' She took a sip of the dark tea.

'And then there's the matter of the permanence of Adrian's disability,' she went on. 'If Adrian recovers, well, the claim would by definition hardly be worth pursuing. Unfortunately there's only one way to find out if he's going to recover, and that's to wait and see. At least another six months, I would have thought. Just getting proceedings started can be a very expensive business, you see, so it's hardly worth going to the trouble before then. One would hope to get legal aid, of course, but that's very far from automatic in civil cases like this.' She took another sip of tea to see if the brew improved with familiarity, but it didn't.

'Then,' she continued, 'just when you might reasonably think you were getting somewhere, you'd face the hardest part of all – persuading the medical experts to agree that the chemical, whatever it was, was indeed responsible for Adrian's illness, and that his symptoms weren't the result of something else altogether, something unconnected with the accident.'

A spark of complicity passed between Campbell and his sister. It was the briefest of glances, little more than a flicker, but the warning lights came on in Daisy's brain.

'What have the doctors said so far?' she asked abruptly.

Campbell's brows shot together and he grunted, a deep growl of a sound, and Daisy was reminded of a large bear.

It was Mrs Bell who answered. 'When they first took him into the hospital – at the outset, it was, for two weeks – they said he would recover, that it was just a matter of time. Then, come September, when he was worse, they wanted him in Glasgow. He was there five weeks. He saw two, mebbe three of the specialists. At first they spoke of the chemical all the time, the likely nature of it. They seemed hopeful. They spoke about gettin' him better. They were kind to Adrian, they couldna' do enough for him. Then . . .' She drew in her lips. 'Then it changed. Adrian was given to other doctors, ones I'd never seen before, ones they never told me about. But even then I didna' realise . . .' She gave a short sigh. 'I didna' see that things had changed . . . Not until Adrian became dis-

180

tressed, not until . . . At first he wouldna' talk to me. An' when I asked the staff, they wouldna' talk to me either. They tried to avoid me. It was as if – ' She broke off suddenly and, looking down at the table, picked harshly at the edge of the formica with her work-stained nails. 'Finally they took me into a room an' told me that, although the chemical might have caused a problem at the start, there was no reason it should now, that Adrian should be better. They said the illness he had now was in his mind. They had a name for it. They called it school phobia. They said it was to do with the death of his father. They said I was – ' She clamped her teeth onto her lower lip. 'They *said* I might not realise it directly, but that I was overprotectin' Adrian . . . that I was encouragin' ma own son to be ill.'

Daisy felt the customary stab of anger that this sort of injustice never failed to arouse in her. She said what she could, telling Mrs Bell that for every doctor who thought like that there was another who was prepared to take chemical damage seriously, but that the science of toxicity was in its infancy, that it was an umbrella science covering an enormous spread of specialities and requiring large teams of scientists which few governments were prepared to fund.

'They sent the education people around,' Campbell announced with a sharp exclamation of contempt. 'Tellin' Meg here to get Adrian back to school or else. I gave them *or else* all right, I can tell you.'

Daisy thought: I bet you did.

'An' the rest – I saw them off too,' Campbell scoffed with pride.

A small worm of alarm turned in Daisy's stomach. 'The rest?'

Mrs Bell answered: 'The social services.'

'Sheep,' Campbell declared. 'Followed the others like sheep.'

Mrs Bell said: 'They wanted me to agree to Adrian goin' back to hospital.'

'What did you tell them?'

Campbell answered for her again, pointing with a dramatic gesture towards the front room. 'That lad leaves here over ma dead body, that's what I told them.'

'Our doctor spoke for us,' Mrs Bell explained quietly. 'He's known Adrian from birth.'

181

'Over ma dead body,' Campbell echoed, slapping his palm on the table.

'And they accepted that, did they, Mrs Bell? Your doctor's opinion?'

'Aye, they seemed to. Although that hasna' prevented them from returnin' now an' again. To see how Adrian is managin' – that's how they explain it.'

'Pushin' their noses in where they're not wanted,' Campbell rumbled menacingly.

Daisy exchanged a glance with Mrs Bell, and saw in her face the knowledge that, but for the actions of the local doctor, things might have gone very differently.

Campbell, leaning forward, stabbed a finger at Daisy. 'Now this compensation business – what about these landowners, the folk makin' the money? Surely in God's name, they canna' escape fault!'

'They might be held liable for a small share of the blame,' Daisy began carefully. 'But even if everything was proved in our favour, they might well plead good faith and get away with it.'

Campbell gave a fierce jerk of his head. 'What about the makers? The chemical people?'

'We don't know who they are,' Daisy pointed out.

'And if we did?'

'If we did, it wouldn't make that much difference.'

'How can that be? They're makin' an' sellin' the stuff, are they not? Is that not negligent?'

'Oh that we could take them on, Mr Campbell. But negligence – or anything else for that matter – would be impossibly difficult to prove, and they'd throw everything they'd got into it – '

'Och, it's the money that talks, is it?'

'Well, yes – I'm rather afraid it is.'

There was a pause. Mrs Bell brought the teapot round again.

Campbell sat back, stretching his arms forward and splaying his broad hands palms-down on the table. His anger seemed to have given way to a genuine if dogged concern. 'So – his chances are na' very good?'

'At the moment, not brilliant,' Daisy admitted. 'Not unless we find more to go on.'

'An' this is what the lawyer people say, is it?'

'Yes.'

'The experts, eh?' He rolled the words round his mouth with contempt and Daisy thought that perhaps this wasn't the time to admit to her qualifications.

'I see, I see . . .' Campbell said musingly. 'So what must be done to start things movin' along the right road?'

'I suppose there are two – no, three – priorities,' she said. 'The first must be to get Adrian the best medical attention. We're not talking about instant cures, I'm afraid, but there's one specialist we usually recommend. I might be able to arrange for him to come up and see Adrian here.' As she said it she wondered how she could swing the expense of getting Peasedale's ally, Roper, to Scotland without Alan finding out. 'After that, well, we'd need to establish the name of the operators – the flying people – and the chemical they used.'

'Right,' Campbell said briskly. 'We canna' arrive before we begin, eh?'

'I'm sorry?'

'You arrange the doctor, fine. The rest, you can leave it to me.'

Daisy looked at him uncertainly. 'The rest?'

'You said – we canna' proceed until we have some facts, correct?'

'Facts would certainly help – '

'Aye, an' I'll be the man to find them.'

Daisy gave a nervous smile. 'And – er – how are you going to achieve that?'

Campbell stood up suddenly, pushing his chair back with a loud scraping noise. 'People not so very far from here know the answers to the question, do they not?'

'I expect they do,' Daisy agreed, thinking of the Willis Bain manager on the next-door estate and wondering what sort of information-extraction methods Campbell could possibly have in mind. It occurred to her that having Campbell on their side was going to be a liability of the most massive kind. 'But how exactly do you intend to persuade these people to tell you what you want to know, Mr Campbell?'

He didn't reply but gave her a long cautionary stare, as if she should have known better than to ask.

From the sidelines Mrs Bell gave an anxious: 'Alistair.'

'An' then?' he exclaimed, twisting round to shoot her an angry glance. 'They canna' be so hard to find, these people.

The flyin' company, they might deny all knowledge. But the aeroplane Adrian saw in the forest there' – he jabbed a finger in the direction of the hill – 'that was real enough, was it not? An' there was a man flyin' it, was there not? They canna' have vanished into the mist. They canna' be so hard to find.' He added ominously: 'One way or another.'

'We did make the fullest possible enquiries,' Brayfield ventured, sounding mildly defensive. 'Throughout Scotland.'

'An' then?' Campbell retorted. 'Scotland is not yet the centre of the planet, is it?'

Despite everything, Daisy found herself warming slightly to Mr Campbell. Whatever his shortcomings he couldn't be accused of being a lily-liver. Having met enough apathy in her time to run even the most inefficient nationalised industry, this threat of red-blooded action made something of a change. It was unfortunate that it was going in such an aggressive and potentially damaging direction.

Plucking his jacket from the back of the chair, Campbell thrust himself into it as if he were about to go and take on the world that very instant.

Taking a card from her voluminous carpetbag, Daisy got up and followed him down the passage. 'If you find anything out, you'll let me know?' she called.

He turned and, taking her card, read it slowly. 'Aye,' he said finally and, pushing the card deep into an inside pocket, opened the door.

Daisy followed him towards the gate. In flagrant violation of Alan's policy guidelines, she said: 'Don't think we won't give Adrian's case our support, Mr Campbell, because we will. I just didn't want you to think it was going to be easy.'

'Aye . . . Nothin's easy in this life.' He stood firm against the wind, a rock in a stormy sea.

Daisy asked: 'Is it far to Glen Ashard from here?'

Campbell turned his head and stared at her, the fierceness glittering in his eyes.

'Not so far,' he said.

Daisy would have asked more but a gust straight from the Arctic blasted up the lane and, with a quick farewell, she hurried back towards the shelter of the house.

But Campbell came after her. 'You know Mackenzie then?' he demanded, catching her at the door.

'A little.'

'You'll be seein' him while you're here?'

'I wish I was,' Daisy said truthfully.

Campbell followed her into the hall, standing so close over her that she had to twist her head to look up at him. 'That's a regret,' he said, 'a real regret.' He hesitated then seemed to make up his mind about something. 'It's the same sickness,' he said.

That took a moment to sink in. 'What is?'

'Mrs Mackenzie. Her sickness. The same as young Adrian's. There's no doubt in ma mind.'

'But she inhaled wood preservative.'

'Mebbe. But she could have inhaled a lot more without the realisation of it, could she not?'

'Why do you think so?'

'Och, the look of her!' he exclaimed. 'The features of the sickness.'

Daisy was doubtful but curious. 'You've seen her? Alusha Mackenzie?'

He looked shifty. 'Not close up, like I am to you, but close enough. She canna' hardly walk. An' thin – she's no more than bones. Aye, it's the same thing all right. There's no doubt in ma mind.'

Daisy must have looked unconvinced because Campbell hurried on. 'Her skin – it has no colour, just like the boy's. An' she sleeps long hours.' He looked mildly embarrassed. 'At least, so I've heard. But most significant' – he paused to add weight to his words – 'she's also right next to Willis Bain forest.'

Suddenly Daisy realised what had struck a chord when Mrs Bell had described the way Adrian mixed up black for white and table for chair. She remembered Nick Mackenzie sitting in Peasedale's window, his elbow on the sill, his eyes screwed up against the brilliant light; she heard his voice describing his wife's symptoms, and the way she interchanged words of quite opposite meanings.

The same illness? The same chemical? It was possible. Of course it was possible. The geography alone was reason for suspicion.

With Campbell's words echoing in her mind, the idea took root and kept her occupied all the way back to London.

*

Dublensky had that wonderful feeling he always got when spring arrived – and the spring came one hell of a lot sooner in Virginia than it did in Chicago. Already the chestnuts were bristling with buds, the birds yelling their heads off. He felt like hollering right back at them, except that his neighbours – and there were a few fellow employees of the Allentown Chemical Company among them – might think he'd finally gone nuts. They already thought he was dangerously close to being certifiable because he cycled five miles to work each day and five miles back, an idea that seemed to sting his car-driving neighbours into nervous confusion.

The journey took twenty minutes on his ten-speed racer and, though the Allentown Chemical Company's works were not the prettiest of sights in the world and the air around it was not perhaps the sweetest, he always felt better for having been out of doors and taken the exercise.

This morning he arrived in his office, feeling like he could conquer the world. Before settling down to work – and maybe even to conquering the more mundane paperwork which seemed to cover every inch of his desk – he sat quietly for a moment, basking in the warmth of his good fortune. Anne had only last week landed a grant to run a marriage rehabilitation project, and would be setting up shop in a couple of months' time. Tad was doing really great in school: he'd made the seventh grade, the junior football team and won a math prize. A *math* prize, for heaven's sake. The boy was going to be a genius. Well, if not a genius, then a candidate for a top college. Perhaps even Yale. Why not? Dublensky had had to sweat his way through Columbia with precious little parental backup and even less money. Tad would have none of those disadvantages.

And Dublensky himself? Well, he was happy – yes, happy. The Allentown Chemical Company might not be the hub of the universe, and the chlorine-based water-purification products the company manufactured might not be of earth-shattering importance, but they were worthwhile, they added something to the wellbeing of mankind, and he had independence, he ran his own department, he was well paid. What more could a man want?

He hummed as he started on the first stack of papers, and was quickly distracted by the latest issue of *Practical Scientist*. There was a four-paragraph item on Morton-Kreiger, he noticed, reporting on the loss of the company's final appeal against the EPA ban on Aldeb. The item closed with a mention of Silveron, and Morton-Kreiger's high hopes for it. Gertholm was briefly quoted as saying he was proud of the company's steady move towards safer cost-effective products.

Dublensky felt amazement and anxiety in equal and bewildering quantities. When he had last contacted Mary Cummins in Chicago just a couple of weeks ago, she had informed him that the results of the new trials on Silveron were due at any moment. Yet here was MKI's own president apparently unaware of what the results must surely contain. Otherwise, how could he be inflating the product like this? It was extraordinary how the company functioned sometimes, like an amorphous monster with several brains, none of them interconnected.

The office came to life around him. Still feeling aggrieved, he put the magazine on one side while he dealt with the day's incoming mail. There wasn't a great deal of it, for which he was extremely thankful, just two or three business letters and the usual collection of circulars, memos and journals. Plus, at the bottom, a typewritten envelope emblazoned 'Strictly Personal' with an Aurora, Illinois, postmark.

The letter was from Burt, the physician who'd been treating the sick workers from the Aurora plant. He was writing to say that one of the original workers had just had a diagnosis of lymph cancer and it was Burt's opinion that this was a direct result of the man's exposure to Silveron. The other two patients were still having severe health problems. Their personalities had changed, their reactions had slowed, their brains were affected in some way that was impossible to measure by any available tests. They also had a multitude of minor symptoms, ranging from eye problems, kidney and liver pain, digestive malfunction, myalgia, severe weight loss – you name it, he said, they seemed to have it.

Dublensky gave a moment's thought to the unfortunate victims. However remote he himself had been from events, he couldn't help feeling the weight of responsibility.

What was more, Burt went on, he was getting new patients from the plant, one who was suffering from similar symptoms, and another three with vaguer ailments that, though not so serious, were still giving him cause for concern. What the hell was going on? he wanted to know. Why weren't the new safety measures at the plant having any effect? And if they weren't effective, why hadn't they been reviewed? Or perhaps there *weren't* any new safety measures? he wrote, underlining the question twice. Perhaps the company had been pulling the wool over his eyes. What did Dublensky have to say about that?

Oh, he'd been given assurances, Burt continued. Dublensky's successor, Dr Mary Cummins, had given him a pledge only the previous week – but now he was damned certain he was being given the run around. Dr Cummins was saying that the product had passed its new toxicity trials with flying colours. How could this be? What did Dublensky know?

Dublensky thought: That's a very good question.

Burt finished by saying he was passing his case notes to the Environmental Protection Agency, and to the workers' union, and that if there wasn't a positive response from Morton-Kreiger soon in the form of confirmation of their toxicity results, he'd be forced to think of approaching the press too.

Dublensky sat back, stunned. Silveron passing its new trials with flying colours? It wasn't possible. He didn't believe it, either as a manager or a scientist. Silveron was trouble, he sensed it, he *knew* it.

He grabbed a piece of paper to draft a letter, a letter that in his mind's eye was going to be so hot that it wouldn't touch the envelope for smoke. Then, breaking off suddenly, he hesitated. Over the last year he'd scorched plenty of paper, he'd fired salvo after salvo of documents and letters in the direction of the MKI management, and look where it had got him. He could almost hear Anne's answer to that one: in Allentown, Virginia, a bought and silenced man.

He wrenched the phone off its cradle and, before he had time to change his mind, dialled head office in Chicago. He had intended to speak to Mary Cummins, but at the last minute found himself asking for Don Reedy.

'What the hell's this with the results on the Silveron trials, Don?' he heard himself bark the moment Don answered.

'The results, John? But they're not available yet.'

Dublensky made a supreme effort to keep his voice low and reasonable. 'According to my information, Mary Cummins already has the results.'

'I don't think that's possible, John. But why don't you ask her?'

'I'm asking you.'

A pause. Reedy's tone hardened. 'Listen, John, we'll let you have the results when they become available, as a courtesy. But I must stress that it's a courtesy. Silveron isn't your baby now, John. You know, it might be a good idea to remember that in future.'

Dublensky said with unusual firmness: 'So when are the results due, Don?'

'Shortly.'

'That's what you told me last time, Don. Everyone keeps telling me that. But when is shortly, Don? And what are the results going to say exactly?'

'Say? How can I know that? What a question, John.' Reedy's voice was heavy with impatience. 'They're trials, for heaven's sake. We can't know the results until they're complete, you know that.'

'But LKY must have given you an intimation.'

Another pause. 'It's TroChem. TroChem are doing the trials.'

'I'm talking about the new trials,' Dublensky explained. 'TroChem did the original trials, LKY Laboratories are doing the new trials.'

'I don't know where you got that idea from. It's TroChem. This time and last time too.'

Dublensky felt himself go cold.

'Listen, I've got to rush, John. A meeting – '

'But Mary Cummins – she told me LKY was doing it!'

'I'm sure there's an explanation. We might have put the job out to tender. Yes, in fact, I'm sure we did. Maybe we considered LKY.'

Might have put the job out to tender. The vagueness was almost laughable. Reedy, more than anyone, knew exactly what job was going to tender.

'Why TroChem? *Why*, Don?'

'What the hell – I don't know. But what does it matter?'

'Why did we choose TroChem again, Don?'

Reedy sighed deeply. 'Because they're efficient, competitive and – oh, for God's sake, John.'

'And because they produce favourable results? I mean, don't they? Nice and favourable.'

Reedy's tone shifted again. 'You're letting your emotions rule your judgement, John,' he said coldly.

189

But Dublensky had the bit between his teeth. He had never realised he could sustain such a level of anger. 'Why Tro-Chem, Don? Could it be because we can rely on them, huh? I mean, because we could be sure the results would be helped along a little, huh? Massaged – isn't that what they call it? Isn't that the right word, Don? Or hadn't you noticed the results came through so good – '

'John, I think you'd better stop – '

'The only reason I kept quiet about this, the only reason I tagged along' – he paused for an instant, aware that his voice had risen unpleasantly, like a fractious child's – 'was because I thought we were going to get some independent data at the end of it. I mean, some data that *meant* something. And all the time – hell . . .' His throat was tight, for a moment he couldn't speak. 'All the time . . . it meant nothing. I mean, if TroChem could make it come right once, they could make it come right again, couldn't they? Wouldn't you say? Christ, Don, don't tell me you hadn't thought about it. Don't tell me it hadn't occurred to you . . .'

He trailed off. There was a silence. Dublensky squeezed his temples in an agony of anger and self-reproach: he'd gone much farther than he'd intended to. Now Reedy would be able to guess the rest; what Dublensky knew about the original trial data – or what he thought he knew. Until half an hour ago he might have been prepared to concede that his suspicions were wildly out of court, that he might possibly be mistaken, but this news had crushed what remained of his fragile faith.

When Reedy finally replied his tone was placatory. 'Now listen, John, you're a fine person. You care, and that's a valuable commodity nowadays. But you *must* keep a sense of proportion. I don't know where you get these crazy ideas from, but there's no truth in them, none at all. You're building mountains out of molehills, and it isn't going to do you any good. I'm saying this because I like you, John, and I don't want to see you end up in trouble.'

'Trouble? Is that where I'm headed, Don?'

A sigh. 'Frankly, yes.'

'I see.' Dublensky screwed up his face into a fierce grimace. 'I see.' He was overcome by moral outrage; his voice wavered, heat pricked at his eyes. 'So what you're saying, Don, is that

I'm going to be in trouble for uncovering the truth. Is that right?'

'The truth as *you* see it, John. As you see it. Though why you see it that way, I really don't know.'

Dublensky asked pointedly: 'And what about the plant, Don? What's happened there?'

'What do you mean?'

'The Aurora plant, Don. You keep telling me safety has been improved, you keep telling me about all these wonderful changes, but what's actually been done, Don? I mean *really* done?'

'Plenty. Plenty's been done.'

'Like?'

'Listen, I'm not on the safety executive at Aurora. I don't know the details. But when the people there tell me that the procedures have been tightened up, I believe them because I trust them. Trust, John. Maybe you've heard of it? I have to say I think you're running a bit low on that just now.'

'Yeah. I think you're right, Don,' he said with elaborate irony. 'I think you're right. Very low. The thing is, Don, what really takes my breath away is how you can let this just happen. How you can let it all pass you by and not stand up and *do* something. I mean – I simply don't know.' Without waiting for an answer, Dublensky put the phone down with a bang and thrust his head into his hands. Disbelief, anger and sadness roared through him in quick succession.

He looked up, his eyes turning instinctively towards the window and the light. The spring sunshine was illuminating the long roofs and tall chimneys of the works with brilliant radiance. Amazingly, it was the same wonderful day that it had been a few moments ago.

He thought of Tad and Anne and their settled lives; he thought of his own simple requirements for happiness. One wouldn't have thought it was too much to ask, a little simple happiness, but it seemed no sooner grasped than lost again.

When he got home, he would go to his desk and take out the file he kept there and study it again. He clung to the idea that this might help him towards the right decision, that somehow the figures would take on a new light. But he knew that this was too much to hope for. The figures would be just the same as before.

He would have to do something. But what? All the possibilities terrified him. He was no coward, but he was no hero either.

Anne would know what to do. Well, he hoped so.

Suddenly the end of the day seemed a long way away; all he could think about was getting home. Bracing himself to look his secretary in the eye while he told her an outright lie, he said he was feeling unwell, and, turning down the offer of a ride home, bicycled off into the sunshine.

At four that afternoon his secretary took an internal call from the office of the chief executive of the Allentown Chemical Company requiring Dublensky's presence, and had to inform them that he was away, unwell. That didn't stop the chief executive from calling Dublensky at home and asking him to come back in. The chief executive, a great one for doing things by the book, took pride in doing his firing humanely, face to face.

TWELVE

As always, there was something to be salvaged, the essence of the theme, some of the harmony, the best of the words. Nick worked all morning, smoking incessantly, phoning through to Mrs Alton for periodic cups of coffee. When he took a break, it was only to walk around the studio, to leaf through a book or read yesterday's paper. He didn't go out. There was a gale raging. For a time he stood at the window watching the trees pulling and straining under the force of the wind. The wind was not southwesterly, as was usual, but easterly, the one direction to which Ashard's park, even the glen itself, lay open, a wind that, if it continued for any length of time, was likely to bring down some of the more fragile and precious trees.

By early afternoon he was finally getting somewhere. He'd abandoned whole sections of the words and replaced them with new stuff which was much simpler, less impossibly pretentious. Now the theme, such as it was, seemed to fit.

At some point Alusha stole in, so ghostlike in her approach that he didn't hear her until she touched his shoulder. She announced that she was going for a walk.

'Very windy,' he said, scribbling down a word before he forgot it.

'But I like the wind,' she said in a curiously flat voice that was devoid of enthusiasm.

'It's easterly. Absolutely freezing.'

'I don't care.'

There was no answer to that. Perhaps a short walk round the rose garden would after all do some good. Walking was the one activity that, against all the odds, she had managed to keep up through the long winter months and which, even on her worst days when the effort of walking almost killed her, seemed to cheer her up.

He turned, intending to give her a brief kiss and return to his work, but there was something about the sight of her that made him pause. The skin of her thin face, already translucent, was tinged with grey, and her eyes, which were remote and unfocused, wore a dull absorbed expression, as if her mind was roaming over quite another planet.

After a moment her attention came back from wherever it had been and she put on a vague smile.

He stood up and put his arms around her. 'Love you,' he said. 'Love you,' she echoed. The smile was there, but he noticed she was smiling with her mouth, not her eyes.

'Crazy to go out,' he said. 'You'll get blown down the loch.' And he wasn't entirely joking; her balance was far from good.

'I'll be all right.' There was a stubborn note in her voice which he recognised only too well.

Releasing her, he said: 'I'll come with you.'

'No,' she said. 'No. I love the wind.' Her voice was at once sharp and unsteady. 'I love it. I want to go on my own.' Two livid spots of colour appeared high on her cheeks, and her eyes were suddenly bright and luminous, gleaming with a strange excitement. This change was so abrupt and so untypical of her that he stared into her face, puzzled and curious, but also alarmed. Her eyes glistened so brilliantly that for an instant he thought he had misread her mood and that she was for some reason close to tears. Then he suddenly knew what it was, and knowing, couldn't think why he hadn't guessed before. She was spaced out. Dosed up. High. The realisation, like so many in the last few months, made him die a little inside.

He knew then that the pain must be very bad.

'I'll come with you,' he repeated quietly.

'No!' She was getting cross.

'But I want to.'

'No! I'm going on my own!'

Maybe it was the strange almost unrecognisable expression on her face, maybe it was simply that the winter had been far far too long, but something closed his emotions down tight as a drum. He knew he should argue, he knew he should prevent her from going out in this weather, but having finally broken through his creative block after so long he was loath to deflect his emotional energy from his work.

She knew she had won. She stood staring up at him for a moment, looking fierce and implacable and oddly emotional all at the same time. Then, pushing herself up on her toes, she gave him a last kiss, a peremptory brush on the cheek, and, turning quickly away, was gone.

He couldn't work after that, of course. Five minutes later he gave up trying and went out into the gale, intending to catch up with her. But though he walked quickly through the rose garden and round the edge of the lawns, there was no sign of her. Completing the circle, he made his way back through the kitchen garden, but she wasn't there either, and he went into the house again, wavering between the urge to search for her and the knowledge that she would bitterly resent any such intrusion on her space.

Leaving the studio door open, making a pretence of working, he kept an ear open for her return. Finally, just when he was getting prepared to risk her wrath by organising some of the estate workers into a surreptitious search party, he heard the banging of a distant door and the murmur of female voices, and felt the tension drain out of him in a rush. He called, and echoing down the long passage came a distant response. By the time he got to the kitchen it was empty, but he saw Alusha's distinctive red scarf thrown across a chair. He thought of going to find her, but knowing she'd probably gone upstairs for her afternoon nap, he decided not to disturb her and, caught up by his work, he went back to the studio, anxious to make up for lost time.

It was two hours later and getting dark before he realised that the voices in the kitchen had been those of Helen and Mrs Alton, and that Alusha had never returned.

He stopped and, gasping for breath, shouted her name, but his call, like all of the calls before it, was sucked away and lost by the wind. He shouted again, straining to be heard over the thrumming and thrashing of the trees, but it was useless, like shouting under water. He shone the torch full circle, then upwards. The forest was alive with movement, the topmost branches contorting wildly, the pines creaking and groaning in loud complaint.

He pushed on fast, climbing steadily up the glen, his feet stumbling and jarring against the compacted earth and rock of the riverside path. He cast the torch-beam rhythmically from side to side, lighting the dead bracken and grasses and boulders on either side, and below, the fast rushing water. There was nothing to see. Just empty forest, and a ringing silence in his brain, and a deadness in his stomach.

He imagined her lying off the path somewhere, cold and barely conscious. Would he hear her if she was calling? Would he spot her? The answer was no, and no again. He'd probably missed her already, probably passed just inches away from her. Despair pulled at him out of the darkness.

With a conscious effort he tried to think logically and dispassionately, to imagine where she might have been making for, the route she would have taken. He realised that he wasn't absolutely certain where she went on her more adventurous afternoon outings. On their morning stroll, which they always took together, they rarely went further than the garden because that was usually enough to tire her out until lunch time. It had never occurred to him that she might go further in the afternoons, although in the past few weeks she had mentioned the glen several times in a nostalgic, thoughtful way, as if something had happened to remind her of it. He had assumed it was the drive they'd taken up the track to the moorlands one brilliant day in early March, but maybe he was entirely wrong, maybe she'd come this way on her own. Maybe.

And today – what had happened today? Had she meant to take a long walk? Or had she simply gone further than she intended, felt tired and stopped for a rest? Or suddenly felt too ill to drag herself home?

He pressed on, the uncertainty and fear clutching at his heart.

Above the low roar of the wind came the sound of thundering water. The fall below Macinley's Rock.

This was crazy – what was he doing here? She couldn't have made it this far, even at her most determined. It was a long climb, even for a fit person: he was panting hard and, despite the cold, the sweat was damp on his back.

He stopped, torn between the need to carry on and be certain of having covered all the ground, and the overpowering suspicion that he was wasting his time. He left the path, fought his way up the bank past rock and scrub and scrambled onto the main track. He forced himself to listen and heard nothing but the awful melancholy of the wind. Closing his ears, he turned quickly away, and realised that, for no reason that bore thinking about, he had decided to turn back.

The realisation brought a new gust of despair. It was so very cold. Even if she was wearing a thick jacket, she'd be almost frozen by now. The thought was like something driven against his heart, almost unendurable, and to suppress the agony, he began to shout her name again, forcing his voice over the rushing and roaring of the wind. His throat grew hoarse, his voice descended to a gasp. Momentarily defeated, he paused, shoulders hunched, and reached for his breath.

Down the track in the distance, through the trees, a light glimmered and flickered, and intensified steadily, growing into the long yellow beams of headlights. Behind it came another car, and another. Duncan's search party.

The first vehicle ground to a halt in front of him, and several people got out.

Duncan's voice said: 'We've a group searching the pastures, Mr Mackenzie. And another going east and south of the house. And a third starting up this way.' He stepped in front of the lights, masking Nick from the glare. 'What d'you think – shall we send a couple of men up the glen? Or just sweep down from here towards the house?'

Nick leant against a tree, his legs unaccountably weak. 'I don't think she could have got this far.'

'Right-ho.' There was forced optimism in his voice. 'We'll get set then. The police should be here soon enough.'

'The police? *Why?*'

'No avoiding it. The village . . .' Duncan indicated the men grouped around the cars. 'Everyone's here.'

Of course. No secrets in the village. Nevertheless the thought of the whole thing becoming public, of all the attention made Nick squirm inwardly. Once the police came thundering up the glen, the press wouldn't be far behind. Alusha would be furious.

Duncan drew closer and said in an undertone: 'The police were asking about kidnap. I said I didn't think it was likely. Was that right?'

Kidnap. Nick hadn't even considered it. *Christ*. He wasn't ready to make room for those sort of possibilities. 'You did right,' he said.

The cars were being backed round, ready to head down the hill again; their lights cut an arc through the trees. Someone came out of darkness offering Nick a cup. A hot drink. Nick put it to his lips, scented coffee, and took a sip. It took him a moment to realise it was laced with whisky. He was gripped by an instantaneous and overwhelming urge to swallow it, along with the rest of the cup, a flask or two, and the contents of an entire distillery. Postponing the decision to swallow, he held the liquid in his mouth, moving it slowly over his tongue. It tasted fantastic. Memories flashed onto the screen of his mind, memories of liquid nights and technicolour days and wondrous oblivion.

He let the liquid fall to the back of his throat. Just one taste would do him good.

The next moment he gagged and spat the stuff onto the ground. It was several moments before he straightened up. A vast heat rushed over him, making the sweat run again.

A close thing. There'd been nothing that close since he'd left New York. What frightened him more than anything was how bloody marvellous it had tasted, and how deep his craving was, even after so many years.

He chucked the rest of the coffee onto the ground and realised he'd spattered someone's feet. He muttered an apology.

'No matter,' returned a voice. He wasn't sure why, but he felt the man had been watching him for some time.

People were moving about, sorting themselves into groups. There were twenty men, maybe more. Nick felt a sudden and savage impatience at the terrible slowness with which they moved. Finally, when Duncan had given a few last instructions, the groups began to start off.

Duncan called Nick towards the nearest car. Duncan plucked something off the back seat and waved it in the air. 'This should help!' It was the image-intensifier which Nick had given him for poacher-catching.

They drove slowly down the track, following the flickering pinpricks of torchlight that had fanned out through the forest.

The next hours were both vivid and dreamlike. Sometimes Nick felt alive and sick with fear, at other times he felt oddly apathetic and detached, as if someone had put the whole thing on film and slowed the projector. For the most part he simply felt ill, his mouth dry, his stomach light and jittery.

Halfway down the glen, they were met by a couple of police vehicles which disgorged men and dogs.

At the edge of the woods where the track looped towards the house, people grouped together again, smoking and whispering quietly, waiting for fresh instructions. Messages from the house brought reports from the other search parties: nothing had been found. The police took the opportunity to put questions to Nick. Gathering around him, their voices deferential but firm, they asked if Alusha always went for walks and how long she generally stayed out and if there was any reason why she should have gone for a longer walk than usual. It occurred to Nick that they were looking for a motive for her to have kept walking – a marital row, an unhappy marriage, a lover waiting at the end of the drive. It was all so ridiculous he didn't know whether to laugh or cry. He answered in monosyllables, if only to prevent himself from letting his rage show, and more than once they had to prompt him for a reply.

It was her illness that impressed them more than anything else. When it came to using police time, illness obviously ranked a long way above marital tiffs. He didn't tell them quite how ill she was. Apart from anything else, he didn't think it was any of their business.

It began to rain, a thin spiky inconsequential rain, then, all too quickly, a more determined rain that spattered against his face and trickled down his neck. He gulped some coffee – unlaced – smoked two cigarettes in quick succession and endured Duncan's well-meaning assurances.

Everything was dreamlike, then all of a sudden he awoke again. The urgency flooded back into him and he pushed forward and began to argue with the police for an immediate return to the glen. The inspector, a soft-spoken man, listened with attention but not, apparently, conviction. There was no indication she had gone up the glen, was there? the inspector argued. It wasn't very likely, was it, not on such a stormy day. Wouldn't she have stayed closer to home? Particularly since she was so unwell.

Forcing himself into a state of exaggerated calm, Nick repeated stubbornly: 'We *must* search the glen!'

199

'The main paths have already been covered, have they not, Mr Mackenzie? Would we not do better to – '

'The upper glen – no one's been there!'

'Why do you think she might have gone up there, Mr Mackenzie?'

'*Because* – ' But he was beyond speech, beyond explanation, his mind a nightmare of half-realised fears and confusions. Catching himself on the point of losing control, he withdrew some way into the darkness and paced back and forth, smoking hard. Just when he thought he'd got himself into some sort of shape, the inspector announced his plans for the search. It would be concentrated on the area around the house and would slowly expand outwards. The denser sections of forest and undergrowth would be left until daylight.

The wind eased abruptly, and a heavier rain began to fall, a drenching pervasive rain that drummed on the roofs of the cars and kicked at the ground, so that people made for the shelter of the trees.

Nick's vision of Alusha shifted agonisingly: he saw the rain seeping into her clothes, saturating her already cold skin, freezing her slowly to death.

He couldn't stand it any longer. Striding away, he jumped into Duncan's car, rammed it into reverse, and, twisting the wheel savagely, executed a tight turn.

As he jammed the accelerator down and shot off up the glen he was aware of someone swinging into the back seat and slamming the door shut behind him. He glanced over his shoulder.

'Duncan?'

'No. It's me, Alistair Campbell.'

Nick considered telling the man, whoever he was, to bugger off, then thought better of it. He might be useful.

The car bumped and leapt up the rough road. Nick didn't slow until he reached the point just below Macinley's Rock where his earlier search had ended. Then he parked and set off briskly up the main track, sweeping the undergrowth with his torch-beam. As if by some previous agreement, the other man cut down to the path by the side of the river and walked in parallel, so that the dull glint of his light was visible through the trees.

Above Macinley's Rock, Nick saw the other man's light fall behind as it flickered slowly round the sides of the Great Pool.

Eventually it came back onto the path and gradually drew level until they were once again in parallel. The wind had dwindled further and now the forest resounded to the steady drum and patter of the rain.

Half a mile later the other man's light rose to meet him as the lower path left the river and converged with the main track. The two men met without speaking and fell into step one behind the other.

To the right the forest thickened: they had reached a dense stand of pines. Nick paused. The stand continued for perhaps half a mile. Beyond it there was nothing but open moor and grazing sheep. It was just possible she had got this far – it had occurred to him that the morphine might have made her feel unusually energetic – but no further. Quite apart from the distance and the climb, she didn't like the darkness of the pine forest any more than she liked the bleakness of the open moor.

Desperate for a smoke, he stepped into the shelter of the trees and reached inside his jacket. His packet was empty. The other man, watchful as some shadowy manservant, stepped forward and held out a packet which he illuminated with his torch. Nick stole a glance at him in the flare of the match, but didn't recognise him.

Their cigarettes lit, the two men started back down the track.

Campbell spoke. 'I could cross the river just by the pool there an' follow down the other bank.'

'No.' The path was rough on the opposite side, the bank very steep. It wasn't a possibility.

'She couldna' manage that, then?'

'No.'

'Not so good at the walkin'?'

'No.'

'Ma sister's lad's the same. Canna' hardly manage to leave the house.'

What the hell was he talking about? Nick grunted negatively and hurried on, swinging his torch-beam purposefully from side to side. The rain dropped over the beam and cut across it like a curtain. He called Alusha's name, and got the constant patter of the rain in return.

'It's the same malady, you know.'

Christ, Nick thought savagely, what a time for obtuse social chat. He walked even faster, determined to shake the other man off.

'It's a chemical,' the man persisted, matching his pace effortlessly to Nick's. 'They were usin' it all over against the beauty moth. The lad, he got a dose of it in June, just before your wife. He's not been right since.'

Despite everything, a small memory triggered in Nick's mind. A letter, something he'd received months ago – other cases, the name Campbell.

There was something else though, something about the man's voice, something familiar which he couldn't quite place.

'Not the same thing,' Nick snapped with finality.

Now it was Campbell's turn to be silent. Eventually he murmured: 'If you say so.'

Suddenly Nick felt a jolt of recognition. The voice, the accent. Even the place. *God*. He swung his torch full onto Campbell. The face was square, with wet hair plastered down onto his forehead. The features were unfamiliar, but the build – oxlike and unusually tall – *yes*.

'You.'

Campbell raised a hand against the light.

'Christ! Christ!' Nick shook with rage. 'It *is* you!'

Campbell lowered his hand. 'I have to say that I canna' entirely deny the fact. But I've not touched a fish in this pool, not since June, an' that's the truth, Mr Mackenzie.'

'Get the hell out of my sight!' Nick turned on his heel and strode off, enraged by the intrusion, furious at the diversion. He went fast, swinging his torch rapidly, shouting Alusha's name until his voice descended into feeble infuriating croaks. It was some time before he glanced back over his shoulder. No sign of a light on the track. Then he saw it, down on the river path once more, a soft pinprick flattened and blurred by the rain.

He pressed on, suddenly aware of how long he'd been out of contact with Duncan and the main search party. Reaching the car, he jumped in and started up. Campbell could damned well walk back. Yet something made him switch off and get out again.

There was no sign of a light. He yelled Campbell's name.

There was only the rushing of the water and the drumming of the rain, then a voice came echoing back. From above, from beyond the invisible bulk of Macinley's Rock.

Nick bawled: 'Hurry.'

The voice came again, rising above the deathly splatter of the rain. A long call that sounded like: '*Here. O-v-e-r h-e-r-e.*'

Nick didn't move. He was gripped by an indescribable fear.

He waited, dreading the words, yet needing to hear them again.

They came once more, as he knew they would.

'*O-v-e-r h-e-r-e.*'

Finally he moved. Each step felt more unreal than the last; his body no longer belonged to him. He broke into an uneven stride, half run half walk, and made his way panting up the track until, abreast of Macinley's Rock, he began to climb down the slope towards the water. Hitting rock, he stumbled and fell, landing heavily on his hip and dropping the torch. Picking it up again, he remembered, by a great effort of will, to shine the beam in front of him. He blundered through undergrowth, past massive stones and across a mossy bank until, finally, he reached the edge of the pool.

'*Here.*' The harsh cry was unexpectedly close.

Nick shone the torch around, then down. The beam caught Campbell's huddled form, crouched at the pool edge. He was cradling a bundle which lay half in, half out of the water.

Campbell raised his head. His face was contorted into a terrible grimace. The bundle unfolded from his lap. First an arm, then a white face fell back over Campbell's knees.

Burning rage came over Nick like a hot sea, his brain exploded with pain.

'*Get off her, get off! You bastard! You bastard!*'

He was aware of screaming, aware of the other man moving away, aware, finally, of dropping to his knees and pulling Alusha onto his lap.

Then the heat left him as suddenly as it had come, cooled by the ice of Alusha's skin.

203

THIRTEEN

The beauty moth didn't live up to its name. Small, little more than an inch from wingtip to wingtip, a uniform and rather drab brown, it had no great claims to beauty although, when Daisy put her nose closer to the glass of the sample box, she saw that the upper wings were marked with an attractive and intricate tortoiseshell pattern.

She commented: 'It doesn't look big enough to eat a whole forest.'

The bugman shuffled his feet. 'Well, the moth itself *doesn't*, of course,' he said with a quick smile. 'It's the larva that's the gobbler.' He pointed to a striped caterpillar impaled on the next pin.

They walked back to the bugman's office, which was situated in a modernish wing of the Edwardian country house that was the headquarters of the forestry research station. The office windows, partially obscured by stacks of files and papers, looked out onto a dense shrubbery and, beyond, to the tall forest that surrounded the grounds.

Daisy asked: 'What would a forest manager do then, if he had a bad outbreak of pine beauty moth?'

The bugman settled in his chair. He was a bearded Welshman with the confident easy-going manner that comes from knowing his stuff and having the happy occasion to impart it. 'You'd have to spray the forest,' he said. 'There'd be no way round that. But we're developing virus applications that are absolutely specific to the moth and therefore very much safer – '

'Developing? They're not in use then?'

204

'Ah.' He gave a sight of regret. 'Still too expensive.'

'So a private contractor would still use an insecticide?'

'At the moment – yes.'

'And what would he use? Can you give me a list of the most likely chemicals?'

The bugman looked surprised. 'A list? Well, I could try. But really, there's only one in common use.'

'Only one?' Daisy echoed, adjusting rapidly to the likelihood of disappointment.

The bugman rasped a hand over his beard and puckered his lip, as if considering the possibility that he might have overlooked something. 'Aerial application, you said? No – there's really only one.'

Fenitrothion. He said the word slowly in case she wanted to copy it down. But there was no need. Fenitrothion was well known. It was an organophosphate that had been around for some time. If it had killed and maimed people on a regular basis the news would have seeped out by now. As it was, it didn't even rate a mention on Catch's 'dirty dozen' of the most dangerous chemicals. Although it was always possible that, despite everything, they had all been missing something.

'And there's really nothing else?'

'Not that I know of.'

There were questions she should ask, but her brain was thick with tiredness and it took a moment for her to grasp them.

'What follow-up studies have been done on fenitrothion?' she asked finally.

'Ah!' The bugman went to a shelf, selected two identical pamphlets and handed her one. The pamphlet was titled *Population, Biology and Control of the Pine Beauty Moth*. On the cover was a glossy photograph of the caterpillar, no longer the faded drab specimen of the show case but a smartly attired fellow in green, brown and white stripes, captured in the act of eating his way down a branch of pine needles.

The bugman leafed through his copy. 'There's a summary of all the major impact studies . . . On birds mainly . . .'

'What about the impact on people?' she asked.

'The operators, you mean? They have to take precautions, of course. Mixing the chemical, filling tanks and so on. They wear full gear – you know, space suits, masks.' The bugman found his place in the pamphlet and read: 'The effect on

205

humans is . . . insignificant. Well, that sounds fairly definite, doesn't it?'

'What about people caught in the spray drift, people on the ground?'

'Um . . .' He referred again. 'Not discussed here. Probably not enough people to study. They're always careful to clear the area, you know, before they start spraying.' He replaced the pamphlet on the shelf. 'No, if you wanted to know more on that, you'd have to ask a toxicologist. Though I have to say I've never heard of anyone having any long-term health problems from fenitrothion.'

'A plane that was spraying the beauty moth – would it have to be specially equipped?'

'If it was using ultra-low-volume technique, yes.'

'What's that?'

'Ah.' He gleamed with quiet pride. 'It's what we've been pioneering. Much smaller chemical droplets, more efficiently distributed. Less chemical used, more effective, less damage to wildlife.'

'So the plane, what would it need for that?'

'Special atomisers. They fit them onto special arms under the wings.'

'And this ultra-low technique, is it in wide use? Would there be many aircraft fitted up for it?'

'Not yet,' he said with the disappointment of an ideas man finding himself pitted against the inertia of the real world.

'Otherwise . . . if a plane was using the old technique?'

'Then the regular spray booms, I suppose. But they give you nasty big droplets, and you miss the larvae who aren't right at the top of the canopy. A high miss rate.'

A high miss rate. Perhaps in Loch Fyne they had suffered a high miss rate during an early spraying, and had needed to dose the forest again in a hurry.

The Metro's heater choked a stream of luke-warm air, and Daisy had turned onto the Farnham bypass before her feet began to defrost. Even then she couldn't shake off a permanent sense of cold which seemed to have rooted itself low in her stomach. The drive back up the A3, far from being an opportunity to think, became a long exercise in staving off drowsiness and failing concentration. Maybe it was just lack of sleep; she had stayed up until one, sifting through the latest batch of case histories from EarthForce in Washington, going through the information from military air traffic control on the flights sanctioned in the Loch Fyne area. Then, when she'd finally got to bed, it had been to lie half-way between wakefulness and nightmare, her brain dogged by images of a featureless woman lying face down in water. Later, when she finally slept, it was to dream that Adrian, like Alusha Mackenzie, was dead.

She found a parking meter at the back of King's Cross, an unheard of stroke of fortune, and, dodging the ladies of the night who seemed to be out in force, she hurried through the litter-strewn streets to the office.

Jenny was perched at her desk, clad from spiky head to booted toe in black, long fringes of jet beads trailing from her jacket sleeves, like the wings of a recently alighted raven. Crouched over the telephone, she waved a batch of papers at Daisy and raised her eyebrows to indicate their importance.

A mug of coffee sat steaming at Jenny's elbow and, taking the papers in one hand, Daisy deftly removed the coffee with the other and headed for her office. Alan's door was partially open and she could hear his cool reasonable murmurings as he talked to someone on the phone. She padded quickly past and slipped into her office, closing her door silently behind her. Alan had been trying to catch her for a couple of days now but, having a fair idea of what he wanted to talk about, she was not too keen to be caught.

She sat down and, swigging at the coffee, glanced over the papers. They were copies of the legal correspondence on the Adrian Bell case which Mrs Bell had arranged for her solicitor to send over, though not without difficulty. Mrs Bell's solicitor had not taken kindly to the idea of Catch's involvement, and had responded to Daisy's phone calls with what could only be described as resistance.

Nonetheless, the correspondence was here, and there was quite a lot of it, including, she noted straight away, a letter from Willis Bain's lawyers.

The first part of the letter contained few surprises. Willis Bain absolutely denied any liability concerning the alleged accident. They also denied having treated the woodland next to the Bell home at any time during the previous June, or indeed in the weeks immediately adjacent to the alleged date in June. The block of forest in question had been sprayed only once during the year in question, in mid May, they said, when every possible safety procedure had been carried out: notifications posted to all neighbouring properties, including the Bells', and the police and local authority informed in accordance with legal requirements. Furthermore, the spraying method had conformed to Ministry of Agriculture and Civil Aviation Authority guidelines. The pesticide used was fully approved for aerial use.

Fully approved. Which meant that, unless Willis Bain were lying through their teeth, they had used fenitrothion.

Daisy went through the bundle once more before turning to her messages. Peasedale, she saw, had called again. Like Alan, he had been trying to get hold of her for the last two days. The reminders to call him, penned in block letters on yellow stickers, sat in silent rebuke on the body of the phone.

'Fenitrothion,' she said immediately Peasedale answered. 'Could it possibly have been involved in the Bell and Mackenzie cases?'

'Listen, it's appalling – Nick Mackenzie's wife.' Peasedale's usual tone of scientific detachment had escaped him and he spoke almost plaintively, interspersing his words with sudden sighs. 'Appalling. Was anything being done for the poor woman? I mean was there any follow-up? Was she under a competent toxicologist? I can't get it out of my mind. I keep thinking about her. Do they know exactly how she died? Was it the effects of some treatment she was getting? I have this awful feeling that maybe I missed something, that maybe I didn't look into it closely enough.'

Daisy told him what he wanted to hear. 'It wasn't you. There wasn't anything you could have done.'

'Do they know exactly how she died?' Peasedale repeated.

'I'm not sure,' she lied, remembering only too vividly the minute details that Simon had relayed to her from the *Sunday Times* news desk, and, by remembering, experienced some of the initial horror all over again.

'You haven't been in touch?' Peasedale asked.

'Hardly.'

Picking up the warning note in her voice, he retreated. 'No, I suppose it wouldn't be the right moment.'

'No. Now how about fenitrothion?'

'Fenitrothion?' he repeated blankly.

'Could it have done this sort of damage?'

There was a silence. She could almost see him sitting there

in his lab, perched on his stool like a stork on a chimney pot. 'My first instinct is no. But let me have a think about it, will you? A day or two? I'd really like to stick with this one. I mean – I'd like to feel that I'd done my utmost. You know.'

Daisy knew. It was all about making oneself feel better about something one felt bad about.

'And Adrian Bell,' she said. 'It could well be the same stuff. When can you can Roper get up there?'

'If you can fly us, I think we could make it this weekend.'

Return flights plus car hire plus meals. She wondered what part of the expense budget could be expanded to absorb it.

Ringing off, she managed to keep out of Alan's way for another five minutes, but it couldn't last. She heard him come off the phone, leave his office to chat to Jenny and then, with the inevitability of a parent coming in search of an unruly child, he was at her door and sidling in.

He sat at the side of her desk and gave her a sympathetic but cautious smile. 'How are you doing?'

'Fine,' she said looking back at her work.

'Listen, the Mackenzie case – you have to look on it as just one of those things.'

Alan took pride in being able to rationalise everything, to take the cool dispassionate stance, to learn and grow, as he liked to put it.

When she didn't respond, he tried: 'These things happen.'

But Daisy wasn't in the mood for banalities. 'They do, do they?'

'You mustn't take it personally.'

She sat back in her chair. 'Sure.' She heard the sarcasm in her voice but was unable to suppress it. 'I could always pretend I'd done a good job.'

'That's not fair. You couldn't have done any more than you did, not when the Mackenzies had shut you out.'

'But I should have *realised*.'

'Realised what?'

'That it couldn't possibly have been Reldane.'

'But how could you?'

'Jeese, it was blindingly obvious, Alan. Or should have been, if I'd had a fraction of my brain in gear.'

'Okay, let's say you should have guessed,' said Alan, at his most conciliatory. 'But would the Mackenzies have listened? Even if you'd had some evidence to back you up? I doubt it. I

209

get the impression Nick Mackenzie had made up his mind about what happened and wasn't about to change it, not for anybody. And even if you *had* persuaded him to listen, d'you think it would have made any difference? I mean, to what happened. I really don't think so.'

She was ready to accept that he might be right, but at the same time she wasn't ready to let the matter go that easily. She was still feeling too angry with herself. She needed time to come to terms with what had happened in her own time, at her own pace.

'It might have made a difference,' she said unrelentingly.

'Come on, Daisy. *If* someone had found out what it was that affected her, *assuming* it was a chemical – '

'What do you mean, *assuming*?'

'Okay, okay.' He held up a hand to signal his unconditional withdrawal. 'Okay, so it was a chemical, and if we'd known which one, *maybe* it would have changed things . . . But we never knew, did we? And we never will, either.'

Daisy picked up some papers and shuffled them noisily. 'Maybe we won't,' she said evasively. 'But then, maybe we will.' She could feel Alan staring at her, trying to work out what that statement might mean in terms of her own involvement.

'Well . . . It would be good to know, of course,' he said dubiously. 'But the cause and effect would be hard to prove. After the event, I mean.'

Perhaps it was the sleepless nights, but she was too tired to argue any more. She dropped the papers back onto the desk with a plop. 'Just so long as Adrian Bell doesn't go the same way.'

Alan looked suitably horrified at the thought. 'Of course not. We must do all we can.'

'Then you'll agree to Catch stumping up the cost for Peasedale and Roper to go and see him?'

Resentment sprang into Alan's eyes, as if he suspected her of having led the entire conversation up to this neat little trap. 'Can't Adrian come down to London?' he suggested weakly. She shook her head.

Alan was not graceful in defeat – he pulled a succession of unhappy faces – but he did at least recognise defeat when he saw it. 'Okay,' he grumbled. 'I'll swing it somehow. But just this once, Daisy.'

210

'Thanks, Alan.'

He grunted and made a hasty retreat. Daisy sat for a moment, staring at the wall, letting the last of her emotions subside. Then, turning with relief towards more positive thoughts, she lifted the phone and called Simon. He wasn't at home, but the *Sunday Times* seemed to think he was somewhere on the editorial floor. While she held, she allowed an indulgent vision to slide into her mind, a picture of herself in Simon's flat having a hot bath and a glass of wine while Simon got dinner and listened to her troubles.

He was sounding rushed when he finally answered. 'Pre-election hysteria,' he explained. 'The latest poll just put Labour five points ahead.'

She made her little plea – or maybe it was a cry for help.

'Dinner?' he echoed, and there was a sudden distance in his voice. She could almost see him calculating the time and effort it would take to shop and prepare the food and cook it. 'I won't finish till late, but I suppose I could pick something up from the Indian,' he suggested eventually, making no attempt to conceal the reluctance in his voice.

The thought of a featureless curry of unknown origin did not enthrall Daisy, but tonight she'd have been happy with a can of beans so long as it was cooked by someone else. 'That sounds fine.'

'The fridge is rather bare,' he mentioned. 'I can pick up some milk, but we'll still need bread. And I think I'm out of fruit . . .' He left the observation hanging in the air, awaiting suggestions. But her suggestions box, like the fridge, was bare, and when she failed to answer he rang off, sounding aggrieved.

Daisy reflected that Simon had many qualifications for the New Man – he related well to women, he made lists, pushed shopping trolleys, cooked adventurous Sunday lunches, consulted her religiously over film and theatre bookings – but this was one occasion when Daisy wished she could trade some of this refurbished masculinity for a burst of wild old-fashioned initiative, even – dare she say it – protectiveness.

It was late, but, unable to summon the energy to leave, she flicked half-heartedly through her mail. Alice Knowles had sent the latest news of her case, adding a note to say that despite the recent setbacks – she had been refused legal aid – she was still determined to go ahead with the legal action,

211

come what may. Doubtless Alan would think Daisy had secretly been encouraging her, which she had not, but then there was nothing Daisy could say on the subject of the Knowles case that didn't bring scepticism into Alan's eyes.

The next note was from Peasedale's assistant, saying that the latest blood samples from the Lincolnshire farmer's wife suffering suspected Aldeb contamination still hadn't arrived. Daisy read the note with disbelief. This was the third time the arrangements had gone wrong, despite the most thorough preparations. When the farmer had replied to her advertisement in the farming magazine, Daisy had persuaded him to agree to a monthly monitoring programme for his wife's blood, whereby Peasedale would measure the samples for enzyme, hormone and liver-function levels. But with the samples continually getting held up, it was making a nonsense of the whole programme. The farmer's wife was called Ruth and she answered the phone in her habitually subdued manner, with a soft almost apologetic greeting.

'What happened to the blood sample, Ruth?'

There was a pause and she heard Ruth inhale a couple of times as if she couldn't quite bring herself to speak. 'I think you should talk to my husband,' she whispered finally.

'But why? What's happened, Ruth? Is there something wrong?'

Another pause, longer this time. 'Well . . . it's . . . I can't say.'

'Ruth – '

She gave a small sigh. 'He thinks it would be best not to go on.'

'Why, Ruth? Just tell me why.'

'They said it would . . .' Then she exclaimed, 'No – sorry! I can't – sorry!' and hung up.

Daisy slumped back in her chair. What had Ruth meant by 'they said'? Who was they – a doctor? An advisor? And what was it they'd said? What could have put Ruth and her husband off a straightforward medical investigation? Daisy couldn't begin to imagine – not just now anyway – and for the moment she gave up trying.

The advertisement stirred memories of another reply, and she called out to Jenny in the outer office: 'Jen, that funny man, Maynard, he hasn't been back, has he?'

Jenny appeared in the doorway. 'Not since the last time,

212

when was it . . .' She pursed up her deep-purple mouth.
'Ooh, November, wasn't it?'

'No phone calls?'

'Nah – I'd 'ave told yer.' Jenny had a habit of lapsing into a
Cockney accent: something to do with her new boyfriend.
'No, 'e seemed quite 'appy with all the bumph.'

'And he didn't ask any odd questions?'

'Nope, not a dicky bird.'

'Not especially nosy?'

Jenny squawked: 'You think he's a spy, don't you!' In her
delight, her Cockney had momentarily disappeared.

'No, no. I just thought he was – odd.'

'Well, he didn't do anyfing exciting. I checked – remember?
No secret mikes under me desk.'

'That's right.' Daisy clasped her fingers to her temples and
shook her head. 'Just going nuts, Jen. Just getting paranoid.'

'Go home. Go on. You look half dead.'

She finally left the office at seven, glad to have the car for
once, but not so glad at the realisation that she'd forgotten to
feed the meter. A parking ticket fluttered triumphantly from
the wiper. Another sixteen quid up the spout, and little hope
of getting it back on expenses.

Simon's bathroom was sparkling white with down-lights in
the ceiling and a scorching hot towel rail and pukka tiles and
a bath with a sloping back so you could fall asleep in it without
getting a sudden snort of water up your nostrils. She poured
the water so hot that it took her five minutes to get in but only
two minutes to fall asleep. She woke when the flat door
slammed and Simon called her name.

'I found some bread,' he called through. 'It's only granary,
I'm afraid. Oh, and some mangy old bananas.'

'Sounds okay to me.'

'Didn't bother with curry though. Thought we could cook
Sunday's chicken a bit early. You'll approve – it's organic –
though what that means nowadays is anybody's guess.'

'Corn-fed, antibiotic-free?' she suggested.

'You'll be lucky.'

'Colonically irrigated perhaps?' She climbed out of the bath
and reached for a towel.

He appeared at the door wearing a disparaging smile.
'Wrong,' he corrected her. 'Only free of continuously fed
antibiotics. As the law stands at present there's nothing to

213

stop the breeders feeding the birds the odd dose of antibiotics on a curative basis. And no guarantee that the birds are even free-range. It's a big con.'

'Why bother to buy it then?'

He regarded her carefully. 'You look washed out,' he remarked.

Maybe it was the sympathy, maybe it was a psychosomatic response, but she shivered violently. She wrapped the towel tighter round herself. 'I think I'm getting flu.'

She might as well have announced a case of yellow fever. Simon stepped smartly backwards, looking alarmed. 'God, I'm due to go to Madrid on Monday. The EEC conference.' Reading her expression, he rearranged his response and put on a solicitous face. 'Can I get you something?'

'Food'll do fine.'

He retreated to the kitchen. 'Then it can't be flu,' he called, not bothering to disguise the relief in his voice. 'You wouldn't be hungry if it was flu.'

'Just starvation then.'

She dressed and found Simon stuffing the bird with a mixture of crushed garlic, herbs and mushrooms. He had a bottle of Pernod out, not her favourite beverage, and she went in search of some white wine.

'Is the paper going to run anything more on Alusha Mackenzie?' she asked, pulling out a bottle.

'Not that one,' Simon cried in horror. He reached past her and grasped another bottle. 'This one. Nice and dry. The other one's an '85.' She wasn't sure which honoured guest he kept the special vintages for, but it didn't seem to be her.

'The Mackenzie story,' she prompted.

'Oh? Nothing, I don't think. Someone floated an idea for an in-depth piece on pesticides, but the editor killed it.'

Someone floated an idea, but not him. 'You didn't push for it?'

'Well – no.' He looked mildly defensive. Wiping his hands, he reached for his favourite corkscrew and began to work energetically on the cork.

'But why not? And why did the editor kill it?'

'You know why, Daisy. Not enough to go on. I mean . . .' He gave her his favourite let's-face-the-facts look. 'She killed herself, and while that's a tragedy it's not a story.' He pulled the cork with a plop.

214

'But you can't say she killed herself!'

'A river. A freezing night. A sick woman. It doesn't take a lot of working out.'

'That's making one helluva lot of judgements, for Christ's sake, one helluva lot of assumptions. God – how would you feel if you were sick and weak and you fell and died and the obituaries all marked you down as a suicide?'

'Fell? Daisy, you don't fall into rivers accidentally.'

She paced the kitchen. 'Sure you do. Sure you do. It happens all the time. People trip, they fall . . .'

'And if it's a poky little river, they climb out again.'

She threw out her hands. 'And what happens if people hit their heads and get knocked unconscious?'

Wiping the neck of the bottle with a professional polish, he poured a glass and thrust it into her hand as a doctor might force a palliative on a hysterical patient.

She took a long swig. 'You're totally pre-judging the issue,' she said. 'Branding someone who can't defend herself.'

'I'm not branding anyone with anything.'

'Oh yes you are! You're saying she killed herself and, whatever people say, suicide's still the ultimate crime – selfish and cowardly and messy.'

Simon poured some cooking wine over the chicken and looked vaguely in the direction of the oven. 'There are worse things.'

'Like?'

He shrugged and, opening a cupboard, rummaged through a collection of herbs.

'Like?' she repeated harshly, feeling ugly and combative.

He selected a jar of marjoram and shook a dusting over the chicken. 'Like, well – being dishonest. Being a drug peddler. I don't know.'

She downed the rest of her wine and reached for a refill. 'There's no comparison. None at all. This woman's dead, and most of her death can be laid at the door of the stuff that poisoned her. You can't even begin to relate it to stealing or drugs.'

Simon gave the chicken a pat, as if the bird at least could be relied on to appreciate a sound argument. Then, waiting for Daisy to move aside, he bent over the oven and absorbed himself with the temperature control.

Daisy resumed her pacing, taking the length of the kitchen in five heartfelt strides.

Simon stood up from the oven, and said suddenly: 'She was doped.'

Daisy stopped dead. 'What do you mean doped?'

'They found drugs in her body.'

Daisy stood still, trying to make sense of it. And yet the sense was clear. He could only mean one sort of drug, otherwise he would have put it differently. But, needing to hear it in cold words, she asked all the same.

'Morphine or heroin or another derivative,' Simon said.

'Perhaps it was for pain. Perhaps it was prescribed.'

'Possibly,' he agreed. 'But apparently the levels were very high.'

'Then – ' She searched his face. 'What are you saying?'

He slid the chicken into the oven. 'It doesn't matter what I'm saying. Or anyone else for that matter. It's what the coroner says.'

'They don't have coroners in Scotland,' she replied mechanically.

'What do you have then?'

'Procurator fiscals.'

'God, what a title.'

'Will there be a hearing, an inquiry, do you know?'

He pulled a dead lettuce out of the fridge and looked at it accusingly. 'An inquest, you mean?'

'I don't think they have inquests. Just inquiries. Can you find out for me? If they're having one?'

'Mmm? Well . . .' He was losing interest. 'If I hear anything.'

By the time a powerful aroma of wine and garlic began to emerge from the oven she had lost her appetite.

'I think it's flu after all,' she said.

The wary expression came back into Simon's face.

Daisy took her cue. 'I think I'll skip the chicken if you don't mind.'

Simon put on a disappointed face, but didn't try to argue her out of it.

The flat was dark and cold when she got in. And a mess. She'd forgotten how behind she'd got with the chores. The ironing board stood in the middle of the room beside a well-filled ironing basket, the floor supported sprinklings of newspapers and magazines and a scattering of music cassettes. Her bed, only approximately made, was strewn with clothes and work papers.

On her way to the kitchen, her eye was caught by a note propped on the mantelpiece. She recognised the neat upright hand of Anthea, her flatmate. Anthea said she was sorry but she was giving two weeks' notice. She didn't quite think the flat was working out, nothing personal. She'd already moved her stuff out, she said, and would send the last two weeks' rent by post.

Despite the inconvenience, Daisy couldn't blame her. If she'd been in Anthea's position, she'd probably have done the same.

In need of cheer, she made herself a hot lemon drink and slid a hot-water bottle into her bed before making a superficial attack on the clutter. She threw the newspapers into a pile behind a chair, hid the ironing board behind the bathroom door and thrust her tapes onto the shelf by the tape player. Something about the shelf made her pause. Though tidiness wasn't her strong point, she liked to keep her tapes in some kind of order, and now she had the sudden impression that something was out of place. She ran her fingers along the ranks of plastic, ticking them off in her memory until she realised that a number of work tapes had got into the wrong slot: recordings of interviews with chemical victims from which she transcribed notes in the evenings. She'd put them between Pink Floyd and Beethoven, where Bach should be. Or was it Brahms?

As she flopped into bed and clutched the blissful hot-water bottle she remembered the answering machine and, reaching out, pulled it across the floor towards her. It was off. Then she realised that it wasn't actually off but incorrectly set. The model was a fairly ancient one; to set it properly it wasn't enough simply to turn the machine on, you also had to flick the control switch away from 'answer set' and then back again before the tape whirred into the correct position. It was a sign of how brain-stormed she must have been that morning to have screwed up this simplest of tasks.

More out of habit than expectation she played back the message tape, expecting to hear a repeat of yesterday's messages.

But she was wrong. There were no old messages, just a

brand new one in the form of her mother's voice announcing the date of her great-uncle Alf's seventieth birthday party, and asking if there was any chance of seeing her before that, like for Sunday lunch. Daisy lay back, trying to work this out. To have recorded that message, the machine must have been properly set for at least some of the day. So what had caused it to unset? It was some minutes before it came to her. Anthea. Anthea must have unintentionally switched it off at the wall as she was moving out, and forgotten to reset it properly. That, or there had been a power cut.

She switched off the light and closed her eyes, ready to let herself lose sleep over far more important things, like what could have prompted the Lincolnshire farmer and his wife to suddenly change their minds about the blood tests.

Hamish Macdonald didn't know what had hit him. One moment he was minding his own business, throwing up outside the back door of The Stag, peaceably wondering why he'd wasted good money on those last four pints only to review them so quickly, when in the next instant he was lifted bodily from the ground. It was a curiously weightless feeling, like flying, or being transported to heaven. Until he hit the wall, that was. Then he knew that he wasn't flying or going to heaven or suffering a malfunction of the brain. The wall was too hard for that; through the considerable haze and uncertainty, he was aware of the brickwork meeting his head with a nasty tap.

The sensation of flying ceased; his body slid a short way down the wall then stopped with his feet still clear of the ground, his weight supported by the grip of two vice-like hands on his lapels. The hands, of course, had an owner, as Macdonald feared they might, and now the owner's voice was hissing in his ear.

'Right, Macdonald, time for a wee chat.'

Macdonald blinked and tried to make out his assailant's identity, but the street lighting of Stirling, such as it was, revealed nothing but the man's black outline. Was he a thief? A man whom Macdonald had offended perhaps? That was always a real possibility. But whoever he was, whatever his business, Macdonald was only too happy to co-operate. Indeed, if only he could get his brain to respond he would tell

218

the fellow so. But try as he might, much as his mouth moved, no words would come.

The other man was very close, his nose almost touching Macdonald's. 'Willis Bain, Macdonald. The sprayin' in the forest, the flyin'. Who did it?'

A memory stirred in Macdonald's mind. This conversation had happened before. This man had accosted him at his lodgings a few days ago and had asked him the same bloody stupid question. There was something about the man that Macdonald knew he should take into consideration, something really important, but for the life of him he couldn't remember what it was.

In the meantime, the thought of co-operating no longer seemed quite such a good idea. This harping on about spraying and dates and places, it reeked of trouble and the law and unpleasant consequences, and no one was going to nail Macdonald that easily, oh no.

The words came at last. 'Och, pish off,' said Macdonald.

He got another tap on the head for his trouble, a forceful push against the brickwork, and then Macdonald remembered what it was about this man he should have taken into account: the fellow was huge, huge and strong.

This called for different tactics. Although he felt no pain, Macdonald cried out, a loud moan intended both to frighten the other man and to vent his own fear.

It had no effect whatsoever. The other man pushed him harder against the wall, repeating the questions in an aggressive tone.

To give himself time, Macdonald moaned again. This, for some unknown reason, seemed to register and the other man relented slightly, letting Macdonald slide down the wall until his feet touched ground. The questions didn't stop, however. Time. Place. Aircraft. Company name. When. What. Which.

'A'right, a'right. Jus' let me go, will ye?'

The hands released him, and Macdonald felt a glimmering of hope that things might go his way after all. Leaving one arm propped against the welcome solidity of the wall, he resentfully shrugged his jacket back onto his shoulders.

'So?' demanded the voice.

'A'right, a'right.' Macdonald ran an unsteady hand over his lapels, both to smooth them down and to show the extent of his affront. Also to give himself time to calculate his chances of making a run for it. The odds were not good, he had to admit, even if by some miracle he could stand unsupported and sprint the five yards to The Stag's back door. No, he would have to rely on a bit of stealth: a smidgen of truth peppered with liberal doses of amnesia.

'When ye say this was?' he asked blearily.

'June last.'

'Tha's a long time. Cannae recall tha' long . . .'

'Try harder.'

The fella moved in again and Macdonald held up a protective arm. 'A'right, a'right. Ye're quick to take offence. So wha' was it agin?'

The explanation came, and Macdonald did his best to recall the circumstances. He remembered making various deliveries to airfields and isolated strips, he remembered seeing planes sitting around. But the names of the two or more flying companies? The names of chemicals? Even if his brain had been clear – and it was thicker than a Gorbals smog – he'd have had trouble knowing the where and when. All he'd ever done in his working life was to turn up more or less on time, pick up whatever he was meant to pick up, take it to the right place, collect his wages and mind his own business.

'I dunno, and tha's the honest truth.'

A massive hand shot out and grabbed his lapel again. 'A wee aircraft,' growled the voice. 'Based out to the west somewhere. A field mebbe. Somewhere handy for the western lochs.'

Nothing stirred in Macdonald's brain.

'The aircraft,' the voice persisted. 'It mebbe had a red band on it. Diagonal.'

Ah, now . . . A bell rang in the back of Macdonald's memory, indistinctly at first, then with greater clarity. Gradually a picture formed; he saw the plane sitting on a piece of concrete, under an arclight, near a portable office. On a farm west of Stirling somewhere. Yes, he remembered all right. The question was, should he speak out? The whole thing reeked of consequences.

Better to be safe. He shook his head. 'Don't remember.'

The next moment it was all happening again, the flying sensation, the thud of his head hitting the wall, and a great deal harder this time, so that he cried with unprompted self-pity. The pain, which the alcohol for once failed to anaesthe-tise, finally persuaded him that enough was enough. This fella wasn't going to take no for an answer, and Macdonald wasn't about to suffer more insult and injury to prove otherwise.

He squealed: 'Mebbe there's somethin' . . . Mebbe.'

'Names, man, names.'

'Lemme think, lemme think . . .' The big man loosened his grip, but this did nothing to clarify Macdonald's memory, which was black as pitch. All Macdonald ever had to do was find the address on the delivery notes – the foreman at the depot near Stirling did all the paperwork, making sure the right chemical went to the right contractor – so how in heaven should he be expected to know the name of the flying company and the stuff they were using all of a sudden?

Seeing the big man looming above, he made an attempt to show willing.

'A field. By the wesht there. A wee plane. But a' never kent the name o' the plashe. Honesh to God, honesh to God . . .'

There was an answering growl and Macdonald cowered, fearing a reorganisation of his face. Then, as if heaven-sent, something stirred in the back of Macdonald's mind, a memory so vague that he couldn't at first grasp it. But realising it offered the only hope of salvation, he begged: 'Hang on, fella. Hang on . . .' and put his mind to concentrating hard, which was no easy task.

Finally it came, and in his haste to get it out before the big man got impatient he jabbered incoherently and it was a moment before he could make himself understood. 'A faerm . . . By a faerm . . . By a faerm name o'. . . name o' Auld . . . Auld-somethin' . . .'

There was a pause. The voice said angrily: 'The name, man!'

'Auldhome . . . Auldhame . . . Aye – *Auldhame*. Honesh to God, tha's all a' ken . . . Honesh to God.'

Having said his piece, Macdonald's stomach threatened to go through its paces again and, to put off the evil moment, he slid further down the wall until he was almost bent double. When he next glanced up he was mightily relieved to see that the big man had gone. He celebrated by sinking the last distance to the ground and having a welcome lie down.

FOURTEEN

The call came at midnight. Susan, surfacing slowly from a heavy sleep, knew there was no point in objecting to the lateness of the call, no point in mentioning that this was the first time they'd got to bed before one in the morning in the last two, maybe three, months. The call would be from party headquarters or a party colleague. Or maybe even the prime minister's office, in which case, even if it was five in the morning, you were incredibly relieved, not to mention pathetically grateful, to be hearing from them at all. It meant that you – or to be precise, Tony – was still up there where it mattered, in the PM's good books.

Through her sleep-drugged haze she suddenly remembered: this wasn't any old night. This was the night the PM was putting the new cabinet together.

She sat up groggily, eyes creased against the light, and tried to read Tony's face as he grunted a few monosyllabic yesses and noes into the phone.

Maddeningly, he wouldn't return her eye signals, and when he turned away to replace the phone, it was all she could do to get him to speak. She had to positively bully him before he finally told her: it was the PM's office. The PM had asked to see him at eleven the next morning.

It took her a moment to take this in, to realise the full implications of what he was saying. Then she knew without a doubt: he'd done it. She gave a great guffaw of delight and grabbed him in a fierce embrace. He didn't respond. He seemed dazed, almost as if he wasn't expecting the call, which was ridiculous because everyone knew he was up for a top job. The PM's office hadn't told him what the job would be, of course – that little morsel would drop direct from the prime minister's lips – but the timing of the call was enough: the senior appointments were always announced first. It couldn't be anything less than full cabinet minister.

'Oh, honey!' She gave him another squeeze. He rubbed his eyes and blinked, as if trying to clear his brain. He didn't seem to have taken the news in at all.

'Are you all right?' she demanded. 'Are you ill or something?'

'What? No. No.' He didn't sound convinced.

'Tired then? Oh honey, you must be *so* tired.'

He gave a small shake of the head.

Susan eyed him fretfully. If he wasn't ill and he wasn't particularly tired, then what the hell *was* wrong? He should be grinning with delight and jumping up and down with excitement. Crying, even.

'Tony – it *has* to be a job! And a cabinet one. Got to be!'

'Yes.'

'Aren't you *pleased*?'

'Yes.' Then, with an effort, he smiled. 'Yes, of course I am.'

'D'you think it'll be Agriculture?'

He nodded absentmindedly.

'But isn't that what you wanted?'

'Yes.'

'*Well*, then.'

He squeezed her hand briefly and reached out to turn off the light. 'We'll see. In the morning.'

She was so baffled by this that it was a long time before she got back to sleep. And even as she finally began to nod off, she was suddenly wakened again by Tony getting out of bed and creeping noisily out of the room. If he slept at all during the night, he couldn't have slept for long because shortly after six, when she got up to go to the loo, she found the other side of the bed empty. She pulled on a dressing gown and, though she was feeling decidedly short of rest, tottered downstairs to see where he was and if she could do anything for him. She thought: Greater love hath no wife.

He was in the room they grandly called the study, but which was actually a ten-by-ten box squeezed out of a half-landing with a desk jammed under the window and a few bookshelves perched on the little available wall space.

223

The door was open and she could see his back hunched over the desk. She paused on the stairs, curious to see what he was up to. The answer was: not a lot. He was quite still, bent forward over the desk with his head cradled in his hands.

She started forward again, on the point of calling gently so as not to startle him, when he reached out a hand to pick up the phone. Something made her pull slowly back until she was hidden by the door frame. She told herself she'd done it so as not to interrupt him, but who was she kidding? His attitude, the stiffness of his body, told her this wasn't a routine call.

Whoever he was calling wasn't in a hurry to answer, but he was obviously prepared to wait it out. He sat motionless, the receiver pressed to his ear, his only sign of impatience a hand rubbed back and forth across his temple.

After what seemed a long time, he stiffened suddenly: he was in business. Susan craned forward.

'It's me,' he said. 'Tony . . . I know . . . I know . . . Yes . . . I'm sorry, but I wanted to be sure to get you.' His voice, already low, dropped to a whisper. As if aware of the dangers, he half turned his head, swinging round to glance over his shoulder. Susan pulled back out of view.

He was closing the door. It swung slowly towards the frame, then stopped short, leaving a small gap. He didn't attempt to close it any more and after a second or two Susan crept forward and positioned herself by the jamb.

'It was the only time I could ring . . .' His voice sounded urgently. 'I know, I *know* . . . Look, I'm *sorry*, I really couldn't call before, I just couldn't. Listen, we have to meet . . . What do you mean? . . . But we *must* – we have to! We've got to discuss this thing! . . . What do you mean? What are you saying? *Christ* . . .' An anguished sigh. 'Listen, we *have* to talk. You can't drop this on me and then say you're not going to talk about it! Christ, it's got to be *discussed*. I mean, what are you planning to *do* about it, for God's sake? No . . . No . . . The only time I have is this morning, in an hour or so . . . No, the only time. Really . . . But I can't. No . . . *Please*. For God's sake, Angela.'

The small worm of jealousy turned in Susan's gut. So she had him crawling, this woman. Well, bully for her. She must be fantastic in bed; there wasn't much else that could reduce

224

Tony to such creeping submission. From the sound of the call, it certainly wasn't her conversation, nor, presumably, her charm when woken at six in the morning.

Fine. In fact, it couldn't be finer. Why should she mind? In the time that Tony had been screwing this woman – at least eight months now – Susan had had plenty of time to get used to the idea. In the beginning she'd ignored it, then, when pretence had become impossible, Susan had entered what might be called her brave and noble phase, and forced herself to face the full facts in all their tacky unpleasantness. But all that had achieved was to make her miserable, tetchy and impossible to live with. Finally she'd learnt the trick: you rose above it. You became the perfect wife. You became sweet, charming and delightful, an absolute cast-iron asset. She had finally worked out that it was not only futile to worry, it was also unnecessary. A sexy number with black knickers and big boobs – or whatever amazing endowments she possessed – was never going to be a serious threat. Not to a marriage that had always muddled along reasonably well, not to a political wife who worked as hard at the job as Susan, not when Tony was on the up and up. It wasn't as if Tony had shown any outward signs of restlessness or dissatisfaction. On the contrary, he'd been sweet and affectionate, and, strange though it seemed, their relationship had if anything improved.

Tony's voice rose slightly, sounding peevish. '. . . But I can't *do* any other time. You don't understand. I'll be getting a new job later this morning. And then – well, it'll be hopeless . . . Angela, *please*.'

Despite herself, Susan got a curious satisfaction from hearing Tony grovel. She wasn't above feeling hurt and vindictive, and there was a part of her that thought: Serves you bloody right for being greedy.

At the same time his tone worried her. What was the urgency? Why was he sounding so desperate?

'. . . No, that would be difficult . . . No, it *has* to be your place . . . *No* . . . Seven thirty . . . No later. No . . . Bye.'

He had rung off. He was getting to his feet. She could hear the chair scraping across the carpet. Too late to vanish. Forward, then, in her mode of consummate actress. She tapped her nails on the door just as it swung open.

Tony gave a start, jerked his head up and stared at her in astonishment.

225

Susan smiled warmly. 'Darling, you're up early. Why didn't you sleep in for once?'

'Couldn't.'

'Darling, are you okay? You look dreadful.'

He gave a great sigh, lifting his shoulders then dropping them in a gesture of hopelessness. He reminded her of a bedraggled storm-tossed bird. The impression was accentuated by his hair, which was uncombed and stood up in feathery spikes around his head. She knew she should feel cross with him, but it was impossible, not when she was so worried.

'What *is* the matter, darling?' He wouldn't tell her, of course, but she had to ask.

'What? Oh, nothing.' He rubbed a hand mercilessly over his face.

When he met her eyes again, she gave him a come-off-it look.

'A problem,' he finally admitted. 'But nothing I can't deal with.' He put on his brave-boy expression, a look that normally worked wonders, as he well knew.

'I can't do anything then?' she asked.

'No.'

'Are you sure?'

He switched to his broad everything's-hunky-dory politician's grin.

'Sure.'

'Well, remember I'm always here if you need me.'

The words seemed to touch him. He looked grateful, almost movingly so, though whether it was because of the offer of help, or because she hadn't pressed him on the nature of the problem, she wasn't sure.

It would be easy to demolish him now. He looked about as confident as a five-year-old on his first day at school. Part of her longed to vent her anger and hurt, to tell him how pathetic his behaviour was, to make him see that he was just another plump menopausal male letting lust overrule his judgement; part of her even longed to point out how wonderful all this would look in five-inch headlines in the gutter press. But she held back. He wouldn't be able to take it. Like most successful men, his ego was paper-thin; he was apt to fall apart in the face of emotional crises.

But *was* this a real crisis? And if it was, what the hell was it about? She was burning to ask, yet loath to bring the whole beastly business out into the open.

She gave him a brief kiss on the cheek and was turning to go upstairs when without warning he caught her shoulder and pulled her back into a powerful hug, squeezing her so hard that her head was forced sideways, almost causing her to wince aloud. The awkward bearish embrace went on for what seemed a long time, and whenever she tried to pull away, he tightened his arms round her.

When he finally let go and she was able to twist her neck gingerly back into position, she looked sharply up at him in questioning astonishment. But, avoiding her eyes, Tony quickly dropped his head and turned to scrabble for a tissue from the box on the desk. He blew his nose with a loud roar. When he turned back, the brave little smile was in place again, though she noticed the moisture hadn't quite gone from the corners of his eyes.

Tony – sorry for himself? Tony – emotional? Never.

Now she knew it was serious.

She considered following him, like some private detective in a TV series, but it would really be far too difficult. Quite apart from the fact that she would have to get dressed in a hurry, something she'd never managed even in times of crisis, there would be the difficulty of finding transport. Tony would, presumably, drive himself in the Rover, so that if she tried to follow in the Golf, which was a most distinctive red colour, he would be bound to spot her in his mirror. A taxi would be more practical, but in this neighbourhood finding a taxi on the street was about as likely as getting the newspapers delivered before ten or finding the pavements litter-free. Even if one ordered a taxi on the phone, it was half an hour before the controller could find a cabbie prepared to penetrate the depths of SE5.

No: there was a better way, and she was rather pleased with herself for thinking of it.

Hearing Tony's splashings in the shower – not unlike the sounds of a large animal at a water hole – she slipped into the bedroom to look for the small wad of belongings – wallet, cards and slim diary – that he always kept in his inside jacket pocket. Usually he left them over-night on his chest of drawers, but for some reason they were not there. She spent some time searching the jackets of his suits before deciding that he must have taken them downstairs.

His briefcase was sitting on the desk in his study. When she tried the clasps they flew open immediately. On top of the thick pile of papers was a black memo book that she had seen many times before, and which she knew he used for his work; but, though she looked carefully in every corner of the case, there was no diary.

She put the black memo book in the pocket of her dressing gown and, closing the case, went down to the kitchen and placed the memo book casually between a directory and a cookery book, as if it had got scooped up and put there accidentally.

Knowing Tony would be getting dressed by now, she prepared some breakfast. He'd already announced that he would be in a hurry this morning. He said he was meeting a journalist in Westminster. He was, she noted, an expert liar.

When he came into the kitchen, it was at the trot. He hung his jacket over the back of a chair, just as she'd hoped he would, and the moment he reached for the orange juice, which she'd carefully placed on the far side of the table, she flipped open his jacket, reached into the inner pocket and, grasping the contents, stuffed them into the pocket of her dressing gown.

Tony drained the glass and turned to say: 'I'll be back to drop the car off at about nine. Could you check with Central Office, to make sure they've arranged transport?'

'Of course.'

He gobbled his toast. 'Must be off.' He patted his trouser pockets. She realised with a lurch of disappointment that he would check his jacket the moment he put it on, and would quickly realise that his wallet and everything else were missing. Stupid of her: she hadn't thought this out properly.

He was glancing towards his jacket; he was going to put it on any minute.

'Darling, do have a vitamin,' she said.

'What?' He looked at her in surprise.

'A vitamin. You're very run down, you know. You don't want to start your new job with flu. There're some in the cupboard over there.'

He looked at his watch. 'Well . . . okay. Where are they?'

He was saying this without enthusiasm, waiting for her to fly past him, find the bottle and shake out a tablet. Tony was used to having things provided for him.

'In the cupboard over there, above the mixer.'

He gave her a questioning glance that revealed his disappointment at her lack of action, then started reluctantly across the kitchen.

As he peered into the cupboard, Susan pulled the bundle out of her pocket. Diary? It was in the middle, between the wallet and the credit card folder. She extricated it, fumbled, almost dropped it, and looked up anxiously. Tony, reading the label on a bottle, was turning round.

With the wallet and credit cards in one hand, and the diary in the other, she moved rapidly behind the chair and dropped both hands behind her back.

Tony was holding up a bottle.

'That's it,' she said.

'One?'

'I should think so. You'll need to wash it down though.'

He gave a small sigh of impatience as he went in search of a water container, eventually taking an upturned mug from the draining board and filling it from the tap.

Quickly, she opened the jacket again and slipped the wallet and credit card folder back into the inner pocket. She was aware of a childish excitement: if this hadn't been so serious, it would have been fun.

He was coming for the jacket now. He pulled it on, patted the lower pockets, then swung open the lapel. She stared as he checked the inner pocket, but the sight of the wallet seemed to satisfy him, and the next moment he was smoothing down his lapels and, with a quick kiss, was on his way.

She needed a couple of stiff coffees after that. As soon as the second cup was on the table in front of her, she set to work. She started with the diary. It didn't cover the previous year, of course, which meant it contained nothing of the Paris–Strasbourg trip, but if he was seeing his piece regularly then there had to be other entries, other trips that would give him away. The diary was pencil-thin, intended simply as an *aide mémoire* to his office diary, and contained only the most cryptic entries. Most had been made in his secretary's neat printed script. Appointments, meetings, dentist: there was nothing that didn't look entirely above board. And the social engagements – dinners, weddings, family gatherings – there was nothing that she couldn't verify there.

Perhaps he'd learnt to be secretive and write nothing down. Perhaps he'd guessed Susan might start getting suspicious. But if he was this careful now, perhaps he hadn't been so careful in the beginning. She wasn't sure where he kept his old diaries; she might have a look for them later. In the meantime, there was still the black memo book.

She went through it twice. Another disappointment. Plenty of names and phone numbers, but all government or party people or political journalists. The few female names were either researchers, identified as such in brackets after each name – Tony was meticulous about categorising people – or well-known MPs or relatives or family. No mysterious initials beginning with A. No initials at all, in fact.

Damn.

She went back to the diary. There was one possibility she hadn't covered; that there was a link between the woman and that grey man Schenker from Morton-Kreiger. He'd been in Paris with Tony, and maybe in Strasbourg too, around the time of Tony's adulterous stay in the château. She found mention of his name quickly enough, first against a daytime meeting in January, then against a dinner, then on a trip to Covent Garden to which she'd also been invited. She flipped back to the dinner. It had taken place in late January. Apparently the two men had had dinner again in early February. And again two weeks later. And yet again just ten days after that. Rather frequent, these dinner meetings, even allowing for Schenker's smarmy little ways. Before she allowed herself a full measure of excitement, she went through the dates a second time, trying to match them to the occasions when her instincts had told her Tony was lying, but her memory wasn't good enough to be certain of the precise dates. Slapping the diary down on the table, she strode up to the study and, starting with the top right-hand drawer, went methodically through his desk. It took half an hour to find the old diaries, which were not in the desk at all, but on the topmost bookshelves in box files, sorted by year, along with all his correspondence, notes and political thoughts. Everything, she realised, for the writing of his memoirs, assuming he stayed

230

in politics long enough and reached a high enough post for people to show interest.

She found the entry for the Strasbourg–Paris trip. There were EEC meetings, a conference. Schenker's name. Then not much else . . . Until, a week later – yes. *Yes!* The initial A. Ha, ha! she thought: Got you. She allowed herself a moment of satisfaction before continuing her search.

In the following weeks and months there were more A's until, in about October, they stopped abruptly. He must have realised he was taking risks, must have decided to get more careful.

But nowhere was there a phone number, or a clue to the woman's name.

Finding the date for the Strasbourg–Paris trip again, she went backwards through the previous months. In April she found an entry for a water conference in the Midlands, and under it for an evening engagement, Schenker's name again.

And in the top margin, a lone phone number. There was no name next to it, and perhaps for that reason she fastened on to it.

Back in the kitchen she thumbed through the memo-cum-address book, but there was no number resembling the mysterious entry in the diary margin. Looking through the current diary again, she went to the blank end-pages, which Tony had filled with densely packed jottings: notes, memos, names, frequently used phone numbers. And there it was at last: the very same number. And next to it, the name A. Kershaw.

She smiled to herself. This detective work was a piece of cake.

The phone book came up trumps, too. There was an A. Kershaw at the same number. The address was a flat in Wandsworth.

Yet, having got this far, Susan couldn't resist the final confirmation. It was getting on for nine: even allowing for Tony having arrived late and overstayed his allotted visiting time, he must have left the woman's place by now.

Before Susan had time for second thoughts or serious nerves, she picked up the phone and dialled the number.

It answered quickly, as if snatched up from its cradle. A sulky female voice. 'Hullo?'

231

Susan realised she hadn't rehearsed this at all. 'Angela?'

'Yes?' The voice sounded grumpy, as if she hadn't had enough sleep.

'This is Naomi. How are you?'

'*Who?*'

'Naomi Attwood.'

'There's been some mistake . . .' She was sounding irritated.

'Oh? Isn't that Angela Kershaw?'

'Yes it is. But I don't know any Naomi. You must have the wrong number.'

'Oh dear. I thought . . . Aren't you Angela Kershaw from Tunbridge Wells?'

'No, I am most definitely not. Listen, you have the wrong number!'

Susan thought: Bad-tempered, too. 'Oh, sorry. I looked you up in the book. I thought . . .'

But there was a click then the buzz of an empty line.

Susan put down the phone, glowing with self-congratulation. In her heyday as a model she'd posed for Bailey, Parks, O'Neill – all the best – she'd even done bit-parts in a couple of commercials, but until now she'd never quite appreciated the extent of her talent to impersonate.

She saw the time. Hastily she phoned Central Office to confirm Tony's car, and, breaking the habits of a lifetime, managed to shower, throw on some makeup and get dressed in twenty minutes flat, so that she was standing at the door to welcome Tony when he finally returned at nine twenty, delayed, he said, by heavy traffic. He looked preoccupied and grim. Two minutes later she was back at the door, the diary and memo book in hand, ready to pass them to him as he flew out of the house again. At the sight of them he looked startled, patted his pockets, and frowned at her.

'You left them by the phone,' she said.

'Good God. Thanks.' He peered into the street to make sure the official car was there, kissed her briefly, started down the steps and turned back. 'I'll call you the moment I get some news.' He grinned suddenly, a pathetic almost apologetic smile. 'Don't get too excited.'

'Ha! No less than the cabinet!'

He managed a laugh, but she could see that he was deep in

some torturous gloom. 'Oh, and Susan – the car. I couldn't find a space for it. Would you?'

He indicated the Rover, which was parked on a yellow line.

'Of course.'

She waved him goodbye. The perfect wife.

Drab utilitarian stuff. Hillyard wrinkled his nose slightly at the Chairman Mao shirt and Castro fatigues, though that didn't prevent him from flicking diligently through the remainder of the hangers. There was only one frock that could be described as stylish, and that was a drapy floral number which would look rather fetching in a country garden, taking tea under an apple tree.

Replacing the dress, he went quickly through the chest of drawers. Cheap Marks and Spencer underwear. Nothing remotely lacy or silly. Except for one nightdress, a present from a rich boyfriend perhaps, although it was hard to imagine Miss Field having friends who even began to verge on the stylish. He ran his fingers over the fabric. Silk: wonderful next to the skin.

There was a clutter of papers by the bed. Kneeling, he went through them methodically, but there was nothing to catch his attention, just periodicals and reports.

He glanced along the shelf of tapes above the tape player. She'd tidied them, he noticed, even rearranged them since his last visit. Put the classics at the far end and the pop music, which accounted for most of the collection, at the near end. While the case-history tapes, the ones he had come to look at, had disappeared. He exhaled crossly and it wasn't until he turned to look around the rest of the room that he spotted the stack of tapes on the desk under the window, perched on a pile of papers. He could almost hear Beryl's gravelly voice saying: Who's a lucky boy, then?

The window, a bay, was tall and uncurtained, the sun hitting the glass and spreading over the film of London grime like gold dust, so that even the most vigilant neighbour would have trouble seeing in. He sat at the desk, slipping the tapes out of their boxes one by one, made a careful note of which tapes belonged in which boxes before exchanging them for the blanks in his pocket. Just as he was restacking the boxes on the pile of papers the phone rang with a loud shrill.

233

Out of long habit he froze until, with the clicking of the answering machine, he could once more hear beyond the flat to the sounds on the communal stairs and the street below.

The answering machine spewed out its message, broadcasting it through the room. *'I'm not here just at the moment, but if you'd like to leave a message . . .'* The caller took up her invitation, announcing himself as Campbell from Loch Fyne.

Hillyard suddenly straightened and strode through to the bathroom. Springing onto the side of the bath, he opened a door set high in the wall and thrust his ear as close as possible to the cupboard inside. The hot water gurgled in the tank below, a pipe expanded with a tick-ticking sound, but even when these extraneous sounds ceased it was impossible to hear the whir of the tape in its hidey hole behind the thick bundles of old blankets and abandoned clothing that filled the available space. The caller rang off. There was a clunk from the answering machine in the main room, but from behind the high-set cupboard there was not the faintest sound.

He didn't disturb the machine – he'd already had it out once to change the tape and renew the batteries – but closed the door and stepped down, carefully wiping any trace of footmarks from the edge of the bath.

As he passed the bathroom wall-cabinet he took a quick look inside on the principle that you never knew what you might find, then, after a quick perusal of the street from the bay window, let himself out. He had obtained a full set of her keys, copied from the spare set she kept in the top right-hand drawer of her desk.

The car was parked in an adjacent street, guarded by Beji. He drove to the heath, to a popular parking place where old dears sat in their cars enjoying the sun and determined dog-walkers set off briskly, chins jutting, into the wind.

Hillyard collected a holdall from the boot, slid the driver's seat back as far as it would go and, settling himself comfortably with legs outstretched, began the time-consuming task of dubbing the tapes. He plugged the tape machine into the 12-volt lighter socket and, inserting the first pair of tapes, set the high-speed dubber in motion. He listened to the senseless jabbering for a moment before turning the volume down and making some cryptic notes in his personalised shorthand. These related to the message he'd heard in the flat. *Campbell, Loch Fyne. May have found (an)? airfield to west of Stirling.* There

234

had been something else noteworthy in the message, but with the distractions of the bathroom expedition, it took him a while to recollect exactly what it was. He wrote: *No luck on the spray.* When the last tape had been copied he put the originals back in his pocket, repacked the holdall and returned it to the boot. As he headed back through Highgate, he hummed contentedly, thinking of the thick body of facts that would go into the next report. Some weeks it had been necessary to pad things out a bit. Then Beryl, exercising all her wicked ingenuity, had massaged the story forward, hinting at the promise of future disclosures without ever quite diverting from the facts, or, indeed, the lack of them. But this week no padding would be necessary, not so long as Beryl got moving on the transcriptions and had them finished in time.

He followed the same route back to Upper Holloway and parked within sight of the Field woman's flat. More from habit than the expectation of seeing anything, he watched the dust-coated windows of the first-floor flat for a couple of minutes before getting out and strolling gently towards the front steps. He was pulling the keys out of his pocket, preparing himself for a rapid entry, when he spotted a man at the far end of the street walking briskly down the hill towards him. At that distance Hillyard couldn't make out his face but he had a sudden and unpleasant suspicion that this was someone associated with the Field woman. A firm disciple of his own intuition, he accelerated into a more purposeful stride and, ignoring the house, kept walking.

Within a few yards Hillyard realised several things simultaneously: that he had been mistaken and didn't recognise the man at all, and that the approaching figure's resemblance, such as it was, had been to the Field woman's boyfriend, the *Sunday Times* journalist, Simon Calthrop, and it was this that had sounded the faint alarm in his mind.

If he'd had more time to think about it, he'd have known a visit from Calthrop wasn't likely. The boyfriend always liked the Field girl to go to him. But better safe than locked up, as Beryl liked to point out.

Passing the man, Hillyard carefully averted his eyes, and reaching the end of the street took a quick look back to make doubly sure that the man was not after all entering number fifty, before turning left and left again, to beat a circuitous path back to the car.

There he waited until there was a nice long lull in the business of the street. Letting himself back into the flat, he replaced the blank tapes with the originals, and stacked them carefully on the pile of papers, exactly where he'd found them.

He was in and out within two minutes. To a casual observer, a resident who'd just popped in for something.

There was a mammoth jam in Park Lane and it took him a good hour to get back to Battersea. He spent the time entertaining himself with Beji, dangling choccy drops above her nose.

FIFTEEN

Normally Schenker never ate alone in hotel suites – he resented the waste of executive time – but today he made an exception and ate breakfast in front of the TV so as to catch the first news of the British government appointments.

Cable news finally delivered at seven, but gave only the top four cabinet appointments. Schenker called Cramm's room immediately to find that his assistant, ever the great anticipator, had at that very moment plucked the information from the Reuters wire service.

Driscoll had got Agriculture.

Schenker beamed. He beamed at himself in the mirror as he adjusted his tie, and he smiled at Cramm as they descended to the Plaza's main lobby and went out to the waiting limo. There were still faint signs of pleasure on his face as they headed downtown to their appointment on Madison Avenue.

'The right man,' he remarked in a self-indulgent murmur.

'Absolutely,' echoed Cramm dutifully.

And the right man twice over, Schenker comforted himself. Not only was Driscoll a friend in the most beneficial sense of the word, but almost any change would have been a vast improvement on the last incumbent, Cranbourne, whose obstructive little ways had been a thorn in Schenker's flesh for a long time. Fortunately Cranbourne had overreached himself and made a slip just before the election. In better times the mistake – allowing the export of some unsafe meat – would hardly have rated more than a brief rebuke in the press, but Cranbourne had failed to realise that for a politician without friends, errors, however minor, were inclined to be fatal. Provided with the appropriate facts – and journalists existed to be fed facts – the media had developed the affair into a minor scandal. The timing hadn't helped the government's election chances of course, but that was a risk that had had to be taken.

'You always knew it would be Driscoll,' Cramm said with suitable admiration.

Schenker shrugged modestly. 'Not *knew*. Just weighed up the chances, and he always came out on top. Not too much of a high-flier, you see. Not too ambitious. Not foreign secretary or home secretary material. And he knows it. That's his strength. Steady, good grounding, solid ability, someone who can be relied on to spare the prime minister unpleasant surprises.'

'He's got a lot to deliver though, hasn't he?' said Cramm delicately. 'The manifesto, those environmental commitments . . . they were pretty heavy.'

'This government will never push Green issues at the expense of its economic programme,' said Schenker with confidence. 'The economy comes first and, whatever the British people may say, however Green they may think they are, the economy will always come first with them too.' Summing it up as he thought rather neatly, he added: 'Food before ideas. Always has been, always will be.'

The Food Bill, which everyone had got in such a panic about, had quickly got bogged down at committee stage, and the more extreme clauses gradually thinned down until, thanks to the snap election, the entire Bill had got killed off. The government had of course promised to reintroduce the legislation, which was only to be expected, but the details had been left acceptably indeterminate. With Driscoll safely in the chair, the insane warning-label idea for food was not likely to emerge again, and with a bit of luck – which, since Schenker left nothing to chance, meant a lot of hard work – the sampling and penalty proposals would lose most of their teeth.

As the limousine undulated down Fifth Avenue, Schenker allowed himself a rare moment of optimism.

Cramm cleared his throat and said: 'That problem at the Aurora works, the health scare – '

'I thought that was under control.'

238

'In so far as it was possible, yes. But there are ripples. EarthForce, the environmental group, are pressing the EPA to investigate the health reports, and a local congressman's got hold of the story and is hammering the press.'

'We don't need this now.' Schenker was thinking of the US launch of Silveron which, after interminable delays, was finally within sight. He was also thinking of the Stock Market, where Morton-Kreiger shares were still under press-ure. 'Who's been talking?' he asked grimly. 'That scientist again?'

'MKI thinks it was this local doctor who's been treating the Silveron workers. Someone called Burt. They're looking into it.'

'I hope they're doing more than looking into it,' Schenker said with considerable irritation.

'Oh, sure. They've obtained some more medical opinions. No sign of chemicals in the blood, run-of-the-mill diseases: that sort of thing. And of course the results of the new toxicology trial are due fairly soon – '

'Soon? I thought they were due yesterday!'

'Technical problems at TroChem.'

'*Technical* problems?' He let his voice rise sarcastically. 'I thought these people were meant to be hyper-efficient. Why the hell can't they deliver?'

'They've given firm assurances that the results will be out within two weeks.'

'*Two weeks?* That'll be too late! Get through to Research while we're in the meeting. Tell them *today*. It has to be today. Or I'll phone McNeill myself.' Perhaps he'd phone McNeill anyway. An opportunity to wave Research's inefficiencies in front of McNeill's nose was not to be missed.

Cramm looked doubtful.

Schenker turned on him. 'You're not trying to tell me there's some kind of problem?'

'No, no. I – ' He faltered uncharacteristically. 'I just thought you should be forewarned.'

Ominous remarks like that had the power to unsettle Schenker. 'About *what*?'

'The environmentalists. The press. Like I said.'

'Not the results?' He examined Cramm's face. 'Not the toxicology trials? God, if McNeill's been holding out on me . . .'

'No, no. Research say the results are going to be fine. As of last night, that is. Shall I check with them again?'

'You do that. *You do that.*' With the launch coming up, any sort of uncertainty frightened Schenker rigid. It took only the smallest scare to rattle the Stock Markets.

By the time they entered the gleaming portals of the advertising agency Schenker's mood was sombre.

Normally he made a point of avoiding advertising agencies, preferring to leave the control of their slick machinations to his executives, but on this occasion he'd been forced to make an exception. The marketing policy at Morton-Kreiger International (US) had been showing less than adequate results for some time and he'd pressed Gertholm into making some big changes in Chicago. The result was a new marketing team who, faced with the challenge of getting Silveron into the three top sellers within two years, had provisionally chosen this Madison Avenue agency for the Silveron account. They had chosen – but were they right? The team was too new, the decision too important for Schenker entirely to trust their judgement.

Advertising agencies, like public relations companies, rubbed Schenker up the wrong way. They always looked too affluent, too polished by half, and he could never quite forgive them for deriving their plump incomes from clients like him.

The agency people and the MKI marketing team were standing in stiff groups, coffee cups in hand, when he sped into the room. Conversation faltered, cups were abandoned as, without breaking his stride, Schenker shook a couple of hands and sat himself rapidly in the centre of the front row, staring pointedly ahead. The account director slipped into his welcoming spiel. The mixture of subservience and arrogance irritated Schenker beyond measure and, without removing his gaze from the screen ahead, he interrupted coldly: 'Let's go.'

There was a stir, a sense of having got off to a bad start, which was precisely what Schenker had intended, and the account executives lurched hastily into their opening routine.

Following normal practice, the presentation began with a summary of Silveron's market strategy, of which Schenker was well aware, but which the agency felt they had to regurgitate to show how brilliantly they understood the product. Finally they came to the proposed selling point: Silveron offered the broadest most cost-effective protection against pests yet.

It was to be a press campaign, the agency said, using saturation coverage in all the major target magazines, starting with a six-page pull-out section in the foremost growers' journals. This campaign would coincide with a free sampling operation, five Hawaiian holidays for the most successful wholesalers, and a $200,000 prize draw.

So far so obvious. Schenker waited to see how they intended to get the message across. The agricultural and forestry journals were bulging with ads, each indistinguishable from the next, each cluttered with facts, exhortations to purchase and glowing testimonials.

Finally they came to the bottom line: the treatment. The advertisement was to be a three-page spread, extended over successive right-hand pages. The first page was to be a tease, a page of solid green bled off at the edges, with just four words in small type in the lower right-hand corner: *Silveron covers almost everything*. Turning over, the reader was then hit by another almost totally green page with a list down the right-hand side, set in equally small type, a restrained, factual catalogue of Silveron's potential targets: *Spruce moth, Tussock moth, Boll weevil, Beauty moth* . . . The list was fifty bugs long. It looked good, Schenker had to admit. Finally, on the third page, came the hard sell: Silveron's cost-effectiveness, on a par with its main competitors; its persistence; the infrequency of application.

'Very good,' Schenker said. They were all watching him, trying to work out if this remark was as promising as it sounded. After a moment, he added: 'But will people really understand what a breakthrough Silveron is?'

The account executive made a show of looking mildly puzzled. 'A breakthrough?' he asked politely. 'We understood it was more of a development of existing products.'

'An *important* development,' Schenker corrected him. 'And we need to tell people that. Perhaps on that first page. Along with *Silveron covers almost everything*. Something to announce it's special. You know – It's new, it's special – something like that.'

There was a silence. They didn't like that, not at all. He'd forgotten how touchy these people got when it came to their words, as if they were Hemingway or Fitzgerald or somebody who could really write.

'Well . . .' the account executive said uncertainly. 'We could certainly examine the feasibility of that.'

'We also need to tell people it's safe,' Schenker continued. The agency people exchanged glances. No one seemed keen to take that one up. It was finally left to the copywriter to offer an opinion. 'Safety's a difficult one,' he said. 'There isn't enough to say.'

Schenker placed his hands in an attitude of prayer and pressed his fingers to his lips. 'Not enough? But Silveron has been cleared – or is about to be cleared – for sale in every country we've applied to market it. What do you mean – not enough?'

'We couldn't make the message sufficiently strong to make it worth saying. To use what you've just suggested would sound defensive. I mean, the consumer will know the product's been cleared by the EPA, otherwise we wouldn't be allowed to sell it in the first place.'

'Morton-Kreiger spends more on safety trials per product than any other major agrochemical company,' Schenker said calmly. 'We should make something of that.'

'That might be a useful selling point in corporate advertising, very useful,' the account executive said smoothly, 'but for a single product – well, it might be thought to imply that the product is in some way safer than its competitors – and that might cause problems.'

Schenker wasn't terribly fond of being told his own business. He said sternly: 'Might it?'

'Problems at our end I mean,' said the executive hastily. 'It would take time to get it past the advertising standards people. They'd want corroborative evidence.'

The copywriter chipped in: 'Even then it would only take one smidgen of bad publicity to make the whole campaign backfire.'

The account executive flinched visibly, as if he'd been stabbed in the back, which, in agency terms, he had. 'Of course that's not likely,' he said hurriedly.

'No one has ever been adversely affected by Silveron,' Schenker said.

Everyone nodded to show they had known this all along.

'Perhaps we could get the safety angle checked out by our

legal department?' the account executive said, trying to paper the cracks. 'And if there's anything we *can* say, we'll find a way of saying it. In an effective and meaningful way, of course.'

This was the usual advertising agency flannel. 'But it should have been a selling point from the beginning,' Schenker argued. 'The company has a fine safety record. We should use it.' He stood up. Those who'd been sitting quickly followed suit. There was a general air of expectancy. The agency were wondering if they'd got the account.

He made for the door. 'Oh, and the teaser,' he said. *'Silveron. It's the greatest yet. It covers almost everything.* That should do it, don't you think?' He flashed a quick smile to demonstrate that, given sufficient grounds for benevolence, he was capable of showing approval, and sped from the room with Cramm at his heels.

Back in the limo Schenker sat staring silently out of the smoked-glass windows. As they neared Wall Street and their next appointment, he said abruptly: 'Those rumours about the Aurora plant, Cramm. They could really hurt us.'

Cramm nodded.

'They have to be stopped.'

Dublensky sat at the kitchen table and drank his after-breakfast coffee. Under the new routine he allowed himself no more than ten minutes for this indulgence before getting into the den and starting work. But today he let the time spin out a bit, not only because it made a change, but because, for all his self-discipline, a minute here or there wasn't actually going to make any difference. Also there was the matter of the mail. He had checked the box but it still hadn't arrived, and he knew he wouldn't be able to settle down to anything else until it did.

He could never get used to being home at this time of day, just as he couldn't accustom himself to the quiet of an empty house. It seemed strange that Anne and Tad should hurry out of the door each morning, leaving him to all this silence. Worse though was the bald unavoidable fact that he had nothing to keep him occupied. In the weeks since the Allentown Chemical Company had dispensed with his services he'd fixed the guttering, the kitchen faucet and Tad's bicycle, none of which had taken more than an hour or two even when he'd spun them out. The other household jobs, like painting the exterior and rehanging the damaged garage door, required money, thus relegating themselves to indefinite postponement.

When his ten-plus minutes were up he washed his cup, dried it carefully, put it away, and went out to the mail box. It was still empty. Returning to the den he started his fifth perusal of the latest issue of *Practical Scientist*. In the first few days of his unemployment he'd applied for nothing but the cream of jobs, but then, as the doubts began their relentless siege on his confidence, he'd started to glance over a few of the lesser jobs, positions he would not normally have considered. Even then it wasn't until he failed two interviews in succession that he began to write a second wave of applications.

The first turn-down hadn't surprised him too much – the job really wasn't his bag – but the second had been a definite surprise. In fact, it would be more accurate to describe it as one helluva jolt. He'd had every reason to think he was in with a good chance: the CV–job specification fit had been excellent, the interview had gone well, he'd established an immediate empathy with the chief executive, but when the answer finally came it had been a flat inexplicable no.

Anne took the news with narrowed lips, knowing eyes and a dark expression. For the first time in his marriage Dublensky avoided discussion with his wife, not only because he had a good idea of what she was going to say but because he wasn't sure he was ready to hear it. The hiatus left him isolated and dejected, yet oddly determined, and when he won an interview with a small corporation in Maryland, he made the decision not to tell Anne until he had the result. He wanted to surprise her. The salary was significantly lower than he'd been used to and he was most definitely overqualified, but it was a position which would allow him to sink into a peaceful kind of obscurity.

The mail man finally appeared, making his way fitfully up the street, and Dublensky ambled down the path to meet him.

There were two letters for him; the one from the Maryland corporation lay on top. He did not open it immediately, but took it into the den and laid it on the desk in front of him. Even then he did not open it immediately. The crisp white envelope seemed charged with all the might and inescapable power of the agrochemical industry. As he reached forward to run his finger under the flap his sense of doom deepened and he realised that, whether from a subconscious need to prepare himself or a sudden faith in his own instincts, he had already accepted the worst.

The realisation did not stop his heart from taking a sharp turn as he pulled the single sheet from the envelope.

Position filled.

'They're nailing you,' Anne said as they lay in bed that night.

'Honey, how could they?' he argued despite himself. 'I mean, this last company, they're only a small outfit. They've no contacts with Morton-Kreiger.'

'Oh no? The references, what about the references? Don't tell me these corporations don't follow them up. Don Reedy may have said some okay things on paper – though they were no more than *okay*, were they? I mean, just *adequate* – but what does he actually say when they call him, huh? Don't tell me a quiet word doesn't get whispered in their ears. You know – Dublensky's a good man but *difficult*. Competent, sure, but slow. I mean, they wouldn't have to say much, would they? They wouldn't have to call you totally incompetent.'

'But why would they bother?' he asked, knowing the answer perfectly well but wanting to hear her say it.

'I'll tell you why,' she said. 'To squeeze you out. To make sure you don't get any kind of position again. To make people think you *are* incompetent. So that if you decide to spill the beans, they can say, well, he's just pissed off, isn't he? Got promoted beyond his abilities. Can't accept his own limitations. Disgruntled employee out for revenge. Who's the world going to believe then?' After a minute or two she added harshly: 'You should have sent that dossier to EarthForce straight away.'

'But Burt's already sent his medical notes to the EPA and EarthForce, for God's sake. And EarthForce are pressuring the EPA.'

'Burt's just a local physician. It's only his opinion. It's not the same.' She clicked her tongue and repeated: 'You should have sent your dossier.'

'But what would it add?'

'Everything. The workers' testimonials. The evidence about safety procedures.'

'But they can get the testimonials direct.'

'And the safety procedures? Since when will they be able to get that from another source?'

'It doesn't prove a lot . . .'

She sighed impatiently. '*God* – really, John! Of course it proves a lot. If Morton-Kreiger are forced to explain away this sickness, they may try to nail it on lax production-line procedures. While you – *you* – know damn well that the procedures were totally okay. Of *course* it proves something.'

'I don't know.'

Anne gave a small grunt of derision and rolled away, turning her back on him, filling the space with one of her expressive silences.

Dublensky thought with a tremor of guilt of the other file, the one that Anne wasn't even aware of, that contained some of the Silveron toxicology results, and the fire which it would bring down on their heads if it were ever published. He had hoped never to have to use it; he hadn't been ready to face those sorts of consequences.

'I could still send them a dossier,' he offered.

'Oh, yeah? *Now?*' Anne retorted. 'And confirm what Morton-Kreiger are going to say about you? That you're just doing it because you're pissed off? That it's simply a case of sour grapes because you can't get another job? That would look great. I told you, I told you right at the beginning, you should have sent it straight away.'

'I thought I'd never get a job if I did.'

'Well, you're not getting a job anyway, so what's the difference? Jesus, John, what was it all for, if it wasn't to get this thing out into the open?'

Over the next days a wretchedness clung to Dublensky. Though Anne said no more, her words prowled reproachfully around his mind, nibbling at his conscience.

Even as he sat at the foot of Tad's bed in the evening, reading aloud from *Kidnapped*, he thought about what she had said. He managed the trick of reading one thing and thinking quite another until he came to some Scots dialect and had to pause and concentrate. His accent slipped from what may have been Irish to what sounded like Italian. Even if it had by some miracle bordered on Scots, he had no means of knowing. He glanced over his spectacles to find Tad hiding his laughter behind the bed covers.

'Okay,' Dublensky said with good humour. 'You try it.'

'No, Dad, you're great. Really. Go on, *please*.' A last giggle, then a straight face.

Dublensky found that he was staring unseeing at the page. He blinked himself back to reality. 'You enjoying this?' he asked doubtfully.

'Sure. It's good.'

'It is?' Dublensky realised he had taken in nothing of the last ten minutes' reading.

Grasping the situation, Tad explained: 'Davie Balfour and Alan Breck have escaped the redcoats and are making for Ben Alder and the Pass of – '

'Who's Ben Alder?'

'Not who – *what*. It's a mountain.'

'Oh. And it's important they reach it?'

'It's a place on their escape route.'

Dublensky frowned. 'I thought Alan Breck was the bad guy.'

Tad gave the sort of impatient sigh that children reserve for parents who are being particularly dumb. 'No, Dad. He's one of the good guys.'

'I thought he was involved in that shooting.'

'He was, sort of. But the guy who died was a traitor, siding with the English, so it didn't matter.'

'Didn't matter?'

'No,' Tad replied with exaggerated patience. 'The English are the bad guys, right? The ones who're down on the Scots. Alan Breck's with the Scots, fighting for freedom. Against the English,' he added just in case his father still hadn't got it. 'Anyway,' he said with a certain logic, 'you can tell Alan Breck's a good guy because he gets the good lines.'

'That makes him okay?'

'Definitely.'

'Isn't he a rascal, or whatever they used to call them?'

'Oh, sure. But he has to do what he has to do, right? And if that includes a few bad things – well, it's okay, isn't it, when he's got right on his side.'

Dublensky nodded slowly. 'I guess so.' And with that he lost whatever concentration he might have had, and put the book away.

The next day he sent a digest of the Aurora dossier to EarthForce. He did it cautiously – that is, anonymously and via his brother in New York, so it wouldn't have an Allentown postmark. He enclosed a covering note, briefly explaining the significance of the information, and would have left it totally unsigned except for a nagging reluctance to cut himself totally off from the prospective custodians of this, his precious and costly information. At the very least he wanted to be able to check that they'd received and understood it and, to do that, he needed a means of identifying himself. Feeling like a character out of a spy movie, he thought up a name and typed it at the bottom of the page. He chose the name Kalisz, after the city in Poland where his mother was born, then almost immediately thought better of it. It was pretty stupid to use a place name with which he had a connection, however tenuous. He briefly considered using an anagram of Tad and Anne's names, but rejected that for the same reason. Thinking of Tad, the answer suddenly came to him and he went upstairs to find the copy of *Kidnapped*.

An eighteenth-century rascal courtesy of Robert Louis Stevenson; you couldn't find a more remote connection than that. He reprinted the covering letter and signed it Alan Breck.

At the last moment, infused with a sudden gust of courage that had him shivering somewhere between exhilaration and fear, he added a postscript. *There is also something seriously wrong with the original toxicology data. Some of it was faked. I have the evidence.*

He hurried to the post before he could change his mind. Then he went and sat in the yard in the sunshine, and, closing his eyes very tight, let the light fall on his face.

SIXTEEN

'You're sure this is it?' Daisy asked, surveying the wide expanse of rough grass.

Campbell leant an arm on the gate. 'Aye,' he grunted laconically. 'It's the place.'

The field seemed large enough and reasonably flat if you ignored the slight rise in the centre which hid the far right-hand boundary. But the ground was neither smooth nor firm. There was a quagmire fanning out from the gate, and, spreading into the distance, a progression of grassy tussocks interspersed with puddles. 'It's rather waterlogged,' she ventured.

'It's dry enough over there.' Campbell gestured towards the centre. 'You could land a jetliner.'

She shot him a glance but it was quite impossible to tell whether he was joking. 'You said there was an access road?'

He pointed towards the left, where a rough road was visible through a ragged boundary hedge. Some way up there was a wide opening in the hedge which led to what looked like a parking area just inside the field. Tucked in beside the hedge was a Portakabin, grey and weather-beaten, so that it blended perfectly with the landscape.

'Shall we get on then?' she said, aware that the morning was slipping away and that she would have to catch the four o'clock train if she was going to get back to London that evening. Officially – which meant for Alan's benefit – she wasn't here at all, but working flat out on a fund-raising campaign proposal due for presentation to Catch's executive committee the day after tomorrow. And she had been working on it, very hard, until Campbell's call had caused her to drop everything and jump on the night sleeper.

Campbell's unearthing of the airfield had sounded so very promising – an airfield would surely be thick with information on planes and flying companies – but now as she climbed into Campbell's battered Ford she reflected on what he had brought her hurrying all this way to see. A long-abandoned airstrip devoid of people and information. A possible interview with the field's owner who, since he wasn't expecting them, might well slam the door in their faces.

She had only herself to blame; too impulsive by half, too easily persuaded, too optimistic. Wasn't that what Alan was always telling her?

Campbell negotiated the car backwards onto the narrow lane, and they started off again. The inside of the car was like a fridge and, still frail from a heavy cold, she leant forward and twiddled with the heating controls.

'Too warm for you?' Campbell asked, rapidly winding his window down.

She stared at him.

'Not *cold*?'

'Well – a little.'

He grunted and, attacking the window again, closed it, though not, she noticed right to the top.

'You work out of doors, do you?' she asked, blowing her nose.

'Aye.'

'Forestry?'

'Fisheries.'

'A fisherman?'

'No.'

She wondered if this terseness was habitual.

'What then?' she persevered.

'Work on a salmon farm. Top of the loch.'

'Ah. A large farm? Successful?'

'Does well enough. But the fish . . .' He shook his head briefly. 'They dinna' compare.'

'To – ?'

'Och, the wild fish.'

They came round a bend and saw an open gateway and a sign for Auldhame Farm. If the name Auldhame conjured up a picture of a quaint dwelling with whitewashed walls and

250

dormer windows, the impression was soon dispelled by the austere greystone house that came into view as they turned in through the gate. The front yard was muddy and rutted with tractor tracks. In a decrepit outbuilding with a tattered metal roof a number of vehicles were rusting quietly. As the car came to a halt, a black mongrel raced from the outbuilding and, flinging itself to the limits of its chain, snarled and snapped at the empty air.

'Friendly place,' Daisy remarked. Picking her way through the mud, she followed Campbell to the grey-painted front door. Campbell rapped vigorously. The dog kept up its frenetic baying and from an open-sided barn on the far side of the yard, beyond a metal-bar fence, a morose-looking cow gave a mournful bellow. The front door remained unanswered.

'No one home,' Campbell remarked unnecessarily. 'We could try again in a wee while. The man'll likely be in for his dinner.'

They climbed into the car and started back along the narrow lane.

'Could take a look at that cabin,' Campbell suggested.

Daisy wished they could find something a little warmer to do. She could feel her throat swelling up and a small thread of pain worming its way through her sinus.

'You wouldn't close the window, would you?' she asked.

Reaching for the winder, Campbell gave a short grunt of amazement.

'I'm soft,' Daisy said. 'I admit everything.'

'Aye, you'd never last up here, that's for certain.'

They came to the access road and turned into it. Reaching the break in the hedge that they had seen from the lane, they drove into the field and onto a large concrete apron sprouting rectangles of weeds. Ahead lay the retreating ribbon of the airstrip, an avenue of smoother grass. On the edge of the apron and roughly three yards out from the hedge was the Portakabin. To one side, a clutter of bricks, wood, chipboard and assorted debris in various stages of decomposition lay in an untidy heap. A couple of oil drums sat under the hedge, a rusting storage tank stood on stilts close to the road and, at the far end of the cabin and partly hidden by it, there was a small wooden hut.

A blustery wind tore across the field, rippling the flattened

251

grass like a fan. A cable rapped a dull tattoo against the side of the storage tank. Pulling up her scarf Daisy went round the Portakabin to investigate the small hut at the far end. Under a leaking roof was a filthy chemical toilet, its seat missing.

The Portakabin was grey and rectangular, about eighteen feet by eight, and raised on breeze blocks at each corner. There were windows in each side and a door reached by three rickety steps. High on the side facing the apron was a pale rectangle of brighter paint where a board or sign had once been. A telephone cable emerged from a hole near the top of one wall, led up to a post and looped off across country in the direction of the farmhouse.

Campbell was trying the door, rattling the handle noisily, apparently without success. Daisy, finding an empty oil drum, rolled it across to the side of the cabin and, righting it, perched herself precariously on the top and took a look through one of the windows. There was not a great deal to see. A bare metal table, a couple of fixed cupboards, a sink unit. There was something on the floor though, and she raised herself on tiptoe to see. Papers, a couple of sheets, lying under the desk close against the wall.

Climbing down, she went round to the steps again to find Campbell bent over the door lock. Ignoring her, he straightened and took a long look around him, taking in the field and the perimeter roads with a single sweep, then listening hard for good measure. The next moment his hand slid into his pocket to emerge with a metal bar flattened off at one end: which, as Daisy didn't need telling, was a jemmy. She was on the point of objecting but something held her back, and she realised that she was rather fascinated by this blatant display of criminal accomplishment and decidedly curious to see the outcome.

Campbell had the jemmy into the doorframe and was levering it forward when he stiffened suddenly and shot a look over his shoulder. The distant staccato of a tractor engine came floating across the field. The tractor must have been coming upwind because it was already quite close, spinning along the lane at a sharp lick, the cab and driver riding high above the hedge, heading in the direction of the farmhouse.

Their presence hadn't gone unnoticed. The white oval of the driver's face turned towards them several times. Then the tractor slowed and, turning abruptly into the access road, came thundering towards them. Campbell came down the cabin steps and stood at Daisy's side. She glanced down and noticed that the jemmy had vanished from his hand.

The tractor came hurtling onto the apron, narrowly missing Campbell's car, and ground to a halt beside them. The driver was a gaunt man with a cadaverous weather-beaten face and a sullen expression. He barked: 'Yer business?'

Daisy stepped forward and, raising her voice over the rattle of the tractor's engine, answered politely: 'We were looking for the people who used to operate from here. The flying company.'

A long pause. 'No flyers here.'

'Are you the owner?'

Another extended pause. 'The farmer.'

'Well, perhaps you could help,' Daisy continued unabashed. 'We're trying to find this flying company. You wouldn't have an address for them, would you?'

An almost imperceptible shake of the head. 'No flyers here.'

'But there was – were – a short while back?'

No response at all. His mouth narrowed into a hard uneven line.

Daisy maintained a pleasant expression. 'We were told they flew regularly from here. Some time last summer.'

'Aye, an' they're away, so y've nothin' tae find oot, have ye?'

She was aware that Campbell was moving, that he was approaching her elbow. She saw the farmer's eyes lock on to him and fire up defensively.

'We just want to locate them,' Daisy said quickly, as much to forestall Campbell as anything else.

'An' why would that be?' the farmer demanded aggressively.

'To hire them,' she said off the top of her head. 'We've got some spraying work.'

He gave her a scathing look. Perhaps he was unconvinced by the idea of Daisy farming, and one couldn't really blame him. 'Recommended, were they?'

She shrugged. 'We heard about them.'

'From a faermer, was it?' He was beating her into a corner, and they both knew it.

Before she had time to think the idea through, she said: 'From Willis Bain.'

'Willis Bain, eh?' A gleam sparked into the sharp face. 'They knew the flyers, eh, but couldna' tell ye the name?'

Daisy thought: I fell straight into that one.

Campbell was agitating his feet, bracing himself for what she suspected would be some ill-chosen words.

Daisy threw in rapidly: 'The man I spoke to couldn't remember the name, only the place.'

The eyes narrowed, and he jerked his head in the direction of the road. Just in case they hadn't got the message, he snapped: 'Ye'll be off.'

Campbell was about to argue, but Daisy pulled at his sleeve and wheeled him firmly towards the car.

As they drove down the access road the tractor roared up behind them, its lights blazing, and hugged their bumper. 'Charming character,' Daisy remarked.

Campbell didn't reply. He was chewing his lip, though whether with fury or the effort of deep thought it was impossible to tell.

They turned into the lane and headed back towards the main road. Daisy watched the tractor stop at the junction. It was still there when she lost sight of it round the next bend. 'He knew all about it, didn't he?' she said disconsolately, blowing her nose. 'But he sure wasn't about to tell.'

'I'd say so, aye.'

'But, look, what about the local village?' she said, trying to salvage something. 'Wouldn't it be worth asking around?' She couldn't help thinking of the hostelries too, and the warmth a brandy would put into her stomach.

'I asked a time back,' Campbell said, rousing himself. 'Nothin'.'

'Not worth trying again?'

'Mebbe, but it'll be dark by six.'

The logic escaped her. 'Dark?' she echoed.

He shot her a conspiratorial look. 'The cabin there.'

Even then it took her a moment to understand. 'No,' she said firmly as soon as she had got his drift. 'Absolutely not.'

'Be in and out in no time.'

'Absolutely not. What about our friend there? No. Really, Campbell, it's out of the question.'

Daisy held the torch while Campbell slid the jemmy between the door and the frame. After a moment he gave a grunt of exertion, there was the sound of grinding metal and the door swung open.

Daisy directed the torch-beam while Campbell went through the cupboards. She had to admit that they made a good team, working over each shelf systematically like a couple of seasoned villains. Their professionalism had extended to leaving the car by the main road in the pitch dark and tramping half a mile across sodden fields.

The cupboards themselves were disappointing. Crumpled chocolate wrappers – mainly Mars Bars – abandoned cigarette packets, paper clips and plenty of dust. Under the sink was an old telephone directory and the last few sheets of a jotter pad which Daisy pocketed in case there was an impression of the last message, like the fatal clues left by culprits in detective stories. The papers she had seen from the window, lying on the floor under the table, were blank.

They combed the crevices behind the fittings, in case they had missed something, but whoever had cleaned the place out had done a fairly good job.

There was a telephone socket, but no telephone and, of course, no telephone number.

They paused. Daisy didn't have to check with Campbell to know that he too had run out of ideas.

They left. Campbell pulled the door to and, using the jemmy, levered the doorlock back into its socket in the aluminium frame, so that to a casual observer the door would look more or less untouched. Close to, the deep dents and scratches around the lock wouldn't fool anyone, and certainly not the tenant farmer.

Daisy flicked the torch-beam across the air space under the cabin. Around the edge of the cabin a fringe of tall weeds reached almost to its base while in the centre a scattering of soft drink cans and unidentifiable metal sent back gleams of silver.

Campbell called her over to the rubbish dump, which he proceeded to pull apart, undaunted by even the heaviest items which he chucked to one side as if they were paper-light. The torch-beam revealed chipboard, formica, breeze blocks, bricks, lumps of concrete, earth and weeds.

They both spotted the red lettering at the same time, buried towards the back of the pile. The style and finish of the lettering was less than professional and the white background paint was peeling off the board in small blisters, but it was a sign all right. Perhaps if Campbell hadn't been lobbing breeze blocks noisily into the hedge, perhaps if she hadn't been humming with premature excitement, then they might have heard the engine noise a bit sooner.

As it was, the vehicle was already out of the lane and into the access road by the time they froze, mesmerised by the approaching lights like a couple of rabbits caught on a vegetable patch.

Daisy was the first to move. Instinctively she turned away from the lights to head down the side of the Portakabin towards the deep shadows at the end. She'd gone only a couple of steps when she looked back and realised that for some inexplicable reason Campbell hadn't moved, that he was bent over the rubbish again, digging at the board with his fingers. She felt a great thump of alarm.

Running back, she grabbed at his sleeve. 'Quick, for God's sake!'

But the big man continued to burrow at the board; he was immovable.

'For God's sake!' she cried.

She saw everything in a succession of frozen images, like a film being run through a projector frame by frame. She saw Campbell hunched over the dump, she saw the car beams back-lighting the hedge, throwing the tracery of branches into lacelike relief, and she saw herself rooted to the spot, like an idiot who couldn't decide which way to run. Yet she knew perfectly well which way to run; it was leaving Campbell that she couldn't bring herself to do, not until the immovable moron got the message. She yelled at him, and kept yelling.

The vehicle had almost reached the break in the hedge. At any second it would turn onto the apron and flood them with light. She felt a terrible rage as Campbell, moving with all the speed of a ponderous animal, finally pulled the board out of the dirt and began to move. Free at last, she sprinted off down the alley between the cabin and the hedge. Half way along she realised she wasn't going to make the end in time: the headlights were sweeping round, and fast. She took a dive onto the concrete. It was a trick she'd never had much reason to try before, and her chin ground into the concrete with an ugly grating sensation.

The lights flooded over her. She choked for air; something

sharp and hard was digging into her ribs. But she kept still, reasonably confident that she'd got down in time, which was more than could be said for Campbell who at this very moment was probably giving the driver a floodlit view of his backside. The lights had swung round and faded. She raised her head and craned round.

No sign of Campbell; the alley was empty.

Under the belly of the Portakabin she could see the head-lights shining out over the airstrip. The engine note slowed, and stopped. She twisted her head up again, but there was no doubt: Campbell had completely disappeared.

There was a pause, then the click of a car door opening. Heavy feet sounded on the concrete, walked a distance then stopped. The feet scrunched intermittently as their owner moved and stopped and moved again.

There was a long silence, then through the space under-neath the cabin, she saw a torch-beam flash on and weave its way over the grass. The beam moved steadily around the edge of the cabin, coming towards the alleyway where she lay. Pushing herself up on her forearms she prepared to crawl under the cabin, but just then the torch-beam swung round and went back the other way, towards the steps.

After what seemed a long time the beam danced back towards the vehicle, the footsteps retreated, the car door slammed, the engine coughed into life and the car reversed into the road and drove away.

Daisy sank her head on to the concrete, took several deep breaths and picked herself off the sharp metal object that had been grinding into her ribs. She felt weak. One thing was absolutely sure: she wasn't cut out for a life of crime.

She rubbed her chin, which felt sore, and brushed ineffec-tually at the grit clinging to her hands and face. Footsteps approached and she looked up to find the dark outline of Campbell standing over her.

'Christ, Campbell, you gave me bloody heart failure!' she declared with feeling.

He didn't reply, but demanded: 'The torch.'

'Why the hell didn't you move! What the hell were you doing!' The torch wasn't in her hand, nor her pocket. She scrabbled about on the ground until she found it some distance ahead of where she'd come down. She fiddled with the switch, but it didn't work.

Campbell took it from her and gave it an almighty thump. It sprang into life. Nothing, apparently, failed to yield to his methods.

'Where the hell did you get to?'

'In the hedge there,' he replied. 'An' when he was past, I went round the road side.'

'Jesus . . . Jesus.' She was still shaking, barely capable of pointing the torch while Campbell led the way back to the rubbish dump. He picked the sign out of the hedge.

It had been quite a large sign, but now half of it was missing. The wrong half. It read: *lying Systems Ltd*.

'Terrific,' Daisy murmured.

She held the light while Campbell searched the rubbish heap for another ten minutes, but there was no more white board, no more red lettering. It was beginning to rain, a thin drizzle which threatened heavier things. She felt deathly cold.

'The village,' Daisy said wearily, thinking of the hot meal and warm brandy they'd had earlier and how she'd like to repeat it, thinking too of the long-departed afternoon train and the overnight sleeper that she really mustn't miss. 'Let's get back to the village.'

The village, two miles away, consisted of a string of low houses straddling a main road. Having tried the larger of the two hotels at midday, they now went to the smaller one, a dreary hostelry with frosted windows, dim yellow lighting, and the sickly-sweet stench of stale beer. The decor was a nicotine-stained sepia, the furnishings a uniform dark brown. Daisy spent ten minutes in the ladies sneezing, coughing and dabbing the blood from the graze on her chin before joining Campbell at the bar and ordering a brandy. She certainly felt she had deserved it. Campbell obviously felt in a deserving mood too, because he had ordered a double Scotch.

The barman was a vast man with a waistline that had defeated the local outfitters. His name was Jock and he tried very hard to help. 'A flyin' company, ye say?' He kept repeating it, as if this might be enough to jog his memory. 'Cannae say I recall a flyin' company. We had a construction company, right enough. Here a couple of months, they was.' He looked hopeful, as if the construction company might prove an acceptable alternative.

The bar began to fill up. The customers had the sly laconic air of regulars. After exchanging monosyllabic greetings they stood silently at the bar waiting for Jock to pull their brew before slapping coins onto the counter and shuffling off to their tables. When Jock questioned them about the flying outfit they looked wary, then thoughtful, then shook their heads.

The atmosphere in the bar became heavy with smoke. Daisy felt her lungs turn raw.

A girl appeared behind the bar. She was about twenty, so far as it was possible to tell beneath the spiky hair and heavy eye makeup. The hair, which came low over her eyes, and the copious use of the kohl gave her the look of a black-eyed terrier.

Jock proudly: 'Ma daughter, Morag.'

Morag's mouth twitched grudgingly into what might have been a smile or a contemptuous pout.

'They're lookin' for an aero company,' Jock explained. 'Based on Auldhame Farm some time back.'

She slid Daisy a look of open suspicion. So much for the freemasonry of women.

Daisy tried to look friendly. 'They used to go spraying,' she said. 'Forests and that sort of thing. Over to the west. There must have been a mechanic. And a pilot. We thought they might have come in here from time to time.'

A sulky shrug and a hand pushed into the spiky mane.

'You've never heard anything about them then?'

Morag picked up a glass and polished it desultorily.

'I thought you'd know everything that went on around here.'

Morage flung her a look of mortal insult. 'I'm no tattler!'

'No, of course not,' Daisy said hastily. 'I just thought you'd have more idea. Than most people, I mean.' She flicked a glance in the direction of the male drinkers.

Morage rolled her eyes and said with feeling: 'Nothin' gets *their* noses oot of their beer, no' the roof fallin' in, no' nothin'.' She stalked up to the far end of the bar and slid a glass onto a shelf. Wandering back, she stopped some way away and looked sulky again, as if to show that she wasn't entirely won over, not by a long chalk. Then, taking her time, she sidled over again and, her back half-turned to Daisy, leant an elbow on the counter.

'There's a person might know,' she said in a bored voice, examining the far side of the room.

'Oh?'

'A friend a' mine. Doon Balinteith way.'

'Oh. This friend knew them then?'

Morag fixed Daisy with a wrathful soot-encrusted stare for daring to interrupt. 'Tha's no' what 'a said.'

Daisy looked suitably penitent, but Morag was not one to be hurried, not when every ounce of satisfaction could be squeezed from a waiting game, and it was another ten minutes and a third round of drinks before she deigned to drop a name and an approximate address.

Even then it was almost nine by the time Daisy managed to prise Campbell off his stool and escape into the cool of the night. After the stench and smoke of the bar, the air tasted sweet and fresh. There was a mist; auras of damp hung around the streetlamps.

Daisy led the way to the car. If they hurried to Balinteith and were sharpish with the interview there was still an outside chance of her catching the overnight sleeper.

Balinteith was ten minutes away along the Stirling road. The home of Morag's friend Jeannie Buchanan was easy enough to find. It lay at the end of a quiet cul-de-sac, a bungalow with pebbledash rendering and square windows adorned with arched frilly curtains in peek-a-boo style.

Jeannie Buchanan's father, a polite but monosyllabic man, informed them that his daughter was out for the evening and wouldn't be returning until after eleven.

Daisy hesitated, thinking of the train and all the work still to be done on the presentation charts. But she couldn't leave this now. Jeannie's father was reluctant to let them come back at eleven until Daisy explained that she was a lawyer and had come all the way from London just to interview Jeannie about the flying company operating out of Auldhame Farm.

As they left, Campbell scoffed under his breath: 'Lawyer!' There was a touch of admiration in his tone, and she realised he was congratulating her on being such an accomplished liar.

'True. Sorry.'

His step faltered, and he moved two paces away, as if she had a contagious disease. 'You didna' tell me that,' he said accusingly.

'And you didn't tell me you went in for breaking and entering.'

'That I do not!'

They got into the car. 'Just a hobby then?' she asked.

He seemed quite upset at the idea.

The Balinteith Hotel provided the sort of dinner that is known as substantial in the North, and solid elsewhere.

At first Campbell was uncommunicative, but by the end of the main course he was becoming almost garrulous, a result very possibly of his fifth double Scotch.

They discussed Peasedale and Roper's visit to Adrian and the progress of his new treatment, which mainly consisted of coming off the numerous tranquillisers, antibiotics and anti-depressants that he'd been on for months. It was too soon to know if there was any improvement. Daisy reached in her shoulder bag, a voluminous carpetbag that expanded to take documents, makeup and overnight things, and pulled out a footballing magazine. 'I thought Adrian might like it.'

'You'll not be passing through on Thursday then?' Thursday was two days away.

'No,' she said, surprised. 'Why?'

'For the inquiry.'

'What inquiry's that?'

'Why, into Mrs Mackenzie's death.'

She lowered her cup carefully into its saucer. 'But why an inquiry?'

'He requested it, so they say.'

'Nick Mackenzie?'

'Aye. Wasna' content with the findin's.'

'You mean there's been an inquiry already?'

'An investigation,' he corrected her. 'By the proc— proc – ' He pursed his lips and took another shot. 'Pro*cu*rator fiscal. An investigation, aye. Just that. No more.'

Daisy remembered that not only were there no such things as inquests in Scotland but that investigations into deaths were held informally and in private, and that their findings were not generally made public.

'I went before him, the proc'ator fiscal,' Campbell said. 'I went an' told him . . . About findin' her. About breathin' into her mouth. About trying to re-vive her. He asked if she felt cold . . .' His voice had got maudlin, his eyes glistened with sudden moisture. 'I told him . . . I said there was nothin' that could have been done.'

'And Nick Mackenzie asked for a public inquiry?'

'Aye.'

'He must be here then? In Scotland.'

'He wasna' just two days back. But by now – mebbe so.'

While Campbell ploughed through a large steamed pudding she thought about Nick Mackenzie being back at Glen Ashard, and wondered how she could manage to get away on Thursday, when that was the day of the presentation to the Catch executive committee. She also thought about Simon, and wondered why he hadn't told her about the inquiry when he must surely have known about it.

Jeannie Buchanan finally got home shortly before eleven thirty. She was a plump pale-faced girl with short cropped hair and large anxious eyes which grew even more circular at the sight of the waiting delegation. But if Jeannie was nervous, it didn't obstruct her memory.

'Aye, I worked there at the airfield,' she said immediately in a soft unobtrusive voice.

'And the name of the flying company, what was it?' Daisy asked.

'Acorn Flying Systems.'

Daisy felt a small chime of satisfaction. 'And where are they based now?'

'Och, nowhere,' came the mouselike voice. 'They . . . stopped.'

'Stopped?'

Jeannie glanced at her father, as if for corroboration. 'Closed down. I think they had some trouble with the bank. In fact . . .' She looked apologetic for mentioning it. 'They still owe me three weeks' wages.'

'When was this? That they ceased trading?'

'Och, it must be September last.'

So much for the easy run. 'What about the owners?' Daisy asked gently. 'The directors and so on – do you have any names?'

'There was a Mr Keen. He was the managing director. I only saw him twice – once when he took me on, and another time when he came out to the airfield and helped us out when we were busy. Then there was Davie, the mechanic. He came from Glasgow. And Reggie, he helped with the navigation system. And of course there was Mr Duggan.'

'Mr Duggan?'

'The pilot.'

Daisy absorbed this for a moment. 'The director, Mr Keen, where did he come from, do you know?'

'The company had an address somewhere in Glasgow, but it wasn't his personal address, at least I don't think so. I tried writing to Mr Keen when the problem with the bank came up but the post office returned my letter. There was a phone number, a Glasgow number. I'd use it to phone Mr Keen when there were any problems. That was maybe two or three times a week. But when I last tried, the telephone people said the line had been disconnected.'

'Have you still got the number?'

Her face, which reflected her emotions like a mirror, immediately fell. 'I'm not sure I still have it. I'd have to look and see.'

'What about wages, paperwork, how was that arranged?'

'With the local branch of the bank. Or through the post from Glasgow.'

'What about other things – supplies – I don't know, whatever planes need?'

'The fuel, that arrived by tanker. It was arranged from Glasgow.'

'And the spray – the chemicals?'

'Sometimes Davie went off to the wholesalers. But most times it was delivered.'

'Who delivered it?'

'That would be Willis Bain,' she said without hesitation. 'Most of our work came from them. They're forest managers.'

'And the chemical used, what was it?'

She wet her lips and cast another glance at her father. 'Och, I'm not sure. There were two . . . They had such names. Long . . . I can't recall.'

'You don't remember a bit of a name?' There must have been a hint of reproach in her tone because Jeannie withdrew slightly. 'I only signed the receipts,' she said defensively. 'I didn't order the chemicals. That was done from Glasgow.'

'Of course,' Daisy said placatingly. 'Was there one that sounded like fenitrothion?'

'Mebbe . . . But . . .' Looking unhappy, she finished in a rush. 'I really couldn't say for sure.'

Daisy sat back. It had perhaps been too much to hope for. Fastening a smile over her disappointment, she asked: 'Duggan, the pilot – what was his full name?'

'Peter. Peter Duggan.'

'And where did he come from?'

'Och, he was from England.' She made it sound like Mars.

'Do you have his address?'

'Och no.' From the way she said it she wouldn't have wanted it even if he'd given it to her.

'You don't even remember the town?'

She was adamant: no.

'And Davie, the mechanic. Was he local?'

'No. He came from up Inverness way.'

'Have you an address?'

She shook her head. 'He said he was going to work abroad. The Middle East, I believe.'

'What was his second name?'

'Robertson.'

It might be possible to trace him, though God only knew how many Robertsons there were in and around Inverness. Daisy tried another tack. 'Acorn Flying Systems – what other work did it do?'

She shook her head. 'None that I know of. Just the spraying – we never did anything but the spraying. The trees, they had a bad disease, the beauty moth it was. We had plenty of work last summer, more than we could handle.'

'Do you remember any jobs up by Loch Fyne?'

She thought hard. 'There were a few. Around and about. But I'm not sure that I remember exactly . . .'

'Up by Inveraray way.'

She shrugged. 'I used to type the schedule and the job sheets and the notifications – but there were so many . . .'

'The notifications?'

'Notices to tell the police, the health and safety office, and the people on the adjoining land.'

'These were letters? Sent out by post?'

'Aye.' She dropped her eyes and started picking at the arm of her chair.

'And they were sent out for every job, Jeannie? To every neighbour?'

She didn't answer at first. When she finally spoke her voice was little more than a whisper. 'Aye.' She had a thread out of the fabric now, and was pulling at it.

Daisy wasn't sure what she'd touched on but it was something Jeannie wasn't inclined to talk about.

Jeannie's father stood up and made a remark about how late it was.

Daisy looked questioningly at Jeannie, hoping she'd elaborate, but she went on staring intently at the thread, weaving it back and forth between her fingers.

Campbell asked: 'This pilot fella, where did he board round here?'

Jeannie looked up; this was an easier one. 'Och, at Mrs Donald's,' she said as if everyone must know Mrs Donald. 'For a while, that is. Then he moved on to Mrs McKay's. Better breakfasts, he said.'

'These places, they're here in Balinteith?' Daisy asked.

'Aye,' she said.

Daisy tried some more questions about the flying schedules, but at the first mention of job sheets, Jeannie was fiddling at the chair arm again, and Daisy retreated.

As they got up to leave, Jeannie disappeared and returned a minute later with the address and defunct phone number of Acorn Flying Systems. 'There,' she said, handing it to Daisy with the formality of an offering.

It was quarter past midnight by the time Daisy drove Campbell's car out of Balinteith, heading west. Having seen the effect Campbell's last whisky had had on him and overcome by a strong desire to live, she had insisted on driving. The Ford was not the easiest car she'd ever tackled. The driver's seat was so low, battered into concavity by Campbell's bulk, that before she could see over the bonnet she had to prop herself up on top of her much-folded jacket and a smelly old fishing bag that Campbell dug out of the boot. The steering seemed only remotely connected to the front wheels, so there was a small but heart-stopping delay before the car responded to the turns.

'I was thinking,' Daisy said when she'd finally got the hang of it. 'That plane must have got serviced somewhere. At an airport, with proper mechanics. If we asked around we might find someone who knows this Keen person.'

There was no reply. She glanced across. Campbell had fallen asleep, his head back, his mouth open wide as if awaiting major tooth extraction. Daisy fiddled with the heating controls and was rewarded with a small but satisfying whisper of hot air.

The road wasn't bad by rural standards: not straight, but

not too bendy either, and with almost no traffic she was able to keep up a good speed all the way to Loch Lomond. Here the road divided: south to Glasgow and the transport network, or west and north to Loch Fyne and Campbell's home. Glasgow was only half an hour away, while Loch Fyne was a good hour over the mountains. South was the obvious choice. If she stayed the night in Glasgow, she could take the early shuttle and still get to the office by morning. There'd still be difficulties, of course. Quite apart from having to justify the wild expenditure on hotels and planes – Catch personnel were meant to stay with friends and travel on cut-price rail tickets – she'd be landing Campbell with a long night-drive in an illegal state of inebriation.

If she took Campbell straight back to Loch Fyne now and stayed somewhere up there, on the other hand, she could interview the pilot's landladies in the morning. But then there'd be absolutely no chance of getting to the office in time to prepare the charts for Thursday. Given enough notice there was no reason why Alan couldn't have done the charts himself, of course. Maybe still could . . .

She had been stopped at the junction for some moments. Now a car was approaching from behind.

With a sigh of dread but also an indefinable clutch of excitement, she turned west onto the Loch Fyne road.

The low cloud that had darkened the sky all day had lifted. On the drive along the west bank of Loch Lomond first one star then another began to gleam through the layers of darkness. By the time she had urged the car up the long pass of Glen Croe to the summit at Rest And Be Thankful the mountains were etched black against a brilliant sky.

They reached Inveraray at one thirty. Campbell, who responded to her prodding with a massive groan, eventually directed her to a white-fronted hotel in the main street. It was ten minutes before the proprietor answered, looking far from pleased, and his displeasure was not mollified by the sight of Campbell, whom he seemed to know well.

Daisy took the key but did not go up to the room. Her brain was suddenly alive, almost feverish; she knew she wouldn't sleep.

She asked for a street-door key, and went out to the car with Campbell. He took some persuading to let her drop him off and keep the car.

'There's nothin' to see, not in the dark,' he grunted, adding superfluously: 'Be light by mornin'.'

'I'll come and pick you up first thing.'

'Is it Glen Ashard you wish to see?'

She gave a shrug, not quite sure of the answer herself.

'I can take you there, you know, right up behind the house. But best wait till day.'

'No. It's not that.' She couldn't explain.

'You could take away some earth, like you did for Adrian. See what it contains.'

'Yes, I know.' She pushed the gear in and moved off.

Campbell sighed, accepting defeat.

'I'll get the car back to you first thing,' Daisy repeated.

'Och no, no,' he declared. 'Keep it at the hotel here. I'll get a ride in, fine.'

His home was a mile or two out of town to the north, on a glen road that snaked up into the high lands. It was a squat cottage sitting on the ledge of a windswept hillside. She had no idea what Campbell's domestic arrangements were, but she rather assumed he lived alone.

As soon as she'd dropped him she headed back towards the town and, rejoining the main road, turned west. The houses thinned to a straggle then ceased altogether as the road ran close by the side of the loch. Though the stars shone as brilliantly as ever, the waters were very dark and it was impossible to see where the loch ended and the hills began.

Soon the road turned away from the water, deflected by high ground, and passed between fields and plantations of conifers. Occasionally there was the twinkle of a light in the distance and once a car came speeding past in the opposite direction, but for the most part the land was as dark as the night.

She briefly thought of turning back, but even as she considered it she knew she wouldn't. It couldn't be far away.

She passed one set of gates on a bend and reversed back to take a look at the sign, but it was some other house. After a mile or two the road left the loch again, passing through an arid landscape of newly felled forest, and she began to think she must have missed it. But then the road dipped into thickly wooded country again, tunnelling under a canopy of giant overhanging trees, and a wall appeared on the right, the sort of proprietorial wall reserved for parklands and large estates.

The gateposts when they finally appeared were prominent enough – fortified mediaeval-style towers, abutted by two gatekeepers' lodges. There was a conspicuous sign: *Ashard House. Strictly Private*, and tall wrought-iron gates which were firmly shut.

She drove slowly on, hoping for a glimpse of the house, but either the screen of trees was too thick or the place was set too far back, because no lights showed above the wall surrounding the estate.

She slowed down, feeling tired and slightly foolish, and looked for a place to turn. Eventually she came to a break in the wall where it curved in two arcs towards an entrance. She turned in and found herself on a rough track barred by a metal five-bar gate.

A point of light blinked through the undergrowth ahead. Switching off the headlights, she got out and went up to the gate, which was heavily padlocked. She stood for a while, undecided, tempted, drawn.

Feeling conspicuous despite the darkness, she climbed over and crept along the edge of the track.

After fifty yards or so the undergrowth became thinner, the trees more scattered until at last she was able to see the house. It was large with numerous tall uncurtained windows, several wings and a turret or two. She had no trouble in making out the size of the place, the number and shape of the windows: the two pinpricks she'd glimpsed from the road had been a mere sample of what was to come. Ashard House was a blaze of lights.

There was something sad in the sight of the bright house. When she crept away, it was in the certainty that she would stay for the inquiry.

SEVENTEEN

'W'ake up, sport.'

Nick, in depths black and heavy, senses obliterated by sleep, brain obliterated by chemicals legal but plentifully administered, heard the voice at the far end of an echoing tunnel.

'Nick, come on. Wakey-wakey.'

Someone was gripping Nick's shoulder, shaking it gently but relentlessly. Focusing on this sensation he used it to haul himself into the light.

It was Mel. Nick closed his eyes again and began to examine the messages his waking body was sending him. None of them were pleasant.

'It's three,' Mel announced. 'David's arrived. And the lawyer.'

Three. It took him a moment to realise it was afternoon. He felt a moment's resentment for not having been woken earlier, then remembered that it had been ten that morning before he had finally slept.

He muttered: 'I'll be down.' When Mel had gone he swung his feet to the floor and waited for his brain to catch up with his body. A nightmare still racketed round the edges of his mind and it was a moment before he was able to shake himself free of it. The half consciousness between sleep and waking was always the worst, worse even than jerking awake in the night, heart pounding, or lying with no hope of sleep, listening to the wailing of the wind.

He took a shower, dressed and went downstairs unshaven. Mrs Alton was in the kitchen, looking flustered. She had risen to the challenge of preparing ready-to-heat food for all-night rehearsals, but she had not quite adjusted to finding Mel and Joe frying steak and chips at seven in the morning. 'Would you like something?' she asked tentatively.

'Coffee and toast, please, Mrs Alton.'

On his way across the hall he saw the envelope propped against a vase on the side table. It was marked urgent, in large letters. He scooped it up and carried it into the drawing room.

He found David and the lawyer either side of a roaring fire. David was sitting in a wing chair with Mrs Alton's full afternoon tea, complete with silver service, on a table in front of him. He had a scone half-way to his mouth but, on seeing Nick, put it down.

'How are you, Nick?' His expression was a blend of concern and faint alarm, and Nick realised that he was reading the full spectrum of bad news into his unshaven bleary-eyed appearance.

The lawyer rose from the seat opposite. He was a Glasgow solicitor called Bennett, a mousy little man with a mild manner and soft deferential voice which concealed a sharp mind.

'I was wondering if you'd given any more thought to what I suggested?' Bennett said as soon they were sitting down. 'It's rather late in the day but, given the circumstances, I'm sure we would find favourable consideration.'

Nick lit a cigarette and said nothing. He'd become adept at silences.

'The inquiry will be exactly what it says it is,' Bennett continued in patient tones. 'That is, a public enquiry. The press will not miss a moment, Mr Mackenzie, and if there's anything' – he paused to choose his words – 'if there's anything worth reporting – well, they will be bound to use it. It will all be very *exposed*. Very trying for you.' He paused then, getting no response, continued: 'I've been looking into precedents and it is perfectly possible that the Lord Advocate might consider withdrawing his recommendation for an inquiry, even at this late stage, since it was you yourself who pressed for it. I don't think he will take much convincing that, despite everything, it is not after all a matter of public interest and concern.' He looked across to David as if for support. 'Then the whole matter could be left to rest, Mr Mackenzie. In peace, one might say.'

They had been over all this before, Nick thought with

bemusement. Perhaps Bennett hadn't listened properly when they'd first discussed it – when was it? A month ago? Two months? Last week? Time had become strangely elastic and shapeless, until whole images were wiped out or transposed. But he could see this particular scene all right: they had been in this room, the two of them, the fire burning brightly in the cavernous fireplace, Bennett sitting on the settee, Nick where David was now. Nick had explained it to him, carefully, at length. Bennett had argued, Nick had held his ground. In those weeks immediately after the accident he had felt a curious energy, he remembered, an extraordinary clarity of mind which had carried him forward, allowing him to tackle things in the most minute detail; he had even garnered an odd sort of pleasure in getting everything done in the correct and proper manner – in the way Alusha would have approved. Her presence had had form then; a bright living speaking thing. It was different now. Her face was fading. He could no longer see it clearly, could no longer hear her voice.

'It's not as if the inquiry would have gone ahead without ourselves specifically requesting it,' Bennett repeated, giving it one last shot. 'It's not as if the Lord Advocate had recommended it off his own bat, so to speak.' Casting an appraising look at Nick, he gathered himself to approach from another tack. 'What concerns me,' he began carefully, 'is the ambiguities that are bound to creep in, the ones I outlined to you.'

'Ambiguities?'

'Concerning the manner of your wife's illness. The differences of opinion. The uncertainties. Would you not agree that they might be best avoided? They could be very – disturbing for you.'

Nick roused himself to an argument for which he had little enthusiasm. 'But the evidence from the Boston man. There's no ambiguity there.'

Bennett dropped his head briefly over his clasped hands. 'I have to say as I've said before, Mr Mackenzie, that I believe it would be unwise to put too much reliance on Gravely's affidavit. Being an alternative practitioner, his opinion will not be viewed in the same light as an orthodox practitioner's. His views may well be – how shall I say? – put into question. And not being present in person, he won't be able to defend those views. It would be a different matter if we had some other opinion or opinions to back him up. Like those of a toxicologist, for example. Without what one might call hard evidence it is going to be almost impossible to establish our theory.' He broke off as Mrs Alton came into the room and put a tray of coffee and toast beside Nick. 'Of course there's always an adjournment,' he continued when the door had closed again. 'I am not sure whether the Lord Advocate would be persuaded to consider such a thing at this late stage, but I could but try. And given some extra time, then perhaps we could renew our enquiries among the toxicologists . . .'

He left the suggestion hanging hopefully in the air.

Nick drew on his cigarette and fiddled with the unfilled coffee cup at his side. 'No. No . . . I don't want a delay. No delay.'

There was a silence. Bennett clasped his hands more tightly and drew breath. 'The procurator fiscal's finding – is it that which concerns you, Mr Mackenzie? Is it that which you feel must not be allowed to rest?'

Hardly trusting himself to speak, Nick said: 'Well, of course, of *course* it is! What d'you expect me to feel when it's *wrong*! Wrong and dangerous.'

'It's natural that you should be upset, anyone would be. It's always hard to accept something like that . . .'

'She didn't kill herself.' The quietness of his voice did not conceal its tension.

'No, no. I accept that, Mr Mackenzie . . .' Bennett used a kindly, humouring tone. '. . . But since the finding was not published, since the procurator fiscal's finding – erroneous though it may be – is to all intents and purpose a private matter, can the whole business not be put behind you?'

'No.'

'Mr Mackenzie, sometimes grief . . . the emotions . . . can colour our better judgement.'

'No.'

Nick was suddenly gripped by such a wave of despair and confusion that he had to get up and stand at the window until he regained the ability to speak. He longed for an enormous drink, a great big golden Scotch, just like the one he'd had yesterday at about this time and had followed with regular top-ups through the night. But he couldn't bring himself to go openly to the drinks trolley, not with David in the room. Already he could feel David's eagle eye on him, sizing up the situation, wondering whether he'd succumbed.

Bennett cleared his throat. 'Even allowing for your very admirable wish that nothing like this should be permitted to happen again, I am concerned that the inquiry will fail to deliver the appropriate sort of warning. I am concerned that the wrong message will come through, that you will be disappointed.'

David appeared briefly at Nick's elbow and pushed a cup of coffee into his hand. Nick stared at it for a moment before nodding his thanks and draining the cup in one gulp. He stared out into the park, towards the wide spread of one of the larger cedars, its branches unbalanced by the loss of a lower limb in a winter gale. At some point he had meant to ask Duncan to prop up some of the more fragile branches, but could no longer remember if he'd ever got round to it. This memory, like so many of the recent and not so recent past, was lost in a haze that seemed to have invaded every part of his brain. The worrying thing was not that the fog existed, but that he had developed a strong need for it. Whenever it lifted he had to take steps to bring it back again; drink or Librium usually did the trick or, more effective still, both.

Bennett came back onto old ground. 'Peace of mind is worth a great deal, Mr Mackenzie.'

Peace of mind? Nick couldn't begin to imagine what that must feel like.

'We go ahead,' he said.

A reproving silence while Bennett regrouped. 'Just so long as you appreciate that I'll have very little control over what might come out in court.'

'What might come out?' There was a roaring in Nick's ears, like being under water. 'What do you mean – what might come out?'

Bennett held up both hands placatingly. 'I meant merely that we will have no control over the evidence that the procurator fiscal might introduce.'

'There's nothing to come out,' Nick retorted, refusing to be mollified. 'Except that my wife was half killed by a dangerous chemical, and that's exactly what I *do* want to come out!' Marching up to his chair, he dropped the cup and saucer onto the tray with a clatter. 'The only thing that can come out is the truth! What did you mean – what might come out? Christ.'

'The London psychiatrist, Carter . . .'

'Just one opinion!'

273

'But that will not stop them from introducing the evidence, will it, Mr Mackenzie! It will not stop those sorts of ideas from being discussed in public.'

'Well, it'll be your job to stop it, won't it!'

His anger was senseless, he knew it, senseless and destructive.

'I'll do my best, Mr Mackenzie, of that you may be sure.'

Sinking into his chair, Nick rubbed a hand over his eyes, and fighting for equilibrium said in a calmer voice: 'I accept the risks.'

Bennett reached for his briefcase and said regretfully: 'Very well.'

David, professional smoother of troubled waters, stepped in and asked Bennett how long he thought the inquiry would last.

Nick's gaze fell on the envelope that he'd carried in from the hall. He pulled it out from under the tray and, opening it, glanced down the handwritten letter. Daisy Field. There was no date and the envelope bore no post mark. He read the letter grudgingly.

An airfield, an aerial spraying programme. She asked if he'd considered the possibility that it wasn't Reldane at all, that Alusha had been affected by another substance altogether? There was a boy with similar symptoms, and a couple of other people who might be affected.

He rapidly lost interest. This sounded like the theory of that man Campbell, or a variant of it. The very thought of Campbell caused him to tighten his grip on the paper.

With time and resources we hope to get firm evidence, she wrote. Which meant she had no evidence at all. Just like the Reldane situation: all wishful thinking and wild promises and nothing to back it up.

She finished with an offer to give evidence at the inquiry if he thought that might help. She gave the telephone number of a hotel in Inveraray.

Bennett was getting up. 'Forgive me for mentioning it, Mr Mackenzie . . .' He gestured a slight apology. 'But tomorrow – a suit and tie might be a good idea.'

Ah, thought Nick, mustn't have the widowed husband looking degenerate.

Seeing the dangerous gleam in his eye, David interposed:

274

'They were rehearsing till six this morning. They've only just got up.'

'Of course,' Bennett said, with an indulgent smile to show that, as a man of the world, he understood the ways of artists.

Nick showed him to the door, grateful both for an end to the discussion and for the chance to slip upstairs and grab a nip of Scotch.

When he came down again he was revived and anaesthetised, and feeling a little more able to face the day, though this didn't stop him from needling David at the first opportunity.

David was standing in the hall waiting for him, wearing that mournful, mildly reproachful expression that Nick knew so well. It was the one he'd used in the old days when Nick had done things like falling downstairs and not getting up again.

'Well?' Nick demanded defensively.

David looked wide-eyed. 'I'm sorry?'

'Why're you looking at me like that? What's the problem?'

'There's no problem, Nick,' he replied, sounding hurt. 'There's never a problem.'

'I've managed to get another three bookings,' David explained, pouring himself another cup of tea. 'Chicago, Detroit and Philadelphia. All cancellations from that Rotten Apple tour. Some tight logistics, I'm afraid, but otherwise good.'

'That's it then, is it?'

'Can't get any more bookings, not at this sort of notice. Lucky to get what we have.'

Nick got up and stood in front of the fire. 'How many's that then?'

'Seven. Start and finish at Madison Square. Well, not quite – actually Detroit will come last.'

Nick stared into the flames. 'It's going to work out, is it?'

What did he mean? David took a guess and replied: 'Sure. The Madison Square dates sold out straight away – I knew they would. We could have filled the Shea Stadium. Well – given more notice we could have. Next time, eh?'

'The material. It worries me.'

'In what way?'

'The new stuff.'

'What about it?'

'Not enough.'

'What – three songs? That's plenty, Nick, for this sort of gig at least. A major tour – well, that would be different. But with a low-scale comeback like this, most of the fans'll be coming for the old numbers anyway, you know that.'

Nick shook his head.

'It'll be okay, Nick, don't worry.'

But he was miles away, wearing the sort of look that rang alarm bells deep in David's memory.

'I'm booking the European tour, Nick. Is that all right?'

'What?'

'I should go ahead, should I?'

Nick pulled himself back from whatever had been detaining him. 'Sure.'

David thought: Give me signals, Nick. Let me know if you're going to make it. Let me know if you're in trouble. He said: 'If you've any doubts, then you only have to tell me.'

Nick ambled back to his seat. 'No – fine. Go ahead.'

'What worries me is the timing, Nick. Will there be enough time to do the album? I worry that you're taking on too much.' He thought: I also worry that you won't be able to deal with it.

'It'll keep me out of trouble.' He grimaced at the platitude.

'So long as it's what you want, Nick. So long as it'll make you happy.'

'It's what I want.' He didn't sound too sure. In fact it seemed to David's sinking heart there was an edge of panic in his voice, an underlying appeal, like a child who can't admit to having made a mistake. Nick had always been stubborn. It was his greatest strength, and his greatest weakness. But desperate though David was to get an accurate grasp of the situation, this wasn't the time to press Nick, not on the day before the inquiry.

'I had an idea,' David said brightly. 'How about a one-off gig in London before you start the European tour. A sort of warm-up welcome-back we're-here date. It'd coincide with the announcement of the UK tour. Great publicity, particularly if it's a charity do – you know, hand-shaking with some royals and all in a good cause.'

'If you think so.'

'Well, I'll leave the idea with you, shall I? Then we'll bounce it off the others. Just thought I'd sound you out first, Nick. You're the boss.'

But he wasn't listening. He was staring at the fire, his hands moving relentlessly on the chair arms, a crossed leg swinging frenetically back and forth. David wasn't surprised when a few moments later he made a show of looking at his watch and, getting up, sidled towards the door in that hesitant way of his. 'Got to call someone. Have some more tea, David. Make yourself at home.' He hovered at the door for an instant. 'Won't be long.' Then he was gone. He hadn't looked David in the eye.

David sank back in his chair, thinking: We've been here before, Nick. I recognise the signs.

Booze. Uppers. Downers. All three maybe. What difference did it make? The whole scene was like a rerun. Everyone knew their parts, everyone knew their lines. Everyone knew they had to pretend it wasn't happening. Everyone hoped it was going to be different but knew it was going to be just the same.

But the ending – that wouldn't be the same. This time there wasn't going to be anyone to catch Nick when he fell.

Mrs McKay's bed-and-breakfast establishment was at the far end of Balinteith, a dark two-storey villa of small proportions but grand design, set back from the road behind a damp garden of tall shrubs. Campbell chose to stay in the car, presumably to nurse his hangover, though Daisy hadn't enquired too closely about that.

A low gate with a broken latch and a short concrete path led to a porch and a glass-fronted door exhibiting a No Vacancies sign and the badges of two bed-and-breakfast associations. The bell sounded deep in the house and was met by a long silence. The glass door panels were draped with thick lace curtains, as were the windows on either side of the porch, and the whole place had a closed-up air to it, as if the owner had gone away. Daisy was hovering irresolutely on the path, searching the upper windows, when a large woman with a shock of white hair pulled back into an extravagant bun rolled in through the gate, a bulging shopping trolley in tow.

'Mrs McKay? Aye, that's me – for my sins. Only one McKay

round here.' She laughed as if it were a great joke and, scrabbling deep in her bag, came out empty-handed and threw up her hands in a theatrical gesture of despair. She reached under the frayed door mat and pulled out a key. 'I've no idea why I bother,' she exclaimed, her eyes dancing. 'The whole place knows where I keep it.'

Parking her trolley in the hall, she waved Daisy into the house with great sweeping movements, like a policeman directing traffic. The hall, dark with ancient furniture and elaborate wallpaper, smelled strongly of lavender polish.

'Now what can I do for you?' asked Mrs McKay, fighting her plump arms out of her voluminous plastic raincoat to reveal a tent-like floral dress that flowed over her bosom like water over a dam.

Daisy explained that she was trying to trace Peter Duggan, and invented an acquaintance who was anxious to find him.

'Come.' The great sweeping movements led Daisy to a parlour with four circular tables laid for breakfast, with overturned cups sitting neatly in their saucers, marmalade and honey jars and solid stainless-steel cruet sets.

'You'll be taking a cup of tea?' Mrs McKay sang gaily, waving Daisy to a table and disappearing into the adjoining kitchen. 'Peter Duggan – aye, he stayed here quite a wee while,' she called through the open door. 'A bit of a rascal if you ask me.' She gave a chortle. 'Not that I've the evidence for that statement, you understand.' She popped her head round the door and winked heavily. 'Just ma canny old instincts.'

'Did he leave a forwarding address?'

'No, no – not that one. Travel light, travel free, no questions asked. They're all the same.'

'Did he ever say where he came from?'

She pulled a thoughtful face and disappeared again, returning with a tray of tea things which she plonked noisily on the table. 'Now that you come to ask, I'm not sure he ever said.' She poured out the tea and sat down, exhaling noisily. 'That's strange, is it not?' she declared, affecting a look of cheerful puzzlement. 'I usually get the entire story, you understand – the *entire* story.' She giggled girlishly, raising a shoulder to her plump cheek.

'You must have some tales to tell, Mrs McKay.'

278

'Indeed. But I'm careful who I tell them to,' she said, her eyes darting up to Daisy's.

Daisy wasn't sure if this was an announcement or a warning. 'Did he say where he used to work?' she asked. 'The name of a company, an airline?'

Mrs McKay shook her head vigorously, so that her bun wobbled precariously on her head.

'Nothing like that?'

'I regret not.' She drained her cup and, under cover of her habitual smile, gave Daisy a long and careful look. 'This acquaintance of his,' she said drawing the words out like beads on a string, 'he just wants to get in touch, does he? Or might it be a she?' She wriggled her eyebrows suggestively.

'The friend simply wants to contact Peter,' Daisy confirmed. 'That's all.'

'Many would find that an unlikely story,' she crowed. 'Many would suspect that this friend might be a woman from his past, or mebbe someone in a wee dispute about money . . .'

'Nothing like that, really.'

'Many would not believe you,' she echoed, 'but then I've always gone where angels fear to tread.' She leaned across the table and tapped Daisy's hand. 'I always go by instinct. It's not let me down yet.'

Daisy ventured: 'So, Duggan – you might have some idea where . . .?'

But the ebullient hands were making flamboyant hushing gestures, the eyes closing, the face, absorbed with sudden concentration, tilting towards the ceiling. A moment of silence then, with a sudden flash of the eyes she announced: 'He had family – ' Her hands described windmills in the air. 'Somewhere in Surrey. Began with a D. Do-Doo-Da – '

'Datchet?'

'Dorking!' she cried triumphantly. 'A sister. In Dorking. His only family, he said. I got the impression he was fond of her. The sister was on her own. She'd married a free spirit.' She lowered her voice waggishly. 'That is, a man who felt free to go off and leave her with three children. Peter played the uncle. He liked that. Fond of the kiddiewinks, he was. Bought them presents.'

'Her name – did he ever mention it?'

'No, no . . . He never told me that.' She tapped her temple. 'Or else it's clean gone oot ma head, which is entirely possible. But Dorking's not so large, is it? The way Peter talked about it I got the impression it was just a wee place. You could ask about, could you not?'

'Well . . .' Daisy didn't know much about Dorking, except that it was one of the larger towns within commuter distance of London.

Her disappointment must have shown in her face because Mrs McKay added brightly: 'Try the pubs. You'll be sure to find him supporting a bar or two. I tell you, I wheeled him to his bed more times than I care to mention.' And she chuckled at the memory, the gleam of old desires in her eyes.

Daisy left her phone number, and as an afterthought Campbell's too, in case Mrs McKay's memory should undergo a sudden improvement.

'Sorry I was not more help,' said Mrs McKay swaying vigorously through the hall.

'It's been a pleasure,' said Daisy.

'You'll give him my warm regards?' she asked, opening the door and leaning coquettishly against it.

'Of course.'

She called down the path. 'I wish you luck.'

Campbell was asleep when Daisy opened the car door. Stretching and unrolling his great frame from the seat, he shot her a bleary glance. 'Anythin'?' he asked.

'Not a lot,' Daisy replied. 'Just Dorking.'

'Eh?'

Daisy shook her head. 'Come on!' she cried, making gee-up-and-go gestures. 'The Stirling road.'

'Eh?'

'We're going to see Jeannie Buchanan at work. It's off the Stirling road.'

Campbell started the engine in silence though she could see all sorts of questions forming behind the lowering brows and narrow lips.

Leaving Balinteith, they drove eastwards through the flat farmlands of the Forth valley, between fields flecked with sheep and young lambs and the occasional white-blossoming tree. Everything was touched with the sharp yellow-green of early summer. To the north, in the far distance, the horizon was broken by soft grey hills that merged into a sky of milky radiance.

'The summer,' Daisy murmured.

Campbell peered through the windscreen as if noticing his surroundings for the first time. 'More colour in the Highlands.'

She smiled. 'Tell me, Campbell, what do Highlanders think of people like Nick Mackenzie, people who buy up the big estates?'

He waved a hand philosophically. 'We've been invaded by the English so many times once more is neither here nor there.'

'But there's resentment?'

'There's always resentment,' he grunted. 'We're still smartin' over the Clearances an' that was two hundred year' ago. The estates would not exist at all if the Scots had not been driven from the land.' He waved a hand. 'But Mr Mackenzie – och, he's all right.'

'No problems with people along the loch? No difficulties?'

Campbell shifted in his seat. 'No,' he said carefully. 'No. Why should you think that?'

'No reason,' she said.

It was one by the time they reached the village where Jeannie had said she worked. The Bonaccord Savings Bank was a modest stone building occupying a prominent position next to the grocery store. Campbell offered to come in with Daisy, but retreated, looking hurt, when she said: 'No, it would only frighten her.' Taking pity on him, she declared: 'You're too big, Campbell! You'd frighten anybody!'

The counter clerk looked disconcerted by the nature of her request, but, after ceremoniously locking his cash drawer, left his window to summon Jeannie. A minute later she appeared through a side door. Her child-like eyes rounded at the sight of Daisy.

'I hope you don't mind,' Daisy said. 'There was just one more thing.'

'More?' she whispered, glancing over her shoulder.

'Last night, there was something else, wasn't there?' Daisy suggested. 'Something you couldn't tell me?'

Jeannie's eyes grew, she seemed to undergo an inner struggle, then, with a sigh that was almost a moan, she began

281

in a sudden and breathless rush: 'Aye, aye. It was the notifications – there was not always the time to amend them. It was not my fault, it was Mr Keen – always sending new instructions, pushing us, changing things, altering dates. There wasn't the time . . .' She paused, misgivings in her face, as if she realised she might already have said too much.

'Amend them – in what way?'

'When the spraying date was changed, when the weather was bad, to tell everyone who should have been told.'

'So you'd send out one set of notifications and then when the date had to be cancelled you were meant to send out another lot with a new date on them?'

'Aye. But there was not the time. It was Mr Keen. Always changing everything. I did my best, I always tried to do my best . . .'

'Not your fault.'

But Jeannie was not to be reassured. 'It was wrong. I knew it was wrong, but what could I do?'

'But were there mishaps, Jeannie – things that happened as a result?'

'Aye.' She closed her eyes for a moment. 'Sometimes I heard Mr Duggan joking about cattle and sheep and how he'd given them a dusting. That's what he used to call it, giving them a dusting. I knew what he meant. He meant he'd sprayed them. It didn't bother him. In fact, he used to laugh.' There was a glint of tears in her eyes.

'Not your fault,' Daisy repeated.

'I should have said something! I should have told someone!'

'How often did it happen – the notifications not getting amended?'

'Four times. Maybe five.'

'On jobs by Loch Fyne?'

The doors sounded and someone came into the bank. They both waited for the customer to approach the counter and begin to speak.

Daisy repeated her question in an undertone.

Jeannie looked imploringly at her, as if she would have given anything not to answer. Finally she whispered miserably: 'Aye. Up there, by Loch Fyne. Once . . .'

'Yes?'

'Once . . . I had no time at all.'

'No time to amend the notification, you mean?'

Her lower lip buckled, a tear plopped onto her blouse. Daisy fumbled in her bag and found a tissue.

'No time to send it,' Jeannie said, pressing the tissue to her eyes. 'Nothing was ever sent, nothing at all . . .' Her voice was almost inaudible.

'And where exactly was it, this forest? Do you remember the name?'

She shook her head firmly.

'It wasn't the Fincharn Estate, was it?'

But try as she might Jeannie was past further remembrance. She thought it was on the north side of the loch, then the south and then maybe up towards Loch Awe.

'I didn't sleep last night for thinking of it,' Jeannie moaned, blowing her nose. 'I knew it would come out. I knew I should have told you.'

'Well, you've told me now.' Daisy squeezed her hand. 'Thanks.' She started for the door and turned back. 'By the way – did Duggan ever mention anything about Dorking?'

'Dorking?' Jeannie echoed. 'Dorking?' She touched her head, as if touching her memory. 'No,' she said. 'No.'

'Or a sister?'

'A *sister* . . . Oh, aye. Aye, he talked of her.'

'What did he say?'

'He talked about getting down to see her. He said he might take her on holiday. At least I think it was a holiday . . .'

'Did she have a name?'

'I never heard it.'

The clerk was pressing his face hard against the counter window in an attempt to get a look at them. 'You'll call me?' Daisy said. 'If there's anything else?'

She nodded effusively.

Daisy was almost through the door when Jeannie called: 'Wait – ' and hurried after her. 'His sister . . . I believe he said she had a wee shop. Clothes, I think it was. Aye, clothes. He said she went to London to purchase things for it. Perhaps it's there, the shop, in that place you said?'

Perhaps it was. But then again, perhaps it wasn't.

Jeannie held open the door and hovered, reluctant to let her go. 'The notifications,' she said. 'I knew it was wrong at the time. But it was the job, you see – there were no other jobs to be found. I was frightened of losing it.'

'I know the feeling,' Daisy said, remembering a phone conversation she'd had with Alan that morning.

Heading west again, Daisy and Campbell took the first road south and spent the rest of the day in Glasgow attempting to trace the elusive Mr Keen. The address of Acorn Flying Systems turned out to be a converted stable at the back of an old house on the northern outskirts of the city. The windows were dirty but not so thickly covered that one couldn't peer through and see that the two interconnecting rooms were empty. There was a patch of hastily applied paint on the part of the door where a company name would have been positioned. The main house had also been converted into offices and was currently occupied by a firm of chartered surveyors who expressed an enthusiastic but resigned interest in tracing Mr Keen over the small matter of six months' rent.

Three aircraft supply and maintenance companies based in and around Glasgow Airport were also anxious to see Mr Keen again. As one manager put it, you could string Acorn's unpaid bills round the passenger terminal and still have enough to paper a house. Out of habit rather than expectation, Daisy called in on the Glasgow CID to discover that Keen's fame knew no bounds and that they too were interested in locating him, this time over a complaint of false accounting and embezzlement brought by an erstwhile co-director of Keen's in another defunct venture, a time-share company.

No one knew where Keen was now, but the police thought he'd moved to the Costa Blanca.

EIGHTEEN

The court officials hadn't allowed enough room for the press. The four seats they had placed behind a single table were already occupied by the local boys, and a group of three journalists stood waiting for the ushers to bring more chairs. The officials hadn't made the same mistake with the public seating however and there was room enough for the eighty or so spectators.

Through the high-set windows the sky was very dark and the rain that had threatened since dawn was already beginning to spill down the glass. The photographers encamped outside would be getting wet, a thought that did not upset Daisy too much. Inside, the overhead lighting was poor and badly spaced, throwing deep shadows which added to the aura of gloom that seemed to pervade the room.

There was a raised top bench where the judge – by Scottish law, entitled sheriff – would sit, and to the right the oddly named procurator fiscal. Daisy had checked her Scottish law: the sheriff would decide the verdict, while the procurator fiscal, a full-time law officer who variously fulfilled the tasks of prosecutor, investigator and coroner, would lead the evidence. Interested parties could be represented by their own counsel. There was no jury. The clerk and a shorthand writer sat to one side of the bench while the witnesses, including Campbell, sat in the hall outside.

Everyone was waiting, and everyone knew what they were waiting for. It was only a minute before ten when a sudden movement of heads marked Nick Mackenzie's entrance. He strode quickly up the aisle, flanked by three men, and took a seat in the front row. He was wearing a well-cut charcoal suit with a white shirt. Only his hair was a little on the wild side. Once seated, he kept his head rigidly towards the front and Daisy could not see his face. The plump dark man sitting on his left turned to whisper in his ear, and she recognised David Weinberg. The man to his right stood up and went to speak to the procurator fiscal; this had to be his lawyer. As the lawyer returned to his seat the usher handed him a note. Daisy knew it was a note because she had written it. As she watched for the lawyer's reaction some people in an intervening row stood up and obscured her view. By the time they sat down again the lawyer was back in his seat and she could no longer see his face. But she noticed that Nick's head was bent forward, as if he were reading the note. When his head came up again, the lawyer inclined towards him and they had a discussion. It was very short.

Then – nothing.

They didn't need her then. In a way she was relieved: her evidence wouldn't have added a great deal, and unsupported guesswork never went down well in court.

The sheriff entered. They all stood. The proceedings were under way.

First to give evidence were the police. It was the standard stuff, delivered in the flat monotone affected by police officers everywhere. The alarm being raised, the layout of the estate, the search for the missing woman, the call to the upper glen, the finding of the body beside the pool.

Nick's lawyer asked some ancilliary questions which were clearly intended to establish that a well-planned search had already been under way when the police arrived.

Next came the police surgeon, who had examined the body on the night of the death. He estimated that death had occurred some time during the day in question. It was impossible to be more precise because of the temperature of the water in which the body had lain. Questioned by the procurator fiscal, he expanded on the methods used to estimate the time of death, and how they were complicated by temperature.

The pathologist was next into the witness box. Daisy braced herself. During her days as an articled clerk she had been to one or two inquests and she knew how clinical and merciless postmortem reports could sound. It had always seemed to her faintly demeaning that someone so newly dead could have the secrets of their bodies, complete in some cases with unmentionable diseases and unfortunate revelations, discussed in public.

The pathologist whipped through the usual preliminaries before stating that the immediate cause of death was drowning. Water had penetrated the lungs fully, indicating that the deceased was alive when she went into the water.

Prompted for his other findings he referred to his notes. 'I found bruising and abrasion on the left temple,' he said. 'The bruising covered an area of four centimetres by three. The skin was broken over most of the bruised area. I estimated that this injury occurred at the time of death or very shortly before. If it was before, then it can only have been a matter of minutes.'

'Could this injury in any way have contributed to death?' the procurator fiscal asked.

'Unlikely. It would not in itself have caused a loss of consciousness, although it could, I suppose, have caused confusion or loss of balance.'

'How in your opinion could this injury have been incurred then?' asked the procurator fiscal.

'It was obviously the result of a blow of some kind, but by what and in what circumstances I could not say.'

'Could it have resulted from Mrs Mackenzie being swept against a rock?'

'Possibly . . .' He sounded rather doubtful. 'If the water was very fast flowing.'

'Or a fall perhaps? Onto a rock or similar hard surface?'

'Yes.'

'Were there any other injuries?'

'No.'

The procurator fiscal indicated that he was satisfied on the point and the pathologist returned to his notes.

'Was the deceased otherwise in good health?' the procurator fiscal asked.

'She was considerably underweight for her height. Less than six stone on a height of five foot six inches. I would describe her as emaciated.'

'Was there any medical reason for this that you could find?'

'I could find no evidence of physiological disease, no. And certainly nothing that would account for the marked atrophy of the muscles. In my opinion the muscle atrophy could well have contributed to death.'

'In what way?'

'The deceased would have suffered much reduced muscle power compared to another woman of her age and build and would have had relative difficulty in swimming or extricating herself from the water. She was likely to have been weak.'

Nick moved then, bowing his head and rubbing a hand across his temple. The sheriff, a grey-faced man with a beaked nose and drooping eyes, peered at him over his half-moon spectacles, before returning to his scribblings.

'You suggest the deceased could have been weak,' said the procurator fiscal. 'But not so weak that she couldn't walk the' – he consulted the papers on the table beside him – 'almost two miles from the house?'

'Hard to say, but walking is not nearly so strenuous as swimming.'

'So it wouldn't have been impossible?'

The pathologist considered. 'Not impossible, no.'

The procurator fiscal waited for the signal from the sheriff that he had caught up on his notes before asking the pathologist to continue. Holding up his pad, the pathologist began to recite a long litany of test results. He spoke in a refined Scottish accent, his voice clear and well-developed like that of a trained actor, an impression borne out by his sense of timing; like a true performer, he left the scene-stealer till last. If the technical terms at the start of his speech had left people behind, morphine was a word they all understood. He had found morphine sulphate in the blood at a level of two hundred micrograms per litre.

'What sort of dose would that be? High? Low?' asked the procurator fiscal.

'For someone of the deceased's weight, high.'

A tiny ripple came from the audience, a collective movement that shivered through the hall.

'Is morphine sulphate a prescribed drug?'

'It is.'

'And what is it administered for?'

'The control of pain.'

'And this dose, it was commensurate with one administered for pain?'

'It *could* have been, but normally such a dose would only be

288

given for really severe cases. As I've already said, I found no evidence of serious disease.'

'And it's normally given for cancer?'

'For that, and heart attack and injury. But as it's an addictive substance it's only given for pain that cannot be relieved in any other way. In cancer, only for terminal cases.'

'Can you say what effect such a dose would have had on the deceased?'

There was a sudden drumming on the high windows as rain pelted against the glass. The sky was so black that the rivulets of water reflected the light back into the hall.

'I can't be certain,' said the pathologist, raising his resonant voice so it could be better heard above the rain, and it occurred to Daisy that he was enjoying his time in the spotlight. 'It would very much depend on the deceased's tolerance to the drug.'

'And what factors would influence a person's tolerance to morphine?'

'The individual's general health, the state of the liver and so on. But also usage – whether the individual was a habitual user.'

Another ripple, a collective intake of breath. Daisy winced inwardly: a disastrous choice of words, not something the reporters were likely to miss.

'I see. So you can't say precisely what effect this level would have had on the deceased?'

'All I can say is that even the most frequent user would have felt considerable effects from such a dose. What I can't estimate is the extent – the degree – of those effects.'

User. Again Daisy flinched, again she was aware of the effect that word would be having on the audience.

'And what are the effects of morphine?'

'Apart from reducing pain, it induces a feeling of well-being and euphoria.'

The procurator fiscal seemed to hover on the point of asking another question before saying: 'You found no other unnatural substances in the blood or tissue?

'I did not.'

'So what is the summary of your findings?'

'Death by drowning. I would add that low bodyweight and high blood-morphine level could have been contributory factors.'

The procurator fiscal nodded towards Nick's lawyer, who positively shot to his feet. First he went over the bruising on the head, clarifying that it occurred at or shortly before the drowning. Then he asked: 'Doctor, you say that morphine is used as a painkiller?'

'It is.'

'So it's widely prescribed by the medical profession?'

'I wouldn't say *widely*. I would say, not infrequently.'

'You mentioned cancer, but is it not also used for other diseases that cause intense pain?'

'Well it *can* be,' the pathologist replied grudgingly. 'But there are not many other diseases that cause such intense pain that they cannot be treated by other means like analgesics. As I have said, a medical practitioner would normally be reluctant to prescribe morphine for anything but the most severe cases, because of its habit-forming nature.'

'But whatever the disease, there's very little else that a doctor can prescribe for really intense and prolonged pain, is that correct?'

'For really intense and prolonged pain that did not respond to analgesics, no. Though, as I've already mentioned, the deceased did not appear to suffer . . .'

'That wasn't what I asked, doctor,' the lawyer cut in rapidly. 'I asked if morphine was appropriate for intense pain.'

The pathologist didn't like being interrupted and looked across to the procurator fiscal as if expecting him to intervene. Finding no support, he rearranged his mouth into a stern line of forbearance.

'You used the terms "habitual usage" and "frequent user" just now,' the lawyer was saying. 'Taking "habitual usage" first, what exactly did you mean by that?'

'Regular and extended usage.'

'And what did you mean by "frequent user"?'

'Someone who uses the substance frequently – often.'

'Regular – frequent – habitual. Aren't these all the same thing?'

'Well – yes.'

'So you might term a cancer victim an habitual user.'

A pause. 'I might.'

'Or an accident victim who suffers prolonged pain?'

A slight shrug. 'Possibly.'

'So the court would be correct to understand that the term "habitual" is interchangeable with "frequent" and "regular" and applies quite properly to someone who has been pre-scribed morphine as part of her medical treatment?'

The pause again, that oh-so subtle suggestion of doubt. 'Yes.'

'Thank you, doctor.'

As the pathologist left the box, Daisy glanced towards Nick, but he was motionless, shoulders back, head erect, and there was nothing to suggest the sort of face he might be showing to the front of the court.

The next to be called was a forensic scientist. Asked about the possible causes of the abrasion and bruising to the deceased's forehead, he ventured the opinion that the blow had come from a large flat surface such as a rock or large stone. He also confirmed that the water found in her lungs matched the water from the River Ashard.

As soon as he stepped down, the usher called Campbell, who, deserted by his usual assertiveness, walked awkwardly to the box and stumbled over the oath. Haltingly, his voice hardly raised above a whisper, he began to describe the search; how he had joined the main party sweeping down the glen, how he had joined Nick Mackenzie to go back and search the upper reaches.

The procurator fiscal interrupted him. 'Why did you decide to search the upper glen?'

'It was Mr Mackenzie. He wanted to go. I joined him.'

'There were just the two of you?'

'Aye.'

'And you left the main search party?'

'Aye.'

'Thank you. Please continue.'

He told how they had driven up the glen as far as the great rock then continued on foot, he by the narrow river path, Nick Mackenzie by the track, and how they had doubled back; how he had stopped by the pool a second time and shone his torch over the surface and seen a touch of white floating near the surface under the great rock, and waded in to investigate.

Campbell faltered, stopped and looked to the procurator fiscal for guidance.

'It was the body of Mrs Mackenzie?' the procurator fiscal prompted.

Campbell nodded.

'Please tell us what you did then.'

With a visible effort Campbell described in a tense hesitant voice how he pulled her to the edge of the pool and onto the bank and tried to revive her, laying her on her stomach and pressing hard on her back, then turning her and breathing into her mouth, and how his efforts had been of no use.

'And then?'

'I called Mr Mackenzie who came down from above. From the track there.'

'Go on.'

Campbell looked nervously about him. He wasn't sure what he was expected to say next.

'What did Mr Mackenzie do when he reached you?'

Campbell looked flustered and didn't reply.

'I'm merely asking what action Mr Mackenzie took when he got to you,' prompted the procurator fiscal gently.

'He . . . er, requested that I move to one side.'

'And then what happened?'

Campbell was silent.

'Did he try to revive her?'

Campbell blinked and ran a tongue over his lips. After some thought he shook his head. Almost immediately he seemed to regret this because he stammered: 'No. That is, he . . . I'm no' certain.'

'Was it dark?' offered the procurator fiscal helpfully.

'That's it,' Campbell exclaimed, grabbing at the idea. 'I couldna' see.' He nodded at the sheriff to make sure that he too had got the point. 'It was dark,' he repeated, the relief evident in his face. 'I couldna' see.'

Daisy closed her eyes and willed Campbell to stop babbling. Not a moment too soon, the procurator fiscal told him to stand down.

Then they called Nick.

In the silence you could hear the wind bombarding the rain against the windows like pellets and the sound of the clerk's footsteps as he positioned himself by the witness box ready to administer the oath.

Nick paused to say something to his lawyer before getting up and crossing to the witness box. He faced the clerk while he took the oath, turning only when it was time to sit down. The women in front of Daisy craned their necks and darted their heads from side to side to get a better view, and it was a moment before Daisy could get a look at him. Skin pale, but not unnaturally so. Thinner perhaps; a little gaunt around that punished face. Eyes weary beneath the hooded lids, and touched with sadness.

The procurator fiscal began by asking him about events on the day the death had occurred – what time his wife had been missed, what form the search took, the return to the upper glen. For the most part he answered in monosyllables. Questions that required fuller answers he kept brutally short and occasionally the procurator fiscal had to prompt him to enlarge on what he had said.

'And when you came across Mr Campbell and your wife's body, what happened then?'

'Nothing,' he said in his quiet voice.

'You didn't try to revive her?'

'There was no point.'

'Why was that?'

Nick pressed his lips together. 'It was obvious my wife was dead.'

The procurator fiscal nodded, and went through some background about Alusha Mackenzie's daily routine and the walks she used to take. Then:

'Can you tell us about your wife's medical condition, Mr Mackenzie?'

'She had been very ill for some time.'

'What was the nature of her illness?'

Nick's glance flickered across the court in the direction of his lawyer. 'She'd accidentally inhaled a poisonous substance.'

'When was this?'

'Last June.'

'This substance – do you know what it was?'

'I believe it was a wood preserver called Reldane.'

'Could you tell us how you came to this conclusion?'

'My wife had been using Reldane on a stable door. She was found unconscious with the stuff – the Reldane – spilled on the concrete around her. She became extremely ill and never recovered.'

'Did you seek expert advice at that time?'

'If you could call it that.'

'You consulted a toxicologist?'

'More than one.'

'And what was their opinion?'

293

'Well, they couldn't say exactly how the damage was done, if that's what you mean.'

The procurator fiscal turned to the sheriff. 'Your honour, in view of the seriousness of the allegation concerning Reldane – a product which is freely available to the general public over the counter – and in view of the court's duty to investigate the matter as thoroughly as possible I will be calling an eminent toxicologist to give evidence about Reldane at a later stage.'

Nick's expression darkened. Hadn't he realised that this was inevitable? Daisy wondered. Hadn't he realised that his word would count for little against the experts'?

The procurator fiscal put his next question. 'Did the toxicologists you consulted venture any opinion on Reldane's role in your wife's illness?'

'Not really . . .' He shrugged it off. It was an unfortunate gesture, giving the impression that he wasn't interested in the question. Perhaps he realised his mistake because he added sharply: 'They all had different ideas.'

The procurator fiscal nodded solemnly. 'Did they not match the known effects of Reldane against your wife's symptoms?'

'They didn't seem to know a lot about Reldane.'

'So they could not be sure it was the Reldane?'

'Not certain, no.'

'You took your wife to America for assessment and treatment, I believe?'

'Yes.'

'And what was offered there?'

'Not a lot. They had no idea about treatment either.'

'But your wife was treated by a Dr Hubert Gravely of Boston?'

'Yes.'

'And he offered a firm opinion on the nature of your wife's illness?'

'Yes.'

The procurator fiscal reached behind him for some papers and announced that he was going to read the affadavit from Dr Gravely of Boston, Massachusetts. He read slowly, pausing occasionally to allow the sheriff to make his notes. The doctor's statement was impenetrable with jargon, but it seemed to boil down to the fact that he had attended Mrs Alusha Mackenzie at various times between November 15th

294

and December 18th of the previous year in Boston, and that she was suffering from the effects of exposure to a highly toxic substance. The toxicity had affected, as far as one could gather, almost every organ in her body, including the heart, the liver, and the endocrinal and nervous systems.

'It appears, then, that your wife suffered a rapid and devastating decline in her health, Mr Mackenzie. Had she been well before the accident?'

'Yes.'

'Both mentally and physically?'

'Absolutely.'

'She was of normal weight?'

'Yes.'

'She had been expecting a baby at the time of the accident, is that correct?'

'Yes.'

'And what happened?'

'She lost it. Two weeks later.'

'What did the doctors say about that?'

Nick cast him a withering look. 'There wasn't a great deal they could say, was there?' It was the first time he had showed anything approaching emotion.

'And her weight loss, did that come soon after the accident too?'

'Yes.' He had pulled the mask back over his face.

'How did it come about? Did she lose the desire to eat?'

'No. She lost the ability to absorb her food.'

'So she ate as much as usual but still lost weight.'

'That's right.'

'What other symptoms did she have?'

'She was in pain nearly all the time.'

'I see. What sort of pain? Can you elaborate?'

'All her joints and – well, all over. And vicious headaches.'

'Did this pain disturb her a great deal?'

'It was unbearable.'

'And she was given drugs for it?'

'Yes. Morphine.' His voice had dropped until it was barely audible.

'And this was prescribed for her?'

He gave the briefest nod of his head.

'By whom?'

295

'The American doctor.'

'This doctor?' The procurator fiscal said, picking up the affidavit. 'Dr Gravely?'

He gave a slight shrug. 'Yes.'

'What dosage did she take?'

'It varied. I don't know.'

'Then she herself determined the dose?'

'Yes.'

'I see.' A pause. 'May I ask, Mr Mackenzie, was your wife depressed at all?'

He didn't reply for a moment. 'What sort of depression are you referring to? Endogenous or exogenous?' he demanded, and there was an edge to his voice.

'Well – I don't think we need to know . . .'

'It's an important distinction,' Nick said defensively, his voice rising. 'If you mean had my wife lost the will to fight her illness – absolutely not. Even at her worst she never gave up, never doubted that she'd get well. But the illness itself – sometimes she felt so bad that it got her down. Physically, I mean. But it was never so bad that – ' He broke off. He didn't need to finish; everyone knew what he had intended to say. But he said it anyway. 'That she would consider taking her own life.'

'On the day of her death, was she particularly depressed?'

'No.' There was a tremor in his voice, as if he were controlling himself with difficulty.

'She didn't make any remark, any comment that could have a bearing on later events?'

'No.'

'There was no note, no message of any kind?'

It was an instant before Nick managed to answer. 'No,' he said with emphasis. 'There was not.'

There was a short pause while the procurator fiscal consulted his notes.

'Your wife didn't have a family doctor here in Scotland?'

'No.'

'Why was that, may I ask?'

'She'd had enough of doctors. And before that she never needed one.'

'Thank you.' The procurator fiscal sat down. The worst was over; but then the damage had already been done.

Nick's lawyer did what he could, going over Alusha's health

296

before the accident and the devastation of her illness, but there was no disguising the fact that, according to Nick's own evidence, the toxicologists had been unable to offer explanations about the cause of Alusha's illness, nor had they been able to support the allegations about Reldane.

Finally Nick was allowed to leave the box. He strode back to his seat, his face set, his expression guarded.

The court adjourned for lunch. The press were up and making for the door before the sheriff had left the court. As the spectators stood up, Daisy looked for Nick but there was no sign of him and she realised he had been ghosted away, perhaps into a side room. She spent the hour rebuilding Campbell's spirits in the nearest pub.

When the court reassembled, the procurator fiscal said to the sheriff: 'In view of the highly technical nature of the affidavit from Dr Gravely I think the court may benefit from some elucidation.' He nodded to the clerk who recalled the pathologist to the witness box.

The pathologist shook his head. 'I find it very difficult to interpret this statement, Mr Procurator Fiscal. Certainly it doesn't match with my findings.'

'In what way?'

'He mentions liver damage. I found no evidence of that whatsoever. He also mentions heart damage. Again I found no evidence of that. And as for hypothalamus malfunction – well, that's impossible to measure; there *is* no test for hypothalamus function. And he talks about T-cell damage of a type unknown to science.'

'So there would seem to be some discrepancy?'

'Yes, and I think I can offer an explanation. I took the liberty of looking up Dr Hubert Gravely in the United States medical register. I could not find him there.'

'You're saying he's not a registered medical practitioner?'

'Apparently not.'

There was a rustling in the room. The two women in front of Daisy exchanged glances at this unexpected turn of events. Nick had a hurried consultation with his lawyer. The two of them seemed to be in some disagreement because, though Nick was strongly arguing some point or another, the lawyer wasn't having any of it and kept shaking his head.

Then the procurator fiscal recalled Nick.

It was obvious that Nick's mood had shifted. The largely

impassive expression of the morning had been replaced by one of guarded belligerence. He no longer sat erect, but hunched forward, one elbow on the chair-arm, knuckle against his chin, glaring at the procurator fiscal with what might easily be interpreted as suspicion. There was something else, too, a heaviness to his eyes, an unfocused look. It suddenly occurred to Daisy with slight shock that he had been drinking.

The procurator fiscal went back to the matter of Alusha Mackenzie's medical care in America. Nick left no one in any doubt as to his dislike for this line of questioning, grunting the briefest of replies, and executing some fairly obvious manoeuvres around direct answers. But it came out all the same.

Alusha Mackenzie had gone to Dr Gravely only after several stays in hospitals in London and New York, where, despite running every possible test, the doctors had been unable to offer an explanation for her illness.

'They could find no abnormalities whatsoever?' asked the procurator fiscal, clearly puzzled.

'Tests don't pick up everything,' Nick snapped. 'They're not perfect.'

'So in the absence of any diagnosis from the physicians, your wife went to Dr Gravely. He was an alternative practitioner, was he not?'

'Yes.'

'Forgive me, but I'm confused on two matters here,' said the procurator fiscal. 'First, what reason was offered by Mrs Mackenzie's physicians for the considerable pain she was in, the loss of weight and so on?'

Even from that distance Daisy could see Nick's jaw muscles working overtime.

'I have to ask, Mr Mackenzie.'

Still Nick didn't answer.

'Was it suggested that your wife was suffering from a nervous illness?'

Nick flinched slightly as the procurator fiscal touched the raw spot. 'She was damaged by a highly toxic substance,' he said bitterly, 'but it didn't fit the textbook, you see, so they were too frightened to give it a name! They couldn't find out exactly how the damage was done and couldn't see a neat list of symptoms, so that was that! They had to dredge their ideas bags and come up with something else – anything else.'

Wrong way to go, Nick. Looks bad. Too emotional, too defensive, too angry.

The procurator fiscal hesitated, as if genuinely regretting the necessity to press the matter. 'So – what was it they finally suggested?'

'Ha!' It was several moments before he managed: 'They said it was depression. But it wasn't true. There's no way it was true.'

The procurator fiscal nodded slowly and for a moment Daisy thought he might let it go at that. But he was too professional to forget the other matter that had been confusing him. She had a good idea of what was coming, and she was right.

'One last question, Mr Mackenzie, you said that Dr Gravely prescribed the morphine for your wife, yet he was not a qualified practitioner. Could you – er – clarify this point?'

'I must have been mistaken,' Nick said impatiently, his face puckering warningly.

'It was another physician then?'

'Yes – what the hell does it matter anyway?'

The procurator fiscal looked a little taken aback at that and for a moment Daisy thought he would drop the point, but he pressed: 'You can't recall the name of this other physician?'

'No.'

'But it was prescribed by a doctor during your stay in the United States?'

Making little effort to hide his exasperation, Nick barked: 'Yes.'

After a last glance at Nick's face, the procurator fiscal allowed him to leave the box.

The next hour was taken up by evidence from the Mackenzies' staff corroborating the events of Alusha Mackenzie's last days. The housekeeper was adamant that Mrs Mackenzie had not been in low spirits; the estate manager, though fiercely loyal, was less certain. She had not looked well, he said. He could not say in what way, and in evading the question left the unfortunate impression that he had seen her looking depressed.

The toxicologist was last on. He didn't say anything unexpected, and he didn't say anything helpful either. Reldane was regarded as a relatively safe product, he stated. Of proven low toxicity, it had never been known to cause serious side effects among people regularly exposed to it.

As the court was adjourned until the next day, a shaft of weak sunlight the colour of amber splashed against the wall of the court, a sudden incongruous shaft of brightness.

Wherever Nick had been spirited to during the noon recess, he did not go there now. Instead, with his companions forming a tight circle round him like soldiers round their warrior king, he ran the gauntlet of the photographers and hurried from the building.

Back at the hotel Daisy called the office. She got straight through to Alan, and she had the strong feeling that he had been waiting for her call.

Having martyred himself on the field of the trustees' presentation all day, he was at his most scathing.

Going her own way, he accused, acting entirely at the expense of everyone else. No allowance for the load she was dumping on the rest of the team, no *consideration*. No pulling together. It was getting to the point, he added ominously, where Catch was becoming unworkable.

Ignoring the spirit of the last remark, Daisy made the appropriate noises: apology and entreaty, a little well-chosen flattery and some overt grovelling. Eventually Alan allowed himself to be placated, though grudgingly and with extremely bad grace so that she was left in no doubt that he was still highly displeased.

It was twenty minutes before she got to speak to Jenny, and even then she had to remind Alan she was calling long-distance before he would remove himself from the line.

'Tried the Civil Aviation Authority,' Jenny murmured, keeping her voice down. 'They don't give pilots' addresses out to the public, but they do forward letters, so I wrote.'

'Good.'

'But they couldn't be sure the address they had for Peter Duggan was up-to-date. It was abroad somewhere – outside Europe, presumably, because they asked for extra postage. I turned on my persuasive powers' – she gave a self-mocking giggle – 'but they wouldn't say which country.'

'There must be other ways to find pilots,' Daisy said more in hope than certainty.

'I'll keep trying.'

'And the mechanic?'

'I've got someone trying all the Robertsons in the Inverness phone book. *Not* a simple task!'

Daisy spent the remainder of the afternoon with the local police, going over the flying notifications for the previous summer. The officer in charge was most co-operative. Acorn Flying Systems had sent out no less than twenty notifications for the Argyll area, but none of them was for any patch of forest adjacent to Ashard, and though they had posted their intention of spraying forest near to Adrian's, the work had been undertaken in July, well after he had been doused.

Dispirited, she took the last stuffy symptoms of her cold back to the hotel for an early bed with an aspirin and a cup of hot lemon. She slept until four, and then listened to the wind and thought of Nick Mackenzie at Glen Ashard.

The next morning it was raining again. The papers had been reasonably restrained. Only a couple of the tabloids had reported Alusha Mackenzie's 'heavy morphine usage', but had refrained from further comment, waiting, presumably, for the findings of the inquiry before running their main stories.

When the court resumed, just one witness was called, a psychiatrist named Carter, as smooth in appearance as he was in speech. He had examined Mrs Mackenzie during the previous October in London, he said, and had run extensive tests.

'And what was your diagnosis?'

'Acute clinical depression.'

Daisy closed her eyes momentarily.

'And what was the treatment you recommended?'

'Antidepressants, graduated exercise, psychiatric therapy. But Mrs Mackenzie was removed from my care before the treatment could begin.'

'Removed?'

'Her husband came and discharged her very suddenly.'

'And this was against your advice?'

'Very much so. I was extremely concerned for Mrs Mackenzie's health.'

'In what way?'

Daisy bowed her head.

'I thought she might attempt to take her own life. I was extremely concerned about it.'

Nick's lawyer did his best to shift the elegant Dr Carter

301

from his position, but he was not be ruffled and not to be drawn. If exposure to chemicals could produce such symptoms, then he had never heard of a single case.

All that remained was for the procurator fiscal to summarise the evidence. He was thorough and meticulous. He recalled the pathologist's statement which allowed for the possibility that the deceased's illness had contributed to her death. But as to the cause of that illness, he believed the evidence to be inconclusive. While Mrs Mackenzie may well have inhaled Reldane, and it might have caused some temporary symptoms, there was no evidence that it could have caused the chronic debilitating illness of the following ten months. The chemical Reldane had been in existence for years; it was considered relatively safe. It seemed an unlikely culprit. And then there was the evidence as to the deceased's state of mind. Dr Carter had diagnosed clinical depression, and had warned of the dangers of his patient's state of mind. And it must not be forgotten that she had experienced a traumatic year, with both an accident and a miscarriage. It was possible, therefore, that her illness and indeed her death were of nervous origin, and did not result from inhalation of the chemical Reldane.

Mr Mackenzie, on the other hand, was convinced that his wife had not been depressed, but if the court accepted that, then it left her considerable physical deterioration unexplained, and could well implicate some as yet unidentified factor.

As to the actual day of the death, he would only summarise the few facts, that no note had been found, that she had been seen to be looking unwell on the day of her death, that she had taken a high dose of morphine. The role which the drug may or may not have taken in the death was impossible to determine.

The sheriff announced that he would like the weekend to reflect, and would give his finding on Monday morning. The tension fell back uncertainly, people stirred discontentedly, as if they had been cheated.

Even before the sheriff had left the room, Nick was on his feet and striding down the aisle so rapidly that it was only by jumping quickly and awkwardly from her seat that Daisy made it to the door first and, passing quickly through, held it open for him. But before she had the chance to speak he had gone, speeding past with the barest flicker of a glance. An instant later his companions burst through the door in hot pursuit, one bumping into her with a muffled apology.

The party had almost reached the main entrance when it suddenly ground to an abrupt halt, the cohorts almost colliding with one another. It was Nick who had created the jam, she realised. He had stopped at the doors. He was turning to David Weinberg.

She hurried forward, aware that if she was going to speak she must say the right thing and in the right words, aware that she would have only a few moments in which to say it.

He saw her, he frowned. Close up, he looked raw, defeated, heart-stopping. Suddenly anything she might have said seemed crass and inappropriate.

Finally she blurted: 'Can I talk to you?'

People were crowding round him. She could sense his panic, his need to escape. With an obvious effort he forced himself to look down at her.

She didn't know why at that moment of all moments she should look at anything but his face, why as she drew breath to ask him if she could come to see him that evening she should look past his shoulder and notice the head of the man passing behind him. But she did, and there was something about the retreating head, the greased-back hair and fat neck, that caught her by surprise. The words died on her lips, and in the second that she was distracted, in the very instant she was about to force her eyes away from the bull-like neck and back to Nick's face, something made Nick take fright because suddenly he was turning and before she realised what was happening he was pushing his way clear and his friends were rapidly closing ranks behind him.

Her heart bumped, she pushed after him, through the crowd, out of the doors and into the rain. Emerging, she realised there would be no second chance. The press were converging for their close-ups. As Nick made for his car they shouted questions, pushed shamelessly in front of him, held cameras in his face. Watching the mêlée, Daisy could only feel glad when he reached the shelter of the car and it tore away in a welter of spray.

She stood in the rain, filled with disbelief. She had let him go. She allowed herself a moment of sharp self-rebuke and something approaching misery, before peering through the sheeting rain, searching for the fat neck and slicked-back hair that had jerked at her memory. She began to half walk, half run along the street, examining the memory as she went. The image of the bull-necked head had been incongruous yet familiar.

It was only when she reached the main street and paused to look up and down its length that it came to her. Colin Maynard. The man from the Waldorf.

The implications confused her. Why should he be in Scotland? Interest in Alusha Mackenzie's case? Interest in Catch? If so, he must have done some serious homework to find out when and where the inquiry was being held.

The more she thought about it the more unlikely it seemed. She was seeing demons, she was having what Alan would call one of her windy phases.

The rain, which was gentle but relentless, dribbled down her face and flattened her hair coldly against her head. A few intrepid people were braving the shops, their heads hidden beneath lowered umbrellas. Two men appeared from a doorway and strode towards her. Both were short with fat bull-like necks, and by the time they had darted into the public bar of the nearby pub, their hair, too, had acquired a wet slicked-back look.

She turned back.

It was Campbell who called with the news on Monday.

Finding undetermined. The matter of Alusha Mackenzie's death was to be left open.

Daisy felt relief, as if Nick had been on trial and found innocent.

But of course it hadn't been Nick who had been on trial, it had been Alusha Mackenzie, the charge, mental instability.

NINETEEN

Dorking, backbone of England, boasted several boutiques, small high-class establishments with two to three racks of tailored suits, floral dresses and glittery evening clothes.

Daisy drew a blank at the first two, but in the third the owner showed some interest at the mention of a pilot brother. She did not have one herself, but she had heard that Jane Ackroyd did, and directed Daisy to a boutique called The Dresser.

The shop was a few yards up an alley off the main street, the sort of place where the rents are only half the price. A door-operated bell sounded as Daisy entered and a well-groomed fortyish woman popped her head round a curtain at the far end of the shop.

'Are you Jane Ackroyd?' Daisy asked.

'Yes.' She was what some people might call faded, with pale washed-out eyes, soft blurred features, and a pair of deep vertical frown lines over the bridge of her nose.

'I believe you have a brother Peter Duggan,' Daisy said, diving in. 'I wanted to get in touch with him.'

A strange expression, half defensive, half curious, came over Jane Ackroyd's face. 'Oh yes? In connection with what?' she demanded.

So Duggan was her brother. Concealing a flutter of triumph, Daisy began the marginally adjusted story she'd prepared on the way down. 'I'm a solicitor making enquiries into the affairs of a company called Acorn Flying Systems,' she explained, 'and in particular one of its directors, a man named Keen. I believe your brother worked for the company last year.'

305

Jane Ackroyd stared. 'You're a solicitor?' she asked doubtfully.

'Yes.' When the disbelief in Jane Ackroyd's face failed to recede she added: 'Though I'm what you might call off-duty today.' She gestured apologetically towards her scuffy clothes. 'I was on my way to the country. Going fishing.'

'Fishing?' She was incredulous.

That was the trouble with lies; they had to be repeated. 'Fishing,' she restated.

Jane Ackroyd gave the sort of nod she probably used to humour difficult customers. 'Who are you acting for, Miss – er?'

'Field. Daisy Field. I'm sorry, I'm not at liberty to reveal the name of my client. I can only say that my client has a direct interest in the matter.'

'Ah,' she said. 'It's money then, is it?'

Daisy shrugged regretfully as if ethics prevented her commenting further, but allowed a small collusive smile to slip onto her face which Jane Ackroyd could take any way she wanted.

She got the message all right. 'Money,' she affirmed knowingly. 'It had to be. They still owe Peter several weeks' salary. It's outrageous when you consider he was doing all the work and taking all the risks. Quite outrageous.' She eyed Daisy one more time, as if making up her mind about her. 'Wait here while I phone, will you?'

'Is he a long way away?' Daisy asked her retreating back.

'Oh no,' Jane Ackroyd called over her shoulder, and Daisy tried not to get too excited at this second unaccountable stroke of luck.

'Peter?' Jane Ackroyd's voice floated out from behind the curtain before dropping to an inaudible murmur. Daisy wandered closer to the curtain, touching the sleeves of the dresses as she passed. Just as she began to catch the occasional snatch of conversation, the street door opened, the bell sounded with a loud buzz, and a customer came into the shop. Jane Ackroyd peered round the curtain and cut short the conversation with a 'Must go now.' She emerged with a smile for the new arrival, then, returning her attention to Daisy, politely but skilfully shepherded her towards the door. 'My brother's on his way into town,' she announced in a low voice. 'He'll meet you at The Saddler's Arms in fifteen minutes.'

It was more than Daisy had dared hope for, and she must have let it show in her face because the defensiveness sprang back into Jane Ackroyd's eyes. She said sharply: 'This business – it's not going to involve Peter in any unpleasantness, is it? I mean, no court cases or anything like that?'

This was a promise that Daisy knew she couldn't make. 'A court case?' she murmured. 'There's no suggestion of that at the moment.'

'You see . . .' Jane Ackroyd dropped her voice to a whisper. 'Peter's been through a bit of a rough patch recently. He . . . Well, he's not too . . .' Then with an abrupt shake of her head, she abandoned her speech and opened the door.

The lounge bar of The Saddler's Arms was empty except for an ancient lady sipping a pint of stout which had left a broad foam moustache on her upper lip, and a couple of jovial salesmen arguing amicably over a sheaf of papers. Daisy bought a Coke and sat at a table opposite the door.

After a few minutes Duggan came in. She knew it was Duggan even before he caught her eye and raised his eyebrows questioningly; he looked like something out of a boys' comic, a parody of a flying man with his spotted cravat, his cavalry twills and blazer, and his longish black hair neatly parted and flattened against his head. The only thing lacking was a moustache.

'Miss Field?'

'Mr Duggan.'

He sat down, rubbing his hands energetically, and glanced in the direction of the bar. 'A drink?'

'No thanks.'

'God, not an abstainer, I hope,' he said with forced heartiness. 'Article in the paper today says all this health talk is claptrap. A little booze does wonders for the arteries.'

Close up, Duggan didn't look quite so dapper. His blazer had seen better days, his shirt collar was frayed, while his hair, which was heavy with grease or dirt or both, had discharged a sprinkling of dandruff over his shoulders. His face, which must have been quite good-looking once, appeared worn: his eyes were red-rimmed with pronounced pouches underneath, his skin was coarse and blotchy, and his teeth were heavily stained. It was no surprise when he lit a cigarette and drew on it with a deep gasp.

'Think I might have a little something,' he said, jerking his head towards the bar and ambling over. The barman seemed to know him well enough because he greeted him by name and, putting a glass unhesitatingly under the gin measure, gave him a double. Duggan returned to the table, cigarette jammed between his lips, eyes half-closed against the smoke. Sitting down, he dashed some tonic into his gin and took a quick swig. 'My sister said you were trying to find Keen.' He had a smoker's voice, deep and throaty.

Daisy ran through her prepared story, though she took care to shift the emphasis away from Keen to the broader canvas of Acorn Flying Systems.

'It was a limited company, Acorn, you know,' Duggan said. 'Can't get anything out of a limited company if it's got no assets. I know. I tried. Not a penny left in the kitty. Stripped bare. It was that bastard Keen, of course. Cunning little shyster. Expensive cars, Italian clothes, that sort of thing. Bled the company dry. Left everyone else to carry the can. Should have known. Nasty common little upstart.' He took another gulp and sucked it through his teeth with a hissing sound. When he wasn't talking or drinking he was drawing on his cigarette, dragging the smoke deep into his lungs.

'How did you come to work for him?' Daisy asked.

'Had a job out in Oman which folded unexpectedly. Needed a job for the summer. Hadn't heard about Keen's reputation when I took it on, of course.'

'Had you done crop-spraying before?'

Duggan's lazy gaze fixed on her with new interest and he narrowed his eyes as if he'd got smoke in them. 'Yup. A bit.'

'It's quite tricky, isn't it? I mean, don't pilots kill themselves regularly?'

He liked that idea. His eyes came alive. 'It happens,' he said, tossing off the remark with a well-practised blend of nonchalance and bravado. 'But then just as many pilots get killed in road accidents, probably more.' The devil-may-care persona was obviously one he enjoyed and had doubtless used to some effect over the years.

He drained his glass and, holding it at chest height, twiddled the stem slowly between thumb and forefinger. Daisy guessed she was meant to notice how empty it was. 'Can I buy you another?' she offered.

He attacked the next drink only marginally less slowly than the first, and she saw that his hand trembled slightly as he

308

reached for the ashtray. It occurred to Daisy that this was not Duggan's first drink of the day. The bad patch Jane Ackroyd had alluded to began to take on a new dimension.

'You don't know where Keen disappeared to?' she asked.

He gave a dry laugh which turned into a phlegmy cough that rattled deep in his chest. 'Christ, no,' he said, recovering himself. 'Don't care either. It's no good knowing where the bastard is if I can't get any money out of him, is it? I just hope he's got his come-uppance. Wrapped his BMW round a lamppost or something.'

'He was difficult to work for, was he?'

'Christ – was he. Always buggering things up. Phoning new instructions through, trying to make me fly over my hours, wanting everything done pronto. It wasn't as if he provided any bloody backup. Just a mechanic, a field operator and an office girl who didn't know her arse from her elbow.' He stabbed his cigarette ineffectually into the ashtray so that it lay there smouldering. 'I must have been out of my tiny,' he snorted. 'Sweating my guts out to finance his flash lifestyle.'

'How long were you with the company in fact?'

'Oh – May till September. Something like that.'

'And the spraying – what sort of jobs were they exactly?'

'Forest stuff. Estates, that sort of thing. Everyone was in a tizz about this beetle moth or whatever it was. They all wanted everything done yesterday.'

'Willis Bain was one of your clients, I believe?'

He took a long slow drink, eyeing her over the rim of his glass, and she sensed a sudden caution in him. 'Yup,' he answered finally. 'Did quite a bit for them. But, um . . .' He hesitated, pulling out another cigarette and lighting it with an old-fashioned steel Zippo. 'Thought you were just interested in Keen? Tracing him and so on.'

'Wish it were that simple,' Daisy said. 'But I need a whole lot of background information. Evidence, facts.'

'You're actually trying to nail him, are you?' he said in sudden admiration. 'What for?'

She gave a shrug. 'Oh, financial irregularities. That sort of thing.'

'Bloody good. Bloody fantastic. Hope you get him!' He drained his glass and grinned congenially, displaying teeth which were so discoloured and unattractive that Daisy couldn't help staring at them.

309

'Only thing I don't understand is what your client hopes to gain.' He said it so casually that it was a moment before Daisy realised the difficulties inherent in the question.

'I'm sorry?'

'Well, it can't be money.'

'No.' Daisy was thinking hard.

'Jail then?'

Daisy spread her hands to show that this might not be so far from the truth.

'My God!' Duggan exclaimed with relish. 'Keen must have upset your client very severely if they want to pin something that serious on him.'

'You could say that.'

'So it might be jail?'

'It might be.'

Duggan gave a long lazy wink that was probably intended to look conspiratorial but which merely appeared lecherous. 'Well, you can count on me.'

Daisy thought: Now I wonder if that's true? For all his affability Duggan didn't seem the steadfast type. Tricky and difficult, she guessed; out for number one.

She offered him another drink. He accepted readily, though not before going through the heavy drinker's time-honoured ritual of insisting that he couldn't possibly drink alone. She ordered a low-alcohol lager and a packet of crisps to soak it up with.

'You don't look like a lawyer,' he said.

'What does a lawyer look like?'

'Older and uglier.' He winked again, and this time the suggestiveness was deliberate though self-mocking.

She said: 'Well, you know how it is, one has to overcome these handicaps.'

He laughed appreciatively, then, just as she was thinking the interview was beginning to go smoothly, he added casually: 'You didn't say what firm you worked for.'

'Didn't I?' Was he trying to catch her out? Or was he just curious? She laughed it off. 'I'll give you my card.' She went through a pantomime of rooting through her bag. 'Well, I *would* give you a card, but I seem to have run out.'

He was waiting.

Aware that she was being forced into open lie, she heard

310

herself give him the name of her old firm, the solicitors where she'd worked before joining Catch. 'Here – I'll give you the phone number.' She wrote down Catch's unlisted number on a scrap of paper. This lie she liked far less than the fishing story she'd told Jane Ackroyd, if only because there was a far greater chance of being found out. Duggan only had to look up her old firm and call their real number to discover she wasn't there any more. Or to call the Catch number before Daisy had a chance to brief Jenny.

But would he bother? It was all too easy to imagine that his mind was as languid as his body. Yet those sharp little questions hadn't come out of thin air.

She asked him about his dealings with Keen, routine stuff about paperwork, how the wages were paid, what money went through the Portakabin office.

'Never saw the cash,' Duggan declared, waving an expansive hand. 'In fact he kept us so tight that we had trouble getting enough petty cash for lav rolls. Not that we used the bloody place at all if we could possibly avoid it.'

Daisy smiled. 'You mean the hut?' The moment she'd said it, she could have kicked herself.

Duggan's glass paused half way to his mouth. 'You've been to the airfield then?' he asked.

'Yes.'

'Why? What for? Nothing to see.'

'I was just passing. On business.'

'Ah.' He nodded sagely, but she sensed him carefully weighing the information.

'Did you ever sign for things?' she asked. 'You know, fuel deliveries, that kind of thing?'

He shook his head. 'Nah. Though I bloody well checked the stuff once it arrived. Didn't trust Keen an inch.'

'In what way?'

'I wouldn't have put it past him to try and give me low-grade fuel.'

'Good God, really? Wouldn't that have been dangerous?'

'Probably.' Duggan chuckled to himself. He was back in the role of fearless daredevil pilot battling against unfavourable odds. All this boyish bravado, not to mention the heavy drinking, made Daisy wonder how Duggan was ever allowed in charge of an aircraft.

Keeping her tone light, she nudged the conversation forward. 'What about the chemicals – the stuff you used to spray the trees with – did you check that out too?'

'No. Didn't have to. Keen didn't have anything to do with the gunk, thank God. Davie, the mechanic, he was in charge of measuring and mixing and all that. The gunk was delivered direct from the customer most of the time anyway. They bought it direct from the manufacturers or whatever.'

'Of course.' Daisy nodded vigorously as if he had just reminded her of something she knew perfectly well.

'That way there was no chance of Keen short-changing them,' Duggan explained in case she'd missed the point.

'Quite. And the stuff you were using – er, remind me . . .?'

He shrugged. 'We used to call it "the usual". I'd say, is it the usual? And Davie'd say, it's the usual. And that would be that. But the name – it was feni – fenitri . . . Christ, never could say the bloody word.'

'Fenitrothion?'

'That's it.'

'Was that the only stuff?'

He brushed at a fall of ash on his lapel and managed to smear it deep into the fabric. 'Mmm – sorry?'

'What other chemicals did you use?'

'Other chemicals? No, that was it. Feni-whatsit.'

'But I thought . . . Hang on.' Daisy made a show of getting out her notebook and flicking through it. 'Something else was used for a couple of jobs near Loch Fyne, wasn't it?' She looked up expectantly.

He wasn't crazy about the question. He took a long sip at his gin, frowning at her over the glass. It was time for another refill, she noticed. She caught the barman's eye and pointed in the direction of Duggan's glass.

'Something else?' Duggan echoed coolly. 'I don't see what the hell that has to do with anything.' His voice had an edge to it, a note of truculence. 'I mean, how can your client be interested in the gunk we used on a particular job?'

'It's a matter of finding out if Keen did what he was contracted to do.'

'But like I said, it was a limited company. It doesn't matter if he delivered the goods, if he did what the client wanted – it's all bloody water under the bridge, isn't it? The only thing you can possibly get him for is fraud, and I don't see that what we sprayed on the treetops of Loch Fyne has got a blind thing to do with how Keen managed or mismanaged the bloody finances.'

Daisy held up a staying hand. 'It may seem that way, but the point is . . .'

The barman arrived with Duggan's refill and another low-alcohol lager. While she counted out the money coin by coin, she tried to think exactly what the point was. 'The point is,' she said finally, 'that if Keen was substituting cheap chemicals then it *was* fraud.'

But Duggan wasn't buying. 'Even if he'd pulled a fast one, it would have netted him a hundred quid at the most. Don't tell me they're going to nail him on a hundred quid!'

'They got Al Capone on a technicality.'

He sank slowly back in his chair, wrists draped over the arms, cigarette and drink in either hand. 'You're on the wrong track,' he announced with finality. 'Willis Bain delivered everything. It never came through Keen.'

'Oh.' Daisy looked disappointed. 'It'd still be useful to have the name of the other pesticide.'

'I never knew it.'

'But surely – you must have seen a name?'

'No. Does it matter?'

'I told you – every detail helps.'

He shook his head, his cat-eyes watching her through the curling spirals of smoke. 'Can't remember.'

Can't or won't, Daisy thought grimly. She took a sip of lager while she considered the way forward. He wouldn't take much more pressing, she sensed, or he'd clam up altogether. Letting the subject drop, on the other hand, would be to lose what might be her only opportunity.

There was a third option, she realised, something quite different. She let the idea grow and sharpen in her mind. She'd have to push hard to carry it off, and it wouldn't be very pretty – and that was putting it mildly – but it might just work.

She put her drink down. 'I need to know the name of that pesticide,' she said.

He picked some tobacco off his lip. 'I told you,' he said with an impatient sigh, 'I don't remember.'

'Or don't want to? Listen, Mr Duggan, I don't like to press you, but according to my information there were plenty of irregularities at Acorn Flying Systems, and they didn't just involve Keen.'

He was very still, the drink and cigarette for once forgotten in his fingers. 'What does that mean?'

'It means that rules and regulations were broken all the way down the line and Keen wasn't the only one responsible.'

His mouth twisted, his voice was hoarse. 'What the hell are you talking about?'

'About notifications not getting sent out. About livestock getting sprayed. About flying hours being exceeded. Shall I go on?' The excessive flying hours was a guess, but Duggan wasn't arguing.

He jerked forward in his chair, his face louring across the table. 'Who the hell *are* you? What the hell's this about?'

'Calm down, Mr Duggan. There's no need to get angry. I'm sure it won't be necessary to let this go any further, not if you can find a way to help me out.' As she said it, she wondered if this was the way practised blackmailers generally put their demands across. 'Just tell me the name of the pesticide, and we'll forget about the livestock.'

She thought: But not about the people. She couldn't make any promises on that. Which made her offer devious, even, if she were in the mood to be utterly scrupulous, dishonest. But remembering Alusha Mackenzie and Adrian Bell, she couldn't feel too heart-stricken about that.

Duggan was rallying from the initial shock. 'It's not bloody true, all you're saying,' he declared belligerently. 'Don't know where you got these outrageous bloody ideas from – '

'Reliable sources.'

Duggan's face contorted with something like fear. 'Christ, you b—' But the rest, which might have included the word bitch, was lost as he sat back in his chair and drained his drink at one go.

'It's a reasonable offer,' she said.

'Sounds like a bloody threat to me!'

'Take it or leave it.'

'But I don't bloody remember the name!'

'Try.'

His mouth was working hard and he looked as if he could cheerfully kill her, but he was thinking all right. 'I don't know – I don't know,' he said fretfully. 'It never had a name, just some stupid code number. ZX-something. ZX . . . P. That

314

was it. ZXP. No name. Well – it *did* have a name, but I only saw it once, about the second time we used the stuff. It was the day Keen actually deigned to come in. We couldn't believe it – never saw the bastard normally. Turned up out of the blue, treating us like bloody lackeys . . . It was all his sodding fault that things went wrong, you know. He pushed us – '

'The pesticide,' she interrupted.

He glared at her. 'Yah, well . . . There it was on the sheet. With the code number.'

'And a name.'

'Yeah, but only that once. The girl, she just put ZXP on the job sheets after that. And like I said Davie and I weren't into gunk names. We just got to call it "the old gunk" or "the new gunk". And that was it. I only saw the name that once, for God's sake.' He lit a cigarette from the butt of his old one.

Her silence finally drove him forward, fumbling resentfully through the remnants of his memory. 'I think it was some trade name or another. You know, one of those catchy made-up words. Something to do with forests. Leaves, needles, something like that . . .' He waited expectantly as if Daisy could in some miraculous way pull the name out of thin air. 'For Christ's sake,' he grumbled, 'it was last year – no one could remember that far back.' He glanced at her to see if this little appeal was going to earn him a reprieve, then lurched on: 'We had a lot of jobs that day. Too many. And Keen slapped on another. What could I say? If I'd caused trouble he'd simply have told me to get lost.' He ran a hand through his hair so that it stood out over his ears like feathers. 'White . . .' he murmured for no apparent reason. 'He was wearing white, Keen. Like a spivvy wop waiter. Top *and* bottom. White shoes too – I ask you! Standing there like some gift from God, ordering everyone around. Changing the schedule. Putting the wind up that stupid girl. Kept threatening us with financial disaster if we didn't pull out the stops.' Catching her expression he pulled himself back to the subject with bad grace. 'Okay, okay.' He shook his head, fretting at the problem. 'White . . . It was something like that. Pale, anyway. No – glittery. Silver maybe. Yes . . .' He flapped a hand. 'That was it. Silver.'

'Silver?'

'The name. The gunk. Silver-something.' He coughed, a

315

loose rattle deep in his chest. 'And that, I tell you, is all I bloody remember.'

He thought she had finished with him, but he was wrong. 'You did several jobs around Loch Fyne, didn't you?' she asked.

He was very still, his eyes creased into a line of watchfulness. 'A few.'

She described the approximate area of Adrian Bell's house. He shrugged. 'Don't remember.'

'And the Fincharn Estate – you were up there, weren't you?'

His face hardened. She could see him preparing a denial. Then his expression lightened abruptly and he laughed. 'Barking up the wrong tree there, dear lady. Quite the wrong tree. Had an equipment failure that day. The job was aborted. Never did get to do it. Bad weather, no time.' He sat back, blinking heavily, lips slack, ash spilling down the front of his jacket. 'Quite the wrong tree,' he said, and smiled.

Jenny flicked her eyes towards Alan's open door, indicating that he was in or waiting to pounce, or both. Taking long light strides Daisy sped past the door and into her office. Plucking the Ministry of Agriculture's pesticides manual off the shelf, she bent over the desk and started to thumb through its 400 pages and 3000 odd products. She started at the trade name index. Sickle, Sierra . . . Silvapron.

Then . . . something called Silveron ZXP.

ZXP. Silveron.

She checked it back to the main register. Insecticide for professional use only, it said. Manufactured by Morton-Kreiger (UK) Ltd. Registration number MAFF 05012.

The registration numbers were allocated historically, the latest products being awarded the highest numbers. The 05000 numbers were the latest and suggested recent registration. She looked for the previous year's manual, searching her shelves and hunting through the most likely bumf dump, which was located on the floor in the corner. Nothing. In desperation she tiptoed to the door and mimed to Jenny. Jenny, looking innocent, pulled her copy off the shelf and sauntered over as if she were making for one of the filing cabinets.

316

Daisy winked her thanks and took the manual to her desk. It was as she thought: last year, no Silveron.

She went back to the current manual. Typically, the ministry in their infinite wisdom omitted to state the type of crops each product was actually approved for, and she had to go to *The UK Pesticide Guide*, a publication of the Crop Protection Council. Silveron wasn't listed. She phoned the Council. Silveron had been approved too late for the last edition. But they had the details to hand. It was a broad-spectrum, contact organophosphorus insecticide. It was approved for use against aphids, weevils, midge, moth, thrips and numerous flies and beetles, for use on a wide range of fruit and vegetables. Forestry use was considered such a low-risk activity that it was not listed.

They gave her the label precautions by reference numbers, which she looked up in the back of the guide. Silveron, so the manufacturers advised, was not to be used by people who were under medical advice not to work with organophosphates (she'd yet to hear of anyone getting this advice until after the damage was done). Silveron was dangerous to bees and harmful to fish, livestock, game, wild birds and animals. It was harmful if swallowed, inhaled or put in contact with skin. Users were advised against breathing vapour or spraymist. Protective clothing was to be worn.

This inventory, though chilling, was nothing out of the ordinary. In fact, if the consumer did but know it, it was typical for most chemicals in daily use on fruits and vegetables. What was almost as interesting were the omissions. No mention of special precautions or dangers, no directions to wear respirators when applying the stuff. In other words no one was treating Silveron like an especially dangerous chemical.

Neither was there any mention of approval for aerial application, she noticed. Which meant that Willis Bain had committed an offence in supplying the stuff to the flying company.

She felt a glimmer of hope. Getting warm, getting warm.

Forgetting the need to lie low, she gave a small whoop of triumph. Through the open door Jenny looked round and, catching the mood, laughed and raised a clenched fist in reply.

As Daisy hastily dialled Peasedale's number, she became aware of Alan striding swiftly into her office, a half-eaten sandwich clutched in his hand.

'Real progress, Alan,' she cried as Peasedale's number started ringing.

'I need to speak to you,' Alan said.

She gave him an unconcerned smile. 'Of course. In a while? I'm rather—' The number answered. 'Peasedale? It's me. Listen – I've got it. The pesticide in the Bell case.'

Alan thrust his face into her field of vision and mouthed an exaggerated 'now', repeating it several times, until his mouth moved like that of a newly landed fish.

Peasedale was making interested noises at the other end of the line. 'Hold on,' she told him and, capping the phone, promised Alan: 'Soon. Really.'

'And when's *that* likely to be?' He was squeezing his sandwich so tightly that the honey was oozing through the bread in dark glutinous patches.

'But I've got the name of the pesticide.'

She might as well have been talking about the latest stationery order. 'Ten minutes,' Alan hissed.

Peasedale hadn't heard of Silveron ZXP, but he promised to ask around and see if anyone else had. She also called an industrial chemist at an independent laboratory who agreed to do an analysis for her. It wouldn't be free, of course, but he always managed to fiddle the hours to the minimum.

Finally, unable to find any more excuses, she made the excursion round the partition to Alan's office.

Alan had trouble in beginning his speech. He opened his mouth several times before sighing: 'For all the good our discussions do I sometimes wonder why we bother.'

'Alan, I'm listening,' she said, settling herself attentively in a chair. 'I always listen.'

'But you don't bloody take any notice of what we *agree*.' His voice cracked slightly.

'Whatever it is, I'm sorry,' Daisy said humbly.

'You can be sorry all you like, but it doesn't seem to make any bloody difference, does it? You disappear to Scotland, you abandon the presentation and leave me to face the trustees, then, just when I think maybe there's a chance of getting back to normal – you know, working as a team again, which is how it's meant to be in case you'd forgotten – you're

318

off again and I'm up until midnight, preparing for the next meeting that I know damn well you won't turn up for.'

'What meeting? I had no meeting . . .'

'If you'd bothered to call in yesterday you might have found out about it. The EEC ban on Aldeb. The British Euro MPs asked for a quick briefing, which seemed a pretty reasonable request. I mean, that is what we're meant to be here for, isn't it, briefing people who have the power, and that sort of thing? So I said yes. I couldn't very well refuse, could I? Even when I knew I wasn't going to get a single iota of backup.' He measured an iota between thumb and forefinger and held it up in front of his face. 'Not an iota!'

There wasn't a lot Daisy could say. 'Alan, I would have been there if I'd known, you know I would.'

Alan raised his glasses and rubbed his hand angrily across his eyes. 'It's not good enough,' he said.

'No, I suppose not.'

He pushed the glasses back onto his nose with such ferocity that the impact made him blink. 'I don't think it's going to pan out, Daisy. You might as well be working for a different organisation. Sometimes I wonder if you're with us at all. I mean – well, it's just not going to work out, Daisy.'

An unpleasant little chill gripped Daisy's stomach. 'What are you saying, Alan?'

'I'm saying that it's hopeless, this doing your own thing. It's not fair to me, it's not fair to Catch.' He pursed his lips and looked unhappy. Eventually he managed to spit it out. 'I think you should think about resigning, Daisy. In fact' – he gave a small shudder – 'I *know* you should think about resigning.'

Daisy stared at him, totally taken aback.

'But I'm just getting somewhere, Alan. Everything's just beginning to happen. Identifying that pesticide is going to make all the difference to the Adrian Bell case.'

'That's it, Daisy. *You're* getting somewhere. Not Catch. Not the campaign. And as for the Bell case – Daisy, how often have we discussed our policy on individual cases? Just tell me, how often?'

'But, Alan – the case is going to expose all that's wrong with pesticide control – '

'Is it?' he said sharply. 'That's your opinion, Daisy. Not mine. Not the trustees'.' *Documenting* the Bell case is fine and useful and good anecdotal stuff and all that. But a detailed investigation – I mean, tracking down the pilot, going to inquests, all that stuff – is *not* part of our strategy.'

'But, Alan, we can't just leave it! Blimey, you might as well walk away from a road accident!'

'Daisy – ' He clapped his hands to his face in a gesture of despair. 'We've been through this before – how many times? It's just not possible to take on every injustice in the whole damned world and fight it personally. We don't have the resources.'

'Well, I do.'

'No you don't, Daisy. You don't!' He stabbed a finger at her. 'It's Catch's resources you're using.'

'Jesus, Alan!' But for once she made the effort to pull herself up short. This wasn't the time for a row, not when Alan was talking of her resigning and looking deadly serious when he said it.

A voice intruded, drifting over the partition from the outer office. Daisy recognised Simon's unmistakably authoritative tones. It was a moment before she remembered that he'd arrived to take her across town to an Arts for the Earth auction at Bonham's.

She said to Alan: 'Listen, I hear what you're saying, Alan. Really. But . . .'

'There's always a but, Daisy.'

'Yes,' she said momentarily defeated. 'I suppose there is.' She cast him a contrite look. 'I don't want to leave Catch, I really don't. Blimey, this is my life, Alan.'

'I think you're in the wrong organisation, Daisy. I think it's as simple as that.'

Daisy took a moment to come up for air. 'Listen . . .' She waved in the general direction of the voices in the outer office. 'Can we talk about this later?'

Alan didn't reply but turned back to his desk with a dark expression. He was still exhaling sharply as Daisy closed the door.

Simon was propped on Jenny's desk, chatting. He turned a smile on Daisy. 'Ready?'

'Can't make it. Sorry.' Another man, another apology.

He glanced at his watch, looking put out. 'Oh?'

'Something's come up,' she explained. 'To be precise – the pesticide in the Bell case.'

'Ah?' A spark of interest. 'What about it?'

'Got the name,' she announced, allowing some of her satisfaction to return.

'And – ?'

'It's something called Silveron ZXP. An organophosphate.'

He frowned slightly. 'Are you sure?' There was a touch of condescension in his tone.

'Yes, I'm sure,' she said, moving out of Jenny's hearing. 'Why?'

He went though the motions of considering her idea in more depth, but scepticism was still written large on his face. 'It just seems a little unlikely,' he said cautiously. 'Just when Silveron's about to get US approval, I mean.' The surprise must have shown in her face because he said, not without satisfaction: 'You didn't realise?'

'No,' she said, adjusting to the fact that Simon seemed to know all about Silveron. 'But then the EPA aren't perfect,' she said. 'They've had it wrong before.'

'They usually get it an awful lot righter than us, though, don't they?'

'You know a lot about Silveron,' she said accusingly.

'It's Morton-Kreiger's new baby. They seem to think it's got a great future.'

'Which means they think it's going to make them a lot of money,' she said waspishly. 'Anyway, since when did a company's opinion of its own product bear any relation to its safety?'

'I could ask around,' he said, putting on his magnanimous voice. 'Shall I? There *was* something, I know – a problem on the production line . . .'

From Alan's office came the sound of a chair leg scraping across lino. Unable to face a three-way discussion, Daisy led Simon outside and up the steps to the street. A fierce wind was blowing from King's Cross, spiralling litter along the pavement. The front page of the *Sun* jammed against Daisy's leg.

'A problem?' she prompted, kicking the newspaper aside.

'It was a scare. Some workers on the production line. A temporary lapse in safety procedures, I think. But I'll dig the cuttings out for you. Ask around. I've got to phone some people in the US anyway.'

'They were sick, the workers – how sick? What sort of symptoms?'

He shrugged as if he couldn't possibly be expected to know. 'Must go.' He pecked her on the cheek. Turning away, he hesitated and looked back. 'Oh, I'm seeing them tomorrow – Morton-Kreiger. I'll ask them what sort of safety margins it has, shall I?'

She laughed disbelievingly. 'They'll never tell you!'

'You'd be surprised. They're very PR conscious, very anxious to show environmentally willing.'

She called after him: 'You won't let on, will you?'

'What? Who?'

'Morton-Kreiger. You won't tell them why you're interested?'

Throwing her an offended look, he spread his hands as if the idea was too insulting to be worthy of consideration and hurried away.

She watched him go and wondered if it had been such a good idea to encourage questions. Much as she was desperate for information, any probing, particularly on the part of an environmental journalist, was likely to alert Morton-Kreiger to the possibility of attack.

Back in her office, she closed the door to deter another Alan-led offensive, and sank into her chair, overcome by a sudden despondency. Never having been asked for her resignation before, it took some getting used to. Had Alan really meant it? Had she really gone too far or asked too much? It wasn't as if she'd asked Alan or Jenny to do anything she wouldn't have gladly done herself.

She said: 'Bugger it,' to no one in particular and sat up with a jerk. On her desk was an update on Jenny's investigations into Acorn's flying activities. Though she had managed to locate several Davie Robertsons in the Inverness region, none of them was or ever had been employed as an aeroplane mechanic, nor knew of a Davie Robertson who was. Further enquiries with the local Health and Safety Executive and the military air controllers had also drawn a blank, at least as far as flying in the Loch Fyne area was concerned.

The other messages did not interest Daisy and her attention returned to the pesticide manual still open in front of her at the Silveron entry. She stared at it for a long moment, then reached for a pile of worldwide environmental literature that she hardly ever had time to read in detail, and went through some of the latest issues. Silveron did not rate a mention on anyone's hit list: no warnings, no news of production-line sickness, no nothing. Abandoning the journals, she worked her way through the bullky contents of her in-tray. From somewhere near the top she pulled out the latest EarthForce bulletin, and there it was in the news section. Silveron ZXP. Sickness at the Aurora production plant in Aurora, Illinois; EarthForce making representations to the EPA; Morton-Kreiger tightening up their production-line safety procedures; a secondary toxicology study which, according to sources, was expected to show that Silveron came within statutory safety limits.

It was six p.m. and the cheap phone rate to the US didn't start until eight, but she dialled Washington anyway. Paul Erlinger greeted her with a cry of delight, as if she were a long lost friend and charged into an effusive stream of questions, before cutting himself ruthlessly short and getting down to business.

'So what can I do for you?'

She told him she was interested in Silveron and what sort of damage it might be doing to people.

'You read our bulletin, did you?'

'I need more. The symptoms, the exposure, how those workers are doing. What *you* think.'

'Listen, er . . .' The line became muted as if he'd capped the phone. 'Listen, can I call you later, at home maybe?'

She gave him the number and they fixed a time.

She took a bus home, stopping at the Patels' to buy fish fingers, bananas and Greek yogurt. The flat was cold: she had left a window open. Her one pot plant had dropped most of its leaves, a victim of gross neglect. The mail consisted of three brown envelopes with windows. There were no messages on the answering machine.

She lit the gas fire and had a quick bath. The water hissed and spat in the tap, percussion to the hot tank's strings section, which sobbed and sighed and gurgled as it refilled.

Lying in the bath, she closed her eyes and the questions swooped in on her, one on top of another.

Silveron. Morton-Kreiger. Within statutory limits. Secondary trials. Was it that safe? How could it be that safe?

And the workers, how sick had they been? Did they have the muscle wasting, the problems in absorbing food?

She thought, too, of Scotland and Nick Mackenzie. Where

323

was he now? she wondered. What was he doing? He wouldn't be in Scotland. He would have gone abroad, America, or a hot climate, the West Indies or Bahamas. Perhaps he was working again, perhaps he was beginning to pick up the pieces, but even as she nursed the thought forward, she remembered his heavy unfocused look during the inquiry, his uncharacteristic belligerence, and she wasn't so sure.

The call came through on the dot of nine. 'I'm sorry to have cut things short there,' Paul Erlinger said immediately. 'But I was with a journalist. Not known for his discretion – are they ever? Listen – is it safe to talk?'

'Safe? What do you mean?'

'I mean, is the line okay? Bug-free?'

The idea was so preposterous she almost laughed. 'I don't think Catch rates that sort of attention.'

'You'd be surprised. Might be worth getting it checked out.'

She couldn't see herself getting the idea past Alan. 'I'm at home anyway,' she reminded him.

He gave her the case histories of each of the Silveron workers, the numerous unexplained symptoms, the general malaise, the loss of weight, the single case of cancer which may or may not have been related to the Silveron exposure. Morton-Kreiger International were admitting absolutely nothing, but had tightened up their safety procedures at the plant 'as a precautionary measure'. He told her about the back-up toxicology trial and how the results, which had been carefully leaked by MKI, would show that there was no cause for alarm.

'And what do *you* think?'

A pause. He exhaled into the mouthpiece. 'I think there's a bad smell hanging around this one.'

'Why do you think so?'

'Just a feeling really. Hard to pin down, you know?'

'Nothing definite then?'

'Nothing *definite*.' There was something in his tone that suggested quite the opposite.

She felt a beat of excitement. 'Come on, Paul! I need this, I need it badly! I think I have two victims here, maybe more.'

'Look, Daisy, I wish I could tell you – but it's not that simple. You see, we took a decision to keep this under wraps, at least until we could be sure of protecting our sources.'

'So there *is* something!'

324

There was a silence interspersed with groans as if he were battling with his better judgement but quite enjoying the process. 'Okay, okay. I'll tell you this much – there could be hard evidence.'

'What sort of evidence? You mean, more victims? Or – *God!* – are Morton-Kreiger covering something?'

He laughed, but it was only to give himself time. 'Daisy, you're a one-woman interrogation machine.'

'Can I have this evidence?'

'Whoa, whoa. We ain't got it yet!'

'When? When will you get it?'

'Daisy, Daisy . . .' He was objecting, but not that strongly. 'Ask me again after the thirtieth.'

Ten days away.

'You're not coming over for the PAN conference?' he asked. 'Maybe I'll have something by then.'

The Pesticide Action Network was a North American umbrella organisation with which Catch attempted to keep close contact. Alan had considered sending himself to the conference in Boston but had decided against it, not on the grounds of expense, which did not anyway seem to pose such an insuperable problem where Alan's foreign trips were concerned, but because of pressure of work, a barb that had been aimed in Daisy's direction.

'Maybe I will,' she heard herself say.

'Hey, but I can't promise anything, Daisy. Don't come specially, will you? I mean, I might have absolutely *nothing*.'

'I was thinking of coming anyway,' she lied, trying to remember what she had in her savings account.

'You were?' He sounded pleased. 'In the meantime, Daisy, take my advice, don't leave anything lying around. You know what I mean?'

Involuntarily, she glanced around the room. Then, feeling faintly foolish at having caught herself taking the idea so seriously, she shook herself free and in her American-cop voice said: 'Listen – suspicion's my middle name.'

TWENTY

Susan waited for the hotel doorman to dart across the pavement and set the revolving doors in motion before sweeping through. She was ten minutes late, but since that was exactly how late she'd intended to be, she did not hurry. Nothing, anyway, could add to the considerable flutter of nervousness already dancing in her stomach, a nervousness that was tinged with an odd kind of excitement, like wearing a revealing dress for the first time.

The bar was dimly lit in the American style, so that it was impossible to see anything until your eyes had got used to the gloom. She stopped inside the door to get her bearings. Almost immediately the figure of Schenker appeared out of the shadows and taking her lightly by the elbow, guided her to a booth and took her coat. She ordered a glass of champagne. He ordered a mineral water with ice and lemon to add to the one already in front of him.

'Will you change your mind about lunch?' he asked her smoothly. 'The restaurant does a lovely *sole meunière*. Or there's smoked salmon in the bar here. Or club sandwiches.' He'd been polishing up on his culinary terms and social graces, she observed. The *sole meunière* was dished up far less obsequiously than before, and with the correct pronunciation.

'I can't, I'm afraid.' In fact she had no other lunch appointment, but Schenker was not her idea of a scintillating lunch companion, and she wanted to be away and free of him the moment the business was over. 'Another time perhaps.'

He asked her some dutiful questions about Camilla and how family life was surviving Tony's appointment. Susan

326

kept her answers polite but short. She had no wish to discuss her domestic arrangements with Schenker, and if he had any brains, he'd realise that too.

He seemed to cotton on at last because he changed the subject, saying: 'And how's the fund-raising going? You've been doing great things for Save the Children.' He probably thought she was on the scrounge for more funds. This year alone she'd asked Morton-Kreiger for sponsorship for a major water project in India and to take fifty seats for a gala concert, and got both.

'You know how it is,' she said vaguely. 'The Third World's a bottomless pit.'

His small black eyes slid up to her face then away again several times. She could almost see him wondering why she'd asked for the meeting if it wasn't to beg for funds. He reminded her of a cautious reptile, waiting motionless to catch passing morsels.

They progressed unenthusiastically over the economic news, the state of the agrochemical industry and other equally thrilling topics until, unable to bear the sheer frustration any longer, Susan fixed him with her best gaze and said: 'Listen, something's come up. And I think you might be able to help.'

The raisin-eyes flicked away then back again, looking flattered, wary and curious all at the same time. 'Of course.' He reached for some nuts from the bowl on the table.

'You know a girl called Angela Kershaw, I believe.'

His hand hardly hesitated in its journey from the bowl to his mouth. He also made a pretty good job of hiding the glimmer of alarm that flashed into his eyes – a pretty good job but not a totally successful one, and Susan felt a tremor of satisfaction at the knowledge that she was on the right track.

He chewed on the nuts, a rapacious chomping. 'Umm . . . should I?'

'You and Tony had dinner with her in France.'

He made a show of trying to remember. 'Oh? Did we? Sorry – one meets so many people.'

Did he think she was going to be taken in by this sort of hot air? He must take her for a total idiot. Her temper rose and ripped away from her with alarming speed. 'Look,' she hissed, 'we can play games and pretend we don't know this woman, or we can get on and save ourselves a lot of trouble.'

He stared at her, taken aback, then, recovering, rubbed the

salt fastidiously from his fingers. 'If you say so,' he said cautiously. 'Go on.'

'This woman. She's seeing Tony. I think she's causing him problems.'

'Ah. I see,' he said unevenly. 'I see.' He was thinking hard, playing for time. 'What sort of problems?'

'I'm not certain. But Tony's looking very worried.'

'And you say you don't know the – er, details?' he asked, picking his way over the words as if they were glass.

'No, but I thought you might.'

A glare of amazement. 'Me? Why?'

'You introduced them, didn't you?' she said.

'No,' he said indignantly. 'I did not. Absolutely not. I only met her the once. I don't know her at all!'

He sounded convincing. Doubt opened up in front of Susan like a crevasse. 'But you know her well enough to remember her name?' she asked accusingly.

He didn't argue on that point. 'I really have no contact with Miss – er, this lady. And I certainly don't know what the – er, details are. Really. No idea at all.'

'But you could find out,' she persisted.

The surprise again. 'I'm sorry?'

'Your company must be finding things out all the time. It can't be too difficult.'

'Difficult?'

'Finding things out. Using investigators, that sort of thing.'

He shook his head. 'Mrs Driscoll, I'm afraid the sort of investigations we undertake aren't anything like that. We commission reports on other companies, City personalities, financiers, that sort of thing. We don't investigate – well, *personal* matters.'

'No?' She raised an eyebrow.

'Besides, what could you hope to achieve? What would you expect to find out?'

'What she's up to, of course.'

'Dear Mrs Driscoll – '

Susan bridled at the dear. Little creep.

' – it would be most unwise to follow such a course on a matter like this. You see' – he dropped his voice and adopted a tone of patient explanation – 'it's not something one could pursue without actually compromising the minister further – without exposing him to the most terrible dangers. Investigators – people like that – one could never entirely trust them. There could be leaks. The press might get to hear of it.' He paused to emphasise the full horror of the idea. 'The risks would be enormous.'

'Risks?' she said briskly, finding her confidence again. 'But you don't seem to understand. He's already at risk. This woman's putting enormous pressure on him, pressure he can't take. She might already be planning to go to the press for all I know.'

Schenker's mask of impassivity slipped a little and he chewed his lip in mild agitation. 'So? What are you suggesting?'

'She's got to be dealt with.'

'Dealt with?'

'Dealt with,' Susan repeated with more conviction than she felt. 'Given what she wants. Told to disappear. Paid off. Whatever it is she's after. And' – she fastened him with the full power of her considerable gaze – 'you're the best person to do it.'

He didn't reply, but she caught a hint of triumph in the staring black eyes. He liked the fact that she was having to grovel to him, she realised; he liked the fact that she'd had to come down to his level.

Schenker raised a beckoning finger and ordered another glass of champagne, and a Scotch and water for himself.

They didn't speak again until the drinks were in front of them and the waiter gone. Schenker took a long sip of his whisky. She noticed that his hair had been blow-dried to give the impression of thickness, the better to hide the receding hairline that reached almost to the bald patch at the back.

'Mrs Driscoll, even if I *could* find a means of helping,' he began in the sort of hushed condescending tone that pastors reserve for their flocks, 'I'm not sure it would be appropriate for me to get involved. In fact, entirely *in*appropriate. Behind your husband's back . . .' He sucked in his breath.

'But why?' she snapped.

'Why? Because quite apart from anything else, you might have misread the situation. Suppose there's no problem – '

'I haven't misread the situation. Believe me.'

He spread a hand, conceding the point reluctantly. 'But wouldn't it be better – more suitable, I mean – if a family friend, the family solicitor – '

'No. You're the only person who can do it. The only person I can trust.' It was flattery, of course, but it was also the truth. If anyone could deal with the matter effectively, it was Schenker. Not only did he have the power and the resources to do whatever should be done, but just as importantly he was a naturally secretive man, someone who could be relied on to keep things quiet.

He seemed affected by her unexpected declaration of trust. '*Dear* Mrs Driscoll, I wish I could help but . . .' A condescending smile, a regretful shrug.

She thought viciously: Don't patronise *me*, you little worm! But with superhuman effort she suppressed the urge to say so. Was he being dense? Had he really not got the picture? Or was he just playing games? She decided to spell it out for him. She leant forward and rested a hand on his arm. He quivered slightly as if, given half a chance, he would have snatched his arm away, and it occurred to her that he didn't like contact with women. Perhaps he was the other way inclined. She lightened her touch.

'Tony could be finished by this,' she said. 'The strain could kill him. And if that doesn't, then the scandal most certainly will – and if this woman's as stupid as she sounds then there *will* be a scandal. Either way, he'll be finished,' she said, hammering the point home. '*Finished*.' She withdrew her hand and added in elaborate parody: 'And then, *dear* Mr Schenker, where would we be?'

His eyes dipped, his face closed down into an unreadable mask, he reached for his drink. Sipping it slowly, he looked at her over the rim of the glass, his eyes sly and pensive.

'Under the circumstances . . .' He hesitated as if giving the matter further thought, though she had the feeling that he had already made up his mind. 'I will do what small amount I can to help . . .' He looked up to catch her reaction, but she kept very still.

'. . . But I can only act in a *private* capacity, as one friend helping another.'

Was she the friend he was putting himself out for? Or was it Tony? The intimacy didn't bear thinking about.

'. . . But I can promise nothing. Nothing. I'm sure you can appreciate that.'

Susan picked up her bag and got to her feet. 'I'm sure you'll do your best, Mr Schenker. I'm sure you always do.' And in the instant that followed, a brief look of understanding passed between them.

When she walked out into the foyer, Susan wobbled slightly on her heels, though they weren't especially high, and it was only when she was safely in a cab that she finally stopped shaking.

Dublensky tapped the corporation name into Anne's word processor, pressed the exit key and gave the print command. The daisywheel churned into life and disgorged the customised letter. A few weeks ago he would have sent nothing but a CV and a short covering note, but now he gave every application the fully personalised treatment.

By starting late and spinning things out a bit, this took him until noon, when he had an early lunch of cold cuts and salad, and set off on his daily bicycle journey to the gym for a workout. He had been making full use of the sports club recently; his membership lapsed in a month's time and, due to economies on the home front, would not be renewed.

A fresh breeze was scudding over the lawns but once out of the shade the patches of sunlight were warm and sensuous on his back. It was the sort of day that would normally have made him outrageously glad to be alive, but in his present mood the coming of spring was dimmed by the reminder that time was passing and jobs were harder to find in the summer. He pedalled at a leisurely pace, saving his energies for the tyranny of the Nautilus equipment. At this time of day the street was quiet. A couple of pre-school kids were riding tricycles in their front yards, a housewife was hosing her car, a truck was making a delivery.

A car overtook Dublensky and, with a soft toot on the horn, drew in to the kerb. Dublensky recognised the green stationwagon of his neighbour, Joe Ankar, and cycled up to the driver's window.

'You got callers, John,' Ankar announced, gesturing back in the general direction of the house. 'A removal company. Arrived just a moment ago. Parked right outside.'

Dublensky automatically glanced over his shoulder. 'Removal company? I don't think so,' he smiled. 'I'm not going anywhere.'

'Well, they're there all right. Just a small truck, so maybe they're just delivering something. Anyways, they went right up the side of your house, like they were expected. Thought you must be in, otherwise I'd have checked it out.'

Dublensky couldn't think what goods Anne could have ordered, not when they were cutting back. 'Thanks, Joe.' Waving, he turned his bicycle for home. As he breasted the final rise he spotted the truck, parked out front just as Joe Ankar had described.

It was a well-worn vehicle, with *ABC Ready Removals* emblazoned on the side in paintwork that had seen better days, and underneath in smaller letters *Dor-to-Dor Express*, with a toll-free phone number.

There was no sign of the driver. Dublensky parked his bike against the garage and walked round to the back of the house expecting to find the driver leaving whatever he was delivering in the yard and maybe wedging a delivery note inside the screen door. But the yard was empty, the door closed. He walked across the width of the house at the back and looked up the other side. Nothing. Returning to the back door, he opened the screen and tried the door handle.

The door swung open. Dublensky felt a sharp chill. Had he left it open? He went over his departure in his mind, reliving his progress through the house. But there was no doubt about it: he had definitely locked the door.

He tried to calm himself, tried to think the thing through. The smartest move would be to go to a neighbour's and call the police, but he hesitated. Suppose he was mistaken? Suppose there was no prowler, suppose the delivery man was even now leaving the parcel or whatever it was at the next house?

Best not to be too hasty; he'd feel a fool calling the police if there was nothing wrong. Best to check things out first.

He hovered in the doorway. Fear held him back, but curiosity finally drove him forward and he stepped gingerly into the kitchen, listening hard. Nothing. Only the muffled sound of a dog barking somewhere up the street. He crept forward, aware of sharp excitement and a crazy disbelief at his own actions which seemed so daring as to belong to someone else altogether.

Measuring each step carefully, conscious of the appalling pounding of his heart, he reached the hallway door and peered through. The hallway was empty, silent.

Then it came: a slight sound, a rustling, like paper. Close by, within the house. *Someone*. Incensed, he felt a great leap of atavistic rage, quickly followed by the equally primitive response to get the hell out. The intruder could be armed. Knife or gun, what did it matter? You ended up dead all the same.

Yet for some inexplicable reason a paralysis gripped him and he held still. It seemed that the intruder was taking a break too because the rustling sounds ceased. Against all his better judgement, hardly believing he was capable of such lunacy, Dublensky inched forward into the hall, propelled by an appalling urge to see the intruder himself. The squeak of his soft shoes on the polished floor sounded unnaturally loud, like he was wearing suckers on his feet.

He crept towards the double doors to the lounge which were latched back against the wall and, squeezing himself hard against the wood, peered slowly round the frame.

It took him a moment to take it all in. The mess, the scattering of papers and books, the books standing up like islands in a sea of white. A dark-haired man dressed in overalls was crouching next to the wall units, searching the shelves. After a moment he sat back on his heels, a sheaf of papers balanced on his knee, and went through them methodically.

Mesmerised, Dublensky stood and watched. The papers on those shelves were Anne's – lecture notes and case studies. What could this man possibly want with them? And why had he made such a mess to get at them?

The intruder flicked through the last of the pile then, as casually as if he were throwing a ball to a child, chucked them to one side so that they fanned out over the floor. He went to the next batch of papers and it dawned on Dublensky that this was no ordinary prowler. What kind of burglar would bother to look through batch after batch of valueless papers, and so systematically?

He didn't pursue the realisation further though he dimly perceived its significance. Instead he unbottled his anger, which was considerable, and stepped into the room.

Disconcertingly, the intruder, absorbed by his task, did not immediately see him. Dublensky drew breath to shout but the words died in his throat as he became aware of a flicker on the periphery of his vision, a movement that didn't belong. He jerked his head round. Too late, he remembered Joe's words. *You've got visitors . . . they went down the side . . .*

A second man was coming from the den. He too was dressed in overalls. He was a Hispanic, olive-skinned with a balding head and thick moustache. He saw Dublensky about the same instant that the crouching man did. Everyone froze, the Hispanic half-way through the door, the crouching man by the wall unit, and Dublensky in no-man's-land, three steps into the room with nowhere to go. They were frozen into a tableau, excepting that everyone's eyes were moving.

'Get out of my house!' Dublensky screamed, astonished at the aggression in his voice.

It seemed that the Hispanic didn't need a second invitation. He moved quickly, accelerating from a standing start to a smooth and rapid walk in no seconds flat. Dublensky retreated slightly, suddenly alert to the risk of attack, but the Hispanic, though coming in the general direction of the door, kept wide, taking a loop out towards the wall as if to establish his non-aggressive intentions.

'Get out of my house!' Dublensky repeated, his attention caught by the crouching man, who had straightened up and was also beginning to move. He came forward at an almost leisurely pace, making no attempt to pretend he was heading for anything or anybody but Dublensky.

Dublensky felt a bolt of alarm, a fresh awareness of his vulnerability, and twisted his gaze back to the other man. Too late he saw that the Hispanic's loop had brought him close up behind him, that, far from continuing through the door, he was reaching out towards Dublensky. Dublensky's heart leapt against his chest, he heard himself cry out, and tried to duck away. The Hispanic's fist came punching forward, Dublensky countered with his forearm, only to find that the move had been a feint. With sickening helplessness he felt the Hispanic's free hand close in on his wrist, grip it brutally, and twist it up behind his back. The Hispanic kept twisting until Dublensky, yelping with pain, was forced to bend forward.

The least physical of men, Dublensky had time for a fleeting reflection on the stupidity of having instigated this encounter before everything was pushed from his mind by the arrival of a fist in his guts.

The top of his body jack-knifed forward and he sank slowly

to his knees. His initial astonishment was eclipsed by ferocious and overwhelming panic as he choked for breath. His lungs were banded in steel, his stomach crushed in a vice, he thought he was going to die. So desperate was he for breath, so focused on the clawing of his lungs, that for an instant his brain failed to register the arrival of the next blow, which hit the back of his head with the force of a power hammer. The impact seemed to drive his skull forward into his head, he was aware of a thunderous roaring, an astonishing weightlessness, then finally, with massive relief, the gathering balm of unconsciousness.

When his brain climbed slowly back to life, it was with a dragging reluctance. He lay motionless, his eyes and ears closed to everything but the needs of his lungs. He reached for breath, pulled at the air like a swimmer saved from drowning, yet when he finally managed to catch a long draught of air, it was only to cough it out again, along with his lunch. It was a while before he could be certain of breathing with any confidence, though it couldn't have been more than a few minutes. Then he lay still again, examining each of his senses in turn, muttering and whimpering with bewilderment and outrage, waiting for the worst of the pain and trauma to pass, half hoping he would slip back into unconsciousness again.

Somewhere outside, a bird sang. There was the hum of a car passing in the road. He opened his eyes and saw a scattering of papers, an overturned chair, an empty bookshelf and a vase of dried flowers balanced precariously on the edge of a table within an inch of falling.

No sounds came from inside the house. The intruders were long gone. He realised with a bitter sense of failure that he hadn't even managed to get the registration number of the delivery truck.

It was another fifteen minutes before he felt strong enough to lift his head, which ached with a nauseating intensity. He had trouble keeping his balance, and it was only by leaning hard on a chair that he managed to climb unsteadily to his feet.

His first instinct, as in any crisis, was to contact Anne. Her office told him she was in case conference, and he had to wait while she was called out. The sound of her voice, tinged with concern, sent him into helpless inarticulate weeping, and it was some time before he was able to explain haltingly what had happened. Anne, who in her determination not to fall into feminine stereotypes had spent a lifetime controlling her emotional responses, couldn't entirely suppress the quiver in her voice as she told him to sit tight.

While he waited for her, he sat in the lounge, staring at the sea of paper, shivering occasionally, murmuring and sighing to himself. When Anne arrived, he cried again and talked incoherently in a great stream of indignant rage. She gave him coffee and headache tablets, dried his tears and over his objections called the doctor and the police. The doctor wanted him straight down to the hospital for a skull X-ray, while the police, who seemed to think a bang on the head quite fortunate compared to some of the alternatives, were more interested in getting the suspects' descriptions and an idea of what was missing.

Anne led the police on a tour of the house. The upstairs was untouched, but the den, like the lounge, was a terrible mess, with overturned table and strewn papers. There were also broken lamps and damaged furniture, almost as if the Hispanic had had a more ambitious burglary in mind.

Even before Anne with her customary thoroughness started to check each item off in her mind Dublensky knew that nothing of monetary value had been taken. The fancy carriage clock Anne had given him one birthday was still on the windowsill. His four-hundred-dollar camera sat in full view on a shelf. Some cash in the top drawer of his desk was untouched.

Rapidly losing interest, the police took down the brief descriptions Dublensky was able to give them and, putting the incident down to a failed burglary attempt, said they'd come back when the inventory was complete.

Dublensky was relieved when they were gone. His outpourings had drained him of speech, his head throbbed mercilessly. At the same time his mind had taken on a curious lucidity. Armed with more coffee and aspirin, and a pile of cookies which Anne insisted he eat for their energy value, he knelt on the den floor and began to sort through the scatterings of papers, books, journals and notes. The shock had worn off, to be replaced by a gathering anxiety, something akin to dread. He had a suspicion that, in one sense at least, the worst of the day was yet to come.

It took him almost an hour to sort the loose papers into rough batches and reorder the files, and another half hour before he was absolutely certain of what was missing. Then it was all he could do not to weep again.

His scientific notebooks going back to his student days were gone – all twelve of them – as well as a number of scientific papers, several diaries and his main correspondence file. A hurtful loss, but bearable.

More difficult to bear was the loss of the Aurora dossier, with its data on the sick workers and the safety procedures at the works. Although, when he really thought about it, it was not perhaps a complete disaster, since much of it duplicated Burt's work.

What was far, far worse than any of these was the loss of the slim unmarked file which he had hidden inside a folder of scientific papers at the back of a lower drawer of his desk. He kept on searching, but there was no doubt.

The secret file on the Silveron toxicology trials, with its ten irreplaceable photocopied pages, was gone.

TWENTY-ONE

They sat by the window, separated from the oppressive midday heat by a chill wall of air-conditioning. The restaurant was Ethiopian, the drinks American, and the food somewhere in between. Daisy ate spiced lamb and couscous, and an unashamedly American salad served with Roquefort dressing. Paul Erlinger was stabbing at some charcoal-grilled chick-pea rissoles with yoghurt sauce.

'Pity you couldn't make it to the conference,' he said between mouthfuls. 'There were some really useful people there, some great new initiatives. What was it, you couldn't get away in time?'

'Something like that.' Something like the fact that Catch was not funding this trip and that she'd got a bucket-shop ticket for a four-day trip sandwiched around a weekend.

'Any other time and I could have shown you a bit more of the town,' he said. 'Washington has great food – Mexican, Cuban, Creole – you name it.' He gave her a lop-sided grin. 'Food's my weakness.'

'I would never have guessed.' She grinned at him. He was far from good-looking, with his round face, snub nose and small mouth, and he was decidedly heavy round the jaw and over the belt, but his looks were redeemed by a beaming affectionate smile and a conspicuous sincerity.

'I could have shown you the Chesapeake,' he said warmly. 'Or the Appalachians. But like I told you, I've an appointment Sunday.'

'Another time,' Daisy said.

'I'll hold you to it.' His eyes sent unmistakable signals.

'That would be nice,' she said, trying to match his affability without offering open encouragement.

Guiding the conversation gently back onto the right track, she ventured: 'This source of yours – he never gave you his name?'

Paul lowered his voice theatrically. 'He calls himself Alan Breck.'

'But it's not his real name?'

'I doubt it. When he wrote us, he put it in quotes. I assume he's a Robert Louis Stevenson fan. It's a while since I read *Kidnapped* – like twenty years. I don't even remember if Alan Breck was a good guy.'

'And you've no idea who he really is?'

'Nope.' The waiter cleared the dishes and gave them dessert menus. Paul made a point of waiting for the waiter to go before continuing in the same confidential tones: 'But he has to be with Morton-Kreiger or TroChem – that was the laboratory Morton-Kreiger used to carry out the official toxicology trials on Silveron. It's just possible he could be with the Environmental Protection Agency, I suppose, but somehow I don't think so. We have our contacts there and – well, we'd have heard if they had something that hot on a big one like Silveron.'

'Why don't they have any suspicions? It seems incredible.'

'Not incredible – oh no. Not when the EPA have just had their funding cut, not when they only have the manufacturer's data to go on.'

'What will it take then, for the EPA to start an investigation?'

He spread his hands. 'Alan Breck's data, maybe.'

'That would be enough?'

'You bet. More than enough.' He picked up the menu. 'You want a dessert?'

She shook her head. With an obvious effort of will, he pushed the menu aside.

'He didn't send you the data itself?' she asked.

'No, I think he wanted to see if we'd treat the information seriously first.' He signalled the waiter for the tab.

'Why didn't he send it direct to the EPA?'

'Listen, the EPA's a government agency. They'd want names, dates, sworn affidavits – I mean, a heavy deal. And this guy may be in a real hot spot. Going public could lay him open to serious trouble. By sending the stuff through us he

339

gets to lie low while we get to put ten times the political pressure on the EPA than he could ever achieve solo.' He paid the bill and they made their way to the door.

Outside, the heat closed around them like a blanket. The air was very still and a heavy bronze light hung over the street, as if there were a storm coming.

The EarthForce office was five blocks away, a broad red-brick converted warehouse on three storeys, between a used-furniture store and a Lebanese deli. The windows were heavily barred, the door faced with sheet metal.

'We take no chances,' Paul explained as he tapped a pass code into the security panel. 'A break-in would be seriously bad news.'

'You have a lot of break-ins round here?'

'Sure.'

'The drug problem?'

Paul led the way in and closed the door. 'Addicts? Oh, they're a problem, sure – but not so much for us. No cash here, you see, no valuables.'

'But you still get burgled?'

'You bet we do,' he said mysteriously. 'We've had a few kids try to hack their way through the windows – you know, just to show that no place in the neighbourhood is beyond their skills. But that's amateur stuff.' He paused, squeezing the suspense dry. 'No, we've had two professional break-ins in the last two years, and both times we've asked ourselves, now why would they bother?'

He led the way up the stairs, panting slightly, climbing crabwise so as not to lose a moment's conversation time. 'And we always came to the same unpleasant conclusion.'

'And what was that?'

'They came to get their secrets back,' he said with dramatic emphasis. 'Oh, they made it look like it was robbery – you know, spread everything around – but when we came to do an inventory, it was very particular kinds of documents that were missing. Since the first robbery we've made duplicates of all the important stuff and stored them in a secret hideaway.'

She followed him into the offices of EarthForce's Land Pollution Division. The layout was open-plan, the decor hi-tech rustic, with bare brick, tropical plants and six Meccano-style work stations.

340

Paul led the way to his work station and dragged over a second chair.

'So what exactly was taken?' she asked, sitting down.

'When I tell you that the Mafia controls the land-dumping industry in this country, you might be able to guess. All our hard-won evidence on illegal dumping – names, places, chemicals which got in the wrong barrels, chemicals which disappeared between destinations – you can imagine. Oh, and some major case files on river pollution – information which was going to nail some big companies. Companies who obviously had friends in all the right places. Pretty weird stuff, huh?'

It could only happen in America, she decided, the links with organised crime, the break-ins.

Paul, far from being disturbed by these incidents, seemed to relish them. 'We decided we were flattered by so much attention,' he announced. 'It meant we were on the right track.'

At last he seemed to remember what she had come for and, assuming a sudden seriousness, pushed himself to his feet and reached up to the shelves above the desk. The shelves had the usual lines of books, files and journals, but unlike the Catch shelves, everything was scrupulously organised so that journals were in sequence and files coded with coloured labels. 'I've got the case histories here.' He reached past the files and pulled down an unused pack of six A4-sized padded envelopes held together by a broad paper band and still in their cellophane wrapping. 'The ones I told you about on the phone – people who're all – or *were* until they got sick – workers on the Silveron production line in Aurora, Illinois. They were sent to us by Burt, the local physician. He's got no doubts about the cause of their troubles.'

'He can prove it?'

'That's the damnedest thing – nothing shows up in tests. Nothing significant, that is. The victims just feel and look like hell. One guy did develop a fatal case of cancer, like I said, but that happened so quickly that Burt thinks that the malignancy must have been brewing for some time, and was just accelerated by the chemical exposure.' He peered into the bundle of envelopes, levering their necks open with his fingers to view the contents. Finding the one he wanted, he pulled it out from between the rest.

'But these people, they lost weight?'

'Like they were starvation victims. And they got headaches, and sick to their stomachs. Some can't eat. Some have bad pain.' He indicated the packet of unused envelopes and grinned. 'My little hiding place. I don't leave this stuff in here at night of course. It goes in the safe.' He pulled a slim sheaf of papers out of the envelope. 'I thought of taking the stuff home every night, but it'd be no safer. I mean, I might get mugged.' He laughed at the thought.

Daisy couldn't help thinking that this obsession with secrecy and persecution was rather overplayed.

The bundle of papers was slim, perhaps ten sheets in all. Paul peeled off the first two and put them on one side. Gesturing her to draw her chair closer, he placed the rest in front of her. It was a report from the physician, Burt, containing a summary of his findings, backed up by the individual case histories of eight people, five male, three female, all workers at the Aurora Chemical Works, Aurora, Illinois. The symptoms were there: profound fatigue, severe weight loss, non-specific often agonising pain, loss of memory and concentration, anxiety and depression. Not every patient had every symptom, but most had the fatigue and weight loss though, confusingly and perversely, one had actually put on weight. All had developed acute sensitivities to chemicals to the point where they had to stay away from even the mildest household products. All but two had also developed severe food allergies and were following restricted diets.

'We talked to Burt several times now,' Paul commented. 'He's pessimistic on the prognosis. He says the condition appears to be untreatable, and that these people don't seem to recover. In fact, four have steadily deteriorated. He thinks the chemical has long-term effects on the immune system, though he can't prove it. Nothing shows in the tests – at least not in the tests he has available to him.'

She read the cases through once again, slowly. When she'd finished, Paul took the report and, with a small flourish, handed her the two pages that he'd put on one side. It was the letter from Alan Breck.

The letter began with: *You don't need to know who I am*, and launched into a summary of what she had already read, listing the ailments of the Silveron workforce, and urging EarthForce to contact Burt the physician direct for detailed case histories.

Morton-Kreiger had been given the facts not once but several times, the writer went on, but had continued to deny the problem. Only recently they had promised to tightened safety procedures on the production line, but the point was, there had never been anything wrong with the procedures in the first place. They had been checked at an early stage and found to be well structured and well implemented. Morton-Kreiger may have gone through with some cosmetic changes in the safety procedures in the last month, but that wouldn't achieve very much. The real point was, if Silveron could do this to chemical workers who were reasonably well protected, then what damage was it going to do the millions of people who'd handle the product once it got on sale?

But it was the postscript that put everything else in the shade. *There is also something seriously wrong with the original toxicology data. Some of it was faked. I have the evidence.* She looked up at Paul Erlinger.

'Dynamite, huh?' He took the letter back and fingered it reverentially.

Daisy tried to keep a sense of caution. 'How could it be faked?'

'Easy. Make up the results.'

'And Morton-Kreiger would do that?'

He made doubtful noises. 'Could be, but it was TroChem who did the testing. They're a so-called independent, but since most of their shares are owned by the agrochemical industry, they're not what you or I would call independent.'

'But why would they want to fix the results?'

'Who knows? Found themselves in deep shit? Maybe they'd set their price too low and had to cut corners, maybe they wanted to please the client.'

'Faked . . .' Daisy's mind worked quickly through the implications. If it could be proved, there had to be a good chance of winning a UK ban. There might even be a chance of bringing Adrian Bell's case to court with Morton-Kreiger in the defendant's seat, if not in the UK, where courts were notoriously resistant to the idea of chemical illness, then here in the States. Then, with a great leap of imagination, she saw possibilities for press campaigns, for bringing fresh attention to the Mackenzie case.

'Your case histories,' Paul interrupted. 'It'd be interesting to compare.'

Daisy, pulling her thoughts back into shape, said hastily,

'Of course,' and dug into her bag for the slim folder that contained Adrian Bell and Alusha Mackenzie's stories, with those of the two less serious cases that had been reported by the union man, Brayfield.

Paul swung back in his chair, reading fast. 'Mackenzie . . . Isn't that Nick Mackenzie's wife? Didn't I hear something about this?'

Daisy was silent.

'Jeese, but I read about it,' Paul exclaimed almost immediately. 'She killed herself, didn't she? Just terrible. But I didn't hear anything about a chemical hit.'

'It wasn't suicide,' Daisy said defensively. 'It was an accident. And as for the spraying, the story just didn't come out at the time.'

He caught her tone. 'Oh,' he said carefully. 'Right. Right.' He watched her for a moment, gauging whether it was safe to continue. 'Has he brought charges, Nick Mackenzie? If anyone has the resources, he's sure the one to do it. I hope you've got him set up right.'

'Set up?' she asked stiffly.

'I mean, in with the right advice. Legal, specialist . . .'

'Yes.' She couldn't bring herself to tell him the truth; or maybe she couldn't bring herself to admit to it. 'But I don't think he'll go ahead. I think he's . . .'

'Not interested?'

'Not convinced,' she murmured. 'He thinks it was something else.'

'That's the way it goes.' Paul heaved himself forward in his chair and read the case history again, adding almost to himself: 'And I guess he's got troubles enough.'

'Troubles enough?' A faint squeeze in Daisy's chest.

'Well . . . you know.' Putting his hand up to his mouth, he spread his palm and made a fluttering gesture.

She chose not to understand.

'Drink troubles.'

'Old history,' she corrected him, feeling combative.

Paul pulled down his mouth, looking doubtful. After a moment's consideration, he rotated himself out of his revolving chair, went to another desk and scooped up a newspaper. Searching through it, he folded a page open and positioned it in front of Daisy.

He didn't have to point out the item. There was a large

photograph. The pose of the three faces was fashionably disdainful, the juxtaposition carefully contrived, the lighting arranged to eradicate signs of age, but the face in the centre was unmistakably that of Nick Mackenzie. For some reason the reproduction had made his eyes unusually pale, almost white, so that they stood out in a disturbing way, like something out of a sci-fi film poster.

The headline was also large. *Amazon No-show Threat*. And the story: Lead singer Nick Mackenzie's health problems had caused the cancellation of a concert in Philadelphia. Disappointed fans had almost started a riot. The tour organiser was quoted as saying that Mr Mackenzie had been suffering from a recurrent chest infection which had necessitated heavy medication, but that he had now recovered and that the last two dates would most definitely go ahead. But the writer of the piece clearly thought otherwise. He reported that the lead singer's troubles had started in Chicago, where he seemed to be having trouble not only with his voice, but in remembering the words of his own songs. He'd made it into the second half, but only just. He'd looked unsteady on his feet and at one stage had almost tripped over.

'Maybe I was reading too much into it,' Paul suggested kindly. 'I mean, maybe it *was* just the flu.'

The rest of the piece was equally disastrous. There was the inevitable mention of tragic circumstances, the raking over of Alusha Mackenzie's death, then, most damning of all, a mention of Nick's former problems with alcohol. Clearly the reporter had few doubts as to the real cause of his so-called illness.

Daisy folded the paper with elaborate slowness. It hurt, and what surprised her was just how much it hurt. She felt a weight of responsibility. More than that, she felt angry at Nick Mackenzie for having shut her out. That's the real trouble, she thought: I believe that I could have saved him from this, if only he'd had faith in what I was doing.

But could she? People in trouble, people with habits they couldn't break, generally had a built-in resistance to being saved.

'So when are you seeing Alan Breck?'

She caught Paul by surprise, so that he didn't have time to prepare his lie and it came out on a false and guilty note. 'Eh . . . soon. I'm not too sure when.'

'You said the end of the month.'

'I did?'

'Paul, that's why I came.'

'Well – ' He fought it, looking unhappy then, catching her expression, gestured defeat. 'Okay – it's Sunday. Look, I would have told you but – well, I promised not to tell anyone. And what am I doing now? I'm telling you! But, listen, I don't even know if he'll show. We fixed it weeks ago when he called to check I'd got his letter. I haven't heard from him since.' He threw open his hands. 'He may not show.'

'But I can come along?'

'Listen, I wish you could, I wish you could.'

'I'll be quiet as a mouse!'

He fell back in his chair, his hands clamped over the dome of his stomach, and stared at her for a long moment. Then he gave a groan of half-hearted disapproval. He had agreed.

He picked her up from her hotel in the Adams-Morgan district shortly after breakfast, and they drove out over the Potomac, heading, she thought, south-west. The sky was hazy and bleached, the colour already leached out by the sun. It was going to be another hot day. The car had no air-conditioning and even as they passed the turn-off for the Arlington Cemetery, rivulets of sweat dribbled down Paul's cheeks and onto his neck.

They stayed on the main highway for over an hour until, just short of a place called Culpeper, Paul slowed the car and peered ahead, looking for landmarks. Sighting a turn-off, he gave a grunt of recognition and a moment later they pulled off the road and stopped in front of an Italian wayside restaurant advertising Budweiser and home-baked pizzas.

The interior was dark and chill and, at first glance, empty. A waitress led them towards a booth. From the ceiling Pavarotti was belting out a Neapolitan love song.

As they sat down Daisy was the first to spot the lone figure seated in a far booth, a silhouette set against the brilliant light of the window. Paul went over and held a murmured conversation. After a time he beckoned her over. Alan Breck had turned up.

He was in his mid- to late-thirties, with dark limp hair, pale skin, anxious eyes magnified by metal-rimmed spectacles and nervous hands that flittered and settled constantly. Daisy sat opposite him, next to Paul. He viewed the two of them with apprehension. Perhaps he'd hoped they wouldn't come. Perhaps he'd almost not come himself. Did he, too, have a persecution complex? Did he, like Paul, believe that he'd stepped into some sort of spy thriller where an all-powerful 'they' were watching his every move?

He did not volunteer his name. Paul launched straight into a speech of thanks and appreciation, sprinkled with reassurances. But though he radiated confidence and professionalism, this did nothing to impress their friend who, looking increasingly uneasy, tried to interrupt a couple of times until, in a final burst of desperation, he held up a staying hand.

'I don't know how to say this,' he said in a sharp off-beat voice. 'But – er' – he took a gulp of air, as if drawing courage from it – 'I think I may have wasted your time. I don't have, er, what I, er, suggested I might have . . .' He glanced up at their faces to see if they had understood. 'I do not have any data for you,' he said, drawing the words out ponderously. 'My, er, contact tells me that the information he had in mind, the data he *thought* was there – well, for one thing it wasn't exactly what he thought it was. I mean, it didn't add up to – what he thought it did. And then – '

He was interrupted by the waitress who deposited iced water and menus in front of them and, in an abrasive monotone, rattled off a long list of specials. Paul, momentarily silenced by the unexpected turn the conversation had taken, rallied sufficiently to order orange juice and eggs and hash browns with waffles and maple syrup.

Daisy ordered doughnuts. Their friend wanted only coffee.

'You never saw this data yourself then?' Paul asked.

Their friend shook his head. Despite the air-conditioning, he was sweating slightly. 'No. I just – heard about it.' He looked at the table, he looked at his hands; just occasionally he looked up at them in a series of darting uncertain glances. 'My contact – the one who told me about all this – well, now it seems . . . he built the whole thing up. You know, sort of misled me. I mean, he didn't *mean* to mislead me, but he kind of put the wrong interpretation on the figures. He thought they'd been fixed, made to look good – like I told you in my letter. But now – well – ' He took another gasp of air. 'He's pretty sure he was mistaken.'

His words settled over the table like a blanket of lead. For a moment Paul looked as though he was going to cry.

'This data, these figures – what were they exactly?' Daisy asked.

He took a sip of water. 'Well, they, er . . .'

The waitress sped up in her soundless soft-soled shoes, slid cups and cutlery noisily onto the table, and poured the coffee.

'You were saying?' Daisy asked as soon as she had left.

He glanced past her, checking that the waitress was well out of earshot but also, Daisy suspected, delaying the moment. 'They were, er, some of the main toxicology test results.'

'And how were they fixed?'

'But they weren't fixed,' he objected with an awkward smile.

'Quite. But when your contact originally thought they might have been fixed, how did he think it'd been done?'

He didn't want to go into that. He glanced at Paul as though for help, then gave a nervous mirthless laugh. 'He thought the results had been massaged . . . helped along a bit. Improved.'

'Is that easy to do?'

He shifted his shoulders reluctantly. 'I don't know about easy . . . But it's certainly possible.'

'Has it happened before?'

'Maybe. No one's sure. But once,' he embarked conversationally, 'oh, years ago – there was a rumour. A product was withdrawn.'

'Your contact – he's with Morton-Kreiger?'

He drew back again, considering whether he should make this most basic of admissions. Finally he nodded briefly but miserably, as if he was already angry with himself for having gone this far.

A door sounded. Some customers came into the restaurant, their voices raucous in the silence. Their friend stiffened and looked around him. Daisy knew then that it was only a matter of time before he made his escape. Outside, the sunlight had intensified, casting hard shadows.

'You were going to tell us something else,' she said, waiting for his eyes to drag back to hers. 'You said, for *one* thing the data wasn't what it appeared to be. What was the other thing?'

He made a show of searching his memory before saying with forced casualness: 'Oh, yeah . . . I was going to say that, er . . . my contact no longer has access even to the *summary* data. He found the file had been, er, removed from its usual place. It's never been returned. There's very little he can do to get it back. Officially he has no reason to call on it, you see.' He spread his hands. 'So . . . That's it, I'm afraid.'

Why, Daisy wondered, has our friend gone to all the trouble of stringing these stories together? Why has he bothered to come and meet us when it would have been so much easier to leave a message saying he'd changed his mind or, even simpler, not to have shown up at all? Why, when he's scared sideways and every which way, has he risked showing his face?

The waitress brought the food and a fresh pour of coffee. The doughnuts were the size of cartoon car tyres and glistening with frosted sugar. Paul, faced by a large plate of eggs and hashed potatoes, dug straight in, though that didn't prevent him from cross-questioning their friend at length, going over each fact in plodding detail as if by sheer repetition he might coax more out of him. Daisy could have told him he was wasting his time. Their friend had already lied himself into a corner and, however uncomfortable he might feel about that, he wasn't going to back down now.

'Wouldn't your contact know if the figures had been massaged?' Paul began. 'I mean, wouldn't it have required collusion between a whole group of people?'

'But MKI didn't carry out the trials themselves,' he explained quickly. 'It was a company called TroChem.'

'Oh,' said Paul, feigning innocence. 'And who're TroChem?'

'They set up about eight years ago, offering specialist toxicology testing. They've earned a reputation for being hyper-efficient and cheap. They've been very successful.' Their friend's hesitation had disappeared, Daisy noticed. And it wasn't just that he was on safer ground; he spoke with the ease of someone who knew exactly what he was talking about. A laboratory technician then? No, he was brighter than that. A scientist.

'There weren't any checks carried out on the work? No independent assessments?'

He hesitated slightly then shook his head and frowned.

349

'So,' Paul continued, 'it'd be hard to tell that the figures had been massaged, would it? I mean, from the outside?'

He liked that question; it gave him another opportunity to pour cold water on the idea of any stray information just lying around. 'Absolutely impossible,' he said. 'You'd need complete access to all the lab results, all the data. You'd need to get full access to TroChem's records.'

'Or you'd need someone to talk,' Daisy suggested gently. 'Someone who'd seen the data and was sufficiently qualified to know what the figures meant.'

His eyes blinked up at her. He didn't say anything.

Paul picked up a waffle and, dribbling maple syrup over the top, used it to break the yolk on his fried egg. 'There's something I'm not clear about here,' he said. 'This contact of yours – he's a scientist, right?'

'I can't say . . . I really don't think I should say.'

'Of course,' Paul said hastily through a large mouthful. 'I just wanted to know if he – your contact – had the expertise to assess the data when he had it in front of him.'

Alan Breck's face was transparent; Daisy could see him fighting his way round his self-imposed obstacles. 'But I told you, he didn't have access to the full data,' he said. '*No one* could have made judgements about anything without having the data!'

'But he saw enough to suspect the possibility of – hell, let's be clear what we're talking about here – *fraud*?'

'I told you – he was mistaken. Really, he got it wrong!' His voice was taut and thin.

Paul nodded slowly. 'Right, right. Well . . .' He mopped up some egg and forked it rapidly into his mouth. 'Maybe we can still persuade the EPA to review Silveron.' He was thinking aloud. 'Approach them another way.'

'The Aurora testimonials,' their friend interjected with something like relief, and Daisy realised that he'd been trying to lead them to this point. 'If you're so concerned – that evidence should be enough, shouldn't it? You're in contact with Burt, aren't you? You only need some back-up – an expert or two – and then you can file for deregistration, can't you?' He looked back and forth between them, like a child seeking reassurance.

'We'll give it all we've got,' said Paul, licking syrup off his fingers.

350

'At the very least the EPA will have to postpone approval. I mean, won't they?' He sounded as though he needed to believe it very badly indeed.

'But if that fails?' she asked quietly. She felt Paul give her a questioning look. 'What happens if the Silveron launch doesn't get postponed? Suppose we have a repeat of the situation in Britain?'

Their friend didn't reply. His eyes were very large behind the lenses of his glasses.

'Britain?' he echoed.

'We've got two sick people, and another two possibles. And those are just the ones we know about.'

In a sudden movement he removed his glasses and rubbed the bridge of his nose. 'That's bad,' he said, and there was a gasp in his voice.

Paul tried to ease the moment along. 'It could be a lot worse.'

Daisy kept her eyes on their friend. 'Let me ask you one thing,' she said, 'do you believe Silveron is a safe product?'

He closed his eyes, then replaced his glasses very slowly and with elaborate care. 'Well, I can't judge – ' He caught her eye. 'No,' he said eventually, with a short baffled sound. 'I'd guess not.'

A noisy family arrived in an adjacent booth. 'More coffee anyone?' Paul asked brightly, looking for the waitress.

Their friend caught Daisy's eye. There were all sorts of messages in that gaze – fear, regret and something she couldn't quite read. A plea for understanding perhaps. As Paul turned back, he quickly looked down at his hands again.

She realised suddenly: it was Paul that was the problem. It was Paul that their friend didn't trust. Their friend had taken the trouble to come and deliver this message personally, not out of the goodness of his heart, but because it was vital for Paul to believe that he could be of no help in the matter, that he knew absolutely nothing, that, most important of all, there was nothing to know. The whole business had been an exercise in disinformation.

Why? Fear? Distrust of security at EarthForce? Or distrust of Paul himself? Did he know something about Paul that she didn't?

'Don't go away,' she said lightly, and went in search of the washroom. From her bag she took one of her visiting cards, emblazoned with the Catch logo, and, balancing it on the side of a basin, scribbled on the back: *If you ever change your mind, please call me,* and added her home number. Then, on an impulse: *Anything you say will be safe with me.*

She went straight back in case he might try to leave while she was gone. He was still there, though she noticed that he had manoeuvred himself closer to the end of the bench.

Paul was talking about the Aurora workers. She slid in next to him, opposite their friend, and, leaning forward on one elbow, slid the card under the table. She found his knee. He looked startled, his eyes swivelling nervously between hers and Paul's, then, as understanding dawned, he moved his hand down to meet hers.

TWENTY-TWO

The clinic was the last word in restrained elegance – or, as Hillyard liked to pronounce the word in his jocular moments, 'elly-*garnce*'. The place was new, built in muted brick with blue window frames, tinted glass, a ruthlessly landscaped strip of garden, and a large splash of flowers around the entrance. No expense spared. And one would hope not, at their prices.

He parked in a space marked 'Doctors only' and, whistling softly, marched into the foyer.

The accounts department was like a small bank, the customer service area separated from the clerk by a glass screen. Two Arabs in full garb were blocking the only window. They were bent over some papers as if they were having difficulty in understanding them. They were probably reading them upside down.

He inserted a shoulder politely between one of the Arabs and the window and said to the female clerk in his most attractive voice: 'Hullo there. I've come to settle Miss Kershaw's bill and I'm a bit pushed for time.' He gave her a collusive wink which she carefully ignored. 'You couldn't just hurry it along for me, could you?'

Turning away, giving no indication that she'd heard, the clerk tapped a code into her computer and looked idly at the screen.

Still smiling, Hillyard thought: Stone-faced bitch. The clerk swivelled in her chair and suspended her hand over a printer. The printer obediently spewed a document into her grasp which she ripped off and passed under the glass partition.

'Is this for me?' he asked with exaggerated surprise.

She gave a brief nod.

'Why, thank you,' he said, clasping his hand to his heart like some dreadful old ham on the steps of Elsinore, when what he really wanted to do was reach through the glass and grab the stupid woman by the throat and give her a good shake.

He went through the bill, item by item. Daily in-patient rate. Operating theatre hire. No mention of the actual operation, he noticed, no mention of that creepy word *termination*. Surgeon's fee, a healthy little three hundred and fifty quid. Now how many such jobs would that guy do in a morning? Six? Ten? It was all right for some; nice if you could get it.

He looked up to find the clerk watching him. He raised his eyebrows and gave her an exaggerated look of surprise, and she quickly looked away. He took the money from his wallet and counted it out. The notes were new and adhered to each other, and he took care to count them a second time. He didn't want to give old Stone-face the satisfaction of pointing out a mistake.

The Arabs, having asked a question and been rebuffed, had fallen back from the window to regroup. Hillyard thrust the bill with the money on top of it half-way under the partition. As the clerk reached for it, he dropped his hand back onto the money, pinning it to the counter. 'You'll tell them upstairs that it's paid, will you?'

'They usually call down.'

'But I'd like you to call up. Then Miss Kershaw will know she's free to leave, won't she?'

She pursed her lips. 'If you like,' she conceded.

He shone her a gracious smile. 'It would be so useful.' He kept his fingers firmly on the money. 'You'll phone immediately then, will you?'

She nodded, but he still didn't let go, not until she'd actually put it in words. Then he released the money with a gay flick of his fingers. When she had given him his change and stamped the receipt, he inclined his head. 'How very efficient you've been,' he said. 'It's been a real pleasure.'

He drove straight back to Battersea. Beji yapped excitedly round his feet as he let himself in, and panted up the stairs ahead of him, pausing hopefully by the flat door, asking for

354

food. Ignoring the dog, he walked straight into the main office.

No Beryl. Cigarette butts in the ashtray, a half-drunk coffee, stone cold with lipstick marks on the rim, a newspaper folded at the racing selections. It was, he noticed, Ascot Gold Cup Day. She'd be locked in the betting shop for the rest of the day, the old bag. He bent over the typewriter to see how far she'd got with the transcription of the last tape. Not far, was the answer. But far enough to cause him a distinct spark of interest. He leafed back through the transcript, then, sliding the earphones over his head, he played the rest of the tape, making notes as he went along.

He looked through what he'd written to make certain he'd got the essential points, then dialled the number of the South Bank office. There was no answer.

After lunch in the flat he took a coffee down to the office. Miss Kershaw would have had plenty of time to get home by now. He dialled her number.

She answered.

'Ah, Miss Kershaw, how are we? All right, I trust. Was the clinic comfortable? It seemed a most pleasant place. As far as these places ever can be, I mean.'

'Leave me alone.'

Now that wasn't very pleasant. He adjusted his tone; friendly but firm. 'I was wondering how we were progressing towards Friday. Travellers' cheques, passports, that sort of thing.'

'Go to hell.'

'I only want to be of help,' he said, ignoring her little outburst and maintaining a cheerful and uplifting tone. 'Your flight's at eight, I believe. Why don't I order a car for five? That'll allow us plenty of time for the Friday-night jams.'

'Christ – ' She was suddenly tearful. 'Just leave me alone – '

'I understand,' Hillyard said, feeling magnanimous. 'Why don't I call you again tomorrow?'

'Listen, just piss off. I don't *ever* want to hear from you again. Not *ever* again, d'you understand?'

'Now, now. I only want to be of help. Make sure you get away for your little break. After all you *have* – ' He was going to say 'earned it', which, considering she was getting a very tidy sum for having got laid by a minister of the crown, wasn't far off the mark. But, checking himself, he said instead: 'You *do* deserve it. And then you'll be wanting me to give you your

355

spending money, won't you? You'll be wanting to buy a nice swimsuit, and the odd frock – '

'Fuck off, you little pimp,' she screeched violently, and the line went dead.

Hillyard dropped the phone gently into its cradle. He said to Beji: 'Talk about the pot calling the kettle black.' The dog, who'd been hovering in the doorway, plucked up courage to come trotting across and sit at his feet.

'She'll be more herself by tomorrow,' Hillyard said to the dog. 'She'll be thinking about the rest of the money.'

Looking at the time, he tried the South Bank number again. This time it answered. He said immediately: 'Got something of interest for you.'

'Yes?'

'That Washington outfit, EarthForce, they're on to something to do with Silveron. I quote their man, Paul something: "We might have some hard evidence." He meant, against Silveron. The Field girl's flown over. They've promised to give her the details.'

There was a silence from the other end of the line, then: 'That's it?'

'For the moment,' Hillyard said, somewhat piqued at the lack of reaction. 'I thought it sounded quite promising.'

'Well, keep me informed.' The interest, Hillyard noted, was not exactly overwhelming.

'I can't say when I'll have anything. The Field girl's due back in the morning. There'll be the usual delay.' Hillyard added peevishly: 'It's not easy having one hand tied behind one's back.'

There was a silence. This was an old argument and not, apparently, one Hillyard was going to be allowed to go into just at the moment. 'And the other matter, the one you dealt with today?' came the voice.

'All on schedule,' Hillyard replied. 'The main event was yesterday afternoon. She's decided to go to the Seychelles with a friend. I'll see her off myself.'

'No problems then?'

'No, all paid up.' Unable to let things lie, Hillyard returned to the old argument. 'You know, it's crazy to leave that office uncovered.'

'You know the policy. Too risky.'

356

'There'd be no risk, not with the new technology. I told you, no one'd ever know they were there.'

A pause. 'We'll see.'

'You talk about risk, but personal visits are ten times riskier.'

'I'll think about it.' He was sounding edgy. He didn't like being pushed.

'What about the boyfriend's place then?' Hillyard suggested. 'I could fix that up, no trouble – '

'No.'

'But she spends quite a bit of time there.'

'No.'

Hillyard gave a biting little sigh of annoyance. 'Right-ho, you're the boss. But don't blame me if I miss something.'

Hillyard replaced the receiver a little too hard so that it jumped out of its cradle and he had to replace it. The dog was still at his feet. He bent down and grabbed its head. 'No imagination, these people, eh, Beji?' he hissed into its ear. 'No imagination.'

The dog looked up at him, its eyes bulging beseechingly, and gave a little whimper. Hillyard pushed its head playfully from side to side, gripping the fluffy ears tighter as it tried to struggle free. 'None at all.'

Releasing the dog, he pushed it aside with his foot.

Daisy thought: Now how did I manage this?

She was standing in the main hall of the Greyhound depot at the Port Authority building, on her own, with a hundred and fifty-three dollars in her pocket, an empty folder of travellers' cheques, and a gaping ignorance of New York. Her homeward flight had left Washington two hours ago, making her return air ticket, which had been a cheap no-swap deal, worth nothing at all. Worse, she wouldn't have time to find a hotel, not if she was going to get to Madison Square Garden by seven thirty.

She looked for some bench space, no easy matter when the little available seating was taken up by sprawling family groups, back-packers, and sinister men with lizard eyes and large bellies. Taking her case to a corner, she laid it on the floor and sorted her way through underwear, a change of T-shirt and a toothbrush. A passing security guard paused to stare.

357

Pushing the bundle into her voluminous shoulder bag, she lugged her case towards a uniformed official. It took a moment to establish that it was not a left-luggage office that she wanted but a parcel check.

The depository was on the lower level, and cost two dollars. Which left a hundred and fifty-one dollars for a non-available ticket for a concert that may or may not happen, and a hotel room she may or may not find.

Outside, the heat was oppressive, and a thin clammy rain was falling, almost as warm and sticky as the air itself. The traffic was heavy and the cabs all taken, and it wasn't until Daisy leapt across the street at a run, yelling at the top of her voice, that she managed to capture a cab offloading a passenger.

The traffic was at a crawl and the ten or so blocks to Madison Square Garden took ten minutes. The cab driver, who spoke almost no English, did not understand her questions about cheap but decent hotels, although she noticed that his English improved dramatically when it came to spelling out the fare.

The Garden was a massive circular building covering two blocks. The entrances were choked with people. When Daisy finally managed to get inside there was no misreading the signs above the ticket windows. Sold Out. No Returns.

Back outside, the touts were asking upwards of a hundred dollars and weren't about to haggle. One laughed derisively when Daisy volunteered an English cheque.

Seven twenty-three. A passer-by directed her to a late-opening bank in a nearby shopping plaza. At the bank she discovered that money was easy to get, but only if you were a paid-up card carrier. Gold card, dispenser card, charge card: the automatic dispensing machine wasn't too fussy. But if you were a non-plastic-carrying foreigner with scruples about easy credit the place was a fortress. Sometimes, Daisy reflected, pursuing one's principles was a pain.

It was after seven thirty. The rain was thin but penetrating. She ran back to the Garden along an uneven and slippery sidewalk. A few latecomers were still rushing for the entrances, but otherwise the street was empty. Even the touts had evaporated.

She walked round the curve of the building until she found the employees' entrance, a dark doorway hidden under an overhang. It was well-defended, a veritable Alamo, with rows of hefty security guards glaring out over metal barricades, looking for hostile forces.

She approached the nearest guard, who was staring at a point somewhere above her head. 'I've come to see someone in the show.'

His eyelids flickered. 'Passes only.' She noticed he spoke without moving his lips.

She nodded slowly. 'Suppose I said that I was expected, but I'd lost my pass – '

The guard swivelled his eyes in her direction. 'Look, lady, no one gets through without a pass, okay?' This time his lips gave the slightest quiver, as if he were exhaling sharply.

'I see,' she conceded. 'Could I at least leave a message?'

His mouth hardened.

'All I'm asking is to write it inside and come straight out.'

'*Lady* – it's no pass, no *pass*, okay?'

'Let's try it another way,' she said. 'Suppose I write the note out here and then hand it to you to leave inside the stage door.'

The guard blinked impassively. 'Lady, you can write an en*tire* book so long as you don't pass this point, okay?'

She eyed him, this fountain of assistance, then smiled to show that she had no trouble in moving her lips.

She retreated. A note – what would a note do? She felt a sudden gloom, a loss of energy. A note probably wouldn't even get through.

In the shelter of the overhang she extracted one of her cards and scribbled a few words on the back. *I'm here in New York. I have some news. I wondered if we could meet* . . . The next moment she groaned aloud as the absurdity of the exercise struck her, as she remembered that she had no number to leave, no contact point. She leant her head against the wall. What madness is this, Daisy? Not thinking straight. Not thinking at all. Ever since the meeting with Alan Breck she had been overcome by a driving compulsion to act; and now it had lost her the last of her judgement.

Dropping the business card back into her bag, she crossed the street to a phone and rooted around for a number Paul Erlinger had given her. It was a friend of his; someone environmental in Greenwich Village. The friend had been out that morning when Paul had called, and now as the line

359

picked up Daisy heard the unmistakable click and blip of an answering machine. Curious sounds came singing down the line, a gentle twittering. At first she thought it was a bad connection but then she realised it was birdsong, a dawn chorus. After a few seconds, a voice came winging over the symphony. 'Hi, this is Thomas H. Raffety, working towards an integrated environment. I can't take your call right now, but I'll get back to you as soon as . . .'

Rain came shafting against Daisy's face. She twisted away from it, and, out of the corner of her eye, saw a figure emerge from the barricades around the employees' entrance.

Tom H. Raffety's machine bleeped in her ear, awaiting an answer. She gave her name absently, her attention fixed on the briskly walking figure who was crossing the street towards her. He was a young man in jeans, pale sneakers and a bomber-jacket with the collar turned up against the rain. As he drew closer she saw *Amazon* emblazoned across the front.

Tom H. Raffety's tape was turning patiently, the bird population silent. She muttered, 'Call you later,' and replacing the handset, hurried to intercept the striding figure.

'Excuse me – are you with the show?'

He cast her a sidelong glance but didn't break step.

'I'm a friend of Nick Mackenzie's. I'm in town unexpectedly.' She was almost running to keep up. 'You wouldn't be able to get a note through for me, would you? I couldn't get past the apes on the gate.'

His face grimaced, he rolled his eyes wearily heavenward. 'Come on, luv, I've 'eard it all before!'

She laughed: his accent was pure East End. And resuscitating the full ear-splitting beauty of her half-forgotten south London accent, she gave her best performance yet; she was the environmental campaigner over on a conference, she'd come to the show because Nick had invited her, but she'd failed to let him know in time, hence the lack of contact. After the long day and the succession of disappointments, the little embellishments came easily.

His name was Les and he was a roadie and he wasn't totally convinced. But he had at least come to a halt and was standing in the rain, listening. The campaigner bit seemed to hold him; he was impressed by the sight of her card. He also took in the fact that she'd had meetings with Nick, that they'd worked on an investigation together. She could see from his face that

360

he'd already worked out which investigation that must have been.

He dithered for a while, his expression swinging between caution and suspicion, then with a decisive grunt he jerked his head towards the barricades and led the way back to the Alamo. After a few minutes he came out with a pass that got her as far as the stage door. As she passed through the barricade Iron Lips, impassive to the end, made a point of looking away.

Tearing a page out of her address book, Daisy scribbled: *I'm here in New York. Wanted to see the show but you're too popular. Have you a moment later? Or tomorrow? Something's come up – extraordinary and important news. Daisy Field (from the Campaign Against Toxic Chemicals). PS Please leave a message at the stage door with a number where I can reach you.*

'It'll be all right to pick up a message here?' she asked. 'I've no contact number, you see.'

Les shot her a doubtful glance, then, looking at his watch, issued a sigh of inconvenience. 'Wait a mo,' he said abruptly and before she could ask him where he was going he'd disappeared into the backstage area.

At the barricades the guards lounged at their posts. Old Iron Lips slid her a knowing look, as if he'd had her number all along. Beyond the canopy, the rain fell steadily. Above the hiss of wet tyres on the street, she thought she could make out the twang of amplified music from inside the hall.

Les was back in five minutes. He had an envelope in his hand. It was unsealed and lying inside it was a ticket.

Daisy laughed with surprise and pleasure. 'How on earth did you manage that? Thank you.'

He was half-way out of the door, resuming his interrupted errand. 'Don't fank me, luv,' he said. 'Fank the boss.'

The sound didn't hang in the air, politely waiting to be heard, it resonated through your body until your bones vibrated and your ears drummed and your brain felt as if it contained a billion megawatts of sound. And just in case that wasn't enough to pulverise you into submission, there were the special effects. Strobes, lasers, kaleidoscopes of garish lights, and a stark fantastical set of girders and reflective metal revolves.

It had been so long since Daisy had been to a live concert

that she found herself jerked sharply back in time, landing somewhere between school and student days, surprised at the vividness of her memories yet unable to relate to them.

The auditorium, a vast amphitheatre, was packed. There were ageing fans in Gucci shoes and designer jeans, jiggling around in their seats like fifteen-year-olds, having no trouble in recapturing the good old days. There were real kids too, who had ten years on Daisy, if not a great deal more, and for perhaps the first time in her life it occurred to her that, to some people at least, she was middle-aged.

From the stage, one number followed another. The band was in two sections: towards the rear a shadowy six-piece backing group, and to the front and bathed in ever-changing light, Amazon – or rather two-thirds of them. Nick Mackenzie had not yet appeared.

On first seeing this, she'd decided that it was part of the act, an old theatrical trick to build up the tension. Though it occurred to her that, in view of the press stories, the suspense might not be of the sort the producers had had in mind.

After a time it seemed to her that the audience was starting to get restive, although this might simply have resulted from the monotony of the music, the sort of tuneless rock that had fuelled a hundred forgettable bands. It was certainly not Nick Mackenzie's sort of music. This was all rhythm and amplification, while Nick's songs had striking melodies and words that you actually listened to, songs about issues, songs about the environment, songs that had been written before most people knew that Brazil had a rain forest. His biggest hits, though, had been love songs. Yet they too were different – sharp and funny, or, when they were sad, seriously sad, so that you didn't play them when you were feeling down.

The set finished. The band took their bow. The lights faded. A shiver of expectation passed through the crowd.

Was this it then? Or was this the big let-down? Had the others been covering for him? Would he fail to show?

There was a pause.

Then quite suddenly, without warning, he was there. No special effects, no drumroll. He simply slipped out of the shadows and stood there in the spotlight, centre stage.

The crowd roared its welcome. He gave a small gesture of acknowledgement, a brief spread of the hands, and launched straight into his first song.

The crowd fell silent. A charge seemed to fill the air, partly expectation, partly, it seemed to Daisy, something a little less comfortable, as if the crowd were daring him to live up to their expectations, to match up to the collective memories of a thousand middle-aged fans for whom, in their imaginations at least, time had stood still. Or maybe it was more sinister than that; maybe some had come in the hope of getting altogether more dramatic kicks by witnessing a spectacular and highly public personal disaster.

Nick was dressed simply, in black jeans and open-necked shirt. His hair looked different – longer, fluffier – and his skin pale. Even from this distance she could glimpse the brilliant blue of his eyes. He wore no jewellery, no gold medallions or bracelets. In fact, there was nothing extraneous about him at all.

The effect was powerful. There was something about the way he stood, self-contained and uncompromising, that made it impossible to drag your eyes away from him. And she didn't try. For some reason she felt a proprietorial thrill, as if she had in some way helped to get him there.

Amazon, finally complete, began with a rock ballad, a hit from over twenty years before. The strobes flashed, the lasers darted tongues of light, the crowd roared its approval. Yet for all the heightened atmosphere, for all Nick's presence, it dawned on Daisy that, while the other two were squeezing every inch of attention from their performance, Nick was withholding something from his, something elemental.

The memory of the courtroom strong in her mind, she watched his every movement, sensitive to the slightest suggestion of hesitation, wary of any step that might remotely resemble a lurch. But it wasn't the drink or, if it was, he was hiding it very well. He moved easily, almost lazily, and she remembered his extraordinary grace, the beautiful hands, the long stride.

More Amazon hits followed, a rock number, a rock ballad: standard stuff from the Seventies. Then a conscience song, one of his early ones, famous for its biting words and powerful message. But now, for some reason, the force, the intensity had gone. The singing of the song seemed to be posing an immense trial for him; she could sense the effort he was making to get through to the end. And then quite suddenly she understood: his heart simply wasn't in it. He was going through the motions all right, moving to the rhythms, creating the appropriate expressions, doing what was expected, but the effect was strained and contrived.

It seemed to her that the crowd's early excitement was also bleeding away. At the end of each successive song, the applause seemed to become less frenetic, more restrained. By the end of the set the air itself seemed cooler.

She noticed that, when Nick stepped back to take a bow, he was frowning slightly.

The applause died away. This was the moment for the opening chat with the audience, the ritual hi-there and how-wonderful-it-is-to-be-back, but the lights, instead of coming up, dimmed rapidly, leaving the stage in darkness. A single white spot grew at the front where Nick had been. It was empty. The silence drew out. The audience was very still, as if no one dared to imagine what might happen next.

Was this another stage effect? If so, it was in danger of being overplayed. The suspense was being pulled out to breaking point. Then, just as the silence became unbearable, he stepped slowly back into the cold white pool of light and up to the microphone, with a guitar in his hands. For a long moment he stared at a point a yard or two in front of his feet, then, coolly, almost absentmindedly, started to play, very quietly, very slowly, and with rapt concentration. After a few bars he began to sing, so softly that his voice was barely audible above the instrument. A verse later and the band came in, muted and unobtrusive. He sang out a little then, but only enough to be heard. It was almost as if the audience didn't exist for him, as if he were singing for no one but himself. The effect was extraordinarily intimate, and the crowd seemed to reach forward to meet him, to try and join him in the intensity of the experience.

A sea-change had come over him, Daisy realised, a shift of mood and focus that had brought him back into his perform-ance. It was almost as if he had decided to reinhabit his emotions. Now it was all there – force and feeling and words and melody. And heart – yes, that as well.

He came to the refrain and suddenly his voice soared high above the music, and the sound was clear and strong, and so full of pain that something squeezed tightly in Daisy's chest.

. . . *Long nights, lying softly in the dark, waiting for you* . . . *lost to me . . . in the long nights* . . .

As the song wound its way effortlessly through her emotions, it occurred to Daisy, with the suddenness of the obvious, that he wasn't singing for himself at all, he was singing for his wife.

By the time he held the last mournful note, Daisy had to dig out a hankie and give her nose a good blow. Music got her like that sometimes.

The sound fell away. The crowd was still for an instant, caught in a short collusive silence, then burst into loud and ecstatic applause.

The lights came up. Nick seemed to become aware of the crowd for the first time. He bowed and gave a brief self-deprecating smile, the sort that comes with all sorts of conditions and apologies attached.

Daisy felt an overwhelming sense of release, as if she had personally delivered Nick from whatever fate had been lying in wait for him.

After that he was all right. Even in the fast rhythm numbers he managed to deliver all the dreams intact, while in the solo numbers he held everyone in an effortless grasp, and the crowd was his, and his alone.

It was after ten thirty when the last applause died away and the crowd surged out into the night.

The rain was still falling. Sheltering inside an exit Daisy searched her bag for the number of Tom H. Raffety and his performing aviary. Deep in the bag, next to her address book, was the envelope that had contained the concert ticket. She drew it out and took another look inside. Nothing. It was only then that she thought of turning it over and looking at the front.

It read: *Hotel Pierre, Suite 1605. Nick.*

365

TWENTY-THREE

Bourbon was smoother than Scotch, and sweeter. It slipped down more easily, like honey, though Nick suspected his liver didn't find it quite so attractive. Sometimes, as now, he mixed the liquor with dry ginger to persuade himself that it lasted longer that way. It was a reasonable deception so long as he ignored the proportionately larger swigs he took by way of compensation.

He took a big gulp now. If a drink had ever been essential, this was it. Well, perhaps the first had been really essential, but this one, his fourth or fifth since the show, was just as deeply deserved. He had abstained since two thirty, five hours before the concert, an exercise he often set himself on performance nights just to prove that he could do it. Though what exactly it proved, he wasn't sure. At the start of the show, just when he needed all the help he could get, he always felt lousy.

Now he sat back in the armchair, bare feet propped on the seat opposite, lit a fresh cigarette and stared out into the Manhattan night, just as he'd stared out into a million other nights across America, drink in one hand, cigarette in the other, waiting placidly for oblivion.

He reviewed his performance, although it took precious little analysis. It had been dishonest, second-rate. He'd faked it – faked the pleasure, faked the climaxes, like a woman deceiving a lover. And they'd applauded him. Which just went to show you could fool a lot of people a lot of the time. Though part of him couldn't believe they'd really been taken in.

Well, what did it matter? He knew all right. He knew that on the times he managed to carry it off – when he managed to carry it off at all – he did so by the skin of his teeth. Far from this uncertainty stimulating the adrenalin, far from providing a welcome edge to things, it filled him with a sickening panic.

There was a knock on the door. He didn't answer. The knock came again and David Weinberg's muffled voice called: 'Nick? Nick? How about dinner?'

Nick got slowly to his feet, walked through to the lobby, flicked open the door and returned to his chair.

David followed him across the room. 'So? How about joining us?'

'No, thanks.'

'Come for a short time. Just one course.'

Nick briefly considered the prospect of dinner with David. He knew exactly how it would be. Somewhere showy, like Sardi's, with a group of grey-faced backers, sponsors or recording company executives, providing sparkling conversation about percentages, contracts and promotional strategies.

'I'm fine,' he said.

David was silent for a moment, and Nick knew he was eyeing the glass in his hand and the bottle of bourbon on the side. 'Nick . . . Take it easy, eh?' There was sadness in his voice, but also a note of censure. 'We've still got a long way to go.'

Nick almost laughed. 'Sure.' There was an album to record in the autumn, and the European tour at the end of the year. Twenty-four gigs in six weeks. A beautiful unimaginable nightmare, and there was no one he could blame but himself.

'Shall I call room service for you?' David asked.

Nick shook his head and, raising a hand, smiled a goodbye. David, taking his cue, gave a small sigh and left.

Nick got up and made himself another drink, but without the dry ginger this time. When David took the trouble to look him out after the show, the pressure was really on. Usually David kept well clear of everyone else's troubles, but when he did make the decision to get involved then he did it wholesale, in full Jewish mama mode, complete with exhortations to eat and doctors armed with vitamin shots.

The problem had begun in Chicago, on the morning when

Nick had failed to put the bourbon bottle away. It had started like any other day on tour, that is bleakly, with a homogeneous hotel room, a nagging hangover and no reason to get up. He'd read for a while, a fashionable and impenetrable novel, then turned on the TV to watch the news. A South American coup, an earthquake in Turkey, a mugging. The mugging was particularly vicious; a young female lawyer attacked and left for dead outside her New York City apartment. By New York standards it wasn't such a special story and probably would never have made the national news if the girl hadn't been the daughter of a senator, yet there was something about the story that affected him. Perhaps it was the girl's picture – she was very pretty – or because she was about to get married, or because she lived just a block away from his and Alusha's old apartment. Perhaps it wasn't anything to do with the mugging at all. But suddenly he found himself holding onto his pillow as if it were a life-belt and he were in danger of drowning, which in a sense he was. When the despair threatened to close over his head, he forced himself out of bed and into a cold shower and paced the room and tried to fight his way out of it until, with an almost laughable inevitability, he reached for a drink. There wasn't a thing he didn't know about himself at that moment, not a shaft of self-knowledge that didn't turn in him, but it made no difference. At that moment there was simply no other way to save his life. The binge lasted two days.

Since then he'd regained some sort of hold on things. Each day had become a precarious walk along a precipice, a contest to maintain his consciousness a notch or two below the critical level without actually falling over the edge. But there were still the dangerous days, the days when he lost his fear of heights.

Another knock came on the door. Mel or Joe, or a message from an acquaintance perhaps. He didn't move; there was no one he particularly wanted to see.

The knock came again, a gentle but insistent tap. Giving in with bad grace, he got up and, drink in hand, went to the door. A girl stood there, most definitely familiar, yet out of context, so that he couldn't immediately place her.

Reading his expression, the girl's smile faded a little. 'You didn't suggest a time,' she said, holding an envelope up in front of her face.

'Ahh.' Recognising his own scrawl, the memory came stumbling back. 'Of course . . . *Daisy* . . .' He touched his head in apology.

'I thought I'd better come straight away,' she said. 'In case you were racing off somewhere.'

He stood back to let her in. 'Racing? No . . . No . . .' He gave a low chuckle. 'Where I was going, it wasn't fast.'

'This is the second time,' she said, walking through to the sitting room and surveying the lavish decor, 'that you've forgotten me, I mean.' She turned and gave him a jaunty grin. 'But I won't take it personally.' Then she laughed, and he realised that, for all her self-assurance, she was nervous.

'Have a drink,' he said.

'No thanks.'

He drained his glass. 'Well, I think I will.' He waved her towards a seat while he went to the drinks corner.

'I met your manager in the lobby,' she said. 'He got me through the security people and told me to come straight up. I hope that was all right.'

'Sure.' So that was it, he thought with a flash of annoyance: David exercising his good intentions, pushing female company his way. Next thing he'd be organising social evenings.

Daisy sank into a deep chair, falling back with a small sigh, before straightening up and sitting rather stiffly on the edge of her seat.

He added some dry ginger to the bourbon and took another look at her. When had he last seen her? In London? Scotland? His memory of that time was poor but he seemed to remember her as pretty and fresh-looking, rather a one-off. She looked different now. Bedraggled, her hair hanging round her face in tight damp curls, and scruffy-looking, with her old denim jacket and worn, mud-splattered trousers.

'I was so sorry about your wife,' she said, her voice very clear. 'I wrote. I don't know if . . .'

There had been hundreds of letters, but he remembered seeing her name, remembered reading something, though he couldn't recall what she had said.

'Thanks. I got it.' He sat down opposite her.

'Thanks for the ticket,' she said.

He gestured that it was nothing. He didn't ask if she'd enjoyed the show; she'd probably tell him anyway. Most people did.

369

'I enjoyed the show,' she said.

'Aha.'

A slight pause. She was smiling at him. It was a generous smile, candid and full of goodwill. 'What about you?'

'Sorry?'

'Did *you* enjoy it? I mean, presumably you don't sometimes.'

Well, there was a question. Lighting a cigarette he pretended to consider for a moment, although there was only one possible answer. 'Not a lot,' he said baldly.

'I didn't think so.' Aware that he might take this the wrong way, she laughed to soften the impact.

He decided to take it the wrong way anyway. 'Why would you think that?'

'Well – you seemed – not quite there. At the beginning anyway.'

He experienced one of the rapid mood swings that characterised his bourbon evenings. 'You're right,' he said abruptly. 'I was lousy, and it showed.'

But she wasn't having any self-pity. 'Not lousy, and it was only at the beginning,' she said firmly. 'Up till "Long Nights". After that you were terrific. Particularly in the slow numbers.'

He almost argued, but got up to get another drink instead.

The bourbon bottle was beginning to look more empty than full. Normally he left the bottle on the side, to maintain some degree of control, but for convenience he brought it across and stood it on the table between them. 'Sure you won't have one?' he asked, speaking with care so as to get the words out right.

She gave a slow shake of her head. Apart from the smile, her expression was unreadable.

He gulped at his drink. He always gulped when he was with strangers; something to do with nerves. 'So how's your campaign going?' he asked to change the subject. He didn't terribly want to hear, in fact it was the last thing he wanted to talk about, but she would be expecting him to ask and he wanted to get it over with.

'Oh, one step forward, one step back,' she said lightly. 'Usual thing. You know.'

He wasn't sure he did know. He pushed himself to say: 'I thought people were coming round. More aware. What with all the scares.'

She considered for a moment. Her back was still ramrod straight as if she were sitting in a hard-back chair. It gave her the prim look of a school teacher. 'The public can only take so much,' she said. 'They're already frightened rigid by the greenhouse effect and the holes in the ozone layer. The idea of being poisoned on a daily basis is altogether too much for them.'

'Well, you can see why . . .' He lost his thread – or perhaps whatever it was hadn't been worth saying – and buried his nose in his drink.

There was a long pause; he was aware that he had run out of conversation.

'Perhaps I'll have a drink after all,' she said. 'Coke if you have it.'

'Sure.' He got up and went over to the side. He took a Coke out of the fridge and began to pour it. He misjudged the flow and some spilt down the side of the glass onto the tray. As he picked up the glass to dry it, it came into contact with a bottle and made a loud clink.

Well, that hadn't taken long. Things were happening fast tonight.

He was aware of her eyes on his back. He took a breath. Concentrate, Mackenzie, get it together.

He carried the drink carefully back to the table. He sat down and watched her sip at the Coke. There was another pause. He wished he could say something appropriate, but his brain was thick and treacherous.

She flicked a thoughtful glance at him, as if she were plucking up courage to launch into something difficult and wasn't sure what sort of a reaction she'd get. Of course. He realised then: she would hardly have gone to all this trouble if she hadn't wanted to ask him something. Everyone wanted something. He decided to get it over and done with.

'So what is it you want?' he asked.

That took her by surprise. She dropped her eyes and gave a nervous grin, as if he'd caught her out in some trick. Her approach, whatever it might be, was not well planned.

'Well . . .' She took a deep breath. 'I could give you all the usual junk. You know – about wanting to get you involved in the campaign. The standard celebrity stuff, about needing your support on the publicity front and all that. Or . . .' She tipped her head to one side and gave him a sidelong grin, half

371

embarrassed, half amused. 'Or I could come right out and tell you what I really want.'

He fiddled with his glass. 'Let me guess – a benefit concert.'

'A concert?' She was genuinely surprised. 'Well, I suppose – I mean, we wouldn't say no. Not if you were offering.'

She had such a gracious way of putting things. He stubbed out his cigarette and lit a fresh one. 'So what is it then? That you want.'

She hesitated. He noticed her eyes, which were hazel with very clear whites. For the first time since she arrived her expression was entirely solemn. 'Money,' she said.

He almost laughed. Most people when they wanted cash, which was often, usually approached the subject casually, as if money was so much garbage that just happened to have attached itself to him and which he was only too glad to be rid of. But Daisy Field said the word with the spiritual reverence of the dispossessed.

This, or something else about her, made him smile. He studied his glass for a moment. 'Daisy Field. There's a name.'

If she was disappointed in the sudden turn of the conversation, she hid it well. 'It wasn't my parents who had the sense of humour,' she said. 'It was my schoolmates. Deeply original, they were. You can guess the sort of thing – Potato . . . Corn . . . Turnip . . . There wasn't a field they didn't try on me. I gave as good as I got, of course, but it made no difference. We called a truce at Daisy. To tell the truth, I didn't mind too much.' She made a face. 'Anything was an improvement on the original.'

'Which was?'

She gave a cat-like smile and shook her head. 'Can't say it. Too shy.'

It occurred to him that she was far from shy, and that no one got anything out of Daisy Field that she didn't want to give.

'This money, what do you want it for?' He had to concentrate to get the words out right. That came from forgetting to eat, a mistake he made two or three times a day.

'A research programme.'

'What kind?' he asked.

'To investigate a pesticide called Silveron,' she said, launching earnestly into her subject. 'Or to be precise, an insecticide. It's been on limited sale in Britain for about a year, and it's

372

due to be introduced here soon. We suspect it's unsafe. It's already caused serious problems.' She told him about some workers at a production plant in Aurora, Illinois, how they were seriously ill, how Morton-Kreiger, the manufacturers, were denying any link with Silveron. There was something about the way she talked, a breathless urgent quality, that made the story sound both convincing and a little unlikely. He remembered their car journey in London all those months ago, and how disturbingly simple she had made everything seem to him then.

'This programme,' he said. 'What would it give you at the en' of –' He took another shot at it. 'At the end of the day?'

'Oh, evidence of toxicity, evidence of carcinogenicity,' she said, as if it was the most obvious thing in the world. 'Evidence that would get the chemical banned.'

'Can't the government people take care of that?'

'Oh, they won't do anything,' she declared derisively. 'Not just like that. Not until we push some proof right in front of them. These new products have a momentum all their own, you see – tests, approvals and launches – and once the bandwagon's under way, it just keeps rolling. You have to produce a bombshell to even begin to stop them.' She gave what looked like a shiver and pulled her arms closer to her body. 'At the moment it would only be our opinion against the manufacturer's, and the way things are, that ain't going to stop anything. Our word carries about as much weight as . . .' She blew out her lips. 'Well, the paper it's written on.'

'Recycled.' He thought that was quite good, particularly for this stage of the evening. Daisy's face lit up and she laughed, a light dancing laugh full of amusement, and he flattered himself that it wasn't just politeness. The evening began to look up; he was glad she had come.

'How d'you know they'll listen? The gov'ment people.' He heard the thickening of his speech, the slurring of his words.

'Oh, our work'll be done under the strictest scientific conditions. They'll have no choice.' Her jacket had fallen slightly open, and he saw a dark crescent of damp down the front of her T-shirt. Through his not inconsiderable haze, it dawned on him that she was sitting so stiffly because she was soaking wet, and that it must have been the air-conditioning that made her shiver. He pulled himself forward in his seat. 'You're wet,' he said.

'I *am* a bit. No, not a bit – ' That laugh again. 'A lot!'

'Give me your jacket,' he said. 'I'll put it to dry.' After a moment's hesitation, she took the jacket off. Somewhere in the process of getting to his feet, reaching for the jacket and turning towards the bathroom, he had to reach suddenly for the arm of the chair. He shot a quick look at her. Diplomat that she was, she was showing a sudden and absorbing interest in the carpet. But she'd noticed all right, and he minded about that. He always hated anyone to see him in this sort of condition. Anyone being outsiders, people who wouldn't make allowances, people who would judge him.

Moving off again, he still hadn't got it right and barked his shin hard against the table and swore, though not so quietly that she could avoid hearing. By the time he got to the bathroom, he was experiencing one of his periodic bouts of anger and self-contempt. He could imagine what she was thinking: another foul-mouthed performer with more money than manners.

He went into the bedroom and picked out his favourite Fair Isle cardigan, some five years old but still in shape. Giving the furniture a wide berth, he negotiated himself back to the sitting room and handed it to her.

'Thanks,' she said. She had to concertina the sleeves before her hands appeared at the ends.

'Shirt?' he asked, seeing just how wet her T-shirt was.

'This'll dry soon enough, thanks all the same.'

'Something to eat?'

'Oh . . .' She looked undecided. Then her eyes sparked with sudden pleasure. 'Something nice and junky? I've been living off ethnic food for three days.'

He dialled room service and passed her the phone.

She took the phone uncertainly, but was soon ordering king hamburgers and fries, with ice-cream to follow. 'What about you?' she asked. He gestured a why-not and she ordered the same again.

She was hungry. She ate like a stevedore at the end of an eight-hour shift, in great gulps, hardly pausing for breath. Her hair was drying now, springing out into a halo of curls round her head, and the freshness had come back into her face. She had a fine clear skin, he noticed, slightly freckled over the nose and almost devoid of lines.

She may have been nervous when she'd arrived, but she

certainly wasn't now. She was perfectly happy to concentrate on her food and leave the conversation to him – which meant that as often as not she was eating in silence – and to throw him the occasional smile.

An uncomfortable thought came to him: Was she so relaxed because she thought he'd agreed to her request?

He tried to get the conversation going again, if only to iron out the possibility of misunderstanding. 'This money,' he said, picking his way through the enunciation. 'How much did you have in mind?'

She paused with the spoon half-way to her mouth, then returned it slowly to the dish. 'Brace yourself,' she said.

'Not suggesting I have another drink?' The wit. If it hadn't been such a joke, he might have laughed.

She grinned fleetingly, then fixed her eyes on him. They were large as lamps. 'It's a lot,' she admitted. 'We'd need at least two maybe three specialists and several assistants to get through all the work. And then there'll be the victims' blood to be monitored for maybe months at a time. That involves a lot of tests. I can't cost it fully until I get back to the UK and phone around and get estimates – '

'The UK?' he asked thickly. 'But . . .' There was a reason he'd asked the question but it took him a moment to remember what it was. 'The people are in Illinois – how're you goin' to test them if you're over there?'

'Oh, we can manage with the victims in Britain,' she said. 'There aren't so many, but there are enough.'

Two realisations began to filter through to Nick, both of which caused his heart to sink slightly. The first and the least surprising was that he was rapidly losing his nightly balancing act with the booze. Normally he put up no fight at all – the sooner it was all over the better – but tonight, just when he needed his brain, it was slipping away from him.

The second realisation, which was slower in coming but just as inescapable, was that she was holding back, failing to tell him something, something that he wasn't going to like.

In a bid to salvage his brain, he pushed his glass across the table out of reach and braced himself to tackle the hamburger. It was spongy and dry.

'What's the rest of the story?' he asked, putting some briskness into his voice. 'Why's all this so important?'

She had picked up the shift in his tone because she started

to speak quickly and urgently, in a level voice, very business-like. 'There are three reasons,' she said, striking one finger with the index finger of the other hand. 'First, all the victims are little people, and the way things are at the moment they haven't a hope of getting compensation, not without scientific back-up from us.'

The meat was too much to swallow and, pushing it out from the middle of the roll, he ate the bread with a filling of onions and ketchup.

'The second thing is that as things stand there's absolutely nothing to stop Silveron getting full approval,' she continued, bending back a second finger. 'That means it'll be used on everything – cereals, vegetables, fruit. A disaster just waiting to happen. Oh, the effects may not be so immediate, but give it a year or two and they'll start to be reflected in the health statistics. By which time the whole bandwagon will be that much harder to stop. Once a product starts to make money, manufacturers and government agencies become that much more reluctant to admit that anything could be wrong with it. Not until millions of people have been exposed to what may be irreparable damage.'

He saw that this kind of speech, with its crisp well-used words and ready-hatched thoughts, came easily to her.

She began to elaborate but he held up a staying hand. 'Got it,' he said. Replacing the last of the bread on the plate, he asked: 'And the third thing?'

'Ahh.' Her eyes shone with suppressed excitement. 'We have good reason to believe that the manufacturers are hiding something. It's even possible that they have falsified their test results, which shows just how desperately unsafe the system can be. But the only way we can hope to prove that is to come up with our own results – '

'Got it,' he interrupted. 'Come up with your own results . . .' He focused on her with great care. 'And?'

'And?'

'Why me? Why should I help?'

She hesitated, her confidence suddenly plummeted. He was reminded of a child caught out in some minor subterfuge. 'We have evidence . . .' she began slowly, fixed those beauti-ful clear eyes on him again, 'to show that Silveron was used illegally on forests in the west of Scotland last year.' She took her time, anxious not to give him too much too soon. Then,

376

with a deep breath, she added in a rush: 'And we have reason to believe it was sprayed on your wife. That it was the cause of her illness.'

He was silent.

Hastily, she reached down and pulled a file out of her bag and put it on the table. 'If you want to read the case histories of known Silveron victims, you'll find the symptoms are almost identical.'

He made no move towards the file, but stretched for the glass he'd carefully left out of reach across the table.

She began to tell him a long and involved story about an aerial spraying company which had been based to the west of Stirling, and a pilot who admitted to using Silveron in the Loch Fyne area, and how he had admitted to an abortive job on the Fincharn Estate. She went through every lead, explained every connection, described with considerable feeling the state of the sick boy on Loch Fyne – though he noticed that she was careful not to mention the boy's uncle, that loathsome Campbell – then jumped rapidly to her conclusions, explained them, interpreted them.

Facts, ideas, connections – they poured out of her like water, and like water they flowed over him and through him until his imagination foundered. Inventing a reason to get up, he went to find some dry ginger. The room swayed. That was a new one. Usually the room got progressively darker, like someone was turning down a dimmer switch.

He didn't realise she'd left her seat until she appeared beside him and touched his arm. 'Are you all right?'

'I'm all right,' he said.

'What about some water?' She reached for a Perrier.

'No.' He turned obstinately away and made his way across to the window and stared out into the night. A welter of sensations bumped and crashed around his head. Even if what she was saying were true, what the hell did it matter anyway? None of it was any use now. Investigations, diggings for truth, they didn't interest him, they were for energetic people like Daisy Field. But then, perhaps that was the point. Perhaps that was why he had let her come here, to let her take charge of it all, to let him work his way free.

He glanced back at her. She was watching him, her gaze steady, patient. Suddenly he warmed to her. Usually when he was the worse for wear people gave him infuriating looks of compassion, the sort they reserved for newly bereaved people and injured dogs.

Manoeuvring himself gently round the furniture, he walked past her and into the bedroom. He dug his chequebook out of a drawer and sat on the bed for a while, letting the emotional dust settle.

He wandered back to the sitting room. 'How much was it then?' he asked.

She stared at him.

He shrugged extravagantly: 'How much?'

'Listen, I – ' She looked trapped. 'I – don't know.'

'Thought you wanted money?'

'But – are you sure?'

He tut-tutted and said with magisterial grandeur: 'Cheque-book's in my hand.' He held it up. 'Pen's in the other. An opportunity not to be missed. Might not come again.'

'Perhaps you should think about it.'

'This is all wrong,' he said, suddenly vastly amused. 'You're meant to be closing the deal. Meant to be standing over me with a gun.'

'Okay.' She ran her tongue along her lips and took the plunge. 'One million.'

She seemed to be reassured by his silence. She added hastily: 'It's possible we could do it for less, but that figure's a reasonable estimate, allowing for contingencies. Of course I'd keep you in touch, I'd provide full accounts – '

'Pounds or dollars?'

'Pounds.'

He took a breath. It was rather more than he'd expected. Even after all these years, he never got used to the noughts on the end of everything. The puritan in him was alarmed by the ease with which money came his way, while the child, the son of the local government official from Chertsey earning ten thousand a year, was terrified it would all slip away.

A million. Well, it wouldn't kill him.

He wrote a cheque.

Daisy kept sighing: 'I don't know what to say.'

'It's for two-fifty thou,' he said. 'More when you need it. Though don' try and cash it, not till I've had words with my accountant.' He sat back in the chair, holding the cheque up between his fingers. 'Two conditions.'

She nodded.

'One, don' ever link this publicly to me or my wife. No talk of this stuff causing her death. Understand? And no talk of me having anything to do with the money. Okay?'

She looked disappointed. 'Okay,' she said.

'If I hear anything, tha's it. No more money.'

She seemed a bit anxious at that, but nodded anyway.

'Two, I don' wanna know. I don' wanna see accounts, reports. Nothing. Just get on with it and do what you think's best.'

'But won't you want to know how we're getting on?'

'Nope.'

'But . . .' She bit back whatever she was going to say, then came in on another tack. 'Your songs – '

'My songs?' he echoed.

'I thought, with everything you've written . . .'

'Jus' songs,' he said stiffly. 'Not the same.' She'd managed to touch something raw in him.

She couldn't let it go. 'Perhaps I didn't explain . . . This research – it could blow the lid off a lot of things, it could be really important for the whole movement.'

'The movement? Listen' – he lurched sideways in his chair – 'I don't actually give a shit – ' This was sounding much worse than he'd intended. He started again. 'No, I . . . I mean . . . Course I give a . . . It's jus' . . .' He trailed off, suddenly uncertain of what precisely he was trying to say.

'Your decision, of course,' Daisy said, edging forward in her seat and pulling her bag towards her. 'But I just thought . . . Well, if you were in touch then at least you'd feel that' – she groped for the right words – 'that something *good* was coming out of the whole horrid business.'

Here was a fine example of instant half-baked wisdom. His blood pressure leapt and he gave an ugly chortle. 'Listen, if I need counselling I can get it from a shrink at two hun'red dollars a throw.'

She stared at him.

He heard the ugly words reverberating through the air and could have bitten his tongue out. He said awkwardly: 'Sorry . . . Sorry. I didn't mean to . . .'

She gave a quick bright smile. 'None of my business.' She picked up her bag.

'Look, I'm sorry . . . Please, don't go, don't go . . .'

She stood up.

'Please. Won't you, er . . .'

'I really must go. God, the time.'

Suddenly he couldn't bear the thought of being alone, couldn't bear her to leave with those ugly words still hanging in the air. He got clumsily to his feet. 'Please stay. I'd like you to stay.' Then before he realised what he was doing, he reached out and grasped her arm. He knew there was some reason he shouldn't, realised dimly that there was a risk of some misunderstanding, but by then it was too late: he'd asked her to stay, he'd grabbed at her, it was late and they were in his hotel room; a scenario not open to that many interpretations.

'I'd love to,' she said, sending out masses of signals to show that she wouldn't love to at all. 'But I really can't. My friends are waiting up for me.'

'Please – I didn't mean . . .' He took a deep breath. 'What I meant was, how about a film? Or a walk?'

She regarded him gravely for a moment, then dropped her head and smiled. She said: 'I thought no one walked in New York late at night.'

Sixteen storeys down, the rain had stopped. The streets were shining like mirrors and the air was heavy and damp so that the lights on the far side of Central Park were smudged and blurred.

They turned north along Fifth Avenue. Nick took several gulps of air and felt refreshed and slightly nauseous all at the same time. Daisy, looking small in his oversized cardigan, bounced along at his side.

They didn't talk much until they got to East 64th. His head was heavy; everything seemed remote and unfocused. But he recognised the block all right. 'We used to live up there,' he said. 'We – ' It was hard to shape the right words. 'Something bad happened.'

She was silent. A cab turned the corner, hit a pothole and sent a spout of water onto the sidewalk a few feet ahead of them. 'Someone attacked Alusha,' he said.

She was staring at him. 'How dreadful.'

'It was stupid, stupid . . .'

'What happened?'

'It was a kid – someone I'd tried to help. I let him do small jobs, deliveries – that kind of thing. But we never thought to check him out . . . He was a schizo. Unstable. Into drugs.'

380

'Oh.'

The lights went to *Walk* and they crossed the street. Nick's legs felt heavy; it was an effort to go on.

'Was she badly hurt?'

'Bad enough.'

Daisy was silent for a moment. 'And then you went to Scotland?'

'Yes.'

'A wonderful place.'

He gave a dismissive grunt.

'You'll go back?' she asked.

'Nope.'

'Never?'

'Never.'

He stumbled slightly and she reached for his arm, letting go when he was back on balance.

How must he seem to her? he wondered furiously. How must he look? Suddenly he felt ashamed and angry.

'It's touring . . .' he said, waving his arm by way of explanation. 'Gets to me . . . I don't mean to . . . I . . . After the show, you know . . .'

'I know all about it,' she said in a reminiscent tone. 'My father was a drunk.'

Drunk. What a word. He winced.

'Don't worry,' she said. 'I'm not going to try to talk you out of it. I'm not going to lecture you. I know better than that. My mum wasted thirty years trying to talk my father round.'

'I can stop.'

'Sure.'

'Any time.'

'Sure.'

He ground to a halt. He heard himself roar childishly: 'But I can!'

She stopped and turned to him and said simply: 'I know that.' She took his arm and they resumed walking. 'My father was a very charming drunk.' That word again. 'Hid it well from the outside world. Said he got early retirement because of his back, though if his back was bad, it was only because he spent so much time lying across the stairs.' She gave the ghost of a chuckle, which was more like a sigh.

He stopped. He felt crushed and dizzy.

'Are you all right?' she asked.

'I'm all right.' But he wasn't. He found a wall and leant against it. Closing his eyes was a mistake; his head spun faster and when he opened his eyes again he had to grip his temples to prevent lift-off. After a time he was aware of Daisy taking his arm and coaxing him into a cab and getting him back to the hotel.

It was midday when he awoke, in need of the bathroom. He was lying on the bed fully clothed except for his shoes. A bed-cover was spread over him and the curtains were closed. There was a glass of water beside him and he remembered that she had made him drink tons of it before she'd let him sleep.

When he finally got up and showered and took his hang-over for a stumble through the suite he found a note on the sitting-room table.

I took the cheque, but won't do anything with it until I've spoken to you. To say I'd be heartbroken if you changed your mind is an understatement . . . A line had been crossed out. He tried to make out what it was. Something like: 'I'd shoot myself', followed by several exclamation marks. *But I'd understand*, she went on. *In the meantime, think again about staying in touch. We need you. Yours gratefully, Daisy.*

He dropped the note back on the table and forgot about it until later, when it was time to move out. Then he scooped it up and, crushing it into a small ball, threw it in the bin.

Three days later, sitting in a rented flat in London, he called his accountant and told him to expect the cheque. Then he called Catch and left a message with the girl there to say it was all right for Daisy to cash it.

When he put the phone down, he felt, against all expectations, as if the shadows were lifting.

TWENTY-FOUR

Schenker had been given a side table for the second time in a week. After three years in the wilderness of the Savoy Grill's centre tables, did this mean he had finally crossed the invisible divide and won the accolade of guaranteed occupancy? One could never be sure. Had Schenker's secretary told them he was going to be lunching with a cabinet minister? That might have decided the issue, of course, though Schenker preferred not to think so.

The minister, when he arrived, strode in at the politician's trot, energetic and fired with purpose, smiling broadly, greeting the head waiter like a valued colleague, acknowledging acquaintances with a regal nod as he motored across the floor.

It was five months since the election, and three months since Schenker had seen Driscoll, though not for lack of invitations. The minister had been too busy for Ascot, Wimbledon, Henley and Glyndebourne. Too busy or, it occurred to Schenker, too intent on quietly distancing himself from old affiliations.

The minister ordered mineral water, a wild mushroom and scallop salad followed by a plain grilled Dover sole. 'My waistline,' he laughed. But he said it with pride, patting his stomach to draw attention to a considerable weight-loss which had left him, if not quite slim, then certainly looking a great deal fitter. Power obviously suited him. He had the air of a man taking his responsibilities seriously but with huge enjoyment.

Schenker commented on how well he was looking.

'Thank you.'

'And how's Susan?'

'Oh, very well.' But it was said with a certain crispness and Schenker got the impression that the conversation was not going to be allowed to drift into more personal realms.

The first course arrived and they talked their way through the economy, the latest food scare and an opinion poll on irradiated food. Schenker would have liked to leave the business of the day a little longer, but he sensed that Driscoll was going to make his escape as soon as decently possible.

'You'll have guessed why I wanted a chat,' Schenker began as soon as the waiter had cleared the plates. 'This extraordinary business about Silveron.'

Driscoll gave a rapid nod. 'My staff have been keeping me informed.'

His staff would have been alerted two weeks ago, Schenker guessed, when items had appeared in *The Times* and *Independent*. Neither story had been more than a couple of column-inches long, but that had been quite sufficient to put the wind up the Morton-Kreiger shareholders. 'The point is,' he said, 'there's absolutely not a shred of evidence to back these claims. Not a shred. This is pure scaremongering of the worst kind. An alarmist campaign dreamed up by the American pressure groups.'

'We realise that,' Driscoll reassured him.

Schenker proceeded delicately. 'So the ministry will back us on this?'

'In what way do you mean?' He sounded guarded.

'Announce that the stories are absolutely groundless.'

'The ministry can't make those sort of statements, Ronald, you know that.' Driscoll's voice seemed to have altered, to have become plummier and more melodious than Schenker remembered, as if he'd been taking voice lessons.

Schenker tried another tack. 'But I can understand, can I, that your people privately condemn this campaign?'

'We always frown on pressure-group hysteria, you know that. Unless there's some basis in fact, of course.' He nodded to some new arrival across the room, his face breaking into a fleeting smile before resuming an appropriate seriousness. 'We certainly have no intention of responding to pressure, otherwise we'd spend all our time reacting, and not doing what the people elected us to do, which is to get on with implementing the government's election programme. No, I understand that my people are in contact with your people over this, and that we're all in contact with the Americans. I've no doubt the experts will sort it out. They usually do.'

Was he being deliberately unhelpful? Schenker couldn't decide.

'The thing is, Tony,' he said, 'this sort of thing can have repercussions out of all proportion – if matters are allowed to get out of hand, that is. If people panic.'

'Panic? *We're* certainly not going to be panicked into anything.' Driscoll spoke with vague condescension, as if he'd been a minister for years and knew the ropes backwards. 'Nothing's getting out of hand at *our* end.'

Schenker, bristling slightly, made the effort to smile. 'At your end, no, of course not. I didn't mean to suggest it was.'

The next course arrived, and they waited while the waiter took the sole off the bone and arranged the fillets on Driscoll's plate. Schenker had ordered salmon, but was no longer hungry.

The waiter finally left. 'But there's still a small problem from our point of view, Tony,' Schenker said, forcing intimacy into his voice. 'I was hoping you might be able to put my mind at rest. Concerning a disturbing bit of news I heard, something to do with a possible delay in Silveron's full licence. And' – he gave an incredulous laugh – 'I even heard that the ACP might be reviewing the *existing* licence. It seemed so improbable I couldn't believe it.'

Driscoll took his time finishing his mouthful. 'You know very well that the ACP go their own way, Ronald. The *Advisory* Committee on Pesticides. And that's just what they are – advisory. They're the experts and I rely utterly on their judgement. They're my ears to the world of science.' He obviously liked the sound of the phrase because he paused to let it reverberate a little.

'But it's an extraordinary step to take on no evidence – '

'Well, not exactly *no* evidence, old boy,' Driscoll said reprovingly. Schenker noticed the *old boy*, a new addition to Driscoll's vocabulary. 'That's the point, isn't it?' Driscoll said. 'All these sick workers at your plant in Chicago – '

'*Three* people, Tony. Maybe only two. And even if it had – '

'I thought it was eight or more?' Driscoll cut in.

'Three,' Schenker persisted. 'And there's strong evidence to show that Silveron is completely innocent. We can show that at least four workers who *thought* their illnesses were chemical-related are suffering from diseases that have absolutely nothing to do with – '

'Of course, of course.' Driscoll waved a hand. 'I'm sure your people have done their homework. They ran a second batch of trials, didn't they, and the product looked fine? I know all that, Ronald. But the fact remains that some people are sick, and the thing has to be looked into. Don't forget the unions, Ronald. I've got them breathing down my neck all the time. They're never happy about these things until matters are properly investigated. And you won't need reminding, I'm sure, that they can do you far more damage than anyone else in the long run, with boycotts and that sort of thing. Far more damage.'

'I respect their anxiety. I do, sincerely,' Schenker said. 'But in this instance it is very seriously misplaced, Tony. Very seriously misplaced.' Driscoll had the blank look of someone who was rapidly losing interest.

Doggedly, Schenker pressed on. 'The Silveron licence, Tony. What I'd like to know is what possible reason the ACP have for taking another look at it?'

Driscoll gave a laugh, the sort people use to skirt around questions they have no intention of answering. 'Ronald, what can I say? As far as the ACP is concerned, my hands are tied. Utterly tied. It's a question of the due processes running their course, and being *seen* to run their course.'

Was this obduracy just a ploy? Schenker wondered. Was Driscoll taking a tough stand merely to make a future concession look doubly generous?

Driscoll pointed a knife at Schenker's plate. 'You haven't touched your salmon. I wonder if it's farmed. We export twelve thousand tons of salmon a year, you know. Amazing.'

Picking up a fork, Schenker began to pull half-heartedly at the fish.

'On second thoughts, probably wild,' Driscoll murmured reflectively. 'The Savoy, you know. Still caters for purists.'

Schenker put his fork down without eating. 'Tony, I don't need to tell you what this uncertainty means to us. A licence review would result in a serious loss of confidence. We've invested a hell of a lot in this product, Tony, one hell of a lot.'

'I know that.'

386

'Then where's the faith in our expertise? Where's the back-up? Where's the support? Delays and uncertainties will cost jobs, Tony. We'll have to lay people off – hundreds, maybe thousands.'

'I'd never let it get that far, Ronald, you know that.'

'But these things can happen overnight!'

Driscoll smiled benevolently and, folding his napkin into a neat square, leaned confidentially across the table. 'Listen, this is what I'll do.' Ah, here comes the concession, Schenker thought; here comes the sweetener. 'I can't make firm prom-ises,' Driscoll began like a true politician, 'but what I can do is to press the committee to consider the matter with all possible speed, and remind them of the inadvisability of proceeding any further without hard evidence.' He sat back looking pleased with himself. 'I think that should do the trick, don't you?' Reading Schenker's face, he spread his palms. 'More, sadly, I cannot do.'

Oh but you can, thought Schenker, his stomach twisting unpleasantly. In view of the favours you owe me, in view of the substantial donations Morton-Kreiger makes to party funds, you can. But Schenker wasn't going to beg, cap in hand, for a few additional crumbs of comfort that a grateful Driscoll might throw his way. That wasn't his style.

'That won't be enough,' he said firmly.

Driscoll looked surprised as well as cross at this lack of appreciation. 'What do you mean, not enough?'

'We need a firm statement, to reassure people.'

'Ronald, Ronald.' He gave a small pitying shake of the head and dabbed his mouth with the folded napkin. 'What do you expect me to do? Stand over the scientists and tell them how to run their committee?'

'I expect you to do whatever you have to do to save Morton-Kreiger from this totally undeserved and highly damaging attack – this victimisation.'

Driscoll pulled himself upright, looking ruffled. He was just beginning to realise that Schenker might be calling in a number of long-standing favours. He didn't reply but but-toned his jacket, ready for a quick getaway.

Schenker spelt it out. 'I saved your bacon, Tony. Now I'm asking you to do the same for me.'

Driscoll looked at him uncomprehendingly and said tersely:

387

'I've said I'll do all I reasonably can. And I will.' Then, casting an eye around him, itching for escape, he added dismissively: 'What do you mean anyway – saved my bacon?'

Schenker made a show of reticence, as if wild horses wouldn't drag such unnecessary details from his lips.

'Saved my bacon!' echoed the minister with a chortle. 'Really, Ronald, that's a little over the top, isn't it?'

He has no idea, Schenker realised, not even an inkling.

He'd probably erased the girl from his memory. Looking suitably reluctant at having to mention it, Schenker helped his memory along a bit.

'That unpleasant business.'

'Unpleasant business?' the minister retorted. 'It'd help if I knew what the hell you were talking about.' He was irritated, but also, Schenker sensed, curious.

Schenker pitched his voice just above a whisper. 'The business with Miss Kershaw.'

Surprise flashed across his face, and he gave a slight twitch as if he'd been attacked by an insect. Recovering, he raised an admonitory finger. 'Don't talk to me about Miss Kershaw. She was one of your least clever ideas, Schenker.'

'*My* idea?' He shook his head very slowly. 'I don't think that's quite accurate, Tony. Remember, I never even knew the girl until I met her with you.' Gesturing to show that the matter was hardly worth arguing about, he went on rapidly: 'But it was certainly my idea to settle her financially and make sure she kept out of your way.'

Driscoll was very still, his mouth sagging, the lower lip full and damp, revealing back teeth gleaming with fillings. When he finally managed to speak, his voice was thin and breathless. 'Settle her?'

Schenker flicked a warning glance as the waiter approached. They ordered coffee.

Driscoll's eyes were fixed blackly on his, waiting for an answer.

Schenker took his time. 'She had – er, ideas. We thought that her ideas were the last thing you needed in your new job. We identified the problem and dealt with it. We also went to some lengths to ensure she would never trouble you again.'

Driscoll's mouth moved. He spluttered: 'You – ' But he

never went on. He closed his eyes as if a lot of half-realised pieces were suddenly falling into place. Then he shot Schenker an agitated glance. '*We*, you said?'

'Sorry – I. Me.'

The coffee arrived. Schenker asked for the bill. Then he fixed his gaze on Driscoll. 'I valued our friendship highly enough to go out on a limb for you, to save you unpleasantness which might have been highly inconvenient to your career. This Silveron business means a lot to *my* career, Tony. I'm asking you to go out on a limb for me.'

Driscoll was recovering fast, the fight bouncing back into his face. He protested: 'I didn't ask you to interfere. In fact, it was a bloody liberty.'

'You would have preferred the business to' – Schenker rotated his fingers, as if plucking the right word out of the air – 'to, er, *progress*, would you?'

He got the meaning of that all right, and mashed his lips together. 'It wouldn't have got that far.'

'No?' Schenker was losing patience. 'Well, whichever way it had turned out, it would have cost you a great deal of worry, not to mention cash. I would have thought you were only too pleased to have that little lot taken off your hands.'

The bill arrived. Schenker signed it without reading it.

'It was rank interference,' Driscoll repeated bitterly.

Schenker could see what the trouble was. It wasn't that he had interfered – Driscoll could hardly be anything but grateful about that – it was injured pride, lost face, and the fact that the revelation had put Driscoll so completely in Schenker's debt.

'I acted as a friend,' Schenker said lightly. 'If I did wrong then I did it with the best intentions.'

That took the wind out of his sails, as Schenker had known it would. Driscoll, his eyes darting rapidly round the room, ran a smoothing hand down the front of his jacket and pulled his shoulders back, soldier fashion. 'I must go,' he said sharply, and got to his feet. Schenker rose and they nodded formally to each other.

'I'll be in touch,' Driscoll murmured, and marched off. This time he forgot to nod to his acquaintances.

*

389

Anne Dublensky gave a long shuddering sigh of exasperation. 'What do you mean, let's be positive?'

'I mean, let's be positive,' Dublensky replied with a short laugh.

'Sometimes you talk so much baloney, I think your head needs attention.' She stalked out into the yard, letting the screen bang behind her. Standing up wearily, knowing what was to come as surely as if they were reading a script, he followed her outside and found her raking the leaves with ferocious energy.

'What do you want, Anne?' he asked, genuinely puzzled. 'I mean, I have this job, don't I? We have a new start. It may not be much, but what am I meant to do – throw it all away?'

'I hate this place,' she hissed under her breath.

Automatically, he turned to look at the house. Okay, it wasn't perfect – truth be told, it was rather a dump – but it wasn't as if they were buying the place. They were just renting it while they waited for the house in Allentown to sell.

'When the agreement runs out we could try another place,' he suggested.

'What?' She looked at him as if he were a fool. 'I meant this place.' She made an impatient all-encompassing sweep of her arm.

Ah, this place. This small town in New Jersey. It wasn't such a bad neighbourhood, at least Dublensky didn't think so. A little too satisfied with itself perhaps, not so friendly as other places they had been, a little too thick with country clubs that had mysteriously few Poles, Italians or Jews among their members, but not to be condemned for all that. There were always good unaffected people everywhere; you just had to go out and look for them. For some reason Anne hadn't shown much interest in meeting people. Nor, for that matter, in applying to join any projects, although in the past she had always complained bitterly when she had been denied the opportunity to work.

Each day seemed to be a burden to her, each conversation a source of profound irritation. Whatever he suggested by way of a diversion – an evening out, a weekend drive – she dismissed with now familiar contempt. And her displeasure, rarely far beneath the surface, was never more intense than

390

when he tried to pacify her. Then, eyes glittering dangerously, she reacted with sharp-edged lunges of scorn.

'I never know what's wrong,' he said plaintively. 'You act like I've done something terrible but you never tell me what it is I'm supposed to have done. I mean, is it the job? Okay, so it's not great, I know it's not great – but I like it, I really do. I know you don't believe me, but it's true.'

'Oh, I believe you,' she said, picking up a sack and stuffing leaves in aggressively. 'Whatever else, you've always had the ability to adapt.'

Was there a touch of sarcasm in her tone? Even after all these years it was never possible to be sure with Anne. Observations, even compliments, were delivered conditionally, with overlays of meaning; she was incapable of seeing the simplest thing without sighting endless complications beyond. His job – as a toxicologist at a new contract research company called Dalton Research International – was an irony in itself, as the fast-growing Dalton had aspirations to become another TroChem, and was even now hungering after a contract with Morton-Kreiger. The position was a step down in responsibility, status and salary, but it was solid employment. Anne, despite her past optimism, her remorseless encouragement, had shown only a glancing interest in this success, her enthusiasm as guarded as it was short-lived.

She stared at him, grasping the rake to her chest with both hands. 'I've lost respect for you,' she declared suddenly. 'Yes,' she repeated more deliberately, 'I have lost respect for you. I need to tell you that. You have a right to know. That that's the way I feel about you now.'

'Anne . . .' He sighed. 'We've been over this so often.'

'Not often enough for me.'

'I can't take the world's burdens on my shoulders. I've got you and Tad to look after. That's my first responsibility – '

'We can look after ourselves, thanks. In fact' – her face hardened – 'I don't know if I wouldn't prefer it that way.'

Their arguments normally followed such well-worn paths, such predictable channels of self-torture and mutual frustration, that this new departure took him by surprise, like a sudden blow.

The pain must have shown in his face because she clutched a hand to her forehead with a groan of self-disgust and said quickly: 'Forget that. I didn't mean it. I really didn't mean it.' She turned back to her work, then paused again and said grudgingly: 'You know I wouldn't mind so much if you'd kept in contact with Burt, if you knew what the hell was happening.'

She didn't always take this line. Sometimes she berated him for not having stood up to the Allentown management and sued for wrongful dismissal, other times she harped on his stupidity in leaving the Aurora documents lying around, waiting to be stolen. Most usually – and this was the nub of her displeasure – she'd rebuke him for hiding the existence of the second file from her, for not telling her about it until long after it was stolen, and worst of all, for having done nothing about it, for not being prepared to get up and tell the whole world what it contained. This was the real crime, the one that could never, it seemed, be forgiven.

'It's not in Burt's hands, I've told you,' Dublensky said sharply, still catching his breath from her unexpected salvo. 'It's EarthForce,' he said. 'EarthForce are the only people who can take the thing forward.'

'Well, they tried, didn't they? They had the publicity campaign, and where did that get them?'

'I don't know, how can I know?' He heard his voice rising; he felt a sudden heat at the back of his eyes.

'You could ask them, couldn't you? Why don't you call them?' she pleaded, her voice swooping low with entreaty. 'Why not? How long would it take – five minutes? Less? Speak to Paul Erlinger. Find out. Oh, this time *do* it, John. For me.'

His shoulders slumped, he gave a gesture of defeat. She'd made this request before and, though he'd genuinely intended to call, he'd never managed to get as far as the phone. At first he'd told himself it was a sensible move against the possibility of bad security at EarthForce, that he was merely protecting himself against a rerun of the burglary and other hostilities, but he knew this wasn't quite the whole story. He clung to the belief that Silveron would never get final EPA approval, that the product would come unstuck long before it got to the marketplace, that someone somewhere would denounce it; that, even on the slenderest of evidence, EarthForce would somehow persuade the EPA to demand a completely new set of toxicology trials.

In the meantime he had managed to salvage a large chunk of his life. His message of non-cooperation with EarthForce had obviously been received loud and clear by the powers that be, because it was soon after his meeting with Paul Erlinger that he had landed this job. And now Anne was berating him for having made the best of things, for picking up the pieces of their lives.

'Okay, okay,' he said, hovering close to the edge of his self-control, 'I'll call, I'll call. But I would like to know if I'm going to be allowed some peace afterwards. Am I going to be forgiven for whatever this crime is that I'm meant to have committed?'

She sighed impatiently. 'There's no crime.'

'Well, you could have fooled me.'

She eyed him. 'If there's a crime it's that you don't seem to care any more. That's what I find hard to take.'

'Don't care! How much am I meant to care? I mean, am I meant to stand up and make these claims and get torn apart in public and go onto welfare, all to achieve absolutely nothing, and then feel good with myself because I've done it for some great principle?'

Shaking her head, she rolled her eyes skyward in an expression of hopelessness, and, rake in hand, stalked off across the grass. Even her back broadcast disappointment.

Two days later he got away from work earlier than usual and, remembering that Anne had gone to collect Tad from swimming practice, finally goaded himself into sitting in front of the phone and calling Paul Erlinger.

In Washington the name of Alan Breck brought Erlinger panting breathlessly to the phone. He betrayed his hopes straight away. 'Your friend – are there developments?'

Dublensky felt a squeeze of shame. 'No.' As he said it, the disappointment at the far end of the line was almost palpable. 'No, I'm sorry. Nothing. No, I was hoping you might be able to tell me about developments. How you're progressing with the medical opinions and that sort of thing.'

'Oh, well – you know. It's slow, like these things are always slow.' His voice had lost its edge of excitement. 'At the moment I'd say it was one step forward, one back. Some of the Aurora workers – four in fact – have gone and gotten themselves rediagnosed with good old-fashioned ailments, non-chemical diseases that make it a lot easier to obtain welfare and insurance payouts. Can't blame them, but it's lowered our data base.'

'You think you still have a case?'

'Not such a great case that we couldn't do with a helluva lot more evidence.' The comment hung in the air, awaiting suggestions.

Dublensky was silent.

'We've been campaigning on Capitol Hill,' Erlinger continued, 'spreading the word. But you can imagine. They all say, where's the proof, let me know when you've got something to show me.'

'And the EPA?'

'Same. Took a second look at the test data, but can't act until there's something to go on.'

'So it's *not* looking good?'

'I wouldn't say that exactly. It's just the difference between catching someone with a smoking gun in his hand and having to patch a case together from circumstantial evidence. You can still get a conviction, but the jury may be out a long time.' There was a pause. 'Your friend – he hasn't regained access to that material?'

'No.'

'He wouldn't be prepared to swear to what he saw?'

Dublensky didn't speak. He was remembering how the robbery had occurred a short time after he had sent the Aurora dossier to EarthForce, how even if it was purely coincidental and there was no security leak at Erlinger's end, he couldn't risk exposure again. Unemployment, once sampled, was not a desirable option.

'No,' he said at last.

Erlinger absorbed this, then commented: 'There've been more victims in Britain, you know. Daisy Field reports three new cases.'

'Three? Isn't that some sort of proof?'

'Not while the British authorities are pretending there's no problem and the cases don't get reported to Daisy until it's too late to run tests.'

'Can't she get publicity?'

'Not enough.'

Erlinger, sensing an opening, pressed home. 'There's only one way to cut the whole thing short, Alan.'

For a moment neither of them spoke.

'If you should ever see your way to getting us that information . . .' Erlinger let the idea hang in the air.

'I know,' Dublensky said tightly, battling with his thoughts. 'I know. I wish . . . I mean, I would if . . .' He pulled back, frightened of what he might hear himself say. He felt as if he was teetering on the rim of a volcano in a strong wind, his balance threatened by each gust of words. Finally he said: 'I'll see what I can do. Maybe there's something I can do.'

'You will?' Erlinger couldn't hide his excitement.

'Please, *please*. I'm not making promises. I'm not in any position –'

'No, no. Of course. I understand, I understand,' Erlinger said hastily. 'But any time you want to call, I'm here. Okay?'

Dublensky rang off, any relief he might have felt at having finally executed his chore more than outweighed by the realisation of what he'd said. Why had he made even that vaguest of promises? But he already knew the answer: it was the thought of the people in Britain, the new cases. That reality couldn't be escaped, and the knowledge reduced him to a new state of wretchedness.

In the last minutes before Anne's return, he forced himself towards some sort of a decision.

He would call Erlinger again in two weeks' time and, if there was no sign of a ban in Britain, he would commit a serious amount of time to rethinking his position. The decision, which he knew wasn't much of a decision at all, gave him a tangible sense of achievement.

The door sounded. Tad's call echoed through the house. Dublensky's heart lifted and, wrapping his mind in thoughts of family and home, he rose to greet him.

TWENTY-FIVE

Daisy awoke to a feeling of anxiety. She lay still, trying to make sense of this, placing herself in time and space. Early, very early, and dark; a homely back room in Mrs Biddows' bed-and-breakfast establishment in Elm Avenue, Chelmsford; the sound of a passing car in an adjacent road. She tried closing her eyes again, but the unease lingered on, cold as a draught. She remembered that she had an early meeting today. It was this, perhaps, which had made her wake. Or the thousand things on her mind. But unease? Fear? That was more difficult to tie down.

She got up and, going to the window, pulled the curtain aside. The row of semi-detached houses in the next road stood out sharply against the sulphurous rays of the street lighting, and the intervening gardens were dark as ink.

She went out onto the landing and listened, though she wasn't sure what for. Dressing, she went downstairs and left a note for Mrs Biddows to say she wouldn't be in for breakfast.

Usually the journey to the laboratory took three minutes, five on the rare occasions when she travelled as late as eight thirty, the height of the Chelmsford rush-hour. Now, in the pre-dawn, it took less than three.

She parked next to the chainlink perimeter fence that surrounded the laboratory and unfastened the padlock on the gates. She stepped through and stood for a moment, listening again. The estate consisted of a single loop road which gave access to twelve or more warehouses and light-industrial workshops. Most of the companies employed security firms –

or so their warning notices proclaimed – but she had never seen guards or cruising vans, not even when she left at midnight, which was often.

Closing the gate behind her, she crossed the apron to the main door of the building. Above the door, illuminated by an exterior light, was the sign: *Octek Ltd*. The name had come from an off-the-shelf name dealer, the sort that registers and stocks company names for customers who want to set something up in a hurry. The name didn't say very much about anything, which was one of the reasons she had chosen it.

She unlocked the single mortise lock. The door was in need of two more heavy locks, top and bottom, but in all the rush she hadn't got round to arranging it. She had, however, ordered key-operated locks for all the windows and heat-sensitive floodlights for the perimeter which were due to be fitted in the next week or so. Ideally of course, the place should be manned by a rota of security guards, but people cost a great deal, as she had spent most of the last two months finding out.

Opening the door, the alarm shrilled a warning until she punched the code into the key pad. Turning on some more lights, she locked the door behind her. Ahead was a passage, with three offices and a washroom off it, and at the end, the laboratory area, entered by two sets of double doors.

Until three months ago the building had been occupied by a health supplement supplier, churning out vitamin and mineral capsules on a number of short assembly lines. The benches and fittings had not met Peasedale and Floyd's specifications however, and everything had been ripped out and replaced by gleaming smooth-edged work surfaces topped by shelving and interspersed with power points, piped water, stainless-steel sink units and specialised refrigerators. She knew the specification of almost every item, and she certainly knew its cost.

In the light from the passage the rows of polished metal fittings glinted darkly, and there was a tang of newness in the air. The place, though quiet, looked businesslike and productive. She knew she should feel some sort of triumph in having got so far in such a short time, but the elation, such as it was, was overshadowed by the worry which had become a permanent feature of her existence. The project had taken on a life of its own, monstrous and unpredictable, like an ungrateful child over whom one has lost control. The only thing that she could absolutely rely on, day after day, was that the money would continue to flood out.

She went along to her office, which lay to the left of the main entrance. She worked on some costings and estimates – figures which looked no better than they had the night before – until seven thirty when, hearing a car, she looked out and saw Peasedale's raincoated figure emerge from a taxi. He glided in on his long legs, soundless as a bird, and settled into the visitor's chair. He peered myopically at his watch. 'Mustn't miss the eight thirty.'

She spread her hands expectantly. 'Well – how did it go?' He had spent the previous evening at Floyd's house, hammering things out.

He considered his answer, canting his head to one side to reveal his long bony neck. 'We reviewed the protocols, and the time allocations . . .'

'And?'

'I think we've broken the back of it.'

A door slammed and Floyd entered, a small stocky figure radiating vitality and goodwill. He had recently joined them as chief scientist. Peasedale had suggested him for the job because, though Floyd wasn't the most highly qualified toxicologist around, Peasedale believed quite rightly that he was the only person likely to take the job. Most scientific staff were on fixed-term contracts and unable to change jobs at such short notice. Also, as Peasedale pointed out, most toxicologists didn't want their CVs sullied by involvement in renegade research projects. Such considerations didn't seem to bother Floyd. Irish-born, outgoing to the point of extroversion, he lived for work, horse racing and conversation, though not necessarily in that order.

'I'm not late, am I?' he said cheerfully.

'We hadn't really started,' Peasedale commented. 'I was just saying that we'd sorted the figures.'

There was a pause. The two of them exchanged glances and Daisy was reminded of a double act, except that no one was feeding the lines.

It was Peasedale who finally said: 'There's a problem.'

She'd rather thought there might be.

'The problem is that we can't finish in the time,' said Floyd.

'It's the enzyme assays. Oh, they're going fine,' he added, waving a confident hand in the direction of the laboratories, 'but we're only scratching the surface. We had a think about it and we decided that, to get a good picture, we should be covering another twenty or so of the major enzymes. But the way things are at the moment it'd mean another two months on the schedule.'

'Maybe more,' said Peasedale.

'We can't extend the schedule,' Daisy said firmly. 'And certainly not by two months.'

'No, no,' Floyd murmured supportively.

'Isn't there a way round it?' she asked.

Peasedale made a pained face. 'Another two technicians.'

'Ouch,' she said.

'Push us over budget, will it?'

'That sort of thing.' She pressed the tips of her forefingers hard against two points over the bridge of her nose. It was a trick based on acupuncture that was meant to relieve stress, but either it didn't work or she always tried it too late. 'These enzymes, we have to have them, do we?'

The two men, tall and short, bony and chubby, serious and sunny, like a couple of comedians paired up for their dissimilarities, nodded in unison.

She sighed: 'I'll see what I can work out. If you're absolutely certain.'

They were certain. Experts were always certain when they were asking for money.

'Otherwise we're okay?'

'With the usual provisos,' Peasedale said.

Floyd gave a short discordant laugh. 'Like getting that permit.'

Six weeks before, they had applied for a Home Office Project Licence but, despite continuous follow-up, nothing had come through.

'There couldn't have been anything wrong with the application?'

She'd asked this before, and now Peasedale gave the answer he always gave. 'Nothing that they could object to.'

'Except perhaps the research itself.' She tried not to voice that particular worry too often. She glanced at Peasedale and saw from his face that the idea had already taken hold in his mind.

Floyd, never a one for pessimism, said brightly: 'We could always move the whole shebang abroad.'

Daisy gave a mock groan. 'The problem is, you may well be right. Perhaps we should have been somewhere else all along.' She dragged her hands down her face. 'Like China.'

'You're forgetting,' Floyd said, 'if all else fails we'll have the cell-line results.'

'But they don't count. You said they don't count.'

'They'll count with the public well enough, I think.'

'But not with the committee. Anyway, it's academic. We don't have any results yet.'

A sly smile spread over Floyd's face. 'But we have things of interest.'

She glanced across to Peasedale for confirmation but found him with his watch pressed up to his glasses. 'My train,' he said anxiously.

Daisy picked up her car keys. 'Let's go then.'

In the car, Peasedale was tense and uncommunicative until they were safely over the first roundabout and clearly in good time for the train.

Daisy asked: 'I suppose it's useless asking what Floyd was on about?'

'What? Oh, the cell-line tests. Best that he shows you himself.' They continued in silence for a while, then Peasedale asked tentatively: 'The budget – you sounded worried.'

Something made her decide to confide in him. Perhaps she'd been grappling with the problem too long, perhaps she was tired of having no one to talk to. 'Quite honestly, I don't know if it's all right,' she said, accelerating past a noisy lorry. 'The money man – I haven't seen him in three months. He's abroad somewhere. I haven't even been able to talk to him. The money's been coming through all right, but . . . Well, you know how it is. Everything's gone way over estimate and . . .' There was no easy way of saying it. 'There's going to be a shortfall.'

'How much?'

'Twenty per cent. Maybe more.'

'So when do we run out?'

'I'm not sure. Some time around March maybe.' She couldn't admit even to herself that it might be as soon as Christmas.

They came to a stop at the end of a slow moving queue.

She saw Peasedale's knuckles whiten at the thought of missing his train. 'Still plenty of time,' she said reassuringly.

'You can contact your – er, man?' he asked cautiously. He knew as well as anyone Daisy rarely answered questions about the source of money.

'Not directly.'

The line of cars was moving again. Ahead, the lights turned red.

'What, no means of contact *at all*?'

She gave a wry laugh. 'Oh, I leave messages regularly. With his accountant, with his – well, with all sorts of people – but I can't put it all in a message. I mean, it wouldn't sound too good to say thanks for all the money, but I need some more already. Not just like that.'

Ahead, the lights turned green. 'So what happens next?' Peasedale asked.

She considered for a moment. For the first few weeks she'd felt sure Nick would make some contact – a phone call, a message, something. But the silence had been as long as it had been absolute. 'I'm not sure,' she said baldly.

They reached the lights at last and got through on the amber. The station came into sight. Peasedale had five minutes to spare. He looked drained. He clasped his overnight bag to his chest, ready for the off.

'So what happens when the money's gone?' he asked.

Daisy turned into the forecourt and drew up in a taxi bay. 'Then we're out of business and it'll all have been for nothing.' She gave a brittle laugh.

Peasedale got out and popped his head back through the open door like an anxious bird. 'You think it could come to that?'

She raised her shoulders. 'Who knows? Don't miss your train.' He craned his head up in alarm and, slamming the door, flew into the entrance, the wings of his raincoat flapping out behind him.

She drove back slowly, thoughtfully, reviewing the decision to set up Octek as an independent operation. It had been a choice between that and waiting for laboratory space in a university, which could have taken as much as six months, and which required the co-operation of academics with both the time and the fearlessness to put their other research funds in jeopardy. The time couldn't be spared, not enough people could be found. So here they were, cobbling the thing together, throwing in people, equipment and commitment, and hoping it would be enough.

And if the money ran out? She couldn't bring herself to think about that now.

In A-Lab, the larger of the two laboratories, Floyd was sitting on a high stool talking to one of the technicians. 'Come on, sunshine,' she said. 'Cheer me up.'

Floyd got to his feet with a grin. 'I'm going to show you some pretty pictures.'

He led the way into the ante-room of B-Lab – commonly dubbed the robing room – where they put on green overalls and washed their hands before passing into the lab proper. Floyd navigated between the benches, exchanged greetings with the two young technicians, and stopped in front of a counter covered with rows of circular glass plates. Picking one up, he passed it to her. 'Salmonella. One of the control plates.' His voice hummed with anticipation.

The agar culture had been scored with bacteria, some of which had mutated and divided to form small colonies, visible as sporadic white dots on the clear jelly.

'And here is the result with ten micrograms of chemical per litre.' Like a magician, Floyd whipped away the plate and gave her another. On this plate the white dots, though still well spread, were clearly more numerous.

'And . . .' He produced a third plate. '. . . fifty micrograms.' Here the colonies had proliferated to such an extent that the dots formed a distinct white ribbon across the surface of the plate.

'What does it mean?'

'It means we have a dose-response effect – that is, the greater the dose of chemical, the greater the mutative response. Of course, it would be nice to know which individual chemical or compound is doing the damage . . .'

'But this is promising?'

'Oh yes. Looking good. Or perhaps I should say bad.'

'But not bad enough for the ACP,' she murmured. Neither the advisory committee, nor any of the government control agencies, accepted cell-line tests as evidence of a product's cancer-producing properties.

Daisy sat back. 'It's a start though, isn't it?'

'Oh, it's that all right.'

She felt heartened, though that didn't stop her feeling renewed anxiety at the delay over the Home Office permit. Without that, they were all set up with nowhere to go.

Coming out of the robing room, she went diagonally across the passage to what was known as Room 4. Here she was met by Vera, the animal welfare assistant. Room 4 smelled of hay or some other sweet-smelling substance. It was brightly lit and warm. The cages were well-spaced, and within each cage the mice and rats had plenty of room and clean bedding. Vera was already well into her morning chores, changing bedding and water, measuring out and recording feed. Later she would observe and log the appearance of each rodent.

It was all done by the book, the animals couldn't have been better looked after if they were pets. Daisy wished that none of this was necessary, but so long as the international safety requirements remained unchanged, there was no escaping the fact that it was. As Peasedale put it: rodents or people; safe chemicals or no chemicals at all. Until there were several billion fewer people in the world then managing without chemicals was never going to be a serious option. Cheap food and safe drugs, or a ramshackle vegetarian utopia: she'd left such stark choices behind, somewhere in her student days. Now she recognised that there had to be an in-between, a place that wasn't impossibly bad, and wasn't impossibly good either, where, though a tiny number of rats had to die to satisfy society's chemical requirements, it was always going to be far, far fewer than the number of cattle and pigs that died each day to make hamburgers. And under Vera's care these rodents, at least, would be given the best in analgesics and anaesthetics, and generally receive far better treatment than veal calves or intensively farmed poultry, which people with a so-called conscience ate every day.

No, there was no real answer, and there never would be.

Anyway, the whole thing was academic without the permit, because without it, they were not permitted to start testing anything on the animals.

When she got to the front office, the phone was ringing. It was Jenny. Jenny always phoned before nine thirty because Alan was rarely in by that time and she could make the call in peace. It wasn't that Alan minded the odd call now that Daisy had officially resigned, it was the extent of the message and information service Jenny was providing that he objected to.

Jenny relayed the messages, which didn't amount to much, followed by a progress report on the anti-Silveron campaign. The Aurora story had got coverage on both sides of the Atlantic, but, as with all such stories, the interest had rapidly fizzled out. In the US, EarthForce were continuing to lobby hard for an EPA review. In the UK, a few reliable MPs had promised to keep up what pressure they could during the long parliamentary recess but, apart from a single bland ministry statement, the government were living up to their reputation on environmental matters by taking the least possible action over the longest possible time.

'What about the rumour of a licence review?'

'Haven't heard anything more,' said Jenny. 'D'you want me to ask around?'

'Yes.'

'Who shall I ask?'

'Try Simon.'

'Simon?' Jenny sounded surprised at being given the job, but managed a tactful: 'Oh – right.'

The rest of the news was domestic. Alan was in a dither over the bill from the security firm who'd screened the office for bugs.

'But he okayed the estimate,' Daisy said.

'Well, he's saying it's extortionate, considering.'

Considering they had found nothing, she guessed. Alan believed in value for money. 'I was sure they'd find something,' Daisy murmured.

'Not a bleep,' said Jenny.

'So are Alan and I not speaking again?'

'Oh, you are, of course you are. But you know how he is.'

Daisy knew how he was, nobly agreeing the cost of her return flight from New York, bravely shouldering all the work while she was gone, and with no more than a muttered reminder every day for two weeks. Despite that, or maybe because of it, she missed having him and Jenny around. It was like leaving school; you couldn't wait to taste freedom, but, once gone, you became nostalgic. Since coming here, she'd got to know all about the loneliness of command.

She'd gone back to Catch a couple of times, but had found the sight of her old desk, cleared of her familiar clobber, disturbing. She couldn't help noticing, moreover, that the clobber of the new girl was a lot more orderly. A pin-board

404

had appeared on the wall where her save-the-whale poster had been, an event chart with a neat array of coloured pins had been fixed over the desk, and the shelf of reference books had a whole new logic to it. Alan had found a soul-mate at last.

'Oh, and the security people,' Jenny giggled before ringing off. 'They even checked the loo.'

'I should hope so too.'

She tried Nick Mackenzie's accountant at exactly ten to eleven. On one memorable morning some weeks before, at exactly that time, she had managed to catch him at his desk and not in a meeting or being unavailable. Today, however, he was in a meeting, and she was forced to leave the standard message with his secretary, saying where she could be contacted for the rest of the day.

At noon she drove to the other side of Chelmsford to see a company about some equipment Floyd wanted. Whenever possible, she went to see people on their own patch because then there were fewer questions to answer about Octek. She had become rather expert at evasions and half-truths. At first she had quite enjoyed the subterfuge; now it was a strain. One became increasingly aware of how easy it was to get caught out.

She got back to Octek at one thirty to find a message from Jenny. It was marked very urgent.

'Thank God,' Jenny breathed down the line when she got through. 'It's your flat, I'm afraid.'

Daisy's first thought was that it had been burgled.

'A big leak from the floor above. The water tank burst in the Greek boys' flat and' – Jenny paused to break it gently – 'they think it poured through your ceiling.'

Daisy swore loudly. She could already see this absorbing great chunks of time that she simply didn't have.

'The Greek boys got a plumber in to fix their water tank, so the leak's stopped, but no one's managed to get into your place yet so . . . What can I do? Do you want me to go and see what's happening?'

Daisy thought through the alternatives. 'No – I'd better go.'

'Shall I meet you there? Would that help?'

'Thanks, but I'll see what it's like first.'

'Are you sure?'

'I'm sure.'

'Oh,' she said hurriedly, 'that Scotsman phoned.'

'Campbell?'

'He wouldn't say what it was about, but he said it was urgent.'

'I'll try and call him now.'

'And there's a letter from Mrs Knowles – Alice. I'll forward it to you.'

'What does it say?'

'Well . . .' There was a hesitant note in Jenny's voice.

Daisy prepared herself. 'Go on,' she said.

'Well – it's about that cancer doctor, the one who promised to be a witness.'

She could guess what was coming. 'He's backed out?'

'Yes.'

It wasn't worth feeling angry. You could never blame these people. When it came to dealing with its own non-conformists, there was no body so ruthless as the medical profession. The man had probably got ridiculed or warned off or threatened with the loss of his job, or all three.

'Any more good news? Tell me while I'm still sitting down.'

'That's it.'

She hoped Campbell's news wasn't going to make it three in a row. She tried to call him but he wasn't in, which at that time of day was no great surprise. More surprising was that Mrs Bell wasn't in and, though the phone was often left next to Adrian when he was alone in the cottage, there was no reply from him either.

She meant to start for London within half an hour but it was three o'clock before she'd made the last phone call and finished priming Mabel, the office typist-cum-fixer, to hold the fort. On her way to the London road she called in at Elm Avenue to pick up some washing things and write another note for Mrs Biddows, saying that she might not be back that night.

As she headed down the A12 she tried to work out when she'd last managed to get to the flat. It had been almost three weeks ago, she realised, for a short weekend. Another two weeks before that, she'd managed less than a day. A neighbour in the flat below forwarded her mail to Catch, and Jenny had popped in now and again to see that the place was all right.

It would be strange to see it again – but not so strange as seeing it with the ceiling spread all over the floor.

She'd forgotten what a pig the journey could be. She got caught behind a pile-up on the M25, then a jam at Edmonton, and didn't reach Holloway until after five.

Ominously, there was a section of ripped-up vinyl flooring lying beside the front door of the house.

She took a deep breath before opening the flat door.

It was bad, but like all these things it could have been worse. The water had poured through the ceilings of all three rooms, but had brought down the plaster in only one, though, with a certain inevitability, it was the main room, containing her few valued possessions. It was as if a small bomb had been detonated close to the ceiling, leaving a long gaping hole. Lining paper hung down from the bulging plasterboard in tattered rags, with shards of plaster still attached.

She spent half an hour removing the larger chunks of plaster from the floor, hanging rugs up to dry, mopping up the remaining patches of damp, turning the mattress on its side. But, like the aftermath of a flood, it was not a situation that could be restored in a couple of hours.

On an impulse, in need of some sympathy perhaps, she dialled Simon. He sounded rather huffy, and she had the feeling she should be apologising for something. 'Sorry not to have called,' she said, trying to remember when she'd last spoken to him. A week ago? No, eight days. 'I've been unbelievably busy,' she said.

He gave a non-committal grunt, and the atmosphere settled heavily, like the plaster-dust.

'I've had a slight disaster,' she said, and explained about the ceiling not being in its proper place. She added, half seriously: 'Don't suppose you'd like to come over and help clear up?'

'Is it right down, the ceiling?'

'No, not completely.'

'What – a half? More, less?'

'A third.'

'Is the rest sagging?'

She looked up. 'Cracked in places. Sagging in others.'

'They'll only take the rest down, you know, when they come to repair it. They'll never be able to patch it up as it is. It's not worth clearing the place up. I wouldn't bother if I were you.'

'But my things – '

'Send them to the cleaners.'

She closed her eyes and took a slow breath.

'While you're on,' she said, opening her eyes, 'you couldn't do me a favour, could you?'

'I'll try.' The cautious tone.

'Have you got a mole at the Home Office?'

'A mole? What sort of a mole?'

A journalist's answer if there ever was one. 'The normal sort,' she said. 'Someone who can find something out.'

A pause, a tinge of resentment. Was he still miffed because she hadn't told him what she was doing up in Chelmsford? Had he, the champion of discretion, taken exception to being on the receiving end of his own brand of secrecy?

'What department?' he asked.

She told him.

'I might know someone. Near enough anyway,' he conceded.

'It's a favour for a friend,' she said. 'He wants to know why there's a delay in issuing a project licence to a company called Octek Ltd.' She spelt out the name and gave him the date and reference number of the application. 'He thinks there's a problem they're not telling him about. He thinks someone might be blocking things.'

His ears pricked up at that. 'Oh? Well, if I'm to have any hope of getting that sort of information, I'll need to know why anyone would want to block it.'

'My friend didn't say.'

Simon sighed fretfully. 'Really, I don't think there's anything I can do with so little information.'

'There could be a story in it.'

'How do you know?' he accused sharply.

A trap, a Simon-trap. 'All right,' she conceded. 'There *is* a bit more to it than I've told you, but I can't say what it is. I'm sorry.'

'This wouldn't be anything to do with your new job by any chance?'

What was one more lie? She raised her eyes towards the remains of the ceiling. 'No.'

'Well . . .' He made dubious noises. 'I don't suppose my contact'll be much use anyway.'

'But he's worth a go?'

'I don't know till I try.'

'The story – if anyone's going to get it, it'll be you, you know. You're the only one who could do it properly.'

That mollified him a bit. He always responded to a bit of flattery. It was one of his more endearing features.

'Okay,' he said grudgingly. 'I'll do what I can.'

'Thanks.' Someone walked across the floor above Daisy's head and disturbed a sprinkling of plaster dust which floated down around her. 'Simon, I couldn't come over, could I?' she asked suddenly. 'I'm a bit homeless, at least for tonight.'

'Look, I'd love to see you, but I can't.' He trotted out a story about having to meet a Euro-MP for dinner then drive straight down to Bristol. She noticed that he didn't offer her the use of his flat, although she still had a key.

'Can't you stay at Jenny's?' he asked, putting some concern into his voice.

'Oh, I expect so.'

'Well, then . . .'

There was a silence, the sort that says almost everything. Mainly goodbye.

She said it. 'Goodbye, Simon.'

It was a moment before he replied, but when he did she could tell that he'd read and absorbed the message in her voice. 'Goodbye, Daisy,' he said.

'I'll drop your keys in some time.'

He didn't put up much of a fight about it. 'Thanks.'

She put the phone down and poured herself another glass of wine and sat in silence for a long while. She remembered Campbell and dialled his number. She was relieved when there was no reply. Half the wine had disappeared before she found the energy to bundle her clothes into plastic sacks, pile up the soggy linen, and scoop the saturated sugar, flour and rice bags from the top of the kitchen units into the rubbish.

One of the few cupboards that was both dry and relatively free from dust was the one in the bathroom above the hot-water tank. Standing on the bath, unable to see into the recesses of the cupboard, she restacked the contents she could reach – the ones at the front mainly – and loaded in her clothes that were still dry and undamaged.

After that, there didn't seem much point in staying. She locked up the flat, lugged the plastic sacks of clothes and linen down to the car, and left a set of keys with the downstairs neighbours, along with a note, asking them to let the repair men in. It was already growing dark. She could go and grab a bath and a bed off Jenny, or she could fight her way across London to her mother's, or she could head straight back to Mrs Biddows'.

There was no debate really and, starting the faithful Metro, she headed north-east, back to Chelmsford.

Removing the earpiece, Hillyard switched off the recorder and pulled out unhurriedly. He remained some distance behind until he reached an arterial road, where the traffic thickened and he was forced to close up. A few miles up the A10, he had an annoying few moments trapped behind some red lights, and thought he would have to rely on the pinger, but he managed to catch sight of her distinctive unmatched rear lights just in time to follow her onto the M25, heading east. After that it was easy. He kept two cars behind her all the way to the turn-off for the A12. Then it was a nice gentle run along the dual carriageway towards Chelmsford with the sound of the direction-finder pinging softly on the seat behind him.

He had just prepared himself for a drive into the depths of East Anglia when she left the Chelmsford bypass at the first roundabout and headed towards the town centre. They came to a straggling suburban high street lined with small shops and pubs. She indicated left, slowed and drew up in front of a Chinese take-away. He went past and, looking in his mirror, saw her get out of the car and enter the shop without looking to left or right.

He parked and waited. Beside him, Beji woke and pulled herself up to peer out of the window. She gave a tentative sniff, then another. He reached across and ruffled her head playfully.

The girl emerged from the take-away with her boxed dinner, got into the car again and drove straight off. Again, she didn't hesitate, didn't look about her. She hadn't used the journey to think too much then, hadn't linked the little water-tank disaster with anything more significant. Hadn't realised she'd been had. Not quite as smart as she thought she was. This idea offered him some consolation for the two months that she had managed to evade him.

As he followed, it occurred to him that she knew her way around this town. There was no hesitation in her driving, no

410

pausing at junctions or craning to look at road signs. She was cutting skilfully across the suburbs with the confidence of someone who had used the route many times. After five minutes they came into a semi-industrial area where there was far less traffic. He dropped back a little and turned up the pinger. Suddenly, with hardly any warning and only the briefest flick of her indicator, she turned left into a slip road.

He slowed as he approached the turning, and took a quick look down it. The road looked more like an access road than a public thoroughfare. Making up his mind, he accelerated past, took another sideways glance, and realised he had made the right decision. It was a private road leading to some sort of industrial estate, and undoubtedly a no-through road. A little further on he turned around and made his way slowly back.

Just short of the entrance he drew into the kerb and twiddled with the dials on the direction-finder. The volume and direction of the pings were constant. He allowed himself a moment of satisfaction.

He gave it a full two minutes before turning into the estate and driving purposefully along, not too fast, not too slow. After a short distance the road forked. He continued along what seemed to be the most likely turning. Fifty yards on, he noticed a light flickering on in a building which lay ahead to the right. Simultaneously he spotted the Metro parked outside the perimeter fence. He drove steadily on, taking a careful look at the building as he passed. Lights were showing behind closed venetian blinds in a front room and in the entrance hall. Above the entrance was a sign: Octek Ltd. That, he remembered, was the name she'd mentioned on the phone, the company she'd asked her boyfriend to look into, though Hillyard would play back the recording later to make sure.

The road formed a loop, coming back on itself at the fork just before the main road. He drove out of the estate and turned right in the direction of the town centre. Plenty of time now. Time for a beer and a sandwich, a walk for Beji, and a call to Beryl. She would be pleased, she would chortle lunacies down the phone at him, she would call him a clever boy. And, he thought to himself, she would be absolutely right.

Too much sweet, too little sour, and some dubious ball-shaped protein that was, presumably, the promised prawns.

Nourishment of a sort. Daisy folded some rice into the glutinous mixture and with her free hand leafed through the pile of papers that had found their way onto her desk.

Turning over an invoice, she found a message in Mabel's upright schoolmarmish script. A Mr Hotstart had telephoned. There was an office number and a home number. Hotstart? She must mean Hopkirk. *Hopkirk*, she said aloud, as if Mabel were in earshot. Hopkirk was Nick Mackenzie's accountant.

A home number – he'd never left a home number before. What did it mean? News? Bad news?

She dialled the number. It rang without reply. It was nine thirty. Out to dinner perhaps. What time would he get back – eleven? Twelve? Well, she would keep trying. There was plenty of work to fill the time.

But her mind kept sliding back to what the accountant might want, to what he might say. That the last instalment couldn't be paid next month as she'd requested? Or, even worse, that there would be no last instalment at all?

Finally, at ten forty-five, Hopkirk answered.

Mr Mackenzie was back, he said casually. If she wanted to see him, he was free at ten on Saturday morning. Would that be convenient? He gave her an address in West London – Mr Mackenzie's new house, he said – and a telephone number.

He rang off and she leaned weakly back in her chair. Did she want to see him? *Did she!* God, she would have trekked to Scotland, flown to America . . . What a question! The relief was warm and sweet. In her mind she was already going through her story with him, already explaining how the budget had managed to blossom, how the project needed this last injection of cash. He might be reluctant to listen, of course, he might be even more reluctant to provide the money, but he'd do it, she felt sure he would. At heart, he was all right. It was just a matter of *getting* to his heart, reaching him one more time. She checked herself, ashamed at such a manipulative thought. It was, she realised, a measure of her desperation.

Somewhere there was a sound. She listened but it didn't come again. She tried to place it. Muffled, from somewhere deep in the building, it had sounded like something falling or banging. A door perhaps.

She went down the passage and, unlocking the door to the labs, passed through and listened again. There was silence.

412

She made her way down to the passage, into B-Lab's robing room and put her head round the door of the lab itself. It was quiet and dark. The windows were closed, the ventilation system whirring softly. Turning back, she looked into each of the store rooms in turn before coming to A-Lab. She switched on the lights and blinked for a moment. Then she saw a high narrow window which had been left open. Finding the pole, she inserted the hook into the ring on the frame and slammed the window shut.

She looked around to see if anything had been knocked over by the wind but nothing had been disturbed. It was very quiet. It didn't sound as though there was any wind at all. The sound must have come from somewhere else altogether, another building perhaps.

She left, double-checking each door before setting the alarm. Barring accidents, she should be asleep by eleven thirty.

She locked the gates, started the Metro, did her customary U-turn and accelerated towards the main road.

If you want to see him. What a question.

It was only when she drew up outside Mrs Biddows', where the dial of the telephone was firmly locked against improvident guests, that she remembered that she had forgotten to call Campbell. Wearily she turned the car around and headed back towards the lab. A half-remembered phone box came into sight in a street radiating from the first roundabout. She took the unfamiliar road and, approaching the box, saw the green sign of a card-operated phone. She stopped and, delving into her purse, found three phone-cards, none of which had more than two or three units on it.

If Campbell had a lot to say, she could always reverse the charges, or even go back to the lab and call again from there.

Campbell's number didn't answer. She left it ringing for a long time in case he was sleeping heavily, but there was still no reply. Then, despite the time, she tried Mrs Bell.

She answered straight away. 'Ahh,' she said flatly. 'I thought it would be you. They're holdin' him for the night. There's a hearin' in the morning.'

'What? *Who?*'

'Campbell. I thought you knew,' she said without surprise. 'There was trouble.'

'What sort of trouble?'

413

'With the therapist woman.'

'What therapist?'

'A psychotherapist, she called herself. Sent by the social services. She came twice in a week, all the way from Glasgow. Said she'd be comin' regularly. Campbell heard what she was sayin' to Adrian. He didna' like what he heard.'

'And?'

'There was an incident.'

'What sort of incident?'

'Well . . . They're sayin' it was assault.'

Daisy sighed aloud. Wonderful, Campbell, bloody wonderful.

The call meter started flashing a nil-units warning. Daisy said hastily: 'Listen, I'll be up. I'll try to get up as soon as I can – '

The line went dead.

Daisy leaned against the side of the box while she worked out what time she would get to Scotland if she grabbed a few hours' sleep and started at four.

Placing the car was half the art. Too far away and you could say goodbye to any hope of a quick bunk, too near and it was like hanging up a sign to say that you were in there, uninvited. There was another alternative, of course, and that was to look like you owned the place. Hillyard used a spike to spring the padlock, then swung open one of the gates and reversed the car close into the side of the building and, returning to the gate, latched it loosely shut behind him.

He marched purposefully up the side of the building until he was in the shadows, then went slowly about his business. He never hurried a recce, especially one like this. In fact, it was possible he might not go in tonight at all. It all depended on the alarm system, if there was one.

There was one. Shining a pencil beam through one of the windows, he sighted a magnetic contact attached to a window frame opposite. After that it was a question of cataloguing the type and location of each security device. It wasn't difficult. The windows around the rear of the building were numerous and large, revealing two laboratories full of equipment but not, as far as he could see, a great deal of security. There was no sign of heat sensors, nor of floor beams. The system appeared to be a fairly primitive mix of magnetic contacts and vibration sensors, though it never paid to make up one's mind about these things too soon.

It took him half an hour to decide that his first assessment had been right, and the system was as basic as he had first thought. It took him another twenty minutes to decide on the best way in. The front of the building was out: too well lit. On the open side where he had left the car there was a side door, but it was solid and well bolted, and all the windows were covered by vibration sensors. On the other side however, reached by a narrow strip between the building and the one next door, there was a frosted metal-frame window which looked as though it belonged to a washroom of some sort. As far as he could tell by peering through the distortions of the glass, the opening half of the frame, a conventional vertically hinged window, had only a single magnetic contact. More to the point, the other, fixed, window had a revolving draught-operated vent cut into the glass.

From his tote-bag he selected some tools and, taking his time, began to work on the vent. In the end he had to cut around the fitting and lift the thing out wholesale. This was not ideal – the refixing would require clips and putty and a lot of fiddling about – but it was safer than trying to drill out the fixings from the wrong side.

Padding the sharp edges of the cut glass circle with his jacket, he reached through up to his shoulder until his fingers touched the latch of the other window. It moved under his fingers: it was not locked. He then checked the alarm fitting to make certain that it was indeed magnetic.

From his bag he took a magnetic contact and, passing it through the hole, stuck the magnet to its brothers on the frame, ensuring that a circuit would be maintained when he opened the window. Then, dropping his hand down to the latch, he levered it upwards.

He pushed open the window. The alarm did not go off.

Climbing through, he came out of the washroom and into the passage and made his way softly towards the front entrance, looking for floor beams or heat sensors. Finding none, he looked into the rooms to right and left – offices, a stationery and equipment store – until he came to the office at the front of the building, the place where he had seen the light flicker on. This looked like the centre of operations: a large desk, a smaller one, two phones, filing cabinets.

He doubled back and went down to the other end of the corridor, to a pair of swing doors, just to check he hadn't missed anything. The doors were locked. He thought of trying to pick them, but it might not be possible and, since they undoubtedly led to the laboratories he had seen through the windows, it was unlikely to be worth the effort.

He returned to the front hall. Tracing the lightweight cable from the alarm touch pad inside the main doors, he found the alarm control box tucked inside a utility cupboard in a corner of the main office. It was a standard if outmoded model. He made a note of the model type, and the number of circuits.

Then he settled down to his main work of the night. Closing the venetian blinds, he draped his jacket over a desk lamp and risked turning on the light. Reading through the files, it took him half an hour to get the picture. Even then, he went back over some of the material a second time, just to be sure. Well, well. Cunning bitch.

He began to photograph everything systematically: correspondence, names of staff and advisors, scientific protocols, weekly progress reports, lists of so-called victims, accounts, bank statements. Everything was here. But just as he allowed himself a small chortle of triumph he realised there was after all something missing. The money: or rather, its source. This wasn't the sort of operation which the shoestring Catch budget could finance, not when the money was arriving in dirty great lumps, a quarter of a million at a time. Oh no, Miss Field had got herself a benefactor from somewhere, a nice little money machine. A rich lover perhaps; a sugar daddy.

In his mind he sifted through what he'd already read and photographed, but he knew the information wasn't there. By three, after a last search through the files, he had to admit defeat. But only temporarily. There were ways, and stuff the low-risk policy.

He hovered for a moment over the choice of items in the specially cushioned box in his tote-bag, and finally went for a small crystal handset transmitter. Better range than the wall-socket variety, and that was the main consideration when he wasn't sure how closely he'd be able to monitor it.

Opening up the telephone handset, he clamped the transmitter's tiny alligator clips to the connections, and stuck it to the inside of the plastic casing using double-sided tape. Neat as pie.

416

Closing the handset again, he tested the transmitter, then tidied up carefully, ready to leave.

He got as far as the door, then turned back as a memory struck him, something he'd seen in one of the files. It was a moment before he recalled the file's pedantic title: Home Office Project Licence Application. He didn't pretend to understand it all, much of it was in scientific-speak, but the relevant parts shone through all right, and a wonderful idea began to simmer and glow in his mind.

TWENTY-SIX

'Y ou look fine, *fine*.' David's smile was the sort fathers use on adolescent children, fond but hesitant, in vague fear of rebuff. 'The rest's done you good.'

'It also drove me crazy,' said Nick mildly, and raised an eyebrow to show he almost meant it.

The waiter arrived with the drinks, a lager for David and a Badoit for Nick.

The restaurant was filling up. It was a nouveau-Italian place in Covent Garden, a cellar done out in neutral pastels with all the plumbing showing. Now and again someone looked Nick's way then just as quickly looked away again.

'She's late,' Nick remarked.

'The traffic. A state visit or something. Do you want to order?'

'No.'

David gave him that soft nervous smile again. He was unusually deferential, Nick noticed, almost as if Nick were some new client who might prove unpredictable.

'You've seen Mel and Joe?' David ventured.

'Yesterday.' Then, because it was what David wanted to hear, he added: 'I gave them a couple of songs to look at.'

David, terrified of overreacting, hid his pleasure behind a frozen smile. 'Stuff you might – er – put in the album?'

'Too early to say.'

David went into immediate retreat. 'Of course. Too early to say.'

'Might not be suitable, that's all.'

'Whatever you say, Nick. Whatever you say.'

Nick's irritation rose. All this eager agreement, all this backing away from the slightest risk of confrontation was getting on his nerves. David was sounding like a yes-man. Somehow, somewhere they'd lost touch with each other. Perhaps it had begun a long time ago and neither of them had noticed, perhaps it had happened during the brief American tour. Perhaps David wasn't even aware of it. Either way, it was a lonely thought.

David rolled his eyes towards the door. 'Here's our lady now.'

Nick glanced round. Some women enter restaurants, others make entrances. Susan Driscoll was not entering unobtrusively.

As she strode towards him and reached out to take his hand he tried to work out how she'd changed since he'd last seen her. It was her hair, he thought, though whether it was the colour or the style he had no idea. Grasping his hand, she kissed him warmly on the cheek as if they were old friends. He wondered if she was remembering their last meeting in David's office almost a year ago. From the breadth of her smile, he guessed not.

'Well!' she cried. 'How lovely it is to see you.' She leaned her chin on her hands to get a closer look at him. The movement caused her heavy golden hair to swing forward from her shoulder so that you couldn't help noticing it. He wondered if she practised the gesture. 'You look so well,' she said. 'Have you been away?'

'I've been drying out.'

Her smile didn't falter. 'Where did you go – Clouds? My friends tell me it's the best.'

'A place in Arizona.'

'Mmm. Sounds lovely. And do you do all that follow-up? AA meetings and all that. They say it's the most fantastic brotherhood. Better than a club.'

'I keep in touch.'

'Well,' she breathed, withdrawing gently from the subject. 'That's wonderful. You look wonderful.' And, giving a soft laugh, she reached out and brushed her fingers lightly against his arm in a gesture that was curiously intimate. His instinct was to pull up his drawbridge and retreat fast, yet there was something so direct in her manner, so well meaning, that he decided to reserve judgement, for the time being at least.

David launched the subject of the restored charity concert.

'It sold out in three days,' Susan said, throwing up her elegant hands in delight. 'Even at the extortionate prices we're charging. And the advertising's gone well. We should clear over a hundred thousand.' She turned her eyes to Nick's. He noticed their colour, a clear grey-green, and a distant memory came to him, of a morning when they had woken up together, long ago. But his recollection of his feelings at the time was strangely clouded, and no clear emotion came through. He knew that he hadn't loved her – though he had liked her well enough for a while – but there had been something disturbing in their relationship, something that had resulted in difficulties and unpleasantness, particularly towards the end, though he couldn't remember exactly what the problem had been. His memory, never brilliant, had faded dramatically during the drinking years.

'It's so inadequate to thank you, but I will anyway,' Susan said in her light dancing voice. 'It's such a nightmare this fund raising,' she sighed. 'Such a hassle thinking of brilliant ideas only to find they've all been done before. But to get you *and* Amazon – well . . .' She gave an expressive little shrug.

'Glad to help,' he murmured.

She fixed him with those eyes again. 'I know it's probably a great bore for you.'

The first course arrived. 'It's just another concert.'

'Of course, but . . .' She paused, tucking her chin down and casting him a long upward look. 'Can I come straight out and ask you something?' She gave a sudden laugh that was self-deprecating and charming all at the same time. 'Then I can get it over and done with, and I won't have to spend the rest of the meal in misery, working out how on earth I'm going to find a way of asking you.'

It was bound to be something he didn't want to do, but at least she was asking. Some charity organisers just sprang things on you at the last minute, on the principle that once the event was under way it was almost impossible for you to make a scene. 'Ask away,' he said.

'It's our main donors – you wouldn't shake their hands at the party afterwards, would you? You know, say a couple of words to one or two of them. It wouldn't take long – fifteen minutes at the most, then you could slip away – through a

420

back entrance or something. It's just so they can go away saying they met you. It makes such a difference.'

David tore himself away from his pasta. 'Can't be done in fifteen minutes. More like thirty. And Nick'll be very tired.'

'They're business people, are they?' Nick asked.

She wrinkled her nose. 'Corporate moguls, I'm afraid. *Seriously* boring. But what can you do? Some of them are very generous.'

'We know the sort,' David said drily, raising his eyebrows at Nick.

Nick smiled. 'They say they can't stand pop music. They say they only came because their kids made them, then admit they quite liked the show. They say it took them back to their youth.'

She laughed again, but her eyes remained on his, watching for his answer.

He made up his mind, though he knew he'd probably regret it. 'I'll come for half an hour,' he said.

David shot him a well-don't-blame-me look. Susan bowed her head and said simply: 'Thank you.' Her voice, soft and low, had a slight tremble to it, and she closed her eyes for an instant, as though saying a little prayer of thanks.

Before today, warmth was not a word he'd have associated with Susan Driscoll – brittle would have been nearer the mark – but he was rapidly opening his mind to the possibility that he had misjudged her.

Putting her salad aside, she began to talk about the old days which she seemed to remember with some fondness. But it didn't take her long to sense his lack of interest. 'So tell me,' she said, shifting onto safer ground, 'where are you based nowadays?'

'Kensington. I've just bought a house.'

'Oh? You've given up the country life then?'

'Kensington's quite leafy.'

She gave a soft laugh. 'But not many cows.'

'Not that I've noticed.'

'But then London has its compensations, doesn't it?' she ploughed on. 'Theatre and concerts and things. I adore London, but it might as well be Siberia for all I get to see of it nowadays.'

There was a small silence.

'Don't you get entertained a lot?' he managed.

'Oh, official entertaining, yes – dreary receptions, the occasional opera if one's lucky. But theatre, dinner parties with friends . . .' She shook her head and a slight frown furrowed the smooth line of her forehead. 'I thought I was in for a quiet life but, well – ' She seemed to become aware of David who, having finished his pasta, was half listening to the conversation. She broke off with a brave little laugh. 'Let's just say things don't always work out the way you expect them to.'

What's this? Nick wondered. Are you trying to tell me that under all this brightness you're unhappy? Since Alusha's death even the most casual of his friends had unburdened their troubles on him as if, having marked him as a fellow sufferer, they felt confident of a sympathetic response. Was the whole world suddenly unhappy, he wondered, or in his years with Alusha had he simply been too wrapped up in his own life to notice?

Aware that the conversation had faltered, he murmured: 'The Ministry of Agriculture, isn't it? Lots of farmers, I suppose.'

She rolled her eyes heavenward. 'Worse.' Her voice was heavy with ridicule. 'Factory openings. Beef federations. Milk marketing boards. Agrochemical giants.' Her mouth twitched with amusement, on the point, he guessed, of doing a sharp demolition job on the agrochemical industry, until the amusement drained out of her face, as if she had remembered something serious. He had a feeling he knew what that something was.

'Your wife – Did they ever find out . . .?' she began cautiously. 'It was a chemical, wasn't it?'

David emerged from a mouthful of veal in cream sauce, looked nervously at Nick and took refuge in a hasty wave at the wine waiter.

'Well, no one's exactly sure,' Nick answered quietly.

'But . . . there was a suggestion, wasn't there?'

'It doesn't really matter now.'

'No . . .' she said uncertainly. 'I suppose not.'

No one spoke for a moment. The restaurant seemed very noisy.

'But you know, if you'd wanted any help . . . access to information . . .' She paused, her fingers lacing an intricate

422

pattern under her chin, her eyes steady and clear. 'I'd have done all I could. Anything . . .' The word hung in the air.

'Thanks,' he answered simply. He caught David looking impressed at the calmness of his response.

Susan eased the conversation effortlessly away onto food, recounting some disaster she'd had with an unknown fish in a foreign restaurant. She was good at smoothing things over, Nick noticed, something she'd probably learned in her years as a politician's wife. As he listened he realised she never mentioned her husband, either directly or indirectly. Was this intentional, he wondered, or a reflection of the discontent she'd already hinted at?

She told her tale entertainingly, with wide graceful gestures and frequent explosive laughter. His mood lifted. Against all the odds, he was enjoying himself, which just went to prove that you could never tell what might come out of even the most unpromising situation.

Yet was it really so unexpected? In the last year he'd been so careful to avoid new people and unfamiliar situations, so in dread of the effort they demanded, that he'd forgotten how refreshing a new face could be. Old friends, fond as they were, couldn't help humping the luggage of the past around with them. Susan represented the best of both worlds, he realised, an old friend with the virtues of the new.

There was something else about her too, an energy, an obvious and unquestioning appetite for life that in his present mood was rather beguiling. She was like a sun, sending out light and vitality in every direction. Her brilliance was a little remorseless perhaps, but with no dark shadows attached.

Catching his eye, she accused: 'You're laughing at me.'

'Not at all.'

'Well, I wouldn't be surprised,' she declared, looking rather pleased at the idea. He noticed her skin which was the colour of pale honey as if she'd been abroad a lot but had taken care to keep out of the sun.

David called for the bill.

'Already? And we've hardly talked about the concert!' Susan gasped in mock horror. 'Aren't there lots of things we should discuss?' she asked, striking a serious pose. 'Things you'll need on the day? Or anything you *don't* need? Mr Weinberg and I' – she indicated David with a slight movement of a long finger – 'we've covered security and transport. But what about home comforts – champagne, food, that sort of thing? I've looked backstage – it's a bit of a tip, but I can do something with the dressing rooms, jolly them up, you know.'

'It's really not necessary.'

'But it's no trouble. It's my living, after all.'

It was a cue. He took it. 'Oh?'

'I'm an interior designer.' She gave a jaunty little bow. 'Newly established but trying hard. All reasonable commissions considered' – she lowered her voice confidentially – 'which means I'll take on anything to get established.'

'You find the time?'

'Oh, I find it.' There was a note of determination in her voice. 'It'll be easier when I get a few big commissions, of course. Less rushing about. And I'll have our new place to practise on. We're moving closer to the Commons.'

She paused, then, with a spark of calculation she could only have intended him to see, her eyes brimming with amusement she asked: 'I don't suppose your new house needs doing up, does it?'

He played along. 'I hadn't noticed.'

'Let me show you some ideas,' she said instantly, her face alight. 'And if you hate them – well . . .' She raised her shoulders to suggest this was unlikely. 'If you like them – then we can take it from there.' She spread her hands like a showman.

Out of the corner of his eye Nick caught David giving him a stare which, if he'd chosen to look, was probably loaded with caution. Maybe in reaction to that, maybe because he'd taken a sudden liking to the idea of change, maybe because Susan had made him laugh, he heard himself agree.

She gave a small exclamation of pleasure. 'I'll need just two things to get started,' she declared breathlessly. 'One's your address, of course.'

He put his hand out to David for a pen. 'And?'

'Some idea of the style you're looking for. Traditional, minimalist, neutral . . . you know.'

An image of Ashard flittered into his mind, the cavernous drawing room, muted and cool, the cosy library with its crackling fire and wood shelves, the bedroom overlooking the park, heavy with silks and soft brocades. 'I don't know,' he said.

She brushed the idea aside with a light twist of her wrist as if it had hardly been worth considering in the first place. 'Fine,' she said, 'absolutely *fine*. We can do it from another angle altogether. Just wander round the house, and you tell me what you *don't* like about the present decor. That'll tell me almost everything I need to know.' She broke off. 'How does that sound? Am I rushing things? Do you want to think it over?' She widened her eyes, giving him a look of apprehension that wasn't entirely convincing.

'No, that's fine.'

She grinned at him and, pulling a pocket diary out of her bag, opened it at a back page and pushed it towards him. He wrote down his address and phone number.

'Now tell me,' she said, 'when would you like me to come round?'

He shrugged.

She laughed, shaking her head as if he was a child whose little foibles were to be indulged as well as enjoyed. 'Well, what about tomorrow? Teatime? I love tea. I'll bring sticky buns.'

He didn't like sticky buns. He didn't like tea much either. He heard himself say: 'That'd be great.'

When he'd finished shaving, Schenker scrubbed a brisk flannel over his upper body, patted himself dry, applied fresh deodorant and put on a clean shirt laundered by Jeeves of Belgravia. He had a sudden doubt about the shirt. Blue medium-width stripe on white – too City-ish? And the style, with its deep collar – too Stock Exchange? Too assertive? Maybe. But did it matter? The days when he stood in fear and trembling of the group board were over. Half of them had come up the hard way, like him, and were unlikely to begrudge him a touch of style, while the others, Establishment to the core, wore shirts with stripes visible at fifty yards. Anyway, with what he had to tell them today, they wouldn't be looking at his shirt.

Passing out of his private bathroom into his office, he found his secretary standing expectantly by his desk.

'Hope it goes well,' she said.

'Thank you. It will.'

She slid soundlessly away and, sitting at his desk, Schenker went over his notes for perhaps the tenth time. The message would be best delivered briefly and low-key, underplayed to the point of understatement. He would merely say that, as of ten o'clock that morning, the Ministry of Agriculture, Fisheries and Food had decided to grant Silveron a licence for general use in the United Kingdom.

The board would show their delight. Then, after a decent interval, they would express a wish for the situation in the US to be resolved as satisfactorily, which would be their way of asking how things were going over there. He would assure them it was progressing, if slowly. He would remind them that the number of new products being granted licences in the US had dropped dramatically in recent years, that product-development times had never been longer, that, product for product, Morton-Kreiger was getting more new lines onto the market than any of their competitors.

No one would could argue with that. No one could say he wasn't on top of the job.

Someone would ask about the Aurora scare, but he would be able to reassure them on that too. All blown over, all illnesses accounted for, no new cases. Merely a storm blown up by the environmental activists.

Twenty minutes to go. In his anxiety to prepare himself properly, he had left too much time. He buzzed for Cramm.

Cramm was even quieter on his feet than Schenker's secretary, and it was a second before Schenker realised he had entered the room.

He waved him to a chair. 'I think I'll probably go to New York for the weekend,' he announced. 'Take tomorrow's Concorde. See friends on Long Island.' This wasn't quite true. The friends he was going to see – the senior vice president of a giant cola company and his wife – actually lived in Connecticut and weren't so much friends as new acquaintances. But Schenker, who'd been watching with growing interest some of the recent and highly dramatic cross-industry career moves of his contemporaries, wasn't about to tell anyone this, particularly Cramm.

'We'll meet in Chicago on Monday,' he said. 'So – is there anything before then?'

Unusually for him, Cramm didn't answer immediately.

Schenker gestured impatiently. 'Well?'

'It can wait,' Cramm said, but his eyes told a different story. They told Schenker it was something he wasn't going to like.

426

'I'll hear it now,' he said.

Cramm stared at him impassively. 'Perhaps we'd better speak outside.'

Schenker made a sound of irritation, already resenting the intrusion into his triumphal day. 'Is this really necessary?' But without waiting for an answer, he jumped to his feet and led the way through the adjoining conference room and out onto the terrace.

'Well?' he said tartly when Cramm had circled round to face him.

'Catch, they're setting up an operation – a whole lab – to run independent tests on Silveron.'

Schenker glared at him while he made up his mind how to react to this. 'So?' he said finally. 'They're going to spend a lot of money for nothing, aren't they? Might be a useful experience for them.'

'So you don't want us to do anything?'

'I don't know – keep an eye on it. Do what you think.' He waved a dismissive hand. 'Whatever. Is that all?' he added impatiently.

'It's the Kershaw woman. She's causing a bit of trouble.'

Schenker took a sharp breath of anger. He didn't want to hear about this, not now, not ever. 'What do you mean – *trouble*?'

'She wants more money.'

'What the hell *for*?'

'Distress and suffering.'

'*Distress and suffering*? She has to be joking.'

'Oh no, she's deadly serious.'

'But she's already been dealt with!' He glared into Cramm's impervious features. 'Hasn't she?'

'To the tune of fifteen thousand.'

'Jees-us,' Schenker hissed. He added: 'Remind me – where did that come from?'

'The Iraqi development budget.'

Schenker blinked. How Cramm managed these things he was never quite sure. 'So what's she after now, for God's sake?'

'Another ten.'

Schenker snorted with contempt. 'Offer her one thousand and if she's not interested tell her to go and jump.'

'What, call her bluff?'

'Why not?'

'She might spill it to the newspapers.'

'So? What's the bottom line? There's no link to us, is there? She has no idea who contributed the funds, does she?'

'No. Oh no, none at all. But Driscoll?'

Schenker fixed Cramm with a telling gaze, and spread his hands in an expressive gesture of helplessness. Cramm read the message and for an instant looked slightly shocked.

Schenker glanced hastily at his watch and made for the door. Cramm got to it first and slid it open.

Schenker paused half-way through. 'No, we've done all we can for Driscoll. If the girl talks, he's on his own.'

Only eight minutes to go. On his way back to his bathroom to recomb his hair, Schenker buzzed through to his secretary to make sure she'd got the Concorde booking. His urge to renew his acquaintance with the cola magnate was growing by the moment.

Daisy followed Campbell out of the solicitor's office, and they stood for a moment looking down on Oban.

Campbell took a dark backward glance at the solid façade of the office, as if to check that he was really free of the law, albeit temporarily, then set off down the street at a brisk pace. Daisy ran to catch up as Campbell led the way down towards the harbour and into a solid hotel on the waterfront.

The lounge bar was gloomy but clean and uncrowded. Daisy ordered toast, marmalade and strong coffee.

'Well?' she asked when they were alone. 'Care to tell me about it?'

Campbell gave a solid grunt and for a while she thought he wasn't going to answer. Finally he declared: 'Wrong. *Wrong.*'

'Are you saying you didn't do it?'

He shot her an angry look.

'Assault's a serious charge,' she pointed out. 'You could get a custodial sentence, you know. You were lucky to get bail.'

'I only tapped her.'

'Blimey, Campbell, a *woman*. Despite everything they're still meant to be *different*, you know. And a health professional! That makes her untouchable, Campbell, as close to sainthood as you can get without running for pope. *And* on official business . . .' She sighed: 'I won't go on.'

He was silent.

The waitress brought the coffee and toast.

She pushed him: 'Well?'

He looked angry again, then his expression relaxed into something more neutral and he gathered himself to speak. 'She struck him,' he said very slowly, to give it emphasis, 'she struck Adrian.'

Daisy settled slowly back in her chair and clasped her hands around her cup as if for warmth. 'From the beginning. Please.'

His mouth contorted with the exertion of memory. 'They said they were sendin' somebody – '

'They?'

'The social services. They said they were sendin' someone to look at Adrian,' he began hesitantly. 'They didna' say it was a – psycho*therapist*. No mention of that, och no.' He gave a caustic snort. 'We thought mebbe it was going to be some expert. Aye, we thought mebbe that they had found someone who could help. We were taken aback when this woman appeared. Och, not because she was a woman,' he added quickly, casting a defensive eye in Daisy's direction, 'but because of her manner. Very grand, she was, very cool. We were nothin' to her, she left us in no doubt o' that – hardly merited a civil word. She wouldna' answer questions, och no. Too high for that, she was. She requested we leave the room – she wanted to see Adrian alone, she said. There was no mention of bein' a psycho*therapist*, nothin' about what she'd come for. Not a shaft of politeness or consideration. Kept repeatin' she wanted to see Adrian alone.' For someone who normally kept things short, Campbell was doing well, stringing his sentences together with only the slightest pauses, though the effort had brought his brows low over his eyes. 'I should have had a notion, of course. I should have seen . . .' He gave a harsh sigh and, draining his coffee, looked towards the bar with transparent longing.

'Go on.'

He dragged his gaze back to her. 'Aye, well, we left her with Adrian for the time she wanted. Mebbe forty-five minutes – which was all too long for the lad, as you know. He can no' manage the talkin', not for that time. Och, lookin' back' – he took a great hissing suck of breath – 'like lambs, we were. Doin' her biddin'. Waitin' for her word from on high. Ha! When I think . . .' He gave a short bitter laugh. 'Well, finally she comes out, cool as you please, an' says she wants to talk

429

to the two of us for a wee while. It was not a request, do you
see, but an order. We agree right enough – we thought she
would be tellin' us somethin'. But she says nothin' about
Adrian, och no, she hadna' come to talk on a level with the
likes of Meg an' me. She had *other* business, do you see? She
begins pokin' her nose around. She asks about Meg an' her
marriage an' the death of Jamie – Adrian's father. Then . . .
then, if you please . . .' A pressure built up behind his face,
his cheeks expanded and his voice, when it came, was tight
and raw. 'She asks about Meg an' me. She wants to know
how we get on, the two of us. If we spend time together. If
we're close . . .' He blinked down at the table in dumb
outrage, unable to meet Daisy's eyes. 'Brother an' sister!
Brother an' sister. Och, I mebbe slow, but not that slow,' he
cried, tapping the side of his head with a great squared-off
finger. 'I could see the way her evil mind was workin'. I asked
her straight out what kind of a doctor she was. We have the
truth then. She's no doctor, she says, she's this psycho*therapist*. Ha! I could have murdered her – ' He clawed his hands.
'Her wicked mind had no place in that house, no place!'
Calming himself, he narrowed his eyes and raised a finger.
'But I didna' let her see a sight of that. I didna' give her the
satisfaction. No, I kept myself still, I said nothin' of my
thoughts!'

'Then?'

'She was gone.'

'Just like that?'

'Eh?' He shifted heavily in his seat. 'Well . . . I told her
there was no point in makin' another visit.' He pulled his
shoulders back grandly. 'I told her Adrian was not in need of
her kind of attention.'

'So she left?'

'Aye. But not for long. She was back just three days later,
an' with no warnin'. I was away on the loch, I didna' hear
until too late. An' this time, she brought another social
worker. Och, but it was well planned, there's no doubt of
that. The other woman, she was come to keep an eye on Meg,
to make certain she stayed away while the dirty business was
done. While the *person*' – he put a wealth of feeling into the
word – 'had Adrian to herself. An' she had him to herself a
long while – an hour, mebbe more – and when she left . . .'
His shoulders rocked slightly, like a fighter's squaring up to

an opponent. 'When she left, Adrian was broken, *broken*. Quiet an' wouldna' speak. An' that night – aye, he wept, wept like a babby. I saw him, but I couldna' get a thing out of him, he was that upset.'

During this last speech he had been getting increasingly restless and now, with what might have been a wave of apology, he lumbered to his feet and went to the bar. He came back with a large Scotch undiluted by water.

He took a quick gulp, his hand twitched, his eyes seemed to brighten. He went on: 'I had no doubts then. I told Meg that this *person* was to be locked out, that she was never again to enter the house. But Meg – she didna' see the sense of that. She said we would do best to make no complaint, not until we had good reason.' He pulled at his drink again and continued at what for him was breakneck speed. 'Good reason . . . Aye, well there was only one way to find good reason. I took the loan of a portable telephone device – you know? – so that Meg could call an' tell me when they returned. An' they returned soon enough. A week, it was, to the day. I went straight to the parlour door and opened it – slow, slow – just a crack at first, an' listened. I couldna' hear Adrian – he wasna' speakin' – but I could hear *her* well enough. Aye, every word, every single evil word there was to hear. An' I heard other things too,' he said, his voice rough and low.

He paused and rubbed a hand mercilessly across his closed eyes so that it seemed he must do them damage. 'I didna' realise at first – what the sound could be. But then – aw – I knew,' he said.

Daisy waited.

'Strikin' him. She was strikin' him.'

The doubt must have shown in Daisy's face because he repeated emphatically: 'Strikin' him, aye. Slow, regular, like some – *machine*. You're not ill, Adrian, she says – *tak* – you know you're not ill – *tak* – ' With each sound he swung his open palm softly through the air, in a wide slapping motion. 'You're not ill, Adrian – *tak* – tell me you're not ill, go on, tell me – *tak*.'

Daisy stared at him, reading the signals in his face. Everything told her it was true; everything warned her it must be an exaggeration.

'It was not the entire time, och no, she had a rest now an' again, to give her time to put other notions in his head. It's attention you want, isn't it, she says, it's attention you want, isn't it, Adrian? – I heard each an' every word, each an' *every* one. You're tryin' to punish your father for havin' died, she says. You're angry with him, aren't you, Adrian?' He had raised his voice in a savage imitation of a woman's voice. 'You're angry that he's not here for you to tell him how angry you are. You're angry at your mammy for letting your uncle take his place.' He broke off and dropped his head for a moment. Daisy gave a sudden shudder.

'That's why you want to be ill, isn't it, Adrian?' he began again, coming up slowly. 'But you're *not* ill, Adrian, an' it's time you told me so. Now, tell me you're not ill, Adrian, tell me . . . Then . . .' His voice lowered, trembling with anger. 'Then I heard it again, the sound, the *sound*. *Tak, tak!* An' I went in an' I saw . . .' He sank the last of his Scotch in one gulp. He said flatly: 'I went in an' I saw what she was doin', an' I struck her right back. An' I tell you – there's not an ounce of regret in ma body.'

'You're not going to tell the judge that, I hope.'

He frowned and was silent.

'Where was she hitting Adrian?'

'The cheek. Here.' He put a hand to his face.

'Was he bruised? Were there marks?'

His mouth moved uncertainly. He looked at her with sudden suspicion. 'Red. The skin was red.'

Daisy sighed. 'Striking is a strong word.'

Campbell, putting a treacherous interpretation on this, became aggressive. 'An' what would you have me use?'

'Were they perhaps nearer to taps or light slaps?'

'Good God!' His eyes bulged with rage and she was reminded of how very frightening Campbell could be. 'Are you tellin' me this word or that would make it right?'

'Nothing would make it right. Don't misunderstand me. Even if she hadn't touched Adrian, it would still have been appalling.'

'Well then, taps, slaps – what's the difference?'

'With you, quite a bit, apparently. You said you just tapped the psychotherapist, but she ended up with a badly bruised eye. I'm just trying to get our vocabulary straight.'

Campbell hunched his shoulders and tried to look penitent. 'Well . . . Perhaps I put a mite more force behind it than I intended,' he admitted reluctantly. 'Will it count against me?'

But he asked it more out of hope than expectation. He knew very well that it would count against him. What worried Daisy was the other ways in which it might count against not only him but Adrian Bell and his mother as well.

'I think we should get straight back to Dermott's,' she said.

He did not look thrilled at the idea of seeing his solicitor again so soon. 'For what reason?'

'We might have to think about protecting Adrian.'

Expressions of alarm, perplexity and suspicion crossed Campbell's face in rapid succession. 'Protection? From what?' But before he had the chance to ask again, she had gone to the desk and paid the bill and was leading the way out into the street. It was how the social services might be taking all this that worried her, she explained as she set a rapid pace up the hill; how they could argue that Campbell's presence constituted a bad influence. At this, Campbell, with a certain predictability, ground to a halt and protested violently.

'I'm just telling you what they might be thinking,' Daisy argued quietly.

She painted the picture even more strongly then: how they might consider taking Adrian into care, how they could apply for a place of safety order on the grounds that Adrian's physical health was in danger from lack of essential medical treatment, or that his emotional health was in danger from unsuitable home influences, or both of these. Overriding Campbell's further explosions of rage, she told him how, unless Scottish law was dramatically different from English, the order could be granted in the absence of family representation, without anyone knowing anything about it – not until the police and social services arrived unannounced on the doorstep, and how Campbell and his sister would be powerless to prevent Adrian from being removed.

For a time Campbell fell into a furious inarticulate silence. 'They can be prevented?' he panted finally.

'I don't know. I'm not sure what the law allows here. In England a family can start ward of court proceedings. That way the social services can't do anything until the story's been heard by a judge. Even then there're risks – the judge might get talked into allowing some of the medical treatment – '

Campbell grabbed her arm, 'Hold it there! *Hold it there!*' he roared, sending a shower of spittle over her. 'You're sayin', you're sayin' . . .' It was a moment before he got a grip on his thoughts. 'You're sayin' we should apply to the court just so they can send that *person* back to torture Adrian?'

She grasped his hand and lifted it gently away from her sleeve. 'Whatever course we take involves risk. But anything's better than having Adrian removed altogether, surely.'

His rage made him speechless. 'But . . . Why should they want to take him?' he said at last in a broken voice.

'Because they want to get their way, that's why. You have to realise, Campbell, that these people are convinced they're right, and there's no stopping people who believe they've got right on their side.'

He couldn't take it in. 'I must talk to Meg. Must talk with Meg.'

A weariness came over Daisy, but also an acceptance. She could see that there was an inevitability to this, that Campbell would never dare move alone, that indeed he had no right to do so. But how long would these discussions take? It was Friday, midday. The legal weekend started early.

She offered: 'Do you want me to come back to Loch Fyne and go through it with Meg, then?'

He nodded doggedly.

She looked away across the water and took stock. Even if everything went smoothly, there wouldn't be a hope of getting anything before a judge before midday tomorrow. And tomorrow was the day of her meeting with Nick Mackenzie. A meeting, she hardly needed reminding, on which the financial future of Octek, if not the entire Silveron project, depended.

In the end she compromised with Campbell. While Campbell agreed to continue up the hill to see Dermott, to get the benefit of his advice on Scottish law regarding minors, Daisy promised to stop for an hour's discussion with Meg Bell before continuing on to London. She would return promptly on the Sunday, to help Campbell and his sister come to a firm decision.

To do the round journey by road would kill her; she would have to fly. But then when would she be able to get back to Octek? Monday night? Tuesday even? When she was away, the problems always seemed to pile up.

Waiting in Dermott's office it occurred to her that there was one further option, and borrowing a phone, she dialled Nick Mackenzie on the London number his accountant had given her. It rang for a long time then, just as she was about to give up, suddenly answered. For some reason, her heart did a leap against her ribs. Nerves.

A voice said: 'Hullo, can I help you?' It was a female voice with a northern accent, not young, probably quite old.

Mr Mackenzie was not at home, the voice said. This was the housekeeper speaking.

Daisy explained about the difficulty of keeping her appointment, and asked if there might be another time when he was free.

'He's going away,' said the voice. 'He leaves tomorrow evening. I'm not sure how long he'll be away.'

'Abroad?'

There was a pause, as if the housekeeper were uncertain whether to impart the information or not. 'Scotland,' she said eventually.

'He's coming to Glen Ashard?' she asked.

Yes, it was to Glen Ashard.

She left a message. She would be at the George Hotel in Inveraray, she said, and would come to Glen Ashard on Sunday at eleven, unless she heard to the contrary.

Dermott found a moment to see them, though in the way of lawyers who are not really very busy, he made it clear that it was not terribly convenient. There was no such thing as wardship in Scotland, he announced. And even if there was, such extreme measures were surely unnecessary. If anything needed to be done – and by his tone he clearly doubted it – then a reasoned dialogue with the social services would be the most sensible course. Everyone, after all, had the child's interests at heart. He spoke with complacency and a confidence that seemed to Daisy to spring more from inertia than good judgement.

In the car Daisy said: 'I think we should move Adrian. Take him to England.'

'You mean hide him away?'

'I mean – ' She sighed. 'Yes, I suppose that *is* what I mean. But not too obviously. Not so we can't pretend that we were just taking him in search of medical treatment.'

Campbell shifted unhappily in his seat. 'Meg will never agree,' he sighed. 'She'll never be wantin' to leave Loch Fyne.'

This thought had also loomed large in Daisy's mind, and she fell silent for the rest of the journey.

It was three when they reached Loch Fyne. After a long chat with Adrian, who was up and sitting in a chair, looking a little fuller in the face but still very weak and with newly acquired liver problems, Daisy gave the idea of removing Adrian to England a first run past Mrs Bell. Later she went through it with her again in more detail. But Mrs Bell was not to be moved, not for the moment at least.

After a supper of thick stew and dumplings Daisy left Campbell and Mrs Bell to talk it through in the kitchen and, lying on the sofa next to Adrian, fell asleep to the flickering of an old movie. She didn't wake till morning.

TWENTY-SEVEN

The massive gates were closed, the lodges at either side apparently deserted, the woodland beyond, impenetrable. High on one of the gateposts was a security camera and, lower down, an intercom with a bell and an integral camera lens. Daisy rang, and a light came on above the lens. She faced the camera and waited. A single low buzz, and the gates swung silently open. She got hastily into the Metro and drove through before they closed again.

The road wove gently through the woodland until, after a long bend, the Metro ground over a cattle grid, its suspension rattling alarmingly, and the shrubs gave way to a wide expanse of rough grassland dotted with large trees that rose like sentinels out of the mist.

It was only when the car had jangled over a second grid that the mass of Ashard House came into view. The place sprang straight out of a Walter Scott novel or an Errol Flynn film: heavily buttressed and turreted, windows not just leaded but mullioned as well, ivy growing dutifully up the walls towards a main tower which sported a tall undraped flagstaff.

In the porch was another security camera with a red winking light, its lens pointing to the spot a couple of feet in front of the door where callers stood to operate the old-fashioned metal bell-pull. But for all the hi-tech, security wasn't that rigid because the massive oak door was lying half-open.

She pulled the bell anyway, and heard an electronic ring echoing through the house. No one came. She checked her watch; she was dead on time. She gave it two more minutes and another ring before stepping inside. The hall was large and baronial, with a lot of dark wood and a wide staircase towards the far end. Someone was moving house. Along one wall a stack of cardboard and wooden packing cases rose three-high.

Several doors led off the hall. She knocked and looked in each in turn.

Beyond the staircase was a passage which led almost immediately to a large and immaculate kitchen. This too was empty, although she noticed that on the table a place had been set for breakfast.

She retreated, feeling indecisive. A sound came drifting down the passage from the far end, a sound so slight that at first she thought it was the buzz of an insect. Then it changed pitch, and she realised it was broadcast music of some kind. She followed the trail to a closed door. She knocked, and again, louder. There was no reply. She opened the door.

The music surged up, amazingly loud, as if someone had suddenly turned up the volume. The light from the three tall windows was very bright, and it was a second before she made out the figure sitting with his back to her, in front of a control panel. His hands were moving over a keyboard, and she realised he was playing along with the music in some way. He stopped to scribble something, and the music sped on, multi-stranded, but incomplete. He put the pencil down, listened for a moment, then reached out and flicked a switch. The music stopped with a squawk and turned into a high-speed caterwauling as the tape rewound.

'Hi,' she said.

Nick jerked round, looking startled, and stared at her for a moment. 'It's not time already, is it? God!' Shaking his head, he twisted back in his revolving seat and flicked more switches until the noise stopped. 'You got my message then?' he said over his shoulder. 'Ten was okay, was it?'

'Yes,' she smiled. 'Fine.'

He hunched over the sheets he'd been scribbling on. 'Always the same,' he murmured. 'Have to stop just when it's going well . . .'

'If I'm interrupting . . .'

'No, no. Got to stop anyway.' He lifted the sheets of music and threw them onto a next-door table. Facing her at last, he shot her an oblique look that was both appraising and cautiously welcoming, before striding across to the window and looking up at the sky. 'Mist!' he exclaimed impatiently. 'No good while there's mist.'

'No good . . .?'

'Can't go till it's lifted.'

She gave an uncertain laugh. 'Go?'

He turned. 'Didn't I say?'

'Not unless the hotel clerk got amnesia.'

'Ah, I didn't say then.' He frowned at her, and it occurred to her that the omission had been intentional. Inviting her to follow he walked out into the passage. She caught up with him in the kitchen as he was coming out of a side room with a cool-box in either hand.

'Well, the important part's ready,' he said. 'Hope you like smoked salmon? And white wine? Otherwise it's mineral water – still or bubbly or in between. But look – would you like some coffee while we wait?' Running out of things to say, he looked down at her, his face pursed into an expression that was wary and watchful and amiable all at the same time.

'What's the occasion?' she asked.

His mouth twitched. 'Ah, well . . . I've got to go and see something. I thought you might like to come along.'

'Surprise time?'

He shrugged. 'If you like.' But he didn't mind the idea.

'Oh, I like,' she declared firmly. 'The surprises I've been getting recently have all been the nasty sort.'

A glint came into his eye, a tiny but unmistakable warning that he didn't want to hear about any of that, not yet anyway.

'You're moving?' she asked, gesturing towards the packing cases.

'Sort of.'

'A pity.' She meant, because the place was so beautiful. But she sensed it was the wrong thing to say.

'Oh well,' he remarked calmly. 'Things change, things move on.' He led the way across the hall and into a book-lined room with an open fire. 'Though I don't know about the house. I might keep it. Sell the rest – the farm, the estate.' He stood in the middle of the room and gave a small shrug. 'It seems to be the only place I can work. God only knows why.' Suddenly remembering his manners, he said abruptly: 'Sit down. I'll get some coffee.'

When he had gone she wandered over to the window,

439

feeling unaccountably ill at ease, then turned and looked back across the room. To one side of her, in an alcove set into the book-shelves, were a number of photographs mounted in silver frames. She moved closer. Nick. Nick and Alusha. Alusha on her own, looking like her newspaper pictures but more so. An unusual face, arresting, beautiful.

The great house, the beautiful dead wife: shades of *Rebecca* – except that Nick had loved Alusha. And had not as yet taken a second wife.

Daisy reached out and lightly touched the frame.

'No time for coffee.' Nick dodged briefly around the door and beckoned.

She followed him through the hall and out onto the gravel. He pointed to a spot just above the trees.

The noise came first, the dull clacking of rotor blades, then a black dot appeared in the distance, coming in over the loch.

'I'll get the lunch,' said Nick, making for the door again. By the time he came back with the cool-boxes, the helicopter had clattered down onto an open expanse of lawn not far from the house, almost blasting the ivy off the walls.

Daisy felt an almost childish excitement. 'I've never been in one of these things before,' she shouted as they walked towards it.

He insisted she took the front seat, next to the pilot, while he sat in the middle of the three seats behind. They took off immediately. Daisy had barely slipped on the headset before the trees were passing under the glass window set into the floor, and the long expanse of the loch was opening out before them, a plate of blue steel glistening through the last smears of mist.

Soon they had left the water behind and were crossing the opposite shore, flying over hills reduced to mild corrugations, like crumpled paper, and forests condensed into strange geometric shapes.

Nick and the pilot were talking, their voices shrill in the headset, but she didn't listen until Nick's arm appeared over her shoulder, pointing towards two fingers of water ahead. 'Loch Riddon, Loch Striven. And beyond – you can hardly see it yet – the Firth of Clyde.'

Clyde. South. The city of Glasgow. But her disappointment was momentary. This was a day to let things happen, to sit back and enjoy.

They followed the right-hand shore for some minutes before cutting across to meet the Firth as it looped back towards the brown haze of the city. The helicopter slowed, and she realised they were coming in to land on the near shore.

The area was heavily industrialised. They came down on a derelict patch of concrete, surrounded by Victorian factories and warehouses, junk heaps and rusting corrugated-iron fencing, and tall blank walls.

As the rotors wound slowly down, a Mercedes appeared out of nowhere, as if by magic, and bounced cautiously over the cratered concrete towards them.

Climbing out, Daisy laughed: 'That was wonderful! *Wonderful!* I didn't want it to end!'

Nick led the way to the car. 'It hasn't. Not yet.'

She got into the back of the car next to him and let the driver close the door for her. The heating was on, the seating soft.

'This could get too much, you know,' she remarked, only half joking.

He almost smiled, and she noticed that a couple of times after that he looked at her surreptitiously, as if to remind himself of what it was like to experience something thrilling for the first time.

After a few minutes the car slowed and turned in at a decrepit security gate manned by an elderly guard who peered at them myopically and waved them through.

They entered what appeared to be a shipyard, one that had seen better times, with rust-streaked cranes, vast sheds with patchwork iron roofs, and barren docks with long empty wharves.

The car picked its way carefully over the ruts, came to the end of a long shed and rounded a corner. The contrast could not have been more dramatic. In front of them was a flash of blinding, brilliant newness: a great, gleaming sea creature, immaculate and dazzlingly white, with shining metal trim and, high on the upper storey, sinister-wrap-around black-tinted windows.

The craft was out of the water, sitting at a backward tilt on a slipway. Maybe it was the low vantage point, maybe it was the sheer height of the hull, but the thing looked enormous, like a vast shark. It must have been close on two hundred feet long. It was sleek in an aggressively modern way, the front very sharp, the lines severe. Two enormously tall masts and a web of rigging rose from the deck, looking like later additions. Daisy supposed the yacht – or maybe it was a ship – carried sails, though from the ruthlessly aerodynamic lines it looked as if it ran on rocket fuel.

'Blimey,' she said. 'What an outrage!'

Nick shot her a quick glance and shifted in his seat. 'It's only a thought,' he said with a slight edge to his voice. 'I haven't decided anything yet.'

Getting a sudden idea of what this was about, Daisy murmured a diplomatic, 'Ah-ha,' and shut up.

A succession of ladders and platforms took them up the side of the vessel to the deck. A two-man reception committee stood waiting for them, like something out of a royal visit. One introduced himself as the agent, the other as the captain. The captain came complete with white uniform and brass buttons and scrambled egg on the shoulder.

The captain led the conducted tour. Not a stereo socket was missed from the inventory, not a built-in TV, heating control or en-suite bathroom. Each stateroom was close-carpeted in a different theme colour, every curtain and bedcover was ruthlessly co-ordinated. Even the loo-rolls matched. The kitchen had everything that baked, froze and chopped. The bridge was straight out of *Star Trek*, with wall-to-wall controls and raised swivel chairs, like the ones on sport-fishing boats. Desalination plants, air-conditioning, ice-making machines: there was nothing this floating palace didn't possess, except, perhaps, the smallest suggestion of atmosphere or heart.

At one point they were asked to admire the Jacuzzi in the master suite, complete with gold taps and built-in stereo. Nick said nothing, but she saw his eyes roll slightly, though whether from disbelief or disapproval she wasn't sure.

When it came to the engine room, Daisy developed information fatigue and slowed down, intending to give it a miss, but Nick, turning back, widened his eyes in silent entreaty and beckoned her forward.

'I need moral support,' he whispered.

'Stay around here, and you'll be needing more than that!'

'Tell me what to say,' he asked in mock panic.

'Me? I don't know a cylinder from a carburettor.'

'Nor do I,' he said and gave a slight giggle.

'Pat the machinery – isn't that the thing? Give it a good stroke!'

He giggled again, a wonderfully infectious sound, before turning a serious face to the sales agent.

The ridiculousness of the vessel, the echo of that giggle, caused the bubble of suppressed laughter to rise in Daisy in ripples, and she had to look away until she had regained some sort of control. But for a time the laughter was never far from both of them, she could see it in the quiver of his mouth, and it wasn't until they returned to the sitting room – termed by the captain, the saloon – that she dared to look him in the eye.

Even then she thought it safer not to face him as they had coffee, and she sat next to him on the sofa while he talked with the captain and the agent. Yet in that moment of laughter in the engine room, something had overturned, had shifted inside her, and she found herself unable to keep from watching him, watching that wonderfully mobile mouth as it went through the motions of looking serious, of contemplating a question, of smiling suddenly, and noticing how these smiles were not always reflected in his eyes. Noticing, too, how beautiful his hands were, and how restless; seeing the way his hair curled on his neck and even, for a moment, seeming to catch the scent of him, woody and warm.

These were signs that even an idiot could read, these were warnings a mile high, and choosing to read them well, needing time to absorb the implications of this sudden bolt of feeling, she unlocked her gaze, leant over on the sofa arm, and paid studious attention to the captain.

Leaving the saloon, the sales agent smoothed his way through some last well-practised selling points, and then they made their way back down to the ground.

'Well?' Nick asked, as they walked towards the car.

'Well what?'

'What did you think of it?'

'Ah. Well . . . I think it's – um – ' she made a show of trying to find the right word – 'I think it's *unbelievable*.'

He cast her a sidelong glance, trying to gauge her meaning. 'I thought I might take off for a year,' he explained seriously. 'You know, get away. Sail somewhere nice. Explore.'

'*Explore?* It won't exactly make it up the Amazon.'

'I wasn't thinking of – ' He made a face. 'You're very hard on me,' he commented without rancour. 'You really didn't like it?'

'I thought it was *dreadful!*' she laughed. '*Really*. I mean, that's one seriously vulgar object, Nick.'

They got into the car. The driver sped round to his seat and they started off.

'The owner went bankrupt in the middle of the refit,' Nick said. 'And now if the yard don't manage to sell it, it could bankrupt them too, put people out of work.'

'But the yard's already broke, isn't it?' she cried, waving a hand. 'I mean, the docks are empty. You can't buy a horror like that just to bail out a boatyard, Nick.'

'But it's something to take into account – '

'Not if they're going down the chute anyway.'

'And I thought you were the idealist, Daisy.'

He had spoken in a bantering tone, but there was a dart of seriousness underneath. 'Ouch!' she said, with feeling. 'But what I do – that's different, that's – ' She creased her face into a grimace. 'Okay, well, maybe it isn't *entirely* different,' she conceded. 'But that doesn't change the fact that the boat's a stinker, Nick. It's for flash-merchants, the sort who drive gold Rollers and wear shades in the dark – retired arms dealers and property developers and men with shiny suits. The kind who buy their friends like they buy their clothes. You're not that loud, really you're not.'

It was out before she could stop it. 'I mean – '

But he was already saying solemnly: 'You don't think so?'

'I mean' – she felt the laughter simmering between them again – 'you're *better* than that.'

'Well, thank you.'

The irony came through in his voice, and seeing that she had made him smile again, she looked out of the window at the rows of gloomy houses in a state of sudden and quite unjustified happiness.

The pilot said he'd stay in the aircraft and have a sandwich there. It occurred to Nick that he was being diplomatic, that he thought the expedition had been organised for some romantic purpose. Realising, Nick almost asked him to join them, but thought better of it. He and Daisy did, after all, have things to discuss, though they would be very far from what the pilot had in mind.

Taking the cool-boxes, Nick led the way across the springy turf towards a small rise. Carrying the rugs, Daisy strode along beside him, all energy and life, her chin set, her face tilted towards the sky, her eyes half closed as if to absorb the light.

Breasting the rise, a vast panorama opened out before them: to the left the hills of Islay, so close that they looked like a continuation of the land they were standing on; far to the right the long craggy outline of Mull, and, ahead, lying dark and low in a sparkling grey sea, the islands of Colonsay and Oronsay, conjoined in a single elongated reef. Beyond them, there was nothing but sea, the vast sprawl of the western ocean, stretching towards an invisible horizon.

'Where are we? Where are we?' Daisy gasped. Then in the next breath: 'No, no, don't tell me!'

He saw a perfect picnic place a short way below, an area of close-cropped grass within a circle of heather, and carried the cool-boxes down. He took the rugs from Daisy and shook them out. Opening a box, he offered her a drink.

She seemed dazed, only half listening. 'What?' she said, tearing herself away from the view. 'I'll have wine, thanks.'

He opened a bottle and poured her a glass.

She sat down on the rug with a long sigh. 'This place . . .' She exhaled, then shook her head, as if words could never adequately describe it. 'Is it an island?' she asked suddenly.

He nodded. 'A large one.'

'Don't tell me the name! Don't tell me anything about it! I don't want to know. I never want to know.' She stretched her arms lazily towards the sea as if to embrace it and gave a low almost sensual chuckle.

He recorked the wine bottle and poured himself a mineral water. He was aware that she had turned and was watching him.

'Not quite like when we last met,' he said, going carefully. 'How did I behave? I mean, was it bad, or just plain embarrassing?'

'You behaved immaculately,' she declared. 'You gave me all that money.'

He gave her a look to show that hadn't been what he meant.

'No, you were fine,' she said, with that quick open smile of hers. 'I mean – considering . . .'

'Not, I hope, *loud*?'

'Ha, ha.' She grinned. '*Not* loud.'

They looked out over the sea, which from this height seemed hard and flat, like steel. Eventually Daisy said: 'You know, you look at all this and you can't believe there's anything wrong with the world – you know what I mean? Everything seems so strong here – so incorruptible. It seems unbelievable that we can screw it up so effectively.'

'I'll tell you what I see,' he said, loading his bread high with salmon. 'I see the sea.'

There was a pause while she thought about that. 'You think I'm bullshitting,' she said, her voice coming alive with the possibilities of a friendly argument.

'No.' He took a mouthful. The salmon was tender as butter. 'But I think you worry too much.'

She gave a short sigh. 'You're right, of course you're right.'

This sunny, reasonable, languid Daisy – was it an act? Even as Nick considered it, he thought it unlikely. She was too spontaneous, too transparent for that. She was like a guard dog whose ferocious exterior hides something quite different beneath.

She sipped her wine and, leaning back on one elbow, arched her neck until her head lay back against her shoulder. She had a long neck, he noticed, long and smooth.

'An island,' she murmured, her voice soft and low. 'Cut off from everything.' She half turned to him: 'Ever fancied an island? I mean, having one all to yourself.'

'I've got one,' he said. 'In the Seychelles.'

She propped herself up on one hand and stared at him. 'God, you've done it all!' she accused. Then, in further horror: 'It must be *awful* to have done it all!'

He thought about that for a moment. 'Not in my work, I haven't. I've still got a long way to go there.'

She accepted that. It satisfied her work ethic. But she didn't let him forget the island, not for a while anyway. She kept looking at him and sucking in her breath gently and shaking her head.

When they had finished eating they went for a walk, striking off parallel to the sea across the hilly moorland country. Daisy was well equipped in Doc Martens, he less so

446

in trainers. They walked between dense patches of gorse and thistle, through knee-high heather, over wind-scrubbed slopes spotted with the occasional black-faced sheep. It was a while before they hit anything that resembled a path, and then Daisy was all for leaving it and making across rugged terrain towards a hill.

'You forget – I'm unfit,' he panted, hearing the wheezing of his lungs.

But she wasn't having excuses and urged him up the hill at a great rate. Twenty minutes later they reached the summit, he gasping, she triumphant. She would have led him down the following valley and up the next hill if he hadn't insisted on returning to check with the pilot.

The walk seemed to exhilarate her. As they retraced their steps she talked easily and rapidly, asking him about his childhood, his early life, listening with concentration, offering occasional comments. Her remarks were perceptive in an oblique off-beat way; they were also kind. The word echoed in his mind: *kind*, and he was aware of feeling a new trust in her. Even when she touched on dangerous territory – Alusha's illness, the inquest – he was able to answer with something like ease.

Back at the picnic site he left her sitting on the rug and went to find the pilot, who said it was all right to stay another half hour. When Nick returned, Daisy had dozed off. The way she lay – head tucked on one arm, mouth slightly open – and the suddenness with which she'd fallen asleep, reminded him of a child.

He sat close by, smoking steadily – too much, as always – watching a hawk hovering head-down over the heather, seeing the way the ocean glittered under the path of the sun.

When he next glanced down at Daisy she was awake, peering up at him through half-closed eyes. She smiled softly at him, and he smiled back.

She sat up and stretched. He said reminiscently: 'That day, the day of the accident. There was a plane. I only remembered it when I was in Arizona. I had a dream one night, and it was there – in the dream. And when I woke up I could see it. A light plane. I don't remember anything special about it, no spraying gear, nothing like that, but then I only saw it for an instant. The plane was coming down Loch Fyne, heading straight for Ashard.'

447

'The plane that dumped its load on Adrian Bell, he saw it clearly,' she said. 'He said it had a red diagonal stripe on one wing.'

'I don't remember a stripe.'

'No,' she agreed quickly as if she hadn't expected him to.

She sat up on her haunches and pushed a hand through her hair. Her brightness had gone. 'One of the reasons I'm up this weekend is to try to find a way of stopping the local authority from taking Adrian into care.'

'Why would they want to take him into care?'

'To give him "essential" treatment – essential psychiatric treatment, that is.'

'Christ . . . Can they do that?'

'Oh yes.' She explained it to him. Her voice was flat and cool.

He remembered Alusha and the enforced swimming and the nameless drugs. 'Well . . . if I can help at all . . . Can I?'

'Ah.' She gave a nervous chuckle. 'You already have. I took some money out of the project – I didn't think you'd mind, it's not very much.' She looked up to him for approval. 'To pay their solicitor.'

He said he didn't mind.

Far below, the sea had softened under a mackerel sky. The breeze had strengthened. Turning to face it, she said in a neutral voice: 'They okayed Silveron for general use this week. MAFF – the Ministry of Agriculture, Fisheries and Food – they think the stuff's okay to be sprayed on food.' She allowed herself a small snort of disgust. 'Morton-Kreiger must have pulled some wires to get away with that one. They probably nobbled that twit Driscoll.'

Driscoll. He thought immediately of Susan, saw her walking through the rooms of the Kensington house, redecorating them with a curl of her hands, and moved the conversation onto different ground. 'What about the project – *our* project?' he asked. 'No results?'

'Not yet. And I'm afraid there won't be any, not for a while.' She sat up on her heels, eyes round and bright, head alert. The guard dog back on duty. 'Maybe months.'

Here was the bad news then, the news she'd been preparing to tell him all day. He began to pack the bottles back into the cool-boxes.

'It's been a combination of things,' she said, forcing some

448

of the lightness back into her voice. 'Unforeseen expenses –
we're running over budget, I'm afraid. But also there's a
problem with a licence. We've got to have this licence to get
started, and there's been a delay. I'd almost believe it was
intentional, except . . .' She trailed off, and the worries of the
world came across her forehead in a sharp frown.

He stood up. 'So?' He knew what was coming, but he
thought he'd ask anyway.

She clambered to her feet. As she rose, he reached down
and picked up the rugs.

'The delay – it's going to cost a great deal. And we were
running tight on the budget anyway.' In her discomfort she
couldn't quite meet his eye. 'There were so many unforeseen
problems, things we couldn't budget for. Everyone's been
great – the staff, trying so hard, working all hours, getting
everything set up . . . But without that piece of paper it's
useless – we can't even begin.'

A flurry of wind caught her hair and lifted it across her face.
She pushed it impatiently away. 'I've tried to find a way
round it – God, I even thought of moving the whole thing
abroad – but there'd be just as many problems.' Her mouth
tightened. 'So near and yet so far isn't in it.' She gave a ragged
laugh. 'You know I've never cared about anything as much as
I've cared about this. It's not just Adrian, it's not just all the
other people, it's the bloody injustice of it all. It makes me
totally wild!' She glared at him, daring him to disagree. 'I know
you think I'm totally obsessed – well, I am, I admit I am – but
why not – why not? If this isn't worth doing, then what is?'

The old Daisy, fiery as ever. She must have caught the look
in his eye because she pulled back visibly. 'I wouldn't ask if it
wasn't important,' she said with sudden gravity. 'I wouldn't
even ask.'

He didn't reply immediately. Giving her the rugs to carry,
he picked up the cool-boxes and started up the rise, using the
time to go through the motions of conducting a brief debate
with himself, although he already had a strong suspicion of
what the outcome would be. His brain was quite rightly
shouting caution: any fool could have told him it was crazy to
let Daisy suck him deeper into what was fast looking like a
doomed situation, complete with financial and organisational
catastrophes. His brain shouted, but his mind wasn't listening. It was tuned to his instincts, and they were saying: To

hell with it. It was partly stubbornness but it was also a fascination with Daisy's uncomplicated view of justice, a need to believe that life could be reduced to basic moral issues. He rather liked the idea of an anarchic one-woman campaign against the world. Daisy and Goliath.

Then of course there was the plane, the plane that prowled around the edges of his memory. The plane heading in over the loch.

He was nearing the top of the rise. He could hear Daisy's footsteps coming up behind. He turned suddenly.

'How much?'

She stared at him. He noticed her eyes, which were flecked with gold. 'Three hundred thousand. Well – ' she grimaced. 'That is – I *think*.'

He put down the cool-boxes and looked back at the sea for a long moment. 'All right.'

Searching his face for confirmation, she gave a low gasp and, dropping the rugs, threw her arms round his neck and pulled him into a large and very tight hug. Her body was small and warm against his. Slowly, not quite sure what he was feeling, he put his arms lightly round her, then just as gently withdrew them and pulled away.

Picking up the cool-boxes, he started off again. The Bell came into view over the ridge. Daisy caught up with him again.

'This licence,' he asked her, 'it'll come through all right, will it?'

'What?' Her face was radiant, her eyes shining. 'Oh yes,' she panted. 'We've checked. Should be quite soon.'

'What is it, this licence, anyway?'

'Oh, it's a permit really, it's – ' She seemed to hesitate. 'Well, we're not allowed to start work without it.'

'Why? What's it for?'

'It's – to ensure that things get done properly.' That suggestion of evasion again. 'To make sure one follows the rules.'

A thought came to him, a thought so appalling and so obvious that he knew it must be true. 'What rules?'

'For the tests.'

Grinding to a halt he looked down into her upturned face. 'What kind of tests?'

'Well . . . the mandatory tests. The ones that have to be done for all pesticides – '

450

He felt cold, the buffeting wind seemed to pass straight through him. 'Like?' he asked sharply.

She was pale, she knew what was coming. 'Like the LD50 test – '

'What's that?'

She tried to pass it off lightly. 'It's to see what dosage is needed to kill fifty per cent of the sample. Though you don't actually *kill* fifty per cent, you can work it out statistically without that – '

'Sample? You mean, animals?'

'Rats. Or mice. Usually rats.'

He stared at her, dumbfounded. *'Animals?'*

'Look, we wouldn't choose to use *any* animals, not in a thousand years, but we're forced to. That's the system.'

'The *system*?'

'Yes! Animal tests are the only kind they recognise – '

He still couldn't take it in. 'Jesus,' he kept saying. *'Jesus.'*

She began to rally. 'Look, every pesticide used on every vegetable has been tested that way. Every time you buy a carrot or a potato or an orange, anything that's not organic, you're condoning the system – '

His anger had been held back by his surprise, but now it surged up in his throat. 'Stuff the system! Christ – ' He could barely speak. 'All my money – *my* money – and you never even *told* me!'

'You said you didn't want to know! You said you didn't want to be involved!'

'Oh, come *on*!'

'Anyway, I thought you'd realise – '

'God!' Unable to handle his rage, he twisted away and strode towards the helicopter. The pilot was already at the controls, his headset on, making his checks.

She ran to catch up with him. 'What do you expect us to do? If there was another way, then we'd *do* it!'

Reaching the Bell, he threw the cool-boxes into the storage compartment and scoffed: 'Just tell me how I'm expected to get up and sing the songs I sing while you're in that lab murdering animals in *my* name. Christ!' – he beat a fist against the side of the helicopter – 'my stuff's all about *not* doing things like that!'

The pilot put his head out of the door and, making a circling motion with his hand, questioned whether he should start up. Nick nodded abruptly. A moment later there was a whine, a cough and the rotor blades began to turn.

'What about Adrian and all those other people?' Daisy shouted above the gathering noise. 'What about your wife?'

'Don't you give me arguments like that!' he roared. 'Don't you bloody dare!'

She pulled back as if he had threatened her. Her lip wobbled, she mouthed air. 'But it's not as if . . . I mean, they're only *rats*! Just rats!'

He slammed the storage door shut and checked the clips. 'And where do dogs and cats come in the okay stakes,' he yelled. 'And monkeys?' His voice sounded ugly; he felt ugly. 'Before people, or after?'

He should have left it there, he felt confused enough as it was. But, pushing past her towards the open door, he couldn't resist a parting shot. 'Just imagine how the kids'd feel,' he cried, his voice rising harshly over the din, 'the kids who buy my music. *Betrayed*. They get ripped off the whole time as it is. Imagine how *they'd* feel.'

'You mean it wouldn't look good for you?'

'Yes – no – *Jesus* – ' But there was enough truth in what she'd said for him to feel rage at hearing it. 'I see!' he proclaimed savagely, 'I see!' having no idea what it was he was meant to be seeing.

Waving her fiercely into the back seat, he jumped in beside the pilot and gestured for them to leave.

She didn't put her headset on and later, when the pilot pointed out something of interest on the ground, she made no response.

TWENTY-EIGHT

T he medical secretary went so far as to admit that Dr
Konrad was somewhere in the city of Reading, either in the
hospital or the nearby university. But his exact location,
whether he had received Daisy's message, whether he'd have
time to see her – these facts were not immediately available.

After an hour Daisy took to hunting the corridors of the
hospital. Dr Konrad, oncologist lion, had the advantage of
perfect camouflage and good cover, but a passing houseman
eventually pointed her towards the right department and she
was rewarded with a sighting of a short hunched figure loping
head-down across a corridor. He was through the doors of
men's surgical and into a side room before she could catch
him, but a waiting game was one she knew how to win and
after fifteen minutes and a brief spurt across the fifth-floor
lobby she cornered him in a staff-only lift.

'Dr Konrad?'

He looked defensive, then, seeing no possibility of escape,
gave a slight nod. He was a stocky man of about fifty with
blunt features, large hands and ruddy cheeks. He looked
more like a bricklayer than a cancer specialist.

She introduced herself. 'It's about the Knowles case,' she
said. 'May I ask why you changed your mind?'

'Changed my mind? I didn't change my mind,' he said
briskly. 'The evidence was quite simply inadequate. Regretfully, there was nothing more I could do.'

'But the affidavit – a year ago you were prepared to swear
to it.'

'No, no,' he said with authority. 'Not swear to it – that's

453

quite wrong. All I said was that I would do what I could to help. If Mrs Knowles and her solicitor thought I was saying something else then I'm afraid they were mistaken.'

This wasn't the impression Daisy had got from his letter to Mrs Knowles last December but she knew she wasn't going to get anywhere by saying so. 'I see,' she said. 'But tell me, do you still believe Aldeb was the causative agent?'

The lift slowed. His eyes flicked to the floor indicator and he was out through the opening doors.

'Aldeb,' she prompted, keeping pace with him as he strode off. 'You think it was responsible?'

'I thought it was the most *likely* cause,' he said cautiously. 'But that was just my opinion. Which isn't worth a great deal, I'm afraid, not without some hard statistics from the epidemiologists, some independent laboratory evidence.'

'The Americans have found enough laboratory evidence to ban Aldeb.'

'That was only with massive doses, wasn't it? Not conclusive.'

'Apparently not.' She tried again. 'Your opinion was worth a great deal, Dr Konrad.'

'Not on its own.'

'Well, the Knowleses' counsel certainly thought so.'

He slowed, his expression yielded into something almost apologetic. He stopped and said confidingly: 'Look here, without scientific evidence I'd have had nothing to back me up, Miss Field. The other side's lawyers would seize on me straight away, they'd demolish me. I've appeared in these cases before. I know what happens.'

'But without you – ' She shrugged. 'There's no case.'

'Look, I'm very sorry, I really am, but there's nothing I can do.'

She nodded reluctantly. 'Thanks anyway. Oh, one last thing, Dr Konrad . . .' She paused, trying to find a way of putting it. 'May I ask – is this your own decision?'

He halted, his head thrust forward. 'I beg your pardon?'

'I meant, did you decide this thing yourself or would it have been – well, something that was discussed?'

He didn't like the question any more than he'd liked it the first time round. 'It was a matter of judgement,' he said sternly. '*My* judgement, although I felt more than justified in sounding out my colleagues on the subject. As it happened, they all agreed with me.'

'I see.'

His eyebrows shot together, his eyes hardened. 'I'm not sure what you were suggesting there, Miss Field, but I take exception to it. I resent the implications – yes, I resent the implications very much indeed. Pressure, undue persuasion – that sort of thing could never happen here, and if it ever did then I'd fight it most vigorously! There *are* such things as ethics, you know, and we stand by them!' Giving a stiff little nod he pushed at the door and was gone.

Daisy sat in the car for a while, debating whether she should go and tell Alice straight away. Alice's place was only twenty miles to the west of the city, but it was twenty miles in the wrong direction and it was easy to persuade herself that she couldn't afford the time. Even as she argued the matter she was aware, with some feeling of shame, that there was more to it than that. She was already giving up on the Knowles case, she realised; she was already allotting it less time.

She drove out of Reading and headed east towards London. There was patchy fog on the M4 and a contraflow system just the other side of Windsor, but she calculated she could get to Catch before it closed at six to pick up her messages from Jenny, and still have time to drop in at the flat to see how the repairs were going before getting back to Chelmsford for a couple of hours' paperwork later in the evening.

Her conversations with Nick kept running and running in her mind, like a cassette player doomed to go on repeating the same tape. She heard every wrong note she had struck, every false comment, every idiotic statement. And hearing them, she was pricked again by uncertainty. Not just uncertainty over the money either – though there wasn't a moment when that particular dread didn't haunt her – it was the knowledge that he must be thinking badly of her, that he believed she had set out to deceive him over the animal testing. She minded about that. She wanted him to think well of her, she wanted him to enjoy her company, she wanted . . . Well, sometimes it was best not to think too deeply about what one wanted.

There had been moments – long moments – that day when

they had been friends, when nice warm indecipherable messages had passed between them, when she had begun to think . . . But then whatever she had thought, it was too late now. It had been four days since the picnic, two days since she had left messages at the Kensington house and his accountant's. His mind was undoubtedly made up. He'd probably already instructed his accountant to cancel the last payment.

I can't talk about it now. She saw him striding rapidly from the helicopter and pausing at the door of Ashard House. *I can't talk about it now.*

It was just after six when she reached Catch to find Jenny and Alan gone, and Daisy's replacement, Candida, nose down at her desk, scribbling hard, beavering, presumably, on another flow chart. From the outer office Daisy gave her an encouraging wave and reached into the bottom of the pending tray where Jenny hid her messages away from prying eyes.

There had been five calls for Daisy, one from Peasedale, marked urgent, saying he'd be in his laboratory until six thirty that evening and could she come and see him on a very important matter; another from Dermott, the Oban solicitor. Dermott's call hadn't been marked urgent and he hadn't left any particular message, but Daisy snatched it up and reached for the phone straight away. It was three days ago, on Monday afternoon, that Mrs Bell had finally arrived at a cautious, irresolute decision regarding Adrian's future. She would speak to Dermott first, she had announced, to gather his opinion, and then, if he couldn't offer sufficient reassurances, she would consider Daisy's suggestion again more seriously.

'Ah, Miss Field,' declared Dermott when she got through to him. 'I had a meeting with the social services.'

'You did *what?*'

'I think we came to a good understanding. They appreciated Mrs Bell's concerns for Adrian's future, her worries about the psychotherapy. But they say that the doctors are unanimous in their judgement that the treatment put forward is, all things considered, the most appropriate. So I suggested a compromise.' His voice resounded with self-congratulation.

'*Why* did you go and see them? *Why?*'

There was a stiff pause. 'I was instructed by Mrs Bell to look into the matter, to take whatever measures I thought necessary to secure Adrian's future,' he said defensively, 'and I felt

456

a conciliatory and reasoned approach would be the most beneficial, as indeed it has proved – '

'When did this meeting take place?'

'What? I don't see – ' He gave a soft tut. 'We met yesterday afternoon, at four.'

'*God . . .*' Automatically Daisy looked at her watch. 'God . . .' Her mind flew over the possibilities, but she could see only one outcome. 'Can you fend them off for a while? Can you keep them talking for a few days? *Please*, Mr Dermott. It's terribly important.'

'I cannot see the point – '

'It would give us time to get Adrian away to England.'

'*Really*, Miss Field, I think I'm best placed to judge the situation, and I cannot advise Mrs Bell to take such precipitate action. It's far better, surely, to keep the matter on a reasonable basis – '

'They've never accepted he was chemically damaged, Mr Dermott, never! Don't you see that this is the perfect excuse, just what they've been waiting for.'

'Excuse? Really, Miss Field. These are professionals – '

'But they won't be happy until they've got him in hospital, they won't be happy until they can try out their theories – '

'You make it sound like some *experiment*, Miss Field! You make it sound as if these people don't know what they're doing.'

'They're trying to say it's psychiatric, Mr Dermott. They're trying to say it's school phobia.'

'I think you're being a little overdramatic, Miss Field. From what I gather, the treatment that would be offered has been successful in the past. Adrian might be better off, you know. In hospital.'

'Did they promise not to take him into care?' she asked briskly.

'No such undertaking was necessary,' he protested, 'because no such suggestion was made.'

'Well, they wouldn't, would they?' Daisy snapped. 'The social services aren't known for sharing their plans with anyone, and certainly not parents. What about Mr Campbell?' she asked in increasing agony. 'Did they make a requirement that he stay away from Adrian?'

'The general advisability of such a move was discussed,' Dermott admitted cautiously.

'But not demanded?'

'No. As I'm trying to explain, Miss Field, it was a most amicable discussion.'

This was a bad sign. If they'd really been prepared to compromise, the banning of Campbell from the house would have been the very least of their requirements.

'Will you at least keep in touch with them, just in case?'

'If the situation merits it, certainly.'

Selecting a tone of exaggerated politeness, she said: 'Thank you for keeping me informed, Mr Dermott. I really appreciate it,' and rang off.

There was no reply from Mrs Bell's number. She tried Campbell, but he too was out. She thought of Adrian alone in the garish front room, propped up on the settee with his eyes fixed on the flickering soundless telly, and dialled again, just to be sure, but there was no answer.

A chair scraped behind her, in what had been her office. Candida was pinning up a wall chart. It was after six thirty. She called Peasedale and found he hadn't yet left. He wouldn't say what the matter was, but sounded relieved that she was coming over. Scooping up her messages she made for the door, only to be called back by Candida who sped out of her office, plucked a hard-back notebook off the top of a filing cabinet and presented it to Daisy. The cover was labelled *Phone Log: Daisy Field*. Inside were columns for recording the date, time, length and distance of calls. Daisy made admiring noises, and scribbled *Local call, 3 minutes. How are you, Alan? Hope the efficiency drive goes well*, and spread a large signature across three columns.

Peasedale was standing wedged against the window, his hair standing up at odd angles against the light.

He cleared a seat for her. He seemed curiously reluctant to start. 'I was summoned,' he said eventually, 'to the Lord God himself. Yesterday afternoon.' He plucked at his hair nervously. 'He said he'd heard that I was doing consultancy work for a private concern involved in speculative research. I told him I wasn't *working* for anybody, that I took no salary, only expenses. But that didn't seem to bother him. What concerned him, he said, was the effect on my reputation.'

'He knew?' Daisy asked very quietly. 'But how did he know?'

'He said my standing in the profession would be affected,'

continued Peasedale, not listening. 'Well, that was the way he put it anyway. He said it wasn't just the fact that I had taken the job on without departmental permission – though that would have been a fair point – it was the ethics of the thing. Ethics – God! I thought my one bit of safe ground was the ethics!'

Daisy was still trying to absorb the fact that an academic, a head of a university medical department, tucked away in an ivory tower far removed from government and media contacts, had heard about Octek.

'How much did he know?'

'Oh, enough. What we were trying to do, the set-up, that sort of thing . . . I told him more, of course, about why we were doing it and so on, but he didn't seem too interested. He said that however good our intentions it was still a maverick project, and as such the results, if any, were bound to be ignored by the scientific community. I must say he got me there. I was a bit shocked. It had never occurred to me that our findings would be done down just because the project hadn't been hatched by the university – just because there wasn't a big name at the top of the letterhead.' He added: 'And I'm still not sure he's right about that, you know.'

'But how did he find out?'

'What? Oh, I have no idea.'

'Did *you* tell anyone?'

He shook his head vehemently. 'Nobody. Only my wife, and she wouldn't have told anyone. We don't mix in university circles much anyway. No – however he heard, it wasn't through *us*.' He pulled an emphatic face.

Who, then, had done the telling? Who had conveyed the information so very accurately to the spot where it would carry the most weight?

A further half hour with Peasedale didn't bring her any nearer to finding out, though it convinced her that, for all the head of department's apparent concern for Peasedale's career, the advice he had dispensed amounted to nothing less than a warning off.

Giving up any ideas of going back to Chelmsford that night, she joined the traffic snaking up York Way towards Tufnell Park. She drove automatically, her eyes locked onto the stream of tail lights and prepared herself to face the flat. A week ago the landlord had promised to send some men over

459

to repair the ceiling absolutely instantaneously, so the chances of any work having been done weren't good.

But she was wrong. Once she managed to find a light that was still working, she saw that someone had been in and pulled down the remains of the ceiling and pinned up a layer of plasterboard. But if they'd gone to the trouble of throwing covers over the furniture, it certainly didn't show. Dust was everywhere, in a cloak far thicker than the original snowstorm. The stuff had penetrated every corner of every drawer and reached into the furthest depths of the highest kitchen cupboards. The shoulders of her clothes wore a white coating, like fine dandruff in a shampoo commercial.

She hunted around for a drink. There was some months-old cooking wine next to the stove, and in a cupboard above, an inch of vodka in a long-forgotten half-bottle hidden behind the Chinese spices. She took a sip, then, dispensing with formalities, knocked it back Russian-style.

Rummaging in a drawer she found a pad of paper, tacky with grit, and taking it to the table by the window, shifted some magazines, dusted off a chair and sat down. She compiled a number of lists: the first, of those who knew everything there was to know about Octek – barring of course the source of the funding. This numbered three: herself, Peasedale and Floyd. The second list, of those who knew some of the facts but not all of them: this contained the rest of the Octek employees, a total of five. Lastly, a list of outsiders, who knew bits and pieces, but not, significantly, the fact of Peasedale's involvement. This included Octek's accountant, Nick Mackenzie's accountant and sundry lawyers. After some thought, she added Simon's name, though again there was no reason for him to connect Peasedale to Octek. It was just possible he'd guessed, but it would have had to be one astonishingly accurate and assured guess. There was also Alan and Jenny, and, presumably, Candida.

None of it made sense. She knew all the Octek employees well. They were all committed; none of them would have talked. While the outsiders were either loyal or simply didn't have the information to know Peasedale was involved.

She tore the piece of paper off the pad and, crushing it, chucked it in the direction of the waste paper basket.

She tried Mrs Bell again. This time she was home. She listened quietly to what Daisy had to say, she seemed to

460

appreciate the growing danger to Adrian, but she would promise nothing, not until she had spoken to Dermott about it in the morning. Then, on the point of ringing off, she added: 'But Dermott did well with the social services, did he not?'

With a sudden swoop of disappointment Daisy realised that she had understood nothing. 'But that's just the point, Meg,' she argued weakly. 'I don't think that the meeting achieved anything at all. I think it would only have spurred them into action . . .'

But it was no good. When it came to the law, Dermott's judgement was to be respected above all other.

Ringing off, Daisy was filled with an acute restlessness. She ranged up and down the room, kicked at the dust, lit the fire, went into the kitchen for coffee and, changing her mind, returned to her chair. A minute later she stomped back into the kitchen and, sweeping up the cooking wine, poured herself a glass. The stuff was dark, almost black, thick with sediment and horribly bitter. But two glasses later it had succeeded in dulling her brain. Not long after that, it brought a thumping tiredness, close to exhaustion. Curling up uncomfortably in the chair, she drifted into an uneasy sleep.

The phone woke her, slicing slowly into her mind from a great distance. She waited for the answering machine to pick up the call before remembering she had turned it off.

She scrabbled for the receiver and raised it slowly to her ear.

'Daisy? Daisy? Hullo – are you there?' It was Simon's voice.

'Hi.'

'You're there.'

'More or less.'

'You should answer.'

'What?'

'*Answer.* Say hullo or something. It helps, you know.'

'Yes.'

'Your friends the Octek people,' he said briskly, as if anxious to keep everything on a businesslike footing. 'I got the information,' he said. 'Or rather, I got all there is to get.'

'Thanks, thanks.' She straightened her legs and knocked over her empty glass.

'The answer, as far as they know, is that it's being processed in the normal way.'

Daisy sat forward in her chair, wishing the wine out of her head. 'You mean – ?'

'No story. Nothing abnormal at all. Frankly, Daisy, I felt a right berk, being so totally in the dark. He didn't believe I didn't know anything. Thought I was holding out. Got shirty.' He added resentfully: 'And he's a useful guy too.'

'What did he think you should know, then?'

'What Octek was about, that sort of thing.'

'You didn't tell him?'

'Well, it would have been difficult, wouldn't it?' he said with heavy irony.

'Yes . . . Sorry.'

'Are you ill or something? You sound half asleep.'

'Uhm – just tired. So what exactly did he say?'

'Well – *nothing*,' he retorted, losing patience. 'That's the point. There was nothing to report. The thing's just going ahead in the normal way.'

Daisy lay back in her chair and closed her eyes again.

After a silence, Simon asked tentatively: 'You all right?'

Maybe the day had simply been too long, maybe her head was too thick with exhaustion and bad wine, maybe she had simply reached the point where she had to tell somebody, but she told him.

She told him about Adrian and her fears of a care order, she told him about the final setback in the Knowles case and, since the entire world seemed to know about Octek, she told him about that too. Why it had been launched, her involvement, the lab set-up, the testing programme.

'Jesus . . . That's a large undertaking, Daisy. You're doing it on your *own*?'

'Sort of.'

'But who – ? What – ? It must cost a fortune. Where's the money coming from?'

'Ah . . .' She gave a soft sigh. 'We had a backer . . . Though, as from this week, he may not be our backer any more.'

'Oh.' A sympathetic pause, and Simon said: 'Look – er . . . I'd, er . . . ask you over, but I've only two eggs . . . no bread. And I've got to go out again at nine thirty.'

'Thanks . . . It was sweet of you.'

'No, well . . . I'm always here, Daisy, you know that. This backer, tell me . . . What happened? Who is he?'

'Who is he?' she echoed dully, seeing Nick against the backdrop of the sea. 'No, I – I can't tell you . . .'

'Daisy, for God's sake, it's *me*.'

It was Simon, and in her exhaustion, in the skewing of her emotions, in her need, finally, to talk it through with some-one, he took on rock-like form, a bastion of security.

Biggs, former detective sergeant, Metropolitan Police Notting Hill Division, in receipt of early retirement on health grounds, crouched in the Transit van and strained to hear. The reception wasn't too good at this distance, but he hadn't been able to park any closer.

He took a stab at the name the girl had mentioned, writing it methodically in his notebook, but though he had a strong feeling he'd heard it somewhere before, he wasn't sure he'd got it right. The tape might tell him when he played it back later. In the meantime he fiddled with the volume control, checked the recorder was running all right, and pressed the cans closer to his head.

The two of them were still talking about the guy, but not by name. It was all 'he' and 'him'. Biggs went on making notes, hoping the name would come up again, but the girl was getting tired of talking, you could hear it in her voice. She wanted to get off the phone and shift over to his place, she wanted a bit of the old how's-your-father. But her boyfriend wasn't sounding so keen, not since he'd heard the name of the character with all the gravy.

Suddenly the boyfriend said the name again. This time it came over loud and clear, and there was no mistaking it.

Biggs wrote it down in capitals. NICK MACKENZIE. No wonder the name had sounded familiar. Just like the rock star.

The girl ended the call and after a few minutes he saw her leave the house and walk past the van.

He took the tape from the recorder, pocketed it and put in a fresh one. He set the recorder to sound-activated operation and, picking up his mobile, dialled Hillyard's number. Hill-yard answered straight away. From the sound of it he was out of doors somewhere. As if to confirm it, there was the sound of a car door slamming.

Biggs gave him a full report, leaving the choicest bit till last.

The moment Hillyard heard the backer's name, he started crowing with pleasure, his voice rising in a series of outrageous sighs, like a tart catching sight of a rich Arab. If Hillyard hadn't been such a regular employer, if he hadn't been such a pro in his work, Biggs would have told him to stuff off long ago. In his Met days Biggs had duffed up lesser queens than Auntie Colin, and for no more than the way they twinkled their little toes.

A car door slammed again, there were voices, and Hillyard's sighs ceased as quickly as they'd begun. In one of his lightning shifts of tone he shut off with a blunt: 'See yer.'

'Shall I bring the tape over?'

A car engine fired. 'Not now,' he snapped as if Biggs had suddenly ceased to exist. 'We're off.' And with an abrupt click the connection was broken.

The room was hot and uncomfortably crowded. Nick looked round for Susan but she had gone. He was startled not only by the fact that she'd vanished, but the speed with which she'd done it. A moment ago she'd been at his elbow, protecting him like a seasoned diplomat, guiding selected guests towards him, cutting off more unwelcome advances, steering people firmly away when their allotted five minutes were up, while at the same time moving him slowly but steadily through the room in a curve that would have brought him to the door – and escape – within fifteen minutes.

Her dress was an unusually vivid blue, her hair swept up into an ingenious and very distinctive topknot, but even from his height, normally a good one for crowded rooms, he couldn't spot her. He looked briefly for David but he, too, seemed to have disappeared.

He tried to calm himself, but he'd forgotten how easily these things rattled him. He tried to move away but someone was pulling at his elbow. He turned, hoping for Susan, and found himself facing a vermilion-lipped woman. She waved a programme in his face. 'I *hate* to be a nuisance,' she crowed, 'but you *did* promise.'

No one had a pen. Someone called for one. A second arm descended, waving a programme, then a third. People pressed in from both sides. Several voices spoke at once. He felt the heat rise into his face and the sweat start on his back, and knew he was hovering close to some limit that didn't bear

464

thinking about. He felt a snatch of bewilderment, a spurt of anger, and finally and more persistently, misery.

Signing, replying as best he could to the questions, he kept looking up for signs of rescue. He saw the distinctive topknot over the sea of heads long before he saw her face. She was shouldering her way through the circle of people like a small but determined tank, apologising profusely as she came, but in a tone of such authority that no one dared challenge her. When she finally burst through and stood in front of him she rolled her eyes in an expression of apology and sympathy.

'God, what animals,' she breathed. 'Sorry, but I had to go and find the *one* person you have to meet.' Taking his arm, she extricated him firmly from the group and led him back the way they had come. She must have sensed his alarm because she said: 'After this, that's it, I promise. The end – *really*. I'll never bother you again.' Stopping abruptly, she smiled: 'Apart from our curtain and carpet sessions of course. There's no escaping that!'

She squeezed his hand, then, releasing it, led him to a less crowded corner where a man stood waiting.

'Can I introduce Ronald Schenker?'

They shook hands. Schenker's grip was cool, like his expression.

'Ronald's a great benefactor of ours,' Susan explained. 'In fact I don't know what we'd do without him.'

Schenker gave a smile, modest but tinged with complacency, as if he didn't really believe he had a great deal to be modest about. He stood in a small man's posture, upright and slightly defensive.

Schenker eyed Nick appraisingly. 'I found the concert very interesting,' he said carefully, 'and far more . . .' He paused to choose his words. '. . . *thought*-provoking than I'd imagined.'

Nick took it as a compliment. 'Thanks.'

A waiter appeared with a tray of food. Aware that he should eat, Nick spiked three pieces of chicken and balanced them on a paper serviette. When he glanced up, he caught Schenker staring at him.

Schenker said in his studied way: 'I noticed that a number of your songs had ecological themes. Harking back to some Golden Age we were meant to have enjoyed when we were cave men.'

'Well, not quite – '

'There never was a Golden Age, you know. Life was tough, life was harsh. It was dog eat dog. It's only civilisation and technical advances that have taken the sting out of the daily grind. No one ever got anywhere by going backwards, and that's truer today than it ever was in the distant past. It'd be extremely dangerous to chuck everything away and start again. We'd be sabotaging our chances of survival. You can't stop progress, you know.'

'Some of us think progress has gone far enough.'

'Oh, it's very quaint to think of turning the clock back, running everything off water power, recycling junk, starting up crafts and cottage industries, but the average person wouldn't take kindly to having his electricity rationed, his rubbish charged by the metre, his food doubling in price. There'd be a revolution.'

'But you can be selective about progress – keep the good, regulate the bad.'

'Ah, regulations!' Schenker bared his teeth in something that approached a smile. 'The present government's fought three campaigns on the issue of the free market economy, and won handsomely every time. I think maybe the public aren't too keen on having their lives regulated.'

'But they're keen on a better quality of life.'

'Quality of life,' Schenker mused as if he wasn't quite certain what that involved. 'To most people I think that means having more of what they want at a lower price.'

'I think most people want to sleep easy in their beds in the knowledge that they're breathing clean air, eating clean food, drinking clean water . . . Creating a healthy world for their kids to grow up in.'

'You make us sound as if we're working against it, trying to prevent it.'

Susan saw the question in Nick's face. 'Ronald's one of the baddies,' she explained in a whisper designed to be heard. 'He makes chemicals. He's chief executive of Morton-Kreiger.'

'Just the Agrochemical Division,' Schenker elucidated.

Susan winked in Nick's direction. 'He's still in charge of billions! Ronald's a corporate star.'

But Schenker made no response to her flattery, he was too busy watching Nick's face.

'Time to go,' Nick said to Susan, sending messages to show he meant it.

One thing about Susan, she was quick. She picked up his signal straight away and, narrowing her eyes in reply, spirited a highly plausible excuse out of thin air and gave Schenker a charming goodbye.

Taking Nick's arm, she cut a swathe through the room and had him outside and into his car before the autograph-hunters looked up from their champagne. Telling the driver to wait, she perched beside him on the seat for a moment.

'You look exhausted,' she said. 'I wish . . .' She didn't finish but leant over and pressed her cheek to his.

She pulled back and regarded him fondly. 'Was it such an ordeal, the party?'

'No,' he lied.

'It meant a lot, that you came.' She gave a little smile and said cheerfully: 'See you tomorrow as usual?'

He remembered something he was meant to be doing the next afternoon, something financial with David.

'I've got a brilliant fabric for your bathroom,' she said. 'Hand-made for a rich Arab with more money than taste.'

'Should be just the job then.'

She laughed as if he'd said something really funny; she was good like that.

'I'll come over then, shall I?'

He nodded.

'I'll bring the buns,' she whispered and kissed him lightly on the lips.

Hillyard drove into the estate on the dot of two a.m. Drawing up outside the Octek building, he killed the engine, wound the window down another notch, and listened. Satisfied, he signalled to the shadowy outline of Len's face in the mirror. He watched a crack of light appear as the van doors opened, and saw the dark figure slip out. Len closed rapidly on the gates. A moment later the padlock was undone and the gates swung open. Hillyard drove through and backed the van up the side of the building into the shadows.

Hillyard checked his pockets to make sure he had everything and climbed out to meet the other three as they emerged from the back of the van, carrying their gear. The four of them went up the side of the building and rounded the corner just as Len smashed the floodlight over the main entrance and plunged the area into a darkness relieved only by the dim light that spilled out from the interior.

They assembled by the main doors. Again Hillyard listened, again there was silence. Len moved into the patch of light thrown out from the glass door-panels, and started on the locks. Soon there was a click, then another, and they were into the lobby, lit by a single fluorescent light.

The alarm buzzed its warning. In a certain time, probably less than a minute, it would go off. Len, moving with soft-footed agility, was in front of the control box, tools in hand, even before the last of them – the boy – was through the door and moving towards his station by the office window.

Hillyard shone a light onto the control box. Despite the surgical gloves, Len worked with extraordinary speed, running wires across three sets of connections, cutting two intervening wires without visible hesitation.

Nevertheless time was getting on. Getting into the box had taken a good ten seconds, while the wire work had taken another forty, maybe more. Still the warning buzzer sounded. If Hillyard hadn't had such confidence in Len, if there had been anyone else to touch him in the whole of south London, he might have said something. As it was he tightened his grip on the torch and kept silent.

Len paused, a third wire held loosely in the jaws of his palm-sized cutters, and checked the connections. Giving an imperceptible grunt, he severed the wire.

The buzzing stopped. The silence closed in, shockingly loud. Hillyard exhaled.

Len peered at him through his spectacles and asked hopefully: 'What about them?' He indicated the doors at the end of the passage.

Locks were a serious disease with Len and it positively hurt him to leave them untried. 'No, my old darling,' Hillyard whispered firmly. 'From now on it's amateur night.'

He went to the door of the front office. The boy was at the blinds, staring out into the night. The remaining two already had the pickaxes in their hands. At Hillyard's nod they went down the corridor and began smashing through the double doors at the end.

The doors gave up without much of a fight. Leaving Len to

tidy up his control box, Hillyard followed the others through the remains of the doors and, overtaking, led the way into the first room, immediately to the right of the passageway. Lighting a path across the floor with his torch, he lowered the venetian blinds at all four windows and shone the torch around the room until he found a desk lamp. Switching it on, he gestured to the others to begin.

They chose the most inviting equipment first: wooden carousels of test tubes which smashed with the satisfying crunch of crushed wine glasses; tiers of jar-lined shelves which bent and crumbled, shooting cascades of glass across the floor; complex electronic equipment with VDU units which imploded on impact.

Leaving them to it, Hillyard explored the rest of the place. Plain unmarked doors to the left of the passageway, one locked, the next – a store room – open, the last locked again. To the right, a small room with rows of white shoes in plastic bags and overalls hanging on pegs that led into another laboratory even larger than the first. He went into this room and, closing the blinds, looked for a small lamp. Finding none, he went back to the door and flicked on one of the overhead lights.

Returning to the first laboratory, he saw that the lads had finished with their pickaxes and were now creating a pile of chairs, papers and miscellaneous rubbish in the centre of the floor.

When they had finished he led them back into the passageway and asked them to tackle the two locked doors on the left. The first door revealed stacks of stored equipment, the second a much larger room whose occupants were announced by the pungent smell that went before them. The room was lined with banks of cages containing an assortment of rodents. Mice and rats; white, grey, piebald, black. There seemed to be hundreds of them.

Leading the two men into the second laboratory to start work there, he returned alone to the cages. 'Now wouldn't Beji love *you*,' he said, dragging a gloved finger across the rungs of a cage of white mice. He tried lifting the cage, but it was fastened down in some way. Squatting, he examined the sides and base of the cage, and saw that it was clipped to the next cage. Once the clips were undone it was a simple matter to lift the cage and carry it out. He took it to the side door which he'd noticed on his first visit. The door was fastened with bolts, but also a bloody great mortise lock. Hillyard looked up the passage and saw Len still tinkering with the control box. Hillyard called to him. Len, perking up like a hunting dog, came hurrying along, pulling his skeleton keys out of his pocket.

It took him about five seconds to get the lock open, a speed which seemed to both please and disappoint him. The rest of the job took considerably longer. Hillyard carried the cages, a pair at a time, out of the building and round to the back area, which, though dark, was the only place that was sufficiently distant from the van. There, having opened each cage, he had to spend more precious seconds getting its inhabitants to leave. The first lot of rats fell out all right, but the mice clung stubbornly to their cages. He had to shake the cage quite violently to get them out. On the second to last trip, shaking out a cage of fat grey rats, one of them fell against his leg and clutched at his trousers. Jumping clear with a cry of repulsion, he landed on something soft which squelched and crunched underfoot. Cursing, he ran back to the side door and scraped his shoe repeatedly on the doorstep. Shivering with disgust he took the last pair of cages to the door and threw them out into the darkness unopened. He turned to go back inside then stopped suddenly, and, retracing his steps to one of the unopened cages, picked it up and threw it into the back of the van.

The others had finished in the second lab and were hovering tensely in the passageway, waiting for him to give the go-ahead for the next stage. Hillyard noticed they had already collected the jerrycans from the front lobby.

Hillyard looked at his watch. They'd been in the building twenty minutes. It felt like a long time. The men's restlessness was infectious, the urge to cut and run almost overpowering, but Hillyard suppressed it. He knew that this job, above all, had to be done properly.

'Not so quick, not so quick,' he flung at them, leading the way to the store rooms.

Only when the store rooms had received the pickaxe treatment and all the filing cabinets in the front offices had been emptied onto the floor did Hillyard finally give the go-ahead for the jerrycans to be emptied over the piles of

470

furniture and papers. 'Not too much!' he barked at one point. 'We don't want a towering bloody inferno!'

By the time he had supervised the fuelling, he was behind schedule. He hurried into the office and, yanking the phone out of its socket, smashed it hard on the corner of the desk. Pulling off the casing, he removed the tiny transmitter that he had put there on his first visit and put it in his pocket. Passing the boy at the window, he went out into the lobby. Pulling an aerosol can from his pocket, he paused at the main doors. On the nod from the boy he stepped outside. He shook the spray can until he could hear the metal ball rattling inside its housing. He chose the long stretch of wall under the windows of the main office for his first effort. Considering the poor light, it wasn't too bad. For his next site he chose the main doors themselves then, as a final offering, a stretch of wall on the side of the building, which, though poorly lit, was nice and large, like a blank page.

As he finished, he remembered that the side door was still open. Finding Len, he sent him to close it again.

When Len returned Hillyard gestured questioningly towards the control box.

'All set,' Len confirmed.

Now it was a matter of getting things in the right order. He sent the boy to the main door, Len to the burglar alarm, and the other two down the passage to wait outside the doors of the labs. When everyone was in position he gave the nod. The first lab went up immediately with a great whoosh and flash of light; the other one he couldn't see, but it must have gone up all right because the man in charge of lighting it came running out into the passage like a bat out of hell. As the two fire-lighters came through the smashed swing doors Len reset the burglar alarm and closed the box. Hillyard would have liked to wait and see the offices go up, but there wasn't time.

He ran out and round the corner and jumped into the van. The boy was already at the gates, swinging them open. Hillyard fired the engine, drove the van out onto the front apron and reversed it up to the main doors. Len was bending over the locks on the front door. The moment he straightened up and moved clear, the other two attacked the doors with their pickaxes, as if they were only just going in. The sound of the splintering wood was horrendously loud, but it was

471

nothing compared to the alarm, which went off suddenly a few seconds later, its bells piercing the darkness. It seemed to Hillyard that the whole neighbourhood must be up and looking out of their windows.

The flames in the front office were filling the window. The next moment there was a great whoomph! as the glass blew out. Hillyard pricked up his ears. Under the jangling of the alarm, he thought he could hear a siren in the distance.

He slid across the seat and yelled through the window: 'Come *o-n!*'

The rear doors of the van opened and first Len, then the other two, jumped in. The boy flung himself into the passenger seat as Hillyard accelerated through the gates. The boy panted audibly all the way to the Chelmsford bypass.

Hillyard was panting too. Reaching across, he brushed his hand against the boy's thigh.

TWENTY-NINE

A log settled noisily in the grate, sending licks of gold up the oak panelling and into the dusty drops of the dark chandelier. The room was warm, the rug soft under Susan's back. Lazily, she rolled over and picked a crumpet off the dish by the hearth. The crumpet, sagging with melted butter, pliant as a sponge, was heavy with the scent of schooldays and other diet-free eras of long ago. She bit into it with a delicious sense of rediscovery. It had been a long time since she'd allowed herself anything so wicked.

Keeping her eyes off Nick – he mustn't feel she was crowding him – she looked casually towards the window. It was a filthy afternoon. Rain splattered against the glass, leaves streamed off the trees, and the sky was darkening rapidly. No sound penetrated the room – the double-glazing was too thick for that – and she was left with the curious but exhilarating sensation that everything that lay outside – London, people, family – was at a great remove, incapable of intruding on the afternoon.

She finally rewarded herself with a look at Nick. He was sitting on the floor with his back against the sofa, the wallpaper book open on his knees, his shoulders hunched, his face creased with concentration, like a student pondering some impossible maths problem. As always when she looked at him she felt a tiny proprietorial thrill, an involuntary spasm of excitement, the precise nature of which it wasn't necessary to examine. It was enough, she'd decided, to experience the surge of feeling, to ride the rush of elation which, after a week

473

of these tea parties, seemed to be spilling over rather pleasantly into every part of her life.

She watched him, and smiled affectionately. He had a way of chewing on the side of his lip, of splaying his fingers over his cheek, of drawing sudden hissing breaths on his cigarette that suggested a bafflement, a mild helplessness that was really very attractive. This hint of vulnerability, and his habit of letting people get closer to him only by the smallest and most tantalising degrees, made him rather a challenge.

She was making progress though, chipping softly away at his defences. She thought, not for the first time, of how satisfactorily things had changed. When they had been together all those years ago there had been passion – on her part at least – but also some beastly misunderstandings.

Nick flicked over a page and pulled at his chin. Unlike Tony, he was one of those men who had improved with age. Lean body, thick hair, intriguing face.

She had promised not to interrupt him while he studied the wallpaper samples – a rather professional-sounding assurance, she had thought – but what had been a reasonable pause had now stretched into an unwieldy silence, and silences were not something Susan felt comfortable with.

'I'm keeping quiet,' she said. 'I hope you've noticed.'

'It's no good,' he said, snapping the book shut and sliding it onto the floor. 'They're all beginning to look the same. You'll have to choose.'

'No problem,' she said happily. 'We could paper one wall and if you don't like it, we can take it down and start all over again.'

He nodded distractedly and she saw that she had lost him. This happened now and again: one moment he'd be there, listening attentively, sliding her the occasional glance in that oblique way of his, the next moment he'd slip away into a part of his mind that excluded her as completely as if he'd left the room.

'You were so brave at the party!' she said, pushing just the right balance of fondness and mockery into her voice.

His eyes flicked towards her but she could see he was only half listening.

'I still can't get over the way those women besieged you,' she went on lightly. 'People with money are the worst of

474

all, I'm afraid. Think they've bought you along with the ticket.'

'Tell me about Schenker,' Nick asked suddenly.

She shrugged. 'Oh, he's just a mogul. You know . . . earnest. And dull.'

'Ruthless?'

'Ooh, that's a strong word!' she laughed. Sensing she had hit too flippant a note, she made a show of giving the question serious consideration. 'I don't know him *that* well,' she said, 'but ruthless – yes, I would think so. Why?'

But he didn't answer. Instead he asked: 'He knows your husband quite well, I suppose?'

Now where was this leading? Generally he never asked about Tony, not directly. 'Oh, they've met . . .' she said casually. 'You know – at functions, in the House. These companies always do quite a bit of lobbying. Oh, and he's taken us to the opera a couple of times. But then all the big companies do that – take us to things.'

Nick absorbed this slowly, staring intently at the fire.

The opportunity of deepening the conversation while at the same time airing the subject of Tony – something she'd been wanting to do for some time – was not to be missed. 'I hardly see Tony nowadays,' she murmured a little ruefully. 'He's in Luxembourg at the moment. Some trade talks, or whatever. But even if he'd been free to come to the party, he'd have persuaded himself he couldn't. In fact since he became a politician – well . . .' She gave a valiant little laugh and, though she didn't plan it, her breath caught rather attractively in her throat. 'We don't really communicate much . . . His work just eats him up. And he's so incredibly hyped up all the time, rushing around like a madman, that we don't have time to talk – about *anything*. So I've rather given up, I'm afraid.' She looked down at the rug and pulled delicately at the pile. 'I'm not complaining, not exactly. Well, perhaps I *am*,' she added, shooting him a fleeting smile. Looking suitably serene, she added: 'But I think one has to try to make the best of things, don't you? Even when they're – difficult. Make do. Muddle through.'

Nick lit a cigarette, propped an elbow on one knee and looked into the fire. He was gathering himself to say something in that cautious thoughtful way of his, but just as he began to speak the phone rang. Usually he ignored it, letting his housekeeper pick it up somewhere in the depths of the house, but now he got up to answer it. 'My direct line. Sorry . . .'

Direct line. She hadn't realised he had one. She certainly didn't have the number for it, and she rather thought she should. It was someone called David. David Weinberg, presumably.

Nick was mumbling a perfunctory apology for having missed some meeting or another. Susan reached for another crumpet. It wouldn't do any harm when she was burning up so much nervous energy.

'*What!*' Nick's voice was sharp and raw.

Susan abandoned the crumpet. Nick was sinking slowly onto the sofa, reaching out a hand to steady himself.

'God!' he groaned, dropping abruptly into his seat and clamping a hand to his face. 'I might have known! I should have known!'

He listened for a few moments longer, muttering the occasional 'God!' and 'Christ!', then, the conversation apparently over, slumped wearily back in his seat, the receiver forgotten in his hand until, looking down, he swung it slowly back into its cradle.

Susan was on her feet. 'What's the matter?'

Almost immediately, the phone rang again. This time Nick ignored it and after a few rings it stopped. He covered his head with his hands.

'*Nick* – what is it?'

He dropped his hands.

'Would you do something for me, Susan?'

'Of course.'

'Look and see if there's anyone hanging around the gate.'

'Of course.' She started across the room.

'Don't let them see you.' Nick's voice followed her.

A chill of excitement squirmed in her stomach; this was rather an adventure.

She approached the window at an angle, keeping away from the glass. The cloud had lifted a little, the rain abated, but now it was almost dusk and the streetlamps were burning a dull orange.

The house was fronted by a short garden of ornamental paving and thin strips of lawn, and screened from the road by a high wall.

476

'I can't see from here,' she called. 'Shall I try upstairs?'

'Would you?' His face was grim.

She went upstairs to the guest bedroom that lay immediately above the sitting room and peered cautiously from behind the edge of the curtain. Someone passed under the streetlamp on the opposite pavement, head down, small dog in train. A car was backing into a parking place. Otherwise nothing. She was rather disappointed. A man got out of the parked car and crossed the street diagonally, heading straight for the house. The next moment she heard a bell sound deep in the house.

She raced downstairs to hear Nick giving instructions that he was abroad and not available for comment.

'Didn't take them long!' he remarked bitterly.

'Nick, what *is* it?'

He lit a cigarette, shut his lighter with an angry snap and sucked the smoke in greedily. 'You're trapped as well, I'm afraid – unless you want to get snapped, of course. They won't leave, you know, not until they get fed up. Or it's near closing time.'

She took a few steps closer to him. 'Who?'

'The papers! The tabloids!' He gestured towards the front of the house. 'They won't give up.' His tone was belligerent, indignant.

'Nick . . .' She made a calming voice. 'What's it all about?'

He gave a harsh chuckle. 'You might as well know. The whole of the rest of the bloody world'll know by the morning, so there's no reason why you shouldn't be the first.'

She went up to him and, kneeling at his side, tugged gently at his arm. After a moment's hesitation, he sat down beside her on the rug, resting his elbows on his knees.

'There's this research project I got involved with, a scientific project,' he began slowly. 'Well, the building – the laboratory they were using – it got burnt down in the night, totally destroyed.' He snorted mirthlessly. 'By animal rights campaigners, of all people. Angry at what the evil scientists were planning to do to the rats and mice. Protesting . . . Funny really . . .' He dropped his head onto his knees for a moment, then flicked a sideways glance at her. 'You see, I funded the place.'

Susan maintained her expression of concern. 'I see,' she said gently, not seeing very much at all. 'You, er – ' She

477

grappled with her available ideas. 'It was a good cause, was it?'

He told her. He explained it fully, from the beginning, although afterwards she realised it wasn't quite the beginning, because he didn't disclose his real interest in the chemical called Silveron, not until a little later.

He told her about Catch and what they were trying to achieve with the Octek project, how the boy in Scotland had got sick, how several other forestry workers had been affected. How he had provided the funds on the condition that no one knew of his involvement.

A million pounds, a hidden laboratory: the extravagant whims of a rich man. The images were like breaths of excitement.

'I asked for total secrecy,' he murmured bitterly. 'I should have known.'

As if to emphasise the press interest, the phone rang. They waited for the unseen housekeeper to silence it. It rang again almost immediately and, with an exclamation of impatience, Nick jumped to his feet and took the receiver off the hook. He returned to the rug.

He went on, his voice thin and rough. He told her, haltingly, circuitously, why secrecy had been so important to him, and finally she understood. It was all about his wife. He thought this chemical had killed his wife.

He lit another cigarette, and she saw that his hands were trembling slightly.

'And now, just to put the lid on everything, they'll brand me a vivisectionist!' he cried painfully. 'Bloody great! Bloody terrific!'

She put a hand on his arm and squeezed it. 'They'll understand, once they know your reasons for doing it.'

He twisted his body away to look at her incredulously. 'Know my reasons?' he exclaimed. 'I'm not bloody telling them. Christ, no! It's bad enough them having this, without giving them . . .' He couldn't say it. 'No, I'm not going to tell them anything.'

She wanted to say: But they'll work it out for themselves. Perhaps he realised the inevitability of it, because all the energy went out of him and, turning back to the fire, he slumped his arms on his knees. His shoulder came up against hers. 'You mustn't tell them anything you don't want to,' she said reassuringly. She stroked a finger across the back of his hand, very lightly, as she had done for Camilla when she was small. 'Poor darling,' she murmured. 'Poor love.' It seemed to pacify him. She slipped her hand over his, and clasped it. He didn't pull away.

'What about a statement?' she suggested. 'To give your version.'

'I've done it,' he said exhaling smoke slowly downwards. 'I just told David what to say.'

'So there's nothing more to be done?'

'No.'

'Well, then.'

But he wasn't quite talked out yet, and it was another ten minutes or so before his despondency finally bordered on resignation.

She said again: 'Well, then.' He was very close. With her free hand she brushed the back of her fingers lightly across his cheek, once, and again.

'Poor love,' she breathed. A warmth hit her stomach, her heart fluttered nervously.

For a moment neither of them moved, then he flicked his cigarette into the fire. He closed his eyes, tightened his lips and, dropping his head, pressed his cheek against her fingers.

'Poor love.' She heard her voice from a distance, deep and uneven.

He twisted his head slowly towards hers, his eyes still closed; she turned her cheek to meet his. They stayed like that for a moment, their cheeks touching, then she reached up and put a hand on his neck and stroked it gently.

'Poor love.'

He moved first; she met his lips as they turned to find hers. He had moved first, and the triumph roared in her ears.

'Miss Field, would you mind?' The inspector leaned in through the open door and beckoned outwards. 'Something I'd like to discuss.'

Daisy pushed the remains of her cold hamburger back in its carton and climbed stiffly out of the police car. The inspector turned and led the way through the slanting rain into the Octek compound, past the last remaining fire engine, the flattened hoses, the piles of charred furniture. A group of workmen were hammering boards over the gaping holes that

479

had been the doors and windows. On the outside walls the taunting graffiti stood out garishly, its lettering untarnished.

Inside, a fire officer was waiting for them. He introduced himself as a senior investigator and led the way into B-Lab, or what remained of it. Half the roof had gone, and most of the contents, blackened, pulverised or otherwise destroyed.

'Very methodical,' said the fire officer. 'Smashed everything first. All the glass, all the equipment, then stacked the combustibles in the centre here. Very methodical. Axes, from the look of it, like they used on the front doors. Then an inflammatory agent – undoubtedly petrol. You can see the way everything burnt outwards from here.' He indicated the concentric circles of water-soaked ash and debris.

'And the animal quarters . . .' interjected the inspector. 'Took every cage out – they were clipped down, you said?' – this to Daisy – 'Now *that* couldn't have been done in a hurry.'

The inspector's name was Brent. At the beginning of the long day, when she was still in a state of numbness and shock, she had misheard his name and called him Bent.

'They took their time,' commented the inspector enigmatically.

He was waiting for Daisy to draw some great conclusion. A gust of wind rattled through the remains of the roof.

'Did they?' she echoed dutifully.

With the air of someone grudgingly revealing a valuable card, Brent said: 'The alarm sounded at 0235 hours. We have a resident on the other side of the main road who can confirm that exactly. In the bathroom at the time, he was. Heard it go off and looked at his watch. Then a couple of minutes later, looked out of his window and saw the glow of the fire. Phoned the fire brigade straight away. Got here in six minutes.'

She still hadn't made the great connection. 'So? I'm sorry . . .'

'The fire was already well away when he looked out. Which means it was already burning when the alarm went off.' The inspector looked at her as if this explained everything. Catching her expression he continued heavily: 'Which suggests our friends got in well before it went off – must have done, to have got all this work done. Unless the alarm was faulty. But you said you had the security firm check it a month ago, so it doesn't seem very likely, does it?'

There was a pause. Rain dripped off a beam and spattered

480

noisily onto a curl of charred roofing felt. 'I'm sorry, Inspector, I don't see . . .'

'Seems like they got in without setting off the alarm.'

She waited.

'Like they had access.'

He was watching her carefully. Ah, she was beginning to get the idea now. It was an insurance job. She herself had set it up for the money.

'There was very little insurance cover, Inspector. Certainly not enough to make it worthwhile.'

He absorbed this impassively, then ignored it. 'It makes the job very professional, Miss Field.'

Wherever this was meant to be leading, she really couldn't guess. 'But I thought animal rights groups *were* professional nowadays,' she said. 'You know, all geared up . . .'

'Not so professional that they'd reset the alarm as they were leaving so as to make it look as though they hadn't got past it in the first place.'

'I'm not sure of what you're getting at – '

The rain had formed a droplet on the end of his nose, which vibrated as he spoke. 'I was hoping you might be able to tell me, Miss Field.'

Guessing games. She shook her head firmly to show she wasn't going to play. 'There's nothing I can tell you, Inspector.'

Perhaps dusk had been coming on for some time and she just hadn't noticed, but when she walked back along the side of the building the firemen had rigged up a floodlight on the forecourt to help the workmen fix the last of the boards to the windows. The cast of the light gave the graffiti on the front wall a new prominence, like an advertisement for a coming attraction. *Animal Liberation! End Experiments!* Looking at it again, she noticed the lettering which, like everything else, was rather professional.

Professional . . . Why shouldn't activists be professional? Wasn't everyone nowadays? Charities, muggers, beggars . . . masters of their various arts.

She noticed that the stringer from the local paper, a spotty-faced young man in a Dick Tracy raincoat, had returned and was loitering near the police car. By the way he perked up at the sight of her, it wasn't hard to guess who he was waiting for.

But Mabel, Octek's office factotum, reached Daisy first. She brought a phone message from Jenny, who had managed to track Mabel down to her home nearby.

The message was succinct. It read: *Adrian Bell taken into care at eight this morning under place of safety order. Social services, police. Nothing anyone could do. Children's panel hearing in a week.*

Daisy felt a lurch of bitter disappointment. Needing to be alone, she walked rapidly through the gate and out of the compound.

'Miss Field, may I have another word?'

She walked on blindly.

'Miss Field?'

The raincoat bounced along at her side; she realised with sinking heart that, leech-like, it had attached itself to her and would have to be driven away. She hissed: 'I've nothing to add to what I said this morning, Mr – Bishop.'

'Brown, actually. Wayne Brown.' He took a couple of skips to get ahead of her as, turning, she went in the direction of her car. 'We've had a report come through, Miss Field,' he said, walking rapidly sideways. 'I was wondering if you'd care to comment. It's about Octek being involved in the unlicensed testing of chemicals – '

Unlicensed? God, where had this come from? 'No, no – I have nothing to say,' she insisted, digging into her pocket for her keys.

'The report says the financial backing came from Nick Mackenzie, the rock star. Is that right, Miss Field?'

She faltered, almost lost her balance, stopped. She stared at him. '*What?*'

'Nick Mackenzie,' he repeated with awful certainty. 'According to the report, he put up the money for this place. Could you confirm that, Miss Field?'

She managed to shake her head.

'Are you denying the story, then?'

'No . . . I mean – no comment. No comment!' Her head was light and bursting. She twisted round, momentarily disorientated, and looked for the car.

'Would you confirm that he was involved?'

'*No.*' She fastened on the car, and made for it, head low, blinking rapidly to clear the smarting from her eyes. Keys – where the *hell*? She scrabbled in her bag.

'It'll be all over the nationals tomorrow, Miss Field. All

over. It'll look strange if you don't comment.' He ducked his head, trying to catch her eye. 'When did Mr Mackenzie become involved, Miss Field? Was it his idea? What were the animals involved? What exactly was being tested here, Miss Field?'

Her throat was dry, her head pounding. Keys, *keys*. Turning her frustration on her bag, she upended it on the car bonnet and shook it mercilessly.

Wayne darted forward ingratiatingly. 'Can I do anything?'

Extricating the keys, she jammed them into the lock and, losing her grip on her temper, told him tersely in words of four letters what he could do with himself. Looking aggrieved, he retreated. 'It'll all be out by tomorrow,' he echoed reproachfully. 'You'll be sorry you didn't give me your story.'

Shaking, still dangerously close to violence, she scooped up the contents of her bag and drove away. A hundred yards up the main road she swerved into the side and stopped, reaching for breath. She jammed her hands against her face and muttered furiously: '*God, God . . .*' as the realisation sank in: this was the end of everything – Octek, Adrian's freedom. Nick.

She groaned aloud as the full horror of Nick's position dawned on her. The papers – she could imagine the sort of line they would go for. *Rock star's secret lab attacked by animal libbers . . . Singer's animal laboratory inferno . . . Protest star silent on vivisection slur . . .* As far as the animal-loving Brits were concerned, they might as well call him a child murderer and be done with it.

All he had asked was silence, a degree of protection, and she had let him down. For some reason she was certain it was she who had let him down. Somewhere, somehow she had let this happen. Somewhere, somehow she had trusted someone too much.

She blew her nose and angled the rear-view mirror downwards. She dragged at her eyes blindly, smearing the dampness away, and thought: *Who?* She realised it hadn't been so long ago that she'd asked that very question in relation to the leaking of Peasedale's involvement in Octek.

Who?

She reached Kensington just after eight. The rain had eased off. It took her a while to find the address, which was near Holland Park. It lay in a dark tree-lined street of ambassadorial residences with well-camouflaged house numbers. Nick's place was towards the end, a substantial house set behind a high wall. Above a screen of tall shrubs gothic gables rose sharp against the sky; no lights showed.

Beside the solid wooden gate there was a video-phone with a glowing buzzer. When she pressed it a light sprang on. She stared resolutely at the camera lens, her heart high in her chest.

The wind rattled the leaves of a nearby shrub, a branch creaked, a walker's heels clacked rhythmically along the other side of the street. The light went off with a slight click. She had the sensation of momentary disconnection, then, coming to, she reached up and pressed the buzzer again.

'Gone abroad.' A voice from behind, bored, knowing.

She twisted round. The man was close, but he had his back to the streetlight and she couldn't make out his face.

'At least that's what they're saying.' He shifted slightly then, stiffening, squinted at her. 'It – er – wouldn't be Miss Field, would it?'

'No comment.'

'No need to be like that,' he chuckled triumphantly. 'No need at all. I'm from the *Sun*. We've been good friends of yours in the past, Miss Field, very good friends, haven't we? *And* of Mr Mackenzie's – I think he'd agree about that, in fact I'm sure he would. Knows we can be relied on to give a fair quote. What about a quote, Miss Field? Can you tell me – '

'Get lost.' She stabbed at the buzzer, then, in a fit of desperation, left her finger on it.

'Miss Field – I'll take your words down verbatim. No aggro. You can say as much or as little as you like. No pressure. I'm good with the human angle. My speciality, you might say. They always give me the victims – '

A voice barked out of the video-phone. Hurriedly, guiltily Daisy jerked her finger off the buzzer as if it had stung her. It was a male voice, staccato, edged with fury. Nick.

For an instant Daisy stared vacantly at the camera before putting her mouth to the grille. 'Daisy. Daisy Field.' As she pulled back the reporter moved closer, coming in for Nick's response. Daisy slapped her hand over the grille as if that could prevent Nick's voice from emerging, and, parting her fingers, added hastily: 'Let me in – ' She almost said *Nick*, but stopped herself. 'There's a guy bothering me.'

A pause, a silence, she thought for a moment that he wouldn't let her in, then the door-release sounded. She pushed her way through into the garden and slammed the gate behind her.

No lights showed at any of the windows, nor at the door just visible at the end of a short path. She waited on the doorstep. A bolt shot back, a lock turned. The door opened and he stood there in a pool of yellow light, barefoot, hair tousled, an open shirt pushed haphazardly into the waistband of his jeans. He didn't speak but moved back a step and indicated with a small jerk of his head that she could come in. His expression was grim.

He pushed the door closed behind her, and stood there, feet apart, arms folded. She didn't have to ask if he'd heard what had happened, it was written all over his face.

'Well?' he demanded, and his tone was like ice.

'I . . . just wanted you to know that I have no idea how the press got hold of this . . . I wanted to say – I'm sorry, *really* sorry . . .'

'Is that it?' he asked caustically. 'If so, then – ' He moved to open the door again.

'No – I . . . Please. I wanted to explain.'

'Explain? You're joking!' He gave an ugly laugh. His gaze was unwaveringly hostile.

'But it's not the way it looks!' she pleaded. 'If you'd just let me explain.'

He hesitated, then, with the heavy air of someone overcoming his better judgement, moved away from the door and briskly refolded his arms. 'So?'

'It was . . .' She grasped at a half-formed idea, something that had taken root during the journey from Chelmsford, and developed it rapidly. 'I think the whole thing was planned. I think they knew all about Silveron, all about what we were doing, long before the raid. And the story about you – they leaked that specially, to get at you. To discredit you – '

'Well, they did a bloody good job, didn't they?' he interrupted bitterly. 'I'm for the slaughter tomorrow, and that's for sure.' He made another move for the door.

'No, no, you don't understand – ' She gabbled slightly in her rush to explain it to him, to get the idea straight in her mind. 'The animal rights people – we were meant to think it was them – but it wasn't! The police said it couldn't have been

485

– too professional. The burglar alarm had been disconnected, and they said the animal people aren't up to that sort of stuff. Disconnected and *reconnected*, in fact – so it wouldn't go off until the fire started. That way they had time to wreck everything and get the fires going and get away before anyone knew . . .' Not certain that he'd absorbed the enormity of what she was saying, she explained: 'There *were* no animal rights people! They never existed. They were just a front, for someone else. Someone who wanted to stop what we were doing.'

Perhaps she was selling the idea too hard, perhaps he simply wasn't ready for it, but his face had become a mask of disbelief. 'These people are really dangerous,' she argued, hearing the desperation in her voice. 'They could have killed someone!'

'But they didn't, did they?' he exclaimed with a bark of sarcasm. 'Except *me*, of course.'

'Okay,' she said in sudden surrender. 'Okay.' She spread her hands wide. 'So it's my fault. Okay, so I fouled up. I take the blame. All right.' She fisted her hands. 'But, listen – if we give up now, then they'll have won. They'll have beaten us – '

'What are you saying?' His face was alight with incredulity. 'What are you suggesting? Are you saying we should go *on*?' He hit the heel of his hand against his forehead in an extravagant gesture of disbelief. 'Incredible! I don't believe it!' He let his voice rip. 'Christ – I've never known anyone with such – such total *tunnel* vision. God – you beat everything. *Everything* . . .' He took a stride closer. 'Tell me – what does it take for you to get the message? How can I get through to you?'

'I think you're getting through to me,' she said quietly.

'I am? Good! *Good!* Well, the message is – it's all over. Finished. *Finished*. I was crazy to agree to this thing in the first place! Crazy to think there was a hope in hell of keeping it quiet! Crazy to think tha. you – that you – ' He took a pace back, then swayed forward again, looming over her. 'I never want to hear about this again – got it?'

He was very close. She had a sudden memory of the island, and the touch of his cheek when she had reached her arms round his neck and hugged him.

She held up her hands in submission. 'Okay,' she said, trying to steady her voice. 'Okay.'

He hovered for a moment, not entirely convinced of victory, then let out a long breath and stood back.

Daisy cleared her throat. 'One thing. The boy – Adrian – he's been taken into care. No warning, the social services just arrived this morning and took him away. It'll take months to get him back. Lawyers, costs . . . The last of the cash – I thought perhaps you wouldn't mind?'

His hands unwound, his shoulders slumped. He was just beginning to focus on the idea when there was a sound from deeper inside the house, a loud clinking of china and a sharp exclamation, quickly followed by a crash, the sort that comes from a catastrophic breakage.

Nick started across the hall, calling: 'Are you all right?' Reaching an open door, he put his head through and said something Daisy couldn't hear. There was a reply, which she missed as well, but she could make out the speaker's gender all right. Female, a liquid voice, a rich laugh.

Daisy thought hastily: Well of course, there was bound to be somebody. There had to be. She did her best to sit hard on her emotions, but some of them bulged out untidily, like air in an unruly cushion.

Nick turned back. Sighting Daisy, his eyes hardened again. Clearly not in the mood to waste any more time, he raced for the door, his hand reaching out to pull it open.

'The boy,' she reminded him as he sped past.

'What?' He yanked open the door and glared at her. Finally he gave a short sharp nod. 'Okay.'

'Thanks,' she said. Stepping out, she turned back. 'And thanks for everything else, for your support.'

'Bye,' he said sharply, and shut the door.

In a state of emotional suspension, hardly aware of what she was doing, she set off in the general direction of Holloway. Nearing King's Cross, she changed her mind suddenly and made for Simon's flat. Yes, *you*, she thought with sudden viciousness. I want to talk to *you*!

But his car wasn't outside, there was no answer to her ring. She crossed the street and looked up at his windows. During his creative phases he had been known to ignore the doorbell, but tonight there were no seams of light showing through the blinds. Back in the Metro, she swore and hit her palm against the wheel. She thrust the key into the ignition and twisted it brutally. The engine turned with an agonised shudder and failed to start. With each attempt, the turns became progressively more half-hearted until the engine lapsed into silence, leaving only the tortuous whine and click of the starter motor.

She sat back and laughed emptily. She was past any other reaction.

Three lads from a nearby pub gave the car a push, but the engine refused to show the slightest spark, and, thanking her helpers, she abandoned the Metro in a meter bay and took a taxi.

The stairway leading to her flat was spattered with dust and debris that crunched noisily underfoot. Inside, the builders had moved the furniture round again, but this time, as if to make up for their previous lapse, had draped almost everything with plastic dustsheets, so that only the rugs had caught the splashes of plaster from the new ceiling.

Mess or no mess, it was still home. Within minutes, she had set up the small table in front of her old red armchair by the gas fire. While she waited for the water to heat in the cistern, she sat down to call Mrs Bell. She dialled the number then, jamming her finger on the rest, cut the line before it had a chance to ring. Mrs Bell could wait. The care order wouldn't be heard for a week, nothing could be done for Adrian tonight.

There was time for six Jaffa cakes and two glasses of wine before the water was hot. When at last she sank into the bath, armed with a fresh glass, her mind felt dazzlingly, dangerously lucid.

There was no doubt: Simon was the traitor. Oh, maybe not in the way she had first thought. Conspiracy and bribery weren't really his style: it was impossible to imagine Simon lowering himself to dealing direct with the opposition. No, it was much more likely that he had trapped himself into an error of judgement. He was egotistical enough to believe he could weave his way effortlessly through his web of contacts, sufficiently vain to think his judgement infallible. He had probably exchanged the information on Nick for something else, had probably used it to impress his editor, and come unstuck. Of course he'd never admit to it, not even to the slightest possibility. Even during the best of their relationship,

Simon had not been able to admit to anything so prosaic as leaving a ring around the bath.

Illuminated by the wine, she saw everything with absolute clarity. Simon had been using her, manipulating her in that dry unemotional way of his. He had looked down on her from his intellectual pedestal, poured scorn on her ideas, then sold her short. Realising this, she felt a wild irrational anger at all the food and creative support she had provided for him.

She slid down in the water and wet her hair. When she came up again, it was with a compulsive desire to tell him to his face. 'Ha!' she cackled aloud, and heard the drink singing in her voice.

After the traumas and confusions of the day, retaliation was a good clear-cut emotion, something nice and straightforward one could get one's teeth into, and wrapped in her old dressing gown in front of the fire, she dwelt lovingly and voraciously on the idea.

She was, she supposed, quite drunk – the bottle, she noted with some amazement, was empty: a whole bottle, for God's sake. But if the clarity of her mind was fading, it was compensated by an almost euphoric determination.

She lifted the phone.

Either Simon wasn't answering or he was still out, because his machine clicked on at the second ring. Drawing breath, she started on her little speech.

In case he'd been in Mongolia, she gave him the news of the fire and the daubed animal rights slogans. Then, her head singing with wine, her heart lurching with harsh excitement, she gave him her new version of events. The police had already established it wasn't animal rights campaigners, she declared, knew it had just been a front. Oh, they might not have the complete evidence to nail the real culprits, but they soon would. Then Morton-Kreiger would have to dig their way out of *that* one! As for the laboratory itself, well – no one was giving up, she said, and certainly not Nick Mackenzie. There were already plans for a new laboratory. She heard herself give a brief bray of triumph, a raucous discordant laugh. She had meant to stop there, but her voice took off, self-propelled, swollen with wine, and she heard herself saying there was more, much more – an immense scandal involving cooked data on Silveron. Picturing the disbelief in Simon's face, just *seeing* how he would be taking this, she said she had the hard evidence right *here*. And what was more she had someone in a key position who could verify it, back it up all the way. Then the lid would blow right off the whole rotten business. End of Morton-Kreiger. Pumph! But there'd be no story until the time was right – until *she* decided it was right – then she'd go public – though she would not, she implied rather subtly, bring the story to *him*.

She rang off with a brief sense of triumph. The feeling of release was soon overshadowed by a sense of futility. What had that proved? What had that done? Simon would merely think her stupid and drunk. And he would be right.

She woke once in the middle of the night, sprawled awkwardly across the chair, in a muck sweat from the fire which was still on at full blast. Switching it off, she lurched across the room, opened a window and burrowed under the plastic sheets onto the unmade bed. After a succession of nightmares peopled by men in white coats and arsonists working in full technicolour, she woke again at dawn, her mouth thick, her head clogged with EEC-approved wine additives. Getting up to fetch water, she passed the empty wine bottle, saw the phone.

In the cold light, she felt a sudden regret.

THIRTY

Nick felt something brush against his shoulder and woke with a lurch that sent his heart racing. In the instant before his memory came plunging back, he felt an upsurge of panic, a stab of something that almost overwhelmed him.

Then Susan spoke.

'Did I wake you? Oh, my love – I'm sorry.' She moved against his back and stroked his arm. He could feel the contours of her body, soft and bony, firm and warm.

He lay still for a moment, absorbing the sensation of female flesh against his, feeling a quaking relief at not, for once, waking alone.

He grappled for his watch in the semi-darkness and couldn't find it. 'What time is it?'

'I think we missed tea,' she laughed. The bed shook slightly as she put on the bedside light. 'Five thirty.' Her head came back against his shoulder. 'Were you dreaming, poor love? You were twitching and muttering so much, I didn't know whether to wake you. I didn't sleep. I always feel dreadful if I sleep in the afternoons – an absolute beast for the rest of the day.' Her hand came down his arm, following it round to his chest, weaving her fingers through his. 'Poor love – a nasty dream?'

He murmured, 'Not so good,' which was true, though he couldn't remember the details. Then, because he didn't want to set too depressing a tone, he said: 'I was being chased by a herd of reporters – or something like that.'

'Oh, those stories! I know you don't believe me – when I

got here today I could almost *see* you thinking that I was only saying it to make you feel better – but they really *weren't* that bad, you know. Not bad at all! None of them said *anything* as remotely terrible as what you were worrying about last night.' She pushed herself up on one elbow. 'Honestly, they were *kind*, darling.' She put her cheek against his, and he caught the scent of her rather overpowering perfume. 'They *like* you, the press, they really do!'

He almost laughed. They may have been kind on one level – no one had openly called him an animal experimenter or an out-and-out hypocrite – but there wasn't a single newspaper which hadn't linked the story with Alusha's mysterious 'poisoning', and suggested, openly or not so openly, that he was involved in some sort of vendetta. And of course the tabloids had been unable to resist rehashing some of the more titillating evidence from the fatal accident inquiry. Yes, they may have been obliging on the surface, but they were still merciless about the past. He had been bracing himself for a frontal assault, only to find that they had stolen up on him from behind and taken him by surprise. Like old wounds, the memories had reopened painfully.

Susan tugged gently at his shoulder, and he rolled half-way onto his back. Leaning over him, she kissed him on the mouth, a fond lingering kiss. Then she smiled the broad contented smile she had been giving him ever since she'd arrived that afternoon. Whether it was the excitement of sneaking out through the garage at three that morning disguised with a scarf and old raincoat of the housekeeper's that appealed to her, or the rapid development of their relationship, he didn't want to guess. It wasn't that he exactly regretted starting this affair – although he wasn't entirely sure about that yet – but he rather wished it hadn't happened at this particular moment, when he was feeling besieged again; he wished he'd had more time to think it over.

But then it was the very fact that he was besieged that had made him turn to her. And perhaps it wasn't such a bad decision. He'd forgotten what a luxury it was to have someone to talk to, someone who wasn't otherwise involved in his life, someone who'd never known Alusha. He'd had the occasional relationship or near-relationship over the last few months – all brief, all highly unsatisfactory, all wanting what he wouldn't or couldn't give. Susan, by comparison, was undemanding. Well, so far. And though the arrangement, with its secrecy and lack of commitment, was far from ideal, it would do for now.

'What about a short break?' she suggested soothingly. 'Get away for a while. Somewhere you can relax.'

'I would, but I need to work.'

'But your European tour – surely you deserve some time off before all that?'

'No – you see, I *want* to work. There's something I have to finish.'

'Can't you work abroad?'

He sat up and stretched. 'Difficult.' He rubbed his face. 'I need a studio.'

'Oh.'

Her hands pushed up his back and started massaging his shoulders. The feel of hands on his skin . . . He closed his eyes.

'And where do you have to go to find a studio?'

He'd been thinking about that, but it was only now that he realised he had made up his mind. 'Scotland.'

'*Scotland.* Not to . . .? But I thought – ' She checked herself and gave a small exclamation, as if to tick herself off for straying into forbidden territory. She was good like that; she never delved too far. 'Well, if it'll make you happy . . .'

Happy? What he felt when he worked was too obsessive for that, but it was a contentment of sorts, and, most important of all, a form of oblivion. Before going on the Arizona dry-out his mind had refused to wrap itself round anything even vaguely creative, but now it was showing definite signs of life. He'd spent a few evenings in a borrowed studio in London trying to push the choral piece forward, but though the familiar slow-burning excitement had begun to simmer away in his brain again, he knew there was only one place where he could really work.

Exhibiting her talents as a masseuse, Susan pushed her thumbs into the pressure points either side of his spine on a level with his shoulder blades. He winced at the perfect blend of pleasure and pain.

'Does all this work mean I won't get a decision out of you on the main guest suite?' she said in mock reproval. 'It was between the peach and the eau de nil, remember.'

He couldn't remember what eau de nil was when it was at

493

home. 'You'd better decide,' he said. 'You're rather good at that.' Coughing, he reached for a cigarette. Smoking too much again.

'When will you go to Scotland?' she asked lightly.

He was suddenly able to make up his mind about that too. 'Tomorrow.'

Her hands paused. 'So soon? Oh. *Oh.*' She kissed his back. 'Wish I could come too,' she added in an undertone, and there was a hint of reproach in her voice that he'd not heard before. Then, in her cheerful tone: 'I'd planned – well, I'd thought I might be able to find out about that chemical for you. What did you say it was?'

'Silveron,' he murmured.

'*Silveron,*' she repeated slowly. 'You know – ask Tony's people to look into it.'

He twisted round and stared at her.

She shrugged slightly, pulling the sheet a little higher over her bosom, and asked charmingly: 'No?'

'I don't think that would be a good idea,' he said.

'Oh?' That hint of reproach again. 'But why not? That's what Tony's people are paid for, digging out information. They've nothing else to do, as far as I can gather.'

'Won't your husband . . .?'

'Oh, don't worry about him,' she said with a dismissive hand. 'He'll agree all right.' It occurred to Nick that the greatest single emotion she felt for her husband was scorn.

Perhaps she was aware that something unattractive was showing in her face, because she grinned suddenly and ran her fingers down his cheek.

But though her lips were smiling and her eyes unswervingly attentive, there was no humour in her expression.

From the past came memories of their earlier relationship. He remembered great outpourings of woe and abrupt emotional upheavals for which she had demanded his complete attention, sometimes for days on end. He couldn't remember what she had been so bothered about. Fitting in? Not being taken seriously? Something like that. And him not loving or understanding her – yes, plenty of that. The details were blurred, but he remembered the emotional exhaustion all right.

Looking at her now, the old and new Susan began to fuse, like one painting being scraped off another that had been painted underneath, until you couldn't be sure what you were seeing any more.

'So,' she said, 'I'll go ahead and ask, shall I?'

'I don't know.'

'But it won't be any trouble,' she insisted brightly. He couldn't help wondering if her eagerness didn't stem from a desire to show off her influence in high places.

He thought suddenly of Daisy – an image that never sprang to mind without a disturbing mixture of sensations – and remembered her conspiracy theories. With some surprise he found himself trotting it out. 'They won't have any information that hasn't been handed to them on a plate by the manufacturer. Might as well ask Morton-Kreiger.'

It was a moment before Susan spoke. 'Morton-Kreiger?'

There was someting in her voice that made him turn to look at her again. 'They make the stuff.'

'Oh.'

'Your friend Schenker.'

'My friend!' she retorted. 'Hardly.'

She moved behind him to resume her kneading and he could no longer see her face. 'My *friend*!' she repeated with a snort. 'Tedious little man!'

Her hands fanned out over the small of his back and found two points that no masseur of his acquaintance had ever found before. He gave a shiver.

'I should have used oil,' she said.

'Doing okay.'

Sighing, she lowered herself down beside him, and her touch lightened into a caress that travelled down his spine and over his backside. 'Next time I'll bring some,' she whispered, and there was something in her tone which told him he wasn't going to get to the studio that evening as he'd planned, not unless he made the effort to move straight away.

An hour later he was still there. But then, if working was one sort of oblivion, making love was another.

In the lazy time before they got up, he lay half listening to Susan's murmured recollections, his mind travelling lightly, soporifically over thoughts of work and Ashard.

'You're not listening.' Susan tipped a finger at his chin.

He mumbled in mild apology.

'You're still thinking of those newspapers!' she accused. 'Why don't you put your side of the story?

495

'I gave them a statement yesterday.'

'No, not a statement – a story. The whole thing, from your point of view.'

'It wouldn't work.'

She stroked the hair clear of his forehead. 'Why not?'

'Telling your story only prolongs the agony,' he explained. 'Then the tabloids would pick out the best quotes and use them out of context. They'd dredge things up, ask questions I couldn't answer.'

'But what could they ask that would be so bad?'

He almost laughed. 'Plenty.'

'You worry too much.'

'Oh no,' he said. 'They'd . . .' He hesitated, and wasn't sure why he hesitated.

'They'd bring up Alusha's death,' he heard himself say. 'And the evidence from the inquiry. They'd ask me about things I wouldn't want to talk about.'

Suddenly he had to move. Disentangling his arm, he sat up.

'You mean – her illness?'

'I mean, the psychiatrist's bloody report!' he retorted with sudden anger, and he realised that after all this time he had come to terms with nothing, nothing at all. And realising this, his anger fed off itself. '*And* the morphine!' he added bitterly.

A pause, then she whispered: 'The morphine?'

He swung his legs to the floor and reached for his shorts. 'It was for the pain. She had terrible pain.'

'Well then . . .'

'They thought the pain was imaginary, like the rest. They thought she had a *habit*. I couldn't talk my way through all that again. Christ.'

'But *would* they ask – '

He stood up and tugged a cigarette from its packet. 'I'm not going to take that risk. They think I supplied her, you see.'

Susan gave a nervous laugh. 'What?'

'Oh, they didn't say so, not straight out, but that's what they *thought*.' Lighting the cigarette, he clamped it to his mouth and pulled on his jeans.

'But that's outrageous! They could never say anything like that.'

'No, well, maybe not – but I couldn't risk it.'

'But, Nick, they'd never *dare*.'

Changing his mind about dressing, he headed across the room towards the shower. He stopped in the doorway. 'You don't understand,' he said, suddenly inexplicably cross with her for failing to understand. 'I *did* supply her. I *did* get it for her.' He was already regretting this, already feeling that old sickness rise in his belly.

He went into the bathroom and closed the door and said aloud to the walls: 'I got it for her because she *needed* it.'

Alice scraped her chair back. 'Another cup?' She was already scooping up the teapot.

'Please.'

Daisy watched her go to the Aga, drop a fresh bag in the pot and stab at it absentmindedly with a spoon.

'I'm not surprised,' Alice announced. 'No . . . it's what I expected really.'

'I'm sorry, Alice, I really am.'

'These things happen.'

'We'll have to think again. Look elsewhere. Konrad's not the only specialist in the world. There'll be someone else. It's just a question of tracking him down.' Daisy heard the tired old reassurances, and wondered if she herself believed them any more. 'I heard about a new epidemiological study on agricultural workers in America . . .'

Alice twisted round and stood facing her, back against the stove, one hand gripping the rail.

'. . . I'm not sure who's doing the study,' Daisy went on, 'But they're looking into something very like Aldeb, something called – oh God, I can't even remember the name. Going nuts at last, Alice, but then it was only a matter of time – '

'Daisy – don't.'

There was a peremptory tone in Alice's voice that made them both pause and look at each other.

'I'm not going on,' Alice announced. 'I'm calling a halt.' In case Daisy still hadn't got it, she explained: 'I'm giving up the legal action.'

Daisy stared at her, not sure that she hadn't been expecting this.

'Why, Alice?'

'John's ill again. They've found two secondaries.'

'Oh, *Alice*.'

'I feel I'm letting you down.'

497

'Letting *me* down? You have to be kidding.'

'Well . . . Whatever, I've no choice. What John needs now is care and support. And a bit of fun before it's too late. The promise of cash in five or six years or however long it takes isn't going to do him much good.'

'Oh, Alice, I'm so sorry. I'm so sorry.'

'He's only twenty-seven.'

'But what do they say? Surely . . .'

'Oh, you know. The usual treatment, then wait and see.'

There was resignation in her voice. She'd seen too many courses of treatment fail on her husband to allow herself much hope.

'Alice, if there's anything I can do. Anything.'

'I feel I'm letting you down,' she repeated.

Daisy went across to her and put an arm round the wide curve of her shoulders. 'Alice, you've been a real trooper. I couldn't have asked for more.'

Alice gave a rueful grin. 'Wish I could have done more. Still makes me mad as hell.'

Daisy hugged her. Her old sweater smelled of animals and other unidentifiable farmyard odours, and her hair, wiry as horse bristles, tickled Daisy's cheek. 'You stay mad as hell, Alice. It's what gives you your get-up-and-go.'

Alice gave her a squeeze, then pulled back to scrabble for a handkerchief. She blew her nose with a loud hoot, then flicked the tails of her handkerchief across her eyes. 'Remember the agricultural show?' she said in a reminiscent tone. 'I promised myself then I'd never give up. Swore it.'

'But we gave them a fright. Don't forget that.'

'Did we?'

'You betcha. You'll be on a file somewhere, Alice. The one who nearly nailed 'em.'

She cheered up a little at that and, sluicing the hot water into the pot, took the tea back to the table.

Talking about her altercation with the law seemed to raise her spirits further. Her only regret, she declared, was that she hadn't been clapped in chains and taken to court, because then she could have aired the whole thing in public. But she wasn't to forget the impact of the hundreds of letters she'd written, Daisy reminded her, the dozens that had got published, and the numerous MPs who'd replied sympathetically. All that had raised public awareness.

498

'Wouldn't have given in,' Alice murmured from time to time, her eyes fixing on Daisy's in the failing light.

'I know you wouldn't,' Daisy said.

Shortly before six the gin came out. Alice produced it with a flourish which almost concealed the slight but unmistakable flash of guilt. 'Does me good,' she said. 'Always have a drop about this time.'

'I should hope so too,' Daisy said.

'You're a good girl, Daisy. I'll miss you.'

'Not half as much as I'll miss you, Alice.'

They blinked at each other.

'You'll have one . . .?' Alice tilted the gin bottle over a glass, her voice gently pleading, as if she already knew Daisy would take this as her cue to leave.

'Actually, I've had a bit of a time in the last few days,' Daisy said, allowing herself a measure of understatement. 'I've got to get back to see a few people.' Like the garage people, who had towed her car away that morning, like Jenny, whose VW Beetle she had borrowed, like the Chelmsford police, the insurance agent, the Octek staff, and various other people who, weekend or not, would be wanting to speak to her urgently.

'You managing all right, Alice? I mean, for money, that sort of thing?'

'Hah!' she exclaimed, waving a vague hand, the gin already trembling in her voice. 'Another mortgage, another bank manager . . . I'll be all right.'

Before leaving, Daisy called Simon's number but there was still no reply. The *Sunday Times* features desk, never particularly well-informed on the whereabouts of its staff, was also unforthcoming until the unidentified voice on the end of the line broke off, capped the phone for a consultation, and returned to announce that Simon was expected back that evening from Prague.

'*Prague?* When did he leave?'

Another conference. 'Friday morning.'

The morning immediately after the fire. She drove away from Alice's in a state of bafflement and alarm. If Simon had left on Friday morning, then he would have had to pass on the information about Nick mighty quick. Impossibly quick. Like straight away, the very night he'd got her message.

But then if she was blaming Simon for revealing Octek's existence to people he shouldn't have, there was another problem. More than a problem – a great yawning gap. It was just after eight that morning, as she had faced her hangover in the bathroom mirror, that the realisation had come to her; she had never told Simon where Octek was located. The set-up, the cell-line trials, the five-month testing programme, and of course Nick's identity – she'd given Simon all of that. But nowhere in the conversation had she given him the city, let alone the street, where it was all happening.

And if she hadn't told him, and he hadn't passed it on, then how had the fire raisers known where to go?

Unexpectedly, there was a parking place bang opposite the flat. She examined it for builders' skips, no-parking cones and upturned nails, courtesy of the local hooligans, but it seemed clear of hidden traps. Parking, she walked round the Beetle and flicked an unthinking glance up at the windows of the flat.

She stopped and looked again.

The lights were blazing.

The scene shook, her heart hammered.

As she watched, a shadow arced across the ceiling and the top of a man's head swelled briefly into the lower corner of the left-hand window.

She started across the road only to pause and retreat, struck by sudden doubts. Confrontation might not be such a good idea. Wait for him to come out then? Call the police?

She hovered uneasily in the road, looking up at the stagelit window.

Another movement. She scrambled back onto the pavement. A tall metal object appeared, glinting in the light, followed by the man's head, along with his shoulders and back. The man levered open the object – a stepladder – and climbed slowly towards the ceiling.

She leant against the car, weak and shaky, and it was some time before she managed to move in the direction of the house again.

The workman grinned down at her when she let herself in. 'You're working late,' she said.

'Didn't want ter 'ang about,' he said. 'Save me 'avin to come back Monday. Nearly done now.' He slapped some sort of filler into a hole in the wall where the falling ceiling had ripped a lump of plaster away.

'You gave me a shock,' she said. 'I thought you were . . .'

'What, doin' the place over? Nah,' he laughed, 'I was lookin' after it for yer, wasn't I?' He smoothed off the filler and climbed down the ladder. 'Just leave it ter dry now. A week, I'd say, to be on the safe side. Oh, yer got some phone calls – seven, as I remember. Three left messages on the machine there. Oh, and a visitor. 'Bout free o'clock.'

Daisy pulled the plastic sheet off the red armchair. 'Who was it, did he say?'

'Nah.' He collected his tools into his bag. ''E just rings the bell. I put me 'ead out the windar and says there's no one 'ome, and 'e nods and goes off. Didn't 'ang about.'

'What did he look like?'

He climbed out of his overalls and dusted his hands thoughtfully. 'Blimey . . . now you're askin'. Brown 'air . . . Well-built. Nah . . .' He shook his head. 'Nah . . . didn't really get a good a look at 'im. Too busy tryin' to get me 'ead through yer windar without gettin' meself topped. You know you got a sashcord broke?'

'I have?'

He manoeuvred his ladder out through the door and came back for the dustsheets which he pulled off the furniture with great flourishes that sent billows of dust mushrooming lazily into the air.

'Only three messages?' she called after him.

'Yup. The other callers – four there were – they rang off when they 'eard the machine.'

'Thanks,' she said.

When he'd gone she played back the messages. A tense Peasedale pleaded for information, Inspector Brent requested in formal tones that she contact him as soon as convenient, and Jenny, in a no-nonsense message strong on emotional support, insisted that Daisy come over that evening for a meal with her and her boyfriend.

She was tempted by Jenny's offer. There wasn't much she could do in Chelmsford until Monday morning, although Inspector Brent probably thought differently, and there was even less to be done for Adrian until she could get up to Scotland, hopefully on Monday afternoon.

501

She called Jenny and said she'd be over as soon as she could. She thought of calling Peasedale, maybe even Brent, but couldn't face either. She felt like the pilot of an aircraft that had crash-landed in the jungle, miles from civilisation, with a plane-load of demanding passengers.

There was a shout of laughter from the street, answered by a raucous exuberant yell. She felt a pang of loneliness, the sort you get when the rest of the world is having a good time and someone forgot to invite you. She scooped up some wine as an offering to Jenny and made for the door. Pausing, she went back to the answering machine and hovered over it uncertainly. No, she'd had quite enough messages for tonight. Leaving the machine off, she hurried out.

Remembering that Jenny was allergic to wine, she drove down the hill to Mr Patel's and picked up some cider. She added some bread and milk for her breakfast next morning.

She'd parked on a corner of the junction, pointing the wrong way. To save herself a trip round the block she backed cautiously out into the wider of the streets, peering through the tiny rear window of the Beetle, and was rewarded by the blasting horn and flashing headlights of a suicidal speed maniac screaming blindly out from behind the row of densely parked cars. Her adrenalin surged, her hands trembled on the wheel, she felt an abrupt exhaustion. Jenny's place suddenly seemed a long way away, the prospect of talking through the last couple of days altogether too much. Better to call it a day, better to get some sleep.

Wearily, she pointed the car up the hill again. Anticipating that the prime parking spot would be gone by now, she took the first space she came to, some way short of the flat on the near side. Getting into it involved a ten-point manoeuvre with a killing amount of wheel winding, but at the end of it the car was more or less parked.

Someone walked briskly past the car, going uphill. As she prepared to open the door, she glanced up and took in a jaunty gait, stocky build, and dark casual clothing. The lighting wasn't brilliant, he was largely in shadow, but something about the back of his head, or possibly his stride, made her pause, something that sparked the glimmer of a memory, and she canted her head to one side to observe him through the windows of the parked cars ahead. After a time the car windows offered more frame than glass, and she lost sight of him.

She opened the door and clambered heavily out. She noticed that the striding pedestrian had disappeared. For some reason, she wasn't sure what, this bothered her, and she took another look, balancing on tiptoe to get a view over the car roofs. Then she spotted him. He was climbing the steps to a house not far from hers. A neighbour, then, which accounted for the familiarity. A close neighbour at that, though from the oblique angle and in the darkness, it was hard to tell precisely how close.

Gathering the groceries, balancing them precariously on one arm, she closed and locked the car door, and made her way slowly up the hill.

She looked over to the prime parking place and saw that, far from being taken, it was still there. Automatically she glanced up at the flat windows.

Light.

She stopped, baffled. What lights had she left on?

But if she wasn't sure about the lights, she was absolutely certain about the curtains. She hadn't drawn them, either when she arrived or when she went out.

She stared at the familiar pattern of the Indian cotton, its peacock design thrown into colour-bleached reverse by the backlighting, the two curtains pulled around the bow of the windows and drawn together so tightly that there was no thread of light between them.

She had the feeling that this was happening at a remove, that she only had to pause for the scene to shift towards something more acceptable. But there was no escape from the curtains and the fact they were drawn.

Walking swiftly back to the car, she unlocked it and quickly restarted the engine. A car came ponderously over the brow of the hill. She knew the look; hunting for a space. 'Oh no you don't,' she breathed, winding viciously on the wheel to extricate the Beetle in fewer than ten moves.

She misjudged the final manoeuvre, clipped the bumper of the car in front with a loud scraping sound, and shot forward just in time to see the approaching car pause by the vacant parking space. She was accelerating, rehearsing reasons why the interloper should give up the space to her, when the car

503

started towards her again, the driver's head bent forward over the wheel, peering at the house numbers. He was just lost.

She slowed down, made a conscious effort to unwind the tension in her hands, and parked quietly, without attracting attention. From here she had a good view of the front door and, when she shifted across to the passenger seat, the flat above. The lights were still on, the curtains drawn.

She settled down to wait, to catch him when he came out. She wanted to see his face.

Was it the man in the dark clothes, the pedestrian who'd passed her when she parked? There had been something about him, some echo of the past. She groped for the memory, but it wouldn't come.

Whoever he was, he was taking his time. How long had he been in there? Ten minutes? No, more like fifteen. She angled her head so she could keep the whole width of the bay window in view. What could he be doing in there? she wondered. What could be taking so long? Perhaps it wasn't the dark-clad man after all, perhaps it was a sneak thief who'd left even before she returned from Mr Patel's. Perhaps there was nobody in there any more.

Suddenly the light went out, the curtains absorbed the dull amber of the streetlights.

Her adrenalin rocketed. Fixing her eyes unwaveringly on the front of the house, she slid back into the driving seat. Her foot caught the edge of the milk carton, it fell. She swore and leant down to right it.

She glanced rapidly up at the window and her throat dried.

The curtains had been reopened.

She looked down at the front door.

It began to open. Whoever was opening it had not activated the time-lapse stair lights so that behind him the hall was in darkness, and she could make out only the barest shadow as he paused ghostlike in the open door, as if to watch and listen, before casually stepping out and pulling the door behind him.

Dark clothes, thick build: yes, the man from before. He ran quickly down the steps, head down.

Look up. I need you to look up.

He reached the bottom of the steps and, moving into an aureole of light, took a quick glance over his shoulder before setting off briskly in the direction he had come.

Got you.

Maynard.

The neck, the tight jaunty walk. *Maynard*. Plastered-down hair, thick lips, stocky build: crawling obsequious Maynard.

He was walking fast, his head and shoulders bobbing rapidly over the line of car roofs. She screwed around in her seat, watching the buoyant head retreating rapidly down the hill, and was fixed with a momentary indecision.

Should she leave it there? Be satisfied with the fact that she'd rumbled him? Or was she going to take it further? Make a complaint. All she had, she remembered, was an address in Hertfordshire, a phone number in Battersea. But suppose Maynard wasn't his real name, suppose the Battersea number wasn't there any more?

Undecided yet loath to lose him, she started the car and, straddling the street in a tight three-point turn, began to follow. Too fast, too fast. She slowed until she could see his head bouncing along at a comfortable distance ahead of her.

Turn off the headlights? No, too obvious. Best to crawl close by the parked cars, like the motorist she had seen earlier, so that if he looked back he would think she was lost.

Reaching a corner he turned suddenly, swivelling his body round abruptly until it was almost facing the way he had come. She resisted the urge to jam her foot on the brake and kept creeping forward, craning her head from side to side, so that, if his eyesight was that good, he would be able to see the dim outline of a face peering up at the house numbers.

When she glanced back he had vanished. She drove cautiously on towards the junction and stopped just beyond the last parked car, so that she could see along the pavement of the adjacent street.

No sign.

Now how had he managed that, for God's sake?

She looked down the hill towards Mr Patel's, then back the way she had come, then across to the other side of the side street again. Nothing.

Hell.

An engine started not far away. She wound down the window to get a direction on it, only for the sound to be drowned by a car lumbering up the hill towards her. The approaching car, a rumbling diesel, made ponderously slow

505

progress and it was a long time before she could tune into the altogether quieter hum of the other car.

She had the sound now: it came from the side street where Maynard had disappeared.

It had to be him. Could it be him? But why, having started his engine, wasn't he moving?

A second later, the red glow of a rear light sprang on, then a second later the white reflection of a reversing light. The car moved back once, then curved out and accelerated away.

Daisy turned the corner and followed. It was a dark saloon, possibly a Rover. But was it Maynard?

Part of her accepted that this was crazy – even if it was Maynard he was probably the sort who'd know instantly if he was being followed – but the other part of her was damned if she was going to give up without a try.

The street led into another that ran parallel to Augustus Road. With hardly a hesitation to see if anything was coming, the dark car turned left, heading downhill through the web of dark residential streets. Reaching the arterial road at the bottom, it stopped in the face of a steady stream of traffic. Daisy saw an immediate problem: to close up or stay back? To invite attention or risk him seeing her in his mirror?

In the end she closed up, lowering the sun visor to hide her face. As she halted behind the Rover she saw with relief that the driver was not looking in his mirror: he was too intent on pushing the car impatiently forward, sticking its nose further and further out into the traffic, his head peering sideways as he waited for a suitable gap. Peering sideways and showing his profile to her.

Maynard. *Maynard*.

He spurted forward, then jammed on the brakes as someone hooted at him. As the brake lights flashed on and off, Daisy realised she was looking at his registration number. For God's sake. How many half-brained witnesses forgot to remember something as basic as a car number?

She got the number into her head just as the Rover finally sprang forward into the main road, accelerating fast. She rolled forward, knowing she must get out soon or lose him. The traffic was thick but tailing off, regulated by some unseen traffic lights. A small gap was coming up, followed, four cars later, by a larger one. She went for the earlier gap, pushing her foot hard down which, in the Beetle, provided little extra speed but some illusion of achievement. The approaching car braked uncomplainingly to let her in.

She was four, no five, cars back. Too far if there were traffic lights. One car peeled off to the left, then, in a straightish section, she risked overtaking another with nerve-racking slowness, hanging out in the centre of the road until she was almost squeezed against a traffic island.

Still two cars between them. The road curved to the right and she got a clear view of the Rover ahead. In the fluorescence of the shop lights it glinted dark red.

The road straightened then, enacting her worst fears, some traffic lights ahead of the Rover turned amber. As the line of cars slowed, she pulled out slightly to get a better view of the junction and waited with a sinking heart for the sight of the Rover speeding away. The lights were a solid red now, yet, though she waited, the car didn't appear. Maynard wouldn't be one to stop at anything short of red. Had he turned off then? She darted a glance to the left, but no car was turning off.

The cross-traffic had started, and she realised that he must have stopped at the amber after all.

Lucky, very lucky. More than she deserved.

Quickly, before the lights changed, before she forgot the registration number, she reached for her bag and scribbled it on a scrap of paper.

When the line started off again, she saw that the leading car was not after all the Rover, that Maynard had been caught behind another more cautious motorist. Now the Rover was jammed up against his bumper, as if this would encourage him to accelerate faster. She waited impatiently for an opportunity to overtake the car immediately in front of her and narrow the gap but they were into the twists of Turnpike Lane, heading north-east towards Tottenham, and it was impossible to pass.

The problem was eased by the car two ahead, which slowed and swooped into the kerb by a parade of shops, leaving just one car between her and Maynard. She couldn't decide whether she should leave it at this, whether the still considerable risk of getting separated at lights was preferable to being spotted. A few seconds later the problem became academic as the Rover suddenly indicated right and rocked to a halt in the centre of the next junction, waiting to turn.

As she drew up behind him she tweaked the sun visor for maximum shadow, and instantly regretted what must be an obvious gesture. But if Maynard had seen her tell-tale movement, if he had recognised her, he gave no sign.

The lights changed, Maynard lurched to the right across the junction, she followed. The road, not one she knew, was relatively clear of traffic, and Maynard accelerated away. She let him pull ahead a little, content just to keep him in sight. She was gripping the wheel so tightly that her nails were digging into her thumbs. Slow, take it easy. It's going well.

Even as she thought it, she drew a mental map and realised they had performed a loop and were now heading south. Perhaps Maynard wasn't sure of his way, perhaps he'd lost his sense of direction. In most people that would have been believable – this part of north London was enough to defeat most map readers – but for some reason she was certain Maynard knew exactly where he was going.

The thought made her pull back further.

'Still with me?'

The walkie-talkie gave a loud crackle, then Biggs' voice came through, gruff and terse. 'Affirmative.'

Hillyard gave a sharp sigh, intended for transmission. If Biggs' police jargon had once had novelty value, it had long since lost its power to amuse. Hillyard asked with heavy sarcasm: 'Does that mean yes?'

A silence. 'Affirmative.'

'Right. Close in. Make it snappy. I won't want to hang about.'

'Received and out.'

Hillyard braked hard and, keeping the radio to his ear, swivelled the wheel with the heel of his free hand and took the car round the corner into a dead-end street that led between banks of dismal council flats.

He continued to the end of the road, where there was a more recent though equally grim development, a series of concrete blocks with slit-like windows and peeling murals, partly raised on concrete stilts and connected by webs of poorly lit footways, halls and flights of high-walled steps.

Hillyard, who had been here before, bypassed the designated parking area and stopped the car under a raised block, between a massive concrete stilt and the blank wall of a service shaft. He parked unhurriedly, taking his time to slip the walkie-talkie into the inner pocket of his trainer jacket before getting out and locking up.

Resisting the urge to look over his shoulder, he sauntered past a sombre light and along the front of the building before disappearing into the shadows of a covered footway.

Daisy parked some way back. This was the sort of place you read about, where grannies locked themselves up at night and women didn't take their babies out for fear of thugs. The ten-storey blocks were ribbed with external galleries lit by row after row of dim bulbs, many not functioning. Several of the ground-level flats were deserted and boarded up, abandoned to the vandals. The wide concrete verges were speckled with litter.

She tucked her bag out of sight under the seat and got out and locked the door. Somewhere high up in one of the buildings, a thin shout echoed along a long empty space.

Ahead, in the dark area under one of the buildings, she saw the lights of Maynard's car go off. A moment later, he emerged from the shadows and strolled along the front of the building. He wasn't looking around him, he wasn't hurrying. He turned and disappeared into some sort of passageway. She waited for a minute to see if he would reappear, then wandered uncertainly forward. She wasn't about to follow him into the maze of walkways – she wasn't mad – but it might be worth taking a quick look at the car.

On the other hand she might just wait right here until he came out again.

You're frightened. *Yes, I know I'm frightened.*

Yet, as at so many times in the past, her old doggedness stirred, she was unable to let the idea go. Maybe it was the memory of Maynard at the Waldorf, his hamster cheeks full of cucumber sandwiches, maybe it was the idea of him poking around in her flat, but she set off along the pavement towards the towering end block, towards the shadows where the Rover was parked. Approaching, she kept an eye on the passageway in case Maynard should reappear, then ducked her head down to look in the rear window.

The back seats were in deep shadow: impossible to see anything. She moved to the front and put her eye closer to the glass.

The roaring snapping mouth reared up at her out of the darkness, aiming at her nose. She jumped back with a cry.

The mouth yapped frantically at the window, its teeth clacking against the glass.

'Jesus!'

She stood still, her heart racing.

The mouth subsided for an instant, revealing bulbous eyes, a flat squashed-back nose, a mane of pale hair, then started its screaming again, yelping maniacally, crashing itself blindly at the window.

She retreated, her pulse still pumping in her ears, and headed back towards the Beetle.

Voices, loud and shrill, reverberated suddenly from the block to her right, and a group of youths spilled out from a doorway, jostling each other in aggressive horseplay. She kept her head down, aiming straight for the car. She sensed them catching sight of her, exchanging remarks. One of them called out something, though she didn't hear what it was. She caught it second time, though. It was the sort of graphic sexual invitation that yobs like to yell at women to make them feel threatened. She slowed a little and tipped her head up to show she wasn't going to be impressed. At the same time she was relieved to see someone coming along the pavement towards her, a man with a coat flapping round his knees: the sort of thin raincoat worn by clerks and insurance salesmen and other safe people.

She reached the Beetle just ahead of the man in the raincoat and thrust into her pocket for the keys. As she went round to the driver's side and bent to open the door, she was aware that the man in the raincoat was no longer on the pavement, that he had achieved some mysterious vanishing act. Then, by some instinct she couldn't name, she realised that he had moved around behind her, and realising it, she instantly rationalised it: he was coming to ask her something, coming to ask if she was all right. She sensed his sudden approach as much as heard him, or maybe she glimpsed a brief flicker of movement, but either way she was turning when he hit her, which was probably why the weapon missed the back of her skull, where it could have been aimed, and caught her on the side of her head, above the ear and across the width of her cheekbone. *Thwack!* The weapon was both soft and enormously hard: she felt its soft edge, she felt its immense force.

Even as it cannoned into her cheekbone, she thought: *He shouldn't be hitting me in the face. No one gets hit in the face.*

The blow threw her sideways and she felt herself sprawling untidily against the car. At some point two of her fingers got caught up somewhere and mangled, possibly in the door hinge, and at about the same time she must have sunk to the ground, where she was eventually found, but at that moment all she was aware of was a vast shock, a loud ringing in her ears, and a sensation that felt like drowning.

'Didn't tell you to brain her,' Hillyard sighed.

'You didn't tell me not to either,' said Biggs, with his usual mindless logic.

Hillyard straightened up and took a quick look around. 'Brought it on herself,' he commented waspishly. 'Trying to switch cars like that. Trying to be clever.'

'Didn't see it was her when she got on to you,' said Biggs. 'Just saw the car. That van's no good for gettin' a view, y'know. Can't see a bleedin' thing.' He gestured down at the girl. 'What shall we do with her?'

'A mugging victim, isn't she?'

They went through the contents of her shoulder bag, then the car itself, examining each item before either pocketing it or putting it back in the bag. Hillyard gave a grunt of satisfaction at finding one piece of paper, but otherwise he was not at all pleased. He had still not found what he had been looking for in that flat.

THIRTY-ONE

Dublensky sat over the newspaper and idly marked off the ball games that were showing on TV later in the day. Although it was ten he wasn't yet dressed and still wore a towelling robe over his shorts. His unclad feet were cold on the floor, his coffee in need of a refill, but indolence made him heavy, and he couldn't summon the energy to move.

The phone rang, a long sombre sound. Gathering his robe around him, Dublensky rose and shuffled over to the wall phone.

The voice wrenched Dublensky back to the past with a speed that left his mind stumbling. *Reedy?* But there was no mistaking the hearty tone, the sheer force of that voice. And then the name itself, announced with warmth and an extraordinary note of expectation, as if they were long-lost college friends due for a congenial reunion.

Dublensky managed: 'How are you, Don?'

'Never better! Never better! I'm in the Big Apple, John! Arrived yesterday. Attending a weekend meeting of the Institute. Dinners, lectures – you know, everyone applauds your speech then secretly tears it apart later.' He chuckled: 'You know the kind of thing.'

But Dublensky didn't know. He'd never belonged to the organisation that he assumed Reedy was referring to, had never made a speech, nor torn anyone else's apart.

What did this show of brotherhood mean? When they had last spoken – it was back in March, shortly before he was fired from Allentown – it was to exchange bitter words over the

Silveron affair. The memory of that conversation still had the power to shrink Dublensky's heart.

'What can I do for you, Don?' he asked tentatively.

'John ... .' Reedy lingered over his name, giving another chuckle. 'I thought we could meet. It's been a long time. How about dinner tonight? There's a conference event I'll be glad to skip. Can you make it? Say you can. It would be really great to see you.'

Dublensky fought for a reply.

'Would it be easier if I came down to you?' said Reedy, cutting into the silence. 'I could grab a hire car and get down by six thirty.'

This willingness to travel seemed to cast Reedy's invitation in a new light. Maybe the forced joviality hid a desire to make amends. Maybe he had come to apologise.

Not entirely free of suspicion, Dublensky found himself asking: 'Er, what is it you want to talk about exactly?'

'Why, nothing, John. I just wanted – ' Reedy paused suddenly, as if he had thought better of this approach, and murmured: 'John, you know how it is, there are things you can never talk about over the phone. I mean, like it'd be real nice to *see* you, John.'

'Is it Morton-Kreiger business?'

'What?' He sounded genuinely shocked. 'Oh no, John, no. This isn't business, this is entirely my idea!'

Dublensky knew then that he would agree. His curiosity was too great, his suspicions too sharp to leave it alone.

It was only after they had arranged to meet at a local inn and Dublensky was back at the table with a fresh cup of coffee, that it occurred to him that Reedy must have gone to a lot of trouble to track him down to this corner of New Jersey. In Allentown only two neighbours had known where he and Anne were moving to, and he certainly hadn't told anyone at the chemical works. Had Reedy traced him through his employers then? And if so, were Dalton now fully informed of Dublensky's background? Were they even now preparing to fire him? The thought filled him with new trepidation.

But then it was probably foolish to imagine that the mandarins of MKI were not aware of the fact that he worked for Dalton. Now and again it had even occurred to him that, incredible though it seemed, MKI might actually have fixed up this job in order to keep an eye on him.

Speculation, increasingly wild and torturous, filled Dublensky's mind until the evening when, telling an uninterested Anne he had a business meeting, he went to meet Reedy.

From the shadowy corner of the inn's bar area, Reedy rose with a smile that sent his chins creasing into the folds of his neck.

'John,' he sighed, taking Dublensky's hand and overlaying it with a fond pat. 'John.' He stood back and surveyed him like a parent eyeing a prodigal child. 'Hey, but it's good to see you.'

By the time they had finished their drinks and moved through to the dining area, Reedy had asked him about life in the town, about Tad and his schooling, about Anne. He did not enquire after Dublensky's work.

His tone was avuncular, though Dublensky thought he could detect a trace of briskness, as if he was anxious to keep the conversation moving at some predetermined pace.

Dublensky, needing to assert himself, if only modestly, made an abrupt interruption. 'What's happening at MKI?' he asked.

Reedy laughed at the question and tipped his fingers into space. 'Oh, you know. Unchanging. The monolith rolls on. Although – ' He shot Dublensky a slyly modest look. 'For some reason they have seen fit to kick me up a step. As of next month I become Executive Vice President, Research.'

'Congratulations.'

'Means getting my arse kicked more often.' He assumed a long-suffering look that wasn't designed to convince anyone.

The food came and they paused to apply relish and sauces to their steaks. Reedy talked again, but more generally now, touching on everything from the national debt to bankruptcy among Iowa farmers. It was a screen of words, Dublensky realised, delivered both as a means of controlling the conversation and of giving himself time to prepare. But for what? There was something coming, of that Dublensky was certain. A formal non-aggression pact? An olive branch? A monetary deal?

He said with unaccustomed boldness: 'Was it about the Silveron affair you came, Don?'

Reedy put down his fork. 'The past is past, John,' he said, affecting surprise. 'That business – ' He waved a hand in the

514

air. 'We all took the stance we thought was right at the time. Now, well . . .' He gave a slight shrug and said magnanimously: 'Let's say there were faults on both sides.' He returned to his plate, forking a lump of steak and lowering his head to push it into his mouth.

'Faults?'

'Mmm? Oh yeah, sure.' He chewed as he spoke, making little effort to close his mouth. 'Safety's the watchword at the Aurora plant now. My Lord, the safety! You can't move in that place for controls and regulations. We would never risk one worker, John, not one.' He pointed his fork for emphasis. 'But those early reports had us worried at one time, oh yes, I won't pretend they didn't.' He used the *we* as if he had long been operating at senior executive level. 'And of course we reacted appropriately. Now that the true facts have emerged we don't regret that. Some people might say that we'd overreacted, but no risk however tiny is worth taking, not where people are concerned.'

Dublensky was struggling to catch up. 'The true facts?' he echoed hesitantly.

Reedy gave him a polite, mildly puzzled stare. 'The people who reported sick – what was really wrong with them.'

Dublensky looked blank and with a sudden exclamation Reedy slapped a hand to his forehead. 'You didn't know?' he asked incredulously. 'About the medical diagnoses?'

Dublensky remembered Burt telling him about the Aurora workers who had got themselves rediagnosed in order to claim welfare, but chose not to say so. Instead he stared across the table, awaiting a fresh interpretation of the facts.

Reedy, relishing his responsibilities, put down his fork and folded his serviette ceremoniously. 'Okay,' he said, holding up the fingers of both hands then folding down two, 'there were eight workers who reported sick in the early days. Except two weren't really sick – one had a nervous complaint from long before, the second was pregnant.' He knocked off two fingers. 'Of the six remaining, *two* had cancer – different forms – and the medics agree that chances are they both had the disease *before* they came into contact with Silveron. Which leaves four.' He spread the remaining fingers wide, thrusting his wrist forward for emphasis. 'Now these were the people we were really worried about – thanks in part to you, of course.' He gave a small bow of acknowledgement.

Dublensky's mind plunged back to the old Reedy, the man who had been indifferent to the Aurora workers, and wondered at how things could change.

'These four people were sick,' Reedy went on, curling his fingers into a fist, 'really sick. There was no doubt about that. But what we never realised – at least not for some time – was that they had not received the best diagnostic advice.' He dropped his voice confidentially. 'That physician Burt – well-meaning, of course – but he hadn't run half the tests he should have run. It seems he made up his mind in advance that it was a problem of toxic exposure and closed his mind to everything else.'

'But, but – ' Dublensky agitated a hand in his anxiety to get the words out. 'He ran all kinds of tests and they showed nothing.'

'Ah!' Reedy, smiling benignly, raised a correcting finger. 'All sorts of tests, but not the *right* ones. When we finally got these people to a top diagnostician, well! Two had identifiable ailments. One was a rare liver disease, I believe. Another an auto-immune problem. I don't know the details.' He gestured his ignorance. 'But I do know they would have gotten a lot more help if they'd come to MKI sooner.'

'To MKI?'

'Sure. We offered the diagnostician for free and were happy to do so.'

Dublensky wondered who this diagnostician was that he could find so much that Burt had missed.

'That still leaves two,' Dublensky ventured.

Reedy returned to his meal, spearing his fork into his french fries. 'Two,' he echoed contentedly. 'That's right. Well now, it's early days, but it seems that one of these people was a malingerer and the other had some sort of mental illness. The diagnostician couldn't be too specific on *that* – not his field, you understand – so he referred him to a psychiatrist. Sadly, this man refused to attend any sessions, diagnostic or otherwise.' He shook his head uncomprehendingly and spread a hand. 'What can you do when people don't want to be helped?'

All kinds of questions hovered on Dublensky's lips. Like why all these illnesses shouldn't have been brought on by the original exposure. Like why the first two victims – the ones with nervous illnesses and pregnancy – should be written off with a wave of the hand. And since when had pregnancy made a woman so ill she couldn't function?

But he did not put these questions. He said neutrally: 'I had no idea.'

Reedy, taking this as a positive response, beamed. 'Nothing to worry about, see. A scare.' He threw a last nugget of meat into his mouth and chewed it lazily. Catching sight of Dublensky's plate, he made a sound of dismay. 'You've not eaten!'

Obediently, Dublensky picked up his fork, only to prod at the food without interest.

Reedy finished his meal and, leaning forward, surveyed Dublensky with paternalistic satisfaction. 'You mustn't blame yourself, you know, John,' he said. 'You did what you thought was right. You followed your principles, and everyone respects you for that.'

Dublensky, stung by the condescension of the remark, was galvanised to ask: 'Is that what you came to tell me?'

Smiling, Reedy made a weaving motion with his hand. 'I came because I wanted to, John. It's been a long time and – well, I was grieved by what occurred. I wanted to check things out, make sure you were okay.'

Dublensky couldn't think of anything to say.

'You're happy at Dalton?' Reedy enquired.

Dublensky shrugged. 'Yeah.'

'Well, it's a company that's going places, that's for sure. They're up there with the high fliers, in line for some major contracts. And you'll get to fly right up there with them.' He drooped an eyelid into a half wink: one winner greeting another.

'It wasn't easy to find work,' Dublensky said flatly.

'But you're okay now,' he declared assertively. 'You're okay now!'

The waitress removed Dublensky's uneaten steak and took their orders for coffee and dessert.

As she left, Reedy leant across and said in a low sympathetic tone: 'Look here . . . There *is* something else, John. I've been debating whether to bring it up and I still don't know whether I should. But, hell – you're a good man, John. I'd hate to see you get the blame for something you didn't do. And as a friend – I hope a friend? – I couldn't let it pass without telling you. Otherwise I'd never forgive myself. You know?'

Dublensky thought: Here it is at last. 'You're making me

nervous,' he said truthfully. 'What is it I'm supposed to have done?'

Reedy made a show of bracing himself, his face creased with regret. 'Please treat this in the greatest confidence,' he whispered, hunching over the table. 'But it seems . . .' He drew a breath. 'It seems that one of the environmental groups has gotten hold of some information, information that is *meant* to show inconsistencies in the Silveron trial data.'

Dublensky's heart bumped. His eyes fixed on Reedy's with ghastly fascination.

Reedy rocked back in his seat. 'Now we know this stuff is fake, we know it's been fabricated. Nothing but cheap disinformation. But the point is, this sort of subversive crap can be damaging – which of course is the intention.'

Dublensky pulled his features into the semblance of interest.

'Now none of this would affect you, John, except – ' He gave a great sigh of disbelief. 'Someone's trying to link your name to all this. Now don't ask me why. It seems incredible. But that's the way it is.'

Dublensky uttered a thin sound half-way to a question.

'They're saying you're the source, John. They're saying that you provided the information. More than that, they're saying you're about to go public on it – to get up and make a noise about all this.' He raised his shoulders and spread his hands in a further show of bafflement. 'Crazy.'

Dublensky hastily pulled his spectacles down his nose and pressed his fingertips into the corners of his eyes in the way he did when he needed time.

What made them imagine he would suddenly choose to talk now, after all these months? Then it came to him. It was his call to EarthForce the other day. It was his conversation with Paul Erlinger. Somehow MKI had got to hear about it, just as they had got to hear about his call to Erlinger back in March and instigated the burglary. They knew about it, and had interpreted that unhappy promise of his, that vague pledge to help, as a firm intention to act.

It had to be. What else could it be? *Jesus*. He knew he shouldn't have made that call.

Dublensky felt Reedy's eyes on him, gauging his reaction. Pushing his spectacles back up his nose, he said: 'The, er . . . the information, it's fake, you say?'

'Oh yeah. The figures were obviously fabricated – '

'How do you know?'

Reedy drew his lips into a narrow line and regarded Dublensky with an air of forbearance beginning to wear thin. A forced note came into his voice. 'Now, John, really . . . We know. We just *know*.'

'But how?' Dublensky interjected quietly. '*How?*'

'How! For lots of reasons I'm not at liberty to divulge. For – ' He broke off and gave a harsh impatient sigh. 'Godammit, John, there's nothing *wrong* with Silveron!'

Dublensky realised then: Nothing has changed, nothing ever would. His anger stirred, a small spot of heat burned on his face. 'What exactly are these fake figures meant to show?' he asked.

'I don't know,' Reedy shrugged impatiently.

'Remember that conversation we had on the phone, Don? When I said I wasn't happy with the Silveron toxicology trials?'

Reedy was silent, his face a mask of disapproval.

'I wasn't happy because it looked like they'd been fixed up by TroChem. I told you about it, Don, but you wouldn't listen. I'd like to know why you wouldn't listen.'

'Come on, John,' Reedy exploded. 'You were irate, you were upset. No one would have taken you seriously under those circumstances!'

Dublensky considered this for a moment. 'Okay,' he nodded gravely, 'okay. But suppose I asked you to take me seriously now?'

Reedy hesitated then laughed awkwardly. 'I'd listen, of course I'd listen. I'm listening now, aren't I?'

'Okay. I'm telling you now. The toxicology results were fixed up, Don.'

'Come *on*! Where's your proof, John? Give me some evidence.'

'It was stolen from me.'

'*What?*' He gave an unnatural laugh then examined Dublensky's face. 'You look at me like it was my fault or something. Oh, come *on*, John. You're trying to tell me these rumours are true? That you're going to go public on this thing and make one helluva fool of yourself? Jesus, what are you thinking of?' He reached over to tap Dublensky's elbow, as if to suggest that the whole thing could still be written off as a joke.

'You're not believing me again, Don.' Dublensky slid his

519

coffee aside. His courage was developing a life all its own. 'Silveron's on the British market, Don. Did you know that? There are people there who've gotten sick after one-time exposure. Who've developed symptoms like the Aurora workers. Some of them are kids – '

'*John*. Unsubstantiated conjecture! Pressure-group propaganda!'

Dublensky's accumulated frustration rose into his throat like a wedge. 'These people are sick,' he repeated with difficulty, 'and you're telling me it's nothing to do with you?'

Reedy waved a hand. 'John, John – ' he wheedled. 'Come on – tell me you're going to give up this crazy idea!'

'I . . .'

'*John*. Not only are you totally *wrong* about all this, but you're failing to appreciate what you're taking on.'

The heat was suddenly very great. 'What am I taking on exactly, Don?'

Reedy gestured exasperation. 'For Christ's sake, John. MKI will eat you alive if you don't approach this reasonably.'

In that instant Dublensky felt himself lifted across some divide and deposited effortlessly on the other side.

'Eat me alive?'

'You know what I mean.'

'I don't think I do.'

'Be reasonable, John.'

'And how should I do that?'

'Well – talk the darned thing through, I guess. Sit round a table in a civilised way. Meet us in a spirit of co-operation – '

'Agree to a deal, you mean.'

'Aw, come on – '

'Agree to keep quiet.'

'We must be able to talk this through.'

'Am I set to lose my job? Is that it?'

'*John*. Come *on*.' He gave a false laugh.

The heat burned so hot in Dublensky that he could hardly keep still. He hovered on the edge of the precipice, the chasm clearly visible below, and, feeling no qualms at all, stepped out into the void. 'No deals,' he said.

Reedy sat back in his seat, his mouth puckered with cold displeasure. 'John . . . What's all this about? What's it about? Just tell me.'

Framing his reply, Dublensky saw the irony of the situation.

'Until you came today I wasn't planning to do anything, Don. Not for sure anyway. But now . . . I guess I don't feel too good about your attitude. In fact' – Dublensky exulted in his own boldness – 'it makes me sick.'

Reedy's eyes narrowed, his mouth slackened, he contemplated Dublensky with something like distaste. Crumpling his serviette and placing it deliberately on the table, he said: 'I feel sorry for you, John. I really do.'

Dublensky nodded blankly. 'You may be right.'

Reedy gave it one last shot. 'You won't see sense? You won't change your mind?'

Dublensky thought of Anne, he thought of Tad, and though he felt a sudden sharp fear for them, he knew that he wouldn't change his mind.

Daisy pushed the door shut behind her and stood, gathering her breath. From above, a muffled thump, the reverberation of a slamming door announced the presence of the Greeks, then the house fell quiet again, stifled by the Sunday morning hush.

She stood, matching the room against her memory of the previous evening. The furniture was still herded together in the same haphazard way, the books lay undisturbed on their shelves, the red chair sat by the fire.

There were no obvious signs of an intruder. But then Maynard would be too professional for that.

Out in the road, a horn tooted lightly and, going to the window, Daisy pushed up the lower sash and, supporting the weight of the frame on her shoulders, waved to the Beetle which was double-parked below. Jenny looked up at her, her face pressed close to the windscreen, and signalled a question: Are you sure you'll be all right? Daisy nodded: I'll be fine.

Jenny shook her head as if to say, I give up, then with a last glance to make sure Daisy hadn't changed her mind, drove away.

Daisy eased the broken sash down and, dropping her jacket over the red chair, went to check the answering machine, only to remember that she had left it off. She continued into the kitchen, still looking for signs of Maynard's presence. There were several mugs sitting unwashed on the draining board, an open jar of instant coffee, a coffee-soaked spoon sitting in the sugar bowl – the plasterer, most likely, making himself at home. Otherwise the jars, shelves and racks were possessed of their usual disorganised clutter.

She put a kettle on, prepared some coffee. A familiar routine: a way of re-establishing her territory. Maynard may not have left any visible trace, but like an alley cat he seemed to have left a nasty aura behind him.

As the kettle heated, she drifted towards the bathroom in search of a bottle of witch hazel which she remembered having put in the back of the medicine cabinet somewhere.

Even after regular glances at Jenny's bedroom mirror during the night, the sight of her face still held a lurid fascination, and seeing it now in the surroundings of her own place, it seemed even more macabre, as if a makeup artist had run riot with the rouge and plasticine. The swelling on her cheek had reduced her right eye to a little more than a slit through which an iris swam darkly and uncertainly in a brilliant sea of blood-red that had once been the white. The skin of her cheek, distended by the hugeness of the swelling, was red and taut and burning hot. The bruising continued into her hair to a point somewhere above her ear, which still rang loudly, like an alarm bell going off after the event. But the ringing, though distracting, was mild compared to the headache, a throbbing girdle of pain which a double dose of Panadol had failed to shift.

She found the witch hazel and dabbed at the bruise. What was really needed was ice, and she pottered back into the kitchen to chip some chunks off the solidified lump that was the ice tray.

The couple who'd picked her up off the ground and propped her against the wheel of the Beetle the previous night had pressed a handkerchief to her head, as if she were bleeding. More welcomely, they had also fed her cheap brandy, produced like magic from the inside pocket of the husband's coat. Being long-standing residents of the estate, they were not surprised when she turned down the offer of an ambulance, and, in their relief at not having the bother of explaining their side of the business to the Bill, took her to their flat and put a call through to Jenny.

Wrapping an ice chunk in a tea towel, Daisy pressed it to her face and, making coffee, went into the main room and rooted around in her bag for the Panadol that Jenny had put there. Breaking two out of the bubble pack, she washed them down. Then, going to the desk, she opened the centre drawer and pulled out a pile of notebooks going back two years or so. These spiral-bound A5 pads were her daily records: pages of names, phone numbers, information and ideas jotted down as meetings occurred, as people called or thoughts came to her. Most of her ideas she later transferred to the relevant files or lists, and the phone numbers to her pocket-sized loose-leaf folder which, despite its striking similarity to a Filofax, she refused to call anything but an address book.

It didn't take her long to find the phone number Maynard had quoted in his original letter all those months ago, the number of the friend in Battersea, the place where he was staying for a while and could be contacted between eleven and twelve.

Before she found reasons to put off the call she took the pad to the phone and dialled the number. There was a click, the usual pause, then a deathly whine. She tried again but there was no mistake: the line was disconnected.

The Hertfordshire address would probably be just as useless, though Jenny was going to dig the letter out of the Catch files first thing in the morning and check it, just in case.

Sitting down in the red chair she began to go through her shoulder bag, compartment by compartment, an exercise she had carried out twice already at Jenny's. Her purse had gone, along with its contents: cash, driving licence, library ticket, Green party membership card. But her address book was still there, also her cheque book, note books, miscellaneous papers and documents. Also, her keys. Didn't muggers usually take keys? If not for themselves, then for friends who might want to knock over your flat while you were in hospital?

But then it was possible that the mugger hadn't been interested in the keys because his friend, Maynard, had already had a good look around the flat. The scenario of the mugger and Maynard as a team had a disturbing ring of plausibility to it.

During the early morning, when her splitting head had woken her and she had lain on Jenny's sofabed, dazed with pain, she had attempted to construct another plot, to persuade herself that the mugging had been pure chance, that she had been the victim of nothing more than bad luck, but when she looked at it the other way round and considered how lucky that made Maynard, then her suspicions took on more life.

Besides, the man had been wearing a raincoat. What sort of mugger wore a raincoat?

But if any one thing was needed to convince her, it was the absence of the scrap of paper on which she'd scribbled Maynard's registration number. Looking again now, the scrap – roughly the size of a supermarket receipt – was definitely not there.

Late last night, while under the influence of brandy and Panadol, Daisy had tried to remember the registration. Now, sitting in her old red chair, her head buzzing with coffee, she had another go, jotting down possibilities and comparing them with her previous efforts. The first part of the sequence looked promising in so far as it came out the same each time – G412 – but the final three letters showed a depressingly variable pattern, and the more she worried at her memory the more uncertain it became. After a time, even the first part of the sequence began to lose conviction and, admitting defeat, she dropped the pad to her knee.

No phone number, an unlikely address, a lost car registration. Got me beaten, Maynard. Had me beaten all along. Ran rings round me, in fact. It must have made you laugh, to find someone this simple.

She thought back over the last few months, to the way everything that could possibly go wrong had gone wrong. Peasedale being warned off, the destruction of Octek, the publicising of Nick's identity. Looking at these events from her new vantage point – a half-closed eye, one might say – she now saw that bad luck had very little to do with it, that, on the contrary, there seemed to be an absolute inevitability to what had happened. Maynard – or his friends – seemed to have a flawless seam of information which allowed them to judge their tactics very finely indeed.

But how? What was this infallible source?

And what had brought Maynard here? What had he been hoping to find?

She went to the shelves. The tapes were undisturbed. The books were in their usual order, pressed back against the wall so that the spines of the differently sized volumes formed an irregular line. Yet when she looked more closely she saw that the dust on the shelves had been pulled into tramlines as the books had been slid out one by one. She ran a finger over the compressed page tops, and it seemed to her that some of them were missing their veneer of dust.

She went over to the desk and stared at the familiar stacks of papers, files and magazines that covered the top. Moving slowly round the side, she peered at the desk's ancient cracked leather surface. Finally she found what she was looking for: a shape made dark by being dust-free, a shape that was clear-edged and right-angled, marking the place where a pile of files had been standing before it was moved.

So he had been looking for papers. Yet what would he find that was on paper? She groped for the significance of this thought, fretted at the edges of it, but this too refused to come.

The phone rang. She reached quickly down and flipped on the answering machine.

It was Inspector Brent, sounding tetchy, wanting her to come in and see him the next morning, *if* it would convenient – a note of sarcasm here – and would she please confirm as soon as possible.

She decided to leave the machine on for the rest of the day. Even when Campbell called ten minutes later, she let his voice feed onto the tape. He sounded subdued, depressed, but though she felt a vague shame at not answering him, she couldn't get to grips with Adrian's case now. Time enough tomorrow when the lawyers were back at work, when she could think about returning to Scotland. When she had thought the Maynard business through.

Why had Maynard come looking for papers? She never put anything on paper.

Her brain finally made the connection. *That was it.* Peasedale, Nick . . . Nothing had been in writing. Their connection with Octek had only ever been mentioned person to person. Or –

She was still for a long moment. Then, lowering the cold compress from her face, she went into the kitchen and found the collection of basic tools she had acquired during one of her self-sufficiency drives. Kneeling on the floor in front of the red chair, she unplugged the telephone cord from the wall, and took the cover off the socket. This revealed a simple array of wires and no space for concealment.

The phone itself then. But what was she looking for? How large were these things?

She removed all the visible screws and lifted the casing clear of its base. The inside of the casing was free of extraneous fixtures. She went over the guts of the apparatus wire by wire, connection by connection, but everything looked as though it had been soldered or welded; the two sealed cubes that had seemed vaguely promising had obviously been fixed on some production line.

She reassembled the body of the phone, dropped the handset back in place and rested her head against the side of the chair for a while.

The phone rang. She watched the answerphone whir into life and, watching it, thought: It's you!

Jenny's voice sang out, demanding to know if she was okay and insisting that she call back *immediately* otherwise she'd worry and have to come over again.

The moment she rang off, Daisy had the answerphone cable out of the wall and, a short while later, the front off the socket.

Nothing.

The answerphone itself, with its tape decks, windows, knobs and composite plastic casing, was more resistant to dissection, but finally yielded with the unfastening of four deceptively small screws in places designed to conceal them. The back, a single sheet of alloy, came away to reveal the interior, a dark conglomeration of electronic clutter. She examined it minutely under the table lamp. There were tape receptacles, circuit boards, sealed units, bunches of bound wires. And absolutely nothing that was loose or extraneous.

When at last the machine was together again, she took a rest, had a herb tea, and felt the effects of the Panadol lifting.

The handset was relatively easy: just two screws and a firm tug and it fell into two halves.

And there it was. An oblong, about two inches in length, half an inch square. Dull metallic black in colour, attached to the inside of the casing with some sort of sticky tape. Two wires coming from the ends, fastened to connections near the mouthpiece by tiny alligator clips.

She looked at it for a long time, but did not touch it. Eventually she put the two halves of the handset back together and screwed them up.

She climbed into the red chair, her legs over one arm, her cheek against the back. The headache had returned, pumping

526

more fiercely than ever, and new shafts of pain darted down the side of her skull and into her neck.

She realised that she'd been far, far too modest. She hadn't thought she was important enough for anyone to bother.

Well, Maynard had bothered all right, and Maynard had been well rewarded. Slowly, working through the drumming in her head, she catalogued the information. Conversations with Peasedale, the call to Simon, the explanation of Octek, the mention of Nick. He'd had it on a plate.

The next realisation came to the surface with a great leap, like a submerged bubble.

I've got hard evidence. I've got it right here!

That was what Maynard had heard, that was what had brought him snooping around the flat. The evidence she'd embroidered for Simon, the proof about the Silveron data, the proof that did not exist.

She felt a flutter of satisfaction; she almost laughed. Serve him bloody right, serve his masters bloody right. Let them panic. With that thought, she wondered if the black bug in the phone might yet serve a purpose, though at the moment she couldn't quite see what.

When she woke the light had shifted round until it was shining in a golden rectangle on the wall above the bed. The answering machine had just clicked on. It was Jenny again. Daisy reached down and picked up the phone.

'Now *listen*, you; are you okay?'

'I'm okay.' She lay back, feeling drugged and heavy.

'You should have an X-ray, I'm sure you should have an X-ray.'

'No point. Can't put it in plaster, can they?'

Jenny made more clucking noises, threatened to come over, and was only placated with promises of doctors if things weren't better in the morning. On the point of ringing off, she said: 'Oh, there's a message from Alan. A call he took late on Friday. A Mrs Ackroyd. Came through on the unlisted line, asking for some company that Alan had never heard of. But also asking for you.'

'Ah.'

'She left a number. Dorking.'

Dorking? Duggan, the *Boy's Own* pilot Duggan. But Ackroyd . . .

But no, wait a minute – Duggan's *sister*.

527

'Keen to speak to you, so she said. Shall I deal with it?'

Daisy remembered the invisible black box under her hand and said: 'No . . . Don't worry. It's nothing important. Just give me the number.'

She had a wash and walked down the hill. She tried the Dorking number from the phonebox a few yards from Mr Patel's, but there was no reply. She went into the shop and bought some supper. Mr Patel, his expression twisted into a comic picture of concern at the sight of her face, popped a packet of marshmallows into her bag when she wasn't looking. On her way back she tried the number again, but there was still no one home. As she started up the hill again, she found herself looking over her shoulder. Was it possible? Would they bother with *that* as well? Surely not. And yet why not?

The thought powered her up the last of the hill and kept her occupied while she boiled up a steak-and-kidney pudding with frozen peas. Then she tackled the area around her bed, shifting furniture, clearing the dustsheets, making up the bed.

It was much later, in what felt like the depths of the night, that she heard the phone ringing from a long way off, as if from another room. The answering machine picked up, she heard a voice, a voice from another age, another world, a voice that had her stumbling awake and groping for the receiver.

'It's me,' she interrupted groggily.

'Daisy Field?' asked a soft male voice.

'Yes.'

'Umm. We met in Virginia. Back in July. Umm, Alan Breck. You remember? With Paul Erlinger?'

She pulled herself up on one elbow, struggling to clear her brain. 'Yes. Of course I remember.'

'I wanted to talk. Is this a convenient moment?'

'Yes, yes.' She sat up and fumbled for the light. There was a short silence and for an instant she thought she had lost him. 'Hullo?' she prompted.

'Look, I'm not sure you can help . . .'

'Please, I can help. I can help!'

He gave a short laugh, nervous, cautious. 'That day we met, you seemed . . . I got the feeling that you understood the, er . . . difficulties . . .' His voice hung in the air, awaiting reassurance.

'Oh yes,' she said hastily. 'I understood. I still do.' She saw the dark figure in the diner, the restless hands, the furtive eyes.

'It's . . . well . . . There have been particular problems with EarthForce. You know what I mean?'

She gathered her wits and plunged in, hoping she was on the right track. 'Security problems, you mean? Yes. Yes, I could see that.'

'You could? You could? But . . .' Another long pause. 'It's all right your end? It's – I mean, I'd be safe, would I?'

Even as she began to make firm reassurances, her mind took off in a great leap of fear and she stalled in mid sentence. The black box! Christ! What was she thinking of! Her heart raced, her mouth was suddenly dry.

'What is it?' he asked sharply.

She was silent, in a momentary panic, but even as she fought her way free, it came to her that if she told him to stop talking and the reason why, then she'd lose any trust he might have, and that would be the end of that. She heard herself stalling: 'Sorry – it's the middle of the night here. I dropped the phone.'

A pause. 'It's a big step,' he said uncertainly, as if debating the matter with himself.

'Of course it is,' she said, trying to urge him gently forward without actually feeding facts to the invisible ear under her hand. 'But I can guarantee you all the support you need.'

He said suddenly: 'Look, if I went ahead I'd need some sort of financial security for me and my family, at least until the worst is over. Maybe other kinds of security as well. Could you guarantee that?'

'I guarantee everything. Whatever you need!'

'And it's safe. You're sure?'

God, forgive me this. 'I'm sure.'

'And if I were to make a statement – go public – could you arrange the right outlets – you know, newspapers? TV?'

'Absolutely. I have contacts, good contacts.'

'But here in the US?'

She'd have to work on that, speak to Simon, but this wasn't the time to show anything less than complete confidence. 'Definitely. You just say the word. Just give me the when and how.'

'The when?' He sounded alarmed. 'But *now*. I mean, I don't think it's safe for me here any more, I don't think it's safe for my family. And I thought you'd have the how. I kind of assumed you'd know.' He was ready to be disappointed in her, she realised, ready to back off at any moment.

'Give me a couple of days,' she said rapidly. 'I'll fix everything. Money, security, media coverage.' Sensing he still wasn't convinced, she insisted: 'You call back in two days and if you're not happy with the way I've arranged things, we'll think again. Fair enough?'

'Okay.' There was still an edge of doubt in his voice. 'Okay. Tuesday.'

'Tuesday. Same time.'

When he rang off, she sat for a long time, waiting for her heartbeat to slow down.

Tuesday. Just two days. God.

And the black box: what would Maynard and his friends guess from all this? Had she already put Alan Breck in danger? Christ.

She slept less than four hours more, and started her day well before dawn.

THIRTY-TWO

Schenker, in rare good humour after a sporting weekend in the Scottish Highlands, hummed the melody from *Top Hat* as he unpacked in his apartment high above Bryanston Square.

On Friday he had been the subject of a feature in the *Financial Times* and he reflected happily on the thought that it would have been read by everyone of importance in the City.

A copy lay in his case and he glanced at it now. The photograph was excellent: it had caught the fire of intelligence in his eyes, made a virtue of his rather thin mouth, given him an aura of tension and energy. The interviewer had also been kind: effortless high-flyer; talented trouble-shooter; tipped for greater things. And he had used Schenker's grittiest quotes: *I consider my learning curve hasn't reached its peak. The day you stop learning is the day you stop justifying your salary. Confidence comes from judgement, but growth comes from a certain degree of humility, from constant re-evaluation.*

Good stuff.

As he picked a suit for the morning, the telephone rang. Unhurriedly, he slid the trousers into the overnight press and laid the jacket over the integral hanger before strolling across to the bedside phone. It was, he noticed, almost one a.m.

'I need a word,' said Cramm.

'We'll have half an hour before the divisional meeting.'

'It can't wait.'

Schenker, who rarely slept more than five hours a night at the best of times, offered: 'Seven then. For breakfast.'

531

'But I'm here. In a box, down in the square. It'll take fifteen minutes at the most.'

As he waited, Schenker wondered if his purple silk dressing gown with quilted lapels wasn't a little too flamboyant for Cramm's eyes and, deciding that no risk, however small, was worth taking when it came to office gossip, he changed it for a black kimono.

Cramm appeared wearing holed jeans, an American-football jacket and a day's growth of beard.

'You look as though you've been sleeping rough,' said Schenker in a tone not totally devoid of criticism.

'I thought I'd better come straight over,' Cramm said in a tone that had Schenker bristling slightly as he waved him forward into the living room. Unexcitability had always been one of Cramm's greatest qualities, and it did not please Schenker to see that it seemed to have deserted him.

Offered a drink, Cramm took a Scotch and drank deeply.

'Well?' Schenker demanded.

'There was a fire – you may have read about it – at a research laboratory run by a company called Octek.'

'I hardly had time to read the papers. I was stalking at Lord Crowborough's. Why?'

'It was the láboratory I told you about, the one set up by the Catch woman.'

Schenker, pouring himself a ginger ale, lowered the bottle soundlessly to the bar top. 'You said it wasn't going to get off the ground.'

'There was a time when it looked like that. But in the end it couldn't be stopped.'

'You surprise me.' The sarcasm had been unintentional but he let it stand. If there were difficulties, then Cramm should have told him about them straight away.

Taking his drink, he sat on the sofa opposite Cramm and studied his assistant. In the past few months he had been leaving a lot to this young man. With a spark of unease it occurred to him that Cramm's eagerness to serve, his dogged pragmatism and his precocious grasp of office politics may not have been matched by a corresponding level of judgement.

'Tell me about the fire,' he said.

'It was an animal rights raid. Octek were using rodents. The activists broke in, liberated the animals and set fire to the place – '

Schenker interrupted with an upheld finger. 'These activists, why did they choose Octek?'

Cramm hesitated, uncertain as to the purpose of the interrogation.

'Why not choose a more obvious target?' Schenker persisted. 'One of our own places, for example?'

Cramm got the idea; they were playing detective. 'The place was unguarded,' he said. 'An easy target.'

'And how would they know that?'

An instant followed, a taut silence in which Cramm's gaze hardened. 'They must have been tipped off.'

Schenker felt his mood descend another notch. 'But it was definitely animal rights campaigners, was it?'

'Yes.' Cramm nodded emphatically, his eyes challenging Schenker to disagree, and in that moment Schenker's heart completed its descent. He was no longer in any doubt that Cramm had got carried away, that the situation, if unravelled, would prove ugly. Absorbing this, he felt a flash of anger, barbed with sudden fears and anxieties. Then just as rapidly, he pushed these feelings aside. Anger served no purpose, not until he could see his way clear.

He put his glass to his lips and sipped his drink. 'Go on.'

'They're going to try to pin it on us.'

'Who are?'

'Daisy Field and her group. They're threatening to go to the press.'

'On what evidence?'

'Apparently the police are saying the job was too professional for animal rights people.'

'That cuts both ways, surely. If it was too professional for one group, then why not for another?' Without waiting for a reply he pressed on: 'Is that all?'

Cramm shifted in his seat and studied his glass. 'No . . . There's something else apparently, some other evidence.'

'That could link us to the fire?'

'Yes.'

'And what is it?'

'We don't know.'

'We don't know,' repeated Schenker heavily. 'Well, what *could* it be?'

Cramm retorted defensively: 'I've no idea! There's nothing for them to know.'

Schenker regarded him carefully. This, he decided, was probably the truth. 'So what's the problem?'

Cramm looked surprised that he should miss the obvious. 'Well, the press could make it look very bad for us.'

'But how? No paper will print a story without some facts to back it up. What facts could they have?'

'I don't know, but the Field woman's boyfriend is a *Sunday Times* journalist.'

'So? He's a professional then, isn't he, with a tough editor. No stories without solid substantiation.'

'But she's got something, so she says.'

'Well, she's bound to say that, isn't she? It's called rattling the opposition. Come on, Cramm, if there are no facts, there are no facts!'

Cramm nodded uncertainly.

Schenker said crisply: 'I suggest you draft a suitably dismissive statement for the press, in case they try to run something.' He moved to the edge of the seat, ready to get up and show Cramm out, but the younger man obviously hadn't finished.

'They're planning to carry on,' he said doggedly, 'to start another lab and continue the work. They say none of this is going to put them off.'

'Did you imagine it would? These people have to martyr themselves,' Schenker scoffed with a wave of the hand. 'Let them! Silveron's okay. Nothing they can do is going to show otherwise. They're just going to waste a hell of a lot of money.' He slapped his knees and stood up. 'That's it?' he asked.

'No,' Cramm replied. 'They say they've got evidence that the Silveron trials were fixed. They say someone in a key position is prepared to talk. They're threatening to go public.'

Schenker had the sudden sensation of having been in this job too long, of seeing events come round for the second or third time, like the rerun of a tired old film. 'It's not that madman again, is it? That toxicologist in Chicago – the one with the name?'

Cramm nodded. 'Dublensky.'

He laughed derisively. 'He's just a nutcase!'

'But there's a chance, a risk – he might have documentation.'

'What do you mean, *documentation*?'

'He might have copied some data,' Cramm said eventually, picking his way cautiously through the words. 'Data that shows that some of the Silveron test results were lifted from another product.'

'Lifted?'

'Identical data, duplicate results.'

'And what's meant to be the significance of this – *data*? What's it meant to show?'

'That the Silveron trials were not carried out properly.'

Schenker let out a harsh guffaw that rang loudly in the quiet of the flat. 'You're not suggesting it's *genuine*?'

'Well . . .' Cramm spread his hands in a gesture of helplessness. 'It *looks* genuine, and that's the same thing.'

Schenker felt a shiver of anger. He slapped his palm down on the table. 'I want that document on my desk first thing this morning.'

'I'll try – '

'By ten. At the latest.'

Cramm looked unhappy but did not say it was impossible.

'So what's the bottom line here?' Schenker snapped. 'A press bonanza? A media massacre?'

'That's about it.'

Schenker got to his feet, fighting for air, and strode to the window. What a cock-up! Christ, and he had trusted Cramm to keep a finger on the pulse! With a swoop of resignation, he saw that he was going to have to take personal charge of this, that nothing would get sorted out unless he did.

'Okay,' he said, turning briskly. 'Let's go through it from the top.' He returned to his seat, leaning close over the coffee table, tapping the surface with a forefinger. 'I want a list of damage containment ideas by the morning. I want to know how this Dubinsky – '

'Dublensky.'

' – how this Dublensky can be effectively discredited the moment the first journalist gets on the line. I want to know how he can be neutralised.'

And, he thought to himself, I want to know how to guard my rear, to cover myself in the unpleasant eventuality that this thing blows up in my face. He thought of the cola magnate, and the discussions on Long Island, and wondered how close he was to being offered a new job.

'You might think of how to clip Miss Field's wings too,' he

535

went on. 'Have another go at finding out where she gets all this money from – '

'You didn't hear then? I thought you'd have heard. It was all over the tabloids. It's Nick Mackenzie, the rock star. He was financing everything, the Field woman's salary, the laboratory.'

'How deep?'

'Must have been well over a million. Now he's going to finance Dublensky.'

'Finance him?'

'Bring him over, dish him up to the press.'

'Oh he is, is he! Jesus, who does he think he is? What the hell does he think he's playing at?'

'Saving the world?' sighed Cramm.

'Christ, these people!' Schenker exploded. 'Think they're a cut above the common herd! Think they've the God-given right to tell everyone how to behave!'

Cramm threw him a shrewd look. 'When it comes to behaviour, Mackenzie's got nothing to boast about.'

'Oh?'

'He's been seeing Mrs Driscoll. Every day.' He paused significantly. 'And some nights.'

Schenker stared unseeing at Cramm, then looked down at the table, gripped by a sudden pang, the nature of which he couldn't identify but which left him off-balance, almost breathless.

'Mrs Driscoll? Mrs *Driscoll*?' He glanced back at Cramm and, seeing that it was true, murmured: 'Well . . .' Then, aware of Cramm's gaze, added: 'What a very stupid woman she is.'

It was the same Rolls that had picked her up on the evening she had first met Schenker, Susan realised. Leather seats, walnut trim, glass partition screening the grey-uniformed driver and, best of all, something she hadn't noticed before, an old-fashioned voice tube with a brass spout.

'Does this thing actually work?' she cried delightedly, pulling the tube from its bracket and whisking off the cap.

Schenker glanced briefly across. 'Certainly.' But his look didn't encourage her to try it, and she replaced the tube with a shrug.

The car was heading up the Brompton Road towards Knightsbridge. 'Where are we going?' she asked brightly.

'I thought we'd drive round the park. Would you like to be dropped back at Harrods?'

'Round the park? How mysterious! I thought you were going to take me somewhere exciting. To the Dorchester at least.' She added teasingly: 'Rather clandestine, isn't it, a drive round the park? People will think we're meeting secretly.' She watched for Schenker's discomfiture, and was rewarded with the sight of his tongue flicking nervously over his lips. What a character he was! She was almost fond of him in a repugnant sort of way. So desperate to succeed, so childish in his anxiety to get things right, applying himself to London society with the same humourless intensity he applied to his business life.

He answered: 'I thought it would be better to talk here.' He was looking ahead, watching the traffic.

'Ooh dear,' she said, making a face. 'This sounds ominous.'

She kept her tone light. Whatever this was about, she wasn't going to be robbed of her mood, which was euphoric.

Schenker didn't respond immediately. It wasn't until they had passed under the Bowater building and were driving along the South Carriage Drive that he began to speak in a flat monotone. 'The Kershaw woman. She's been asking for money again. Additional expenses, was how she put it.'

Susan regarded the sky which until an instant ago had looked unblemished, and, despite her intentions, felt her euphoria deflating. She looked accusingly at Schenker but his profile was unreadable. 'And so? Will you give it to her?'

'We already have.'

She felt a flutter of relief. Of course he had. Schenker knew which side his bread was buttered on.

'Unfortunately it's unlikely to finish there,' said Schenker. 'She'll come back for more.'

What was Schenker trying to do to her? She shot him a furious look. 'Oh?' she replied stiffly. 'And why do you think that?'

He was examining the traffic with concentration. 'Well, it's rather an attractive proposition, isn't it? A limitless supply of cash.'

'She can't be that stupid, surely. I mean, she can't think it'll go on for ever.'

'She's already making noises again,' he interrupted smoothly.

A tremor of annoyance passed through Susan. Schenker was playing games with her, trying to undermine her happiness.

'But she can be stopped, can't she?' said Susan, unable to suppress a hint of desperation in her voice. 'I mean, it's ridiculous. The woman's behaving like a criminal.'

'And how would you suggest she be stopped?' He threw her a questioning glance, and she caught a glint of something unfamiliar in his eye, a coolness, a spark of hostility. It was another side of Schenker, one she had never seen before.

'There must be a way,' she argued. 'I don't know . . . I mean, can't she be threatened with legal action or something?' This, she well knew, was not a realistic proposition, but then she could hardly be expected to provide serious answers. Problem-solving was Schenker's province, and she was surprised, not to say annoyed, that he should want to consult her about it. He had seen to all the arrangements, had struck the deal, whatever it was, and now he would have to see the matter through.

Schenker said: 'Sadly, I really don't think there's much more I can do.'

Susan looked at him sharply. 'What do you mean?'

Schenker turned his head towards her, his black button eyes unblinking. 'Simply that I have done all I can and if this woman comes back . . . Well . . .' He lifted his shoulders slightly.

'What are you saying?' She almost prodded him on the arm, she was so irritated with him.

'That there'll be no more money.'

Susan stared at him, trying hard to interpret this. Did he simply mean he was going to get tough with the woman, keep her quiet in some other way? Or did he mean what she feared he meant, something so unpleasant she could hardly bring herself to think about it?

'But what happens if this woman gets difficult?' she asked, feeling her way forward. 'What happens if she threatens to go to the press?'

Schenker's eyes dropped slowly to the floor before coming back to her face to resume their steady gaze; his mouth curved down at the corners. She realised this was his way of showing regret.

538

'You'd let her . . .?' she asked incredulously. 'You'd *let* her?'

'Hopefully it won't come to that.'

'*But you'd let her!*'

He turned a palm upward. 'I'd really have no choice.'

It was a moment before Susan could speak. 'But what about Tony?' she cried. 'What about everything he's done for you? God, you have an odd way of showing gratitude! After all he's *done* for you!'

'I'm not quite sure what you mean. We've enjoyed a pleasant working relationship, your husband and I, but I wouldn't have said we owed each other any favours. On the contrary, the minister has gone so far out of his way to avoid showing partiality since he's been in office that, if anything, I would say my company has suffered from our association, rather than the other way round.'

Was this what it was about, then? Sour grapes? Or was he after favours from Tony, in exchange for which he would find more money for the Kershaw woman? Was this an elaborate way of exerting pressure? Susan felt as if she had been plunged into a pit blindfold.

'But you're implicated in this business as well!' she protested. 'If the woman talks to the press, you'll get dragged into it too!'

'Oh? And how would that be?'

'Well, you introduced her to Tony for a start.'

'Hardly,' he murmured in a tone of mild distaste. 'They met at a party. I didn't even know the girl.'

'In France then. That weekend.'

'No, you're quite wrong. Your husband made all the arrangements.'

It came to her then: he was prepared to let Tony sink without trace.

But perhaps he wasn't quite so clever as he thought he was. He'd forgotten one rather important point. She rang triumphantly: 'Well, what about the money then? She'll say who gave it to her, won't she? She'll tell them it was you!'

With forbearance, in the tone of a teacher explaining basics to a child, he said: 'She has no idea where the money comes from. She certainly has no reason to think it comes from us. And even if she were to get the idea, she wouldn't be able to substantiate it.'

'Oh, come on! Who else could it come from?'

But even as Susan finished asking the question, she knew the answer. Tony. Of course. Tony.

She turned hastily to stare out of the window, trying to absorb the implications of this terrifying development. The car was approaching Speakers' Corner, passing the row of parked tourist coaches that lined Park Lane even in late October. In that moment Susan grasped what she should have understood from the beginning, that Schenker had thought this out very carefully, that he had left nothing to chance, that if there was a scandal then one person at least was going to emerge unscathed.

'You'd *let* this happen?' she repeated weakly, feeling herself close to tears.

'Really, we did what we could.' It seemed to her that he was suppressing a sigh. 'Under the circumstances . . .' He waved a hand as if it wasn't worth explaining all over again.

Lifting her chin, she asked bravely: 'So why are you telling me all this? What d'you want?'

'Want?'

'From me.'

'From you? Why, nothing. Nothing at all.' He seemed surprised and mildly offended. 'No, no. The only thing I wanted was to warn you about the wo— about the situation. To tell you I could do no more.' But his tone was a little too emphatic, his surprise a little too polished to be entirely convincing, and she knew she wouldn't feel any confidence on this point until the drive was over. But if he was planning to say anything he wasn't in a hurry, and they sat in silence as the car swept into the north carriageway.

Finally Schenker said: 'Things are very tough at the moment.'

Was this her cue? Maybe. But she wasn't in the mood to make things easy for him.

Schenker, seeing he wasn't going to get any help, went on: 'Your friend Mr Mackenzie's causing me a few headaches.'

Before she could prevent herself, she had jerked her head round to stare at Schenker. Of all the lines he might have taken, of all the approaches, this was the last she had expected. For an awful moment it occurred to her that he might know about her and Nick, but in the next instant she

540

rejected the thought. No one, and especially not Schenker, could possibly know about that. Much as she'd wanted to shout it from the rooftops, much as it had killed her to suppress her exhilaration, she hadn't told a soul, not even her best girlfriend. But then, unless you wanted the entire world to know, you never told your best girlfriend.

No, it couldn't be that. What could he mean? Then it came to her. 'The laboratory, his project . . .?'

Schenker twisted in his seat to face her. 'He has this obsession with one of our products. I don't know why. He seems to think it harmed his wife. Though at the beginning the villain was meant to be something completely different – a wood preserver named Reldane. But when that proved harmless, he lighted on Silveron. Frankly, we're mystified as to why he should go to these extraordinary lengths to try and prove that there's something wrong with what is basically one of our best products, a substance that's been tested to within an inch of its life.' He leaned closer and, resting his arm along the seat back, extended a finger as if to touch her shoulder. 'Oh, don't misunderstand me. I'm sorry he was the victim of those animal rights people. But at the same time I can't pretend I'm actually crying about it.'

Here was the confident approachable Schenker again. It was as if the unpleasantness of the last few minutes had been an unfortunate interlude which, now it was out of the way, could be ignored. She realised how little she understood this man, and how much he alarmed her.

'Well, he's finished with all that now,' she said. She added quickly: 'So I understand anyway.'

'Finished? Really?' His tone was polite but unbelieving. 'I'm reliably informed that he's already setting up a second laboratory, that he has every intention of continuing with this obsession. More unfortunate for him, I also understand that he and these Catch people have fallen victim to some forged laboratory data and are planning to make allegations to the press that they cannot possibly substantiate. We would have to sue, of course. It would be an ugly business, do him a lot of harm. As well as causing us a great deal of trouble.'

She had got the idea. Somewhere in here was the bargain, the price of Tony's safety. She heard herself say: 'Perhaps I can help . . . Speak to him . . .'

He considered: 'Well . . .' he said doubtfully. 'I hardly think an appeal to reason is going to have much effect, even coming from you.'

Even from her? Did he know after all? The thought bewildered her. And what did he want if he didn't want her to speak to Nick? A small worm of dread curled in her stomach.

The car was heading south through the park towards the Serpentine. The driver half turned his head. Schenker, catching the movement, picked up the voice tube and told him to carry on. So there had been a plan to stop, a plan which was no longer necessary. Schenker obviously expected to finish his business before they reached Harrods.

Unable to bear the uncertainty any longer, she asked: 'What do you suggest then?'

He put on a show of faint surprise, shrugging slightly. 'Suggest? Why, nothing.' He waved a hand into space. 'No, I'm just surprised that Mackenzie should want his life subjected to scrutiny, and by a press which holds nothing sacred. It's a rare man who has nothing to hide.'

Susan was very still. A chill crept up from her stomach.

Schenker interleaved his fingers and pushed out his lips, his movements drawn out, almost languid. The dark eyes travelled slowly across to Susan and stared at her with a look that, while pretending to be quizzical, was deeply knowing. 'And Mr Mackenzie has a great deal to hide, so I believe.' Any last doubts she might have had as to his meaning were dispelled by the glint of personal contempt that he couldn't quite conceal.

She looked quickly out of the window before her face crumpled.

He knew. The realisation was only marginally less shocking than the knowledge that this was no idle disclosure, that at the end of the day this dreadful little man wouldn't hesitate to make use of it, to betray her in the same way that he was preparing to betray Tony.

Chemical-campaigning pop star and agriculture chief's wife. The papers would have a field day. Tony's career would never survive it. She leaned her head against the glass.

They were in the traffic queue at Alexandra Gate before she felt steady again.

'I could talk to him,' she offered, gaining strength as she said it. 'Persuade him that publicity wouldn't be a good idea.'

542

'Mmm?' Schenker seemed almost bored. 'And d'you think he'd listen?'

'Yes,' she said defensively. Then she remembered Nick and his principles and felt a sudden doubt. If it came to a choice between her and his beloved project, how would he decide? Publicity about their affair wouldn't frighten him at all, she realised bitterly. He wouldn't care, he would tell her to go to hell, just like he'd told her to go to hell all those years ago. Nothing would frighten him. Nothing except . . .

The answer came to her then. Part of her was shocked and repulsed by the idea, but another part of her reached out for it avidly. There was a sort of justice in it, an awful sort of satisfaction.

A last instant of uncertainty, then she said: 'There's something he wouldn't be happy about, something he'd hate the world to know.'

She could feel Schenker watching her. 'Oh?' he said casually. 'And what's that?'

Susan told him and for the first time during that dreadful drive she felt a glimmering of hope.

Hillyard whistled as he bounded up the stairs two at a time. In this sort of quiet he reckoned it was less obvious to make a bit of noise than to creep around surreptitiously. As he came up the final flight he switched the tote-bag he was carrying to his left hand and prepared to let himself into the flat, spinning the door keys round his finger as if he owned the place. On the landing he paused for a moment, listening hard, before resuming his whistling, more softly this time.

There were footsteps on the stairs, coming down; males gabbling in some foreign language. He was sliding the key into the lock when they turned onto the landing. He took his time before looking round, his lips still pursed into a whistle, and smiled briefly and impersonally at the two swarthy men approaching. They fell silent, eyeing him liberally as they passed. Well, they might not know what to make of him, but he had their mark all right. A pair of queens, and no mistake.

He let himself into the flat without looking back. By this time he knew his way around the place so well that he could see at a glance what had changed. The furniture was different – she had moved two chairs round – a dust sheet lay in a tangle on the floor, and a new pile of papers had appeared on

543

the desk. And then there was the ceiling. The fresh plaster was dry in the centre but still damp at the edges where it met the cornice, and a right mess down one of the walls where the water from the tank had got behind the wallpaper and bubbled it away.

He went straight to the phone and, careful to weight the rest so it would ring if someone called, unfastened the handset with a screwdriver and eased the halves apart. He looked at the microtransmitter for a moment, remembering the sounds on the tape recording, the clunks as she had unscrewed the fastenings, the creaking of plastic as she had removed the casing, and then the long silence. She must have seen it: she couldn't have missed it. And if she hadn't been looking for this, what else could she have been looking for?

She had seen it, but she had left it in place. She hadn't told anybody, she hadn't called the police. Clever girl. Well, almost.

The transmitter was fixed with double-sided tape, and now he pulled it free, and unclipping the tiny alligator clips slid it into his pocket.

He put the halves back together and refastened the screws. Then, going to the main telephone socket on the skirting board, he removed the socket plate and replaced it with a new one from his bag, his work interrupted only by a squawk from his walkie-talkie, which gave him a moment's fright. He checked with Biggs down in the van, but there was nothing brewing; just interference.

He had a quick look through the new pile of papers on the desk. Insurance claim forms, magazines.

Then the final task. He took some time mulling over the exact location for his little present. He went through her hanging cupboard and bathroom drawers, but lingered longest over the underwear in the top drawer of the chest in the main room. All in all, it would be the most fitting place. He fingered a pair of panties and dangled them in the air, both repelled and fascinated by the thought of catching her bodily scents. Then he ran his hand up inside the chest to make sure there would be no gaps once the drawer was closed again.

He pushed the drawer closed except for an opening of about three inches, then went back to the tote-bag. Shuddering with physical excitement, unable to suppress a crow of anticipation, he pulled on a glove and slipped his hand carefully into the

544

holdall. After a moment's scrabbling, he had his prey. A big beauty who went into the drawer good as gold.

Hillyard was all finished and out of the place in eight minutes flat.

THIRTY-THREE

Nick buzzed for Mrs Alton and looked at the house phone accusingly when it failed to respond. He peered at his watch. Nine. Could it be that late? He looked up and realised it had probably been dark for some time. Rolling his chair clear of the console, he leaned back and stretched, pushing his arms high over his head and giving a long shuddering sigh. Eight, no, nine hours he'd been here.

He had completed – what? He leaned forward to count the pages – ten pages of manuscript; maybe five minutes' finished music. It had come with breathtaking speed. The orchestration was still a bit rough, of course, definitely in need of refinement, but it had begun to develop the sort of texture he was after and he didn't think he'd be too ashamed to hear it performed in its present form. Since Sunday he had finished one complete section, or, to be more accurate, a movement, though that was rather a grand title for something that was just eight minutes long. It was a lyrical section entitled *In a Summer Garden*. Next would come *Dawnlight*. The movement he had been working on today, an allegro section which would come before both of these, had not yet found a name. Something that suggested life or joy, he thought. The whole thing was going to be called simply *Thanksgiving*.

The structure of the piece, with its elegiac choral tone, was loosely that of a requiem, but he wasn't going to call it that, not only because it would sound presumptuous and people would think he was trying to put himself up there with Mozart and Fauré, but because he didn't want to be

546

constrained by the conventions of the form. Also, and even more to the point, the requiem mass was about death in its direst sense, quite the opposite of what he was trying to achieve in this celebration of life.

Perhaps *Thanksgiving* was too bland; perhaps *Last Song* would be better. While he considered this he got up and went down the passageway to the kitchen, suddenly ravenous.

Mrs Alton, who knew him only too well, had left a large notice on the table, directing him to the various dishes in the fridge and larder, with instructions for microwaving.

The sounds of the night, inaudible in the heavily clad studio, now wafted softly against the dark window. Irrationally, he felt conspicuous in the light, as if someone were out there watching him from the rising land beyond the window, and he went to lower the blind. He paused to take a look into the darkness. He could just make out a tall beech, caught against the glimmer of the sky. It moved gently, the last of its thin leaves causing the stars to wink uncertainly. From somewhere a long way off came the faint whistle of a night creature.

That morning he had walked to the western woods. The smell of autumn was strong, the air sharp and damp. He had felt a great surge of feeling, something close to exultation. It was partly the work, of course, the humming of the music in his brain, but something else too: a sense of liberation, a growing feeling that he was breaking free of the old patterns of despair and hopelessness.

Eating in solitary splendour he listened to the silence, feeling the emptiness of the house around him, and decided that, in spite of everything, he might learn to love the place again. When he wasn't here he might offer it to other people, make it into a retreat for composers and musicians, set up a special trust named after Alusha.

The ideas kept him occupied to the end of the meal. Soon his mind was darting back to his music and, restless, he scooped up some fruit and started for the studio again.

At the kitchen door a faint sound caught him and he stopped to look back over his shoulder, thinking the fruit must have overbalanced in the bowl. But the room was quiet, the fruit undisturbed. He tried to pin the sound down – the microwave cooling? The contents of the dishwater settling? – but the sound had been too indistinct.

He thought of security. Had Mrs Alton locked all the doors when she left? Were the sensors on?

He hovered indecisively before depositing the fruit back on the kitchen table and beginning a round of the house.

The passage beyond the studio was dark, the estate office darker still. The outside door which led from the office into the courtyard on the east side of the house was securely locked and bolted. Retracing his steps, he checked the front door then, skirting the packing cases which still lined the walls, went to the door of the drawing room. Switching on a light, he glanced towards the french windows at the far end, then continued into the boot room, which had been a gun room in another life. Here another external door gave out on to the western side of the house, close to the rose garden. He didn't bother with a light, but felt his way past the coats in the half darkness, watching his own outline approaching in the dark reflections of the glass-panelled door. As he tested the locks he looked out into the night, but the sky seemed darker on this side and he couldn't make out the shapes of the trees.

Back in the kitchen he picked up the fruit before remembering the last and most frequently used door. Biting off a piece of apple he went through the small hall at the rear of the kitchen into the scullery, which served as a back lobby. It was a large room and dark, its shadows pierced by the green eyes of three giant freezers. From the boiler room next door came the low hum of the heating plant.

Next to the door was a narrow window. As he reached for the door handle he peered through it and saw that the starlight had faded and the outline of the beech had become less distinct: a deeper blackness against an uncertain sky.

Then the darkness shifted.

He thrust his eye closer to the glass.

Something had moved, but what?

Suddenly his eye was brought down to the splash of light falling from the bottom of the kitchen window. A foot had come into view. A booted foot, heavy, large. It was placing itself cautiously on the flagstone. After a moment, the other foot appeared, feeling its way forward. The figure above was in darkness apart from the side of the leg, the shadow of a hand.

Not Duncan: Duncan would come straight in. Not one of

the estate workers: they'd ring at the courtyard door. No: this person was too furtive, this person was hoping not to be heard.

Pulse racing, Nick abandoned his apple, threw the banana on the floor, and reached for the door to throw the lock. The next instant he wavered and pulled back. No, let the bastard come in, let him get the appropriate welcome.

Reaching down to the door again, but stealthily, he tested the key to make sure the lock wasn't set, then, trembling and hot for battle, he went on a feverish hunt for a weapon – a stick, a metal bar, anything that would carry some weight.

Panting fretfully, cursing under his breath, he worked his way rapidly round the room, feeling for implements, long, sharp, heavy – he would have taken anything – and found nothing but cans, sacks of potatoes, catering-sized coffee tins.

A knock. Soft, like a tap.

He froze. It came again, a little louder.

He tiptoed along the front of the freezers until he was in the shadows to the far side of the door, the best position from which to spring an attack. An elbow locked around the throat should do it. If not that, an arm-lock up the back. His hand-to-hand technique wasn't too hot, but he mentally rehearsed the grip and twist needed to immobilise his enemy.

The knocking came again, a louder more confident rap that was designed to be heard. It figured: he'd want to be sure the house was empty, he'd want to know he wasn't going to be disturbed.

A scrunching of feet as the man shifted his weight, then a thunderous rap that had the door bouncing on its hinges. Through the window the outside light sprang on; the man's rapid movements must have triggered the vibration sensor.

Nick felt a moment of doubt. Could it be friend rather than foe? Should he take a look? But no – what friend crept up to one's door so as to avoid activating the security lights?

In the ensuing silence, the sound of the handle turning had his stomach barrelling up into his ribs. He retreated slightly, to get a better run at it.

The handle ground on. The sound ceased. It was a moment before he realised that the door was already swinging open, coming rapidly towards him. Then it stopped. In the light from the kitchen, the man was clearly outlined as he stepped into the room. Large, heavy.

The man paused, as if to listen, then pulled the door closed behind him.

Perhaps Nick made a sound, perhaps the other man suddenly sensed his presence, but the next instant he was spinning round with an audible gasp.

Nick, himself startled, went in a split second too late. He knew it was too late because as he went for the man's arm to try for the arm-lock he saw the arm curling upwards to block his strike.

Having missed his move, he went for anything he could get, scrabbling to get a grip on his opponent's shoulder, flailing for the wrist of the blocking arm. At the same time he tried to hook a foot round the intruder's ankle and knock him off balance. The man was shouting something, but whatever it was Nick didn't hear and pressed on. The advantage of surprise was gone, and the other man was recovering fast. He kicked Nick's foot away as easily as if it were some mild obstruction, and, neatly reversing the position, hooked his leg behind Nick's.

Nick might have been able to cope with that if it hadn't been for the hand that came from somewhere under the cover of the blocking arm and splayed itself against the underside of his chin, snapping his head backwards with a nasty jerk. Abandoning all thoughts of attack, Nick tried to twist away, at the same time pulling the iron-clawed fingers away from his chin. But as his weight was driven back, he came up against the man's leg and, feeling his balance going, pushed out a hand in the direction of the man's head to grab what he could.

The man was trying to speak again, but Nick was too busy finding hair and part of an ear to listen. Getting a firm grip, he twisted hard. He heard the other man yelp with pain, but any triumph he might have felt was shortlived when the pressure on his chin failed to lessen; if anything it intensified. He made a last effort to twist away, but somehow the intruder had got a vice-like grip on his shoulder. God, he was strong. It was like tussling with a machine.

Finally Nick felt his weight begin to topple. Determined not to go down alone, he held on grimly to the patch of scalp. The other man came down all right; his weight – what felt like a good eighteen stone – landed right on top of Nick. But even as the man was on his way down, he must have been planning

550

his next move because he quickly straddled Nick's body and, letting go of his chin, pinned his shoulders effortlessly to the floor with one arm, while conjuring up a spare hand from somewhere to bolt itself round Nick's throat. One didn't have to be a martial arts enthusiast to realise he had done this sort of thing before.

One feel of those steely fingers closing round his neck and Nick felt a punch of real fear.

'I'm not here to harm you!' came a deep voice. 'Just let go ma head, for God's sake.'

For an instant the hand around Nick's throat increased its pressure, to show what it could do if it really tried. Not needing a second hint, Nick loosened his grip on the man's scalp and immediately felt the hand withdraw from his neck.

For an instant neither of them moved, their panting loud in the gloom.

'Aye, but you gave me a shock!' came a deep voice.

'Who the hell – ! Get the fuck off me!'

'Sure. Sure.' His tone was surprisingly contrite. He moved hastily, rolling clear and clambering to his feet. 'I didna' mean to go fightin' you. It was just the shock. By God, but you were like a devil there.' He gave a low gasp. 'You nearly had me . . . And no mistake.'

Nick, recovering fast, scrambled to his feet. 'Who the hell – !'

In the gloom he saw the man leaning against the wall, gathering his breath. 'It's Campbell,' the voice said. 'Alistair Campbell.' He held up a defensive hand. 'Now don't go mad, Mr Mackenzie. You'd best listen to me, or you may regret it. I came specially to warn you, do you see?'

'Jesus,' Nick howled angrily, still feeling the fingers at his throat, 'I could get you arrested for this. Trespass, for Christ's sake . . . You've no right to go creeping about, scaring the shit out of people. What the hell's wrong with ringing the door bell like everyone else?'

'What, at the gate there? You mightna' have let me in.'

'Up here then, for Christ's sake!'

'I didna' want to meet with the police.'

Nick, suddenly exhausted, propped himself against a freezer. 'The police?'

'That's what I came to tell you, Mr Mackenzie. They're on their way. At this very moment.'

'What the hell are you talking about?' He felt like a drink. No – not a drink. Coffee. Striding shakily past Campbell, he tottered into the kitchen and made for the percolator.

'They're comin' right now, Mr Mackenzie,' said Campbell, hurrying along behind. 'I have it on good authority' – a tone of confidentiality came into his voice – 'a friend at the local police. I thought you might need to know.'

Nick wasn't in the mood for this obtuse conversation. He was still smarting from the speed of Campbell's victory. 'Look, I don't know what the hell you're on about,' he retorted, pouring his coffee.

'It's a squad from Glasgow.' Campbell drew in his lips. 'From the drug squad.'

Nick guffawed. 'The drug squad? Don't make me laugh. I've never touched the stuff. No, laddie,' he wagged an irate finger, 'you've got things wrong! If anyone's going to get into trouble tonight, it's going to be you!'

Campbell shuffled, his face creased into an expression of almost childish alarm. 'Mr Mackenzie, you have to believe me. This is no joke.'

There was an earnestness about the man that caused Nick's anger to subside a little – his anger, but not his incredulity. 'No joke, eh? Well then, they're in for a big disappointment, aren't they?'

'They've a warrant, Mr Mackenzie.'

Nick paused, the coffee half-way to his mouth. There was a certainty in Campbell's tone that was beginning to unnerve him. For the first time he considered the possibility that there might be some truth in what he was saying.

While he was trying to make sense of the idea, there was a loud buzz from the far side of the room.

The two men exchanged glances.

Nick slowly put down his cup. 'The gate,' he said.

Campbell bounced forward on the balls of his feet, poised for action. 'Shall I hold them off? Keep them busy?'

Nick didn't dare imagine what Campbell had in mind. 'But I tell you, there's nothing here!' he said harshly, striding across to the videophone and looking at the screen. Two cars, two men standing in the foreground, both in plain clothes. He felt a sudden unreasoned panic, as if he had something to feel guilty about.

On the screen one of the men reached forward, his hand

552

growing disproportionately large in the distortions of the fish-eye lens. The buzzer sounded again.

Nick lifted the handset. He saw the two men cock their heads as they heard the click.

Suddenly the scene lurched in front of him, the heat drained from his face.

'What is it?' Campbell's hoarse whisper sounded at his elbow.

Nick fell back, staring dumbly at the wall as he tried to fight himself clear of the thought that was ricocheting round his brain. '*God . . .*'

'Here.' Campbell took the handset from Nick's faltering grasp and barked a peremptory. 'Hullo?'

It took Nick a few seconds to gather his wits, about as long as it took Campbell to have a grudging conversation with the men at the gate and, capping the receiver, to turn questioningly to Nick. 'They've a warrant all right. Shall I . . ?'

Nick gave a dazed nod, already retreating. By the time Campbell had pressed the entry button, he was beginning to run, sprinting into the hall and up the stairs. In the bedroom, he pulled open the wardrobes, now largely empty, and progressed rapidly through the drawers, scrabbling through the contents and slamming them shut again. At Alusha's bedside cabinet he pulled himself up short, thinking: Slow, slow. Don't miss anything. Crazy to hurry now.

Her clothes had gone months ago, donated to charity, but smaller belongings remained, things he hadn't got round to clearing away. He dropped to his knees and went through the main compartment, a wide cupboard with two shelves. Books, Walkman, tapes, magazines. As he moved to the drawer above, he was aware that Campbell had entered the room and was hovering at the window.

Jewellery, Panadol, face cream, hairbrush, hairbands, pencils, tissues, cotton wool . . .

Campbell made a warning sound, but Nick had already heard the scrunch of car wheels on the drive.

His hand closed over a small jar half hidden by the bag of cotton wool balls. Rapidly he unscrewed the top and put his nose to the white powder. Sticking a finger in, he took a lick, resealed the jar and jammed it in his pocket. There might be more somewhere. *Where, Alusha?*

A car door slammed. He caught Campbell's eye as he sped

past him into Alusha's bathroom and started on the double stack of drawers either side of the dressing table. Eye makeup, skin makeup, lotions, creams.

The front door bell sounded deep in the hall.

'I'll keep them busy, shall I?' called Campbell from the bedroom.

'No!' He shot a drawer home and wrenched out the next. Belts, scarves, trinkets, haircombs. The travelling drawer next: sun lotion, fly repellents, stomach remedies.

The door bell sounded again.

Straightening up, he lunged for the corner cupboard. Nothing. *Where, Alusha?* Feeling the sweat on his ribs, he brushed past Campbell and hurried into the dressing room that he had shared with Alusha.

The door bell rang again, but this time someone was leaving his finger on it.

Her cupboards were empty, the shoe racks bare. He began to lose hope.

'Let me search!' hissed Campbell, grabbing his arm. 'Just tell me where – '

'I don't know! I don't know!' he replied fretfully. '*Somewhere . . .*'

The police were hammering at the door now, their shouts floating up through the window.

'I don't know!' Nick cried as much in anguish as exasperation.

'They'll break the door.'

Nick slouched, his energy gone, and realised he had resigned himself to giving up the search. He made for the stairs, turning sharply at the top so that Campbell almost bowled into him.

'Get rid of this,' he said, thrusting the jar into Campbell's hand. 'And I mean, get *rid* of it.'

Campbell gave a fierce nod and slipped soundlessly away, heading, it seemed, for the back stairs whose location he seemed to know as well as he knew the rest of the house.

Nick's story about having been in the soundproofed studio unable to hear the doorbell and the staff having inexplicably disappeared did not impress the police, and certainly not the detective inspector, a fiftyish man, short and overweight with heavy jowls and a broken nose, nor his second-in-command, a young detective sergeant who, with his black leathers and

554

razor-cut hair, looked like something out of *Mad Max*. The rest of the men immediately fanned out and, though he couldn't be sure, he had the feeling some of them made straight for the lavatories to see if they could find evidence of recently flushed drugs.

He thought suddenly of Campbell. Would he – ? Dear God, let him have had more sense. Anywhere but the lavatories.

There were seven or eight officers altogether, sullen men with hard staring eyes, all Glaswegians as far as he could make out, their accents as impenetrable as their expressions.

They were thorough, or at least he assumed they were, because they were there a long time. After calling his solicitor, a privilege grudgingly permitted half an hour after he'd requested it, he sat in the library, looking into the fire, trying very hard not to think of the snooping hands going through Alusha's things, occasionally glancing up to find the sergeant's eyes boring into him. Despite himself, aware that he shouldn't be rattled by such transparent bullying, he felt unnerved.

What had triggered this little visit? It was no accident, that was for sure; they wouldn't have gone to all this trouble without a tip-off. His first thought was that the dealer had talked. Going by the unlikely name of Ned Sunshine, he was supplier of drugs to the aristocracy and other branches of show business, and had been recommended by Joe. But why now? Why after so long? And why single out Nick?

After a time the inspector came back into the library and began a plodding question-and-answer session. Was Nick in possession of illegal substances? Had he ever purchased illegal substances? Had drugs ever been used on the premises?

Nick kept his voice level, showing what he hoped was the right degree of indignation without actually losing his temper, although as the inspector's questions grew more asinine and repetitive his control became patchy.

A knock on the door brought a welcome if astonishing interruption. It was all Nick could do not to stare as Campbell appeared, preceded by a hazardously balanced tray of mugs, and came cautiously across the room, eyes fastened on the drinks as if his life depended on it. He managed the transition onto the persian rug all right and, after a moment's alarm, successfully negotiated a protruding table, then, his breath rasping audibly, his mouth puckered with concentration, he lowered the tray to the inspector's elbow. His old tweed jacket, visibly frayed, a large and mysterious stain on the hip, added a certain distinction to the idea of Campbell as a butler, and Nick watched in fascination as he straightened, set his sights firmly on the mugs again, and advanced across the hearth.

As he lowered the tray, he looked directly at Nick and dropped a heavy wink. Nick, needing more reassurance, raised a questioning eyebrow. Campbell gave an imperceptible nod. 'All gone,' he whispered.

The mug contained coffee, not bad coffee at that. As Campbell paused at the door, Nick called: 'Thank you, Campbell.'

Tucking the tray under his arm, he gave a slight bow. 'Not at all, sir.'

After that Nick allowed himself some optimism, which, as he should have known, was bound to be fatal. Five minutes later a young officer came jauntily into the room and, with an unmistakable flourish, handed the inspector a small screw-top jar.

'A bag in the bottom of a wardrobe, sir.'

The inspector unscrewed it and sniffed. He held out the open jar and said: 'And how do you explain this, Mr Mackenzie?'

THIRTY-FOUR

Number nineteen Linden Gardens, the home of Jane Ackroyd, sat at the end of a road of identical bow-fronted houses with pebbledash rendering and steep gables, distinguished from each other by the colourful paintwork of the mock-Tudor beams on the gable ends and the various sugary hues of the pebbledash.

Daisy walked up the path an hour late. There had been a morning meeting with Mrs Bell's new lawyer in Glasgow which had overrun, a long call to Jenny in London to check on progress on the arrangements for the arrival of Alan Breck, and, as a final hurdle, a delay on the Glasgow shuttle. But then it was an achievement to have reached Dorking at all.

In Chelmsford the previous morning, Inspector Brent had kept her for over an hour, asking questions about insurance cover, business associates, and – his favourite expression – those who might wish her *harm*. He floated concepts that would have been quaint if they weren't so unlikely – a spurned boyfriend? A disgruntled former employee? The possibility that there might have been an entirely different sort of villain didn't seem to occur to him, and she hadn't bothered to put him on the right track. At each mention of *harm* his gaze invariably travelled to her swollen and multi-coloured eye until, unable to contain his curiosity any longer, he asked in his deathless style if it was possible that the circumstances surrounding her injury might have a pertinent bearing on the damage to the laboratory.

The insurance assessor kept her another half hour. Then it was back into Jenny's car – borrowed again at six that morning

– and a hasty drive to the Glasgow shuttle via Hertfordshire. She found the address given by Maynard in a parade of shops on the outskirts of St Albans. It was a print and duplicating shop which rented out accommodation addresses by the week. They did not keep a record of past transactions and, even if they had, would not have been prepared to reveal them.

From Glasgow she had taken a hire care to Loch Fyne and spent a challenging hour persuading Mrs Bell to dispense with Dermott and use a Glasgow lawyer named Munro, an expert on family law. A hurriedly arranged meeting with Munro followed, then, aided by some legal muscle from Munro, the three of them gained permission to go and see Adrian in hospital. They found him grey-faced, subdued, unresponsive to everything but the sight of Daisy's black eye, which produced a stare of amazement. He hadn't been able to say what drugs they were giving him, only that they made him sick. The physiotherapy was hurting him, he said, and he felt very weak.

Later in that long day, perched in her Glasgow hotel room Daisy tried a few press contacts to see if she could drum up some local interest in Adrian's case. But she had underestimated the opposition: Munro called to tell her that Strathclyde Council had been granted an injunction banning all publicity. Such was the power vested in the authorities: the power to remove a child and the power to prevent the world from hearing about it.

Suddenly Monday was almost over, and Alan Breck's call was only twenty-four hours away. Jenny, working alone and under pressure in the Catch office, had found a firm to cover security, had looked into flights and accommodation. But the media deal hung insecurely in the air. Simon wasn't back, an opposition newspaper was showing only limited interest. No guaranteed coverage; no money. Daisy didn't need telling that Alan Breck wouldn't come for that.

The door of number nineteen was painted Cambridge-blue to match the gables. Bypassing the heavy Victorian-style brass knocker, Daisy pressed an electric bell set into a ceramic plate under a reproduction carriage lamp. At once a dog barked, a woman's voice shouted 'Quiet!' and the door was pulled open by Jane Ackroyd in a dark blue suit with white-edged lapels and rows of chunky jewellery.

'Oh, it's you!' she declared more in relief than irritation, holding on to the collar of a snapping Jack Russell. 'I was beginning to think you weren't coming.' She peered closer as Daisy came into the hall. 'Good God! What *have* you done to your face?'

'A car hit me. Well, a car door.'

'Oh,' she murmured, already losing interest. She closed the door and released the Jack Russell which immediately jumped against Daisy's leg and bared its teeth.

'Listen,' Jane Ackroyd said, dropping her voice conspiratorially, 'I think you should know – I only told Peter a couple of hours ago. That you were coming. And he's still a bit – well, *unhappy*.'

'I thought it was his idea. I thought it was urgent. You said it was urgent.'

'Oh, he's keen, oh yes! Absolutely! It's just – well, he wasn't too happy to hear it was *you* that I'd phoned.'

Daisy didn't attempt to hide her annoyance. 'Perhaps I should go then?'

'Oh no! Please don't go.' She gripped Daisy's wrist, her jewellery jangling in agitation. 'He's talking about going to South America. Apparently they're desperate for pilots – and not too worried about the state of one's licence.' She released Daisy's wrist and took to twisting her rings. 'He'll get work, I've no doubt he will, but all those mountains. The bandits. No spare parts. No, I couldn't stand it, I really couldn't.' She glanced over her shoulder. 'He went back to the medical board to ask for a review, you know,' she said, whispering again, 'but they wouldn't reconsider. It was that Scotland job, he's sure of it. Never been the same since. When I saw your name in the paper and I realised you were with – what is it?' She gestured forgetfulness. 'The Campaign For . . .?'

'Against Toxic Chemicals.'

'Then I guessed you might know what to do. It's a scandal.' Her colourless eyes showed a pale outrage. 'He was only doing his job. An absolute scandal.'

Through a closed door came the sound of a muffled cough and the energetic shaking of a newspaper. 'You'd better come in . . .' She led the way into a living room, small but grandly decorated, with a pale carpet and matching curtains, a chintz drop-arm sofa with extravagant gilded cords, silk-shaded standard lamps, and a fake open fire.

Duggan was sitting in a high-winged chair to the right of the fire, a newspaper on his knee and a cigarette dangling loosely from the fingers of one hand. Taking his time, he folded the paper, balanced the cigarette on the rim of an ashtray and lumbered to his feet. He was still dapper in a boy-flyer sort of way, but it seemed to Daisy that his blazer, resplendent with brass buttons, hung loosely on him, and that his cheeks had lost some of their fullness. His hair still sported its razor-line side parting, but his eyes were watery and his skin had a dry spongy quality to it.

He shook hands, but his gaze harboured old grievances and as soon as his sister had left the room he couldn't resist taking a stab at her. 'Someone hit you back, did they?'

'Someone who couldn't take the truth when he heard it,' she smiled.

He sat down again, looking defensive.

Daisy asked after his health.

'Bloody awful.' By the way of illustration he gave a terrifying cough, the sort that anti-smoking campaigners would be glad to have broadcast to every schoolkid in the country. 'But not so awful that they had the right to take my licence away.' She noticed his hands were trembling.

'What grounds did they give?'

'No grounds. Don't have to give grounds. Like bloody insurance companies.'

'And you think your health was affected by chemicals?'

Resting his elbows on the chair-arms, he brought his cigarette in front of his mouth and regarded her through the spiral of smoke. 'You lied to me,' he said. 'You said you were with some solicitors' firm or other.'

'Did I?'

'You know bloody well you did.'

'Perhaps I thought you'd be less than forthcoming if I said I was with Catch.'

'Too right.' He took another drag, sucking so hard that she could almost feel the smoke biting into his lungs. 'Could have your licence revoked as well, perhaps?' The thought appealed to him and he creased up his eyes with malicious amusement.

'Maybe.'

It didn't satisfy him. 'Bloody cheek, you know. Bloody cheek. And those threats – ' He stabbed a finger at her, eyeing her down the length of it, like someone sighting along a rifle.

560

'I don't take kindly to threats, you know. Not on. Not on.'
His voice shook slightly.

'You had important information. I needed to get it.'

'Bloody cheek.' But the venom had gone out of his voice.

He got up and poured himself a liberal glass of Scotch. 'So
what can you do for me?' he demanded truculently.

'Hard to say. What sort of thing did you have in mind?'

'Why, compensation. It was that damned gunk I worked
with, I'm sure of it. Felt off-colour ever since. That blighter
Keen. Took no precautions, you know. Hired fools like Davie.
Couldn't read a label to save his life.'

'When you say off-colour, what do you mean exactly?'

'Well . . .' He waved an impatient hand. 'You know, *low*.
Can't bloody concentrate. Hands all over the place. Head feels
woozy, that sort of thing.'

Putting down his drink, he reached for a packet of cigarettes
and lit one, steadying one trembling hand against the other as
he operated the lighter. Daisy could see that there might be
difficulties in persuading a court that this trembling was
purely the result of chemical exposure.

'Any particular chemical you had in mind?' she asked.

He gave a series of short coughs which he dampened
greedily with a drink. 'Pretty obvious,' he declared sullenly.
'That stuff you were so curious about – '

'Silveron.'

He wagged his cigarette in confirmation.

'Did you come into direct contact with it then?'

'When the wind was in the wrong direction.' He glared
morosely into space from under drooping eyelids. Then his
eyes dipped back towards hers and his voice rolled on
reminiscently: 'Gunk slopped all over the place when we were
filling the tanks, too. Couldn't help it, not with that prehistoric
equipment.'

'And the spray, did it ever land on anyone else accidentally?
I mean, that you know of?'

His mouth hardened. 'What sort of question's that?'

'It'd help to know.'

'I'd bet it would!' he said in a voice suddenly vicious with
injustice. 'Trying to trap me, eh?'

Daisy, her patience already frail, stood up and said briskly:
'Obviously I can't be of help.'

'So what d'you want me to say?' he bellowed as she made

561

for the door. 'We've all made mistakes, for God's sake. You show me a spray pilot and I'll show you someone who's made a cock-up!'

She paused at the door and looked back at him. He threw out an expansive arm, slopping his drink in the process. 'What the hell difference does it make anyway?'

'Everything,' she said.

'Christ Almighty!' he spluttered. 'I'm meant to incriminate myself, am I?'

'No.' She came back into the room. 'Just tell it all to a newspaper.'

'Just!' His eyes darted imploringly around the room, as if seeking the sympathy of an invisible audience. 'And that's not incriminating myself?'

She sat down again. 'You could stay anonymous.'

'Ha. That's what *you* say. The licensing department of the CAA would bloody know. I tell you, they'd soon bloody work it out.' He snorted vaguely until, with a sideways glance, he said coolly: 'And what'd be in it for me?'

'We'd find the right lawyers and experts to help you fight your case. If that's what you decided to do.'

He gave a non-committal grunt and eyed her leerily over his glass. Finally, after a last thoughtful glance, he chucked his cigarette onto the fake coals. 'I did my best, you know. Never knowingly hurt a fly. Never.' He looked up at her mournfully.

'But there were cock-ups?'

He tensed and looked into his drink. For a moment she thought he wouldn't answer. Then he drew in a slow breath, hissing it through his teeth. 'The bloody guidance system . . . sometimes didn't work. Or the flow line – that jammed once. Not my fault. It was the no-good ground staff. Bloody incompetent. Keen's fault. Wouldn't pay a decent rate.' He reached slowly for a cigarette, spinning out the movement so that he could avoid looking into Daisy's eyes. 'One day . . .' He hesitated and said with sudden anger: 'Shit, I don't know – '

'This is off the record,' she murmured.

He risked a look at her and nodded unhappily. Perhaps he knew that what he was about to say wasn't going to sound too good. Perhaps the memories had been bothering him for some time. He lit his cigarette and started to play with his lighter, swivelling it on the arm on his chair.

'The time with the flow line. Bloody thing seized up. Then suddenly got going at the wrong moment.' He held the cigarette in his fingers like a peashooter, drawing short puffs from it. 'Doing a patch near a big house. Loch Fyne, it was. Thought I saw someone. Couldn't be sure though. There was a horse. Saw that all right. And a hut, a stable. Thought I saw something else. Behind the horse. But then I had to turn away fast. Impossible to go back and see. Fairly sure they must have got a pretty good whiff though.' He gave a joyless chuckle. 'Surprised not to hear anything about it, if you really want to know. Thought all hell would break loose.'

'And the other time?'

Baring his teeth, he sucked in his breath. 'Think it was a boy.' His fingers tightened on the lighter so that it stopped turning. 'Not absolutely certain . . . Only saw him for a flash. Standing in this field at the end of the run, he was. So close couldn't have missed him if I'd tried. Flew right over him.' He grasped the lighter and squeezed it hard. 'Turned back and took a look, but hard to see. Hidden behind the animals or something . . .' He blinked rapidly. 'Flew straight back to the strip, sent a telex to Keen telling him to stuff it. Told him that if I wasn't given proper recce time I'd be off. Same bloody answer. He'd see to it. He was always seeing to things that never bloody happened.' He glanced at her, gauging her reaction. 'Felt bad about it,' he said in a rough voice. 'Just a kid. Often wondered if he was okay. But it was too late by then, wasn't it? No good telling everyone. What good would that have done?'

Daisy spent a moment examining her hands. She said: 'Can you remember what you had in the tanks that day?'

'Yup. It was that stuff of yours,' he offered gladly. 'Silver-whatsit.'

He peered at her through the wreaths of smoke, his lids drooping knowingly. 'Did I say the right thing?'

Jenny was waiting in the Catch office with good and bad news. The good news was that Simon was due back from Prague at any moment and that she'd managed to arrange a meeting in the editorial office of the *Sunday Times* for seven that evening. The bad news was that she'd got a price from a security firm for guarding Alan Breck and it wasn't going to be cheap.

As bad news went, it could have been a lot worse. There was still something left in the Octek kitty.

Then Jenny showed her the day's newspapers, and Daisy saw it was going to be worse after all. The story took up a quarter page in the tabloids, a more restrained side paragraph in the qualities. Charged. Bailed. In possession of drugs at his Highland castle. All the tabloids called it a castle, which suggested they had got the story from a wire service. In the absence of other facts, they had rehashed the usual history: Alusha, the financing of the laboratory, the fire.

She wondered: Can it be true? Then in the next instant: What the hell difference did it make anyway? They should leave him alone. He doesn't deserve this.

It was nine before the Alan Breck deal was struck. Simon delayed the final agreement, worried by the apparent lack of documentation, throwing up what seemed to Daisy to be unnecessary obstacles. The offer wasn't as good as she'd hoped – travel expenses and a ten-thousand-pound fee – but with foreign rights the money could double. Would it be enough? Would Alan Breck be hoping for more? And what about all his other expenses? She had the feeling he would be expecting her to find them, along with the cost of the security people.

The flat was cold when she got in. As she bent down to light the fire something made her pause. She listened for a second or two. A sound, a gentle scraping, like a leaf on the window, except it hadn't come from the window. The kitchen then? She went in. The kitchen window returned her reflection dustily, like a sheet of black metal. Outside it was very dark and, though she put an eye to the glass, she couldn't make out anything in the small patch of paved garden below. Above, the yellow oblongs of lighted windows hung in the blackness.

Whatever the sound was, it had gone, or else it was lost in the ringing that was still buzzing like a run-down alarm clock in her ear. She switched on the kettle then heard the sound again.

It was more distinct this time, coming in clearly over the chiming in her ear, not so much a scraping as a scratching, emanating, so it seemed, from the main room. She crept soundlessly towards the door, but as she stepped into the room it stopped. She waited, cocking her good ear from side to side. For perhaps half a minute there was nothing but the murmurs of the street, the faint beat of reggae music from the flat below and the humming of the heating kettle. Then it sounded again, but so soft, so vague, so lost in the insistent caterwauling of her singing ear that she was no longer sure that it was inside the room. She crept into the centre of the room and stood still, preparing to wait it out.

When the scraping came again it was so sharp that it seemed to be very close by, and she started slightly. A grinding noise, as if someone were running his nails over a rough surface. She'd got the direction now – close by the kitchen door and lowish – but by the time she had inched forward the kettle was rumbling to the boil and if there was any other sound she missed it.

When the kettle had clicked off and grumbled into silence there was still nothing, and after another couple of minutes she gave up and went and made herself a coffee.

She unpacked her bag, hung up some clothes.

In the flat below the reggae music stopped and a door slammed.

She went to the chest to throw a jersey into the bottom drawer. As she leaned forward she caught a whiff of an acrid almost fetid smell.

She pulled open the top drawer to drop in some clean clothes and the smell rose up in a wave. At the same time her eyes were drawn to a series of yellow stains and black dots scattered over her underwear.

'What the hell – ?'

She reached into the drawer. As her hand closed over her one and only pair of silk panties, the clothes at the back of the drawer gave a distinct twitch. She stared, immobilised. She looked into the shadows at the back of the drawer and was met by a single shining dot. Yellow, glistening. An eye.

She jerked back, and in the same instant her clothes burst into movement; there was a violent scuttling and scrabbling, and a missile thundered wildly round the drawer. She gave a shriek that sounded unnaturally loud in her ears. The missile, brown and trailing a low tail, leaped at the side of the drawer, propelled itself over the edge, landed on the ground and, its claws skittering furiously on the floorboards, shot past the red chair, across the hearth and disappeared under the bed.

She stared mutely at the bed then back at the ruins of her underwear. Suddenly and without warning, something folded inside her, the tears leapt hotly against the back of her eyes.

'Shit,' she murmured. '*Shit*.'

It was a moment before she realised the door bell was buzzing.

The route to the window – her normal vantage point for the inspection of callers – would take her too near the bed and other dark places. She backed towards the door and pressed the entry. Opening the flat door she heard the street door open and close, she heard footfalls in the hall.

Then, inexplicably, the footsteps ceased. A second later the stair lights clicked off. Darkness and silence.

Something rose up in her, something close to panic. She roared: 'Who is it?'

There was the heavy sound of someone stumbling, and a muffled oath.

'Who is it?' she yelled, her throat raw.

'Daisy? Where are the lights, for God's sake?'

That voice. That *voice*.

She reached out onto the landing for the push button and the lights came on. She went to the stairs and peered over the banister.

'God!' she cried.

Nick, climbing the stairs, began to speak but, looking up, the words died on his lips. 'Jesus . . .' He came to an abrupt halt. 'What the – ?' His expression was so astonished that she slapped a hand over her black eye to cover it.

Coming up the last few stairs, he said: 'Daisy . . . What *have* you been up to?'

He laid a hand against her bruised cheek and murmured a sympathetic: 'Ouch, ouch!'

The lights clicked off and for a moment Daisy thought she'd landed in heaven.

She found him a rolling pin, part of a set of kitchen implements she'd bought off a stall in Camden Lock. Clearing the furniture away from the bed he advanced slowly.

'Careful. It's enormous,' she warned.

'Not nearly as big as I am,' he said.

'I'm not so sure.'

He looked back over his shoulder. 'Whose side are you on?'

'The winner's.'

'I'd better not let him get away then.'

He slid the bed slowly away from the wall, one end at a time, then crept round behind it. He poked the rolling pin into the assortment of luggage, scrolled paper and plastic-wrapped bundles that made up the subterranean clutter under the bed, then moved with sudden speed as the creature scuttled between a suitcase and a roll of paper. He took a swipe at it, missed by a tail, and chased it to the other side of the room, tripping and almost sprawling over the rug as he scrabbled round the end of the bed in hot pursuit.

The creature was fast, but he finally cornered it by the bathroom and dealt it a blow. Finishing it off quickly, he wrapped the carcass in newspaper and took the parcel down to the dustbins. While he was away Daisy hastily sponged her face and daubed some makeup over her bruise.

She came out of the bathroom to meet him. He was still catching his breath. They stared at each other for a moment.

'I'm not too practised at rat-catching,' he said.

'Oh, you'll do,' she said. 'Believe me.'

'Thanks.' He smiled but distractedly.

'Please – sit down.' She straightening the red chair and brushed a hand over it. 'Coffee?' she said brightly.

He stopped just in front of her and said: 'How *did* you get that face?'

'Ah! That's another story.'

He raised his eyebrows slightly and she could almost see him thinking: If this was a boyfriend, he must be something else.

'I'll make the coffee,' she said and turned quickly towards the kitchen.

His voice drifted in from the living room. 'What happened to the ceiling?'

Tapping the coffee gently into a mug, she went and stood in the doorway. 'I was wondering about that too.'

He was looking mystified, trying unsuccessfully to fit this into the boyfriend scenario.

'I think they did it on purpose, when they came to install the bug – ' Her hand flew over her mouth. 'Hell,' she breathed and, going back into the kitchen, found a screwdriver. Putting a finger to her lips, throwing him a significant look, she stabbed a finger towards the instrument. Kneeling, she unscrewed the handset and pulled it apart. Her heart skidding, she peered inside, held it up to the light, ran two fingers along the casing and sank slowly back on her haunches. 'It's gone,' she gasped.

He slid forward onto his knees beside her and peered at the handset. 'What's gone?'

'The bug. The microphone. The thing they were listening with.' Her voice was flying high, sawing all over the place.

'What are you saying?'

'They were bugging this place. Listening to everything.'

He hesitated as if he needed to understand it correctly. 'Listening?'

'Yes! It was a bug all right, otherwise they wouldn't have gone to all the trouble of removing it, would they?'

He nodded uncertainly.

'They must have realised I'd found it, you see,' she argued. 'They must have been frightened that I'd use it as evidence.'

'You're shivering,' he said. 'Are you okay?'

'I'm okay.' But she wasn't, not quite yet, and he seemed to realise it, because he got up and went into the kitchen and came back with the coffee.

He sat hunched forward in the chair above her, watching over her as she drank. 'All right?'

'I'm glad you're here.'

He smiled, and the tiredness seemed to go out of his eyes for a moment.

'Tell me about it,' he said, sitting back in the chair. 'The rat, the ceiling, the bug.'

'Not overlooking the eye,' she said.

'Not overlooking the eye,' he said gravely.

She sat on a cushion at his feet, her profile outlined against the fire, her bruised cheek turned away from him. Her hair was untied and swelled out in a cloud from her neck. It was the sort of curly pre-Raphaelite style much favoured by models, but which in Daisy's case was almost certainly achieved without a hairdresser. She had a fine profile, with a straight nose and arched brows, and he noticed the outline of her lips.

When she began to speak her voice was hesitant and low-pitched.

The Greeks' water tank was the first real clue, she said, the first thing that should have made her stop and think. But she had too much on her plate, too many things to organise; it simply never occurred to her that it might have been intentional. Why should it? But looking back she could see that they must have been desperate to locate the laboratory, and that the tank was the only sure way of getting her back to the flat. If anyone had tried to tell her people would go to those sort of lengths, she wouldn't have believed them. But now . . .

She gave him a quick sideways glance. He smiled briefly by way of encouragement. She looked back to the fire.

She told him about the succession of things that had started to go wrong, small things, not-so-small things, and her feeling that she was constantly being outmanoeuvred, that however hard she tried, someone was always there ahead of her. The problems with the licence, Peasedale being warned off by his boss, Adrian getting made a ward of court, the disintegration of Alice Knowles' case . . . Always something. Looking back she couldn't be sure what was inevitable, what might have been prevented. All of those things perhaps, or none of them; it was impossible to know.

The fire, though, that was something else. She arched her head back and gave a laugh of disbelief. He noticed the long smoothness of her neck, and remembered having noticed it once before. Animal rights! she scoffed. You had to hand it to them. The slogans, the freeing of the rats and mice – well planned. And they did a brilliant job at destruction, nothing left intact. And the burglar alarm: disconnecting the thing, then setting it to go off when they left and it was too late to save anything.

She was silent for a moment, then shifted on her cushion. For an instant her leg came against his, but she moved it quickly away.

Then there was you, she said, her voice calm now. Only three people knew about your involvement, she said. You yourself – she ticked him off with a solemn gesture in his direction – and me – she pressed a splayed hand against her chest – and your accountant. Until the night of the fire, that

569

was. Then – yes, she had to admit there had been someone else – Simon Calthrop of the *Sunday Times*. But he wouldn't have told, she added; she was certain of that. And even if by some wild chance he'd gone against everything he believed in and told someone, it certainly wouldn't have been another newspaper, not in a thousand years. No, no, the point wasn't that she'd *told* Simon; the point was that she'd made the call from *here*, from this phone. She looked back to him to make sure he'd grasped the significance of what she was saying.

Then she gave an exclamation of disgust, directed at herself. She should have guessed then. Why she hadn't, she couldn't imagine. So stupid, so stupid. She said it over and over again, screwing her eyes down and shaking her head.

'But why should you have guessed?' he said.

She began again: Friday night, the night after the fire, the night she had come to see him in Kensington . . . She faltered uneasily, as if this was a part of the story she'd rather not relive.

'Sorry I got mad,' he volunteered.

She spun round. 'No, no. I don't blame you!' she said. 'Really. Really.'

Then, looking back to the fire, she continued, speaking in a pedantic un-Daisyish fashion, all bare bones and no emotion, running briskly through facts like so many on a file: how after she'd left him in Kensington she'd gone home and drunk too much and left the wild overblown message on Simon's machine, how next evening she'd spotted Maynard leaving her flat and followed him into the dead-end trap of the north London estate. She skimmed over the attack itself with a cartoon-strip 'Then, pow! That was it!' and was on to the discovery of the bug in the phone before he could pull her back to the mugging.

'It must have been one hell of a clout!'

'Don't remember much. Just that he wore this unlikely raincoat. More like a flasher.'

He leaned forward and turned her face towards him, tracing the bruise across her cheek and into her hair, feeling the lump above her ear.

'God,' he said.

'Don't be too sympathetic.' She laughed feebly. 'Might feel sorry for myself.' She spoke lightly, but not so lightly that there wasn't a trace of emotion in her voice.

'Can you hear all right?'

'What did you say?'

'Ha, ha. He could have killed you, you know.' He dropped his hand. 'And the rat?'

'A charming little thought of Maynard's, I'd guess. Probably one of the ones from our own lab!'

He thought suddenly: And I killed it. And with no compunction at all. Daisy had obviously appreciated the irony of the situation already, because she turned and gave him an oddly flustered look.

'Is that it?' he asked.

'Not quite.' She twisted around until she was facing him and, laying an elbow over the chair-arm, told him all about the man known as Alan Breck and how she needed to get him over to Britain.

'Can I help?' he said.

She looked questioningly at him.

'I mean, money?'

'Amazing.' She was laughing with disbelief.

'Well, it's about the only thing I'm good for, isn't it? Money.'

'Not true!' Impulsively, she knelt forward and, reaching an arm round his neck, pulled his cheek against hers. He felt the softness of her, felt her warmth. But after a reciprocal squeeze he disengaged himself. He was in too uncertain a state of mind to be embracing someone like Daisy; he might cling to her, a piece of buoyancy in the wreckage.

Sitting back on her heels, she regarded him gravely. 'Why did you come? Was it . . .?'

'Something happened.'

She said quickly: 'I read about it.'

He murmured: 'And that was only the half of it.' He thought of Susan and felt a lurch of bitterness, but he didn't want to talk about that, and certainly not to Daisy. 'My manager's having hysterics,' he said instead. 'Our European tour starts in two weeks and with this drugs thing the insurance people are threatening to withdraw cover, which means if anything goes wrong I could get wiped out financially.' He snorted with an amusement he didn't feel, then added: 'I won't put up a defence, you see. They'd want to know where I got the stuff. They'd want to rake over old ground.'

She didn't say anything.

He said: 'No, why I came was . . . I talked to Campbell.'

'You did what!'

'He dropped in on me. Unexpectedly. He told me about Adrian.' And all about you, he almost added.

'Adrian,' she echoed.

'I realised . . . Well, anyway – I've come to offer my help. *Again*. If you want it.'

'Even after everything?'

'*Especially* after everything.' He thought: Oh, you have no idea!

'You won't regret it.'

'I don't expect you'll let me.'

She grinned, her bruise like a carbuncle on the side of her face.

'Your Mr Breck, you said he's calling? Shall I wait?'

'Would you? *Would* you?'

He went down to his driver and sent him for a pizza, which they ate sitting on the floor in front of the fire.

They talked. He stretched out in the big red chair with the creaky arm. After a while he felt drowsy; he hadn't slept the previous night. Without meaning to, he dozed.

'Sorry,' he said, waking suddenly.

She couldn't resist it. 'Like old times.'

'Ha, ha.' He smiled.

When he woke next it was midnight and the phone was ringing.

THIRTY-FIVE

A brilliant Sunday morning. Daisy stood waiting by the window. It had stormed and blown for three solid days, the media had talked about a repeat of the 'eighty-seven hurricane, but by now the air was still, the last few leaves hung exhausted in the plane trees and a strong yellow light was touching the chimneys of Augustus Road.

Seven twenty. She made her calculations again, working backwards from the time Simon would need to leave for Heathrow to the latest he could reasonably get up. It was possible he'd got up early to work on the novel of course, but as she knew from many a gruff encounter it was safer to interrupt his work than his sleep.

Finally, worried that she might have miscalculated and missed him altogether, she dialled his number fifteen minutes early. The telephone was answered at the first ring: she could almost see him snatching it up.

'Yup?' His brisk tone.

'I checked with the airport,' she said. 'The flight may be early.'

She could imagine him pursing his lips, putting on a look of forbearance. 'I'll be there in good time,' he grunted.

'Terminal 3. Jenny'll be waiting from nine thirty – '

'Yes, yes.' He was openly impatient now. Stress was not kind to Simon.

She asked: 'The US agreement, it got signed?'

'There were problems, they wanted one of their own people to take over the story. In the end we agreed to split it.'

Of course you did, she thought, because this story will

573

make your name and the US deal will make your newspaper some money. 'Well done,' she said.

But he wasn't to be deflected from his bad temper. 'This secrecy's ludicrous, Daisy. I *cannot* go away without leaving a number. The office have *got* to be able to get in touch with me.'

'I told you – it's not possible, not at the moment anyway.'

A sigh of exasperation. '*Really*. You've been seeing too many films, Daisy. Life isn't like this.'

'Maybe not, but I promised.'

'*Jesus* . . . Anyone would think I was going to broadcast it from the rooftops!'

But Simon had lost the power to intimidate her. 'Jenny'll tell you at the airport,' she said mildly. 'Like we discussed.'

Another sigh, some more huffing and puffing, but he rang off without further argument.

She drove down to Hammersmith by a circuitous route, stopping several times just past tight bends, taking detours through drowsy streets. By the time she was onto the Great West Road she was sure she was quite alone.

At eight thirty only a few dedicated Sunday travellers had ventured onto the roads and the M4 seemed unnaturally wide and empty, like a runway. Soon she was turning off and running along the road skirting Heathrow's northern perimeter, with fifteen minutes to spare. She decided to use the time on a last check, a final look for fellow travellers. She circled a roundabout, turned into a cul-de-sac, parked for a few minutes outside a garage. She watched, but the scene, like the morning, was fresh, clear and innocent.

After that it would have been tempting to take a few shortcuts, but she stuck to her plan and, avoiding the Airport Inn and its car park, left the car at the next hotel along and walked back, taking a couple of rearward glances as she went. These precautions, which would have seemed ludicrous a couple of weeks ago, were now a bare and reasonable minimum, and never mind the scorn that Simon would pour on them if he knew.

The hire car, a grey-green Escort, sat on the far side of the Airport Inn car park, in the tight space she had found for it at eight the previous night.

It was a moment before she got it started, a moment that

574

brought the time up to nine exactly. She drove round to the front of the hotel and peered under the canopy.

Campbell must have been watching for her, because he came straight out and, throwing his bag into the back, sank wordlessly into the seat beside her. He was wearing his usual tweeds, she noticed, though as a gesture to town life he had forgone the headgear he had been sporting when she met him off the flight – a countryman's narrow-brimmed hat of great age and uncertain shape. What Campbell thought of her costume he wasn't saying. She had deliberated long and hard over the choice of clothes that would achieve both transformation and anonymity, finally borrowing from Jenny some loose charcoal-grey trousers, a black cossack jacket and a deep-brimmed grey hat, turned back at the front in Paddington Bear style. She had tied her hair up inside the hat and added tinted glasses: a student traveller, an artist, a would-be actress on her way to New York.

At Terminal 3 she stopped in one of the drop-off lanes and instructed Campbell on the various manoeuvres that would be needed to elude traffic wardens: moving the car a few yards along the lane, hovering at the far end, in the last resort making a circuit of the traffic system.

Leaving Campbell, she went to the arrivals hall and, having established the flight was on time, took up station in an ill-lit corner furnished with two lines of bucket seats and a wide pillar. There was a dense crowd at the barriers around the customs exit. Shortly after nine thirty she saw Jenny arrive with the two security men, who looked like everyone's idea of bodyguards, large, with jackets that sat uneasily on their shoulders and heads that swivelled continuously. Led by Jenny, the three of them took up a position at the corner of the barriers, where Jenny's hand-held sign was visible to the emerging passengers. At ten, when the 'landed' sign lit up next to the American Airlines New York flight, Simon was nowhere in sight, and when he still hadn't arrived by ten fifteen it occurred to Daisy that he was putting them through this uncertainty on purpose.

It was ten twenty when Jenny and the two security men finally pushed their way free of the crowd and closed around a family negotiating their trolley out of customs: Alan Breck, instantly recognisable behind his owlish spectacles, and next to him his wife, a dark-haired, intense-looking woman, and their son, ungainly and sullen in a football jacket and cap.

As Jenny shook their hands Simon appeared as if by magic with a photographer at his elbow, and, in his effortlessly dominating way, took charge of the party and guided them towards the exit.

Now, Daisy. Use your eyes, stay back, don't hurry, don't lose them, stay back.

She started forward, then halted at the edge of the flowing crowd which was dense with relatives and high-stacked trolleys, sometimes three abreast. Through the heads she saw Simon lead his group down the concourse towards the side exit.

She manoeuvred into the crowd, scanning faces, heads, clothes, people who might be making for the side exit, people who might be hanging back. There was nobody. As the party disappeared out into the light, she doubled back and made as rapidly as possible for the only other exit, inexplicably located at the far end of the building. Getting out at last, she made her way to the corner and looked down the side of the building to see that the group had wandered in her direction and were close enough for her to see that Simon and Jenny were in urgent and visibly acrimonious discussion. Alan Breck and his family were looking on apprehensively, the security men were hovering, the photographer was diplomatically observing airport life.

Daisy inwardly raged, and had to restrain herself from striding down and taking Simon by the neck. What *was* he up to? What did he think he was playing at? She deflected her frustration into rooting for Jenny. Come on, she shouted silently, don't let him talk you down, girl. Stand firm, tell him where he gets off, ease the moment over. Come on, Jen. *Come on.*

At last Jenny turned her back on Simon and went over to the Brecks. Daisy was so intent on their reactions that she almost forgot her watching job, and twisted hastily round to scrutinise the steady trickle of people continuing to ooze from the building. A bus drew up with a screech of brakes, a child screamed inconsolably; no one looked her way.

The security firm's car, an excessively showy limousine with darkened windows, had drawn into the kerb beside Jenny. The bodyguards loaded the baggage for the short journey to Terminal 1. Simon, having struck his journalist-of-the-world stance, all weariness and tested patience, now roused himself to talk to the photographer and gesture in the direction of the other teminal. A moment later, he set off on foot with the photographer in train. There wasn't room for everyone in the car, but it wasn't that which had annoyed him, she guessed. No, it was Scotland. He wouldn't have taken kindly to having such an out-of-the-way destination sprung on him, particularly when he knew it had been planned by Daisy. Well, he would survive. The fresh air would do him good.

Daisy lowered her head and, skipping across the traffic lane, walked hurriedly to where the Escort was waiting. As she climbed in Campbell gunned the engine like some geta-way driver.

'Easy, easy,' she murmured.

They watched as the limousine drew out ahead and, threading itself into the flow of traffic from the other lanes, turned into the one-way system and disappeared around the side of the multi-storey car park. Daisy mentally logged the traffic that followed: a transit bus, a beat-up pink jalopy, a black cab, a Volvo estate, two more cabs. None of which, from what she could see, had started its journey from that side exit, or even hovered near by.

'Anything?'

Campbell shook his head and they started off, resighting the limousine as it set itself at the Terminal 1 ramp and snaked its black body up to the departure level. Coming over the lip of the ramp, they saw the limousine at the far end of the car lane, a security man stationed on either side as a porter unloaded the baggage.

In the adjoining lanes there was no Volvo, no beat-up jalopy, nothing that might be hovering at a careful distance, only travellers wheeling their trolleys over the crossings and the usual procession of buses and cabs.

Campbell leaned forward and rested his arms over the wheel. 'What about the red car there?'

It wouldn't be red; whatever colour, it wouldn't be red. But she followed his gaze anyway to see a business-suited man get out and pull on a thick camel coat.

'No,' she said.

Jenny and the Brecks were negotiating the passenger crossing, the porter ahead, the security men back and front; the limousine was pulling away. Reaching the terminal building, Jenny led the way towards domestic departures.

In the drop-off lanes taxis squealed to a halt, cars came and went, people humped bags onto trolleys and kissed each other and hurried away; only two cars showed no signs of activity, but neither had been following the limousine when it came up the ramp.

'I'll watch them to the gate,' said Daisy with a baffled sigh.

She went into the building by a central door. This terminal was a little less crowded, and she took care to walk briskly across to the far side of the concourse and place herself between a roundel of postcards of the Royal Family and a sock shop before looking round. She spotted Jenny immediately, standing at one of the British Midland check-in islands, in conversation with the ground staff. Her flock was gathered moodily around her. Alan Breck looked a little more relaxed, though that wasn't saying a great deal, but his wife still wore the thunderous expression she'd acquired during the altercation outside Terminal 3, and Daisy knew whose feathers were going to have to be smoothed once they arrived at Glen Ashard.

After five minutes the walking party arrived, and Simon, characteristically impervious to atmosphere, chose to stand and talk to Alan Breck in a close shoulder-hunched way that conspicuously excluded the wife. Even at that distance Daisy could pick up her resentment which flashed like so much dark electricity across the hall. More of Simon's winning ways and the party would be in danger of falling apart.

Watching Mrs Breck's grim face, Daisy almost missed the raincoat. It was on the near side of the same island, standing by a closed check-in point. The wearer, a shortish man with cropped gunmetal hair, was turned towards her but his head was bent over an information leaflet, so that only a wide forehead and the tip of a flat fleshy nose were visible.

Nonetheless there was a familiarity, an echo, to him – or was it just the raincoat? In her present state of nervousness she had no trust in her jittery memory. She saw again the striding jaunty walk of the man approaching her on the housing estate, the raincoat flapping around his knees. Was he short like this? Was his nose squashy and flat?

578

Jenny was shepherding everyone towards the domestic departure area. Typically, Simon, engrossed in his conversation with Alan Breck and apparently in no mood to hurry, was slow to move. Mrs Breck began to follow Jenny then, realising her husband wasn't with her, hung back to let him catch up, while the son, looking mutinous, arced off in the direction of a newsstand. As the party fragmented, the security guards showed their first signs of agitation, fanning out on either side, as if to round up a dissipated flock.

The man in the raincoat glanced up from his timetable. He looked in the direction of the straggling group and his stare did not waver. From this angle the blunt face looked unfamiliar.

He put the timetable on the counter and, leaving it there, sidled round the island and spoke to the check-in clerk. Head on, he was suddenly promising again; there was a squareness to his face, a set to the jaw, that could have belonged to the murky figure of the council estate.

The raincoat man was gesturing, pointing towards the departure area. The clerk leaned forward to follow his gaze, then nodded and jerked a hand in the same direction. He asked her another question and seemed satisfied with the answer he received because, with a brief nod of thanks, he set off towards the departure area.

Daisy moved clear of the postcards and watched him crossing the concourse. That stride – cocky, jaunty. It looked right. Even from side on, she could see the roll in his walk, the swagger in his shoulders. His image slipped effortlessly into its night-time guise.

Making her way along the fronts of the boutiques, her eyes on the striding figure ahead, she felt the unaccustomed sensation of sweat against her shirt.

The departure hall was L-shaped. The short arm led to the domestic departure gates by way of a waiting and information area. Reaching the corner, Daisy saw the raincoat man come to an abrupt halt half-way across the area and stare up at the information board. Reaching into an inside breast pocket he pulled something out and began to write on it.

Another man stopped beside him to look up at the board. The raincoat man, without any sort of acknowledgement, held out a scrap of paper to the second man, which he took and

579

read. The second man – fiftyish, balding, draped in a shapeless waterproof jacket – said a few words then went off towards the departure gate.

She was still watching the balding man when the raincoat man turned and walked straight towards her.

She stood still, transfixed by the suddenness of his movement, unable to unfasten her gaze from his face so that, when his glance flickered onto hers, their eyes met. In a reflex that seemed to come far too late, she managed to drag her eyes to a point a few feet above his head, to the information board which she read with apparent concentration.

He was coming quickly, his step showy, purposeful. The rain-coat flapped around his knees. *Muggers don't wear raincoats.* He gave her another brief glance as he passed. He did not appear to recognise her. But now it seemed to her that she recognised him very well indeed.

She kept on staring at the board for what seemed a long time but which was only a half a minute or so, then turned very slowly and fumbled in her bag as if searching for something. Keeping her head down, she looked out over the top of her dark glasses. He was not in sight. Sweeping the concourse more openly, she began to walk unhurriedly towards the nearest exit, then, remembering the speed with which the raincoat man had been travelling, more urgently.

Move, she thought; take it slow. Mustn't lose him; mustn't rush it. *Hurry. Slow.* He might be waiting outside, watching for her to burst out and give herself away. *Careful.* Think this through. Take your time.

Unable to decide on the most sensible course, she swerved towards another door, wrenching the hat off her head and pulling the elastic bands out of her hair as she went. She was still pushing the hat into her bag and agitating her hair into some sort of frizzy disorder when she came through the doors. The scene was cluttered: in the first lane were coaches and buses and cabs; in the next cars; and close by on the pavement, a large group of package-tourists blocking her vision. She couldn't see the raincoat man. She couldn't even see Campbell.

She ran across to the pedestrian island, then, conscious of the risk of exposure, held back and shifted sideways instead. Take your time, take your time. She had got Campbell now –

he'd been hidden by a black cab. He was standing beside the Escort talking to a traffic warden. She kept moving, following the edge of the pavement, dodging past a hotel bus, peering into blind spots. A knot of people stood at the taxi rank. Beyond them were two isolated figures searching vacantly for transport. Neither was raincoated.

With a growing sense of futility, she crossed to the island and looked along the line of cars, then across to the car park.

She walked disconsolately back towards Campbell who was easing himself gently away from the warden and into the car, bowing slightly, fingers tipping a salute against the brim of his absent hat. The warden, a small woman with violently bleached hair, was looking charmed and had just placed her pen firmly back in its holder. Immediately ahead of the Escort a second warden had found a less amenable citizen in the form of a black-cab driver, who was arguing vehemently over some transgression. His passenger stuck his head out of the window, trying to intervene.

The head was square-shaped with a gunmetal crop. The wrist, appearing suddenly over the sill, was wearing a raincoat. He turned slightly and she saw his face. It was the raincoat man.

She dropped into the seat beside Campbell while he was still completing his conquest of the warden through the open window. 'I'm supposed to be meetin' ma granny,' he hissed at Daisy out of the side of his mouth.

Ahead, the argument ceased, the driver slammed his door and the black cab roared off.

'Tell her Granny's been delayed.'

They followed, staying on the cab's bumper until they were safely into the airport tunnel, falling back when they came onto the motorway proper. Campbell, in a state of grim concentration, did not speak. Daisy too was silent as she plodded morosely through a sudden burst of doubts. That walk, that stride, had they really been so familiar? And the face, she'd never really got a good view of it that night. Even the interest the man had seemed to show in Jenny and her group could have been innocent. And while she had been watching him, had there been someone else? Someone she'd never seen, someone who'd seen her?

While Campbell stared stoically ahead, she changed her

clothes, swapping the cossack top for an old donkey jacket and the loose trousers for some jeans, and tied her hair back with a band.

They were forced to close up on the cab at Chiswick because of the lights, and, except for the run over the Hammersmith fly-over, had to stay close all the way to the junction with the Earl's Court Road, where the cab peeled off to the right and headed south.

The Earl's Court Road was jammed. They inched forward, one car between them and the cab. Daisy checked the batteries on the pair of walkie-talkies that she had hired from the security company and, sliding one into her shoulder bag, laid the other on the seat where Campbell would be able to reach it.

In the next lane was a black cab with an illuminated for-hire light and no one hurrying to bag it.

'Feeling brave?'

Campbell raised his eyebrows uncertainly.

'Remember,' she said as she prepared to open the door, 'stay with him until I tell you.'

She did not look back as she wove between the cars to the free cab and climbed in. Only when she was in the darkness of the interior did she peer forward, but if the raincoat man was looking back he wasn't doing it just then. Neither was the driver, whose face was just visible in the wing mirror.

'You want to follow that cab?' Daisy's driver repeated phlegmatically. 'Well, I'll tell you straight off, it ain't so easy as it looks in the films.'

The traffic was moving now, filtering slowly down to two lanes in the narrow section by the tube station. Campbell was three cars ahead and two behind the raincoat man. Approaching the junction with the Old Brompton Road the lights turned red and Daisy watched in sudden tension as the raincoat man's cab sped over the junction into the beginning of Redcliffe Gardens. The car behind also scooted across on the red and then, to the sound of indignant hoots and a near collision, the Escort.

'See what I mean?' the cabby called as they ground to a halt.

Daisy thrust the walkie-talkie to her ear and when after a few seconds Campbell hadn't come through she called him up. Finally there was an answering crackle, and Campbell's voice informed her he was at the next lights, with the cab just ahead, looking as though it was going straight on. She described the next junction and how, once over it, he would come to the river and curve round to the left and that he should call her if the cab showed any signs of turning off. Whatever happened, he was to stay as close as possible.

When the traffic moved off again, the cabby put his foot down, skilfully cut up a couple of cars and gained three places. They beat the next two sets of lights, so that they caught up with the Escort on the Embankment just as Campbell's voice winged over the radio to tell her that their quarry was indicating right to turn over the river.

On Battersea Bridge they overtook Campbell and came up behind the cab. Daisy checked the registration number and, once her tension had subsided a little, she radioed to Campbell to drop back.

Over the bridge they survived two more lights before plunging into the web of back streets that was Battersea. There was no order to the streets, just one-way systems with sudden twists and roads squeezed in beside tall railway arches, and row after row of squat two-up two-downs. Daisy relayed the route and street names to the invisible Escort until Campbell, with panic in his voice, declared himself confused, and after a short pause, lost.

Ahead, the other cab turned into successively smaller streets. 'Hold back,' Daisy commanded the driver sharply.

'I'll lose 'im!' he declared in an injured tone.

'We're too close!'

The driver shook his head and slowed down. Ahead, the cab turned a corner. When, after what seemed a long time, they also turned, it was to find themselves in a road of terraced houses, and to see the other cab fast approaching the far end of the road where it formed a T-junction with a street of shops.

'Too far back now,' Daisy urged. 'Get a bit closer.'

With an admonishing sigh the cabby pushed his foot down. The taxi was starting to accelerate nicely when the vehicle ahead swerved unexpectedly into the left and stopped, just short of the junction.

'Drive past, don't slow down,' Daisy said sharply. She drew back from the window and did not look out until they were past the stopped taxi and turning left into the shopping street.

Then, glancing quickly back, she saw that the raincoat man had been very quick off the mark; he was already across the pavement and stepping into a doorway set into the side wall of the corner building.

Daisy stopped the cab a safe distance along the main road and radioed fresh directions to Campbell. Then, paying the cabby off, she walked slowly back and examined the front of the corner building, which at street level contained a cycling shop. On the floor above were some sort of offices. The two windows were labelled Reynard Associates in the sort of gold-block lettering much favoured by solicitors and accountants. This firm, however, gave no hint as to its function.

She walked on, crossing the side street – its name was Peregrine Road – and continuing along the main street until she was well out of sight of the bicycle shop.

The Escort appeared soon after, approaching cautiously from the north. Campbell's head swivelled from side to side as he looked for shop numbers and street names. Spotting her, he broke into a brief grimace, and pulled in.

They parked the car in a street on the other side of the main road and walked back to a baker's shop which stood on the corner diagonally opposite the bicycle shop. Daisy, looking obliquely through the double thickness of the baker's side and front windows, watched Campbell continue alone, crossing into Peregrine Road and ambling down the long side wall of the bicycle shop.

He paused at the door in the wall, gazed intently at whatever information it had to offer, then, glancing up as if to admire the architecture or perhaps to check for windows, he continued on his way down Peregrine Road. He reappeared five minutes later from a parallel road, having cut across the back somewhere, and, keeping largely out of sight of the bicycle shop, rejoined her, looking for all his tweeds like a thoroughly urban animal. It would be all too easy to think the two of them were getting to be rather good at all this.

'It's a firm called *Rey*nard Associates,' Campbell announced, drawing the words out in a long string. 'Investigation an' security.'

'But what now?' she murmured. 'We can't very well walk in and ask them to own up, can we?'

Campbell threw her an odd look, both shrewd and innocent.

'No, Campbell,' she warned, getting his meaning. 'Are you nuts? Far too dodgy.'

He looked away. 'If you say so.'

'I do. All I need is to *see* Maynard. That's all. Just to make sure.'

Before starting the watch, she went in search of a phone box to call Scotland. As she dialled, a slight heat came into her face, a butterfly of anticipation, and it was with disappointment that she heard the housekeeper answer and say that Nick was out on the estate. The helicopter bringing the party from Glasgow was not expected for another hour. Daisy left a message saying she would try again later, but that she and Campbell might not make it up to Ashard until the morning.

She found some take-away tea and sandwiches and, making her way back to the baker's shop, thought of Nick. Thinking of Nick had taken up quite a lot of her time in the last few days. Since he'd left the flat on Tuesday night, they'd spoken, what? – eight or nine times, and met once, for a quick meal. She had gained his support and goodwill, but had she gathered a bit more along the way? Was there something to be read into his willingness to talk when the business was done, his near-confidences, his subtle teasing?

It was two hours later, as Campbell was preparing to go in search of pizzas, that the raincoat man suddenly emerged from the side door and, striding a short way down Peregrine Road, stopped by a car and got in. When the car drew out from the line of parked vehicles, it was pointing the other way and there was no chance of seeing the registration number as it drove off.

After that she and Campbell split up. While Campbell stayed by the baker's window and called in on the walkie-talkie every half hour, Daisy took the Escort and, circling the backstreets, came up Peregrine Road and parked in the slot vacated by the raincoat man, just fifty feet from the doorway. When she leaned across the passenger seat, she had a good view of the side wall and the rear of the property: three storeys of grimy brickwork with a two-storey extension pushing back into the yard to create the long outside wall.

The stillness of the morning had given way to a sharp breeze and the clear sky to a succession of bold black-rimmed clouds. Daisy pictured Alan Breck and his wife in the warmth of Ashard, perhaps in the room Nick called the library, with a roaring fire and a hot meal, and wondered if Simon would have tried to begin the first session yet. It would be nice to think he wouldn't rush things, but that might be hoping for too much.

Would he let Nick sit in on the sessions? She tried to imagine the two of them in conversation, tried to guess what they'd make of each other. Journalists were not among Nick's favourite people, not even when they were on his side, while Simon would, she guessed, try to be amenable. Like many people who publicly distrusted excesses of money and power, Simon was at the same time fatally attracted to them.

The day slowly wore on. A couple of dogs met, bristled and briefly scrapped. The traffic increased to a steady trickle, a few residents of Peregrine Road dawdled out, returning with Sunday newspapers under their arms. Regretting the tea, Daisy at one point went in hasty search of a loo, finally inveigling a newsagent into letting her use his.

Towards four the thin winter sun began to settle over the roof of the bakery, there was a brief flare of rich buttery light, a moment of glory for the houses of Peregrine Road, then twilight came quickly and the streetlamps began their uncertain flickerings. Taking pity on Campbell at his windswept station, Daisy offered to swap places. While they were talking, there was a sudden movement at the door in the wall. A dog appeared.

The animal was fluffy and low-built, a Pekinese maybe. She wasn't too good on makes. It seemed to be unaccompanied. It raised its nose to the air then snuffled along the base of the wall, the model of a well-trained pet.

But we know better, don't we? Daisy thought with a stab of savage excitement. We know what a vicious little agitator you are! In dark cars, under tower blocks, in well-laid traps. She saw again the white shape as it hurled itself against the glass, the bared teeth, the goggle eyes.

The walkie-talkie crackled and she realised she was still pressing the transmit button. She released it to hear Campbell repeatedly calling her name. She was about to answer when the dog acquired an owner in the shape of a hunched female figure with high heels and thin legs beneath an over-short coat that did not quite cover her knee-length skirt. She was

586

pulling the door shut with one hand, locking it with the other. A cigarette hung from her lips. Her hair was blonde or grey – it showed white-rimmed against the shop lights in the main street – and was styled into a tall starched beehive rolled into a sausage at the back, like well-moulded candy floss. But if the beehive was enjoying a fashion revival and could have belonged to a young woman, the legs could not. They were thin and slightly bandy and, in the way of older women who lose weight, her feet looked a little too large for her body.

The woman dropped the keys into a handbag and stood watching the dog, puffing on the clamped cigarette while she buttoned her coat more closely.

Campbell's voice was becoming increasingly agitated.

'I'm okay,' Daisy whispered. 'There's a woman – ' She broke off as the woman strolled towards her.

Daisy shifted rapidly across to the driving seat and prepared to engross herself in something on the opposite side of the road. The woman halted alongside the Escort, one foot resting coquettishly out to one side like a model's in a fashion still, one elbow tucked tightly into her waist as she alternately pulled on the cigarette and let her hand swing wearily away to the side. Her face was long and angular and adorned with heavy makeup; in the fading light, her arched eyebrows and mascaraed eyes were like black ink strokes, and her thin mouth, painted with some deep colour, made a dark gash across her face.

She stared along the length of Peregrine Road for a minute or two then turned and strutted slowly back, stopping once to call the dog.

Daisy eased herself back into the passenger seat and watched as the woman paused by the door in the wall, called the dog to her and snapped a lead onto its collar. Then, walking as briskly as her heels would allow, she disappeared around the corner into the main street, jerking the loitering dog after her.

Daisy gave a report to Campbell. A few minutes later he came over and got into the car beside her. 'She locked up as she left, did she?' he asked.

Daisy didn't answer. She knew where this was leading. But since she knew it, she had to ask herself why she had allowed this watching exercise to go on for so long, and why indeed

587

the two of them were here at all if she didn't intend to let Campbell progress the thing to, what was for him at least, its natural conclusion.

Campbell tried again. 'No lights at the front. None at the back either, eh?' He had taken several looks at the rear windows, but now he craned forward to stare again. 'No one home at all.'

'Campbell, this isn't like breaking into Portakabins. No talking our way out if things go wrong. No hedges to dive into.'

'Och, I wouldna' be so sure of that.' His confidence had driven him to an unnatural heartiness.

The place seemed crowded suddenly: a couple came round the corner and walked briskly past; a hunched man shuffled slowly over the junction; a lone cat trotted by. The long wall, black with shadows, its upper features lost against the dark mass of the buildings, was beginning to pick up dull reflections from the shop lights, and the door itself, far from getting lost in the gloom, seemed remarkably prominent.

'I don't like it,' she said.

'Have I led you wrong in the past?'

'Our criminal partnership hasn't lasted that long, thank God.'

'But what could happen, eh? No one home. All closed up for the night. And a Sunday at that.'

'Why am I so bloody scared then? My hands are shaking.' She held them up accusingly.

He laid a rough hand on hers and patted it briefly. 'You'll be all right once we're in.'

'I'll be better once we're out.'

'I could go on my own,' he suggested.

She looked up at the dark walls of the building, towards the invisible windows and the offices beyond.

'No . . .' she said. 'You might miss something.'

'Don't go sayin' I didna' offer.'

'I'll tell the judge,' she sighed.

'A helicopter? Go on.' Hillyard removed his gaze from an intriguing smooth-skinned creature on the far side of the restaurant and, addressing his dessert once more, dragged curls of ice-cream off the top with a spoon.

'Couldn't find out where it was going,' said Biggs defensively. 'Tried a touch of financial persuasion, but no go. Too few in the know, and they weren't talking.'

'So what's Phillips doing now?'

'Asking around some more.'

'Well, that's not very bright, is it?' Hillyard said, larding his voice with exasperation. 'Glasgow Airport's a small place. Don't you think it's just possible people might notice someone asking the same bloody stupid questions time and again?' He clicked his tongue and gave a harsh sigh. 'Pull him off, for God's sake. Get him on the next plane.'

'But – don't we need to know? Where they was going?'

Hillyard slid him a pitying look over his spoon. 'We do indeed, Biggs. But luckily for you and Phillips it doesn't take a master brain to work it out.'

Biggs looked reproachful.

Hillyard glanced up to see his lunch companion, whose seat Biggs was temporarily occupying, emerging from the gents. An old partner in crime – crime, it had to be said, of a youthful and entirely different nature – he made a face when he saw that Biggs was still in his chair. Hillyard signalled to him to stay away a while longer, and watched him stalk sulkily off towards the bar.

'And the Field girl?' Hillyard asked Biggs.

'I told you, she wasn't with them.'

'But she was at the airport?'

'She saw them off.'

'Then what did she do?'

'Drove back to London. Well, I suppose.'

'You didn't follow her?'

'I tried.'

'Doesn't make sense.' Abandoning the delicate scrapings, Hillyard scooped up the last of the ice-cream in a single mound and jammed it into his mouth. He had a sudden certainty that Biggs was lying. 'She was on to you, was she?'

Biggs' eyes gave him away immediately, a sharp dart of resentment. It was a wonder he'd ever made inspector. Not for the first time Hillyard regretted the boom in business that had forced him to take on staff in the shape of incompetents like this.

'On to me?' bleated Biggs. 'I told you – I lost her, that's all. Blimey, what do you expect on me tod? Bloody miracles?'

'When did she suss you?'

'Oh, for Christ's sake – '

He gave a squawk as Hillyard's hand closed over his wrist, an exclamation of outrage which subsided into a slow hiss as Hillyard's grip tightened. He looked wildly across to the neighbouring tables to see if people were watching, which one or two of them were, then brought his affronted gaze back to Hillyard. Hillyard could see what Biggs was thinking, that in the Met no one would have dared treat him in this way without dire consequences to their health. Hillyard almost said aloud: But it's me you work for now.

Hillyard dug his nails into the other man's flesh and whispered: *'Don't bugger about with me, you little sod.'*

'The airport,' he admitted furtively.

'And then?'

Biggs wrenched his arm free but made no reply.

'I'll be grabbing more than your wrist next time.' Hillyard smiled sweetly.

Biggs stared morosely at the glass of wine in front of him then, seeming to focus on it for the first time, knocked it back in one. 'She tried to follow me.'

'Tried?'

'She lost me.'

'Where?'

'Battersea Bridge.'

'You're sure?'

'Sure I'm sure,' he said, his voice rising with fresh indignation. 'I got the driver to hook round the houses. No way she could have stayed the course without me clocking her.'

'What was she in?'

'An Escort. Greenish.'

'Got the number?'

'Oh, no chance,' he replied with overblown sarcasm. 'I twiddled my thumbs all the way from Heathrow, didn't I? Never even *looked*. Why would I ever think of something that obvious? Christ Almighty . . .'

But Hillyard wasn't listening any more. One section of his mind was rehearsing the call he would be giving Cramm in a few minutes' time, hatching the phrases he would use to break the bad news of the American scientist's arrival while managing to convey the impression that there was still plenty of useful work to be done on the ground. Reynard Associates' turnover – not to mention Hillyard's lifestyle – wouldn't look so rosy if there was a withdrawal of Cramm's very considerable custom.

The other section of his mind was working on how he was going to tell his lunch companion that the meal was over, and that he was about to leave with this plodder Biggs on rather more urgent business.

THIRTY-SIX

Dublensky walked down the broad staircase and paused to get his bearings.

Whatever he'd imagined about his arrival in Britain, it had involved nothing like this. The strange mansion in the northern wilds somewhere; the shadowy servants who slid in and out without a word; and the owner, a singer – a rock singer, for heaven's sake. Dublensky remembered his songs from college days. They had been all the rage. For all he knew, they still were. The whole thing was very strange.

The girl Jenny had tried hard to make them feel at home, but with that ring through her nose and her weird makeup and crazy clothes, her appearance only added to his feeling that he had landed in the middle of a TV drama, an Agatha Christie perhaps. In his present mood, maybe even a Munsters.

He hadn't asked Anne what she thought of the day so far; he could read it in her face. While Tad, disgusted at not being in London, had decided to sulk in his room.

He entered the room to the left of the front entrance.

Simon Calthrop the journalist was there, also Nick Mackenzie. There was no sign of the photographer; perhaps, having got his pictures, he'd left.

'Ah!' Calthrop jumped to his feet. 'All ready, Mr Dublensky?'

Dublensky wasn't certain he was ready for this and perhaps it showed on his face because Mackenzie said: 'Maybe you'd prefer to rest, Mr Dublensky?'

Calthrop threw Mackenzie a sharp look before saying to Dublensky: 'I really don't think we have the time for that. I need to get back to London by Tuesday at the latest. We've a great deal to get through.'

Unseen by Calthrop, Mackenzie raised his eyebrows kindly at Dublensky, as if to say: I'd make up your own mind if I were you.

Dublensky asked: 'Miss Field, has she arrived yet?' knowing that he wouldn't be reassured until she did.

Calthrop shrugged as if it wasn't a matter of great interest, but Mackenzie looked worried, which only served to add to Dublensky's feeling that something wasn't quite right.

'I'd really like to see Miss Field,' Dublensky echoed dully.

'Is it the contract?' Calthrop demanded, moving in front of Dublensky. 'Are you worried about something in the contract?'

'Not exactly. I . . .'

Calthrop motioned him towards a chair, holding the gesture until Dublensky had sat down. 'Well, what is it then, Mr Dublensky?' He dropped into the seat opposite and fastened Dublensky with a firm gaze.

'I just . . . I guess I would have liked to talk things through with Miss Field.'

'Well, that doesn't seem possible just at the moment, does it? So I suggest we get on, and then when she turns up you can talk about anything that's still worrying you.'

'It's what'll happen when we leave here,' Dublensky said, putting a shape to his anxieties. 'No one's told me what's going to happen.'

From the fireplace Mackenzie said: 'You'll be looked after, Mr Dublensky. I guarantee it.'

His voice was reassuring, his manner amiable, yet how far could a rock singer be trusted? 'Perhaps a rest might be a good idea,' he muttered indecisively. 'I'm really very tired.'

Calthrop pressed his lips together. 'I think it might be best to start now, Mr Dublensky.'

'Well, I . . .'

'Simon.' Nick Mackenzie beckoned to Calthrop, and the two of them went into a huddle by the door. Dublensky couldn't hear what was being said, but he knew they were arguing. Finally Nick Mackenzie came back and crouched on the edge of the opposite chair. 'How about a walk before it gets dark, Mr Dublensky? I rather wanted to show you something.'

They took warm coats from a cloakroom and went out of the house by a side door which gave on to a hedged garden with neatly delineated rectangular beds. It was cold, but not unpleasantly so. Patches of white cloud skated across a low winter sun. Mackenzie began again: 'You mustn't let them persuade you into doing anything you don't want to do, you know.'

'No, but . . . Well, I've burnt my boats. There's no turning back, that's for sure.'

'But take it at your own pace. Don't let them pressure you.'

They turned out of the garden and joined a path that led upward between shrubs.

Mackenzie slowed a little. 'You were worried about the future . . . Well, I just wanted to say that there's a job waiting for you if you want it.'

Dublensky looked across at him in surprise. 'There is?'

'It's a trust, a research charity. It's going to be set up in the next month or so. They'll be needing people.'

'But . . .' He floundered for a moment. 'Will they want to employ me?'

He gave a small smile. 'Oh yes.'

'What kind of research are we talking about?'

'Research into the effects of chemicals, how to help people recover from them. That sort of thing.'

Dublensky paused. 'Well . . .'

'No interference. No strings.'

'Sounds . . .' He was going to say unbelievable. 'Unusual.'

'It might mean being based over here.'

Dublensky, who a minute ago would have considered any suggestion of moving abroad with dismay, now found himself turning the idea over in his mind. 'This trust, could I present research proposals?'

'Sure. Anything you liked.'

They continued until, breasting a rise, they reached a paddock surrounded by a wooden rail with a stable on one side.

'We could look at Silveron, for example?'

'Oh yes.'

They stopped and leant on the paddock rail. 'This trust,'

Dublensky said, 'it's yours, right? You yourself would be setting it up?'

Mackenzie gave a slight shrug which was an admission, but not so much of an admission that it invited further comment.

'Well . . .' said Dublensky. 'It sounds . . . interesting.'

They stood in silence as if all had been agreed between them, which in a sense it had.

The wind seemed to bite suddenly, and Dublensky felt the cold. 'You were going to show me something?' he prompted gently.

Mackenzie was staring up the slope of the paddock, towards the forest. 'What?' He came out of his thoughts with difficulty. 'Was I?' He blinked at Dublensky in mild surprise. 'Of course.' Turning, he raised a hand to the panorama below. 'I was going to show you the view.'

Now and again during that long evening Dublensky's words would dwindle and his eyes travel from face to face as if to be sure that he had people's attention. Strange that he should be in doubt: it seemed to Nick that the room was held in a breathless hush of concentration, broken only by the settling of the logs on the fire and the clinking of Anne Dublensky's coffee cup. But then Nick realised: it was not attention that Dublensky craved, but belief.

Simon Calthrop, hunched over a glass of best claret, armed with two tape recorders and a large note book was taking Dublensky painstakingly through the procedures used in toxicology trials: the day-to-day recordings, the tests and examinations.

Nick found he was able to listen to the statistics of rodent extermination with a new and undreamed of detachment. It wasn't just the ease with which he'd clobbered the rat in Daisy's flat, it was the realisation that, when all was said and done, people like Dublensky hadn't been able to find a better way.

He also recognised that moral dilemmas belonged to a world of hard practicalities and uncomfortable truths, a world in which he felt poorly qualified to make sweeping judgements. Alusha had died because the safeguards had failed; perhaps that was all he needed to know.

Calthrop was leading Dublensky firmly onwards. 'So when did you begin to suspect irregularities?'

'Oh, not straight away. I mean, not until the Silveron texicology results had been in for quite a while, like over a year.' Dublensky was crouched forward on the sofa, arms resting on knees, hands pulling nervously at each other. 'Then one day I was looking through the full set of data. Not many people bother with that, believe me. It runs to five or six heavy volumes: computer printouts, daily observation sheets, test results – and here you're talking about maybe five, six specialities: immunology, oncology, dermatology, histology, pathology. I mean, these things can go on for ever. Anyway, my particular interest is haematology. That's because I'm a chemist and I don't know a darned thing about it.' He smiled wrily. Beside him on the sofa, Anne Dublensky shifted in her seat and frowned at him.

'Blood,' continued Dublensky, drawing back into himself. 'I always look at the blood tests, because it's there that you often get the first hint of trouble. Anyway, there I was flicking the pages and I stop at this one page – a computer analysis of standard haemoglobin tests with statistical significance calculations – and I see that the figures have thrown up this strange pattern, a succession of three identical numbers. Like on a roulette wheel you'll occasionally get a number repeating itself. Mathematicians will tell you these things can happen quite easily and that it's well within the normal range of probabilities, but it still seems sort of strange when it appears. So I see this row of identical numbers and I think, hey, what a crazy set of figures, then I notice another oddity, a really low figure in the first column. It could be a testing error, of course, or a statistical error. Then, again, it might be a genuinely low result, just like it seems. Nothing really unusual about any of that. In fact if you didn't get the occasional crazy figure, then things really *would* look strange, like too good to be true, you know.' He jerked his head from person to person, searching out reactions, then paused modestly to recount his moment of glory. 'Except that I suddenly get this feeling I've seen these figures before,' he explained. 'Now this isn't possible – I mean, that's what I tell myself. It's just a trick of my mind. But the more I think about, the more uneasy I get. And you have to remember that by this time the production line at Aurora is pumping out Silveron for export and I've already had the first letter from Dr Burt. So I don't need all that much encouragement to think unhappy thoughts.'

Calthrop, keen as ever to get his chronology right, interjected with a request for dates. While Dublensky leafed through some old diaries he had brought, Nick helped Jenny to stack the supper plates onto a tray. As he bent over the table he became aware that Anne Dublensky was staring at him.

'Where's Daisy Field?' she asked tensely.

'Something important must have come up,' he said.

'Important?' Her tone demanded to know what on earth could have been more important than this.

Returning to his chair Nick too wondered what could be so vital that it could keep Daisy away from this meeting which she had fought so hard to stage.

'I thought and thought, but it didn't get me too far,' Dublensky was saying. 'So I got methodical. I went through all the test data I'd read in the last three years or so. Quite a job. Even then, I missed it first time round because the 8,3,5-Q file was never on my official reading list, so to speak. Picked it up by chance and zoomed through it, you know.'

'What product was that?' asked Calthrop.

'8,3,5-Q? It was an insecticide that never got beyond development stage. It was in initial development at the same time as our big seller Bulwark – was quite similar to it chemically in fact – but once it was realised that Bulwark was the more effective product, 8,3,5-Q was put on what turned out to be permanent hold, and the data buried, forgotten. But not' – he made a sound of fresh surprise – 'by TroChem.'

'TroChem had carried out trials on 8,3,5-Q?'

'They had.'

'So when you looked through the 8,3,5-Q data you found what?'

'I found that many of the haematology results between Silveron and 8,3,5-Q were identical.'

'When you say identical . . .?'

'I mean identical. Ten sheets of results that were the same in every respect. Coincidence wasn't in it. I mean the chances were so remote as to be mathematically incalculable. No – TroChem had simply lifted the data and reused it.' With this, a dreaminess crept over him as if he were reliving the moment of discovery. It was a moment before he responded to the next question. 'Why would TroChem do it?' he echoed. But he'd obviously thought about it a great deal because his reply flowed easily: 'Commercial pressure. Lack of staff. Human nature. The temptation to take short cuts. A desire to please the client. A belief that no harm would come of it.' He spread his hands. 'Any of those. All of them. Who knows.'

'But how could they expect to get away with it?' Nick chipped in.

'Oh, easy. It goes like this. They sincerely believe the product's okay – I mean, it's been developed by Morton-Kreiger, hasn't it? All the expertise, all those expensive labs – they think the trials are just a question of waving things through, of rubber-stamping something that's bound to be okay. They've no reason to think the data will ever be queried. So they cheat things – or maybe only one man cheats things, an overworked head of department, a guy who's under pressure to hurry things along, who's got problems with his budget. He just slips in some ready-made data that no one's ever seen – or he *thinks* no one's ever seen, stuff from a defunct product. No problem. End of story.'

'Were no genuine tests done at all then?'

'Oh, I've no doubt TroChem got the trials under way; it was just the analyses they didn't get round to doing.'

There was a silence. Dublensky rubbed his eyes, Calthrop shuffled thoughtfully through his notes, Anne Dublensky watched, looking worried.

'Can we move on to your dealings with Morton-Kreiger then?' murmured Calthrop. 'How you reported your worries to them and what sort of a reaction you got?'

Just then Mrs Alton buzzed through to say Mr Weinberg was on the line and needed to speak to Nick 'very urgently'. Nick took it in the hall.

'Where the hell are you?'

'I'm here, David.'

'You're meant to be bloody rehearsing.'

In all their years together Nick couldn't remember David swearing at him, however mildly.

'A couple of days won't make much difference.'

'The tour starts in one *week*, Nick! Not only can't it wait, it's beyond a bloody joke. I never thought I'd get this sort of prima donna shit from you, Nick. Never! Joe, Mel – I've never expected anything but grief from them, but *you* . . . Christ, the entire band managed to turn up at the studio at ten sharp this morning, just like yesterday and the day before, and what

598

do they find? What are you trying to do to us, Nick? Just tell me? Mmm? *Mmm?*' Words temporarily failed him.

'I'll be there, David.'

'But *when*? Listen, I've been on the phone the whole bloody day getting these lawyers to pull out the stops and get these charges dropped. The rest of the time I've been telling the underwriters it's all a terrible mistake and you've never touched drugs in your life and the newspaper stories are crap and begging them on my hands and knees not to pull out the rug from under the tour, and all to no bloody avail because their hearts are made of concrete, and I find I'm wasting my breath anyway because I'm getting shot in the back by my own team. You're killing me, Nick, killing me. Tell me, just tell me, *why* are you trying to stymie the whole goddam thing? Huh? Is it that you don't want to do this damn tour?' He sounded close to tears.

'David, I'll be down tomorrow.'

There was a silence. 'You promise?'

'I promise.'

'First thing?'

'Well . . . No. Can't do first thing. Later, David, later.'

A weary pause. 'Nick, you're the one person who can kill me, you know that?'

'Tomorrow, David, I'll be down tomorrow.'

'Suppose there's an alarm?'

But Campbell, having pocketed a torch, was already hoisting himself up the low wall at the back of the property and hooking his heel over the lip. After a great deal of heavy breathing he heaved his bulk onto the top and for an instant lay there, face down, limbs hanging loose, like a lion resting on the branch of a tree.

Someone came round the corner: a leather-jacketed youth in a hurry, hands thrust in pockets, head down. Daisy glanced up to warn Campbell, but he was already gone. She passed the youth at a stroll, face low. Rounding the corner she went a few yards along the main street, looked in the window of an electricity showroom then sauntered back. Reaching the door in the wall, she gave a sharp tap. Someone came out of a house in Peregrine Road. Moving quickly away from the door, she went to the car and pretended to let herself in. Two minutes later she returned to the door and tapped again.

There were two bells by the door, she noticed, a large brass-mounted one next to the engraved plate of Reynard Associates, and above it a small plastic type marked by a blank label stuck into a cheap metal surround. Campbell hadn't mentioned a second bell. A second bell meant a flat, a flat with occupants who came back at all times of the day and night. She began to feel jittery again.

There was a sound, a scraping scrabbling noise to her left; quite close. A movement took her eye up to the top of the low wall, and she watched Campbell's dark bulk appear over the top and drop untidily to the pavement.

'Couldna' make it up the back. Nowhere to get a grip,' he panted as he dusted himself off.

'Well, we tried.'

The sweat shone on Campbell's temples, he blew out noisily through his lips. 'We're no' finished yet.'

'But how?'

He jerked his head towards the door in the wall.

'Jesus, Campbell.'

He was already sliding the jemmy out of the warren of pockets and compartments that lined his jacket.

'Isn't there another way?'

'Eh?' he answered distractedly, already moving towards the door.

'What about keys – can't we use those skeleton things?'

He threw her a protesting look. 'I dinna' carry stuff like that!'

Now you tell me, she thought as she took up station to one side of the door, trying to shield Campbell from casual observers in the main street, a fairly ludicrous exercise when she was half his size.

'Isn't it going to show, the damage?' Daisy called nervously. 'The Bill always check doors.'

In reply, there was a grinding sound, a vicious groaning of timber and an almighty report, so loud it was like a pistol shot. A pedestrian on the far side of the main road paused and looked across. When he didn't move on, Daisy uttered a loud yelp of laughter. Behind, Campbell gave a startled exclamation and grabbed her arm. 'What is it?' She laughed again and jerked her head towards the pedestrian who, convinced he was hearing nothing more than a couple of people returning from an alcoholic afternoon, gave one last look and moved on.

Inside, Campbell found a light switch and Daisy held the door while Campbell wedged it closed with a stack of telephone directories sitting on the floor. The door was severely damaged, the wood badly splintered around the lock and jamb so that, even when it was closed, a large chink of light showed through from the street outside. No bobby in his right mind would miss something that obvious, but she tried to close her mind to that as Campbell led the way through the narrow hall to a flight of stairs which wheeled round a blind turn to a first-floor landing.

Daisy's back crawled, she felt a deep foreboding: what Campbell would probably dismiss as first-time nerves, and he would be right.

Campbell found the next switch and the landing was flooded with light from an array of spots splaying out from a central ceiling rose. There was new carpet, bright paintwork, a prosperous look. The area contained five doors and no windows. Campbell took the left-hand doors, Daisy the right. The first door on the right was marked 'Private' and opened onto a continuation of the stairs. Here the stair carpet was very far from new, the paintwork visibly worn, and a musty aroma of ancient damp and old cooking fat wafted down the stairs, mixed with an odd animal odour, like wet fur.

She moved on. Next was a toilet, the door labelled with a cheap stick-on sign. Last was an unmarked door, also open, that led into the rear extension that she had seen from the street.

From the sound of rattling door handles, it appeared that Campbell was having less success with the two doors at the front of the house. One was a frosted glass-panelled door with 'Reynard Associates, Investigation & Security' in concentric arched gold lettering and on the rail underneath, a stick-on sign: 'Please Enter'; the second had ribbed glass, and was marked 'Private'.

Daisy called: 'This one's open.'

Abandoning his rattling, Campbell swept past her into the back extension. She followed and in the light from the hall saw what appeared to be some kind of conference room with easy chairs, a low table, a coffee-making machine and a tall metal cabinet in one corner. An odour of newness mingled with the strong smell of stale cigarettes. There was a large spill of some dark liquid on the carpet near the door.

Campbell switched on the light, cutting off her objections with a gruff: 'Might be keys.'

'Keys?'

'The office there.' He indicated the door he had left, and started to search the filing cabinet.

Daisy went to the window to watch for signs of approaching danger in Peregrine Road but, feeling conspicuous, pulled back.

Campbell, tiring of his search for keys, went back across the hall to the office door.

'Try not to make so much noise,' she called as Campbell grew more ferocious with the door handle.

He made a sound, a non-committal grunt before punching a hole in the glass with his elbow. Daisy sucked her breath as the sound reverberated into the night.

She warned: 'No lights, Campbell' as he reached through and slipped the latch.

There were blinds at the windows, venetian blinds with knotted cords and jammed pulleys which she closed before allowing Campbell to switch on his torch. Then, with Campbell angling the light, his body masking any stray beams that might find their way through the blinds, they went to work.

The offices consisted of two rooms separated by a chipboard and frosted-glass screen. The first room contained two cluttered desks, a photocopier and a wall of filing cabinets, the second, reached through a connecting door stamped 'C. Hillyard, Director' or by means of the locked ribbed-glass door from the hall, had one much larger desk clean of papers, two easy chairs, an exercise bike and four gleaming filing cabinets.

It was a mistake to start at the filing cabinets, but she didn't realise that straight away. In its time, Reynard Associates seemed to have dealt with large numbers of clients. Each drawer contained dozens of files, and while the file tabs bore numbers which suggested some sort of system, the files themselves appeared random, and she began to realise that, approached this way, the job could not be done in a single night.

One of the cabinets in the inner office refused to open, and leaving Campbell to pick the lock – which in Campbell's repertoire meant to break it – she went back into the outer office and, by the light from the hall, searched the tops of the desks. The larger desk was the more obviously occupied, with in- and out-trays, two telephones, piles of papers and files, a couple of unemptied ashtrays and a stack of tape cassettes. She picked up a cassette and, holding it up to the light, read the label. There was a date – it was five days back – and the word 'Jackie'. The rest of the cassettes – there were twenty or more – seemed to relate to Jackie as well, with the exception of two labelled 'Charlie'. On the windowsill beside the desk there was a cassette player with headphones. Dropping one of the Jackie tapes into the slot, she sampled the buttons until, hitting the right one, the machine gave a click and began to play.

The voice when it sprang into life was both strange and familiar. She recognised the inflections and flat south London vowels and other oddities of her own voice, even recalled the precise conversation – she'd been speaking to Jenny early one morning – yet at the same time the voice sounded disconnected and alien, grotesquely so. Partly it was the recording, which was distorted, partly it was the sheer surprise of hearing her unguarded words relayed back to her in this unlikely place.

Slowly, calmly, she sorted through the stack of cassettes. The most recent was dated yesterday. She jammed it into her pocket, along with three others picked at random.

Campbell reappeared and she beckoned him across to shine his torch over the desk while she searched the papers.

A file also marked 'Jackie' was on top of the largest pile of documents. She might have thought this was a lucky find if she hadn't spotted the next file, which was also entitled Jackie, and the one beneath that. Examination of the bottom file – no surprises on the title – gave her the picture. The transcriptions in the files were rough, the typing erratic and littered with errors, but they faithfully recorded every telephone conversation she'd had over the last few months, in many cases word for word.

Then her gaze lit on a report which read: 'Conversation with painter?? Workman?? Tells her she got some calls, also that she had a male visitor who left no name. Painter couldn't give a description. *Who's a lucky boy, then?* NFI.'

So obvious, thought Daisy. So obvious, and I missed it.

Why should they restrict their listening to phone calls? Why not bug the entire flat and record every conversation with visiting house painters, repairmen, friends, and lovers? Catch every private moment, and, if they were lucky, a few intimate ones as well to relieve the boredom and give them a few laughs. Well, they would have been disappointed on that score. No lovers in her bed for a long while, nor anywhere else in the flat for that matter. Only that long conversation with Nick by the chair. She thought abruptly: Did they get that too?

She glanced at the report again. NFI. No further investigation? No further interest?

'We should have brought a camera,' she muttered, eyeing the photocopier and wondering how long it would take to copy a complete file.

'What for?' Campbell declared as he went through some of the papers she had cast aside. 'Just take the stuff. It's not as if they will na' be knowin' we were here, nor what we came for.'

With Campbell life had a certain simplicity. She tucked three Jackie files into her capacious carpetbag and went through the remaining papers on the desk. They yielded little: surveillance reports on errant husbands, security reports on business premises, bills, invoices, VAT forms.

Campbell disappeared into the inner office. Outside, a lorry thundered past and slowed with a long piercing squeal of brakes. She held still, listening, and realised that for the last few minutes at least, she had forgotten to be frightened. As if to punish her, one of the phones began to ring.

After half a minute the ringing stopped. She returned to the desk top. Her hand settled on the invoices again and she held them up to the light one by one. Each one had the name and address of the creditor typed into the appropriate box with an invoice number above and a reference number below. In the main section came the itemisation – hours of surveillance, office expenses – and the amount owing plus VAT. In some cases there were no details, just the statement 'paid on account' or 'paid in advance against expenses'. Roughly half the invoices were made out to individuals, the other half to companies, and the majority were for between £100 and £500. Only two were for significantly more, one, for the amount of £5575, made out to Workham Overseas Holdings Ltd, covering 'security for the month of October', the other for £2310, made out to PKL Electronics, covering 'employee security'. Workham Overseas Holdings Ltd had an address in the Cayman Islands, and a postal address care of a bank in London.

She made a note of the two reference numbers on the invoices and, after briefly checking the drawers of both desks and the stacks of papers on the windowsills, returned to the filing cabinets. But the gloomy light from the hall defeated her and she had to summon Campbell, torch in hand, before she could make progress through the files. The reference numbers seemed to bear some relation to logic and sequence and, working her way along the wall of cabinets, she found the drawer with the numbers most closely related to that on the PKL Electronics invoice, and then, an instant later, the PKL file itself, more or less in the right place. From what she could see PKL was everything it purported to be, an electronics company, indulging in a little surreptitious spying on its employees. There was no mention of Jackie, nothing relating to agrochemicals.

The locating of the Workham file took a little longer. In the place where the file would most logically be found – two cabinets away in the top drawer – there was a gap, a large one, as if several very bulky files had been removed.

Outside in the street a siren screamed and Daisy stiffened, senses reaching out beyond the room.

'Try next door,' suggested Campbell, his voice cracking with something that might have been tension.

In the inner office, in the top drawer of the filing cabinet Campbell had forced open, they found a mound of papers, none of which referred to Jackie or Workham Overseas Holdings, while in the lower drawer there was a batch of eavesdropping equipment: recorders, batteries, and foam-lined boxes containing small black oblongs like the one she had found in her phone. As Daisy squatted to search the lower drawers there was a resounding *crack!* She twisted round to see Campbell at the desk, manoeuvring his way into the drawers with the jemmy.

'For God's sake!' she cried weakly.

A moment later she forgave him as he called her over to inspect the contents of the top right-hand drawer. The Workham file – or rather the first of three – was sitting on the top.

Surveillance reports, digests of the Jackie transcriptions, a study of developments at Catch and Octek, even – she drew Campbell's attention to it – a report on the fire.

She muttered excitedly: 'Bloody hell.'

'Aye, well, take it an' let's be off then!'

She pushed the file into her now bulging bag. 'There's more,' she said, shining the torch on the files underneath.

'You've enough,' Campbell whispered, his voice alive with sudden anxiety.

The second file contained detailed expense sheets covering the rental of cars and vans, the salaries of two 'operatives', sometimes three, along with equipment hire, phone calls and numerous incidentals.

The third file was a bit of a mystery. Though it had the same reference number and must presumably relate to Workham Overseas Holdings, it concerned someone called Angela Kershaw who lived in Wandsworth, and contained a number of surveillance reports, some hospital bills, a few scribblings and not much else. One of the scribblings said: *Paid in full. Subject has agreed not to see M again.* Then underneath: *Cramm – But will Driscoll stay away from her?*

'Campbell . . . look at this.'

But Campbell wasn't looking. 'Hurry,' he said in agitation. Daisy snapped the files shut and threw them back in the drawer. Then something made her draw the last one out again.

'Come on!' urged Campbell.

But she was taking another look at the note. '*Driscoll* . . . You realise who that – '

Campbell made an abrupt hushing sound. His fear transmitted itself across the darkness, and she felt a creep of alarm. The street had gone quiet, the traffic had fallen into one of those inexplicable lulls that occur from time to time. Inside the house there was a deep stillness. It was broken by a faint sound, a muted ticking. Expanding metal. 'The heating,' she whispered.

She sensed him relax. Sitting the torch on the desk she stacked all three Workham files and tried to force them into her over-stretched shoulder bag, but there wasn't room. Even the surveillance file on its own was a squeeze, and reluctantly she put the other two back on the desk. Even then she couldn't bring herself to leave them and, ripping the contents of the Kershaw file from its covers, tearing five specimen sheets from the expenses file, she rolled them up and pushed them into her belt. This, she immediately realised, was not ideal either and, removing them again, she thrust the bundle at Campbell who, after some complaint, jammed it into an inside compartment of his jacket.

'That's it,' she said.

Campbell didn't reply. He seemed to be listening again. Abruptly he moved towards the outer office, waving at her to turn off the torch. Following, she came into the hall as he reached for the switch and killed the lights.

In the darkness all she could hear was the soft rasp of Campbell's breathing and the vibration of the traffic humming against the windows.

A creak, a flow of sounds billowed into the stairwell: someone had opened the street door.

Suddenly the lights in the lower hall sprang on and spilled round the turn in the stairs, and Daisy's hand gave a slight involuntary spasm. Campbell touched her arm and jerked his head towards the blind spot between the toilet and the door that led to the floor above, where they would be hidden from anyone coming up from below. Having installed her there, he advanced slowly towards the head of the stairs, setting his feet down with such caution that in other circumstances he would have looked comical, like an actor in a farce.

A floorboard creaked beneath his foot. She could almost feel him wince. He paused and tried again, but as he shifted his weight the wood creaked again.

No sound came from below, no shout, no footfall.

Reaching the top of the stairs Campbell put his eye to the corner and peered cautiously down the first flight, ready to spring out at anyone who came up. The silence ticked on. Numerous thoughts jostled in Daisy's mind: the absurdity of the situation, the weight of the files dragging at her shoulder, the desire for something – anything – to happen, the urge to make some appalling noise, to shout or maybe even laugh.

Just as it seemed the silence would go on for ever the lights went off below, plunging them into darkness again. A moment later there was a scraping of mauled wood against a frame, and an uneasy silence rippled up the stairs.

It was perhaps two minutes before Campbell reached back and touched her arm and whispered: 'Stay here.' In the darkness she sensed rather than saw him move. A couple of treads creaked as he made his way down the stairs. With each sound Daisy's foreboding returned.

There was no way of knowing how far he had got when the loud thud rumbled up the stairwell. It was a deep and solid sound, like the thwack of a bat hitting a ball, like –

She saw again the open door of the Beetle and the raincoat man's arm raised above his head.

A shuffling, a grunt, the sound of a scuffle. The dull thwack again. A crash, then silence.

She opened her mouth to call Campbell's name but the word died on her lips. Someone was already speaking. The murmur of a voice, not Campbell's.

After a moment the lower light sprang on again.

She felt a moment of overwhelming helplessness, then the options spread themselves out before her: the conference room with its sheer drop to the yard below, the office with its windows that might or might not open, the toilet with its tiny window and no way out at all.

From below, the voice rose, the words indistinct. The sound seemed to be coming up the stairs towards her.

Catlike, her instinct cried out for height and, reaching for the knob beside her, she pulled open the door that led upstairs, and, stepping silently around it, closed it softly behind her. Feeling her way up the narrow stairs in the darkness, she stepped on every second tread, using the edges where the wood was least likely to give her away. Her back prickled with the heat of pursuit, she felt the terror of every small girl's nightmare – the man panting at her heels, the weights pulling at her limbs – and it was with difficulty that she suppressed the urge to hurry.

Rounding the dogleg in the stairs she heard feet pounding up to the floor below. Under cover of the noise, unable any longer to control the need to run, she made it to the top floor in three swift strides, two steps at a time. She stopped to listen, her heart hammering in her chest.

The pounding feet were not following. Not yet anyway. She felt her way softly round the edge of a small hallway to an open door. Lights from the main street cast a fan of rectangles over the ceiling of a kitchen. In the next room, which was charged with the odours of ancient meals, tobacco and animals, the street reflections outlined chairs and the glint of glass-fronted pictures. To the back was a room in pitch darkness. Here the scent was of stale sweat and aftershave.

She felt her way across the room to a sliver of night light showing through curtains and peered out. Below was the black bulk of the rear extension. Was it a flat roof? For all the times she had looked up at it from the car, she couldn't remember. And what sort of a drop was it? A few feet? Six at the most.

Slipping the bag off her shoulders, she opened the curtains a short way, hearing the clink of the rings sliding along the rail, and tried the window. It wouldn't budge. She felt along the top of the lower sash for a catch, and finding one, slid it open. Still the frame wouldn't shift. 'Come on!' She heard the desperation in her voice, felt the cold dampness on her forehead. The upper sash was a little more forthcoming and, after she had swung her weight on it, finally permitted itself to be lowered a grudging twelve inches or so. From somewhere in the house came the sound of a banging door, rapidly answered by the thudding of her heart. She thought: Dear God, I'm no good at this. Not without Campbell.

She pulled at the window again, to see if she could open it further, but it was solid, and she realised there were security stops on the frame.

A strange sound rose from below: a faint scratching. Hurrying now, she zipped up the bag, heaved it onto the lip of the open window then, giving it a firm shove, watched it bump past the sill before disappearing into the darkness and landing almost immediately on the roof below with what seemed to be a grossly amplified thud.

A dog barked, a sharp furious yapping. The sound was coming from inside the house. A voice yelled for it to shut up. The barking continued. Claws scratched frantically against wood. After a moment a door was opened and she knew instantly which one it was – the door to the stairs. A male voice came floating up the stairwell: 'Fuck off, Beji.'

She heard the skittering of the animal's paws as it scrabbled up the stairs. She made for the door, intending to slam it shut, but even before she stumbled over the bed she realised she had left it too late. The dog was fast; it was already racing across the hallway. Her brain, acting on its own initiative, was making a few simultaneous calculations: if she lunged for the door and pushed hard she might catch the animal against the jamb, while if she held back, the dog would get in and try for a chunk of her leg. Either way someone was going to get hurt. The question was, who would make the least noise?

She held back. The dog shot in, braked hard and spun round to get a run at her. She kicked out a defensive foot but the animal had seen plenty of those and was past it in a flash and under the cover of semi-darkness was coming in to her leg from the other side. Daisy tried to grab at the mass of fur, but it was surprisingly hard to grip. The animal snarled and wriggled and howled, its snapping teeth grabbing at her legs. Any last self-control she might have felt vanished in the heat of her panic and, letting the teeth get to grips with her jeans, she caught the animal by the scruff of the neck and yanked it screaming into the air and clamped a hand round its throat. She wasn't sure how much pressure was needed to kill, but she soon found out how much was needed to cut off the noise. When the animal stopped screaming, she eased the pressure, and cocked an ear towards the door, straining to pick up sounds over the dazed gasps of the dog.

The silence reached out, unsettlingly quiet.

She dropped the snuffling rasping dog onto the bed and looked longingly towards the window. There might still be time. But even as she assessed the precarious climb onto the sill and the impossibly narrow squeeze through the high opening, she heard the creak of a tread on the stairs.

She was very still.

And again, faint but unmistakable.

I don't think I can deal with this, she thought; I want to scream.

A light came on in the hall beyond the open door.

She moved deeper into the room. The window was out of the question now. Under the bed? She felt an anticipatory lurch of something like claustrophobia. In the wardrobe? It stood to one side of the door, a narrow old-fashioned free-standing wardrobe in dark wood. Too small. To the other side of the window then, in the corner, a door to what could be a walk-in cupboard?

There had to be a better way.

Bluff it out? Stand her ground?

The dog began to whimper. In the light from the hall she could see it clearly – two globular eyes in a squashed face, a

610

mass of pale fur – and then it came to her with sudden certainty: this was *his* room.

For a moment she was the child again, fear panting at her heels, limbs dragging in water, unable to move.

Another sound. Much closer, almost at the door. She moved at last, stealing deeper into the room, towards the far corner and the narrow recessed door. It pulled open soundlessly. She met hanging clothes, a floor covered with shoes and soft unidentifiable bundles. Easing her feet through to the boards beneath, she stepped into the dark sweat- and musk-scented world of Maynard's shirts.

The long journey and the time change were finally taking their toll on Dublensky, and his memory was giving trouble. It wasn't the contents of the memos he'd sent to the MKI management that were failing to come to mind – he remembered them quite clearly – nor even the responses he'd got back – they'd been few enough – but the order and timing of these events, which Calthrop was determined that he should recall. But with each new effort of memory Dublensky's mind was only becoming more confused.

Mackenzie suggested a break. Calthrop didn't look too happy about that, but then matters were brought to a natural halt by a buzz on the internal phone which had Nick Mackenzie leaving the room like a rocket. The girl Jenny followed immediately, then a few minutes later Mackenzie put his head round the door and summoned Simon Calthrop as well, leaving the Dublenskys alone.

Anne said: 'There's something bad going on, I know there is. And they're not telling us.'

'Why d'you say that? I thought it was going well. I mean, they've done everything they said they would.'

'I meant something else.'

'Like what?'

'How do I know?' she said impatiently. 'That's what they're not telling us.'

They sat in silence for a while, aware of the murmur of urgent voices wafting through the partly open door.

Dublensky got to his feet. 'I'll go and make sure Tad's okay. Should he be in bed?'

Anne shrugged. 'He's half-way through a video.'

Dublensky decided to go anyway. Reaching the door he

pulled it open to see Mackenzie, Calthrop and the girl in the centre of the hall. Calthrop was saying in a fast low-pitched voice: 'I can't possibly get involved with this! Christ, you shouldn't even be telling me. It's *crazy* to tell me. If the paper gets a whiff of this, they'll have hysterics. *God.*'

Dublensky would have moved then if he hadn't heard Mackenzie say: 'But what about *Daisy*?'

Calthrop held up both hands and said with a chilly little laugh: 'I'm sorry – I'm really not listening to this. I've gone totally deaf.'

'She could be in trouble!'

'Daisy's a resilient girl. She'll be all right.'

Calthrop began to retreat, but Mackenzie grabbed him by the shoulder. 'What do you mean, *all right*? Suppose she's been beaten up like Campbell? Suppose she's lying somewhere, hurt?'

'Listen, Mackenzie, perhaps I'm not making myself clear,' interrupted Calthrop smoothly, shaking his shoulder free. 'I won't – I *can't* – have anything to do with this.'

Even from where Dublensky stood he could see the set of Mackenzie's jaw, the anger in his face. 'I see,' he hissed. 'So Campbell's beaten up and Daisy's missing and you're not prepared to help?'

'Now wait a minute,' Calthrop argued virtuously. 'Don't let's forget what they were doing to get into this mess, shall we? A *burglary*, for God's sake. What do you expect me to do, find a tame policeman to help out?'

'You must have contacts!'

'Nobody could have contacts that good,' Calthrop scoffed. 'They were committing a criminal offence, and my paper can have *nothing* to do with it. *Nothing.* And' – he raised an admonitory finger – 'nothing to do with the perpetrators, either. Daisy's finally gone over the edge this time. Killed her chances. If this comes out she'll be finished, believe me!'

'They were only looking for evidence,' Jenny chipped in defensively.

'What evidence?' Calthrop jeered. 'We could never use that sort of evidence, it's useless!'

Mackenzie hunched down into his shoulders. 'What do you mean?'

'I mean we can't use stuff which has been stolen in a bloody burglary. God, we'd be bombarded with writs and injunctions, not to mention arrest!'

There was silence. Mackenzie glowered at the floor, then, sensing Dublensky's presence, swung round to stare at him. Dublensky tried to pretend he'd just that minute come into the hall.

'Fine,' Mackenzie said to no one in particular. 'Fine.'

And with that he strode over to Dublensky. 'I've got to leave,' he said in a rough undertone. 'You won't go away, will you?'

'What's happening?' Dublensky asked in agitation.

'Nothing that need bother you.'

Dublensky protested: 'But I think I should know.'

'Just don't go away, that's all!'

And he disappeared up the stairs at a run. The next morning the housekeeper told Dublensky that Mr Mackenzie had been driven south the previous night. She thought he had gone to London.

THIRTY-SEVEN

The silence closed in around Daisy, steady and tantalising, and at that moment she might have been able to convince herself she was alone in the building if it hadn't been for the sickly scent of Maynard's clothing, the blend of hair gel and unidentifiable body scents that were like a presence in the darkness.

She had eased the hanging clothes away from her face and was standing propped against the wall, her ear close to the door, waiting and listening, though for what she wasn't sure. More silence? Some sign that it was safe to get out? Even perhaps a sound in the room outside.

The pipes ticked gently, and a muffled sound, something like the banging of a car door, drifted up from Peregrine Road.

How long had she been here? Ten minutes? No, longer, much longer – more like twenty. It had taken a good five minutes for her heart to regain its rhythm after she'd stepped into the cupboard and discovered that not only were there no means of pulling the door closed after her, but it was threatening to swing open again. Gripping the edge of the door with her fingers she had run a hand over the inner surface and eventually located a clothes hook which had given her sufficient leverage to pull the door gently into the jamb. Then, just when she thought the worst was over, the spring-loaded ball closure had given a slight click as it went home. The sound, no louder than a breaking matchstick, had seemed to reverberate across the silence, gathering volume in her brain. Her throat dried, her heart squeezed against her chest.

There had been no sound from the other side of the door.

It was another five minutes before she convinced herself that it was silence that she was hearing in the room beyond, that the rustlings of her own movements, the sound of her own breathing were not masking some other breathing or the creep of footfalls on the carpet or the soft snorts of the lurking dog.

There had been no one moment when she had realised the dog had gone, no one moment when the snuffles had stopped; rather the sounds had faded imperceptibly, probably early on, when she was still listening for something much closer, like a touch on the door, a sudden pull on the handle.

Once the snuffles had faded there had been no other sound. Whoever had come up the stairs had come and gone silently.

Now the silence was long and seemingly uninhabited. She would have to move sooner or later, and this was as good a time as any. She slid her hand to the edge of the door and began to exert pressure on it by degrees. It resisted her first efforts and, realising she'd have to push a little harder, she felt for the hook so that she could restrain the door from flying open once it sprang past the catch.

Finding the hook, she was on the point of giving the door a solid push when a sound came, catching her by surprise.

Loud, close, just beyond the door. Her hand jerked away from the hook.

Loud, close. The bitter complaint of wood sliding against wood, the squeal of ancient pulleys: the window.

But if the loudness was startling, so was the realisation that someone had stolen into the room without a sound, had crossed to the window without the creak of a floorboard. Had even – the thought unnerved her – been there all the time.

Her knee gave way, she jerked it taut. She realised she was holding her breath and exhaled rapidly. She shifted her weight and put her head closer to the door. Had he realised why the window was open? If so, why was he closing it? Then it occurred to her that the frame was complaining so much not because the window was being closed but because the upper sash was being opened further; either that, or somehow he'd managed to prise open the solid lower sash.

There was only one reason he would be opening the window further: to search the roof below. He must think she'd got out that way. Or maybe he was checking to see if she was trapped there, unable to get down.

Whatever, he would see the bag. The realisation came to her with sickening certainty, and she grimaced in silent frustration. Stupid. *Stupid*.

She pressed her ear back to the door. Faint scrabbling sounds, a soft rasping like clothes dragging over the window-sill.

That was it then, she thought, adjusting to the full weight of her disappointment: he'll have seen it by now. She pictured him leaning out of the window, torch in hand, casting the light over the roof until the bulky shape of the bag caught in the beam. In a few minutes he would climb out and retrieve it. Then he would discover the bulging files and, knowing she would never have left them behind intentionally, he would realise that she couldn't have got very far after all.

She listened for the sound of feet on the sill, for knocks and scrapes as he climbed down onto the roof. She prepared to open the door and run while he was out on the roof, but though she waited, nerves beating at her throat, the pause stretched on and on until, finally, it was broken by an abrupt and unexpected sound: the screaming pulleys again, louder than ever. The window being closed. And not just one sash either: there was the thud of a second sliding home, and the click of a clasp.

What did it mean? He couldn't possibly have had time to get out onto the roof and retrieve the bag and climb back in. Maybe he'd decided to leave it till morning. Maybe he didn't have a torch. Maybe – it seemed too much to hope for – he hadn't spotted the bag at all.

But hope comes cheap and she allowed herself a large ration. She almost persuaded herself that he'd given up on her, that he thought she'd escaped. From there it was a short step to an even more promising thought: that he didn't realise she was there or had ever been there, that he believed Campbell had come on his own. The open window could after all have been Campbell's doing, while the dog, catching Campbell's scent, could have become hysterical and run itself into the door.

Arguments that didn't bear much examination; but they kept her going while she waited breathlessly in the darkness. The silence was worse this time because she knew he moved soundlessly, and, while he might well have left the room, he could just as easily be inches away, his hand reaching slowly for the door, or, worse, just standing there, waiting.

The silence stretched out. The sounds in Peregrine Road, now stifled by the closed window, were barely audible: a dog barking, the occasional car, a jet rumbling over on its descent to Heathrow. After a time she persuaded herself that the room was empty again. When ten minutes' silence had passed she murmured inwardly, *This is ridiculous*, and reached for the door again, one hand to the hook, the other to the door edge. She pushed gently but the door didn't shift. She tried harder. It was very stiff. She ran over her memories of the door: the soft click when she had pulled it shut, the operation of the simple spring-ball arrangement, the knob on the outside which had been of the fixed non-turning variety, the impossibility of a latch or anything heart-stopping like that.

She pushed again, really hard this time. And again.

And then for an instant her heart really did stop, because as she put her whole weight against the door, she realised it would never open. It had been locked from the outside.

'Are you sure?'

'Sure I'm sure. Over the bicycle shop. An' look, the hire car's still there. Three down, behind the white one.'

Nick looked at the Escort, then surveyed the building. It was on the opposite corner, on a junction with a small street called Peregrine Road, whose name, set on a plate on the side wall, was just visible in the streetlights. A single white light glowed dimly in the window of the shop. The windows above were in darkness.

'The door, it's at the side there.'

Campbell's voice tightened oddly, and Nick took a quick look at him. He sat stiffly in the passenger seat, his head pressed back against the rest, his lower lip pushed out fiercely, like a bulldog's. In the thin light it was hard to tell if he was in pain or just exhausted.

'You all right?'

'Huh? I'm a'right,' he replied testily. It was the answer he'd given at the hospital when Nick had picked him up from the casualty department an hour before. His only visible signs of injury, then as now, were a puffy left eye and a long cut over the lid which had been fixed with Elastoplast, giving him the look of a boxer after a choppy fight. The nurse had mentioned something about concussion, but Campbell had brushed the idea aside.

Nick turned off the engine and peered forward to take another look at the building. Was Daisy still there? He tried to imagine her somewhere behind the dark windows. Was she lying unconscious? But no, why would they have attacked her? There wouldn't have been any need to subdue her, not like with Campbell. Trapped then? But why would they have kept her there, why would they bother?

He sighed fretfully: 'We should have gone straight to the police. There's nothing we can do here!'

'Ha!' Campbell brayed his contempt. 'An' what would *they* be doin' that we canna'?'

'Having the law on their side,' Nick replied.

'Aye, an' they'd just listen like lambs, would they? They'd just come along an' do as we asked, would they?'

Nick, remembering that he was up on drugs charges and Campbell on bail for assault, reluctantly felt himself giving way, though it went against his better judgement.

'But why would she still be here?' he argued.

'Huh? Well, she didna' come out, did she?'

'How do you *know*? You were in the gutter unconscious.'

'But she'd have made a call if she'd have got out, would she not? She'd have taken the car. She'd have called Ashard.'

There was no denying that and, momentarily silenced, another idea came to Nick: that she'd had an accident, tried to climb out and fallen from a window. The idea, dramatic and unlikely though it was, began to fix itself in his mind.

'Perhaps we should ask at the hospitals.'

'Eh?' Campbell dismissed it with a blow of his lips. 'But they'd have brought her to the emergency there' – he gestured over his shoulder in the general direction of the hospital they had just left – 'I would've seen her.' He moved his bulk towards the door, impatient for action.

But Nick had a good idea of the action Campbell had in mind, and he didn't want any of that, not if it could possibly be avoided. 'Wait,' he insisted firmly. 'Let's decide what we're going to do – to say.'

'Say?' Campbell sucked in his breath disapprovingly. 'Best to go straight in' – he thrust an arrowlike hand in the direction of the building – 'take a look around, see if she's there, an' talk later.'

'That's a sure way to get into trouble!' Nick snapped. 'They might call the police.'

Campbell threw him an incredulous look. 'What? They'd no more call the police than I would!'

'We don't know that,' Nick argued, zipping up his jacket with finality. 'But whatever happens violence isn't going to help.' He was aware of sounding sanctimonious, but he didn't know how else to dampen Campbell's insatiable appetite for action.

'Stay here,' Nick instructed, and before Campbell could argue he got out and strode across Peregrine Road to the entrance in the wall. It was barely six and still pitch black; there weren't many people around yet, just the occasional car in the main road. The door was in a bad way, splintered and bent around the remains of the lock. It had been patched up with pieces of plywood, nailed roughly into place. A square of white card had been pinned to the door. Peering at it closely, he read: *Reynard Associates are temporarily closed for staff holidays.*

Nick pressed the bell, waited, then pressed the second bell. After four tries he left his finger on both bells.

No one came.

He returned to the car with a sense of anticlimax.

'Should a' gone straight in,' mumbled Campbell, a note of censure in his voice. 'Now they'll know we're here.'

Nick clenched the wheel. 'I want to find her, Campbell, just as much as you do.'

His remark seemed to trigger something in Campbell for, without a word, he got out of the car. Nick shouted, but there was no stopping him.

Nick watched half in agitation, half in fascination as Campbell strode up to the door and beat on it with both hands. Ignoring the stares of a passer-by, he then kicked viciously at a point half way up the door where the lock should have been. When that failed he ran the full weight of his shoulder against it, and looked surprised when the door withstood his advances. He was rallying himself for another go when a man on the corner of the main road started shouting and gesticulating at him. Then Nick saw that the gestures weren't aimed *at*

619

Campbell, but *towards* Campbell, as if directing someone towards the scene. Suddenly appreciating his danger, Campbell abandoned the door and, looking over his shoulder, half walked, half ran back to the car. Nick, falling into the required role of getaway driver, had the engine running and the car moving even as Campbell climbed in. Braking to turn out into the main road, he saw a uniformed policeman pounding up to the passer-by, who was pointing towards the car.

Nick shot out into the road and accelerated away, his ears singing, his heart pumping, feeling the policeman's eyes burning into the illuminated car registration. The car lights – he should never have turned them on! What a stupid mistake! Then, when the worst of his panic had subsided and he'd got things into some sort of proportion, he realised that it wasn't the lights that had been the mistake, but allowing Campbell to talk him into such a crazy idea in the first place.

He wasn't capable of speech for some time and it was Campbell who broke the silence as they crossed the river.

'A regret,' he said with feeling. 'A real regret. I was almost there!'

Nick pressed his lips together and parked in silence just the other side of the King's Road. Using the car phone he called Jenny at Glen Ashard, but there was no news. They walked back to a café-brasserie that was just opening up, ready to catch the yuppie breakfast trade.

Nerves partially restored by strong coffee, Nick made Campbell go through the whole evening again in more detail, from the time he and Daisy had got inside the place until the moment he woke in the street with the ambulancemen leaning over him. Campbell, speaking haltingly, got as far as the tape recordings and the invoices and the Workham Overseas Holdings files when his ruddy cheeks turned ashen and he clutched a hand to his injured head.

After that he wasn't much good for anything. Nick offered to deposit him at a doctor but with some predictability Campbell wasn't having any of that and lay back in his seat, pale and uncommunicative, as they drove through the first knots of rush-hour traffic to Scotland Yard.

'What was she doing there exactly?'

The inspector's manner was deceptively benign, making it only too easy to overlook the directness of the question.

Nick replied carefully: 'She went there for information.'

'What kind of information?'

How much to tell? 'Information about the illegal bugging of her telephone – and other things.'

The inspector smiled blandly and raised an eyebrow to show that he was prepared to be moderately impressed. Having become something of a judge of policemen over the last months, Nick put him down as shrewd rather than bright, a man who had carved out a niche that exactly suited his talents. Greying and pouchy, he seemed poured into his seat. The benevolence, the unhurried speech, the apparent sloth were, Nick suspected, part of a well-practised approach, designed to lull, lure and, quite probably, to drive people to confession through sheer frustration. It was almost an hour since Nick had announced himself at the desk downstairs, and forty minutes since he had been ushered in to see this man Morgan. Yet far from responding to the urgency, it seemed to Nick in his present mood that Morgan was taking pleasure in slowing things down.

Morgan asked: 'And what makes you so sure she's still in there?'

'I told you – the car. And she would have called if she'd managed to get out. It's the first thing she would have done.'

'So why would she be having trouble in getting out? Why would anyone want to prevent her?'

At Campbell's insistence, Nick hadn't mentioned the fact that Campbell had been there, hadn't suggested that Daisy was anything but alone. 'These people had been spying on her,' Nick offered. 'They knew she was on to them, they knew she was going to expose them. They would have had good reason to shut her up.'

'But she hadn't called us in?' Morgan murmured. 'She hadn't thought it serious enough for that?'

Watching the inspector, Nick was suddenly reminded of the roomful of doctors he'd faced during Alusha's illness and how they had worn the same look of condescension and quiet disbelief. Goaded by tiredness and old anger, Nick added testily: 'You don't seem to believe me.'

'If I didn't believe you, Mr Mackenzie, I wouldn't have sent a car to go and look, would I?'

'But can they get in? Can they search the place?'

'Not without a warrant.'

'And will you get a warrant?'

'Not without some evidence.' He gave a humouring smile. 'Which is the purpose of these questions, Mr Mackenzie.' He took a long languid breath. 'Now this company, Reynard Associates – you say they're private investigators?'

'I told you . . . Look, can't we do this later?'

'But why not now, Mr Mackenzie? Is there some difficulty?' The ingenuous smile.

'Because – ' Nick could almost hear Campbell's voice, telling him that this was just what he had warned him about, all talk and no action. 'Because there's no time!'

The inspector dropped his eyes slowly to the desk and examined his pen. When he looked up there was an obdurate look beneath the benevolent gaze. 'We'll hurry as best we can, Mr Mackenzie. In the meantime, Reynard Associates – would you mind?' Nick saw that there was to be no escape, not for the time being at least, though that didn't stop him from burying his head in his hands. Then, drawing a deep breath, he started to go through it again.

It was nine fifteen by the time Nick called an exasperated halt. The patrol men sent to ring on the side door in Peregrine Road had drawn a blank, and the inspector was showing no signs of trying for a warrant. Leaving Morgan to dig up what he could on Reynard Associates, Nick got down to the car to find Campbell half asleep in the passenger seat. He was grey-faced and groggy, but that didn't stop him remarking: 'What did I tell you, hey?' with a glint of satisfaction.

Nick called Jenny at Ashard again, but there was still no news.

Intending to drop Campbell off into the care of his house-keeper in Kensington, Nick headed west. His route took him close by David's place in Knightsbridge and, realising David might still be at home, he diverted into Montpelier Square.

David emerged from the door of his immaculate town house and stared at Nick disbelievingly before his face lit up like a child's for whom a long-heralded promise has unexpectedly come true. 'Nick! You made it! You made it!' He must have been shaving because he was still in his dressing gown and there were smudges of foam on his ears.

Nick remembered his promise of the previous afternoon. 'David, I'll try to get into the studio later, I promise.'

David's expression underwent a painful transformation from open joy to the sort of dull hurt shown on the faces of ill-treated dogs in advertisements for animal charities.

'David, a favour. Could you trace a company for me? It's called Workham Overseas Holdings.'

With a sigh David turned away and padded off across the hall and down the stairs. Nick followed him into the basement kitchen, a mock-German-farmhouse affair with a dazzling ceiling of recessed spotlights, walls of dark oak fittings and a central island that sported hanging copper pans which gleamed from lack of use.

'It's based in the Cayman Islands,' Nick prompted.

David flicked on a coffee percolator, filled it with water and, opening a cupboard, pulled out two cups and deposited them noisily on the work surface. His movements were slow and heavy, as if he was suddenly very tired. 'Can't be done,' he said laconically.

'Why not?'

'Half the reason people put their companies in the Cayman Islands is so that people like us can't trace them.'

'But haven't I got a company in the Caymans?'

'Exactly.'

'But there must be a way surely.'

'You asked me, and I'm telling you there's no way. Zilch.' He made a chopping movement with his hand. This was David at his steeliest, the David encountered by record companies trying to negotiate contracts.

Nick persevered: 'Have we no contacts?'

David turned slowly to face him, his emotions hidden behind layers of hard-won impassivity. 'Contacts are only as good as the favours they owe you.'

'But you could ask, David?'

'Asking'll get me nowhere,' he drawled. 'Secrecy's sewn into the system tighter than the coins in my grandmother's hem when she escaped the Russian revolution.'

'But *asking* . . .?'

A slight pause which Nick took as a hopeful sign.

'When can I tell the others you'll be coming to rehearsal?' David replied, apparently changing the subject but not, as they both knew, changing it at all.

'David, as soon as I can. This afternoon. Maybe sooner. Look, I wouldn't ask if it wasn't important.'

David filled the cups and, taking them across the kitchen, plonked them saucerless on a rustic wooden table that matched the dark oak units. 'Everything's important with you, Nick, everything except what you're meant to be doing at the time.'

Smarting under the unprecedented rebuke, Nick sank onto a stool.

'Someone's gone missing,' he tried to explain. 'Daisy Field, the campaigner from Catch. You remember . . .?' He began to tell him about the weekend's events but a veil of indifference had dropped over David's eyes and Nick recognised the look he usually reserved for the stream of hard-luck stories that regularly came his way each working day.

'Not your problem, surely,' David murmured at last.

'But it *is*. She was— She's— I have to find her, David!'

'I see,' he said, and his eyes carried a wealth of meaning.

'It's not like that,' Nick replied sternly. 'It's not like that at all. It's just – I feel sort of responsible. I feel . . .'

He trailed off, aware that David was watching him with open puzzlement. He repeated: 'I can't leave it, David.'

David reassumed his world-weary mantle.

'Okay,' he conceded with a slow sigh, 'okay. I'll do what I can, but I promise nothing, you understand, *nothing*. I'll have to ask a lot of favours, serious favours I have no right to ask. It could take time.'

'How long?'

'Well there's the time difference for a start, five hours, and favours never come quick. Several days, at the least. But even then I can't promise a *thing*, Nick, not a *thing*.'

'I thought . . .' What had he thought? That it would be a question of lifting a phone and getting a quick answer.

'Having got that out of the way,' said David heavily, 'can we now discuss a few small items like this tour we're meant to be starting next week? I won't begin to tell you what I'm going through with the insurance people – '

'I was fixed up, by the way.'

David's eyelids drooped lower. He didn't speak.

'The drugs. Someone set me up.'

David kept all expression out of his face. 'Who'd want to do that, Nick?'

Nick downed his coffee and got ready to leave. 'People who wanted to warn me off.'

This was too much, even for David, and a sort of regretful wariness came across his eyes. 'But, Nick – do you mean they *planted* the drugs?'

Nick stood up. 'I mean someone tipped them off.'

'Who?'

A vision of Susan slipped into Nick's mind, and, as always when he thought of her now, it was against the backdrop of that South Kensington flat all those years ago. Whether from an improvement in his memory or some trick by which his brain had patched in conversations from other times, he seemed to hear the very words she had used in the argument that had finally broken their relationship, words that were uniformly violent, bitter, and ugly. It occurred to him, as it had occurred to him soon after the drugs raid, that she had hated him then, and probably still did.

But this wasn't the moment to deal with that. There would never be a right moment. Thoughts of vengeance and recrimination had never formed an important part of his repertoire. It was quite enough that he was rid of her.

Yet as he went out to the car and half turned to wave to David it suddenly struck him that Susan, far from being someone to avoid, was probably the very person he should go and see. Much as he loathed to admit it, much as it infuriated him to think of facing her again, Susan might just be able to wave a magic wand: Susan with her knowledge of Schenker, her many dealings with him, Susan who liked to show off her contacts, Susan the perfect messenger. Even – it wasn't totally impossible – Susan with a sense of shame at what she had done.

Campbell raised his eyebrows expectantly as Nick got into his car.

Nick fought an increasingly miserable battle with himself before starting the car and driving round the square.

'Well? Anythin'?' Campbell demanded eventually.

'What? No, nothing.'

'So?'

'We're going to see Mrs Driscoll. Well, I think so.' And saying it he realised he still hadn't made up his mind.

'And who is she?'

'The wife of the agriculture minister.'

Coming into Eaton Square, Campbell gave a sudden peremptory exclamation, half-way between a grunt and a shout, and seemed to clutch his stomach. Imagining sickness or worse, Nick swerved in to the kerb. 'What is it?'

Campbell made an odd sound, and it was an instant before Nick realised it wasn't a bark of impending nausea but of gruff excitement. He was brandishing a half-rolled bundle of papers which he had extricated from the inner reaches of his jacket.

'Daisy, she had no room for them, she gave them to me. That name, that name – it's in here!'

Nick shuffled through, reading quickly. 'I don't see . . .'

'Look – *Driscoll*!'

Nick stared at the papers for a long time, reading and rereading them until their meaning was both clear and confused in turns. Workham Overseas Holdings. The Cayman Islands. Expenses. Operatives. Vehicles. And then hospital bills. The name Angela Kershaw. And: *Cramm – But will Driscoll stay away from her?* Who was the her? The Kershaw woman? And Driscoll, could it really be the same . . . Yet if all these papers came from a Workham Overseas Holdings file, if Workham was in fact Morton-Kreiger, then why on earth not? Reading the cryptic message again, he tried to imagine a situation where a man in a prominent position couldn't be relied on to keep away from a woman, and ended up with a sexual scenario. The hospital bills sent him further along the same path. He tried to push his mind in other directions – hate, guilt, debt – but nothing else rang with anything approaching conviction.

He threaded the car back into the traffic, aware of two simultaneous and equally disturbing thoughts: that this might be something extremely valuable, and that he hadn't the first idea what to do with it.

He remembered that Susan had moved to a place somewhere off Vincent Square but had to call his housekeeper on the car phone for the exact address. He found the house at one end of a narrow and uninspiring street of variable architecture. The place was a dark-bricked Georgian town house with newly painted window frames, a royal-blue front door that shone like glass and baggy-knicker curtains in the upstairs rooms. Waiting outside was a black car with a uniformed driver.

Nick hesitated a moment, struck by nervousness and an odd beating excitement that, in an ancient reflex, had him momentarily longing for a drink. Leaving the car keys with Campbell, he went up to the house and rang the bell. The door opened instantly as if someone had been waiting behind it, and a soberly suited man in horn-rimmed glasses stepped forward. The man had clearly been expecting someone else because an expression of surprise darted across his face. Deciding that Nick was harmless, exercising a politician's versatility, he recovered quickly with a brisk enquiring look.

'Good morning,' he said, angling his head as if to catch some airborne clue as to Nick's identity.

'I've come to see Susan.'

'Of course, of course.' The professional smile, broad but bleak, flashed across his face. He looked like his photographs but smaller and plumper, and, despite his vigorous manner, less intimidating.

'One of her interior people, are you?' Driscoll said. He allowed himself a moment to enjoy his turn of phrase before deciding that his time was too valuable to be spent hanging around on the doorstep. Retreating into the hall he shouted Susan's name up the stairs while shrugging on his coat. Picking up a battered ministerial dispatch box, he advanced on the door again.

'With you in a moment.' He ground to a halt on the threshold, faced by the impropriety of leaving Nick in front of an open door, and yelled over his shoulder: 'Susan, your guest's waiting. Mr – ?' He turned questioningly.

'Mackenzie.'

Driscoll repeated it up the stairs without visible recognition, then, assuming the benevolent but preoccupied look of someone with good works to do but not enough time to do them in, he scuttled across the pavement to his waiting car.

When Nick looked into the house again it was to see Susan standing on the stairs. She was wearing a Japanese wrap, long and flowing, in a blue which intensified the colour of her eyes. Her skin was pale and luminous and apparently bare of makeup, her hair a shining gold. Her loveliness shocked him, it seemed so inappropriate; and for a moment he was bowled back in time and remembering all kinds of things he would rather forget, like the warmth and suppleness of her body, and the long afternoons in Kensington, memories now inextricably mixed with anger and remorse.

She gave an abrupt laugh. 'Well, talk of the devil!'

'Were you?' he asked.

'What?' She took his hand and drew him inside the house and closed the door.

'Talking of me.'

'Not exactly,' she said, kissing him chastely on the cheek. 'But I was *thinking* of you, which was a hundred times better.' Still holding his hand, she stood back and examined him carefully, like a fond and long-lost friend. He looked for signs of embarrassment or shame in her face, but apart from the peculiar concentration of her gaze there was nothing to give her away, and she wore her confidence brilliantly, like a piece of jewellery. She thought she was safe, he realised. She thought she had got away with it.

'Now why would you be thinking of me?'

She caught the edge of sarcasm in his voice and for the first time a glint of doubt darkened her eyes. But it didn't trouble her for long; with a small chuckle, she started across the hall, gesturing for him to follow. When he didn't move, she looked back and asked in mock reproach: 'What, no coffee?'

'I won't stay,' he said tautly, knowing he mustn't antagonise her, yet unable to prevent the disapproval from showing in his voice.

She caught the message all right because her eyes lost some of their sparkle and she said a small 'Oh.' Then some sort of realisation came to her and, clapping a hand theatrically to her forehead, she came back and gripped his arm. 'Of course, forgive me . . . The papers, that beastly story. I was so glad to see you that I almost – ' She made a face of suitable mortification, her eyes already inviting forgiveness. 'Listen, I tried to call you several times. I left messages, but they told me you were in Scotland.' She gave a soft groan and pressed a hand against his cheek. 'Poor, poor Nick – the *last* thing you needed. But they can't charge you with anything, surely – can they? I mean, *drugs*. It just isn't *you*, anyone could have told them that.'

The anger rose suddenly, without warning, and then he couldn't stop himself. 'They knew what they were looking for.'

She looked surprised then puzzled. He had to admire her: it was really a very good act. 'Knew?' she asked.

'Someone tipped them off.'

'Oh?' Her forehead crinkled gently into a frown.

'Told them about' – he couldn't say Alusha's name – 'the morphine in the house.'

She searched his face, and read there the meaning he had intended her to see. Her mouth twitched, her eyes narrowed and then came understanding, disbelief and hurt.

'You think . . .' She gave a soft gasp. 'You think *I* . . .'

She looked so appalled, so genuinely hurt, that his certainties uprooted themselves and swam around, dissolving the moment his mind touched on them. He couldn't think of anything to say.

'Well!' She was sawing away at her mouth, biting back tears. 'Well!' Her eyes brimmed suddenly, and she drew away.

'I think you'd better go,' she choked, hiding the contortions of her face with a splayed hand.

There was nothing he would have liked better than to go, to be free of the swooping and churning of his emotions, but there was still the business of Daisy. He said: 'That wasn't why I came.'

'It wasn't? I see!' she retorted in a sudden fury. 'That was just a little aside then, was it? My God, you're making me wonder what's coming next!'

He plunged in, desperate to get the whole thing over and done with. 'Daisy Field's gone missing,' he said quickly. 'We think your friend Schenker might be able to find her.'

She stared at him for a moment. '*What?*' She made an exaggerated gesture of disbelief, stabbing the fingertips of both hands against her chest. 'You want me to – ?' She rolled her eyes expressively. 'You came to ask me *that*?'

'We think she might be in danger.'

'But' – through the tears came an incredulous laugh – 'God, you've got a nerve! Schenker's nothing to do with *me*. Why should you think he's anything to do with me! If you need to ask him, why don't you go and do it yourself!'

'I thought the request would come better from you.'

She shook her head slowly. 'I can't help you. And now I think you really must go.' Her voice rose suddenly.

'He'd listen to you.'

'Oh yes! And what would I tell him!'

'That we have evidence to show Morton-Kreiger have been involved in dirty tricks, that we know who was responsible. That we know about Workham Overseas Holdings.'

629

Waving this aside, she stood up suddenly. 'You'll have to find another messenger boy.'

'You don't understand –'

'Oh, it's not that I don't understand,' she cut in sharply. 'That's not the problem. The problem is that you've just accused me of the most incredible breach of trust, and now you expect me to do you some sort of favour. My God.' She laughed outright, a bark of disbelief.

She's acting again, he thought suddenly, and in the tilt of her head and the twist of her mouth he caught the profile illuminated by the sunlit South Kensington window all those years ago, saw again the fierce expression, the white rage, the mouth distorted with the stream of bitterness; and seeing them, his intuition and anger took fresh shape.

He said abruptly: 'You could give him the name Angela Kershaw as well!'

There was a moment of startled silence. Susan was absolutely motionless, her eyes round and enlarged as she stared up at him.

'Schenker's been paying some of her bills.'

Her mouth opened slightly and she was so still that she seemed to have stopped breathing. Then her eyes narrowed, she blinked rapidly. 'I'm sorry . . .?'

He might have hesitated then if it hadn't been for her tightly fisted hands and the chalkiness of her skin, which betrayed her shock.

He said: 'There's a file on her.'

'A file?'

'We've seen it.'

But he didn't have to elaborate. This was quite enough for Susan. Her mouth set into a grimace of despair. She sank back onto a chair. 'Oh God, oh God.' She looked as though she'd been punched in the stomach. In that moment he realised – if there had ever been any doubt – where her loyalties really lay, where they had always lain.

She recovered a little. 'How did you come to see it?' she asked. Then, in horror, as if it had only just occurred to her: 'Who else has seen it?'

'All sorts of facts about Schenker are going to come out,' he said, 'facts that Schenker won't want the world to hear.'

'Facts? You mean, evidence, documents?'

'Yes.'

'And there's evidence' – she braced herself to say it – 'about Angela Kershaw . . .'

'Yes.'

She gripped her forehead as if to contain her agony. 'But this evidence – it's not out yet?'

'No.'

A glimmer of hope dashed across her face. 'So we've got time!'

We? The assumption was so brazen he let it pass. 'Possibly.'

'So? *So?*' She was taut with impatience.

So? What came next? He thought of the thin sheaf of papers in the car, of what they would represent to Susan if she knew about them, and what she would give for them; and the next move loomed up in front of him, obvious and horribly enticing. Yet he balked at the thought. However one viewed it, however many excuses one larded over it, it would be blackmail, ugly and repugnant. Even looking at her now, even knowing without a doubt that, finding herself in his position, she wouldn't hesitate to use whatever weapons were to hand, just as she hadn't hesitated to bargain away his most precious and painful secret, he couldn't bring himself to do it. He didn't like the idea of sinking to her level. He had enough of a bad taste in his mouth already.

'Can't we do something?' Susan pressed, beginning to recover her fighting power. 'Get hold of this file?'

He hesitated, playing for time. 'It's possible.'

'Can you get hold of it? *Can* you? I'd do anything,' she said, '*anything.*' Then, realising this might have revealed too much, she pulled back a little, adding: 'It's not fair, you see. Whatever Tony is, whatever he's done, he doesn't deserve this.' She consolidated her selfless image with an appealing, pathetic smile. 'This thing's been hanging over his head for ages, it's been making him ill. That dreadful woman . . . It was nothing, *nothing*. But she's made his life an absolute misery ever since. *No one* deserves that sort of thing.'

He was silent.

'If there's any way of getting the evidence back, any way . . .' She was going more carefully now, concealing her determination. She must love Driscoll a lot, Nick decided; or she must love being his wife, which probably added up to the same thing.

He heard himself say: 'There might be a way,' and realised

631

that she had presented him with an easy way out, and that he was about to take it.

'There might?' She brightened visibly. 'So what do we have to do? Is it a question of money?' She had no trouble using the word.

'Not money.'

'Something else then?' She was bargaining eagerly, and he saw that the doing of deals, the trading of favours, were the only currencies she really understood, that for her everything had a price, that everything – and that included people – only had value in so far as they contributed to her own wellbeing. Where had he come in her grand reckoning, he wondered? Well, it didn't matter. He had little doubt where he stood now.

She was waiting.

'Daisy has the file.'

'Ah!' She let out a long breath of comprehension. 'So if we find Daisy, we find . . .' She smiled collusively, and he shrank from the new and ugly intimacy in her eyes.

'That's about it,' he said.

'So you want me to approach Schenker?'

'Yes.'

'I see, I see.' Her mind was working overtime, the effort visible in her face. 'He'll know how to find her? Are you sure?'

'I'm sure.'

'Doesn't it . . .? Why shouldn't . . .?' Thinking better of whatever she was going to ask, she gave him a searching almost suspicious look. 'You *have* been busy,' she commented, and it wasn't entirely a compliment. 'So how much should I say?'

'Say that we believe that his associates know where Daisy is and that we want her back. And that they'd better make sure she turns up quick. Mention those company names.' He went through them with her.

'I see, I see.' She was painfully anxious to get it right. 'But what about Schenker, aren't we going to promise him something too?'

He didn't understand immediately.

She explained with slight impatience, as if it should have been obvious: 'The facts you were talking about, the ones he's not going to like – can't we get hold of those files as well?'

The machinations of her mind were quite amazing, they

quite took his breath away. 'No,' he said vehemently. 'That's different, totally different. Schenker's not going to get off the hook. There are things that have got to come out, things that Daisy's worked on for months. Things that' – he didn't know how to express it to her – '*matter*.'

'Right,' she said at last, having come to some sort of decision. 'I see.' She got to her feet and pulled the lapels of her robe together and drew herself up, as if she was about to step out on a stage and play a great role. 'I'll phone now.'

'Don't say anything about getting any files back,' he reminded her. 'They might think we're willing to do a deal and we're not.'

'Right.' Preoccupied, already rehearsing what she was going to say, she turned away and went down the hall and disappeared into a back room, closing the door behind her.

Nick went to the front door and looked out. He could just make out Campbell in the front of the car, his head slumped to one side, asleep.

Susan was gone about five minutes. He spent the time circling the hall, thinking of Daisy, imagining where she was now, remembering all the work she had put into the Silveron case and what an uphill struggle it had been for her. Looking back, he felt a sort of dazed admiration for her. Her perseverance seemed to run like a constant thread through the upheaval and horrors of the last year or so, a point of light in an otherwise murky sky.

He had treated her badly, and he minded about that.

A click of a door and Susan reappeared, coming swiftly up the hall. Her expression was withdrawn, unreadable. 'I gave them the message,' she said.

'Them?'

'Schenker's man – his assistant.'

'And?'

'I imagine they'll look into it.'

'Imagine?'

'Oh, he bleated about not knowing anything about your friend,' she explained quickly, 'but he understood all right.' She came closer, and her face was hard with new questions. 'Tell me' – and she paused to fix her eyes firmly on his – 'how is it that you know all about the Kershaw woman when your Daisy friend still has the file?'

He started for the door. 'Listen – it doesn't matter.'

633

'What do you mean it doesn't matter?' She caught his sleeve and jerked him round again, her lips tight with suppressed fury. 'You'd better be telling the bloody truth!' she hissed. She looked older now, older and not at all lovely.

'Don't worry, Susan, you'll get what you want.'

Her fist twitched as if she would punch him with anger.

'I'd better,' she said bitterly. 'I'd better or . . .'

Something overturned inside him. 'Or? Or what, Susan?' he said brutally. 'Or you'll tell your friends even more things about me? Well, I've news for you. There's nothing more to tell. My real secrets I keep for my friends.'

Her mouth opened to speak but nothing came out. Instead she shut the fury neatly away and reached out a hand towards him, as if to take back what she had said. Perhaps she thought he might change his mind and she wouldn't get the Kershaw papers back after all.

But she needn't have worried. She could have them. He didn't care any more. He was already opening the door, making for the fresh air. He didn't look back.

Hillyard turned up the volume and angled the cassette player to carry the sound further into the room. The music blared out. It was a Forties-style big band number with plenty of brass and a noisy vocalist, one of three tapes he'd given Beryl for Christmas because they took her back to her youth.

Moving softly back to the door he picked up the broom that he had brought from the kitchen and went to the window. With the arrival of the music, the beating had started again on the wardrobe door, an irritating thud-thud, rising after a moment to more aggressive thumps as she took some hard object to the wood – a shoe, he imagined. She'd better not be using one of his new shoes or he'd thwack it right back at her. Or better still, give her a taste of what Beji had suffered, a twist to the throat and some hair out of her scalp.

Thankfully the music spared him the sound of her voice, or maybe she'd simply run out of volume. Throughout the evening no sooner had she shut up than she'd started again, disturbing his work and his rest, bash bash, yell yell. Finally, partly to teach her a lesson, partly to give Beji some satisfaction, he'd opened the flat door and let the dog race upstairs to bark herself silly at the vibrating door.

Now, in the early morning, he slipped the catch on the

window and raised the lower sash. Feeding the broom out, brush-end first, he found he could just reach the bag. Hooking the broom under one of the straps was more difficult. The bag was much heavier than he'd thought and kept sliding off. Clicking his tongue at this tiresome development, he went in search of the small stepladder from the office and manoeuvred it out of the window and onto the roof. The roof was pitched, making the firm positioning of the base tricky, and he had to run a rope from an upper rung over the sill and across the bed to the door handle. This extra work did not please him at all, not after the many aggravations of the long evening, during which he had had to patch up the street door, barricade it from the inside, and then feed endless files into the shredder. What with one thing and another, he hadn't got to his makeshift bed on the back-office sofa until two, and then it was to have his fitful sleep interrupted shortly after six by someone who had first rung, then hung, on the bell, and finally tried to break the door down. From the vibrations that had resounded through the building he had no doubt it was the girl's muscle man again.

There had been more callers at a quarter to eight. Stationing himself at the blinds in the front he had seen the marked police car pull out into the main street.

It had occurred to him then, with some force, that he didn't have a lot of time.

Now with the benefit of full daylight he clambered onto the ladder and climbed cautiously down to the roof. Hitching the bag over his shoulder, he remounted the steps and made his precarious way back into the room.

He went through the contents immediately, there on the bed. As far as he could tell, nothing was missing – or was it? Retrieving the ladder, he took everything downstairs and double-checked each file as he put it through the jaws of the shredding machine, sheet by sheet. Nothing seemed to be missing from any of the files – the girl would hardly have had time to remove individual pages – but were all the files themselves there? Had the cow stuck any in her pockets?

He made himself a coffee and, sitting at Beryl's desk, made a mental list of the files he had shredded last night, along with the files he had found in the bag, and matched them against his memory. He went next door into his own office and went through the smashed drawers of his desk again.

It was then that he saw something that he had missed during the night, lying on the floor in the desk well: the edge of a file. Pulling it out he saw it was a Workham file. It was empty. He certainly hadn't shredded the contents. He muttered: 'Cow, bloody cow,' and, returning to the main office, he went through the cabinets and the clutter on the desktops. The papers weren't there. At one point his mobile phone rang, which he chose not to answer. A minute later the desk telephone rang. Turning up the volume on the answering machine, he tilted the blinds open and gazed across the street to the opposite roof. He watched a couple of seagulls shrieking and raging over a scrap of booty while he half listened to Cramm's voice asking him to call 'very urgently indeed'. With a sigh he lifted the receiver just before Cramm rang off.

'The Catch woman, have you got her?' demanded Cramm. The voice had a nervy ring to it, a note of panic.

Hillyard replied harshly: 'She was here but she's gone.'

'*There*? What do you mean she was there? What *happened*?'

'She was hiding upstairs. I didn't realise.'

'Christ – how long was she there?'

'All night.'

'Jesus – and she's gone?'

'I said. She's gone.'

'Christ, but what the hell did she take with her? What did she find out?'

'Nothing. She took nothing.'

'That's not what I bloody heard! They're on to us, you fucking idiot! They've got some of your bloody files!'

'Not possible. Guesswork. No proof.'

There was a new stream of invective which Hillyard cut off by putting the phone down. He muttered: 'Stuff you, Cramm.' As for the girl, she wasn't going anywhere, not until he'd finished with her, and he hadn't finished with her yet, oh no.

In the hall Beji was whining softly, agitating to be let out.

'Shut up.' He aimed a quick kick which, despite the animal's wild evasions, managed to meet its rump. As usual the screams were out of all proportion to the pain. 'Anyone would think I'd killed you, you bitch.' Shutting the creature on the other side of the flat door, he mounted the stairs on light feet and crossed the landing to the bedroom. On the cassette player a female vocalist was trudging her way through some dirge about true love. Rapidly, he stopped the tape and, flipping it over, restarted it on the other side to ensure a reliable half-hour's musical accompaniment. As the music started again, so did the knocking, but much fainter now, as if she'd lost enthusiasm.

Taking his time, Hillyard closed the window, fastened the latch and drew the curtains, tugging the edges meticulously across each other to obliterate the daylight.

Then, treading carefully around the one creaking floorboard, he approached the cupboard door and slowly and soundlessly turned the key in the lock.

THIRTY-EIGHT

'The plane was late, then?' Schenker's secretary asked, rising fluidly to her feet and following him to the door of his office.

'A little.' In fact it had been on time but Schenker had spent half an hour in the first-class lounge at Terminal 4 talking to his American lawyer at home in Greenwich, Connecticut, hearing the words he had banked on hearing, the words which had finally put him out of the nervous agony he had endured ever since leaving New York.

Everything had gone through, the lawyer reported: the final terms were agreed, the contract was signed. Some ground had had to be given away on profit sharing, termination pay and perks, but no more than Schenker had reckoned for, and this morning, as his car had eased its way through the jams from the airport, he had allowed himself a measure of euphoria, ready to carry him through the considerable challenges of the day, which would mainly consist of ensuring that it was his last at Morton-Kreiger.

'Orange juice? Coffee?'

'Coffee.'

His secretary retreated and he entered his office alone. It looked strange to him, as if he'd been away a long time. The river, grey and sluggish, had a decayed air about it, and the city in its wash of rare sunshine wore the unreality of a picture postcard. He realised that in his mind he had already left the place behind.

His secretary reappeared with the coffee. 'The chairman asked you to call him straight away, before anyone else.'

Schenker pressed the internal number.

'What's this additional agenda item?' said Sir Harry without preamble.

'I thought it was self-explanatory, Chairman.'

'It sounds like a no-confidence motion in McNeill to me.'

'That would be accurate, yes.'

'Ah.' A thoughtful silence, then: 'You'd better spare me five minutes then.'

Rising from behind the desk, Sir Harry gestured Schenker not to the chairs by the floor-length windows which, as a devotee of the informal avuncular approach, he usually chose for his confidential chats, but across the desk to the chair in front of him.

'This sounds serious,' he said.

'It is,' Schenker confirmed briskly. 'Bad news from Chicago. We've been seriously let down by Research.'

'Explain, if you will.'

'It's very simple. McNeill's people have been holding out on me – on *us*. The toxicology trials on Silveron could, apparently, be unreliable after all.'

He sat up at that. 'On what evidence?'

'A former MKI toxicologist and – '

'But I thought there was no substance in that rumour.'

'So did I!' said Schenker with a bitterness that was perfectly genuine. 'Research consistently denied the possibility, as you know, but now it seems that his little man might have been right all along. Apparently TroChem took *shortcuts*. Duplicated a bit of data here and there. Adjusted a few results. What can you *do*, for Christ's sake?' He got to his feet and started pacing the room. 'McNeill's never allowed anyone *near* Research. Never allowed anyone to question the controls . . .'

He paused to ensure that the chairman absorbed the full implications of the last remark.

'And the controls were at fault?' said the chairman.

'You bet your life they were!' He came up behind his chair and gripped the back. 'McNeill finally admitted it yesterday at MKI. We were fed a pup by TroChem, data which was – *is* – highly dubious. If anyone had taken the care to lay down proper protocols, to install proper control mechanisms, none of this could have happened! Any confidence one might have had in Research has been totally destroyed!' He slapped his hands down on the chair to add resonance.

639

'Oh dear,' said the chairman, who liked to see things running smoothly. 'That bad?'

'Most certainly.'

'But what are you saying – that Silveron is back to square one, that the trials are invalid?'

'Yup.'

'My God.' The chairman was not much given to expletives, but he repeated this several times. 'There must be a way to salvage the situation, surely?'

'Possibly, but I really don't feel able to take it on. This thing has made my position untenable. All my work has been totally undermined. I've put everything behind Silveron – *everything* – both publicly and privately, and now I find myself stabbed in the back. How can I continue to support the product?' He made a wide gesture. 'How can I defend it in public?'

'But will that be necessary? To defend it publicly?'

He thought: Of course it will be, you stupid old fool. But perhaps this wasn't the time to tell Sir Harry of the press storm that was about to blow up under Morton-Kreiger's feet. Instead he said: 'Yes, I very much suspect it will be.'

'But surely it will be possible to reassure, to tell the world that we're looking into it and doing everything in our power . . .'

Schenker came round the front of his chair, tweaking the knees of his trousers, sat down again. 'In all conscience I couldn't do that.'

'You couldn't?' He seemed surprised.

'No.'

'But . . .' Sir Harry's shaggy brows shot down, he seemed to swell at the enormity of what he was hearing. 'You feel that makes your position untenable?'

'Yes.'

There was only one direction in which this conversation could possibly lead – and indeed only one direction in which Schenker had been leading it – and Sir Harry, who in matters of this kind was sharp as a razor, was not slow in recognising it. 'You intend to resign?'

'I can't see any alternative,' Schenker said with as much regret as he could muster.

Sir Harry leaned slowly back in his chair and, making a cage of his hands, puckered his mouth into a tight oval and regarded Schenker over the arch of his fingers. 'You can't be persuaded?'

'No.'

'I see.' He gave a brief smile of regret, but it was a mere token. 'You would not consider a – er – bridging period. Getting us through the crisis. With your expertise – ' Seeing the expression on Schenker's face, he broke off and said sombrely: 'I see.' He drew a deep and troubled breath as a new thought occurred to him. 'There could be – er – difficulties,' he murmured.

Schenker was well aware of the difficulties he had in mind, but it would not be appropriate to say so. 'Oh?'

Sir Harry assumed his favourite role, that of the senior diplomat feeling his way slowly over treacherous ground. 'The difficulties would surround – er – the timing. There must be no doubts about Silveron, no perceived link with your departure, no *rumours* – not until the matter has been properly investigated.'

'Of course not. I see that.'

'You do?'

'Absolutely.'

'There would have to be assurances . . .' He hesitated delicately.

'Of course!' Schenker looked marginally offended at the implication that he would have objected to any such suggestion.

'Good. Good.' Sir Harry gave a small self-satisfied smile, as if he had brought about this most satisfactory understanding singlehanded. 'These assurances would have to be a condition of – any arrangement.'

'Yes.'

'A sad day for Morton-Kreiger, a sad day indeed.'

Sad enough for the board to decide that his departure could be judged to have occurred by mutual consent? He didn't ask, although the answers would be worth an extra two hundred and fifty thousand on his golden handshake. He didn't ask because the extra money hardly rated beside the importance of being free to take up the cola job at short notice.

He had an hour before the board meeting, an hour to prepare for what would be a much tougher version of his interview with Sir Harry, complete with merciless attacks from McNeill. His preparations certainly did not involve Cramm, who was waiting for him in his office, looking grim and, unless he was mistaken, doom-laden.

'Later,' he announced sharply before Cramm could speak.

'It can't wait.'

He glared: 'You'd be surprised,' and sat down, glancing rapidly over the lists and messages that had been arranged neatly over his desk.

'The Kershaw business,' Cramm rushed in. 'It's about to get out.'

Schenker sighed impatiently: 'I'm sorry, but really, that has nothing to do with us any more, does it?'

There was a pause and Cramm said painfully: 'There are other things that might have got out as well.'

'Like?'

'Our connection to a security firm in south London, people who undertook some investigations for us – '

'Not my problem, Cramm.' He fixed Cramm with a hard stare. 'Though if you intend to stay on here, I suggest you make it yours.'

Cramm looked like a man being stoned, with missiles flying at him from all directions and no idea which part of himself to protect next. 'Won't there be dangers?'

'For us? You've always told me not, Cramm. You've always said there would be no difficulties for us.'

Cramm's throat moved soundlessly.

'If you're worried about it, Cramm, I suggest you make certain the story gets told in the right way.'

Cramm craned his head uncertainly. 'I don't understand.'

Schenker raised an eyebrow.

'You mean – leak it?'

Schenker shrugged gently as if to deny anything quite so extreme. 'I would just point out that once a story's got fixed in the public mind in a particular way, then it's almost impossible to change it again later, isn't it? Better for people to think it was Driscoll who dealt with the whole unsavoury matter himself – the payments and so on. Better for Driscoll, that is. Looks more gentlemanly.'

Cramm seemed confused.

'Better for you, too,' added Schenker with an emphasis which was not lost on Cramm.

Recovering, Cramm managed: 'I'll draw up some ideas and come back to you.'

'No time for that.' Schenker's mind was already on the board meeting, his eyes scanning the papers in front of him.

'You don't want to check – '

'You'll handle it very well, I'm sure,' he replied crisply.

Cramm finally moved uncertainly towards the door. 'Containment,' he said, making a painful stab at humour.

Schenker looked up for the last time. 'Very good, Cramm.'

The daylight vanished quite suddenly. Daisy had watched it creep under the door barely half an hour ago, a lozenge of grey which had slowly rimmed the heel of her shoe with a curve of light. Putting her hand to the base of the door, she had watched the smudge of grey harden into a sliver of brightness against her fingers.

When the music suddenly blared out it had sent a tattoo of adrenalin knocking against her ribs, and half in reflex, half in fear, she'd picked up a heavy shoe and started beating on the door again. When she gave up, which was quite soon, she had looked down and seen dark beams flowing across the splinter of light, as someone moved back and forth across the window. After a time the flickerings stopped. When they returned a minute or so later, it was only to cease again almost immediately, and this time the dart of light stayed unbroken for a long time, leaving nothing but the tinny bray of the music and the taunting swoops of the singers' voices, pounding through a heavy refrain.

Adjusting to the possibility of another wait, Daisy settled back on her makeshift cushion, a coat she had taken from its hanger and folded twice to soften the impact of the floor, and leant back into the corner, which she had also padded with clothing. Not too uncomfortable if one ignored the lack of leg space. At the beginning, the possibility of claustrophobia hadn't entered her mind, but during the long night, flutterings of something like panic had struck her, and now she was aware of it loitering not far away, like a giant mugger in the shadows. Strangely, it wasn't the lack of space that seemed threatening, nor even the darkness, but the air, which sometimes seemed so viscous that it was an effort to breathe.

During the earlier part of the night she'd had other distractions, first the cold which had necessitated pulling one of Maynard's jackets over her, later the demands of her bladder, a mild annoyance which rapidly grew into a major crisis. Nothing, she decided, was worth doing damage to herself and when her kidneys began to ache she reached out a hand to examine the selection of receptacles on offer. Tempting though it was to leave Maynard with a lasting memento of her stay in the form of a fluid-filled Chelsea boot, she finally chose a plastic bag which she found bundled up in a corner. Thankfully it proved to be watertight. In films, she reflected bleakly, the leading characters never encountered problems like this.

After that, at what seemed like midnight but which was probably much earlier, she exercised herself by throwing her weight against the door, partly in the genuine hope of breaking out, partly to remind Maynard, if he was still there, that she wasn't about to give up, and partly to break the sound of the silence, which seemed to stretch out endlessly. But lack of space prevented her from gaining momentum and the door didn't budge. Pressing her back against the rear wall and punching her heel against the lock was more promising, but the door, seemingly made of steel, continued to stand firm. After a short rest she began a new assault which was interrupted by the yapping and screeching of the dog on the other side. She thought briefly: I should have silenced you more permanently. Then she realised the dog was a message from Maynard, telling her that he was still out there, that it would be futile for her to try to escape.

She retreated and thought again. Perhaps in the morning . . . Perhaps he would simply open the door and let her walk out of the house. Why not? Why not? If she said it often enough, it acquired a sort of credibility. After all, what else would he do? Well, that certainly didn't bear thinking about.

After a time the dog stopped yapping and she thought she heard it pad away. Raiding the hanging clothes to fold into cushions, she settled down on the floor. If this was to be a waiting game, then she'd learn to play it her way, and rest while she could.

She thought of Campbell again, and wondered where he might be. Lying unconscious downstairs? Trussed up perhaps? Or dumped miles away, unable to remember what had happened, incapable, for some other reason, of getting help?

And everyone at Ashard, what would they be thinking? She pictured Nick in the book-lined room wondering where on earth she'd got to. Feeling let down perhaps, thinking she was tricky and unreliable, regretting his change of mind. She allowed herself a few moments' pure fantasy, a scene in which all this was long over and everything they had fought for had been vindicated, and she was standing at the door of the studio, waiting for him to finish whatever he was doing. This time when he turned it was to smile. Then . . .

Best not to let the reel wind on.

The picture of the others at Ashard was even more confused. Was Simon managing to coax the story out of Alan Breck? Was he doing it sympathetically or was he steaming ahead in his usual oblivious way? Only one thing seemed fairly sure, Simon wouldn't notice her absence except to remark on the inconvenience and added difficulties it was causing him. And Alan Breck? He would be closest to the truth, she suspected. He would be seeing disaster at every turn.

At some point she must have dozed because her mind filled with dogs that pulled at her legs and grasping hands that reached out of the darkness to drag her down. She woke with a start, and stared with blind relief into the darkness. She didn't mean to sleep again, but it stole up on her and she found herself dreaming quite another sort of dream in which the Nick fantasy came alive. This time, after turning to smile at her, he got up and reached an arm round her shoulders and pulled her against him, just like he had at the flat, but this time he kissed her, and, needing no encouragement, she kissed him right back. Then, in the maddening way of dreams, the scene shifted and the two of them were standing close to the burning laboratory, which somehow seemed to be located close to Ashard, though it wasn't the equipment that was burning, but her carpetbag with all the hard-won evidence against Morton-Kreiger.

She had woken, disturbed at the reality of it, not quite persuaded it wasn't true, wishing the dream had stayed firmly on Nick. Then she had looked down to watch the lick of dawn light creep onto the shoe.

The music must have been going for half an hour when it stopped in mid-song. Pulling herself hastily up, putting an ear to the door, she heard a mechanical click and the music

645

started again. She hammered on the wood, though not so hard that she couldn't hear what was going on outside. '*I see the moonlight, baby, and I dream of you* . . .'The music was louder than before. She sighed with frustration, and the wardrobe was suddenly uncomfortably hot, and the mugger in the shadows moved several inches closer. Finally she sat down again and did some breathing exercises, and it was then that she looked down and realised that the splinter of light had gone. She ran her fingers along the crack and leant her face lower to the floor, but there wasn't the smallest whisper of light. She stared at the place where the light should have been, and a chill crept into her stomach. The curtains had been drawn. Or – a ridiculous overblown thought – something had been pressed against the outside of the door, something designed to seal the cracks and prevent the air from getting in.

She fought down the nudge of panic. She thought: Get a grip! Ten deep breaths, slow and steady; count to five, hold five, exhale five.

She stopped abruptly on an in-breath. Beyond the door one song had finished, another, a slow mournful number, was starting. And in the slight pause in between – what? Nothing she could be sure of, nothing she could pin down, yet –

What? A faint rustling?

Her senses reached out into the darkness, she forgot to breathe, resuming abruptly with a gasp. Slowly she got to her feet and, resting her hand against the door, put her ear to the edge. The dog? No: too quiet, no snuffling. Something else, something huge and furtive.

The female voice sang: '. . . *nothin' ain't the same without you* . . .'

Daisy flattened her hand against the door and applied a minute amount of pressure. The door seemed to give a little. She felt very hot suddenly, and when she reached up to find the hook, her hand was trembling.

The slow song ended, there was a short pause, and the band crashed into a swing number screeching with brass. The sound seemed to pulsate through the darkness, smothering everything in its path. Gripping the hook, she increased the pressure on the door. Finally she gave it a distinct push.

A slight resistance, then it gave suddenly and opened with a plop.

Reflexively, she yanked on the hook to prevent the door swinging out too far and in her anxiety pulled the door back against the jamb so that it almost closed again.

She waited for the thumping of her heart to subside. She felt the heat inside her shirt, the looseness in her stomach.

Part of her was crying: *Stop!* Suppose he hasn't gone. Suppose it's a trick. Something elaborate and unpleasant, something –

She forced herself on. No good wasting time over questions without answers; no good hanging about.

Gripping the edge of the door, she pushed it slowly open. She saw a faint thread of light reflected vertically down a wall, revealing the edge of the drawn curtains. Another faint dusting of light showed against the ceiling.

She stepped over the threshold. The curtains must have been very thick or lined with a particularly dense material because almost no light permeated the room. It was impossible to make out the position or shape of the furniture. Keeping a hand on the open door, she took another tentative step forward, senses reaching out into the darkness. She strained to hear something – anything – over the shrilling trumpets; she strained to see, but the blaring music seemed to intensify the darkness.

The scent came suddenly, a distinct smell like the one in the cupboard but sharper. It wafted towards her as if blown from some invisible source, and she had the impression that it was coming from close by. She half turned. She sensed him before she saw him; his closeness was like an unbearable heat. Then he seemed to loom above her, huge, suffocatingly close, a giant black shape against the greater darkness of the room. The fear shot into her throat. Instinctively she tried to step back, but he was very quick. Somehow his arm came up from behind and, before she could dodge aside, it looped around her neck with a force that pushed her head back with a snap. Reflexively, her hands flew up and tried to pull his arm away, but he was massively strong. Even as she clawed ineffectually at his arm, he was forcing her forwards, over and down. She struggled to keep her footing, to try to get some leverage from the floor, at the same time twisting violently to free herself from the stranglehold. But his power was remorseless, like a massive weight pressing down on her. He caught her unimpeded arm and twisted her wrist round and backwards.

She felt the screaming deep-seated fear that comes from complete helplessness, and opened her mouth to cry out. No sound came. She lost the last of her balance, her foot skidded away, her leg twisted over, the bed came up and pressed into her face.

His weight continued to bear down on her, crushing into her back, while he slipped a hand round the front of her throat. She thought: He's going to kill me. Somewhere in the far distance the music had paused, and she heard ragged gasps which she dimly recognised as her own.

Another number started, a duet with a sickly violin accompaniment. The pain was excruciating as he twisted her wrist inwards over her back. Something breezed against her ear. It was only when he spoke that she realised it was his breath.

'Where are the other files, you little cow?' His voice was high and uneven. The odour of his breath hit her, pungent and stale. 'Where?' he repeated in a hiss, giving her throat a squeeze.

Her head throbbed, the blood pounded in her ears, she felt herself choking. Perhaps he realised he was half killing her because he suddenly eased the pressure.

'Where?'

'Gone,' she gasped.

'Gone where?'

'Gone.' A realisation nagged at her; she couldn't think it through.

'Gone where?' He gave a savage twist to her wrist.

'Away.' Most of her mind was registering pain, but another part was working overtime, trying to read the message her brain was attempting to deliver.

Suddenly he jerked at her throat, and his hand was tight as a noose. She couldn't breathe. The fear rose up and burst like an explosion in her head. She fought for air, her lungs heaved, a loud drumming filled her ears.

He let go suddenly, and she sucked in a long shuddering breath. The blood came back into her veins with a roar.

'Where?'

He didn't know. It came to her suddenly: he didn't know where the other papers were, which meant he didn't have Campbell, had never searched him.

648

'Campbell. With Campbell,' she managed.

He couldn't have heard her properly, or perhaps he wanted to hear it a second time because he wrenched her wrist backwards and snapped: '*Who?*'

Through clenched teeth she told him again and he gave her a great shove of rage. 'In that case,' he said in a vicious tone, 'we're going to have to get them *back*, aren't we?'

'He'll have contacted the police,' she said.

'I don't think so, somehow.'

The tones were harder, none of the solicitousness remained, but it was unmistakably Maynard's voice, complete with sing-song and that strange indefinable accent, and she saw again the table at the Waldorf and the fat neck beneath the pasty cheeks and the stomach pushing against the shirt and his lips folding daintily over the scones and the pale eyes following the spinning dancers.

She coughed; her gullet was raw. 'I know he'll have gone to the police,' she rasped.

He didn't reply. She tried again. 'He'll have handed the evidence in by now.'

'No time.'

'He won't agree to hand the files back – '

He snapped: 'Shut up,' and his voice sawed higher.

He had stopped the music but left the room in darkness. She was sitting on the bed, facing the dim outline of the curtained window, following his movements around the room by the sound and scent of him. He was behind her now, somewhere on the other side of the bed.

'*Shut up,*' he repeated savagely for no apparent reason, and she felt a fresh flutter of fear. His hand came from across the bed and grasped the back of her neck loosely, almost caressingly. Her flesh crept, she longed to recoil. She spoke, as much from the need to break the spell of fear as to argue with him.

'Keeping me here won't do any good,' she said. 'It'll make things far worse, worse than anything – '

He shook her slightly. '*Shut*' – his grip tightened on her neck and he shook her again, more violently – '*up.*'

She kept very still then, looking blankly ahead. His hand stayed on her neck and she sensed that he was considering his next move. The following moments were very long; there was only the closeness of him and his sickly scent and the deadness in her stomach and the ache in her throat.

'Don't turn round,' he announced at last.

When she didn't answer he gave her neck a shake.

She agreed quickly: 'No.'

His hand fell away.

Snap! A light came on, a low lamp on the other side of the bed which threw her shadow large against the curtains. An instant later the outline of Maynard soared massively up behind her shadow, filling the whole wall.

'Strip.'

'What?'

'You heard.'

'But . . . *why?*'

He exhaled impatiently. His voice came in a vicious sing-song. 'You could be *lying*, couldn't you? *Hiding* things!'

'I'd have given them to you.'

'I don't think I'm going to believe that. Why should I?' His voice rose sharply. She decided quite suddenly that he was unhinged. 'Don't turn round,' he added quickly. 'Clothes on the bed. Nothing on the floor. *Now.*'

Several thoughts converged on Daisy's mind: how he would react if she refused, what he would do when he discovered the tapes in her pockets, whether she had time to hide them.

Although he wasn't touching her, she gave a large involuntary shudder as if to slough him off. She realised she had decided what she must do and, feeling faintly sick at the thought of going through with it, she got to her feet and began to undress. As she unzipped her jacket and pulled it off she reached into one of the pockets and, grasping a tape, hid it in one hand as she passed the jacket backwards onto the bed with the other.

She heard him begin to rummage through the jacket. She slipped the remaining tape down the front of her jeans.

'Bitch!' he yelled suddenly, and she heard him rattle one of the cassettes. Then: 'What else have you got, *bitch*?'

She went on undressing. As she unzipped her jeans she pushed the tape down the front of her pants. When she was down to her underwear she stopped and waited, watching his shadow on the wall as it swayed and billowed against the light, thinking of the times Maynard must have been in her flat, realising he must have searched through her clothes before.

'Bitch!' he echoed. He stopped moving. 'Where's the rest? *Where's the rest?*'

'There isn't any more.'

His shadow shot upwards, growing huge. She ducked but he was too quick and, grasping her hair, he pulled her down. Gasping, she threw her hands back to stop herself sprawling flat on the bed, but she still fell far enough for him to see down the front of her body.

He uttered a bark of rage; the sound reminded her of the dog. He gave her a small punch of fury and reaching down grabbed the tape from the front of her pants.

'What do you think I am – *stupid?*' The exaggerated singsong had an oddly mesmeric quality to it. *'Mmm? Stupid?'*

She sat up again, moving slowly so as not to attract his attention, then remained very still. She realised she was behaving like a victim. She made herself speak. 'You were right about Campbell. He won't have gone to the police – '

'Shut up!'

She could hear his breathing; it was coming in shallow angry pants.

She said: 'He's got form, he wouldn't dare – '

'Shut up.' She felt a movement of air on her back. *Don't show your fear, don't let him see.* The telephone was dropped onto the bed beside her. The hand came back onto her neck. His voice had a malevolent slow-beating rhythm to it now.

'All right,' he said, 'call your friend, but no silly business!'

'He's – I don't know where he is.'

'Then you'll have to *find* him, won't you?' On the *find*, he jabbed a finger in her back.

'The number – it's in my bag.'

He gave an exaggerated sigh of annoyance. *'Wait.'*

His shadow expanded and shifted; he left the room. While he was gone she stared at the phone, unguarded beside her. Tempting, but not enough time, nothing to be gained, too frightened: more to the point, no number.

He returned quickly, throwing her carpetbag onto the bed. His hand came onto her neck again.

Moving with care, willing her hands not to tremble, she found her address book in the outside pocket of her bag. She began to tap out the Ashard number and got one digit wrong.

651

She cut the call. The fingers squeezed, biting into the sides of her neck. 'Come on, *darling*, he hissed. 'Get it right.'

She waited grimly until he eased the pressure, then wriggled her neck free. 'Keep off me,' she protested. 'Or no call.'

'Or no call,' he mimicked in a piping voice. 'Ha! You break in, you half murder Beji, then you start bitching. Jesus . . .' He came at her suddenly, put two hands round her throat and dug his fingers briefly and savagely into her windpipe. '*Make the call.*'

She choked, bent double and coughed herself dry. When she could breathe again she pulled herself up and started again.

She did better this time. The number connected and began to ring. Jenny answered with a squeal: 'Where *are* you?'

'Never mind. Where's Campbell?' She heard her own voice, gruff and raw and strange in her ears.

'He was beaten up. He was –'

'Is he all right?'

'I think so.'

'Where is he now?'

'With Nick. He's with Nick.'

'What, in Scotland?'

'No, London. Are you all right? You sound –'

'London?' She hesitated. It was a mistake; a thumb pressed hard into her flesh.

'Daisy? Daisy?' Jenny was sounding worried.

'Where are they?' she managed.

'I'm not sure. Look, is everything all right?'

'You *must* know where they are!'

'Daisy – there's something wrong. What is it?'

'I've got to find Campbell.'

She could almost hear the thoughts rumbling through Jenny's brain. There was a heavy pause then, catching on, Jenny said briskly: 'You could try Nick's house, but you might have more luck with his car phone. Have you got the number?'

Daisy reached into her bag for something to write with. Out of the corner of her eye she caught the blurred outline of Maynard's head against the light, and, more clearly, his left hand resting loosely on his bent knee. His hands were blunt, she noticed, blunt and very white.

She took down the number and rang off before Jenny could

ask any more questions. She dialled the car phone. The line produced a strange screech, and she had to try again. Maynard made sounds of irritation, sharp sucking noises. His hand was clammy on her skin.

Her fingers were stiff; she dialled with concentration. The line connected, the number rang. It went on ringing. And on, and on.

'No answer,' she whispered.

'Try something else then!' The thumb bit deep into the sensitive spot at the side of her spine.

She still had the phone to her ear. As she moved to cut the line and dial Nick's house, the ringing tone stopped suddenly. Perhaps, being a car phone, it had disconnected automatically. Her finger was moving to cut it off again when a voice grunted: 'Yus?'

It was a moment before she realised. 'Campbell? Campbell!' She gave a shrill cry of relief. 'Oh, for God's sake.'

'Daisy? Is that you? Where are you?'

But she wasn't allowed to answer that, and the warm moist fingers closed on the back of her neck as a reminder.

The day had not kept its promise. The sky, which had been darkening as Nick gunned the car away from Victoria, became positively black as they crossed Chelsea Bridge and ran down the side of Battersea Park. Rain came suddenly, falling in long perpendicular lines like pencils, drumming loudly on the roof and bouncing off the bonnet in a dense ridge of spray that obscured the Mercedes insignia on the front and much of the road besides.

'The *western* entrance?' Nick asked Campbell.

'That's what she said.'

They reached the south-western corner. Here the black iron gates were closed. Was there another entrance on this side? He couldn't remember. Or had she meant them to wait here? He turned right, along the western side of the park, heading for the Albert Bridge. The spray from the other vehicles had him slowing to peer at the line of parked cars and railings marking the edge of the park. Finally he saw an entrance, black gates again but open this time.

They drove in. There was a circular turning area, various roads spoking off, all of which sported barriers against traffic, and, to the right, a large parking area. Nick stopped on the circle beside a sign warning against stopping at any time, and looked through the trees towards the river. A woman ran head down along a path, dragging a small stiff-legged dog in her wake. A bent figure stood beneath a tree, huddled under an umbrella.

They went on into the car park.

'A blue Vauxhall?' Nick asked Campbell.

'That's what she said.'

'What the hell does a Vauxhall look like?'

A slight shrug. 'The name'll be written on it someplace, will it not? We can look as we pass.'

'What, in this?'

Nick heard the edge in his voice, and knew he was sounding unreasonable.

They rounded the circle and headed into the car park, a long thin rectangle of hard-packed gravel interspersed with deep potholes and landscaped with trees. The blades flipped fluidly over the windscreen at double time, the rain continued its pounding. There were a cluster of cars at the near end. Further down there was just a scattering of vehicles: a Range Rover with steamed-up windows, a Fiat disgorging dogs, a saloon of indeterminate make, undoubtedly blue – also, on closer examination, undoubtedly a Honda and unoccupied. The fourth car was a metallic-grey Volvo, the fifth an ancient black Mini.

Suddenly the wind came with a vengeance, picking up the rain and slamming it against the car, so that the wipers were momentarily overwhelmed. A car appeared out of the blur, parked at the far end of the parking area. They both craned forward. The car was canary yellow: the shape unmistakably that of an old Renault.

Nick sank back in his seat. 'Too early anyway, isn't it? How long? Ten minutes?' He knew perfectly well how long there was to go. Campbell looked at his watch and grunted in confirmation.

'Definitely the western entrance?'

'That's what she said!' He could hear the tension in Campbell's voice. He remembered Campbell's voice as it had sounded on the phone in the CID office high above Victoria Street, when Campbell had called up from the front desk and interrupted Nick's second meeting with Inspector Morgan.

654

There had been a bark of concealed excitement in his tone, and Nick had turned away in case Morgan should hear it or see the mixture of relief and alarm on his own face.

Nick drove back towards the top of the parking area and pulled in at a place where they could see the western entrance.

The rain eased, the drumming melted into a mild tattoo. Only the wind kept up its racketing, spiralling the rain upwards through the stands of black trees, buffeting at the doors of the car.

Campbell broke the silence. 'Suppose these people try some trick or other?'

'What do you mean?'

'Suppose Daisy's no' there?'

'Then – ' The thought, which had been lurking with others at the back of Nick's mind, pulled at him. 'We leave it to Morgan.'

For once Campbell did not argue.

Pulling his jacket tight around his neck, Nick got out and walked up to the circle and looked out through the gates, then wandered a short way along a path towards the river. The mist had thinned and the trees stood out in ranks, like a waiting army. The thin suspension cables of the Albert Bridge were like long strands of cooked sugar falling towards the white haze of the river.

He returned to the car. Time was up. Absurd fears flew through his mind. That this was just a game for some sick mind, that the car phone would ring and he would hear someone laughing down the line and telling him to go jump; that Campbell had got it totally wrong and they shouldn't be here at all but in Hyde Park.

Campbell made a sound. Following his pointed finger, Nick saw the car coming in through the gate. It stopped on the edge of the circle. The bodywork was dark; it could have been blue.

It started off again, rounding the circle and heading into the parking area. It was definitely blue. He felt a lurch of excitement. He tried to make out how many people were in it, but it was hidden by the line of cars as it passed down the far side and when it emerged at the end he couldn't see properly through the streaming side windows.

The blue car continued towards the less inhabited end of

the parking area and, executing a sudden U-turn, stopped on the near side, quite a long way down, facing the way it had come.

In his eagerness to turn and follow, Nick stepped a little too hard on the throttle and the wheels spun. He eased off but not enough to prevent the car executing a flamboyant turn. He was aware of another vehicle, a large saloon of dark but indeterminate colour, emerging from between the lines of parked cars and braking in plenty of time to let him pass. He accelerated away.

Passing the blue car on the far side, he made another much slower turn to come up behind it. He stopped five yards short.

It was a Vauxhall Cavalier. Its exhaust was spewing vapour. Its back window was rain-soaked but demisted. There was only one head visible above the outline of the headrests.

Nick put out a hand to Campbell for the documents.

'But she's no' there!'

Nick gestured again for the documents.

Campbell glared at him. *'But she's no' there!'* he shouted as if Nick were deaf.

Nick glanced away to the right and saw that the dark saloon was trundling slowly down the far side of the parking area. There were at least three people in it. He said to Campbell: 'The documents! Don't bloody argue!'

With a rasp of exasperation, Campbell pushed the roll of papers into Nick's hand and reached for the door. 'I tell you,' he said threateningly, indicating the car ahead, 'this fella's no' going any place till *we* say so!'

Paying no attention, Nick got out and looked back at the dark saloon, which was turning itself round and parking twenty yards behind. Jamming the papers inside his jacket out of the rain he walked towards the Vauxhall with Campbell at his heels. As he came up to the driver's door, the window opened. Nick bent down and saw a dark-jowled man with hooded eyes and a weary expression.

'Maynard?' Nick asked.

Ignoring the question, the man drawled: 'The delivery, is it?'

'Are you Maynard?' Nick pressed.

'Look, I'm just the messenger boy, right? Like I take the delivery and radio through that I've got it. Right?'

Nick, aware of Campbell hovering at his elbow, said: 'What guarantees do we have?'

The man shrugged. 'Look, I've just been told to radio through, haven't I?'

Campbell had lowered his head and was glowering into the car. 'I know you!'

'Shut up!' Nick hissed out of the corner of his mouth.

'The one at the airport,' Campbell growled in Nick's ear. 'The one we followed.'

Nick motioned him silent with a sharp movement of his hand, and handed the roll of papers through the window. The man in the car spoke into his walkie-talkie, listened for a moment, then signed off. Throwing the radio on the seat, he reached forward to engage the gear lever. At about the same time he also opened his mouth to speak but before he could say anything Campbell, seeing treachery in the movement, roared, 'An' where d'you think you're goin'?' and, elbowing Nick aside, pushed a hand through the window.

But the other man's reflexes were quicker; he had the gear engaged and his foot down before Campbell could get at the keys. The car jumped forward, Campbell was nearly pulled off his feet. For a few surreal moments he managed to stay with the accelerating car, his legs wheeling and kicking into the air like a racing cyclist's, before his feet got mixed up and he nosedived towards the gravel. He saved himself with an astonishingly effective roll, all roundness and no arms like a barrel, and was already struggling to his feet as he came out of it.

Nick loped forward, eyes on the disappearing car, choking with disbelief and fury. He was about to bawl at Campbell, to give him a small but furious taste of his mind, when the blare of a horn had him twisting round and jumping instinctively to one side as a car tore past, shooting out a heavy wedge of spray. It was the dark saloon.

Nick ran back to the Mercedes and, jumping in, roared after the others, rocking briefly to a stop to let Campbell scramble in beside him.

'Who're that?' gasped Campbell, barely articulate.

Foot hard down, Nick blasted towards the exit without replying. Slowing to negotiate the bend at the entrance he shot out into the circle in time to see the tail of the dark car disappear through the gates, turning left. He accelerated across the circle and slewed out into the Albert Bridge Road as a car nosed its way across the junction from the opposite direction, turning south. Missing it by a couple of feet, feeling a brief surge of fear, Nick ignored the agitated bleats of the car's horn and, straightening up, accelerated once again.

The rain and spray mingled into curtains of moisture which closed in and lifted like drifting fogs. The dark saloon, lost one moment, reappeared the next. He saw that it was jammed up behind the Vauxhall's bumper, flashing its lights. At the corner of the park, the two cars swerved in beside the closed gates.

'Who is it?' demanded Campbell.

'Morgan,' Nick said, adding firmly to crush any argument: 'My idea. I asked him along.'

By the time they pulled in behind the dark saloon, Morgan and his men had the driver out of the Vauxhall and into a tight box of tall backs. As Nick ran up the man was showing his driver's licence and protesting rapidly: 'Just delivering a message, lads! That's all! Just doing a favour for a friend. Listen, the name's Biggs, ex-Notting Hill CID.' Turning to Morgan he added with forced camaraderie: 'Don't I know you?'

'The message,' Nick interjected, shouldering his way past the coppers and pushing his face close to Biggs. 'What was the message?'

'The message?' Biggs had a ghastly smile on his face.

'What you were meant to tell me!'

Biggs looked at the waiting policemen imploringly. 'I was just pickin' up and deliverin'. I didn't know what it was about. I was just told to – '

'The *message*.'

'Yeah, well. It was "Albert Bridge", wasn't it? That's all I know. Just doing a favour . . .'

Nick didn't hear the rest. He was already running back to the car.

Susan threw the swatches of fabric onto the sofa and paced over to the window. Restlessly she turned away and went down to the kitchen to make another cup of coffee, then changed her mind and poured herself a drink. Only midday, but what the hell.

It was the waiting that was killing her. Would Nick ring as

soon as he'd retrieved this beastly file or whatever it was? On the whole she thought not; he was too puffed up with wounded pride, too self-obsessed, too self-righteous. Should she try Cramm's man then? God only knew what sort of a reception she'd get from him. Or Schenker himself? No, she hated the thought of grovelling, and however mildly she couched her request, it would be self-abasement of an odious kind.

Taking her drink, she went up to the bedroom and combed her hair and repencilled her eyebrows. The sound of a closing door echoed up from the hall. The front door? It couldn't be. The daily had gone for the day. Camilla was away at college. She strode out and hung over the stairwell. 'Who's there?'

'It's me.' Tony's voice, flat and sombre.

Balancing her drink, she hurried down the stairs. 'Good God, what are *you* doing home?'

He was very still, his face set, his eyes black and staring.

'*Well?*' she demanded, suddenly irritated at him for taking her by surprise.

'I have to talk to you.'

There was something about his tone and the oddness of his expression that infuriated her. 'What *is* it?'

He dropped his gaze, ran a hand up his cheek and over his forehead, and turned towards the drawing room. He walked untidily, as if he had just got out of bed.

She followed at his heels. '*Well?*'

He reached for a drink, lifting the gin bottle then letting it fall again. 'I'm afraid – it's bad news,' he said with difficulty. 'I've made rather a foolish mistake.' He made the effort to look at her, but his gaze slid away again. 'A stupid error of judgement.'

Susan clutched at his arm. 'What? *What?*'

He looked back at the bottle and began to unscrew it slowly. Stopping again, he said suddenly: 'There was a girl. It was nothing, absolutely nothing, believe me. She was just . . . Well anyway, it all got out of hand, I'm afraid.' Abandoning the bottle, his hand dropped wearily to his side and he said in an abject tone: 'I'm sorry, Susan.'

'What do you mean? What's happening?' In her agitation she yanked on his lapel, pulling the shoulder of his jacket awry.

'I'll have to resign.'

'*Resign?*' She heard the shriek in her voice. 'But why, *why*?'

Grasping the gin bottle again, he poured himself a large one. 'No choice. Money changed hands. She was a tart. They know all about it.' He took a large swig.

Before Susan could think, she had exclaimed: 'But it wasn't you! It wasn't *you* who gave her the money!'

Tony's head jerked back, he almost spilled his drink. He stared at her in astonishment.

'You mustn't resign!' she rushed on. 'Why should you! Lots of people have women, half the cabinet are bloody divorced, for God's sake – why should *you* have to resign?'

He couldn't take it in. 'You *knew*?'

'Of course I knew! Of *course* I knew! Just as I know that you *don't need to resign*!' She spaced the words out so that he would understand. 'It's all under control, you see. It's not going to come out after all. By the end of the day we'll have all the evidence back – all of it!' She saw the amazement in Tony's face. In her anxiety to convince him she gave an odd laugh, almost a shriek. 'Trust me, trust me! All of it – *back here*! Every single bit. Then no one can touch you! No one!'

She went on – she couldn't stop – while he stared at her half in shock, half in something like wonder. Finally, keeping his eyes on her face, he put his drink down. 'Susan. *Susan!*' He touched her hand. She fell quiet, gripped by a fear she couldn't name. 'Susan . . . it was the *press* who called.'

She felt a stab of terrible cold, for a moment she couldn't speak. '*Why? How?* They couldn't! They *couldn't!* Was it that woman? But it's just her word against yours! It's just – '

'They've got the whole story.'

'How *can* they? How *can* they?' Susan heard her voice rising and knew her face was ugly. 'She's just making things up, she's got no proof!'

'They've got details of hotels.' His tone dropped to one of near despair. 'And of three separate payments. And . . .' His face creased into a mask of anguish. 'A hospital visit.'

'No! No!' She pulled her hand free with a jerk and in her rage almost punched him. 'No! They can't! They *can't!* It's all in the file! All in the file!' She gave a cry and stumbled away, making for the hall.

He caught her at the telephone. 'Susan – don't!'

'I'll call that bastard Schenker! How *dare* he? *Bastard, bastard!*'

'Susan – don't. It's all over.' He grasped the receiver and

660

for a moment they both pulled at it before she released her grip and burst into tears. 'It's not fair!' she cried. 'It's not fair!'

He put the receiver firmly back in its cradle and put an arm round her shoulders.

But her rage was vast and inconsolable and, punching him on the chest, she struggled free and screamed at him. She was still hurling invective as she ran up the stairs and raced into the bedroom and fell raging onto the bed.

The towers of the Albert Bridge rose like ornate candles out of a damp mist. The rain had eased a little, more of a steady drizzle than a downpour, and the wind had died right away, although as they came onto the bridge it produced a last fleeting gasp that pattered the rain against the side of the car.

The traffic was heavy and when Nick slowed down he got an impatient horn from behind. There were a couple of pedestrians and a jogger braving the pavement on this side of the bridge. All of them were men. The tooting car overtook, sounding its horn again as it passed.

They went on steadily, they crested the rise of the bridge. Campbell made a sound and pointed to the far end of the bridge on the opposite side, to an old-fashioned red telephone box just visible beyond the neat hexagonal band box which housed the cable anchor. A figure stood huddled against the box. Jeans, jacket, slight build, hair flat against the head. A boy. Or maybe not a boy. With shoulders hunched high and head dropped low as if to ward off the rain, it was hard to tell. Then the figure moved, folding its arms together as if in disgust and there was something in the movement that was so completely Daisy that Nick jabbed the accelerator, pulled out into the fast lane and roared towards her.

She saw him coming. She straightened up, she bent to peer at the car, she moved forward and, reaching the kerb, began to gesticulate or wave or both. Nick stopped in the middle of the road, indicating right, and met a fresh volley of abuse from the vehicles behind. Seeing a tight gap in the oncoming traffic he stepped on the throttle and bolted across, causing one driver to stand on his brakes and flash his lights in rage.

He shot onto the pavement ahead of Daisy and had to brake suddenly as she ran towards him, swerving round the bumper. He jumped out and they nearly cannoned into each other. She was already talking: she must have been talking

661

even as he opened the door. If he hadn't been so alarmed by the look of her he would have laughed. Her skin was very pale, her eyes dark with shadows, her hair plastered onto her head by the rain.

He grasped her tightly by the shoulders. 'God – are you all right?'

But she was gabbling insistently: 'You didn't give him the files, did you? You didn't, did you? *Did* you?'

'Slow down! Slow down! It's all right.' She was shivering under his hands.

'You didn't, did you?' Her voice was wobbling dangerously.

He spread his lips into a grin. 'Not quite everything.'

'Not everything?'

'I gave them what we didn't need,' he said truthfully. 'And kept the rest.'

'Kept the rest, kept the rest.' She was taut as a wire, humming with a furious electricity. 'Maynard – he took it all back, everything. I couldn't stop him. I couldn't – ' She broke off. Her eyes had a dark and empty look.

'Morgan'll be after him by now.'

'Morgan?'

'From Scotland Yard.'

She seemed to take that in. 'Alan Breck – is he all right? Is he – '

'He's all right.'

'Must get to him. Must get to Scotland. Must – ' She tugged at his sleeve in agitation and looked around as if some airborne transportation might at any moment manifest itself.

'Daisy, it's all right. Slow down.'

She froze. She had caught sight of Campbell getting out by the passenger door. For an instant she stared at him blankly, then she hissed: 'Campbell!' and from her tone one might have thought she was cross with him.

She looked back at Nick and then at Campbell and her expression folded inwards. She dropped her head against Nick's chest and gave a great shudder and said: 'Oh, I'm so tired.'

Hillyard's hands were wet on the wheel. Furiously he rubbed them one at a time on the side of the seat. Turning a corner into the Wandsworth Bridge Road, he almost clipped a parked car. Christ, he thought, I'm falling apart. Get it together, get it together. The cow won't talk, not when her big friend has form, not when she herself could get debarred or whatever they did to lawyers caught breaking and entering.

No, she wouldn't talk. But hearing himself repeat this, he realised he was far from persuaded. *Christ*. He must think this through, must get his story fixed up. He'd say that if the cow got trapped in the flat then it must have been accidental. He'd say that on discovering the burglary he'd taken a quick look around, repaired the door – the hammering would have covered any sounds from upstairs – and gone to Beryl's to sleep. He would flatly deny the rest. Beryl would back him up. She'd provide an alibi for the evening. Biggs and his lunch companion would cover for the earlier part of the day.

Would it be enough? Yes, yes, of course it would be enough. The girl could never prove otherwise, not without incriminating herself. The thought calmed him, and he indulged in a different scenario, one in which he was above all suspicion, and the police, on the strength of his evidence, were forced to charge the Field bitch with burglary.

Approaching Battersea, he tried Biggs on the walkie-talkie but either he was out of range or he was already back inside the office because there was no answer. Parking, he looked for Biggs' car but couldn't see it. He approached the door in the wall and saw that the door which he'd wedged tightly shut was now slightly open. He prodded it with his finger. It swung open further. He listened. Somewhere upstairs, Beji began yapping, but without enthusiasm.

Hillyard stepped inside. He heard a voice drifting down from the office. He recognised the inimitable sound of Beryl gabbing on the phone. He felt a mingling of relief and anger. He did not need Beryl in her shrewish mode, carping at him for screwing up, telling him exactly where he'd gone wrong, going hysterical about the carnage to her beloved files. At the same time the sound of the old trout's voice was oddly reassuring.

As he began to trudge upwards, Beji appeared on the turn of the stairs, growling softly. 'You can shut your face for a start!' he hissed. The dog bared its teeth. Continuing past, he aimed a blow in the dog's direction, a blow which, as his hand travelled through the air, took on all the considerable force of his pent-up fury and caught the animal a clout that sent it sprawling against the wall.

He was seven steps up and almost onto the landing when two unpleasant sensations hit him one after the other. The first was a sudden, sharp pain in his lower calf which, as Beji's teeth cut deeper into his flesh, grew to such excruciating proportions that it was a moment before he could find the breath to scream. The second sensation was of a dark shape coming up the stairs behind him, a shape that wasn't Biggs. As he twisted round to beat Beji away from his leg the shape was no more than a blur, a snatched impression of a tall figure stepping round the bend of the stairs, but by the time he had torn the dog's teeth quite literally out of his calf he had recognised the confident step and heavy expressionless gaze of a CID man. Seeing the second one coming up behind, Hillyard realised they must have been waiting for him. He fell back against the wall sobbing and spitting, and it wasn't entirely because of the pain in his leg.

THIRTY-NINE

It was a day of brilliant light and deep winter shadows. Snow lay on the hills and across the floor of the pass and on the north-facing slopes where the January sun couldn't reach. The landscape seemed to reflect itself upwards into the whiteness of the sky, but as the road dropped down towards the loch the colours came back into the earth, rich and golden, and the sky turned a pale crystalline blue.

The potholed road to nowhere wound its way upwards through the conifers towards the low roof of the Bells' cottage. As Daisy turned the last corner Campbell's figure came into view, waiting motionless by the gate. It was just as they had planned: no one else at all.

In the back of the car, Meg Bell said prosaically: 'Well, here we are then.' But the calmness of her voice could not entirely conceal her emotion. Daisy glanced in the mirror. Adrian was staring ahead, holding the dazed, gravely incredulous expression he had worn since they had picked him up from the hospital.

She drew up at the gate. Campbell opened Adrian's door and helped him out and when Daisy looked again Adrian was enveloped in Campbell's awkward hunched embrace.

Daisy looked away over the broad landscape. There was no wind, and in the stillness it seemed to her that there were strange imperceptible sounds echoing softly from the hills, sounds that had always been there but which she had never heard before. She looked away towards the west, to where the head of the loch lay unseen around the bend of the hills, and thought of the parkland and the empty house beyond. In

665

her mind the house was cold and barren. He would sell it eventually, she thought; he would sell it and move on to another life.

She turned. Campbell, one arm around Adrian, was helping him up the path and into the cottage.

The four of them ate in the front room, sitting around a table in front of the small open fire. Daisy had syphoned off some cash from the legal fund to install four dimple radiators and put something aside for the fuel bills, and now the cottage was warm and dry and free of fumes.

Adrian seemed to wake to his freedom by slow degrees until, fired with something approaching energy, he gave a sudden smile. Daisy's pleasure was tempered by the lingering frustrations of the seven-week legal battle, and the knowledge that, though Adrian was out of hospital and clear of the place of safety order, he was not completely free, since the local authority had obtained a supervision order. Adrian would not be able to travel or start new medical treatment without the social services' permission, nor could his case be publicised in any way. Daisy reflected that, when doing battle with the authorities, there was no such thing as a good clean win. The best that could be hoped for – at least until Adrian reached sixteen and had more hope of establishing his right to refuse medical treatment – was a truce, albeit an uneasy one.

On the plus side, the whole process could have taken a great deal longer. Six months, or even more, was not uncommon in child-care cases. And Adrian, though he had been virtually comatose on the heavy drugs given him in the early weeks and had lost a great deal of the weight he had fought so hard to gain, seemed at the same time to have acquired a fresh determination, a new resilience to his disabilities, exhibited by his insistence on leaving the hospital on foot under his own power.

No amount of will-power could sustain his energy for long though, and at the end of the meal he lay on the settee, looking drained. But he was not so tired that he didn't want to inspect the book of press cuttings that Daisy had brought with her.

'The show that runs and runs,' Daisy remarked, not without a certain satisfaction. The *Sunday Times* had made Silveron a lead story for three consecutive weeks, then, after a break for Christmas, had picked it up again for another two. They ran

Dublensky's story for the first two weeks and the anonymous pilot's the next, with appropriate responses or evasions from Morton-Kreiger, politicians and pressure groups. The rest of the press had been forced to cover the story – giving due credit to the *Sunday Times* – because numerous questions had been asked in the Commons and the new Minister of Agriculture had been forced to make a statement. Coming on top of Driscoll's sudden resignation for 'family reasons', with attendant rumours of unsuitable women, blackmail and late-night parties – rumours subsequently confirmed by Angela Kershaw who had sold her story to the *News of the World* for £45,000 – the ministry had been pushed firmly out of its complacency and into the political spotlight, and there was talk of a major rethink, of imposing more stringent regulations on all pesticides, of having data independently analysed. There was even renewed talk of splitting Food from Agriculture, and creating two separate ministries with non-conflicting aims.

But the item that thrilled Adrian more than anything was the *Sunday Times'* New Year lead feature. The cutting had been smuggled into hospital to him, he had already read it twice, but now, looking proud and embarrassed in turns, he could not get enough of it, and who could blame him, since he himself was the star of the piece. Well, the unacknowledged star. To work its way around the injunction on publicity, the newspaper had been forced to use pseudonyms, to move the Bell home to 'somewhere in western Scotland', to alter all other facts that could in any way identify Adrian. But for all that, the story was very much Adrian's, some of it told in his own words, courtesy of a tape recorder and a list of questions that Daisy had taken into the hospital when posing as an assistant to the Bells' solicitor.

But if Adrian was intoxicated by his stardom, Daisy got most satisfaction from the two items that had appeared in last Sunday's paper. First, the bald front-page news that Silveron's UK licence had been suspended; and that in the States the EPA had announced an urgent and thorough investigation into Silveron and all other chemicals tested by TroChem.

The second item, another massive four-page leading article, was the exposure of the dirty tricks and surveillance campaign mounted against Catch and its sometime employee Daisy Field by Reynard Associates at the behest of the mysterious

Workham Overseas Holdings. There were facsimiles of the expense sheets detailing the operatives and vehicles used to keep tabs on 'Jackie' (no suggestion of how this and other material had been acquired, Daisy noted), an invoice made out to Workham Overseas Holdings showing the accommodation address in the Cayman Islands, a photograph of the bug like the one found in the phone socket at Daisy's flat, a calendar of the long series of unexplainable and violent events culminating in the Octek fire, and a detailed re-examination of the facts surrounding the fire itself.

The newspaper also noted the arrest of the managing director of Reynard Associates, one Colin Hillyard, on certain charges which, being *sub judice*, were closed to further comment.

Then, just when it seemed that no more revelations were likely to be squeezed out of the story, came the punch, the point where the newspaper, at possible risk of an injunction and almost certainly amid the violent screams of its lawyers, had taken the plunge and stated that Cayman Islands sources had linked Workham Overseas Holdings to an offshore subsidiary wholly owned by Morton-Kreiger. These sources, as Daisy knew, had first consisted of friends and contacts of Nick's manager David Weinberg, but the information had subsequently been corroborated by the newspaper's own investigations, the nature of which Simon wouldn't reveal to her.

Significantly, Morton-Kreiger had neither confirmed nor denied the allegations. The company seemed to be in much-denied turmoil. Their chief executive (agrochemicals) had left in early December to join one of the big cola companies, their head of research had taken early and abrupt retirement just before Christmas and then, with the breaking of the Silveron story, their share price had taken a very nasty bump on the stock market. Although just days ago Daisy had noticed that, with the announcement of better-than-expected profits and with high contingency reserves, their share price had recovered to within a few points of its previous level.

Adrian had fallen asleep. Leaving him, they went into the kitchen, Mrs Bell to prepare tea, Campbell to thirst after a celebratory drink of a stronger nature, which he satisfied by spiriting a flask out of his jacket. For someone who in less than two weeks faced an assault hearing, he was extraordinarily sanguine. But then Daisy suspected he was making the not uncommon mistake of believing too heartily in his own defence – a defence first suggested by Daisy and subsequently endorsed by his lawyers. The plea was to be guilty – no escaping that – but with lashings of mitigation: emotional strain, an over-developed protective instinct – which was one way of putting it – and a misreading of modern psychological techniques which had resulted in Campbell's not unreasonable belief that Adrian, far from being helped by the psychologist, was actually being attacked by her. The lawyers reckoned that, with luck and a good performance from Campbell – patent regret and no aggression, he would get a hefty fine or maybe three months suspended.

'Well then! Very fine! Very fine!' Campbell beamed across the table in a surge of bonhomie. He insisted on pouring a large measure of whisky for Daisy, and his sister as well, although she never took more than a sip. 'Everyone home, everyone well and good,' pronounced Campbell with magisterial pomp, an emotional wobble in his voice. Everyone home. Everyone well and good. Contemplating this, Daisy thought of Adrian and a future in which his hopes of recovery had improved little, at least in the short term, but which promised a much better chance of compensation, although the fight would undoubtedly be long and bitter, a grind through the courts which might well take five, six, even ten years. She thought, too, of Dublensky and his family setting up home near the new trust headquarters in Oxford, a Dublensky who, delivered of his moral burden, blossomed with pride and zealous energy, who, far from retiring from the fray, had offered to visit Washington to testify publicly before a congressional committee on the Silveron affair.

But there was someone Campbell had forgotten. Nick was not back yet. His European tour had closed in Amsterdam just the previous night. He had last telephoned a few days ago, wanting to hear the news, agreeing proposals for the trust, confirming that he'd seen the latest *Sunday Times*. He had been surviving the tour reasonably well, he said, had even, to his surprise, enjoyed parts of it. As always during his irregular calls she had, to her slight shame, listened for traces of drink in his voice, for small signs of despair, but he had sounded happy, and if anything caught her attention, it was perhaps a hint of preoccupation in his tone. He had apologised for not phoning more often, but he'd been very tied up. At which Daisy's imagination had bounded off in new and unwelcome directions.

He had been vague about when he was coming home, murmuring about studio time and a recording that he must finish. He hadn't even said which home he would be coming to.

But Campbell knew. 'Ashard,' he declared. 'It's been readied.'

She looked away through the window then back at Campbell. 'You're sure?'

Campbell waved a hand, as if to indicate that his sources were impeccable. 'Aye, expected this mornin'.'

She thought of phoning but changed her mind. Ten minutes later as she was on her way out, Campbell called: 'And tell Mr Mackenzie I'll be after my jacket directly. Tell him it was never in the wood store, though I must have searched a dozen times.'

The gates were open, the housekeeper let her into the house. The hall was warm, there were displays of flowers. But it was not until her knock on the studio door went unanswered and she pushed it quietly open that the dream from the long night in Hillyard's flat came back to her. Nick sitting at the console, music pouring from the amplifiers, the strong white light at the windows: the scene was a mingling of old and imaginary images, so that she wasn't sure if this hadn't already happened and she wasn't in some extraordinary way reliving it.

But then, with a certain inevitability, the reality diverged. Though she waited several moments he didn't realise she was there, he didn't look round, and after standing uncertainly for a while she went and sat on the arm of a chair.

The music was rich and orchestral, with an overlay of voices, sometimes in chorus. Most of it was taped and he seemed to be adding strands of sound on the keyboard as he went along. After a pause which was no more than a beat, he came in with a solo written for a voice much higher than his own. First he hummed the melody, then he sang in a strained falsetto. The words were from a poem, she thought, or maybe a lament. Despite the odd pitch of his voice and the patchwork of different sounds, the effect was unusual and rather lovely.

670

She tried to imagine how it must feel to create something like this, and felt a thrill of excitement for him.

He stopped suddenly, flicked the tape off, and made a small grunt of dissatisfaction.

Standing up, she said: 'Sounds beautiful.'

He swung round, not at all startled, and a slow grin spread over his face. '*Daisy*.' He got up and came over and kissed her firmly on both cheeks. He looked wonderful.

Holding her lightly by the shoulders, he pulled back and stared at her. 'Daisy,' he murmured again. He appeared pleased, though whether with her or with life in general, it was hard to tell. 'What, no black eye?'

'Not today.'

He dropped his hands from her shoulders. 'No one left to fight, huh?'

'Oh, I wouldn't say *that*. But I was thinking of giving up hand-to-hand combat.'

'Getting soft?'

'Just thought I might try a quiet life. You know – for a change.'

He made a disbelieving face and grinned again. 'Adrian's free anyway. That's great. Well done.'

'Adrian's out,' she agreed. 'But then Campbell might well be in, and the place he'll be going to has a lot more bars on the windows.' She explained how Campbell was finding the idea of public repentance difficult.

'Can't you coach him?'

'A gorilla with stage training would be more receptive.'

'Oh well,' he laughed, refusing to take the threat too seriously. 'I'll keep him company. Two old lags doing our time.'

'I thought they were dropping the charges. I thought they understood why you had the stuff – '

'Bad joke. Sorry,' he said rapidly, grimacing an apology. 'They *do* – they *have* dropped the charges. But what about you? There was a time when I thought we'd all be inside together. The Three Musketeers up shit creek.' The idea entertained him.

'Oh, Morgan knows I did it,' she said blithely. 'I mean, he knows that I know who broke Hillyard's door down, and I know he knows. And I know he knows that I was in there

671

when I shouldn't have been. But we don't talk about any of that. I just say I knocked on Hillyard's door and got invited inside and we ended up making a deal over the documents. No unlawful imprisonment, no kidnap, nothing nasty. That way I don't get to perjure myself and Campbell keeps out of further trouble, all at the same time. Well, that's the theory anyway. Hillyard's busy pushing his side of the story.'

'Which is?'

'That I sent some thugs to break into his place, and he found me there next morning.'

'Are the police buying that?'

'They're doing their best to overlook it. They're rather keener on getting Hillyard for breaking and entering my flat, for illegal surveillance and assault and a few other things.'

'And will they get him? I mean, on all of that?'

'Enough. Though' – she bared her teeth – 'I'm not sure anything could be enough.'

'Nightmares?' he asked, and she saw his own nightmares reflected in his eyes.

'A few.'

He reached for her hand and squeezed it.

She put on a look that said it was all right really, which at that moment it most certainly was.

'Come on,' he said suddenly, 'let's go out before it gets dark. I haven't seen around the place yet.'

Pausing at the door he jerked his head in the direction of the console. 'You really liked it?'

'Oh yes.'

'Well, it's finished,' he declared, making a broad arc with his hand as if to encompass an enormous volume of music. 'At least *nearly*. I worked on it almost every day while I was away.'

She couldn't help asking: 'You had the time?'

'Sure. In the afternoons before the show . . .'

'You said you were tied up.'

His expression changed from puzzlement to wry amusement. 'Now what else would have tied me up, Daisy?'

'Will you be performing it soon?' she said rather too quickly.

He was still laughing at her, trying to catch her eye as they went into the hall. 'I'll get a rough on tape first. Then . . . well, we'll see.' He added more thoughtfully: 'Once maybe.

With a full orchestra and choir. Yes, just the once. Who knows.'

'Why not more often?'

He led the way into a small room that was entirely given over to coats and boots. 'I don't know . . . Hearing something once, sometimes that's enough.' He held up a quilted jacket for size before helping her on with it.

She sensed he wasn't ready to explain further, and she didn't press him. 'Oh, Campbell wants his jacket back,' she said.

'What?'

'He says he's looked for it in the wood store a dozen times.'

He frowned as he searched his memory. 'A jacket?' Then he gave a short laugh. 'Oh *that*. He wants it back, does he? Ha! He'll be bloody lucky.' But going to a hook behind the hall door he rooted through a pile of coats and, with a grunt of satisfaction, emerged with a well-worn tweed jacket. He held it at arm's length. 'This,' he said scornfully, jerking it up and down until it danced, 'was used to wrap me up one night. Campbell bloody *tucked me up* with it!' For a moment he was lost in the past somewhere, but then he turned and looked at her, and there was nothing of the past in his smile. 'Come on,' he said.

He threw the jacket on a bench and they went out of the side door and into a formal garden. The air was fresh, the hills were so finely drawn that they seemed to be etched into the sky. They stood looking out over the water for a minute before taking a well-trodden path that led across the park towards the trees.

'I won't be staying here,' he said.

'Where will you go?'

'There's a place in Oxfordshire I thought I might go and look at.'

'Nice?'

'Could be.'

'A farm? Land?'

'Just a bit of land.'

'Quiet?'

'Quiet enough. But much more convenient, much closer to everything.'

Closer to the trust headquarters, to London, to *me*, she thought.

'Will you come and look at it with me?' he asked, almost shyly.

'Yes! Of course I will!'

'I want to be sure it's not too *loud*, you see.'

Daisy clasped her chest as if she had been stabbed. 'Who-ever *said* that word!'

They started off again. She asked: 'The tour – how did it go? Was it all right?' But he wasn't going to miss that opportunity either.

'Rather tied me up,' he said.

'You're victimising me!' she complained.

He said more seriously: 'No, it went well. In the most important way anyway.'

'The most important way?'

'It made money.'

'Ah.'

'Well, I have to keep you and your projects in the manner to which they've become accustomed, don't I?'

'In that case,' she declared, 'I hope it made pots and *pots*!'

And then the dream converged. He gave a hoot of laughter and, pulling her into the curve of his arm, squeezed her close against him.

WOLF WINTER

For Roma Schapiro

My thanks to the many friends, old and new, here and in Norway, who helped me research this book.

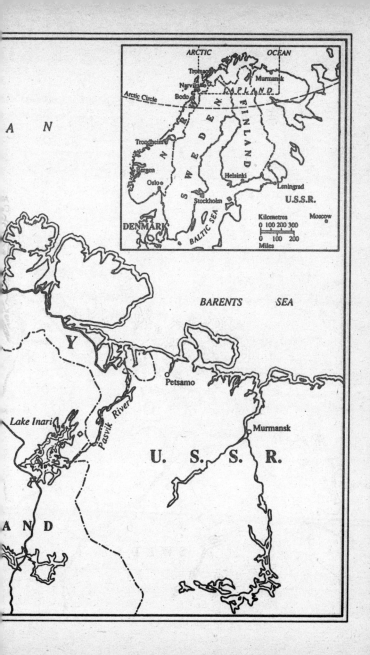

ARCTIC OCEAN

Tromsø
Narvik
Murmansk
Arctic Circle
Bodo
LAPLAND

N
O
R
W
A
Y
S
W
E
D
E
N
F
I
N
L
A
N
D

Trondheim

Bergen
Oslo
Helsinki

Stockholm
Leningrad

DENMARK
BALTIC SEA
U.S.S.R.
Moscow

Kilometres
0 100 200 300
0 100 200
Miles

BARENTS SEA

Y

Petsamo

Lake Inari
Pasvik River

Murmansk

U. S. S. R.

AND

Prologue
North Norway, January 1945

The night was cold and brilliantly clear. You could see for miles: peak after peak of ice-mountains rose into the dome of the sky, jagged crystal teeth squeezed between the deep inroads of the jet-black fiords.

High in the mountains the near-full moon cast long shadows and lit the snow with transparent brilliance so that visibility was particularly good. Which was just as well for the two young men who were making a quick but properly cautious descent of the mountain known by the Lappish name of Goalsvarre.

At 4,230 feet the peak was not the highest in the Lyngen Alps – there were several higher, many of which were tantalisingly unclimbed – but Goalsvarre was close to the village of Lyngseidet and convenient for the bus and ferry ride back to Tromso.

Most people, had they known of this expedition, would have considered it foolish. It was irresponsible enough to go mountaineering in the depths of a winter night, but to do so when the place was thick with Germans was asking for trouble.

But no one did know. And even if they had, the young men would have argued that winter was the best time to go mountaineering – the snow was firm and powdery – and that at sixty-nine degrees north, well within the Arctic Circle, the long hours of darkness at this time of year made night climbing more or less unavoidable.

And as for the Germans – well, the Occupation had lasted five years and if one waited for it to end one might wait for ever.

The descent of the upper slopes went smoothly and by seven in the morning they had regained their camp on a bluff below the main ridge and were eating a spartan breakfast. They made desultory but contented conversation. It had been a good hard climb and they had done it in record time with the minimum of equipment.

Taking to their skis, they began the descent of the lower slopes. The moon was setting but the snow was vibrant with reflected starlight. Above the northern peaks the polar sky flickered with the ghostly radiance of the northern lights.

As always, Hal led and Jan followed. They travelled in silence; there was no need to speak. It was enough to hear the soft hiss of the skis on the virgin snow, and the resonant hush of the frosty air.

A frozen lake discharged into an equally frozen stream, its course discernible only by a slight depression in the thick snow. As the young men followed it downward Lyngenfiord began to open out before them, a narrow black gash between the glistening mountains.

Hal gestured and they came to a stop.

From deep in the fiord rose a low hum. The two listened for a moment then skied on until they could see across the distant water to where Route 50, the German Army-built north–south highway, snaked its way tortuously down the far shore of the fiord. They paused again and stared, transfixed by the sight of a procession of glimmering pinpricks of light creeping slowly southward.

'Retreat?' Jan asked, unable to keep the excitement out of his voice.

'This far, anyway,' Hal said cautiously.

'But surely they'll keep going. They're bound to.'

'Well . . .' Hal said doubtfully. 'It'll depend on the Russians.'

'That's what I mean. The Russians'll chase them out!'

Hal was silent for a moment. 'I hope so,' he murmured finally.

The German 20th Mountain Army had been on the retreat from the Russian border for two months, dragging themselves across Finland and the top of Norway to this, the Lyngenfiord. During the retreat along the Arctic coast, the German Army had been pursuing a ruthless scorched-earth policy, evacuating civilians, burning towns and villages, destroying livestock. For weeks evacuees had been arriving in Tromso by coastal steamer, many of them to be sent further south. Now over a hundred thousand German soldiers of the 18th and 36th Mountain Corps were encamped at Lyngen.

Hal tried to imagine what this retreat must have cost the Germans, floundering first through the forests and lakeland of northern Finland then across the vast emptiness of the high plateau until they reached this, the deeply indented coastline of northern Norway – and all in the depths of winter, on primitive roads that were often closed by avalanche and drift snow. And with the Russian Army on their heels.

It must surely rank as one of the most difficult retreats ever undertaken. Hal knew how impossible it was to move a heavily equipped army quickly, even in ideal conditions; at the age of twelve he'd had a taste for military history, and had read his way through a detailed account of the Napoleonic Wars. For a while he'd even wanted to be a soldier. But then at fourteen he'd discovered the glory of the mountains, and that had spoilt him for everything else.

Now he was almost eighteen and his old ambition to be a soldier had returned. Like every other boy of his age he wanted to get hold of a decent weapon and have a shot at the Germans and force them to get out of Norway.

But *would* the Russians come? There were rumours: it was said the Russians were already deep within the northernmost province of Norway, named Finnmark, and advancing fast on Lyngen. But Hal doubted it. No army would risk getting trapped on this coast, hemmed in by the fiords and open sea on the one side and the mountains on the other.

No: the Russians would hold off. And the Germans, having abandoned Finnmark, would stay here at Lyngen until the bitter end.

'Come,' he said to Jan, and they refastened their hoods and adjusted their gloves and set off once more.

As they continued downward the night retreated a little and the outlines of the mountains lost their sharpness and became soft and blue-tinged as the winter day, which would grow to no more than a dim twilight, glimmered slowly to life.

Lyngseidet came into view beneath them. Pausing, they looked down. The small village on the edge of Lyngenfiord

3

was choked with German vehicles that hadn't been there the previous evening.

'Better keep clear,' Hal said.

They turned away from the village and headed towards a pass through the mountains. This led to a small fiord called Kjosen, a finger of water that almost dissected the forty-mile-long Lyngen peninsula. A narrow snow-packed road led over the pass towards the Tromso ferry. Even this road, though far from busy, had more traffic than usual.

Hal decided it would be risky to take the bus, even if it was running, which was doubtful. Their papers were in order, but with all this activity the guards at the checkpoints might be over-zealous and ask questions about the unusual amount of food and survival gear in their rucksacks. The guards were always on the lookout for young men fleeing over the mountains to Sweden to avoid *Arbeidstjenesten* – known as AT – the so-called 'labour service' introduced by the Quisling government in a thinly disguised attempt to force Norwegians into the German Army.

Hal led the way down into the pass and, when it was safe to do so, on across the snow-packed road and up the opposite slope. Keeping high above the road and the checkpoints, they made their way along the mountainside, parallel to the road, until the pass was left behind and Kjosen Fiord lay below and to their left, a dark gash between the steep blue-lit slopes. Along the shore an occasional farm nestled darkly in the snow, the windows blacked out, the buildings dead-looking.

The hillside got steeper. Hal looked up, trying to remember the formation of the hidden upper slopes. There was a hanging glacier, he knew, and at least one deep snow-filled gully: avalanche country.

Finally they were forced to descend on to a gentler slope covered with sparse birch scrub. The road was now only a hundred yards away. Occasionally a German military vehicle sped past, throwing up clouds of snow but, screened by the scrub, the two skiers remained unnoticed, striding along in the long sliding gait of practised cross-country skiers.

A valley opened out to the right. They curved into its mouth to distance themselves from the road.

Suddenly Hal stopped dead so that Jan almost ran into him.

Motionless, they listened. The air was very still. For several moments the silence was deep and unbroken. Then a muffled sound floated across the snow.

A human voice.

Hal stiffened. He saw them now: a group of skiers about half a mile away, coming straight for them on a reciprocal course. There were six of them, uniformly dressed in white parkas with rifles slung over their shoulders: a German patrol. And travelling fast.

Why ski-troops should be down by this road Hal couldn't imagine, but they were. And there would be no escaping them.

It would be best to look casual and unconcerned when first seen. With a sigh of resignation and anger, Hal gestured to Jan and led the way forward again.

Just as it seemed the patrol must spot them, the leading soldier halted and trained his binoculars up the narrow side-valley. He appeared to see something for, with a sudden movement, he grabbed his rifle and put it to his shoulder. Then, just as abruptly, he lowered it again and, beckoning excitedly to his men, led the way into the valley, skiing briskly.

The opportunity was too good to miss. The moment the patrol was gone Hal and Jan thrust rapidly forward in a rapid kick-glide movement that was almost a run, and crossed quickly behind the disappearing Germans.

As he ran Hal glanced sideways. The reason for the soldiers' excitement was now clear. High in the head of the valley were two black dots, plainly visible in the blue light. Men on skis. Climbing slowly up the steep slope at the head of the valley, like two ants on a white wall.

Reaching the comparative safety of a thick clump of birch at the far side of the valley mouth, the two young men paused.

Jan whispered: 'Who can they be?'

Hal gave a shrug. The two figures couldn't be Lapps – the Lapps were miles inland on the plateau at this time of year – and they weren't likely to be mountaineers – it wasn't exactly a popular sport. They were probably AT evaders. Hal wished there was something they could do to help, but short of side-tracking the patrol and getting themselves arrested or shot in the process, there was nothing to be done.

5

The Germans had now reached the head of the valley and were striking up a deep gully, climbing awkwardly and slowly. It was hard to be sure from such a distance, but to Hal's eyes the gully looked heavy with drifts, bulges and hummocks of snow. Some distance above the gully was a steep snowfield, with a thick cover of snow, smooth as a cake topping, which gleamed ice-blue in the late-morning twilight.

The gully looked tricky but it was nothing to the snowfield. That looked wildly unstable. Only fools or men untrained for these mountains would have chosen that route.

But the two black dots higher on the mountain knew their stuff all right, for they had bypassed the gully and were now making short work of a ridge well to the side of the pregnant snowfield. Soon they would reach the safety of the high mountains. Hal put up a silent cheer.

Half-way up the gully the soldiers were making heavy weather of their climb. They had slowed down visibly and the leader was stationary, as if undecided about the route ahead.

Suddenly the silence was broken by the distant sound of a shot, echoing once, faintly, through the valley.

Hal stiffened, thinking: They're mad.

There was a long and deathly silence.

Another shot rang out, reverberated once, feebly, and was quickly absorbed by the snow.

Jan gasped audibly.

A small puff of white had appeared at one side of the snowfield. Slowly, almost leisurely, more delicate puffballs ballooned out, like cannon smoke from a broadside.

The sound came seconds later, a low rumbling of distant thunder. Denser clouds blossomed out from the bottom of the snowfield which lay curiously pristine and untouched in the centre. Yet this was an illusion, for the whole face was in fact sliding, the bottom already voiding itself like some vast ponderous waterfall, a white cataract disgorging tons and tons of compacted snow into the gully beneath.

The surface of the snowfield cracked and heaved and segmented, and was slowly obscured by the billowing snow which rose up and outward in a vast cloud.

The six soldiers below seemed rooted to the spot. Then, as if at a signal, they moved at once, racing down the gully in jerky

6

zigzags like insects fleeing a fire. Two figures collided and one fell. The others pressed on, their progress in the heavy snow painfully slow.

It was a race that couldn't be won. The avalanche poured remorselessly into the gully. Hal winced as the dense white cloud engulfed the first man and the next and the next, until four had been overcome. For a moment it seemed that the last two might escape – they appeared to be keeping ahead of the advancing wall – but then they too were enveloped in the rumbling cloud.

A German Army truck passed by on the road behind. It did not stop.

It was a full two minutes before the last thundering echo died away. A pall of blue cloud hung in the valley like morning mist.

Hal and Jan exchanged brief glances. They both knew what the other was thinking. Had the buried men been Norwegians they would have gone for help and tried to dig them out. But it was impossible to feel pity for Germans. It had been a long war and few families had suffered more than Hal's. In 1941 his elder brother had been lost at sea in a torpedoed cargo ship and a year later his father had been deported to Germany.

Without a word they turned away.

Hal set off at a smart pace: the sooner they were clear of the scene the better. In the absence of anyone to blame, the Germans would doubtless arrest them.

Jan made an exclamation and, calling to Hal, gestured back up the valley. Following his gaze, Hal saw with surprise that the two fugitives had reappeared. Their tiny figures were heading downhill again, back into the valley.

Jan raised his eyebrows questioningly at Hal.

Hal thought for a long moment. 'They might need help.'

His words hung heavily on the air. If the men were wanted by the Germans the risks would be considerable. The penalties ranged from deportation to a forced labour camp to a bullet in the head.

There was no discussion. Hal and Jan turned and skied into the valley. A short way up the valley they stopped and waited in the cover of a thicket of dwarf birch.

The figures had reached the lower slopes at the head of the valley. But instead of hurrying towards the valley mouth, they

7

made a long traverse, heading for the vast pile of avalanched snow at the foot of the gully. Halting on top of the white burial mound, they went first one way then the other, as if searching for something.

After a while they seemed to find what they were seeking, for one moved across to the other and they both crouched in the snow. They remained in the same spot for some time, and Hal thought he could see them digging.

Finally, after a good five minutes, the two figures stood up, their task apparently completed, and began to ski down the valley.

Hal let them get quite close before emerging from the thicket.

The two men stopped dead. One slid an automatic weapon quickly off his shoulder.

Hal called a casual: 'Good morning.'

There was a long silence, then: 'Who are you?'

'Friends.'

They murmured to each other then moved cautiously forward until the four of them stood face to face. The two strangers were hooded and muffled, but Hal could see from their eyes that they were young, roughly his own age, he guessed.

Hal decided on the direct approach. 'We saw what happened. We thought you might need help.'

The taller of the two pulled the hood down from his mouth. 'Help? You could say that. You could tell us how to get out of this place!'

'Where are you going?'

There was a pause while the tall one eyed Hal thoughtfully. He seemed to make up his mind. 'North.'

Hal blinked with a mixture of alarm and admiration. Only desperate men would try such a thing. The new German lines would be almost impenetrable. And even if they got through they'd have to run the gauntlet of the demolition squads before they could hope to reach the relative safety of the Russian lines.

'Not easy,' Hal said.

The tall one gave a short harsh laugh, the sound uncomfortably loud in the silent valley. 'Well, we know that, my friend!'

Hal flushed. Recovering quickly, he tried to think. 'All I could do is direct you to a place where there are boats. Someone might be able to take you a few miles up the coast, past the lines.

Though it's an awful risk.'

The two exchanged glances. 'We'll give it a try,' said the second one. 'Anything's better than freezing up there.' He indicated the mountains.

'We need food, too,' said the tall one. 'As much as you can find.' It was the request of someone accustomed to getting what he wanted.

'You're welcome to what we've got,' Hal offered solemnly.

Another German vehicle passed along the distant road. Aware that both the fugitives had highly visible automatic weapons over their shoulders, Hal added urgently, 'We must get away from here.'

He led the way out of the valley and along the side of the fiord, keeping as high above the road as possible. Finally the narrow strip of lowland by the shore opened out into a wide flat plain and, hugging the edge of the mountain, they curved away from the road until safely out of view of passing vehicles. They stopped and made camp, waiting for the cover of the deepening afternoon twilight.

The two fugitives ate ravenously, consuming all Hal and Jan's remaining rations. While they ate Hal examined them. They were both about eighteen, he guessed; twenty at the most. The taller one had a handsome face, with regular features, a thatch of thick yellow-blond hair and vivid blue eyes. But what one noticed most was his taut energy: a sort of driving force that commanded attention. He talked in great bursts, as if his energy could barely be contained, and his eyes were charged with a restlessness which only fell away when he laughed; then he seemed exhilarated, almost euphoric.

His friend, who was dark with a pleasant round face, was altogether quieter, appearing strangely unaffected by the day's events.

They didn't offer an explanation of how they had arrived in Lyngen or where they had come from, and Hal didn't ask. But their accent was not a local one. It was from further south, though Hal couldn't place it exactly.

It was Jan who asked: 'Have you come far?'

The first one shot his friend a warning glance, but too late to prevent him saying: 'Trondheim.'

There was an awkward pause, then the conversation switched

to the avalanche. The two strangers discussed it with great amusement, even pride. With a slight shock Hal suddenly realised that it was they, and not the Germans, who had fired the shots. He stared at them, slightly awe-struck. Finally he asked: 'You meant to start the avalanche?'

'Well, we didn't mean to, exactly. But we certainly caused it!' said the tall one. He gave a brittle laugh, his blue eyes sharp and shrewd, and Hal had the feeling that he had known exactly what he was doing with those shots. 'We did well out of it too,' he added. He patted the sub-machine-gun propped against the rucksack beside him. 'A Schmeisser,' he said proudly. 'Now we have one each.'

'And ammo, and a knife, and new gloves, and goggles, and a warm fleece-lined cap!' his friend added, pulling article after article out of his rucksack.

'And look at this,' the tall one boasted, producing a pair of field glasses, rubber-jacketed and overpainted with flaking white paint. 'The Germans are very good at making binoculars. They make the best lenses in the world, did you know that?' He put the glasses to his eyes and twiddled with the focus. 'Excellent!'

Hal wasn't so sure this booty was excellent at all. He murmured: 'If they catch you with it ...'

The tall one gave his short snorty laugh. 'If we're caught, we're dead anyway!'

Hal wondered what they had done that was so serious. As if reading his thoughts, the tall one indicated his friend and said: '*He* beat up an officer, *I* –' he paused – '*I* executed one of their lot!' He said it with a bright mocking smile, as if he didn't care a damn, but his quick eyes darted straight to Hal's face, searching for a reaction.

There was a moment's silence. Hal was meant to be impressed, he realised, but he could only feel a stab of concern. When one of their number was killed the Germans always exacted terrible reprisals, executing dozens of civilians – sometimes even women and children.

The tall one sensed his dismay. 'Sometimes these things have to be done,' he said defensively. 'We did everyone a favour, believe me. We're heroes back home. Or at least I hope so!' He laughed again. The sound was sharp and discordant in the silence. No one spoke. After a while the two strangers settled back in the snow and dozed. Hal and Jan kept watch until gathering clouds brought an early darkness. Waking the sleeping men, they packed up and set off again.

Luck was with them: the cloud thickened and they were able to travel across the flatlands with little fear of being seen.

Hal led them along the wide shore of Ullsfiord until they were safely past the checkpoint at the ferry link to Tromso. Then he explained the way to the isolated settlement where they might find a boat.

'One favour,' the tall one said to Hal.

'If I can.'

'Your skis. You see, one of my bindings is almost off. I can't fix it without tools, but it wouldn't take a moment in a workshop. You don't mind, do you? I'll return them or at least repay you – I promise. Though I can't say when!'

Hal's face fell in the darkness. His skis were new. It had taken him two years to get hold of some seasoned spruce and hickory, and another year to persuade the local ski-maker to make the skis to Hal's own design: spruce upper with laminated hickory sole; narrow and very fast. They had proved to be everything Hal had hoped they would be, and more.

'You can't fix yours?' he asked, hoping for a miracle.

'Afraid not. And we've a long way to go.'

Hal sighed inwardly and, wishing he didn't mind quite so much, bent down to remove his skis. He thrust them quickly into the other man's hand and took the damaged ones in exchange.

The tall one murmured to his friend in the darkness: 'Yours all right, Petter?'

'Yes.'

The four of them parted, shaking hands gravely in the darkness.

On impulse Hal said, 'If for any reason you can't get away and you find yourselves in Tromso, ask for the Starheim house.'

'Thanks,' said the tall one in the distant tone of someone who never expects to have to take up an offer. And then the two of them were gone, and Hal and Jan turned back along the path to the ferry and the faint hope of a bus ride home.

Two days later the news flew around Tromso: a boat had been stolen from Ullsfiord the previous night and gunfire had

11

been heard in the fiord.

No one knew anything more. But in Hal's imagination it was only too horrifyingly obvious: the two boys had been captured and were already in Gestapo headquarters in Tromso. The memory of his father's incarceration in the grey forbidding building on Bankgata was still vivid in his mind. It was said that everyone thrown into its notorious cells talked in the end.

His friends on Ullsfiord would be betrayed and punished – probably executed.

But those fears were nothing to what he felt when he remembered he'd told the two young men his family name. His *name*!

He couldn't believe what a fool he'd been. His mother, his sister, himself – they would all be taken and shot.

Two days passed with agonising slowness. Then another day, and another. Still the Gestapo did not come. Neither was there news of any arrests at Ullsfiord.

Gradually Hal began to hope. Perhaps, despite everything, the two boys had got away.

After a month he finally allowed himself to relax and, far from minding about the loss of his lovely new skis, grew quite fond of the other pair. Not that they were any use: quite apart from the damaged binding, one ski had a long crack down the length of the grain.

Had the fellow known about the crack when he suggested the swap? Probably. But in a strange way Hal didn't mind. In the same position he liked to think he would have had the nerve to do the same thing himself.

On examining the skis closely he saw that something had been carved into the tips then scratched out. From time to time he made desultory attempts to decipher the markings.

Then, several months after the German capitulation, when no harm could possibly come from knowing, he took a soft pencil and thin paper and did a rubbing.

Initials, faint but distinguishable.

R.B.

After that Hal put the skis in the cellar and forgot about them. Only now and again, when he was climbing in the Lyngen Alps or passing the insignificant valley off the Tromso–Lyngseidet road, did he wonder about the skis' owner and whether he had got through.

He still liked to think that he had. But, on consideration, he thought not. The Russians had stopped short many miles to the north-east. It would have been an impossibly long journey across the devastation of Finnmark, and without supplies in the harshness of Arctic January.

No, the fellow probably hadn't made it. Hal was sorry.

PART ONE

February 1960

One

The major pulled up the hood of his parka and stepped out into the night. The cold snapped him awake as he'd hoped it would and, though his body was still warm from sleep, he stamped his feet and clasped his gloved hands to get his circulation moving.

He wandered idly away from the hut. It was four in the morning, but the dawn, such as it was, wouldn't come for a long time. Even then the day would be over almost before it had begun. What a godforsaken place this was! Too remote and lonely for his taste. Even the cold felt different – harsher, unforgiving, like the landscape.

The north had a sort of fascination, of course – he wouldn't be a good Norwegian if he didn't believe that – and on a night like this he had to admit that it had a stark, if severe beauty.

The air was astonishingly clear. The outlines of the surrounding hills and distant mountains were hard-rimmed against the night sky. To one side the main body of the camp lay quiet, dark except for the perimeter lights and sentry posts, the huts clearly outlined against the soft reflections of the snow. Below, he could just make out the rough winter road from the Arctic coast running up the floor of the valley, a ribbon of white through the sparse birch wood. The road was, of course, quite devoid of traffic. It continued southward past the camp until, somewhere deep in the interior, it rose clear of hills and trees and disappeared into the wilderness of the plateau.

The major had never been on to the plateau. On the rare occasions when he came up here to Finnmark he went straight to some garrison or military installation on the coast. It was such a distance – the best part of a thousand miles from Oslo

17

to the Arctic coast of north Norway – and travel was so difficult and very time-consuming that, once his business was finished, he usually wasted no time in getting back.

He shivered and checked the time: 0410. Five minutes to the weather forecast and forty-five minutes to the off. He stamped about for another minute then went back into the hut to see what was going on.

In the mess the two travellers and their driver were eating breakfast, talking quietly. The major did not join them. He was too tense to eat, and would anyway have felt out of place: the three had already formed themselves into a group, friendly but exclusive.

Instead the major asked shortly: 'All right?'

Jan Johansen, the leader, looked up and smiled. 'Fine.' It was a reassuring smile and the major took comfort from it. The success of the venture lay with these men, yet the major was only too well aware of where the blame would fall if anything went wrong.

In the passageway a door banged. A staff sergeant appeared with a written forecast. Strong northerly winds and a sharp drop in temperature. The major passed it to Jan Johansen who gave a slight dismissive shrug. The major, however, felt a twinge of concern: it didn't sound too good to him. He found himself wishing that Starheim were still around to discuss it.

Aware that he was hovering over the breakfasting men, the major went outside again. Two soldiers from the local battalion were loading the Land Rover.

'Is that the lot?' the major asked.

'Apart from the skis.'

The major inspected the gear. There didn't seem very much of it. 'Has this been checked?' he asked.

The soldier nodded. 'By Major Starheim.'

'Starheim? Oh you mean – yesterday?'

'No, about an hour ago.'

The major hid his surprise. 'I see.' Starheim had left after the briefing the previous afternoon, giving every indication that he wouldn't be returning. Yet here he was again, unannounced. The major should have been annoyed – if it had been anyone else he would have been – but in truth he was rather relieved.

'Where is Starheim?' he asked.

'Gone skiing, major.'

This time the major blinked visibly. 'When is he expected back?'

The soldier pointed up the hill behind the hut. 'He just went to the top. He said he wouldn't be long.'

The major scanned the slope above. He couldn't imagine climbing it in less than half an hour. But then he was neither an Arctic explorer nor a mountaineer.

He sauntered off until he was clear of the lights and sounds of the hut. The night was swathed in silence. Nothing stirred save the wisps of snow drawn from the peaks by the hard cold breeze. It was difficult to believe that anything existed on the wind-scoured slopes. Yet he didn't doubt that Starheim was up there somewhere. The major pictured him, moving silently and invisibly across the snow, a mountain man in his element. He tried to imagine himself like that: inured to cold and hardship, self-sufficient to the point of total independence, at home in the most desolate of places. But his imagination failed him, and he gave a sudden violent shiver.

*

Halvard Starheim stood high on the hill and looked down the length of the valley, towards the north and the distant mountains that stood above the Arctic fiords.

The air was cold, and it was going to get even colder. All the signs were there. The night was hard and clear. The surface of the snow, glowing luminously in the brilliant starlight, was powder-dry. And now a wind had sprung up, as yet no more than a sharp breeze, but already frost-cold against his skin.

He turned his face to it. Northerly. With perhaps a touch of east in it. Ice-bearing wind from the Arctic Ocean and the Pole beyond; a wind that was capable of taking the temperature down really low. Not a problem in itself – he and Jan had been through minus seventy °F overwintering in the Northwest Passage – but something to be borne in mind all the same.

He wished it was the only thing there was to worry about.

Over the Arctic horizon the northern lights shimmered in an iridescent curtain and, even as he watched, the aurora leapt outward until the sky was filled with silvery radiance. Instinctively he thought: Radio contact will be bad. Then he remembered that there wasn't going to be any radio contact and he exhaled harshly, his breath vaporising in a milky cloud.

He liked nothing about this expedition, as the major from military intelligence insisted on calling it. He disliked clandestine activities at the best of times. But most of all he disliked not having had a bigger say in the planning of it. Weather, ice, blizzard, terrain: he could deal with those. But this, with all its politics and subterfuge – this was distinctly tricky ground.

Sounds drifted up from the camp below. There were lights and movements outside the hut. Time was getting on. He pulled the drawstrings of his hood tighter over his face, checked his ski bindings, and looped his sticks over his wrists.

Out of long habit he paused briefly for one last look around before setting off. Then he began a long traverse, the narrow skis hissing softly through the deep virgin snow, occasionally rasping noisily as they touched some unseen rock. Approaching a bank of what might have been soft drift, he prepared to turn. Pushing his uphill ski well out, he made a long sweeping telemark turn, then straightened again for the next long traverse.

As he dropped fast towards the hut he came on to hard crust and risked a jump turn, a difficult manoeuvre when wearing narrow cross-country skis and soft boots attached by the toe alone. But the turn went well and he allowed himself a moment of satisfaction.

He came to a neat stop on a knoll just above the hut and bent down to unfasten his skis. The quiet was disturbed by the sound of an engine whirring. The Land Rover warming up. Fifteen minutes to go.

More sounds: the crunch of hard boots on snow. Hal looked up and saw a figure shrouded in a parka making his way carefully towards him. He recognised the man from military intelligence: Major Thrane.

Hal picked up his skis and went to meet him.

'How was it up there?' the major asked pleasantly.

'Oh – good.'

'The weathermen seem to think it's going to get cold.'

'I've no doubt they're right.'

'But that won't be a problem?'

Hal suppressed a wry smile. Desk men always fretted about

the wrong things. 'No, not on its own,' he replied.

The major nodded. 'I wasn't expecting you back.' His voice was friendly but curious.

'I thought I'd come and see them off. I hope that's all right.'

'Of course,' the major said quickly. 'Glad you stayed.'

They walked slowly towards the waiting vehicle.

The major cleared his throat and said a little awkwardly: 'Last night I had the feeling you were still unhappy about something. Was I right?'

Hal hesitated. He often made the mistake of speaking too plainly. It was his greatest failing, at least as far as his career in the army was concerned. It had made him at least one enemy in high places. And he couldn't afford that at the moment.

The major waited expectantly. 'Please feel free,' he pressed. 'Say what's on your mind.'

Hal stopped and faced him. Thrane was in his early thirties, about the same age as Hal, with sharp watchful eyes suggesting a deep intelligence. 'Well, if you really want to know,' Hal said finally, 'I don't like the idea at all.'

'I see,' Thrane said stiffly. 'Well, I'm sorry about that.' There was a pause. 'Obviously if there'd been another way ...'

'It *can't* be right to use civilians on a military operation.'

'But it's *not* a military operation. It's an intelligence expedition – operation.'

Hal gave him a hard stare. 'Come on.'

The major conceded the point with a reluctant shrug. 'Well – all right. Semi-military, then.' They began to walk again.

'In which case *I* should be going,' Hal said.

'You know that's out of the question,' Thrane said in a soft patient voice.

Hal gritted his teeth. Whether on exercise or one of his own expeditions he was used to being up there with his men. Staying behind went right against the grain.

Thrane murmured: 'You're a serving officer. You know you can't be found – outside.'

'Outside?' Hal echoed, shaking his head. Like all intelligence personnel, the major had a gift for euphemism. 'You mean, it would be embarrassing if I were caught, but all right if *they* are?'

'They're civilians and more importantly Lapps – or part Lapp

21

at least. They have a right to be there.'

'They'll still be spies.'

Thrane winced at Starheim's choice of word. 'Hardly. In fact, no, definitely not! No one would call them that.' He sounded quite hurt. 'Besides, no one will ever know they were there.' There was a finality to his words and he changed the subject briskly. 'Now, about this cold – it isn't going to slow them down, is it?'

They came to a halt some yards from the Land Rover. 'Maybe. If it falls below minus forty.'

'But they'll be able to keep going?'

'Difficult to say. Other things are more likely to slow them down – strong winds, heavy snow, a sudden thaw. It's not *just* the cold. But we've allowed for it. They've got time to spare.' Hal added, almost to himself: 'I'd be more worried about the other chap getting there on time, if I were you.'

Someone was gently revving the Land Rover's engine, so that clouds of vapour spewed out of the exhaust into the night air. Thrane murmured: 'Well, one can only make plans and assume everyone will do his best to carry them through.' He exhaled sharply, and added with sudden intensity: 'Look, he's important to us, this man. Believe me. Otherwise we wouldn't be going to all this trouble.'

Hal thought: I'd love to know why. But he didn't bother to ask. Secrecy was Thrane's stock in trade. Like the others, Hal had been briefed on the need-to-know principle. In his role as survival expert Hal had needed to know where Jan and Mattis were going, and that was about all. He'd been told nothing about the man that Jan and Mattis were to meet and bring back – not his name, age, language or nationality, nor even his ability as a skier.

Hal disliked secrecy because in his experience it always led to misunderstandings and mistakes. On his own expeditions he always insisted on each man being fully aware of what he was doing and why.

A door opened. The soldier who was to be the driver for the first leg of the trip emerged from the hut and climbed into the vehicle.

While they waited for the others the major stamped his feet, making a full circle, and said in a conciliatory tone: 'My God,

I'd hate to be up on the plateau when the weather's bad. How on earth do you survive it?'

Hal gave a small smile. 'We survive.' People from the south always thought of the northern interior as empty and hostile, but then they had been fed on the richer diet of forests and pastures, and couldn't see the plain beauty of simple things. The north might be relatively bleak, even harsh, but it certainly wasn't the barren uninteresting place people believed it to be.

'I first came up here in '45,' Thrane was saying. 'Helping to rebuild things. There was nothing left. I was posted to Alta. Hardly a house standing. At the time I wondered if people would ever bother to come back. But they did, of course.' He shot Hal an apologetic glance. 'But of course you come from this region, don't you?'

'Not quite. From Tromso.'

'Ah,' the major grunted. 'I read that somewhere.' He added almost accusingly: 'It's impossible not to read about you nowadays. All the magazines and papers. Doesn't it bother you?'

'Not any more.' It wasn't quite true, but Hal didn't feel like going into that now.

'And you're planning another expedition, I suppose?'

'Yes.'

'The North Pole again?'

'No.'

The major wasn't going to be put off. 'What sort of expedition then?'

'A mountain.'

'Ah.' The major smiled. 'A tall one no doubt.'

A figure emerged from the hut. It was Mattis. Hal went to meet him, grinning broadly. 'Okay?'

'Okay, Hal.' They had known each other a long time. Mattis was a nomadic Lapp from a family that wintered in the middle of the plateau at Kautokeino and summered at Kaafiord, not far from Tromso. He was also an ex-army cross-country ski champion. Like many nomadic Lapps he was small, barely a couple of inches over five feet, with characteristically bandy legs. He was dressed in traditional winter costume, a *luhkka* of reindeer-fur, reindeer-skin leggings and *finnesko*, large grass-lined moccasins.

He climbed into the Land Rover and laughed: 'We'll be there

too soon in this weather!' Hal didn't doubt it. Mattis had once skied ninety miles in twenty-four hours.

Hal wandered back towards the major, who immediately picked up the conversation again. 'So where's this mountain?'

Hal took his time. 'In the Himalayas.'

'Not Everest!'

Hal tried not to feel annoyed at Thrane's astonishment. 'Yes. The West Ridge.'

'Ah. Is that difficult?'

'It's never been climbed.'

Thrane nodded as if he'd known all along. 'An army expedition?'

'No.'

'Oh. I assumed – '

'The army gives me leave, that's all. And the odd piece of equipment when it wants something tested. I get no financial help.' He was always explaining this. Outsiders seemed to believe that money for expeditions grew on government trees.

Thrane considered for a moment. 'Tell me, I can understand doing the Northwest Passage – in the footsteps of Amundsen and all that – but why did you try for the Pole?'

This was a popular question. Hal pretended to consider his answer, although he knew it by heart. 'Because I wanted to show that, if one was sufficiently well prepared, it was possible to travel fast and light to anywhere in the Arctic, even the North Pole.'

'There were just the two of you, you and Johansen? And dogs?'

'Yes,' Hal said patiently.

'But the supply plane didn't find you?'

'Well – something like that.'

Their radio had packed up and, reaching a drop zone three days late, they'd found that the Canadian Airforce plane had been and gone, having dropped a few supplies blind. Though they'd managed to retrieve some of the scattered packages, they didn't have enough supplies to continue the attempt. Just a hundred miles from the Pole they'd been forced to turn back for Ellesmere Island.

But then you couldn't expect to win them all.

Jan appeared at last, much taller and looser-limbed than

Mattis. Jan wore an entire outfit of reindeer skin, complete with leggings and *finnesko*, while on his head perched a stylish and gaily coloured Lappish hat. Hal screwed up his face and laughed: 'A real Lapp!'

'My grandmother would have been proud of me.' Jan smiled and in the reflection of the lights it was possible to see in his features a hint of the high cheekbones, smooth skin and dark eyes that mark so many Norwegians from within the Arctic Circle. Jan was a quarter Lapp and, unlike many, proud of it.

He glanced at the sky. 'It's going to get cold, eh? But no snow, I think. So – nothing to slow us down.'

Hal chuckled. Jan had a way of seeing the positive side of everything. During the winter of '54 when the two of them had been iced up in Prince Albert Sound in northern Canada and the blizzards had kept them hut-bound for three weeks, Jan's quiet optimism and ingrained good humour had never flagged. Hal had needed that; it counterbalanced his own darker, more impatient nature.

'Good firm going,' Hal agreed. 'The luck of the devil.'

He pulled open the Land Rover door. The two men stood for a moment, smiling at each other.

Hal indicated Mattis. 'Have you warned him about all the chattering you do in your sleep?'

'No, but then he hasn't told me about his snoring.'

It was an old joke, but they both grinned anyway, and a dozen memories of shared laughter echoed through Hal's mind. Memories, too, of the bad times, experiences they had survived together. It was as a team that he and Jan had developed Arctic travel and survival techniques.

Now, suddenly, they weren't a team any more.

A wave of affection caught Hal and, overcoming his usual reserve, he reached out and embraced Jan awkwardly. Jan, after a momentary surprise, returned the embrace. The two men pulled back a little and patted each other's shoulders.

Hal said with forced cheerfulness: 'See you then.'

Jan climbed in and Hal slammed the door. The engine roared. Jan gave a brief wave and then the Land Rover was pulling away, its tail lights weaving red traces across the astonishing clarity of the night.

Hal watched until long after the lights had disappeared. He felt depressed.

The major shuffled up. 'Well, they seemed happy enough.'

The two men made their way back to the hut.

'Incidentally,' Thrane said, 'will you be in contact with Johansen's wife?'

'I'll be seeing her. The day after tomorrow.' A vision of Ragna swept into Hal's mind.

'She's been told some story, has she?'

'What? Oh, yes. That he's field-testing some new equipment for me.'

'Good.'

'Though I doubt she believes it.'

Thrane ground to a halt. 'What do you mean?'

'Well, she's not stupid.' Hal pulled open the hut door and after a moment Thrane followed him into the warmth of the interior. 'Jan can do field trials on his own doorstep, in the Lyngen Alps. He doesn't have to disappear into Finnmark for the best part of a week.'

'Oh,' the major said heavily. 'Well – I trust she's discreet.'

Hal thought of Ragna. She was many things: funny, bright, irreverent. And discreet: yes, that too.

In the mess there was coffee and a basic breakfast of rolls, cheese, and cold meat. The two men helped themselves and sat down.

Hal buttered a bread roll, and eyed Thrane across the table. He'd come across plenty of office men in his time, ambitious types who sat safely behind desks, determining other people's actions, taking the minimum of risk, and expending the larger part of their energies on plotting their own advancement. Certainly Thrane had all the polish and self-confidence of a man who expected early promotion.

Hal was irritated by him on principle. He asked suddenly: 'What happens if anyone finds out about this operation? Like the Finns, for example.'

A flicker of what could have been annoyance crossed the major's eyes, but he recovered well and said evenly: 'Why should they?'

'That's not an answer.'

'They won't find out,' Thrane said firmly. 'Anyway that's

26

our problem, not yours.'

Hal persisted: 'But these men have no protection if anything goes wrong.'

'I don't see what you mean,' Thrane said lightly. 'The men are merely going into Finland to meet someone. They won't be breaking any laws. And they certainly won't be crossing any other borders, will they? There's nothing that can go wrong.' He smiled soothingly. 'Besides, they volunteered. They weren't forced to go.'

'Not forced, maybe. But heavily persuaded!' As always when Hal showed his considerable anger, he instantly regretted it. He added more reasonably: 'Well, that is my opinion.'

Thrane eyed him tolerantly. 'One has to be practical. There are certain jobs that have to be done. Grey areas which have to be covered. In an ideal world it wouldn't be like that, but as it is . . .' He trailed off.

Hal drained his coffee and got to his feet. 'I have to go or I'll miss my transport.'

The major stood up. 'It's been a pleasure.'

Hal searched for a hint of sarcasm, but there was none. He softened a little and gave the ghost of a smile. 'You'll let me know?'

The major said smoothly: 'But I won't know much, if anything at all, until it's over. I've no doubt you'll hear direct from Johansen before you hear from me.'

A typically evasive reply. Hal thought crossly: I should have known.

Quickly, before he said something he might later regret, he turned on his heel and left.

*

Thrane wandered over to the window and watched Starheim stride off into the darkness towards the main part of the camp. It was a pity they had parted on less than amicable terms. Under different circumstances the major felt sure they would have hit it off. Starheim had a sort of prickly independence that Thrane always admired.

That independence was the trouble, of course. Starheim resented someone from Oslo telling him what to do. He was

27

used to running his own show. No cloudy issues in Starheim's operations. Thrane doubted Starheim had appreciated his allusion to grey areas. Men like Starheim saw things in black and white, which was ideal for the front line or expeditions to the North Pole. But in the real world the areas of dark grey were just as vital, otherwise you lost the battle before it had begun. And Norway being where it was, there were plenty of grey areas to attend to.

Besides, the operation couldn't misfire. Starheim was over-reacting.

Although it would be embarrassing if anyone found out. Starheim was right about that.

Two

It is best known by its romantic name: the land of the midnight sun, and in midsummer it is indeed a land of continuous light and sudden, abundant fluorescence.

But it is also the land of the Dark Time, as the Lapps call it. For two months in midwinter the sun never rises above the horizon, and the day, such as it is, passes in a few brief hours of twilight. February is an improvement: the sun shows above the horizon for a brief hour or so with long periods of twilight on either side. The extra light is, of course, welcome, but it brings little relief to the inhabitants, for the winter is still tightening its grip and will not let go for another two months.

But this northern land within the Arctic Circle is two worlds. There is the coast, its fiords and attendant valleys successfully if sparsely inhabited; and there is the interior – which might as well be another planet.

The interior is mostly high plateau, or *vidde*, a great wilderness which reaches from the coastal mountains across northern Scandinavia to Russia, a stretch of tundra flowing into the wastes of the Siberian Plain.

The plateau is not completely flat; its surface is covered by a maze of low hills and shallow valleys interspersed with small lakes. The land consists of moor and bog and to the inexperienced eye appears barren, especially in winter. But hidden under the snow are lichen and moss and berry-yielding plants, waiting to blossom thickly during the intense but brief summer. Towards Finland and Russia, the plateau falters and drops away to silent lakes, or is cleaved by a deep-running river, and there dwarf birch and willow grow.

But now, in the depths of winter, everything is covered in

29

ice and snow, and even the most adaptable of the plateau's inhabitants lie low.

For there *are* inhabitants: arctic fox, ermine, wolverine, the rare lynx, wolf.

There are men, too. The nomadic Lapps have wintered on the plateau for centuries and made a living from this most unpromising of lands. For it is here that the reindeer come to scratch away at the wind-scoured snow to find the frozen lichen and moss that is their winter fodder. Their summer pastures on the coast, though less cold at this time of year, are covered by deep drift snow which make foraging impossible. The herds of reindeer, long domesticated by the Lapps, still range free, and the Lapps follow them on their migration to the winter pasture.

But the pastures cover hundreds of miles, the herds are widely scattered and the Lapps are few. So to the traveller the wilderness appears featureless, a rolling desert of snow stretching into an endless distance, a hostile land where man is out of place.

And the traveller is wise to see it like this: the plateau is no place for people who don't know or understand it. On the vast unbroken plain the temperature had been known to drop to minus fifty or more. Animals, including man, can tolerate this sort of cold, but the wind is more difficult to survive. The long winters are punctuated by savage storms which drive heavy snow into the long fiords and steep mountains of the coast, then rise up on to the interior, where the winds tear unchecked across the bleak plateau, ripping at the snow cover and blowing it God knows where.

Yes, as everyone will tell you, it is the wind which is your enemy, for unless you have shelter the wind can freeze you to death.

*

From the army hut at Porsangmoen, the army Land Rover headed inland, climbing steadily on to the high plateau. As the land became flatter the driver kept an eye on the marker posts, for the wind was blowing a fine drift across his path and the posts were his only reliable guide to the course of the road whose snow-packed surface was indistinguishable from the

30

surrounding whiteness.

Eventually, after several hours, they came to the Lapp town of Karasjok, formerly the winter quarters of nomadic Lapps but now a permanent settlement and a spiritual centre of Lapland. Perched in the middle of the plateau, it was the only real civilisation for fifty miles.

On the outskirts of the settlement, by a single-storey wooden house, the Land Rover came to halt. The two passengers got out and removed their gear. The vehicle disappeared in the direction it had come from.

The two men went into the house, unmistakably a Lapp dwelling with its roughly built outhouses, sledging equipment, carcasses hanging from the eaves, and racks of drying reindeer skins. Inside, the men were given coffee and bread and cheese. Half an hour later a rather battered truck drew up outside and an old Skolt – eastern – Lapp got out and entered the house. After further refreshments and some exchange of news the two men followed the Skolt Lapp back to his truck and, loading their gear, clambered in.

The truck set off. In the town – though town was a rather grand term for it – the road forked. One road turned left, to skirt the northern border of Finland for two hundred miles until, at the most easterly corner of Norway, the road came to the Soviet border and an abrupt halt.

The battered truck did not take this turning, but took the right fork that led across the Karasjok River and, ten miles later, to the Finnish border.

The Skolt did not anticipate any problems at the border. The old man was a trader who went through about twice a month. Often the border guards waved him straight through. Only very occasionally did they glance at the contents of the vehicle or ask for identification.

This occasion was no exception. When the truck drew up at the frontier a guard strolled out and peered at the vehicle. The old man wound down the window. The guard saw the distinctive Skolt costume the old man wore and nodded in recognition. The guard did not bother to ask him where he was going or why; the Lapps were a law unto themselves and naturally secretive. Besides, apart from certain restrictions on goods, there was free passage between Norway and Finland.

With a brief smile, the guard waved them through.

As he drove off again the old man started to talk, telling the younger men how his grandfather had remembered hearing from *his* grandfather about the days when there had been no such things as borders in the far north. Lapland and much of northern Scandinavia had been inhabited entirely by Lapps, and they had ranged freely across hundreds of miles of country. But then the land that had been theirs for thousands of years had been parcelled out, becoming part of Norway, Sweden, Finland or Russia. Slowly and inexorably the Lapps were driven further north; many gave up their wanderings and settled by the coast to become farmer-fishermen, others became non-migratory herders; many had their land taken from them.

The two younger men found the old man's curious eastern dialect difficult to understand and missed a word here and there, but they understood the underlying message well enough, and sympathised, not just because the Skolt was older and venerable, but because among their own generation there was a growing awareness that one way and another the Lapps had lost out.

For mile after mile the road snaked across the lonely snow-swept plateau of north-eastern Finland. Finally it descended towards the lowlands that stretch up from central Finland to Petsamo on the northern coast: a strange and unexpected region of primeval forests and silent frozen lakes.

The men could see from the snow flurries that the wind had freshened and that the temperature, already minus twenty, must still be dropping. But they were not concerned: one took the weather as one found it, and as the truck spun onward the snow was thick and firm beneath the wheels, the visibility adequate, and they knew they were making good time.

*

It is two worlds, this northern province. There is the plateau, and there is the coast.

On the coast the winter is a miracle. The miracle is that the weather is not far, far worse. At this latitude the sea should, by the normal laws, become ice-locked for months on end, and the land seized by a deep and unbearable cold which no summer could entirely thaw nor many creatures survive.

32

Yet animals and men survive pretty well. For the real miracle is the Gulf Stream, whose long arm reaches up the Norwegian coast from the south, keeping the sea ice free and the air temperature bearable even in the depths of winter. The summer, when it arrives, comes quickly, so that oats grow as far north as North Cape, and thick forests grow in protected valleys.

The ice-free sea is used by sealers, whalers, travellers and traders as an open all-season road to the Arctic. A blessing indeed.

But, as with many blessings, there's a dark side to it.

Norway is not the only country to rely on the Gulf Stream waters. There is also her vast neighbour to the east. Like a powerful genie trapped in a bottle, the Soviet Union has no year-round outlet to the Atlantic Ocean except through the bottleneck between Norway and the Arctic pack-ice.

She guards these waters jealously and uses them continuously, sending the ships of her Northern Fleet out through the neck of the bottle into the Atlantic, to cover her western flank.

And what a fleet it is. At this time, in 1960, it is growing rapidly; they say it will soon be the largest in the world. A massive collection of warships and submarines and auxiliaries, backed up by vast dockyard and technical facilities grouped around Murmansk and the Kola Peninsula. Murmansk: the only ice-free port in northern Russia, and, uncomfortably for everyone, very close to Norway, a Nato country.

They call the Kola Peninsula the most valuable piece of real estate on earth.

But it's the sea lane that's beyond price.

And whoever controls Norway controls the sea lane. Norway is the key. And, not to put too fine a point on it, she rather wishes she wasn't.

So the warming waters of the Gulf Stream are a blessing, but rather a curse, too.

*

Hal reached the boat in mid-afternoon as the twilight deepened. Across the water the peaks of the snow-covered island were hard and clear against the dark incandescent blue of the sky.

Almost home. He felt better already.

He ducked down the companionway to the engine compartment and, giving the Volvo Penta diesel a firm pat, bent down beside it. Releasing the valves, he gave it a few hand cranks to get the oil moving, sprayed it with Easy Start then pressed the starter. The cold batteries turned the crank with agonising slowness until with a loud splutter the diesel coughed once, twice, and chugged sluggishly into life.

Hal shook his head. The damned thing always did that – sounded like death, made his heart sink, and then proceeded to clatter away happily as if it were used every day.

He returned to the wheelhouse and waited for the engine to warm up a bit. Then, tightening the hood round his face, he stepped out on to the deck and went forward to let go the mooring.

The wind was fierce now. It blustered across the sound, solid and heavy with Arctic cold, sending sharp-ridged waves hissing against the hull. The cove, sheltered from most winds, was exposed to northerlies, and the deck pitched and jerked beneath his feet.

The mooring safely away, Hal made his way back into the wheelhouse and, slamming the door, pushed the engine into gear and pointed *Skorpa*'s nose out into the open water. It was three miles across the sound to the island and in the clarity of the dying light he could already see the twinkle of Arne's lamp balanced on the rim of the far-off shore.

The diesel settled into a steady throb as *Skorpa* found the rhythm of the waves and surged forward. She was a good boat, *Skorpa*. A modern fishing cutter of thirty-five feet, she couldn't fail to be an improvement on the small petrol-driven boat he'd inherited from his father, which had specialised in spluttering to a halt half-way across the sound at dead of night.

The snowy peaks of the island were clearly visible ahead, gleaming palely against the sky. Its lower outlines were indistinct though, merging into the mass of the islands that surrounded it. For the island was only one of a long chain of islands, rocky islets and barren skerries that formed a massive natural barrier to the ocean beyond.

This particular island was in fact twelve miles by five and its name was Revoy. Fox Island. Though Hal had discovered that it also had an ancient long-forgotten Lappish name – Gumpe

Fuolo. Wolf Island.

Whether there had ever been foxes, let alone wolves, on the island Hal very much doubted. The only wildlife there now were hares and ptarmigan and, in the summer, eider and mallard ducks, oyster catchers and sandpipers.

Skorpa buffeted her way into the short choppy sea until finally the island provided some lee and she rode more smoothly. It was four in the afternoon. The journey had taken almost twelve hours. First an army transport had taken Hal as far as Alta Fiord, then, after a two-hour wait, he'd caught a seaplane to Tromso. Taking a ferry across Tromso Sound – the new bridge connecting the island of Tromso to the mainland was not yet open – he'd picked up the Land Rover and driven the twenty miles to the cove where he kept *Skorpa*.

In just over twelve hours he would be leaving again. It was a lunatic way to live, but this was the only home he had and he felt a need to come here when he could, if only for a few hours.

The twin peaks of Revoy loomed higher. Nestling between them, deep in a valley, glimmered a soft golden light from an oil lamp placed in a window: the house. Down by the shore was the sharper whiter light of the hurricane lamp on the boathouse, its reflection glinting in the dark water. As he closed on the shore, Hal turned the boat westward until he caught the silhouette of the mooring buoy in the flickering reflection. Then he drove *Skorpa* straight up the path of light, ducking away at the last minute to turn a half-circle and bring *Skorpa* to a stop with her nose above the buoy.

As he secured the heavy chain there was a hail from Arne on the shore, and he returned a brief shout before going aft to stop the engine. As he lowered the dinghy into the water, a steady barking echoed across the water and he grinned to himself.

He jumped into the dinghy and rowed in long steady sweeps to the shore. Arne caught the boat and the two men pulled it well up the beach. A nose thrust itself into Hal's hand. Bamse. Hal took the dog's broad head in his hands and fondled it roughly, saying, 'You devil! You old devil!'

The dog growled softly and thrust his weight against Hal's legs.

Arne grunted in the vague direction of the wind: 'A northeaster. Cold.'

'It's a lot colder up there.'

'Ah, *there*,' Arne said, understanding immediately that he meant the plateau. 'Ha! I don't doubt it.' To Arne people who ventured on the plateau in winter were crazy. Nearly everyone – and certainly everyone Arne knew – lived on the coast. Only the Lapps belonged on the plateau.

Arne was sixty and looked eighty. A farmer-fisherman all his life, he had more lines on his face than a mosaic and his expression was fixed in a permanent frown. A widower for fifteen years, he lived alone a mile along the island shore, and looked after Hal's place when he was away, which was nearly all the time.

'I've lit the stove,' Arne said. 'And put something on the table.'

'Thanks, Arne.'

Arne took the hurricane lamp down from the side of the boathouse and extinguished it. They trudged up to the snow-covered track that was the only road. 'I have to leave early in the morning,' Hal said. 'About five.'

Arne nodded. 'I'll come for the dog.'

With a brief wave, the two men parted. Hal started up the valley. Bamse danced around him like a young dog, which he wasn't any more, then, remembering his dignity, scouted ahead, nose firmly to the snow, his limp less pronounced than usual, his tail wagging in a circle of pleasure.

The valley was two miles long and half a mile wide, its sides rising abruptly to the mountains on either side, giving it the name of Brattdal – steep valley. The valley floor rose quite steeply too, so that it was a brisk climb to the house.

As Hal left the sea behind, the hushed murmuring of the waves receded and he was met by the rushing of the wind swooping down from the mountains and hissing across the snow.

The house was hidden behind a slight hump in the valley floor, and it was not until he had been climbing for some minutes that it finally came into view. His stomach tightened with pleasure. He held his breath for a moment, savouring the powerful sense of homecoming.

The place always had this effect on him. Which was why he kept coming back.

The house was distinctive – some people called it extra-ordinary. It was the sort of house that wealthy nineteenth-century merchants built for themselves – in towns. A tall two-storey wooden house embellished with high old-fashioned gables and ornate carved vergeboards and architraves, and fronted by a long veranda with fine latticed arches. It was a far cry from the simple functional dwellings that the fishermen built for themselves along the shore. Far from blending into its surroundings, the house sat proud and erect on the rising ground, like a grand old lady who, refusing to move with the times, still wore her most extravagant crinoline.

The light of the oil lamp burned large and gold in the window. Arne had lit the stoves well, and a wall of warmth met Hal as he entered the house.

A pungent scent of burning birchwood mingled with the elusive smell of age the house had always possessed, ever since Hal's childhood. The panelled rooms, their wood darkened by time, reflected a soft glowing light. A familiar sense of peace and security settled over him.

He stoked up the stoves and checked the woodstore. He put dried fish down for Bamse, who was still outside re-establishing his territory, then cut some cheese and bread from the supplies that Arne had left on the kitchen table. He took the food and sat in his favourite seat at the desk in the living room.

Most of his childhood had been spent at the family home in Tromso, but Brattdal was his spiritual home, the home of endless summers and happy family holidays. It had never occurred to him that those days would end. But his sister had married and gone south, his brother had been lost at sea, and both his parents were dead.

The old roll-top desk had been his father's. Hal remembered him sitting there, late in the bright summer evenings, reading aloud from Egge or Hamsun. On the wall above was a photo-graph of his father taken in 1930 when he was thirty-three, a year older than Hal was now. Dressed formally in a three-piece suit and dark hat, he looked every inch the successful merchant he had become. Yet, if one looked carefully one could see a warmth in the eyes, hinting at the man beneath, the man who read extensively and spoke four languages and had great com-passion for his fellow man.

His compassion had not been appreciated by the Nazis however. They had objected to his attempts to save some young men from reprisal executions. At the end of the war his father had come back from the concentration camp alive – but only just. He died two years later. Hal's mother had died of a tumour four years after that. Hal still missed them a lot.

Bamse scratched at the door. Hal let him in and cuffed him affectionately. Bamse was half Laphound and half Husky, although his parentage was by no means certain. Hal accused him of having wolf blood. He had a long nose, a shaggy grey coat, white jowls and sharp pointed ears. Normally Bamse stayed with Arne on Revoy, but occasionally, when no one was looking, Hal took him on training operations.

Bamse growled and, taking Hal's arm gently in his teeth, pulled at it.

'No time for games, you!'

Hal finished his meal, then, with a sigh, found the pile of post that he had picked up in Tromso. With Bamse at his feet, he began reading. There were letters concerning the new expedition, which, thankfully, he could hand over to the newly appointed expedition secretary. But there were others that could not be got rid of so easily: young climbers wanting advice on training, clubs wanting him to come and visit them; even a request from a group of Lapps asking him to support a Lapp rights movement.

He was curious about that one. Why had they written to him? He read the letter thoroughly. The Lapps wanted him to support their campaign for the reintroduction of the Lapp language in their schools and to protest about the use of some of their lands for a military training area.

Privately he sympathised on the language question. The Lapps' culture was dying and it was wrong for the government to force the Norwegian language on them. But it was a political issue and he couldn't possibly become involved in it.

As for protesting against a military training area – he gave a wry smile: that would be a quick way of getting fired.

In fact he'd thought about leaving the army a lot recently – though preferably not by getting fired. It had become increasingly obvious that something in his life would have to go, and the only part of his life he could spare was his military career.

He'd only kept at it this long because the army were tolerant of his long absences, and he needed the pay. For years he'd ploughed his earnings from lecture tours, books and articles back into his expeditions, with the result that he was permanently broke.

He thought of the time it would take him to draft a suitably polite letter to the Lapps, and wished he had someone to deal with this sort of thing. He could do with a housekeeper too. Arne was not exactly the most adventurous provisioner and, as for the cleaning, that probably hadn't been done in weeks.

On a sudden impulse, he got up and threw open the doors of the cast-iron stove. The light leaped out and licked the panelling with flickering tongues of amber. It almost made the place seem lived in. Almost. The past rushed forward, and for a moment the room contained all the love and warmth of family evenings.

Would he grow old here? He hoped so. One day he would like to start a proper farm at Brattdal, and go fishing regularly, and write books during the long winters.

Hal stared thoughtfully at the flames. It would be no good on his own, though. He had been thinking about that a lot recently. When he looked at Jan and Ragna, so happy together, he couldn't help feeling a pang of envy.

In his twenties he'd carefully avoided long-term involvements. Looking back, he'd been rather too ruthless and single-minded about it. Then, four years ago, there'd been a serious girlfriend. He'd gone out with her for almost two years, he'd liked her a lot, but in the end something had held him back. A last urge to keep his freedom, perhaps, or a feeling that she wasn't quite right – he wasn't sure. But, whatever the reason, he had failed to write to her from the Polar expedition and when he returned, she had gone.

Since then there'd been others. There was a girl in Tromso he saw quite regularly. She was pretty, cheerful and very sweet, but ... But what? He wasn't sure, that was the trouble. All he knew was that he didn't want her to come and live at Brattdal.

Now he was aware of time slipping away and a loneliness that crept up on him, reaching under his guard, troubling him even here, in this house, where he had always felt happy. The feeling had nothing to do with the exhilarating aloneness you felt on the Arctic ice or hanging on a rope from an ice wall. This was different – a forlorn kind of feeling, an ache of the spirit.

Bamse stirred briefly from his sleep and gave a loud yawn.

Hal said: 'You're no good to me!' Bamse lifted his head and stared at him.

Hal said affectionately, 'Go to hell, you!'

Bamse yawned again and curled into a ball. He was a law unto himself, Bamse. That was why Hal liked him so much. He'd been a working dog most of his life and didn't have a lot of time for people – apart from Hal, of course. He'd belonged to a farmer over on Lyngen. Hal had found him one spring day, high in a valley, half dead, caught by the foreleg in a vicious leghold trap. His owner had wanted to shoot him. Hal had brought him back to Revoy.

Bamse was a good companion. But one shouldn't get too fond of a dog.

He closed the stove with a bang and, going into the front lobby, threw on a coat and, bracing himself against the wind, stepped outside on to the veranda. A new moon had risen and, in the transparency of the night, he could see across the water to the promontory where the cove and *Skorpa*'s mooring lay, and beyond, to wide Ullsfiord and the jagged peaks of the Lyngen Alps. The view, though familiar, never lost its power to move him. Neither could he look at the Lyngen Alps without remembering that there were still a couple of good unclimbed peaks among them. He had marked them down for his retirement.

But for once his mind wasn't on the mountains. He was thinking of the wind.

Hal peered at the thermometer nailed by the door. Minus twelve: cold for the coast. It would be colder on the plateau – it was always colder on the plateau – maybe minus thirty with another ten or fifteen degrees of windchill.

Jan and Mattis would be well into Finland by now, perhaps even as far as the lake. The weather wouldn't bother them, there was no reason why it should. He thought: So why am I uneasy then?

But he had no answer to that.

After some minutes he roused himself. Time was getting on. Tomorrow would be a busy day. Reluctantly he went back into the house to face the pile of unanswered post.

Three

Rolf Berg tore the paper out of the typewriter and stared blankly at his living room wall. These articles were such a balancing act. Too much alarmist talk and people began to ignore what you said. Too little and you might as well not bother. He hadn't got the balance right on this one yet, not by a long chalk.

He focused on his latest acquisition: a painting by an up-and-coming Swedish artist. It was a remarkable piece of work. He felt a glow of satisfaction: he had been right to buy it. Quite apart from being a thing of beauty – and he very much liked having beautiful things around him – it would be a good investment.

He fed another piece of paper into the machine and typed his name at the top. He concentrated hard, turning more ideas over in his mind, but none of them gave him the attention-grabbing start he needed.

After a couple of minutes he exhaled noisily and decided, not for the first time, that fate hadn't intended him to be a journalist. Too much impatience. Too little self-discipline. As if to prove the point, his mind wandered. He remembered that he had a meeting later that evening, a meeting he was not looking forward to. He'd been hoping there might be some way of avoiding it. But there wasn't. He would just have to grit his teeth.

His mind then wandered to something far more pleasant: an Italian girl called Isabella, a warm vital piece of sunshine in the drabness of the Oslo winter, and very new – he'd only met her a couple of weeks ago; but then new relationships were the only kind he really enjoyed.

The blank paper stared up at him. Berg pushed himself out

of his chair and strode over to the window. The outlook was bleak: an early darkness had settled over the quiet residential road and a veil of fine snowflakes whirled past the streetlamps, blurring the outlines of the apartment buildings opposite. A pedestrian walked cautiously along the icy pavement, his head bowed against the wind.

He forced himself back to the typewriter. He really had to get this piece done. It was important. The subject was nuclear weapons, and the issue whether or not they should be allowed on Norwegian soil. He was reasonably confident that the Labour government would make the right decision, but a powerful article might just help to consolidate opinion.

He retrieved the screwed-up sheet from the floor and reread it: In 1958 Norwegian Airforce planes started carrying American Sidewinder missiles. Last year US ground-to-air missiles, operated by American personnel, were installed on Norwegian soil. Next, if the US have their way, these Nike missiles will carry nuclear warheads.

The Soviet government have made it clear that they will be forced to draw only one conclusion from this progression of events – that Norway's intentions are aggressive. Putting ourselves in their place, can we blame them?

Berg shook his head. Wrong: far too pedantic and opinionated. Though the same could be said for most articles in the Norwegian press. He must think of something punchier. Finally it came to him and he wrote: Norway is fast approaching a vital decision. Whether to step into the front line of the Cold War.

Not brilliant, but it got the point across.

For three hours he sweated away at the body of the article until he felt it struck the right note of balance and reason, giving the idea that he might have come down on either side if the evidence had justified it. He read it through once more, then put it to one side.

He would come back to the article later and give it a final polish before handing it in the next morning. But it had taken him much longer than he'd realised; it was almost five. Damn. Now he'd hardly have time to see Isabella. He should have got down to work earlier.

He changed out of his Levis into a pale blue cashmere sweater and grey flannel slacks – both picked up on assignment in Paris –

and wound a long white scarf round his neck.

Pulling on a cashmere coat he hurried out of the flat to his car. There was a bit of traffic along the park, but then it eased and he was away: the Oslo working day finished at four and the rush hour was over. He stopped at a florist as it was closing and bought some roses. He loved gestures, however banal: anything that added amusement to life which, if one wasn't careful, could be frighteningly serious.

A traffic light was turning red. He shoved his foot down and drove through it. Very un-Norwegian.

As he pulled up outside Isabella's flat, he suddenly remembered that he hadn't phoned to say he was coming. But he'd told her he might drop in: she would probably have waited around just in case.

She hadn't: the doorbell remained frustratingly unanswered. He left the flowers standing up against her door and scribbled a note: *Where were you?*

As an afterthought he took off his tie and pushed it into the jaws of the letterbox. He put a PS on the note: *For the rest of me apply 74 72 29.* Now she'd have to phone him. It would be a test. If she took it in the right spirit – lightly – she'd be okay. Okay to Berg meant fun while it lasted and no hard feelings afterwards.

When he got back to the car it was only five-twenty. He didn't want to be early for his next appointment. He decided to take the long route and use the time to get into the right mood.

Adjusting his mood wasn't easy. These meetings were always a strain. They'd been going on a long time – in fact, how long was it? He tried to think. A year. No, fourteen months. Good Lord.

It was beginning to feel like a life sentence.

He reached the suburb of Vinderen at five-forty. As usual, he parked some way away from the house and in a slightly different spot from the last time, to avoid being noticed by neighbours. It was all a bit cloak-and-dagger, but he rather liked that. It gave a *frisson* to the evening, and it needed it.

He waited in the car for fifteen minutes, smoking a cigarette, then, with a weary sigh, he got out and began to walk. The house was five minutes away. The evening was very cold, but

44

pleasantly so. The snow had stopped and the air was dry and fresh against his skin. He rather enjoyed the climb through the avenue of tall pines, which sighed and moaned as the strong wind ripped at their tops. He should spend more time out of doors, he decided. One of these days he would go ski-touring again.

As he approached the house he paused for a moment, waiting in the shadows of the trees. As usual she was there before him, her car parked in the driveway and a light showing in the living room window. As he watched, a light came on upstairs. He knew exactly which room that was.

He stood a moment longer under the firs then strode up to the back door and tapped with his fingers. After a while he heard the sound of her footsteps. The door swung open and she stood before him.

Fat, frumpy, fiftyish Sonja.

He smiled.

She gave the small laugh she always gave and stepped back to let him in. She closed the door and took his coat and hovered expectantly.

He embraced her and managed a reasonably enthusiastic kiss, saying: 'How's my girl?'

She looked embarrassed and pleased all at the same time. 'I'm fine.'

'You look well.' What she looked, in fact, was her age.

'You too,' she replied with a shy smile. She stared at him for a moment, then, replacing her spectacles carefully on her nose, said in a light voice: 'I've got salmon tonight. I hope that's all right.'

He followed her into the kitchen. The evening always followed a pattern. She would offer him a drink – Scotch, which she knew he preferred – and she would cook and they would chat in a general sort of way. After the meal they would go upstairs. That was the bit he quietly dreaded. In the beginning her body had had a perverse sort of attraction for him, but that had long worn off.

The evening was generally over quite early. He'd never had to stay the night, thank God. The house was theirs only until ten-thirty when its owner – a friend of hers – returned.

He sat down at the table and waited for her to pour his drink.

He let her pour until the glass was almost full. She gave him a questioning look. 'Hard day?'

'Very.'

She went to the stove and rattled some pans about, talking in that smoothly reasonable way of hers, which he found rather irritating. At least he wasn't expected to reply until he'd finished his drink. He took the opportunity to eye her over the rim of his glass.

Her name was Sonja Bjornsen, and she worked for the Norwegian Intelligence Service, known as FO/E.

In the beginning it had been so easy – amazingly easy. He'd been doing an article about Norway's involvement with the CIA – an article doomed never to be published, of course. He'd been watching the offices of FO/E in an attempt to prove that the Intelligence Service did exist – a fact no one in authority would admit. She was among the people he'd seen leaving the building on Platous Gate. She'd looked just the right type: a spinster in a senior secretarial position. It had been a simple matter to follow her home. A week later, on her weekly visit to the cinema, he'd bumped into her – well, not quite accidentally.

After that things had progressed extremely satisfactorily. He'd had to take risks, of course, far greater risks than he'd ever taken before, but it had been worth it. She'd turned out to be a veritable goldmine, though it had taken several months for him to realise just how valuable she was. In the last year he'd got two front-page exclusives on defence policy, in addition to a steady stream of pointers and hints which he'd built into nice little stories.

Yes, a goldmine.

Then she'd got promoted.

When she'd told him he'd barely been able to conceal his delight. She's been made queen bee: secretary to the Director.

But within a month his euphoria had faded. The lady had taken her new responsibilities very seriously indeed. Instead of dropping bigger and better morsels into his beak, she'd given him little more than crumbs. All he got nowadays was office gossip and interdepartmental politics.

He looked at her now with irritation. He was bored with having to make all this effort for nothing, he was bored with being patient. If she loved him so much why on earth didn't she give him what he wanted?

She had stopped talking and was smiling gently. 'I'm sorry, I'm chattering on. Poor Erik, you look shattered.'

Yes, thought Berg, poor Erik. Poor Erik Leif.

*

Sonja always forgot how beautiful he was. It was odd to think of a man being beautiful, but there was really no other word to describe Erik. Whenever she opened the door to him, the sight of that face always gave her a small shock of pleasure. During the long days they were apart she thought about him a lot – even when she was working – yet her memory never quite did him justice.

Leaving the cooking for a moment, she sat down and prompted him to talk so that she could examine his features one by one. Straight nose, wide mouth and blue eyes. But it was his hair that one noticed most of all – it was very thick and very blond. So many Norwegians were mousy-haired or pale blond, but Erik had really yellow hair.

He had stopped talking and was looking bored. She said hurriedly: 'I'll get the food,' and went to serve up.

She'd met him in a cinema queue. When she'd realised he knew exactly who she was she'd been rather alarmed, but as soon as he'd introduced himself properly everything had become clear. He was in the 'other' department – the Security Service, known as FO/S.

She'd checked up on him of course. That was automatic. She'd phoned Anna, her opposite number in the Security Service, and Anna had confirmed that Erik Leif worked in FO/S. The hair colour, height and age had matched.

Which had left Sonja with just one concern: why someone as wonderful as Erik should be bothering with her. But he'd explained that as well. In fact he'd been quite open about it, rather endearingly so.

What Erik wanted was a little inside knowledge.

And for a reason she could appreciate. Between their two departments there was some not-so-friendly rivalry which occasionally led to what was euphemistically called 'difficulties'. Erik wanted to cut through the ponderous inter-service liaison

47

machinery to, as he put it, help things along. Which really meant: help his career along. Because Erik was ambitious. One only had to look at him to see that. But Sonja didn't mind; on the contrary, she loved being close to such drive. It made her feel young.

And so the affair had begun. She'd had a few short-lived affairs in her twenties, but nothing like this – nothing remotely like this. She'd had no idea she could feel so – powerfully. His body, the things he did to her – he was like an addiction. She couldn't help herself at all; she wanted more and more of him.

She didn't fool herself about their relationship, of course. She was perfectly aware that she was no beauty. In her youth she'd looked quite pleasant, many people had thought so, but in recent years she'd let herself go. There was an awful lot of weight in unsightly places. But looks weren't everything. In his own way Erik cared for her, she knew he did. He gave small signs of fondness now and again. He obviously respected her judgement. That was enough...

Their relationship was essentially a bargain, of course. The inside gossip in exchange for this time together. But she didn't mind the idea of a bargain. In fact, she rather preferred it; it gave her a sense of worth and self-respect, it gave the affair balance.

She chatted as she put the food on the plates. She always tried to accumulate a little store of amusing anecdotes and stories during the week, hoping they might interest and amuse him. She was careful to keep off certain subjects that bored him though. Her mother, for instance, who lived with her and was virtually bedridden. But then Sonja liked a rest from her too.

Sonja brought the meal to the table. 'How's your drink?'

Without a word he drained his glass and held it out for a refill.

'Things must be bad,' she said with a short laugh.

He shrugged. 'Just rather a lot on at the moment.'

'Really?'

His mind seemed to be elsewhere this evening. 'What? Oh, there's a lot of manœuvring going on for the Deputy's job, that's all. Which means that a lot of work is getting off-loaded on to us.'

She was surprised. She'd thought the Deputy's job at FO/S

was filled. But maybe it hadn't been announced yet.

She began to eat. Erik pushed the food half-heartedly round his plate.

'I hear the Head of E Branch might be next,' she said, smiling in expectation. He should be interested in this one. 'E' was his own branch: Protective Security.

'I'd heard,' he said shortly.

'Oh, have you? Tell me, what's the real story behind it?' And she paused with her fork half-way to her mouth to stare at his lovely face.

*

She was waiting for an answer. This sort of office gossip was always the trickiest part of the evening. He had to remember exactly what he'd told her the previous week – she had an excellent memory – and outline a plausible series of developments. Once or twice in the past he'd tripped up quite badly, and had a few adrenalin-charged moments extricating himself. But he usually managed pretty well. In another life he liked to think he'd have made a good actor.

'I think there was a row,' he said.

'Oh?' She sounded surprised. He must be on the wrong track.

He said briskly: 'But look, I really don't know. And to be honest, I'm not terribly interested. Office politics bore me to tears.'

She dropped her eyes; the subject was over. She never pressed him.

She wasn't a stupid woman, Sonja. Just gullible. The Erik Leif deception had grown quite naturally. But the name hadn't come out of thin air – he wasn't that stupid. There was a real Erik Leif in FO/S, a low-ranking diplomatic protection officer whom Berg had come across some two years before when the man was guarding a visiting Nato minister.

After that Sonja had believed the lot. Everything they said about middle-aged spinsters was true: age made them desperate, grateful and blind. Sometimes he'd felt almost fond of her, in the way that ugly things have a curious and compelling fascination. But disenchantment had set in.

She cleared away the food and brought the coffee.

He thought: Last chance, Sonja.

Toying with his cup, he acquired a distant troubled look.

Sonja picked it up immediately: she was very quick on atmosphere. 'Anything the matter?' she asked gently.

A slight hesitation. 'Well...'

Her eyes blinked rapidly behind her spectacles. 'What is it?'

Berg smiled fleetingly, then assumed a deep frown. 'Something's come up, Sonja. I—' He broke off, apparently unable to continue.

She looked suitably alarmed.

'The thing is—' he took a deep breath – 'I've got a new job.'

Sonja froze. She knew it was bad news.

'It's a sort of promotion,' he continued. 'I'm heading a new team. It'll involve a lot of travelling at short notice. The team'll work very closely together. We'll have to keep in permanent contact with each other – in fact, the others'll need to know where I am at all times. So' – he stared her firmly in the eye – 'it may not be possible for us to see each other very often ... if at all.'

She was staring, her face pale, her mouth slightly open. 'But – surely – you'll have some free time.' Her voice was gruff and uneven.

'I can't have a secret life, Sonja. And *you* are most definitely a secret.'

'But surely there must be a way?' She was trying very hard to be brave.

'It's a permanent job.'

She blinked a few times then gave a small quivery smile. 'Well. We always knew it might come to this, didn't we? We mustn't complain, I suppose.' Suddenly she pulled off her glasses and clamped a hand over her eyes. 'Sorry ...' she said with difficulty. 'Sorry ...'

He went round the table and, pulling her to her feet, let her cry against his shoulder. It was, after all, the least he could do.

After a long while she pulled away and, drying her eyes decisively, said: 'Just such a surprise, that's all. I'm all right now. Really. Just such a surprise.' They sat down again. He poured her a stiff drink. She took a gulp and asked with forced calmness: 'I still don't understand. Why – what – tell me about the job.'

Berg had planned his answer. 'Well, we're trouble-shooting really.'

'Oh? What sort of trouble?'

'We think there may be a leak somewhere, and ...' He shrugged. 'We've got to sort it out.'

'A leak?' Her tear-filled eyes sharpened.

'Maybe.'

'Where?'

'If we knew *that* ...'

'What sort of material's been leaked?'

This was developing in a promising direction. Taking it slowly, Berg frowned, as if considering whether to tell her. 'We're not absolutely sure yet. But it seems to involve CIA-linked operations.'

Horror leapt into Sonja's face. 'Oh. *Oh*.'

'I told you, it's only a whisper.'

'But – we haven't been notified! Why haven't we been notified?'

Sonja was keen as a ferret when her curiosity was roused. He'd have to go carefully. He said: 'The leak seems to be from a Norwegian source and – look, I've already said far too much. Even to you, Sonja.'

'What're you saying?' she cried. 'That the leak may come from *us*?'

'It's a possibility.'

Behind the thick lenses Sonja's eyeballs were round as orbs. Berg felt as if he'd thrown a snowball and started an avalanche. She leaned across the table and said in a low urgent voice: 'Erik, this is very serious. I –' She stopped abruptly and gave him an agonised look, as if she wanted to tell him more but couldn't.

Berg felt a *frisson* of interest. He prompted: 'Yes?'

Her mind was hard at work. She said at last: 'It just couldn't have come at a worse time.'

Berg tried to decide whether she was playing games or not. In his experience women – even docile women like Sonja – were capable of almost anything when clutching on to a failing relationship. 'Why's it a bad time?' he prompted.

She hesitated for a long while, then shook her head decisively: she had decided not to talk. Instead she began to cry again.

He stood up.

She jumped to her feet, a panicky look on her face. 'Wait! Please don't go yet. I couldn't bear it. I couldn't bear you to go just like that.'

'Look, Sonja, it's best not to string things out, don't you think?'

'No, *no*! Please. *Please* ...' She made a big effort to be calm. 'Please. Whatever happens, I – oh, I couldn't bear it. Erik, *please*. I can still be of help to you, I know I can.'

He raised an eyebrow. 'Oh?'

She stared at him for a moment, then came slowly and humbly towards him and, putting her arms round him, laid her head against his chest.

He longed to walk out, but his curiosity was pricked: he had to know.

He made the necessary mental adjustment to the idea of going to bed with Sonja one more time. Difficult, but it probably wouldn't kill him. He'd managed often enough before.

He began to stroke her hair.

Yes: if he concentrated very hard he might be able to make the incredible leap of the imagination needed to pretend that the plump body in his arms was that of Isabella.

*

Sixty miles inside Finland the truck came to a halt in the darkness beside a vast frozen lake. Here the three men unloaded the vehicle, removing rucksacks and skis, a bundle of birch poles, a roll of thick cloth and several boxes of provisions. A short distance below the track, in a sheltered hollow among the trees bordering the lake, they made camp.

They built the curved birch poles into a domed tent frame and stretched the thick woollen cloth around it. They added a floor of birch twigs covered with reindeer skins and within twenty minutes the tent was completed.

It was a long time since either Jan or Mattis had erected a traditional Lapp tent, known as a *lavo*, but the old Skolt Lapp remembered the method well enough, although he himself hardly ever bothered nowadays. There was a perfectly good wooden hut ten miles up the lake that he normally used. But in this instance it was best to stay off the beaten track. The Skolt

Lapp was well known in this region – but the other two men were strangers and would attract attention.

The men retreated gratefully into the tent. The wind was blowing hard down the sixty-mile length of the lake; wind-torn clouds raced across the new moon and, to the north, the stars had vanished behind an advancing mass of deeper darkness. Mattis lit the pressure stove – their only concession to modernity – and prepared a hot meal from dried fish and potatoes, followed by hard unleavened bread and cloudberry preserve with real butter, a delicacy in these parts. This was followed by coffee and, for the old man, a swig of aquavit.

The old man loved to talk and for a while the younger men listened politely, though it was hard to follow his rapid and mumbled dialect. He talked of pre-war days, when his community had lived in the Petsamo region, an area trapped between east and west and the subject of eternal border disputes. Then it was Finnish; now it was Russian. Like many of his generation the old man wanted to return to his homeland. Yet he wasn't allowed to, and he still found it difficult to understand why.

He didn't like life here on Lake Inari; the fishing wasn't as good, and the hunting was poor, and the Finnish settlers were hostile to the Lapps. What was the answer?

There was no answer and the younger men fell asleep, leaving the old man to have another slug of aquavit and contemplate the fishing next day, and decide where on the frozen lake he would try his luck.

Eventually he too slept and the only sound was the insistent soughing of the wind as it blew the first swirls of snow against the side of the tent.

*

Sonja knew he was awake, but she didn't speak. At times like this it was best to leave him alone. Neither did she move, though as always she had a strong urge to touch him. She loved the texture of his hair, so rich and heavy; she liked to stroke his arm and feel the astonishing smoothness of his skin.

But she held back. Self-control was essential. Clever women never gave anything away, she knew that. They were careful not to show their feelings, careful not to make too many demands. And she'd been careful, so careful. And it had really paid off.

Until now.

What had gone wrong? She couldn't imagine. She had done nothing to upset him.

But then a part of her could imagine only too well what was wrong – he was bored with her. He was trying to get rid of her. The thought was agony.

This new job was just a pretext, she was certain of it. If he really wanted to go on seeing her he would find a way. After all they'd managed this long without anyone finding out. Not a whisper of their relationship had ever got out into either department.

It was Erik who'd insisted on secrecy. He'd said it would damage his career. Deep down she suspected there was another reason – he was ashamed of her. She could see how some people might find the relationship ridiculous. They wouldn't understand, they wouldn't realise how dependent they were on each other.

Had been ...

Torture.

She felt tears well up again, and held them back. So undignified, like that exhibition downstairs. What had she been thinking of, showing her feelings like that!

She'd been so happy with the way things were. In her twenties she'd expected too much – that had been her mistake. At thirty-five she'd still been waiting patiently for the right man, but suddenly there weren't any more available men, right or otherwise. It dawned on her that she'd been far too choosy.

Then Mother had got ill and Sonja had moved in with her and suddenly her last remaining social life had evaporated to a once-weekly trip to the cinema.

Now she was fifty and it was all far far too late.

Erik stirred at her side. She held still, longing for him to speak, but he rolled away from her, his breath slow and steady. Outside, the wind sighed in the trees.

She thought: I'll do anything to keep him.

Erik rolled on to his back again and she held her breath.

His hand touched her arm and patted it.

A rush of love and longing surged through Sonja. She pressed

54

herself against him. He swung his arm behind her neck and pulled her to him. With infinite slowness she stroked his arm and touched his hair, concentrating on each sensation so that she could store it carefully in her memory.

He murmured: 'You know, Sonja, I'm really very fond of you.'

She held still, eyes firmly closed, teeth gritted.

He sighed. 'It's just that ... I'll be working all hours and ... I just won't have time.' He added shortly: 'This job's really important, you see.'

Forcing her voice to be immensely reasonable she said: 'I understand.'

'Well, I'm not sure you do. It could be a big feather in my cap.'

'Can I help at all?' Her words hung in the air.

He was silent for a moment. 'Well ... I shouldn't think so.' He sounded very doubtful. 'Unless there's anything you think I should know about. I mean anything sensitive that could be – well, easily jeopardised.'

She knew exactly what she should tell him, but she wanted to be absolutely sure. She asked: 'This leak – it might involve joint operations, you say?'

'Yes –' he sounded annoyed that she'd asked for elaboration – 'anything involving operations with the NSA or CIA.'

Still Sonja hesitated. There were joint operations with the US National Security Agency and the CIA, certainly, but she had never given him details before. General policy decisions, details about intelligence-gathering installations – they had seemed harmless.

But never operations. And why should she now, when he was leaving her?

Erik bent over and kissed her, then, drawing back, looked down at her without speaking. In the dim light his expression seemed almost gentle. 'You know,' he murmured, 'I *would* miss you.'

'Don't leave me.'

'Sonja, I –'

'You won't regret it.'

'Well, I don't know ... Perhaps there might be a way.'

'I can help, I really can, Erik.'

A pause. 'I'd begun to think you didn't want to help me any more, Sonja.'

'Oh I do, I *do*, Erik. It was just that – it was so difficult deciding what was safe for you to know.'

'Dear Sonja.' Another pause. 'Perhaps we could meet now and then...'

She let the words sink in slowly. Did he mean it? She wept openly, burying her head against his chest and whispered in a sudden burst of honesty: 'Erik, I can't help it, I do love you so.'

He gave a short laugh. 'Sonja, Sonja ... I love you too.'

And then, so that he would never live to regret those words and because she wanted to please him so much, she told him.

She was extremely careful *not* to give him the names of those involved or the precise location, but she told him the rest. About the two Lapps on their way to the border, about the meeting with the agent from Murmansk, the man who was buying his freedom with information from the Murmansk shipyards.

And then they made love again, and, overcome with relief, Sonja made a vow. That she would never disappoint him again.

Four

Ragna Johansen stared at herself in the mirror and saw a cabbage. Not a bad-looking sort of cabbage, admittedly, but in the eyes of her former friends a distinct vegetable none the less. A woman who had thrown away her early promise for the vice-like grip of domesticity.

She'd given up nothing worth having, of course – but the idea amused her all the same, because in the old days the thought of being an ordinary housewife would have appalled her.

But then the old days hadn't been so brilliant. In fact, they'd been pretty awful.

She brushed her hair and held it in a bunch at the back of her neck. Tomorrow night she'd be seeing two friends from the old days – but good friends, not like the rest. Yet they'd still be curious to see what time and the north of Norway had done to her.

She eyed herself in the mirror, smiling in a self-mocking way. Not bad for almost thirty. There were faint laugh-lines round the eyes, but her skin was good, her eyes clear. She'd always thought her eyes were her best feature, but it was her colouring that usually attracted attention. It had been a joke among her friends that one of her ancestors must have been a Greek or Italian sea captain. Both her parents had been fair-haired, but either her mother had had a lover – a distinct possibility – or the genes had skipped a few generations. Ragna's hair wasn't brown like many Norwegians', it was dark and glossy, and her skin had that smooth sheen that usually went with sun and olive oil.

She hovered over her meagre assortment of make-up. Since living in Tromso she had hardly bothered with it, but now she felt the need to look especially good, partly to bolster her confidence, partly to show her friends that she hadn't entirely lost her sparkle.

She put on eye shadow, mascara and lipstick, and clipped on some bright earrings. The effect made her pause; there were echoes of the past in that painted artificial face. For a moment her confidence faltered; part of her suddenly didn't want to go to Oslo at all.

She'd been brought up in Oslo – if brought up was the right description; and there she'd spent some of the worst years of her life.

Her early childhood had been unsettled, disturbed and disjointed. When she was fourteen her father, a writer and enthusiastic alcoholic, had left Ragna's stepmother – his fourth wife – and disappeared, leaving Ragna to be sent to her mother, a wild and unconventional poetess and former actress who lived with an eighteen-year-old labourer in two rooms overlooking Oslo harbour. At sixteen Ragna had run away with a film producer twice her age to become an actress, a career which led at the end of the war to Stockholm and leading roles in three low-budget films memorable only for their mildly shocking eroticism.

At nineteen she met her true Svengali, an avant-garde director, and made a film with him called *Chance*, which won prizes at two film festivals. She also made a baby with him, a little girl named Anne. There were several more films, and plenty of money. It was a golden time. It lasted – how long? Difficult to remember now. And hard to tell when it began to fall apart. But by the time she realised what was happening it was too late, and everything had turned sour ... her lover, rotting and unproductive and ugly on hard drugs; herself, sunk in an uncreative unemployable mess, and then ... Then little Anne. Even now her mind remained tightly sealed around the events of those dark days, unable to grasp completely that Anne had died from meningitis.

She called the years that followed the black time. She'd tried to escape in the only way she knew, travelling a lot, surrounding herself with noisy people – lots of them – at parties, in communes, in fringe theatre groups; never alone but always alone. There were men – and too many of them – and the more they liked her, the greater and more barren was the emptiness around her.

Jan picked up the pieces. Why he'd done it she still wasn't sure. Jan: quiet, patient and fathomless, a Norwegian of the sea and mountains – everything her artistic friends dismissed as faintly ridiculous and dangerously non-intellectual. But for her, a rock in an ocean of uncertainty. The marriage had been a success because it had given her things she had never had: stability, tranquillity, love and a humdrum existence.

She exhaled sharply. Memories of the past still had the power to cause her pain. She turned firmly away from the mirror.

Outside, the glimmering twilight revealed a dark and stormy morning. Maddening. The flying boat would probably be delayed.

She finished her packing, throwing in some designer clothes she hadn't worn for years. They were a bit out of date now – fashions had changed, waists were disappearing, skirts getting shorter – but they would still wear well. And she'd included a smart dress. You never knew. She might get invited to dinner at Blom's, like in the old days.

There was a sound at the bedroom door. A small child tottered into the room, rubbing his eyes.

Ragna sighed. He was meant to have slept for another hour at least.

'Hello, you.' She picked her son up and looked at him quizzically. His name was Kristian, known as Kris or Krisi, and he was almost two.

The child suddenly focused on her mouth and, frowning, prodded a finger at the unfamiliar lipstick.

Ragna smiled. 'Funny, heh?'

Seeing that it was a joke, Krisi giggled. Then, ever curious, he looked round and saw the case on the bed. Ragna watched his face change. He knew very well what cases meant. They meant people – usually Jan – going away.

'I told you, darling,' Ragna said calmly, 'I'm going to Oslo for a few days. Not long.' A small lie: she'd actually be away for ten days.

Krisi clung to her and began to whine. Ragna took him into the living room and tried to distract him with a few toys, but his arms stayed firmly locked around her neck. She loved him to pieces, of course, but he was just at the stage when he threw mighty rages, and from that point of view this short break wasn't coming a moment too soon.

Her mother-in-law, Sigrid Johansen, finally arrived. Ragna plopped a screaming Krisi into his grandmother's arms, and went to collect her case. When she returned Krisi was quiet. The moment he caught sight of her he started crying again. Ragna pulled him on to her lap and gave him a cuddle.

Mrs Johansen shook her head. 'Going to Oslo alone. Such a long way.' Mrs Johansen had lived in Tromso all her life. She didn't see the necessity for people to travel.

'Well I have to go, I want to go. It's part of my new job, after all.'

'But Jan away *too*,' the older woman tutted.

'But if he hadn't been away he'd only have come with me to Oslo. So . . .'

'But why is he away? What's he doing?'

Ragna shrugged. 'Trying out some new piece of equipment. I'm not sure what.'

'Well, it's a pity,' her mother-in-law said firmly. 'What about the shop? Who's looking after that?'

'That runs itself.' Jan had a sports shop in Tromso which the small staff could run perfectly well on their own.

'Mmm. Well, I hope you're not taking on too much. With Kristian still so small.'

Ragna ignored the implied criticism. She was looking forward to starting her new job. Expedition secretary: Everest West Ridge, 1963. The grandness of the title tickled her; it sounded better suited to a man of great distinction and mature years, rather than a former actress with little previous experience. But she was good at organisation – the chaos of her early life had given her a mania for order; and she had a way with people. She was sure she'd make a success of it.

She went to collect her briefcase and paused at a window. The house stood among birch trees on the southern tip of the island of Tromso, and looked down a wide sound towards Straumsfiord, with wonderful open views of mountains and water. On clear days at this time of year the whole scene was bathed in delicate pastels, the light so transparent you could see thirty miles or more.

Today, however, the weather was bad. Yet was it her imagination or had the blizzard eased a little? The wind sighed in the birches, and she could see its force in the swirl and bluster of the snowflakes, but the visibility seemed to have improved and the fiord was slowly emerging from the pall of darkness.

She gave a thought to Jan, somewhere up on the plateau. The weather might well be different up there; it often was, so they said. But even if it were blowing a blizzard he'd be perfectly at home. The harsher the conditions the more he seemed to like it.

The doorbell rang. The taxi. In the hall Sigrid Johansen and Krisi were waiting to say goodbye. Ragna tried to make her farewell to Krisi as optimistic and firm as possible, but he howled all the same. She got into the taxi and waved with guilty relief.

It was five minutes to the centre of Tromso. The 'Paris of the North', they called it. The boast always amused Ragna. It was a long time since Tromso had been on the trade route to northern Russia, and even longer since the sea captains had brought the latest Paris fashions back for their wives. The place still had quite a few restaurants and nightspots left over from the whaling boom, however, and for that Ragna was grateful. Compared to other Arctic towns Tromso was almost bustling.

The taxi dropped Ragna at the waterfront. The visibility had definitely improved, and she was relieved to see that the seaplane was already there, tethered a short distance off the quay.

The girl in the small airline office said a little reproachfully: 'No, the plane won't be leaving late.' She glanced at Ragna's ticket. 'Oh, there was someone asking for you. Another passenger.' The girl busied herself with the paperwork. 'I believe it was Halvard Starheim.'

*

Returning from a stroll along the quay, Hal came in and spotted her straight away. You couldn't miss her. The dark hair, the way she stood, the well-cut clothes.

He made his way towards her, aware of a slight nervousness.

Turning, she spotted him and smiled broadly. Hal thought: I always forget how lovely she is.

Ragna declared: 'Well! If it isn't my new boss.'

Hal smiled a little uncertainly. He had the feeling he was being teased.

She said: 'I thought you were already in Oslo.'

'I had to stay on another day. Unexpectedly.'

'Ah! On the same jaunt as Jan?'

The question caught him unawares. 'No, I – it was something else.'

She gave him a look of amused scepticism, and he thought: I'm a bad liar.

'You two are up to something,' she said. 'If I wasn't so nice, I'd be cross that you hadn't told me about it.'

'Didn't Jan explain?'

'Well – he gave me some story or another. But I can always tell when he's skirting the truth. In fact, if you really want to know, I didn't believe a word of it!'

Because the subject needed changing and he couldn't think of anything else to say, he replied: 'But you should always believe what your husband tells you.'

She threw back her head and laughed uproariously. 'Oh, Hal! You do make me laugh sometimes!'.

He examined her face: what did she mean by it? He decided finally that she was making fun of him in a perfectly harmless way. Yet with Ragna he could never be absolutely sure, and for that reason she always made him feel slightly off balance.

She laughed again. 'With ideas like that you'll have to find yourself a very old-fashioned girl.'

Hal made the effort to enter into the easy banter that was so characteristic of conversation with Ragna. 'I've tried old-fashioned girls – but they always expect *me* to be old-fashioned and work regular hours and come home every night.'

She was pleased with that. 'Then you'll have to put your foot down.'

'I'm too nice.'

She put her head on one side and stared at him thoughtfully. 'Yes,' she said, 'I think you probably are.'

Hal looked away. She was teasing him again.

The passengers were called to the door: the Catalina was ready to leave. Hal picked up Ragna's hand luggage and led the way out. Darting flurries of snow crystals scythed across the quay and Ragna gave a small gasp. Hall took her arm and she leant against him as they climbed down the steps to the waiting launch.

After a bumpy but mercifully short sea journey they reached the plane and climbed in. Ragna exclaimed: 'I can never get used to the damned wind in this place. I don't think I was cut out for the north.' They settled in their seats. She asked: 'Doesn't it ever get you down? The wind, I mean?'

No one had ever asked him that before; they usually asked him about the cold. He considered carefully; he wanted to give her a proper answer. 'The wind's just a part of it all – the terrain, the snow, the place. I can't separate the wind from the rest. So I don't feel strongly about it.'

She shook her head. 'You really love it, don't you?'

'What?'

'Oh, those wide open spaces, pitting yourself against the elements and all that. I could never stand the isolation!'

'Well – I only love it for short periods. I'd hate it *all* the time. When I've a particular objective, something to aim for, then it's great. Everything becomes very simple and straightforward – it's just *you* and *it*, whatever *it* may be. And I never have time to feel isolated. Too much to do, too much burning ambition to achieve the objective.' He was going to add that he'd felt lonelier in crowds than he'd ever felt in the middle of the ice, but that might lead the conversation into more personal areas, and he'd rather avoid that. He added: 'But I'd go mad if I was in the middle of nowhere for too long. I need people, just like everyone else.'

She gave him a sidelong look. 'You surprise me. You always seem so – well, self-sufficient.'

He smiled wryly. 'Perhaps I'm not what I seem.'

'A lamb in wolf's clothing?'

He shot her a quick questioning glance.

She wrinkled her nose and smiled. 'No. Just a lamb.'

She'd done it again: thrown him slightly. He decided that Ragna marched to a different and quicker drum.

'I can understand the attractions of simplicity, of course.' She was nodding sagely now, a furrow of concentration between her brows, to show that she was giving his answers the serious consideration they deserved. 'I think that's the part that Jan loves too.' She added with a snort of fond amusement: 'You two are a real pair.'

It was true and he smiled. 'But you don't seem to mind,' Hal said. 'I mean, that Jan still wants to go on expeditions. That ... well –'

'That he doesn't want to stay at home with me? No, why should I?'

'Most women would mind a lot.'

'Well, I'm not most women.'

Hal thought: I know that.

'I like him the way he is,' Ragna continued. 'Besides, he was already a mountaineer when I married him. He'd only be unhappy if I locked him up at home.'

Hal pictured Jan and Ragna together and, though he tried hard to suppress it, was stabbed by the familiar pang of envy. Why didn't he have a marriage like that?

The Catalina revved its engines and taxied downwind, keeping in the lee of the shore. Finally it turned to face the buffeting wind and, engines rising to a scream, slowly accelerated, bumping and vibrating over the waves. Ragna held her breath and laughed: 'I can never get used to this crazy business!'

With one last bump, the plane rose into the air and, after seeming to hover motionless above the water, banked towards the south and gathered speed.

*

Ragna thought: Sometimes I don't know you at all.

She observed Hal covertly. He was pleasant-looking, with strong well-formed features, a long straight nose and a rather nice expressive mouth. His hair was brown and short and slightly curly, the sort that's nice to touch. His eyes could be extraordinarily warm and kind when he let them, but most of the time they were dark and serious, and shadowed by a frequent frown, giving him an absorbed intense look.

Beneath the serious manner Ragna suspected he was rather a honey, but in the four years she'd known him she'd never managed to get under his guard and there'd always been a slight awkwardness between them.

It was disappointing. Not only did Ragna pride herself on

getting on with people, but she liked to think she could strike up a spontaneous and open friendship with anyone she liked. But Hal was a dark horse.

When she'd first met him she'd suspected that he was merely a man's man, one of those unattractive breed who secretly fear and dislike women. Certainly he was more at home discussing an expedition with his team-mates than making small talk in a mixed gathering – though there were plenty of men like that, God only knew. But with Hal it was different. She'd noticed how other men looked up to him – mainly because of what he had achieved, of course – but also because he had that indefinable quality of leadership, a sort of iron resolve and detachment which men always admired. As far as the members of his expeditions were concerned he could do no wrong.

Yet there was more to Hal than a simple man of action; something he kept in reserve, something he didn't choose to reveal to anybody. She tried to decide exactly what it was. A sensitivity maybe ... Yes. And there was a passionate side to him, too. She suspected he was rather a romantic. Ah, that was it. And if he was a romantic he was vulnerable, and he wouldn't like that at all. No wonder he took such care to hide it.

Lots of women had tried to crack him, of course. They'd all failed.

She wondered what held him back. A broken love affair? A secret unrequited passion?

Something.

Yes. Sometimes she felt she hardly knew him at all.

*

She handed him a set of beautifully typed notes.

He was impressed: she had it all worked out. There was a diary of appointments with possible sponsors, plus a fall-back list of companies and individuals who might be approached if the first list failed. Also a guest list for the press conference, due to be held on Wednesday morning. And he noticed that, despite earlier problems, she had been able to arrange a meeting with a senior government minister who might be able to push their case for a government grant.

'Well done,' he said over the din of the engines. 'But I think we should try to see all these companies, even those on the back-up list.'

'Oh. But surely we should try the ones who are interested first.' She indicated the main list.

Hal shook his head. 'Believe me, getting a murmur of interest is one thing. Getting a firm commitment is quite another.'

'You're wrong! You're established now. Everyone knows you. Everyone knows what you've *done*. They'll be glad to sponsor you!' She stabbed a finger in his direction and said: 'You'll see if I'm not right!'

She made it sound so easy. But it never had been, and he couldn't see any reason why it should be now. He remembered all the times he'd had to sell himself and his ideas like some salesman trying to sell an unknown and unwanted commodity: no one had wanted to know.

When he'd first tried to get an expedition off the ground he'd known it would be tough, of course. This was a country where everyone, man, woman and child, was something of a mountaineer and skier. A lot of people believed that, given the opportunity, they too could climb high mountains and traverse arctic wastes. It was a hard job to convince them that you could climb higher and endure longer than they could. Though once they *were* convinced, and provided they knew and understood your motives, then they did give you their respect.

But respect didn't translate itself into cash. Norwegians, especially northerners, were generous and warm-hearted when times were hard. But they were also fiercely independent, self-sufficient, stubborn and tight-fisted. They found it convenient to believe that, in some magical way, expeditions financed themselves.

Hal felt no bitterness. On the contrary, he understood their attitudes only too well. One only had to remember the rugged coast hidden beneath the thick cloud, the settlements and isolated farms clinging to the narrow band of fertile soil between mountains and sea, and the hard-working women who ran them, and the men who went fishing winter and summer, gale or calm, to appreciate what a hard and tenuous life it still was for so many. In the past there had been terrible poverty, even famine. Now there was a growing prosperity, but memories were long, attitudes deep-seated, even in the wealthier south.

No, it wouldn't be easy. It never was.

Ragna was reading her own copy of the week's diary. He noticed there was a handwritten entry on her schedule which he hadn't remembered seeing on his. He checked: no, it wasn't there. He glanced back at the copy in her lap. He could see the entry was for Thursday and that there was a time written to one side of it.

'What's that?' He pointed towards it.

She looked faintly defensive. 'Oh. A meeting of mine. I just put it on there to remind me.'

He leaned over and peered more closely. She made a slight movement as if to slide the papers away, then thought better of it.

He deciphered the handwriting and looked up at her in surprise. 'The justice ministry? Why on earth are you going there?'

'Ah.' She gave him a long appraising look as if she was making up her mind what to tell him. 'Well, I'm going on behalf of some friends of mine really. It's a sort of favour.'

'Oh?'

She shrugged and murmured something which he missed in the loud drumming of the engines.

He leaned his head closer to show he was waiting for her to repeat it.

A look of resignation came over her face. She said: 'Some Lapp friends. They want me to go and ...' She pursed her lips in annoyance, as if she'd been caught out in some way. 'And ... well, ask some questions for them, represent them if you like.'

A small but powerful suspicion flew into Hal's mind. He hesitated, thinking he must surely be mistaken, but the suspicion had lodged too firmly to go away. Finally he had to ask: 'It wouldn't by any chance be something to do with a military training area?'

Her eyes flashed darkly, and he knew he was right. His heart sank. 'What sort of questions?'

'We want to know how the military can possibly lay claim to land which doesn't belong to them! And, if they insist on going through with this, how they expect to compensate the Lapps for the considerable disturbance to their herds. And a few things like that!'

'That's fighting talk, Ragna.'

'Too right it is.'

It was the actress in her, Hal decided: all zeal and big-heartedness. It was just a pity she'd chosen such a sensitive cause. Successive governments had been very good at closing their minds to Lapp rights, and he had a feeling they wouldn't take kindly to having objections forced down their throats.

He drew a deep breath. 'Ragna, this is most –' he searched for the right word – 'unfortunate.'

'Oh? Why?' Her tone was defensive.

'It's a political matter. And we can't be involved in anything political.'

'But it's me who's involved, and I happen to think this is important.'

'Yes, but you're part of the expedition now. Your involvement would be misunderstood.'

'By whom?'

'Government officials. Newspapers. You name it.'

'But it's something I can do quite separately. I can use my unmarried name. I won't even mention the expedition.' She added proudly: 'You see, I can't let them down.'

Hal sighed: 'But why you, Ragna?'

'Why not?'

'Well you're not a Lapp for a start.'

'But that's just the point! No one listens to them. They need someone like me, someone who can get them heard. Anyway,' she added with a shrug, 'Jan's a quarter Lapp.'

'And what does he think about this?'

'He respects my point of view.'

There was a long pause. Suddenly they hit some turbulence and the small plane bucketed and lurched. He saw that Ragna's knuckles were white on the seat arm.

Hal touched her wrist. 'Okay?'

She gave a tiny nod, but her lips were set in a hard line, and her eyes were round and very dark. He wasn't sure if her anger and fear were directed at him or the plane.

Finally they flew into smoother air, and began a gentle descent to Bodo where they would change to a DC7C for the last two legs to Oslo.

Conversation became possible again. Hal prepared himself. He couldn't possibly leave this matter unresolved.

'Norway's a small country,' he began and immediately thought how horribly pompous that sounded, as if he were treating her like a fool. 'I mean, everyone in government knows each other. People talk. There's no possibility of your association with this – *issue* – going unnoticed. The press – at least some of it – will sit up and take notice. People will find it strange, government officials won't be quite so helpful...'

'What are you saying exactly?' she asked stiffly.

'That – it would be an embarrassment to the expedition. And to me.'

'But I can't just let them down.'

'I wish you'd talked this over with me before.'

'I didn't think I had to!'

'Well – yes, you had to. Everyone has to discuss things with everyone else. That's how a team works.'

'This sounds like a lecture.'

He dragged a hand across his forehead. The discussion was not going well. His instincts had failed him and he merely seemed to be antagonising her. He said simply: 'I'm sorry.'

'You're forbidding me to go, is that it?'

For several moments he didn't answer. She wanted him to state things too baldly. 'Well, I wouldn't have put it that way...'

'But it boils down to the same thing!'

There was a wilfulness, a stubborn intransigence in her, and he knew that one way or another she'd force the admission out of him. 'All right,' he said finally. 'If you like.'

A flush stole up her face and her lips narrowed. She turned away and stared doggedly out of the window.

He had an urge to reach out and touch her arm, to show he regretted the incident. But something held him back and then the moment had passed.

*

The distance across the lake was eighteen miles, a journey of three or four hours in good conditions. The two men had planned to set out well before the first glimmering of dawn, but a fierce blizzard kept them in their tent. There was no hurry. If necessary they could travel at night. One had to be adaptable. Only the foolish went out in minus thirty and a full gale unless absolutely necessary. It wasn't just that the visibility was down to less than five yards, it was the wind. Not only did it take energy to walk against it, but it was energy one needed to maintain body heat and prevent one's extremities from freezing in the vicious windchill.

So the men waited and by mid morning their patience was rewarded. The wind began to moderate; the snow, though falling steadily, was not so dense; and Jan's pocket-thermometer registered a small but distinct rise.

They ate a last meal of hot reindeer stew, cheese and coffee, then donned their outer garments, rucksacks and skis, plus an extra pair of skis which Jan strapped to his back. With a brief farewell to the old man, they made their way down on to the lake. Then, using a compass bearing to guide them to their first landmark, an as yet invisible island some two miles out, they set off, settling into the long sliding lope of practised cross-country skiers.

Jan kept his bearings by keeping the wind at an angle to his left cheek, only occasionally checking his compass. As soon as they had found and skirted the first island, they headed for the next islet another two miles away. Jan noticed that the wind was shifting slowly through north towards the west.

Once the men stopped to drink from the water flasks they kept close to their bodies. Dehydration was always a problem in intensely cold dry air.

Otherwise they kept going, thrusting through the soft snow in rhythmic strides, travelling surprisingly fast. The long narrow wooden skis were light and flexible and bowed. The ends were polished and slid forward easily on the forward thrust, while the middle section, which only came into contact with the snow on the back thrust, was carefully waxed to make it sticky and permit no back-sliding. The boots were light and soft, made of reindeer skin, and fastened to the skis by hide bindings at the toe, allowing the heel to rise on the stride. The Lapps needed no lessons in the art of skiing; they had been practising it for over three thousand years.

Another island reared up ahead, its side speckled with dwarf birch and dark patches of bare rock.

There were no more islands after that, and they headed out across a five-mile stretch of open lake towards a promontory as yet invisible on the opposite shore. Once there, they would follow the shoreline another six miles into a deep bay, and complete the crossing of the lake.

They would then stop at an isolated hut – if they could find it. The old man had told them that the *hytte* was situated a few hundred yards up a low fell heading off a tongue of the lake, but in the poor visibility and falling darkness they might well miss it. If they did, it would be unfortunate but not disastrous. They would merely dig themselves a snow-hole for the night, and, instead of enjoying a strong fire in the *hytte*, they would make do with the rather thinner warmth of the pressure stove.

Thereafter it was not far to their journey's end – in a straight line only six miles. The route would be relatively straightforward, taking them along a series of valleys and watercourses. But if the visibility was poor they would have to watch their distance: there was a border close by, a border they weren't intending to cross.

In the centre of Lake Inari, meanwhile, the wind dropped away and the swirl of snow thinned to a few desultory flakes. From a cocoon of grey, the world slowly opened out before them. Dark specks showed in the whiteness ahead, hinting at rocky outcrops: the promontory. It was a welcome sight in the approaching night. Jan turned his head and raised his snow-crusted eyebrows to Mattis. The Lapp nodded back. They were both thinking the same thing: no cold discomfort in a claustrophobic snow-cave after all; now they would find the hut and enjoy a relatively luxurious night.

Five

As a newspaper story it was useless.

Berg pulled the sheet of notes out of the typewriter and read it through. A fantastic and explosive story – but no newspaper would touch it with a barge pole, not even if he veiled it so heavily as to be almost completely obscure. The Norwegian press, for all its self-righteous talk about freedom and rights, was desperately hidebound and law-abiding. Even his own paper, the *Sosialist Dagens Post*, which prided itself on its liberal roots, rarely printed anything controversial. All it did, as Berg knew only too well, was to reinforce its readers' deeply entrenched opinions.

Well, there was more than one way of killing a cat. It was just a question of deciding which way.

He wandered restlessly around the flat, thinking hard. He'd already sat on this for over a day. He must do something soon or risk losing everything.

Trembling slightly, he lit a cigarette and inhaled deeply. This was the big one, the jackpot; no doubt about that. A coup. Beyond his wildest dreams. Beyond anything they had ever expected of him.

He calmed himself. He had to get it right. And right meant exposing the full extent of the CIA's involvement in Norway, so giving the lie to the idea that Norway was totally autonomous. Christ – what a balloon that was going to send up.

But exposing the truth wasn't going to be easy. He knew that the operation must be under the direct control of the CIA, simply because the third man, the man who was to be met at the Finno-Russian border, was an American agent. He had to be because Norway had no agents inside Russia – Norway had no agents anywhere.

He knew the truth all right – but how to convince the world?

And then there was the matter of Finland. The operation was being carried out on Finnish soil without that country's knowledge or consent. Handled correctly, that too would raise a monumental stink.

Berg could guess why the Finnish route had been chosen, of course. An operation on the Norwegian–Soviet border would have been far too difficult: the border was short and, Norway being a member of Nato, relatively well guarded. The Finnish border, on the other hand, was hundreds and hundreds of miles long and less heavily guarded, not only because Finland was neutral, but because any Russian defectors who did manage to reach Finland were immediately handed back.

So – the possibility for double embarrassment.

Incredible. And as a bonus, the furore might just tip public opinion further against the nuclear missile issue.

He stopped his pacing and sat down abruptly. He knew what had to be done. In fact, he'd known all along; he'd just put off the moment of decision, hoping there might be another way, a way which would leave him total control.

But that had been too much to ask for: sometimes one just had to take a back seat.

Besides, he was looking forward to seeing the look on Alex's face. He wouldn't have long to wait: he'd arranged to meet him for lunch.

It was eleven-thirty. Berg went into the bathroom, a brilliant box of a room lined with mirrors and sparkling starlike lights. The room had been featured in a leading home design magazine. Berg kept a copy on the coffee table in the living room, open at the appropriate page.

This morning, however, the lighting assaulted his eyes and tinged his skin a rather unhealthy grey. He splashed cold water over his face and rubbed it dry. He looked up into the mirror. Lines, a hint of bags under the eyes: tired, older. Lack of sleep.

He ran an electric razor over his chin and combed his hair. Better.

Excitement churned in his stomach and his spirits rose again. He grinned broadly at his reflection and thought: *What a hell of a thing this is!*

Gathering a coat and his notes from the typewriter, he went out. The weather was vastly better: the sky was clear and the sun, making its brief midday appearance, made the snow sparkle and the buildings glow.

He drove slowly for once, letting the car pull itself up through the hilly suburbs to the restaurant on the high point of Holmenkollen. Berg hardly ever came here – he preferred Blom's or the Theatre Café – but Alex liked it. He said he liked it because of the spectacular view over the city, but Berg suspected he got a perverse amusement out of sitting among the other diners who, more often than not, included diplomats and Nato personnel.

Alex was already there, by the window, his plump jovial figure beaming with goodwill. 'This view!' he said immediately. 'What a day to be up here! What a day! I never get tired of the view.'

They went to the cold table and helped themselves from the unchanging selection of pickled and smoked fish, meat and vegetables. Alex's plate was piled so high that slivers of pickled cabbage fell to the floor as he returned to the table.

Berg watched him stuff large mouthfuls into his already well-padded face. 'Hungry?'

Alex smiled. 'Always. It comes from starving as a child. Those memories never leave you. We used to boil up shoe leather, you know. And catch rats – those that survived the cold, of course. I was the champion rat-catcher of Leningrad. Did I tell you that?'

'You told me.'

'Ah. One forgets.'

Berg thought: You never forget.

Alex took a mouthful so large that he had to leave his mouth open to chew it. Berg averted his eyes and took a small bite of pickled fish. He put down his fork – sometimes he despaired of the Norwegian mania for pickling everything – and began to give Alex some of the latest gossip.

Above the relentless grinding of his jaws, Alex was quietly absorbing every word. Berg had a reputation for knowing all the latest scandals and whispers, and for recounting them amusingly. And Alex, a GRU (Soviet Military Intelligence) officer with the Novosti Press Agency, was keener than most to keep

74

abreast of events in the Nato community.

Berg finished with a little tale of a trade delegation visiting Sweden from a well-known Far Eastern industrial country and getting caught in a brothel, quite literally with their trousers down.

Alex laughed until he almost choked. His face scarlet, he held up his hand in protest. 'Stop, stop!' he sobbed. 'I can't bear it.'

Berg watched him coolly. He suspected Alex would already have heard the story from his own sources, in which case he was putting on a good act.

Only the mention of dessert brought a halt to Alex's laughter. He collected a double helping of apple tart and cream from the cold table. Before plunging in, he asked: 'Did you see that Polaris story in *Time* magazine?'

Berg nodded.

There was a pause. The two men exchanged glances.

It had been a jewel of a story, and it had been largely unearthed by Berg. It had concerning the secret building of a US navigation station on the north-west coast of Norway, for use by Polaris submarines carrying nuclear weapons. The story had been cleverly disseminated by Alex. It had first appeared in an East German paper, and then been picked up by a Finnish left-wing daily. Variations of the story had subsequently appeared in other European papers until, finally, a Norwegian paper had plucked up courage to run a highly modified version.

The Norwegian government had squirmed and wriggled before finally admitting that a defence establishment was in the process of construction on the north-west coast. The affair had caused the government some embarrassment, particularly after the now-famous Bulganin Note of the previous year, in which the USSR had given Norway a strong warning of the consequences of Nato bases appearing on Norwegian soil.

'Mmm, the *Time* piece was all right,' Berg said casually, 'but it never made banner headlines in Tromso.'

Alex looked worried, then, as the joke dawned, laughed heartily. 'No banner headlines! Tromso! You're cruel! Cruel! One day, one day!'

Berg smiled to himself. It was easy to make Alex laugh. One merely had to remember that his sense of humour was as subtle as a sledgehammer.

There was a short silence.

Alex spooned the last of the cream from his plate and sat back in his chair, focusing benevolently. 'Well, what can this humble fellow-journalist do for you today?'

'I wanted to sound you out on the official Soviet response to the presence of nuclear missiles on Norwegian soil.'

Alex nodded slowly. This was the official reason for meeting openly – always openly – for lunch every few months or so. Many political journalists had professional relationships with Soviet officials and diplomats. No one thought anything of it.

If Alex remembered that Berg had asked him this question before, he didn't show it. 'Sure. Sure,' he said. 'It's quite simple. The Soviet Union would take the arrival of nuclear weapons on Norwegian soil as a totally unprovoked act of aggression on the part of Norway against the Soviet Union.' He threw a chocolate into his mouth and beamed. 'Will that do?'

Berg didn't answer. A large party was entering the restaurant, a group of about twenty Nato personnel: Norwegian, American and British naval and army officers. They walked rather stiffly and formally to a long table nearby.

Berg gave it a moment and murmured very quietly: 'And how does the Soviet Union feel about clandestine activities by Norwegian agents on the Finnish–Soviet border?'

The chocolate-chewing stopped. Berg felt a leap of pleasure; he had taken Alex totally by surprise.

'Ah,' said Alex. 'That's something else of course.' He sucked at his teeth. 'Now why would they be wanting to do such a thing?'

'To meet someone.'

'Someone one knows?'

'Someone with valuable information, someone from Murmansk.'

Alex swallowed abruptly. 'Oh dear, oh dear. Now what is one to make of that?'

'It hasn't even happened yet. But it's going to happen very soon. I have all the details.'

Alex's jaw dropped open. 'My friend, what can I say? You are really most – efficient.' His eyes firmly on Berg, he jabbed a finger impatiently into his mouth in an attempt to dislodge some food stuck in his teeth. Then, giving his lips a brief

76

wipe, he said breathlessly: 'How will the world react to this, I wonder?'

'It depends on how quickly the story breaks.'

'Yes, yes.' Alex's eyes were shining greedily. His colleagues were very skilful at feeding information into the Western news system so that no one was ever quite sure where the original story came from.

'But what we need is some questions in the Storting,' Berg said. 'And quickly, to get the best out of it.'

'Questions in the Storting? That's not so easy.'

'Of course it is, Alex. Don't tell me you can't do it.' Some members of the Norwegian parliament had affiliations with trade unions and other left-wing groups, in whose ranks were several converts to the cause.

'Perhaps you overestimate me,' Alex said carefully. 'Unfortunately I don't get to enjoy delightful meals like this with members of the Storting.'

'But you know people who do.'

Alex dropped his eyes. Berg raised a finger and wagged it at him. Then, taking the single typewritten sheet out of his pocket he passed it openly across the table.

Alex stared at the paper as if it would bite him. His face went a pale shade of yellow. Berg thought: He can't believe his luck. Alex's hand shook as he reached out and, with exaggerated care, picked up the paper and put it into his breast pocket. 'You know, Rolf, these things should not be done this way. It is very dangerous – for *you*, I mean.' As if to emphasise the point he swivelled his eyes in the direction of the Nato personnel.

Berg's face hardened. He didn't blame Alex for being nervous – he himself felt rather tense, though in a decidedly stimulating way. No, what he disliked was the road the conversation was taking. Unless he was mistaken, he was in for the set lecture.

Reading Berg's face, Alex looked as if he wished he could get out of it too.

'Rolf, listen,' Alex began tentatively in a low whisper, 'you are very valuable to us. Very *very* valuable. Sometimes I don't think you realise just how important you are – not at all!' He made a gesture of exasperation.

Berg gave a heavy theatrical sigh. 'Come *on*, Alex.'

'But, Rolf, things cannot continue like this.'

'Why not?'

'It's asking for trouble.'

'Nonsense. Unless you're about to defect, of course.'

Alex raised an eyebrow and let that one pass. In his younger days he'd probably considered it several times. He persisted: 'We should take basic precautions!'

'I'm no virgin, Alex. I can look after myself.'

'But if you run risks long enough, you get caught out.'

Berg made a face. Bureaucrats to the last, Alex and his friends were longing to get him locked into the system. But Berg wanted no part of dead-letter boxes, clandestine meetings and sordid financial arrangements. He wanted to do things his way or not at all.

'But at least let us look after you,' Alex pleaded.

These attempts at entrapment were always childishly transparent. The Alexes of this world thought they could manipulate almost anyone with flattery, money and gifts. That was because they judged people by their own standards.

Berg looked at the fat obsequious man before him, and thought: Does he really believe I'll swallow it? He laughed, and said: 'Alex – come on! Can't you do better than that?'

Alex made a gesture of hurt surprise. 'But we do want to take care of you. Anything you want. Just say!'

'I want nothing, Alex. Nothing. You know that, so why the hell do you keep asking?'

Alex sat back, momentarily defeated, and looked thoughtful. A sly calculating expression came over his face, and he leant forward again.

'An old friend was asking after you,' he said meaningfully. 'He's coming to Oslo soon. He was hoping to see you.'

Berg's stomach tightened. 'There's no one I want to see, Alex –'

'But this is your old comrade-in-arms,' Alex interrupted smoothly. 'He wants to see you for old times' sake.'

A sudden anger came over Berg. 'Don't, Alex.'

Alex opened his hands in a gesture of incomprehension. 'Don't what?'

'Don't go on. Do you understand?'

'Understand? My friend, I'm baffled! What harm can there

be in meeting an old friend?'

A vision stole into Berg's mind, a vision of Nikolai Andreevitch, his uniform dirty and unkempt, his cap sitting jauntily
on the back of his head, his face young, yet faded by time and
light, like the tints of an old photograph. Behind Niki was the
camp just to the east of Murmansk, its outlines shaded in pale
greys, like the snow, the mountains, the people. And somewhere
in the foreground was the thin shadowy figure of himself: sick
and cold and bitter because there was no war left to fight nor
any home he wanted to return to.

He owed Niki a lot. He'd never begrudged the debt – but
he'd repaid it many times over.

He didn't want to see Niki. What he did now he did because
he wanted to.

'Piss off, Alex.'

A conciliatory smile flickered across Alex's face. 'Please –
don't take offence. You are my friend. The last thing I want to
do is upset you!'

Berg pushed back his chair. 'Well, you can shut up then. And
get busy.' He waved his hand in the direction of the Russian's
breast pocket. 'I expect the works on this one, Alex. Don't balls
it up, eh?'

He got up and walked abruptly away, almost bumping into
two uniformed officers, one Norwegian, one American, manoeuvring with loaded plates from the smorgasbord. Berg apologised. The two officers smiled and passed on, talking with the
forced cheerfulness of military allies.

*

Press conferences were invented by sadists, Hal decided. The
sort of people who liked bear-baiting. And today he was in the
pit.

He took his seat behind a table at one end of the hotel
conference room and faced the congregating journalists. Many
smiled in his direction – though was it his imagination or were
their smiles rather cool? Several came up and shook his hand
with what seemed excessive politeness. Some just eyed him, like
piranha.

He remembered with nostalgia the journalists he had met on

his American lecture tour, and their energy, toughness and openness. By comparison the Norwegian press were conservative and cautious, with a decidedly puritanical streak. Hal never quite knew what to expect from them, except that they seemed to make up their minds in advance.

Hal glanced down the room to the door where Ragna was crossing off the journalists' names against a list. She looked up and caught his eye and grinned, a cheerful sort of 'don't you worry' grin. He smiled faintly back.

When everyone had arrived, the president of the Geographical Society rose and made an over-long and rather pompous introduction.

Then Hal was on his feet, outlining his plans for the expedition. He was aware of starting uncertainly, his voice sounding strangely flat and dead in his ears, but after a minute or two he got into his stride and when he sat down again twenty minutes later he felt confident he'd covered everything rather well.

The president invited questions.

A hand was raised and someone asked about the difficulties of high-altitude climbing. Hal described the training schedule planned for the run-up to the expedition, and how it would include oxygen-assisted and high-altitude ascents. Someone else asked about the food, another about team selection.

Then a woman Hal didn't recognise raised her hand and, after giving her name and newspaper, said: 'Your previous experience is mainly in Arctic survival. Do you think you have sufficient experience for Everest?'

Hal resisted the temptation to give her a short sharp answer, and said reasonably: 'I'm first and foremost a climber –'

'But you've never climbed at high altitude?'

This lady was definitely hostile. Hal felt his temper rising. 'It's difficult to get to the Himalayas every day!' He let his anger subside a little. 'I agree that I'm best known for my Arctic survival work, but climbing's my first skill. Those who understand mountaineering would consider Everest a natural progression for someone like myself.'

The woman was silent. Another hand was raised. A man this time. 'What is your motive for undertaking this expedition?'

'I explained. The fact that this ridge hasn't been climbed

before. And it's a great challenge.'

'But you've already navigated the Northwest Passage and tried for the Pole. Most people would find that more than sufficient. By adding Everest, your career begins to look like a quest for personal glory.'

The anger swept over Hal in a red-hot wave. He'd never tried to hide his motives, yet here he was having to defend them. Only in your own country could you be made to feel guilty for your ambitions. He answered with elaborate care: 'Some people work solely to survive, others for money. I, fortunately, work for personal satisfaction. I admit that that makes me a lucky man. As to the glory, well, I don't think such a remark deserves an answer. I do what I do because it's my life. It's in my nature to try for harder and harder things. How people interpret that is their own business.'

The questioner stood his ground. 'But is this expedition really necessary? Everest has already been climbed. And in these days of economic stringency, when the Norwegian people are striving hard under difficult circumstances, can the expense be justified?'

*

Ragna thought: Come on, Hal!

He'd started off far too modestly. He really wasn't the best person to sell himself; someone else needed to do it for him – and not the president of the Geographical Society, who was a hundred and five if he was a day, and couldn't sell an orange to an Eskimo.

Anger had improved his delivery. The actress in her had applauded the last few answers: they had contained just the right amount of punch and dramatic effect.

Now, inexplicably, he was faltering again, sounding tired, almost apologetic.

She had a sudden thought. Hurriedly, she scribbled a note: *Tell them about rival American and Japanese expeditions. Other countries think expense IS justified.*

Before she had a chance to change her mind, she made her way up to the table and placed the message in front of him. He paused, read it, looked vaguely puzzled, then nodded slightly. 'There are several other expeditions lined up to try for Everest,'

81

he announced. 'And at least one – an American team – is going to attempt the West Ridge the year after us.'

Ragna willed him to go on and make the logical point, that if the challenge was worth it to other countries, why not to Norway?

But Hal was silent. Groaning inwardly, Ragna scanned the journalists' faces. Already she could imagine the sort of cautious moralistic articles that would appear: We think Starheim is courageous but is his expedition soundly based?

People were looking restless. The president pushed back his chair, preparing to close the meeting.

As he came to his feet, a voice came from the other end of the room. 'If I may ...'

Heads swivelled. Ragna craned her head and saw a man detach himself from a group near the door. He came forward, a tall, blond figure, immaculately dressed, with an easy confident walk.

On reaching the table he grinned broadly at Hal before turning to face the room.

'Well! I think we have been very privileged today to learn about the new plans of Halvard Starheim. We belong to a nation with a glorious tradition. We produced the two greatest names in polar exploration – Nansen, the first man to cross Greenland and tackle the Arctic ice; and Amundsen, the first man to reach the South Pole and sail the Northwest Passage. These men created a tradition of which we are justly proud. Thanks to Halvard Starheim that tradition is not only being continued but enhanced.'

Ragna stared. Whoever this man was, she loved him!

'It's very easy to find reasons *not* to undertake great challenges,' the stranger continued. 'It is also very easy for other people to criticise –'

Ragna took a triumphant look at the sniping journalist.

' – but it takes a very special sort of man to set off into the unknown not just once but several times, to succeed in nearly every instance, and without the loss of a single man – and then be ready to undertake something even more challenging. Norway may be famous for polar exploration, but there is absolutely no reason why it shouldn't be famous for mountaineering too.'

Hal was looking studiously at the table, a frown on his forehead, his lips clamped tightly together. But Ragna could see that he was pleased.

The speaker hadn't finished either. 'We are a nation of individualists, proud of our self-sufficiency and independence, but also proud of our generosity to each other in times of hardship and need. Hal Starheim cannot mount this expedition on his own. He needs the help of the Norwegian people and, I'm sure you'll agree, he deserves it.'

People were relaxing. The atmosphere had shifted. Even Hal seemed to have sensed it, and a ghost of a smile hovered on his lips.

The speaker glanced at Hal again. He had a fine, handsome face with vivid blue eyes. There was something very attractive in his smile, a sort of mischievous complicity.

'In 1954,' he was saying, 'I spent two weeks with Hal Starheim and his crew in Arctic Canada during their two-year journey through the Northwest Passage.'

With surprise Ragna realised that this man must also know Jan.

'I went expecting to find a battered boat with an even more battered crew, but both the men and the boat looked ready to do the whole trip all over again. Spending that amount of time with someone in exceptionally tough conditions, you get a pretty good idea of what he's really like. Well, I can tell you that Hal Starheim is everything he seems to be. An inspiration to his men. And to us all.' He paused for effect. 'Join me now in wishing him every good fortune in his new venture.'

Some got straight to their feet; others followed. The stranger approached Hal and, with elaborate formality, shook his hand and said loudly, 'Good luck!' Then, unseen by everyone in the body of the room, he gave Hal a distinct wink. Ragna thought: What a character!

There was a spontaneous movement towards Hal, and, one by one, people shook his hand. The room filled with the babble of easy conversation.

Ragna sagged with relief then shot to her feet as she remembered that she should be at the door, handing out information to the departing journalists.

Later Ragna found Hal having a drink at the bar with the tall blond man.

Hal took her arm. 'Ragna, my expedition secretary – Rolf Berg, from the *Dagens Post*. An old friend.'

'So I gathered!' Ragna laughed.

They shook hands. His smile was just as attractive at close quarters, although she had the feeling he was well aware of the fact. He had very blue eyes, and a wide mouth, but it was his hair that one noticed. It was thick and unusually golden, and he wore it longer than was fashionable, to the collar.

A veritable Viking god, Ragna decided with a jaundiced eye. She had a long-standing suspicion of good-looking men.

'I'm delighted to see that Hal has a woman in the team,' Rolf Berg was saying. 'There are apt to be too many men on these things.'

'I couldn't agree more,' Ragna replied lightly. 'But then he would have been mad not to have me. I was by far the best person for the job, you see.'

Hal laughed: 'Ragna's not one to be modest.'

Berg looked amused.

'Thanks for what you did today,' Ragna said more seriously. 'I thought for a moment Hal was going to be eaten alive!'

Hal sighed audibly.

Berg gave a small dismissive shrug. 'I was just saying that people get worried about success. They're nervous in case someone they admire turns out to be a fraud. They protect themselves by asking stupid questions. But wait and see,' he said directly to Hal. 'They'll end up by saying they thought it was a great idea all along.' Berg flicked Ragna a sidelong glance. 'Isn't that right?'

He had a way of making you feel you'd known him for years. Ragna liked that. 'Of course!'

Hal said gravely: 'I hope you're right.'

'I am,' Berg said. 'Just like you're always right about the weather.'

It was obviously an old joke, for they began to talk about the Northwest Passage and frosted eyebrows in minus fifty falling fast. Masculine reminiscence time; not Ragna's favourite sort of conversation. But Berg was an accomplished and amusing raconteur and, despite the irritation of knowing she might as well not be there, she found herself smiling at some of his more elaborate stories.

Someone came up to talk to Hal and the conversation ended. Berg looked disappointed.

She asked: 'Are you going to cover this expedition too, Rolf Berg?'

He shook his head. 'Can't stand heights.'

'And you're going to let a little thing like that stop you?'

He bit his lip in mock shame. 'Ah, I have a great weakness, you see. I'm a coward.'

Ragna decided that, despite his good looks, Berg might be all right after all. She'd always had a soft spot for people who didn't take themselves too seriously.

'What about *you*?' Berg asked. 'Are you going to Nepal?'

'Ah no! One climber in the family's enough.'

He looked puzzled.

'Jan, my husband, will be going.'

'Your husband?'

Good Lord, thought Ragna, did he think I wasn't married?

'Yes,' she replied. 'Jan Johansen.'

'A-a-h,' he said, very slowly. 'I see.'

'But there's nothing to see,' Ragna said a little defensively. 'I'm here in my own right.'

'Of course.' But he didn't look as convinced as Ragna would have liked. He drained his drink as if preparing to leave, then hesitated. 'Didn't I hear your name yesterday? Weren't you lobbying the justice ministry on some Lapp issue?'

'Oh!' Ragna flicked an anxious glance in Hal's direction to see if he'd heard, but to her relief he was still talking. She looked back to Berg to find him regarding her curiously. Trying to laugh it off, she said: 'I'm surprised you heard that. No one was meant to realise it was me, you see. I used my unmarried name.'

At that moment Hal finished his conversation and turned back, looking from Ragna to Berg, waiting for them to continue their talk. If Berg noticed the warning signals emanating from Ragna's eyes he chose to ignore them.

'Well, even if people weren't meant to realise,' he said, 'they knew it was you all right. As I heard it, you were objecting to the location of a military training area. Or have I got it wrong . . . ?'

He knew perfectly well he'd got it right. There was a stony silence. Ragna could feel Hal's eyes boring into her.

'Possibly,' she said lamely. 'But it's not something I discuss when I'm working.'

Hal put his beer down on the bar. His mouth was set in a thin hard line. Ragna could feel the icy chill of his displeasure.

He said to Berg: 'I'll see you, Rolf.'

'We'll have that meal.'

'Sunday.'

'Sunday.'

Without a word to Ragna Hal turned on his heel and was gone. Berg raised an eyebrow.

Ragna took a deep breath and said coldly: 'He wasn't meant to know about my visit to the ministry. It was strictly forbidden, you see.'

'Then why did you go?'

'I couldn't let them down.'

'Who?'

'The Lapps.'

'Why?'

'Why? Because they're being trampled over and it's scandalous!'

Berg's mouth twitched with amusement, as if he found her answer touchingly naïve.

Ragna bristled. 'Someone's got to stand up for them.'

'But why you? Can't the Lapps represent themselves?'

'No! Yes ... I mean ...' She drew a breath and started again. 'Jan's part Lapp. So I have a direct involvement.'

'Ah. I'd forgotten. Of course.' But the amusement was still there in his eyes.

He said: 'I'm sorry not to see Jan. Is he away?'

'Yes. On field trials.'

Berg gave an elegant shiver, as if feeling the cold. 'In this weather?'

'Oh, they'll be holed up in a tent somewhere, just like a pair of Mountain Lapps. Living off dried reindeer and foul compo rations, happy as anything.'

Berg looked at her strangely. 'They're up north, are they?'

'Somewhere on the plateau, yes.'

A slight pause. 'Have they been there long?' His voice was very smooth.

It suddenly occurred to her that she shouldn't be talking about this. Yet the question was harmless. 'Since early this week. Sunday.'

Berg nodded, but his expression was curiously distant and thoughtful, as if his mind were already on other things.

The next moment he was saying a polite but brisk goodbye.

As he walked away Ragna made her judgement on Rolf Berg: charming, amusing – but tricky. Then, because she had met plenty of men like him before, she hardly gave him a second thought.

Six

The position was a good one. They had made camp on sloping ground on the western side of the frozen lake. From here the two men could see across the snow-covered ice to the gully between the hills on the opposite side, and down to the southern end of the lake which narrowed like the neck of a bottle. Anyone approaching from the south-east would use one of these routes.

But no one had come, not yet.

They had arrived two days before and dug themselves a snow-hole in the lee of a rocky outcrop some way above the lake. Below, sparse scrub stretched down to desultory clumps of pine and birch which obscured the immediate foreshore.

Now, as the short day began, Jan kept watch while Mattis slept. Misty cloud hung low over the valley, casting a flat shadowless light over the landscape. The temperature had risen slightly – it was no more than thirty below – and the wind had dropped away, leaving the air deathly still. In the silence the valley seemed completely devoid of life. Yet every now and then Jan swung his binoculars on to the slopes beneath to look for signs of wildlife. After an hour his patience was rewarded by the sight of an arctic fox weaving stealthily through the scrub hunting for vole and shrew in their burrows beneath the snow.

Later Mattis awoke and, lighting the paraffin stove, filled a pan with snow. While waiting for the water to heat, the two men sat in silence, looking out over the lake.

It was Mattis who gripped Jan's arm and pointed. Jan squinted across the valley, then put the binoculars hastily to his eyes.

They were a long way off, further up the lake on the opposite side, among the trees. Their form and gait were unmistakable.

Wolf.

Five of them, trotting fast, heads thrust forward – hunting, moving with purpose, as if following a strong scent or a well-trodden trail.

The two men watched closely, for wolves were a rare sight nowadays. Mattis was filled with regret, for if things had been different he might have used his rifle and there would have been two fewer wolves on the far shore, maybe even three. To the Lapp the wolf, the tireless stalker and killer of reindeer, could never be too rare.

But to Jan's eye the rarity of the animal gave it a certain beauty, and he felt no desire to kill. Though he remembered the winter of 1942, the coldest in living memory, when the wolves had come down from the *vidde* into some of the valleys in search of food, raiding farms and terrifying people. Then, despite the German ban on weapons, his father had taken his rifle from its hiding place and gone out to hunt them down.

People said that nothing like it had ever happened before, but Jan's Lapp grandmother had shaken her head and said there'd been other wolf winters far far worse.

The wolves were almost level with them now, just half a mile away on the opposite shore. Suddenly the leader raised his nose to the air and the pack came to an abrupt halt.

Jan glanced questioningly at Mattis. 'Us?'

'Not us,' said the Lapp. 'Too far away and no wind.'

The animals remained motionless for several seconds then moved off again, though more slowly and with greater caution, their bodies closer to the ground, taking only a few steps at a time before stopping to sniff the air once more.

They had definitely scented something. Jan scanned the area immediately ahead of them, but could see nothing in the tangle of snow-heavy birch and willow.

'There!' Mattis' voice hissed at his shoulder.

Jan followed the Lapp's gaze to the southern end of the lake. Then he saw it.

A grey speck against the stark whiteness: the distant figure of a man.

Jan jumped to his feet and, grabbing his rifle, put it to his shoulder and adjusted his sights. He hadn't much hope of hitting the pack leader at this range, but the sound of the shot might be enough to deter it from starting an attack.

The wolves were motionless: he held his fire.

The pack leader turned away, then twisted back again, nose to the scent, as if he couldn't make up his mind. This was repeated several times like a ritualistic dance. Keeping the leader firmly in his sights Jan steadied his finger against the trigger.

The leader sniffed the air once more, then turned for the last time and, with the pack on his heels, loped quickly away in the direction it had come from.

Slinging their rifles over their shoulders, the two men hastily packed away the cooking gear and placed it in the snow-hole with the stores and bedding, sealing the entrance with snow.

Then, with a last look at the vanishing wolves, they skied down through the trees towards the man on the lake.

The three skiers converged across the snow-covered lid of the lake, the two at a fast gliding stride, the third at a slow plod. The stranger stopped dead in his tracks, apparently seeing the others for the first time.

Jan reached him first. Beneath the hood of a dirty white parka was a man of about thirty with a haggard face and eyes half closed with exhaustion. Offering the man water, Jan asked the question he had been told to ask.

He said in Norwegian: 'Don't I know you? Aren't you Tor?'

The man was meant to answer: 'No, that's my brother. I'm Erkki.'

But the man said nothing, and there was silence except for the low rasping of the man's breath.

Jan repeated the question in Lapp and then Finnish. The man said nothing but dropped his head and leant heavily on his ski stick. Jan exchanged glances with Mattis and said: 'Let's take him to the camp.'

As they went to take the man's elbows he slowly buckled at the knees and collapsed into the snow.

Without discussion, Jan and Mattis started to revive him, one removing his skis while the other patted his cheeks. After a while the man opened his eyes and for the first time seemed to focus on his surroundings.

He spoke what was clearly a question. Jan frowned in alarm. He did not understand what had been said, but he certainly recognised the language. Russian.

There was a cold silence.

The man spoke again, this time in the only language that he correctly guessed they might have in common: English. 'Where am I?'

'Finland.'

A small flicker of what looked like relief passed over his face and he closed his eyes again. Then he stared at Jan and murmured: 'Who are you?'

Jan paused before answering: 'We're hunters, from near Karasjok.'

'Please – you come to find my friend?'

Jan did not reply. This wasn't going to plan at all. There was meant to be only one man, a man who spoke some Norwegian – enough to answer the set question at least. Now, suddenly, there was this other man, the wrong man: a Russian who spoke no Norwegian at all.

Finally Jan said, 'What friend?'

With an effort the stranger sat up. 'He comes to find you. I come with him. I have maps, skis ... I want to come to West too. My friend said you meet us here. My friend try very much. But he is not good. The cold ... too hard for us. We stop. Now he cannot come.'

'What do you mean?'

'He is not good. He is sick.'

Jan said roughly: 'But what's wrong with him?'

'Very tired. *Very* tired. And bad foot. He hurt the foot.'

Jan sighed. 'But where is he? How far away is he? How far away?'

The man shrugged. 'Two miles. Maybe more. Not so far.'

Jan questioned the man for a long time, but there was nothing more to learn. He got angrily to his feet and stared blindly into the distance, furious with the stranger, furious with himself for not knowing what to do. The briefing had covered the possibility of a no-show, but it had covered nothing like this, nothing.

The decision was impossible, yet he had to make it.

Finally he decided: he and Mattis would accompany this man to the border. Then – then he would think again.

*

Hal slid a finger inside his collar and tugged at it. He never felt at ease in a suit and tie, and his new shoes were compressing his toes like pincers.

The austere office of the Minister of Cultural and Scientific Affairs was heated to the pitch of a sauna, and Hal's hands were slippery against the chair arms. The chair, a gleaming example of modern Scandinavian design made of bent steel tubes and shiny black leather, creaked loudly whenever he shifted in his seat.

Hal exchanged glances with Ragna who gave him a small conspiratorial wink.

The minister, a severe bony-faced man in his sixties, was reading the proposal slowly, his elbows on the polished pine desk, his fingertips touching to form a perfect arch under his chin.

A fly walked sleepily up the treble-glazed window. Hal thought: The minister wouldn't approve of that.

Looking up, the minister's gaze went from Hal to Ragna, and he smiled. It was impossible to tell if this was a good sign. 'I'm afraid cash is definitely out of the question,' he said with an apologetic shake of the head. 'It would be impossible to justify it to the taxpayer. But I'm sure something can be arranged on the matter of the equipment and stores. Although we *would* need to be certain that sufficient money had been raised to get the expedition off the ground.'

'And then you'd be able to make an announcement?' Hal pressed.

'I would think that there's a reasonable possibility of that – once I have approval, of course.'

Hal wondered if that meant a definite-yes or a maybe-yes.

Ragna asked ingenuously: 'Does that mean yes?'

The minister blinked rapidly. 'I would hope so.'

Hal tried another tack. 'When might this approval come through?'

'In two weeks – roughly.'

Hal tried to hide his disappointment. Two more weeks of uncertainty; two weeks of lost momentum. 'I see,' he said tightly.

He was aware of Ragna shooting him a quick glance. She said sweetly to the minister: 'Obviously our sponsors will be most encouraged by a generous government offer. The press will give it a lot of coverage –'

A flicker of alarm passed over the minister's face and he cut in hastily: 'But it would be extremely premature to announce anything.'

'Of course,' agreed Ragna reasonably. 'We wouldn't dream of it. However –' she sighed regretfully – 'it will be difficult to prevent speculation.'

'Oh? What speculation?'

'Well, everyone's expecting an announcement, obviously.'

Clearly this was news to the minister. Hal tried not to look as though it were news to him too.

'I wasn't aware of this,' said the minister.

'Oh? Weren't you?' asked Ragna with obvious surprise. 'Well, only this morning the *Aftenpost* – and, indeed, the *Dagens Post* – were asking me how large a contribution the government would be making. They seemed to be expecting a substantial cash grant.' She frowned suddenly, as if the consequences of this had only just occurred to her. 'Rather unfortunate.' A slight pause, then she added brightly: 'Of course, once they hear about your offer I'm sure they'll realise it's most generous ... As these things go.' She repeated vaguely: 'Once they hear.'

Hal suddenly had to examine the view outside the window very seriously indeed.

The minister stared at Ragna with narrowed eyes as if grasping some illusive and not entirely pleasant interpretation of what she had just said. 'Well,' he murmured eventually, 'let's hope they don't get the wrong idea.'

Ragna nodded vehemently. 'Quite.'

The minister stood up and came round the desk with elaborate care, as if negotiating treacherous ground. He extended a hand to Hal. 'I can say, in all sincerity, that it has been a great honour.' To Ragna he added: 'And – er – most illuminating.'

Ragna gave him the benefit of her loveliest smile. 'I knew you'd understand how important this was to us, minister. And I assure you that I'll do my best with the newspapers.'

She's overdone it this time, Hal thought, closing his eyes for a moment. Steeling himself, he risked a quick look at the minister.

A weak smile hovered uncertainly on the man's face. Then,

held by Ragna's innocent and unblinking stare, he cocked his head to one side and conceded a wry grin. 'Have you ever been in politics, Mrs Johansen?'

My God, Hal thought, she's got away with it!

Hal waited until they were in the taxi before murmuring: 'Ragna – sometimes.'

'Sometimes what?'

'Was there a rumour?'

'No,' said Ragna blithely, 'not exactly. But he didn't know that, did he? So he'll make sure the papers get wind of the right story and appreciate which generous and far-sighted minister arranged it. That way he'll come out of it smelling of roses. And by Monday morning everyone will know we're getting government support.'

'Ragna – it was blackmail!'

'Nonsense. It was politics, like he said.'

Hal shook his head. 'I don't know . . . I don't know.'

She patted his shoulder. 'Hal, believe me, it's all for the best. We have to strike while the iron's hot.'

The coverage had been astonishingly good, Hal had to admit. The expedition had made the front page of every paper and, apart from the odd cautionary remark, the response had been entirely favourable. Yet he didn't want a reputation for deviousness.

Sensing his doubt, Ragna said firmly: 'Hal, listen, when I was an actress you either sat back and let your talents go unnoticed, or you kept yourself in the public eye and got lots of work. What I'm saying is that you have to *push* a little. We're not going to get good marks for being patient.' She patted his arm. 'Look at the money we've been promised already. Government support will put the seal on everything.'

He couldn't deny Ragna's success so far. She had tied down an amazing number of sponsors in an incredibly short time. In fact, a few more promises and the expedition would be guaranteed. *Guaranteed*. The idea was so new for Hal that he could hardly adjust to it.

The taxi was approaching the flat where Ragna was staying. 'All right,' he said finally. 'But Ragna, do try not to ruffle people's feathers. We don't want to make enemies unnecessarily.'

'Enemies! I thought the minister rather liked me!'

He tried to give her a reproving look, and failed.

She looked sorry and repentant and quite lovely all at the same time. 'Don't think too badly of me,' she said suddenly. 'I always mean well.'

'Mmm. Like with your Lapps.' He hadn't quite forgiven her for going to the justice ministry behind his back.

'I said I was sorry. But I just couldn't let them down.'

It was impossible to be cross with her. 'I know,' he said, and, on a sudden impulse, leaned over and gave her a peck on the cheek.

The taxi ground to a halt. He suddenly thought how nice it would be to take her to dinner. 'Are you –'

She looked at her watch and exclaimed: 'Good Lord! Is that the time?' She jumped out of the cab. Popping her head back inside, she declared: 'I need extra time to get ready, you see!'

'Oh?'

She smiled impishly. 'Got to look extra good. I'm going out with an old flame and I want him to be sick at what he's been missing all this time.'

Hal was still smiling when the taxi drew up outside his hotel.

*

The men halted. They had come about two miles from the lake. The border lay just ahead, though it was impossible to be absolutely certain as to its position. There were no posts or fences; the landscape looked like any other stretch of snow-covered taiga. The only certainty was that ski troops regularly patrolled its far side and that beyond lay many many miles of forbidden territory where interlopers, Russian, Lapp or otherwise, risked instant arrest or worse.

Jan wrestled with indecision. The choice was impossible. Was it a trap? Was this man genuine?

Impossible. But then if he was going to be wrong whatever he did, he might as well try to save the man he had come to meet.

Torn with doubt yet keen to get the matter over and done with, he waved the others forward and the decision was made.

They were crossing the border.

The two Norwegians were uncomfortably aware that each stride was a step away from safety; a step, furthermore, that would have to be retraced. They were also acutely aware of the stillness and the growing clarity of the light and how conspicuous they must be, and how even the sleepiest patrol would be able to track them with ease.

Jan had wanted to leave Mattis at the lake, but according to their strange companion the sick man was too weak to ski, so Mattis had come after all, armed with a makeshift litter made of birchwood and padded with sleeping bags.

The Russian led the way, following his outward tracks which were etched deeply into the snow.

Easy to follow.

For anyone.

Jan knew they must be approaching the Pasvik River, an area which would be heavily patrolled. Nervously, he called a halt and questioned the Russian again. The man was adamant: his companion was very close now.

They continued through sparse woodland. With a cold sense of foreboding Jan noticed that the Russian's tiredness seemed to have mysteriously vanished and that his outward tracks were very straight for those of an exhausted man.

New doubts gnawed at his stomach. He thought of questioning the man again, but the Russian turned excitedly, indicating a point just ahead.

Motioning the others to halt, Jan went cautiously forward. As he approached the brow of a hillock he crouched low on his skis and peered over.

Below him was a slight hollow in which grew dwarf willow and low scrub. Under a gnarled bent willow something protruded from the snow. A sort of bundle. Covered in what looked like a dirty white anorak.

A man?

To one side of the bundle was a rucksack and a pair of skis, and to the other an area of well-trampled snow where people had walked in boots. He thought he could see a set of tracks leading into the hollow from the east in addition to the tracks coming out to the west. But that proved nothing: it was impossible to tell how many pairs of skis had used them.

He made a half circle round the hollow, his ears straining,

his eyes scanning every inch of terrain. Towards the river the trees were taller and denser: anything could be hidden there.

Taking a last look round, he beckoned to the others and skied down into the hollow.

He went straight to the half-buried shape in the snow.

It was a man all right.

Removing his skis Jan knelt beside him and pulled the hood back from his face.

He stared. Realisation came instantly. There could be no doubt: the eyes were only partially closed, the skin was marble-grey and strangely smooth, as if the man had never had a worry in his life. But he went through the motions all the same, feeling the pulse at the neck and wrist, lifting the eyelids to examine the pupils.

Jan put his fingers against the man's cheek. The skin yielded, not yet frozen by the air temperature which was at least minus twenty. He hadn't been dead long then, probably less than half an hour.

A suspicion began to form in Jan's mind. He rolled the body on its back. Then he saw that he was right: the anorak and the snow beneath were stained brilliant pink; there was a large wound in the chest.

He examined the man's clothing and found the neat entry mark of a high-velocity bullet in his back.

Jan spun round and grabbed the Russian by the collar. 'What happened! *What happened?*'

The Russian stared at the figure in the snow and his face crumpled in despair.

Jan shook him violently. '*What happened?*'

'At the river. They shoot at us. We escape in the night. We come back on our track and we walk close to the river. We travel all night. Then he cannot travel no more . . .' He bowed his head.

'Why didn't you say?'

'I think you will not come . . .'

Jan closed his eyes in exasperation.

Suddenly he became aware of the silence again. It seemed alive, as if some mysterious movement were taking place within it.

Gesturing to Mattis, he began to search the body.

They went hastily through the rucksack, then the anorak, shirt and trousers. Because they knew only that the man was carrying something important, but not what it was, they pocketed everything they could find: a map, a knife, a pistol, a bar of chocolate, a wallet, a pair of binoculars. They left the clothing with the remaining food.

Jan glanced at the dead man's face and paused. A distant memory stirred, so faint, so indistinct that he shrugged it off. And yet ...

He stared down at the empty grey features and tried to picture the face as it must have been ...

The memory fluttered again, faint yet persistent. He tried to place it but failed. Yet there was no doubt: the features were vaguely familiar. Or maybe they reminded him of someone else?

There was a loud hiss. He spun round.

It was the Russian, standing on the hillock, gesticulating in the direction of the unseen river, a look of panic on his face.

Jan and Mattis exchanged glances. Hastily they refastened their skis and grabbed their sticks. Mattis tapped Jan's arm. The Russian was leaving fast in the direction of the border, ducking and twisting away, poling off with rapid jerky arm movements, like a rabbit on the run.

Jan and Mattis did not follow him. Instinctively they made a fresh trail well to the north of their old track. They purposely chose difficult ground, through frozen marshland covered with myriad hummocks and waist-high scrub. They used other tricks, too, skirting even the smallest hills to avoid putting their profiles against the sky, keeping close to denser cover where it existed, forcing themselves to their limits, pushing forward in long thrusting strides, faster than their pursuers could ever achieve.

And they listened.

The endless landscape was shrouded in silence, a silence broken only by the steady swish of their skis and the sucking and panting of their breath.

Minutes passed. Jan made calculations. They must be within a mile of the border.

Softly now, softly.

The scrub was thinning. Ahead it petered out altogether and gave way to the openness of a frozen lake.

Jan conjured up the area map from his memory. The border –

98

it must be on the far side of this lake.

Both men gave a sudden start and paused like animals scenting the wind.

A single *crack!* floated on the air, muffled by distance and snow. Then again and again. *Crack! Crack!*

They listened for the last echoes, trying to gauge distance and direction.

Then they poled forward again, but swinging to the left, to skirt the terrible nakedness of the lake.

The silence pressed in, heavy and vibrant.

The horizon beckoned, the landscape opened out, wide and bare and naked around them.

They went on. They had no choice.

The border. So close, so close.

Even as Jan thought it, he froze in his stride and jerked his head up, his senses reaching out. He felt a moment of animal fear. His hand went to his rifle.

A movement. Away, away to the right.

The two men crouched and watched.

Suddenly they saw them.

A group of men, as yet tiny grey dots, but approaching fast.

Jan and Mattis raced off again, instinctively arcing further to the left to diverge even further from the patrol, creating distance.

But distance had little meaning, for there was no cover.

There was a muffled shout, a distant call. The two men's hearts lurched but they did not turn.

A sudden *crack!*, very loud, the bullet very close; then the echoing *thump!* of the detonation.

The two men sped on, their lungs rasping with pain.

More shots: *crack! crack! thump! thump!*

They were half-way round the lake. Ahead was a dip in the fold of the hills: freedom. So near.

Another volley of shots. But though Jan braced himself, his skin alive with fear, nothing came near. It occurred to him that the shots might be intended to miss ...

More calls echoing feebly across the empty air.

The two men sped on. So *near*.

Another shout.

A new leap of fear. The sound came from the *left*.

Jan couldn't see them yet. Where were they?

He pressed on, the slow-burning terror pushing his aching limbs forward, forward.

There were no more shouts. For some moments there were no more shots either. Just the pounding of their hearts in their ears.

Then – *thud!*

A cry split the air. A moment of disbelief. The voice was his own, shrill and unrecognisable. The breath was knocked out of him. A terrible pain pierced his lungs.

He was not aware of falling, only of the burning pain and breathlessness, and a lightness in the head, like he was floating.

The snow pressed into his face. His mouth was liquid. A pink stain spread slowly across the whiteness. He coughed and cleared his mouth.

A part of his brain registered the *crack! crack!* of continuous shooting.

A cloudiness was creeping up on him. Fighting it back, he coughed and swallowed and tried to clear the choking in his throat. With a vast effort, he called Mattis's name. His voice was infuriatingly faint.

There was no response. Silence. Even the shooting had stopped. He tried to turn his head. It was heavy, heavy. He twisted his body a little so that he could see past his feet.

He stared, blinked, refocused and stared again.

For the first time he was overwhelmed by despair.

Mattis. He lay crumpled in the snow, his legs twisted under him, a ski protruding oddly into the air.

Struggling for breath Jan called again. Mattis remained infinitely still.

The cloud closed in again. The liquid rose inexorably in his throat; he fought for breath. He heard a gurgling sound. He knew he was drowning. His head was filled with a hot sweet roar.

One further moment of dim awareness ... Voices murmuring, a sensation of hands turning him.

He made a last effort to open his eyes but saw nothing but shadows and the approach of a greater darkness.

Seven

Hal smiled. 'You're not trying to get me drunk by any chance!'

'Drunk?' Berg looked at him in mock astonishment. 'Hal, you're one of my oldest friends.'

'So – no mercy for me.'

They both laughed. They had dined at the Theatre Café. The meal had been good – no, thought Hal, excellent – with glorious food and a bottle of incredibly expensive French wine.

Now he accepted the glass of clear liquor that Rolf offered him, and sat back on the sofa, feeling content.

The flat was typically Rolf: very smart. Even the clutter of the work area looked well arranged and stylish. Most of the furniture was modern; Hal seemed to remember Rolf saying it was Rastad and Rilling designed. Whatever, it was very striking. Around the living room were various pieces of exotica, presumably collected during Rolf's travels: a large Persian rug, an Eastern-style rattan chair, a Venetian mirror, jade ornaments, a Chinese vase filled with dried grasses. The heavy glass in Hal's hand was of finest Waterford crystal and the drink cupboard was well stocked with highly taxed spirits. A Bang and Olufsen hi-fi played Mozart in deep resonant tones.

Rolf lived well; Hal was pleased for him. He said with a smile: 'I'm surprised you left such a pleasant life to come and see us in the Northwest Passage.'

Rolf sat down in the opposite chair. 'Anything for a good story.'

'And it was, the way you wrote it.'

He acknowledged the compliment with a nod, adding drily: 'It was, of course, very sensible of you to let me write it.'

Hal smiled. It was typical of Rolf to make an ambiguously

arrogant remark.

'But you're sticking to political stuff nowadays?' Hal asked.

Rolf shrugged. 'I seem to stir up the establishment satisfactorily. Better than anyone else anyway. The *Dagens Post* was a bit nervous to begin with – they'd hardly publish anything. But in the last year or so they've got much more daring. By their standards, of course.'

'Where d'you get all your stories?'

Rolf threw back his head and laughed. 'Hal! Only someone outside the business could ask a question like that! Journalists don't reveal their sources except on pain of death.'

Hal grinned. 'What a loyal lot you are.'

'Actually the editor sometimes asks me the same question,' Rolf said more seriously. 'He says he hopes I'm not getting anything from "irregular" sources. What he means by that I'm not certain. But I suspect he thinks that tip-offs from government officials and civil servants are irregular. In which case he's a fool. Where else would I get my information from, eh?' His eyes glittered with scornful amusement.

'Perhaps he worries about small details like breaking the law.'

Rolf rolled his eyes. 'Oh! Probably. We're so damned lawabiding that sometimes I think we're more self-righteously puritanical than even the Germans.'

Hal hesitated, then ventured: 'Some people – well, people in my line of work anyway – feel the *Dagens Post* does go a bit far. That it's unnecessarily antagonistic to the military. And blatantly anti-defence.'

Rolf corrected him. 'No, no – anti-*Nato*. Which is quite different.' He sat forward in his seat. 'Surely you can see it would be disastrous to have nuclear weapons on Norwegian soil, Hal. If there was another war the Soviet Union would crush us like – like – glass' – he clenched his hand into a tight fist – 'and they wouldn't wait for us to explain how we'd never actually meant to use the weapons.'

'But surely it's right to be part of Nato.'

'Why? *Why*? Far from saving us, it would merely make us a target. No, I think we should be neutral.'

'We'd be a target anyway, Rolf. Our geography makes sure of that.'

He shook his head. 'War's all about submarines and long-range missiles nowadays. They won't bother with us unless we've let ourselves be turned into an American base.'

'You're sounding anti-American, Rolf.'

'Perhaps I am.' His tone was light, but Hal knew he wasn't joking.

'I thought you enjoyed your time in America.' Rolf had been there for a couple of years immediately after the war.

'I did. But that doesn't mean I want Norway to be America's pawn.'

Time to talk about something else. This was a subject on which they'd never agree and Hal didn't want to spoil the evening. 'D'you ever see any friends from your American days?'

'No.'

There were certain subjects on which Rolf couldn't be drawn. His time in America was one. Their first meeting was another. They'd known each other properly for – how long? Six years. Since the Northwest Passage, when they'd been amazed to realise that they'd met once and so dramatically before. In all that time Rolf had given Hal only the scantiest outline of those events. Rolf was a master at deflecting questions he didn't want to answer.

Hal knew that Rolf's wartime experiences had been very painful. He didn't want to reopen old wounds. And yet they were old friends. Wasn't friendship all about openness and trust?

The aquavit pushed any remaining doubts aside and Hal found himself saying: 'You still owe me a pair of skis, you know. Yours were quite useless. We ended up using them for firewood.'

A faint but unmistakable flicker of displeasure passed over Rolf's face. Getting up, he went to the sideboard to top up his drink. 'Skis,' he murmured, clunking bottles around. 'I still haven't got a decent pair. But listen' – he turned and flashed a smile – 'why don't we go trekking one of these days, eh? I'd really enjoy that.'

'Good idea.' Hal thought: He's done it again. But he wasn't going to be so easily deflected this time. Doggedly, he returned to the subject. 'You never really told me what happened, Rolf. After you got away. You told me what happened to your friend. But that was all.'

Rolf paused for a moment then, picking up his glass and a full bottle of vodka, returned to the sofa. He placed the bottle on the coffee table in front of him and eyed it thoughtfully. Finally he said, 'There's really not a lot to tell.'

'But I'd like to hear it.'

He considered for a moment. 'It's hard for me to talk about it.' He spoke slowly, his voice low and pensive. Suddenly he gave a short self-deprecating laugh. 'You see, I hate the thought of other people knowing how – dreadful it was.'

'You know it would never go any further.'

Rolf stared at him for some time, his eyes sharp and startlingly blue over the rim of his glass. Finally he seemed to make up his mind.

'Well, it's not much of a story,' he said, settling back in his seat. 'We stole a boat that night, as you know. Naughty, but we didn't want to get your friends into trouble. The only problem was, someone must have reported us.' He raised his eyebrows. 'Charming, eh? Anyway before we knew what had happened a gunboat came scooting around looking for us. We hid behind an island, among rocks. Bloody frightening, I can tell you. The rocks, I mean. Much worse than the gunboat. Anyway the boat fired into the darkness for a while – to make themselves feel better, I suppose – then went away.'

'So they never spotted you?'

'No.'

'What happened after that?'

Berg took another gulp of his drink. 'Did I never tell you any of this?'

Hal shook his head.

He gave a short bitter laugh. 'Well, it was hilarious. Hilariously awful, that is. We ran up against a German death and destruction squad, slaughtering livestock and burning everything in sight. For several days we couldn't get past them. Then, when they finally left, there was no food. Nothing. We camped in the remains of a village. It was empty. Not a soul left. Not a scrap of bread. We began to starve. And freeze. God, the cold ... Then we were incredibly lucky. We went hunting and shot a reindeer up in the hills. We got very excited. We thought we'd go on finding reindeer. We set off across the plateau ...'

He clenched his lips together and stared at his drink. 'But

that was disaster ... There were no reindeer. We couldn't find the Lapps. When the meat we had with us was finished, that was it ... The cold was terrible – I can't tell you.' He gave a small mirthless laugh. 'But of course you would know. Anyway, I could see my toes freezing one by one. I was convinced I'd lose the lot of them. Petter did. The lot. Then he got sick – I never knew what was wrong with him. I suppose he just froze up slowly. Anyway, he couldn't move. He sort of gave up.'

There was a pause. The Mozart had finished. The silence stretched out.

Berg looked up suddenly, his eyes hard and distant. 'Then he died.'

Hal felt the pain of it and sucked in his breath. 'I'm sorry.' For something else to say, he murmured: 'Petter. I'd forgotten his name.'

'If Petter *was* his name.'

'Oh. I thought you knew him well.'

'By then. Not before. But we stuck to first names so that we'd never get our families into trouble. For all I know he might have lied about his first name.'

There was a haunted look in Rolf's face. Hal said: 'But you don't blame yourself surely? For his death.'

'One always blames oneself.'

Hal thought: What a burden to carry all these years. 'What about you?' he asked. 'What happened after that?'

'Mmm? Oh, somehow or another I made it back to the coast, to Alta Fiord. I thought I'd find the Russians there. But of course they never got that far. Still, I found some Sea Lapps, thank God, and they fed me on fish. I survived.' He shrugged. 'So.'

'Well, at least you escaped the Germans.'

He gave a vague nod. 'I told you it wasn't much of a story.' Shrugging the subject off, he sat up abruptly and reached for the bottle of vodka. 'Come on,' he said with forced cheerfulness, 'you're not keeping up with me.'

'But I wasn't drinking vodka!'

'You are now.'

It was a drinker's challenge, and Hal didn't drink, at least not in the Scandinavian way – that is, to oblivion. But there was something in Rolf's face, a loneliness, that made Hal want to keep him company.

'Rolf, you're a bad influence on me,' Hal said affectionately. Knocking back the last of his drink, he held out his glass.

*

Berg poured the vodka and sat back. Thank God that was over and done with. He'd done rather well, he thought: almost faultless in fact. Hal hadn't even asked what happened next.

Best to get on to something else though, just to be on the safe side. 'You should have brought Mrs Johansen along tonight,' he said. 'She's quite a character. No chance of your project being ignored while she's around.'

'Yes, she's good news, isn't she?' Hal grinned like a rather amiable puppy, and Berg realised the drink had taken effect.

'Odd that she married Jan.'

'How do you mean?'

'I would have thought they had little in common.'

Hal gave him a slightly pitying look as if he had missed something blindingly obvious. 'But they compliment each other perfectly. It's because they're so different that it's such a success.'

'Ah, I see.' Berg said no more; he was a cynic on these matters. 'Got a girl in your life, Hal?'

Hal made a rueful face. 'Too busy to get serious.'

And too honourable, thought Berg. Hal was the sort who'd want love and commitment before getting seriously involved. Not that Hal hadn't played the field until quite recently – once he'd actually pinched a girl from Berg, though Berg knew he hadn't realised it at the time: an extremely beautiful Swede who was very choosy about her men and had been much keener on Hal than she'd ever been on Berg. Berg hadn't felt the slightest rancour; he wasn't the possessive sort.

'Katya liked you a lot,' Berg remarked.

'Ah.' Hal gave a long slow smile of reminiscence. 'She *was* lovely. But what about you, Rolf? Anyone special?'

Berg gave a short conspiratorial laugh. 'There's always someone special.'

'Until the next one turns up?' The disapproval was gentle and affectionate.

'Yes, until the next,' Rolf admitted with a shrug.

The telephone rang. It was after ten. Isabella maybe. But

more probably the office. Apologising with a wave of the hand, he went to his desk to answer it.

A firm male voice said: 'Is Major Starheim there?'

Berg glanced at Hal in surprise. 'Yes. One moment.'

Hal made an is-it-really-for-me face as he crossed the room. 'I didn't think anyone knew I was here.'

Berg thought: Nor did I.

Hal took the phone from Berg's hand. 'Hello ... Yes ... Thrane! How –'

Berg went back to his chair and picked up his glass.

'What?'

Berg sipped his drink and stared at one of his best lithographs. 'No ... No ... My *God!*'

It was a cry of horror. Berg swivelled in his seat. Hal had crumpled on to a chair, his head bent, a hand clamped over his eyes.

Berg got rapidly to his feet and walked over.

Hal was groaning, like an animal in pain. Only his mouth was visible below the hand, twisted back in a ghastly grimace. The hand that held the phone was white at the knuckles.

Berg thought: Somebody's died.

Finally, after a long while, Hal spoke again, his voice rough and unsteady. 'Yes. I'll come ... What? ... Yes, I'm leaving now.' Slowly he replaced the phone. His face was deathly white.

Berg put a hand on his shoulder. 'Hal? *Hal?*'

He rose awkwardly to his feet. Berg had never seen such an expression of blank despair. Hal shook his head slowly from side to side, his mouth open and moving soundlessly. Finally he cried out, a bitter cry of rage and anguish.

'*Hal!* What is it!'

The reply was a long time coming.

'Jan ... *Jan*. And Mattis.'

Berg turned the possibilities over in his mind. An appalling accident? An avalanche? A car smash? Or ...

He took Hal by the shoulders. 'I'm so very sorry. What happened?'

Hal didn't reply, but staggered towards the hall. Rolf followed him and helped him on with his coat.

'What happened?' Berg repeated.

Hal shook his head again, as if he didn't trust himself to

speak. He reached for the door. At the last moment he paused and seemed to hear Berg's question for the first time. 'They're ... they're dead. Shot. But why? Why?' He searched Berg's face for the miraculous answer he knew he would never find.

It took a moment for the words to sink in.

Then it was Berg's turn to feel a jolt of horror, and he had to twist quickly away so that Hal wouldn't see the shock in his face.

*

Berg paced off along the dark quay, hands thrust angrily in his coat pockets, and came to a sudden halt. Spinning on his heel, he stamped back to Alex and said through clenched teeth: 'But how could they have been escaping?'

'I know little more than you, my friend – just what was contained in the official protest,' Alex replied. 'The men were on the Soviet side of the border, heading for Finland. One assumes the guards thought they were common criminals – defectors to the West.' He spoke with the weary regret of someone who half expects men to do foolish things. In the distance a large brightly lit ferry manoeuvred into its berth. Alex watched it doggedly, as if it was his purpose for standing on the quay.

The man's nervousness was almost palpable. Berg thought angrily: The sod wants to be rid of me. As if to confirm it, Alex kept glancing over his shoulder, apparently obsessed by something at the far end of the quay.

'What the hell're you looking at? You weren't followed, were you, for God's sake?'

'No. No.'

Berg felt helpless, as if he were drowning in mud. He exclaimed: 'For Christ's sake, Alex.'

Alex glanced over his shoulder again. 'I told you. I know nothing.'

'You're lying!'

The Russian looked miserable. 'My friend, what can I say? I merely do what I'm told. That's all I ever do.'

Berg succumbed to impotent rage; he had a strong desire to squeeze the life out of that big fat throat. 'That's it then, Alex!

No more meetings. No more cosy chats.' He could hardly speak. 'One of them was my *friend*, you bastard!'

'Friend?' Alex repeated vaguely. He was staring openly towards the square. Suddenly he stiffened and, gripping Berg by the arm, said in a voice heavy with relief: 'Look, *I* cannot tell you much, but ...' His eyes flicked to the right and with a small apologetic wave he sidled away.

For a moment Berg didn't understand, then he saw someone walking briskly towards him, someone Alex nodded to as he passed, and he realised this man had been sent to talk to him.

The man approached.

The feeble light from a nearby warehouse fell on his face.

Berg's stomach gave a violent twist of recognition.

Niki.

The Russian stood before him. The two men stared at each other for a moment.

Niki chuckled gently. 'Fifteen years. You look just the same.'

But *he* didn't. He looked quite different: plumper, affluent. He was beautifully dressed in a well-tailored double-breasted coat with deep lapels, a pale cashmere scarf and fur hat.

But the intelligent knowing eyes were the same.

Berg suppressed a fierce anger: how dare they do this to him? How *dare* they?

And yet – Niki must know the truth of what had happened: why else would he be here? And there was one thing Berg had to know: a question that gnawed at him continuously, like a wolf snapping at his heels. Now, without preliminaries, he spat it out. 'Why did they die?'

'Ah. The Norwegians?' Niki's voice was a sigh of regret. 'An unfortunate accident.'

Berg made an effort to keep his voice calm. 'How? Why?'

Niki drew a deep breath. 'Believe me, it would have been infinitely preferable to have got the two of them alive. Then there would have been a proper trial and – well, shall we say we would have come out of it looking a little better.'

'So what the hell went wrong?'

He made a wide gesture. 'Rolf, the guards had orders to stop anyone trying to cross the border. They saw two men. They warned them. The warnings were not heeded. They shot them. It was regrettable. But it happened.'

Some of the tension went out of Berg's body. 'But why were they on the wrong side of the border? *Why?*'

Niki shrugged. 'We'll never know. The point is, they were. It was their own doing.'

Berg examined his face. His expression was unreadable. Berg said resentfully: 'How do I know it's the truth?'

'You don't.' His voice was sweetly reasonable. 'But did I ever lie to you in the past, Rolf?'

Berg gave a small mirthless laugh which turned into a violent shiver. 'That I certainly don't know.'

Niki touched his arm. 'Come. Walk. It's too cold to stand around.' They began to walk towards the far end of the deserted commercial quay. 'You must think positively, Rolf,' the Russian said calmly. 'Despite the – er – unfortunate aspects of the affair, it is already a major incident. It will strike a hard blow. I'm pretty sure it will bring this government down, you know.'

'What?'

'Our official protest will be on the front pages of newspapers all over the world. Finland will be up in arms at the violation of her territory. In due course the CIA's involvement will be revealed, and then the government will have to answer for it. The incident will grow and grow. There's going to be an enormous row, Rolf.'

The news charged around Berg's head. He felt as if he'd unleashed a mad tiger which had run amok. Yet Niki was too damned confident by half. There was one rather important aspect of the affair he seemed to have forgotten. Berg pointed out caustically: 'Shooting two men in the back isn't going to endear you to the world.'

Niki gestured with upturned hands. 'We can't be blamed for shooting two foreign agents caught on our territory in the act of breaking every imaginable law. No, it is the country responsible for training and sending the agents who must bear the consequences. And that is Norway – in partnership with the CIA, of course.'

Berg stared out across the black water towards the wide expanse of Oslo Fiord. Navigation lights gleamed and winked in strange rhythms like glow-worms in a darkened garden.

'They weren't agents.'

'What? Well – agents, spies; these are words. The men were

110

recruited and trained ... They were paid. They were dressed as Lapps, I know. But even if they were Lapps it doesn't change the fact that they were agents going to meet a spy.'

Berg shook his head. Niki didn't know everything after all. He said, 'You're wrong.'

Niki gave him a long stare. 'Oh?'

'They were amateurs. It was a one-off. One was a Lapp called Mattis Hetta and the other was an explorer called Jan Johansen. Did you know that?'

Niki shook his head.

'Johansen's well known here, Niki. He was a climber, an explorer. No one will believe he was an agent. They'll think he crossed the border accidentally – innocently – and got ruthlessly shot in the back.' He added sarcastically: 'I assume it *was* in the back?'

'They'll know the men were recruited, Rolf, they'll know.'

'They won't believe it! Johansen was Starheim's right-hand man. They did the Northwest Passage together. No one's going to believe he was a trained agent!'

Niki thought for a moment. 'Why do you think they chose him, Rolf? Because he wasn't in the military, that's why. They wanted the whole episode to look innocent.' He wagged his finger. 'That's almost worse than sending a trained agent, don't you think?'

A chill wind whistled across the water. Niki looked across the wide basin to the dark high walls of ancient Akershus Fortress, behind which were the headquarters of the Norwegian Defence Command. He stared for a moment, as if contemplating the vast array of Nato secrets it contained then, waiting for Berg to fall into step beside him, began to wander back the way they had come.

Niki made a small exclamation. 'But of course – you must have known him, this Johansen?' He raised a hand to forestall Berg's reply. 'I've read all your articles, Rolf. I've followed your progress.'

Berg pursed his lips in annoyance. He had the feeling Niki knew more about his life than he did himself.

Niki paused under a lamp. 'Look, I'm sorry Johansen died.' He shrugged to emphasise his regret. 'But blame those who sent him.' A speculative look came into his eyes. 'Perhaps it was

Starheim himself, eh? What do you think? Am I right?'

Berg hesitated, realising with a slight shock that he was probably right.

Niki nodded knowingly. 'But of course it was. Of course.'

A hot anger came over Berg. There seemed no limit to Niki's probings, as if he was intent on reasserting his power over Berg. 'Don't drag more people into this, you bastard! Don't spin your bloody webs.' Making the most of his indignation he thrust his face close to the Russian's. 'In fact, I've had enough. Enough. I don't believe your accident story. I don't believe that the whole thing was bloody accidental. No more, Niki. I've had it.'

He sensed Niki's alarm and felt a moment of vicious satisfaction.

'Had it, Rolf? In what way?'

Berg's confidence rose. 'In the way that there'll be no more little meetings with Alex, Niki. Oh, I'll go on writing my stories, don't worry. But I'll never trust you with something like this again.' Berg thought: They'll soon learn not to pressurise me again. He felt a weight begin to lift from his shoulders.

'I'm sorry you feel badly about this, Rolf. After all that we've done for each other.'

Berg almost laughed. 'Stuff you, Niki.'

The Russian dropped his eyes and inclined his head. 'Rolf, may I explain one thing to you. May I explain that our actions in this matter were directed by one overriding consideration – our need to protect a vital asset. Now, when I talk of this asset I am not speaking of the paltry secrets this spy was trying to trade. The man was of little importance – he had access to only minor classified information. But he is relevant to what I want to say, so I will tell you about him.'

Niki started to walk again. Berg hesitated, not wanting to know, then, driven by a powerful curiosity, fell into step beside him.

'He was an electronics design engineer in a Murmansk shipyard, working on submarines,' Niki said. 'Quite talented. Not in a top position. But still in a position of trust. Generous on our part considering he was foreign-born, a guest who had come to us at the end of the war.'

Niki reached into his pocket and, bringing out a packet of cheroots, stuck one in his mouth. The elaborately elegant clothes, the cheroot, all seemed faintly ridiculous: he looked like a cheap gangster in a bad movie.

'So how did this guest repay us? Mmm?' Niki paused, sparking a lighter behind the shelter of his hand, and drawing deeply until the cheroot-end glowed red. 'So how does he repay us? He decides he doesn't love the Soviet Union after all. In fact, he discovers his heart lies back home. He re-establishes his love of his homeland by passing oddments to the CIA through an agent in Kiev. Not a nice way to repay hospitality, was it? But we find out all about him, Rolf.' His voice warmed. 'In fact, we made good use of him. We used him to pass on a little nonsense from time to time. Everyone was happy. No problems. Then, suddenly, he makes this deal. He will escape in exchange for a package of information. We could have had the last laugh, of course, and fed him a marvellous bundle of nonsense to hand over on arrival.' A pause. He added significantly: 'But we couldn't let that happen, Rolf. We couldn't.'

They were approaching the end of the quay and the Town Hall Square, where small fishing boats came to sell their catches direct to the public. A short distance away, two lovers braved the cold on a bench, giggling loudly. The boy was saying: 'It's warm under my coat! Come on, it's really warm!'

The two men turned back into the shadows. A taxi sped by on the main waterfront road.

'We couldn't do it, Rolf, we had to stop him. He was a Norwegian, you see. He had come over in 1945. He had travelled across Finnmark – an epic journey of hardship and deprivation, one gathers – to meet up with the Red Army near Kirkenes.'

Berg faltered and gave the Russian a sharp look.

'The soldiers took him in and fed him, though they had little enough to offer him. The young man was grateful. He joined the army for the last of the fight. He stayed on in Russia after the peace. He wanted to learn the language and complete his technical training. His new country was generous. He was given every opportunity, every advantage. Nothing was too much trouble –'

Berg felt slightly sick. He held up his hand, but there was no stopping Niki.

'He had tuition,' said the Russian, 'a nice place to live ... He was bright, you see, gifted.'

Petter. He was talking about Petter

Niki paused. 'So you see, Rolf, when it came down to it we couldn't let him go. He would have nailed you. Nailed you in his first breath. Your name, your happy time with us – everything.'

Berg broke into a hot sweat.

'So you see, he had to be stopped.'

The realisation hit Berg like a blow. 'You mean –'

'Stopped from crossing the border. That's why the guards had their orders.'

'And –'

'Oh, he was stopped.'

Berg stared blankly at the Russian.

'For you, Rolf. All for you. You see, *you're* our vital asset.'

Then Berg knew. He'd never been free. And now he never would be.

Eight

Sonja. He had to fix Sonja.

He found a phone box near the harbour and called her flat.

The number rang and rang. It was almost midnight; Sonja never stayed out late. And where was the sick mother? He felt his first pangs of alarm.

He kept trying, first from another call box, then from his flat.

He must speak to her. Otherwise her imagination might make two and two into five.

Unpleasant possibilities seeped into his mind: that she already knew about the Soviet protest and had been called to her office for an emergency meeting; that she had told her colleagues about him, that at this very moment they were hearing about the second Erik Leif.

He built himself into a rage of indignation. Niki should have given him more time to protect himself!

He dialled Sonja's number continuously. Twice it was engaged and his hopes rose. Then it didn't answer again and he realised someone else might be trying to call her too. The flat became stifling and he went out again.

He found another phone box. Should he try her office? No, that would be madness – or would it?

He dialled her flat again.

It answered almost immediately.

Sonja's voice. 'Hello.'

He regained his breath.

'Hello?' she repeated.

'It's me. Where've you been?'

'Erik!' She sounded pleasantly surprised. 'Oh, we went out to a cousin's at Drammen and the car wouldn't start on the way back. I've left Mother in Drammen and –'

'You've been out all day?'

'Yes – why?'

He felt limp. 'I have to see you. *Now*. I'll be waiting at the university. Outside the administration building.'

'What's wrong?' Her voice was low and panicky.

'I can't talk now. But, look, if anyone else calls, do nothing, say nothing until after you've spoken to me.'

He rang off before she could argue, and drove straight to the university. The moment he arrived he wondered if he'd chosen the right place. The modern university buildings were set in open parkland and, apart from the traffic on the main road, it was very quiet. There was nowhere to hide.

He got a grip on himself: he was thinking like a marked man.

He parked round the side of a building and walked back to where he could watch the approach road.

She was late.

He waited, thinking furiously, yet trying not to think.

Five minutes ... ten. His mouth was dry, his skin cold. He forced himself to stay calm.

At last. Lights. Coming slowly. Hesitantly. Drawing in to the kerb.

He gave it a moment, waiting in the shadows. No other lights appeared. No strange sounds.

He stepped out and went quickly over to the car. He opened the passenger door and got in.

She was looking frightened, her eyes round and white, her chest rising and falling like bellows. He realised: she knew.

He said immediately: 'We were too late. We couldn't prevent it. The operation in Finland went wrong.'

'I know,' she cried. 'They called me immediately after you did. But what happened?'

Berg realised: this thing could be turned to his advantage. For once he had all the facts at his fingertips. Putting a gentle hand on her shoulder, he gave her the outline of the story, carefully omitting details of the man from Murmansk.

Equally carefully, he managed to mention the names of the two Lapps. A small demonstration of his inside knowledge.

She looked miserable. 'I can't believe it.'

He examined her face, the tone of her voice.

He realised: She hadn't a single suspicion.

The relief was so great he could have laughed.

He should say something. He sighed aloud. 'Given time we might have managed to stop it ...' He shook his head. 'I'm sorry.'

'But why did it happen, Erik?' she asked imploringly. 'What went wrong?'

'The Russians knew, that's what went wrong. They were tipped off by their friend in high places, whoever he is. The only good news, if you could call it that, is ... well, we can't be sure ... but the word is that the leak's from the American end after all.'

She threw him an agonised look. 'What I can't understand is why they were *shot*, Erik. *Why?*'

He looked her straight in the eye. 'We'll probably never know.'

She pushed up her glasses and rubbed her eyes fiercely. 'Oh, Erik, what a mess! It's the worst thing that's ever happened.' Her voice broke and he saw that she was near to tears. 'I feel those men were our responsibility. I feel we've – failed them. Oh dear, this is awful ...' She found a handkerchief and blew her nose loudly.

'You mustn't blame yourself,' he said briskly. 'It really isn't your fault.'

He leaned over and gave her a long hug.

'By the way ...'

Drawing a long shuddering breath, she gave a sharp little nod to show she was listening.

He suddenly felt very confident.

He asked: 'Was Starheim involved in this?'

*

It was morning, Hal realised. There were people in the streets, cars parking, defence staff entering the castle.

Thrane touched his arm. The two men made their way out and into the back of the waiting car. The car threaded its way out of the Akershus compound and down towards the harbour, heading west.

A fine sleet fell, spinning in desultory yellow whorls around

117

the streetlamps. A bus hissed past, its passengers grey and blank-faced behind the steamy windows.

Hal stared, unseeing. His anger was temporarily exhausted, burnt out by the all-night meeting. All he felt now was a bottomless despair, a chilling hopelessness that engulfed him in a fog-like apathy, dulling everything, even the pain.

The rush hour wasn't yet in full swing and in no time he recognised the street before hers, then, all too soon, the final corner.

The moment had almost come. Dread pulled at his stomach. Friday – the taxi-ride, the hasty goodbye, the last sight of Ragna dashing into the apartment building – seemed so long ago. How long? He couldn't think.

They turned into the street.

The car slowed.

Hal said to the driver: 'It's further along.' Something caught his eye; he looked past the driver. There was a knot of people standing half-way up the street. As the car approached, some of them spread out in a fan. But it wasn't until the waiting group started peering excitedly in the direction of the car and aiming their cameras that Hal finally realised.

He exchanged glances with Thrane and said in horror: 'What the hell –'

Thrane jumped forward and said to the driver: 'Accelerate! Don't stop! Quickly. Back to the Akershus.'

Hal grabbed Thrane's arm. 'No! No! We stop here! I'm getting out! D'you *hear* me?'

Thrane threw him a fierce look, seemed on the point of arguing, then gave a sudden nod. 'Driver, stop as planned!'

The car accelerated then ground to a halt in front of the apartment building. Immediately the newsmen pressed in around the car. Faces were thrust against the windows.

Thrane pushed the door open and led the way out. As Hal followed there was a crackling of flashbulbs and a babble of voices. 'Major Starheim – please, do you have any comments on the border incident?'

'Major Starheim, had Johansen been on one of these expeditions before?'

He ran up the steps. The voices cackled on, intrusive, hideous, bellowing Jan and Mattis's names like so much public property.

'How do you feel about Johansen and Hetta's deaths, Mr Starheim?'

How did he feel?

He jerked around, ugly with rage, wanting to hit out at them.

Thrane hissed, 'Don't!' and, grabbing his arm, pulled him inside the building. 'You mustn't talk to them, you *mustn't*!'

'The bastards!'

Thrane led the way up the stairs. 'They're just doing their job.'

'They seem to know a hell of a lot!'

Thrane's head jerked up, and he paused in mid-stride. 'Yes, they do, don't they?' He looked shaken.

Hal grabbed his arm. 'How do they know?'

He shrugged. 'Soviet sources.'

'But the identities. How do they know *that*? Christ, this whole thing stinks!'

Thrane didn't reply but started up the stairs again.

They reached the second-floor apartment and rang the bell. The door was opened as far as the chain. Eventually they were let in by a woman wearing jeans and an artist's smock. The woman said: 'She's ready. I hope you're going to keep the press away from her. They've been pestering us for hours.'

The woman disappeared. Hal waited, his heart like lead.

There were murmuring voices, a door opened, the woman-friend came out.

Then, in one fluid movement, with hardly a sound, Ragna was in the room.

She stood before them, very white and very still. Her clothes looked too big for her.

Hal stepped forward.

Tentatively he reached for her hand. In a small but distinct gesture of refusal, she pulled it away. She said in a flat monotone: 'I don't want to talk. I just want to get home as soon as possible.'

Hal dropped his hand awkwardly. 'We've come to take you to the airport.'

She waited passively, looking at the wall. Thrane picked up the suitcase that stood by the door. The woman-friend took a handbag off a chair and hooked it over Ragna's arm, then embraced her strongly. The two women clung together for a moment, then pulled back. The woman-friend turned away, crying gently.

The party made its way slowly out of the apartment and down the stairs. As they came into the hall Hal said: 'The press are outside, I'm afraid. Just walk straight towards the car and ignore them completely.'

She said nothing but he could see that she had understood.

Hal gripped her arm and, as Thrane opened the front door, led her out.

The pack was waiting.

A few flashguns popped. Some reporters looked as though they were about to speak. Hal looked daggers at them. They stood back in respectful silence.

Some decency at least.

But the moment Ragna bent her head to climb into the car, they closed in again.

'Major Starheim, did the men have orders to cross the Soviet border?'

'Please – could you tell us if the men were trained for this work?'

Hal followed Ragna into the car.

As he twisted into his seat one voice rose above the others.

'Major Starheim, could you confirm your part in the operation?'

Hal reached for the handle to pull the door closed.

The hectoring voice shrilled: 'Major, can you confirm that you were involved in the operation? That you were in charge –'

Hal slammed the door shut. The car shot off.

The last words hung heavily in the silence. A vice seemed to close around Hal's heart.

Slowly, he turned to Ragna.

She was staring at him, a troubled look in those enormous dark eyes. As he met her gaze her eyes narrowed slightly, as if she had read something from his expression; something that confirmed her inner thoughts.

She dropped her eyes suddenly and looked away.

PART TWO
January 1963

Nine

Thrane crossed the hotel lobby and peered through the plate-glass window. Very dark; strong wind; snow swirling down the street. Tromso by morning. He turned back to the taxi driver. 'It doesn't look that bad.'

'The boat won't be running.'

'But are you sure? Can't we find out?' For the tenth time that morning Thrane wished he was on official business and had military transport at his disposal.

'The boats don't run in bad weather,' the man said obstinately.

It was the first time Thrane had heard of a supply boat not running. He tried another tack. 'Well, how *do* I get there then?'

Looking shifty, the driver pulled on his cigarette. He said suddenly: 'He won't see you, you know.'

Thrane looked at him in astonishment. 'What?'

'Starheim. He won't see you. You'll be wasting your time.'

Thrane relaxed. So that was it. 'I'm not a journalist. I'm a friend of his. He'll see me.'

'That's what the last one said. It didn't make any difference.'

'Good Lord,' Thrane commented, 'they still bother him, do they?'

'Now and again. But they never have any success.'

'Look,' Thrane said patiently, 'I'm an army officer, a former colleague of Starheim's.' He took out his ID and passed it briefly in front of the man's face. 'Believe me, he'll be happy to see me. Now I'm told you can take me to the boat. So how about it?'

The man thought for a long time. Finally he made up his mind and, with a shrug, indicated grudgingly that Thrane might accompany him out to the car. But not without a last passing

123

shot. 'Well, don't blame me if he won't see you.'

'How long will it take?' Thrane asked as they set off.

There was a long pause. 'Depends.'

Thrane gave up – he knew a brick wall when he saw one – and settled back in his seat. No doubt the fellow's intentions were good. Hal's name still had the power to arouse strong feelings and fierce loyalties. Hal's name, and that of Pasvik.

Pasvik.

Three years ago it had been nothing but a river that happened to flow along a border.

But international incidents need names, and so the Pasvik Border Incident had been born, or 'Pasvik' for short. People would say: 'After Pasvik.' Or 'in view of Pasvik'. Or 'If it hadn't been for Pasvik'. A part of the nation's vocabulary.

Although to Thrane's secret relief it had been overshadowed a few months later by another event. The U2 Incident. That, too, had been a nasty shock to the country. The fact that US spy planes had been using Norwegian bases was awkward enough, but for the Norwegian government to have to admit it hadn't been aware of the flights was a national humiliation.

At least the incident couldn't be laid at FO/E's door. Which made a change.

They came to a jetty. After a long wait, a ferry loomed out of the greyness and they drove on. It started across the main lead towards one of the larger islands. Thrane guessed the supply boat must leave from there.

The driver lit a cigarette and the car interior filled with smoke. Thrane got out for some fresh air. He had no problem finding it – it was forced down his throat by the buffeting wind.

The temperature was icy. He pulled up the collar of his jacket and walked to the boat's side. The sky had lightened a little. Looking up the lead to the north, Thrane could just make out the end of one island and the beginning of the next. If he'd got his geography right, Revoy must be just beyond that.

By screwing up his eyes he thought he could distinguish land in the right place: an indistinct shadow, a faint suggestion of darker grey in a slate-coloured sea.

But then the weather closed in and everything blended into a dense twilight.

Hal scraped the snow aside and examined the base of the sapling. Quite dead. He sat back on his heels and looked thoughtfully at the blackened upper stems of the aspen. He decided, finally, that the topsoil must be too thin at this spot. He refused to accept Arne's prediction that the valley would never support anything but birch. Birch grew fairly easily; Hal wanted something different: a delicate varied woodland of rowan, aspen, bird-cherry and willow. This aspen hadn't survived, but he would plant another in a better place, and make it grow, even if he had to wrap the entire plant in sackcloth every winter.

He hadn't been so stubborn about the shrubs near the house. He had admitted defeat over the lilac and flowering cherry killed by frost two winters ago. But a cluster of six young willows had taken well in the hollow to the west of the house, and he had walled in a plot where, in addition to the usual potatoes, carrots and turnips, he had grown leeks, lettuce and maize. Most farmers didn't bother with such difficult crops, and stuck to root vegetables, cattle, hay, and fish, but Hal enjoyed the challenge of growing a wider variety of things.

His neighbours thought he was mad.

But from the moment he'd come to live permanently at Brattdal he'd wanted the place to be more than just a self-supporting farm. It gave him immense satisfaction to think he was creating something special, something beautiful and lasting. And why not? The mixed woodland, once established, would stop the wind howling down the valley and provide shelter for a whole range of plants and flowers. Slowly he would extend it, adding new shrubs and trees in fenced enclosures, until in the summer, the whole valley would be ringed with greenery and colour.

Most of the trees were coming along all right. Making the farm self-supporting was taking a little longer.

He cut down the dead aspen, checked the animal defences round the remaining saplings, and whistled for Bamse. The wind ripped the sound from his lips.

He looked up towards the head of the valley. The col was obscured by low cloud racing over the ridge and pouring down the slopes, like water flowing over a dam. He whistled again, and Bamse finally appeared, a small grey shape floundering through a patch of heavy drift, his nose close to the snow. Game was scarce, but Bamse never gave up hope.

Hal walked slowly down towards the house, stomping through the thick snow. The snow had come very early this year, with several exceptionally heavy falls since November. The temperature had been unusually low too, down to February levels over Christmas. Now, with the worst of the winter still to come, he was beginning to worry about the fodder. He had a variety of stock: a flock of thirty Steigar sheep, a dozen cows, and six goats. Normally he would let the goats out to forage during the short day, but the snow was too thick even for that.

The only animals who didn't need to live in the barn were the ten musk-oxen. Hal could see them now in the bottom pasture near the water's edge. These strange creatures were Hal's greatest experiment and his greatest success. Dark and primeval, with long low-curving horns and skirts of dense shaggy hair which brushed the ground, looking at a distance like small American buffalo with trailing coats, they weren't oxen at all, nor even cattle, but overgrown members of the goat-sheep family.

Once, a long time ago, they were thought to have ranged northern Scandinavia, but now they were found only in eastern Greenland and Arctic Canada. Hal had imported them specially.

It was impossible not to develop a liking for the beasts. Not only because they were thriving – for which Hal was extremely grateful – but because they were fiercely independent. One ram had charged him three times. The score was two escapes to Hal and one hit to the ram. The hit had taken the form of a powerful butt, a decidedly painful encounter which had left Hal with a two-inch scar on his backside.

The musk-oxen were a success. But there had been failures and a number of ventures which had fallen somewhere in between: an attempt to grow highly prized cloudberries had succeeded, only for the goats to knock down the fencing and consume the entire crop; wild strawberries had flourished one season and failed the next; an unusual strain of oats had failed to ripen in the lower valley but managed to seed itself in a couple of patches half-way up the hillside. You never knew

126

what would work, but it was a hell of a challenge to find out.

He paused just above the house and looked down the valley. He often paused like this to contemplate the weather, the sky, the light. The scene was never the same. Today the waters of the wide sound were steel-grey, and the sky dark and streaked with long strands of wind-torn cloud. Angry, cold weather.

But then in summer the days were long, the light continuous, the growth abundant. Infinite variety; he never tired of the place.

Bamse caught him up at the door and they entered the house together. The midday meal never varied: cheese, cold meat, bread, bottled fruit or, if Arne had been to town recently, fresh fruit. Bamse had dried fish and, when Hal was feeling generous which was nearly all the time, a ration of cheese. Hal took his main meal at six in the afternoon. The evenings varied according to season. In winter he spent long hours at his desk working on his research papers. He had two projects in hand at present: a study of survival clothing for the Army, and a study for Oslo University into the feasibility of introducing musk-oxen to Arctic Norway on a commercial scale. In summer he tried to keep the written work to a minimum, and spent the long daylight hours on the farm, or fishing, or tinkering with *Skorpa*'s engine or improving the farm buildings.

Recently he had started another project which took him into the boathouse for hours at a time.

Now, as always, he spent a bare ten minutes eating before going back to work. He never sat idle for long. Idleness led to introspection which never did any good. Life had to be lived with the minimum of self-indulgence, and he arranged his time accordingly.

He strode up to the barn and began to muck out the cattle. He worked at a fast pace, shovelling the manure into a barrow and carting it to a small silo for rotting down in the summer. He worked fast and energetically, pushing himself hard, so that his body would feel well used and dog-tired at the end of the day. It was the only way he could be sure of a good night's sleep.

After an hour the job was finished and, sweating well, he paused at the barn door to pull on his jacket and think about the remaining chores.

Something caught his eye. He became very still. A figure was climbing the path up to the house. And it wasn't Arne.

A sudden hot anger rose in Hal's throat. Strangers meant only one thing.

Bamse ran on ahead, growling. Hal strode down the hill, round the house, and emerged at the front, ready to repel boarders.

The approaching figure circled the growling Bamse warily, then looked up and waved. There was something familiar about him.

Recognition suddenly came.

Thrane.

Hal's first reaction was one of surprise and pleasure, quickly followed by vague alarm.

Thrane wouldn't have come all this way for a social call.

Nevertheless he managed a brief smile as Thrane strode up, panting hard. 'Welcome,' Hal said. 'Not many people come to Revoy in January.'

They shook hands. Thrane said: 'I was just passing – if you could call it that. On my way back from Kirkenes. I would have let you know but –'

'I know. I'm not on the phone.'

'I did try your neighbour. There was no reply.'

'He's been in Tromso.'

Thrane sighed. 'Wish I'd known. He might have given me a lift.'

They turned towards the house.

'Quite a place you have here,' Thrane said. 'I didn't realise it was quite so – well, extensive.'

'I added the large barn two years ago. There was only the *stabbur* before.' Thrane admired the ornate wooden food store which stood just above the walled vegetable garden.

They climbed on to the veranda and Hal held the front door open for him. 'In fact I am having a telephone installed. This summer. I already have electricity. It's made a lot of difference. Wind-up gramophones can lose their charm.'

They hung up their coats and removed their boots. Thrane wandered into the hall. 'What a beautiful place,' he said admiringly.

'Thank you. Will you have some coffee?' Hal led the way

into the kitchen and put the kettle on. Thrane sat down at the table.

Impatient with the niceties, Hal broached the subject that Thrane must surely have come about, saying: 'Thanks for your last letter.'

'I wish there'd been more to report.'

'I was grateful for what you could tell me.'

Silence. Hal waited expectantly, but despite the cue Thrane seemed happy to wait for the coffee to appear.

Had he come about something else then? Surely not.

The original FO/E inquiry into the Pasvik Incident had taken place more than two years before. Not having been in FO/E, and worse still, having resigned his commission, Hal had not been permitted to know the result. Thrane, technically sworn to secrecy, had taken quite a chance and dropped Hal enough pointers for him to build up a picture of the findings.

An accident, the inquiry had concluded. Resulting from misjudgement on the part of the two men, which had led them to cross the border.

The political judgements had been much more public, of course. There had been an outcry, rows in the National Assembly, endless recriminations in the press. When the U2 Incident occurred a few months later it had seemed as if the government must surely resign. It had survived in fact – just. But there had been a distinct shift in public opinion. Though still pro-Nato, the Norwegian people were no longer in favour of limitless co-operation with the US and Nato. In a popular move, nuclear weapons had been banned from Norwegian soil.

Now, almost three years later, the fuss had died down. It was all over.

Except that Pasvik would never be over for Hal, because the doubts never went away.

And Thrane had doubts too, Hal was sure of it, although he never voiced them openly. That was why he kept the file open. That, Hal had presumed, was why he was here.

Hal put the coffee on the table and sat down.

'I didn't come about that,' Thrane said, reading his mind.

Hal shot him a questioning glance.

But Thrane wasn't ready to talk yet. He said conversationally: 'I gather you still get unwelcome visitors.'

'What? Oh, you mean, journalists? Yes. Now and then. There was an American writing a book on the CIA. Came all the way up here. I didn't see him though. I don't see anybody. It's easier that way.'

Thrane nodded. There was a slight pause. 'How about the farming then?' he asked pleasantly. 'How's it going?'

Hal gave a wry laugh. 'Nothing wrong with it that two more pairs of hands and endless money wouldn't cure.'

'So how do you manage?'

'With difficulty. A place like this isn't really designed to be run single-handed. I manage with Arne's help, and a couple of students in the summer. But it's hard, I don't pretend it isn't.'

They talked on for a while. Hal laid out a meal of smoked fish, smoked meat, cheese, jam and bread.

'You're most kind,' Thrane said, and looked as though he meant it. Hal began to wonder if he'd got it wrong, and Thrane had come simply out of friendship. Yet they weren't close – impossible under the circumstances. Just united by events.

Thrane said: 'Don't you find it hard here in the winter? It must be very lonely.'

'I write a lot, I read, I listen to music. I go to Tromso sometimes. Or friends come to visit me here.' He gave a dry laugh. 'I think it makes them feel adventurous.'

Thrane buttered some bread and asked quietly: 'But no more adventuring for you?'

Hal's heart squeezed uncomfortably. Time never softened that question. Especially when an American expedition was poised to conquer the West Ridge that very summer. His own expedition had been cancelled immediately after Jan's death. Even if he'd had the heart to go ahead with it, which he hadn't, the project would have foundered: the sponsorship offers had evaporated overnight.

He stood up and refilled the coffee pot. 'No. No adventuring for me. I don't want it any more.'

Hal brought the refilled pot to the table.

'How's Ragna Johansen?' Thrane asked. 'I wrote to her some time ago, but she didn't reply.'

Was this leading somewhere? Hal answered cautiously: 'You mustn't mind her. She tears up letters from the military.'

There was a pause. 'But not letters about the proposed installation near Kaafiord?'

Hal looked up sharply. Now he had a very good idea of why Thrane had come. 'Ah. Probably not,' he agreed. 'But then she feels very strongly about what's happening there.'

Thrane frowned. 'And er – so do you, I gather.'

Hal thought: Ah, now we have it. 'I have no argument about the installation itself,' he said evenly. 'Just its location.'

'But it's got to go somewhere, Starheim. If another valley were chosen, then another lot of people would object. Nowhere's perfect.'

'Do you know the site at all, Thrane?'

'No-o-o,' he conceded.

'Well then.'

'What's so special about it? Tell me.'

Hal eyed him sharply. Did Thrane really not know? Or was he feigning ignorance in order to probe Hal's stand on the issue?

Hal decided to give him the benefit of the doubt. 'It's located several miles up the main valley of Kaafiord,' he began. 'And then a short distance up to the right, in the mountains bordering the plateau. I imagine it was chosen because of an old track that leads to a disused iron mine – easy to build up into an all-weather road, I suppose. But they didn't do their homework, Thrane!' He gave a small exclamation of disgust. 'Planners behind desks! Doubtless they looked at a map and saw 'wilderness' and thought there couldn't be anything there. Well, I tell you, they're wrong. And if they'd bothered to consult the Lapps they would have found out. But they didn't. Oh *no*.'

Thrane had the resigned look of someone who was going to hear a lot more whether he wanted to or not.

'The Kaafiord Valley and the hills around it are the spring and summer pasture for two families of Lapps,' Hal continued. 'Their reindeer calve there. At calving time does are disturbed by the slightest thing – the smallest noise, other animals, certainly people. Imagine how it'll be when the road's being built – all those heavy trucks and all that terrible noise. And later there'll be the constant toing and froing of personnel.' Hal shook his head. 'It can't be right, Thrane. It can't. I'm not interested in what the installation is for, or why they want to build it in such a remote spot, but they really can't ignore the Lapps' rights.

The people have been using that area for hundreds and hundreds of years.'

Thrane stared at him thoughtfully. 'Why this sudden interest? You were never interested in Lapp issues before, were you?'

He had a point. Hal conceded: 'No ... But then it was impossible for me to get involved in anything – controversial.'

'But now it's all right? Could it be because' – he stared fiercely at his coffee cup – 'because one of these Lapp families are cousins of Mattis Hetta?'

Ah, Hal thought, so he *has* done his homework. 'That did make me more inclined to look into the matter, I suppose. But after that – it made no difference.'

'Are you sure about that?'

Was he? In the sense that Thrane was suggesting, yes. Mattis was dead and gone. He wasn't trying to exact retribution from the military. He said: 'I'm sure, Thrane.'

'So why all this badgering of the authorities?'

That was very simple: a very persuasive woman called Ragna. But Hal didn't feel like telling Thrane about Ragna. He said: 'I became more aware, that's all. Perhaps I'm more inclined to see the underdog's point of view nowadays.'

Thrane gave a loud sigh. 'You wrote to the minister of defence.'

'And two other ministers. *And* the prime minister.'

'And now Ragna Johansen is in touch with the press. Did you know that?'

'Yes.'

'That sort of thing gets you noticed.'

'Ah. Does it now?'

Thrane looked unhappy. 'Listen, I came here as a friend, not in an official capacity. Because I wanted you to – understand just what was involved. You must realise that this installation is not something that can be brought into question and discussed openly like a site for – well, a village hall. Not to put too fine a point on it, it's secret. If this matter becomes an issue –'

'It will, Thrane. It must do.'

Thrane's lips narrowed into a thin white line. '*If* it becomes an issue, then your opposition will be seen as – well, political.'

Hal was silent for a moment. 'I think I can live with that.'

'The people of this country are still pro-Nato,' Thrane said with exasperation. 'They'll see your stand as anti-Nato. They won't like it. They won't understand it. You're going to lose yourself a lot of friends.'

Hal laughed ironically. 'I'm not sure I've got that many friends to lose.'

Thrane leaned back in his seat and shook his head, as if Hal were already a lost cause. 'You'll be marked as –'

'Yes?'

'Someone to keep an eye on.'

'You mean I'll go on a list somewhere. Well – that's another sort of fame, I suppose!'

'They'll wonder who your friends are.'

'Oh, will they?'

'You seem very well briefed on the exact location of this installation. Some people might regard the possession of that knowledge as rather unpatriotic. I don't suppose you'd care to tell me where you got it from?'

'Believe it or not, I don't know.' Hal could look Thrane straight in the eye: it was the truth. 'But I can't see that it matters one way or the other. It doesn't change the fact that the Lapps, who were here a helluva long time before *us*, are in danger of having their rights taken away.'

The major shook his head. 'If only it wasn't an installation, Hal.'

There was a silence. Thrane was beaten and he knew it. Hal felt a sudden sympathy for him; he had meant well. In a spirit of conciliation, Hal said brightly: 'Have a drink!'

Thrane looked at his watch and said wearily: 'No thanks, I've got to get to the jetty to meet the supply boat.' He drained his coffee and stood up.

They walked in silence to the front lobby.

Hal said: 'I appreciate your coming, you know.'

Thrane leant down to pull on his boots. 'You can't win this one, Hal. It's a pity to lose your good name for nothing.'

'My good name! I haven't got one!' Hal exclaimed, trying to keep the bitterness out of his voice.

'You're wrong!' Thrane said crossly. 'Quite wrong.'

But Hal knew he wasn't. People hadn't been able to turn their backs on him quickly enough. They'd crucified him once. They could do it again for all he cared. He didn't care a damn.

Buttoning his jacket Hal opened the door and stepped out into the cold. The wind had dropped a little, the cloud lifted off the sea. The view had opened out, revealing water, light, distant land.

Thrane joined him and, led by Bamse, they walked down the path towards the shore. Thrane was frowning, lost in thought. 'Look,' he said after a while, 'there was something else. Though –' He stopped suddenly. 'Can I trust you, Starheim? Absolutely? I must be sure it won't go any further.'

Hal felt a leap of excitement. 'Of course.'

Thrane nodded as if he'd expected nothing less, and walked on again. 'It may mean nothing, it may not tell us a lot but – well, some very reliable information has come our way ... About the third man.'

Hal almost stopped in his tracks.

'Apparently he was a Norwegian by birth.'

Hal absorbed the information greedily – and immediately felt a keen disappointment. He couldn't see how it was going to help.

Thrane continued: 'As I say, it's probably neither here nor there. But for us it's a clue to his identity. There can't be that many Norwegians resident in the Soviet Union.'

'Very few, I would have thought.'

'They must have gone there at the end of the war,' Thrane went on. 'We're checking the records to see who disappeared at that time. We're also working with a lawyer called Sorensen who specialises in tracing collaborators and Nazi war criminals. He's got an amazing set of files.'

Hal almost stumbled, his mind far away. Eventually he said: 'Thanks for telling me.'

They reached the track. Thrane turned to face him. 'There was a fourth man too, a Russian defector, trying to get out at the same time. They travelled together.'

'And? What happened?'

'Both died. At or near the border. That's confirmed now.'

For some reason Hal thought: Nobody left to talk. 'Thanks for telling me,' he said again. 'You'll let me know? If there's anything else.'

Thrane gave him a reproving stare, like a headmaster eyeing a wayward pupil. 'I can't promise.'

They shook hands and Thrane started along the shoreside track.

Bamse raced ahead of Thrane, making for a distant figure plodding steadily towards them. It was Arne. He and Thrane converged, greeted each other with a brief nod, and passed on their way.

As Hal waited for Arne, he turned Thrane's information over in his mind. It was maddening, but he couldn't see how it was going to help. Just as all the other things hadn't helped: retracing Jan and Mattis's route to the border, finding their camp, sifting through their gear, writing countless letters to intelligence experts.

And yet any piece of the jigsaw, however small, was better than nothing. Or was he wasting his time? Would there ever be a finished picture? And if so, would it show anything? Perhaps it had been exactly as they'd said – a stupid misjudgement, an accident.

Even if it had, even if there was no one to blame, it would be a relief to know.

The snow gleamed feebly. To the east the low cloud had parted in hard horizontal lines, as if cleaved by a knife, revealing gashes of pink light, like layers of a cake. For a moment the wavetops caught the faint colour, but then the speckles of pink faded into the grey of approaching night.

Automatically Hal looked towards the Lyngen Alps, but they were already lost in a heavy band of darkness. When the visibility was poor like this he always missed the sight of their jagged peaks. He remembered what he'd told Thrane about not caring. It wasn't strictly true. There were still days when he hungered for the snow, for the bare simplicity of the old life.

But there wouldn't be any more expeditions. Because nothing was that simple any more. Only perhaps his life here, at Brattdal.

Arne arrived. Not one to waste energy on conversation, he grunted a greeting and handed Hal the post.

Hal glanced quickly through it. Something from Oslo – official by the look of it, a couple of bills, a handwritten envelope which made his heart sink slightly. And –

Ah. A letter from Ragna.

He tore it open and, holding it close to his face, tried to read it. The light was bad, but Ragna's writing was worse.

'. . . *The journalist was a wash-out*,' he managed to make out. '*I almost threw him in the snow! He only wanted to talk about you-know-what. Can you think of any other journalists we could try? And have you heard a single word from the ministry? They are incredible! Aslak and I should be back from Kautokeino on Tuesday night. I'll let you know how we get on. Though I'm sure the Lapps will be disappointed at the lack of progress. Can't blame them. I am.*'

It was signed simply: 'R.'

Underneath was '*P.S. I promise to take care of the Land Rover. Nearly forgot – wrote to that friend of yours, Rolf Berg. Good idea? Only met him that once, but he seemed all right.*'

Arne was wandering off again, talking gruffly to Bamse. Hal considered for a moment, then called: 'Arne, could you look after things tomorrow? And call Ragna Johansen to say I'll be down in the morning?'

Arne raised his eyebrows. 'Tomorrow morning?'

'Yes.'

'It's not Sunday.'

Hal said heavily: 'No, Arne, it's not Sunday. It's Wednesday. But could you tell her anyway?'

Back at the house Hal opened the rest of his mail, leaving the handwritten envelope until last. Eventually he tore it open. The paper smelled strongly of perfume.

It said: 'Shall I come up on the weekend? I could bring food, music, books. Or why don't you come and stay here – there's a party at a friend's house. I'm on my own this weekend. I'd love to see you. Anna-Kristin.'

Hal pushed the letter to one side. He didn't want to deal with it, he didn't want to decide. In fact he hadn't the first idea what he wanted where Anna-Kristin was concerned. He'd met her two months before. She was good-looking and vivacious and he enjoyed her company. But . . .

But he didn't want to pursue it any further.

He went to milk the cows. By the time he'd finished it was six. There were more chores to be done, but his mind kept going to the morning and his trip to Tromso and Ragna and little Kris. Because Ragna had been away he hadn't made his usual Sunday visit, and he'd missed it. And he knew Krisi would have too.

He normally took the boy a small present. What could he take tomorrow?

He had a sudden thought. There was always the project in the boathouse – a rather large present he'd been planning to surprise Krisi with for some months.

Yes, why not? It was almost finished. It would be an awful sweat to get it finished by morning – he didn't dare think of what remained to be done. But it'd be worth it for the expression on the boy's face.

The chores would suffer, of course. He went through the pretence of wrestling with his conscience, then strode down to the water's edge. Throwing open the door to the boathouse, he lit the lamp and surveyed the beautiful sight before him.

Six hours should finish the job. Rolling up his sleeves, he set to work.

Ten

Ragna wiped the tears from her eyes and coughed until her lungs rasped with pain. The Lapps, who seemed totally immune to the choking wood-smoke, glanced at her with good-hearted amusement.

The tepee-like tent, the *lavo*, was ten feet across and about as high, with a floor of birch twigs and, in the centre, a ring of stones in which a fire smoked profusely. Ragna eased herself away from the fire until her back was against the tent side. While the Lapps talked on in their sing-song voices, she pulled a map out of her pocket and peered at it in the semi-darkness, trying to work out exactly where they were.

She and Aslak had come up from the coast in the Land Rover the previous day, driving up the long road into the interior, coming first into Finland and then, via a lesser road which was more of a track, back into Norway. It had been an awful journey, the visibility poor and the road covered in drifts. But finally they had arrived at the town of Kautokeino, perched in the middle of the plateau and, like Karasjok to the east, a traditional winter gathering-place of nomadic Lapps.

They had expected to find the head of the Hetta family, Aslak's uncle Isak, at the wood-built family house. But only the women and children were there. The men, they were told, were away with the herd. After much uncertainty and some exasperation on Ragna's part – the Lapps were not known for their decisiveness – another relation of Aslak's had offered to take them to the herd.

Ragna had looked forward to the journey – she had never been on the plateau in mid-winter before – but when they set out early the next morning it had been dark and viciously cold with a strong wind blowing. Worse still, not having skied since the previous spring, she was rather unfit and had slowed the others down. Finally she had been allowed to ride on the reindeer-drawn sledge – a distinct improvement – but she had become almost rigid with cold. Her romantic image of the plateau in winter had rapidly faded.

After three hours they had finally got here.

But where was here? She made a guess and, putting her finger on the spot, showed the map to Isak. The old man peered at it, frowned deeply and spoke to one of his sons in his own language. Then there was silence. Fighting back another spasm of coughing, Ragna asked Aslak: 'What does he say?'

Aslak kept a straight face. 'He says that maps are not very useful.'

Ragna clamped her lips together. She tried another tack. 'Could he show me the route the herd takes to the spring pasture?'

Aslak looked away, the two sons and the sledge-driver sipped their drinks.

'Well?' Ragna demanded.

The old man turned to her. 'The herd choose the way. I follow,' he said in Norwegian.

'Yes, but – well, it would help tremendously if I knew your *route* into Kaafiord Valley. D'you see?' Her eyes burned so fiercely she had to bury them in her hands for a moment.

When she looked up the old man's eagle-like face was beaming at her and he was holding out a dish of food. She took the food, asking: 'What will you do if they go ahead and build this thing? Can you take the herd somewhere else?'

Too late she remembered that Lapps – or at least remote Mountain Lapps – did not deal in hypothesis; in their opinion it was completely pointless to consider something that had not actually occurred.

The old man was busying himself with his meal. She had the feeling that the conversation, such as it was, was over. With a sigh of resignation, she peered at the contents of the dish. It was impossible to tell what it was. But it could only be reindeer, stewed or stewed. Oh well, she *was* hungry.

She accepted a piece of hard bread. She'd heard about the Lapp bread and how it kept for over a year, and the moment her teeth came to grips with the stuff she knew it must be true. Barely pliable and slightly sweet, it tasted like old leather doused in syrup.

No one talked. Instead there were loud sucking and smacking noises as the Lapps got their mouths round some large bones. Through the gloom Ragna watched, fascinated yet slightly repelled, as they tore at the flesh with their teeth, chucked the bones outside to the waiting dogs, then sucked their fingers. Was it true that the Mountain Lapps never washed? She couldn't believe it, yet a small suspicion remained. It was one of those things one longed to know but could never ask. Like whether they still practised black magic and invoked the devil to put a hex on their enemies.

Old Isak said something in Lappish and, throwing back his head, gave a high-pitched cackle. The others joined in the laughter. Ragna smiled politely.

Whatever these people's customs, she was determined to respect them. Most Norwegians patronised the Lapps, laughing at their *yoiking*, the strange high-pitched, and to the Norwegian ear tuneless, singing, ignoring Lapp history and culture, branding the Lapps primitive and uneducated and unreliable, even pointing out to foreigners that Lapps were 'racially different, you know' as if that established their own superiority. Ragna never let comments like that go unchallenged and had earned herself a reputation for being outspoken and argumentative.

Nothing wrong with that. In fact she was rather proud of it.

She peered at the stew and swallowed a few mouthfuls. It was watery and curiously tasteless. Gagging slightly, she put it hastily aside. The atmosphere was suffocating; she needed to get out. Pulling on her anorak, she dived for the flap, ducked outside and drew in great gasps of freezing air.

Better. After a while she walked away from the tent, eyes half-closed against the wind, and stood looking at the great herd of reindeer scattered far across the wide landscape, hooves scraping at the snow, mouths pulling and chewing at the vegetation beneath.

She tried to estimate the size of the herd. That was another thing old Isak wouldn't tell her. It was too personal a question, Aslak had explained, like asking someone how much he had in the bank. She'd given an ironic laugh at that; she wouldn't mind telling Isak how much she had in the bank, because it was precisely nothing.

After a time Aslak came out to find her.

She said wearily: 'Isak seems to think I'm prying. But I'm only trying to help.'

'I know,' he said. 'Isak does appreciate it, believe me. It's just that old habits die hard.'

'Well – there's not much point in staying. We might as well get back. Or am I hoping for too much?'

'Just wait for them to finish their meal.'

They wandered back towards the tent and sat on the sledge, their backs to the wind, looking out across the plateau. 'My aunt had ten children,' Aslak told her. 'Six of them were born up here in winter, in a tent just like this, in temperatures as low as minus thirty or forty.'

Ragna shivered, pulling her hood closer round her face. It felt that cold now, though she knew it wasn't. 'And they survived?' she asked.

'Seven out of ten did. Not bad for those days. But now my aunt stays in Kautokeino in the winter. Nearly all the women and children do.'

'I don't blame them.'

'No.' There was a note of regret in his voice.

'Isn't it better that way?' Ragna asked.

He shrugged. 'It's inevitable, that's all. Along with TV sets and snow-scooters. One of my aunt's neighbours already has a TV. Soon everyone'll have them. And the Sami will be that much closer to losing their identity.'

Sami. It was the Lapps' preferred name for themselves. 'The answer's to have the best of everything, isn't it?' Ragna suggested carefully. 'To have TVs and snow-scooters, yet keep the culture and traditions ...'

'But you can't do that while the Sami have no pride in themselves and take Norwegian-sounding names and allow Norwegian to be spoken in their schools. Not when all they get for trying to be good Norwegians is to be called *finnfaen* – peasants.' He brushed some snow briskly, almost angrily, off his trousers. 'You may find Isak hard to deal with, but at least he's a true Sami and unashamed of it.'

'Of course!' she said hastily. 'Really – I *admire* him for it!'

141

Aslak stood up. 'I know. Here, give me that map of yours. I don't promise anything, but I'll see what I can do.'

He went back into the tent, leaving Ragna to stare at the endless monotony of the plateau and to feel glad that she'd seen it in winter just this once – and to feel even more grateful that she wouldn't have to see it again.

*

It was late the next day when she dropped Aslak at his home on Kaafiord and drove towards the ferry that would take her across Lyngenfiord. Once across the fiord she would have more driving and two more ferries to catch before reaching Tromso. She was already dog-tired; by the time she got home she'd be dead.

And for what?

She hadn't got a great deal for her three days' hard travelling. Aslak had managed to draw her a line on the map, so she had a rough idea of the migration route, but she still didn't know how many reindeer were involved, just as she didn't know how many calves were born in the mountains above Kaafiord Valley each year. She could just imagine the men from the ministry seizing on her lack of facts with undisguised glee.

She drove dangerously fast along the side of Kaafiord, following the curve of the shore round into Lyngenfiord, only to see the ferry pulling away from the landing-stage.

She swore aloud. And again, harshly. It would be at least an hour and a half before the next ferry. If she hadn't been so tired and if the roads hadn't been so snowed-up she would have turned round and taken the much longer road route.

She parked at the landing-stage and closed her eyes. Within seconds she was sound asleep.

Much later an insistent tapping woke her. She rolled her head round. A smiling face loomed at the window. She vaguely recognised a woman from Tromso. Behind the woman was the local bus, blazing with lights, disgorging foot passengers for the ferry.

Ragna slid back the window and said without enthusiasm: 'Hello.'

'Going to Tromso?' the woman asked brightly.

Well, she wasn't likely to be going anywhere else. 'Er, yes,' she admitted. 'Why don't you join me?'

The woman, whose name was Karen – Ragna couldn't remember her other name – was not someone Ragna would normally go out of her way to talk to. But then that went for a lot of people in Tromso. When Ragna had first arrived she'd thought how very friendly and open and uncomplicated the people were compared with down south. Now she saw them quite differently: as provincial, nosy and opinionated.

It was the last three years that had lifted the wool from her eyes. After Jan's death people had reacted in one of two ways. Either they'd been too embarrassed to talk to her, or they'd positively swept her into their circle of friends, like some rare exhibit or trophy, and then debated the Pasvik Incident right in front of her, just as if she wasn't there. The arrogance of it!

But then what could you expect?

She was sounding jaundiced. She thought: But then I *am*.

She managed a pale smile as the woman – *was* it Karen? – got into the passenger seat.

'This is Halvard Starheim's car, isn't it?' the woman asked.

'Yes.'

'Ah,' she said, managing to sound knowing and faintly surprised at the same time.

Ragna turned away and rolled her eyes in irritation. The whole of Tromso had her and Hal virtually married off. It was that damned party line of Arne's. Everyone on the surrounding islands listened in, she knew they did. And to their simple minds, twice-weekly phone calls and regular Sunday visits meant only one thing.

Infuriating. Her relationship with Hal wasn't like that, and wasn't likely to become so.

'At one time I heard you were thinking of moving back to Oslo,' Karen said, in a chatty tone. 'Did you change your mind?'

'Not exactly.'

'Oh. So you're still thinking of going?'

'One of these days.'

The ferry came into sight at last, its lights emerging from the gloom of the fiord.

'Well, I suppose Tromso must seem very quiet compared to Oslo.'

Ragna almost smiled. She could say that again.

'And I suppose having been an actress you like the theatre and that sort of thing.'

'Yes, I do rather.' What she liked was the idea of being in touch with the rest of the world, and the possibility that she might meet intelligent people and have interesting amusing conversations: she loved the idea of feeling alive again.

'A bit of a change for your son. How old is he now?'

'Five.' Ragna made a show of shivering. 'Sorry it's so cold in here.' She restarted the engine. With a bit of luck the noise might deter further conversation.

But no.

'Five's a lovely age,' she said. 'Kristian's his name, isn't it? Who does he take after?'

Ragna didn't answer for a moment. She didn't like speaking Jan's name to people she hardly knew. In fact she had a complete phobia about it. She said: 'No one in particular.'

'Well, it'd be a pity to see you go. Your shop's been quite a thing for Tromso.'

The shop. The albatross round Ragna's neck. Just thinking about it made Ragna feel depressed.

The woman continued: 'We'd all be sorry to see it close.'

'Oh, really?' Ragna replied, genuinely surprised.

'Yes, of course. Such wonderful clothes. Fashion's never got to Tromso so quickly. Those sack dresses you had in – quite fantastic. So modern.'

'Did you buy one?'

'Well – no,' she said, adding hastily, 'you didn't have anything in my size.'

It seemed that most of Tromso had failed to find anything in the right size: quantities of unsold sack dresses still littered the rails.

The ferry nudged against the landing-stage at last and lowered its ramp. A van and a car drove off. A small group of foot passengers made for the waiting bus.

Ragna drove on and switched off the engine. As soon as the ferry was on its way, Karen started chattering again. Ragna realised she was a gossip of the first order, the sort who acquired information like a sponge and dispensed it like a fountain.

Ragna barely listened. The time dragged. The lights of Lyngseidet seemed to get no closer at all.

Then a name sprang into the air, and Ragna woke up.

The woman had mentioned Hal.

'Sorry?' Ragna murmured.

'Oh yes, he was there, at her party.'

Hal going to parties? 'Oh.'

'She gives wonderful parties, of course.'

She? Ragna felt a small pang of – she wasn't sure what. 'Does she really?'

'Oh yes. She's made a lot of friends in no time at all.'

'Sorry – who? I didn't catch the name.'

'Anna-Kristin Dahl. I thought you must know her.'

'No, I don't think so.'

'Oh.' There was a hint of relish in her voice. 'She's such a good friend of Halvard Starheim's, I thought ...' She gave a nervous laugh. 'I thought you must know each other.'

'Halvard leads his own life. There's no reason why I should know all the people he knows.'

'No, quite. Exactly so. No reason at all.' Ragna was aware of the woman trying to read her face in the darkness. 'Such a nice man,' she rambled on. 'And so is she, of course. They seem to get on very well.'

Oh, do they? Ragna thought with sudden fury. Why the hell don't I know about this? Why hasn't Hal told me?

'I saw them at that recital last week. You know, the quartet from Oslo. Bach, it was. And some Mozart. We should have more music like that.'

Recitals now. Ragna tried to bite back the question hovering on her tongue but failed. 'Oh?' she said in a casual voice. 'I must have missed that. When was it?'

'A week ago. Er – Wednesday, I think. Yes ... Wednesday.' Now there was a triumphant note in her voice, as if she'd succeeded in catching Ragna out.

Which she had, damn her.

Hal had come to Tromso without telling Ragna – twice. He'd come without even phoning her. And he'd always said that he hated coming to town.

Things had obviously changed, and rather abruptly, and he hadn't even had the decency to tell her. She felt distinctly put out about that.

Yet why should she mind? Did she mind? No, of course not. How could she? It was just that – what? She was used to knowing when he was coming to town. She was used to him visiting Krisi. Yes, that was what surprised her: that he hadn't come to see Krisi.

'And what about you, Ragna?' the woman said. 'Anyone special in your life?'

Ragna gripped the wheel. 'Me?' she said with a light laugh. 'No. No time for all that.' And she suppressed the rush of anguish and self-pity that swept over her.

*

She couldn't avoid driving past the shop. The windows were plastered with sale notices. Stopping for a moment, she peered at the racks visible in the display lights. They still looked jam-packed with clothes.

She drove on, feeling depressed. The shop had been a failure from the word go. She'd got a bit carried away with the fitting-out and the stock-levels, admittedly. But it was the Tromso women who had defeated her: they just didn't buy.

And she'd been so certain it would work. As a sports shop it had been just one of three in the town, but as a clothes shop it had been the only high-fashion store for several hundred miles. You would have thought the women would have fallen over themselves to make use of it.

A few had, of course. But not enough. The outgoings were terribly high – and the income nearly always lower.

At the beginning she'd looked on the business as a welcome challenge, something that she could get her teeth into while she decided what to do with her life. Well, she'd decided what she wanted to do with her life – move to Oslo – but instead of selling the shop at a nice profit and setting herself up in a new life she was trapped here in a morass of debt.

It made her sick to think about it.

The house came into view at last. It was in darkness. Krisi was staying at his grandmother's.

Parking the Land Rover, she slipped and slithered down the icy path. It needed clearing: yet another job to add to a long list that didn't get done.

146

She let herself in and turned on a few lights. There was a pile of mail neatly stacked on the hall table. Her mother-in-law must have been in.

She took the mail into the kitchen and put the kettle on. She glanced through the envelopes. Her heart sank: one from the bank. She put it to the bottom of the pile.

Then an Oslo postmark. Curious, she opened the letter and glanced at the signature. Fred: one of Jan's old climbing friends. She thought: How sweet of him to write. Not all of Jan's friends had bothered to keep in touch. Losing your husband was only half of widowhood, she'd discovered: you also lost status and friends; you became an awkward reminder.

Fred asked after her and trusted she was well. He told her what he had been doing, and how he hoped to raise an expedition to K2 in two years' time.

The letter continued: 'However we're still looking for a leader, someone the climbers will follow and someone the backers will have faith in. There's only one person who fits those requirements, and that's Hal. We've been writing to him for months now. He said he wouldn't consider it, but don't you think he should? He's the only one we want ...'

Ragna narrowed her lips; she had a very good idea of what was coming next.

'... The point is – would you have a word with him? We feel certain he'll change his mind once he realises how much people really want him. His exile is purely self-imposed, you know. I feel he's wasting his life unnecessarily, don't you?'

Ragna slapped the letter down on to the table and, snatching a mug off the shelf, made herself a strong coffee. Impulsively she added a large dash of aquavit.

So, she was to persuade Hal to go off and make something more of his life, was she? That was rich. Hal was the one who was free as a bird, the one who could do just as he pleased. He didn't have to live on that bleak island. For some extraordinary reason he actually seemed to like it there. Well, lucky him. Doing what he wanted. Why should she try to persuade him to do something else?

No, if anyone's life was a waste it was hers.

She poured more aquavit into her coffee and, taking a long gulp, sat down, feeling empty and tired and hopeless.

She also felt ashamed. There had been a touch of envy in that reaction of hers. Hal had talents which were in demand and she couldn't help wishing that she had too.

She thrust her head in her hands. It was this place that got her down. The place and the everlasting winter and the lack of money and the loneliness.

The loneliness.

The first year hadn't been so bad: her fierce determination had kept her going. That and the memories, the feeling that Jan was still somehow there, still loving her, still on her side . . .

But time had worn her down; time had cheated her, removing the warmth of the memories, leaving only emptiness. Now she tried not to think about Jan; she pushed him from her mind. She had learned to think of only one person apart from Kris: herself.

Now she was aware of life passing her by.

Tears dripped steadily through her hands into her coffee cup.

She kept thinking: I'm thirty-two. These are meant to be the best years of my life.

Eleven

Sonja felt sad, of course. But she also felt reborn.

That day she had thrown the last funeral flowers into the rubbish and cleared out her mother's room. She'd packed away everything: ornaments, bedlinen, even the curtains. Then she'd scrubbed the place from top to bottom.

She would give the room a new colour scheme, she decided – pale pink perhaps: so fresh and young, and much more suitable to a spare room.

It would be nice to have people to stay, though she couldn't immediately think who. And of course she'd be able to entertain. Little supper parties, friends dropping in for coffee.

The possibilities opened out endlessly before her, though, like any prisoner suddenly released from a long sentence, she also found the new freedom a little frightening.

But she had no problem about what to do with the money. Mother, who'd always pleaded poverty, had had a surprising amount tucked away. Sonja, rather hurt by this deception, had spent the whole of the previous day in the shops, buying clothes. On her bed lay a wonderful black silk dress with a red jacket.

Passing the bed, she stroked the dress lovingly. By her standards it had been extremely expensive, but it had been worth every penny. She looked marvellous in it.

Seeing the time, she hurried to her desk to scribble a note.

She wrote simply: *Dear One. Worst over. Feeling much recovered. Can't wait to see you. How about a holiday? Love.*

Popping it in an envelope she carefully printed the name 'Lundquist' – a false name of their own invention – and the address on the front.

She'd already written to Erik twice in the last ten days. The first note had been simple but to the point: *Darling, Mother is dangerously ill. I have to be with her. Phone if you can.* The second had been stark: *Mother died this morning. Need you. Call as soon as possible.*

It was the first time she'd pressurised him to call, but her need for him had been so great that she'd thrown caution to the winds.

Sadly, he hadn't called, which meant he must still be out of town. It had been a great disappointment.

She'd been very brave without him, of course. But she couldn't help imagining how much better it would have been with Erik at her side. She enacted little scenes in her mind all the time, scenes where she was being extraordinarily serene and composed, containing her grief with dignity, while Erik looked on admiringly.

Maybe it wouldn't have been exactly like that, but the experience would have drawn them closer together, she knew it. However there was no point in fretting over what might have been. She had the future to think about.

A future without Mother.

She couldn't help feeling a vast and rather wicked relief. She had loved Mother, of course she had. But the last two years had been a nightmare. Mother had said she'd rather die than go to a nursing home, so a nurse had had to come in daily, with Sonja taking over in the evenings. And Mother had become hysterical if Sonja tried to go out too often. Her meetings with Erik had been reduced to one every two or three weeks. Agony.

Now all sorts of delights opened out before her: bringing Erik here to dinner; having him stay all night; maybe even going on holiday together abroad. Why not? Yes, why not!

She almost laughed aloud.

She suddenly saw the time. Six. She mustn't be late. She flew to the bathroom, showered, brushed and lacquered her hair, and carefully applied some make-up.

Then she put on the black dress and red jacket. It looked so smart she almost burst with pleasure.

She left the flat at six-forty, posted her letter to Erik, and got to the National Theatre in plenty of time to meet Elsa in the foyer.

It had been months since she'd been to a theatre, and years –

she couldn't remember how many – since she'd been to a first night. She'd forgotten how overwhelming it was: the bustle, the noise, the feeling of not quite belonging. She felt intimidated by the chattering people, the familiar yet strange faces of actors and politicians, the proximity of fashionable women in their gorgeous clothes. Then she remembered how smart she looked and realised she was being rather silly. She could hold up her head with the best of them.

She was a little disappointed to find their seats were in the upper circle, and right over to one side. But she was determined that nothing was going to spoil the evening. She concentrated hard on the play, a new-wave drama (so the programme told her), full of long involved monologues about the agony of family relationships. She felt sure she must be getting a lot out of it.

During the interval the crush in the bar was so great that they retreated into the auditorium and stood at the front of the circle, looking down on the audience slowly filtering back into the stalls below.

The bells went. The trickle of people turned into a steady flow. Elsa nudged Sonja and pointed to a woman in the moving stream below.

'Hildegard Lindman.'

Sonja nodded. She knew the name. Hildegard Lindman was a famous actress who made films with a top Swedish director. Beautiful, expensively dressed, she was the sort of woman who quite naturally stood out from the crowd, even when one could see little more than the top of her head.

Sonja exchanged a quick grin with Elsa.

The actress seemed to be in a group of several people, all talking, their heads turned to each other, their hands moving expressively.

Beside her was a man with rich blond hair just like Erik's. The man reached out and put a hand on the actress's shoulder. Hildegard Lindman turned and smiled up at him so that Sonja could see her face. The smile was wide, warm, almost a smile of love. The man bent his head to hers and said something which made her laugh.

They stopped at the end of a seat row and waited for people to let them in.

Sonja caught her breath. The man's bent head, the obscured

face – there was something shockingly familiar about him.

Suddenly she went very cold.

The man shuffled along the row, pulled down his seat, settled.

Then he took a sweeping look round the auditorium, his face raised, his expression languid and aloof.

Sonja gaped.

Erik.

The lights began to dim. Elsa whispered: 'Come on!'

He had turned his head away. Sonja gripped the rail, waiting for another glimpse of that face – desperate to be sure, yet horribly certain.

Elsa pulled at Sonja's sleeve. 'The curtain's going up!'

Sonja dragged herself away and, following Elsa, stumbled back to her seat.

The rest of the play passed in a daze of babbling voices. The moment the final curtain dropped Sonja jumped to her feet, pushed her way past the row of applauding people and ran for the stairs. She arrived in the main foyer and paused, breathless, to adjust her glasses. After a moment she decided the stairs would offer the best vantage point. She stationed herself half-way up and waited.

The applause died away, the doors opened, the foyer filled with people queuing for their coats. Sonja kept her eyes glued on the main exit from the stalls. After a time the stream of people thinned. She grew desperate. She couldn't believe she had missed them.

Suddenly it struck her: They would have gone backstage!

Or would they?

Miserable with indecision, she waited a little longer then went to claim her coat. Elsa rushed up to her. 'What on earth's wrong, Sonja? Are you ill?'

Sonja pulled on her coat and, shaking her head, mumbled, 'I have to go . . .'

Leaving the startled Elsa, she hurried round the side of the theatre to the stage door. A group of five or six young people were hovering outside. Sonja retreated across the road to the porch of the Continental Hotel and waited.

Five minutes passed, ten. Now and then the odd person emerged: backstage people, she thought.

It was cold. Her feet began to freeze. She glanced nervously around, aware that she must look conspicuous. Yet she couldn't bring herself to leave.

At last more people appeared, people with loud well-modulated voices and animated faces. Sonja recognised a couple of the actors from the play.

Then *she* was there. Hildegard Lindman. Standing in the doorway, swathed in fur, head turned, waiting for as yet invisible friends. Sonja stared, immobile.

A couple joined Hildegard Lindman and they strolled out on to the pavement. Beautiful people, totally at ease with themselves and the world.

Then *him*. Smiling, coming forward, taking the actress's elbow with easy familiarity.

Erik. There was no doubt.

Sonja pulled back into the shadow of the building, grimacing with humiliation and pain.

The party of four made off briskly towards the bare trees and snow-covered gardens of Eidsvolls Plass, the sound of their high brittle laughter echoing on the air.

Sonja crossed the street and followed, keeping close to the side of the theatre in case they should turn round.

The foursome passed the statue of Ibsen, and headed diagonally across the area in front of the theatre. Sonja hesitated at the corner of the building.

There was a shout. Erik's party paused. Sonja ducked behind the wall, her heart hammering against her chest. She peeped out. Two men had joined the foursome. There was a short animated conversation, then loud goodbyes. The two men were waving and walking towards Sonja, leaving the others to resume their walk.

Suddenly one of the two men stopped and shouted back: 'Hey, Hildegard!'

The actress turned. Her companions stopped.

'Will you be in Stockholm for Ingmar's first showing?'

She called back: 'Yes! Will you be there?'

'We hope so! Bye. Bye, Rolf!'

Erik raised his hand and waved.

Sonja stared, not understanding.

The party set off across the gardens. Sonja followed at a safe distance. They walked briskly, purposefully, crossing the street

153

on the north side of the square and heading into a building. A bright blue sign read: Blom's.

Erik led the way, holding the door open for the others, then they were gone.

Sonja halted, suddenly feeling deflated. What now? She couldn't wait here.

But she couldn't bring herself to leave either. She found a bench under the leafless trees and sank on to it.

How could he?

But he could, very well indeed. That was what hurt the most. He must have been doing this all along. Telling her he was away, while he was actually with women like Hildegard Lindman.

And she knew why, of course. Because the Hildegard Lindmans of this world were beautiful and polished and desirable, and wanted him in return.

She'd always known there must be other women. She'd always known he was too wonderful to be true. Well, here was the proof. She shouldn't be surprised, she shouldn't mind.

Why then did she mind so much? The pain was so great that she actually hurt inside.

Tears slipped down her cheeks. She didn't try to wipe them away.

She suddenly remembered the notes she'd written, the pathetic heart-rending little notes. What must he have thought of them? He'd probably found them childish and over-dramatic. Had he torn them up? Her stomach gave a lurch of humiliation and pain.

Had he ever cared?

She didn't want the answer to that. Standing up abruptly, she wiped the tears roughly from her cheeks. It was her own fault. It served her right. She'd got her just deserts. She should have faced this all along.

Time to go home.

She walked a few steps, then hesitated. Something held her back, and she tried to think what it was.

But of course she knew: burning curiosity. A need to know. Jealousy. Agony.

She walked up to the café at the far end of the gardens, opposite the Storting. They were about to close, but allowed her in for a coffee. She sat in a corner where she could just see the entrance to Blom's. Twenty minutes later the café turned out its lights and she left.

She walked back past Blom's on the opposite side of the road. It was ridiculous to wait: it was already after midnight. Yet she'd come this far – somehow a long cold wait didn't seem to matter much either way.

She waited on the bench, her toes like ice, her body numb.

After a time a taxi drew up in front of Blom's. Some people emerged from the restaurant and got in.

It wasn't Erik and his friends. But that was what they'd do. Order a taxi. And she'd be left like a fool, watching it drive off.

But then she'd need a taxi at this time of night anyway. With a groan, she realised what she should have done right at the beginning. How much money had she? About a hundred kroner, she thought. Enough – maybe.

Running breathlessly to a taxi rank by the theatre, certain that Erik must have chosen this moment to leave, she jumped into a taxi and told the driver to park just short of Blom's. Then she waited, miserable in case she had missed Erik, trying not to hear the remorselessly expensive click of the meter.

Forty-five minutes later a taxi swished past them and pulled up in front of Blom's.

Some people emerged from the restaurant.

Them.

Sonja felt slightly sick.

The foursome paused on the pavement, kissing each other's cheeks, gripping arms.

Then they split into two couples.

Erik and Hildegard Lindman got into the taxi.

Sonja leant forward, clutching the front seat. 'Follow that taxi!'

The driver threw her a strange look, but started off without a word.

They threaded their way through the narrow streets in the centre of town, heading north, then west. Every time they approached a junction Sonja's heart froze in case the lights should turn red just at the wrong moment. One light turned amber as they sped towards it, but the driver kept going. Sonja breathed: 'Thank you.'

155

The driver snorted: 'One second longer and I'd have had to stop.'

Sonja got her bearings. The Royal Palace was to the left; they were heading along the north side of the park. Erik's taxi had drawn slightly ahead. Sonja said anxiously: 'Don't let him get too far away.'

'He's speeding,' the driver said virtuously. 'I'm not going to risk my licence, you know!'

Sonja's heart sank. The other taxi was getting further and further away. At the corner of the park it turned left then right again and she lost sight of it. Then, as they came round the right turn, it came into view again.

Suddenly it slowed and turned off into a side street. Sonja gripped the seat again. It seemed an age before they reached the turning.

They entered the street. The other cab was there in front of them, stopped by the kerb. Its back door was open. Erik was already on the pavement.

Sonja's driver braked. She realised with horror that he was going to stop, right there behind Erik's cab. She cried in his ear: 'Go on! Go on!'

He hesitated, then accelerated. As they pulled out to overtake the stationary cab, she realised that Erik's white face was turning towards them. For a moment she couldn't take her eyes off him, mesmerised as if by a snake. Then, just as his eyes were about to lock on to hers, her heart gave an almighty thump and she came to her senses. She jerked her head down and pushed a shaking hand over her face.

She could almost feel Erik's eyes drilling into the back of her head. When they were past she scrabbled for her glasses which had fallen on to the floor and, jamming them back on her nose, twisted to look out of the back window. Erik was walking casually across the pavement, his arm round Hildegard Lindman.

Sonja's shoulders sagged weakly.

The driver stopped. She got out and told him to wait. He grumbled about it not being 'policy' to wait.

She thought: I don't think I can stand an argument! Then she realised that he was worried about the money. She thrust all she had into his hand.

The place was a newish apartment building, three storeys high, set a little way back from the road. Expensive, she guessed. This was a nice area.

She approached cautiously. Lights suddenly blinked on in two of the first-floor windows and she drew back a little.

Finding a courage she didn't think she had, she went up the short pathway to the main door. There were six apartments, each with their own bells and illuminated name cards. She thrust her face closer. *Eyvind Vorren. Prof. Hermann Dahlberg, Karen Dahlberg. Rolf Berg. E. Nettum ...*

She pulled back, then read the list again.

There was no Erik Leif.

She looked up again. The lights on the first floor continued to blaze, while the rest of the building was in almost complete darkness.

The first floor. If there was any logic to the list of names then that must belong to either the third or fourth name. Professor Dahlberg and his wife. Or Rolf Berg.

Rolf Berg. She kept staring at the card, remembering the man outside the theatre, the shouted conversation, the last goodbye.

Rolf. He had called out: *Rolf.*

And it had been Erik who had waved back.

Twelve

It was six when he set out. The morning was pitch-black with occasional snow and a strong gusty wind. The temperature was about minus ten. The sensible thing, Hal knew, would be to change his plans and take *Skorpa*. But he had worked until past midnight to finish the job and he was loath to give up now.

It was tricky launching the boat from its makeshift trolley on his own, and in the end he had to float it off, getting water over one of his boots in the process. He pulled the boat's nose up on to the beach while he raised the gaff. The mainsail flogged furiously, creating a deafening clamour which shook the boat as if to death. Anxious to be off and put an end to the din, Hal raised the jib and, pushing the nose out, got ready to shove off.

Then he remembered Bamse and called impatiently: 'Come boy!'

Eventually a low skulking form slid unhappily towards him. Hal laughed: 'Coward!' Bamse was not fond of the sea and even less fond of small boats. Eventually Hal had to grab the trembling dog and pull him into the boat by the collar. 'Coward,' he repeated, laughing again.

Hal poised himself with one foot in the boat and one in the water then shoved off hard, deftly swinging his body inboard as he did so. Now came the difficult bit. As the westerly wind carried the boat away from the shore Hal took the rudder from where it lay in the bottom of the boat and lifting it outboard, attempted to slide it into the gudgeons on the sternpost. As he felt beneath the water for the lower gudgeon a gust swooped off the land and filled the sails with a low booming sound. The rigging strained and creaked, and the little boat careered off downwind like a mad thing. Hal pushed the rudder round by brute force and the boat came up into the wind again, sails shaking and rattling, pausing bewildered in her forward charge.

At last the rudder pintles went home and, grabbing the tiller with one hand and pulling his padded gloves on with the other, Hal settled on his seat, found his course and pulled in the sheets.

The boat surged forward and flew headlong into the darkness, the water hissing along her hull. The wind came pouncing off the land in great gusts and then, almost as quickly, fell away again in sudden lulls. As each icy blast bowled down on to the boat she heeled, shivered slightly, then, gathering herself up, surged forward like a wild thing. The wind was coming from the west, off the outer islands, so that here, close under the shore, the sea was flat and there was hardly a wave to check the boat's headlong race.

Hal clung on to the tiller in sheer exhilaration. From time to time he crowed or laughed aloud. Bamse, curled under the centre thwart in a tight ball of consternation, gave an occasional low whine.

'You don't know what you're missing, you old devil,' Hal cried. 'You should come up here!'

Hal patted the boat's side, sliding his glove over the glassy smoothness of the varnish. What a creature! He'd bought her for almost nothing from a fisherman on one of the outer islands. She was an eighteen-foot gaff-rigged fishing smack, built at the turn of the century for cod fishing off the Lofoten Islands. She was made of pine and spruce, clinker-built so that her planks overlapped, and had the sweeping lines, the high stem and stern, the low freeboard of a miniature Viking ship. She had lain neglected in a boatshed for at least fifteen years. Hal had had to replace part of the keelson, recaulk all the seams, find a new mast, and remake all the rigging. He had also made a new removable rudder so that the boat could be beached. The only thing he had not attempted was the sailmaking, and a new set of tan canvas sails had come from an old sailmaker in the Lofotens.

He had named the boat *Lillebjorn*. Little Bear.

A squall came through, heeling the boat until she quivered, as if in fear. Hal sat out on the gunwale to keep her steady. Sleet drove down, obscuring the shore lights on either side of the sound. Hal pulled his hood more tightly round his face, ignored his freezing hands and feet, and peered into the gloom ahead.

He became aware of Bamse scrabbling about in the bottom of the boat. Spilling some wind from the sail, he sat inboard again. Bamse's shadowy form clawed its way desperately towards the stern. He realised what the panic was. The bilges were awash with water. Hal chuckled: 'Oh, you miserable old devil! What a life, eh!'

It was the seams. He should have left the boat filled with water for at least a week, so that her planks took up moisture and swelled and closed the seams tight. But he hadn't, which didn't matter too much in itself, except that he'd forgotten to bring a bailer. He shrugged the problem off: if necessary he'd use his hands.

'Sorry, Bamse, you're going to get wet.'

It was over twenty miles to Ragna's on the southern tip of Tromso Island. It seemed no time before the sound opened out to the south and he was almost half-way there. It had taken two hours, which meant the little boat had been doing a good five knots.

Sheer bliss. Hal had quite forgotten how it felt to be content and carefree. In the old days he'd known nothing else. What was it they said? Youth was wasted on the young.

Determined to keep his mood, he ignored the increasing sluggishness of the boat. But finally there was no getting away from the considerable quantity of water sloshing backwards and forwards inside the boat.

'Bamse, where's the bailer, hey? Why didn't you remind me?'

From his refuge in the stern the dog gave a whine. Eventually Hal pulled off a damp boot and used it to bail. After fifteen minutes' hard work he'd made some impression and, leaving three or four inches of water in the bottom, returned gratefully to the tiller.

Buoyant again, the boat rushed on happily. Hal listened to the sound of the waves slap-slapping against her bow, the water swishing noisily down her sides, the wake gurgling behind. Around them, the first grey light of dawn crept up, gradually diffusing the darkness so that the boat, the sea, gained form and space.

It was two hours later that Ragna's house finally came into

view. Hal sat on the aft thwart, his feet like blocks of ice, his hand frozen to the tiller. A bedraggled Bamse shivered at his side, his wolf-like face a picture of misery. Despite constant baling the water was well over the thwarts and almost lapping at the gunwale. Hal reckoned they had five minutes at best. He patted Bamse's head. 'That's called timing, hey?'

The boat moved forward like a barge, solid and stately and exceedingly low in the water.

Ragna's next-door neighbour appeared in front of his house and stared. Hal waved graciously. The man waved slowly and hesitantly back, then stood motionless, as if glued to the spot. Hal understood: the arrival was beginning to look rather interesting to him too.

A delicate manoeuvre could no longer be avoided – a gybe, which was always a little tricky at the best of times. Hal moved himself across the boat, hauled on the mainsheet and thrust the tiller over. Filled with a sudden wild excitement, he yelled: 'Here we go!'

The little boat turned, the wind crept behind the mainsail and, with an almighty whack, slammed the sail across to the other side. Hal ducked to avoid the boom as it whistled over then thrust his weight out on to the gunwale to hold the boat upright as she began to heel over. But as he struggled to balance the boat a gust of wind defeated him and the lee gunwale dipped under.

The shore was not far away; Hal could see sharp waves breaking on the shingle. But any remaining doubts about the outcome of events vanished as the water rose to his knees. There wasn't a hope. Hal giggled and, overcome by a ridiculous euphoria, kept the boat going as she slowly and majestically sailed under.

'Time for a swim, Bamse!' he shouted as the water – almost warm after the icy wind – rose rapidly to his chest.

Bamse, his nose high out of the water, was already striking out for the shore. Hal attempted to swim the boat in, but she slowly capsized and lay dead and heavy in the water. Paddling round to the bow he got hold of the anchor warp and, with one end in his hand, swam to the shore.

'And what on earth do you think you're doing!' It was Ragna, hands on hips, looking very cross and very lovely.

161

Hal waded out of the water, like a dripping rat, and grinned. 'Well, I thought I was having a sail!'

'You're mad! What's *this*, this – *thing*?' She jabbed a finger at the wallowing hull.

Hal began hauling the boat towards the shore. 'It's a Lofoten fishing smack from the turn of the century –'

'No, I mean, what are you doing with it?'

'Well, I was going very fast.'

Ragna sighed impatiently. 'Really! You might have had more consideration. You've upset the whole of my morning! I only just got your message. Why didn't you call me yourself? As it is I've had to hang about and let Sigrid take Krisi to kindergarten and –'

Hal felt a keen disappointment. 'Kris isn't here?'

'No, of course not!' she cried indignantly. 'Really, Hal, sometimes!'

Hal smiled amiably. His spirits were too high to be quashed easily. Today he found her anger a distinct challenge.

'Well, if it's not convenient I shall call again another day. Goodbye,' he said solemnly, adding in deep theatrical tones: 'Back into the maelstrom!' he turned and walked back into the water, wading past the capsized boat until the sea was up to his shoulders.

'Come back!' Ragna screamed. 'You're crazy!'

Hal continued until the water lapped his chin and the waves buffeted his head. This time it felt a lot colder. Just as he was beginning to think it wasn't such a good idea after all, he heard a loud shriek from the shore and turned to see Ragna hugging herself with laughter, staggering idiotically from side to side.

He thought triumphantly: Got you!

He prolonged the performance a little longer, standing upright and straight-faced as the waves broke over his head, until a large wave knocked him off his feet and he had to swim for it. She was still laughing as he righted the boat and beached it. She helped him bail it out and pull it up on to the shingle.

Seeing his chattering teeth and white skin, she declared: 'Well, you'd better come and have a hot bath.'

'Please –' Hal held up his dripping hands in mock politeness. 'Don't feel under any obligation!'

'Ha!' She glared at him. 'You might get pneumonia and then

you'd be a real nuisance.'

'You've such a kind heart!' They began to walk up to the house.

Ragna snorted: 'Kinder than you deserve.'

Her mood, though abrasive, was improving. He gave her a sidelong glance, but she was looking thoughtfully ahead, a frown on her face.

'Look,' she said abruptly. 'I really do have lots to do today. I should be in town already.'

'Of course. I've things to do myself. But first I'll have to borrow some clothes. You wouldn't have a little number in my size, would you?'

She said archly: 'What did you have in mind?'

'Oh, one of those shapeless outfits will do. The ones like a sack with four slits in it that you sell for a fortune.'

She ground to a halt, looking cross again. 'You *are* in a funny mood today. What's the matter?'

'The matter?'

'All this smiling and joking. It's not like you.'

Hal absorbed that one. She was right of course: he didn't find a lot to laugh about normally. 'Well, I'm feeling rather happy today, that's all. Just came over me.' His teeth clattered like castanets. He began to move off towards the house again.

But Ragna stood her ground. 'What's happened?' she demanded.

Hal suddenly felt very sure of himself. 'Happened? I sail miles in a sinking boat, almost drown, get sent back to the sea – all to visit you. And you ask me what happened?'

His tone, he suddenly realised, was breaking new ground: he was flirting with her, something that had never somehow been appropriate before.

She eyed him coolly and said in a flat voice: 'I'll find some of Jan's old clothes for you.'

Hal flinched inwardly and looked away. He thought: Ah, I got that message all right. It'd been as clear as a slap in the face. He turned and strode up to the house, his good humour evaporated.

He bathed quickly, rinsed out his salty clothes and wrung them hard. Opening the bathroom door he found some clothes neatly folded on the floor outside.

Jan's. He reached for them, an odd constricting sensation in his throat.

When he got downstairs Ragna was standing by the front door, coat on and keys in hand.

She pointed to the hall table. There was a large parcelled box on it. She said levelly: 'I'd forgotten – that's been sitting in a cupboard for ages. They sent it some time ago. The army, I mean.' Her eyes slid to the parcel, then back to his. 'Jan's things. Could you deal with them?'

She went out, calling over her shoulder: 'Get rid of it all, will you?'

Ragna struggled into the house with two heavy bags of groceries. She called 'Hey-ho', but there was no reply.

She dumped the shopping in the kitchen and went through into the living room. It was empty, but the coffee table was littered with sheets of paper and coloured pencils. She bent over the table and looked at a large picture of a farmhouse in a valley surrounded by mountains, shaggy black-haired animals, and flowers. No prizes for guessing where that was.

She went to the window. There they were, in the very place she'd known they'd be. By the boat. She watched them for a moment, the man and the boy and the dog, huddled together in the twilight, as thick as thieves.

She went outside and shouted: 'Anyone hungry?'

They looked up, conferred with each other, and a faint 'Yes!' floated across the air.

She prepared a hot meal of salmon and potatoes, with cheese and fresh green apples to follow. Krisi rushed in first, noisy, red-cheeked and overflowing with excitement.

'Have you seen *Lillebjorn*, Mama? Have you seen my boat?'

'Your boat?'

'Yes, *my* boat! My boat!'

Hal came in and, passing behind Krisi's chair, ruffled the boy's hair affectionately. She noticed that he was wearing his own clothes again.

'Ah! before I forget!' His voice was bright – he was back in that extraordinary sunny mood of his. He came up to Ragna and she felt a moment's surprise as he took her by the shoulders and looked into her eyes. 'We have an urgent request, Kris and I. A matter of great importance.' His tone was ironic, his look roguish and amused. She thought: My God, you can be charming if you try!

Krisi was giggling furiously. 'Of course,' she said, rather looking forward to whatever he was about to say. 'What is it?'

He narrowed his eyes. 'It's my feet. They'd stay a lot drier if you could find me a bailer.'

Krisi rolled off his chair, helpless with laughter. Hal smiled that quiet smile of his. Ragna sucked in a long breath before managing a pale smile. Her sense of humour was not in good shape today. 'I'll see what I can find.'

Recovering, Krisi jumped to his feet. 'And Mama, can we go to Brattdal on Saturday? *Please, please.* You promised. *Please.*'

Ragna made an indecisive face. They'd last been in the summer, in June, and Krisi had been badgering her ever since.

'One day soon, darling,' she said vaguely, putting the food on the table.

'But I want to see the *mo'kusokse* again,' Krisi whined.

Smiling at the mispronunciation, she said: 'The musk-oxen won't go away, Krisi.'

Hal said quietly: 'I could come and pick up Kris on Saturday and have him back by six on Sunday. How about that?'

Ragna was taken aback. Hal had always asked the two of them before. Immediately she thought: It's that woman – she's changed everything.

She frowned at him. 'I don't know. I'll think about it.'

Hal and Krisi exchanged conspiratorial looks, and Ragna sighed audibly.

They ate in silence.

Then Ragna said: 'I had a letter from Fred. He wants you to lead his expedition.'

Hal made a face of affectionate exasperation. 'They won't have any luck. I do wish they'd stop trying.'

'He seemed to think I'd be able to persuade you. He wrote pages and pages.'

He examined her face. 'I'm sorry he bothered you. I'll write and tell him I'm definitely not interested.' He added almost to himself: 'Although it might do me some good.'

Ragna stared at him. His capacity to surprise her seemed limitless today. 'Ah, so you might be tempted after all!' she said, hating the waspishness in her voice.

'Ragna – you're the one who's always telling me that I'm cut off at Brattdal.'

Ragna opened her mouth to contradict him, but thought better of it. Standing up, she cleared the dishes away. 'Well, you are, aren't you?' she said defensively.

There was a pause. Hal asked quietly: 'What do you think? Should I consider going with Fred?'

'Don't ask me!' she said sharply. 'What you do with your life is no affair of mine!'

The muscles in Hal's cheeks worked furiously, a sign she had learnt to recognise. She thought wearily: Now I've gone and made him angry.

Hal said suddenly: 'I must be going.'

'Don't go!' wailed Kris. 'Please don't go, Uncle Hal! Please don't go!'

'It's already dark, Krisi, and I have a long way to go.'

Hal took him by the shoulders and, leaning forward, whispered in his ear. The child nodded violently and scampered off in the direction of the living room. 'He's gone to finish his picture of Brattdal,' Hal explained. 'We need to have a quick talk.' His voice was cool and his eyes had regained all their usual seriousness. 'You never told me how your trip went.'

She gave him a brief account of the journey to the plateau and what little she had learned about the migration route.

He listened then said: 'I should tell you that Major Thrane came to see me. You remember ...?'

She remembered him all right. Cool, clever, too smart by half: she hadn't liked him at all.

'He came to warn me off.'

Ragna stared at him in amazement. 'What do you mean?'

'He came to warn me off the Kaafiord protest.'

'What a cheek!'

'He said I'd ruin my good name.' Hal gave a short derisory laugh. 'I told him I wasn't too bothered.'

'Good Lord! What a nerve!' Ragna felt her blood pressure rising. 'That's typical – thinking they can push you around.'

'But Ragna, he did come as a friend. He thought he was doing me a favour.'

'Huh!' Hal always put great store by friendship, as if friends could never let you down.

'He was quite curious to know where the information had come from. He seemed to think we must have fallen into bad company.'

'He would.'

'I told him I didn't know where the information was coming from.'

'Which was the truth.'

'Yes, but ...' Hal was wearing his responsible expression, the one he kept for admonishing people. 'Ragna, it's wrong – not knowing.'

'I've told you, it's all above board,' she said emphatically. 'Nothing illegal or sinister. I promise.' It was best Hal didn't know about the Friends for Peace or one of its founder-members, an old acquaintance of hers, who regularly phoned with little snippets of information. By any standards the group was left-wing, and she knew Hal wouldn't be very happy about that.

She said: 'You're not going to take any notice, are you? Of Thrane's warning.'

He gave her a thoughtful look. 'No.'

She smiled, suddenly pleased with him. 'Good!'

He got to his feet, preparing to leave. 'But what about this journalist you saw? Why wasn't he any good? Didn't he think it was a good enough story?'

'He thought it was "too sensitive". Ha! No guts!' To her mind, lack of guts was the worst sin of all. 'But I'm sure Rolf Berg will be a better bet. By the way, I said in my letter that you were involved in the protest and would be – well – happy to give him an interview. I hope that was all right.' She added: 'Or is he an untouchable, like all the rest?'

She could have bitten her tongue off: a flicker of pain crossed his face. He was remembering the savaging some of the newspapers had given him three years before.

He said quietly: 'No, of course I'll talk to Rolf. If he thinks it'll do some good.' He was out of the room before she could soften the moment.

167

Her shoulders sagged; she had been unkind. In fact, she didn't like herself very much today.

They tramped down to the beach in the dim light, Hal with the bucket she had given him for a bailer, Krisi and Bamse dancing ahead amid whoops and shouts of joy.

'What about the Land Rover?' Ragna asked.

'I'll pick it up some time at the weekend. Have you thought about Saturday?'

Ragna frowned. 'Krisi's awfully young to go away ... And the weather ...'

He exhaled harshly. 'I'd look after him, you know that.'

She didn't want Krisi to go away, and she wasn't quite sure why. 'Well ...'

'It'd give you a break,' said Hal. 'A chance to be on your own.'

She thought: But I don't want to be on my own!

Suddenly she remembered the woman. 'Will there be anyone else there?' she demanded.

'Only Arne.' There was surprise in his voice.

'Ah. No – friends?'

He looked at her sharply. There was a long silence. She thought: So it's true!

He said finally: 'No friends, Ragna. Just Kris and me.'

Hal rigged the boat, carefully explaining the name and job of each rope to Krisi. The child nodded furiously, as if memorising every word. Ragna watched, feeling sad, though she wasn't sure why.

When the boat was ready they all helped push it into the water. Hal stowed something carefully under a seat. Ragna recognised the beastly army parcel.

Hal gave Ragna a firm impersonal kiss on the cheek, then swept Krisi up into his arms. The boy laughed as Hal held him high in the air. The two figures were etched black against the last of the glimmering light, a shadow-play framed by the wide sweep of sky and mountains. Something about the scene made Ragna's heart give a curious twist.

The two silhouettes merged as the child sank gently into the man's arms and embraced him.

Ragna heard herself call: 'Come on, you two!'

She and Krisi stood for a long time watching the boat sail

clear of the land. After a while the little vessel tacked into a silver pool of reflected light. The sails, the man and dog in the stern, were ink-black against the pewter sea. The boat seemed to glide over the darkly glittering water, as if drawn by magic.

The boat passed through the pool of light and merged into the darkness.

Hal cut the cords that bound the parcel and took a deep breath.

He hadn't realised there'd be more.

Jan's personal belongings had been recovered from the Porsangmoen Camp at the time of the incident. Following orders, Jan had left them there before setting out. A wallet, photographs of Ragna and Krisi, some money, a pocket diary with names and addresses.

Then there was the stuff they'd discovered at the camp by the lake. The hidden snow-hole hadn't taken long to find – Hal had guessed where to look – and there they had found food, spare ammunition, and signs of a meal hastily abandoned.

It'd never occurred to him that there'd be more.

He drew a deep breath and opened the outer packaging. Inside was a heavy cardboard box. He opened the lid.

A thick brown envelope lay on the top. It was sealed. He slit it open. From deep within came the gleam of gold. He slid the contents into his hand.

A gold chain with a cross on it. A gold wedding ring.

He stared. This must have come back with the body. Why hadn't he known? Why hadn't they told him? But then he remembered: they had told Ragna.

He cradled the jewellery in his hand, a tightness in his throat.

Eventually he replaced it in the envelope, and put it on one side. It would go to Kris when he was older.

Next there was a knife, the one Jan had always carried, a Lapp knife, curved, with a distinctive carved horn sheath and a handle bound in leather. Jan had always kept it razor-sharp. He'd been able to skin and gut a hare in thirty seconds flat.

The knife, too, would go to Kris.

He saw to his surprise that there was another knife in the

169

box. Hal picked it up curiously. He recognised the type – he'd seen dozens like it before. It was a dagger-knife, straight and long with cross-arms and a leather sheath designed to lace on to a belt. Even before he saw the swastika emblem stamped on the grip, he knew it was a standard German Army-issue dagger from the war.

Determined not to be caught unarmed or unprepared again, half the men in Norway had mementoes from the German surrender: daggers, pistols, rifles – even the occasional machine-gun.

Yet Hal couldn't remember Jan having one.

He put it down on the floor and returned to the box.

Binoculars. Small light-weight ones with Polaroid filters for alpine use. He knew them all right. He and Jan had each been presented with a pair by the manufacturers – ironically, a German company.

These joined the items to be kept for Krisi.

There was a pouch. Hal had last seen this at the final briefing at Porsangmoen. Then it had contained bank notes, he remembered. Norwegian kroner and Finnish marks. Not very many, just enough to buy food or transport if necessary.

The pouch was empty. That would be Thrane's lot, reclaiming their government-issue cash.

The Russians had kept the rifles and guns, he supposed, and they would have taken the maps, too, as so-called evidence. The clothing would probably have been destroyed.

Even as he thought it he spotted a handkerchief, a pair of gloves. Good God, why had they put those in? He gulped awkwardly.

He reached hastily into the box for the last item and brought out a case containing another pair of binoculars.

He glanced over them but suddenly didn't have the stomach for any more. Getting hastily to his feet, he went outside for some fresh air. He stayed on the veranda for some time, staring into the distance.

When he returned he put the jewellery in a fresh envelope, wrote Kris's name on it and placed it in a drawer of the old roll-top desk, along with the hunting knife and the snow-binoculars.

After some thought he added the gloves and handkerchief,

170

although he wasn't sure they were the right sort of thing to pass on.

That left the dagger-knife and second set of binoculars.

He examined the binoculars. Zeiss 20 × 30s. Covered in flaking white paint, as though they had been adapted for military use.

Yes: there was a tiny swastika stamped on the body. And an engraved name: Schirmer. And some scratchings alongside: numbers and letters.

Perhaps the things had belonged to Mattis. But if so Hal was sure he would have remembered seeing them.

He sat by the flickering light of the stove and let thoughts turn freely in his mind.

Some people might like to carry two knives, but why should anyone want to carry two sets of binoculars?

The explanation was probably obvious and mundane, yet he was curious.

He returned to his desk and wrote a letter to Mattis's family.

And just in case they couldn't help him and because he never liked to leave any stone unturned, he also wrote a letter to Oslo, to someone he knew at the Military Archives.

Thirteen

Berg carefully negotiated the doors of the *Sosialist Dagens Post* and made his way gently across the marble hallway. The lift door was just closing. He thrust a shoulder in, the door jerked open, and he stepped inside.

A woman's voice said: 'Morning.'

Berg recognised a girl from the advertising department.

'You look terrible,' the girl said, suppressing a giggle.

Berg narrowed his lips and turned away.

As soon as he reached the editorial floor he went to the men's room and stared at himself in the mirror. Eyes a bit red, a touch of puffiness underneath, skin a little mottled. But he still looked all right. Sour grapes on the girl's part.

But he should have gone easier on the wine. Judging by the ache in his head it must have been second-rate. He should have stuck to vodka or Scotch: you never went wrong with them.

He stood back and smoothed his hair and straightened his lapels. The problem was overtiredness and overwork. Nothing a good holiday wouldn't cure.

But the headache needed immediate attention. He fished in his pockets for an aspirin and, failing to find one, went across the floor to Ingrid, who always had a supply. Ingrid defended the editor from unwanted callers.

'Meeting in half an hour,' Ingrid said, handing him the aspirin. 'You don't look well,' she added with a knowing look.

He made a face.

She wagged a finger at him. 'You burn the candle at both ends.'

He raised a tolerant eyebrow. He got on with Ingrid. 'Is there any other way?'

172

She retorted: 'Not for you, apparently!'

Taking a strong coffee from the machine, Berg wove his way through the modern furniture and tropical plants of the open-plan office to his desk in a far corner. With one foot he pushed a weeping fig across to hide the front of his desk – he didn't want social calls – and, washing the aspirin down with coffee, stared unenthusiastically at the mound of paper sitting in his in-tray.

The two prices of success: a hangover and a large post-bag.

Since he'd got his own by-line the post had been coming in steadily. People holding strong opinions – and, this being Norway, there were plenty of them – seemed to feel it was their duty to express themselves at length. Most of it went straight to the editor of the correspondence page, but Berg couldn't afford not to glance through it first, just in case there was a tip-off.

The first mail had come with Pasvik, the next with the U2 Incident. Berg had nearly resigned over the U2 story. The day after the Russians had announced the capture of Gary Powers, he had written a strong piece suggesting that the US had been operating spy flights from their Norwegian bases for some considerable time, and without Norway's knowledge. The editor had been hysterical about publishing it, but when Berg had threatened to walk out, he'd run the story, though watered down.

Putting the mail off a little longer, Berg phoned his message service. Though message service was rather a grand title: it was in fact a grubby tobacconist's shop run by an Estonian. But appearances didn't matter: the Estonian had never met Berg, nor did he know Berg's real name, and only two people used the service: Alex and Sonja.

The Estonian answered almost immediately and Berg announced himself as Lundquist. The Estonian read out the latest message from Sonja.

Berg rang off with a sigh of irritation. Yet more family dramas. Why on earth Sonja wanted to saddle him with all this he couldn't imagine: he'd never even met her mother.

And a *holiday*. He pictured Sonja lying on a beach, large and whale-like, and gave a small snort of incredulity. An evening

173

with Sonja was survivable, but a week would be a prison sentence.

He'd have to be careful about wriggling out of it though. Sonja was bound to be emotional at the moment. And emotion was one thing he couldn't cope with.

He'd have to phone her some time, though. Tomorrow. Yes, if he had the time.

Lighting a cigarette, he drew on it deeply and, as the coffee and aspirin took effect, began to feel better.

Supported by a second coffee, Berg finally reached for the mail.

He opened envelopes steadily, glanced over the contents, and chucked them on one side. The usual stuff.

One letter made him pause. It was typewritten but headed with a handwritten 'Dear Rolf' in a round feminine style. There was a Tromso address. The letter was long and he had to flick through three pages to find the signature.

He felt an uncomfortable little twinge. Ragna Johansen.

What on earth could she want?

He stared at the name for a moment then went to the beginning and started to read.

It quickly dawned on him that she wanted a favour. He was vaguely flattered, yet also defensive. He didn't like having to put himself out.

But by the second page his natural scepticism had been overtaken by curiosity.

Kaafiord.

He read on then went back to the second page and reread it twice.

Kaafiord. Yes, he knew about that. Sonja had mentioned it when she'd been talking about security at installations and how new ones were to get extra protection. New ones like Kaafiord, she'd said.

She hadn't told him much about the installation itself or what its function would be, and he hadn't pressed her. He never did. With Sonja patience was the key.

She'd tell him eventually. She always did.

A number of secret installations had appeared in Norway in the last few years, and they generally fell into three categories: early-warning radar installations, Nato communications systems, or, most recently of all, a new navigation system for submarines.

This last category interested Berg most of all because the navigation system – Loran-C – didn't guide just any old submarines, but Polaris subs carrying nuclear weapons. Norway being a non-nuclear nation, this was by any standards highly provocative stuff.

Now if Kaafiord was anything to do with that ...

But of course Ragna Johansen didn't know.

Ragna Johansen was interested in Kaafiord for a quite different reason. The Lapps.

Berg weighed up the possibilities. Would it make a good story as it was? His instincts told him yes, though the Lapp issue was always a difficult one.

Mention of the Lapps brought out all sorts of guilts and neuroses in the Norwegian public. Quick to condemn racialism abroad, Berg noted that his countrymen were considerably less vocal on matters close to home. This was because they'd persuaded themselves that the Lapps were well treated. The truth was somewhat less comfortable. Frequently regarded as inferior, primitive and a little crazy, the Lapps had had a raw deal for a long time.

Nevertheless when it came to protecting the Lapps against a US-built and -financed installation public opinion might well rally round. The underdog versus the American goliath. It might just work.

And then Berg could take a stab at the real target.

Who controls these installations? (The US.) *Who benefits from them?* (The US.) *How will they help Norway?* (They won't: they'll merely provoke the Soviet Union and intensify the Cold War.)

Yes: the story had potential.

But he'd have to know what the installation was for.

That meant seeing Sonja sooner rather than later, which was a nuisance.

Glancing up, he saw Ingrid gesturing him towards the editor's office. Lighting another cigarette and searching half-heartedly around his desk for a pencil and notebook, he followed the rest of the staff into the meeting.

The editor, a nervous thin-faced sixty-year-old on the wrong side of a heart attack, gestured Berg in and said immediately: 'Something's come up that might interest you.'

Berg sat down. 'Oh?'

'A whisper. About an item that's about to appear in a British left-wing magazine – the *Examiner*. About Pasvik.'

Berg's heart missed a small beat.

'Apparently a KGB man has defected to the British and told all. Including information about the third man at Pasvik –'

Berg's stomach did a leap. He kept his face in a mask of passivity.

' – apparently the third man got as far as the border – might even have met Johansen and Hetta – but was shot also. And – listen to this – the report says this third man was a Norwegian, and that he'd been living in the USSR since the war.'

There was a silence. Everyone looked at Berg. He raised his eyebrows. 'Is the third man's identity known?'

'Er – no. It isn't.'

Berg hid his relief behind a frown. 'Is that all?'

The editor shuffled through the papers on his desk. 'I think so.' He reread his notes hurriedly. 'Ah, wait . . .'

Berg drew on his cigarette, holding an expression of professional interest.

'Wait . . .' the editor stumbled, '. . . got it wrong. The defector to the British was a *GRU* man, not KGB.'

If that was all . . . Berg breathed again and forced himself to think calmly. There really was nothing to worry about.

The editor looked at him. 'So, what do you think?'

Berg thought quickly. There were so many different ways to play this. Eventually he said: 'Well, it brings up all the same old questions that were never properly answered at the time of Pasvik, doesn't it? Like the extent of the CIA's involvement. And who planned the mission to the border. More to the point, it reveals an attempted cover-up, doesn't it? That idea put about by the government that the purpose of the mission was to meet a Soviet refugee.' He gave a derisory laugh. 'That's obviously nonsense. If this man was a Norwegian, then he must have been a fully-fledged CIA agent all along.'

The editor looked unhappy. 'But this story's unsubstantiated. We can't get into the realms of – conjecture.'

Conjecture. Berg liked that. 'But this story's going to get

picked up all over the place. All the foreign press'll run it. We can't just ignore it.'

The editor looked undecided. 'Well ...'

Berg was about to try a slightly different angle when someone said: 'Aren't we missing something here?' It was the political editor. 'Isn't there a story in how a Norwegian came to be living in the Soviet Union? I mean, I'd like to know how many arrived there at the end of the war. And, more to the point, how many might still be there against their will. Imprisoned, or whatever.'

Another voice chimed in and Berg recognised a young staff reporter. 'If you take it one step further, you wonder how many went to the Soviet Union and came back to Norway as model citizens, but with their loyalties ever so slightly adjusted.'

Berg drew calmly on his cigarette. Somewhere deep inside he had a dreadful urge to laugh.

The editor was looking daggers at the young man who, because he was standing in for an absent superior, obviously wasn't fully familiar with editorial policy. Policy was never to be unpatriotic. Critical of government, yes. And, after centuries of domination by Denmark and Sweden, critical of foreign (which nowadays meant US) influences, but this sort of suggestion smacked of stabbing oneself in the back.

The editor said icily: 'We can't go off on wild tangents when we have no real facts. No, we'll keep this as a straight news piece. And short at that.'

Berg wouldn't argue with that, he decided.

But the editor hadn't finished. He tapped his pencil thoughtfully on the desk. 'Berg – you might just look into the idea of Norwegians kept in the Soviet Union against their will some time. No hurry. That lawyer Sorensen – the one with all the stuff on collaborators and war criminals – he might be able to shed some light.'

Berg looked doubtful, then, with a small dismissive shrug, nodded an okay. Better that he should do it than someone else. Far better.

The meeting moved on. Ideas came and went. When it was Berg's turn he put forward the Kaafiord story, carefully couching it in attractive non-alarmist terms – land rights, the future of reindeer herding as a whole, bureaucratic insensitivity.

When he'd finished the editor considered for several

moments. Then, blowing out his cheeks, he slowly nodded.

Berg had got his story.

'Good morning.'

Sonja looked up from her desk with such a start that her glasses slipped down her nose. It was Major Thrane. She hadn't heard him come in. He must have entered through the Director's office. She realised she was looking foolish, her mouth open, her glasses askew. She straightened her glasses and attempted a smile.

'I'm so sorry about your mother,' Thrane said.

She put on a brave expression. 'Sometimes these things are for the best.' She added more brightly: 'Have a good trip north?'

'Yes, thanks.' He hovered, watching her carefully.

'Anything I can do for you?' she asked.

He pulled up a chair and sat beside the desk, leaning thoughtfully on his elbow. 'I wanted your advice.'

'Of course.' Major Thrane was number two to the head of security, a post he'd taken up three years before. He was one of the few people who were allowed unlimited access to information.

'We had a few chats during the security review, didn't we?'

Sonja was very still. She didn't want to talk about the review, she didn't want to talk about anything. She could hardly deal with the simplest things. Her mind had almost ground to a halt.

She managed: 'Yes.'

'Do you remember all the things we discussed? About new procedures?'

'Er ... Yes.'

'Well, how do you think we're doing? Have we done enough?'

What was he getting at? She thought of the photocopier and felt rather cold until she remembered that he couldn't possibly know about that.

She said abruptly: 'I would have thought so, but then I'm no expert.'

Surprise flickered across Thrane's face. She realised her voice had sounded shrill and edgy. She thought: Get a hold, get a hold!

His expression changed to one of understanding, as if he'd momentarily forgotten the strain her mother's death must have put her under. He said pleasantly: 'Well, you're not an expert maybe but – well, you know better than anybody how things work round here.'

She tried to summon up some interest in the subject. 'Let me see . . . I think the regular screening's a good idea. And the more restricted access to information.'

He nodded sagely. 'We're thinking about more comprehensive screening for top personnel.'

She thought: Why are you telling me all this? She moved some papers around her desk. 'It can't do any harm.'

'Mmm . . .' He pondered for a while. 'Trouble is, it takes time and a great deal of money. And it may cause bad feeling.' There was a pause. She looked up to find him staring at her. 'I mean, how would you feel about having your life put under a microscope?'

'It would be a nuisance, I suppose. But I could hardly object.'

Thrane did not reply, but rubbed his fingers slowly over his chin. Then, smiling abruptly, he got to his feet. 'Well, thank you. You've been most helpful.'

Sonja nodded a faint goodbye, and he was gone.

For several minutes she stared at the closed door, a dreadful aching feeling in the pit of her stomach.

What had all that been about? Did he know something?

The next moment she got a grip on herself. She was imagining things. Major Thrane often wandered about. He often dropped in on people and asked questions. It meant nothing.

She sat back, feeling weak, and rested her head on the back of her chair.

The buzzer sounded. She jumped again.

The Director. Ready for his meeting. She hurriedly patted her hair, picked up her pad, and went into his office.

It was a long departmental meeting. She surprised herself by managing quite normally. She took the minutes, typed them, and went to the photocopier in the secretarial office next to her own. Ten copies were needed.

She turned the dial to ten, put in the first page, and pressed the start button. The copies churned out. The machine fell silent.

She stared at the copier. One of the secretaries walked past her on the way to lunch. Then the office was empty.

Sonja swallowed nervously. She examined the first copy, decided it wasn't good enough, and, resetting the quantity dial to one, pressed the start button again. The extra copy came out.

She hesitated, not wanting to pick it up. Why was she doing this? There was no reason to, not any more.

And yet ... She wanted to keep the upper hand. She wanted to keep her bargaining power.

She wanted *him*.

The thought made her want to cry.

She decided: One last time. She'd do it just one last time.

She repeated the process for the second and third pages of the minutes. In each instance she examined the first copy, decided it wasn't good enough, and made an extra one.

She picked up the copies and the originals, collated and stapled them, entered the document and file number in the photocopy ledger along with the number of copies – she was careful to put down the correct number, which was three times eleven – and signed it.

Then she slipped three blank sheets of photocopying paper behind the sheaf of minutes.

Going to the shredder, she turned it on, and carefully fed the three blank sheets into its jaws.

She made a neat entry in the destruction ledger: Three sub-standard photocopies. And added the document number and her signature.

Returning to her desk, she marked eight copies of the minutes for distribution and retained two plus the original for the files. The extra copy she slipped into her handbag.

Finally she took her shorthand notes to the shredder. Before feeding them in she read through them one last time, just to make sure she had missed nothing.

But no, she had understood it all perfectly. Every detail of Project Bluetail: the building of a new intelligence-gathering installation in the north.

Back at her desk, she got out her sandwiches and put them on the desk in front of her. She didn't eat. Instead she waited until the Director buzzed through to tell her he was going to lunch.

She gave it another minute then reached for the phone. First she rang Anna, her opposite number in FO/S.

Anna was expecting her call. 'I had a look at the file for you,' she said immediately.

'I hope it was no problem.'

'No! Like I said yesterday, he left us – let me see – six months ago. He's a security adviser for the railways now. I can tell you that all right. But why are you asking me, Sonja? I thought you knew him anyway. You asked me about him before, didn't you?'

'Yes,' Sonja said lightly. She'd rehearsed this bit. 'I was just curious because he was talking so freely about "work" and I thought for an awful moment he was still with you.'

'No, no. He's not with us any more,' Anna said emphatically. 'Besides, he was always a great one for security. Always went by the rules.'

'You knew him well then?'

'Well, a little. He was very quiet. I can't say I ever exchanged more than a few words with him.'

'Oh? He seemed quite – outgoing – to me.'

'Goodness, I must have missed something then. He seemed mouselike to me. He was good at his job, such as it was. But he was never going to go far. That's why he left.'

Sonja made herself laugh. 'We have got the same man, haven't we, Anna?'

The other woman didn't laugh. Sonja realised she'd overdone it: one didn't joke about identities in the security services. Anna said: 'Aged just over thirty, married, three children. Fair hair, six-two, round face, glasses, a bit thick round the middle. Bookish, a bit puritanical, I'd say; non-drinker, non-smoker. How'm I doing?'

'Oh, that's Erik all right,' Sonja lied. 'Thanks, Anna.'

The sick feeling returned to Sonja's stomach with a vengeance.

Trembling, she pulled open a drawer and took out a newspaper. She leafed through it until she came to an article on a centre page.

The article was written by the owner of the second-floor

apartment, the journalist called Rolf Berg.

She picked up the phone again and dialled the number she'd written on her jotter pad.

The number rang.

'*Dagens Post,*' said a voice.

Sonja gripped the receiver more tightly. 'Rolf Berg.'

A pause, a click, background noise. The blood pounded round Sonja's head.

A *female* voice. 'News.'

'I wanted to speak to Rolf Berg.'

'He's not around at the moment, I'm afraid. I'll just check ... No. Can't see him. Is there a message?'

'No, I –'

'Hang on! Hang on!' the female voice called. 'He's just coming.'

There was a clatter as the receiver was put down, the sound of voices, then –

'Berg.'

Sonja held on tight, feeling weak.

'Hello? Hello?' A sigh of annoyance, then an aside: 'There's no one here. Who was it, do you know?' A pause and a bored: 'Hello ... hello ... hello.'

Slowly, Sonja put the receiver back in its cradle. She'd heard enough.

It was him.

Shakily she got to her feet and went to the ladies' room. She doused her face with cold water, and again and again.

Finally she looked up into the mirror.

A reporter. All this time, a reporter.

And she'd told him everything.

A final door closed, a last set of high heels tapped down the corridor, and there was silence. Thrane waited a little longer, then strolled out of his office.

It was four-thirty in the afternoon – the Norwegian working day finished at four. The evening staff would already be on duty in the first-floor duty-room. His own security men would have started their rounds. Apart from that, the building should be empty.

He locked his door and went towards the Director's offices. He stopped at the door of Sonja Bjornsen's office and knocked. After a moment he took a bunch of keys from his pocket and, finding the correct one, unlocked the door and went in.

Her desk was neat and tidy, with no papers on it. He checked the drawers, just in case, but there was nothing.

The files in daily use were kept in a special strongroom to one side. He had collected the keys earlier, and now opened the door. He found the file he wanted, marked IG-FR 61: Project Bluetail.

The minutes of the meeting held that morning had been filed in their correct place, on top. Thrane glanced through the three typewritten pages, then took careful note of the entry on the top of the document. This showed the number of copies that existed, and where they had gone to. 1 + 10: three in the files, eight distributed. Thrane noted the document number and, replacing the file, went through to the secretarial office next to Sonja Bjornsen's and looked at the photocopy ledger. He felt a moment of excitement. *Eleven* copies of each page! He checked the other photocopy entries for the day. Sixty-two in addition to Sonja's thirty-three. A total of ninety-five.

Kneeling, he unfastened the side of the photocopier and peered at the small meter inside. He compared its reading with the one from the day before, and did the mental arithmetic.

Ninety-five. It tallied.

Next, he went to the shredder and examined the ledger there. There was the entry: three spoilt photocopies. But had she really put them through? He opened the sack of shredded paper waiting for disposal, and taking an ultra-violet penlight from his pocket, shone it into the sack.

Several shreds of paper glowed back at him. He checked the ledger to see if any other spoilt photocopies had been shredded that day.

No. So the photocopying paper, which had been marked with ultra-violet-sensitive ink, must have been put through by Sonja.

He felt a pang of disappointment. He'd had such a strong instinct about this one.

He spent two hours checking that every copy made by the

183

photocopier that day had gone to its proper destination. Then he returned to his office, puzzled but not defeated.

He would just have to put some extra thought into it. There had to be an explanation for the fact that five times in the last four months extra copies had been made on that machine. Extra copies which had been entered as spoilt copies and shredded.

In every case they had been signed for by Sonja Bjornsen.

Fourteen

The office of Lars Sorensen was a model of Scandinavian order and cleanliness: white walls, modern tubular furniture and gleaming filing cabinets. Berg guessed no papers stayed unfiled in this place for long.

'So this is a general piece you're writing?' Sorensen asked. He was a thin-faced, sandy-haired man of about sixty, bounding with youthful energy, sharp-eyed, and, Berg suspected, even sharper-minded.

'I don't know if it'll make a story yet,' Berg said. 'I'm after background really.'

'Oh yes? What sort of background?'

Berg didn't answer but peered at the wall of cabinets. 'You specialise in finding war criminals, I gather.'

'Not in finding them, no. In accumulating evidence, yes. Evidence of crimes committed on Norwegian soil and against Norwegian citizens. Mind you, it's almost eighteen years since the war. Evidence isn't so easy to come by nowadays.'

'Nor are war criminals presumably.'

The sharp eyes glittered. 'Oh, I don't know about that. You'd be surprised how many are still hiding in the woodwork.'

Berg said admiringly: 'And you're ready to nail them.'

Sorensen jumped to his feet with surprising agility. 'Here, I'll show you.'

He beckoned Berg into an adjacent room. Here the ranks of filing cabinets filled all the available wall space.

Sorensen began to talk with the enthusiasm of the dedicated specialist. 'I have everything cross-referenced by victim's name, district, type of crime and, of course, the criminal, where known. There is no serious crime of the Occupation that isn't here in these records, in some form or another.'

Sorensen added in a flat unemotional voice: 'My son was murdered by the Gestapo, you see.'

Berg was silent. He was staring at the sheer quantity of information. He'd had no idea the records would be so extensive.

'Look, each village, each town.' Sorensen pulled open a drawer full of index cards categorised by place names. 'I have a record of what happened in even the smallest village. I wrote to each *kommune* immediately after the war, you see, while people's memories were still fresh.' He commented with pride: 'It was a mammoth task.'

Berg stared at the rows of place names. It occurred to him that somewhere deep in these files was a place and a name he knew very well indeed. The knowledge did not please him at all.

He said briskly: 'I was actually interested in Norwegians who might have been detained in the Soviet Union at the end of the war. I don't know if that's your field ...'

'But of course it is!' Sorensen exclaimed. 'In fact, it's my main task nowadays.'

Berg was incredulous. 'Looking for Norwegians in *Russia*?'

'No, no. Missing persons generally.'

Berg recovered his composure. It had been eighteen years. No reason to get rattled now.

He asked: 'And are there any in the Soviet Union, do you think?'

Sorensen hesitated. 'Why do you want to know, may I ask?'

Berg assumed a smile. 'My paper's picked up a story about a Norwegian who lived happily in the Soviet Union for some years. We wondered how many others there might be.'

The lawyer shook his head. 'Ah, you have me there. Impossible to say for sure, I'm afraid. One can only guess. A boy might have been last seen near the Russian lines, or in a forced labour camp later overrun by the Russians. But even then – who can tell? The boy might not have got into Russian hands at all, but been killed by the Germans and put in an unmarked grave.' He shook his head.

'So you don't have much luck with your missing persons?'

'Oh, I wouldn't say that,' he replied firmly. 'It depends on where and how the person disappeared. If the subject was in a camp I can often trace the person who last saw the subject alive. Surprisingly often I find someone who actually saw the subject die. Even that's a great comfort, you know.'

'A comfort?'

'To the relatives.'

'Ah.'

'They rarely come to me expecting to find their sons alive. They just want to know the truth.'

Berg flicked through the index cards in the open drawer. 'So they come to you, the parents, and hire you to find their sons?'

'Yes. I do charge them a little, I have to – I give up a lot of commercial work for this. But I ask hardly anything. It gives me a lot of satisfaction, you see.'

Berg said warmly: 'I'm sure it does.'

'I don't get so many requests nowadays, of course –'

A female voice called from an adjacent office. Sorensen hurried out, gesturing towards the cabinets. 'Have a look if you want to. Please. Have a look round.'

Berg stared fiercely at the rows of cabinets. He wished Sorensen hadn't issued the invitation. On the one hand he was drawn by a terrible curiosity, on the other, a strong desire to leave well alone.

He examined the drawer markers. The open drawer beside him was labelled Har–Hau. Two cabinets further along he saw Por–Pu. The T's must be just beyond.

He took a step forward, then stopped, thinking hard.

Suddenly he relaxed and, reaching into his pockets, found a cigarette and, lighting it, drew deeply. He must be mad even to consider looking. Why bother himself with all that? The information might be there – in fact, it probably was – but if so, it had been successfully buried for sixteen years or more. No one would find it now, not unless they were looking for it.

And why should they look?

Nobody was hiring Sorensen to search for *him*.

When Sorensen returned it was to find Berg flicking through the entries for Ber–Bor with the slightly bored expression of someone who has seen quite enough.

*

Thrane stared at the blank sheet of paper on the desk in front of him, lost in thought. His assistant, a young man called Jensen, had given up trying to get anything out of him since arriving for work at seven-thirty.

'How much longer?' Thrane demanded suddenly.

'Any moment now,' Jensen replied. It was the fourth time Thrane had asked in the last half hour.

'What the hell's taking them so long?'

'I'll go and see.'

Five minutes later the internal phone rang and Jensen's voice said: 'Got it!'

Thrane walked casually out of his office and down the stairs. But once in the basement he almost broke into a run. Passing the incinerator room he rapped on an adjacent door. Jensen let him into a large storeroom, and jerked his head towards a tall brown paper sack. 'The collection was a bit late today,' he explained. 'They were short-staffed.'

Thrane cut open the neck of the sack and shone his ultra-violet penlight on to the contents. A few shreds of paper gleamed back at him. Thrane sagged with relief. At least they'd got the right sack. The roar of the incinerator could clearly be heard from next door: all the other sacks were already going up in smoke.

It took thirty minutes to pick out all the ultra-violet shreds. That was the easy bit. Spreading them out and examining both sides of the minute strips took much much longer.

The answer had come to Thrane at three in the morning. He'd realised it was the only way she could have done it. No record was kept of the amount of blank paper stored and used – a near-impossible task. But she'd had to use something. She'd got to be seen turning on the shredder and she'd got to be seen feeding paper into it.

Clever girl.

Thrane tried not to get excited too quickly, but half-way through the job he knew he was right. The feeling of triumph was glorious.

When the job was almost finished he left Jensen to it and ran upstairs. Within minutes he'd got the go-ahead to apply for a phone tap. It took an hour to get the application rubber-stamped and another two hours to get the tap in operation. He also put someone on to her office phone, although he knew he wasn't likely to get anything there.

He spent the rest of the afternoon in closed session with a tight-lipped Ekeland, Head of Security, and a shocked and disbelieving Director. Thrane pressed for complete and immediate surveillance, but the Director delayed a final decision until he'd put it to an emergency meeting of the security committee that evening. Thrane's argument for haste was overruled.

After that, everything seemed rather an anti-climax. Thrane worked out a detailed surveillance schedule with Ekeland, then went through Sonja's security file, only to find exactly what he'd expected to find – precisely nothing.

Finally he forced himself to face the fact that nothing much was going to happen at the moment. It would be a waiting game. In fact it might take weeks, even months, before they got what they needed. It wasn't just a question of proving Sonja was removing information, it was a matter of establishing what she was doing with it. Who was she passing it to? Was it going direct to the Russians, or through an intermediary? Was she passing it knowingly to the Soviet Union?

Was she a fully trained agent, for God's sake?

As the full implications filtered into Thrane's mind he felt quite sick with anger.

Sonja had known almost everything. She was likely to be the greatest disaster to Nato security in living memory.

And the only proof he had was a few shreds of paper.

He began to fret again. He didn't know if he'd be able to survive a waiting game.

After everyone had gone home he sat down and went through Sonja's security file again with a fine-tooth comb. Nothing. Everything desperately normal. Sonja had led an exemplary life.

But a woman like Sonja Bjornsen didn't start spying just like that. There had to be something, there had to be.

There was, but it wasn't in the file.

His phone rang at 18.45. It was Jensen. 'The phone tap. The subject got a call at 18.34. A male who didn't give his name. They made a date for tonight. No time, no place given.'

'Got the full script?'

'Yup. The man said: "It's me. I've only just got back. Any chance of tonight?" She said: "I don't know. It's very short

189

notice." He said: "I'm away again at the weekend. I can only manage tonight, that's the problem." She said: "I see." He asked: "Something the matter?" She said: "I was so hoping to hear from you." "I told you. I've been away. But I am sorry about your mother. Really. Now how about tonight?" She said: "I'll try. I can't promise. It'll be very difficult." He said: "Good. See you later then."' Jensen added: 'She sounded distinctly cross with him.'

'Get the tape up here as soon as possible.'

'There was another call. The subject made it.'

Thrane urged: 'Yes.'

'She called a woman called Monika. The subject asked if she could have the house for the evening. Monika wasn't at all keen and made a bit of a fuss. But our girl talked her into it. Monika's vacating the house between 19.30 and 21.30.'

Thrane looked at his watch. Almost ten to seven. 'Christ.' He hesitated, remembering the Director's ruling.

To hell with it. He ordered: 'Get someone round to her place. No, damn it – go yourself, Jensen. Fast.'

An hour later Jensen called in.

'I've been here since 19.10. She'd already gone. No lights, no sounds. Nothing.'

Thrane groaned and buried his head in his hands.

Sonja was late arriving at the house in the pinewood. She saw with relief that Monika's car had gone.

There was no sign of Erik.

She let herself in. She hadn't brought food; there hadn't been time to buy any. Besides she couldn't have eaten a thing. She'd remembered the Scotch though, and, pouring herself a glass, she took a sip.

Normally she didn't drink hard liquor, but tonight she didn't care what she was meant to do or not do. She needed it. She took a more substantial sip. It tasted good. So it should: it cost a great deal. In fact, liquor was taxed so heavily that a bottle was about the same price as a new dress. She stared at the amber liquid thoughtfully. Sometimes Erik drank half a bottle in an evening.

She gave herself a small shake. What was she doing sitting

around drinking? Everything should seem as normal as possible. Finding some cheese in the fridge she put it on the table then, catching sight of herself in a mirror, hurried to the bathroom to tidy up. She did what she could with her hair, which wasn't a lot, and glanced at the overall effect. She stopped and stared at herself for a long time. Her face seemed quite different from before. Older, less attractive ... defeated.

Tears sprang to her eyes. Turning hastily away, she returned to the kitchen and sat at the table, motionless.

After half an hour she heard a sound and stiffened, but it was only a car going to the next house.

He was very late.

Perhaps he wasn't coming.

The thought was agony and she could hardly bear to imagine it.

When the knock finally came, her heart hit her ribs with such a thump that for a moment she couldn't stand up.

Finally she went and opened the back door. He came in. She searched his face. She couldn't believe it: he looked just the same.

He gave her a quick kiss. His breath smelled of alcohol and stale cigarettes. She heard him say: 'The traffic was bad.'

He went straight into the kitchen and poured himself a large drink. He looked around. He seemed restless and distracted.

He spotted her drink. 'Good Lord, Sonja, taken to hard liquor?'

'Yes.'

'Oh, your mother. Of course. I am sorry.' He came and put an arm round her shoulder.

'Didn't you get any of my notes?'

'I only got them today, I'm afraid.' He gestured regret. 'I really couldn't come till now.'

She thought: Such lies. Why such dreadful lies?

He dropped his arm. 'So, how are you bearing up?'

'I'm better now,' she said eventually. 'Managing quite well, really.'

'Poor darling,' he said briskly, swigging at his drink.

That was the total sum of his compassion, she realised. He wasn't going to ask another thing about her ordeal. She realised: **he didn't care in the slightest.**

191

But she wanted to be sure. She said: 'I don't know why I told you that. It's not true. In fact I haven't managed at all. I don't know if I'm managing even now.'

He looked vaguely surprised. Sonja rarely complained about anything, and never about herself. His face assumed a mask of concern. 'Oh dear, how awful for you. Poor darling.' His voice was cool, carefully establishing distance in case this marked the beginning of an emotional outburst.

She knew then that he really didn't care. Had she ever really believed he did?

He said: 'How long have we got the house for?'

'Two hours at the most. No, much less now.'

'Oh, what a pity.'

There was relief in his voice. She knew why: because there wouldn't be time for love-making. The knowledge turned like a knife in a wound.

Her heart thumping, she asked: 'How's work?'

He gave her a quick look. 'Oh, all right. But I have to go away again this weekend.' He sat down at the table.

'The department are sending you?'

He frowned. 'Yes. Who else?'

'I don't know.' She realised it was a stupid question: he was suspicious. She added quickly: 'I thought you might have been seconded. There's quite a lot of secondment going on at the moment.'

He was looking at her as if she were mad.

She sat down opposite, and burbled: 'Where are you going in fact?'

There was a pause. She never usually asked such bald questions. Eventually he answered: 'To Kaafiord, actually. To have a look around the site of the new installation.'

'Oh.'

'Trying to protect FO/E's interests as usual. Though – also as usual – I'm not allowed to know what they are.'

Sonja thought: My God, but you're brazen.

He raised his eyebrows, waiting for a response. That was what it had come to, Sonja realised: a prompt from him and a gush of information from her.

Suddenly Sonja wanted to kill him. She wanted to squeeze a trigger and dig a knife into his ribs and tear all that lovely thick hair out of his head.

She jumped to her feet and, going to the fridge, pretended to look inside. 'I didn't have time to buy food.'

She heard the snap of his lighter and the suck of his breath on a cigarette. 'No matter.'

In the shelter of the fridge door she closed her eyes, wanting to postpone whatever ghastly confrontation lay ahead. She dreaded challenging him.

She said: 'We'll just have cheese then, shall we?' and went to the cupboard to find some plates.

Suddenly she knew she couldn't face a confrontation. She couldn't face the arguments, the denials, the derision, the final scene when he would walk out. Because he would walk out, there was no doubt about that.

She could bear almost anything but that.

No, there wouldn't be a confrontation. The decision was a relief, an enormous weight off her shoulders. She felt almost happy again.

She dug in a drawer for some knives.

Of course she'd have to decide what to do eventually. She couldn't let things go on as before.

Suddenly it occurred to her – she could. Things could go on just as before – except for one thing.

The germ of an idea crept into her mind. At first she couldn't quite grasp it and, to give herself more time, said: 'The cheese looks pretty old. D'you mind?'

He shrugged.

She put some of Monika's tomatoes on the table and a bowl containing some rather old fruit.

At last the idea came into focus and sharpened. She grabbed at it. Suddenly she knew what she was going to do.

She sat down rather abruptly.

Erik looked at her questioningly.

Rubbing a hand over her forehead, she said, 'The drink – it's gone to my head.' She added in a matter-of-fact tone: 'So you're going to Kaafiord. We had a meeting about it only today.'

'Ah.' He displayed only the mildest interest.

Sonja thought of the minutes in her bag and tried to remember all the details of the installation. 'It's something quite new,' she said truthfully. 'And very sensitive. So I'm not surprised they're sending you up there. Security will be quite a problem.'

His eyes were like a cat's, blank but watchful. He was probably thinking how easy this was proving to be.

'And they really haven't told you anything about it?' she asked.

'Really.'

She looked puzzled. 'I don't know why, darling, with your – seniority. Anyway – Kaafiord is to be the first of a new navigation system. The system's called Delta. It's far more accurate than Loran-C. Apparently it can fix a submarine's position to within a few hundred yards.'

'And Loran-C can't do that?'

She must get this right. 'Not unless the sub's on the surface. And even then it isn't nearly so good. Only to within a mile or so.'

'And Delta?'

'To within yards.'

'When the subs are down?'

'Yes. Not too deep. But definitely down.'

He appeared to be absorbing it all. He looked up suddenly. 'But the site isn't on the coast.'

'What? Oh – no,' she agreed. She hadn't thought this far. He was waiting for an explanation. At last inspiration came. 'It has to be installed high up, away from interference.'

'Ah.' Finally he nodded and said lightly: 'Oh well, all *I* have to do now is make it secure, don't I?'

He'd swallowed it. She felt weak. What a minefield lies were.

For a long while she sat limply, hardly hearing what he was saying.

Then she brightened up. Everything was going to be all right after all.

Fifteen

Skorpa ploughed steadily across the sound, her bow cleaving the water into two neat white curls. The sky was transparently clear and, though the sun was well hidden behind the mountains, the light was unusually bright. Or so it seemed to Hal. He stood beside the wheelhouse, peering at the jetty ahead, screwing his eyes up against the electric-white of the hills, suppressing a slight queasiness.

The hangover was no more than he deserved. Having been abstemious for weeks, he'd got involved in beer and aquavit with Arne, and hadn't remembered anything including when to stop. A gold medal performance. He wasn't feeling very proud of himself.

The jetty was drawing closer and he spotted two figures starting down it hand in hand: Ragna, in the bright blue woollen jacket she often wore, and Kris, small and well wrapped at her side.

He waved. At first they didn't see, but then Kris pointed and, jumping up and down, waved back.

With more than his usual concentration he nudged *Skorpa* alongside. Ragna took the lines, looped them over the bollards, and strolled up. 'Hiya,' she called cheerfully. There was a warm glad-to-be-here smile on her face. Hal looked at her curiously. She looked exceptionally happy – something must have happened.

Ragna caught his look and answered with a small laughing shrug.

Climbing on to the jetty he kissed her dutifully on the cheek. 'Are you all right?'

She made a face of mock surprise. 'Yes – why?'

Something *had* happened. She'd sold the shop. She was moving to Oslo. She'd met a man. He hesitated, wanting to know, yet unable to ask. Finally he murmured: 'Nothing,' and, leaning down, said a grave manly hello to Kris. 'Where's your bag, young chap?'

'With Mummy!'

Ragna had gone to pick up a couple of holdalls. It seemed a lot of baggage for one small boy.

Hal took the bags from her. 'I hope it's all right,' she said, 'but I thought I'd come too.'

For a moment he didn't understand what she meant.

'It's probably the only good day we'll have for the rest of the winter,' she explained. 'It seemed a pity to waste it.'

He took it in at last: she was coming to Brattdal. For a moment the suspicion entered his mind that perhaps she hadn't trusted him to look after Kris on his own.

'I could have managed.'

'Oh, it wasn't that!' she exclaimed.

He still felt uncertain; she'd taken him completely by surprise. 'There's nothing special to eat. And the stove's not lit in the other room. I wasn't expecting you . . .'

'That makes us quits then!'

'What?'

'On surprise visits. One each.' With a smile, she pressed the palm of her hand against his cheek. He turned quickly away. He wasn't as immune to her as he liked to think. Not yet.

He helped Kris on to the boat. Ragna made her own way on board. Her visit was obviously settled: he was pleased. It would give their new relationship a good start. She didn't know about this new relationship yet. But she soon would.

He'd finally realised that waiting for a change of heart from Ragna was a hopeless cause. The sailing visit had revealed the situation very clearly – she was angry and impatient with him, she was irritated by his devotion, she wanted to go to Oslo to 'escape' – and he was beginning to suspect she meant from him.

So he'd come to his decision. He would give up all ideas of winning Ragna. The two of them would become trusted old friends.

Hard, but not impossible, not if one was determined enough. He'd already taken the first step: he'd asked Anna-Kristin to

Brattdal the next weekend.

As soon as they were under way he stood Kris on a box in the wheelhouse and pointed out the sights, because that was the way he had planned it. Ragna did not join them, but stayed on deck in the shelter of the wheelhouse, leaning against the window, tendrils of hair twisting and snaking around her face.

From the mainland jetty it was four miles across the sound to Revoy. The island gave a good lee and, once *Skorpa* was safely moored, the transfer to the dinghy was relatively easy. The only awkward moment came when Hal lifted Kris over *Skorpa*'s side and down into Ragna's waiting arms. Then, as he let go of the child, he lurched foolishly and grabbed for the rail.

'All right?' Ragna asked, swinging Kris down on to a seat in the dinghy.

'Nothing a hole in the head wouldn't cure.'

She looked at him curiously. 'You've been hitting the bottle!'

Hal grunted: 'The bottle hit *me*.' He forwent his usual athletic leap into the dinghy, and made his way carefully over the bulwark.

'Don't tell me you're a secret drinker!' She looked pleased at the idea.

'Not so secret,' he said with a sheepish glance. He slid the oars into the crutches and began to pull towards the shore.

Ragna's eyes widened in surprise. 'Oh ... I see. A party.'

'That would be rather an exaggeration.' He gave a hard pull on the oars so that the dinghy creamed through the water.

She murmured: 'The social whirl of Revoy, eh?' and settled back on her seat, watching him closely, her head tilted, her eyes half-closed.

Hal realised that her imagination was probably running away with her, but let it ride.

The dinghy crunched gently on to the shingle beach. Bamse met them with low barks and wild convolutions of his tail.

For fun, Hal had brought the tractor down for the short journey up the valley. But three people and two bags were going to be a problem in a one-seater.

'I can see that this expedition is man's stuff,' Ragna said tactfully. 'I'll walk.'

'I can come back for you,' Hal volunteered.

'No, it'll do me good.' And she set off at a brisk walk.

Kris was wide-eyed and silent at the sight of the enormous tractor, whose rear tyres towered high above him. Hal put the bags in a corner of the cab and started the engine. It fired with a roar. Kris screwed up his face. Hal climbed into the cab and pulled Kris up on to his knee and they set off, trundling and lurching up the hill. They caught up with Ragna, who stood to one side and waved as they passed.

Kris clung to Hal as the tractor took to the steepest part of the hill, its body rocking and jarring over the uneven surface of the hard-packed snow. Glancing down, Hal saw the boy's face alight with excitement, and he felt a sudden burst of happiness.

He thought: Why can't it always be like this?

Ragna came round the curve in the track and saw the tractor, empty of passengers, parked to one side of the house. Then the house itself came into view. She paused for a moment, head on one side, and took a fresh look at it. She'd forgotten how striking the place was. On her last visit in mid-summer it had rained all day and the place had seemed as bleak and grey as the weather. But now in the pale winter light the mellow wood had a subtle warmth which was almost welcoming.

She walked on. Away to the right a number of shaggy, long-haired creatures stood noses to the snow. The famous musk-oxen. To the left of the house were clusters of fragile saplings and, behind, a walled area. The much-prized vegetable garden. It all looked very ordered.

She reached the top of the path and paused to look at the house from close quarters. She'd forgotten how ornate the carvings and ornamentations were, and how pretty the veranda was, with its latticed arches. It was a ridiculous house for such a remote spot, of course. A monument to some overblown nineteenth-century ego. Yet in a strange way it belonged here, like some grand dame lording it over her country estates.

If you felt like burying yourself alive, it was probably the perfect spot.

The front door opened and Hal and Kris and Bamse came out in a rush of shouts and barks. They were on their way to see the musk-oxen. Kris begged Ragna to join them, but she smiled a refusal and watched them dance off across the snow.

She strolled into the house. There'd been many changes since her last visit, she noticed: bright rugs on the pine floors, new curtains, old wooden farming tools and copper cooking utensils hung on the walls as ornaments; more furniture, most of it antique and rather beautiful; photographs, paintings, mementoes; and dozens and dozens of books arranged on shelves, in bookcases and in high stacks on the floor.

Hal had been busy.

She peered at the photographs. Several of expeditions, a few of Jan and Hal in the old days, a series of formal poses from the last century, soft-focus family portraits from the 1930s.

On a long table under the window a large number of papers, books and pamphlets were spread out. She peered at them. Research papers, notes, technical magazines, letters.

Her eyes focused on a letter which lay openly on the top of a pile.

'My dearest Hal,' it said in large scrawling handwriting, 'Just a quick note to say yes to next week. I've missed Brattdal very much. And you. It's good news that you'll be on the' –

On the what? Ragna flipped the letter over.

– 'telephone soon.' Ragna blinked: he hadn't told her that.

The letter finished: 'Are you interested in trekking on the plateau at Easter? love, A-K.'

Ragna replaced the letter carefully in the position she had found it.

Anna-Kristin.

Coming to Brattdal. Going trekking.

Fine.

Not fine. She minded. Which was ridiculous. Why should she?

But she knew why. It was the feeling that Hal's life was bowling onwards, while hers was standing still.

Yet there was more to it, and she wasn't sure what it was. But she had a sudden acute feeling of loss.

Her good humour deflated, she half-heartedly continued her tour. The kitchen was simple and old-fashioned, with a large stone sink and scrubbed wood surfaces. The table had been laid with two places, complete with neatly folded napkins, and dishes of meat and cheese, conscientiously covered in muslin.

If she hadn't been so preoccupied, she would have thought the preparations rather touching.

Next to the kitchen was a box room, spartan and with the musty smell of a room that is never used.

On the upper floor was the bathroom, such as it was, and three bedrooms. The main bedroom and the guest bedroom were at the front of the house on either side of a hallway. At the far end of the hall next to the bathroom was a room that connected with Hal's. This was obviously Kris's room, for the bed had been made and turned back, and his bag placed at the foot.

She went in. The window, decked with bright check curtains, overlooked the vegetable garden. She peered down and saw symmetrical rows of canes protruding from the snow. On the bedside table were some picture books – two of them brand-new – a jug of water and a glass. On the centre of the pillow lay a stuffed rag-toy, a horse with one eye missing. It looked old and well loved.

The scene was very ordered – what was the word – snug. It left her feeling vaguely excluded, almost as if she were an intruder.

The connecting door to Hal's room was open. She paused and, drawn by a glimpse of the view, walked in, aware that she really was an intruder now.

She went straight to the window. The view was magnificent. The valley walls and the falling ground created a frame for the expanse of dark glinting water that extended towards the shores of Ullsfiord. In the distance the Lyngen Alps rose in pink-tinged peaks, like icing on a giant cake.

'I've missed Brattdal very much . . .'

Ragna pursed her lips. She had, had she?

There was a distant sound. She put her face to the window. She could just see the boys on the hillside. They were heading slowly back.

Turning to leave, she took a quick all-encompassing look at the room. Something made her pause. There were photographs by the bed. She recognised one of herself and Kris, another of Hal's family. But her eye was caught by a tiny picture stuck into the frame of the family portrait.

She padded silently over and peered at it.

It was a full-length colour snapshot of a woman on skis, an extremely pretty woman in a sky-blue all-in-one ski outfit. Ragna wasn't quite sure what irritated her more – the woman's prettiness or the incredibly smart ski outfit.

The woman was laughing. She obviously liked a good time. Well – she'd be disappointed in Hal.

Or would she?

Perhaps Hal did give her a good time.

She gritted her teeth and hurried downstairs. When the others came in, noisy with chatter and stamping feet, they found her sitting thoughtfully at the window. Kris threw off his outdoor clothes and rushed up, ruddy-cheeked and bursting with life. It made her heart lift to see him so happy.

During lunch she observed Hal. He seemed very relaxed. She pictured him with the laughing woman, and thought: Sometimes I feel I don't know you at all.

After the meal they went out to enjoy the last of the afternoon light, climbing up the valley to one of the new plantations, where they examined the saplings and learnt their names and guessed how tall they might grow. Later they climbed even higher, though Kris found the going difficult and hitched a lift on Hal's shoulders. The air was hard and fresh, crisp with the dry cold of winter. They found the tracks of a ptarmigan in the snow. Bamse, driven into an instant frenzy, floundered through the snow and disappeared over the ridge at a determined canter.

On the way back Kris insisted on Ragna seeing the musk-oxen at close quarters. She had to admit they had a certain charm, with their thick black coats falling in shaggy fringes almost to the ground and their long old-man faces with the unexpected frosting of white round the muzzle, as if they'd just licked cream.

But most of all she liked the way the thick black hair grew so suddenly and densely from the smooth forehead, rising in a high coiffure from a distinctive hairline.

'They look as though they're wearing wigs,' she laughed.

Kris gave her a fierce look. 'It's not pretend hair, Mama!'

When the steely night-cold crept down from the mountain they headed home. The sky had a luminous radiance, all baby colours, pink and violet and silky blue, while beneath, the snow seemed almost transparent. Ragna had to admit it was lovely, magical almost. But the prospect of getting back to the warmth of the house was lovelier still.

Hal, with Kris on his shoulders, told the boy what his grandmother had told him: about the *huldrefolk* – the hidden people – who were meant to live in the valley, and of the trolls who had inhabited the mountains long ago and left giant footprints on the rocks, and of the ghosts, the *deildegast*, who until recently had jumped out from behind rocks and frightened people to death. Then he laughed and said the ghosts had all been chased off by the musk-oxen, and Kris giggled with relief.

Later Hal cooked an early supper: halibut steamed with herbs, potatoes, carrots in butter, followed by Arctic cloudberries.

Afterwards they played a game of happy families, but Kris, tired and difficult, made a fuss about losing, and Ragna hauled him upstairs to bed.

They had their customary bedtime hug. Tonight she looked down at him nestling contentedly on her lap and felt a sudden surge of emotion for this child of hers. It wasn't that she didn't love him all the time – of course she did – it was just that, coming on top of all her other worries, he sometimes wore her down.

She tickled his cheek and he made the funny little grunting sound he always made when he was content.

Hal came up as she was tucking him in. For a moment they stood either side of the bed, looking down at the child. A happy family group, thought Ragna, except that this wasn't a family. Ragna said abruptly to Hal: 'Why don't you read him a story?' and, kissing Kris firmly on both cheeks, walked briskly from the room.

It was half an hour before Hal came down. 'Would you like a drink?' he asked. 'I'm having a beer myself.'

'The hair of the dog?'

He made a wry face. 'Quite.'

Ragna was about to refuse the drink when she suddenly thought: Why the hell not? And had an aquavit.

They sat in the living room, either side of the blazing stove, in long low armchairs with cushioned seats. The room was filled with the scent of pine. The light of the oil lamps made the wood gleam with a rich reddish hue, like mahogany.

The cosiness suddenly irritated Ragna. 'You know, if you get much more comfortable here you'll forget the outside world altogether.'

Hal replied with a soft smile: 'Ah. I don't forget the outside world, Ragna. I just do without it most of the time.'

'But not all the time, I hear.' It was out before she could stop it. A horrid shrewish remark.

He shot her a questioning glance.

Too late to back out now. She said lightly: 'I heard you had a new friend.'

Understanding came over his face, and he looked quickly away, frowning. She'd caught him by surprise. 'Ragna –' he began and closed his mouth abruptly. Finally he looked up again. 'It means nothing. She's just – a casual friend.'

'Oh, don't misunderstand me,' she said hastily. 'I don't mind what sort of friend she is. None of my business. It's just that I seem to have been the last to hear. And I think I mind about that.'

'Yes . . . I'm sorry.' But he looked curious rather than apologetic, and she found his steady stare rather disconcerting.

'At least it'll put paid to the rumours,' she added.

'Rumours?'

Was he being slow on purpose, she wondered? She thought she caught a glint of mischief in his eye.

'You know what I mean,' she said firmly.

He looked mystified. She felt sure it was just a ploy.

She resisted answering, then said in mock irritation: 'Us.'

'Oh – us!' he exclaimed, feigning surprise. 'Now why would they think that?'

He was definitely making fun of her; his eyes were full of laughter.

'Why?' she repeated drily. 'It's that damned party line, that's why. They all listen in, I know they do.'

'In which case you'd have thought they'd have got it right.'

'Huh! You know what they're like around here.'

'Pretty accurate, normally.'

He was in an unusually gay mood. She couldn't work it out. 'Not so accurate in this case,' she pointed out.

'Well,' he said easily, 'perhaps they sensed the way I felt about you.'

She was completely taken aback. He'd never talked like this before. She stared, for once speechless.

He got up. She realised he was coming over to her. She held her breath: she couldn't deal with this situation at all. He stood before her and put out his hand. 'Want another drink?' he asked lightly.

She exhaled weakly, and handed him her glass.

He went to the corner cupboard where he kept the drinks. 'Don't worry, Ragna. This isn't a declaration.' He threw her a brief smile of reassurance.

She found her voice. 'Oh.'

He brought the drink and sat down again. 'There was a time when I hoped we might become more than friends, but ...' He shrugged. 'That doesn't seem very realistic now, does it?'

Ragna didn't know what to say. Hal's presence – his devotion – had been part of her life for three years, something undiscussed and unquestioned. She'd got used to it, even reliant on it. Now here he was – what? – withdrawing it?

'You want to move to Oslo, you want lots of people around you,' Hal went on. 'And that desire is very strong in you, I can see that. Personally, I don't think crowds of people are ever the answer. But that's just me.'

She said: 'I could never live in a place like this, Hal.'

He seemed to hold his breath. 'I understand that. Well, now I do.' He smiled so nicely that she wanted to hug him.

Hug him. She thought: That's the drink talking!

She said: 'You've been very good to me.'

'Good!' he exclaimed with a shudder. 'I've just tried to be a friend, that's all. And because I wanted to be, Ragna. Because I admired and respected you. It wasn't just – because of Jan.'

The drink gave her the courage to say something that had been unsaid for far too long. 'I never blamed you, you know.'

He stiffened visibly.

'Not for a moment,' she said. 'But I've never been sure you believed that.'

He got up and, taking the poker, crouched in front of the stove and stoked the fire so that clouds of sparks flew up the chimney. He sat down again, frowning at the flames, then looked at her with sudden intensity. 'I still blame myself for not having prevented it, and nothing will ever change that. Nothing.

But my – feelings for you are quite separate.'

She nodded, feeling strangely inadequate and oddly guilty. Hal would never forget about Pasvik – he didn't want to forget – whereas she couldn't wait to leave it far, far behind.

'I would have wanted us to be friends whatever had happened,' Hal continued. 'You do see that?'

She smiled, pleased.

'Anna-Kristin is something different,' Hal went on, and Ragna's pleasure dimmed a little. 'I – well, you know how it is – it's nice to have someone around now and then.'

Nice? Ragna was sure it must be very nice indeed.

She imagined the woman here with Hal, and felt a small pang. Did they make love? Of course they did! What else would they do? She pictured Hal making love, and the picture was vivid, disturbingly so. He would be passionate – yes, very – but kind and gentle too.

She shifted restlessly in her chair, uncomfortably aware that she had not made love to anyone for three years. It suddenly seemed a very long time indeed.

Hal was saying something. She made the effort to concentrate and realised they were still on the subject of Anna-Kristin.

'Our relationship isn't going to change. I would never ask her to come and live here, for instance. Not that she'd come anyway, I shouldn't think.' He gave a brief self-deprecating smile. 'I'm not perhaps the easiest person ...'

She decided he was probably right about not being easy, but that it was nothing to be ashamed of. Difficult people were generally far more interesting. She murmured: 'It's just a matter of finding the right person at the right time.'

They talked about choices then, choices between career and relationships, and how difficult they were to make. And how easy it was to make mistakes which could never be undone.

As they talked it seemed to Ragna that some barrier had lifted and there was a new bond of frankness and affection between them. Hal had yielded up something important to her. Trust, good will, but most of all his natural reticence, as if he'd decided to lay his most precious possession at the feet of their new friendship.

She was flattered. She was also intrigued – she'd never seen him so relaxed or expressive before. He seemed – unfettered. It suddenly occurred to her that he *was* unfettered – he was free of his feelings for her.

She should feel relieved. But she wasn't sure she did.

It was the drink. Or was it?

They talked for a long time and whenever he smiled – which was often – she thought how very nice he looked when he was happy, and how very attractive he looked when he was serious, and how very much she wanted to kiss that mouth of his.

Later he said: 'You were so happy this morning. Has something happened?'

It all seemed a long time ago. 'No. I was just determined to enjoy the day. I've been thinking that I don't perhaps –' she paused, searching for the right words – 'live for the moment enough.'

'Live for the moment?'

'Feel alive!'

He smiled.

She felt alive now – oh yes. Her worries seemed far away – even the debts seemed unimportant. She'd never told Hal about those; she felt too ashamed.

Whatever was happening, he was aware of it too, because now and then he would smile at her for no particular reason, and she would hold his gaze, and feel her heart move with excitement.

When it was really very late she asked suddenly: 'Do you think one should live for the moment?'

'It depends on whether you can live with the consequences.'

'You're so wise!' she laughed.

'Ah, I'm good enough at the theory. It's life that doesn't follow the rules, damn it.'

She could have stopped it a dozen times, but she didn't want to. She kept thinking: It won't do any harm. Life's too short. I've been so lonely. I need somebody – I want him – just for tonight. I want to feel really alive.

And then she couldn't have stopped it anyway. Some embers settled noisily on the grate and as he leant forward to throw fresh logs into the stove, she thought how fine his profile was and how much she wanted to touch his skin, and the next moment she had knelt beside him and brushed his cheek lightly with her fingertips and sighed: 'Oh Hal.'

Hell.

Nothing had changed at all! He'd never stopped hoping. He still loved her – he'd just got better at hiding it. Who'd he been trying to fool?

The flutter of her fingers almost paralysed him with shock and exhilaration. The softness in her voice caught at his stomach.

Slowly – he made sure it was very slowly – he turned his face towards her and smiled a conspiratorial smile, as if her gesture had been the most natural thing in the world. Then he reached for her hand and pressed it against his cheek.

She knelt beside him on the rug, her face turned up to his, and he bent forward and brushed his lips against hers in the ghost of a kiss.

Then he smiled again because, whatever happened now, he mustn't frighten her away. And she responded with a small be-witching movement of her lips, and then they kissed – different kisses now: endless, deep, needful kisses, and Hal thought his heart would burst with wanting her.

Eventually he actually said it. 'I want you.'

She pulled back a little, and for a heart-stopping moment he thought she was retreating, but then she put her mouth to his ear and whispered softly about how important it was to stay friends afterwards and not let this change anything, and was that all right with him? He agreed – he'd have agreed to *anything* right then. She asked again, was he sure? Of course he was sure – he was sure of everything. He even managed to make light of the moment by saying: 'What are friends for?'

They kissed once more, then Hal pulled her gently to her feet and, with a small step, made the first move towards the doorway. Her eyes dancing with dark excitement, she came into the fold of his arm and let him lead her to the stairs.

The silence seemed to roar in his ears. He couldn't believe what was happening.

He repeated: 'What's the matter?'

'I'm sorry ... I'm *sorry*.'

'Ragna, what is it? Tell me, tell me.'

'I can't explain. I just can't. I'm sorry.'

They were standing by the bed in the darkness, their arms round each other. He hugged her tighter, feeling the wonderful warmth of her body against his, unable to believe she wasn't feeling that warmth too. But it was happening again: she was pushing gently against his chest, trying to escape. He was chilled by this incredible change around, this sudden appalling reversal. He held firm, unable to let her go.

'Ragna, Ragna, don't ... don't *do* this.'

'Hal, it wouldn't be any good. It wouldn't. I'm sorry – I'm *sorry*. It's all my fault. I should never have ...' She moved in his arms, gently but insistently trying to free herself. 'It wouldn't be – I mean, this isn't – oh God ...'

A sudden rage overtook him. He gripped her roughly by the arms and almost shook her.

'Ragna, talk to me about this. Talk to me.'

She gave a short sharp sigh which was almost a sob. 'Hal, it just – wouldn't work.'

'Why?' He tried to read her face in the darkness.

She was shaking her head miserably. 'I don't know – I need time to think –'

'Ragna – we were talking about one night. Not a bloody lifetime. You were the one who wanted to live for the moment – remember!'

'But it wouldn't be like that, would it? I mean, it wouldn't be that simple.'

He cried: 'But I agreed to your rules, remember. I *agreed*.'

'I know, I know. But – perhaps the rules were – no *good*.'

He pushed her away. He was trembling with anger. 'You wouldn't know what you wanted if you had the whole bloody world, Ragna. You've *never* known what you wanted. Christ ...'

He sat down abruptly on the edge of the bed and put a hand to his forehead, completely lost for words.

'Oh, Hal ...' She could hardly speak. He suspected she was crying, but he didn't terribly care. She said in a small voice: 'I don't know what to say.' With a small sigh she bent down to pick up her sweater where it had fallen on the floor.

He realised she was going.

Suppressing his anger, he said flatly: 'Just tell me why.'

A silence. She began to move towards the door. Finally she paused. 'I don't know, Hal. I don't know.'

And then she was gone.

He breathed: 'Go to hell. Go to hell!' and threw himself on the bed.

Sixteen

There were good mornings, there were bad mornings. Thrane had no doubt which this one was, and not just because it was a Monday.

The *Sosialist Dagens Post* lay open on the desk in front of him. There was a news item on the front page. It announced that, according to unconfirmed reports, the third man at Pasvik had been a Norwegian.

He cursed inwardly. How had they got the damn story?

Thrane's Director had already had a word with the editor, who'd mumbled the usual rubbish about protecting his sources, then, as a softener, had dropped a hint that the source was foreign.

Thrane dismissed the idea. He knew who the source was: Sonja. He just couldn't prove it. Not yet.

After three days of round-the-clock surveillance costing a lot of men and even more money he had nothing that would survive in a court-room.

Pushing the newspaper aside, he went through what little he did have.

Sonja went to work, she returned from work, she went shopping, she went to the cinema with a girlfriend on Saturday nights, she went for a walk, she talked on the phone to friends – all women – about the weather and the holiday she was planning in the Canaries.

The search of her apartment had revealed nothing out of the ordinary. Her bank account showed no outside earnings and her spending was modest, although she'd gone on a bit of a spree after the death of her mother, possibly in anticipation of an inheritance. The model of a quiet middle-aged woman.

But a woman with a secret lover.

He was the link man. He had to be. He was the only part of her life that didn't fit.

He'd give anything to know when she was due to meet the lover again. Thursday perhaps, if it was a regular weekly meeting. But he guessed not. The lover had said he was just back in town. It was possible he travelled a lot and their meetings were spasmodic.

So there was nothing for it but to keep the surveillance going and hope that the next meeting would be sooner rather than later.

In the meantime he could continue with the damage assessment report. It was looking very black. Sonja wasn't just a deceiver, Sonja was a full-blown subversive.

He'd spent the first part of the weekend matching what Sonja had known to what had been leaked to the press. The connections were not always obvious. Sometimes a story would appear in the East German press first, sometimes in the Finnish, or Bulgarian, or Soviet, or French – agents of influence from many different countries were used to launch the stories. Yet the stories always did appear, and, in the case of Nato secrets, they appeared between five days and five weeks after Sonja had gained access to the information.

There was also the matter of Pasvik itself.

Sonja had been in the perfect position to leak that.

In which case he'd personally see to it that she got locked up for life.

Along with the mystery lover, of course.

Now all Thrane had to do was catch him. And her. Preferably together.

Restless, he left FO/E headquarters and went to the special operations room they had set up in a safe house nearby. He'd already spent most of the weekend there in session with the security committee and the Director, who was still looking shocked at the activities of his trusted secretary.

They'd examined the most recent secrets to which Sonja had had access. It was a depressing exercise. The minutes she'd so carefully copied just four days ago had covered the building of some highly sensitive COMINT installations for the US National Security Agency.

If the Americans discovered that all the details of their new installations had got out ...

It hardly bore thinking about.

Thrane went into the ops room and took a first-hand look at the surveillance team's latest report. It was just as they'd informed him first thing that morning: Sonja had got up at the usual time and gone to work.

Exciting stuff.

Then he called FO/S, to find out if their field operatives had noticed anything unusual around the installation sites in north Norway. A long shot if there ever was one, but it was a case of leaving no stone unturned.

He hung around for a while, trying for the hundredth time to think of aspects of Sonja's life they might not have covered.

Finally, at eleven, when he was sure nothing was going to happen, he left to keep an appointment with Lars Sorensen, an appointment he'd made last week when his mind had been on other things – namely, the third man.

The lawyer was based near the town hall, in the centre of town. Though it was freezing cold, Thrane decided to walk.

Oslo looked very grey at this time of year, the buildings dark and sombre, piles of grimy snow deposited along the roadsides, the people unsmiling and with long-suffering expressions. Only the trams added light and colour as they jangled gaily along.

The brisk walk did Thrane good, and he felt more cheerful as he climbed the stairs to Sorensen's office.

As always, Thrane was shown into Sorensen's inner sanctum precisely on time. The lawyer shook hands formally, and the two men sat down. Thrane couldn't help noticing that a single sheet of paper lay on the desk in front of Sorensen. It didn't look very promising.

'You've seen the *Dagens Post* this morning?' Thrane asked. 'The report on the third man at Pasvik being a Norwegian Well, that's our man.'

Sorensen nodded. 'I guessed as much.'

'Well? Have you had any luck?'

Sorensen settled in his chair. 'I have some rough figures for you. But first I'd like to tell you exactly how I've arrived at these figures so you'll understand how and why they must inevitably be imperfect.'

'I see.'

'In a country of only four million people with a highly regulated system like ours, missing people generally get noticed, although during and immediately after the war, it all got very confused, as you can imagine.' He paused. 'My information on those who went missing comes from a wide range of sources – *kommunes*, population registers, central military records, regional police forces, and so on. It's relatively simple to find the total of all reported missing. But matching them to unnamed dead is much much more difficult.'

He stood up and wandered over to a filing cabinet. 'Over the years I have obtained copies of all the Nazi records relating to Norway that I could beg, borrow or steal from archives all over the world, from America to those behind the Iron Curtain.' He opened a drawer and pulled out a file. 'The Germans kept immaculate records for much of the time, as you know, and in many cases I've been able to match a dead concentration camp victim to a missing Norwegian citizen. However, the Gestapo here in Occupied Norway were less orderly – not only because they were naturally more secretive but, more to the point, because they didn't always know the names of their victims.'

He opened the file. 'For example, here is an entry for Tromso dated 23rd November 1942. Three men were shot early in the morning and put into an unmarked grave. Now –' he prodded the file – 'these were not Tromso men. It's probable they were three young men missing from the Bodo area since the previous August. Though why they were brought to Tromso we don't know.' He closed the file. 'You see the problem?'

Thrane sighed. 'I'm beginning to.'

'Then there's the problem of those who died right at the beginning, resisting the German invasion, but whose bodies weren't identified. And those who went to fight with the Soviet Army and never returned – maybe they died, maybe they didn't. Needless to say, the Russians have not been forthcoming with figures or names. The only interest they've shown is in Nazi collaborators.'

'So we have no way of knowing how many stayed on in Russia?'

'No.'

'Do you think there were many?'

Sorensen shrugged. 'Impossible to say. But there must have been a few. You know how it was. After four years of German occupation, the Russians seemed like angels to the people in Finnmark.'

'So – where does all this leave us?'

'With a rather inaccurate picture, I'm afraid.'

If Sorensen intended Thrane to feel discouraged, he was succeeding.

'The post-war records were quite useful, of course,' Sorensen went on. 'National service records and so on. A surprising number of people turned up who'd been thought missing. There were a number who'd spent the war in Sweden and managed to evade registering with the authorities there. And of course there were some in Britain, in the army-in-exile. But – let's look at what you're interested in. The shortfall.' He picked up the piece of paper. 'Five hundred and sixty-five.'

Thrane put a hand to his forehead and groaned aloud.

'We can discount a number on grounds of age. You said the man you were looking for was likely to be between thirty-three and fifty at the present time. So ... that would leave four hundred and – let me see – forty-three.'

There was a silence. Thrane stood up. 'You've gone to a lot of trouble.'

'But this is no good to you?'

'Not really. I'll come back to you when – if – I ever get any more information.'

'The list will be here when you want it.'

Sorensen walked him to the door of the outer office. 'By the way, someone else was asking.'

'What?'

'A journalist from the *Dagens Post*.'

'Oh.'

'He was after background information. About how many Norwegians might have been detained in the Soviet Union against their will.'

'Mmm.' It was, he supposed, inevitable that they'd come snooping around. 'But look, let me know if they start ferreting again, will you? And I'd rather they didn't get any figures or anything like that.'

'Of course.'

'In fact, I'd be grateful if you could keep me informed of any requests that might relate to this business in any way at all.'

When Thrane had gone Sorensen returned to his desk and picked up a letter that had been forwarded to him by the Military Archives. It was a request from Halvard Starheim for information on a German name and wartime identity number.

He had almost mentioned it to Thrane just now, but had thought better of it. On consideration, he was glad he'd said nothing. Though he had never met Starheim, he respected and admired him, and had sympathised with him over his unfortunate involvement in the Pasvik affair. He had no wish to bring the man to Thrane's attention unnecessarily.

Besides, the request was completely unrelated. There was no risk of having done the wrong thing.

Rolf Berg's nightmare goes like this:

The school gates loom up. The boy's father has him by the scruff of the neck and is hauling him up the path. The classroom windows are lined with the jeering faces of the boy's schoolmates. The boy is suffocating with humiliation. He wants to strike out and kill this man who is his father, this man whom he hates more than any person in the world. Most of all he wants to die.

The whole school is assembled. They turn to watch the boy being dragged to the headmaster's dais. Their eyes are filled with contempt.

The father deposits the boy in front of the headmaster and says shortly: 'He won't run off again!' He turns on his heel and is gone.

The boy stands alone, burning with shame. This is worse than anything he can imagine. Worse even than the beating his father gave him that morning. *Please let me die.*

With a few gruff words the headmaster sends him to his place.

Now he must survive the day. Many of his schoolmates choose not to speak to him at all, but he can endure that. It is the jibes, the vicious whispers, that hurt.

'Traitor ... Traitor ... Informer ... Murderer ...

They are talking about his father, of course. But the shame is as bad if not worse, because what they say is true, and there's nothing the boy can do about it.

Except hate. Hate his father with all his heart. Hate and plan revenge.

He is fifteen. Soon he'll be taller and stronger than his father. Then he'll kill him.

But the nightmare is static, claustrophobic. However hard he tries he can't move it forward in time. He remains fifteen. He is doomed to stand in front of the school for ever. Their voices scream in his ears: 'Informer ... Nazi traitor ...'

And he dies of shame. Again and again and again.

Berg woke with a start and looked around him.

A hotel room. Somewhere – Tromso. He remembered now: the journey had taken all day.

Damn. He'd overslept.

He pushed the remnants of the dream from his mind and, sitting up, checked his watch. Eight. He stumbled into the bathroom and, splashing his face with cold water, tried to muster his thoughts.

He had phone calls to make – to the office, to people in Oslo, to Ragna Johansen.

He swore again. If Ragna Johansen went out to work, he would have missed her by now. Damn!

He showered and shaved quickly, feeling cross with the world and himself. Then he tried Ragna Johansen's number. No reply. She hadn't been there all weekend either. It would be just his luck if she was away. But unlikely, he decided – January wasn't a time to go visiting in these parts.

Going down to the dining room he had a quick breakfast of black coffee, half a roll and two cigarettes, and returned to his room to try the office.

Nine was a bit early for a daily and it took minutes before the switchboard could find anyone to answer an extension, then several more minutes while a young journalist went to Berg's desk and checked it for messages.

None.

Then he called the Estonian tobacconist.

'One message,' came the reply. 'For Harri. It reads: *Very*

interested in your latest. More detail would be useful. That's it.'

Alex.

Berg put the phone down.

Alex, wanting more information.

What a bloody cheek.

Still ... It meant Kaafiord was important. It meant that someone – which meant Niki – had considered it sufficiently important to want more.

Well, they'd have to be patient. Putting the request to the back of his mind, he set about getting hold of Ragna Johansen. He thought it might take a long time, but he'd forgotten how easy it was to find people in a town the size of Tromso. The telephone operator not only knew who he meant by Ragna Johansen, but had a very definite idea of where to find her.

Ragna sat in the cubicle that served as her office and stared unseeing at the accounts ledger in front of her. She cradled her head in her hands and closed her eyes. From the front of the shop came the murmurings of customers' voices. The staff would be expecting her to give them a hand.

Leaning over, she pushed the door closed. She couldn't cope with customers today.

She shook her head slowly from side to side. The small voice was still there. And it kept saying the same thing over and over again.

What have I done?

Every time she remembered the events of Saturday night she felt sick. What a fool she'd been! He'd never forgive her. And she didn't blame him. She certainly wasn't feeling very proud of herself.

Sunday had been a terrible ordeal. He'd been as cold as ice. Polite, but chillingly distant. The day had passed with agonising slowness.

What a mess.

If only she'd been able to explain. But she hadn't. Not at the time.

It was only later that she'd understood the stifling panic she'd felt at that awful moment in the bedroom. It was as if she were standing on the edge of an abyss of pleasure, about to enter an entrancing prison which, like a golden cage, would close around her and keep her trapped for ever.

She'd realised quite suddenly that it would be impossible to have a casual affair with Hal. He was an all-or-nothing man. Whatever he'd pretended to agree to that night, it wouldn't have worked. He'd have expected all sorts of things from her – commitment, time, love. She couldn't live up to those kinds of obligations, not at the moment. Perhaps not ever.

She'd given commitment and love to Jan, and then he'd gone and – not been there any more. She was no good at dealing with that.

She had a need for darker things now: frivolity, laughter, the stimulation of different people; irresponsibility.

God – why had she let it happen?

Even as she thought it she knew the answer.

Loneliness: it wore you down and made a fool of you. It made you reach out blindly.

Oh, she'd wanted him badly enough. She'd wanted him far too much. That was the real trouble.

She clenched her fists at the still-vivid memory of him, at the touch, the feel of him, and sighed aloud. She knew – it would have been so good.

Yes: that was the real trouble.

And now he'd never understand. What must he think of her?

The telephone rang and she started violently.

She became aware of the office again, and the open ledger, and the sounds outside in the shop.

Pulling herself together, she answered with a brisk: 'Yes?'

'Ragna Johansen?' came a strange voice. 'I was beginning to think I'd never find you.'

'Who is this?'

'Rolf Berg. You wrote to me.'

Ragna tried to take it in. Rolf Berg. She heard herself blustering: 'Oh, hello – *hello*. You read my letter? You're interested in the story then?'

'Yes. In fact, I'm here in Tromso. Can I come and see you?'

'Oh!' She thought quickly and groaned aloud. 'I can't get away. Not until three or so.'

'Ah.' A slight disappointment in the voice. 'Well – I can use the time to get some background, I expect.'

'You could go and see one of my Lapps,' she said quickly. 'A nephew of one of the Kaafiord families.'

'Yes.' He sounded pleased. 'That's exactly what I could do.' She gave him Aslak's work address, and he rang off, saying: 'I'll come to your shop at three then.'

Ragna went to a mirror and dragged a brush through her hair and put on some make-up, thinking: He's come all this way for my story! It was an exhilarating thought. Rolf Berg and his newspaper were influential, and the fact he'd come to Tromso showed that her judgement had been right all along. It *was* an important issue.

She could hardly concentrate on her work, which did nothing to endear her to the customers, who arrived in an unexpectedly steady stream from the late morning onwards.

And then he arrived early, just when she was flustered and exasperated, trying to deal with a belligerent woman determined to squeeze into a dress two sizes too small for her.

Ragna came out of the changing room and he was there, standing by the door, looking surprisingly at ease in a women's dress shop. Ragna was suddenly aware of the scowl on her face and her make-up which she hadn't retouched for hours, and her hair which had fallen over her eyes.

Undaunted she pushed the hair back from her face and strode across to him, thinking: I'm going to impress you!

He shook her hand. 'How are you?' His tone was intimate, as if they'd been friends for a long time.

'Fine!' she said briskly, taking in his confident stance, the immaculate grooming, the smart clothes. She'd forgotten what a sophisticated man he was.

'Give me five minutes, will you?' she said. 'And then perhaps you'd like to come to my house. I've got all the papers there.'

He gave her a long unhurried look and she sensed that those lazy blue eyes missed absolutely nothing. 'Of course,' he said.

She found him waiting outside. He held the door of her car open for her, a gesture that most men in Tromso would think absurd, but which he carried off quite naturally.

As she drove, he told her about his visit to Aslak. He talked in a detached almost bored tone, but she guessed it was his normal manner. She took an occasional glance at him. He was a good-looking man, with that thick blond hair and long straight nose, although the face was harder than she remembered, with deeply etched lines either side of the mouth and across the forehead. An interesting well-lived-in face, with experience — and probably the wrong sort — written all over it.

'I tried to find the reindeer migration routes on the map,' he said, 'but Aslak wasn't sure.'

'Oh, none of them can read maps,' Ragna replied. 'Because they never need them, you see.'

'But he said you'd be able to show me?'

'Oh yes!'

As soon as they got to the house Ragna put some logs in the stove and turned on all the lights so that the room looked welcoming. She prepared a tray of bilberry jam, bread, biscuits, coffee and aquavit. On the way into the living room she paused in front of a mirror and checked her face.

She found him in front of a framed photograph of Krisi. He gave her an odd glance. 'I'd forgotten.'

She put the tray on the table. 'He's five now. He spends the afternoons at a neighbour's house.'

They sat either side of the low table and she poured the coffee. He also accepted an aquavit, a large one, then lit a cigarette and drew on it deeply. He smoked like he drank, she noticed, with determination and long practice. That explained the slight bleariness of the eyes, and the hint of puffiness beneath; imperfections which saved his face from being too handsome, she decided.

She started in a businesslike way. 'Right! Where would you like to start?'

Ignoring the question, he reached into his pocket and handed her a small package. 'A little something for arriving out of the blue.'

She opened it and found a box of handmade chocolates. 'Well, you'll make me change my opinion of journalists yet!'

'Are we not in favour?'

'Hah! I think you're wonderful,' she said emphatically. 'Just as long as you're never allowed to ask the questions!'

He laughed suddenly, a nice deep laugh that transformed his face. She was rather pleased: she guessed that few people were clever or quick enough to make him laugh.

Unfolding a map, she showed him the position of the installation and the migration route of the Lapps who used the valley above Kaafiord.

'At this time of year they're way up on the plateau,' she explained.

'Can we find them?'

She grinned impishly. 'If you've several days to spare and some good skis.'

'What about the installation site. Can we go there?'

'Yes. It's not that far.'

'Could you fix it?' The question was asked charmingly, but she had the impression he was used to people doing exactly what he wanted.

She considered for a moment. 'I would think so.'

Then she showed him the correspondence she and Hal had had with the various government departments. He leafed through it, and asked casually: 'How did you find out about the installation in the first place?'

'Ah.' She wagged a finger at him. 'You should know better than to ask for my sources.'

He smiled, but his eyes were cool, and she thought: He doesn't like being ticked off.

'I just wanted to know how accurate your information was,' he said.

She hadn't thought of that. She felt somewhat deflated. 'Oh, I see ... Well, supposing I said I had friends with friends in the right places. Would that do?'

He didn't look entirely happy, but went on: 'What about the function of the installation – do you know that?'

'No. Wish we did.'

He drained his glass and, leaning forward, helped himself to another drink. He was making himself very much at home, she noticed, but she didn't mind that.

'A pity,' he said. 'It would be better to wage your campaign fully armed. If you knew the function of the installation then you could suggest alternative sites and spike the military's guns – so to speak.'

'Well, we just assumed it was a defence installation ...'

'Ah well, there are installations and installations.'

He ran his fingers over his mouth, looking pensive. She noticed what beautiful hands he had.

Finally he gave a small shrug. 'As far as I understand it, the place is more offensive than defensive.'

'Oh. *Oh.*' She absorbed this startling new information. 'So — it's all nonsense. What they've told me, I mean. About these places being essential for defence.'

'Well . . . it depends on how you define defence.'

'Do you know what this place is for, then?'

He shook his head and, changing the subject, said quickly: 'Will you take me up to the site?' He gave her a slow winning smile. She thought: He's used that before.

But she wasn't going to be put off that easily. She demanded: 'Why won't you tell me about the installation?'

A flicker of irritation passed over his face. 'Because I honestly don't know.' His tone was very soft, very reasonable, and very final. For some reason she was convinced he wasn't telling her everything.

He repeated lightly: 'Come up to the site with me.' He made it sound like an invitation to get to know him better.

She hesitated, wanting to press him on the unanswered question, yet not wanting to alienate him. Finally she left it alone and said: 'Yes, of course I'll take you. Wednesday would be the earliest, if I'm going to organise it properly.' She gave a light laugh. 'I'm no great skier, I'm afraid. But then every event needs a liability. We'd better have a guide though, in case the weather's bad. It's quite a trek up there. Aslak will be happy to come with us, I'm sure.'

'How about Hal?'

Hal. Her heart thumped. A jumble of sensations tumbled into her mind, some exquisite, some painful, but all of them disturbing.

Rolf was watching her closely. He seemed to be reading her mind. She flushed and gave a non-committal shrug.

He said: 'It would be very good for the story if Hal came along. His name still means a lot – both to the editor and to the readers. Besides, I'd very much like to see him again.'

Ragna pictured herself in the mountains with both Hal and Rolf Berg. It wasn't a very happy picture. But she couldn't see any way out of it. She nodded slowly. 'I'll phone him.'

'And tomorrow – can you suggest any more people I should see?'

'Certainly. I'll take you round, if you like.'

'Please.' He was getting to his feet, smiling that lazy smile of his. 'I'm afraid I'll have to ask you to run me back now. I've arranged to have dinner with a local journalist.'

Ragna was disappointed. She'd rather hoped he would stay for the evening.

'But how about dinner tomorrow?' he asked.

'Yes, that would be nice.'

'Assuming I wouldn't be – er – keeping you?'

'Keeping me?'

'From the man in your life.'

He was fishing. Was this a declaration of interest? She almost smiled: it was an intriguing thought.

She heard herself say: 'I can spare the time.'

Then for some reason she thought of Hal and felt incredibly guilty.

Seventeen

Thrane ordered a second search of her apartment, more to convince himself he was doing something useful than in the hope of finding anything concrete.

Immediately they gained entry he was glad he'd come.

Things had changed. Sonja's high standards had slipped. The flat had been scrupulously tidy before. Now there were clothes draped over the bedroom chairs, a mug of half-drunk coffee beside the bed, and a couple of dirty plates soaking in the sink.

Why the change of behaviour? Was she worried about something? Did she know they were on to her?

Or, worst of all, had the lover flown, leaving her lovesick and forlorn? His heart sank at the prospect.

The four of them split up and searched different rooms. Thrane and Jensen chose the main bedroom. Wardrobe, dressing-table drawers, cupboard, bedside table, bed – a difficult one this, they had to be careful to remake it in exactly the same way – light fittings, curtains.

There was nothing. Thrane couldn't help feeling disappointed. One always lived in hope..

Through the hall to the kitchen. The other two were ploughing their way through every pot, pan, screw-top jar and cubbyhole.

Back into the hall. Cupboard with raincoat, light jackets, ski anorak. And on the top shelf a holdall and a handbag. Thrane went through the holdall, which was empty, then the handbag, which was empty too.

He closed the doors and turned away.

He ran a hand lightly over the antique table near the front door, and opened the single shallow drawer. Keys, tram tickets, a lipstick, pens, pencils, paper-clips – unwanted items from a handbag, perhaps. And papers: a receipt from a plumber, a theatre season guide, a letter and, at the back, a thicker batch of papers.

He reached for the thicker papers, unfolded them and almost choked with excitement.

The missing minutes.

It took him a second to work out what it meant.

It meant she hadn't passed them on yet! She hadn't made her contact!

He allowed himself a moment of triumph.

He gave the papers to Jensen to read, then, carefully replacing them in the same position, he slid the drawer closed.

Berg sat in the car beside Ragna and stifled a yawn. It had been a decidedly dull day. They had visited the Tromso museum where an expert on Lapp culture had explained at great length the significance of the reindeer migration routes and how the various groups of Lapps laid claim to their pasturelands.

They had gone to one of the local newspapers only to discover that Lapp affairs hardly made local news at all. Neither the files nor the journalists had much to offer in the way of opinions or facts.

Then a local politician had made a brilliant job of simultaneously professing interest in the Kaafiord issue while backing off rapidly.

In fact the only bright thing about the day had been Ragna herself. He took a glance at her now, as she drove back to the hotel. She was a good-looking woman; her profile, white in the reflection of the headlamps, was quite enchanting. And she had the sort of wry humour that Berg liked. Yet he suspected that her sharp mind and vivid energy concealed a strong will. In the old days he'd liked women on the fiery side, but now he wasn't so sure. The more independent, the more difficult they were to deal with.

He realised he was already regarding an affair as a foregone conclusion.

He cast another look at her and knew he wasn't mistaken. If

she wanted it, it would happen.

She caught his look and said: 'Sorry it wasn't the most exciting afternoon.'

He gave a dry chuckle. 'Did I look that uninterested?'

'Yes,' she said bluntly, and laughed.

They came into what passed for rush-hour traffic in Tromso, a queue of three cars at a junction. He noticed that Ragna was tapping the wheel impatiently.

He said: 'Do you enjoy living in Tromso?'

'Enjoy? Well – I suppose so ... *No,*' she corrected herself irritably, 'what am I saying? No, I don't. Except when I'm in the mood for a quiet life. And that isn't very often!'

'I always understood Tromso was full of life.'

'Compared to where?' There was sarcasm in her voice.

'So why do you stay?'

The traffic started to move. Ragna shoved the car into gear. 'Believe me, I'd like nothing better than to get away, but I've had trouble with the shop and I can't get rid of it.'

'Ah.' So he'd been right. Ragna wasn't the sort to stay in a place like this. He'd known she had too much style for a parochial town. He wondered why she had married Jan Johansen, and remembered wondering that once before, a long time ago.

'You used to be an actress, didn't you?' he asked.

She didn't answer straightaway, but concentrated on man- oeuvring into a parking space in front of the hotel. Finally she said lightly, 'Way back, far too long ago.'

'You don't talk about it?'

'Not often. It ...' She hesitated and pushed out her lower lip. 'It wasn't a good time for me.'

'But that was your sort of world, surely. More than –' he gestured: here.

She pursed her lips, as if he'd uncovered some unwelcome truth.

'I'd like to hear about it over dinner,' he said and surprised himself by meaning it.

'I don't promise to talk about my past, but I'll take the dinner off you anyway.' She said it with a casual shrug, but he thought she looked rather pleased.

'You're sure you don't have a lover?'

Her eyes flashed at him darkly, and he realised he'd touched a sensitive spot. She give a light laugh, followed by a small shrug. 'I'm sure.'

He thought: I wonder why not.

He asked: 'Do you have to go home first or –'

'My mother-in-law's there. She'll look after Krisi.'

They got out of the car. 'I suppose we'd better eat early,' Berg said. 'What time did you say we've got to start in the morning?'

'Five.'

He grimaced. 'Ouch! Usually I only see five when it's at the far end of the day.'

She wasn't going to miss that one. 'Mm,' she said, giving him an amused look. 'It shows.'

He smiled as he took her arm and led her into the hotel. He found himself looking forward to the evening.

He took her up to his room and offered her a drink from the two bottles he had there – normal social practice in a country where drink was prohibitively expensive. He poured himself a large Scotch, downed it in three and felt himself come slowly alive.

He made a phone call to the office. Ingrid told him the editor wanted to know when he'd be free to go and cover a defence story in Bonn. Berg said hopefully never. Ingrid said she'd arrange it for Friday then, unless he wasn't going to be back from Tromso in time.

Berg dropped the receiver into its cradle with a crash and swore under his breath.

Ragna said: 'I've never seen a telephone glow before.'

He almost snapped at her, but, seeing her good-natured smile, stopped himself in time. He took another drink and his anger melted away. It always did with the second drink. 'It's my newspaper,' he said. 'Always asking the impossible.'

'That's probably because you're too good at what you do. You should deliver a few dud stories.' She wagged a finger at him. 'But not yet!'

He took a shower while she talked to her son on the phone. Then they went out, walking slowly through the brightly lit centre of the town, following the road that ran parallel to the waterfront. It was six. The restaurants were opening up, people were strolling along the snow-packed pavements talking, linking arms, laughing.

'Where shall we go?' he asked.

'Well, the food's pretty much the same everywhere. Fish. Or fish and potatoes.'

He chuckled. 'Don't tell me. Boiled.'

'Or fried! But there is a place with a nice atmosphere. Nansen used to stay there before setting off on his Arctic expeditions. Or was it Amundsen? I always forget.'

'Speaking of explorers, what about Hal? Shouldn't we have left a message at the hotel to tell him where we've gone?'

There was a silence. They stopped at a crossing. Berg noticed that a small frown had appeared on her forehead.

'He wasn't too sure when he'd get here,' she said, avoiding his eyes. 'He'll probably arrive too late. But yes, of course. We'll phone from the restaurant and leave a message.'

She looked firmly ahead but he noticed that her lips were thin and tense and her eyes were narrow like a cat's. He thought: Now, I wonder what all that's about?

Hal realised he'd never make Tromso in time for dinner. Everything had gone smoothly until late morning when he made his last rounds and found a young musk-ox in the high pasture, lying in the snow, sick and weak. It was a one-hour job to rig up the tractor winch, haul the creature on to a litter and down to the barn. The animal was obviously in distress but there was no way of telling what was wrong with it. All Hal could do was ask Arne to keep an eye on it.

Then, on a quick trip to pick up a batch of extra fodder from the supply boat, the tractor decided to get stuck in a drift. By the time he'd got it free, dropped the hay and got back to the house it was late in the afternoon. It would be a good three hours before he got to Tromso. Ragna and Rolf would probably have finished dinner.

As he threw equipment into the trailer a powerful image of Ragna sprang into his mind: Ragna across a candlelit dinner-table, Ragna laughing, Ragna looking wonderful. He extended the scene to Ragna making love, and almost slammed his finger in the cab door.

He was about to set off when he realised he'd forgotten the spare rucksack for Rolf and the compo rations. He ran down to the basement storeroom, angry at being so disorganised: he really had to get a grip.

When he returned, Bamse was waiting by the tractor, barking excitedly.

'If you think I'm taking you . . .'

Bamse wagged his tail furiously. Hal said crossly: 'You'll be a nuisance, you old fool.'

The dog whined and growled in a frenzy of happiness. With an exaggerated sign of resignation Hal gestured towards the open trailer and Bamse jumped up. 'You'll need feeding, I suppose!' He made one final dash into the house for some dried fish.

It was six and very dark by the time he'd ferried the equipment to *Skorpa* and had a last word with Arne. He pushed the engine to maximum revs for the journey across the sound, but it still took far too long. He unloaded at the jetty, took *Skorpa* to her mooring and, collecting the Land Rover, set off at a furious pace, throwing up clouds of snow on the road behind.

He was mad to be going at all, of course. He still couldn't think why he'd agreed. She'd taken him by surprise, that was the problem. When Arne had given him the message to call her, he'd imagined she wanted to talk, to explain – even – agony to think of it now – even to say that she'd made a dreadful mistake and would he forgive her.

Laughable.

Oh, she'd sounded sheepish and miserable all right – a couple of times she'd seemed on the point of saying something – but she'd managed to restrain herself without too much difficulty and keep to the subject of the call, which was to ask him to come to Kaafiord. And he'd heard himself agreeing because he was damned if he was going to show her how bloody hurt and angry he still was.

He was sounding bitter. He *was* bitter.

It would pass. He was determined that it should. He was not only going to survive this, he was going to emerge with total immunity to Ragna, so that she could never ever do that to him again.

From that point of view the trek wouldn't be a mistake after all. It would help the recovery process along. He couldn't help thinking that it would also be a perfect opportunity to show Ragna that he didn't give a damn.

Yes. He drew a childish satisfaction from the thought, and, giving a grim laugh, pushed his foot down. A moment later the Land Rover bucked over a ramp of drift snow and swerved into the beginnings of a skid. The adrenalin kicked into his veins and, with a sense of perfect control, he steered carefully out of it.

As the car's speed dropped, a lot of his tension suddenly fell away.

He reviewed his earlier thoughts. They had been very childish. Scoring points off Ragna would achieve nothing except to make himself look petty and foolish.

Far better to show nothing, reveal nothing, remain coolly polite; take things as they come. There'd be Rolf to talk to, news to catch up on. If he put his mind to it, he might enjoy the trip after all.

The new and as yet unopened bridge to Tromso Island came into view, arching across the dark water towards the glittering lights of the town. It was eight-thirty. He might yet be in time to join Ragna and Rolf for dinner.

He pictured the candlelit table again, and saw her laughing her extraordinary laugh, a soft chuckle which came from somewhere deep in her throat; he saw her lips, moist and soft, and felt the warmth of her body and her powerful sensuality, and experienced a rush of feeling so strong that he gripped the wheel until his knuckles turned white.

He was the sort of man that she and her schoolgirl friends used to call a wolf. And in the old days she'd certainly had the sense to keep well away from the Rolfs of this world. But now? She didn't care: one had to live for the moment – wasn't she always saying that? – and at this particular moment she was enjoying herself.

There were two sides to Rolf Berg, she discovered. A serious side which expected a lot: well-informed opinions and quick

230

answers. He was ruthlessly intolerant of sloppy thinking, and it was a challenge to pull herself up to his level. But the effort paid off: slowly her sluggish brain began to pick up and tune into his thinking, until she was arguing with him, point for point. By the end of the meal they had talked their way through the politics and ethics of the Cold War, the newly erected Berlin wall, and Nato defence strategy. She sensed that she had earned his approval. It pleased her; she guessed it wasn't something he gave very easily.

Their politics differed, of course: she was middle-of-the-road while he was left-wing and noticeably anti-American, but he was too sophisticated a man to be intolerant of someone else's opinions, and she had the feeling that he argued simply to exercise his considerable mind.

The other side of him was also challenging, but in a completely different way. He was sensual, charming, attractive and spoilt. She guesssed he'd had dozens of affairs: he had the slightly jaded air of someone who'd always got what he wanted and wished it wasn't quite so easy.

He produced a flow of amusing, sometimes provocative conversation, sprinkled with anecdotes which she guessed he'd used a thousand times before; yet more than once she managed to cut through the polished delivery and throw him off balance, and then he really came alive, laughing suddenly with obvious delight.

There was also a sense of uncertainty about him – even danger. Or did she mean excitement? Whatever, it was very attractive.

Ah, she thought: Am I thinking about him like that?

Yes, she was. It was impossible not to.

'You haven't told me about your acting days,' he said over coffee.

'No, I haven't,' she said with bright finality.

'Ah,' he said, accepting her refusal calmly. 'You may have a point. The past's only a millstone round one's neck, isn't it? Or at best irrelevant.'

He signalled for the bill. When it arrived, he looked up suddenly and said: 'I wonder what happened to Hal.'

She felt a flutter of guilt. 'The farm, the animals. Anything might have delayed him.'

231

Rolf was giving her a long look. She thought: He knows.

He said softly: 'You look – cross.'

She laughed it off. 'It's the idea of having to get up at four.'

His eyes rested on hers a moment longer, then he pushed back his chair and said abruptly: 'Well, let's go and see Tromso by night, then.'

'What?'

'A night club. Doesn't everything start early round here?'

'Not that early. It's not even nine.' Suddenly she had an idea. 'There's only one thing that begins early.' She led the way out to the car.

As he got in beside her he raised his eyebrows questioningly. She shook her head to show that the surprise, whatever it was, would be ruined by more explanation.

She drove up a winding road that led up the hill behind the town. When they reached the highest point on Tromso Island she parked. They walked a short way to the brow of the hill, and looked out.

There was no moon but the night was washed with diffused silver light. A sprinkling of stars shone dimly. A mist hung over the sea, soft, translucent and so deep that it was impossible to see where the water ended and the sky began. To the north the mist rose towards the source of the silver glow – the northern lights, the aurora, which hung across the sky, brushed with soft colours, trembling and undulating like a vast crown of glistening thorns.

'There,' she said.

He looked in silence.

She said: 'I usually wave at them.'

'What?'

'Wave at the lights. Up here they say you mustn't. It's meant to be very unlucky.'

'So you do it to prove they're wrong.'

'And because I can't stand superstition. But surely you'd heard of that superstition?'

'When I was a child I remember some old woman saying: Don't stay out late or the northern lights will take you.'

'Did that frighten you?'

He thought for a moment. 'The only thing that frightened

232

me was the idea of being stuck in a small town for the rest of my life.'

Ragna gave a short laugh, then realised that he was intensely serious. 'Was it so bad? Where were you brought up?'

He didn't answer. Instead he shook his head in the direction of the panorama. 'I'm afraid that I don't very much like beautiful places. They tend to depress me.'

'Most people find them inspiring.'

'Most people don't know what life's really about.'

She laughed. 'That's what I like about you. No false sentiment.'

'Nothing false about me at all.'

'Oh?' said Ragna archly. 'In that case you're very unusual.'

'Absolutely. I don't deny it.' He shrugged, and she had the feeling he was only half joking.

He indicated the aurora. 'It's caused by magnetism, you know. Electrons charging into the upper atmosphere at up to twelve hundred miles a second. The friction makes the atmosphere glow. Oxygen glows red and green. And I think it's nitrogen that produces the bluish purple.'

'Oh dear. That explanation rather lacks romance, doesn't it?'

She felt his eyes on her. He reached out and, turning her face to his, kissed her softly on the mouth. She was so surprised she didn't respond at first, then, just as she was about to kiss him firmly back, he pulled away.

She gave a short and rather nervous laugh, aware that he had thrown her off balance. She rallied with: 'Was that the missing romance then?'

He laughed and they began to stroll back to the car. He put his arm round her shoulders. The gesture was oddly familiar, as if they'd known each other for years. Almost, Ragna couldn't help thinking, as if they were lovers.

Lovers. Ragna turned the idea over in her mind. As a distant prospect, it wasn't unattractive. No – she glanced up at him – not unattractive at all.

'Perhaps they've already been and gone,' suggested the waitress. 'Do you want to order?'

233

Hal looked at the time. Nine. The waitress was right – he must have missed them. 'No thanks,' he said.

He paid for his beer and made for the door. A diner smiled at him as he approached and leaned out to touch his arm. 'Off on another trip soon, eh?'

Hal looked at him blankly. He'd never met the man before in his life. With a brief shake of the head, he passed quickly by. From the sound of the muttered exclamations behind, he'd obviously caused offence. To hell with it: he wasn't answerable to the public. He wasn't answerable to anyone any more.

Nevertheless he was angry with himself as he walked briskly through the streets to Berg's hotel. The receptionist shot him a white toothy smile. She was sorry but Mr Berg had not returned. Did he want to wait in the adjoining café?

Hal shook his head. Someone in the café was bound to want to talk to him and he wasn't in the mood for small talk.

He waited impatiently near the main door, then sat restlessly on a sofa by a large spiky tropical plant. There was nothing to read. He stood up again and wandered over to the window. Taxis and the occasional bus went past, their studded tyres scrunching softly on the snow. A family party came in from the street, chattering loudly.

Hal felt his anger simmering up again.

He was about to turn away when a car swooped in to the kerb. A woman was driving. She had rich dark hair. He recognised the car. Ragna.

She turned and, smiling, opened the door and climbed out. Rolf Berg appeared from the other side and came round. Taking Ragna's arm, he paused and put his mouth to her ear. With a wide smile she cocked her head slightly to one side so as to hear him better. They pulled back, laughing at some joke, and came towards the hotel doors.

Obviously Ragna was having no trouble enjoying herself. An unpleasant feeling spread through Hal's stomach.

He stood back and waited for them to come in.

Ragna was breathless and flushed, her eyes dark and sparkling. Seeing Hal she stopped with a tiny gasp and put a hand to her chest.

'Hal!' Her expression cleared and, coming up, she gave his arm a small hug then automatically offered him her cheek. He leaned down to kiss it. It was cool under his lips.

Rolf was smiling broadly. 'Hal!'

Hal said: 'We're very honoured.'

Rolf retorted: 'I'll bet!'

Rolf had changed, Hal noticed; he looked tireder and rather unfit. Or was it simply that they were both getting older.

Ragna said hastily: 'We missed you at dinner.'

'I was there just before nine,' Hal said quietly.

'We must have only just missed you then! What a pity!' A smile fluttered across her lips. She seemed flustered.

She chattered on. 'We've just been to see some of the local sights.'

'Tromso by moonlight,' Rolf said, with a touch of irony.

There was a short silence. Ragna made a show of looking at her watch. 'Well, if we're really starting at five ...'

'What are the arrangements?' Hal asked.

'Oh, didn't I tell you?'

'No. That's why I've been waiting.'

She looked embarrassed. 'Sorry –' She ran quickly through the morning's arrangements, her eyes darting everywhere except up to his face.

'We meet here then,' Hal agreed.

Rolf commented: 'I hope you aren't going to be too talkative at five. It's not my best time of the day.'

'Don't worry,' Ragna said. 'Our lips will be sealed.'

She was having no trouble looking Rolf straight in the eye, Hal noticed, and very warmly at that. He remembered the two of them getting out of the car, the smiles, the extraordinary intimacy of their movements. His heart sank. She couldn't ...

He said abruptly: 'I'll see you to the car.'

Ragna blinked at him.

Hal put a hand on her shoulder. It was a deliberately proprietorial gesture. Faint surprise registered on Rolf's face, followed by a mildly questioning look that went first to Ragna then to Hal.

Hal stared back at Rolf and gave him his answer: Keep off.

A flicker of understanding crossed Rolf's face, he smiled faintly and said to Ragna: 'Good night, then.' He leaned forward and kissed her lightly on the cheek.

Ragna murmured: 'Thanks for the dinner.'

Outside, Hal pulled open the car door and waited for Ragna to get in.

She hesitated by the door, on the point of saying something. He cut in: 'Good night, Ragna.'

She said softly: 'You've got somewhere to stay?' It was a polite enquiry, not an invitation.

'My friend's expecting me.'

She caught his meaning and dropped her eyes.

As soon as she was in the car, he walked off, heading for Anna-Kristin's.

Eighteen

The route of the old mining track was just visible in the grey morning twilight, zigzagging its way up the side of the valley to the unseen plateau above. Hal led the way towards it, with Aslak at his shoulder and Rolf and Ragna following up behind. Bamse raced ahead, nose to the ground.

They had driven up the rough road from Kaafiord and parked the Land Rover beside the track. Now it was only three miles to the site as the crow flew, but the valley side was steep and the real distance, allowing for the snake of the track, was over four miles and four tough uphill miles at that. Hal set a pace that wouldn't tire Ragna and Rolf, settling into an easy plodding rhythm that was echoed by Aslak, so that the rasp and fall of their skis merged into one.

They left the thin dark stubble of the birch scrub behind and started up the valley side. Around them hung the steep, near-vertical slopes of the mountains, steel-grey and wind-blasted where the snow had failed to find a grip on the hard, ridged gabbroid rock. On the track, however, the snow was thick and full, and Hal automatically looked around for signs of avalanche danger.

It grew noticeably colder. This side of the valley was north-facing and remained untouched by direct sunlight even in mid-summer, for it was too steep to catch the low trajectory of the Arctic sun. Now, in the brief winter day, the twilight barely penetrated the thick cloud which hovered above the flat-topped mountains, and the hillside was cast with an oppressive gloom.

Hal reached a bend in the track and halted to allow the last two to catch up. Aslak stopped beside him, and, rolling his eyes towards the sky, murmured: 'Snow.'

He could be right – the cloud was certainly heavy enough. With inexperienced people in the party there was a case for turning back, but something made him want to press on. He realised what it was: he didn't want to have to repeat the expedition another day.

The others were closer now. Their pace was almost leisurely. Clearly they didn't feel the need to hurry. They were too busy talking happily. As he watched, Ragna's head jerked back, and a shout of laughter rose up and was swallowed by the stillness.

Pressing his lips into a hard line, Hal gripped his ski-sticks and set off again. This time he went at his own pace, which no one but Bamse could match. It took a moment to find his rhythm, but then he experienced that extraordinary release that came from pushing himself hard, through and beyond the point of resistance, until his body slipped into the slow effortless burn that could carry him for miles, even days.

After a while he came to a reluctant stop because he dared not lose sight of the others who were already some way back. He saw with satisfaction that they seemed to be finding the climbing harder, for they had dropped into single file, their heads down and their bodies bent over.

No bright laughter now.

He surveyed the weather again. The cloud layer seemed to be lifting slightly – or was it his imagination? He looked down into the deep valley below. The visibility had definitely improved. It was possible to follow the line of the snow-road back the way they had come, down the floor of the valley towards the fiord, six miles away. Immediately below him the parked Land Rover looked toylike, even at this distance. The road went on up the valley, running alongside the frozen river, until it disappeared in the curve of the hills. But it only went for a few miles, he knew. After that it petered out into a foot trail as the valley rose rapidly on to the expanse of the plateau.

Aslak caught up. Finally the others drew nearer and Hal prepared to set off again. As he adjusted his gloves a tiny distant movement caught his eye, and he paused.

Something deep in the valley: a vehicle on the snow-road, coming up from Kaafjord. Hal watched for a moment, wondering who on earth would be coming up here at this time of year. He looked questioningly at Aslak who gave a small shrug.

'Hunters?' the Lapp suggested without conviction.

There was the scrunch of approaching skis and a long feminine sigh.

'Goodness!' came Ragna's voice. 'I'm not as fit as I ought to be!'

Hal pulled at his gloves again, harder. 'There's still quite a way to go,' he said. 'Are you up to it —'

'Oh yes!' she said hastily, her breath shooting out in white clouds which vaporised instantly in the frozen air. 'I'm fine! It's just a few leg muscles I'd forgotten I had!'

'And how about you, Rolf? City life catching up with you?'

Rolf gave a wry smile. 'Any moment now.'

'Not on for a race to the top then?'

'Ah . . .' Rolf made an exaggerated gesture of regret. 'Another time.'

Hal led off again slowly. A moment later a pair of skis caught up with his. It was Rolf. Hal smiled a welcome and the two men began to talk. After a while Hal found himself relaxing; Rolf had always been good company.

Men were so straightforward and uncomplicated. He thought: Why can't women be the same?

The path was getting steeper. Ragna concentrated on the climbing, trying not to fall too far behind the two men who, lost in conversation, were striding ahead with Aslak at their heels. She wasn't up to this, she decided: her boots were chafing and her legs were aching and her skis were back-sliding. Also her hands and feet were freezing, while her body was raging hot. The correct thing to do was to remove a few layers of inner clothing, but she couldn't face the effort. She wasn't up to this!

It was all right for Hal. He was in his element, that was clear from the way he strode out, welcoming the challenge, relishing the steep climb. For some strange reason she'd never been trekking with Hal before. On holidays she'd always been with Jan or other friends, and then, when Krisi arrived, they'd kept to small excursions close to home.

Now she was glad that he'd come, very glad. She'd forgotten how eerily quiet it was up here, and how rapidly the weather could change, and how very easy it was to feel suddenly and unpleasantly alone.

Hal. Thinking of him she felt a renewed pang of – what? Remorse. Yes, and confusion. She did so wish they could talk.

Some time later she looked up and realised Hal had slowed down, leaving the other two to go on ahead. He was waiting for her! She felt a leap of nervous excitement.

But on reaching him, panting hard, she found him staring intently through binoculars. Her breathless greeting went unacknowledged.

She realised he hadn't stopped for her at all. She adjusted to the idea with difficulty.

Following the line of his binoculars she saw he was looking downwards. The valley floor was almost lost to view behind the bulge of the hillside, but it was just possible to see the Land Rover, which showed as a tiny grey dot against the whiteness. Next to it, she noticed, was another vehicle, also stationary.

Was this what Hal was staring at?

There was a click as Hal replaced the binoculars in the pouch at his waist and, without a word, started off again, leaving her standing.

She hurried to catch up with him. 'Whose car was that?' she gasped.

He was frowning. 'What? I don't know.'

She struggled to keep up. He was moving fast.

Finally she exclaimed in exasperation: 'Hal . . . Please.'

'What?' He slowed down a little.

'Don't let there be bad feeling between us. I can't bear it.'

He was silent. But she could sense the suppressed anger in his movements.

'Hal –'

'Ragna, I have absolutely no intention of discussing this now!'

Angry, Ragna stopped abruptly and let him pull away from her.

When she finally started off again she saw that Rolf was waiting for her.

'All right?' he asked.

'Apart from not enjoying myself very much, yes.'

'It's not so far to the top.'

They trudged on for a moment in silence. Ragna was glad to

see that the track ahead was less steep; perhaps the worst of the climb was over.

Rolf, who didn't seem nearly so out of breath, said: 'This story. Once I've written it, how will you use it?'

'How?' she panted. 'I don't understand.'

'How will you capitalise on it?'

'Oh.' She hadn't thought about that. 'I don't know ...' She trailed off, partly to catch her breath.

'You should go and see some members of parliament. Get pledges of support.'

'Oh, I see....' Suddenly she had to rest. She stopped, and Rolf waited with her, the two of them leaning on their sticks.

She said: 'The problem is money. I don't have any. Certainly not for trips to Oslo anyway.'

'It wouldn't take more than a day or two.'

'But the travelling – I don't have the fare. Anyway, which politicians would I go and see? And supposing they didn't want to see me?'

'I've a pretty good idea of who's likely to be sympathetic. I can get you the introductions. It would definitely help. So would another round of letters to ministers.'

'Oh.'

He heard the doubt in her voice. 'Is that a problem?'

'Hal's the best one for letter writing.'

'So?'

'I don't know if he'll – want to.'

The blue eyes shot her a questioning glance. He said carefully: 'Hal's a great asset to your campaign, you know.'

She shivered; it was suddenly very cold. A keen wind seemed to have sprung up out of nowhere.

She murmured: 'Yes, I know,' and they set off again. With sinking heart Ragna saw that there was another steep section ahead.

Behind, Kaafjord Valley seemed to drop away like a precipice. Ahead they glimpsed the sides of austere mountains and the beginnings of a shallow valley, a valley that led to the plateau.

Ragna was struck by a sense of desolation and emptiness.

Even Rolf was frowning and silent, and she guessed he was oppressed by it too.

God, he knew this place all right.

The plateau did not change. Still godforsaken, cold, empty.

After all this time Berg had thought it wouldn't have the power to touch him, but the sights and sounds of the place triggered astonishingly powerful images in his mind.

He remembered the sound of the silence – he remembered that better than the howl of blizzards or the whine and rasp of wind-torn snow, better, even, than the endless drip-dripping in the snow-cave. But he'd forgotten the incredible pervasiveness of it, and how its soft deathly absorbency enveloped everything. A permanent reminder that life and hope ended here.

For him it nearly had.

He couldn't remember the pain of the frostbite, though he knew it had been appalling, he could barely remember the sensation of hunger – but he did remember the cold. Oh yes, he remembered that all right. It was the sort of cold that ate into you, seeping through flesh, then bones, and finally into your very guts. Given enough time it even consumed your hunger.

He was beginning to regret coming. At the same time he took a perverse satisfaction in being reminded of how appalling and precarious the other side of the coin of life could be.

Too much alcohol, too much good living had made him soft. This was sharpening him up.

So was the cold. He felt it now, embedding itself in his cheeks, and paused to draw the hood of his anorak tighter round his face and up over his mouth.

Ragna did the same, sighing: 'God – this place.'

He thought: You should try it at minus fifty.

The ground was levelling off. The old mining track – if it was still there – was invisible beneath the snow. Hal led the way unhesitatingly up into the shallow valley until, after another twenty minutes, he finally stopped and dropped his rucksack on to the snow.

By the time Berg joined him, Hal was bent over a map with Aslak. The Lapp pointed to the head of the gently rising valley where it divided into two passes between the surrounding hills 'We camp up there in the pass, away from the herd, so we make no sound that would disturb them. Down here' – he made a wide gesture that encompassed the body of the valley – 'here the calves are born. The lichens, the grass, they are good in early May, you see. The air from the fiord, from the sea, is warm and the snow leaves early and everything grows well.'

Berg pulled his hood back. 'Where exactly will the installation be?'

Ragna panted up and collapsed breathless on a rocky outcrop.

Hal pointed at the map. 'If they're going to use the remains of the mining track then they'll probably site it around here, or over by the mine itself.'

'Where is the mine?' Berg asked.

Hal pointed across the valley. Berg examined the various possibilities and decided that, though buildings might be located in the valley, the long cables which seemed to be an integral part of modern navigation systems would have to be suspended between two high peaks, possibly even across Kaafiord Valley itself.

'But why have it up here at all?' Ragna chimed in. 'That's what I don't understand. Why not have it in a more accessible place?'

No one knew the answer to that except Berg, and he didn't speak.

Hal said: 'We should eat.'

Taking off their skis, they sat down on the rocky outcrop to drink coffee and eat sandwiches.

Berg asked Aslak: 'Is there really no other valley where the reindeer could calve?'

The Lapp looked vaguely surprised that anyone should not know the answer to such a question. 'The does were born here,' he said. 'Nearly all the herd were born here or very close to here. They do not know any other place. Their instincts bring them back.'

'What would happen if you herded them into another valley?'

'If you herd reindeer you put them under stress. We'd lose half the calves that way. Normally we just follow the reindeer, let them lead the way. We only herd them once a year for marking and slaughter.'

'What about the miners when they were here? Didn't they disturb the reindeer?'

'It was long ago. But they came only in summer, when we were down in the low pastures.' Aslak described the seasonal migrations, and the food needs of the reindeer at different times of the year.

He fell silent. Hal stood up suddenly and reached for his skis. He jerked his head towards the head of the valley. 'I'm just going to take a look around.'

They watched him pole off rapidly, then Aslak strolled across to his rucksack to find a cigarette and Ragna went to take photographs, leaving Berg to take a long look at the map. He realised it wasn't that far to the Finnish border. He worked it out on the scale: ten miles.

When Ragna returned, she peered over his shoulder. 'Jan and I came trekking up here once. If you take the road right up to the end of Kaafiord Valley, then it's only a few miles until you're right on the plateau.' She traced a route into a wide empty expanse of Finland. 'There's a lovely ice fall' – her finger hovered over the map – 'here. And a couple of huts, I can't remember where. We went for three days.'

'I thought you didn't like the plateau.'

'But that was at Easter. It was sunny. And warm.' She sank down beside him. 'And I was fit! Not like *this*.'

She hunched down, pulling her hood round her face, and said: 'Well, what d'you think?'

'About what?'

'The story.'

'Mmm. Promising.'

'Surely you've enough.'

'No.'

'What else d'you need then?'

He stared into the distance. 'The source of your information.'

She hadn't been expecting that. 'I can't!' she exclaimed. Then an idea seemed to come to her. She grasped his arm. 'Although – well, we might be able to do a deal.'

'Oh?' He looked down at her. She had the gleam of mischief in her eye.

'You could tell me what this place is going to be used for,' she said.

She was a trier, he had to give her that. 'And even supposing I could, what would you do with the information?'

'I'd use it to suggest another site. I'd use it to impress those politicians.'

'Then you *are* coming to Oslo?'

'Maybe,' she said meaningfully.

He considered. The information would help her campaign only if she handled it properly – that is, with discretion. Ragna was lots of good things, but not, he suspected, discreet.

Yet an idea was forming in his mind. He pushed it around for a moment, looking for pitfalls, assessing risks. He thought he saw a way of turning the situation to his advantage.

He might well give her the information. Not out of the goodness of his heart – in matters like this he didn't have any heart – but as a way to leak the information out into the press. It was far too risky for him to use the information himself – too many hard facts like that in his articles and the Security Service would soon start sniffing round – but if he gave it to Ragna and she bombarded the government with the information, it would soon leak out. Her lack of discretion would do the trick.

Then he could pick up the story and give it wider coverage.

One problem remained: how to let her have the information without implicating himself.

But he was beginning to see a way in which that too could be achieved.

'Okay,' he said, 'tell me then, what was your source?'

She hesitated. 'Promise it won't go any further?'

Berg almost smiled. She was like a child. 'Promise.'

'All right,' she said with due solemnity. 'Well – some friends in Oslo told me. A group called Friends for Peace. They told me it was phoned to them anonymously.'

Perfect. He asked: 'And how did you get to know them?'

'From the old days. A writer friend of mine helped found the group. I've known him for years.'

Even better.

She asked: 'You know about the Friends then?'

Berg knew them well. Left-wing intellectuals involved with the World Peace Movement, and various anti-nuclear groups, and, more often than not, with the Communist Party too. He had been careful to keep his distance from them.

'They're rather left-wing, of course,' Ragna said, huddling

down even further out of the wind. 'But their hearts are in the right place.' She looked at him expectantly. 'Well?'

It would work so long as he could trust her. *Could* he trust her?

Removing his glove, he touched her cheek. Her eyes widened, then, understanding that his gesture marked some important turning point, she returned his gaze with mischievous frankness, one eyebrow raised challengingly, a smile on her lips.

He decided. Careful that Aslak shouldn't overhear, he said softly: 'You have to promise me one thing.'

She nodded.

'You must never under any circumstances say how the information came to you. Because if you do, not only will my source realise I broke his trust, but no one will ever let me have any information ever again. Also, and more to the point, my source would get arrested.'

Her expression was suitably serious. 'I promise. Absolutely.'

'Okay –' He drew a deep breath. 'It's part of a new navigation system.'

'Navigation.' The disappointment showed on her face.

'Hold on, hold on,' he said irritably, raising a hand to show that he hadn't finished. 'The system has been designed with a very specific purpose in mind – to penetrate beneath the surface of the sea, up to ten yards down, to reach American Polaris submarines.' He could see that she didn't understand the significance of this. He explained patiently: 'Polaris submarines carry nuclear weapons – offensive nuclear weapons – and just two years ago Norway declared herself to be a strictly non-nuclear country.'

Enlightenment dawned. 'My God! I see.'

'The system's called Delta. Not only will it give Polaris submarines their precise positions instantly – something they've never had before – but, because they won't have to come to the surface to find out where they are, they'll be able to obliterate Moscow without any fear of discovery. It gives the US an immense advantage in the Cold War.'

She was taking it in.

'By the way, if it's anything like the Loran system it'll involve a massive array of long aerials which'll stretch from here' – he gestured towards the mountains – 'probably all the way across

Kaafiord Valley itself.'

'And I can use all this?'

He chewed his lip thoughtfully, as if making up his mind. 'Yes.'

'Thank you, Rolf,' she breathed reverently. 'Thank you.'

Berg gave a modest shrug, and looked satisfied, which he was. It was all rather neat. Doubtless FO/S had been keeping an eye on Ragna for some time and knew all about her links with Friends for Peace. They would assume, reasonably, that she had got this new batch of information from her usual source.

And they would assume that Berg had got his information from Ragna.

Yes, all rather pleasing.

Before replacing his glove he rubbed his knuckles affectionately against Ragna's cheek.

Hal headed for the old mining camp on the far side of the mountain valley. It was a relief to be on his own, with only Bamse weaving irregular patterns in the snow ahead. His senses expanded towards the silence and the absolute stillness and the certain feeling that he was happy in places like this. The snow lay fresh and soft on the undulating ground, absorbing the faint hiss of his skis, so that the sound barely touched the vast silence.

Nansen had described the Arctic as a place 'high under the heavens ... the air was clear and life was simple ... Back to solitude – silence – greatness ...'

That summed it up perfectly.

He broke into an energetic lope so that the backs of his skis rose in sharp little kicks at the end of each stride. He pushed hard, as if the exertion would obliterate unwanted thoughts.

When he reached the ruins of the mining camp and found there was nothing to see, he resigned himself to having to turn back.

It would have been nice to push on over the brow of the next hill – he always wanted to find out what was on the other side of things. But it was almost midday. The light would soon fade, making the downward journey tricky for Ragna and Rolf.

He enjoyed a last few moments of isolation, then started off.

Instead of heading straight back, he decided to make a triangle that would take him down the near side of the valley, and then across the valley mouth at the point where the land began to fall steeply towards Kaafiord Valley.

He took the first leg at a slow plod, not wanting the excursion to be over too quickly. Before starting the final leg he paused to look out beyond the deep chasm of Kaafiord Valley to the mountains beyond, which were just emerging from the cloud. The weather would hold off all right.

His eyes swept across the vast panorama, dipped down towards Kaafiord Valley and finally swung up to the three small black dots near the rocky outcrop.

It took a moment for his brain to absorb what his eyes had registered. Then he cranked his head back with a sudden jerk.

There had been a tiny anomaly, something out of place –

He redigested the visual information, trying to pinpoint the spot.

It had been something small, something moving, a shape that didn't quite fit ...

Somewhere *there*. Near the top of the mining track, where it was steep and narrow.

Sensing the tension, Bamse whined at Hal's side.

Hal hushed him and, pulling the binoculars from their pouch, made a slow sweep.

He looked over the ground again and again. Nothing.

But there had been something.

Hooking the binoculars round his neck, he set off, heading for a point above the first zigzag of the track. The ground was hardly more than slope yet; he had to go into a frantic kick-glide run to make speed.

Bamse went bounding ahead. Hal summoned him to heel with a sharp angry whistle.

At last he reached the point where the ground began to fall away more steeply and he could gain momentum. Even then he dug his sticks in hard to gather speed and yet more speed, until he was careering headlong downhill towards the steep drop ahead. He almost came to grief on an unseen snow-covered rock – one ski skidded from under him, the other shot into the air and he had to flail his arms in a desperate attempt to regain his balance. More by luck than design he landed on one ski

248

and, with one final jerk of his arms, managed to find his footing.

His heart thumped with relief. He was out of practice.

The floor of Kaafiord Valley came into view below and finally the track itself, snaking away beneath him.

He halted and crouched down, very still, to watch.

Nothing. He felt a sharp disappointment.

Then suddenly –

There!

Movement.

A figure – a skier – on his way down the track, negotiating a bend.

Putting the binoculars hastily to his eyes Hal examined the figure as it cruised out of the bend, accelerated down a straight, and then dropped from view.

He straightened up, frowning deeply.

He was still frowning when he returned to the others and led them slowly down the track, heading for home.

The figure had been wearing familiar kit.

White from head to toe. Except for the rifle, ammo belt, goggles.

But he'd recognised them too.

Norwegian Army-issue, the lot of it.

Nineteen

Hal stood on the veranda and peered at the thermometer. Minus fifteen. And still dropping. The night was clear and cold. Stars carpeted the sky, but they shone palely as if they, too, were dulled by the cold.

The wind was from the north-east. Everyone knew what that meant: a high-pressure system over the Arctic and the risk of a big freeze.

It had been some time since they'd had a real north-easter – three years, in fact. Since the time of Pasvik. The high pressure hadn't properly established itself then and the freeze had only lasted a few days. But on the plateau it had dropped to minus forty.

Whenever he remembered the weather at that time an old torment returned, worrying at him like an aching tooth: that Jan might have died slowly. The picture was vivid and sickeningly familiar: Jan lying in a desolate windswept place, alone and bleeding, dying slowly, knowing he was dying, feeling the cold creep over him ...

Hal shook himself free. There was no reason to think it had been like that. Yet the suspicion remained. He could only hope it wasn't true; he could only hope Jan had never realised what had hit him.

Turning abruptly, he went back into the house and closed the door firmly behind him.

It was seven. The end of a long day; the end of three long days since the trek.

Hal went and slumped by the stove. He was feeling very low. First the sick musk-ox had died. The vet had come from Tromso at great expense, only to declare that he had no idea what had

250

caused the sickness. The man had taken some blood and tissue samples for analysis, but hadn't been very helpful. Hal had been upset; he was fond of the animals. It was almost like losing a family pet.

Then there'd been the extra work caused by the weather: feed to be doled out, constant mucking out because the barn was overcrowded, a musk-ox to be dug out of a drift, an injured goat to be dealt with.

As a result the paperwork was piling up horribly. A report for the Army on a new ski design was overdue. In his advisory capacity to a scientific expedition to Greenland, he had three equipment inventories to check over. Finally, as ever, there was the post.

Rousing himself, he ate a quick meal, put on Beethoven's Fifth, and sat at his desk with a ration of aquavit to help things along.

He'd already opened some of the post, and now flicked through it to remind himself of the contents. Putting the bills and business letters to one side, he re-read a carefully hand-written and rather formal note from Mattis's family. They said that Mattis had never possessed a pair of binoculars of the type described. The only ones he had ever had were the ones given him on the Alpine Expedition of 1951. They were sorry they could not be of further help. They sent kind regards.

Hal would pen a short note of thanks later.

He didn't need reminding who the next letter was from. No one else had handwriting like that. It was a large hasty scrawl, liberally sprinkled with punctuation that defied all known rules.

He re-read the last sentence.

'... *Hope you'll come on Sunday – Krisi wants to go tobog-ganing –* would *you??*'

Sunday was tomorrow. He hadn't made a final decision about this yet, but he had the feeling the visit wouldn't be a good idea. Though the invitation was clearly a peace offering, he wasn't quite ready to make peace. He'd miss seeing Kris of course, but better to leave it another week and give things a chance to settle down.

And they would settle down, he was sure of it. Rolf had gone. He'd flown back to Oslo on Thursday with no plans to return. For Hal it had been a considerable relief. It was bad enough to be turned down by a woman like Ragna, but to watch another man win such obvious favour was like a slap in the face. The memory still made him wince.

But what really staggered Hal was that Ragna couldn't see what sort of a man Rolf was. Rolf was an accomplished journalist, a warm and generous friend, but he was impossible where women were concerned.

Ragna surely had better judgement than to get mixed up with someone like that. It made him despair to think about it.

With difficulty, he forced himself to go back to the beginning of Ragna's note and concentrate on the main body of the message. It was dated Thursday a.m., the morning after the trek.

'... *Incredible information from my contact in Oslo – it's a navigation system called Delta – there'll be massive aerials, loads of maintenance men coming and going all day long – but, most incredible of all, it's for use by Polaris nuclear submarines – i.e. not defensive, but offensive – for use in a nuclear war!!! Would you write to the minister of defence and ask him how the Norwegian government can possibly allow it to be built on Norwegian soil???*'

Hal shook his head. Sometimes Ragna could be wildly unrealistic. He couldn't possibly ask that question. He couldn't even mention submarines. If he objected to the installation on anti-Polaris grounds, he'd be labelled even more of a subversive than he already was, and that would lead to a very quick cancellation of his Army contracts. No contract, no money. It was very simple.

At the same time he must continue to help Aslak and his people who, he never forgot, were also Mattis's people. Their rights were being overridden, and he couldn't let that go unchallenged.

He sighed harshly: 'Ragna ...' and, pulling out some paper, attempted to draft a letter to the defence minister which would make everyone happy.

Half an hour later he thought he'd achieved something which would further the Lapps' cause without, hopefully, putting himself in too subversive a light.

Though whether the watchdogs at FO/S, the Security Service, would see it that way was debatable. Doubtless he was already labelled a danger and had been given a file all to himself. Thrane hadn't said as much, of course, but Hal knew how the system worked. The US insisted on rigid anti-Communist procedures where their interests were concerned.

As he typed the letter he thought of Thrane. He had the feeling the major wouldn't be at all happy when he heard about this latest lapse on Hal's part.

But he couldn't help that. He signed and sealed the letter, and put it ready on the ledge by the front door.

Then he sat and listened to the last magical strains of the symphony. The Fifth always cheered him up. He put on some Mozart after that, because Mozart put him in a businesslike mood. Then he braced himself to start on the batch of unopened post that Arne had brought up that afternoon.

There was a typewritten envelope from Oslo. He slit it open.

Bamse suddenly leapt up and, rushing to the door, barked furiously.

Hal heard Arne's distinctive stamp on the veranda outside and wondered what was bringing him out so late; he was usually in bed by nine.

Hal pulled the letter out of its envelope and glanced at it as he rose to his feet, intending to go and meet the old man at the door. He paused, staring at the letter-heading.

'Cold,' the old man remarked as he stamped the last of the snow from his feet and came in. 'And it will get colder.'

Hal hardly heard; he was too busy reading.

The letter was from a lawyer called L. J. Sorensen. He skimmed through the four paragraphs, then went back and read it again more slowly. The binoculars. This man had discovered who they had originally belonged to.

The old man was hovering.

'One moment, Arne.'

Nodding, the old man disappeared in the direction of the kitchen.

Hal read the letter a third time, rubbing his lip thoughtfully. Then he went to his desk and, pulling open the lowest drawer, started to search through it.

At last he found what he was looking for, an old dog-eared notebook, and flicked quickly through it. This was his diary from the early days, a record of all his early climbs and excursions.

He was trying to remind himself of what had been going on in the winter of 1944-5.

He saw that Jan and he had been on a couple of climbs. Yes: Blaamannen, Goalsvarre. But the knowledge didn't jog any other memories. If Jan had acquired a pair of German binoculars at that time Hal certainly didn't remember it.

Arne returned, carrying a warm drink, and sat down by the stove.

Hal gave him a brief smile. 'Sorry, Arne.'

'There's a message.'

Hal murmured absently: 'Yes?'

'Ragna Johansen. She telephoned. She said she's sorry, but she won't be there tomorrow.'

Hal looked up sharply. 'Oh?'

'She's gone away.'

Hal's throat went dry. 'What? Where?' But even as Arne opened his mouth to reply, Hal knew.

'Oslo. She went to Oslo.'

PART THREE

Twenty

In the dream the cold was closing in on him. Berg opened his mouth to cry out, but no sound came. He tried to fight his way out of the blackness, but his arms were limp and useless and his legs heavy as lead. A weight seemed to press down on his body and he thought he'd never move again. He felt an immense surge of self-pity and impotent range. He wanted to curl up and cry.

But Petter was shaking him by the shoulder, chivvying him, calling out his name again and again. 'Raf! Raf! You must get up! You must get up!'

The same words, over and over again, harsh and strident, invading his darkness when all he wanted was to be left alone.

The scene changed abruptly. He was being forced to move, hauled to his feet, but the effort was appalling and he cried out with the agony of it. When he tried to open his eyes a vicious whiteness assaulted them and sent an excruciating pain bursting inward on his brain.

Petter's voice again: 'Come on! Come on, you son of the devil! Not much further!'

The scene shifted. He was lying on the snow surrounded by reindeer, a vast herd that swarmed and stamped and snorted around him, their feet dancing closer and closer. He was overcome by terror: the animals were about to trample him, yet the stupid Lapps were doing nothing to prevent it. He tried to call out, but he was strapped down in some sort of sleigh and for some reason his mouth, like his limbs, would not move.

The panic rose in his throat.

Someone was shaking him again. Insistently.

This time he was really angry with Petter.

He moaned a long, loud 'No-o-o!'

The sound of his voice came winging in from far away until it was suddenly very loud and very close.

He awoke with a violent start and looked straight into Ragna's face.

She was looking startled. 'Are you all right?' she said. 'I hated doing that, but you did ask me to wake you.'

He took everything in – his bedroom, the grey light, Ragna bending over him – and flopped back on the pillow. He mumbled: 'Okay.'

He was aware of Ragna padding quietly out of the room. How had she got into the flat? Of course: he had given her a key so she could come and wake him.

He reviewed the dream. It had been awful. It was that damned trek to Kaafiord – it had stirred up his memory.

He peered at the time: eleven.

He swung his legs out of bed, ignored the tiredness and the dull headache, and went straight into the shower. He ran it hot, then cold, and came out feeling more human.

Throwing on a robe, he followed the smell of breakfast to the living room and saw that Ragna had put out a steaming pot of coffee, squeezed orange juice, bread, cheese and honey.

Very domestic. Not, therefore, to be encouraged.

As he sat down and poured his first cup of coffee she emerged from the kitchen. She was looking marvellous, he noticed. She'd obviously used the last few days to go shopping and have something new done to her hair.

She asked: 'Did you get the article finished all right?'

He nodded. 'At four.' It'd been a stinker: a five-thousand-word piece on the Bonn Conference, and he'd only got back from Bonn at nine the previous evening.

She gave him an appraising look. 'Feeling alive yet?'

He made a face. 'Just about.'

'In that case ...' She advanced on him, put a hand on either side of his face, and gave him a forceful kiss. 'That's a thank you!'

'Ah. It appeared then?'

'You bet!' She passed him the *Dagens Post*. The editor had given his Kaafiord article a full inside page.

Berg said cautiously: 'Well, we'll see what it produces. Don't hope for too much at this stage. But I'm sure this won't be lost on the man from the justice ministry. What time are you seeing him?'

She sat down at his feet. 'Two.'

'You'll go easy on him, won't you?'

She looked offended. 'Well – I'm not going to hit him over the head if that's what you mean.'

He smiled. He rather enjoyed teasing her.

She pretended to give him a fierce look. 'You'll see – I'll have him eating out of my hand.'

Berg said seriously: 'He'll certainly sit up when he realises you know what the installation's for. But be careful, won't you? I mean, don't say too much – just mention that you know what it's going to look like. And slip it in casually, as if it was common knowledge. Don't make a speech about it.'

'I'll be careful.' She had a grave expression, like a child trying to show how grown-up she was.

He sat forward on the edge of his chair and, reaching out, gently brushed his fingers against her hair. It was beautiful hair, dark, thick and shining with colour.

A tantalising smile appeared on her lips. He leaned forward and kissed her. Her mouth was very soft. He thought: Tonight. We'll become lovers tonight.

His mood darkened suddenly: he remembered that he was due to meet Sonja that evening. He sighed peevishly. 'Damn! I've just realised, we can't have dinner tonight.' He thought for a moment. 'But we could meet later, at about ten.'

Ragna pursed her lips and looked at him through half-closed eyes, as if she was considering whether to accept. But he knew she would: her laughing eyes gave her away.

That was what he liked about her: she made everything fun.

He gave her a lift to the flat of some friends of his where he'd arranged for her to stay, then went on to the office.

As soon as he appeared Ingrid said brightly: 'Well? Wasn't Bonn exciting like I promised? Weren't you glad you went?'

He raised a sarcastic eyebrow and dropped the Bonn article on her desk with an exaggerated flourish.

The pile of mail in his in-tray was visible from half-way across the editorial floor. Flopping into his chair, he pushed the tray to one side and, lighting a cigarette, started leafing half-heartedly through the telephone messages. Contacts, minor politicians, pressure groups ...

He remembered that he hadn't called his message service for some days, and immediately dialled the number of the Estonian tobacconist.

There was one message.

It was from Alex: *Contact me urgently.*

Berg replaced the phone, suppressing a vague feeling of alarm. He'd never had a message like that from Alex before.

He drew heavily on his cigarette, thinking hard, his mind skittering over possibilities, almost all of them unpleasant.

Leaving the office, he went to a public phone box and, dredging his memory for the special number Alex had given him, dialled it.

It answered straight away.

Berg said: 'It's Harri.'

A strange voice said: 'Go to the Hotel Bristol, the Library Bar, in half an hour,' and rang off without waiting for a reply.

Berg muttered contemptuously under his breath. Back to the cloak and dagger stuff. Yet as he walked briskly back to the office his stomach was jittery, his mouth dry.

He arrived at the Hotel Bristol thirty-five minutes later.

Taking off his coat, he went straight across the main lobby, past the giant stuffed bear that glared out from a corner, and into the Library Bar. The bar was busy, most of the book-lined alcoves occupied by the writers and artists who liked to frequent the place. Berg recognised a couple of journalists he knew. Finally he saw Alex sitting in an alcove at the far end.

As Berg approached, Alex stood up and greeted him with a show of surprise, as if their meeting were accidental.

Berg played along with the pantomime and suggested a drink.

'Why not!' Alex exclaimed loudly and ordered beer.

When the waiter had gone Alex said in a low urgent voice: 'There's a small – er – query, Rolf.'

The fear rose in Berg's throat. 'Oh?'

'The story you gave me. It's been looked into and –' Alex swallowed nervously and Berg noticed he was sweating.

Berg knew then: it was going to be bad.

'– we think there's something not quite – right with it, Rolf.'

'What do you mean?'

'It doesn't fit with what we know, Rolf. Oh, there is a new navigation system. But we're pretty sure it's called Omega, not Delta. And the Omega installation is already under construction. But much further south. At Aldra.' He added unhappily: 'We know this information is good, Rolf.'

'But – perhaps the one at Kaafiord is a second site, part of a string.'

Alex shook his head. 'It doesn't work like that. Apparently a single installation is enough to cover the whole of the North Atlantic. It would make absolutely no sense to have a second. Also' – he took a deep breath – 'the site itself, there at Kaafiord, would not be right. Surrounded by mountains, and with those tall alps, the – er?' He searched for the name.

'Lyngen Alps.'

'That's it – the Lyngen Alps. With them in the way, between the site and the sea ... Technically, it isn't right, Rolf. They wouldn't put such an installation there.'

There was an ugly pause.

Berg said harshly: 'So what the hell's the place for then?'

Alex raised his hands in a gesture of bewilderment. 'We don't know.'

'You seem to know everything else –'

Alex leaned a little closer. 'Listen, Rolf, when I say we don't know, we don't know for sure. But when we first discovered that this site was to be developed, our people took a small guess at its function. They decided that, because of its location, it could only be something else.'

'What else, for God's sake?'

Alex didn't like having to spell things out. He lowered his voice still further. 'A monitoring station designed to pick up emissions from the upper atmosphere.'

Berg rolled his eyes in exasperation; he wasn't in the mood to extract information by degrees. 'What do you mean, emissions?'

Sensing Berg's anger, Alex said in a rush: 'Well – signals from satellites. Our satellites – the Vostoks, the Luniks. The US wouldn't miss an opportunity like that, would they? And apparently Norway is the obvious place, and this site, up in the mountains, is the ideal spot. Because – let me get this right – yes, something to do with other radio signals. Apparently it's essential to site such a place well away from interference.'

A bell rang in Berg's mind. Sonja. She'd spoken of – what were her exact words? – needing to be away from radio interference.

She'd said it, but for the moment he couldn't work out how significant that was.

He said savagely: 'But you don't know for sure.'

'No,' he conceded. 'And of course we would very much like to know. But one thing, Rolf –' He shifted his considerable bulk in his seat and looked unhappy again. 'Our people think it most unlikely to be a navigation system.'

'I see,' Berg said icily, suppressing his anger.

He gave it a moment, then said with a calmness he didn't feel: 'So what does this mean, Alex?'

Alex made a feeble attempt to look reassuring. 'Maybe nothing. Maybe nothing at all, Rolf.'

They stared at each other. They both knew what it could mean. It could mean that they were on to him.

Berg found himself glancing round the bar, then jerked his head back. This was ridiculous. He was letting it get to him already.

He got to his feet and, in a half-hearted attempt to play out the pantomime, said brusquely: 'Bump into you again soon, I hope.'

He walked the length of the lobby, past the main entrance, and down the stairs to the men's toilets.

He needed time to think.

Locking himself in a cubicle, he sat down on the closed lavatory seat, lit a cigarette, and put his head in his hands.

Be calm, be calm. Think it out.

He went through it, step by step.

Sonja. Start with Sonja.

First: she might have made a genuine mistake.

Possible but unlikely. Her memory had never failed before. When it came to her work, she was razor-sharp. She'd got the bit about the radio interference right, why should she get the rest wrong?

Second: the false information was a plant.

The thought made him ill. Yet it made no sense. They would never have planted such blatantly false information, for the very reason that it would be revealed for what it was.

Third ...

He couldn't think of a third explanation. Except, perhaps, that Sonja had simply gone mad. It was possible. The death of her mother, her age ... perhaps she was going through the menopause.

He tried to remember the details of their last meeting: had she behaved differently? She'd knocked back the booze a bit. And she'd been unusually jumpy. But that was easily explained by her mother's death. There was something else though. She hadn't seemed to mind about the lack of love-making; normally he'd have expected her to be more disappointed. Yes – that had been unusual.

But it was no good. He could think himself stupid without getting an inch nearer the truth.

He was sure of only one thing – that he was not going to the meeting with Sonja tonight. It would be madness. That house was a perfect trap. The thought was enough to make him shudder.

He forced himself to consider all the possible consequences, coolly, rationally.

Supposing they were on to him, then what was the worst and best he could expect?

The worst was simple: they already knew his identity and had enough evidence to convict him.

The best was also simple: they had no idea of who he was and no idea of how to find him.

The more he thought about it, the more optimistic he became. After all, he'd been very careful. It was very unlikely that they knew enough about him to have him under surveillance, and even if they'd been watching him he was sure he'd have spotted them. The only direct link was Sonja, and Sonja didn't even know his identity. There was no other way they could link this rubbish information to him.

Except –

Christ –

He jerked his head up.

Ragna.

The time. He thrust his watch-face up to his eyes.

One-thirty.

Leaping to his feet, he shot out of the cubicle and ran up the stairs and across the lobby to the telephone booths.

He called the flat. She had gone.

He waited until just before two, then rang the office of the man at the justice ministry.

The secretary told him to hold, then Ragna's voice came on the line, a little breathless, rather surprised, saying: 'Oh, it's you!'

And the relief flooded through him, cool and sweet.

Ragna ran a hand over her hair and stood back to take a critical look at herself in the mirror.

All right. More than all right.

Everything had come together perfectly: the striking aquamarine dress, slim and waistless and right up to date; the stranded jet necklace and matching earrings; the new shorter hairstyle, which hung smooth and sleek to just above her shoulders.

And her make-up was okay too. Dramatic, with strong colour on her lips, because that was what suited her best.

She was dressed to kill. And kill she would. Mr Rolf Berg. She grinned at the thought.

They were having dinner together after all. He'd managed to get out of his meeting and they were going to the Theatre Café.

Perfect.

She was filled with a childish euphoria. The moment she'd arrived in Oslo she'd known she'd done the right thing. It was as if she'd finally come home. She belonged in places like this – she always had – in cities surrounded by energetic creative people, people like her – people who appreciated her. For the first time in three years she felt completely alive, and she'd forgotten how very good that feeling was.

When she thought how she'd dithered about coming! That had been because of the money of course. But she'd managed to borrow some from her mother-in-law. Old Mrs Johansen had been rather disapproving, which was no surprise. But really, what were families for?

The doorbell rang. Her throat was suddenly dry.

Rolf.

She hurried to the door and, swinging it open, gave a small

exclamation of pleasure. 'You're early!' she said warmly.

Berg paused for a moment on the threshold, his eyes hard and glittering. Then his expression softened and, stepping forward, he kissed her on the cheek. 'You look stunning.'

She laughed: 'Thank you.'

He led the way into the living room, and, going straight to the drinks trolley, helped himself to a large drink.

'No one else in?'

'No.'

He began to pace up and down. 'Are you all right here? Comfortable?'

'Yes.'

'They look after you?'

She gave a small shrug. 'Of course.'

He seemed restless, almost preoccupied. She supposed he'd had a hard day. She made a mental note to ask him about it later, when he'd had a chance to relax.

He stopped abruptly and asked: 'How did the meeting go?'

'Brilliantly!' She threw out her hands in an expansive gesture of delight. 'He'd read your article. It'd made quite an impression on him, I think. Though he didn't admit it, of course. Anyway, he heard me out and promised that the minister would look into the matter of land rights and that he'd produce a full written answer to all my points.' She added happily: 'It was more than I expected.'

'I'm sorry I had to call you like that.'

She sat down on the sofa. Berg chose to stand by the fireplace. She noticed that his mouth was set in a hard tense line.

'Why didn't you want me to talk about Delta?' she prompted.

He looked down at her. 'I discovered that the information was completely false. My source got it wrong. Someone had fed him a load of nonsense.'

She tried to absorb it. 'You mean – you mean, there's no Delta?'

He gave a shake of the head.

'It's not for Polaris submarines? It's not a navigation station?'

He said firmly: 'No.'

She gave a sigh of disappointment. This was a setback. 'Then we're back to square one.'

He sat down beside her. 'Let's look on the bright side. There's no harm done.' He gave her a quizzical mirthless smile. 'Or is there?'

She blinked. 'What do you mean?'

'You didn't tell anyone? You didn't use the information?'

'No. I haven't had the chance.'

He looked relieved. 'Good. Then everything's all right then.'

Ragna nodded vaguely.

Then she remembered.

Hal. Her note to Hal. She'd told him all about it. And she'd asked him to write that letter to the defence ministry.

She looked at Rolf uneasily. She had the feeling he wouldn't be pleased.

Perhaps she needn't tell him.

But that was silly. It would be far better to get it out in the open. And straight away.

She was opening her mouth to speak when Rolf said: 'It's a good thing we found out in time. You see, someone's out to get me. Trying to make me look stupid. You might even say he tried to set me up.' He fixed her with those intense blue eyes of his. 'It would have been extremely embarrassing if the information had been traced back to me. But it can't now, can it?'

'No.' That was true enough. Hal didn't know it came from Rolf.

He seemed partially reassured and went to refill his glass.

Ragna thought frantically. Would Hal have written that letter yet? She pictured him alone at Brattdal, doubly angry and hurt now that she had left Tromso; she couldn't imagine he'd be in the mood to do her a favour. But she decided to phone Arne first thing in the morning and leave an urgent message, just in case.

Yes: no sense in alarming Rolf unnecessarily. If Hal hadn't written the letter then Rolf need never know.

If Hal had . . . Well, she'd cross that bridge when she came to it.

Rolf was draining his glass. 'Let's go to dinner.'

Pushing everything out of her mind, she smiled at him. 'Lovely.'

He glanced at his watch, frowned momentarily, then led her to the door.

Eight-ten. There was a sinking feeling in Thrane's stomach.

He took another look at the luminous dial of his watch and groaned inwardly.

He had been over-confident. And now he was paying the price.

It had all looked so promising: the sudden break in routine, the shopping for dinner, the drive to the love-nest in the pine-woods and then ...

Nothing.

But Sonja had been expecting her lover, no doubt about that.

Thanks to the Norwegian custom of never drawing down-stairs curtains, Thrane and his team had had a perfect grand-stand view from the pinewood.

They had watched her preparing dinner, laying the table, looking at her watch, peering out of the window, pacing ner-vously back and forth.

Now, after two hours, she was sitting at the kitchen table. She had long since stopped peering out of the window.

He put the binoculars back to his eyes and focused carefully on the brightly lit interior. She was sitting motionless, her back to him, a drink at her elbow which she hadn't touched for some time. He wondered how a woman like Sonja could sit for so long, doing nothing.

Almost as he thought it, she jumped to her feet and dis-appeared from view. He picked her up again as she crossed an adjacent window, then lost her again. Making his way softly through the pines, he skirted the house until he found her in the living room.

She was on the phone, dialling rapidly.

She held the receiver to her ear without speaking. After a time she jiggled the cradle and dialled again.

Thrane thought: I'd give anything to know that number.

She waited for about a minute then crashed the phone down and buried her head in her hands. A handkerchief appeared and was clamped over her eyes.

Sonja had been stood up.

Thrane felt the full weight of his disappointment.

There was always a chance that the lover might turn up

another time, but somehow Thrane didn't think so. He had the nasty feeling that something rather final and irreversible had occurred.

No evidence for that, of course, just his intuition and the way Sonja was hunched forward, rocking visibly, crying her silly eyes out.

He dropped the binoculars and waited.

An hour later Sonja finally emerged and made her way to her car. She drove off slowly. Thrane and his men followed in two cars.

At first Sonja seemed to be heading straight for home, but then she turned east, and Thrane felt a flicker of interest.

For a while he thought Sonja was on to him, for she suddenly accelerated and shot across a junction. But then she slowed, hovering close to the pavement, and pulled in to the side. Thrane overtook and risked a quick glance.

She had her head in her hands again.

He pulled in and waited. After five minutes she moved off, turned right, then right again. Back the way she had come.

Sonja had changed her mind.

She was going home after all.

Ragna looked across the restaurant table at Rolf Berg and thought: He'd be the perfect lover.

He was talking seriously, about politics. She had a suitable expression of interest on her face, but she was really picturing his naked body – cool, hard, smooth – and imagining the way he'd make love – with immense skill and experience. He'd know exactly how to give pleasure to a woman, how to build that pleasure up slowly, and then wait until just the right moment ...

A delicious warmth spread through her and, suppressing a smile, she dropped her eyes for fear her lascivious thoughts should show in her face.

He had stopped speaking. When she glanced up, he was looking quizzically at her. 'Did I say something funny?'

'No. Do go on.' Recovering her serious face, she asked him a question about the trend towards socialism.

He gave her an odd amused stare, as if he wasn't quite sure if she was serious, then began to answer.

Ragna watched him again, and decided he would be the perfect lover not only in bed, but out of it as well. He would treat love-making as a simple pleasure between two people, something to be enjoyed, with no stifling obligations on either side. He wouldn't expect her to be around all the time. He wouldn't be cross if she had her own life. He would understand her need for freedom. Certainly he would never talk about *love*.

She pictured her life once she'd moved to Oslo. She'd get a small flat, put Krisi into a local kindergarten, find herself a job, and see Rolf twice or three times a week. They'd go to the theatre a lot, dine out in restaurants like this; she'd get to meet his friends who, she felt sure, would be just her sort of people: artists, writers, actors.

She became aware that he was silent again. From the expression of mild amusement on his face she knew he'd seen through her question on socialist trends. His earlier pre-occupation had obviously passed.

'Oslo suits you,' he said. 'You should move here.'

Ragna made a wry face. 'I know!' She looked round the restaurant. 'I love it all.' The Theatre Café rippled with conversation and laughter and continuous movement. The spacious room looked like the interior of a Renoir café: all dark wood and soft golden lights and turn-of-the-century décor. Up in the gallery the pianist smoothed light melodies out of a grand piano.

'I love it all,' she repeated. 'The only problem is, what would I do? Look at me. I'm not qualified for anything.'

'I'm looking at you.' And he was. It was a frank expression of interest. She grinned and a look of complete understanding passed between them.

'Ah – if looks were everything!'

He burst out laughing. It was a wonderful deep laugh and she found herself thinking: I could love that laugh.

The bill arrived. He said: 'But really, you'll have no trouble getting work. You're very unusual. Most important' – he touched her hand softly and thoughtfully – 'you have life in you. That's a very rare and beautiful quality.' He added firmly: 'But then I'm not telling you anything you didn't already know.'

He caught a waiter's attention and handed him the money.

'But it's all wrong, you know.'

'What is?'

'That you should be alone.'

Ragna's heart lurched. 'Ha! Don't give me sympathy,' she said, putting on a bright voice. 'I'm not used to it. I dissolve into a jelly!'

He gave her a gentle look. 'You must have been very unhappy.'

On the verge of feeling sorry for herself, Ragna covered the moment with a harsh rather unnatural laugh. 'Stop it, you'll have me crying in a moment!'

'I apologise.'

'I should hope so! If you go on like that I'll run out on you!'

He liked that, and grinned. 'On no, don't run away, Ragna. Don't do that, whatever you do.' He got up and held out a hand to her. 'Let's go home instead, shall we?'

Home.

It was all decided then. She felt a delicious suffocating anticipation.

She had one brief moment of doubt.

They had walked into his flat and he had pulled her gently towards him and started to kiss her. His lips were soft and teasing, brushing across hers, exploring the shape of her mouth, then pulling back a little to start again. She responded, opening her mouth under his, moving closer, pressing her body against his.

He kissed her more deeply then, and she felt that delicious warmth again, more powerful now, and her body responded, growing warmer still ...

He pulled away and took a step towards the bedroom and stood, gently tugging at her hand, waiting for her to follow him in.

It was then that she looked at him and felt a flicker of doubt. His face: it was an impenetrable mask – his eyes hard and glittering, his expression empty of warmth or feeling. A sudden chill came over her, and she hesitated.

He seemed to sense her doubt for, with obvious effort, he

broke out of his mood and smiled.

Yet there was something bleak and lonely about that smile. Still she hesitated, searching his face, thinking: I don't know you at all!

Then he stepped closer and exclaimed: 'Oh Ragna, don't say you're going to run away after all!' And he laughed so charmingly and with such sudden warmth that she couldn't help laughing too, and her doubts dropped away, and all her need for him came back in a rush.

This time he didn't stop kissing her, not until they were standing by the bed and he was slipping her dress off, and even then his lips moved quickly back on to hers.

She felt shy, a little nervous. It had been such a very long time. She was aware of trembling slightly.

He pulled her gently down on to the bed. His mouth moved down on to her body, his lips pulling at her skin, probing, licking, exploring, until she couldn't have stopped even if she'd wanted to. He left no pleasure untried. He took her over completely, guiding her hands, whispering his demands, until he carried her over and beyond the last restraints.

And then she didn't want him to stop ever again.

Berg had thought that nothing could relieve the deep sense of unease that had nagged at him all day, but he was wrong. She did, for a while.

He'd also thought that no woman had the power to really excite him any more, but he was wrong about that too. For a while.

She was shy at first, almost as if she were inexperienced, and it suddenly occurred to him that she hadn't had a lover since her husband had died.

The thought was strangely arousing. So too was her curious mixture of reticence and sensuality. She seemed uncertain, even nervous; he felt her tremble. He had the urge to reawaken her, to see her lose control and cry out and beg him to satisfy her.

He took it slowly, gently, one step at a time, finding each sensitive point, touching, licking, kissing, closing his mind to everything but the sensation of her.

Then, quite suddenly, her reticence vanished, and her movements were urgent, demanding, knowing. He felt vaguely disappointed, even let down. Had the shyness been a pretence?

Pushing the thought from his mind, he concentrated on taking his own pleasure, losing himself in the sensations of his own body. He whispered a demand; she hesitated slightly, then obeyed. He whispered a second demand, adding soft words of affection, and she did that too. And then he knew there was almost nothing she wouldn't do for him, and he abandoned himself to the rapacious hunger of his senses that, much as he fed it, was never satisfied.

When it was over, Berg fought off the sense of emptiness and futility that he dreaded, but it crept up on him surreptitiously, pulling him down and down, until he thought bitterly: Why does it always have to be like this?

Ragna stirred beside him, soft and acquiescent and slightly damp from their love-making. He thought: She wasn't different after all. He felt disappointed, even slightly resentful.

Yet he hadn't had enough of her, not by a long way.

There was also the matter of the Delta business. She wouldn't break his trust, he knew that. At the same time it would be best to keep an eye on her until this little problem with Sonja had sorted itself out.

Sonja.

He'd had her on his mind all evening.

Tonight he'd failed to show up, but that was no solution. He had to know the truth. He had to find out if they were on to him.

The question was: how?

Twenty-one

Lars Sorensen's meeting had overrun and he got back to his office at five with the prospect of at least an hour's paperwork ahead of him.

He went in through the side door that led directly into his private office. To his surprise his secretary popped her head round the door, though she usually left at four.

'There's someone waiting for you,' she said. 'It's Halvard Starheim. I suggested an appointment, but he wanted to wait.'

Sorensen blinked, adjusted to the news, and, feeling a mixture of pleasure and curiosity, headed for the outer office.

The man who rose to his feet and shook Sorensen's hand looked just like his photographs, except taller, more impressive, with a fierce gaze from dark intense eyes.

Sorensen said warmly: 'I hope you haven't been waiting long.'

Starheim shook his head briefly, as if such trivialities were unimportant. 'I would have made an appointment except I came to Oslo at short notice.' His expression was serious, contained, yet he seemed full of suppressed impatience.

Sorensen invited him to sit. He noticed that Starheim carefully tweaked up the legs of his formal grey suit and adjusted his shirt cuffs. The clothes seemed incongruous in a man with such an athletic frame and work-hardened hands.

'You received my letter?' Sorensen asked.

'Yes. I was amazed.'

'Amazed?'

'That you could discover so much.'

Sorensen shrugged it off. 'It's not so hard. The National Archives have some information, stuff which relates directly to the Occupation. But they're not geared up to individual requests

273

like yours, which is why they pass them on to me.'

'You're certain about this Schirmer though?'

'Oh yes. Wait a moment, please.' Sorensen went into the inner office and returned with the file containing Starheim's original request.

'Now, let me see,' he said. 'You gave me the name Schirmer and the markings: III/GJR 218. Etched on a pair of binoculars, you said. Well, it's very simple. GJR stands for *Gebirgsjager* – mountain troops. III was for the Third Battalion. And 218 for the 218th Regiment. Now the 218th Regiment was part of the 7th Division, at least towards the end of the war. It had been converted from the 199th Infantry Division –'

Catching Starheim's expression, he said: 'Sorry, I'll try to keep it simple. The 7th Division was part of the 18th Mountain Corps. Now the 18th Corps had been on the Russian Front at Kestenga, but during "Northern Light", the German retreat of the winter of 1944–5, they drove back through Finland and into Norway as far as Lyngen, arriving between November of '44 and January of '45.'

Furrows of concentration appeared on Starheim's brow.

'So much for the regiment,' Sorensen continued. 'Now this man Schirmer. That was simple too. I merely contacted the German Military Archives at Breisgau in the Black Forest, and they looked him up under 218th Regiment, and there he was. A lieutenant, full name: Hans Schirmer. But then I'd guessed he'd be an officer.'

'Why?'

'Having his name on the binoculars. It meant that they had to be his own property. And only officers carried their own binoculars. The name was properly engraved, I take it, rather than scratched on?'

'Yes.'

'There! That's what I thought.'

Starheim had been listening restlessly, tapping the tips of his fingers together. Now he prompted: 'But this Schirmer died?'

'Indeed.'

'Do you have a date?'

'Yes – didn't I give that to you?'

'You said January 1945.'

'In fact, he was reported deceased on –' Sorensen referred to

274

the papers in front of him. 'Yes, on 21st January 1945.'

'Where was that? And how did he die?'

Sorensen shook his head. 'I can't say. And it would be difficult to find out. Although . . .' He did his thinking aloud. 'It's unlikely he died in action, not on that date. There was no fighting going on at the time. Not at Lyngen, anyway. It's possible that he was injured at some earlier date, at the Russian front for instance, and invalided to a military hospital.'

'But he died in Norway?'

'Ah no, we can't be sure of that. Is it important?'

Starheim gave a harsh sigh. 'I don't know.'

There was a pause. The lawyer asked: 'Can you tell me why you need this information?'

Starheim's dark eyes gave Sorensen a hard appraising stare, as if trying to make up his mind about him. Then he shook his head, a sudden sharp movement. 'It's rather complicated. I can't really explain. Except . . .' He frowned deeply. 'It's a personal matter, something that goes back a long way.'

Sorensen said: 'I understand.' Although he wasn't sure he did. So-called personal matters usually concerned the unfortunate by-products of war, such as sexual liaisons with the enemy. Only this week a Norwegian woman had decided after all these years to try to find her German soldier lover, to tell him his son was nearly fifteen.

Obviously this didn't fall into that sort of category. Sorensen was rather intrigued.

Starheim asked: 'Look, is there any way to find out where and how this soldier died?'

Sorensen hesitated. It was a tall order. It was a job for researchers, who would need to go through archives in Breisgau and Bonn. It might even be necessary to contact some of Schirner's old comrades. The job could take anything from a day to a week. Even then, they might not come up with the answers. He blew out his cheeks. 'I can't promise anything. And it would take a lot of time.'

'If it's a question of money I'll be glad to pay,' Starheim said firmly.

'Well –'

'Please. Will you put it in hand for me? If there's the slightest chance.'

Sorensen understood: this really was important. He made up his mind. 'All right. I'll see what can be done without incurring too much expense. If there's a problem, I'll come back to you. Are you in Oslo for long?'

Starheim hesitated: 'I'm not sure. Two days. Maybe three.'

'Where can I find you?'

'I'm staying with a climbing friend for a couple of days, then returning to Tromso.' He gave Sorensen the telephone numbers, and explained about leaving messages with Arne.

The lawyer stood up and led the way to the door. 'Are you off on any expeditions?' he asked pleasantly.

There was a short silence. The frown on Starheim's face had deepened visibly. He clearly wasn't one for small talk.

Then they both spoke at once. Sorensen said: 'Well, I suppose you're too busy –' just as Starheim rallied himself to say: 'No, not at present.'

They paused on the threshold.

Starheim forced a smile, as if realising how distant and forbidding he must seem. 'Thank you. I appreciate it very much.' He hesitated. 'Of course – this thing, it might be nothing . . .'

Sorensen nodded. 'You don't have to explain. I understand. Sometimes one just has to find out, one way or the other.'

It was bitterly cold. The streets were empty of taxis, and Ha. couldn't remember which route the trams took. He jammed a hat on his head, wound his scarf tighter round his neck and began the long walk along the icy pavements.

He thought about Sorensen and what he'd told him. He thought even more about what he hadn't been able to tell him and felt a momentary despair. It wasn't that he held out much hope of getting useful answers, he was just tired of uncertainty. Uncertainty wore you down. He sometimes thought it wa. worse than bad news itself.

And there was quite enough bad news to be going on with.

He had reached some important decisions in the last few days, decisions which were extremely painful but necessary.

Brattdal would have to go. As a working farm, at least. He'.

been crazy to think he could run it on his own. He could always hire a farmhand of course – though it was unlikely anyone would want to come and live in such an isolated spot – but the cost would be high and the whole operation would become even more unprofitable than it already was. One thing was certain, he couldn't go on trading on Arne's generosity.

Neither could he go on living there alone. He'd been trying to prove something that wasn't worth proving: that he didn't need anyone. It wasn't true. He did need people, and, more particularly, he needed a woman in his life. He'd been hoping that person would be Ragna. But he'd been wasting his time; she hadn't been worth waiting for.

Now he had an urge to make up for lost time, to cast off the past and rejoin the human race, preferably in large numbers.

For a moment he remembered all the work – the vegetable plot, the animals, the musk-oxen – and felt a crushing sense of futility. But he forced himself out of it. Regrets were useless. The chapter was closed.

He arrived at the Hotel Bristol at six-fifteen and came face to face with his partners in the other major decision he had made. Fred; and another old climbing friend, Carl.

Carl's grin stretched from ear to ear and he shook Hal's hand so hard that Hal pulled it away with a theatrical wince.

'Hal! Hal!' Carl cried. 'This is wonderful news! Wonderful!'

'I haven't promised yet.'

Carl winked, to show that it was only a matter of time. 'You'll be with us, I know you will!'

Hal thought: He's right. And the idea cheered him. He slipped out of his coat. 'How long before the meeting?'

Fred glanced at his watch. 'Ten minutes.' Fred had set up a meeting with a wealthy shipowner interested in financing the expedition.

Leaving Carl and Fred in the lobby, Hal went to a phone booth and called Arne's number seven hundred miles away.

The Tromso operator gave the two long, one short ring that was the code for Arne to answer. After a pause Arne's voice sounded down the line. Hal could almost hear the neighbours picking up their phones to listen in.

'A calf's sick,' Arne began. Hal knew immediately: a musk-ox, and his heart sank.

They discussed it briefly. The animal had sores round its mouth, but its general weakness suggested the same infection as before. Until the vet's report came through there was nothing that could be done.

'Ragna Johansen called,' Arne continued and Hal couldn't stop his stomach from doing a small hop.

He said: 'Oh?'

'She wanted to speak to you urgently. I told her you were in Oslo. She wanted to contact you, but I said I wasn't sure where you were.'

Hal felt a savage delight: that would keep her guessing. Good old Arne.

'I have a telephone number. She said it was very urgent.'

Hal wrote the number in his notebook. 'Thanks, Arne.'

'You'll be back soon?'

'Soon, Arne.'

Hal went back to the lobby to join Carl and Fred. They started to walk into the main lounge. Carl was saying: 'I told you, Hal, didn't I, about the Geographical Society?' when Hal suddenly stopped in his tracks.

Reaching for his notebook he found the phone number Arne had just dictated to him and, leafing through his combined diary-address book, compared it with one he had there.

It matched.

The number was Rolf's.

For a moment he stared at the page, then, snapping the notebook shut, he clapped Fred on the shoulder and said firmly: 'After the meeting, my friends, we are going to have a reunion party.'

Berg came out of the phone box, looked briefly up and down and walked off, suppressing the urge to hurry.

The *Dagens Post* office was only fifty yards away, just round the corner in Akersgata. He had plenty of time. He picked his way across the mound of hard-packed snow by the kerb, crossed the road, and walked briskly along the street and round the corner into the brightly lit entrance.

Nodding to the night porter, he strolled up the first flight of stairs until he was out of sight. Then he accelerated, passing the editorial floor at a smart trot.

A door led on to the roof. He extricated the key from the small glass-fronted box marked 'In Case of Fire' and, unlocking the door, went out.

The roof of the *Dagens Post* building was flat and covered in a thick layer of crusty snow. He crossed it rapidly, following the tracks he had made half an hour earlier on his reconnaissance. The next roof, being considerably lower and steeply pitched at the sides, was trickier, but it was fronted by a parapet and, once he had lowered himself gingerly down on to the flat ridge and climbed down the incline on the fixed metal rungs that ran down one side, there was an easy path along the wide snow-filled gutter.

This was the last building in the block, and he approached the corner cautiously, at a stoop. Crouching behind the parapet, he raised his head over the edge and took a long look.

He was above a square called Aschehougs Plass, which was actually a small triangle formed by the junction of three streets. In the centre of the triangle was the phone box he'd just used.

It was eleven thirty-nine. He had made it from the phone box in under five minutes.

From beneath his padded anorak he pulled out a small pair of binoculars and began to search the scene below. He could see straight up the main street that led off to the west, and up the narrow street that came in at a diagonal to form the triangle. By sticking his head over the parapet he could also see the street immediately beneath him that went eastwards. There was only one blind spot: the south side of the square, which was hidden by a protruding building.

A tram jangled along below, turned into the square, and disappeared up the narrow street that ran off at the diagonal.

Otherwise nothing. A pedestrian, the occasional car, the sudden whooping shout of an unseen merrymaker.

His mouth was a little dry, his stomach tense. He calmed himself; whatever happened he would be safe up here.

The streets fell quieter. He could feel the cold biting into his hands. Beneath his padded clothing sweat was cooling fast on his skin.

He put the binoculars back to his eyes and made a slow sweep

279

from the top of one street, down into the triangle, up the next street and down again.

Nothing.

Only ten minutes to go.

If she came.

She would, he was sure she would. She had been angry of course, her voice ice-cold and reproachful, but he knew Sonja: obedient, loyal, curious. She would come.

But the question was: would anyone else?

He sat up.

A car. A car in the narrow street was stopping at the kerb. Its lights died. No one got out.

Berg's hands shook slightly as he grasped the binoculars.

Watchers.

He felt a moment of childish triumph.

An instant later he uttered a sigh of disgust.

A door of the car had opened, a woman had emerged. Waving to the driver, she walked off. The car lights flashed on again and it pulled away.

Berg's shoulders sagged and he sucked in a long breath.

Time passed. Another tram appeared and rounded the square, the rasp and rattle of its wheels unnaturally loud in the frozen air. Berg blew on his aching hands and tried to suppress a sense of foreboding. Supposing nothing happened? Supposing Sonja wasn't followed? Then he'd be no wiser than before. He almost wanted to catch the watchers in the act. It was uncertainty that really frightened him.

Suddenly he spotted Sonja's ancient Volvo.

He jammed the binoculars to his eyes. The car was coming hesitantly into the square from the main street. It slowed, stopped, then started off again. Typical Sonja. Wondering whether she dare park in a restricted area.

She disappeared for a moment, lost to view in the blind spot. Then she reappeared, still driving indecisively.

Finally she seemed to make up her mind. Rounding the square, the Volvo headed back into the main street and pulled in to the kerb. The lights were switched off. Sonja remained inside.

Berg swept the binoculars back and forth.

He couldn't believe it. Nothing.

Unless —
There.
This time he didn't allow himself to get excited. Another car had drawn up some distance further up the main street, too far away to see clearly. But it looked dark-coloured, maybe even black, and fast. Its sidelights were on, but then they too died. No one got out.

Back to Sonja. She, too, was waiting.

The minutes ticked slowly by. No one moved.

Eventually, the door of Sonja's car opened and she emerged. Pulling her coat closer around her, she picked her way across the icy road to the centre of the triangle. She looked up the narrow street, then began to pace slowly back and forth. He could almost sense her agitation.

He swung the binoculars back to the parked car. Nothing.

Sonja left the triangle and, wandering into the beginning of the narrow street, began to pace up and down again.

Berg suddenly realised that if the occupants of the car *were* watchers, they couldn't possibly see Sonja from there.

Which meant there were others. Somewhere.

He looked hard, but couldn't spot them.

Another five minutes passed. Sonja was still at the far corner of the square. She had stopped pacing and was standing still. Then, suddenly, she was on the move again, but fast this time, recklessly half walking half running across the street.

She had given up on him. Doubtless she was in tears.

Suddenly he held very still.

She wasn't heading for the Volvo. She was coming straight for *him*.

He watched in vague horror as she drew nearer and, turning into the street below, crossed the road and marched along the side of the *Dagens Post* building. He craned over the edge of the parapet.

She had the determined stride of someone who knew exactly where she was going.

Crouching low, he ran along behind the parapet until he reached the end of the roof, then peered over again. She was rounding the corner of the *Dagens Post* building.

Ignoring the fact that he might be horribly visible from the street, he scrambled up the metal rungs on to the ridge and levered himself up to the roof of the newspaper building.

He ran lightly through the snow to the front of the building. Crouching, he pushed his head over the edge of the coping.

He froze with disbelief.

She was there, just short of the entrance to the *Dagens Post*, standing still. Then she began to walk forward again, hesitantly, looking over her shoulder, as if she hadn't finally made up her mind what to do.

Where was she going?

But he knew. He knew with dreadful certainty even before she got there, so that when she reached the *Dagens Post* building and stopped again, it was like a rerun film, a nightmare he'd already enacted in his mind.

He ran at a crouch to the corner and looked back towards the square. His stomach jolted savagely.

They were there. Out in the open.

Two of them.

The first walking briskly down the side of the newspaper building. The other coming more slowly from the direction of the parked car.

He jerked back to Sonja, as yet invisible to the approaching watchers.

She was still there. Standing. Looking up at the building.

Indecisive.

He felt a small spark of hope.

She was looking around. Turning her back on the newspaper building. Bending her head. He focused the binoculars. She was searching her handbag.

He looked back. One watcher strolled up to a tram-stop and tried hard to look as though he was waiting for the last tram, though it had long gone. The other was immediately below Berg, and rounding the corner. The watcher, seeing Sonja stationary before him, did the only thing he could, which was to keep walking and go straight past her.

Sonja was still standing there, her head swivelling between the newspaper entrance and the corner.

Finally she made a few tentative steps.

Back the way she'd come.

She took another few steps, looked back over her shoulder, almost hesitated again then, head down, quickened her pace.

282

She was heading back towards the square.

The relief washed over Berg in a hot wave.

He watched her walk briskly round the corner, down the street, and across the triangle.

But it wasn't over; she was going into the phone box.

The watcher who'd been waiting at the tram-stop had retreated towards the black car.

Sonja stayed in the box for several minutes. Berg had the ghastly feeling he knew exactly what number she was calling. His own.

At last she came out of the box, slamming the door behind her, and made for her car.

The lights came on, the Volvo pulled away and disappeared.

A second later the dark car came into view, doing a U-turn, and went off in the same direction.

Berg sat on the freezing roof for a long time, vicious with rage, trying to absorb the awful truth.

Sonja knew who he was.

Sonja knew.

How? How? He racked his brains.

No – forget how. That wasn't important now.

Much more important: did anyone else know?

Them. The watchers. Did they know?

If so they'd already be tapping his phone, watching silently, biding their time, waiting ... He felt violated and enraged. His mind lurched towards nightmare visions of captivity.

With a vast effort, he pushed the images aside.

He clutched at a single powerful thought.

They couldn't have evidence. Not hard evidence. They couldn't prove he'd used the information for anything but his journalism. It suddenly occurred to him that they couldn't even prove he'd received the information in the first place.

They only had Sonja's word for it.

And it was possible they didn't even have that. Yet.

He progressed the idea. Suppose Sonja hadn't talked. Suppose they knew nothing about him. Then they'd be doing exactly what they'd done tonight: watching Sonja like a hawk, hoping she would lead them to him.

He became excited by the idea. It made perfect sense. If they had been on to him they would have been watching him tonight

283

in the same way they'd watched Sonja. Yet there had been no sign of a second surveillance team. He would have spotted it, he knew he would. And if his phone had been tapped, there would have been a giveaway, a click or something.

The more he thought about it, the more convinced he became that Sonja hadn't yet blabbed.

As long as the watchers hadn't read too much into that determined walk of hers to the entrance of the *Dagens Post*, as long as they didn't realise the significance of that pause in front of the building, then he might just be all right.

Now – how to stay all right . . .

A thought came into his mind. He grasped at it, turned it over in his mind, warmed to it, and felt the beginnings of hope.

Three hours later he sat in a parked car with Niki.

Niki was tapping his fingers on the wheel, staring across the icy waters of Oslo Fiord. They had driven out on the Drammen road, past Fornebu Airport, to the end of a road of quietly affluent houses set in thick woodland. A snow-covered jetty, redundant until the spring, stretched out into solid ice. In the ice-free channel beyond, the lights of a small vessel glided across the fiord.

Around them few lights showed; there was silence.

In the faint silvery light, Niki was looking unhappy. He said stiffly: 'Who is this woman?'

'Her name's Sonja Bjornsen. She works in the Defence Ministry.'

Niki's head snapped round. 'What? You're not serious –'

'But I told you, she's totally unimportant. She's nothing but a ledger clerk. I stupidly thought she had access to important stuff. But she doesn't. Would you believe it, but she works in accounts! I just got it wrong, that's all.' Berg gave a small shiver. 'Not only did I get it wrong, but she gives a whole new meaning to hell hath no fury.'

'And she could really blow you?'

Berg gave Niki a long haggard look. 'Yes, I'm afraid so. What's more, the timing couldn't be worse. I'm just on the point of getting some wonderful stuff, Niki.' He paused for effect. 'I've been working on this for a long time. If I lose it now it'll be a bloody tragedy.' He gave a bleak laugh. 'Quite apart from the fact that I don't want to go to prison.'

The Russian said impatiently: 'We wouldn't let that happen. We'd take you out.'

Russia. A prison by any other name.

There was a silence. Niki was clearly in the throes of an inner struggle. 'You don't know what you're asking, Rolf. It's –' He shook his head. 'It's much more difficult than you might imagine.'

'But possible?'

'Possible,' he agreed, 'but crazy. This woman works for the defence ministry. It's going to get noticed. They'll look into her life –'

'And find nothing.'

'How do you know that?'

'I've made sure.'

'Rolf, Rolf . . .' Niki sighed with exasperation. 'Things aren't done this way. Maybe defectors, our own people who've sold out. But this . . . I mean, if suspicion came our way . . .'

Berg said a touch irritably: 'Surely you can deal with all that.'

Niki's mouth was set in a stubborn line. 'Better to take you out, Rolf. We could do it now. Tonight.'

He had to be joking. It was so ludicrous Berg almost laughed.

He realised he was going to have to spell a few things out. He said gravely: 'Niki, look at the choices. They are – well, blindingly simple. Either you protect me and my principal supplier and I get this fantastic new stuff for you and you earn yourself a fat promotion. Or . . . I get blown and my contact with me and you never get another foreign posting in your whole life.'

Niki looked upset, which was just what Berg had intended. He was thinking of life in a backwater of the GRU without the foreign perks, the nice Moscow flat and the pass to the foreign-currency shops. He started tapping the wheel again. 'This information your contact's producing – you say it's good.'

'I said so, and it is.'

Niki hated having to ask, but he overcame his reluctance. 'Well! Give me an idea!'

Berg had prepared this; he had simply chosen what he

imagined Niki would most like in the world. 'Nato's 1964 Strategy for Northern Europe.'

The Russian froze for a moment, then licked his lips. His eyes glinted hungrily. 'Rolf, you never fail to amaze me.'

'Good. Well, now amaze *me*. Give me what I need.'

There was a pause. The Russian looked away, his face contorted with thought. Then he sighed gently, a sigh of resignation, and gave an almost imperceptible nod.

Berg realised it was all settled. He felt a rush of relief.

'You're certain they're not on to you already?' Niki asked.

'Certain,' Berg lied.

'Good. But you should go away for a while. Somewhere out of town – abroad maybe – and don't tell anybody where you're going.'

'How long for?'

He considered. 'A week – I don't know. But keep in touch. We'll let you know when to come back.'

As they drove back towards town Berg considered where to go. Sweden? Finland? No, too far away to keep in touch easily. There were things he still needed to keep an eye on.

Then, suddenly, he had it. He knew exactly where to go.

Twenty-two

Sonja Bjornsen sat by the telephone in her living room, fighting down a bad case of nerves. She glanced at the clock: it was past seven.

Now.

She reached for the phone, hesitated, and pulled back.

She took a walk around the room and sat down again. She wanted a clear head, but lack of sleep had fuddled her brain. She'd got to bed at one, dozed fitfully for three hours, then woken, gripped by a single obsessive thought: that she had to contact Erik.

Time and again she imagined the moment when he answered the phone. The confirmation that he was indeed Rolf Berg, the stunned silence when he realised who she was, the denial that he was Erik, the pretence that there was some mistake. Then the realisation that she had caught him out, the grudging admission and, finally, the agreement to meet.

And this time he'd turn up. He'd have to.

Sonja squirmed with a mixture of anticipation and misery. Why had he failed to turn up a second time? Why hadn't he phoned to explain? What on earth was going on? Underlying all her fears was the suspicion that something dreadful had happened – though she couldn't make up her mind what.

Perhaps it was that stupid Delta story she'd given him. He'd discovered it wasn't true; he'd been made to look a fool and he was angry with her. Yes, that must be it. She could kick herself. Why had she made it up? Why had she been so stupid?

She had tried to call him last night from the phone box – it had been easy to call then, when she was hurt and angry. But he hadn't been at home. And they'd said he wasn't in his office.

Now she regretted not having marched into the *Dagens Post* building; the staff might well have been able to tell her where he was and avoided the necessity for this.

It had to be done.

She made herself sit down calmly. Rehearsing her words over and over again, she lifted the phone and carefully dialled his home number.

The number rang. She gripped the receiver.

It went on ringing ... Her hopes began to fall. He wasn't going to be in.

Then, suddenly, it answered.

'Hello?' A woman's voice.

Sonja held her breath.

'Hello?'

Slowly, Sonja replaced the receiver.

She exhaled sharply. She should have known! Probably Hildegard Lindman. Or another. He probably had dozens of them. The thought cut her like a knife. Damn him!

Sharp bitter tears sprang to her eyes. She didn't mean to cry but somehow she couldn't prevent it and the tears fell in a steady stream.

A moment later she pressed her lips together, blew her nose and stood up purposefully. This was no way to carry on. Crying was the first step on the long slippery slope to depression and despair. She'd spent twenty years learning how to avoid that.

The smooth balm of self-control spread over her.

She noted the time. She must leave for the office; life must go on as normal. She would call Rolf Berg at the *Dagens Post* during the morning.

Before leaving she put on make-up and examined herself critically in the mirror. She'd lost some weight, something she'd always longed to do, yet she wasn't sure it suited her. Her face looked lined: older.

At the front door she paused, a faint memory nagging at her. There was something she should have remembered and hadn't. She searched her foggy mind in growing frustration until, suddenly, it came back to her. She pulled open the drawer of the hall table and found the sheaf of photocopies. It had been very careless of her to leave them there, just lying around. Quickly, she took them into the living room, placed them in the grate and, putting a match to them, watched them burn until there was nothing but ashes.

The journey to the office was so familiar that she made it without thinking: first the commuter train, then the tram, finally the quarter-mile walk. Only when she arrived at Portous Gate did she force herself to consider the day ahead.

She showed her pass and walked towards the lift, her head down, trying to concentrate. There was the weekly departmental meeting at nine, she remembered. Then two further meetings scheduled for later in the day. She would be taking the minutes: somehow she mustn't let the tiredness affect her work.

The lift started up, disgorging people on its way. The doors opened at her floor, she walked out.

Someone approached her. It was Major Thrane. She managed a small polite smile. She realised he was going to speak to her.

'Sonja, could I borrow you for a moment? Before you go to your office?' He gestured that they were to go in the other direction.

She blinked. 'Er ... yes. Of course.'

He led the way along the passage to the stairs and started down them. A small alarm sounded in Sonja's mind, she almost spoke, but something about the major's brisk manner made her hesitate.

They continued downwards to the basement, then along a passage. Sonja wasn't familiar with this part of the building. She tried to remember what it was used for. Whatever, she couldn't imagine what Thrane could possibly want with her down here.

Thrane stopped outside a door and, opening it, stood aside for her to go in.

She stepped over the threshold, taking in the bare walls, the metal chairs, the windowless room, the people waiting for her.

Then, in the next instant, she realised.

It was all over.

She glanced at Thrane. His eyes confirmed it.

It was all over.

Before her sat the Head of Security. To his right were two of his staff, one of whom had a notepad and tape recorder ready on the table before him.

Thrane rubbed a hand over his eyes. He was tired, which wasn't surprising since he'd had three hours' sleep in the last twenty-four. It was almost one. He'd been interrogating Sonja Bjornsen for four hours. The Head of Security had left as soon as Sonja had made her first admission, which had been within five minutes. Now only Thrane and a colleague remained.

Sonja sat opposite them, a plate of sandwiches untouched on the table in front of her. She was ashen-faced, yet oddly composed, as if she didn't believe she had done a great deal of harm.

Thrane found her calmness infuriating. He had the urge to shake the life out of her, to force the silly woman to understand what she'd done. He couldn't be absolutely certain how bad the damage was, not until he went through everything with her, item by item. But she'd made the most important admission.

She had been passing information, and she had been doing it for some time.

As she'd talked he'd got the nasty feeling that the final cost was going to be heavy.

And they hadn't even discussed Pasvik.

He was purposely keeping that until later.

He switched on the tape recorder once more, throwing the switch across with a loud snap. His colleague leant over his pad.

'Right,' he said sharply. 'So let's go back to the beginning again. Did you honestly never suspect him?'

'No. Not until very recently, like I told you.'

'Yet you checked up on him? Right at the beginning.'

'Yes.'

'So you had a suspicion?'

'No. It was just a sensible thing to do. To check.'

'What about his appetite for information? Didn't that make you suspicious?'

'It seemed natural to chat. Departmental gossip.'

'Gossip? But it wasn't gossip, was it, Sonja? It was hard information.'

She was silent.

'And you expect me to believe you never suspected him? That

you never realised he wasn't Erik Leif?'

'I told you. I had no idea until recently.'

Thrane took a deep breath. 'Okay, so what finally made you suspicious?'

The eyes slid away. 'I don't know ... lots of things. Small mistakes. Things he should have known and didn't. His secretiveness.'

'So you checked up on him more thoroughly?'

'Yes.'

'And discovered the truth?'

She nodded.

'Then why in hell didn't you come to me?'

She licked her lips nervously. 'I wanted to be sure. I –' A look of what might have been pain flickered across her face.

'You wanted to protect him?'

'No.'

'Then what?'

'I wanted to – talk to him. I felt sure there must be a reason, an explanation. I was sure he'd tell me about it.'

'What sort of explanation did you think there could be?' Thrane asked in disbelief.

She replied levelly: 'You're wrong about him, you know. He didn't pass anything on to a – third party. I mean he wasn't a –' she tripped over the word as if it were distasteful to her '– a spy.'

'How do you know?'

'I just – know. He ... couldn't have been.' She put a hand to her eyes.

Thrane wanted to exclaim: You've been completely fooled, you stupid woman! Instead he pushed back his chair with an angry shove and took a walk round the room, still incredulous that such a sensible woman could have deceived herself so thoroughly. She had sold her country down the river for what? Not ideology. Not money, not immortality.

No, for what she called love. A furtive sordid once-a-month whiff of it; an infrequent roll in the hay with a virile young lover.

It was staggering – no, pathetic – that sex could reduce a woman to such complete gullibility.

Returning to the table, he said: 'And you've never had the

chance to confront him?'

She shook her head.

'So what made him run for it?'

She looked startled. 'What do you mean?'

'Disappear. Vanish. Run for it.'

Doubt and alarm crossed her face. 'He hasn't disappeared,' she said.

'He failed to turn up not once but twice. A fairly clear indication, I would have thought.' Thrane didn't add that the second time had all the signs of a set-up. As if the lover and his friends were checking up on Sonja, to find out if she was under surveillance. Well, they had checked up and now, presumably, they knew. Which was why Thrane had decided to bring Sonja in.

'What other explanation could there be?' he prompted.

She was about to speak, then changed her mind, her mouth moving soundlessly. Finally she took a deep breath and said in a rush: 'I gave him some false information, stuff I made up – and I think he may have found out. It's the only thing I can think of.'

Thrane thought he must have misheard. 'What do you mean – false information? What are you talking about?'

'It – concerned Project Bluetail, the installation at Kaafiord. He wanted –' She broke off.

Wanted to know all about it, thought Thrane savagely.

'He asked about it,' Sonja continued carefully. 'I told him it was a new type of navigation system. A system which could be used by submarines when submerged. I even gave the system a name – a made-up name. I said it was called Delta.'

'Delta? But why did you tell him all this?'

'Because – I knew he wasn't who he said he was. I couldn't tell him anything – true.'

Thrane was puzzled. 'But I thought – I thought ...' He suddenly felt a leap of triumph. 'You've lied to me!' His words went pouncing across the table. 'You said a few moments ago that you never had the chance to confront him!'

She blanched. He had caught her out. 'I – I was angry and upset. I needed time to think. To work out how to tackle him. In the meantime I didn't want him to have anything – useful. So I told him lies.'

'And warned him off in the process!'

'No, I'm sure I didn't!' she said with unexpected intensity. 'I'm sure he'll come back!'

Thrane stared at her. There was something very peculiar here. It just didn't make sense. She was too certain. 'Why?' he asked quietly.

She shook her head. Clearly she wasn't going to answer. He returned to the subject they'd already covered several times.

'Surely you must have got some clues as to who he might be?'

The slightest hesitation. 'No.'

There it was again, something furtive. Something to hide.

'You tried to phone him last night, you said. After he stood you up.'

'Yes.'

'At your friend Monika's house, at the place you normally met.'

She nodded. 'I thought I might have got the meeting place wrong. That he was waiting there.'

'I don't believe you. I think you know how to contact him directly. We'll check, you know. On whether you really did call your friend's house.'

She dropped her eyes. He thought: Ah, she doesn't like that!

He tried again. 'So, you don't know who he is,' he said, letting the sarcasm show in his voice. 'He must have let something slip though, about where he lived, what he did, how he amused himself. After all, this' – he flicked his fingers across his notes – 'is not very much, is it? Tallish, thick blond hair, blue eyes, early thirties. I mean, that's half of Oslo!'

Her face had gone blank. The shutters were down. She had closed off again.

Thrane thought: Right. You've had your chance. Now we do it the other way.

'Okay, Sonja. Let's go through it item by item, complete with dates, documents and all the details. I have a list of events to help jog your memory. But we'll start with something you'll have no trouble in remembering. Pasvik.'

*

'You're wrong!' Sonja was so appalled that she repeated it twice, her voice tearful and shrill like a child's. With an effort she calmed down and said more reasonably: 'You're wrong. He never knew the location, he never knew the names. I didn't tell him. I *never* told him things like that! He wasn't responsible for ...' She couldn't bring herself to say anything but, '*this*.'

'But you told him the rest, didn't you?'

'I ...' She stopped abruptly, torn between a desire to tell the truth and the lurking fear that in telling it she might step into some awful trap.

'I told him there was an operation on,' she began slowly. 'I told him that we were meeting a man near the border –'

'Were you specific?'

She tried to remember: what *had* she said? 'I said the meeting was to be in the Inari region. But I was no more specific than that. Really.'

'And?'

It was such a long time ago. She racked her brains. 'I told him the third man had done a deal with us. Information in exchange for freedom.'

'Go on.'

'I can't remember.'

'I think you can.'

She buried her head in her hands and cast her mind back to the evening when Erik had almost left her, the pain of it and the relief when he'd changed his mind. What *had* she told him? ... That one of the men was a survival expert. Yes, she remembered telling him that. And she had the feeling she'd told him the other was a Lapp. And that the third man came from Murmansk. Not so much, but if she told Thrane he'd jump on it and draw those dreadful conclusions again. And he'd be wrong.

Whatever Erik-Rolf was – over-ambitious, manipulative – he was nothing more sinister than a journalist. He may have used the information to further his career, but he couldn't possibly be responsible for the catastrophe at Pasvik.

She decided to stay silent. Because Thrane would never ever understand, not unless she told him the truth about Rolf, and she wasn't going to do that. When she'd first denied knowing

Erik's real identity she hadn't been sure why she'd done it. She'd only been certain that it was the right thing to do.

But now she understood why she must go on lying. It was essential to prevent this ghastly thing from growing. She must keep her hand pressed over the hole in the dam or the poisonous water would gush out and drown everything, everybody – her whole world. The moment she told them Rolf's name they would go and arrest him, and she'd lose any chance of seeing him again.

Aaah. The thought stabbed at her.

Avoiding Thrane's hard unyielding stare, she said: 'I told him nothing else about Pasvik. Nothing.'

'I don't believe you.'

She didn't reply.

'I believe you told him everything. I believe he was a Soviet agent, and that you told him everything, Sonja. And that he acted on that information, just as he's acted on all the information you've given him. What's more, I think that in the last week he somehow got wind of trouble and skipped it. Disappeared. Left the country. Leaving you, Sonja, to face the music. All on your own. A real friend, eh?'

'You're wrong.'

'Why, Sonja?'

'I just know.' She felt the beginnings of desperation. This continuous badgering was wearing her down. But he'd never stop, she knew that; these awful questions would just go on and on.

The germ of an idea came into Sonja's mind and she snatched at it. She realised it would give her the two things she desperately needed – time, and an opportunity to see Rolf. The idea blossomed and consolidated. She said to Thrane: 'Look – perhaps there's a solution, a way I can prove he's – not what you think. A way you can find out who he is. Let me go on as if nothing had happened. Let me continue at work, let me go home each evening. Then I'm sure he'll contact me again.'

'You're sure? Why are you sure?'

Sonja realised she would have to lie again. One lie seemed to lead inexorably to another. 'Because he's done this before. Not turned up.'

'You didn't tell me that!'

295

'Oh ... well, it's true. But you see, he always comes back again.'

Looking unconvinced, Thrane hesitated, as if on the point of challenging her, then seemed to think better of it. 'So,' he said finally, 'let me get this absolutely right. You'd be prepared to entrap him for us?'

The bluntness of it took Sonja back. But he was right: it would be entrapment. Could she do it? She imagined the scene: Erik-Rolf coming to a meeting place, responding reluctantly to her quiet questions, becoming faintly concerned and finally, in a crushing moment of realisation, staring at her in surprise and horror. The vision was bitter-sweet.

She whispered: 'Yes, I'd do it,' and felt tears prick her eyes. 'But only –' She gathered her courage in both hands. 'Only if you give me a chance to talk to him. In private. For some time. Hours, I mean. I must have that!'

Thrane shifted in his seat, full of suppressed rage. He finally spluttered: 'This isn't a game we're playing for your gratification, you know!'

She said quietly: 'It would have to be a condition of the – arrangement. You'd have to promise.' The tears poured down her cheeks, falling in a steady stream on to the table.

A succession of expressions crossed Thrane's face – frustration, disapproval, then thoughtfulness, as if he were giving the idea serious consideration after all.

He got up and paced the room for a while then, pausing beside her, said with a harsh ironic laugh: 'How do I know you won't just tip him off?'

'You have my word.'

There was a silence. She looked up to see his face contorted by a black derisive smile. 'Your *word*, Sonja?'

'Yes.'

Eventually he dropped back into his seat, looking weary and said with a heavy sigh: 'I'll think about it.' He raised an admonishing finger at her. 'But only when we've been through everything, and I mean everything, item by item.' He shuffled his papers. 'Now, where were we?'

She knew the answer. And her heart sank.

Pasvik.

Thrane faced the Director and told him: 'She will not budge!'

'But she knows his identity?'

Thrane said emphatically: 'I'm sure of it! Or at least how to find him, which boils down to the same thing.'

'This deal she's offered, it's quite attractive.' The Director was a believer in expediency.

'I don't know ...'

'Well, she hasn't asked for much, has she? I mean, most people in her position would ask for a deal on the sentence.'

'Well, we certainly couldn't promise her that.'

The Director was grim-faced. 'That bad?'

'Pasvik, I'm sure of it. Though she swears she never gave him the exact location or the names of our men. But it has to be her. It all fits.'

'Our priorities are quite simple,' the Director said firmly. 'The first is to find out where the stuff was going. The second is to get proof, and I mean hard evidence, against both Sonja and her contact. This deal she's offering would give us both. So – I think we should agree.' He spotted Thrane's frown. 'Why not?'

'I'm certain the bird has flown.'

'But it must be worth a try.'

'I'd rather wear her down and get it out of her directly. She knows, damn it!'

The Director retorted: 'But an allegation isn't enough, is it? You know perfectly well that we have to catch the contact accepting information or, even better, passing it. It's useless just having his name!' He considered for a moment. 'We'll give Sonja two weeks.'

Thrane knew a decision when he heard one.

It was eight at night. He went back to his office and arranged for the surveillance cover on Sonja to be increased so that there would never be less than three men watching her at any one time. Then he went and told her that the deal was on and she was free to go home.

He retired to his office, tired and dejected. This exercise was a waste of time, he was sure of it. The lover had flown, and the knowledge was driving him mad. He couldn't help thinking that if he'd only got on to Sonja sooner – just a week sooner – then the lover would have walked straight into his arms.

Jensen came in. 'There're a couple of things you should look at before you go.'

Go? Did Jensen mean home? Thrane hadn't even considered the possibility. Home, like sleep, seemed to belong to another life.

Jensen placed two sheets of paper in front of him.

Thrane rubbed the tiredness out of his eyes and focused. The top sheet was a surveillance report from FO/S. Location: Kaafiord Valley. Future site of Top Sec ELINT PROJECT BLUETAIL ...

Thrane skipped to the body of the report. A party had been observed climbing up to the site and taking photographs. The party had consisted of four persons on skis, plus a grey dog resembling a wolf. (FO/S were nothing if not pedantic, Thrane noted.) The party had arrived by Land Rover, later identified as belonging to – Thrane sighed aloud as he read it – Halvard Starheim.

So. Hal hadn't taken the slightest notice of his advice. Some people never learnt, however often they were told. Thrane was disappointed: he'd thought Starheim would have known better. Well, from now on Starheim was on his own. Thrane felt under no further obligation to help or defend him.

He turned to the second sheet and realised angrily that this also concerned Starheim. It was a copy of a letter from Starheim to the defence ministry. He read impatiently. The usual thing. Lapp rights. Historical associations. Disturbance to the reindeer. Size of the installation.

Size?

Thrane read with more concentration.

... *this Delta navigation system, with its long aerials and maintenance requirements, is likely to cause considerable disturbance.*

Thrane clutched a hand to his forehead and stared, horrified.

Take your time, take your time. . . . Think.

Delta. Delta system.

Sonja.

Sonja had mentioned the name Delta. She'd told him she'd made it up.

Hell —

Think. Think.

But however hard he thought, there was no escape from it.

Delta. *Delta*.

Sonja had made it up for the benefit of her lover. She'd *invented* it.

So where in God's name had Hal got it from?

For a moment Thrane rested his head in his hands, then he said quietly to Jensen: 'Neither of us will be going home tonight, I'm afraid. Get on the phone. Tromso police first. Find out if Hal Starheim's at home on Revoy.'

Twenty-three

Hal let himself into Fred's flat and saw that the debris of the
party was still strewn around the living room: dirty glasses, beer
bottles, and an empty bottle of aquavit.

Hal dropped his coat on to a chair and, flopping down on
the sofa, closed his eyes. He'd felt worse, but he couldn't
remember when. The headache was the sort that pummelled
the back of your eyeballs, and stultified your brain. He rubbed
his aching temples and wished for the hundredth time that he'd
never suggested a party.

At nine that morning when he'd gone out to a meeting at the
Geographical Society he'd still felt drunk – the party hadn't
finished until four – but by midday the hangover had set in with
a vengeance. Now, late in the afternoon, he was still suffering.

He was disgusted with himself. Why had he done it? He'd
known perfectly well that he'd regret it. He'd always hated
the whole sordid business of drinking Norwegian-style, not
knowing – or caring – when to stop, forcing the drink down as
if there were no tomorrow.

Well, this was tomorrow, and the hangover was a stinker. It
served him right.

Eventually he roused himself and, after clearing away the
glasses and bottles, went to Fred's desk to work on a draft
proposal for the K2 expedition.

Finally, at six he decided on some hair of the dog. Aquavit.
He drank it like medicine, his nose crinkled up, his eyes closed.
After a time he felt a little better, which was more than he
deserved, and, turning on the radio news, let the distant voice
of the newscaster wash over him.

De Gaulle had vetoed Great Britain from membership of the

Common Market; at a Communist congress in East Berlin the Chinese had attacked Kruschev for withdrawing Soviet missiles from Cuba; and the US and Britain had affirmed their determination to build a Nato Polaris submarine force.

On the home front, the freeze continued ...

Hal pricked up his ears.

Oslo temperature: minus twenty. In the north there had been heavy overnight snow, with exceptionally low temperatures ... Tromso, minus eighteen; Kautokeino, minus forty. Outlook: unchanged.

Hal snapped the radio off and went to the dark window. The outer panes of the double-glazed window were frosted with glittering white lace. Beyond, the snow-drenched trees and snow-decked roofs of the suburban landscape gleamed palely beneath a night sky that was hard and brittle.

Hal thought of Brattdal and the recent snow and the exceptional cold, and was immediately haunted by visions of Arne struggling with drifts, broken-down tractors and sick animals. What a fool he'd been to leave! He should have known something like this would happen. It was almost February: just the time for difficulties and disasters.

Well, he'd get back as soon as possible. Yes – tomorrow.

In the meantime Arne should be phoning at any moment. Hal glanced at his watch, suddenly impatient for news.

While he waited he went through the pretence of convincing himself he wasn't going to have another drink, then weakened and poured a beer.

Normally he never drank on his own, but Fred wouldn't be back for another half an hour or so, and he needed the company. He was overcome by a deep despondency. Oslo and its mass of people always depressed him; he had the feeling people could live and die here without anyone noticing. And here he was, about to give up Brattdal to live in Oslo for months at a time while he organised this expedition.

Give up Brattdal ... The thought was very painful. Like stabbing a friend in the back.

The phone rang. He answered it hastily.

Arne's voice sounded a long way away. But his words were immediate. Three more musk-oxen were sick, with great swellings and sores round their mouths. The vet had phoned to say

301

he thought it might be contagious ecthyma, a viral infection common in sheep and goats, in which case the only hope was to segregate the sick animals. Arne had tried to get the sick animals down to the lower pasture, which was fenced, but he had been defeated by the heavy snow. With the temperature as it was, the old man expected the affected animals to die that night. However, he was going back immediately to see if there was any more he could do.

For a moment Hal couldn't speak. Finally he said weakly: 'I'll be back as soon as I can, Arne. Tomorrow, the first plane.'

'One more thing,' Arne said. 'It's getting colder.'

The instant Arne had rung off Hal called the airport. The first flight north was at 6.40 the next morning. He packed his bag immediately, then lay back on the bed, filled with a restless aching despair.

All futile: the musk-oxen, the farm, the new trees, Ragna, the ridiculous search for the owner of the binoculars. His life. Yes, that too. A bloody waste of time.

The phone jangled in the living room. One of Fred's friends no doubt. He considered leaving it unanswered but thought better of it.

'Halvard Starheim?' a voice said. 'It's Sorensen. You're in luck.'

Hal thought: I am?

'I've got something for you. It's very unusual to get this sort of thing so quickly. But we have my good friend Christina at the Breisgau Archives to thank. She's a bright girl, good at following her nose and taking a few well-chosen short cuts.'

Hal realised what he was getting round to. 'You've found out how the soldier died?'

'Yes. Christina found his family, or at least his brother, still living in the same town – Muhldorf – in Bavaria. Getting the original address was the hardest part – she had to go to the Bonn archives with his name and regiment. But once she had Muhldorf it was simple. She got a local telephone directory and started phoning people in the town who had the name Schirmer.' He added with a triumphant chuckle. 'Very lucky.'

Hal controlled himself with difficulty. 'And?'

'He died at a military hospital in Lyngseidet of injuries received in an accident. Apparently – according to the brother, that is – it was an avalanche.'

Hal didn't speak. After a moment Sorensen added: 'I hope that gives you the information you wanted. I'll have to charge you for some of Christina's time, I'm afraid. I hope that's all right ... Hello? ... Hello? ... Are you still there?'

Hal finally murmured: 'Charge me anything you like,' and rang off.

Ragna let herself into Rolf's flat, deposited the groceries in the kitchen and ran a bath. She sank into it, topped up with hot water, and lay back, letting the heat soothe her.

The day had been frantic, trying to cram two days' appointments into one, but in the end it had gone extremely well. Three months ago when she'd tried to interest the press in the Kaafiord issue they had been mildly attentive but distinctly unhelpful. Defence stories made them nervous, but security matters frightened them to death. Rolf's article had changed all that; suddenly the Kaafiord Lapps were news and everyone wanted to interview her. The foreign press, too. It had been Rolf's idea to get them involved.

It had been a long time since the press had wanted to take Ragna's photograph. In her far-off Swedish filming days she'd become quite well known – people had come to recognise her in the street – but she hadn't given a damn about the press then; she'd been arrogant enough to sweep past photographers in dark glasses. Not now. Now she took the trouble to get the pictures right. With Aslak's help she'd found a young Lapp at the university who was vaguely related to a Kaafiord family, and had persuaded him to become a fully-fledged Kaafiord Lapp for the day – a slight realignment of the facts justified, she felt, by the need to strike while the iron was hot.

And so the campaign was bearing fruit: a respected senior politician had promised to take the matter up in the Storting. And she'd received the detailed letter she'd been promised from the justice ministry – without the answers she wanted, of course – but it was a start.

Ideally she needed more time in Oslo, but she'd have to manage the follow-up from Tromso. Rolf was flying north first thing the next morning and wanted her to go with him. Since he'd offered to help out with her ticket, she couldn't afford to miss the opportunity.

She smiled to herself. Who was she fooling? She'd have gone with him anyway.

The thought of him filled her with wonderfully impure thoughts and she sank lower into the bath and closed her eyes. As a lover he'd been perfect, just as she'd known he would be. Confident, knowing, generous; taking her body into long-forgotten areas of delight. He was a very sensual man.

At the same time he maintained that iron detachment of his. But she liked that – he put no pressures on her, asked nothing of her except what she was extremely happy to give.

The only thing she found unsettling about him was his moods. He had the ability to leap from cool to warm in one breath-taking moment. The previous night he'd come back very late, at four in the morning. She hadn't asked him where he'd been – she wasn't going to fall into that old trap – but she hadn't been able to ignore his tense preoccupied mood.

At first nothing she'd said seemed to reach him, and he'd lain there at her side, awake and restless. Then, for no apparent reason, he'd moved over and started to make love to her with such haste and intensity that he'd taken her by surprise. She'd called softly 'Hey, wait for me!' and he'd paused and, sinking his head against her shoulder, had murmured: 'Ragna – I need you, I need you very much.' It was the only time he'd ever shown anything approaching emotion. She'd felt a sudden wave of tenderness and, taking his face in her hands, had kissed him softly, over and over again. Afterwards, when they lay apart, she was aware that he had drawn the shutter over his emotions again, and that she was once more excluded from his thoughts.

She was careful to remain detached too, of course – it was an essential part of her newly established freedom – yet she was left with a curious sense of loss. She didn't love him, she didn't want to love him, yet she couldn't help feeling that their relationship was lacking in some vital way.

She sat up suddenly and jumped out of the bath. It was almost seven. Rolf had said he'd be back at eight. She must hurry. She needed to get herself ready, phone Krisi to tell him she'd be returning the next day, and cook the supper. She also needed

304

to pack because there wouldn't be time in the morning.

She put on a loose sweater and jeans and brushed her hair. She didn't bother with make-up; she was quite satisfied with her face as it was.

She got through to Tromso just as her mother-in-law was putting Krisi to bed. Krisi was tired and grumpy and, apart from telling her that the sea at the bottom of the garden was so icy that people were walking on it, she couldn't get much out of him. But he sounded pleased that she was coming home.

She put down the phone and felt a small pang of love and remorse. She missed Krisi. Sometimes he drove her mad, sometimes she wondered if she'd been born with a short measure of maternal instinct, sometimes she ...

It was painful to progress the thought, and she paused.

Sometimes she resented him – no, not him, she could never resent him – but she resented his emotional hold on her. Was it that she was terrified of losing him too?

In her brave new mood she could almost admit to that possibility.

Perhaps the problem was that she loved him too much.

She hurried into the kitchen and started making dinner. Cooking wasn't her favourite pastime, but she tackled the preparations with something like enthusiasm. She'd spent a lot on the food – cantaloup melon, fillet steak, peppers and spices for a sauce, French cheese and a gâteau to follow. It was the sort of sophisticated meal she imagined Rolf would like.

After cutting and decorating the melon, she carried it through into the living room with the cutlery and glasses, and laid the table.

The door-bell rang.

She looked at the time. Seven-thirty. Rolf without his key? No, he wasn't the sort to forget. A friend dropping by perhaps. It crossed her mind that it might even be a female friend. Well, she was a big girl: she could handle that.

She went to the door, glancing in a mirror as she passed. She opened the door and swung it wide.

She gaped, astonished.

Hal.

Trying to recover, she made one or two ineffectual attempts to speak, and finally managed a weak: 'Hello, Hal.'

His face was ice-cold. 'Where's Rolf?'

'He'll be back at about eight.'

He half turned away, looked at his watch, hovered indecisively, then came across the threshold. 'I'll wait.'

She closed the door and followed him into the living room, saying: 'I hadn't realised you were coming down to Oslo too, otherwise we could have travelled together . . .' It was the wrong approach; she was burbling, sounding guilty. She started again. 'When did you come down?'

Ignoring the question, Hal strode to the side, began to unscrew a bottle of aquavit, changed his mind, and poured himself a mineral water. As he took a gulp, he looked round, his eyes sweeping over the table laid for two. His face seemed to harden and for a moment she thought he was going to speak but then he went to the window and stared resolutely out into the darkness. He was wearing a smart grey suit, Ragna noticed. She couldn't help thinking how well it looked on him.

The silence stretched out. She found it disconcerting, like an accusation. Searching for something to say, she said brightly: 'Have you seen the coverage we've been getting?'

He didn't move; his profile was unyielding. She realised he had no intention of making conversation. It occurred to her that he was doing it on purpose, to make her feel uncomfortable. And what was more, he was succeeding.

Suddenly she remembered – the message, the need to speak to him about the mixed-up information.

In a small burst of indignation she demanded: 'Didn't Arne tell you to phone me?'

'What?'

'To call me. It was urgent.'

'Oh . . .' Without turning from the window, he gave a small confirmatory nod.

'Well?' Ragna made the effort to suppress her annoyance, and explained levelly: 'It was about Kaafiord. The installation. Unfortunately I was given the wrong information. It's not going to be a Delta navigation system at all. The place is nothing to do with it, apparently.'

He showed no interest. Suddenly she was angry: he was sulking like a spoilt child. 'Did you use the information?' she demanded. 'Did you write to the defence ministry?'

He half turned, frowning. 'I may have done.'

'Well, *did* you?'

'Yes. I mentioned the name of the system. And the fact that it would have quite a few aerials.'

Her heart sank. Rolf would not be pleased. In fact, he'd be very angry. Rolf was not one to suffer fools gladly. He'd want to know why she hadn't mentioned it before. He'd be furious because it was too late to cover himself. Quite rightly, he'd put all the blame on to her.

She groaned and sank down on to the sofa. 'Oh Lord ... Look, Hal, could you write to them and explain? Explain that you've made a mistake and now realise it isn't going to be a Delta installation. I know it's a lot to ask, but it *is* important –'

'Ragna, I'm not going to discuss this now.' He turned and looked at her at last, and there was a deep well of coldness in his eyes.

'But it's important!'

'I couldn't care less at the moment.'

Her mouth dropped open; he was treating her like an idiot. Overcome by a sudden fury, she jumped to her feet. 'Why have you come, Hal? Why do you want to see Rolf?'

He looked away again, his lips set in a thin determined line. She was almost speechless with exasperation.

'Really, Hal! This is ridiculous! Whatever you have to say to Rolf you can say to me!'

He glanced back at her, raising an eyebrow. 'Oh? Why should that be?'

'Well ... presumably this concerns me in some way.'

He gave her a crushing look. 'You flatter yourself, Ragna.' 'Believe me, you are the very *last* subject I would bother to discuss with Rolf.'

She didn't believe him. 'Really?' she asked sarcastically. 'Then why are you so angry? Why are you here?'

He shot away from the window in a sudden startling movement and came and stood in front of her, full of suppressed anger.

'What I discuss with Rolf is my business, Ragna. But I can assure you that women have never loomed large in our conversation. With Rolf's voracious appetite, it would be too tedious and time-consuming to go through his conquests.'

Ragna spluttered: 'My God! You're behaving like a jealous child, Hal!'

He'd begun to turn away. Now he spun back, his eyes glittering with anger. 'Jealous! You've got it wrong, Ragna. There's never been any jealousy between Rolf and me. We've shared women in the past, you see! Or at least passed them on. Doubtless we'll do it again. It hardly merits discussion.' Ragna retreated under the downpour of his words. He laughed mirthlessly. 'Besides – this doesn't qualify as sharing, does it? Since you weren't mine in the first place. No, Ragna, it really doesn't bother me! And I'm sure it doesn't bother Rolf!'

She gasped aloud and felt the heat rush into her face. She couldn't speak.

Hal was gathering himself for another broadside. She braced herself.

'If you want to make a fool of yourself, that's your business, Ragna. But I'd rather not know or hear about it.'

'How dare you! I'm not making a fool of myself.'

'With Rolf you are! He – eats women up, then spits them out when he's finished with them. Usually it happens so fast they hardly know what's going on.'

'So what?'

He stared at her, astonished.

'Who said I wanted it to last?' Ragna cried. 'In fact it's rather nice knowing it won't. Then I can enjoy it for exactly what it is. An affair. Nothing more, nothing less. I don't want commitment and marriage. I just want – fun.' She stabbed a finger at him. 'And God alone knows, I need it!'

He was very still. 'So ... fun makes it all right?'

Ragna growled: 'You men and your double standards! You think nothing of sleeping around when it suits you. I'm free and over twenty-one, and there's been nobody in my life for a long time. So what's the problem?'

'The problem?' His jaw muscles worked furiously. 'What about feelings, Ragna. What about caring and small things like that?'

'I can't handle all that.'

'You can't handle it –'

'That's right.'

'Hah! So I see!'

'But that's what *you* wanted, Hal, and I couldn't ... couldn't ...'

He closed his eyes for a moment in disbelief. 'What did I want?'

'A – deep relationship.'

'Since when?'

'Oh, always!'

Hal coloured slightly.

She almost retreated then, but her anger pulled her inexorably forward. 'You expected things of me! You wanted me to be there and bury myself at Revoy ... I wasn't ready for all that ... I'm not ready for it now!'

'No,' he said with sudden calm. 'You're absolutely right. That is not in dispute, Ragna.' Without another word he turned on his heel and went back to the window.

Ragna breathed: 'Oh shit!' and sank down on the sofa. To her disgust she felt tears well up and fall hotly down her cheeks. She lowered her head and arched her hands over her eyes, determined he shouldn't see her cry.

I don't need to feel guilty. I don't have to care about what he thinks.

But even as she thought it she knew that she did care.

From the window Hal said flatly: 'Ragna, whatever happens, Krisi's very important to me. I'd hate not to see him any more.'

She managed a gruff: 'Of course.'

There was a pause. Through the arch of her hands she saw his feet come into view. She masked her eyes still further. A handkerchief was thrust in front of her nose.

She hesitated, then took it with a firm: 'Thanks.' The feet withdrew a little. She blew her nose and said simply and quietly: 'I'm sorry, Hal. I – I'd hate to lose you as a friend.' She looked up.

He stared down at her for a long time before saying with a deep weary sigh: 'You haven't lost me, Ragna. But – you can hardly expect it to be the same.'

Ragna thought: *But I want it to be the same.* As a small conciliatory gesture, she offered: 'I'm going back to Tromso tomorrow.'

He said: 'So am I. All my damned animals are sick.'

'What? Oh no. Oh Hal, I'm so sorry.' She jumped to her feet. 'Not the musk-oxen?' She could see from his face that it was. She couldn't bear it. Her heart went out to him. 'Oh Hal ...'

He gave a dismissive shrug. 'I've decided to give the place up anyway. So it makes no difference ...'

Ragna reached for his hand and clasped it. 'You can't.'

'Oh can't I?' He gave a bitter laugh, but his expression was grave and he carefully avoided her eyes.

She squeezed his hand. 'Hal, if there's anything I can do –'

A voice said: 'Well, well!'

Ragna jumped. Hal dropped her hand.

Rolf stood in the doorway. He walked easily across to Hal, a grin on his face. 'You old devil! I didn't know you were in Oslo!'

Hal smiled back. The two men began to talk.

Ragna retreated into the kitchen and, pouring herself a generous glass of wine, began to chuck ingredients into a saucepan. After a moment she stopped abruptly and, sinking on to a stool, leant her head in her hands and closed her eyes.

Berg watched Hal's face carefully. He could see that this wasn't a social call. Pouring himself a large Scotch, he sat down and asked: 'So what brings you to Oslo, Hal?'

Hal dropped into the opposite chair. 'Oh, business. Climbing business mainly.'

'Nothing I can help with?'

'Not really. Thanks anyway.'

They talked for a while. Hal was tense. Berg had the feeling he wanted to broach some subject but hadn't yet found the right moment.

Eventually they lapsed into silence.

Hal drew a deep breath. 'An extraordinary thing happened. I thought you might be interested.'

Here it came.

'It's the most remarkable – well, coincidence.'

Berg didn't like coincidences; they smelled of trouble. Neither did he like the cold watchfulness in Hal's eyes. 'Oh yes?' he said amiably.

'A friend of mine has a pair of old binoculars. The other day he told me about them. It's quite a story. In fact, Rolf, it's extraordinary' – he shook his head at how extraordinary it was – 'but I think that at one time the binoculars might have belonged to you. To you – or to your friend Petter.'

With difficulty Berg held an expression of polite interest.

'Petter?' he asked smoothly. 'I'm sorry, I'm not quite with you.'

'The fellow with you at Lyngen all those years ago. The one you went north with.'

Berg played for time. He said: 'Ah, poor mysterious Petter. Of course ... And – er – there might be a connection?'

'Yes. This friend of mine bought these binoculars some years ago. They're German, dating from the war. They had a name and serial number on them and, being a curious sort of person, he traced the original owner. He discovered they'd belonged to a soldier who died. He died, Rolf, in January 1945, at Lyngen. We' – he indicated the two of them – 'saw him die. In that avalanche, Rolf.'

Berg's mind was racing. Binoculars? The avalanche? Petter? Christ, what was the connection? And what did Hal know about them? In a flash of vicious anger Berg realised Hal had been digging around behind his back.

Hal said: 'I thought maybe the binoculars might have been the ones you or Petter acquired that day.'

This required caution. Berg gave an indifferent shrug. 'Good God, I've no idea. What an extraordinary thing. Where did this friend of yours find the binoculars?'

'He bought them from some Lapps up on the plateau. They didn't say where they'd found them, and at the time my friend didn't think to ask. But I immediately thought of you and Petter. I mean, you were up on the plateau, weren't you? And Petter died there, didn't he?'

Berg hesitated slightly. 'Yes.'

'So maybe the Lapps found them at the place where he died. I thought you'd want to know.'

Berg blew his lips out and looked incredulous, which he was. 'Well, what an extraordinary thing.'

'Unless they were yours, of course.'

'Who can tell? Maybe they were.'

Berg could have kicked himself. That was a stupid slip and Hal was straight on to it. 'You both had a pair then?' he asked in surprise. 'I mean, you dug *two* pairs out of the snow that day?'

'No. Just the one pair. But I honestly can't remember who ended up with them.'

'So you don't know what happened to them?'

His tone was calm but persistent. Suddenly Berg knew: Hal was on to something.

Berg tried to think: where *had* those binoculars got to? He knew where his own gear had ended up, and it certainly wasn't on the plateau. But these binoculars, which were undoubtedly Petter's – perhaps something had happened to them. Perhaps Petter had dropped the damned things. He tried desperately to remember, and couldn't. He had the nasty feeling it was very important.

He stalled. 'But there were several soldiers in that avalanche. Presumably they all had binoculars.'

'Apparently not. Only two of them at most. This pair belonged to the young lieutenant in charge of the patrol we saw that day.'

You've got it all worked out, haven't you? Berg thought savagely.

The question was: Why?

Berg went into the attack. 'This friend of yours, when did he buy them?'

'Oh ... about three years ago.'

'Who is he?'

Hal frowned. 'He lives up in Alta. A fisherman.'

He was lying, Berg was certain of it. Time to nip this thing in the bud. 'Well, if he can't shed any more light on it ...' He shrugged to show that he was losing interest in the subject. 'All this was a very long time ago, wasn't it? And *I* certainly can't remember. For all I know, the Lapps who rescued me might have taken them.'

Hal searched his face then, frowning, sank back in his chair and stared moodily into the fireplace.

Berg gave it a minute before asking: 'Now, why don't you tell me what this is really about?'

Hal's eyes locked back on to his and gave him a long appraising stare. Berg prompted gently: 'Journalists can always smell a story, Hal.'

Hal looked thoughtful. He said carefully: 'Really – there's nothing more to it. I just thought you'd be interested. I thought you might like to find the spot where your friend died. To tell his family. And get him buried properly.'

Berg quickly adjusted to the new tangent and realised with a shock that this was a clumsy ineffectual attempt to trick him.

Grimly triumphant, Berg replied: 'Family? But I told you before, Hal, I never knew Petter's name. I have no idea where his family came from.'

Hal gave a slow nod. 'Ah. I'd forgotten.'

Berg thought: Like hell.

Hal stood up. 'I must be going.'

Berg got slowly to his feet and fixed Hal with one of his best smiles. 'Wish I'd been able to help, but there we are.' He added: 'But won't you stay for dinner? Ragna and I would love it if you did. I'm sure the food will stretch.'

With satisfaction Berg saw Hal stiffen at the 'Ragna and I'.

'No thanks.' Hal made for the door. 'I've an early start in the morning.'

'Oh?'

'I'm going back north.'

'Perhaps we'll see you on the plane then.'

Hal frowned with surprise. 'What?'

'Ragna and I are going to Tromso in the morning as well.'

Berg followed him into the hall and opened the front door.

After some hesitation, Hal asked: 'You're doing more on the Kaafiord Lapps then?'

Ragna came out of the kitchen, wiping her hands on a towel. Berg looped an arm round her shoulders and pulled her towards him. 'No. I'm just taking a bit of a break. I thought I'd help Ragna put the shop and the house on the market.'

Hal looked at Ragna, then back at Rolf. A small spark of mutual hostility flashed between the two men. Hal gave a perfunctory nod and left, pulling the door sharply behind him.

Berg spun on his heel and went to the drinks tray for a large refill. He had to think.

He became aware that Ragna was talking about musk-oxen and Hal having a bad time. He wished she'd shut up. He flung her a fierce glance and she got the hint, saying briskly: 'Dinner'll be in ten minutes if that's okay.'

He made an effort to be civil. 'Could you make it twenty?' Barely waiting for her nod, he headed for the shower.

He plunged under the water, running it alternately hot and cold, occasionally reaching out to the adjacent shelf for a gulp of his whisky.

What had it all meant? What did Hal know? How the hell had those binoculars turned up?

He turned the possibilities over and over in his mind. Hal might have been telling the truth, the things might have been found on the plateau, the Lapps might have sold them . . .

But that would have been *too* much of a coincidence.

No, there had to be a reason for Hal's terrier-like interest.

He swore with exasperation. It would help if he could remember whether Petter had still had those damn binoculars in Petsamo. But his memory wouldn't deliver.

He went over scenes and images from Petsamo, magnifying and distorting them, trying to see beyond the dirty clothing and wind-burnt face that was his lasting image of Petter. Trying to look to his waist, to the belted anorak, to the rifle and ammo . . .

Suddenly he went very cold. Leaving the water running, he stepped out of the shower and stood naked and dripping, staring blankly at his blurred image in the steamed-up mirror.

He remembered.

He remembered going hunting with a group of soldiers from one of the camps surrounding Petsamo – crazy hard-drinking lunatics from Kirov. He remembered Petter showing them how to stalk hare, climbing a low hill, crawling on to a ridge, sweeping the landscape for signs of game. In this vision, which grew ever more vivid, he saw, quite clearly, a picture of Petter.

He had the white-painted binoculars in his hands.

In Petsamo, behind the Russian lines.

His mind raced through the implications.

The binoculars could not possibly have been lost on the plateau. They'd never been found by any Lapps.

Hal had been lying.

The water drummed noisily on the floor of the shower, the steam billowed out.

But there was worse – much worse.

The binoculars could only have turned up in one way.

He sank down on to the edge of the bath.

Pasvik. At Pasvik. With Petter.

The full implications came winging into his mind.

They must know Petter was the third man. They must know that Berg had lied about Petter's death.

They must know that Berg had been in Russia too.

Which meant –

Standing up, Berg reached into the shower and turned off the water. Slowly, methodically, he towelled himself dry and pulled on some clothes.

They. He was thinking of a 'they'. Perhaps there was no 'they'. Perhaps it was just Hal.

Just Hal.

He nursed the idea. After a while he made a small exclamation of triumph.

Of course it was Hal alone. Hal had no ties with the military any more. If the Security Service had been on to Berg, they would never have let Hal come and warn him off.

No, somehow or other Hal had got hold of these damn binoculars and worked things out for himself. Quite on his own.

He thought of his forthcoming trip to Tromso and suddenly the problem didn't seem so insurmountable after all.

Twenty-four

The driver peered anxiously through the windscreen and slowed to a crawl. A wall of fog loomed up and enveloped the taxi in a dense grey cloud that the headlights failed to penetrate.

Hal chafed with impatience. At this rate he was going to miss his plane.

'One can always tell how cold it is by the fog in this valley,' said the driver. 'Believe me, it's cold. But we're almost out of it now.'

And then miraculously they were, and the road ahead was brilliant white in the headlights, and the car picked up speed, the wheels making a drumming sound on the hard-packed surface.

When they finally turned off to the airport it was six-twenty. Hal relaxed a little. Twenty minutes; he'd make it after all.

He sat forward in his seat and showed an envelope to the driver. 'I need this letter delivered to a house over in Kolsas as soon as possible. Can you do it?' He also flourished a hundred-kroner note. This seemed to catch the driver's eye better than the letter, and he gave a grunt of agreement.

They drew up outside Departures. Hal reminded the driver: 'Drop that letter as soon as possible, won't you?' and sprinted for the check-in desk.

Thrusting his ticket forward he said to the girl: 'I'm not too late, am I?'

The girl glanced up, a professional glazed expression on her face then, with a flash of recognition, gave a nervous smile. 'Ah. Mr Starheim. Could you wait one moment please.'

'But the flight,' Hal said impatiently. 'Am I all right or not?'

She looked mildly apologetic and gestured to one side. Following her gaze, Hal became aware of someone standing close by.

Thrane. Thrane?

'Starheim.' He gave a brief nod of greeting. 'I need to talk to you.'

Hal replied firmly: 'Look, another time, Thrane. I've got to get this flight.'

'This won't wait.'

'It's got to, I'm afraid.'

Thrane slowly shook his head. 'The next flight. Possibly.'

Hal felt his temper rising. If this was just another ticking-off ...

He was about to argue, but something about Thrane's expression made him pause. His anger gave way to curiosity. Perhaps there had been developments ...

He asked: 'It really can't wait?'

'No.'

Hal rebooked himself on the next flight, and followed Thrane across the concourse and down a long corridor. He suddenly noticed that two men had fallen in behind them. So – it was just as he'd first thought: this was to be a ticking-off! His anger rose again.

Thrane led the way into a conference room with a long table surrounded by plastic chairs.

'They belong to you?' Hal demanded, indicating the silent followers.

Thrane closed the door. 'Yes, but they stay outside.'

Hal sat at the table, tense and angry. 'So! I have the distinct impression that this isn't going to be a friendly chat.'

'Starheim, if I was following the rules I'd have you down at Mollergata with the OP making a formal statement. As it is I'm giving you the chance to co-operate like this – informally.'

'It sounds pretty formal to me.'

Thrane narrowed his lips and sat opposite. 'Very well. I won't beat about the bush. You have quoted certain information in a recent letter to the defence ministry, information concerning the site at Kaafiord. You said the installation was to be a navigation system called Delta. Now I must know where you got that information from.'

Hal thought quickly. It was Ragna. Ragna had put it in that

scrawled note ... *from my contact in Oslo ...*

Then last night she had said that the information was no good after all. She'd seemed rather upset that he'd used it. She'd asked him to write to the ministry to correct it. What else had she said? He hadn't really been listening.

He said: 'Look, Thrane, I have only ever used the information in that letter. And I have no intention of using it further. And I certainly wouldn't give it to the press or anything like that. So you really don't have to worry about the security risk.'

'But where did you get it from?'

Hal had rather suspected Thrane was going to stay on that tack. 'Ah. That I really don't know.'

'Don't know?'

'Really. I have no idea.'

'Or you won't say!' retorted Thrane in a burst of anger. He got to his feet and strode to the window. Returning, he leant forwards with both hands on the table. 'Let me get this right,' he said. 'Am I to understand that you intend to protect your source?'

Hoping he could live with a slight distortion of the facts, Hal said unhappily: 'The truth is that I honestly do not know the source.'

'This information came out of thin air then, did it!' Thrane exclaimed with heavy sarcasm. He sat down again and gave Hal a long appraising stare. 'How long have we known each other?'

'Three years.'

He said with quiet bemusement: 'In all that time I've always felt sure that you and I – shared a common purpose, that we – stuck out for what was right, cut through the nonsense – cared about the truth, damn it. But now – now you're forcing me to think I must have been wrong all this time.' He gave a small gesture of amazement. 'Have I been wrong?'

Hal shook his head and said with a heavy sigh: 'No, Thrane. You're not wrong.'

Thrane cheered up a little. 'So?'

Hal made a face. 'It's difficult ... A matter of trust.'

'Ah.' That was something Thrane could understand. 'Well, I think you'll find your loyalties are misguided. Listen – I'm going to stick my neck out a million miles and tell you that the

318

information you were given, this Delta thing, leads straight back to an enemy of Norway. A traitor, Hal. Someone who's caused the most appalling damage. Do you understand what I'm saying? D'you see – there's a direct connection between this information and the traitor.'

Hal looked into his face and saw that it was true.

'Now ...' Thrane said with heavy emphasis. 'I've trusted you. Trust *me* now. Tell me – where did this Delta information come from?'

Hal tried to absorb the full implications of what Thrane had said. His instinct was to help Thrane all he could, yet he couldn't bring himself to drop Ragna in the dirt without talking to her first. He heard himself being sucked into a lie. 'All I can tell you is that the information came from Oslo. It was phoned through ...'

There was a heavy silence. Thrane's face was a mask of cold fury. 'I don't believe you,' he said eventually. 'What's more I think you're deliberately hiding the truth. You don't seem to realise what's involved here!' He hunched forward over the table and pointed a finger. 'Or perhaps you do. In which case I can only draw one conclusion. That you're deliberately being obstructive.'

The conclusion was right, of course. Hal saw now that this was one fence that could never be sat on. He said: 'Okay. The truth is that I personally don't know, and you'll have to take my word on that. But what I will do is to try and find out.'

Thrane searched his face and seemed to make up his mind that he was telling the truth. He relaxed a little. 'Ragna Johansen wouldn't by any chance be the one who can tell you?'

Ragna might well have been a fool, but Hal didn't want Thrane judging her in advance. Hating the lie, he said: 'No.'

Thrane looked doubtful but let it pass. 'This'll mean letting you go.'

Hal realised with a slight shock that Thrane had seriously been thinking of locking him up.

'No one knows about this security leak yet, Hal. If it got out I'd be crucified.'

Hal began to appreciate just how far Thrane had stuck his neck out. 'It won't go any further. I promise.'

Thrane stood up. 'Look, this thing's very urgent. How soon

can you find out?'

Hal pushed back his chair and joined Thrane by the door. 'I'm not sure. A day – maybe two. I'll do my best.' A disquieting image of Ragna arguing fiercely for the right to protect her source popped into his mind. Ragna was a girl for sticking to her guns; he had the unpleasant feeling that nothing was going to shift her.

As if sensing his doubts, Thrane gripped his arm. 'Hal, this leak's been going a long time. Over three years.' There was a message in Thrane's eyes: Hal was intended to read something significant into what he had just said.

Three years. There was only one thing he could possibly mean. Hal's stomach gave an ugly lurch, and he stared at Thrane, his heart racing with savage excitement.

Thrane gave a quick nod. 'There's a direct connection, Hal. Whoever your informant is, there's a *direct* connection. *Now* d'you see why it's so important?'

It was the longest weekend of Sonja's life. They spirited her away for six hours' interrogation each day, then returned her home in the evenings in a state of exhaustion and despair.

Yet she'd stuck to her story; she'd never altered a word.

But now was the hardest part; going through the pretence of going to work again. And she was going to be late. She was never late. Yet she saw that her lateness was just another symptom of the terrifying disintegration of her life. Like the sleepless nights, the growing despair, the chilling loneliness.

It was a quarter to eight when she hurried out of the flat and along the road. The lighting was poor and she peered intently at the slippery pavement ahead. Suddenly she was on top of some ice and her boot was skidding out from under her. With a loud gasp she tottered backwards, wheeling her arms, and just managed to regain her balance.

Flushing hot and cold, she paused for a moment to regain her breath.

She wondered what the watcher was making of it. He was there somewhere, she knew he was. Someone from FO/S. Or would he come from the security section of FO/E itself? She didn't look back.

Now she could see that the pavement was gleaming with ice. She went slowly. After all, she thought wearily, what did it matter if she was late? There would be nothing for her to do. She wouldn't be allowed near her office, she wouldn't be allowed to talk to anyone. She would be put in an empty room again, in disgrace. The disgrace depressed her more than anything, more, even, than the growing realisation that she would be punished.

She'd been thinking about the punishment. What would they do to her? When they discovered that no real harm had been done they wouldn't try to send her to prison. Surely not. They couldn't. She hadn't done anything really terrible. No, she'd surely get away with summary dismissal, which wasn't so bad. Not *so* bad. Yet she was haunted by the fear of losing her pension; it was all she had. Could they really be so cruel? But she knew they could and, if Thrane had any say in it, they would.

No job, no security. No Erik.

Unbearable.

She almost lost her footing again, gasped, and found herself on the brink of tears. Sometimes she just couldn't take it all in. She felt as if she was being sucked down and down into a quagmire.

Only one thing could save her. Finding Erik. He would tell them, he would explain.

Finding Erik ...

They'd let her keep a telephone at the office, of course, in case he called. But he wouldn't. She knew that now. She would have to contact him.

As she neared the end of the road a train drew out of the station nearby. It would be ten minutes until the next.

That made up her mind for her.

There was a phone box on the far side of the station, on a filling-station forecourt. She crossed over the bridge, went up to the main road and, reaching for the change she had ready in her coat pocket, stepped into the box.

There: she was committed now.

She could imagine Thrane's questions. Who were you calling?

321

Why didn't you make the call from home? It was him, wasn't it?

She hadn't worked out what she would say to that yet. She didn't call from home, of course, because the line was tapped. Closing her mind to the consequences, she began to dial. Clamping the receiver to her ear, she made a silent prayer: Please let it answer. Please.

It began to ring. It rang on and on, drilling rhythmically into her head, until there was no possibility of a reply.

He was away. On an assignment. Or staying overnight with a woman. Or ...

She hung up. She'd slip out and try his office later. The other journalists would know where he was. In Paris or Berlin or ... She'd find him, somehow.

Even as she thought it she couldn't shake off a small but persistent suspicion that she would never see him again.

She made her way back across the bridge to join the group of heavily muffled foot-stamping passengers gathering on the platform. When the train finally arrived it was very crowded and Sonja found herself crushed between two tall men in the centre of a compartment.

The train gathered speed, rocking and grinding over the rails. Someone was saying: 'It's the coldest winter since '46, so they say.' A voice replied: 'No, '42. It was '42, the really bad one.'

Holding tight to a post, Sonja let herself be rocked by the press of swaying bodies and, momentarily lulled, closed her eyes. Immediately the worries that had obsessed her during the long night returned: how to lure Erik-Rolf to a meeting, what to say when she finally confronted him ... the need to see the expression of horror and – yes – respect on his face as he realised that she'd outsmarted him. She thought: Is that all I want – revenge?

No – yes – she wasn't sure. She wasn't even sure she wanted him to be caught. She could warn him, prevent him from incriminating himself, give him time to wriggle his way out of it. Was she capable of doing that? What a sacrifice! Was she that brave and unselfish? She couldn't believe she was. But the knowledge that she had it in her power was extraordinarily precious, and she savoured it.

At the same time she relived other nightmares: the chilling

accusations Thrane had made in that icy voice of his. At first she'd drawn comfort from the certainty that he was wrong. He was mad, mad to try to blame her for Pasvik – how dare he? But as the time had passed tiny doubts and uncertainties had burrowed into her mind, and eaten away at her confidence, until the idea had acquired shape and substance ...

Please. Let Rolf Berg be in his office today.

The train grated to a stop, restarted and stopped again, winding its way through the western suburbs towards central Oslo. Gathering speed downhill, it dived into an underground section. The sudden inrush of air buffeted Sonja's ears, the crush seemed worse. A man's shoulder pressed hard against her face. Pushing against him, she stepped back and tilted her face upwards to get some air. Suddenly she realised she was standing on what could only be someone's foot. Hastily shifting her weight, she said 'Sorry', and glanced round.

A face turned away with a jerk. She looked down. The foot could only have belonged to the owner of the averted face, a man wearing a black coat and black astrakhan hat with ear-flaps.

She murmured another 'Sorry' in his direction, but he turned his back and the apology was lost against the broad bulk of his coat.

Finally the train clattered to the end of the line at the National Theatre and disgorged its passengers. Letting the crowd go ahead, Sonja plodded wearily up the stairs to street level. She thought of walking all the way to Platous Gate, but the freezing air was knife-sharp against her cheeks and she couldn't face it. Changing direction, she went and joined the long queue at the tram-stop on Stortings Gata.

As she waited she looked across to the National Theatre, and back to the dark façade of the Theatre Café, and felt a sudden piercing longing. It took a moment for her to understand: it was a longing for all the good times she'd never had – would never have – for close friendships and easy comradeship, for the gaiety and passion that seemed an integral part of bright-lit places; for all the things which seemed to belong, quite naturally, to more beautiful people; for everything that she had touched in Erik ...

A tram ground to a clanking halt. Sonja let herself be carried

323

forward by the jostling crowd. She was about to step on board when, full to capacity, the tram closed its doors. The unlucky passengers fell back stoically, saving their energies for the next attempt.

She turned her eyes back to the façade of the Theatre Café and to the bright neon lights of Stortings Gata beyond.

She thought suddenly: They'll lock me away and I'll never see any of it again. And with that thought she realised that she had made room for the possibility of going to prison. Even for the idea that she might have done something very terrible after all.

A tram appeared at the top of the street. People began to manœuvre gently for position, shouldering forward surreptitiously.

A vision of Erik walking gaily towards Blom's restaurant flashed into Sonja's mind: Erik with that woman on his arm, admired, indulged, getting what he wanted, and she suddenly thought: Why should he have it all?

Leksand had been with FO/S for two years and had his sights on early promotion. Surveillance was important, he realised, and he appreciated that it had to be carried out punctiliously, but it could be incredibly dull. Standing around in hedges and sitting in cars didn't make full use of a bright mind like his.

Of course it wasn't so bad when one was on the move, tailing a subject. But in this case the tail wasn't much of a challenge – the whole team knew exactly where the subject was going. To FO/E headquarters on Platous Gate.

Nevertheless the team consisted of three men on foot and two in a mobile. Heavy numbers by any standards. But then if the subject worked at FO/E she was bound to be important.

Leksand stood in the tram queue and, as the line shortened, manœuvred gently round the outside so that he was behind her and slightly to one side, with two people in between. At the briefing they'd said she knew of the surveillance, but that she must be watched for attempted contacts.

That meant getting reasonably close. She might pass a note or a package. She might whisper. And if she was going to do any of those things she would do it in a crowd.

He moved himself further forward until he was to one side of her, with one man in between. He glanced sideways at her. Her gloved hands were in front of her, her eyes staring intently across the street.

He followed her gaze. Nothing to see.

He looked back.

A tram came into sight at the top of the street, jangling loudly round a corner.

The subject continued to stare into the distance.

What a noise these trams make, Leksand thought: why don't they oil them or something?

The tram was coming fast. People craned forward to see how full it was. Its tall narrow carriages vibrated heavily over some unevenness in the track; the headlights quivered angrily, holding their fierce gaze like an animal with prey in its sights.

Sonja was still thinking about Erik-Rolf, but now she was thinking that she'd probably get all the blame and he'd escape, because he was clever and she was not. In no time he'd be back with his women, sitting in Blom's or the Theatre Café, while she was locked away in some dreadful place. She thought with sudden resentment: Why should he get away with it?

In a surge of bitterness she decided she'd not only trap and incriminate him, but she'd give Thrane every ounce of evidence she could.

Immediately she was struck with shame and self-loathing. How vindictive she was! How low she'd sunk! She lowered her head.

God help me, I love him so. I love him so.

The tram began to brake with an ugly grating sound. People shuffled forward. Sonja felt someone come up behind her.

A sudden weariness came over her. For an instant she closed her eyes.

The tram was ten feet away, still braking hard ...

The person behind was very close. Sonja turned her head slightly and saw a pair of staring eyes topped by an astrakhan hat.

She frowned with vague recognition and instinctively made to move away.

It was then that she felt hands grip her waist.

What was he doing? Her instincts screamed violently, she sucked in her breath to cry out, she flung back a hand to grab at him.

Then it came. A powerful punishing jab in the back, a solid push. She felt an incredible surprise, a vast disbelief, a great leap of panic.

She felt her body arch, her stomach jerk forward –

Then her whole *body* was falling.

Dreadful heart-stopping fear surged into her brain. Images of childhood flashed before her ... falling from the apple tree, falling fast, the ground rushing up, her mother's scream ...

The ground was rushing up now, ground cleaved by a shiny metal rail.

She thrust her hands forward, landed heavily, bumped her head with a sickening crack, felt the breath hiss out of her, fought for air.

A deafening grinding and screeching enveloped her.

Sick fear tore at her stomach.

Move. She had to move. It wasn't too late.

She pushed up with her hands, turned her head a fraction, and in one appalling moment of realisation knew –

It was too late for everything.

She opened her mouth to scream, but no sound came.

A bundle shot forward. It looked like someone's coat. It took an instant for Leksand to realise.

Her.

Everything happened slowly at breath-taking speed. The woman fell spread-eagled across the track. The tram wheels screamed. The driver's face contorted with horror. Leksand stared aghast, wondering if the tram could ever be stopped in time, willing it to brake harder. But despite the screeching of locked wheels, the heavy beast had a sickening momentum and Leksand knew that nothing could stop it.

The woman's head came up and turned slightly just as the

deflector-bar hit her. Leksand felt a moment of hope – the bar must push her aside – but the hope died instantly as he realised the deflector-bar was riding over her, and over and over. It happened with such slowness that Leksand had a last un-reasoned urge to shout: Move!

He saw an arm come up, her head fall back, and then she was right under the tram and the nearside wheel was rolling on to her.

The tram finally halted, its front wheels astride the body.

Leksand closed his eyes. Women screamed. Men gasped. Leksand reopened his eyes to see the driver shouting soundlessly.

The crowd shrank back. Women were still screaming. Men's voices were loud and ugly. The driver was spewing. Someone moved away, bumping Leksand's shoulder, his face blank as he elbowed past.

Leksand suddenly came to his senses and looked quickly about him. What should he be doing? Where should he be looking? God – could he have prevented this?

He ran forward to look at the woman. Her head was sticking out, a wheel over her neck, blood pouring from her mouth, a garish look of pop-eyed surprise on her purple face. Completely dead.

He spun back to look at the crowd. Horrified faces, staring, covering their eyes. Towards the back, one of his colleagues, his eyes round with disbelief.

Quieter now. People moving further back. The hushed murmur of stunned voices, the occasional sounds of weeping.

Leksand felt the urge to talk to someone, to say how dreadful it was, to share the horror, but he forced himself to think. Everything he'd learnt in his training seemed to have vanished from his mind.

Be observant. Look around you. Don't miss the obvious. Photograph the scene in your mind. Remember everything, everybody. What was out of place? What was so normal that it was abnormal?

He went back over it – the tram, the bundle shooting forward.

Shooting forward.

It came to him in a flash.

She'd been pushed.

He felt a moment's elation at his own cleverness. Then, in

327

the next instant, bitter self-reproach at his stupidity. He hadn't seen the one thing he should have seen – who had done it. And now he was too late – the crowd had moved back, people had shifted.

He searched the crowd, examining each face.

No one looked suspicious, everyone looked suspicious.

He turned, doing a complete circle. A larger crowd was forming on the pavement, along the street, their grey faces contorted with horror.

A small memory pulled at him.

Right at the beginning, a bumped shoulder, someone moving off, someone with a blank face.

A *blank* face?

Who the hell would be unaffected after something like that?

Then he moved fast, diving out of the crowd, half running half walking, searching desperately for – what?

Hat. A dark hat with ear-flaps. Heavy face. Over six feet tall.

He skidded to a halt on a corner. To his left paths crossed the dark tree-studded square, to his right the pavements of Stortings Gata ran alongside well-lit shop fronts.

Nothing.

He forced himself to stand still and keep looking both ways. The bastard couldn't have got that far.

He began to lose hope.

Then – there! Across the square, walking briskly towards a corner. Was it him?

Leksand started off at a cautious walk then, realising that he had committed himself, ran gently across the square. The hat disappeared round the corner. Leksand accelerated, bolting across the street, dipping out of the way of an approaching car, slipping once on ice and then, reaching the corner, grinding to a halt.

There. Not far away, going strong, black astrakhan-type hat on bull-neck head.

Leksand fell in behind.

Black Hat looked round, eyes missing nothing. Leksand quickly looked down at the pavement. Leksand thought: He's a pro. He felt a small leap of triumph – he *must* have got the right man.

Black Hat crossed the street. Leksand did not. Coming to a

junction Black Hat turned a corner, looking over his shoulder as he did so.

Leksand carried on, head down, eyeballs swivelled so far to the side that it hurt. Beyond the junction, Leksand crossed the road and doubled back, trying to ignore the possibility that he might come face to face with his man.

He peered round the corner.

Black Hat was still walking.

Oh no he wasn't.

He was getting into a car.

Automatically, Leksand looked for the licence number.

Too far away to see.

There was a risk of being spotted but, ignoring it, Leksand dived out from behind the corner and ran towards the car, weaving his way through pedestrians, fighting to keep his footing on the treacherous surface, keeping an eye on that licence plate.

The car pulled out.

Leksand stared hard at the number.

The car roared off and disappeared. Leksand pulled out his notepad and wrote the number down.

Then he hurried to a telephone. The longed-for promotion might come sooner than he'd hoped.

He'd been briefed on that number some time ago.

Unless he was very much mistaken, the car belonged to a Bulgarian import-export company.

Twenty-five

It was official: it was the coldest winter for twenty years.

The high-pressure system over the Arctic Sea had deepened. The nights were long and cloudless and the frosts exceptionally hard. At high altitudes the air was incredibly clear while in the valleys the air was so still that thick mists formed, plunging everything into a white gloom. At night the mists froze, covering everything with hoarfrost and decorating branches and twigs with fine webs of white lace.

Trains no longer ran on time; some trains no longer ran at all where lines, brittle with cold, had fragmented under load. In the inner reaches of the fiords fishing boats were frozen in. Wildlife perished, domestic animals sheltered, and in Oslo twenty people a day were admitted to hospital with bones broken on icy pavements. No one stayed out longer than they had to. People compared it to 1942 when, so it was said, the cold was so intense that your nose was at risk of dropping off – but this was recognised as a bit of an exaggeration.

In the north no one bothered to exaggerate; they were too busy trying to get on with their lives. On the coast, where the temperature was minus twenty, the men sailed for the Lofoten Banks to go cod fishing because they always did in February, while the women stayed home and ran the snow-locked farms, because that was what they always did at this time of year.

Up on the plateau, where it was minus forty, life for the Lapps was a little harder than usual – water stored inside their tents froze overnight and had to be remelted every morning, food had to be thawed, and extra peat and wood found for the fires. But with two thousand years' accumulated knowledge, the fierce weather meant no more than a bit of extra work, and, in conditions that would defeat most other people, babies continued to be born, meals cooked and the herd watched.

And it was getting colder . . .

Each night the frost bit more deeply into the earth, each day the ice in the fiords crept further out from the shore.

The country gritted its teeth and waited for a respite.

But it isn't the cold that's the real enemy – it's the wind. At present the wind was faint, no more than a frozen whisper, but its touch was like a whiplash.

Hal climbed steadily up the side of the valley, the dry snow squeaking gently under his skis. When he'd gained sufficient height he continued along the side of the slope, skirting the herd, until he was to the west and downwind of them. Then he closed in.

A coward's approach.

The herd stood in the blue light, watching him curiously. Only six remained out of the original ten. They stood pressed close together, shoulder to shoulder, heads low, in a solid black mass of shaggy hair and thin legs.

When he was five yards away he stopped. Checking that Arne was in position to the right and Bamse well away in the rear, he swung the .22 up to his shoulder.

Scenting danger the musk-oxen stamped around, snorting anxiously, their black eyes glaring and fearful. Yet they didn't run. They had become too trusting for that.

Hal thought bitterly: Trust misplaced.

He looked for the mother and calf, but the other musk-oxen, in the age-old instinct of the herd, had surrounded them.

Nothing for it then.

Slipping off the safety catch he sighted carefully on the wide shoulder of the large bull. Yet he was forced to pause – there was a lump in his throat, he could hardly see – and he had to close his eyes for a moment.

Opening them again, he sighted and, before there was time to hesitate, squeezed hard.

A faint thud as the silenced shot found its target, and the beast crumpled soundlessly into the snow, its great head lolling to one side. The other musk-oxen skittered sideways in alarm, then paused to eye their fallen leader.

The mother was clear of the others now, the calf at her side. Hal sighted quickly and felled the mother. The calf screamed and brayed. Clamping his teeth, Hal took the calf hurriedly, but knew even before he saw the fallen creature kicking and jerking that he'd made a mess of it. Cursing himself, he poled quickly over and, trying to ignore the eye-rolling terror of the young animal, finished the job.

The remaining three musk-oxen were bolting. Arne took one, the unsilenced shot cracking loudly across the valley. Bamse blocked the other two and wheeled them back. Hal dropped the first as it cantered towards him. The last, a barren cow, paused, breath steaming from her nostrils, eyes wild with fear. Raising his rifle for the last time, Hal took it through the chest. The beast crumpled, knees first, into the snow.

The valley was silent, the snow stained butcher-red.

Hal dropped his rifle and stood, staring at the slaughterhouse. A deep ache constricting his chest, his throat was dry. After a time Bamse crept up and sat beside him.

The roar of the tractor split the silence. Arne drove up and, turning, reversed the trailer up to the bull.

Shivering himself to life, Hal wiped some iciness from his cheeks and, hoisting the rifle over his shoulder, skied down to the tractor. Wordlessly, the two men tied ropes to the creature's hind legs, hooked up to the winch and hauled the dead bulk up the ramp on to the trailor, ready for its short journey to the makeshift dump where the frozen carcasses of the other four animals lay covered in snow.

As Hal took the second load he noticed the supply boat running close along the shore below. Normally it dropped the post and supplies at the other end of the island then passed much further offshore. Today he guessed there must have been a special delivery for himself or Arne which the boat would have dropped at the cove just beyond Arne's place. Hal waved to Arne riding on the footplate and, catching his eye, pointed towards the boat. The old man nodded.

On the third trip they loaded the carcasses of the mother and her calf. The calf's forehead, nostrils, eyelids and mouth were covered in puffy yellow-red swellings. The animal could only have had a short time to live. The mother, on the other hand, seemed unaffected. Then Arne pulled back the animal's lip and Hal saw the burgeoning nodules inside the mouth.

Hal drove down to the dump in a mood of black despair and it wasn't until Arne leaned in from the footplate and touched him on the arm that he realised the old man was trying to attract his attention. Arne pointed down the hill.

Then Hal saw. Three figures. At the side of the house, making their way up the hill towards them. The light was dim and the figures heavily muffled, but Kris's small figure was unmistakable. Suppressing a rage, Hal slammed the tractor to a halt, killed the engine and jumped out.

Aware of the carcasses in the trailor and his own blood-smeared overalls, he shouted down to them: 'Stay there! Don't move!' Tearing off his gloves, he climbed out of the loose white army overalls which covered his anorak.

Rolf and Ragna stopped obediently, but little Kris ran forward, puffing and panting up the hill. Ragna shouted after him, but the boy kept coming.

Kicking the blood-stained overalls away, Hal hurried down to meet him and, sweeping him up in his arms, planted a rough kiss on the boy's nose.

Kris recoiled. 'Ouch! Your face is all prickly.'

'Haven't shaved.'

'Ughh! You're no good for kissing!' And wrinkling up his nose, the boy giggled, his little face breaking into an impish grin. Hal's heart twisted with love and he hugged the boy hard against him.

Then, with Kris in his arms, he strode down to the others, his mood darkening.

'What are you doing here?' he demanded fiercely.

Rolf said firmly: 'I thought you might need an extra pair of hands.'

Ragna pulled the tightly-wound scarf down from her mouth. 'We came to see if we could help, Hal.'

Hal didn't know what to make of this kindness – if kindness it was. 'Why didn't you call, for God's sake! I could have told you not to waste your time!' Then to Ragna: 'And Kris – why bring him?'

Kris wriggled in Hal's arms, and Hal could feel the boy's

hurt and bewilderment.

'We did phone,' Rolf cut in smoothly, 'but there was never any answer. So we thought we'd better come over, just in case. The skipper of the supply boat seemed to think you had an epidemic on your hands.'

'All the more reason not to come.'

Ragna asked fearfully: 'The musk-oxen – is there any hope ...?'

Aware that Kris was soaking up every word, Hal shot her a warning look. But it was too late. In the way of all children Kris understood immediately that the news was bad, and buried his head against Hal's shoulder.

Hal shot Ragna an accusing look.

Ragna whispered: 'I just couldn't leave him behind – really.'

'Well, you should have! This is no place for a child!'

Kris began to cry. Hal groaned. Putting a hand on the boy's cheek, he said softly: 'It's nothing to do with you, Kris. You know I love having you here. But it's the animals. They're sick, you see.'

There was a short silence. Then a snuffly: 'Will they get better?'

He couldn't bring himself to tell the whole truth. 'Some of them will. But some of them won't, Krisi.'

Rolf said briskly: 'Why don't you tell me what I can do? Shall I go and help up there?' He indicated the tractor with Arne waiting beside it.

Without answering Hal dropped Kris on to his feet and said to Ragna: 'Take him down to the house and be sure to keep him inside.' He leaned down and whispered to the child: 'Will you and Mummy warm up the house and make some food for us?'

A small nod and, looking a little happier, Kris took Ragna's hand to walk down to the house.

Hal called after them: 'Leave your boots outside the house – you'll see a box there – and wash your hands carefully.'

Ragna mouthed an 'Okay' over her shoulder.

'Is this thing dangerous to people then?' Rolf asked as they climbed the hill. He didn't sound quite so willing to help all of a sudden.

Hal retrieved his overalls from the snow. 'Highly unlikely.

334

But until we get the final vet's report I'm not taking any risks.'

'Tell me what I can do then.'

Hal wanted to say: Not a lot. He resented this unexpected intrusion, as if Rolf's arrival had violated Brattdal in some way. More than that, he resented Rolf himself. He suspected Rolf had not been telling him the truth. Now he felt a division between them, an unspoken chasm of distrust.

Yet why be churlish? This was a stinking job, and another hand would get the job finished all the sooner.

He said with heavy humour: 'Want some practice at shooting sitting ducks?' He gave a mirthless laugh. 'Or rather, penned sheep. Can't miss.'

Rolf shot him a sideways glance. 'Why don't you take a break? The old man and I can deal with it.'

They reached the tractor. Hal pulled on his overalls and gloves and swung himself rapidly up into the cab. Suddenly he was too tired to be angry any more. 'No. With three of us the job'll be done that much quicker.'

As Hal fired the engine he was aware of Rolf's eyes on him, hard and cold and watchful. Then he knew that for Rolf, also, their conversation in Oslo was neither finished nor forgotten.

Ragna had done her best with what she had found: dried fish, onions, carrots, potatoes, flour, milk, cheese – but no herbs. She tasted the finished pie and made a face. What she could have achieved with parsley and thyme ...

She found herself examining the kitchen critically, rearranging it in her mind, installing jars of dried herbs and spices, stocking cupboards with tins of unusual vegetables and fruits, and rice, pasta and preserves.

Then she remembered. Hal was giving the place up. Had he really meant it? Could he ever bring himself to leave? She pictured the kitchen devoid of warmth and clutter, the house silent and deserted, the cold slowly penetrating the empty rooms. She couldn't help feeling it would be a dreadful pity. All that hard work of Hal's, all that passion and determination. No one else could have done so much in such a short time.

But now he was bitter and defeated. She hated to see him like that. Hal of all people, who'd never given up on anything in his life.

Kris charged into the room and cried: 'I can't find Lilli.' Ragna gave a small sigh. Kris had been very difficult since her return from Oslo, throwing tantrums, demanding attention and generally trying to wind her up. Making an effort, she asked kindly: 'Who's Lilli?'

'*Lilli! Lilli!*' he repeated with a stamp of the foot, as if she should know.

'Really, Kris,' she retorted, chopping vegetables energetically. 'You insisted on coming, so now you have to make do. I don't have time to find this Lilli, whoever she is.'

'I want Lilli. I want Uncle Hal! I want Uncle Hal!'

'Well, you know he can't come now. He's busy.'

There was a silence. She looked round. Kris's face was contorted with misery, and he was taking a deep gulp of air, ready to bellow.

With a sigh of fond exasperation she went over and kneeled down and put her arms round him. The bellow, when it finally came, deafened her.

'Oh Kris!' she cried.

He was inconsolably unhappy, screaming and beating his fists against her chest. She tried to hold on to him, but he fought his way free and stood before her, his face red and tear-streaked, his small body shaking with fury. 'I hate you! I hate you!'

She held out her arms to him but he ran off, sobbing wildly, and stamped loudly up the stairs.

She felt bemused. What had happened to her lovely boy? Where had her easy acquiescent child gone? She thought guiltily: It's my fault, I've been neglecting him. And realised it was true. First there'd been the distractions of the shop, then the sudden trip south, then the arrival of Rolf. Worst of all, only that morning Kris had glimpsed Rolf leaving her bedroom. She felt terribly guilty about that.

And now, on top of everything, there was the loss of the beloved musk-oxen.

She stiffened: gunshots sounded from up the hill.

Abandoning the food, she ran quickly up the stairs and found Kris in the small end room, lying curled up on the bed, his body shuddering to the spasms of deep sobs. As she approached,

336

something outside the window caught her eye. In the gathering darkness, beyond the far wall of the white-clad vegetable garden, the snow had been heaped into a large circle. In the centre was an amorphous mass of black. Black animal bodies. A figure clad in overalls was adding the bodies of sheep to the sorry pile.

She realised then: Kris had looked out and seen the gruesome burial ground.

The shots continued to echo down the valley.

She whispered: 'Oh Kris,' and, lying down beside him, put her arms round him and hugged him tight. 'Oh, poor, poor darling. Poor darling.'

At last the distant shots ceased. After a time the sobs, too, subsided.

She said: 'I'll help you find Lilli if you like.'

He said nothing but, reaching for something that had been buried in his arms, he pulled it out: a battered rag-horse. Of course – why hadn't she remembered? She said: 'Hello, Lilli.'

The animal disappeared into his arms again, the warm little body snuggled closer, then a small unsteady voice asked slowly: 'Is Uncle Hal cross with me?'

Ragna squeezed him to her. 'No. He's not cross with you, darling, not in the slightest. He's just ... upset ... about other things. He still loves you just as much as ever. Honestly.'

There was a pause while this was absorbed, then: 'Why do things get ill?'

'Because – well, just now and again a nasty little bug comes along which the animals can't fight against and then ... Very occasionally they die. Like now.'

Another pause. "Is that why Daddy died?'

Ragna tried to adjust to the astonishing switch. 'What?'

'Did bugs make Daddy dead?'

'No, darling. Daddy died in an accident, like I told you.'

'What's an accident mean?'

'It's – something that happens suddenly. So suddenly you know nothing about it. It never hurts you, it's too quick. It just – happens.'

A long pause this time. 'Like falling over and bumping your head?'

'That kind of thing.'

337

'Did Daddy fall over and bump his head?'

She closed her eyes. 'Like that, but worse.'

Silence. She felt him relax against her. She savoured the peace, gently stroking his hair, enjoying the warmth of his dear body against hers, thinking: Beautiful child, I love you so.

He moved again. She prepared herself for another question.

'Uncle Hal – is he going to die too?'

She gave the ghost of a laugh. 'No, darling. Absolutely not.' Sensing he was unconvinced, she added: 'Promise.'

'I don't want Uncle Hal to die.'

'No, darling. He won't. Honestly.'

She stroked his cheek and kissed his forehead. The strength of her love for Hal had always left her with a mild feeling of exclusion and – yes, if she was honest – resentment. It had given Hal a claim on her that she didn't want him to have. But now she was glad, glad that Kris had a man like Hal to love and admire.

She kissed the small forehead over and over again, glowing in the warmth of her love for him.

A voice broke the silence. 'Oh, there you are.'

Ragna looked up with a start.

Rolf stood outside the open door. She hadn't heard him come up the stairs. He said briskly: 'I'm going down to the old man's house to find the telephone.' He shook his head with irritation. 'Why Hal doesn't have one beats me.'

'Are the others coming in?'

'In a while. But tell me, will you? Where the hell does Hal keep his drink? I can't find it anywhere.'

'In the corner cupboard. In the living room.'

'And towels – I need a good wash. It was like a slaughterhouse up there. All blood and guts ...' He gave a shudder. 'I got covered ... I've washed most of it off, but ...'

Appalled, Ragna looked down at Kris. His eyes were wide open; he had taken it all in. His face slowly crumpled, and, clutching at her, he began to cry again.

Ragna shot Rolf a horrified glance, but he was staring at Kris, a frown of annoyance on his face. 'The towels?' he prompted finally.

Controlling her anger with difficulty, Ragna managed: 'The cupboard by the bathroom.'

338

As she quieted Kris down again she heard water running in the bathroom, then footsteps as he went downstairs. Finally a door banged; he was gone.

The silence blossomed out. Ragna settled her head back on the pillow. Interesting how small things could be so revealing. He obviously didn't care for children at all. What was more, he wasn't even prepared to pretend he liked Krisi for her sake.

It didn't surprise her. It just made her wonder. Why had he come back to Tromso? An interest in her welfare? It was flattering to think so, yet a part of her couldn't quite believe it. For that matter, why had he been so insistent on coming here to Brattdal? She couldn't believe he was that concerned about Hal's welfare either. Were he and Hal still bosom friends? It didn't seem so.

No: there was something strange going on. She couldn't work it out at all.

Krisi sniffed. She dried his eyes and blew his nose and read him a story.

Sounds rose from the kitchen.

Were the others back? She remembered the pie and groaned; she hadn't even put it in the oven. 'Come on, darling,' she murmured to Kris and, picking him up, carried him down to the kitchen.

Hal was there, stripped to the waist, bending over the sink up to his elbows in soap and water. The muscles of his back were strong and firm. A vivid memory of embracing that back, that body, leapt into Ragna's mind; she remembered the smoothness of his skin and the hardness of his body and the gentleness of his touch. The memories affected her oddly, almost as if . . .

Half turning, Hal said: 'You wouldn't pass me the towel, would you? Has Rolf gone down to the phone?'

'About half an hour ago.' Sitting Kris on the table, she found a towel hanging beside the stove and passed it to Hal. He started to dry himself vigorously, then, spotting Kris's downcast face, went and sat down in front of him.

'Hello, old chap. . . .'

Leaving the two of them talking in low voices, Ragna went to the stove and, sprinkling some grated cheese across the top of the pie, slid it into the oven, and chopped more vegetables.

Behind her the murmur of voices ceased. She turned to see Kris scampering happily out of the room. Hal came and stood before her. 'I need to talk to you, Ragna.'

He had missed a smear of soap above one eyebrow. Taking a corner of the towel he still held in his hand she dabbed at it, suppressing the urge to smooth away the deep frown from between his eyebrows.

His mouth twitched slightly. Firmly, he pulled her hand away. 'Listen, this is important. I have to ask you something – something which is absolutely vital. I can't explain why – and it may not be easy for you to believe how important it really is, but ...' He chewed at his lip, searching for the words. 'Sometimes things have to be taken on trust, don't they? And I'm asking you to believe that this is vital ...'

Ragna couldn't think what he was working round to, but she had a nasty feeling it would be something awkward. 'Go on.'

'That information about the installation – being a navigation system called Delta and being used for Polaris submarines – Ragna, please tell me where it came from.'

Ragna's heart sank. She had so wanted to avoid more difficulties between them. But this was the one thing she could never tell him. She'd promised. She'd sworn faithfully. With a soft groan she said: 'I can't tell you that.'

'Ragna – I wouldn't ask if it wasn't important.'

She gripped his arm lightly, wanting him to understand – what? – that she would have helped if she could.

Reaching for her hand he grasped it and squeezed it hard against his chest. 'I'm asking you this one thing, Ragna, as I've never asked you for anything before. Trust me, please.'

'Hal – I promised. And *that* was a matter of trust. I wish could, but ...' She shook her head.

'One day I'll explain why –'

She unfastened her eyes from his and extricated her hand and leaned back against the counter, her silence giving him hi answer.

'Ragna!' He rubbed a hand savagely across his eyes. Finall he gave a deep sigh and said gently: 'It's not for my sake that ask. It's for Jan's, Ragna. For his sake.'

She looked up, startled. 'I don't understand.'

'I can't say any more. But, believe me, it's true.'

What was he trying to say? That this concerned Jan in some way? How could it? She bristled with indignation. How dare he use Jan's name like this? What a cheap tactic!

She said coldly: 'Please don't bring his name into this.'

'But it directly concerns him, Ragna!'

She thought angrily: Ah! Got it now! It was Hal's army contacts. They were behind this – trying to discover her source, trying to stop any more information getting out. And Hal had invented this imaginary connection with Jan in order to twist her arm. Doubtless he would tell her it was all to do with Soviet agents and national security.

She wanted to say: Well, pull the other one!

'I can't reveal my source,' she said coldly. 'So there's nothing to discuss.'

The effect of her statement was quite different from the one she'd expected. Instead of arguing, he slumped visibly, and suddenly looked very tired. He murmured almost to himself: 'If only . . .' Then, shaking his head, he sat back on the edge of the table, looking defeated.

She felt a twinge of doubt. Cheap tactics and manipulation had never been Hal's style; would he really have stooped so low? And Jan's name – Hal of all people would never use it lightly. She began to wonder if she hadn't been too hasty.

'It really concerns Jan?' she asked tentatively.

He looked up, his expression open, his gaze direct, and said simply: 'I wouldn't lie to you.'

And she realised instantly that it was true.

She gave a long sigh. She knew then that she would have to choose.

The long walk down the hill had been a complete waste of time. No Alex. No message from Alex.

The previous day Berg had called from Bodo airport on the journey up from Oslo, he'd then called twice from Ragna's, and now, a fourth time, from the old man's house, but there had been nothing.

Berg stalked angrily away from the old man's place.

Could Alex be away? No: Alex never went away. He was a

desk and drink man, far too lazy to set foot out of Oslo. Perhaps, then, something had gone wrong with the contact system.

But someone had always answered that special phone number in the past. Always.

Head down, Berg walked rapidly along the track then, still going fast, struck up the hill towards Brattdal.

He decided to give Alex's special number one more try the following day. If it still didn't answer he'd call the Novosti switchboard and leave a message for Alex from 'Harri'. It wouldn't do any harm just this once. But even as he thought it he wasn't so sure. These remote islands had primitive telephone systems. Doubtless the operator listened in to every call. Well, he'd just have to be careful, that was all.

He climbed rapidly and, nearing the brow of a hill, caught a glimpse of a light from the house. The silence was deafening, the mountains tall and sombre in the last of the twilight. It was so cold his breath was freezing round his nostrils. He thought: This was the last place God made.

Yet, he reminded himself, it had its advantages. No one knew he was here and no one would think of looking for him here - his newspaper thought he was taking a few days' holiday in Denmark. And if he wanted to get out, there was the sea plane twice a day and Bardufoss airport and the Finnish border a matter of hours away.

The house loomed large, a single light glowing in a front window. Berg considered the evening ahead. He must broach that unfinished business with Hal, find out what the hell he knew. But how to tackle it? Casually, he decided, just as if he'd been thinking about it and was curious to know more about the extraordinary appearance of the binoculars. Then, once he'd got Hal talking, he'd simply trip him up. It shouldn't be too difficult. Hal was a bad liar.

He climbed the steps to the veranda, hot under his thick clothing, impatient for a drink. He took off his boots and opening the door, paused abruptly. The murmur of voices was coming from the kitchen.

Moving with care, he closed the door silently behind him, left his jacket and boots in the lobby, and padded up the passage towards the kitchen. He stopped short of the open door and listened.

The voices ceased. The silence stretched out.

He thought: Pity.

But he remained motionless, listening hard, just in case.

Ragna agonised. Jan ... It concerned Jan. Yet she'd made a promise to Rolf – a strict promise. He'd been adamant about the importance of keeping it. If she broke the promise he'd be beside himself with anger. He would accuse her of ruining his career. She'd never see him again – though the prospect wasn't quite as upsetting as she'd imagined.

Perhaps she could hint at Rolf's involvement without actually giving him away, simply by referring Hal to Rolf. But the thought of the ensuing row made her feel quite weak.

There was an alternative, of course. To tell Hal and make him swear not to mention a word to Rolf. As long as they both kept quiet, then Rolf would never know.

It was the coward's way out. It was very attractive.

She made her decision and instinctively moving closer to Hal so they wouldn't be overheard, opened her mouth to speak.

Suddenly there was a sound, so slight it was no more than a break in the silence. She paused and looked questioningly at Hal. He gripped her arm and sent warning signals with his eyes. She closed her mouth.

They looked round. There was a pause.

Silently Rolf appeared in the doorway.

Hal and Ragna. Hal gripping Ragna's arm. Yet again. They seemed to make a habit of touching each other when he wasn't around.

They looked startled and guilty, like two children caught stealing sweets. But what really interested Berg was the look of defiance that flashed briefly across Ragna's face.

He thought savagely: Now what have *you* been up to, my love?

And he knew then: he could no longer trust her.

343

Twenty-six

Thrane sat in the hot seat and thought fleetingly: Now I know how it feels. Being on the wrong side of an interrogation was uncomfortable enough, but facing people whose minds were quite made up was distinctly unpleasant.

He had been asked to give what the Director called 'a full account'. By any other name it was a carpeting. On the opposite side of the table sat the Director flanked by the Deputy Director and Thrane's immediate boss, Ekeland, the Head of Security.

The Director gave him a look of disbelief. 'So you actually told Starheim. You told him there was a major leak?'

'Indirectly – yes.'

'Didn't it occur to you that you were breaching security?'

'Yes.'

'Good God – why did you do it then?'

'I had to find out where he'd got that Delta idea from, I had to give him a reason to tell me – or rather, to find out for me I trusted him. I still do.'

'But he hasn't come up with any information.'

'Not yet. But I'm sure he will.'

The Director dropped his eyes. 'And you still believe your trust is well placed, even after what's happened?'

Thrane said tightly: 'Yes.'

Ekeland leaned forward and tapped the table. 'It was an extremely serious and unjustified breach of security.' Thrane thought: Now that statement gives a whole new meaning to departmental loyalty. 'And,' Ekeland continued, 'we must face the possibility that this breach led directly to Sonja Bjornsen's death.'

'You can't say that!' Thrane exclaimed. 'The opposition were already on to Sonja. They were already watching her.'

'We don't know that at all, Thrane,' said the Director in the slightly exasperated tone of someone going over old ground. 'There's no hard evidence, is there?'

'There's the fact that her lover failed to show not once but twice, and the second time had all the signs of a set-up.'

No one looked convinced. The Director rubbed his forehead.

Ekeland said: 'Now I'd like to play devil's advocate for a minute and see where it gets us.' He made a show of rearranging his notes. Thrane thought: I know where it's going to get us – to you smelling of roses, and Starheim in deep trouble.

'Now, we have the following ... *Fact* –' he tapped a finger on the table – 'you, Thrane, let it be known that we are on to a major leak in high places. *Fact* – two days later, Sonja Bjornsen gets pushed under a tram –'

'But you can't connect the two things just like that!' Thrane exclaimed. 'There are absolutely no grounds –'

'Please,' Ekeland interjected in the patronising tone of a headmaster addressing a difficult pupil. 'We've taken note of what you have to say. Now, if you would let me continue? *Next* ... we have Sonja Bjornsen's assurances that she never revealed the names of those involved in the Pasvik affair. If we believe her we must ask ourselves, who did have this information? Who could have passed it on?'

'No one need have passed it on,' Thrane argued. 'It's possible that either or both of the men were interrogated before they were shot, and volunteered their names in the process.'

'Possible,' Ekeland conceded. 'But unlikely. The Russians may have overreacted at Pasvik, but I don't think anyone believes they actually interrogated the men then executed them in cold blood. Besides, the Soviet protest came only hours after the event. They could hardly have had time for interrogations. It's much more reasonable to assume that the Soviets knew the names in advance, don't you think?'

There was a silence. Thrane shook his head. Ekeland returned to his notes. 'Next ... the exact location of the Pasvik operation. That was obviously leaked –'

Thrane interrupted wearily: 'Not obviously. They might have followed the third man to the border. They might have been watching him for months beforehand. We can't possibly be sure that they knew the exact location in advance.'

Ekeland and the Director exchanged glances, one sceptical, the other troubled.

Ekeland continued with the air of someone who's been interrupted unnecessarily. '*Next* ... you tell Starheim that the third man was a Norwegian. And very shortly afterwards this gets into the press. Not of direct importance, but still interesting, you must agree.'

Thrane sank back into his chair and crossed his arms.

'*Next* ... Starheim writes all these anti-Nato letters to various government departments and politicians. He's seen up at the installation site, snooping, taking photographs. *Finally*—' he paused for effect — 'we have this Delta business. Which reveals a direct link from Sonja Bjornsen through her contact to Starheim.' He pushed away his notes in the self-satisfied way of someone who's proved his point.

Thrane gave a short incredulous laugh. What could he say? Ekeland needed a scapegoat and, now that he'd found one, he obviously wasn't going to get deflected by the facts. 'If you seriously believe that Starheim is working with the Russians, then you're' — he was going to say 'completely mad' but settled on — 'mistaken!'

Ekeland conceded: 'It's possible he doesn't have *direct* links — He may just be in contact with a front organisation — a political group, a peace group, or whatever. But then he must know what these groups are all about. He must know they have strong Soviet links. He's been trained in all that, for God's sake!'

The Director gave a loud sigh. 'The whole thing may be much more straightforward than all this. He's a man of strong principle, isn't he? Well, he may simply have decided his principles are more in accord with another country's. Who knows? Anyway the point is, all these — facts — lead back to him. We must follow the thing up.'

There was a heavy silence. Thrane decided it would be a waste of breath to start arguing again.

The Deputy Director said: 'We should mount a surveillance.'

Thrane exclaimed: 'What — on Revoy!'

'Well — intercept the mail, tap the telephone.'

'He uses a party line in a neighbour's house. Rather public

for sending messages to the Russians, don't you think?' Thrane murmured.

The Director flung him an icy look. 'We've got to cover it, Thrane. We can't afford any more blunders. We've made quite enough in this affair as it is.'

'I agree,' Thrane replied with sudden relish. 'And our greatest blunder was to let Sonja Bjornsen go. If we'd locked her up I'm certain she'd have blabbed and led us to the lover. And then we'd have been able to expel half the Soviet Embassy instead of a single Bulgarian heavy!'

The Director suddenly looked tired and worn. Thrane imagined the sort of pressure he was under, with both the Cabinet and the Americans at his throat. But that was no excuse; the man had to face facts.

Ekeland looked uncomfortable, but then he'd never liked hearing the truth. 'Certainly I think we can give up the idea of finding the contact,' he said carefully. 'Which means we should concentrate on finding the knave in our own pack. We should bring Starheim straight in for questioning. It's too late for surveillance.'

'But then you ruin our only hope,' Thrane cried.

Three pairs of eyes regarded him with guarded interest.

Thrane continued: 'Okay, I admit there's a connection between Starheim and Sonja – though I'll bet anything you like it's a very tortuous one. But let's concentrate on that connection. Let's find out what it *is* –'

'I agree,' said Ekeland.

'In which case let's leave Starheim to come back to us with that information he promised. Remember, he's the only one who *can* find the connection.'

'You're assuming he's prepared to find out. You're assuming he's not withholding the information.'

'That's right! That's exactly what I'm assuming!' Thrane said, holding his temper with difficulty. 'If we have to put the tabs on Starheim, okay – I suppose we must. But don't let's bring him in and ruin our only chance of getting the people behind all this. Who knows, we might catch the lover after all.'

'On the other hand we might just succeed in sending the whole lot to ground,' said Ekeland.

'What are you suggesting?' Thrane asked darkly. 'That

Starheim is merely going to tip them off?'

'Directly or indirectly, it must be a possibility.'

Thrane gave him a condescending look. 'Well, in that case he would have done it already, wouldn't he? And they – whoever they are – would have hopped it two days ago, so we wouldn't have a hope of finding them anyway, would we? Which just goes to prove we have nothing to lose by trusting Starheim. In fact, we have everything to gain.'

Ekeland looked as though he'd been made to appear stupid, which he had.

The Director considered. 'All right,' he said wearily. 'But I want some hard information from Starheim within two days.'

Nikolai Andreevitch Yurasov stared at the heavy polished door and knew what real fear was like. Fear was imagining life without diplomatic privileges, fear was demotion and a poky little flat in an outer suburb of Moscow.

Fear was waiting to see the Navigator.

This nightmare had haunted him all his working life; the terror that only a senior GRU officer can know when, after twenty years' service – which meant twenty years' patient and, as Yurasov used to congratulate himself, highly skilful manoeuvring through the minefield of GRU politics – he suddenly blows it.

He still couldn't believe it. Agent 173 – *his* protégé – had taken him for a ride and done it so effortlessly that even now the memory of it made Yurasov want to weep.

The question for Yurasov was: could he survive it? Did he have enough friends at the Aquarium? Enough people to put in a good word for him? Enough people to remind the First Deputy of all the wonderful stuff he'd pulled in over the years?

He stared straight at the solid bulk of the polished mahogany door and felt extremely unsure of the answers to these questions. The only certain thing was that there'd be no champagne sitting on the Navigator's desk, not like the time when 173 had started coming up with pure gold, and Yurasov had basked in the glory of having recruited him, and the Navigator had beamed with delight at having probably the most important agent in Europe under his control. Congratulations had come direct from the First Deputy.

No, there definitely wouldn't be any champagne – but would there be a syringe? They always sedated you before evacuation. He knew the procedure well enough: he'd helped evacuate plenty of his colleagues over the years.

When he thought about the nasty events of the last few days, which he did constantly, he could almost feel the needle in his arm. The news about the woman had been the worst, because then he'd known precisely what lay in store for him.

The woman Rolf had identified as a threat, the woman he had dismissed so lightly as a nobody, far from being an accounts clerk, had been – he still blanched at the thought – personal secretary to the Director of FO/E.

And he – Nikolai Andreevitch – had stuck his neck out and obtained authorisation for his Bulgarian neighbours to take care of her. Provocation was too mild a word for what he had done. Norwegian Intelligence would never forgive such a thing. You didn't suddenly go and beat your fencing opponent round the head with a blunt instrument. Because then he got angry and refused to play by the rules – rules which the GRU had learnt to use to enormous advantage.

Of course it wouldn't have been so bad if the truth had never come to light. After all, middle-aged women did occasionally fall under trams.

But had his Bulgarian friends used tact and skill and finesse? Had they used their eyes? Had they used their minute brains?

Of course not. Although the surveillance must have stood out a mile, although a blindfolded child would have spotted it, they'd managed to avoid the use of either their limited vision or their pea-sized brains.

Moreover, just to ensure complete disaster, they had been seen in the act. Seen, followed, and identified.

The disaster was total. Yurasov, even from his viewpoint, could see nothing to ameliorate it. Sweat trickled from his temples. His mouth was dry. He couldn't think. He resigned himself to the inevitable; it would be the syringe. No more foreign postings, no more well-cut clothes, no more surreptitious meetings with Valya, a colleague's wife he was rather in love with.

And all because Rolf had tricked him.

He'd kill him if he ever got hold of him. Rolf had wanted it both ways, and Yurasov had been too trusting to see. Rolf had used him, manipulated Yurasov's need for success – and he had fallen right into the trap.

The minutes ticked by. No sound permeated the two-foot thick reinforced concrete walls of the embassy basement. No voices, no sound of ringing telephones could be heard through the heavily soundproofed door of the Navigator's office. Only a faint hum filtering down from the air-conditioning vents.

Yurasov thought about Rolf and how he could cheerfully murder him.

But of course Rolf would survive. He would be allowed – no, encouraged – to remain *in situ* as a valuable agent of influence, writing his articles, travelling the world, acting the playboy-journalist. The man who had it all. The thought cut Nikolai Andreevitch to the quick. Why the hell *should* he have it all!

An idea sprang into his mind, a ridiculous idea for revenge, whereby Rolf would have to skip the country and go and live in Moscow, condemned to spent the rest of his life in a seedy flat, suffocated by ugliness and mediocrity. Yurasov savoured the idea – it would be the perfect irony – but then, with a weary sigh, he pushed the idea aside. This wasn't the time to indulge in such luxurious thoughts.

He must concentrate on more important matters – saving himself.

A shaft of light. The heavy door swung open on silent hinges. Nikolai Andreevitch's heart catapulted into his mouth and he shook as he'd never shaken in his life before.

He got to his feet and forced himself to walk smoothly across the thick carpet into the room.

The Navigator sat behind his massive desk, his hands on the polished wood, palms down, his face unreadable. To Yurasov's surprise no one else was present, nor, he quickly noticed, was there any sign of a syringe. He allowed himself a small flutter of hope.

The Navigator said: 'The Centre has ordered your recall.'

The flutter of hope died. Yurasov closed his eyes and fell

350

sick. There was no doubt then: it was evacuation.

'However, this order will not be executed immediately.' Yurasov looked up at the Navigator in surprise. 'Not until the matter of 173 is settled.'

Yurasov stuttered: 'I'm most grateful, comrade colonel.'

'Save your breath. You will be staying merely to help salvage this calamitous situation.'

'Of course, comrade colonel.'

'The Centre are talking of pulling 173 out.'

Through his misery Yurasov almost laughed.

'They are convinced he must be blown.' The Navigator leaned forward urgently. 'But is he blown, Yurasov? *Is* he?'

Yurasov pulled himself together. 'There is no evidence for it, comrade colonel. He reported no surveillance. He seemed convinced that he was clear—'

'Exactly. Now – if we can show this, if we can show he's not even burnt, then it will be clear that our action in protecting him was fully justified. And then . . .'

He didn't need to say more. Yurasov was way ahead of him. 'So, comrade colonel,' Yurasov said carefully, 'we give 173 every indication that it is safe to become operational again?'

'That is so. I appreciate that he may not be so – er – forthcoming. But as an agent of influence he would still be extremely valuable, and the situation would be immeasurably – improved.'

Improved? For Yurasov it could mean salvation. And when he looked into the Navigator's eyes he knew that he, too, was thinking of his own skin.

'We must give him every support,' the Navigator continued, 'every encouragement to return to normal as soon as possible. Reassure him, give him whatever he wants.'

'We will have to be cautious, comrade colonel,' Yurasov said unhappily. 'He does not respond well to control.'

'I wasn't suggesting pressure, merely encouragement.'

Yurasov made a show of nodding at the wiseness of the Navigator's words. Then, because it was something that really had to be discussed, he ventured: 'What if he *is* blown, comrade colonel?'

The Navigator didn't want to hear about that. He said gruffly: 'Then we pull him out. Evacuate him.'

'He wouldn't come willingly, comrade colonel. I feel he'd

rather do anything than come over to us.'

The Navigator was alarmed. 'You didn't put that in your reports!'

'No, comrade colonel, no,' Yurasov said hastily. 'It was only a suspicion, no more. I thought it wisest –'

'Yes, yes.' The Navigator relaxed a little. Such observations did not look good on a report.

'But I am sure I did not misread these suspicions of mine,' continued Yurasov. 'He regards retirement in Moscow as an unacceptable option. As I think I've indicated to you in the past, comrade general, 173 is without scruples, without true principles. I believe he would do a deal with the Norwegians rather than come over.'

'That must not happen!'

Yurasov understood the Navigator's fears only too well: the colonel was terrified of a second scandal coming quickly after the first. It would mean certain disgrace for him as well.

'Then we would evacuate by force if necessary?'

The Navigator gave him a strange look, as if suspecting the motives behind the question. 'If necessary.'

Yurasov's vision of Rolf living out his days in a dreary Moscow flat suddenly didn't seem so far-fetched after all.

'But first we must try to bring him back to life,' the Navigator said firmly.

'By all means, comrade colonel.'

'And if he should manage to produce something useful, so much the better. You understand me?'

A pipe-dream, thought Yurasov. He was convinced the woman had been 173's only source. But he certainly wasn't going to say so now. Instead he said firmly: 'Indeed, comrade colonel.'

The Navigator rubbed a hand harshly across his eyes. 'So. We must restore communication.'

Yurasov blinked. 'Er – communication? Is it in need of restoration, comrade colonel?'

'Yes. The line to Savin's people has been left unmanned. A precautionary measure.'

Yurasov couldn't believe it. How could the Navigator have been so foolish? Despite Yurasov's many and detailed reports the Navigator obviously hadn't understood Rolf's nature. Rolf would not take the lack of contact well. Yurasov could picture his frustration and anger. He might even misunderstand the silence – take it as a warning. It was too uncomfortable to contemplate.

Yurasov said unsteadily: 'Ah … I imagine that will have been very – er – unsettling for 173. How soon will the line be manned again, comrade colonel?'

'Within a day.'

'Er – not sooner, comrade colonel?'

The Navigator regarded him coolly. 'Savin has been evacuated. Another precaution. Also the safe house was vacated. Time is needed to set things up again.'

'Of course, comrade colonel.'

'I want you to compose a message for 173. So that he knows you are still around and with his best interests at heart. But you yourself will remain here in the Residency.'

Yurasov stood up to attention. 'Yes, comrade colonel.' He walked quickly out of the room before his legs gave from under him.

Outside, three of his colleagues stared at him in surprise, as if they hadn't expected to see him again.

Yurasov managed a brave self-confident smile.

But he knew perfectly well it was only a reprieve.

Lars Sorensen had spent a whole evening searching his files, and had come in this morning – Sunday – just to have another look. But it was no good. Starheim was going to be disappointed. No German had been murdered in Trondheim during the period in question. It was inconceivable that such an event could have gone unrecorded, if only because of the terrible reprisals the Germans had always exacted when one of their own men was killed.

He'd looked at the files on other towns in the region of north Trondelag, just in case, but nothing had fitted.

Starheim's note had been specific enough: the killing had taken place some time in the autumn or early winter of 1944–5 in Trondheim. Two young men had been involved and had gone on the run, one whose Christian name was (probably)

Petter. Aged about eighteen at the time. The other whose name was Rolf Berg.

Sorensen had raised his eyebrows when he'd read that second name. His first reaction was to think it couldn't possibly be the *Dagens Post* journalist, but Starheim's footnote had confirmed it, adding; 'That's why it is so very important to keep this confidential.'

Sorensen took the point. At the same time it made the whole thing rather intriguing.

Which was why Sorensen was loath to admit he was beaten. This sort of challenge was right up his street.

But now he must think about giving up for the day; his daughter and grandchildren were coming for lunch and he mustn't be late.

He paused a moment longer, leaning an elbow on the desk and chewing thoughtfully on his knuckle.

On an impulse he riffled through his address book, looking for a half-remembered name. Not finding it, he went to the back section, where all the names were cross-referenced by places, and found what he was looking for. Many useful names were recorded in the large red book, people who had been helpful in the past or might be in the future, people he had barely met as well as those he knew well.

The man he was calling had been mayor of Trondheim from 1940 to 1942. After the preliminary greetings, the former mayor sounded a little insulted at Sorensen's question. A murdered German in the winter of 1944–5? Of course not. He would have remembered, he would have known, it would have been on record.

A German who'd died for any reason at that time? Well, that was a tall order. Ordinary soldiers, troops always on the move ... He couldn't possibly know what Germans might have died. But he'd think about it and call back if he came up with anything.

Sorensen hesitated on the brink of asking him if he knew Rolf Berg, but decided that even someone as pedantic as the former mayor would put two and two together, and that wouldn't do. Sorensen thanked him and rang off.

Next Sorensen called a journalist who'd once interviewed

354

him about his work, a man who worked on a Trondheim daily newspaper. The man was out.

Giving up for the moment, Sorensen went home to lunch, ate too much of his wife's excellent fruit pie, dandled his grandchildren on his knee, had a snooze, and finally caught up with the journalist early in the evening.

It was difficult to ask for information without being able to give anything in return, especially when the request involved Rolf Berg, whose name the journalist would undoubtedly know. But he eased the way with: 'I'd tell you all about it if I could, but I can't, and that's that. But when and if I am free to do so, believe me, you will be the first to know.' The journalist gave a wry laugh, because Sorensen had spun him the same line before, but agreed instantly because once not so long ago Sorensen *had* come back to him with a good story.

It was the next morning, just after eleven o'clock, when the Trondheim journalist called back.

There was no trace of anyone called Rolf Berg in Trondheim.

Not in the school registers, not in the *Folkeregister* – the local population register.

Rolf Berg had never lived in Trondheim.

But far from being discouraged by the discovery, Sorensen's interest quickened. This warranted a completely different approach.

During his brief lunch break he went to work, starting with the Oslo telephone directory. Of course it was possible Mr Berg wouldn't be listed, but in Norway's informal open society only one or two really famous people found it necessary to be ex-directory.

Berg, Rolf. There were three entries under that name. He took a guess at the one with the most expensive address then, to check it, phoned the *Dagens Post* and, saying he was a lawyer trying to deliver Rolf Berg an important letter, asked the personnel department to confirm the address, which they did. An important letter ... it was near the truth. He always was – well – near.

Next he called a man called Willy Minge. Minge's son had vanished during the war. Sorensen had helped to establish what had happened to the boy – he'd been shot and his body dumped in a fiord. But Minge had been grateful to know.

Minge was a policeman, a sergeant of many years' seniority, in the Kripos, the criminal police, based at the central police station on Mollergata.

Minge greeted him warmly, then, when the pleasantries were over, asked helpfully: 'Now, what can I do for you?'

Sorensen told him, adding: 'I know this is a little – out of the ordinary. But it's not for any nefarious purpose, I assure you, Willy. It goes back to the war.' He purposely left it vague, hoping that Minge would put a purely humanitarian interpretation on his interest.

'There is no way it would ever ... er ...' Minge's question hung in the air.

'Be traced back? Oh no!' Sorensen declared. Minge was nearing retirement. Understandably, he didn't want to blot his copybook.

'Just checking!' he said cheerfully. 'Give me an hour.'

In fact it was twenty-five minutes.

Rolf Berg had a driving licence issued in his name at the address given in the phone book. Minge read through the details – the date and place of issue, the date of expiry. Then – and Sorensen stiffened – the date and place of birth.

Bergen. Rolf Berg had been born on the 5th April 1927 in Bergen.

Sorensen got it all down and thanked Minge profusely.

Sorensen became aware of the time. His lunch break was over; he should be studying a difficult case that was going to court next week. But because he could never bear to conceive a plan without immediately putting it into action, he picked up the telephone again.

Sigi was a rumbustious lady at the local office of the *Folkeregister*, the register where births, marriages, deaths and current and former addresses – it was compulsory to notify a move of house – were recorded. Sorensen had been carrying on a mild flirtation with Sigi for twelve years, mainly over the telephone. Now they spent a couple of minutes asking fondly after each other, exchanging news and enquiring into the health of their respective grandchildren. Then he made his request.

It would be a simple matter to find out, she assured him. After all he was only requesting what was a matter of public record.

He rang off, thinking what a nice woman she was, and got down to work. He thought she was an even nicer woman when she called back at two-thirty.

Rolf Berg had been born on 5th April 1927 in Bergen. He had gone to school in Bergen until 1937. Then his family had moved. But not to Trondheim.

Sigi's voice said clearly: 'His family emigrated to the United States.'

Sorensen was surprised. 'America? But with him? With Rolf?'

'Oh yes,' she replied.

He began to thank Sigi for her help when she lowered her voice. 'Because it's you, and I thought you might be interested, I looked back through his past addresses.'

He dropped his voice to a whisper. 'Ah.'

'His card goes back to 1947 – he's moved twice in that time, both times in the Oslo area. Before that – before 1947, that is – he was in America. He reapplied for – and got – a Norwegian passport.'

'You mean – he was in America throughout the war?'

'Looks like it.'

Sorensen thanked her and rang off, his mind racing. There was some mistake here. Starheim must have got his facts wrong – and yet ... His letter had been so definite.

If Starheim wasn't mistaken then ...

Well, it was really very simple. Then in January 1945, Rolf Berg had been in two places at once.

Sorensen tried to suppress a growing excitement. He loved a good mystery.

He thought hard, then decided that, despite Starheim's request for confidentiality, he would throw a little caution to the winds.

He made another call. A cool female voice informed him that Major Thrane was not available and was not likely to be available for some considerable time. When pressed, she admitted it could be a matter of days. Sorensen left a message because there was nothing else he could do.

Some minutes later, as he sat drumming his fingers on the desk and wondering where else he might get the information, his secretary announced that Major Thrane was on the line.

So – not so unavailable after all.

'Is it a quick one?' Thrane asked impatiently and Sorensen could hear the tension in his voice.

Sorensen made his request.

There was a hesitation on the other end of the line and Sorensen guessed Thrane was fighting his natural curiosity. Finally he said abruptly: 'I'll get someone to call you,' and rang off.

The call came shortly after. The crisp young male voice identified himself as Jensen, Thrane's assistant, and announced that he had the information he'd requested.

Sorensen knew what the young man had open in front of him. A military service file. Every male over the age of seventeen had one. 'Yes ... date and place of birth, Bergen, 5th April 1927. Height six foot one, weight 150 pounds. Hair blond, eyes blue, no distinguishing features.' A pause. 'Oh, he did no military service. Exempted because of war service.'

'War service?'

'With US Bomber Command. Posted missing October 1944.' Papers rustled as the file was searched. 'Mmm. That's all. Presumably he was shot down or something. But his parachute obviously worked okay. Is that what you wanted?'

'Yes. It doesn't say where he went missing, does it?'

'No. But a bomber ... Over Germany perhaps?'

'Yes. I would think you're probably right. Thank you so much.'

For ten minutes Sorensen sat staring into space. Then he decided.

The way did not lie forward, but back the way he had come.

Twenty-seven

A faint rushing sound; a murmuring, soft but sinister. At first
Berg couldn't work out what it was. Then he realised: the wind.
He shivered slightly. This place ...

He was sitting alone in the living room, a drink in his hand.
Hal was outside doing some final chores or whatever con-
scientious farmers did. Overhead, floorboards creaked as Ragna
moved about on her way to bed.

The three of them had eaten together. It had not been the
happiest of meals. Hal had looked as though he were about to
put a gun to his own head, Ragna had seemed guilt-ridden, as
if the animals' disease were her own fault, and Berg's attempts
at conversation had met with limited response.

The back door slammed, there was a stamping of feet and a
scuffle of paws. The scruffy mongrel came trotting into the
room. Sighting Berg it halted and growled, its hackles raised,
its head down. It looked like a wolf. Berg met its eyes and stared
it out. The dog backed away and sloped off. He and dogs
understood each other perfectly: complete and instant dislike.

Hal came in, a wild unhappy expression on his face. Doubtless
he had been tormenting himself by looking at dead animals
again. He hesitated for a moment then came and threw himself
down in the opposite chair.

'Have a proper drink,' Berg said lazily. 'You look as though
you need one.' Hal shook his head, but Berg got up and poured
him one anyway. At first Hal waved it away then, with an
abrupt change of heart, took it.

Berg sat down again. 'This is a hell of a blow for you. Will
you be able to replace the musk-oxen?'

Hal stared into the open stove. 'I won't bother.'

359

'Oh?'

'I won't keep animals at all.'

'That bad?'

'I'd already decided. Before.'

'Ah ... Why?'

Hal made a dismissive gesture. 'The place is uneconomic.'

There was a silence.

Berg murmured: 'I'm sorry.'

Hal's jaw muscles worked furiously. He looked up suddenly. 'Why did you come, Rolf?'

'Ragna was concerned –'

'I'm not talking about Ragna,' he interrupted. 'Why did *you* come, Rolf?'

Berg eyed him over the rim of his glass.

'Was there something bothering you?' Hal pressed. 'Something you wanted to discuss?'

Berg wasn't quite ready for a head-on collision. 'Discuss?' he asked innocently. 'On the Kaafiord story, you mean?'

Hal uncoiled himself from the chair like a spring and shot past Berg to the far side of the room. The sound of a drawer opening and shutting, and Hal came back and stood in front of him.

He was holding an object in his hand. A pair of field glasses, faded white, wartime German Army issue. 'You didn't by any chance want to discuss these, did you?'

Berg thought: I'm hardly likely to admit it, am I? He raised an eyebrow and, taking the binoculars, examined them casually. 'No. Why on earth should I –' He gave a short laugh. 'Hal – I can see you're obsessed with some idea about these things, something which concerns me. So why don't you tell me about it?'

'You recognise them?'

As if to humour him, Berg turned the binoculars over in his hands and looked at them more closely. 'I can't say I remember them. But if you say they're the ones ... ' He smiled ingenuously.

Hal glared at him, clearly in the throes of some inner struggle.

Berg asked reasonably: 'Look, Hal – there's obviously something on your mind. Why don't you spit it out?'

The words, when they finally came, flowed quickly and smoothly, and Berg realised Hal had rehearsed them.

'They were found with Jan at Pasvik, Rolf! These binoculars were returned with his effects! But they weren't his. They didn't belong to him. He acquired them. How do you explain that? Mmm? How do you think that happened? When Jan left for Pasvik he had one pair of binoculars with him, a pair I knew very well. When he died he had two pairs, Rolf. *Two*. He also had an extra knife. How do you think that happened? Where do you think these extra things came from?' He stood over Berg, quivering with deep controlled anger.

Berg forced his face into an expression of mild astonishment while he absorbed the information. It was bad, no doubt about that. At the same time it was a curious relief to have discovered, at long last, what Hal knew.

He was about to shrug it off when Hal cut in: 'Oh, and don't give me that rubbish about some Lapps finding them. Don't even try giving me that!'

'But that was what you told me, Hal.'

'I — didn't want to cloud the issue.'

'You mean you didn't trust me enough to tell me the truth?'

'I didn't want you to know it concerned Pasvik.'

'I see. So what's the reason for telling me now?'

'The facts don't fit. They don't fit with what you told me.'

'Ah. Is that another way of saying I lied to you?'

A pause. 'Possibly. Yes.'

Berg gave a small mirthless chuckle. 'Now why do you think I'd do that, Hal?'

A cautious expression came over Hal's face. He retreated back into his chair and eyed Berg for a long moment. 'I think that the third man was your friend Petter.'

It had to be a guess, pure and simple. He couldn't possibly know for sure. Berg said levelly: 'But Petter's dead.'

'Now. But he wasn't then.'

Berg sighed like a parent dealing with a naughty child. 'A pair of binoculars, and you jump to these incredible conclusions?'

'They can't be so incredible otherwise you wouldn't be here.'

'What do you mean?'

'I mean you didn't come here out of the kindness of your heart, Rolf.'

'I came because we're friends. I came because Ragna was worried.'

'Don't give me that either.'

'What?'

'That you came out of regard for Ragna.'

'I'm very fond of Ragna.'

'I don't think so.'

Berg opened his mouth to argue, then shrugged and let it pass. He realised that his silence was an answer in itself.

Hal persisted: 'You still haven't answered my question. How did these binoculars come to be with Jan's stuff?'

Enough was enough: it was time to get indignant. 'Okay, Hal. If you're determined to believe there's something sinister in all this, then please yourself. But I strongly object to being cast as the villain. How the hell can I explain completely inexplicable things? How the hell should I know how the damned binoculars got there?'

'Suggest something. Put my mind at rest.'

'I take exception to being called a liar.'

Hal's eyes were hard as ice. 'Try, Rolf. Try to put my mind at rest.'

Berg replied heavily: 'Petter died on the plateau, Hal.'

'Is that all you're offering me?'

'Yes. I don't see any damn reason why I should offer you more.'

'You don't? What about Jan and Mattis?' Hal stabbed a finger at him. 'I think they died because of your friend.'

He gave a sigh of disbelief. 'Christ, what next!'

'I think it was a set-up.'

'You're obsessed with Pasvik,' Berg scoffed. 'You just haven't learnt to live with your own guilt, Hal. Grow up. Two men died. You sent them. So – tough.'

Hal, instead of rising to the bait, went on remorselessly: 'I think your friend is the key to the whole thing, Rolf. I don't think he died on the plateau. I think he went to live in Russia. What's more, I think you know what his name was. I think you've always known.'

Berg got slowly to his feet. 'Hal – really. I think you're rather tired and overwrought.'

Hal stood up. He said deliberately: 'And I think you're a liar, Rolf.'

'Oh no!' Berg corrected him with sudden viciousness. 'Let's

get this right! You're not saying I'm a liar – what you're saying is much *much* worse than that, isn't it, Hal?'

Hal looked away. Berg scented the advantage. 'You've gone mad with this idea of yours, Hal. You're trying to find scapegoats, even after all this time. Well, if you want a scapegoat, then I suggest you look a little closer to home.'

There was an ugly pause. Hal said quietly: 'I'll find out the truth, Rolf. One way or the other.'

'And if you don't?'

'I'll keep trying.'

Berg felt a sudden upwelling of bitterness. What had he done to deserve this wolf at this heels? Hal wouldn't give up. He'd keep at it, darting in, snapping away at the flesh until he pulled Berg to earth.

He thought viciously: God damn you! Why the hell do you have to get in my way?

Ragna pulled back into the shadows of the staircase, her mind racing.

Rolf's voice was suddenly much closer. He was making for the door.

Hastily Ragna picked up the skirt of her nightdress and tiptoed upstairs, keeping to the edge of the treads, praying no loud creak would alert Rolf to her presence. She got back into her room and, closing the door softly, slid into bed.

She lay rigid, thinking hard, trying to make sense of what she'd heard. Pasvik. Why was everyone suddenly talking about Pasvik? First Hal with his mention of Jan, then – this.

It was like a nightmare which one pushed to the back of one's mind, almost banished, only for it to pop up again, as vivid and ugly as ever.

Accusations. Talk of scapegoats and lies. Lies?

She felt confused and angry. She also felt betrayed. Why had she been excluded from all this? What was it they knew that they couldn't or wouldn't tell her?

And Rolf – was this why he had been so keen to come to Brattdal?

She had to know what was going on. She would demand an

explanation from Rolf.

But even as she thought it she knew she wouldn't. She wouldn't dare. For one thing he probably wouldn't tell her the truth, for another – the realisation came to her suddenly – she was frightened of him.

She adjusted to the idea. Yes ... Hidden behind that easy manipulative charm was something cold and hard, something pitiless ...

A sound outside the door. She stiffened. There was a soft click as the door handle turned.

Rolf.

Her heart sank. She didn't want to share a bed with Rolf tonight. Not here at Brattdal ... Perhaps not anywhere.

He approached.

She made herself relax and breath more deeply as if she were asleep. Ridiculous to be in this state. After all it was only Rolf – Rolf, her lover.

There was the sound of undressing, of rustling clothes, then his weight sank on to the other side of the bed, the quilt moved slightly, and he got in.

He settled himself then lay still. He didn't touch her. She felt a vast relief. After a time his breathing steadied into a soft rhythm.

She lay awake for a long time, going over what she had heard, trying to make sense of it all, trying to decide what she should do.

An image of Hal sprang into her mind. *I wouldn't lie to you, Ragna.*

She felt a fluttering of relief. She knew, then, what she had to do.

She stayed absolutely still for several minutes, listening to the rhythm of Rolf's breathing and the sounds beyond. Apart from the soughing of the wind in the eaves, the house was silent. Faint starlight filtered in through the unshuttered window.

With infinite slowness she began to move, first a leg, then an arm. Eventually she had her body on the edge of the bed. She paused motionless. The breathing from the far side of the bed continued.

Gently, she pushed back the quilt and swung her legs to the floor. Bit by bit she moved her weight on to her feet, aware of the mattress lifting behind her.

She froze. Something had changed. The breathing had stopped.

She half turned.

A sudden movement. She gave a start.

His voice, shockingly loud in the silence of the night. 'Where are you going?'

She expelled her breath with a slight laugh. 'Oh, you gave me a shock!' She stood up. 'To the bathroom. I was trying not to wake you.'

His hand found her wrist and gripped it hard. 'Come straight back, won't you?'

Her heart thumping against her ribs, she crossed the room and went out, closing the door behind her. She paused, her eyes screwed up against the light burning at the far end of the passage, outside Kris's room.

Facing her was Hal's door. It was closed. She turned away and passed up the passage to Kris's room. She looked in through the open door. He was sleeping soundly. The connecting door to Hal's room was closed. She hovered uncertainly. Was there time? She imagined creeping through, waking Hal, explaining why she'd come, telling him what he wanted to know, having to repeat it, having to elaborate . . .

Losing her courage she hurried into the bathroom and splashed her face with water. She came out and hesitated again.

Was there time?

She thought of Rolf, waiting. Waiting and listening.

Reluctantly she went back down the passage and into her room.

She climbed into bed. He lay still at her side yet she sensed that he was wide awake. With a feeling of hopelessness, knowing she would never sleep, she closed her eyes.

He shifted, the bed shook slightly. His hand reached across and touched her. Her eyes flew open, she tensed. He moved closer. His lips found her mouth, his hand began to explore her body.

She said with a small laugh: 'Oh Rolf, I'm tired.'

He raised his head, searching her face in the faint light.

'Tired or – is there something the matter, Ragna?'

There was something chilling in his voice.

'The matter? No, of course not.'

'Good ...' He moved across her. 'Good ...' His mouth touched hers and then moved down on to her body, his lips beginning their soft skilful exploration ...

Her body responded – she couldn't prevent it, she wasn't entirely sure she wanted to – but her heart was lonely, lonely and cold.

It was hopeless. He was never going to sleep tonight.

Hal snapped on the bedside light and reached for a book. He read a few pages then realised he hadn't taken in a word. He put the book back on the table and looked at the time. Two.

With a sigh, he turned off the light again. The darkness slowly gave way to soft starlight, and the familiar shapes of the room formed themselves into soft shadows. Outside, the wind whispered against the front of the house, gentle but insistent, as if gathering its strength.

It was an east wind. The fishermen likened it to the Russian bear, because it snapped coldly at their heels, blowing them out to sea. For Hal it merely darkened his already cold mood.

He was certain Rolf was lying. He felt it – he knew it. Why otherwise hadn't he admitted the possibility of a connection between Pasvik and the man Petter? If Petter had really died on the plateau surely Rolf would have got Petter's full name and address from him as he lay dying, so as to inform the family? Yes ... *yes.*

It just didn't fit.

A creak. He half listened. The house always creaked after the stoves were turned down for the night or when the wind came up or when the place was full of people.

He tried to avoid thinking about the occupant of the room opposite. Or was it occupants plural?

Curiously he felt no anger at the thought of Ragna with Rolf, just a dull ache, like the familiar twinge of an old wound.

The only thing that concerned him was the questions Rolf had avoided answering. He realised with dismay that Rolf had succeeded in outmanoeuvring him yet again, slipping agilely past awkward questions then turning the tables on him.

Another creak. A distinctive one. In the passage.

He raised his head. Kris looking for Ragna? Someone going to the bathroom?

He'd heard someone moving about before, but much earlier.

Another sound – a rustling. Then a slight metallic noise. He sat bolt upright, his senses reaching out into the darkness.

A click. A door handle. *His* door handle.

He felt a leap of fear.

... Rolf?

Christ.

Hal rolled out of the bed, landed lightly on his feet and went softly into the shadows of the wardrobe.

The door was resisting, but then gave suddenly, with a slight sound.

He peered round the wardrobe.

The door was open, a figure was silhouetted against the light from the passage, then it was entering the room, closing the door behind it.

A figure in a long pale nightdress.

Hal exhaled with relief.

Ragna.

She began to creep across the room.

He stepped out from behind the wardrobe.

She gave a loud gasp and, staggering backwards, almost fell.

'It's all right,' he said hurriedly. 'It's me.'

She put a hand to her chest and, leaning back against the wall, let out a long sigh.

'All right?' he asked.

She was shivering violently. He took her by the arm and guided her across to the bed and made her sit down.

'Here.' He pulled the duvet up round her shoulders.

She seemed to come to her senses. She looked quickly at the door, then turned back to him. Her skin was translucent, almost ghostly in the pale light; her eyes glistening softly. She seemed unreal.

She whispered: 'Would you tell me, please, what's going on.' Her voice was thick and rough, and it struck him that she had been crying. She went on: 'I overheard you talking down there. About Pasvik. You were arguing. Why?'

He considered how much he could safely tell her. Choosing

367

his words carefully, he said: 'I think Rolf may – know some-thing – something that might help – explain what happened. But for some reason he won't tell me.'

'Why not?'

'I don't know.'

'You mean – he's purposely not telling you?'

Hal hesitated. 'It's possible, I don't know.'

She stared at him for a moment, searching his face; then, with a faint nod of acceptance, looked down at her hands so that her face was hidden in shadow.

'Hal ... I've been thinking about what you asked me. About the installation, and that Delta thing.' She spoke with an effort.

Hal held still. 'Yes?'

The words came slowly. 'It was Rolf.'

'What?'

'He told me the place was going to be a Delta navigation station for Polaris submarines.'

It took a moment for Hall to understand.

Rolf.

The knowledge hit him like a punch in the stomach. Yet at the same time he had the strange sensation of having known all along. A cold anger swept over him, closely followed by a feeling of bitter satisfaction.

Got you, Rolf! Got you! There was no escape now. Let him try and wriggle out of this one!

With a sudden shock he understood more. The Delta infor-mation ... Thrane had spelt it out. It was a direct link to Pasvik.

That made two links. *Two.*

Rolf was more than a liar, Rolf was ...

But he hesitated. He couldn't quite grasp the enormity of what Rolf might be.

'Now will you tell me,' Ragna was whispering. 'Tell me what it all means?'

With difficulty he focused on what she had asked. Tell her? What would he tell her? That Rolf was connected with Pasvik? That Rolf was somehow mixed up in her husband's death?

How could he tell her that? He could never tell her that.

He suddenly felt protective, tender. Putting an arm round her, he pulled her gently against him. 'I don't know. Honestly.'

'But – surely ...'

'Ragna. I don't know.'

She was silent, as if she understood that it was necessary to lie to her.

More realisations flowed into Hal's mind, took shape, hardened . . . Chilling realisations. Instinctively he squeezed Ragna's shoulder.

She stirred. 'Don't tell Rolf I told you, will you? Will you?'

'No. I promise.'

'I must get back now.'

'Don't.'

She escaped his arm and stood up. 'No, better if I do.'

Hal couldn't bear it. 'Go and sleep with Kris!'

She paused for an instant then shook her head. She took a step towards the door then on a sudden impulse turned back and embraced him quickly, pressing her cheek against his. The next moment she was gliding soundlessly across the room and opening the door. She didn't look back.

The young man raised the rifle to his shoulder. It felt very light, almost toylike, as if it were made of wood. He pressed himself against the wall and sighted on the door of the house across the road. He waited. Whatever happened he mustn't take his eyes off that door.

Then in the next flash of awareness he found himself facing the opposite way, not concentrating at all. He looked for the door he was meant to be watching but in some curious way it had become obscured by low snow-covered trees. He tried to move but found himself floundering in deep snow. In a burst of frustration he fought his way out and along the wall until the house came into view once more.

He was almost too late. The door was opening.

In a panic he fumbled for the rifle which had inexplicably fallen into the snow. It was even lighter than before and seemed to have shrunk.

The man he was going to kill was already walking down the path. He tried to sight on him but the man was walking too fast and however hard he tried the rifle barrel would not catch up with the moving figure.

A woman appeared in the doorway. Everything slowed down. The man on the path stopped and turned questioningly to the woman. The woman was saying something.

Here the picture was exceptionally vivid.

His sights settled on the centre of the man's broad round back, half-way between the shoulders and just below the bull-like head with its ridiculous hat.

Bull-like. An animal. A beast to be slaughtered.

Now. He must do it *now.*

His hand was limp and ineffective. He couldn't press the trigger, he couldn't shoot.

The woman stepped backwards into the shadow of the doorway. The man on the path turned towards him again.

Ah. Now he could do it. It had been the woman's fault, it'd been the woman who'd prevented him!

He sighted with fresh concentration.

The man was approaching the gate.

Now.

He squeezed, the trigger gave under the pressure, the gun fired – *he'd done it!*

Or had he?

No sound – just silence. He looked down at the rifle in his hand – it had turned into a wooden toy pistol. Yet the man had fallen. Yes – *definitely.* He was lying crumpled in the snow.

He'd done it! He felt a wild elation coupled with a vast relief, as if some terrible blight had been removed from his life and nothing could prevent him from being happy for ever.

Laughing, he turned his head to Petter, but Petter had disappeared.

Suddenly he was lying face-down in the snow although he'd been standing just a moment before.

Then – his throat filled with horror – he couldn't move, his limbs were like lead. A terrible weight was pressing him down into the snow. *Someone was standing on his back.*

He tried to look round. A hard object struck him a vicious blow on the head. There was no pain, just a memory of pain. But he felt the searing sickening humiliation all right, *that* was always real; the agonising shame tore at his guts. To his disgust he couldn't stop himself from crying, just like he had as a child, loudly and pathetically, whining hideously through his tears.

Finally he was able to turn his head.

His father stood over him, a long leather strap in his hand.

The young man cried: '*But I just killed you!*'

His father gave a low chuckle and, his face contorting with pleasure, raised the strap.

A vicious blinding rage swept over the boy in a red-hot sea and he knew then that he would kill him with his bare hands.

Maddeningly the vision faded. He almost choked with frustration. He wanted to finish it, finish it once and for all!

A strange sound impinged, coming from far, far away.

Somewhere in his unconsciousness he realised the sound was pulling him towards reality, that if he concentrated on it he would wake. He clutched at the possibility and, fighting his way out of the darkness, rose and rose towards the light. Finally he pulled himself into consciousness with a jerk.

He opened his eyes.

Ghastly. He hadn't had a dream like that since –

Suddenly he remembered the strange sound.

He spun his head on the pillow.

She wasn't there.

He sat up, his ears straining. He went back over the memory of the sound, trying to put it down. A creaking floorboard?

Yes! Ragna creeping off. Sneaking off. Behind his back.

To Hal? It could only be to Hal!

Well, he'd soon put a stop to that.

He was about to swing his legs to the floor when it came again – the sound. A creak. Someone moving in the passage. He paused, as tense as a spring.

The door opened. He leant back on one elbow.

She came in, a tall slim figure in a nightgown, closing the door behind her. She began to creep towards the bed then, seeing him, uttered a small exclamation.

He said nothing.

'You're awake,' she breathed nervously, getting into bed. 'I went to see Kris. He had a bad dream.'

She really expected him to believe that?

Berg said nothing. There was no point.

She was lying, he knew she was lying.

He lay back, thinking hard.

Twenty-eight

Sorensen was woken by pins and needles in his right leg. Apart from a faint slit of light under the door, it was pitch dark and he had to peer at the luminous hands of his watch to establish that it was morning.

He swung his legs stiffly to the floor and decided it was high time he got a longer couch; this wasn't the first time he'd spent an uncomfortable night in the office.

He went to the men's room for a quick wash and a scrape at the stubble on his chin. It was seven. He had an hour before the staff arrived.

Another hour to find – what?

The previous evening he'd spent five hours looking through his files, interrupted only by the brief appearance of his wife bearing sandwiches. At two he'd finally given up.

He'd established that during the winter in question there had been the odd skirmish between Germans and partisans, between mountain patrols and young men escaping labour service; but actual murder? He'd looked through every major town, including Bergen, and every smaller town as well, looking for evidence, but apart from the usual Gestapo activity – the sudden arrests, the indiscriminate cruelty – nothing had fitted.

It had got him nowhere.

And yet, and yet . . .

He couldn't let it go. He itched to speak to Starheim, to see if he could clarify the matter. He'd tried the Tromso number twice the previous evening but had got no reply. Now he tried again. There was a lot of clicking on the line and operators saying they were trying to connect him and finally a distant voice which informed him that the line was engaged and would he try again later please?

Sorensen sat back. A small but persistent thought had been ticking away in the back of his mind and now he gave it some air. It was a possibility so faint that he might normally have ignored it. But the mystery of Rolf Berg's military career was too absorbing to leave alone.

He glanced at his watch. Seven-thirty. He could spare another half hour, then he really must do some work on that new case. There was an important meeting on it later in the morning.

At the risk of irritating the former mayor of Trondheim, he called him again.

The mayor told him he hadn't been able to think of any other German deaths that winter, murder or otherwise.

Sorensen put his new question: had there been two young men in trouble around that time? In trouble for any reason at all, either with the Germans or the local police.

He almost added their first names, but decided against it.

There was a long pause on the end of the line, a grunt, then a hesitant: 'Well ... there were quite a few who went into the mountains, you know, to avoid labour service.'

'Yes, of course. But what about more specific sorts of trouble? They'd have been about eighteen.'

'What kind of trouble? You mean murdering a German?'

'No, forget that. I must have got that wrong. Forget that completely.'

'Ah.' Another pause. 'Mmm. Well, I'll have to think about it.'

Sorensen was used to being patient. 'Of course. In the meantime I might try the police. But thank you anyway. I appreciate it very much.'

'Wait –' The mayor's voice was slightly resentful. He wanted to be the one to help Sorensen, not the police. 'Let me think ...' A silence, until Sorensen began to wonder if they had been cut off. 'There *was* something,' he said finally. 'A boy. And his friend.'

'Yes?'

'They disappeared that autumn.'

'What was the story?'

'Well ... The boy's father was a collaborator. The boy had a tough time of it. This is a small town and in school – well,

I'd imagine he wasn't allowed to forget it.'

'What was his name?'

'The father – his name was Carl Blakstad.'

Sorensen wondered if he had this Blakstad on file. He prompted: 'And the boy, what was his name?'

A pause. 'Mmm ... You must give me a moment to remember. It's fifteen – sixteen – years ago now.'

'The boy – did he get into any sort of trouble?'

'There was a rumour, a whisper ... most people didn't believe it, some people did believe it but kept quiet to protect the boy.'

'Yes?'

'Well ... it was suggested that the boy had come back and killed his father.'

'Killed him?'

'Shot him. Coming out of his house one day. No one was too sorry, believe me. The man was a bully. Quite well educated – a lawyer, I think – but with a nasty streak, very nasty. Anyway, he was shot. The Germans never found out who the killer was – but then they never made much of an effort with collaborators. Besides, I can't imagine he was that much use to them. I mean everyone knew he was a collaborator so everyone kept well clear of him.'

'But it was the boy – it was the boy who came back and did it, you say?'

'Ah, now I wouldn't like to state that for a fact. If memory serves me, he disappeared some weeks before the shooting. If he did come back – well, there was never any evidence for it. Only rumour. Though you know how people are – they do have a way of getting it right ...'

'What happened to the boy?'

'Afterwards? Can't say. He disappeared.'

'He was never seen again?'

'Never. Nor was his friend.'

'Ah – what was *his* name?'

'That I remember. Axelsen. His name was Petter Axelsen.'

Petter. Sorensen felt a small *frisson* of excitement. 'And Blakstad – you still don't remember his name?'

'Hang on ... let me think ... Ah, wait ... Something – ah! Yes, I think it was Roar. But he was known as Raf, I don't know why. Yes – that's what it was – Raf Blakstad.'

The moment he'd rung off Sorensen hurried into the records room and went to one of the cross-index files. War Criminals: Dead. No Blakstad there. Not surprising. Although the index contained the names of many collaborators, they were people who had committed serious crimes of betrayal leading to arrests and deaths. Blakstad obviously hadn't qualified.

He tried the voluminous missing persons files.

Blakstad ...

His fingers hurried over the cards, impatient for the prize.

There.

Blakstad, Roar. Official list of missing persons: Trondheim *Folkeregister*. Registered missing, June 1945. Certified missing, June 1946. Last seen September 1944.

There was nothing else on the card. No sightings. No information from the Red Cross.

And no enquiries from the family.

He slammed the drawer shut and went to the drawer above, with the As.

Yes, the other one was there too.

Axelsen, Petter. But the Axelsen family *had* enquired, because there was a Red Cross reference.

Sounds came from the outer office. His secretary put her head round the door with a cheery: 'Good day!'

It was eight. He tried the Tromso number again. After several minutes a rough elderly voice answered and said abruptly that he would take a message. Sorensen remembered: Starheim had told him the phone was some way from his house.

He considered what he should say in the message. Then decided he would put as much into it as possible. Why not? He began to dictate. The line crackled and faded, a tenuous seven-hundred-mile link to the icy north. The voice of the old man repeated the message back to him, word for word, and rang off with the promise that he would pass it on within the hour.

Sorensen forced himself back to his desk, to the enormously fat file whose contents he must fully absorb before the ten-thirty meeting. But try as he might, he could not concentrate.

He kept thinking about Rolf Berg. Was he on the right track? Could Berg really be the same man as Raf Blakstad?

If so, one could understand the fellow wanting to change his name – anyone would if he'd had a collaborator for a father.

In Norway people had long memories for that sort of thing.

Yes, a change of name was understandable.

But if the two men were the same it wasn't just his name he'd changed – it was his entire identity. And he hadn't chosen a false identity either; he'd acquired a real one.

Now the question was: how on earth had he managed to do a difficult thing like that?

Berg let himself silently out of the bedroom and listened hard. An occasional sound, faint and muffled, rose from the kitchen below.

He padded softly up to the child's room and peered in. A dark head was visible on the pillow.

Downstairs a chair scraped, a voice murmured.

Hal. Talking to himself. Or the dog.

Berg forced himself to wait. His patience was quickly rewarded. Below, a door opened and closed, then there was silence.

He went to a back window and looked out into the darkness. A well-wrapped figure, dull grey against the paler luminosity of the snow, was stomping up to the barn with the dog at its heels.

No time to lose. Berg went swiftly into the child's room. As he approached the bed the child popped its head up, blinking sleepily.

'Hello, Kris,' Berg said, trying to sound friendly. 'Mummy's having a lie-in. But she asked me to take you for a walk.'

The child looked suspicious.

'We're going to see Arne,' Berg said firmly. 'Don't worry, we'll be back in time for breakfast.'

The child rubbed his eyes and sat up. Grabbing some clothes off a chair, Berg thrust them at him. The child didn't move.

'Come on now,' Berg said coaxingly. 'Mummy wants you to go straight away.'

With excruciating slowness the child began to move. Berg waited impatiently while he puffed and panted out of his pyjamas and battled with vests and sweaters and socks and quilted dungarees. It was all taking too long. With a sigh of exasperation Berg stood the child on the bed and finished the job with brutal efficiency.

As the last sweater was pulled forcibly over Kris's head his lower lip began to tremble. 'I want to stay with my Mummy.'

'I told you. She's asleep and doesn't want to be woken up.'

'Can't I go with Uncle Hal?'

'He's out with the animals. He asked especially if we'd go down to Arne's for him, to see if there were any messages. He said it was quite important.'

The child almost looked convinced. Making the most of it, Berg led him quickly downstairs. Pulling on boots, anoraks, gloves and hats took more precious minutes, but then at last the two of them were ready.

Berg hurried out of the front door, pulling the child so fast behind him that Kris's feet barely touched the snow. The wind scythed into Berg's unprotected face and he lowered his head defensively. Glancing back he saw that the light in the right-hand bedroom had come on. Ragna was awake. She would discover Kris had gone and assume he was with Hal. She wouldn't realise her mistake until Hal returned which, with a bit of luck, wouldn't be for some time. Then she'd do her mother-hen bit and run around looking for Kris.

One thing she wouldn't do was sit down and have a cosy chat with Hal about Berg.

Kris. His small but comforting insurance policy. He tightened his grip on the boy's hand.

The path became steeper and icier. Berg skidded. As he jerked his arm to regain his balance he pulled Kris off his feet. The child fell face-down into the snow. Berg picked him up, dusted the worst of the snow off his face and started down the hill again. The child whimpered and whined, tottered a few steps, then ground to a halt, crying: 'I don't want to go! I want to go back to my Mummy!'

Berg swore under his breath. He wasn't in the mood to deal with a spoilt child. But he made a supreme effort and said cheerfully: 'Come along, there's a good boy. We promised Uncle Hal, remember?'

The child moved forward again, but reluctantly, snivelling loudly. The old man's house seemed a long way off; the wind was vicious and sharp, freezing Berg's face and creeping down his neck. He might have been able to stand it if the child's thin voice hadn't risen to a high-pitched wail. A terrible fury rose in Berg's gullet. It was all he could do to stop himself from shouting at the child.

Finally, shivering with rage, he hoisted Kris roughly into the air and, gritting his teeth, sat him on his shoulders. The child quietened down.

Suddenly he was alert: something moved in the darkness ahead. A dumpy figure. Coming towards them, head down, stomping heavily through the snow.

The old man.

They drew level. 'I'm just going to use the phone,' Berg said.

Kris whined and, wriggling hard, reached his arms out to Arne.

Quickly, before the old man could say anything, Berg moved off fast, saying loudly for the old man's benefit: 'It's all right, Krisi. No need to be afraid of the dark!' The child struggled, drumming his feet against Berg's chest, and burst into violent sobs. Berg could feel the old man staring into his back.

Berg hissed 'Shut up!' through clenched teeth and pinned the child's ankles hard against his chest.

After a while Berg risked a backward glance. The old man had continued his journey.

The noise from the child subsided, and there was only the rhythmic rumble of the waves on the foreshore, and the hiss of the wind.

At last they reached the old man's small single-storey house. Berg stamped inside and let the boy down. The child pulled itself free and, running into the kitchen, slammed the door behind it. Berg made straight for the living room and the telephone.

He lifted the receiver, listened and swore under his breath. There were voices on the line, talking slowly and incomprehensibly in heavy dialect. 'What the hell –'

Christ – a party line. He hadn't realised that the previous evening.

Berg dropped the receiver in its cradle and waited, picking it up again from time to time. The conversation dragged on. Finally he let his impatience rip. 'Get off the line! There are people waiting!'

The voices paused, then to Berg's disbelief, resumed their

maddening drone as if nothing had happened. They were doing it on purpose. Berg was incredulous yet not that surprised: it was the sort of behaviour one would expect from northern peasants.

Finally the droning voices exchanged interminably slow goodbyes and ceased. Berg jiggled the telephone rest until the operator finally answered. He gave her the emergency number in Oslo, thinking: At last.

After what seemed a long time the connection was made and the number rang. Berg waited tensely.

The ringing went on and on, a long lonely sound. It wasn't going to answer.

He jabbed at the rest again while he leafed rapidly through his address book. He muttered: 'Come on! Come on!' The operator finally came back, a condescending tone in her voice, as if she were doing him a favour. Making an effort to sound polite, Berg gave her the number of the Novosti office.

Not quite eight. Was it too early for them?

It answered: a woman's voice. Berg asked for Alex.

There was a pause, then: 'He does not work here.'

Berg's stomach gave an ugly lurch. 'What do you mean?'

'He has been transferred. Is there someone else you wish to speak to?'

'*Transferred*? Where's he gone?'

'Another posting. Thank you for your enquiry.' The line clicked and Berg realised she had hung up. How could they do this to him? But he knew: they could do it all right.

Okay, he thought savagely, if that was the way they wanted to play it.

Going to the back of his address book, to the list of embassies and consulates he kept there, he found another number.

He jiggled the cradle. Nothing. He tried again. Where the hell was the operator? He kept jiggling the phone.

'Yes?' the operator said coldly.

She took an age to connect him, only to announce that the number was engaged. She said she'd try again in a few minutes if he liked.

He vacillated – was it wise to make the call at all?

He heard himself asking her to try again.

While he waited he lit a cigarette and wandered around the

house. The tour didn't take long: there were four small rooms and, behind a fifth door, dark steps leading down to a cellar, which he didn't bother to investigate. In the kitchen the boy was sitting at the table, chewing on a piece of bread.

'All right?' Berg smiled.

The boy looked up at him with large round eyes, his lower lip drooping resentfully.

The telephone jangled a sort of code: two long and a short ring. It must be for him.

Berg strode into the living room and snatched up the phone.

The operator announced that she was putting him through. A cool male voice replied.

Even as Berg asked for Niki he had a premonition, a sudden chilling certainty of what he'd hear, so that the words, when they came, were like an echo.

Second Secretary Yurasov is on leave. Did you wish to be connected to the third trade secretary?

Berg tried to understand what this meant, and failed.

The voice said: 'Hello? Hello?'

Berg almost rang off, but something made him pause. He said harshly: 'I have a message. That Harri called. Harri called. Okay?' Hastily replacing the receiver, he sat for a long time, staring at the wall.

He constructed a theory. Niki and his colleagues must have found out about Sonja. They must have discovered Sonja was no clerk. But surely it couldn't matter that much? Not when his safety was at stake. Surely he was more important than Sonja any day.

So he'd lied to them – so what? That wasn't any reason to freeze him out.

Crass idiots.

But then he had another thought: Perhaps the silence was a warning. A warning to keep away for a while.

That pulled him up short.

There was only one thing they could possibly want to warn him about, only one thing that could possibly have happened.

Sonja hadn't been dealt with after all. Sonja had talked ...

The fear crept up on him, chipping away at his confidence. He knew then that he must get away from this place. It was beginning to feel more like a trap than a bolthole.

He swept into the kitchen. Seeing him, the child jumped up and ran into the corner.

Berg tightened his lips. 'Come on, old fellow. We're leaving.'

The phone rang in the other room.

Berg hesitated.

He recognised the sequence: two long and one short.

Turning abruptly on his heel he went back into the living room and said into the telephone: 'Yes?'

'Is Major Starheim there?'

'No.'

A pause. 'But he's there on Revoy?'

'Yes.'

'Can I leave a message then? It's Major Thrane here.'

A small shiver of alarm went up Berg's spine. Thrane? He knew that name. He said calmly: 'By all means.'

'Who am I speaking to?' The voice was suddenly wary.

Berg put on the semblance of a northern accent. 'A friend of Arne's.'

'Ah.' The voice relaxed a little. 'Well, could you tell Starheim that I am desperate for that information he promised me. Could he please call my office as soon as possible?'

'I will tell him.'

'Tell him it's even more important than before.'

'Right-oh.'

'And ...' A hesitation. 'Tell him – tell him I'm doing all I can this end.'

Berg dropped the receiver slowly into its cradle, feeling very cold.

Thrane – he had placed the name.

Sonja had mentioned it several times.

Major Thrane was at FO/E. Major Thrane was in counter-intelligence.

... Desperate for that information. Berg thought: I bet he is!

So Hal hadn't been on his own after all. Hal was working with FO/E.

The realisation flooded over Berg in an ice-cold wave.

Immediately following it came the reassuring thought that Hal hadn't yet delivered his information.

He moved fast then, running into the hall, searching shelves, pulling open cupboards and rummaging into corners. Nothing.

381

But there had to be at least one.

He tried the kitchen next, ignoring the child as he looked wildly round. Ah! He let out a small exclamation of triumph.

There behind the door. Set on brackets on the wall. A rifle, a Lee Enfield .303. He took it down and felt along the top of cupboards and yanked open drawers until he found the ammo. He loaded his pockets with clips and, grasping the rifle in one hand, reached for the cowering boy.

'Come on! We're going back to Mummy!'

Thrane paced the room impatiently.

Would Starheim get the message all right? More to the point, would Starheim have the information? Had he had time to find out?

There was nothing to do but wait and see.

But time was running out. One more day, then – then both of them would have had it.

The door opened; someone entered without knocking. Only one person did that: Ekeland.

The Security Head was wearing the grave expression he reserved for moments of extreme self-importance. Thrane had a sudden sinking feeling.

Ekeland began: 'It may interest you to know that a Russian is boarding an Aeroflot flight for Moscow at this very moment. A member of the Novosti staff in Oslo. Name of Aleksander Savin. Heavily escorted, heavily sedated.'

'Savin?' The name rang a bell.

'GRU, according to FO/S.'

'Could he be –'

Ekeland was already shaking his head. 'Not unless she lied to us. He isn't blond-haired or blue-eyed. And he had a heavy Russian accent.'

Thrane wasn't too disappointed. He'd hardly expected Sonja's lover to be a fully accredited Russian.

But why was this boy being sent home in disgrace? He must have been involved in a cock-up, and there was only one cock-up it could be. Sonja's death.

Developing the idea, he said aloud: 'I bet this fellow arranged

Sonja's death without permission. Or without realising her importance. Without knowing how badly we'd take it.'

'That's purely conjectural. No facts,' said Ekeland.

Thrane couldn't argue with that one. Damn, damn. Thrane felt the connections unravelling and slithering away from him like snakes in the grass.

'The timing could be significant, don't you think?' Ekeland remarked with heavy emphasis, and Thrane realised he was going to squeeze every ounce out of his point, whatever it was. 'One might think there was a tip-off involved.'

'Purely conjectural. No facts,' replied Thrane facetiously.

Ekeland licked his lips, savouring some as yet undisclosed gem. 'Not when we put it together with the telephone call which was made from the island of Revoy yesterday ...'

Thrane tensed himself.

'... The call was made to an Oslo number. We traced it. The number belongs to an apartment which is frequently visited by Soviet citizens. According to FO/S it is in fact a safe house.' Ekeland paused for effect. 'One of the most frequent visitors to the apartment was a member of the Novosti staff.'

Thrane closed his eyes.

Ekeland finished triumphantly: 'This member of the Novosti staff was, so FO/S tell us, the assistant to one Aleksander Savin.'

It took a moment for Thrane to take it in, then he sank into a chair, empty of all emotion except a deep sense of bafflement.

Incredible.

Starheim. Of all people ...

After a time Thrane glanced up at Ekeland and said in a weary voice: 'Okay. You were right. I was wrong – God, *was* I ... But let me go up there, will you? Let me go to Tromso. I want to be the one to bring him in.'

Twenty-nine

The goats at least were still alive. Hal had no idea whether he really cared or not. He closed the barn door and, pulling his hood up over his mouth, started back to the house.

The wind surged up the hill, kicking up hard snow-particles which pattered against his clothing. Bamse trotted down the path ahead, head low, ears flat, dead on target for home.

Hal went in through the back door. Ragna was at the stove, cooking.

She gave a wan smile. 'Hello. I thought you might like a good breakfast.' Her eyes had shadows under them, he noticed, and her wonderful skin was slightly blotchy.

'Thanks.' He took off his anorak and boots.

'Are the others behind you?' she asked, returning to the stove.

'The others?'

She gave him her full attention. 'Kris. Rolf.'

'No. They're not with me.'

She stared at him.

Suddenly Hal understood. 'You mean they're not here?'

She shook her head wordlessly, fear and alarm spreading across her face.

'You're sure?'

'Yes!'

Shaking with anger, Hal grabbed his anorak and boots and, running to the front door, shot out into the darkness, yelling 'Kr-i-s!' Hopping along the veranda, pulling on his boots, he kept shouting Kris's name at the top of his voice.

After a time he stopped, straining to hear beyond the rushing wind, trying to pick out sounds in the silence beneath.

Nothing. He shouted again.

A sound floated above the hissing gusts. A hail, a shout of greeting.

Hal recognised Arne's distinctive call. He yelled: 'Have you seen Kris?'

'Yes,' came back on the wind.

Hal thought: Thank God! He went down to meet Arne on the path. The old man panted: 'They're at my place. The boy and – him.'

Hal's relief gave way to suspicion. Why? What possible reason could Rolf have for taking Kris?

Spotting Ragna hovering anxiously on the veranda, Hal shouted the news to her. She disappeared back into the house. He found her in the kitchen, looking very thoughtful. She said to Hal: 'But why would he want to take Kris down to Arne's?'

'I don't know. Perhaps Kris wanted to go.'

She looked unconvinced.

He had a need to reassure her at any cost. 'Perhaps they both woke early and wanted something to do.'

Ragna said firmly: 'Will you go and get him for me, please?'

He nodded. 'I'll go now,' he said, and headed for the door.

Arne called him back. 'A message. Important.' Hal took the piece of crumpled paper and, striding off, took a quick glance at it.

Half-way down the hall, he ground to a halt. He skimmed over the words, then went back to the beginning and read them again, carefully.

When he had finished he stared blankly at the paper, thoughts flying off at tangents, realisations building, hardening ...

Then it came to him.

Rolf worked for the other side.

The conclusion came directly, forcibly, like a punch in the stomach.

Yet it was such an appallingly final judgement that he forced himself to stop and go through it all over again. Slipping into the living room, he sat weakly at his desk, taking each thought slowly and logically.

The man he knew as Rolf Berg could not possibly be Rolf Berg; in the winter of 1944–5 the real Rolf Berg was a US Air Force flyer who had been shot down in a bomber somewhere over Europe.

Meanwhile the young man who had killed a collaborator in Trondheim, the young man who had run north with a companion named Petter Axelsen – this young man had not been Rolf Berg, but someone called Blakstad. And he had vanished, never to be seen again.

Was it the same person? Was Rolf really this Blakstad?

If so, he had managed to take on the identity of another man. But how? How does a man acquire a whole new identity?

But then Hal could guess the answer to that: with help from his friends. And there could be no doubt who his friends were.

In 1945, when Hal had sent him on his way after the avalanche, Rolf had been heading north-east. But instead of getting no further than Alta, as he'd told Hal, he'd obviously kept going.

There could be no doubt: Rolf worked for the other side. But how far had his treachery gone?

Hal remembered Thrane's words.

A direct connection to Pasvik.

And Petter, the third man.

He knew then: there was no limit to Rolf's treachery. Rolf had betrayed Jan. Rolf had betrayed them all.

Another equally unwelcome thought came into his mind: he was the only one who knew.

He had to remedy that, and quickly. He had to let Thrane know. But how? He agonised over it for a moment, then, hearing the murmur of Ragna's voice, went back into the kitchen.

Ragna and Arne looked up, startled. Ragna said in alarm: 'Is anything wrong? I thought you'd gone –'

Hal almost said something but, thinking better of it, shook his head and beckoned Arne into the living room. He scribbled a note, folded it and put it into the old man's hand. 'Listen, Arne. I want you to take the tractor and go down to your place. Tell Rolf that breakfast is ready and that we're all waiting for him and Kris, and that they're to use the tractor. Understand? But as soon as they've gone I want you to get on the phone. Call Major Thrane – I've written the number on the top here. It's urgent, Arne. Whatever happens you must make the call. But be sure the tractor's safely gone before you do it.'

The old man frowned deeply, as though he didn't like the sound of the idea at all.

Hal explained: 'Arne, I'd do it myself except – I don't think Rolf would be happy to leave me alone with the telephone. Do you see?'

This caused a flash of amazement then indignation to cross the old man's face; for the first time he seemed to understand the nature of the problem. He nodded his agreement.

Hal went to the lobby to collect Arne's jacket, glancing out of the front door as he did so. Dim grey light, rushing wind; nobody.

Ignoring Ragna's questioning stare, he led Arne through the kitchen and up to the tractor shed at the side of the barn. When the tractor was started and Arne was perched on the seat ready to go, Hal shouted over the engine noise: 'If you can't find Thrane, then get his superior, d'you understand? Just hang on until you get the right person.'

Arne nodded and, putting the tractor into gear, started off down the hill.

Ragna was waiting for Hal at the back door. 'What's going on?' she cried.

He couldn't begin to explain. Instead he said: 'Arne's gone to fetch Kris and Rolf. I couldn't go after all – there's something I have to do.' He backed into the hall. 'I'll explain later ...'

She set her lips, he thought she was about to argue, but then she retorted with a sharp sigh: 'All right!'

Hal left her and, running down the stairs to the cellar, went to the gun cupboard. He took out his Walther, loaded it and slipped it into a pocket, along with four spare clips of ammunition.

He let himself out by the cellar door which led directly off the stairs, and emerged into the grey wind-whipped morning. Stationing himself by the corner of the house, he watched the track leading up from the shore, and settled down to wait.

Berg strode doggedly along the track, the child silent and cowed on his shoulders. A phalanx of white-topped waves marched across the sound and pounded on to the pebble beach, breaking like thunder. The wind was scorching in off the sea, buffeting

him, dragging at his hood, pulling tears from his half-close
eyes.

He paused suddenly. A sound rose above the rumbling of th
surf. An engine ...

He saw it then, coming over a slight rise in the ground. Th
tractor. Instinctively, he felt for the rifle at his shoulder.

The child began to fidget with excitement. He let the bo
down but held firmly on to his collar. Then he waited, his bod
turned a little sideways so that the rifle wasn't immediatel
visible from the approaching vehicle.

Hal. It had to be. Berg felt the tension spring through hi
body.

It wasn't until the tractor was slowing to make a half-circl
and come up alongside them that Berg realised his mistake. I
was the old man. He exhaled gently.

The old man brought the vehicle to a halt beside them
climbed down and, raising his voice to be heard above the rattl
of the engine and the thunder of the turf, shouted: 'You're t
take the tractor. Breakfast is ready.' He didn't wait for a
answer but turned away, only to do a double-take which almos
jerked his head off his neck. His eyes fixed on a point just abov
Berg's shoulder. Berg realised: he had seen the protruding rifle
barrel.

The old man frowned, moved his lips soundlessly, then
clamping his mouth firmly shut, turned abruptly and stompe
off in the direction of his house.

Frowning, Berg watched him go for a moment before liftin
the boy into the cab and climbing up after him. Grasping th
boy in his lap, he thrust the tractor into gear and started of
His foot rested lightly on the throttle; he didn't want to go to
fast. He was too busy thinking.

The tractor pulled up and over a slight incline. Berg glance
behind; the old man was out of sight. Berg took his foot off th
throttle. The tractor rolled to a halt. He pulled on the handbrak
and had another think.

Why had the old man said nothing? He must have realised i
was his own rifle.

Worrying. Very worrying.

He came to a decision.

Sitting the boy in the driving-seat he stopped the engine an jumped down. The boy began to fret. 'Stay there! D'you hear?' Berg tried to imagine the boy's worst fears. 'Otherwise you won't see your mummy again for a long time, d'you understand?'

The child's face creased up in horror and he shrank back into his seat. Berg turned on his heel and began to run back down the track. With the wind behind him and only the rifle to carry, he made good time despite the cumbersome snow-boots on his feet. Soon he was over the rise and going downhill. Rounding a slight bend, the house came into view.

There was no cover and the snow either side of the track was thick and soft; he had no choice but to stay on the hard-packed road and hope he wasn't seen. He pounded on, breathing hard, sweating beneath his thick clothing.

A last spurt and he was there. He ran softly up the few steps to the door and paused to catch his breath. Gently he turned the handle and slipped inside, closing the door swiftly behind him.

Silence. Only the rattling and murmuring of the wind. He listened hard.

A sound. More than just a sound – a voice. Berg's heart hit his ribs.

He moved out of the tiny lobby into the hall, tiptoeing awkwardly over the resonant wooden floor.

The voice again. From the living room.

The telephone.

Berg moved up to the door and listened.

Silence again. Then: 'Yes? I want Major Thrane. No ... I see ... When, then?'

Berg felt a surge of relief – it wasn't too late. The relief was quickly replaced by grim anger.

Taking the rifle in both hands he stepped forward into the room.

Why hadn't they arrived? Hal looked at his watch and worked it out again. Ten minutes at the very most for Arne to get there, five minutes for the others to pull on their outdoor clothes, then ten minutes for them to drive back. Thirty minutes at the most.

But it had been forty.

He considered his original plan again; to wait for Berg and Kris to enter the house, to creep in behind them and, using the momentary surprise, to pull Kris safely to one side before challenging Rolf – or not challenging him. He hadn't made up his mind about that.

Now the whole plan was hopelessly irrelevant anyway.

He chafed and fretted, and finally could bear it no longer. Leaving his cold perch at the side of the house, he strode round to the front and collected his skis from the veranda. He thought of going in to reassure Ragna, but decided against it. She'd only get worried, and he wanted to spare her that.

He poled away, gathering speed down the slope. He realised Bamse was on his tail, and halted abruptly.

'No – stay, boy. Stay. Look after Ragna. D'you hear? *Stay.*' The dog hovered reluctantly, hoping for a change of heart, but, receiving an angry hiss from his master, knew an order when he heard one. With a reproachful look, he sloped back towards the house.

Leaving the track, Hal made for the valley wall and, maintaining as much height as possible, kept to the hillside, following it towards the sea, around the curve of the valley mouth until he was running parallel to the shore. All the time he kept an eye on the track on the foreshore below, but there was nothing.

Later the hillside lost some of its steepness and he had to lose height in order to maintain speed. He calculated that he would come down on to the track long before he reached Arne's.

He rounded a bulge in the hillside. A stretch of track opened out before him. He spotted the tractor immediately. He frowned. Now what on earth was it doing there?

He headed straight for it, dropping fast, his skis rasping and kicking over the protruding stony surface of a scree.

As he approached he looked for signs of life, but there were none. Yet the tractor was facing Brattdal – Rolf must have been on his way back when it had stopped. Had the tractor broken down? Had he gone back to Arne's for help? Had he –

Trying not to speculate, he pressed forward, forcing the last ounce of speed out of his skis.

Almost there.

Something on the tractor caught his eye – a pale blob behind the windscreen, a small shape . . .

It looked like –

Dropping on to the track, he skated the last few yards.

A small face –

It *was*. Kris.

He shouted. The small figure jumped up and, as Hal came to a halt, leapt into his arms. Kris clung to him tightly, like a small limpet. Hal squeezed him and patted his head.

'It's all right now. It's all right. Everything's going to be all right.' Then he asked: 'Where's Rolf?'

The boy was silent. Hal pulled back and looked down at him. 'Where's Rolf, Kris?'

The boy's mouth pulled down. He seemed on the point of tears.

'Krisi – where is he?'

'Went.'

A tear spilled on to the boy's cheek. Hal wiped it away with his glove. 'And he left you here?'

'We – were – coming for breakfast – an' he just went away!'

'Where?'

'Back.'

'To Arne's?'

A nod.

'Why? Was there a reason?'

Kris's lip trembled. This was a question he couldn't answer.

Hal tried another tack. 'Perhaps he'd forgotten something and had to rush back for it?'

'He – just went.' Reliving the fear and indignation, Kris began to sob quietly.

'It's all right. Promise.'

Gently untwining Kris's arms Hal popped him back into the cab and slid his skis in behind him. Then he went and started the engine. It fired first time. Not a breakdown, then.

He considered what to do. He would have liked to take Kris back to Brattdal, but he was filled with a deep sense of urgency and foreboding. Why had Rolf gone back? Had something made him suspicious? Had he guessed Arne might be going to use the phone?

He decided – he must go to Arne's.

391

With Kris on his lap, still hugging him tight, he turned the tractor round and drove flat-out for Arne's, the vehicle clattering and jumping over the uneven snow. At last the house came into view.

Hal stopped well short. He decided to leave the boy in the tractor, at least for the moment. Doing his best to reassure Kris, he climbed down and walked the last few yards to the house.

Everything looked normal; the door was closed, everything was in its place. Yet he felt horribly conspicuous, almost as if he were being watched.

He climbed the steps to the door. As he reached for the handle the door rattled suddenly and he hesitated. But it was only the wind.

Reaching into his pocket he gripped the pistol and entered. The wind leapt past him, sending whorls of scurrying snow into the lobby, causing the row of coats to shiver and stir.

He shut the door quickly, and listened.

There was no sound. Only the wind hissing angrily against the closed door behind him.

He called tentatively: 'Arne? Rolf?'

He stepped into the hall. Nothing. He went towards the kitchen. The door was wide open. He peered in. Empty. He turned towards the living room.

The door was ajar. He stopped abruptly.

Had there been a sound? A faint knock?

He called again: 'Arne? Are you there?'

Silence. His mouth was dry; he licked his lips.

He approached the living room. He pulled the gun from his pocket. Reaching out with his free hand, he pushed at the door with his fingertips. It swung open.

For an instant he thought the room was empty. Then his eyes travelled downwards and his heart stopped.

Someone lay sprawled on the floor, the upper half of his body hidden by the table.

Arne.

Hal raced over and knelt beside him. The old man's face was turned away; Hal leaned across.

The mouth was open, slack and sagging, and stained red black with fast-congealing blood from the stream that had drained from his body and formed a dark pool on the floor

The eye was half-open and unblinking.

Automatically, Hal put a finger on the jugular. Nothing.

He sat back on his heels, fighting down outrage and grief.

A sound. Abruptly his mind cleared; he was suddenly aware that he hadn't been listening. He looked over his shoulder. No one. Yet the bastard couldn't be far away. He glanced back at Arne's body and his anger hardened.

He tightened his grip on the pistol and stood up.

His senses reached out into the vibrant silence of the house, and then beyond, to the murmuring wind.

A gust hit the house with a low whooshing sound. Wood creaked under pressure. The gust subsided. He crouched forward a little, his weight on the balls of his feet, gun-hand forward, his finger lightly on the trigger: old training remembered.

He stepped out into the hall, sweeping it rapidly with his eyes. He ran lightly to the kitchen door, paused, listened, then put an eye round.

Still nothing.

He sprang inside, pushing the door back as he did so.

Quite empty.

The bedroom next. The door was closed. He flung it open, took cover, then cautiously looked in. Nothing. He checked the room more thoroughly then went back into the hall.

Only the lavatory and the cellar to go. They too revealed nothing.

Where the hell had he gone then?

He had to be outside.

Outside –

Kris.

He prayed: *Dear God, don't let anything have happened to Kris.*

Racing for the front door, he flung it open.

The tractor stood there. The cab was empty.

His heart sank.

He looked rapidly about. There was nobody in sight, nobody racing down the track, no sound above the muffled crash of the surf.

No Kris.

He felt a surge of ferocious rage and launched himself down the steps.

The bastard couldn't have got far.

A sound. He ground to a halt a few paces from the steps, and crouched, his senses taut.

Direction – left. He swept the hillside above.

Again, a sound. Much closer.

Where from? He got it at last: from the side of the house.

He ran to the front wall and, keeping close in, approached the corner.

Then he heard – a sniffle. A child's sniffle.

He put his head round the corner.

Kris! *Kris*.

The child stood there, small, white-faced and very still.

Hal let out an exclamation of joy and relief and stepped forward.

The boy pulled back, his expression changing, contorting. Almost like horror ... For a split second Hal stared at him, uncomprehending.

Then three things happened in quick succession. There was a sound from a completely different direction; he caught a fast-moving blur on the periphery of his vision; and his mind found time to log the fact that this moving object was the cause of Kris's terror.

Last – and far, far too late – came his reaction.

He tried to twist his body, to yank his head round, to throw his arm up and protect his head. But even as he contorted his body and raised his arm and jerked his head reflexively to one side, he knew it was too late. Something was swooping viciously inexorably towards him. He felt a split-second of frustration and rage.

The blow, when it came, caught him on the side of the head a massive sickening blow that exploded inside his brain. He had the impression of falling – but forever, as if from a great height. A screeching filled his ears, then everything closed in around him and he sank into a sea of blackness and nausea.

Agonising pain brought him round. A violent stabbing pain that screamed through every nerve-end, like a blunt knife jabbing at an open wound. He opened his eyes, saw nothing and tried again. One eye registered snow very close up, the other a dense reddish veil. He put a hand to his face to push the blood away, but however hard he tried his right eye continued to transmit an impenetrable red fuzz.

His self-defensive instincts took over. He reached out, moving his hand over the surface of the snow, searching for the pistol. No pistol. He turned his head a little.

His good eye saw a foot. Rolf's foot.

He tried to lift his head and instantly regretted it as his brain did several appallingly painful circuits of his skull.

When the nausea subsided he opened an eye again.

Rolf stood above him, looking down the barrel of a .303.

Hal felt a brief moment of disgust at his own stupidity. In the next moment he was working out the odds of grabbing Rolf's foot and pulling it from under him; of snatching the rifle; of feigning unconsciousness then jumping at him.

'Don't do it.' Rolf's voice was very smooth and very sure. He added: 'We want Kris to be safe, don't we?'

And then Hal remembered the boy and knew that he could never endanger Kris's safety, and he groaned with bitter defeat.

'Get up.' Rolf had stepped backwards and lowered his rifle to chest height.

'Not – sure – I – can...' Hal's tongue felt large and swollen in his mouth.

'Get up.'

Very slowly, Hal raised his head and rolled on to one elbow. The nausea welled up and he deposited the meagre contents of his stomach in the snow. When the spasms had passed, Rolf's voice repeated: 'Get up!'

Finally Hal staggered to his feet. He still couldn't see out of one eye.

'Into the house.'

Through his dim half-vision Hal saw that Kris was close by. He reached for him, but Rolf stepped smartly round and dropped a protective hand on Kris's shoulder. 'I'll look after this young fellow. Won't I? We're chums, aren't we?'

Kris stared at him, round-eyed.

Clutching his head, Hal staggered off, leaning against the wall for support. The pain was overwhelming. Finally he made the steps. Rolf gestured him through the hall towards the living room.

Remembering Arne's body, Hal hissed: 'Not the child!'

'Of course.' Rolf's tone was approving. 'Into the kitchen, Kris. And stay there, there's a good boy.' He propelled the boy towards the door. Kris walked stiffly, as if in a dream. He did not look back.

Hal made his way into the living room and sank into a chair, cradling his head in his hands. His good eye registered Arne's foot protruding from behind the table.

'You didn't —' Hal's voice came out as a dull, barely audible croak. He took another breath. 'You didn't have to kill him, you bastard.'

'He was trying to deliver your message, Hal. I couldn't let him do that.'

'But you didn't have to kill him.'

'But *he* was trying to kill *me*.' His voice was sweetly reasonable. 'What else could I do?'

It was a lie, but then that was probably the case for everything Rolf said.

'Tell me, Rolf ... One thing.' Hal peered up at him through the veil of red. 'Why? Why – all this?'

There was a long pause, and Hal thought he wasn't going to answer. But finally he said: 'They gave me a name, a new life, Hal.'

'Christ – is that all?'

'All? You try living with a name that's – filth.' The bitterness broke through into his voice.

'I don't understand.'

'My father. He was a collaborator. I killed him.'

'You could have changed your name.'

'But it wouldn't have altered the fact that I was his son, that I'd killed him, would it?' He shifted his weight, suddenly restless, and waved the rifle towards Arne. 'Move him!'

'But is a name worth all this, for God's sake?'

Rolf gave a cold derisory laugh. 'You don't seem to understand, Hal. It's not just a name now. I'm highly valued. You might even say, exceptionally important.'

'You're not important any bloody longer.'

'Ah – I think I am. I know I am.' He said it with calm understated pride.

The boast was chilling. Hal knew then that Rolf's conceit was boundless.

He also knew, with sudden certainty, that Rolf was going to kill him.

Hal said: 'Thrane already knows – about you.'

Rolf shook his head. 'I don't think so. Now, come on' – he jerked his head at the body – 'I want him down in the cellar.'

'Listen to me – Thrane *knows*.'

A flash of anger. 'Don't give me that, Hal!' he said viciously. 'He doesn't. Because you haven't had time to tell him. Now, get that body into the cellar!'

Rolf retreated to the other side of the room as Hal made his way unsteadily across to Arne and, taking the body by the ankles, began to drag it towards the door. Hal tried not to look at Arne's lolling head bump-bumping over the floor into the hall.

The exertion made him feel faint and he had to stop. After a moment Rolf gave him a prod. Outside the cellar door he lowered one of Arne's legs to open the door. Steps led downwards into pitch darkness.

Rolf ordered: 'Turn on the light!'

'I don't know where it is.'

'Find it!'

Hal knew where the switch was: inside, tucked up behind the door frame. He made a show of searching for it, then gave a single shake of his aching head.

'Go on down!' Rolf said through narrowed lips.

This was the real Rolf, Hal thought fleetingly. No charm now.

Hal retreated down the steps, pulling the deadweight of Arne's body after him. His head felt as though it would crack open at any moment. A single light suddenly blazed on above his head; Rolf had found the switch. Too much to hope that he wouldn't.

Hal pulled the body beside a stack of storage crates and sank on to one knee, exhausted and vaguely nauseous again. Rolf was coming slowly down the steps into the pool of light.

Hal panted: 'Are you going to kill me now?'

'What would you do in my place?'

Still crouching, Hal felt around the concrete floor with his left hand, looking for something – anything. 'It's true – what you said – about Thrane. He doesn't know about you.'

Rolf paused on the second-to-last step, looking curious. 'Ah.'

'But the researcher knows about you, Rolf. The one who found out about your early life.'

Rolf cocked his head to one side, listening hard.

'He's someone who works closely with Thrane. He'll have reported this by now. To Thrane himself . . .'

For the first time Hal felt that he'd got Rolf's full attention. He went on talking, working his hand up the stack of shallow wooden crates as he did so. Each crate had wide ventilation openings in the sides. Holding Rolf's eyes, he began to ease his hand into one of them.

He said: 'The man's an expert on missing persons. He uncovered your identity straight away. He knows you're really Blakstad . . .' His hand closed over a rough oval object the size of a large egg: a potato.

'. . . He also knows that Blakstad disappeared in the direction of the Russians . . .' He tried to withdraw his hand: it stuck. He shifted his grip on the potato.

'. . . and that you acquired the Berg identity. He'll realise you must have had help . . .' His hand jammed again; he pulled hard. Gradually it became to scrape through, then came out suddenly, like a cork. His body swayed.

Rolf's eyes darted suspiciously.

Hal put his right hand to his head as if he'd just had a fit of dizziness, and slowly got to his feet. 'You're finished, Rolf.'

'I prefer to think not.' The handsome face hardened. He brought the rifle up under his arm.

Fear leapt into Hal's throat. He thought: *He's going to do it now.*

Hurriedly, he flicked the potato at Rolf's head. A look of surprise came into Rolf's eyes, he gave a start, the potato missed him, and the rifle went off with a deafening *boom!* that filled the room.

Hal gathered himself to spring for the single naked bulb, but even as he uncoiled himself he saw Rolf recover, hastily operate the bolt and swing the rifle back on to him. He froze.

Rolf's mouth set hard. His trigger-hand seemed to tighten.

Hal shouted: 'I can prove it!'

A pause. 'What?'

'That they know about you!'

He hissed: 'Prove it then.'

Straightening up, Hal reached slowly into his jacket and pulled out the note that Arne had brought up the hill first thing that morning. He held it out, then, seeing Rolf wasn't going to come and get it, threw it at his feet.

Keeping his eyes on Hal, Rolf picked it up and unfolded it with one hand. He held it up to the light and began to read, flicking his eyes back to Hal as he did so.

Suddenly the note took all his attention. 'Sorensen ...' He looked shocked, his mouth turned down into an ugly grimace, the rifle barrel dropped slightly.

This time Hal didn't hesitate. He sprang for the light and, taking a wild swipe at it, smashed the bulb. His momentum carried him on through the sudden darkness. He threw up a hand just in time to break his fall against the wall.

There was another *boom*!, the explosion so close that Hal flinched, instantly deafened. It was only as he pushed himself off the wall that he felt a burning sensation on his cheek. He launched himself forward, reached out, hoping to grab a foot or a leg. There was a scuffling sound, as if Rolf had momentarily lost his footing. The bastard was close, *close*. Wildly searching for contact, Hal dived forward again. His foot met concrete, he pitched forward and landed sprawled on a lower step.

He staggered up. Dimly – so dimly – he saw an outline, a silhouette against the light filtering down from the hall above. The indistinct form was scrabbling up the steps, trying to gain height and distance.

For a split second Hal thought it was hopeless – the dark shape was moving so fast. But then his good eye seemed to see a leg, a foot, not *so* far away. Summoning his energy, he made one last leap. His hand caught a boot, he reached – stretched – for the ankle, touched it, grappled for it, gripped – gripped harder as Rolf tried to jerk it away. Rolling on to his side to gain leverage, Hal gave an almighty heave.

With wild, vicious kicks Rolf tried to pull his foot free. Hal held on with grim determination, trying to reach forward and upward and get a grip on another part of Rolf – an arm, the rifle, anything. In his determination he never saw the other boot

399

shooting towards him. He knew nothing until the heavy savage kick smashed into his nose with a sickening crunch. He yelped with shock and pain and fell back against the wall.

Then, unbelievably, his head took off again as the rifle butt swung into his skull. A deep *thud!*, a vicious pain in his temple, and he was spiralling downwards. He saw stars, the ringing sound in his ear became a roar, and he pitched backwards into the darkness.

Berg approached cautiously, rifle at the ready, and peered at Hal's crumpled body in the dim light. Blood was streaming from the cheek and nose; the head was bent at an odd angle. It occurred to him that Hal might be dead after all. Crouching, he felt for a pulse at the wrist.

A distant sound came from above: a faint whooshing. He jerked his head up, listening hard. The wind?

He longed to go and find out, he longed to get away, yet he had to be sure about Hal. He felt for the pulse again. Nothing. He tried the neck, jabbing his fingers impatiently into the flesh, searching for the jugular. Nothing. Then – he moved his fingers again – yes: a faint throb. He cursed under his breath. Now he'd have to finish the job.

He stood up and operated the rifle bolt. The ejected shell clattered noisily on to the floor.

The silence closed in again. He aimed the rifle, prepared to fire, then hesitated, his mouth dry. He didn't want to have to do this. Damn Hal!

He gripped the rifle once more. A sound broke the silence. Berg gave a violent start. It had come from above: a loud rattle. The wind again? The child? Or – God forbid – Ragna?

For a split second he hovered indecisively, his finger on the trigger, then, turning abruptly, sprinted up the steps. At the top he ground to a halt and paused, his ears straining. Eventually the rattle sounded again. He located its source – the front door – and, striding through the lobby, flung it open.

No one. He exhaled sharply.

He closed the door and, returning to the hall, paused at the cellar steps. He should go down and finish Hal, yet he resented the necessity. Then it occurred to him that there *was* no necessity: Hal would die anyway. In this cold, with those injuries, he'd last no more than a few hours. And there was no risk of his being rescued: it would be days, maybe weeks, before anyone came.

By that time Berg would be long gone.

With relief, he pulled the cellar door shut, turned the heavy lock and tested the door with his shoulder. Then he headed for the kitchen to deal with the child.

Thirty

Ragna peered out of the window into the murk. Still no sign of them. Bamse sat patiently on the veranda, ears up, nose to the wind. Why were they taking so long? Kris would be starving by now. So would Hal, wherever *he* had got to. And the ham and eggs were rapidly congealing in the oven.

The more she thought about it, the more she could have kicked herself for not having gone with Arne. How much better that would have been! Then, if Rolf had been busy on the phone, she could have given Kris – and everyone else – breakfast down there.

As it was she was waiting here uselessly, missing Kris, missing that funny little face of his. The moment his small figure appeared over the rise she would run down the hill and scoop him up and almost squeeze the breath out of him.

And where was Hal? Why hadn't he told her where he was going? And why had he looked secretive?

It occurred to her that he might have gone down to Arne's to join the others – perhaps even to challenge Rolf, as he had last night. They might argue again. She had an unpleasant thought. What if in the heat of things Hal gave her away and revealed what she'd told him last night?

The fear she'd felt the previous night returned and she gave a slight shudder. She sensed that Rolf, for all his cool exterior had a temper, well controlled but fierce. He was impatient and intolerant of anything that got in his way. Ambition and achievement were everything. With sudden insight she realised he was no different to the so-called friends she'd known in the black time, the people who'd pulled her down, the ones she'd run away from. Did she really want to be part of that again?

She sighed sharply. What a muddle!

Straining her eyes, she peered out into the dark grey morning once more. Where was Hal? If he was here she'd know what to do. If he was here she'd feel – safe.

She strode into the kitchen and looked at the clock. She decided to give Hal another ten minutes, then she'd battle her way down to Arne's. She poured a cup of coffee and switched on the radio.

The news came on. She listened with half an ear. A Bulgarian diplomat was being expelled from Norway for activities inconsistent with his diplomatic status. The big freeze continued. Strong winds in the north were causing severe drifting and several villages were cut off. A woman had been killed under a tram in Oslo. She had been named as Sonja Bjornsen, a civil servant in the defence ministry.

The voice droned on. At one point Ragna thought she heard something outside and turned the volume down. Had there been a sound? She thought of going to the front window, but decided it would be unlucky to go again so soon – it would be asking for them *not* to be there.

She listened hard. Wood creaked. Outside, a whooshing sound which reverberated round the house. She gave a contemptuous laugh. Of course! It was that dreadful wind; it fairly howled up this valley. Well, it had almost caught her out – but not quite. With the satisfied air of someone who isn't so easily fooled, she reached for the radio and, turning the volume up again, let the newscaster's voice fill the room.

Berg strode up the hill, panting hard. Coming within sight of the house he paused for breath.

The tractor had damn well failed to start, so he'd had to make the journey on foot. He'd spent the first part of the trip cursing and raging at his appalling luck. To be blown, after all he'd done – it was incredible. He couldn't believe it. Nor could he believe that the damage couldn't somehow be repaired.

But it couldn't. He knew that. The note that Hal had shown him, the message from Sorensen, it had been genuine, he was convinced of it. Sorensen was on to him.

Then, as he'd turned away from the shore to plough up the hill, he'd realised he owed Hal a debt of thanks. Hal had warned him; Hal had saved him from arrest. He thought bitterly: Good old Hal. Reliable to the end.

He continued towards the house.

As he started up the last slope he looked up and saw the dog.

It was standing in front of the steps, head down, ears flat, hackles raised. Berg tried staring it out, but realised that, on this occasion, it wasn't going to work. The dog bared its fangs and growled ominously. The creature could obviously smell something – blood? Berg looked anxiously down at his clothing then up at the windows of the house.

No blood. No sign of Ragna.

He considered for a moment.

'Here, boy.' He stepped closer. The dog's growl rose to a fierce roar.

He went down on his haunches. 'Come on, boy. You know me.'

The dog snarled and snapped on empty air.

With rising anger Berg realised the animal meant business. He cursed. If Ragna hadn't been within earshot he would simply have blown the damned thing's head off.

'It's all right, boy,' he said in a friendly voice. 'I'm not going to hurt you.' He gave the animal a wide grin and wandered innocently off towards the vegetable garden. He glanced over his shoulder. The beast was following, its head down, its teeth bared.

He headed for the corner, intending to go up the side of the house and round the back, but the dog suddenly accelerated and, overtaking him, stationed itself in his path.

Berg sighed deeply. 'I see.' He slipped Hal's pistol out of his pocket and held it out for the dog to see. 'Come and get a mouthful of this, boy.'

A long low growl sounded in the dog's throat. The animal began to advance, but very slowly, placing each paw in front of the last with infinite care, as if walking on ice. Berg goaded it. 'Come on, boy. Come on. Let's have you! Let's have you!' Finally the dog could bear it no longer and poised itself to spring. As it leapt forward Berg stepped neatly to one side, swung his arm high, and brought the pistol butt savagely down

It hit the dog's head an ineffective glancing blow. The dog landed heavily, a little off balance, then, recovering, twisted its body round for another attack.

But the animal wasn't so quick this time – perhaps the blow had made some impact after all. As the creature came in again Berg crouched well down and threw his left forearm up in front of his face. The dog took the bait just as Berg knew it would. Sighting the forearm, it adjusted its stride, opened its jaws, and was about to embed its teeth in his arm when, too late, it saw his right arm coming winging down. It made a desperate attempt to escape the trap, reopening its jaws, contorting its body to one side, but Berg had the trajectory right this time. The pistol met the animal's skull with a satisfying crack, and the dog fell.

Berg stood up and glanced over his shoulder. Still no Ragna. Lucky. He looked down at the prostrate animal. It was rolling its eyes and floundering its legs. Slipping the rifle off his shoulder Berg raised the butt high in the air.

Just as he threw his weight into a long downward thrust there was a sound.

From the house. Reflexively, he tried to pull up, to reverse the momentum of the blow, but it was too late to stop it altogether. His weight carried the butt down on to the animal's head, though not heavily.

Ducking quickly, Berg glanced round, listening hard.

Nothing. False alarm. No one in sight. Lucky. He grabbed the animal's back legs and dragged it rapidly up the side of the house and under the wall. He glanced back. There were a few bloodstains on the snow, but they wouldn't be visible from the door.

The dog was still twitching. It was more dead than alive. He didn't have time to deal with it properly. He murmured derisively: 'Sorry old chap,' and, straightening his anorak, walked quickly round the front of the house towards the veranda.

A movement. Ragna came out of the house, tying her hood, preparing to go somewhere. Seeing him, she started visibly and pulled the hood down from her mouth. 'Where did you come from?' she shouted over the wind.

'Oh, I came up another way.'

'Where are the others? Where's Kris?'

Berg strolled up the steps. 'They're fine. They've gone off on an expedition.'

'*What?*'

'Hal thought it might take Kris's mind off the musk-oxen. They've gone to look at some rare birds or something.'

'Hal's down there?'

'Oh yes.'

This seemed to reassure her. Then she frowned again. 'An expedition in this weather? And what about breakfast? I've got it waiting for them!'

'They've had some. At Arne's. But I wouldn't say no. I could eat a horse.'

She sighed sharply. 'I don't understand. Hal *knew* I wanted Kris back here. He knew I'd made a hot breakfast!' There was a fretful worried tone in her voice. For the first time her eyes focused on the rifle slung over his shoulder.

Berg took her arm and guided her into the house. The smell of food made his mouth water. 'The problem was Kris,' he explained gently. 'He was starving. Arne offered him some bread and cheese and he gulped it down. Hal decided he may as well eat too.'

Ragna turned and said accusingly: 'Why did you take Kris with you this morning? Why did you take him without telling me?'

Berg unslung the rifle and propped it up in a corner. 'You were asleep, my love, and Hal was off somewhere, up at the barn. Kris was bored stiff. I thought he might enjoy the walk down to Arne's. And he did.'

She was half-way there, wanting to believe him yet not quite convinced.

He pushed the hood back from her face and, stroking her cheek, said cheerfully: 'Honestly, we had a wonderful time. He's a great little boy.'

The pride showed in her face and she gave a ghost of a smile. Berg thought: Almost there.

'Now can I eat some of that breakfast?' he asked charmingly. 'Then we'll talk about the rest of the day.'

*

He ate nearly everything: four out of five eggs and three slices of ham. Ragna poured him another coffee and sat down expectantly. 'Well?' she asked. 'You wanted to talk about the rest of the day?'

'Yes. I have to get back to Oslo. The office is frantic. They need me to go to Washington tomorrow. I have to leave straightaway, I'm afraid.'

'Oh.' Ragna hid an immediate sense of relief. It would be a good thing. Rolf was a disturbing influence. He didn't belong up here. Neither did she want him up here – not at the moment, at least. Not until she understood what the problem with Hal was all about.

Rolf continued: 'Hal's offered me the fishing boat.'

Ragna was surprised. '*Skorpa*? But – what? Take it on your own?'

He looked a little offended. 'It's not far across the sound. I think I can manage. Hal's letting me have the Land Rover too. That reminds me ...' Abandoning a last mouthful he shot rapidly to his feet and began to hunt around. 'Where does Hal keep the keys?'

'In the hall, I think. On the table there.'

He went off and reappeared with a bunch of keys. He searched through them. He seemed to find the ones he wanted, for he chucked them in the air and, catching them with a neat swipe of the hand, slid them into his pocket. He was full of suppressed energy, she noticed, a sort of nervous impatience, as if he could hardly wait to leave.

'One thing,' he said. 'Could you come out to *Skorpa* with me? Apparently the engine won't start unless there are two of us. There's some sort of a problem. Hal explained it all to me.'

'Me? But – it's so windy. I couldn't possibly. I can't row.'

Leaning over the table, he took a piece of bread, wiped the last remnants of egg from his plate and popped the morsel in his mouth. 'But I'll row on the way out. And on the way back you'll be going downwind. It'll be easy. Honestly – the wind'll blow you straight to the shore.'

Ragna was appalled. The sea terrified her. 'I *couldn't*.'

'You must!' His eyes flashed with sudden anger. 'Otherwise I'll be stuck here.'

'But – why can't Hal do all this?'

He gave her a long look, as if deciding whether to tell her something. 'Listen.' He sat on the edge of the table. 'To be perfectly honest, Hal and I are not exactly the best of friends at present.' He shrugged it off as mildly ridiculous. 'And – well, I think he'd rather avoid my company on the trip. He's got some wild idea that I know something – ' he paused, choosing his words carefully – 'on a matter that he's obsessed with ...'

'Pasvik.'

His brilliant eyes flashed darkly. 'Oh. You know?' His expression became more veiled, more thoughtful. 'What did Hal tell you?'

Why had she said that? Why? 'Oh, nothing really. Only that he thought you might know something ... He didn't say what.'

'I see.' He gave her an odd look, and she could see he was unconvinced.

She murmured: 'He just can't let the subject go. He's never been able to – leave it alone.' She added hurriedly: 'But it's all a waste of time, of course. I know that. I mean, there's no more to find out, is there?' Standing up abruptly, she took his plate to the sink. She could feel his eyes boring into her back.

Hurriedly she returned to the subject of the journey. 'But if you take *Skorpa* we won't have a boat. We'll be stuck here.'

'What? Oh, Hal said he'd put you on the supply boat tomorrow.'

'But that takes hours, and it goes miles.'

'He said he'd arrange for it to call in at the end of its round.' She sighed. 'And what about the Land Rover?'

'I'm to leave that at Bardufoss Airport. He'll pick it up next week.'

He seemed to have it all worked out. She had no more energy to argue.

If only she didn't have to do this beastly rowing.

She tried one last suggestion. 'Can't we wait for Hal to come back – just to get *Skorpa*'s engine started, I mean?'

There was a pause. Rolf's attention seemed to have wandered for a moment. He was staring thoughtfully out of the window. 'No,' he said suddenly, 'they'll be gone for some time.'

*

408

'I don't think I can do this!' gasped Ragna as she tried to stand up in the little boat, fighting to keep her balance as it bucked and yawed at *Skorpa*'s side.

'I'll give you a heave!' Rolf chucked his bag on to *Skorpa*'s deck and, turning back, took Ragna's wrists and hoisted her over the gunwhale. She landed awkwardly and stumbled against the wheelhouse.

And to think she had to go through all this again. She was already soaked to the knees from helping to launch the dinghy through the surf. She found her feet and, feeling *Skorpa* pitching under her, held tight to the rail.

Rolf went aft to tie the dinghy on to the stern and, returning, went straight into the wheelhouse. Shivering with cold Ragna looked in through the open door. Rolf was searching impatiently for something.

He demanded: 'How do the electrics turn on?'

'I don't know.'

'There must be a master switch. Surely you've seen where Hal turns it on?'

'No. Didn't he tell you where it was?'

Rolf didn't reply but disappeared down the companionway. A minute later he reappeared and twiddled one of the switches by the wheel. A red light came on. He disappeared again. Ragna waited to be told what to do.

There was a loud sluggish whirring as the engine turned over. The whirring went on and on, then stopped. Ragna looked down the hatch. Rolf was crouched beside the engine, his face very grim.

Suddenly Ragna remembered something. 'He usually sprays something into the middle of the engine when it's cold.'

'What?'

She shrugged. 'I'm not sure what the stuff is. Spray. In a can. Something to get it going.'

Rolf hunted around. Ragna looked towards the shore, and thought longingly of Brattdal and the others.

Rolf stood up, holding a can of Easy Start for her inspection. 'That's it.'

He went to work then, opening up levers on the top of the engine. He seemed to know what he was doing.

After a time he shouted: 'Turn the starter, will you?'

She looked at the instrument panel and, recognising a large black switch she had seen Hal use, turned it. The whirring began again, but this time it sounded distinctly brighter. Rolf dashed up and waggled the throttle back and forth. The engine coughed once, twice, Rolf dived down the hatch again, then slowly, painfully, the engine chug-chugged into life.

Ragna sighed with relief. Thank God! Now she could think about starting back.

Rolf reappeared and played with the throttle until the revs settled to a satisfactory level.

She rebuttoned her hood. 'I'll go back now.'

'Sure.' He went to fetch the dinghy.

After a moment she went out on to the side deck and looked aft to see how he was getting on. He was walking back towards her, empty handed. Why hadn't he got the dinghy?

He came up to her. 'The dinghy's gone!'

'*Gone?*'

'The rope was rotten. It's blown away.'

The full implications of what he had said struck her. 'What — Oh, God! But I must get ashore. How am I going to get ashore? You *must* put me ashore!'

'But how?'

'At Arne's. At the other end of the island. *Anywhere.*'

He made a show of looking at his watch. 'There aren't any landing places for miles.'

'There's the cove where the supply boat landed us!'

'Have you seen the surf?' he said derisively. 'I'm sorry, it's impossible. Look, Kris'll be fine with Hal. It's best you come with me. Then you can take the supply boat back in the morning and go and fetch Kris yourself.'

'No —'

'I tell you. There's no other way.' His lips were tight with determination. 'Really.'

She felt a momentous helplessness. She gave him a pleading look but he turned away and, lowering his head against the wind, made his way carefully up to the bow. Then she realised: he was preparing to leave.

She couldn't bear it.

Clutching the rail for support she made her way forward along the pitching deck. Rolf was unwinding chain from a fastening post. She shouted 'Rolf!' but the wind whipped the words from her lips. She ran the last few feet and lurched into him.

'Please –'

With a great heave he threw the chain and the bright red marker buoy over the bow and turned away. She clutched his arm and yelled, 'Rolf, please get me back somehow.'

Pausing for an instant, he gave her a disapproving look, as if he couldn't believe she would make such a fuss. 'Don't be hysterical, Ragna. You'll see Kris tomorrow. It's not that long to wait, surely.' His tone was final. He pulled his arm free and hurried into the wheelhouse.

Ragna stood motionless, grasping the rail, overcome by a dreadful suspicion.

He'd done it on purpose. He'd let the dinghy go on purpose!

The boat pitched into a wave and almost jerked her off her feet.

Slowly, unsteadily, she made her way down the length of the deck to the stern, and stared towards the empty shore.

'The number is out of order.'

Sorensen put the phone down and stared crossly into space. No wonder Starheim hadn't called him back.

But what was he to do now?

For once he was finding it almost impossible to come to a decision. If it had been a legal problem, a matter of weighing up this factor against that, he could have dealt with it – his work, after all, consisted of nothing but problems. But this was different: this was a moral dilemma.

Should he break Starheim's trust and honour the assurance he had made to Thrane? Or should he stay quiet and risk allowing a serious matter to go uninvestigated? Because the more he thought about it, the more certain he was that it must be serious. A man might go some lengths to hide his past – but not that far.

One thing was sure: whatever he did he was going to break one of the two promises he had made.

If only he'd been able to talk to Starheim.

His secretary put her head round the door and said: 'The taxi's waiting.'

He frowned. 'What for?'

She gave him a look of affectionate rebuke. 'You've forgotten! You have a meeting at the fishermen's co-operative.'

He groaned and made a face. 'Two minutes. Just give me two minutes.'

Suddenly he made up his mind. It was a matter of conscience, and such matters could not be allowed to rest. May the Lord strike him down if he was doing the wrong thing, but do it he must. He reached for the phone.

Thirty-one

A long black tunnel yawned before Hal, sucking him down, floating him along a stream of unconsciousness to a place where there was no more pain. He yielded to it, allowing it to rock him gently along.

Yet something nagged at him, a single persistent thought that darted out of his conscious mind and wouldn't let him rest. He pushed it away, but the thought returned, more insistent than ever.

With a vast effort he tried to isolate the thought. Finally it came to him: unless he woke up he was going to die. Dying itself didn't seem so important, but there was some vital reason why he mustn't die, though he couldn't work out what it was.

Inch by inch, he fought his way out of the tunnel, until, with a last effort, the darkness released him and consciousness returned in a sudden rush of pain.

He opened his eyes. Blackness. He listened, but all he could hear was a loud ringing in his ears. He moved his hand and felt the rough concrete floor. He wasn't dead yet.

He moved his head. Terrible. He moved again, raising himself on to hands and knees, feeling his way along the floor until he reached the wall.

Forcing himself to sit up, he took an inventory of the damage. His right cheek, deeply scored and still wet with blood. His nose, a bloody swollen mess. And his skull – God only knew. As far as he could make out, the rifle butt had struck him twice, once behind the right ear – which accounted for the high-pitched ringing – and a second time on the left temple.

But it was his eyes that really worried him – they registered nothing. Not even a suggestion of light. Maybe it was just dark.

A sudden panic overtook him. How long had he been lying there? Hours? A few seconds? Rolf might be on his way back to finish him off. And Kris – where was *he*?

Pulling himself up, he felt his way along the cold walls of the cellar, bumping into crates, tripping over something large and soft ... He felt down: Arne's body. He must be going the wrong way. He was about to turn back when something made him pause.

A tiny sliver of grey. Light. He blinked; the image was very blurred. Then he realised: he could see with his left eye but not his right. Still – better than nothing. He worked out where the light must be coming from – the loading-door high up in a side wall.

He felt his way back along the wall until his foot met a step. He climbed until he came to the door. He felt for the latch and lifted it. Solid. He pulled at the small handle, but the door was firm as rock and, he seemed to remember, about as thick.

The loading-door. It was the only other way out.

Slowly, carefully, he felt his way back down the steps and across the room to the sliver of light. The door was set well up in the wall. How to reach it? He felt for a pile of crates and dragged them across. The effort made his head throb with deep-seated pain.

He climbed up, feeling unsteady, and ran his hands over the rough wooden surface of the door. No handle – a bar. He gripped it. It refused to budge. He struck it with the heel of his hand. It seemed to shift – or was it his imagination? He gave it another shove, then, overwhelmed by dizziness, clutched at it for support.

Recovering, he had another go. This time it gave. Sweating, he pulled it open. His left eye registered a flood of grey light, his right eye, darkness.

Turning back into the cellar he rooted around among the crates and storage racks until he found an iron bar. Tucking it into his belt he climbed up and through the door, out into the snow. For a moment he lay on the soft whiteness, regaining his breath, then clambered up the bank.

He made for the front of the house. To his surprise he saw that the tractor was still parked where he had left it. Was Rolf still in the house then?

He couldn't work it out. Retreating, he went round to the other side of the house and, pulling himself up the wall, risked a quick look in through the lighted window of the living room. No one. He did the same at the kitchen and bedroom windows.

Nothing for it but the front then.

He approached the door cautiously and turned the handle. It was locked. It was never locked. He rattled it, then put his shoulder to it. Nothing budged except his brain, which did a couple of sickening circuits of his head.

Using the iron bar, he hacked at the door, then levered the bar in between the door and the frame, and put all his weight behind it. Finally there was a sound of splintering wood and the lock gave.

'Kris –'

Silence.

He went into the kitchen, the living room, then the rest of the house. Nothing. He almost wept.

'Kris –'

Silence.

He called again and again, thinking: Dear God, *please*.

He stood in the hall, shoulders sagging, momentarily defeated.

Then he heard it: a faint baleful cry.

The kitchen. But –

He hurried back.

It came again ... From behind the door. Hal swung it closed. The boy stood there – alive, *safe*.

Hal's throat constricted; he couldn't speak. He reached out his arms.

Kris stared at him, opened his mouth and screamed, a long ear-splitting sound.

Hal scooped the child into his arms and carried him to a chair and pulled him down on to his lap by the still-warm stove. He held him tight and rocked him and stroked his hair and murmured soft words until the screaming stopped.

Eventually he stole a look at him. The child's face was blank with shock, his eyes staring vacantly downwards, his body stiff. Hal wondered what terrors the boy had lived through.

'Kris. I'm here.' Hal rubbed the circulation back into the boy's hands. 'You're all right now! Come on!' Nothing. He added much louder: 'Hey! Wake up!'

The child blinked, his gaze sharpened. His eyes locked on to Hal's face and grew round with horror again.

Hal put a hand to his face and realised: it was his face that was the culprit. 'Come and help me wash.'

Sitting the child on the draining board, Hal washed his face rigorously, flinched violently when he touched his nose. It hurt like hell, especially when the loose bone moved. He put disinfectant on his cheek, so that that too hurt like hell. Drying off, he asked: 'Better?' From Kris's expression he guessed not.

He hugged him again. 'Sorry I look so horrible, but I'm the same inside!' He smiled to show it was a bit of a joke.

Carrying the boy, he went into the living room and picked up the phone. He jiggled the cradle. Dead. He looked for loose wires, but couldn't see any. Then he peered out of the window and, even with one bad eye, saw plenty. Cables drooped uselessly from the post.

He found a clock: it was three in the afternoon.

'Come on. We'll go and find Mummy.' He instantly regretted the words. Perhaps they wouldn't find Mummy. In fact why hadn't Ragna come looking for them hours ago?

He hunted rapidly through the kitchen. Arne's .303 had gone but unless he was going to be very unlucky there should still be an old Webley revolver and box of ammunition hidden on top of the dresser. Reaching up, his hand touched the cold metal of the gun and he pulled it down triumphantly. It was about time something went his way. But then he corrected himself: something *had* gone his way – he had found Kris, and that had been the most important thing of all.

Loading the weapon, he stuffed it in his pocket with a handful of spare rounds. He cut bread, spread it with butter and jam, and gave some to Kris with a glass of evaporated milk. He ate and drank, too, though chewing was painful. The food made him feel a lot better.

Wrapping Kris in a thick down jacket of Arne's, he hoisted the boy on his back and prepared to leave. 'All right?' No answer, but the arms encircling his neck gave an answering squeeze.

He made straight for the tractor and, sitting Kris down, tried it. The engine gave a couple of feeble turns and died: the battery was flat. He tried the hand-crank. And again, and again. Nothing. He opened the engine-casing.

He could see nothing wrong. He tried cranking it one more time without success.

With resignation, he settled Kris on his back once more, and set off on foot, bending into the force of the wind. The wind had shifted even further to the east, he vaguely noticed, and was ice-cold. The surf crashed loudly on to the beach, retreating across the pebbles with a powerful sucking and clattering noise.

As he crested the rise in the track his eyes automatically went to the point just off the shore where *Skorpa* lay at her mooring. But he couldn't make her out; he couldn't make anything out in the general blur.

He walked on and tried to focus again without success.

It wasn't until he was almost at the boathouse that he finally got a clear if one-sided view of the mooring. His stride faltered. He looked again. But he wasn't mistaken – she wasn't there.

He groaned inwardly: Of course! What else would Rolf have done but take the boat? He scanned the sound and the distant fiord for sight of her, but the gathering darkness pressed down greyly on a grey white-flecked sea, so that, to his cloudy vision, colour and detail were indistinguishable.

Wearily, he began the long climb up the hill to Brattdal. His head throbbed viciously; he felt nauseous again. He plodded on, closing his mind to everything but the need to reach the house. Finally it came into view, its lights shining into the dusk, calm, almost as if nothing had changed.

Hal climbed the steps up to the veranda and walked straight in.

The silence was very deep.

Kris said: 'Where's Mummy?'

Hal had a strong feeling that she wasn't going to be there. But he said cheerfully: 'I'll have a look for her.'

Leaving Kris in the kitchen he searched the house. Rolf's things had gone. But Ragna's bag, her clothes, her toothbrush were still there. His heart filled with dread.

He searched the rest of the house before returning to the boy. He tried to think of something to say. 'I think Mummy's had to go, Kris. Back to the mainland. To – see to things.' He trailed off. 'I think we should go to the mainland too, don't you?'

417

Kris began to cry inconsolably. Hal put an arm round him. Turning his good ear towards the hall, he kept listening. For what he wasn't sure.

Suddenly he went cold.

Bamse.

He leapt up. 'Just got to take a quick look outside.'

Kris's face was a picture of despair.

Hal pleaded, 'It's the animals, Kris. I've got to go and see to the animals!' and left before the child had time to speak.

He went out and whistled long and hard. Nothing. He climbed the hill to the barn, whistling as he went. On opening the barn door he was met by hysterical bleating and bellowing from the animals. No Bamse. He hoisted several days' supply of feed into the goats' stall and split the sacks open. The goats couldn't believe their luck. He did the same for the cattle, checked their water and went outside again.

He scanned the darkening valley, and whistled long and loud. He strained to hear an answering bark, but there was no sound, just the rustling of the snow as it was lifted and sifted by the wind.

Ragna. Bamse. He felt a flicker of hope. It might be significant that both of them had disappeared. Ragna might have gone to get help and taken Bamse with her. But how? If she'd gone overland to the nearest farm she'd have had to pass Arne's place, and she wouldn't have done that without searching for Kris. And the boat – Ragna could never have got Bamse on board by herself.

The hope died.

No: Ragna and Rolf had gone with *Skorpa*. And Bamse?

He decided on a quick circuit of the house. Skirting to the north and east he searched for signs of fresh tracks, but in the sombre ebbing light the snow had lost all contrast and even Bamse's favourite well-worn paths were hardly visible. He came round the front of the house well below the veranda, still whistling, scanning the grey valley walls, just in case the familiar wolf-like figure should come loping into view. Giving the last corner a wide berth, he went to the vegetable garden and peered over the wall.

Nothing. He headed back towards the front of the house. He stopped. Something caught his eye; something on the snow just in front of him. He crouched down to see better. Marks: dark splodges – stains – on well-trodden snow. And from here a width of smoothed snow led away towards the side of the house, as if something had been dragged over it.

He followed the swathe.

Then he spotted it – a dark shape close under the wall of the house, hidden in the deep shadow of a lighted window.

He couldn't make out what it was. He approached cautiously, creasing up his good eye, forcing himself to see.

At two yards he saw.

And stopped. Not wanting to go on. Not wanting to be right. Dear Lord.

He cried aloud: 'No –' and it was a cry of despair.

He moved the last few steps, dropped to his knees and ran his hands over the coarse fur. For an instant he felt a wild euphoria: the flesh was pliable and slightly warm. Inside the deep rib cage the heart still fluttered.

But then his searching hands found the indentation in the top of the skull, and the euphoria died, and he felt a wild and savage anger, because however he ran his fingers over the indentation, however he tried to pretend it wasn't deep, the thing was a bloody great cavity – a sickeningly deep hole – and in his heart he knew that terrible damage like that could never ever be undone.

With infinite care he picked the dog up and moved him into the shaft of light from the window and laid him in a soft bed of fresh snow. Gently he felt over the fine intelligent head again, still hoping that the furrow would be less of a bloody cavity – but it was still there, deep and savage, and his throat constricted with grief and pain. He pulled back the eyelids and saw the dead unresponsive eyes and, putting a hand to the powerful chest, felt the shallowness of the breathing.

He laid his head against the dog's and stroked the long back, feeling the richness of the fur, murmuring, 'Silly old fool. Silly old fool,' and tears fell hotly across his nose on to Bamse's ear.

Then, his cheek still pressed against the warm head, he pulled the revolver from his pocket, cocked it, and held it hard against the back of Bamse's head.

With a sharp intake of breath, he jerked his head abruptly away and squeezed the trigger.

The Aeroflot advertising manager lay on the sofa, bored and frustrated. He'd read all the newspapers and the book he'd brought with him was unreadable.

The safe house, an apartment in the Frogner region of Oslo, was as still as the grave and just as depressing. The manager – a lieutenant in the GRU – went to the window and looked out. An old woman shuffled carefully along the icy pavement, a delivery man unloaded a large box from a van, a car trundled past. He sighed. He had another four hours of this, and only some sandwiches and the occasional coffee to break the monotony. And monotonous it would be. Nothing, unfortunately, was likely to happen. It never did on his shift.

The phone rang.

He jumped violently and stared at the instrument as if it had gone mad.

Then, pulling himself together, he sat down beside it and marshalled his thoughts.

He started the tape recorder and lifted the receiver. 'Hello?'

'It's Harri – where the hell have you been?'

'I was hoping you'd call.'

The voice floated in from a great distance. 'Well, you don't have a very good way of showing it, you bastard!'

The young GRU man raised his eyebrows; this was going to require tact. 'There was a slight logistical problem, that is all,' he said. 'The telephone line had a fault.'

'A fault? Well, why the hell didn't you fix it?'

Ignoring the question, the advertising manager said smoothly: 'How are you? Is everything well?'

'No, it bloody isn't. Things are very – unwell.'

The Russian absorbed this. 'Oh? I'm sorry to hear that. Are you ill?'

'Yes.'

'And there's nothing that can be done?'

'Nothing, you sod.'

'Do you need anything?'

'Yes – a holiday. And soon.'

'You can't come back to the office first?'

'No!' The voice was tight with anger.

420

'I see.' The GRU man thought fast. He had instructions for this eventuality, but he must remember them precisely. 'Do you want help with tickets?'

'Not yet. But I will.'

'That will be no problem.'

'I want to go on a real holiday. To South America or somewhere like that.'

'Of course. How nice.'

'That can be arranged?' The hostility had gone.

'Most certainly. Just as soon as you decide where you want to go.'

A pause. 'I thought I'd go and see some relatives first. A cousin on my mother's side.'

The advertising manager felt relief. Harri had just made things a lot easier for everyone. He had chosen to go to Helsinki.

'You'll phone me when you arrive?'

'Will you be there, you sod?'

'Someone'll be here. All the time.'

'And from my cousin's I want to go straight on holiday – understand?'

'Of course. Oh – and Harri?'

'Yes.'

'A special friend sent his very warmest regards.'

'Stuff him.'

The phone went dead.

The advertising manager exhaled sharply. He had the feeling his superior would be extremely disappointed to hear about this. The news that the subject was making for Helsinki would, on the other hand, provide some solace. It was only a five-hour bus ride from Helsinki to Leningrad. Tourists made the trip all the time. The Winter Palace and the Hermitage were great attractions.

The operator said: 'There seems to be a fault on the line.'

'A fault?' Ragna clutched her forehead in disbelief. 'But when will it be repaired?'

'Out there? It could be weeks.'

Ragna rang off and put her head in both hands. This was

getting more dreadful by the moment. If she allowed her imagination full rein it seemed so dreadful she could hardly bear it.

Kris. Hal. What had happened to them? Were they all right? Had they really gone on an expedition?

Had Rolf lied? Had he let the dinghy go on purpose? If so, why?

She was sitting in her living room, but it seemed strangely unfamiliar, as if an enormous time had passed since she'd last seen it. One of Kris's toys lay on the floor. The sight of it made her want to cry.

If only she'd stayed at Brattdal. If only she'd gone down to Arne's. If only Hal had come back.

Hal. She felt a powerful need of him, a sudden longing for him. Why wasn't he here?

Rolf's voice sounded from the hall. 'Still no reply?'

She didn't answer.

He put his head round the door. 'Come and help, would you?'

She rose, thinking: Anything. Anything to humour him. Anything to get rid of him. She rose and followed him into the hall.

She found him pulling clothes out of the coat cupboard on to the floor. 'What on earth are you looking for?'

'Warm clothes. Rucksacks. Oh, and I'll need skis and boots, just in case the car gets stuck. I suppose you've got some?' He stood back, waiting for her to sort out the clothes, as if such a task was too menial for him.

'The road to Bardufoss isn't that bad!'

'We're not going to Bardufoss.'

Ragna stared at him. 'We?'

'We. I need you to come along.'

'What. But where to?'

'Finland.'

Ragna gaped. It was miles to the border, but that was nothing to the distance beyond it. And the road. It ran high over the plateau for miles and miles. In this weather it might well be closed. And where could he possibly be aiming for? It was at least twenty-four hours to any real sort of civilisation.

She managed: 'But why?'

He whirled past her into the kitchen and threw open some

cupboards. 'We'd better take food. Collect some tins, would you?'

He headed back for the door but she blocked his way and demanded: 'Why?'

'Just got to, and that's all there is to it, sweet one.' He chucked her under the chin and smiled that charming empty smile of his.

She thought: I'm going to scream. 'But where in Finland, for God's sake?'

He moved past her into the hall. 'Helsinki, probably.'

'That's at least two days. I can't be away that long! You'll have to go on your own. I'm sorry. Rolf, do you hear me? You'll have to go on your own!'

He shook his head. 'No, I'm afraid I need you. To help with the driving.'

The argument had a nightmarish quality to it, like when you try to tell some vital truth and no one listens. She made an effort to sound sweetly reasonable. 'Look. Suppose I find someone else to go with you. Someone –'

'No.'

'Rolf, this is ridiculous!'

He turned on her, his blue eyes very hard and very cold. 'What's ridiculous, my love, is wasting time when we should be on our way!'

A shudder ran down Ragna's spine. She thought: I don't know this man at all.

He grasped her chin in one hand, his fingers pinching her cheeks. 'Now, the quicker we leave the quicker you'll be back. Eh?'

He turned away and bent down to stuff some clothes into the holdall which he had brought in from the car.

Sticking out of the top was the long barrel of the hunting rifle.

Shaking slightly, Ragna went into the kitchen and began taking food off the shelves.

Hal made Kris sit well down in the stern and covered him with a piece of canvas. He shouted over the crash of the surf: 'Keep wrapped up!' Checking that his rucksack was well wedged under the helmsman's seat where it wouldn't get wet, he prepared to launch.

It was not going to be easy, not when the waves had a clear seven-mile run from Lyngen and were steep and short as small walls, and almost as hard; not when it was full night and pitch dark and he still felt rough as hell.

He hoisted the mainsail, which flogged viciously, hell bent on self-destruction; then the foresail. He checked that the rudder was ready to hand, and the tiller. Then, putting all his weight into it, he hauled the boat down the shingle into the water. The water lapped coldly against his boots, then, with the next heave, to his knees; finally, as he floated her off, a large wave broke against his legs, soaking him to the groin. The boat's bow rose and fell piston-like in the breaking surf.

Gripping the gunwhale to keep the boat's nose into the wind, Hal worked his way down towards the stern. Reaching the stern he grabbed the rudder from inside the boat and tried to guide the pintles into their sockets, but every time they were almost home the breaking surf bounced the rudder out of alignment.

Cursing silently, he tried again, only to feel a wave skew the bow off to one side. A second wave caught her; he heard it break into the boat. He waded forward and hauled the bow back into the wind again. As he returned to the stern he saw the pale oval of Kris's face peering over the gunwhale. He shouted: 'It's all right, we'll be off soon!' The face disappeared.

This time he held the rudder rigidly in alignment by brute force and guided the pintles into place. The rudder dropped home. At last. He jammed the tiller into the rudderhead then pushing the boat out as far as he could before the waves broke over his legs, he let the bow fall away until it pointed straight out to sea. As the sails caught scent of the wind and *Lillebjorn* made her first tentative lunges at the waves, Hal hoisted himself over the gunwhale and dropped head first into the boat, scrabbling to hoist his dripping legs in after him.

He pulled himself up, grabbed for the tiller, and hauled in on the main sheet. The sail filled and *Lillebjorn* responded with sudden forward surge, setting herself resolutely at the waves. Her bow rose to the first, but the wave was too steep for her and its breaking crest foamed in over the port bow, poured heavy torrents over the triangular foredeck and down into the boat.

The boat picked herself up, shook the last of the water off her deck and, straining at the bit, pointed herself at the next wave. This time she had a little more speed and Hal was able to nudge her bow up into the fast-approaching wave so that she took it cleanly, cleaving its breaking crest neatly in two.

Two more steep breaking seas advanced on them – one of them curved a hissing crest into the boat – but *Lillebjorn* battled her way through, and then at last they were through the worst and into the regular pattern of the longer deep-water waves. Hal got his bearings on the faint lights on the opposite shore and altered course. He sheeted in the little foresail, trimmed the mainsail to the beam wind, and felt *Lillebjorn* rocket forward, quivering at her freedom.

Now it was the sheer boat speed that made the going wet; sheets of spray rose into the air and flew back over the bow and into the boat. Hal reached for his newly acquired pump, checking Kris as he did so. The boy seemed quiet enough, and fairly dry: he was above the level of the slopping bilges, and had curled himself into a ball and pulled the canvas over his head.

Hal pumped energetically until the sound of sloshing water subsided, then took a rest. He wiped some stickiness from his eyes. It dawned on him that it was blood. He felt his head; he was bleeding from the bruise on his temple. He ignored it, but the blood continued to dribble sluggishly down his face. Unwinding the strip of towelling from his neck, he pushed back his hood and wrapped it several times round his head.

His neck now felt very cold. But the sensation was soon eclipsed by the coldness of his body as the piercing wind penetrated his waterproofs and, finding his sodden clothes, tried to freeze them on to his body. His hands ached with cold, then throbbed, then began to lose all feeling. He slipped them inside his jacket one at a time in an attempt to keep the circulation going.

Half-way. Lethargy crept over him; he wanted to sleep.

He came to with a start and grabbed the tiller with both hands. Not a moment too soon, as a violent squall blasted down from the distant mountains, wailing like a demon, throwing

425

Lillebjorn over on her beam ends. Hal quickly eased the sheet, spilling wind from the main. Slowly – heart-stoppingly slowly – *Lillebjorn* tottered up again, as if recovering from a blow, and, gathering herself, cannoned forward into the blackness, her half-filled sails flogging violently, her shrouds humming, her mast shaking so hard that the whole boat vibrated. Hal clung on, holding her steady because there was nothing else he could do.

Almost as quickly as the squall had struck, it was past, and the shore lights, blotted out by the racing cloud, slowly reappeared. *Lillebjorn* resumed her upright posture and slowed, settling herself sedately in the water like a ruffled seabird.

Hal relaxed and focused his good eye on the shore again. With only one eye it was hard to judge distance, but he guessed it was no more than two miles away. Less than half an hour.

He fell into the numb mindlessness induced by sea and intense cold and, hunching his body over the tiller, keeping his back to the wind, stared blankly into the darkness, steering over the waves by feel and instinct. The only time he moved was to check Kris, curled motionless at his feet. Otherwise he remained immobile, instinctively trying to conserve his body heat. It was an impossible hope, and after a while he began to shiver uncontrollably.

He blinked himself into concentration. The shore lights were much closer now and the sea was already calmer as *Lillebjorn* came into the lee of the land. He blinked again: some of the shore lights were moving. Then he realised: headlights. A car.

The lights slowed and stopped at a point dead ahead of *Lillebjorn*'s bows. Could it be the Land Rover? Rolf would have the Land Rover by now, he knew that because the keys had been missing from the hall at Brattdal.

But why would Rolf come back?

Perhaps it was another car. A strange car. His hopes rose. If so, it would be a godsend. He prayed to the unknown vehicle. Don't go away.

Using the lights of a nearby farmhouse to guide him, he looked for the jetty. Then he realised that the strange vehicle was parked on or near the jetty, and that all he had to do was head for its lights.

The wind, deflected by the land, went fluky and dropped

Lillebjorn's speed slowed to a gentle dribble. Hal chafed with frustration.

He watched the car: it still had its lights on. Something showed in the beam – a mast, a superstructure. A craft alongside the jetty.

Skorpa.

A small gust caught *Lillebjorn*'s sails. She shot forward; the jetty was drawing closer. Hal saw a figure climb down on to *Skorpa*'s deck. Who? The nearby farmer, curious to know why *Skorpa* hadn't been left at her mooring? Yet that was impossible: no one round here – and certainly not a humble farmer – had cars.

Rolf? Why would he bother?

Hal gave up trying to make sense of it. Instead he reached a stiff hand under the seat and into his rucksack. After a moment he found the revolver and pushed it inside his jacket.

The wind seemed to have abandoned him again. He willed it back. It must have heard him, for after a couple of false starts it came swooping in along the land, catching him unprepared. He retrimmed the sails and *Lillebjorn* surged forward again.

Skorpa loomed up in front of him. He saw now that there was more than one person on board. A hope sprang into his mind: Ragna. She'd managed to get help. They were on the point of setting out for Revoy. How wonderful that would be!

Yet some instinct made him keep out of the beam of the headlights and make for the far end of the jetty, where it was dark. Once there, he rounded up and, bringing *Lillebjorn* neatly alongside the wooden piles, lunged for the main halyard and let go. The mainsail dropped into the boat with a loud clatter. Kris's face appeared from under the canvas. Hal whispered: 'Stay there!'

A dark figure silhouetted by the headlights was visible advancing along the jetty towards them. Taking the revolver from his jacket, Hal tried to cock it. He swore under his breath: his damn fingers were too cold!

Fumbling, he put both hands to it and finally heard the hammer click back.

The beam of a torch sprang out of the darkness on to *Lillebjorn*'s mast. The torch-holder came to a halt above him.

'Identify yourself.' The voice was not Rolf's.

Hal felt a momentous relief. He dropped his gun-hand down by his side and stood up, saying weakly: 'My name is Halvard Starheim and I need some help.'

There was a pause. The dark figure said: 'Come up here.'

Hal didn't need any encouragement. At the same time he didn't want the gun to go off and frighten everyone. Bending down into the shadows he managed to uncock the revolver and stick it back in his jacket. He made *Lillebjorn* fast on a long line, then climbed up on to the jetty and said urgently: 'Is there anyone on *Skorpa*? On the fishing boat?'

The torch flashed full into his face. The voice said cautiously: 'No.'

It had been too much to hope for. Hal said to the shadowy figure: 'Listen – it's a miracle you're here, whoever you are. There's an emergency. It's too complicated to explain, but first I must get to a telephone, then I must get into Tromso. Can you take me? I can't tell you how important –'

'Herr Starheim,' the voice interrupted heavily. 'I am Sergeant Christiansen of the Tromso Police. You have to come with me.'

'The police?' Hal echoed. Then, realising what he was hearing, he laughed with stupid relief. 'Oh, thank God! Ragna – Ragna's told you! That's why you're here. She told you.'

A pause. 'We are here because you are required to come to Tromso.'

Hal's relief evaporated. 'You haven't heard from Ragna Johansen?'

'Come!'

'You don't understand!' Hal said in frustration. 'Listen – something very terrible's happened, a –' He almost said that a man was dead, but stopped himself in time; the sergeant would probably arrest him for murder. 'A woman's missing. We have *got* to get to a telephone. The borders – the airports – they must be watched. I have to –' He tried to clear the fog in his brain. 'I have to contact Thrane. Yes – Thrane, and –'

'You must come with me,' the heavy voice repeated.

'What do you mean?' He couldn't believe what he was hearing.

'I have orders. You are to come to Tromso.'

'Why?'

The plodding voice repeated: 'You are to come with me to Tromso.'

'And if I refuse?'

'I am a police officer, Herr Starheim. These are strict orders. You would be best not to argue.'

'But there's a woman in danger of her life! We have to go and look for her, for God's sake!'

'You will be able to make the appropriate representions at the station. But now you must –'

Hal knew what came next: *Come with me!* Visions of long hours shut in a police station with dozens of Sergeant Christiansens flashed through his mind. Like hell he'd come!

A second figure was walking towards them, coming from the direction of *Skorpa*. Another bovine representative of the Tromso police force, no doubt.

Hal said hastily: 'I've got to get the child first.'

'The child?'

'In the boat.' Before the sergeant could object, Hal swung himself down over the edge of the jetty. The sergeant stepped forward to have a look and, failing to see the boat, which had floated clear on her long line, shuffled closer to the edge.

That was his mistake. Hal, still hanging on the side of the jetty, reached up, grasped the sergeant's ankle, and in one powerful movement yanked his leg outward and downward. The officer tottered, windmilling his arms, then fell forward. He must have been a heavy man for he hit the water with a resounding splash.

His partner arrived at a rush.

'He's fallen in the water,' Hal said helpfully.

'What? Oh!' The second officer sounded young, dazed, and not entirely sure of what he should do.

Heavy splashing noises sounded nearby: the sergeant was obviously something of a swimmer, though winter bathing was probably quite new to him. Hal called reassuringly to the young officer on the jetty: 'I'll go and get him.'

A pull on the long line brought *Lillebjorn* gliding in alongside the jetty. Hal jumped lightly in. The splashing sounds were slowly and breathlessly approaching.

Untying the mooring line, Hal pushed off and hoisted the mainsail. There was a cry from the jetty. Hal shouted back: 'I'd climb down and help him out if I were you.'

Another cry. Hal did not answer. He pulled in the main-sheet, the wind caught the sail and *Lillebjorn* shot off into the enveloping darkness.

Thirty-two

Thrane got stiffly out of the car, stretched painfully and walked into Tromso Police Headquarters.

The journey from Oslo had been one long delay: a missed seaplane connection at Bodo, a transfer to a Bardufoss-bound turboprop which had required two hours' repair before take-off, and finally, a slow tortuous drive over the snow-swept road to Tromso.

Seven hours in all. But he should be grateful: getting anywhere in the northern winter was a miracle.

Now he must deal with the local police. From previous experience he guessed they would be a little defensive, a touch suspicious, and that some diplomacy and tact would be required on his part.

But he was wrong: the Tromso police chief was immediately and unreservedly co-operative. This, Thrane soon realised, was because he was in a state of shock. Not only had one of his officers been thrown in the sea, but he'd been chucked in by a man who until the previous day had been Tromso's very own local hero.

But that wasn't all. According to the Security Service's man-on-the-spot, a fellow called Krog, three phone calls had been made from Revoy that morning, one to the same Oslo number as the previous day; the second to the Novosti Press Agency, asking for Aleksander Savin by name; and the third – God, it seemed incredible – to the Soviet Embassy.

Now it was Thrane's turn to be stupefied. Here was proof, if more proof were needed, that Starheim was with the other side. Yet the whole thing was beyond belief: how could Starheim have deceived him on such a massive scale? How could Thrane have been so wrong about the man?

Yet a part of him still couldn't help thinking: I don't believe it.

Thrane was given a desk, complete with a list of messages. Most of them demanded that he call Ekeland. One, however, was an urgent request to call Lars Sorensen.

He put them all aside. They could wait for a while.

He had only one priority now: find Starheim.

Krog said: 'The Fortress approved a special watch on the borders and airports about an hour ago. It should be in effect by now. For back-up, a couple of MP units are being called in.'

'Yes, but isn't our man at sea?'

'He can't get far in a small boat,' Krog pointed out. 'Not in this weather anyway. And we've put a guard on his fishing boat, the *Skorpa*.'

'What about other people's fishing boats? He might well borrow one of those.'

'Around here something like that would be missed pretty quickly. What is definitely missing, though, is his Land Rover. He might well have hidden it somewhere.'

Thrane got up and looked at the wall map, thinking hard. 'Okay. Let's ask our friends for some road blocks. One just north of Kaafiord, and one to the south – they'll know where best to put them.'

He considered: that would cover the north–south road. There was already a watch at Bardufoss Airport and the road over the border to Finland. That left – what? With mountains on one side and sea on the other, not much. Unless you were a magician.

Or Halvard Starheim.

He couldn't help thinking that Starheim was the one man who would be able to find another way. What Thrane had to work out was: which way.

He had a sudden thought and stabbed a finger at Tromso Island. 'We should keep a watch on the Johansen woman's house too. He might well go there.' Turning back to Krog, he added: 'D'you think our friends will be able to manage all this?'

Krog shrugged.

Thrane said: 'Well, we can but find out.'

*

The Land Rover ground to a halt. Pulling on the handbrake Rolf said, 'You drive,' and started to move across.

She realised that she was to be the one to get out and walk round to the other side. As she got down she was met by a sharp blast of icy air which whipped the hood off her head.

She climbed in the other side and, adjusting the seat, started off. The headlights reached out ahead, illuminating the brilliance of the road and the gleam of the mountains, accentuating the blackness of Lyngenfiord as it widened darkly to the left. Suddenly the car slewed and shook, buffeted by a powerful gust. Ragna slowed down.

'Only the wind,' said Rolf. 'Keep going!' His voice was tight, and a little condescending.

Ragna bristled. Yes – why not drive dangerously? With a bit of luck they might have an accident. She pressed her foot down. The wheels spun then took a grip. The Land Rover accelerated, jolting over small drifts and bumps of snow. The speed rose to fifty then sixty.

A corner loomed up, unexpectedly tight. Ragna's heart went into her mouth, she turned the wheel, the Land Rover seemed to hover on the brink of leaving the road, then, with no more than a slight skid, they were round.

She slowed down, her heart beating against her chest. It was no good, she didn't have the nerve to have an accident. She wanted to get back to Krisi and Hal in one piece.

The road swung to the right, into the mouth of Skibotn valley, and then curved left to cross the frozen river. Ahead was a fork in the road. Straight on, the highway continued along the sides of the fiords for hundreds of miles, all the way round the Arctic coast. Right, however, was the turning for inland and the long bleak road over the plateau.

The last time she'd come this way had also been in the Land Rover – but with Hal driving and Rolf in the seat behind – and then they'd gone straight on, heading farther along Lyngenfiord, making for the next valley – Kaafiord – and the installation site. The trip seemed a very long time ago now. But she had a clear memory of Hal at the wheel, silent, thin-lipped, his profile full of unspoken reproach, and her heart squeezed painfully. She had behaved badly towards him. And now she felt as though she had failed him, let him down in some vital way.

She slowed at the junction. Rolf took a long look around, glancing over his shoulder and peering carefully through the windscreen. Then he gestured – right.

Ragna turned the wheel, her heart sinking at the thought of the long hard drive ahead.

Hal pulled a glove off with his teeth and put a hand down to the boy's face. The skin was cold, though quite how cold he couldn't tell.

The boat yawed across a wave. Hastily regloving his hand, Hal pulled her back on course. They were heading southward, running down the mainland shore with the wind on the port quarter and going fast – too fast – carrying too much sail, so that *Lillebjorn* surged and slewed about, rolling heavily in the following seas, threatening to broach in the strong gusts. He should reef her down, but he kept putting it off, loath to waste valuable time, reluctant to undertake what might be a tricky manoeuvre.

He got his bearings. They were approaching the northern tip of Tromso Island. He reckoned they still had another eight miles to go. At this speed, an hour and a half.

For ever.

The lights on the mainland shore were tantalisingly close. It would be a simple matter to beach the boat and knock on a farmhouse door. The people would be helpful and generous. Unfortunately they'd also be exceedingly curious. They'd want to know how he'd acquired a squashed nose and a bloody face and a blind eye and a permanent headache. They'd insist on fetching help in the form of doctors and policemen.

He considered the alternative – to carry on. It was blowing like stink – a full-gale he guessed – and the wind was cold and hard as a sledgehammer. In summer this kind of sailing would have been exhilarating. In February, soaked to the skin, it was a grim matter of survival.

His body temperature was well down, he knew that from the loss of feeling in his feet and hands, the pain in his joints, and the sluggishness of his brain. It crept up on you, a frozen brain

434

If you weren't careful the thought processes became so slow that the brain couldn't appreciate the danger it was in – and then of course it was too late to do anything about it.

Somehow he must keep alert, and certainly awake. He remembered hearing of a fisherman shipwrecked in midwinter on one of the outer islands who'd rubbed tobacco into his eyes to keep himself awake, and therefore alive. But Hal had no tobacco, and he could think of nothing which would have a similarly irritant effect.

To exercise his brain, he tried to work out yet again why the hell the Tromso police had come looking for him in that decidedly belligerent fashion. He kept coming up with a single answer.

Thrane. It could only be Thrane. But why? What had happened to make Thrane decide that Hal was an enemy of the people?

Hal had been under the impression that they'd trusted each other. And they had – hadn't they? So much so that they'd made a deal, or so he'd thought.

So what had gone so terribly wrong?

Hal decided: as soon as he got ashore he'd try to contact Thrane on the phone and talk to him. Persuade him to start looking for the right man before it was too late. On the other hand he mustn't fall into the trap of trusting Thrane too much. Thrane may well try to entice him into another meeting with the Tromso police, and that had to be avoided at all costs.

He needed Thrane – but he wasn't quite sure if Thrane was still on his side.

Where the hell did that leave him?

Nowhere.

He leant down to touch the boy again. Was it his imagination, or was the child becoming hypothermic? He hadn't uttered a sound since they'd made their hasty retreat from the jetty. Hal couldn't decide whether he was half frozen to death or deeply asleep.

Without warning, a violent downdraft dropped out of the sky and hit *Lillebjorn* with a heart-stopping roar. The boat leapt forward like a frightened animal. Hal tried desperately to hold her but her rolling became more violent until she took a wild lurch to leeward, shooting her nose towards the shore, then flipped back and took an equally wild roll the other way, then back to leeward again, this time broaching uncontrollably, pressed hard over, her boom hitting the water with a mighty hiss, her lee gunwhale almost under, her mainsail flogging thunderously.

Fighting to bring her back, Hal clambered up the steeply sloping seat and forced his weight up on to the windward gunwhale and pulled the tiller even harder towards him. At last he felt her respond, her nose dipped away, the lights of Tromso reappeared over the bow, she came upright, the squall died away, and Hall dropped back inboard, shaky with relief.

It took him a moment to realise that Kris's pale face had appeared from under the canvas.

'Kris?' he called above the rushing wind. 'Are you all right? Kris?'

A faint 'Yes' floated up. The boy settled again, pushing himself further under the seat. Hal tucked the canvas in around his body.

'We'll go on, shall we, Kris? We'll go home to Tromso. Would you like that?'

'Yes.'

It was decided, then. It was the only place Hal really wanted to go anyway. He had a vision of Ragna watching and waiting for them, a slim figure standing in a lighted window, the room behind suffused with warmth and soft beds and hot food.

Then he had another vision. The house was cold and dark and empty. And it was this picture that stayed firmly in his mind.

Thrane leafed through the transcripts of the calls. There was the one to the safe house in Oslo – a no reply. Then the one to the Novosti Press Agency, asking for Savin by name. The caller – he still couldn't quite bring himself to think of him as Starheim – hadn't had much luck there. Then the one to the embassy. No joy there either. And he'd left a message saying that 'Harri' had called.

It seemed as though his Russian comrades didn't want to know.

No wonder Starheim was trying to run for it.

There'd also been Thrane's own call which had been answered by the anonymous friend of the old man. That was an odd one. Thrane remembered the voice: very cool, strangely smooth for a fisherman—farmer from such wild parts, and, unless he was mistaken, young. He mused on that as he flicked back through earlier transcripts.

He sat up abruptly. There had also been a call from Sorensen. Good God. He glanced at the date and time. That morning. Early.

He read quickly through the message that Sorensen had dictated to Arne, tried hard to understand what it meant, failed, and read it through again.

Rolf Berg – he knew that name all right. He should do. Rolf Berg was a leading journalist on the *Dagens Post*. Left-wing, anti-Nato, usually anti-government, someone who could always be relied on to stir things up.

More to the point, he was the writer of the piece on the Kaafiord installation.

Now why, oh why, did Starheim want to dig into Berg's wartime activities? They'd worked together on the Lapp story, so presumably Starheim knew and approved of the fellow. So why should he be interested in his past? It was not as if there was anything remarkable about Berg's story: he'd emigrated to the US, joined the Air Force and got shot down.

And then there was this second person, Blakstad, first name Roar. What had he got to do with anything? The man had disappeared back in 1945, along with one Petter Axelsen.

Disappeared ... Thrane was interested in people who had disappeared.

Lars Sorensen had been trying to contact Thrane. Was it to do with this? And if so, was it connected to Starheim's activities? He couldn't immediately think how. Yet he noticed that a small knot of excitement had formed in his stomach. You never knew; in this business you never knew at all.

He reached for the telephone and asked for Sorensen's office number. While he was waiting Krog put his head round the door. 'Sergeant's Christiansen's here.'

Thrane looked mystified.

'The swimming policeman,' Krog explained.

Thrane nodded and gestured Krog to bring him in.

As Sorensen's number began to ring, a well-built, broad-faced police sergeant came stiffly into the room and sat down. He looked pink and well scrubbed as if he'd just had a hot bath.

Sorensen's office number rang and rang without reply. Realising it was well after office hours, Thrane asked Krog to try the lawyer's home number, then turned his attention to Sergeant Christiansen.

'Stop for a moment!'

Ragna put on the brakes and brought the Land Rover to a halt. Removing her gloves she squeezed her hands together and blew on them hard. The heating, though full on, was barely adequate.

Rolf got out to refuel from the jerrycans in the back. They had come about twenty miles from the coast at Skibotn, up through the long valley, slowly gaining height, rising above the tree line, until the towering mountains had diminished and fallen behind and the road had emerged on to the high undulating plateau.

She gave a sudden shiver. Stationary like this, the bleakness really hit you. Wind-whipped snow swirled and danced in the lights, the road, visible only by its marker posts, stretched forward into an endless distance and she was struck by a sense of appalling emptiness.

Then she remembered the border. They must be very close.

She reached for the map Rolf had been using and tried to read it in the reflection of the dashboard lights.

Rolf opened her door, letting in a blast of frozen air. 'I'll drive,' he commanded. As Ragna moved across she saw Rolf take something from the back and slide it down beside him.

The rifle.

All Ragna's helpless terrors returned. Not trusting herself to speak, she folded the map away and stared rigidly ahead.

Rolf jammed the car into gear and they moved off.

They came over a slight rise and there before them was a cluster of bright lights.

The border. Rolf had known exactly where it was.

As they drove towards it Rolf shifted tensely. She noticed he was biting his lip, pulling roughly at it with his teeth. He was very nervous. Dread sucked at her stomach.

A heavily muffled figure strolled out of the customs post and stood waiting for them.

Rolf stopped short of the barrier so the guard had to walk towards them. A second guard came out and, after examining their number plate, went back into the guardroom. Through the brightly lit window Ragna saw him consulting a clipboard.

Rolf had wound down his window, letting in a blast of cold air. The first guard leant down and asked for his driving licence. Rolf reached one hand over into the back and felt around in his rucksack. Ragna noticed that he kept his eyes firmly on the guard.

The second guard re-emerged and called to the first. The first looked up, hesitated, then strolled back. The two men went into a huddle, glancing in the Land Rover's direction.

A movement. A third guard appeared from the guardhouse and stationed himself behind the barrier. He had a large automatic weapon in his hand.

Ragna was instantly alert. She'd never heard of three guards on a border post before.

Rolf, too, had noticed. He had stiffened visibly, his expression fierce and livid.

The first guard broke away and came back to Rolf's window. Peering closely at Rolf's face he said: 'You'd better come inside. This may take a moment.'

The slightest pause, then Rolf said casually: 'Okay.'

The first guard stood back a little, the second returned to the guardhouse and could be seen lifting a telephone, the third remained behind the barrier, the weapon in his hands. Rolf leant forward, as if to turn off the idling engine.

Then everything happened at once. Rolf jammed the car into car, it shot backwards, Ragna was thrown forward against the dashboard, hit her head and cried out. The car rocketed backwards, weaving wildly from side to side, the engine screaming. She thrust out a hand, grabbed the door handle and clung on. The first guard was gesticulating and shouting soundlessly. The third guard dropped into a crouch and levelled his gun at them.

Only when she heard a distant *crack! crack!* over the shriek of the engine did Ragna realise they were actually being shot at.

She screamed and ducked her head between her knees.

A sudden swerve knocked her sideways. She was dimly aware of the car skidding to a halt, of Rolf winding viciously on the wheel, of the car shooting forward and accelerating.

They were heading back the way they had come.

Hal picked Kris up in his arms and started towards the house. He felt exceedingly despondent. There was a snow-reflected glow from the porch light at the front, but the rest of the house was in complete darkness, the windows staring blackly across the water.

Hal gripped the child more tightly. Yet again no Mummy.

Trying to think positively, Hal thought of what they *would* find. A telephone, fires waiting to be lit, some food and, with a bit of luck, Ragna's car. In which case he would drive Kris over to his grandmother's.

He trudged heavily up the side of the house, praying that the front door would be open. Ragna sometimes locked it, though few people bothered round here.

The corner of the house loomed ahead. He strode towards it, nearing the pool of light.

As he stepped out he froze in mid-stride.

On the road, a dark gleam. Metal. He focused his good eye. A car. Parked on the road.

Very slowly, very quietly, Hal retreated, one step at a time, sliding back into the shadows.

He leant back against the wall.

He should have guessed.

A sound. From the front of the house. Lowering Kris, Hal risked putting his eye to the corner.

A dark figure. At a window. A police officer. Nose to the glass and peering in.

Kris pulled at his sleeve. 'Where's Mummy? Where's my Mummy?'

Hal shushed him with a rapid shake of the head and a

gloved hand over the boy's mouth. The boy's eyes popped with surprise. Hal risked another quick look around the corner.

The officer had stopped looking in the window and was wandering slowly towards the door. He didn't appear to have heard Kris's voice.

The officer stopped under the porch and rapped loudly on the front door. As he waited he suddenly glanced in Hal's direction.

Hal jerked his head back. The silence stretched out.

Hal considered walking straight out and trying to explain. Perhaps the man would listen.

Then again, perhaps he wouldn't.

He couldn't risk it.

Footsteps crunched on crisp snow. Distinctly at first, then growing fainter.

Hal dared another look. The officer was walking away down the path towards the car. A door slammed. Hal waited. The car started up, its engine idling. The engine note remained low. Then Hal realised: the car wasn't going anywhere. They were merely keeping warm while they watched and waited. For him.

He thought longingly of the garage on the other side of the house and Ragna's car that was very probably inside.

He put his head down to Kris's ear and whispered: 'We've got to play hide and seek for a minute. Then we'll go to Granny's.' Time for the unpalatable truth. 'Mummy's not here, you see.'

The boy was getting used to bad news. His face showed nothing.

Keeping to the shadows Hal made his way back down the garden and helped Kris over the wattle fence into the next property. Five minutes later the two of them emerged on to the road some three hundred yards beyond the watching car.

Ignoring his throbbing head, Hal hitched the boy on to his back and set off at a brisk walk. It was twenty minutes to Sigrid Johansen's house, maybe more.

He was painfully aware that time was racing away, time that Rolf would be using to the full.

*

Ragna clung to the door handle as the Land Rover tore back towards Skibotn at breathtaking speed.

This was what bad dreams were made of, except that in this nightmare she wasn't allowed to wake up. She'd had a wild hope that the Land Rover would skid and turn over, but it stayed firmly upright. She'd prayed that they would run out of petrol. But between wild lurches of the vehicle she'd managed to get a look at the faintly illuminated gauge and seen that it was still half-full.

Approaching the junction at Skibotn she thought Rolf might slow down, but, the road having fewer drifts, he merely accelerated. And turned right.

To the north.

Ragna's heart sank still further. Away from Tromso. She couldn't bear it.

In rising panic she considered escape: throwing open the door and rolling out, but at this speed the snow bank at the roadside would be harder than concrete. Perhaps if she begged – pleaded – he'd stop and let her out. She'd promise anything if she thought it'd do some good.

Then it occurred to her: perhaps if she made a nuisance of herself he'd stop and throw her out anyway.

She examined the idea: she'd have to make a really terrible nuisance of herself if it was to have any chance of working. It took a long time for her to screw up her courage. The road had turned right on its ten-mile detour into the deep indentation of Kaafiord before she blurted: 'Let me out!'

He flicked a glance at her and, without replying, turned his attention back to the road.

She raised her voice. 'Just stop and let me out!'

'Shut up, Ragna. I need you.' His profile was implacable in the reflection of the lights.

'I'll scream! I'll scream and shout and scratch your face and kick and yell until you let me out!'

He didn't answer.

She'd never screamed in her life – never really screamed. She didn't know if she could do it. But she'd damn well try. She filled her lungs and opened her mouth.

Then out of the corner of her eye she saw Rolf move, so quickly that the scream died on her lips and in one reflex action she pushed herself against the door.

But he wasn't reaching for her at all – he was diving for the dashboard. She realised – he'd switched off the lights. The road ahead had disappeared, swallowed up into the surrounding snow.

'What –'

He kept looking out of his side window. Then she understood. He had seen other lights – a cluster of them. On the far side of the gash of black water that was Kaafiord. Beams of light, stationary.

A group of parked cars?

Her spirits leapt. The police! The border guards must have alerted the authorities. And the police had blocked the road! No need to scream now.

As she watched, a pair of lights detached themselves from the cluster and began to move along the opposite shore. She could see both rear and front lights of the vehicle as it ran parallel to them.

Perhaps this too was a police car. Yes – why not? In which case they would meet it on the road – they couldn't avoid meeting it – for both of them were converging on the top of the fiord. She allowed herself to hope.

Then the doubts came. Why, if this car could so easily be a police car, was Rolf driving like a maniac towards it?

The Land Rover gave an almighty bump. Ragna almost hit the roof. She cried out. Rolf swerved to avoid something. The car seemed to be off the road – there was a terrible jolting and shuddering – Rolf fought the wheel, then they were on to a smoother surface again.

Clinging on tightly, bracing herself for the crash that might come at any moment, she tried closing her eyes, but that only made her sick. Looking ahead was no better. Road markers loomed up and whooshed past with terrifying speed. Desperate, she finally fastened her eyes on the headlights across the black water.

The beam of gold was moving steadily along the steep-sided northern shore. But slowly, so slowly. Barely keeping pace.

Rolf was still racing, hunched forward over the wheel, peering intently through the windscreen.

Yet the two cars must still meet.

443

Or must they?

Suddenly Ragna realised why Rolf was racing.

He was racing for a prize. The prize was the road at the head of the fiord. The turning which led up the valley and into the mountains, past the installation site and up to the plateau. A road which led nowhere, a road no one would bother to search – the perfect place to hide.

In her mind Ragna egged the distant car on, willed it forward, compelled the driver to look across the expanse of water and see the unlit vehicle racing him to the top of the fiord.

But after a time it was clear that the lights were slowly, inexorably falling behind.

Rolf was winning.

As the water narrowed between the converging mountains, and the head of the fiord drew nearer, her hopes died. Even the night-glow seemed to have intensified to make the road markers more visible. Rolf wouldn't make a mistake now.

As they neared the head of the fiord the road curved into the valley mouth. The Land Rover went into the bend fast, lurched and skidded, and for a moment Ragna thought they'd crash after all. But Rolf fought the wheel, the vehicle slewed from side to side and straightened up; he regained control. Ragna suppressed her disappointment.

They came to the frozen river that emptied out of the valley; they flew over the bridge. There, just ahead, was the turning.

Ragna looked for the headlights on the northern shore. They were closer – but not close enough.

She resigned herself: there was no chance now.

Rolf slowed a little, turned up the valley road and accelerated again. The Land Rover bumped noisily as it hit roughly compacted snow.

Aslak's house was half a mile along on the left. Ragna stared longingly towards the golden ornamental lights hanging in its uncurtained windows, hoping against hope that Aslak might be looking out.

They swept past. Twisting, she peered back through the plastic rear window, but the house was lost in the dense snow-cloud whirled up by the wheels.

She looked ahead. Ahead was nothing but darkness.

To her disgust, she began to cry.

Aslak Hetta pressed his nose to the window. He was peering out because he always peered out whenever he heard something on the road. It was his business to know what went on in Kaafiord Valley. Hunters out of season, reindeer poachers, officials snooping: you never knew.

This time his curiosity was fully aroused.

No lights. Who was mad enough to drive around with no lights?

And the vehicle – a Land Rover. Just like Hal's. He was sure of it: he'd seen its silhouette against the snow; and the lights of the house had for a moment reflected on its high grey metal sides. Yet Hal wouldn't drive past without stopping to see him – it was inconceivable.

Much more worrying, what possible reason could Hal have for wanting to go up into the valley on a night like this? It was freezing, the coldest night for years. No one in their right mind was out.

Could it have been someone else? He dismissed the idea: a few people lived higher up the valley, but none of them had cars. And no one else in the entire area had a Land Rover.

Hal. It had to be.

He couldn't understand it.

After a few minutes' thought, he pulled on an anorak, snow-boots, gloves and hat, and, calling to his mother, went out.

Thirty-three

The police chief admitted: 'Nothing, I'm afraid.' He shifted in his seat and looked uncomfortable and faintly resentful, as if the whole business had been invented by Thrane to make his life difficult.

'So he's disappeared?' Thrane tried to sound calm.

'We sent a car up from the south. And one down from the road block at Kaafiord.' The police chief shrugged. 'No sign.'

'But a Land Rover can't disappear.'

'No. Either he stopped somewhere or –'

'Yes?'

'We missed him.'

There wasn't a lot one could say to that. Getting up, Thrane said as pleasantly as possible: 'Thank you. I'd be grateful if you'd keep me informed.'

He found Krog outside their makeshift office. Krog nodded towards the half-open door of an adjoining interview room and raised his eyebrows doubtfully. 'He says he's got more.'

Thrane strode in. The swimming sergeant sat hunched over a sheet of paper, scribbling hard. Seeing Thrane, he said earnestly: 'I think I've got it now.' He gathered himself to talk at some length. Thrane sighed inwardly – the sergeant was not the most succinct of speakers. 'I definitely remember,' the sergeant began, 'that he seemed to think I must have heard from the Ragna Johansen. Then, when I said I hadn't, he talked about having to look for a missing woman. I think that maybe' – he paused to lay proper stress on his words – 'maybe he was talking of the same person. I mean, this Ragna Johansen. Meaning she was the missing woman.'

'Yes, possibly,' Thrane cut in restlessly. From the corner o

446

She felt a surge of self-disgust. Never again! Never again. No more ruining other people's lives. No more selfishness.

And she'd make amends – oh yes. To Kris. But most of all to Hal. She'd find her way out of this place if it killed her. She'd get help. The thought of failure was unbearable.

Finally, after what seemed a long time, she slipped into an exhausted sleep.

Much later she woke with a start. A sound – there had been a sound. From outside. What was it? The silence thundered in her ears. She strained to hear.

There!

A distant sound like –

Her heart hammered against her chest. It couldn't be –

It came again. Faint. Distant. Muffled ... Yet unmistakable. The howl of an animal.

A baying ...

She gave a deep shudder and pressed herself closer to Hal. Trying not to listen, yet unable to prevent herself, she braced herself, eyes closed, waiting for the awful sound to come again.

The silence stretched out. The sound did not come again.

She must have dozed, for she came to with a start, aware that quite some time had passed – maybe as much as an hour. She remained still, not wanting to move, not wanting to think about getting up to check the weather. But the darkness wasn't entirely dark. She looked up. Through a tiny gap between the tarpaulin and the rock she saw a single star.

Easing herself out of the bag she pushed back the corner of the canvas and looked out. A new world stretched before her: the fog had vanished, the night was hard and clear; a slight wind had sprung up.

She hesitated for one moment, remembering the chilling sound in the night ... But already it seemed distant, like a half-forgotten nightmare.

Without another thought, she hastily got herself ready. Relighting the candle, she packed her rucksack with a compass, map, one box of matches, her portion of the food, and two sticks of ski wax.

She placed Hal's food supply next to him within easy reach and made sure his water flask was in the bag where he would find it.

The gun – a revolver – lay where she'd left it. She examined it cautiously then, going to the shreds of Hal's anorak searched the pockets and emptied the ammunition into her own anorak. Picking up the gun again, she tried to see how you loaded and cocked it. She managed to break it open. All the chambers were full. She shut it again; it went home with a loud metallic click.

'Ragna ...'

Her head spun round.

Hal's swollen eyes blinked at her over the edge of the survival bag. He seemed more awake – even a little better.

She smiled at him. 'How do you feel?'

'Okay.'

But then he would say that. She found the water flask and made him drink. He was very thirsty. She wished she'd melted more water.

'How is it?' he asked.

'Clear. And only a little wind.'

'Watch out ... for cloud ... Snow. Find shelter in good time.'

She nodded.

'Got the revolver?' he asked.

She crawled up beside him. 'Could you tell me exactly how to use it?'

He explained slowly, breathlessly, about the double action and how if you pulled on the trigger alone you had to put a lot of pressure on it, but how, if you first cocked the hammer back with your thumb, the trigger pressure was considerably lighter. He told her it would kick quite a bit, and that she should try to count the rounds, so as not to run out at an awkward time.

'And ... the ammo? You've got that?'

'Yes.'

'Good.' He closed his eyes for a moment, then reopened them. 'Won't need to use it ... but best to be safe.'

She didn't tell him about the baying.

'One thing ...' He frowned at some disturbing thought. 'Don't go too quickly ... whatever you do. Don't risk .. catching Rolf.'

'He'll be miles away by now.'

He panted: 'Can't be sure! Can't be sure! Please!' It seemed very important to him.

The risk of catching Rolf seemed very small compared to th

risk of going too slowly and getting caught in another storm and not being able to get help. But she nodded firmly because she knew it would reassure him.

He wasn't fooled. His hand came out and felt for her arm. 'Ragna, you must stay clear. You *must*. He ... He'd do anything ... He'd kill you. D'you understand?' He peered at her for a moment, then added bitterly: 'He killed Arne!'

She stared at him.

'Now do you understand? Say you understand.'

She managed: 'I understand.'

And she did. After the initial shock it was surprisingly easy. Somehow killing seemed a natural extension of Rolf's character. Poor Arne ...

She shook herself free. She didn't want to leave without a look of unshakeable confidence on her face; she wanted Hal to believe that she would bring help soon.

More than that. She wanted to leave Hal with ... Her heart tightened.

She leant forward and pressed her cheek against his battered face. 'I love you,' she said. 'I love you with all my heart.'

He was silent. When she pulled back she saw he had screwed his face up into a mild grimace. He gave a small exclamation of something between fondness and exasperation. 'Ragna ...' And opening his eyes, he smiled faintly. 'Just be careful.'

'I will.'

'Sure of the route?'

'Sure.'

There was a silence. Impulsively, she added: 'I meant it.'

'What?' But he knew.

'That I loved you.'

'Tell me ... when we're back in Tromso.'

'I will.' She looked away. 'Time to be off,' she said brusquely.

'Yes.'

'I've put food here – and the water flask's in there with you. And the matches are by the candle.'

'Yes.' He gave her an I'll-be-all-right look.

She pulled on her anorak. Then, fiddling with her gloves, she asked: 'Tell me one thing, love, before I go. Tell me – what did Rolf have to do with Pasvik?'

He didn't answer at first. She stole a glance at him. He was frowning again.

'I need the truth, Hal,' she prompted.

He narrowed his lips and turned his head to one side. After a time he seemed to come to a decision. Turning back, he said slowly and deliberately: 'Rolf's ... a spy. He leaked Pasvik to the Russians. Jan ... Mattis ... walked into a trap.'

Thirty-seven

The police truck whined up the road in four-wheel drive and emerged from the thick mist that filled Kaafiord Valley into a clear starlit night.

It was Aslak who first spotted the saloon car and pointed it out to the driver. They drew up beside it. It was impossible to see what colour it was for it was completely covered with thick frost which glittered and sparkled in the starlight. But Aslak recognised it. He told the police sergeant: 'It's Ragna Johansen's.'

They forced open the doors and looked inside, but there was nothing to be seen.

Two miles further on they found the Land Rover. That too was empty.

Soon afterwards the condition of the road began to make the police driver decidedly nervous and, within sight of the hut by the lake, he drew up and turned his vehicle round, ready to start straight back. Aslak and his cousin, Erkki Hetta, climbed out and, donning their skis and rucksacks, waved at the departing truck and started southwards, pausing only to take a brief look inside the hut.

Aslak set the pace, a fast one. If Hal had been travelling at full speed Aslak knew they hadn't a hope of catching him, but if as Aslak suspected he had been slowed down by his injuries, if indeed he was in trouble, then they might just have a chance of finding him.

Aslak remembered the route they had traced on the map before Hal left, and it was this one that he followed.

It was three in the morning, the air was clear with only the lightest wind. The temperature was very low, making the snow dry and powdery under their skis. Ideal. While it lasted.

Thrane kept himself awake with strong black coffee and the stimulus of growing bad temper. The army had finally mobilised itself. A unit stationed near Skibotn had put up a road block on the Finland road, while another was hanging around in Kaafiord, though what for, God only knew. It was all too little too late. The crack mountain troops were cooling their heels in Skibotn.

In the meantime Ekeland had called from Oslo to report that things were moving very slowly on the diplomatic front. The Finns wanted to know whether a warrant had been issued for Berg, and if so, on what grounds. On receipt of the information they would consider holding the man. But, they clearly implied, not before.

The Norwegian ministry of foreign affairs had subsequently requested an official search for two other people believed to be up on the plateau. This had confused the Finns considerably — were these other people also wanted? Were they in some way connected with the man Berg? Why had they gone up on to the plateau in these conditions?

But despite having received few answers, the Finns had agreed to mount an air search at first light, weather permitting. It was a matter of pride that search and rescue was always offered immediately, without question.

They had also agreed to send a patrol up along the road towards the Norwegian border, in case the subjects had made it that far.

Ekeland asked if Thrane had any news from his end. Thrane told him what little there was to report, carefully failing to mention that the two Lapps, Aslak Hetta and his companion were on their way up on to the plateau. No point in confusing the issue, not when Hetta had been planning to go anyway.

Ekeland rang off. Thrane noticed he made no apology for having wrongly accused Starheim. In Thrane's absence he was doubtless taking full credit for identifying Berg.

Thrane didn't awfully care. The important thing was that something was being done at last. Yet he was haunted by the fear that it wasn't enough.

He paced the room restlessly, then stopping to look at the wall map for the fiftieth time, going over the route again and again – the route that he would take if he were trying to get from Kaafiord to Finland. And not just to Finland – that was easy – but to safety.

From the top of Kaafiord Valley there was a natural trail that led over the border, through shallow valleys, along watercourses, heading south for some twenty-five miles until one reached a small lake. Then there was a choice – to turn west and make straight for the road, which was only about eight miles away, or to carry on south until one hit the road at a more oblique angle, which was a distance of thirteen miles.

Thrane always chose the shorter route, mainly because there was no advantage in the longer one. Neither brought one out near any sort of civilisation. Whichever Berg chose, he would be forced to wait for some passing transport. Since the Finns were patrolling the road, this might well result in his being held, if only for a short time.

On the other hand Berg might be wary of the short route. It would bring him on to the road only a few miles south of the very border post he'd tried so unsuccefully to pass. He might guess there were patrols looking for him. He might keep out of sight of the road until he was many miles to the south. He might ... do anything.

Thrane paced to the window, to the desk, and back again, fretting unhappily. The worst thing was being stuck here, just waiting for news, while everything was happening miles away.

Krog arrived with a sandwich, which looked almost as tired as Thrane felt.

Thrane chewed on it moodily, hardly registering its flavour, which was probably just as well.

He paused in mid-bite and shot a look at Krog. 'Got a car?'

'Er – you want one? Our friends here can arrange one for you, I'm sure.'

'No, I mean *you*. Have you got a car?'

'Yes.'

'Good.' He stood up.

Krog said hurriedly: 'When I say it's mine, it belongs to the department.'

'But I assume it hasn't got FO/S written all over it.'

Krog blushed slightly. 'No.'

'In that case I'll have it off you, thanks.'

'But –'

'You stay here and keep the shop. I'll keep in touch.'

'Right.'

'And if anyone phones, I've gone to Skibotn.'

'And if the CO at Skibotn calls?'

'I've gone to Kaafiord.'

Krog grinned. He'd got the idea.

Berg stopped impatiently for a de-icing. With his gloved hand he scraped clusters of ice from the front of his head-warmer where his breath had frozen on to the wool, then rubbed at his eyelids, which were heavy with ice beads. Finally he checked his skis, which were gliding badly. No snow had accumulated on them: he decided the cold was the problem – it had made the snow hard and grainy and slightly sticky.

He adjusted his hood. The night was alive with faint whispers of sound: vague cracklings and squeakings from the frozen bogs beneath, as if the very ground were expanding.

He set off again, relieved that the earth-sounds were drowned by the squeak and crunch of his skis. He loathed having to stop, he hated the sound of stillness and the menace of an unchanging scene; he always felt that the snow was rising up around him, trying to swallow him up.

But being on his way – that exhilarated him. Because he knew now that nothing – and certainly not this godforsaken place – was going to beat him. It wasn't far to the lake, and there he would turn west and head straight for the road, no more than ten miles further on. Twelve miles in all – four hours at the most.

His optimism was in stark contrast to his mood during the long hours in the fogbound hut. The place had been empty of fuel and food. Using up almost the last of his stores, he'd eaten a half-frozen can of meat and a bar of chocolate which had been so hard he'd almost lost a tooth on it. For water he'd been forced to suck snow. Even wrapped in his sleeping bag the cold had been appalling and he'd hardly slept. And when he'd finally dozed into an uneasy sleep, it was only to find himself locked in a cell, no more than a few feet square, a cell where he was doomed to remain for years – which to him was for ever. The sense of claustrophobia, of desperation, was overwhelming. But it was nothing to the curious emotion he felt when the dream allowed him to look out through the grilles and discover that his prison was not in Norway, but in Russia.

When he'd finally awoken with a terrible start, it was to find that the fog had lifted and had probably been gone for some time. He'd cursed himself for wasting time.

But now he was on his way and going well, fuelled by the certainty that he was going to make it. His only worry was what to do once he reached the road. Would they be looking for him? Would there be a reception committee? Presumably Hal had told someone – the Norwegian authorities. What Berg couldn't work out was how Hal had known where to find him. It was extraordinary. Perhaps the Land Rover had been seen going up Kaafiord Valley. It was the only thing he could think of.

But even if the Norwegians were on to him, would the Finns agree to search for him? And if they managed to find him, would they hold him? A lot would depend on what the Norwegians had told the Finns they wanted him for.

If only he'd managed to talk to Niki. Niki would have fixed it.

If only he'd got the Land Rover through that border post.

If only – yes, the real foul-up – if only he'd finished Hal off back at the island. Then he'd have been all right.

That's where a little kindness got you.

Well, Hal was dead now. Even if he hadn't been dead when Berg left, he would have been shortly after. No one could have survived a night in the open.

Berg checked his bearings. The lake should be coming up at any moment. He peered ahead. There was no moon, and the stars that had lured him from the hut had vanished. Nothing to worry about though – it was only a haze; there was no sign of the fog returning. Nevertheless navigation was difficult: the snow was featureless and appeared to blend straight into the sky. He could just make out hills on either side, but it wasn't

503

until the ground gently dropped away that he realised he was entering some sort of gully.

His skis lurched and rasped over rocky ground – a frozen brook probably. He guessed it must feed into the lake. His spirits rose even further.

He came up against a small boulder and moved round it.

Then –

Aow-ooo!

An animal cry. Close.

The sound screamed at him, he started violently, the adrenalin leapt into his veins, his arms jerked into the air, he thrust his right arm back, grappling wildly for his rifle.

Then his ski slipped.

Fear grabbed at him.

He was *falling*!

He flailed his arms, clutching the air for something solid. He tried desperately to regain his footing.

But the ground wasn't there.

He was falling and there was nothing *there*.

He went backwards, fast. The end of one of his skis caught on something and twisted round.

Then he hit the ground, his head jerked back, his skis were catapulted upwards, almost yanking his legs out of their sockets, and one struck him hard in the face.

But he was on the ground – winded, stunned – but down. He was aware of enormous surprise and relief; the next moment, of pain. His winded stomach was in spasm, his shoulder had taken a bad knock, his face was stinging – but that was all; his rucksack seemed to have taken most of the impact.

He sat up slowly, still very dazed, and took stock. Face – just a bruise, shoulder twisted and painful, then there was his neck – that had been whipped backwards and was very stiff. Nothing else.

Lucky.

Rifle okay, which was just as well because he'd chucked Hal's away to save weight.

He gathered his wits and looked around. He saw now he had fallen straight over a sheer drop of about fifteen feet. Reaching out, he touched long thick icicles.

What cursed luck. A bloody waterfall.

Then, as he regained his breath, he remembered – that sound. What had it been?

A fox? A wolverine or lynx – hell, a wolf?

But there was no sound now. Whatever it was had gone.

He levered himself weakly to his feet and checked himself over again. Okay.

The silence seemed alive. He felt the familiar panic closing in on him. Time to press on.

He set off. His right shoulder was very painful; almost impossible to move. Dragging his right stick uselessly, he put all his weight on his left.

It was only when he had fought his way through a dense patch of frosted brushwood and emerged on to clear snow that he realised there was something wrong with his right ski.

He bent down to examine it.

Split.

He swore aloud, long and viciously. The front section had split longitudinally, from the tip almost as far as his boot. When he lifted the ski one side sagged away. In a furious anger, he ripped off the loose wood, roughly halving the original width, and started off again, plodding awkwardly but determinedly.

Nothing – *nothing* – was going to stop him from reaching that road.

Ragna realised she was going to make it. And the knowledge spurred her on.

It had been hard at the beginning. Her muscles had been painfully stiff, her legs heavy as lead, and a couple of large blisters on her feet had burst and smarted with pain. She'd thought she'd never warm up. But slowly, slowly, she'd come alive.

Now she was feeling good – not tired at all – and her limbs were moving fluidly: she felt as if she could go on for ever.

It was amazing how the miles slipped by when you had the right wax and a binding that didn't flip off every few strides. She'd found the hut within an hour of leaving Hal. She'd also found Rolf's tracks leading away to the south.

She'd followed the tracks for a while, until the sky had

clouded over and she could no longer see them. Now she was going by her own navigation. Every so often she stopped and checked the luminous hand of the compass and looked at her watch and worked out how far she had come. It gave her a strange thrill to realise how logical, how simple all this navigation was – and how well she was doing it.

An extraordinary and rare confidence filled her. It sprang from pure determination: nothing and no one was going to prevent her from reaching that road. Not wolves – in fact she had stopped worrying about them a long time ago. They were frightened of men, weren't they? She'd read that often enough. They wouldn't harm her unless they had to.

And not Rolf – certainly not! *He* should fear *her*. Ah – for the chance to catch just a glimpse of him.

And yet . . .

Hal was right. An encounter would be disastrous. Rolf had killed Arne. Perhaps he'd killed others.

Would he kill her if he had to?

Probably. If she didn't kill him first. The thought gave her a savage satisfaction. She imagined the scene: she had a gun – a large one – she held it steadily. He was standing in front of her, unarmed. Though he tried to stare her out, she held his gaze unwaveringly. He came towards her, smiling that glittering smile of his, saying those soft oh-so-reasonable words, thinking she'd never do it . . . And she pulled the trigger. Just like that.

The next moment she saw the idea for what it was: ridiculous – she'd never be able to kill anyone – but also unworthy. She was merely allowing herself to be dragged down to Rolf's level. Nothing would ever bring Jan back. Certainly not more violence.

All the same, it was just as well Rolf was ahead and getting further ahead all the time.

Just as well.

Another fifteen minutes passed. Her eyelids felt heavy and it took her a while to realise they were almost iced up. Without stopping, she brushed the ice away. Her nose had lost feeling, her cheeks were smarting with cold, her feet throbbing dully. But nothing could be done; she must keep going. It couldn't be far to the lake. And then it was only eight miles to the road.

To her disappointment she began to feel tired. Just a little.

Perhaps she had been going too fast after all.

Steady, steady.

The hills closed in, the ground fell slightly. She realised she was in some sort of narrow valley. The going got rough. She went very carefully, picking her way round the snow-thatched stones and boulders. For one heart-stopping moment she almost stepped over a great ledge, but managed to pull herself back in time. When her pulse had stopped racing, she made her way to one side and side-stepped carefully down.

In the bottom of the gully she ran into stunted bushes, completely white with hoarfrost and invisible against the soft night-glow of the snow. They reared up in front of her, swiping at her face, catching at her clothes until she despaired of getting free.

But then the scrub was behind her and the snow was smooth and even once more.

She had reached the shores of the lake.

She made her calculations again – with the map this time – and there was no doubt.

West. Just eight miles.

Turning, getting her bearings, she settled into her stride, closing her mind to everything except the rhythm of her body, thinking only of the next step, and the one after that, and the one after that ...

Did Hal think like this – taking each step as it came – when he had a long way to go? Yes, somehow she was certain this was exactly how he thought, and the idea warmed her.

An image of the lonely shelter in its vast expanse of emptiness flashed into her mind, and she pressed forward, the tiredness almost forgotten.

The interior of the smart new Volvo saloon was warm as toast. It was hard to believe it was minus thirty-five outside. Kari Falta glanced across at her husband. He was frowning slightly as he concentrated on his driving.

'Want a rest?' she asked.

'No, I'm all right for the moment.'

She looked down at the map on her knees. Shining a penlight

507

on it she remarked: 'Only twenty minutes to the Norwegian border.'

'We've made good time then.'

'Yes.'

They had left their home in the suburbs of Helsinki at three the previous morning and had been travelling for twenty-four hours, with only the shortest of breaks to stretch their legs and put snow-chains on the wheels. The snow-chains were a nuisance – they reduced speed and made a nasty drumming sound – but they prevented delay on the uncleared sections of the road. Generally, though, the snowploughs had been doing a good job and, until they had reached this last section over the plateau, the roads had been fairly clear.

Mikko Valta asked: 'Where's the next settlement?'

'According to this, there is an isolated house of some sort in about five minutes.'

'We'll stop there then.'

'Yes.'

'Unless you think we should press on.'

'Oh no.' Kari rarely disagreed with her husband. That was why they made such a good team.

After a few minutes she checked the mileometer. 'Any moment now, on the left,' she said.

Sure enough the dark shape of a dwelling appeared. They slowed and stopped. The house, such as it was, was completely dark.

'No one at home,' Mikko Valta observed.

'No.'

'I'll go and check anyway.'

'Yes.'

He was back within two minutes. 'Closed up,' he said and started off again.

'Nothing until the border now.'

'Right.'

She stared intently ahead, continuously scanning the area either side of the headlights, not losing concentration for so much as a moment.

But there was nothing to see. After a time she glanced at the mileometer. 'Nearly at the border,' she said.

'Tell me when, then.'

'A little further.' After a minute she said: 'Now.'

He pulled up and put on the handbrake. 'Want to drive?'

'Sure.' They changed places.

As soon as they were settled again she did a careful three-point turn – this was no time to get stuck in the soft snow at the sides of the road – and set off back the way they had come. 'I'll keep our speed down.'

'Yes.'

He reached down to the floor. 'Hungry?' he said.

'I am rather.'

He pulled a large plastic food box on to his knee and took out some sandwiches, two apples and two pre-wrapped pieces of cake.

He replaced the box on the floor and, almost without thinking, ran a hand under his seat to check that the Luger P08 was still clipped safely to the underside. It was.

Sitting up, he began to unwrap the sandwiches.

Thirty-eight

The road wasn't where it was supposed to be. Ragna couldn't believe it. And after all her careful calculations.

She stood, staring stupidly around her, longing to sink into the snow and get the weight of the rucksack off her back, yet refusing to, knowing that the road must be so near.

It was eight in the morning, she'd been going for five hours and according to the map she should be there. Yet in the clinging darkness she could see nothing but endless rolling snow. Worse there was a hill ahead. Not a large one; in fact, it was probably no more than a slight bulge, but, tired as she was, it might as well have been a mountain.

Turning right to skirt the hill, she started off again at a heavy plod, slipping back into the numb mindlessness that had carried her forward for so long. Had it really been five hours? She'd lost all sense of time; when she looked at her watch the reading seemed to bear no relation to what was going on around her. Even her present vaguely defined misery seemed removed from her body, hardly to do with her at all.

A distant note – like a far-off insect – hovered in her ears. That too was unreal.

But it wasn't unreal. Suddenly she jumped awake and pulled her hood away from her ears.

A humming – an engine.

She looked about wildly.

Above the hill the dark sky glowed with light, whitening steadily, until the rim of the hill became a hard black line. The light became intense, throwing up rays like the spokes of a wheel, then it was past, dimming rapidly. The engine sound rose, then fell away; the unseen vehicle had gone.

Ragna felt a momentary disappointment, then optimism — there'd be another car. The point was: she'd found the road.

Abandoning the circuitous route, she set herself straight at the slope.

An official vehicle, either police or army; it was impossible to tell.

Berg watched its tail lights curve away into the darkness and realised: they were probably looking for *him*.

Well, at least he knew. At least he hadn't run into the road asking for a ride and got a nasty surprise.

Suddenly he felt very depressed. What had he done to deserve this unending run of foul luck? Hadn't he run circles round the precious Norwegians for years? Hadn't he outdone them at every turn?

And Niki. Jesus — hadn't he done enough for him? Why hadn't Niki protected him?

His anger mingled with a deeper tiredness. What he needed was a long rest. A nice holiday in the sun. The more he thought about it the more he fancied Australia.

Niki'd be arranging that now.

The thought cheered him.

All he had to do was get out of this place. Stop a civilian car, hijack it, or get into a house — there must be one somewhere — and use the phone ...

He'd find a way. He always had.

In the meantime he huddled back into the snow and shifted his shoulder until the sharp pain eased. He closed his eyes. Sleep. Just for a while. Then he'd get on his way again.

South.

Ragna sank back into the snow at the roadside. It was unimaginable bliss to take the weight off her legs, to lean the heavy rucksack on the snow, not to have to make any more effort. She wouldn't stay long — an icy wind had sprung up and was swirling down the exposed road — but for a while, just a while ...

Intending to have no more than a moment's rest she closed her eyes and let her head drop forward, and immediately slipped into a light doze.

It was the creeping fingers of cold that eventually woke her, sucking at her body, drawing out the hard-won warmth. Rousing herself, she looked up. She realised she had been asleep for some minutes.

She peered about her, trying to take stock. The snow was lit by the first glimmerings of sombre light and it was possible to make out the shapes of the hills, the line of the road, which stretched away into an empty distance in both directions.

How long before another car came?

It struck her that it might be a very long time. It was already nine. Suddenly she was furious with herself. How could she have let so much time pass! No good waiting. She must get going.

Pulling out the battered map she peered at it in the feeble light. One house was shown some miles to the south, but there was a strong possibility it was uninhabited at this time of year. To the north, however, was the border. That was most certainly inhabited. She remembered the three guards, and the one with the rifle, and the shots he'd fired; it all seemed a very long time ago.

She estimated the distance – ten miles. Another three hours, maybe less. She could hardly imagine keeping going that long. But she would, because she had to go somewhere, and it was the only place to go.

She pulled her last ration of chocolate out of her pocket and, breaking the rock-hard pieces off with her teeth, got wearily to her feet. She decided she'd go much faster without skis – the snow on the road was hard-packed and quite good for walking – so she left them at the roadside. Keeping her sticks, she hoisted her rucksack higher on her back and, shivering in the vicious little wind, began the long trudge north.

It was uphill for as far as she could see, which was to a bend some half mile away, but the gradient was slight. Nevertheless she divided the distance to the top of the hill into sections – half-way, three-quarters – and concentrated on one milestone at a time.

Head down, eyes fixed a few yards ahead, she was aware

nothing but the panting of her breath and the scrunch of her boots on the snow and the patter of tiny snow-grains driven against her legs by the scurrying wind.

She didn't see the car. Not until it was well on its way down the hill. Then the lights caught her eye and she jerked her head upwards.

For a moment she stared, not daring to believe what she was seeing.

Then she let out a joyful shriek and, moving into the centre of the road, began to wave both sticks frantically in the air, shouting wildly and ineffectually through the muffling layers of her hood.

The car approached, slowed, and drew to a halt.

Ragna went round to the driver's side and leant down.

A woman wound down the window. In the seat next to her was a man. They both stared at her curiously.

Pulling the hood down from her mouth, Ragna said tearfully: 'Oh, I'm so very glad to see you!'

'Where have you come from?' The woman spoke in Swedish, the language educated Finns used to communicate with other Scandinavians.

'I've been ... I've been ... I can't –' Ragna clamped her mouth shut and, mustering her Swedish, began again. 'Please – *please* – could you take me to the nearest place that has a telephone – it's desperately urgent – someone needs help – I can't explain –'

The woman exchanged glances with the man.

Ragna hovered, expecting the woman to agree rapidly, to invite her in, to reach behind and throw open the rear door.

Instead the couple had a low-voiced discussion. Ragna couldn't believe it – how could the matter be in doubt? In this sort of wild country no one discussed whether to give help – it was given automatically and without question.

The woman turned back. 'Who is this person who's in trouble?'

'You mean – you want his *name*?'

'Yes.'

Ragna stared incredulously. 'What difference does it make!' she shouted.

513

The woman's face was unyielding in the grey light. 'We want to know.'

Ragna threw her head back in disbelief. 'His name is Starheim. Halvard Starheim! Now are you going to help save his life or not!'

The woman looked back to the man. He muttered something then broke off suddenly and leaned forward in his seat, as if to take a better look at Ragna. Did he think she was a madwoman or something? Did he think she was going to – what? Her imagination failed. 'For God's sake!' she cried.

The man's eyes were hidden in shadow but he was still leaning forward, staring hard. The woman too was staring – but past Ragna.

Past?

The tiniest suspicion darted into her mind.

She began to turn.

Something grabbed her.

She jumped violently and shrieked.

An arm had encircled her chest. Hard. The arm yanked her backwards until her back was arched over her rucksack, her body pinned hard against the arm's owner.

Rolf's voice said in her ear: 'Darling, I've been looking for you everywhere.'

Berg smiled hard at the woman in the car. 'Dreadful weather to be out, isn't it?'

The woman did not return his smile. Berg suddenly remembered his bruised eye – he probably looked a sight.

He said loudly to Ragna: 'Darling, you really mustn't wander off like that. Really. I wasn't badly hurt at all. No need to get hysterical. It was only a fall.' He cast an eye at the woman in the car. She was lapping it up all right. He said to her: 'We were stranded, you know. The most ridiculous thing.'

Berg sensed Ragna coming alive again, gathering herself to squawk. He moved his grip on to her arm, squeezed really hard and, wincing at the pain in his shoulder, drew the pistol out of his pocket and dug it hard into her ribs, whispering: 'One word ...'

She gave a slight gasp and became absolutely still.

'Well, can we have a lift?' Berg asked brightly.

The woman conversed with her companion. 'Are you this man Starheim?' she asked.

Berg thought quickly. 'Yes. I'm Starheim.' And, pushing Ragna towards the rear door, he let go of her arm and tried the handle. It was locked. What were these people up to?

He leant down at the open front window. 'What's the problem?'

'We thought you might be someone else. We were looking for a friend.'

They were *what*? Berg's patience was fast running out. He snapped: 'Too bad! We're here and he's not!'

'His name is Harri.'

'Well, you can –' Berg broke off and gaped at the woman. 'Harri . . .' he repeated stupidly. Then in a wild upsurge of relief and joy he laughed, a wild crowing sort of a laugh. 'Harri. *I'm* Harri!'

The woman looked a little dubious. 'We have a mutual friend then.'

Berg realised: they wanted a name. There was only one name he could think of.

'Niki,' he said.

It was the magic word. The woman smiled and, leaning back, unlocked the rear door.

Though Ragna was looking ahead, she registered nothing of the Volvo's progress over the long white road. She saw only the back of Rolf's head as he leaned forward to talk to the two in the front; she saw the thick blond hair, the hair she had thought so beautiful, the hair she had stroked. And she saw his hand clutching the pistol; the hand that had touched every part of her, made her body come alive, the hand that had killed Arne and shot Hal.

She couldn't take her eyes from that hand.

Rolf glanced back at her from time to time, keeping the pistol pointed in her direction. He glanced at her as if she weren't here.

It occurred to her that he was planning to kill her.

The man in the front said: 'This is it.'

They were approaching an unlit house set just back from the road. A deep dread gnawed at Ragna's stomach.

'It's empty,' said the man. 'I checked it earlier.'

'Okay,' Rolf said. 'I won't be long.'

'Can you manage?' said the woman to Rolf, glancing in Ragna's direction.

'I'll need help to get in.'

'No trouble,' said the man.

Rolf took a moment to slip his rucksack off his shoulders. Ragna noticed that he held his right arm oddly, as if he'd hurt it, and that he winced slightly as he moved. There was a heavy bruise on his face, too, as though he'd been in some sort of accident.

'Open the door, Ragna.' He gestured with the pistol.

She reached for the handle and manoeuvred herself out pulling her rucksack after her. Rolf got out, saying: 'You wai just over there.' She went and stood where he had indicated.

Keeping the pistol on her Rolf waited as the man went roun to the boot and, opening it, removed a rope and some tools.

Rolf took the rope from him and, looping it over his shoulder came up to Ragna.

She said: 'Is that for me?'

'Yes. We can't possibly take you with us, you see.' He gav her that slow smile, that intense look she knew so well – th one he used to charm people. She stared, trying to reconcile th smile with the Rolf who killed so easily.

She said: 'You're not going to kill me then?'

The smile changed into something colder. 'No, of cours not.' He sounded offended.

'I suppose I should be grateful.'

His lips narrowed, his eyes flashed with anger. 'I've only don what I've had to do, Ragna.'

'Oh?' She let the bitterness show in her voice. 'You had t shoot Hal, did you?'

'Yes. It was him or me.'

'And Jan?'

She'd caught him there; she saw the surprise in his face. H said in an injured voice: 'I had nothing to do with it, Ragn

Hal always had that stupid idea it was me. Always. But it just isn't true.' His eye had an open frank look; his voice invited confidence and trust.

'I see,' she said. And she did. She saw that he was a compulsive and well-practised liar.

The man came up, a crowbar in his hand, and Rolf gestured Ragna towards the house.

It was a small, single-storey building with boarded-up windows. The man went to work on the door with a crowbar. There was a splintering of wood and the door swung open.

Rolf indicated that Ragna should lead the way.

It was very dark inside. Someone switched on a torch. The beam sprang out and weaved around the walls, revealing a narrow passageway.

'I'll keep watch,' said the man's voice. 'Here.' She realised he was handing the torch to Rolf.

Rolf shone the beam up the passage. 'Go ahead,' he said.

Ragna went forward. There were three doors at the end of the passage. Choosing the one that was already open, she turned left. Rolf's torch flashed into the room, revealing a table, two benches on either side, a tall cupboard.

Ragna went in and, lowering her rucksack on to the floor, turned to face Rolf.

'Make yourself comfortable,' he said. 'You might be here for some time.' He shone the torchbeam on to the walls and, finding a light switch, flicked it on and off several times. It didn't work.

'How long?' she asked quietly.

'Some hours. Maybe a day.' He was hunting around the room.

'How will anyone know I'm here?'

'I'll phone.' She'd heard that before – several times. The gnawing dread returned.

He gave a small exclamation of triumph and, going to the table, put down the torch and struck a match. He put the flame to a candle and a flickering yellow light filled the room. She realised he had put the pistol down to light the candle. Too late: he was already picking it up again.

She must think. She must *think*.

Slipping the rope coil off his shoulder he started to fiddle with, but awkwardly, because of the pistol. His face was in shadow.

517

She had less than a minute. In a minute he would have tied her hands.

Panic clawed at her; she had to do something.

It was now or never.

Her heart thumped against her ribs.

Now.

Slowly, carefully, she bent down and reached for her rucksack. Her hand found one of the straps. She unhitched it. The clasp made a faint clinking sound.

His voice sprang out: 'What are you doing?'

'My sleeping bag. You said to –'

'Wait!' He came up and waved her away. She backed off. 'Anything in here?' he demanded. 'Anything that shouldn't be here?'

'What do you mean?'

'A gun.'

She was frozen into silence, her mouth moved soundlessly, she looked nervously towards the rucksack.

He read her face in the candlelight and gave an exclamation of fury. '*Christ, you – !*' Dropping on to one knee beside the rucksack, he began to pull at the second strap, saying viciously: 'You don't know when you're well off, Ragna!' He gave a derisive laugh. 'And you were going to reach for it, were you. My dear girl, I would have killed you in a second!'

He jerked at the strap with his free hand, but it wouldn't yield. He said in cold rage: 'Come and undo this!'

She couldn't move, her throat was dry, she wanted to scream. He *would* shoot her.

Then she thought of Hal and forced herself forward. She knelt down on Rolf's left, she undid the strap. Still kneeling she straightened up.

Rolf started to pull things out of the bag.

The fear was so bad she had to bite her teeth together to prevent them from chattering.

He waved the pistol at her and she realised he wanted her to move away again.

She started to get to her feet, she slid her hand into her pocket she gripped the bulky handle of the revolver, she began to pull it out. Rolf's head turned a little. She froze. But then he was bending over the rucksack, rummaging through it with his left

518

hand. His gun hand sagged away, the pistol pointing at the floor.

She straightened up. She couldn't bring herself to pull the revolver right out of her pocket. She felt ill; the blood roared in her ears. She tried to speak. Nothing happened. She croaked: 'It's in the bottom.'

'What?'

'The gun.' She tightened her grip on the revolver.

He gave an exclamation of impatience and plunged his hand further into the rucksack, twisting his crouching body slightly away from her.

She pulled the revolver out of her pocket. Now. Her senses screaming, her limbs shaking, she darted quickly behind him and, with both hands, thrust the revolver against the back of his neck.

He gave a violent start, jerked his head sideways, and began to twist his body and his gun arm round, trying to bring the pistol to bear over his left shoulder. His neck was slipping away; Ragna felt the barrel of the revolver losing contact. The fear stabbed at her. She followed his neck as it twisted, thrust her hands forward, found the neck again and jabbed the revolver even harder into his flesh.

His body stopped twisting but his gun arm was still moving, whipping round. *Coming for her.*

She stepped further behind him, keeping his body between her and the pistol.

'D-o-n't!' she screeched.

The arm, the pistol, were still coming.

'D-o-n't!'

He gave a sudden hiss of pain: the gun stopped coming. He grasped his shoulder and bowed his head, as if in agony.

Was he really hurt? Was it a trick?

There was a moment of silence, broken only by the panting of their breath. Ragna was shaking so badly it was all she could do to keep the gun pressed against his neck.

Slowly he twisted his head round again, trying to get a look at her. *Trying to work out how to grab her.* His bared teeth glinted in the light.

'Ragna ...' he said softly.

She jabbed at his neck and cried: 'D-o-n't, *don't, don't!*' Why

519

didn't he shut up?

'Listen . . .'

She said: 'I'll – I'll kill you – if – you – move.'

'Ragna –'

'Don't – move or I'll do it.'

'Ragna – you don't want to *kill* me.'

'Don't move.' She felt weak. What happened now? She didn't know what to do.

'My love, you'd regret it, you'd regret it terribly. It's me, remember? *Me*. Don't we mean something to each other? Weren't we good together? It was special for me, Ragna. Very.' His voice was soft and low: the voice he used in bed.

She tried to shut the voice out, to think – to *think*.

'Ragna, remember the way we made love. It was good, wasn't it? Not something we could pretend about. Ragna, believe me, I wouldn't dream of harming you. I was only going to tie you up. It was going to be so simple. You'd have been found in a few hours. So why this, Ragna?'

'Stop! Get up! *No!* Stay there! *Don't move!*' She pressed the gun even harder against his neck. God, she was going to die of terror.

'But why all this?' Rolf asked reasonably. 'What's the point?'

Ragna froze: a sound in the passage. The man! He was coming back to find out what was happening.

She knew Rolf had heard the sound too.

'Ragna,' he went on carefully, as if explaining something to a child, 'I'm going to stand up now, and I'm going to take your gun away and I'm going to tie you up – very gently – and then we'll be able to stick to the original plan, and no one'll come to any harm. Okay?'

He began to move.

She pushed the gun at his neck.

He kept moving.

More sounds from the passage. A voice calling: 'All right?'

Ragna hissed: 'Tell him it's all right!'

Rolf was getting slowly to his feet.

'*Tell him!*'

Rolf hesitated, then called: 'All right.'

'Don't be long!' The sound of retreating footsteps.

Rolf began to straighten up.

She kept the gun on his neck. She felt paralysed, unable to decide what to do.

'Can't tie me up!' she declared.

He was standing up. 'Won't be for long.'

'Got to rescue Hal.'

A pause. 'Hal will be dead by now.' He began to turn.

'No!'

He kept turning. *He'd grab her at any moment.*

She leapt backwards – getting distance, *distance* – and pointed the gun at his chest, finger hard on the trigger. 'Don't!' And this time her voice was a low growl.

He hesitated, then kept turning. In the flickering light she saw his gun hand coming round, she saw that beautiful ruthless face.

And then her uncertainty dropped away as if it had never existed. With a sense of being outside herself, of watching herself from far far away, she squeezed the trigger.

Nothing. The trigger didn't move.

A moment of horror. She remembered – she must press much harder.

A sudden movement. Rolf. He'd realised. His arm – the pistol – was whipping up.

She squeezed with all her might.

The gun gave an almighty kick, an explosion filled the room, she was deafened.

She opened her eyes. Rolf was falling backwards, backwards. Gently, as though in slow motion, he crumpled on to the floor.

For a moment she couldn't move. She stared. Sounds encroached on her ... Small moans. It took her an instant to realise: it was she who was moaning. She moved forward a little way, stopped, moved again. Looked down. Stared.

The sense of unreality returned.

There was a red mess where Rolf's left eye had been. Blood spread across his nose and dribbled on to the floor.

She couldn't understand it: she'd aimed at his chest.

A sound from the passage.

The man.

Instantly alert again, she backed away into the shadows of the room.

'Hey!' the man's voice called. 'Let's go! Come on! Let's go!'

Ha! She thought: Wrong person! Wrong person! It's me! It's *me!* I did it!

'Hey?' It was more of a question now. A squeak of boards: he was coming down the passage.

Ragna gripped the gun again. Then she remembered the double action, and finding the hammer, pulled it back with her thumb.

'Hey?' The voice was doubtful now. He began to appear round the door – an arm, a shoulder, finally a head. He paused, half-way in. He'd seen Rolf.

He looked down; he looked up; he saw her.

For a moment they stared at one another. Then, baring her teeth, she levelled the gun and squeezed.

His head vanished, the shot roared out.

When she opened her eyes he'd gone.

She ducked into the shadow of the tall cupboard, just in case the head popped back round the door. She thought: No one'll catch me now! No one! No one'll stop me now! And she raged with savage delight.

Silence. The rage began to die in her. Where was he? Her senses expanded.

A motor revving. The car. They were going.

Might be a trick. *Yes!* Couldn't fool her that easily! She laughed inwardly. She wasn't such a fool as to fall for that!

The motor revved to an even higher pitch, and drew away, fading rapidly.

Had they gone?

Then another sound. A second car. Idling.

The last of the rage ebbed out of her and she lowered the gun.

Thrane drove with the heating turned low. This was a severe form of punishment – he was half-frozen – but it was the only sure way of keeping awake.

He'd seen nothing since leaving the border. He didn't know what he'd expected to find, but he couldn't help feeling rather disappointed. And now it was beginning to snow. That was all they needed! If it got any worse the Finns would have to call off their air search almost before it had begun.

He'd already passed the point he'd marked on the map, the point where he'd have joined the road if he'd been Berg. He'd slowed, had a good look round, and seen nothing. Now he was five miles on and heading for the second mark on his map, the only other place he could imagine Berg joining the road.

Coming over a slight rise he blinked and took notice.

A car, parked on the road with its tail lights on. Next to a small dwelling. He peered through the wipers.

Travellers. But it might be worth having a word with them. They might have seen something, you never knew.

They might even have picked up an extra passenger.

One could never be too careful. He slipped his Colt pistol out of his jacket and on to the seat beside him.

The car was a Volvo, quite a new one by the look of it. Its engine was running. He drove up slowly, trying to get the whole picture.

Someone was sitting in the driver's seat. The door of the house appeared to be open.

Thrane drew to a halt some yards behind and looked at the car registration. Finnish. He memorised it.

The person in the car was agitated: a head kept peering round, then the figure gesticulated urgently towards the passenger window, towards the house –

A man shot out of the house at a run. Thrane grabbed his pistol and, opening the door, jumped out.

The man bolted into the car and even before the door was closed, the car was spurting away in a cloud of snow.

Thrane stared after it, momentarily indecisive. To search the house or to follow?

Thrane had never seen the running man before in his life. He decided on the house.

He made his way through the falling snow, the Colt in his hand.

A movement. He paused. A woman appeared in the doorway, a revolver dangling from her hand.

He blinked. Under all the heavy clothing it looked like –

It *was*. Ragna Johansen.

523

He hurried towards her.

She recognised him and a wild ragged grimace of a smile spread across her face.

Thirty-nine

The area of high pressure was shifting at last, moving east over the Barents Sea. And as it moved, the wind swung slowly round to the south-east. This brought a slight but welcome rise in the temperature – on the plateau, up five degrees to thirty below. But the shifting wind also brought something far less welcome: banks of snow-carrying cloud curving in from the Siberian plains. At first the snow came in a whisper, a thin veil of small flakes so light that they danced and swirled in the air. But gradually the flakes thickened, falling more resolutely, settling on the ground, covering the wind-razed surface of the plateau with a layer of soft snow.

And for once there was no howling gale to rip the snow away.

The visibility made an air search impossible. It was called off at ten that first morning.

At about the same time Aslak and Erkki Hetta reached the half-way mark of their journey and decided to press on quickly before the visibility deteriorated any further. They kept their eyes open for signs of life, of course, but the tracks they had been following had long since vanished under the quietly falling snow. From time to time one of them gave a loud cry, a high whoop, in case an answering shout should filter back through the whiteness.

But they saw, they heard, nothing, and as they hurried on through the empty land their hopes began to fall.

If the snow had eased a little, if the light had been a little clearer, they might have seen the marker, the two crossed skis that Ragna had left standing in the snow beside the boulder. But the two Lapps passed some yards away and never saw them.

Erkki gave one of his regular whoops a minute later, but this, like all the calls before, went unanswered. Having no reason to suspect someone might be near, the Lapps did not repeat the call for some minutes, and by that time the boulder was long past.

They sped on. After a few miles they came to the second hut. In it they found an empty food can and a chocolate wrapper, which could well have been left recently – and could equally well have been left some time before. The two men could not decide.

Continuing their journey, they came to a gully then a lake. Here they turned west, taking the shortest route to the road, resigned to the likelihood that they would find no one, anxious to reach safety before a wind should whip up a blizzard and force a halt.

In the increasing gloom they eventually found the road more by accident than design, and began the weary plod back towards the border. To their relief the Finnish military found them half an hour later and gave them a lift as far as the border post, where they sent a telephone report to Tromso. Four hours later they got a lift down to Skibotn.

It was about then that the wind came up, a heavy snow-laden wind which sent the flakes streaking horizontally across the landscape, blotting out everything, causing would-be rescuers to retreat to warmth and safety.

The two Lapps were the last people to venture on to the plateau for four days.

Hal was woken by a combination of pain and raging thirst.

The thirst was the more urgent sensation. With his right hand he felt about inside the survival bag for the water flask. It wasn't there. He dimly remembered drinking from it before – how long ago? And what had he done with it? He had no idea. With an effort he unfastened the top of the survival bag and, pushing his hand out, searched the area near his shoulder. His fingers touched the ice-cold flask. He grasped it. The cap was hanging loose; he had left it unfastened. Even before he tipped it up he knew from its weight that it was empty.

These manoeuvres had tired him and, abandoning the flask, he closed his eyes again.

A drop of water fell on his face. Drips ... He was vaguely aware that it was the drips that may have woken him.

Water. He had to do something about a drink.

Reaching behind his head he touched snow and, clawing some off, pressed it into his mouth. He repeated this several times: the chilling effect of the snow on his mouth and stomach was a lesser evil than the thirst.

He rested again – he was incredibly weak – and tried to think how long it had been since Ragna left. A day – two days – more? He had been drifting in and out of consciousness; it was impossible to tell. But from the thirst he guessed it might be as long as two days.

He had an overwhelming urge to sleep again, but resisted it. Reaching out, he touched the food, felt his way across it, and found the candle and matches. Gripping the matches in his teeth, he removed a match and struck it.

It went out immediately.

He tried again, more successfully this time, and turning his head painfully, screwing his good eye up against the light, he put the lighted match to the candle. He held it there for several seconds before he realised he was nowhere near the candle wick. At the third attempt he made contact and the candle finally flamed.

This completely exhausted him and he was forced to rest again. He looked up at the dark rock just above his head. The surface was covered in ice. One icicle was dripping on to him. This had some significance, though for the moment he couldn't think what.

Ignoring the hum in his dead ear, he tried listening for sounds from outside, but nothing permeated the roof of the shelter.

Finally he roused himself and chewed at some dried fish. He soon gave it up: the stuff was hard as rock, and salty. The can of meat looked more inviting, but he couldn't have opened it if he'd tried. Heating anything was out of the question; the primus would need pumping, priming, lighting, and he couldn't manage that. He settled on dried apricots – not quite as hard as the fish, and definitely not salty – as well as some glucose tablets.

As his senses slowly came to life he grappled with the sig-

527

nificance of the icy rock. Finally he had it: no ventilation. No air was getting into the shelter. Which probably meant snow. Only a hermetic seal of snow could prevent the air getting in.

He groped behind his head to the point where the tarpaulin met the rock and pushed his hand out through the gap. He touched snow, and more snow. He pulled the tarpaulin away from the rock side and agitated his hand, pulling in snow, until he felt a slight draught on his face.

He settled back, drawing in the cold sweet air.

Better, better.

But there was still the pain, a continuous and painful throbbing in his left hand. No other part of his body hurt, just the hand. As he chewed away at the apricots, he thought about the sort of pain it was and decided he should take a look at it.

However, the meal, such as it was, had worn him out again, and he allowed himself another rest before finally pulling his left hand gingerly out of the survival bag. He knew it must be in a bad way even before he unwound the stained bandage. He had to pull away the last layer bit by bit where it had stuck to the flesh beneath. Such flesh as there was. The first two fingers were a write-off, almost severed near the base. But that wasn't what caused his heart to sink quite so painfully. It was the sight of the swelling, the inflammation, the yellow pus: the rampant infection.

Bringing his hand close up to his eye, he examined the damage from every angle.

He thought about all sorts of things, like how long he might stay in his ice-cave and, if it was a very long time, how he would like to die. As he saw it, he had a choice between the quick agony of blood-poisoning and the slow business of starvation.

He didn't know which was worse, but since one offered time and therefore hope and the other didn't, the choice was made.

Reaching for his rucksack he pulled it towards him and took out Aslak's hunting knife. He rubbed his thumb lightly over the blade. Sharp enough. He put the blade over the candle flame for some moments, let it cool, then, holding both hands up in front of his face, he positioned the blade carefully against the side of his first finger, below the damaged section.

Closing his eyes he began to saw the blade back and forth.

It took an instant for the pain to hit him. He gritted his teeth

528

and kept sawing until the pain rose to a sweeping wave of agony and, crying out, he stopped.

Gasping, the sweat starting from his body, he peered at the hand. The first finger was almost off. Bracing himself he drew the knife sharply across and down once more, and it was done. He tossed the bloody remnant away.

Moaning quietly, he screwed up his eyes until the worst of the shaking and shivering had passed, then gathered himself for the rest of the job.

After roughly binding the first stump, which was bleeding profusely, he examined the second finger. This should be easier, since the bone was almost completely shot away. He decided to try and do it in one go. Bracing himself, grimacing in anticipation of the pain, he made one savage cut which was so unexpectedly easy that he had to pull up short to prevent the knife driving into his third and healthy finger.

He gasped and sobbed with pain, and almost slipped into unconsciousness. But he knew he had to make one more effort if the whole exercise wasn't to be in vain. First he squeezed the bleeding stumps to push out any remaining pus, then, fumbling in a pocket of the rucksack, he found the primus fuel – paraffin – and dabbed some over the wounds. The stinging made tears come to his eyes.

Rebinding the hand tightly in the rough bandage, he refastened the survival bag, closed his eyes and slipped into a dim half-world where the only reality was pain.

There was only one word for it: cruel. Five days. Five whole days of almost continuous snow. A search party had set off on the first day, but when conditions worsened it had soon returned. Since then – nothing.

For four days Thrane had waited at the Finnish command post, staring out into the gloom, watching the angry snow battering itself against the windows.

Now, on the fifth day, the strain was taking its toll. It was bad enough imagining what Starheim must be going through – even if he was still alive, which Thrane was beginning to doubt –

but that was as nothing compared to facing Ragna Johansen each day.

He'd never seen anyone disintegrate in front of his eyes before; he'd never imagined it could happen quite so fast. She was like a ghost, with dreadful staring eyes and sunken cheeks. That first day when the search party had returned she'd at least cried her eyes out. But now she just sat in a chair and stared. She wouldn't eat, she hardly slept, she spoke to no one unless she had to.

The only time she spoke to Thrane was when they yet again offered her a room at a nearby house, or when the doctor muttered about shock and hospital rest, but then it was only to grasp Thrane's arm and turn her large imploring eyes on him, and beg him to make sure that they allowed her to stay.

He had done what he could and so far they had not insisted. But in view of her deteriorating physical condition he wasn't sure he could put them off much longer.

And then there was the questioning. The last time the Finnish security service had gently put some questions to her she'd completely forgotten what she was meant to say, had blurted out entirely the wrong thing, and had almost sunk herself and Thrane without trace. During the earlier interrogations she'd had it word-perfect, repeating the story just as Thrane had drummed it into her, recounting how the mysterious couple had taken her and Berg to the empty house and tied her up and shot Berg and driven off when they heard Thrane's car approach.

During his own interrogation Thrane had regretted not having seen the car registration, but was under the impression it was Finnish. He didn't mention anything about the revolver, though he knew perfectly well where it was, which was carefully concealed in the seat of his car. Nor did he offer a motive for Berg's killing, though he did suggest that the mysterious couple most probably worked for the same people as Berg – the Soviets – and might therefore have had professional differences.

As an explanation of events it was workable, and certainly the Finns had found no reason to doubt it – just as long as Ragna stuck to the right set of facts. He had reminded her of what would happen if the truth leaked out – her removal to Helsinki, long questioning, a possible judicial hearing – but he wasn't sure she was capable of taking it in. If they questioned

530

er again he had the awful feeling she would tell them the truth.

And now it was the fifth day. And still they waited.

During the morning he avoided the room where he knew Ragna would be sitting. It was only after he'd been to the mess and picked at a meal and spent a good half-hour on the phone to Oslo that he went to find her, bearing a plate of sandwiches in case he could persuade her to eat.

She was standing by the window. The moment she saw him she rushed up and fixed him with those enormous luminous eyes. 'The snow,' she breathed, 'it's stopping! It's stopping!'

He looked out of the window. The sky was certainly brighter and, apart from a few desultory flakes floating in the air, the snow had ceased.

'Don't raise your hopes.'

'But they'll go and look now – surely!' Her voice rose to a moan, her mouth trembled. Thrane realised she was finally at breaking point.

He grasped her arm and led her to a chair. 'They'll certainly leave as soon as they can. You stay here. I'll go and find out what's happening.'

'Let me come too.'

He didn't argue – he had the feeling the slightest thing would finish her – but helped her back to her feet and led her to the ops room. The Finnish CO came out and said: 'We're sending a helicopter. Take-off shortly. There's room for both of you. And we'd certainly like you to come along, Mrs Johansen, to help us pinpoint the spot.'

She didn't speak. The tears streamed down her face.

Ragna sat behind the pilot and peered over his shoulder. The snow stretched out endlessly below, a vast grey desert under a heavy metallic sky. There was nothing to be seen at all – no hint of vegetation, no shadows, no suggestion of lakes or streams or valleys. Nothing.

The dread that gripped her heart grew into even more vicious forms. They would fly over him, they would hover over him, they would fail to find him! And in another hour or so it would be too dark and the helicopter would be forced to turn back –

turn back without him.

The prospect was torture, unbearable and, closing her eyes, she put up yet more desperate prayers.

Someone touched her arm. It was the navigator. He pointed downwards then at his chart. Ragna craned forward, looked down, but saw nothing. The navigator passed the chart over and pointed at a tiny dot.

The second hut. They were over the hut!

She nodded stupidly and gratefully at the navigator. He tapped his watch and held up one finger. One minute, one minute to the estimated position, to the cross she had helped put on the chart. She exchanged glances with Thrane who gave her a thumbs-up.

The helicopter reduced speed and began to descend. Ragna looked desperately out of the window.

The snow came up to meet them. They hovered, went forward again, hovered and finally descended on to the snow.

The two soldiers who'd been sitting in the rear of the machine helped her out and escorted her clear of the blades. She walked on, wading through the thick snow, trying to get her bearings, realising with a growing sense of panic that she recognised nothing – *nothing*.

Thrane and the navigator joined her, waiting silently as she turned and turned again, and finally looked at them in dumb helplessness.

Raising his voice above the helicopter's din Thrane said: 'Remember the snow's made it look entirely different!'

But this different?

The navigator shouted: 'We're definitely on the trail as marked on the map. If we're out, it's only on a north-south axis. If you can work out whether we're north or south of the spot, then we can go back to the machine and take another hop.'

She understood. She looked at the map and tried to identify the slight hills, tried to make out whether she might have passed this way before Hal had been shot or after.

After. Her instincts told her after.

She pointed north.

They returned to the helicopter and made a short hop to the north.

They got out again and Ragna scanned the soft white landscape once more.

There was a slight hill to the west of her and another to the
north. Something about the one to the north made her pause.
Could it be the one Rolf had sent her to climb? Might the rocky
outcrop she'd reached be hidden under a slight hump half-way
up?

The more she stared, the more hopeful she felt. Just as she
was about to shout the news to Thrane, one of the soldiers
signalled towards the north. Ragna lumbered through the snow
towards him. 'I think I can see something up there.' He passed
her his binoculars. She twiddled the focus and, following his
direction, peered hard. A faint stick-like object. Very straight.

A ski. She hardly dared believe it.

No one spoke as they trooped back to the helicopter and
climbed in. The machine revved, took off, and slowly advanced.
The navigator talked rapidly into his mouthpiece, the pilot
nodded his head, looked down through his side window, nodded
again and lowered his machine once more.

They jumped out.

There, some ten yards in front of them, was a single ski
standing upright in the snow.

Someone patted Ragna on the shoulder. It was Thrane.

They advanced. The soldiers had shovels in their hands. As
they drew near Ragna noticed that the second of the two crossed
skis had almost completely fallen over. She mentally chastised
herself for not having driven it deeper into the snow, then
realised it didn't matter any more.

Perhaps nothing mattered any more.

They halted in front of the snow-covered mound that was
the boulder. To Ragna's mind the white mound seemed to
have transposed itself into an ice-tomb, cold and still, and she
hesitated, in the vice-like grip of a terrible fear.

Then one of the soldiers leaned forward and swept some
snow away with his glove, and she saw the fabric of the
tarpaulin. Shaking off the fear, she joined the others, scraping at
the snow, working feverishly until the tarpaulin was completely
exposed.

It was Thrane who reached up and cut the thin rope holding
the tarpaulin to the boulder. She stood back then. She stood

533

back because she couldn't face the next few moments of uncertainty. She wanted Thrane to look, she wanted Thrane to establish the situation, she wanted him to turn to face her.

And then she'd know. She'd know by the look in his eyes.

They pulled the tarpaulin away. Thrane climbed in over the ice wall and stooped down. He stayed down a long time. He must have said something to the soldier, for the soldier nodded and hurried past Ragna.

Ragna could bear it no longer and stepped forward.

As she did so Thrane put his head up.

Then she knew.

The tears spilled down her cheeks. 'He's – ?'

'Just about. He managed a smile anyway.' And then Thrane smiled too.

Epilogue

For eleven months of the year the house stands empty, the valley deserted. In the winters the west wind comes swooping over the land as fiercely as ever, disgorging snow that piles against the windows and doorways, snow that remains uncleared until the spring thaw.

No wood fires warm the cold house; no lights shine out over the valley. The vegetable garden has long since grown wild, died back, and been overgrown by tougher vegetation. The paddocks are empty, the barn unoccupied except for an old tractor which has seen better days.

But the trees! They are truly remarkable. Admittedly there are one or two gaps where the harsh winter of 1963 took its toll, but in the subsequent five years those that survived have flourished – by Arctic standards at least.

A grove of willow stands near the house: also a solitary lilac which was long since given up for dead. Above, there is rowan, aspen, ash and bird-cherry, and higher still, pine and spruce which have finally grown tall enough to break some of the force of the wind.

But you have to come in summer to see the trees at their best. Then the sudden wealth of light and warmth causes the whole valley to burgeon with growth and colour. In the shelter of the trees there is dwarf rhododendron and azalea, on the more open slopes, purple and white heathers, and tiny white and pink pine flowers; even wild orchids. The lichens and mosses spring up, the grasses in the lower meadows grow tall, ready for the harvesting that will never come.

It is when the valley is at its most lush and beautiful that the eleven months' silence is finally broken. Then a boat motors close in to the shore and a party is ferried to the beach, complete with luggage and large quantities of stores.

Last year the party numbered four, but this year it's five, young Jan is almost four months old.

Immediately the party has landed, the valley is filled with noise – a great deal of it – as the two elder children streak off in search of adventure. Kris, a very grown-up ten, deigns to let his young sister Elise enter the boathouse and, though she's only four, allows her to help with the removal of the cover. She's not a lot of use, of course, but she tugs willingly and, once the cover is off, looks suitably impressed at the sight of *Lillebjorn*.

'Got no mast!' Elise remarks.

'Of course it has!' Kris scoffs. 'It's lying down over there. There isn't room to put it up in here, is there?'

Elise studies the height of the roof and frowns. After a time she says: 'Does it fall over?'

'Does what fall over?'

A pause. 'The boat.'

'What do you mean?'

Elise struggles with the effort of explaining this complex thing. 'In the sea. Does . . .' she purses her lips, '. . . does it get blowed over in the wind.'

'No!' Kris laughs. 'Never!' He says it in the dismissive sort of way brothers reserve for younger sisters. 'Hal and I sailed in a gale once, in the middle of winter. And it didn't capsize then. Nowhere near it!'

Elise has heard this story before. As always she doesn't quite know what to make of it. Particularly when Kris has recently hinted that Daddy's missing fingers and his eye-that-can't-see have something to do with the boat episode. Yet Mummy definitely told her that Daddy lost his fingers in an accident with a gun.

It's all rather mystifying and she's glad of the distraction of the shiny wood of the boat. She runs her finger over it and watches Kris as he sorts through the ropes in a knowledgeable manner.

A call sounds from outside and Elise scampers off to find her mother sitting on the grass, the baby on her lap, surrounded by luggage. 'Oh there you are,' Ragna says, smiling. She adds 'Daddy's gone to see if he can get the tractor going.'

Elise vaguely remembers the tractor from last year and how very noisy and bumpy it was, and how frightened and thrilled she was all at the same time. 'Can I sit on your lap, Mama? In the tractor?'

'Mmm.'

A movement catches Elise's eye, the bright fluttering of a tiny white butterfly, and, forgetting her fear of the tractor, she runs off to investigate.

Ragna closed her eyes and let the sun beat against her face. Ah, how she loved the summer! How she loved the days that never ended and the sun that never set. How she loved leaving the south behind for these four precious weeks – leaving the daily rush to get the baby fed and changed, and Elise dressed, and Kris to school, and Hal off on one of his consultancy jobs, or up to his study to write. Leaving that for – peace. Up here here was no timetable, no hurry; with twenty-four hours of continuous light the day just happened of its own accord.

She loved to see the children running free – dirty, of course, and more than a little wild – but happy and, when they weren't happy, tired and ready for bed. She loved to watch Hal and Kris setting off on a fishing expedition in *Lillebjorn*, to follow the white sails as they glided away across the gentle blue water, to wait for their return and meet them at the shore and admire the catch.

Ah, the peace, the peace.

Most of all, she loved the long evenings on the veranda after the children were in bed, when she and Hal sat and talked, or read, or listened to music floating out through the open windows of the living room.

Now and again they did none of these things, but sat in silence, looking out over the mirror-calm water towards the white-capped mountains. And then he would swing his arm round her shoulders and she would reach for his hand and squeeze it hard.

They never tried to forget what had happened – it would have been quite impossible – and occasionally, when they felt the need, they talked about it. Then they always reminded each other – though reminder were hardly necessary – of all the good things that had come out of it, their new life, three beautiful children, and most of all, each other. Also justice of a sort. Yes: that was important too.

And Ragna would lean back on his shoulder and sneak a look at him, at that face she knew so well, with its bent nose that had never got fixed and the scar on one cheek, and think how very lucky she was to have him.

But then there wasn't a day when she didn't think that.

A bird sang high in the sky above, a piercing song of such sweetness that she looked up to search for it. The baby pulled at a button on her blouse and gurgled. The scent of flowers, of grasses and soft abundance rose up around her.

Ah, the peace, the peace.

The silence was shattered by the roar of the tractor's engine descending the valley.

Ragna gave an exclamation of pleasure and admiration. He'd got it going! But after all these years she should have known he always did.

She stood up and called to the children. The tractor emerged over the brow of the hill and came down the track, the trailer rattling in its wake.

Hal drew up and jumped out. 'Where are my helpers then?' He grinned at the children.

As soon as the last bag was in, Hal helped Ragna up into the trailer with the baby and Elise, then climbed into the cab with Kris. As they bounced up the hill Kris whooped with joy, Elise clung to Ragna's trousers and the baby fell asleep.

Once they reached the house it was quite a business to unload everything, find the food, get the perishables into the fridge – luxury Ragna had installed – then feed the baby, put him down to nap, and prepare a meal for the rest of the family. By the time Ragna had got the food on the table everyone had disappeared. She shrugged it off: situation normal.

But she had a good idea of where Hal would be.

She ran lightly down the veranda steps and walked round to the front of the old vegetable garden. There he was, crouching by the wall, pulling gently at the tall grass growing over a small plot marked with stones. She didn't disturb him until he stood up.

'Hi,' she called, strolling up.

He gestured towards the plot. 'I'll have a go at this first thing in the morning,' he said. 'And the sign too.' He had the marker in his hand, its inscription so faded that it was barely possible to make out the single word: Bamse.

'Have we got any suitable paint?' she asked.

'I think so.'

They walked back to the house.

'I thought we might go to Ringvassoy early next week,' he said.

'Yes.'

Ringvassoy was the large island close by, where Arne was buried. Once a year they took flowers and tidied the grave and cleaned the gravestone.

He asked: 'And what about going to see Aslak? Have you decided?'

'Yes.' She looped her arm through his. 'I won't bother. It's such a way. And we can just as easily discuss things on the phone.'

Undisguised relief came over Hal's face. He'd given her every encouragement in her continuing campaign for Lapp rights, he'd been proud when, despite losing the battle over the location of the Kaafiord installation, she'd won assurances that the disturbance to the Lapps would be minimised. But, supportive though he was, he didn't like the campaign to impinge on their time together, especially here at Brattdal.

And he was right, she decided. Nothing must be allowed to interfere with the peace, the perfect peace. She squeezed his arm, overcome by the wonderful prospect of having him and the children all to herself for a month.

They climbed the steps to the veranda and, pausing, looked out over the valley.

After a time she murmured gently: 'There's a meal on the table.'

He turned his head, a small frown of annoyance on his face, the frown he always wore when someone spoke in his poor ear and he failed to hear.

She repeated it.

He nodded. 'Where are the children?'

'Oh – vanished.'

'Ha! Situation normal.'

'Yes.' And, catching his eye, she threw back her head and laughed.